NEPHILIM'S DESTINY

THE COMPLETE SERIES

TESSA COLE

Gryphon's Gate Publishing

Nephilim's Destiny: The Complete Series

Copyright © 2021 Tessa Cole

Gryphon's Gate Publishing

550 King St. N.

PO Box 42088 Conestoga

Waterloo, ON

N2L 6K5

Print ISBN 978-1-990587-26-9

DESTINED DARKNESS

NEPHILIM'S DESTINY, BOOK 1

ESSIE

I recognized the freeze in the air the moment I opened the pharmacy's door. Fear. A fear so cold that, if the chill got any stronger my weird next-to-useless empathic magic would manifest it in full and I'd see my breath — while no one else would see theirs.

I fought a shiver and swore under my breath. I hadn't even gotten to the precinct to start my shift, but it looked like my patrol was starting right now. This kind of fear could only mean the pharmacy was being robbed.

The cashier, Pam, a middle-aged woman who'd been happy to see me from the moment I'd moved into the neighborhood two years ago, flashed me a smile. It lit up her heart-shaped face and crinkled around her eyes like it always did. She was completely oblivious, which meant whatever was happening had to be at the back of the store.

"Essie, the usual?" she asked, reaching for the box of nicotine patches on the shelf behind her.

"Yeah, but I need to get something from Abe first." Maybe the pharmacist was worried about something else, or maybe he was angry. Sometimes a person's rage manifested to me as cold. But it was stupid to try to convince myself that the cold biting my cheeks was anything but fear. Sometimes I had no idea what the change in temperature meant, but this was perfectly clear.

Except I couldn't just tell Pam to leave the building and call 911. Not without having to explain how I knew about the robbery. And no way in hell was that going to happen. Which meant I had to call it in where Pam couldn't see me, and keep control of the situation to ensure she, Abe, and anyone else in the pharmacy were safe until backup arrived.

"I'm glad you quit," she said, "but maybe you should consider weaning yourself off of these, too?"

"I'll ask Abe about that," I said as I hurried to the farthest aisle, so she wouldn't see me pull out my phone to call for backup.

"Two years is a long time," she called after me.

And it would be if I'd actually been using the patches to quit smoking, but I wasn't. They were the only thing that seemed to partially ease the constant, painful buzz in my body that had manifested two and a half years ago. It was like I was always in contact with a low voltage electric fence or something. Weaning myself off the patches wasn't even close to being an option. I'd go crazy within the week. Hell, probably a few days.

When the buzz had first started, I'd been terrified it meant I was developing another magical ability, something I wouldn't be able to hide. But when nothing had appeared — thank God — and the hum had lasted more than two weeks, making it impossible to concentrate, or sleep, or do my job, or have a normal conversation with anyone, I'd started looking for a cure, anything to make it stop.

I'd tried everything legal and illegal — not going insane was worth jeopardizing my job with the Union City police department — but nicotine was the only thing that helped, and thank God I'd stumbled across it.

I also had no idea why it had started and couldn't just search the internet for answers since I was a nephilim, half angel and half human, and even if I was supposed to exist, there was little to no information on my type of supernatural being. And I didn't want to start poking around and raise suspicion. I didn't know what the agents of the Joined Parliament would do with me if they found me. Probably lock me up or execute me as a war criminal for a war that had happened twenty-three years ago that I hadn't even been involved in. Hell, I'd barely been seven twenty-three years ago. Or worse, they'd lock me in a laboratory and test me like a lab rat because I wasn't like the other nephilim.

Twenty-three years ago, Michael and Rafael had freed Lucifer and led an uprising of angels to cleanse the earth of the human parasite and — unbeknownst to humans — all non-angel supernatural beings as well. They had found a dark magic that ensured the unnatural conception and rapid maturation of thousands of nephilim, and had grown their army within months. Because of the magic creating them, these nephilim were ferocious, mindless soldiers, more beast than human or angel.

The fact that I wasn't a mindless beast had to prove that I wasn't *made* during the war, that I was somehow conceived naturally even if the angelic powers-that-be claimed it was impossible. Except I wasn't sure that little detail would be enough to protect me, and I wasn't planning on revealing myself just to find out.

The nephilim had slaughtered thousands of humans and angels before Gabriel, the leader of the Angelic Defense, decided to make a deal with the supers to join the fight. No more living in the shadows, representation in government, and, as along as they abided by the laws they helped create, they'd be left to live in peace.

So now everyone knew about supernatural beings.

And nephilim were the new monster-in–the-dark to be hated and feared.

Leaving me to live my life as a normal nothing-to-see-here human who only wanted to serve and protect.

Just, jeez, did it have to be before I'd had my first coffee and replaced my nicotine patch?

I pulled my phone from my purse and eased up to the end of the aisle near the back of the store. I wasn't carrying my off-duty sidearm — my neighborhood was pretty safe so I usually didn't — but that didn't mean I couldn't monitor the situation or talk to the robber and buy time for backup to arrive.

In the convex overhead mirror, my aisle and the store's two others stretched toward the front. The pharmacy counter sat forty-five degrees to the aisles, recessed to my left with its narrow shelves, and a door to the stockroom leading to the only other exit in the store. A rake-thin man with pale grayish skin, ripped jeans, and a dark blue hoodie — the hood down revealing greasy brown hair — pointed a revolver at Abe, Pam's middle-aged, balding husband.

My empathic cold billowed, making my teeth chatter, and the buzz in my body grew stronger, now tiny nips under my skin indicating it wouldn't be long before I really needed a new patch.

"Come on, come on," the guy said. He jerked a step closer to the counter, his movements twitchy, his breath fast, and a sheen of sweat on his forehead catching the glare of the fluorescent light. It was either nerves or he was coming down from some kind of high. Probably both.

Great. Served me right for thinking whatever trouble I found myself in while off duty wouldn't require a weapon.

I inched back from the edge of the aisle, hoping a few feet would make a difference and he wouldn't be able to hear me, and called in the armed robbery. Then I shoved my phone into my pocket, set my purse on the floor, and slunk back into position.

"The Divifend, too." The guy raked a hand through his messy locks and glanced over his shoulder — thankfully not thinking to look up at the mirror. "I don't see Divifend."

Shit. If his high of choice was zip, a concoction of the magical immune enhancing drug Divifend combined with an amphetamine, the situation just got more dangerous. The mixture of upper and magic gave the user an incredible high heightened with the exhilaration of spurts of magically enhanced strength, speed, and vitality. But the low, if it didn't kill you, came with aggressive mania and sometimes violent halluci-nations.

"We didn't receive our order yesterday," Abe said, shoving a plastic bag over the counter toward the robber. It was likely true. Divifend wasn't easy to make and with a slew of recent robberies in town, it likely meant the supplier was working double-time to make up for the lost dosages. And that still meant some cancer patients right now were going without and that pissed me off as much as this idiot pointing a gun at Abe.

"This is all we have," Abe added.

"No, you're lying." The guy waved his gun, his breath coming faster, his movements jerkier.

"I'm not. We didn't get it." Abe's fear deepened, so cold now it felt like my skin was burning.

"Where is it?" The guy slammed a hand on the counter, his voice screeching and desperate. "Where's the Divifend?"

He was going to lose it and no way in hell was I going to let him shoot Abe.

"Hey." I rounded the corner and raised my hands. It was one of the stupidest things I could have done given that I was unarmed, but all I needed was to buy time. Less than seven minutes.

The guy wrenched to face me, pointing the revolver in my direction, but his hand was shaking too much for him to keep his aim. His eyes were bloodshot and wild, his face sunken and pockmarked. Definitely zip. And definitely coming down.

"He has to have it," the guy said.

"How about you put the gun down and we talk about that."

"Talk about *that*?" The guy's breaths were now short, desperate gasps, and he slapped his head with his free hand. "I'm not going to talk about that." His gaze whipped back to Abe. "He's hiding it."

The guy leaped over the counter, faster than humanly possible, grabbed Abe around the neck, and shoved the gun's muzzle against Abe's temple. "Tell him to tell me where it is."

Frost formed on the backs of my hands, Abe's fear so strong the emotion was manifesting on my body. I forced myself to stay put. I didn't have a gun and jumping in to tackle the guy risked Abe getting shot. Seven minutes was all I needed. Hell, probably six minutes now.

"How about you let the pharmacist go," I said. "I can get you help."

"I don't want help. I want Divifend." The guy's grip around Abe's neck tightened.

The pharmacist gasped, fighting to breathe, his wide eyes locked on me, begging me to save him.

"I want the drug now or I swear—"

"I'll get it for you," I said, telling him what he wanted to hear and praying it would calm him down.

"You better," he snarled.

"But you have to put the gun down."

"Do you think I'm stupid?"

A girl could hope — even if it was ridiculous to think that without a weapon I could convince him to put his down. But I still needed to get the gun off of Abe, so I did another stupid thing in the "don't be an idiot cop" book. I took a step forward and said, "Point your gun at me, then. You can only keep it pointed at one of us and I know where Abe's shipment is."

Abe's fear grew, frosting over my wrists, and I ground my teeth, fighting to keep my expression even. This guy could mistake any twitch as an attack and lose his shit, and I didn't want a chance of that happening until I had him in the alley behind the store. Six minutes? Probably more like five and a half. Of course, more cops showing up might set the guy off, so the faster I got him into the alley, the better.

"I saw the delivery guys drop it out back just before I arrived," I said.

The guy dug his gun's muzzle into Abe's temple. "I knew you were a liar. I should shoot—"

"Abe doesn't know about it," I said as fast as I could to stop him from shooting. "He was in here with you when it arrived. I can show you." *Oh, please work. Just get away from Abe.* I took another step toward him. "Point your gun at me and I'll show you."

"You better." He shoved Abe, slamming him against the narrow shelves with a force that made the pharmacist cry out in pain before sagging to the floor gasping. "Show me."

The gun jerked back to me and the buzz in my body crackled stronger, stinging under Abe's frost, now up to my elbows.

"It's out the back." I eased through the half-door at the end of the counter while the guy glared at me, his body trembling, then opened the door to a small, packed stockroom. "Through here to the back door."

"Come on. Come on." The guy jerked forward, his magical speed snapping him a step then stalling out, making him stagger the final two. "Stop moving so fucking slow."

He shoved me into the stockroom, the force knocking me off my feet and crashing me to the concrete floor.

"I said move faster." He clawed at his scalp and the gun dipped away from me.

I scrambled to my feet. If I jumped now, I might be able to disarm him. There was still at least five minutes before help could arrive and I'd hoped to stall him here in the stockroom, since once we were out in the alley he'd know I'd lied about the delivery.

But another burst of speed hit him before I could lunge at him and he shoved me again. I struggled to keep my balance, slamming into the back door and managing at the last minute to hit the crash bar. I stumbled into the alley, smacking against the concrete wall opposite the door, with the robber close at my heels, and a blast of cold hit me so hard the frost swept over my face and neck, defying the early morning sunlight and late-spring warmth.

I wrenched around and my thoughts stuttered, unable to fully comprehend what I was looking at. Swirling, viscous smoke roughly in the shape of a man churned a few feet away, and a body crushed almost beyond recognition lay on the ground before it. Blood pooled around the corpse and painted the alley walls. A sickening sense of power and darkness swept over me, making my stomach want to instantly reject this morning's cereal, and the buzz in my body ignited into an inferno.

The robber screamed, his eyes wild, and he fired three shots at the—

I had no idea what it was. It didn't look like any supernatural being I'd ever come across. Best guess was that it was a demon, but it didn't have the telltale heat, which meant casting a divine light strike might not work. And from its size and emanating power, if this was a demon, it should have been radiating heat like a furnace.

The guy's shots went wide, his panic making him shake, and the monster lashed out a smoky tentacle. It snapped around his neck, slammed him against the pharmacy's wall, and smashed his skull with a sickening crack. The gun dropped from the guy's hand, clattering to the asphalt at the edge of the blood pool. For a ridiculous split-second, I actually considered going for the weapon. If it had been fully loaded before the guy had fired, then there'd be three rounds remaining. But I didn't even know if normal ammunition would hurt this thing, since I doubted the robber's was enspelled. Hell, I had no idea if an enspelled bullet would hurt it.

I turned to run, but a whip of darkness snapped for me. I twisted out of the way, somehow managing to avoid a pile of rotting boxes and not trip, and forced myself to run faster. Another whip flew toward me. I twisted again, lost my balance, and careened into the alley wall. The creature howled, the sense of nausea deepening, making me gag, and three whips shot toward me.

Oh, shit.

I dodged one, but two more seized my leg. I hit the asphalt, managing to protect my face with my hands, and was tossed back down the alley toward the monster's two victims. Half of my back and right shoulder slammed into the alley wall and searing pain screamed through my chest and neck. My knees hit the ground and I fought to stand and run. Hell, I fought to just breathe past the agony.

The monster swept toward me, and I scrambled back, unable to get up on my feet, and instead falling onto my butt. My hand slapped into something warm and sticky. The blood from the crushed victim. Bile burned my throat, but now I was within grabbing distance of the gun.

Two more tendrils swiped at me. I threw myself to the side and snatched the weapon as the tendrils seized me around the chest. The monster jerked me up and agony screamed through me, threatening my consciousness. I gasped for air. The buzzing in my body joined the screaming pain and I felt like I was going to light on fire.

The monster jerked me closer, its writhing mass licking against my body, curling around my neck, and sliding over my face. I gasped out the spell that summoned a divine light strike. My very human level of power warmed the palm of my free hand and I slapped it against the tentacle around my chest.

White light snapped from my hand.

The monster hissed, the blast not even strong enough to make it cry out, and it slammed me against the alley wall, shooting more agony through my chest, then jerked me close again. Its sense of power and darkness grew, and so did the buzz within me.

I fought to breathe, to think past the pain, but I couldn't break free. What little divine power I possessed wasn't strong enough. The only thing I had left was the gun. At least I was at point blank range. *Please, God, let a normal bullet kill it or something, anything.*

I fired.

The darkness screamed and more smoke swept around me, pouring into my mouth, suffocating me. I fired again and again and again, pulling the trigger even though I knew I was out of ammo, but the thing kept pouring into me, choking, engulfing, and making me want to scream and vomit. Except I couldn't get enough breath for either.

Far away, someone yelled.

A gunshot roared.

The monster screamed and jerked.

Three more shots, louder and closer, and the monster howled.

The darkness surged out of me, dropping me to the ground, face-first into the viscous puddle of blood, and flew away.

My stomach churned, the creature's nausea and darkness clinging to me, and the alley around me spun.

Two sets of feet pounded toward me, but I couldn't raise my head high enough to see who'd come to my rescue.

"Shit, Shaw." That sounded like Brant Keels, an officer in my precinct. "I couldn't see you behind it. If I'd known you were there, I wouldn't have fired."

Brant's partner, a rookie whose name I couldn't remember, knelt beside me and called for EMTs on his radio. His pale eyes were wide. He reached to touch me, his hand shaking, but stopped as if he was afraid to. "What was that?"

"I have no idea," I gasped. And I had no idea why it hadn't bashed my brains out like it had with the robber. Which scared the shit out of me.

ESSIE

TEN MINUTES LATER AN AMBULANCE ARRIVED AND SO DID A HORDE OF officers from my precinct — it being the closest one to the pharmacy. They swarmed the area, my captain sending out teams to search for the monster while Detectives Snyder and McLellan examined the scene.

Shaking and sliding in and out of consciousness, I was lifted onto a gurney. My chest was on fire, my stomach queasy, and my head spinning and spinning and spinning as I was rushed to the hospital.

I flirted with unconsciousness and didn't try to fight it. If I was unconscious, I wasn't feeling pain and I couldn't feel the buzz. It had eased, back to its normal non-nicotine level, but that was still painful.

I wasn't sure how I ended up in a hospital gown, but one minute I was in my blood-soaked clothes, the next I wasn't, and I was fuzzy on if I'd had X-rays taken or not. All I really remembered was feeling gentle hands, hearing a soothing voice, and looking into warm brown eyes in a devastatingly handsome face.

I woke with what felt like the worst hangover of my life — and I really wished it had been because I'd been an idiot and partied too hard last night. The buzz crawled in my skin and pain stabbed me in the chest and neck every time I took a breath. I was in a hospital bed, an intravenous needle in the back of one hand attached to a bag of something clear — saline? — with my other hand captured in a sling immobilizing my arm. My light brown hair hung loose, tickling my cheeks, and I was grateful someone had taken pity on what was probably a tangled half-ponytail and taken out the elastic. Above and beside me, a heart monitor beeped, sure and steady, and beside me sat the most gorgeous man I'd ever seen. Correction, demon. Little horns poked through his stylishly disheveled hair, indicating he was a supernatural being from the Realm of Celestial Darkness.

He slouched in the bedside chair, one leg up — ankle on his thigh — his attention on a folder of papers in his lap, his posture doing nothing to diminish his aura of lithe sexual danger. He reminded me of a cat, sprawled and half asleep but ready to pounce. From what I could see of his face, he looked young, mid-twenties, but being a demon, he could be much older. His black hair hung low, veiling his eyes and curling around his ears and the base of his neck, the color a stark contrast to his pale skin. He wore a black T-shirt stretched tight across a chiseled chest and muscular arms, leaving little to the imagination save for maybe what all that muscle would feel like under my hands or wrapped around me—

His gaze rose as if he could hear my thoughts. Heat flooded my face, and I was captured by his warm brown gaze, so unlike a typical demon. My pulse stuttered and the heat turned sultry, sinking low into my chest.

And then I remembered those eyes had been with me when I had entered the hospital, and I was certain now that he wasn't a doctor. Had he been there for my change of clothes? I shifted, trying to secretly determine if I still wore underwear. Had he seen me naked? I didn't know if I'd been in that blood pool long enough for it to seep through my pants and into my undies. God, that would be mortifying. If he was going to see me naked, I wanted to be conscious for it.

Which, jeez, shouldn't be something I was thinking.

It had to be the buzz, and the pain, and whatever medication I was on.

"You're awake," he said, his voice sliding over me like silk.

My brain stalled.

He closed the folder and leaned forward. "Officer Shaw, I'm Kol, an agent of the Joined Parliament."

...

"I need to ask you a few questions."

...

...

He pursed his lips and my brain jerked back into gear.

"Questions. Right. Yes." It made sense the Joined Parliament would take over the investigation into whatever it was that had attacked me.

At least three rounds of department-issued enspelled ammunition hadn't taken it down. The officers in my precinct weren't prepared to deal with anything like it. My division had less than ten percent of supers living within its boundaries, and the most we had to deal with was the odd witch or minor demon causing trouble.

The door eased open, revealing an angel, the soft glow in his eyes giving away his divine nature. His wings were hidden, somehow absorbed into his body — that was part of the magic that made an angel an angel — and he wore a pale blue button-down — matching his eyes — and black slacks. His blond hair was perfect, not too short to look military, but not too long to look sloppy, and his chiseled jaw was clean-shaven. With broad shoulders — broader than the hot-as-hell demon — and narrow waist, he looked like the poster boy for angels: handsome, strong, divine, even if most of the angel population wasn't blond-haired and blue-eyed.

"Finally," he said, his tone brusque and edged with frustration. He strode into the room and turned his attention to Kol. "Has she said anything?"

"I was just about to," I said, pissed that he didn't bother to ask me. Typical angel. I knew they'd risked everything to save humankind, but they still acted like dicks around us. I was still an officer of the law, even if I didn't make everyone follow the rules as strictly as an angel did. Sometimes there really were shades of gray on the spectrum of right and wrong. Good thing most of the angels had returned to the Realm of Celestial Light after they had ensured the war was over and the humans and supers were playing together nicely. "And gee, sorry I got the shit beaten out of me and couldn't answer your questions right away."

Kol smirked, a hint of red hellfire flickering in his eyes.

The angel glared at me. "Ms. Shaw—"

"Officer," I corrected, unable to stop myself even though it was smarter not to draw unnecessary attention to myself.

"Been a beat cop for five years," Kol said. "She's not a rookie."

The angel shot him a dirty look. "Could have fooled me. What made you think you, a human, could take that perp on your own?"

"I hadn't been given much of a choice." I bit the inside of my cheek, yanked my gaze away from him, and glared out the window. Clearly the angel was a part of Kol's team, probably the boss, and I wasn't an idiot. I didn't just jump into danger thinking I was invincible. I'd already learned that lesson the hard way. That was why I'd taken the advanced combat training for dealing with supers and discovered I could summon a bit of divine light with one of the combat spells — and yes, I realized there was a risk of someone discovering my true nature by my being able to summon any kind of magic. But after a disaster that had nearly gotten me and my partner killed four and a half years ago, I wanted every tool in the toolbox so that never happened again.

The training had only taught me that I hadn't wanted to go up against that thing. And while my nephilim nature let me heal a little faster than the average human, it wasn't *that* fast.

I was also smart enough to remember to not piss off JP agents, even if the buzz and the pain and nausea were making it hard to concentrate. Especially if that agent was an angel.

Outside, it was bright, but there was almost no sunlight streaming through the glass onto the floor. Which meant the sun was high and it was around noon. Almost six hours since I'd walked into the pharmacy and thought I could stall a junkie long enough for backup to arrive.

I drew in a breath, trying to calm myself, but pain sliced into me, forcing me to take shallow, quick gasps. "I was in the alley before I knew the perp was there," I said through gritted teeth. "I'd been working on getting a hopped-up junkie with a gun away from civilians when things went sideways."

"That was the second body in the alley?" the angel asked.

"Yeah." I shuddered, the memory of the monster's essence churning my stomach.

The angel looked like he was trying not to roll his eyes at me, probably thinking I was shuddering over the gore. If I was smart, I'd let him continue believing that, no matter how much it grated on my nerves. Honestly. I was smart.

"You know you're lucky to be alive," Kol said, his voice tender and sensual and drawing my attention back to him. He leaned even closer to me. The warmth in his eyes and the heat gently radiating from his body made my heart flutter.

My thoughts stalled and for a second there was only him, no pain, no angel, and no worry about being discovered, then everything evened out. I could think, and while both the buzz and pain were still there, they'd been relegated to the back of my mind.

"That better?" he asked.

"What did you do?"

"Nothing you need to worry about," the angel said before Kol could answer. "Now I need you to give a detailed description of the perpetrator. The other officers didn't get a great look at him, but you were up close."

"Him? It could have been female for all I knew. I'm not even sure what it was." And God, I'd had it pouring down my throat.

I shuddered again, making myself gasp in pain.

"Stop thinking about the bodies and concentrate on the killer," the angel snapped.

"I'm not thinking about the bodies," I snapped back. "I'm thinking about the smoke tentacle monster who cracked a man's head open with one swing and crushed someone to a pulp. I'm thinking how I have no idea how the hell I'm still here, how it didn't rip me apart or crush me or just beat me to death against the wall when it had me in its grasp or when I managed to shoot it."

The angel's eyes widened. "It held you? For longer than a few seconds at a time?"

"Yeah." Why hadn't it killed me?

Someone knocked on the door, opening it without waiting for an answer, and a massive man entered. He was bigger in every way than the angel, with shoulder-length light brown hair pulled back at the nape of his neck. The intensity in his dark eyes was breathtaking, captivating me as much as the demon beside me but in a different way, and his black calf-length duster made him look just as dangerous but more like a Wild West outlaw than a JP agent.

He moved to stand beside the angel, allowing another man behind him to enter, and my heart skipped a beat with a stuttering bleep on the heart monitor, my breath stolen.

"Marcus."

My thoughts stalled on his name. It had been four and a half years since we'd worked together. And four and a half since the biggest mistake of my life, which had gotten Marcus bitten by a werewolf, and the reason I'd taken the advanced training for supers.

There'd been a one in a million chance that he'd be susceptible to lycanthropy, so the odds had been in his favor that he'd gotten through my fuck-up okay, but he'd still demanded a transfer and left. He hadn't even cleaned out his locker or said anything to me. Not a word after the incident. But then I'd been the rookie who'd nearly gotten him killed. I wouldn't have wanted to talk to me, either.

His beautiful green eyes narrowed, a muscle in his jaw twitched, and the temperature in the room rose.

Yeah, four and a half years wasn't enough for forgiveness, and given that my empathy had instantly connected with it, his anger toward me was still strong. Not that I deserved forgiveness. The next time, if I hadn't outright killed him, he could actually have been infected or enspelled with something that would have taken his humanity and turned him into a super. And while there was a small percentage of the population who wanted that, most didn't, and Marcus hadn't struck me as someone who did.

He eased his lean-muscled body against the doorframe and crossed his arms, not even willing to step all the way into the room. God, he was just as handsome as I remembered, rich skin tone, piercing green eyes, his perpetual five o'clock shadow darkening his cheeks and making him mouth-wateringly sexy. Not to mention the way his gray T-shirt stretched across his muscular chest and his jeans hugged his narrow hips.

There'd been something between us. Hell, there'd been a whole lot of something. An attraction that had sizzled and stolen my breath the moment we'd first met. Every time we'd worked together the temperature had always been a little too warm, a little too sultry, whispering to me that he felt the connection, too. But he'd always kept his emotional and personal distance, and I'd messed everything up before fully establishing a working partnership, let alone the intimacy the attraction promised.

Except that sizzle was still there, instantly flaming a need for him within me that I thought had long been snuffed out, as if four and a half years and the biggest mistake of my life had never happened.

"Are we done here, Gideon?" he asked, his attention turning to the angel.

"No. We need to transfer Ms. Shaw—"

I glared at the angel. "Officer."

"—*Officer* Shaw," Gideon said. "We need to transfer her immediately to Operations. She's survived extended contact with the perp, which means we can examine her memories and get his essence."

My pulse picked up, the heart monitor revealing my fear. Shit. If I went into the Joined Parliament Operations Building and let them read my memories, they could learn the truth about me and I might never come out. "I'm a human. I can't sense magical essence."

"You don't have to," the Wild West guy said, his voice a deep rumble, his gaze jumping from me to the heart monitor and back again. "You're alive, so your memories are, too. The lethe demon will be able to sense details your mind isn't able to register."

"A memory demon?" I made my voice crack — I didn't have to work too hard at it — hoping it would make them think that was what I was afraid of, and then pulled the heart monitor's sensor from my finger.

The monitor squealed.

Marcus winced. But at me or the monitor? "She's clearly refusing consent."

"You saw what this thing can do," Gideon said, and a hint of emotion, fear and need, seeped through his chilly expression. The emotions weren't enough to shift my empathy from Marcus's anger, but it did surprise me. Angels were warriors who knew how to lock their feelings away and do what needed to be done. It made them efficient officers of the law, but not overly compassionate. Which meant whatever this monster was, whatever it had done, was enough to break through his icy emotional shield.

"She said she doesn't want to do it," Marcus said, his voice low.

Why was he trying to protect me? Except the moment I thought that, I was sure he wasn't protecting me, he was probably trying to get the hell away from me. Taking me to the Joined Parliament Operations Building meant spending more time with me and he'd made it perfectly clear after that horrible night that he wanted nothing to do with me. Which, if I was being honest, still hurt.

"Technically she hasn't refused, just had a panic attack about it." Kol turned off the screaming heart monitor, leaned forward again, and captured my hand. Heat pulsed from his grip like a heartbeat, sending a wash of warmth up my arm, adding to the heated emotion in the room that no one else could feel. "The lethe demon isn't that scary. It won't hurt. It's just like—"

"It's not consent if she doesn't have free will," Wild West guy said.

"Jeez," Kol said with a huff. "I'm not even doing *that*. I'm just trying to calm her."

Gideon's gaze dipped to our joined hands and Kol huffed again and released me.

"I've been a part of this team for over a year. When have I ever mixed business with pleasure?"

"There's always a first time," Gideon said.

"And you did insist on being the one to sit here until she woke up."

Wild West guy raised an eyebrow, clearly not believing Kol. "You've never been interested in watching over a damsel in distress before."

Marcus snorted. "She's hardly a damsel."

"Dude, you seriously need to have your eyes checked," Kol said. "And yes, I did, because this guy has dropped three supers in five days. We need to get on top of this."

And now that I knew they were after a serial killer, refusing to have my memories examined only made me look suspicious. I was a cop. I was supposed to want to do anything within the law to save people.

And I did. But I couldn't let them know the truth about me.

"It doesn't hurt. You'll even feel better about what... happened." A hint of sadness crept into Kol's gaze, and he slid it over my body, warming my insides and confirming that Kol had been there when they'd stripped me down and assessed my injuries. "And the lethe demon won't look at anything he's not supposed to."

Yeah, right. I didn't believe that for a second. Lethe demons fed on the emotions around memories. Technically they fed on the whole memory, but since they could survive on the emotion alone, the law prevented them from full consumption. Some people actually used them as a form of therapy to purge the emotions around horrific events, but that didn't mean this lethe demon wouldn't take a sip from other memories with strong emotions while in my head. And I had some strong emotions, particularly from my childhood, where I was terrified of someone learning what I was. Hell, I was still scared about that. I was just better able to compartmentalize it so I could hold down a job.

"Will you consent?" Gideon asked.

"I—" I was torn. Saying yes could save lives. It could also end mine.

"Will you?" Gideon's eyes narrowed, as if he was trying to will me into compliance without breaking his precious rules.

"Give her a moment to think about it," Wild West guy said. "She's probably still in shock."

Gideon jerked his attention to him. "We both know we don't have a moment. We've already wasted hours waiting for her to wake on the slim chance she has a lead. Well, she does." More emotion seeped into his voice. This felt like it was more than just an angel determined to find justice. It felt personal.

Gideon's gaze swept back to me, his pale eyes icy with determination. "I *can* get a court order."

The temperature in the room dropped, but I couldn't tell what it meant or who it came from. Useless stupid empathy.

"Whoa." Kol straightened, his expression shocked.

The angel pulled his phone from his pocket, likely to call a judge to get the order.

Marcus jerked a step into the room. "Gideon, really?"

"It's safer for everyone if you consent," Gideon said.

Except it certainly wasn't going to be safer for me. And now it pissed me off that he hadn't even given me a chance to say yes... not that I would have. Jeez, couldn't he wait until my head wasn't throbbing and I could think straight?

"Officer Shaw—" The pain in Gideon's eyes was shocking. This was deeply personal for him. "People are dying."

Which is what it came down to. Whatever had attacked me scared me to death. I didn't doubt that with its strength it could murder any number of powerful supers, maybe even an angel, and if it was on a killing spree and I could help stop it, I had to let the lethe demon see what had happened and get the monster's magical essence. The God damn angel in me couldn't let the murders continue even if it meant putting myself in danger.

Another shiver swept through me, slashing agony through my chest. Maybe I'd get lucky and the lethe demon wouldn't find out I was a nephilim. Without a doubt he was going to know that thing had poured down my throat.

Jeez, I wasn't even going to think about what these JP agents would do when they learned that. Would they consider me lucky or become suspicious because I wasn't dead? What it really came down to was that I couldn't live with myself if more people died.

Fine. God help me.

"I'll do it."

ESSIE

Marcus glared at me, the heat in the room growing, and I met his glare. He was just going to have to put up with me for however long it took for the lethe demon to reveal my secret. Then he could have a party when Gideon arrested me.

My insides churned at the thought. This was a nightmare. There wasn't a way out of this and I could be spending my last free minutes with a man who hated me.

"Let's get this over with," I said through gritted teeth.

"Kol, arrange Officer Shaw's release from the hospital and let Amiah and Yadveer know we're coming. Jacob, a word." Gideon jerked his chin to the door and Wild West man turned to leave. "Marcus, keep an eye on her."

Wonderful. Now I was going to be left alone with him and his rage, which was so strong it burned.

Kol, Gideon, and Jacob left, closing the door on me and Marcus. His presence filled the room, more masculine and powerful than I remembered, almost ferocious. There'd always been something overwhelming about Marcus. That had to be why I'd screwed up all those years ago. I'd been distracted by him. A part of me had wanted my attraction to him to be purely physical. The guy was hot with the sexy scruff along his jaw and those eyes that could capture my soul. But there'd been something else with him, something deeper. I couldn't put it into words then, and I couldn't now.

The buzz inside me bit into my skin and the heat in the room continued to grow. I fought the urge to push the sheet back to help cool down. I didn't know how little clothing I had on and I didn't want him to think my sudden rise in temperature was because I was attracted to him. Even if part of it was. Nothing was ever going to happen between us. I'd screwed up while working with him. We weren't friends, we didn't really know each other, and from his emotional heat it was clear he didn't want that to change.

His gaze dipped down my body, making the heat of desire billow within me. The sense of ferocious power about him grew. "Five broken ribs, a broken collarbone, and most likely a concussion," he growled.

"No wonder I feel like I want to throw up."

"Kol says you did. Nearly got his boots." A hint of a smile curled Marcus's lips. "Serves him right for trying to enthrall away your pain so he could interview you before the doctors dosed you with painkillers."

So Kol had tried to enthrall me. That meant his demonic nature gave him some kind of mind magic. Probably, given his looks, he was an incubus who fed on sexual energy. No wonder just looking at him turned me on. I shuddered, spiking pain through my chest, and gasped.

The muscles in Marcus's jaw twitched, his smile gone, and the heat turned humid. Sweat pricked on my forehead, under my arms, and between my breasts. Jeez, I was going to turn into a puddle and then evaporate with this heat. And God damn it, I needed a nicotine patch. It was so hard to think past everything. Easing the buzz would at least help. Easing the heat would as well.

Fine. To hell with how much clothing I did or didn't have on. I couldn't handle this on top of the pain and the nausea. I tugged the sheet up just past the knee of my left leg, praying that uncovering even this little bit of skin would help cool me.

Marcus's gaze leaped to the massive bruise on my knee and the temperature in the room jumped to sweltering. God, he was so mad at me.

"What the hell were you thinking in that alley?" he said, his voice low, his body tense.

"What?"

"What were you thinking?" His hands clenched. "Haven't you learned anything since you were a rookie?"

"This wasn't like what happened to us." No. I'd been smart this time and tried to run. The monster just hadn't let me.

"They said you didn't even have your sidearm."

"I hadn't started work yet."

"So you just decided to confront a super who could squash a human without breaking a sweat before you started your day? God, Essie—" He raked a hand through his black locks. "What is wrong with you?" Accusation and frustration filled his voice, making me feel just like I'd had that horrible night four and a half a years ago.

And I deserved his anger. I'd screwed up and he had a right to confront me about it whenever he was ready. I had called and left over a dozen apologies on his voice mail when I'd realized I wasn't going to see him again, but he'd never called back. And even if he had, I could never have made it up to him for almost infecting him with lycanthropy and nearly killing him. The problem was, if he'd returned my calls and demanded answers, I wouldn't have had any for him, just like I didn't have any now.

"Well?" he growled. "You're going to get yourself killed."

"You mean I'm going to get someone else killed."

"That's not what I said."

The door opened and Kol entered, pushing a wheelchair. "A chariot for the lady. Oh, and some pants." The incubus held up a pair of green scrub pants.

Marcus held his glare at me, as if daring me to say something. But I didn't know what to say. There wasn't anything I could say. All I could do was not screw up so badly with any other partner.

"Fine." With a growl, he turned and shoved past Kol. "I'll get the car." He strode from the room, taking his ferocious heat with him and leaving me cold and a little empty.

"Don't mind him. It's just getting close to that time of the month," Kol said. "Makes him ornery. I'll go get the nurse to help you change." Kol flashed a wicked grin. "Unless you want me to stay?"

As much as a part of me really wanted him to stay... "The nurse, please. But I think you've forgotten something."

"Clothes and a wheelchair. Pretty sure that's everything." The playfulness softened out of his expression and turned to sympathy. "The clothes you arrived in were covered in blood and the docs cut them off you. I didn't think you'd want them back."

"I don't. But I could use a shirt." I didn't want to be walking around in a hospital gown for who knew how long.

"Until Amiah mends your broken collarbone, I'm pretty sure you don't want to be pulling on a shirt. Trust me." He shuddered and a hint of darkness clouded his expression before he flashed a heart-pounding smile. "But that's your first stop at Operations, so you'll be out of the gown soon enough."

He hurried out the door and I contemplated sitting up. The bed was at a bit of an angle, but I wasn't sure if I was forward enough for my battered body to pull me up. If it hurt to breathe, it was going to hurt sitting up, and I only had one good arm to help me.

A nurse entered, her face flushed and her eyes bright, and I couldn't help but wonder if that was what I looked like every time Kol talked to me. She helped me slide on the pants — and yep, I'd lost my underwear. Then she sat me up so my legs hung over the side of the bed and unhooked the IV from my hand. My body screamed in agony, every gasping breath as shallow as I could make it. The room spun and the contents of my queasy stomach sloshed, but I managed to not pass out or throw up. Somehow I fought through the pain of just moving and got into the wheelchair. God, I had no idea how I was going to manage getting into a car, let alone getting out of it or anything else.

The nurse helped me put on my running shoes and turned me to push me out as Jacob opened the door, as if he'd known we were ready to leave. Gideon stood a few feet away, gave a tight nod, and headed to the elevator without waiting for a response. Jacob dismissed the nurse and took over pushing me, while Kol bounded down the hall toward us, leaving a group of nurses at the floor's station desk flushed and excited.

Gideon rolled his eyes. Not the response I expected. But then, if they'd been working together for over a year as Kol had said, the icy angel would have had to accept the incubus's nature or kicked him off the team.

The elevator doors opened. We took it down to the parking garage, where Marcus waited in a running chunky dark gray SUV.

This wasn't going to be fun.

I tried to take in a deep breath to steady myself and was painfully reminded that a deep breath was a terrible idea. The pain sent the parking garage spinning and my stomach churning. *Oh, Lord, was it too late to go back and ask for stronger painkillers or hell, something to just knock me out?*

"Get the door," Gideon said to Kol, then he bent, slid one arm under my legs and the other across my back, and picked me up. His strong arms held me with ease and cradled me against his muscular chest. The scent of springtime enveloped me, the air after a rainstorm, fresh-cut grass, and sun-warmed skin. His scent was warm and comforting. There was nothing frozen about it.

He set me in a seat in the middle row as gently as he'd picked me up, a stark contrast to how he'd talked to me earlier. Of course he hadn't said anything to me or looked at me, so he wasn't acting completely out of character. He took the front passenger seat ahead of me, while Kol slid into the seat beside me. Jacob folded up the wheelchair, put it in the back, and took a seat beside it, then Marcus drove us out of the parking garage, his emotions simmering around me again.

The hospital wasn't far from the Supers' Quarter, but it didn't cater to supers. They had their own facility, which was probably a good thing. I couldn't imagine the average human doctor or nurse trying to help a vampire or werewolf or even demon in medical distress. They might be living out in the open now, but that didn't mean they were any less powerful or dangerous. And while some humans were adjusting well to this new norm, most hadn't. Just under a quarter of a century had passed since everything humankind knew had been turned upside down. Being happy that your new next door neighbor only came out at night and preferred a diet of O negative was still a long way away.

Of course, the supers weren't thrilled to be living beside neighbors who started growing wolf's bane or installing silver door handles, and even adding all the supernatural species together, they were still a small percentage of the earth's population and outnumbered by the humans — the very reason they'd been living in secret for so long. So the Joined Parliament had expropriated areas at the edges of a few of the largest cities and created neighborhoods catering to supers. Most had at least one high rise apartment/office building with UV filtering glass and a park covered with a UV filtering glass canopy for vampires, as well as dense forested areas for shifters to release their beasts and help their children deal with the first five or so years of their transition.

Not all members of the supernatural community lived in the Quarter, but most did, and it was enough to maintain a peace between humans and supers. Of course, it hadn't hurt that the supers had come to humanity's defense when half of angelkind had tried to eradicate us.

What the members of the Joined Parliament hadn't expected was for the Supers' Quarters to regularly draw human visitors — the few of us who'd embraced the idea that supers lived among us — and an eclectic mix of businesses had moved into our city's Quarter, catering to all kinds. For those humans who were brave or didn't care about the Supers' dangerous natures, the area was a pretty happening place and had a rocking nightlife. Or so I'd been told.

I'd never crossed through the park surrounding the district, which ensured a clear separation between humans and supers, as agreed upon by the Parliament. I hadn't wanted to run into one of the few angels living in Union City.

So much for that.

Now I was going into the heart of angel central where every angel in town — thankfully not many, but still every angel — lived and worked. The Joined Parliament Operations Building.

Marcus turned a corner and headed to the park at the end of the street. The delineation from towering residential high rise and park ring was almost shocking, as if the city had just stopped at the edge of a forest. No series of strip malls leading out of town or farmers' fields. Just blam, mature maples and oaks and blue spruce right up to the chain link fences at the edge of the last properties. But that was part of the magic that made the Supers' Quarter. I didn't know what super had made the trees rapidly mature, but my mother said that within six years, the park ring had looked as if it had always been there.

Sunlight filtered through the canopy above, sending bands of light cutting across the road and into the SUV for a few minutes, and then we were through and the metropolis continued. This had been an older part of town, since the city officials hadn't been willing to let the Parliament expropriate newly built properties, so most of the buildings didn't tower as high as the rest of the city. Artistic scrollwork and wide ledges ornamented the façades of the buildings on either side of the street. The bricks were stained with age, but modern signs hung above the doors of the ground floor businesses and the roads and sidewalks were in good condition.

People drove, rode bicycles, and walked up and down the sidewalk, coming or going from stores, window shopping, and just looking everyday normal. Save for the few demons with horns, onyx skin, or tails, and the odd person with features that didn't look quite human, this could have been any street in the downtown core.

Marcus turned at the first intersection and pulled into the short driveway of a converted 19th century two-story warehouse with a five-story high rise added to the back. The big garage door ahead of us rose on silent tracks and we drove inside, parking in the first spot. There were two other SUVs parked a few spots down as well as about two dozen other vehicles, mostly sedans and hatchbacks.

Much to my surprise, Gideon picked me up and eased me back into the wheelchair, his fresh, warm scent wrapping around me again. Not surprising, though, that as soon as I was seated, he marched away, expecting everyone else to follow.

"I'll go check on Yadveer," Marcus said, also storming away.

The temperature in the garage dropped, the air cooling but still holding a hint of dampness. I hadn't realized how hot Marcus had been making me feel until he was gone, and, if I was being honest with myself, the heat was from both his mood and his body.

"And I'll find you that shirt." Kol darted after Gideon and Marcus, and I was left with Jacob, once again my chauffeur, pushing me toward the door.

One of the chair's wheels squeaked. I hadn't noticed it in the hospital, but in the quiet of the garage it was nerve-gratingly clear. That, along with the buzz, the fear of being discovered, and Jacob's silence, and I was squirming by the time we reached the door only a few feet away.

"So... ah... have you been a JP agent for long?"

"Since its inception," he said in his soft rumble. He hit the button to automatically open the door and we waited for it to slowly... draw... open, then he wheeled me into a long institutional hall with white walls, a frosted-glass sliding door about twenty feet down, and pale gray flooring.

Silence again.

The buzz continued to nip at me and my nerves tightened until I wasn't sure if it was the concussion nauseating me or not, and the squeaky wheel cr-creaked, cr-creaked, cr-creaked—

Oh, my God! This was a terrible idea. I needed a distraction and damned if I wasn't going to force Jacob to be one.

"What makes a—" I had no idea what kind of super he was. "—a super become an agent?"

"I fought in the war. It was a natural transition."

"I'm not sure soldier to investigator is a natural transition." Sure, in the case of being an agent of the Joined Parliament, it wasn't as much of a leap as a human soldier becoming a detective, since often criminal supers were more aggressive than humans and military training would likely be used more often. But I was trying to distract myself before I went insane.

Jacob shrugged. "It's as natural as anything else about me."

I wasn't sure if that was self-deprecation or a clue about the kind of super he was. If he wasn't a natural super, that meant he'd been made, and the pool of possibilities shrank to a shifter of some kind, a witch who'd made a demon-deal, and a vampire. There were a few other kinds of supers that could be made instead of born, but those were the top three.

I tried to get a better look at his face, but couldn't turn my head far enough with the agony of my broken collarbone. With his bulky size and tanned complexion, I'd guess shifter. I'd heard that the JP liked to make their teams diverse to help ease tensions among the various communities. Marcus was clearly the human on the team — as rare and dangerous as it was for a powerless human to be on a JP team — Kol the demon, Gideon the angel, which left Jacob.

Yeah. He had to be the shifter.

We reached a T-intersection, and Jacob pushed me around the corner and through the first door on the right into an office. The room was packed with books and papers and plants with just enough room for the wheelchair and Jacob. An angel sat behind a desk covered with paperwork, the papers and folders and notepads piled on top, on the floor against the legs, and on the chair beside it. She could have been Gideon's sister with her long blond hair, sharp blue eyes, and sculpted features, and a part of me wondered if I'd been told a lie all my life and all angels really were blond-haired, blue-eyed beauties. But then that would have made my mother a liar. She'd said my father's hair had been brown with a hint of copper if the sun hit it just the right way and his eyes were brown with flecks of gold. And while I had the brown hair with a hint of copper, my brown eyes were just brown. Boring and thankfully very human.

The angel closed the file she was reading and her expression turned icy. "Officer Esther Shaw."

"I'll wait outside," Jacob said.

"No need." The angel stood and strode around the desk. "I'm Amiah, and Marcus Diaz has told me all about you."

Just great.

ESSIE

AMIAH CROSSED HER ARMS AND STOOD JUST OUT OF REACH, LOOKING DOWN at me. "The humans agreed to protocols regarding supernatural criminals. This is at least the second time you've ignored that, Officer Shaw." She raised an eyebrow, but I didn't get a sense of angel iciness about her, more of an anger under tight control. The temperature in the room didn't change, so under very tight control. "If I looked at your service file, would I find more disregard for protocol?"

"No." And the incident with today's monster hadn't been on purpose — neither really had been the one with Marcus. But I was smart enough not to say that out loud. That would only start a fight, and I didn't want to draw any more attention to myself than necessary. What was it with everyone assuming I was stupid enough to think I could have taken that thing on by myself? Or at all?

Jacob cleared his throat and Amiah's attention jumped to him. "We're in a bit of a hurry. If you would?"

"She doesn't deserve this," Amiah said, but she stepped forward and clasped my broken shoulder. Lightning shot through me, white hot agony. It turned the buzz into an inferno, screaming in a dissonant resonance to Amiah's magic.

I clenched my teeth against the grating vibrations and every muscle jerked taut. It was like that time we had to go through Taser training and each of us had to experience what over 1,200 volts felt like surging through our body. I couldn't move and couldn't breathe. There was only agony and my whirling thoughts. And at the forefront was the fear that somehow, by using her healing magic on me, Amiah would know I was a nephilim.

Then she jerked her hand back. I sagged in the wheelchair, my muscles twitching, but was unable to tell if the agony of broken bones was gone. The nausea certainly wasn't, and now my buzz was stronger and the room was spinning.

"Healing her like that wasn't necessary," Jacob said, his voice low.

Amiah strode back to her chair behind the desk and sat. "You said you were in a hurry."

"Gideon wouldn't have been impressed if you'd damaged her mind while fixing her bones."

"I didn't." She flipped open the file she'd been reading. "Now get her out of my office."

A hint of a growl rumbled from Jacob, but he pulled me out into the hall and shut Amiah's office door.

"She shouldn't have done that," he said, leaning closer to me. "Are you okay?"

Even with only seeing him from the corner of my eye, the intensity radiating from him made me shiver.

The hall twisted, but the pain in my chest was gone.

"I think I just need a moment."

"You can have a moment when you're done with Yadveer, the lethe demon," Gideon said. He stood in a doorway at the end of the hall.

I opened my mouth to protest then snapped it shut. The sooner I dealt with this, the sooner I could get out of there. Maybe if things moved quickly enough, Gideon and everyone else wouldn't notice the truth about me. This monster was killing supers and if the crack in Gideon's icy angel emotions was an indication of anything, capturing this monster was personal.

And maybe I had nothing to worry about. Maybe I didn't have enough angel in me for anyone to notice. Amiah hadn't, and I was sure she'd have said something if she had. Maybe the lethe demon wouldn't either.

Which only provided a stronger incentive for hurrying through this. In and out and I could go back to being a beat cop in my mostly human neighborhood.

Jacob pulled the wheelchair back, drawing me closer to him and making my long hair brush against his clothes. "She can have a moment."

Gideon stiffened. "Which of us do you think he's hunting next? Prudence and Javan could have been a coincidence, but now Paul is dead. That's a pattern."

"And we won't get anything if her mind shuts down," Jacob growled. "You've more patience than this."

Gideon gave him a withering look, only adding to my impression that this investigation was personal.

Here was hoping that would be enough to distract him and dismiss me.

I drew in a shallow breath to try to steady the whirling room and confirmed that yes, I could breathe without pain.

"Let's just get this done." I considered standing and walking the distance between us but thought better of it. I didn't want to collapse halfway there and draw out my stay at angel central.

I glanced up at Jacob. His expression was pinched, but he gave a tight nod and pushed me into a dimly lit room, past Gideon standing near the door. It was twice the size of Amiah's office, but the walls, floor, and ceiling were painted black, and it didn't have any furniture except for four long benches, one tucked tight against each wall.

Kol and Marcus sat on the one to my right, and the temperature plummeted as my empathy locked onto someone, probably Marcus. He still looked angry, ready to start a brawl, his body tense, his muscles bunched, and his rage had probably swung from heated fury to cold and calculating.

Beside him, Kol leaned against the wall with a folded shirt in his lap, his posture relaxed and sensual, but a sense of tension radiated from him as well.

An elderly man sat in the center on a black pillow, the fabric satiny, reflecting the illumination from the single-bulb light fixture above him. Shadows accentuated his lined and weathered features and a prick of red hellfire glowed in his dark eyes.

"Sit." He pointed to the floor in front of him.

My insides lurched at the idea that I was actually going to go through with this. Not that I had much of a choice, but inevitability didn't necessarily do anything for nerves. And as much as I'd tried to fool myself that if I rushed through this no one would notice me, I doubted it would work.

I unhooked the sling, slid my arm out, and grabbed the wheelchair arms to help ease myself from the chair to the floor in front of the lethe demon. The room still spun, but not nearly as much as before, and I tried to focus on that, not the fear thrumming through me.

He held out his hand. "Give me your hand."

"It's a very recent memory." The words blurted out before I could stop them from revealing my fear that this demon could see things I didn't want him to see.

"Marcus made that very clear." He extended his hand a little closer to me, and I could feel his demonic heat radiating from his skin.

Behind the demon, Marcus shifted on the bench. Now he looked uncomfortable on top of itching for a fight. I'd never seen him like that before. When I'd been his partner, he'd always been in control. His control hadn't been rigid like an angel's, but it had been there. I'd always felt like he'd be able to handle anything. At least until I'd screwed up and we'd ended up in a fight for our lives with four werewolves on a night of the full moon, when they were the most volatile. Now he looked like he was barely holding it together.

"Your hand."

I wrenched my attention back to Yadveer and took his too-warm hand before I could change my mind. His fingers clasped mine and heat trickled over my wrist and up my arm.

It seeped across my chest, up my neck, and into my head, soothing me. It wrapped around me like a blanket, soft and fuzzy, whispering into my soul and taking me to that warm, lazy place between awake and asleep. I lay on a blanket in my mom's backyard. Dappled sunlight, dancing among the leaves of the maple tree above, warmed me, and a gentle breeze caressed my cheeks and forearms. Beside me was a thin chapter book, the kind I had started reading in first grade, but the cover was out of focus. I couldn't tell what I was reading.

I frowned. Was that part of the concussion? It hadn't made anything else out of focus, and the leaves above and the weave of the blanket were perfectly clear.

So why the book—?

Because that detail had faded from memory.

I jerked up and my mom's backyard rippled, as if it were a reflection in water.

No. This wasn't right. The lethe demon was too far back. Way too far back.

"You don't get to take this one." And oh, God, in a few minutes my mother was going to walk onto the deck and tell me we were moving again. A team of angels hunting the last of the fallen angels had established a temporary base in our small town and we had to leave.

My pulse jerked into a rapid tattoo. I had to leave this memory. Now.

My mom had always been honest with me about who I was and why she did the things she did. My angelic nature had to have come up in that conversation. And I wasn't going to try to remember if it did or not and risk Yadveer seeing it.

"Get out." Think of something else.

I heard the back door slide open and my mom's footsteps on the deck.

"I said get out!"

Everything went black. The room flickered into view, Yadveer clutching my hand, eyes closed and brow furrowed in concentration, and Marcus's cold rage stinging my skin. Then darkness jerked me back and I crashed into the alley wall. Blood was everywhere, more than what I was sure I'd seen that morning, as if my subconscious had glommed onto that detail and exaggerated it.

The robber screamed and the monster broke his neck and shattered his skull, the sound sickening, emphasized like the blood.

I jerked away to get the hell out of there, tripped, was grabbed, tossed, and slammed into the alley wall. Then the monster seized me, its viscous smoke thicker, stickier than I remembered, the darkness and power oozing evil. Its tentacles squeezed agony through my chest and it poured its essence into me, drowning me with its darkness. I fought to breathe, gasped a trickle of air, and choked on its smoke again.

Reliving that terrible moment crystallized the horror into sharp detail. I was on fire, but I couldn't tell if it was from pain or emotion or something else. My lungs screamed for air, my body grew heavy, unconsciousness threatening to take me.

It felt like an eternity before I wrenched the revolver up and fired, and another eternity before I fired again. I heaved in the monster's grasp. I had to get free and get it out of me. I had to get—

Something cracked against my cheek and pain stung my face. I opened my eyes and found myself lying on the floor. I must have collapsed and smacked my cheek on the black tiles and Yadveer hadn't tried to catch me. He clutched his throat as if he struggled to breathe and stared at me in horror. If he'd fed off my emotions, he was probably close to having a panic attack. Except I was still terrified, my pulse still racing, so the emotions were still in me. In fact, I think I was more scared now than I'd been before.

Two sets of booted feet hurried across the floor, but one set stopped before reaching me.

The other set drew close and Kol knelt beside me, placing a hand on my shoulder. Warmth slipped into me but it didn't ease the panic clutching my heart.

The stopped set of feet shifted away. That had to be Marcus. He'd been sitting beside Kol and had jumped up to help me, then had thought better of it. I couldn't blame him, but a small part of me was disappointed.

"Did you get his essence?" Gideon asked from behind me.

"It doesn't fit with what she saw." Yadveer's voice trembled. "I can't make sense of it."

"I'm not doing that again so you can figure it out." No way in hell.

"You shouldn't have to," Kol said, helping me sit.

"Shouldn't? That doesn't inspire confidence." And I didn't want to risk Yadveer seeing any of my other memories.

Gideon strode toward us. "Show me."

Yadveer pressed his palms to Gideon's temples. The angel's eyes rolled back and he gasped, coughed, choked on something, and gasped again.

I pushed away from Kol and stood, needing to get farther away from my memory even though I wasn't reliving it with Gideon. My stomach churned, the clinging thick smoke too fresh in my mind, and my buzz began to roar under my skin.

Gideon jerked away from Yadveer and his gaze jumped to me. His eyes were dark as if a cloud had passed over their summer-sky blue and dimmed their angelic glow, and his icy demeanor was arctic.

His intensity drilled into me and my pulse froze. I couldn't tell if he knew I was a nephilim or if the danger radiating from him was because the monster had tried to drown me with its essence.

I staggered back a step, needing to put more distance between us, but he jerked forward and his hand clamped around my biceps. Pain burned into my skin where he held me.

"What was that?"

I wrenched against his grip but he held tight and the burning intensified.

"You're hurting her," Marcus growled.

"I'm not holding her that tight."

And he wasn't. So why the hell did I feel like I was being branded with a hot poker?

"Why didn't that wraith possess you?" Gideon asked. "And why didn't it have a wraith's essence?"

"How the hell am I supposed to know?" I yanked at his grip again. "For the love of God, if you don't let go I'm going to start screaming in pain or pass out."

"You shouldn't have an injury this painful," Jacob said. "Amiah can't pick and choose what she heals. Her magic heals the worst first, even if she doesn't complete the healing."

Gideon grabbed my wrist with his free hand, keeping hold of me, and yanked up the sleeve of my hospital gown. An angry red welt in the shape of a sigil looked like it had been burned on the inside of my left biceps, just above my elbow.

"What is that?" I asked, my voice cracking.

Kol's eyes widened. "Is that an angelic mating brand?"

"A mating what?" Oh, God. Was it something an angel got when they were ready to have a family? Did this give me away as a nephilim, since my essence clearly wasn't that of an angel?

"It's rare," Jacob said, drawing closer from his position at the door.

"It's a mark that binds an angel's soul to another soul, mating them. It's usually between angels, but it can be between an angel and a non-angel," Kol said.

My thoughts stuttered. I was already mated? How the hell was I already mated? And with who?

"The connection is deep," Kol said, "intimate. It can make an angel do crazy things to protect their mate."

"That's because their souls are so intertwined they're compelled to protect each other," Jacob said.

"It only looks like a compulsion to those who've had no experience with it." Gideon glared at Jacob. "If you're in the bond, you don't feel compelled at all. It's beautiful."

"We've seen differently during the war," Jacob said.

"That couldn't have been a true bond, or it had been so twisted with evil intent that it was permanently warped. But this..." Gideon's attention turned back to my arm. "I know it's a mating brand, I can sense it, but the magic feels wrong. It doesn't even feel like that twisted brand we came across during the war," he said to Jacob. "Not to mention a true mating brand would be gold, not red."

My gaze locked on the painful welt. I had to get rid of this. I couldn't be bonded with anyone. I couldn't have anything to do with the supernatural world.

"So what does this mean?" Marcus asked. "There wasn't anything in her chart indicating she had the brand before, and you," he said to Gideon, "are you branded?"

"I would have felt it if I was," Gideon said.

"The only other angel she's been in contact with is Amiah and Essie isn't her type. So does this mean our killer, this wraith, has an angel's magical essence?" Marcus asked. "And did he brand her?"

Gideon's gaze grew unfocused and he frowned. "According to Officer Shaw's memory, he did."

ESSIE

"That thing branded me?" This wasn't happening. It couldn't be happening. The words whirled in my head over and over again. "It can't be true." I couldn't be caught up in a supernatural anything. I had to get out of there before Gideon realized what I was, before—

God, no. No no no no.

I staggered back a step, but Gideon's grip on my wrist tightened, keeping me captive.

"Just take a breath," he said. "We can protect you."

"Protect me?" From an intimate magical connection with a monster that would compel me to protect it? "I want you to get rid of it."

A shadow passed over Gideon's expression, just a flicker but I saw it and my throat tightened.

The racing, screaming panic inside me froze into icy fear. "You can't get rid of it."

"Of course we can get rid of it," Marcus said.

The muscles in Gideon's jaw flexed.

Jacob drew closer, but his attention wasn't locked on the brand like everyone else's. It was on my face and the intensity of his gaze held me captive, as if he were trying to help me fight my panic. "It's not a true brand, so anything is possible."

"Don't give her false hope," Gideon said. "This is an angel brand. The only way this kind of soul bond is broken is when one member of the bond dies. And even then the remaining half usually dies soon after or goes insane. Our best bet to help her is to capture the wraith and magically put it in permanent forced hibernation. It would still have a connection to you, but you might be able to have a normal life with it."

"Might?" This was getting worse and worse. The freeze around my panic cracked, but I mentally clung to the ice. I wasn't sure if an angel's icy demeanor was genetic or not, but I was going to pretend it was. I couldn't let my fear continue to control me. I needed to think. And as much as I wanted to just run and scream and curl into a ball and hide, that wouldn't help me.

Jeez. Some cop I was, panicking the moment something terrifying happened.

Except that wasn't true. If I wasn't the victim, I'd still be calm and collected and working on a solution. Because that would have meant I'd have been able to leave the supernatural world whenever I wanted to.

Now? I was pretty sure even if Gideon could capture this wraith and put it in hibernation, he was going to be watching me for the rest of my life.

Which could end sooner rather than later if Gideon's team found that monster and was forced to kill it.

"How hard is it to capture a wraith?" I asked, but I had a sneaking suspicion I wasn't going to like the answer.

"Challenging at the best of times," Kol said. "But this one has ripped apart two angels and a weretiger. That's more powerful than any wraith I've heard of."

"And his essence doesn't feel like a wraith's," Gideon said. "He's enhanced somehow."

"Yeah, with an angel's magic," Marcus said, his attention still locked on the brand.

"I'll be blunt with you," Jacob said, his voice a soft rumble. "It would be easier to kill it."

"We're not killing it," Marcus growled. "We just need a plan."

"We can't even find it," Kol said. "How are we going to *capture* it?"

"You said the brand creates an intimate connection." God, this was the stupidest thing I'd ever done, but I was in the middle of this whether I wanted to be or not, and I didn't do well just sitting on the sidelines. "Can the wraith use the connection to find me?" And I still wasn't convinced it was a wraith.

The temperature in the room turned frigid and Marcus jerked closer. "You're not using yourself as bait."

A hint of frost tickled the back of my hand and I tugged against Gideon's grasp, hoping he'd release me before he noticed it.

His grip remained firm. Shit. "I agree with Marcus. I can't endanger you like that."

"Except he's branded her for a reason," Jacob said. "He's going to come after her. We should use that to our advantage."

"We might do a lot of things, but we don't use humans as bait." Gideon shifted close to me, pulling me against him as if he wanted to protect me. Heat from his body warmed my back and the frost on my hand evaporated. His scent wrapped around me and for a moment I wanted to forget who I was and who he was and take comfort in his presence.

But that was just as terrible an idea as volunteering to be bait.

I turned to face him, forcing myself to put a few feet between us. "You saw that thing." A hint of panic shuddered in my chest. "You felt it. It's going to keep killing and it's going to come after me. The smart move is to pick the battleground and have the advantage."

"She's right," Jacob said. "And she's not completely helpless. She has some training."

"The Union City PD isn't trained to deal with a super like this," Gideon said. "She didn't even know it was a wraith."

"That's why I'm just the bait." I bit back a huff of frustration. "I'm not spending the rest of my life under this thing's influence. Come up with a better plan and I'll happily oblige."

Gideon glared at me and I refused to break eye contact. It was a dangerous game, but I was already on his radar and bonded with a monster. My situation couldn't get much worse.

Light radiated from his eyes, white, crystalline. Icy. A shiver swept over me and his gaze dipped to my arm, the brand covered again by the sleeve of the hospital gown. I had no idea what he was thinking and I had no idea what he saw when he looked at me.

Please let it be a normal, boring human.

But not quite so normal that he thought I couldn't handle this... as much as I worried that *I* couldn't handle this.

"Fine. But we're not doing this without protection." He released me and strode from the room.

"I'll, ah..." Kol shifted from foot to foot, looking at a loss for what to do and only knowing that he needed to take action. "I'll get a room made up."

"I'll arrange for proper clothes and your personal affects to be sent over from the hospital," Jacob said.

"I can go get my purse myself." I wasn't helpless. And I really needed a patch to ease the buzz.

"It's safer if you stay here for now," Jacob said. The intensity in his gaze softened. "This won't be for long. You'll get back to your normal life soon enough."

He, Kol, and Yadveer left. The moment the door clicked closed Marcus turned on me.

"Bait?" he growled, the room's temperature flickering between hot and cold. "Now I know you're crazy."

"I didn't see you coming up with a better idea." I turned to leave and catch up to Kol or Jacob. I wasn't going to be able to figure out what Marcus's emotions meant, and I didn't want to deal with hot flashes.

He grabbed my wrist and yanked me around to face him, but I jerked free and opened the door.

With a growl, he slapped his hand against the door and slammed it shut. I turned to face him and he leaned in and slapped his other hand against the door, capturing me with his body, his arms on either side of my head.

The temperature jumped to sweltering and stayed there, a stark contrast to the cold metal door pressing against the parts of my skin exposed by the hospital gown. His clear green gaze locked with mine and a shiver of desire slid down my spine. The sizzling attraction between us burned so hot it made my breath catch in my throat. My thoughts stuttered, going blank. All I could think about was his lithe-muscled body and how close he came to pressing it against me, closer than he'd ever done before. Jeez, something about Marcus Diaz made me lose all sense.

His breath caressed my cheeks, and I bit back a groan. I had no doubt he knew how he affected me. He wouldn't be standing so close if he wasn't trying to use it against me. Gideon had already agreed to the plan and left. I was pretty sure that meant the discussion was over. But that meant if Marcus wanted to get rid of me, the only way to do that was to get me to back out of the plan.

Except without the plan, the wraith was free to murder more supers and come after me.

"Why do you do that?" he said, his voice low, dangerous. His pupils dilated and a hint of humidity thickened the air. "Why do you throw yourself into the most dangerous situations?"

"I only did that once." Guilt twisted in my chest. Over four years, and I still hadn't forgiven myself for that. "I learned my lesson."

"It doesn't look like that to me."

"Do you honestly think I wanted this?"

"I think you don't consider the consequences." He leaned closer, his lips curling back in a snarl. "And now you're branded by a serial killer."

"Yeah, no shit." I needed to get out of this conversation. If he got any closer, I was going to scream or kiss him, and both would draw unwanted attention from the rest of the team.

I planted my hands on his sculpted chest and shoved.

He didn't move and his snarl deepened.

"God damn it, Marcus. What do you want?" And a tiny voice hoped he'd say me.

"For you to gain some sense of self-preservation." His breath came fast and he squeezed his eyes shut, as if struggling for control. But over what? I had no idea. "Let the team find the wraith. Don't use yourself as bait." His eyes opened and while his snarl was gone, the sense that there was something ferocious inside him remained and all that power was focused on me. "We can't protect you if you do."

"I know that."

"*I* can't protect you."

My pulse stuttered and a mix of emotions churned within me. I wanted that to mean he felt the same attraction to me as I did to him, but I also feared that. "Marcus—"

A phone rang and Marcus jerked away, turning his back to me and pulling his phone from his pocket. He answered, gave a grunt of affirmation, and hung up.

"Your room is ready," he said, the sense of ferocity vanishing, leaving him tense and suddenly cool toward me. He jerked his chin to the door. "I'll take you."

"Sure." I opened the door and stepped into the hall.

Marcus stalked past me and headed deeper into the building, his walk liquid and powerful, as if there were something dangerous inside him. His stride had always been confident, but there was something more to it now, something that matched the ferocity I'd just seen. If he'd transferred right away and became an agent of the Joined Parliament, then what I was seeing was four years of experience on a job that was seriously dangerous for a human.

We reached an elevator just past the threshold between the original warehouse and the new high rise addition, and took it up to the fifth floor. The door opened into a plain hall with a utilitarian gray carpet, cream-colored walls, and wooden doors stained a dark chestnut. Each door had a card reader like the kind found in hotels, and the third door down on the right had a card sitting in the holder.

Marcus used the card to unlock the door and strode inside. The room looked very much like a hotel room done in blue-grays, creams, and sky-blue accent pieces. It had a door leading to a bathroom, a queen-sized bed against the left wall — the T-shirt Kol had picked up for me lying at the foot — and a panel TV on the wall across from it. A small seating area — also against the left wall — of couch, chair, and coffee table lay beyond that. Behind the chair stood a massive window that took up almost the entire back wall, the curtains drawn open revealing a spectacular view of the park ringing the Supers' Quarter.

"Jacob will be up in a bit with your purse and clean clothes." He tossed the keycard onto the bed. "There's a cafeteria on the first floor. Continue past the elevator and you won't miss it."

"Thank you."

His gaze jumped to me then jerked away and slid over the room, looking anywhere but at me. "Gideon doesn't like to drag things out, so be ready to go within the hour."

"Go?"

"If he means the kind of protection I think he means, you'll need to come with us. The witch who makes the best protection charms doesn't leave her apartment."

He left, the door clicking shut behind him and the temperature dropping to normal. Which now felt chilly.

I hugged myself, trying to fend off the cold and all my other churning emotions. The sun still sat high in the sky and the clock on the bedside table read just after 2 p.m., so I hadn't spent a lot of time having my memory read. My stomach growled, reminding me I hadn't eaten since that morning and I was more hungry than nauseous now.

I contemplated heading down to the cafeteria while still in my backless hospital gown and borrowed scrub pants. To hell with what anyone thought. I'd just had the shit beaten out of me by a wraith and now had the monster's brand on my arm. Marcus already thought I was crazy. It didn't matter if everyone else here thought I was, too.

Except I wasn't sure if Marcus really thought I was crazy or not. One minute he was yelling at me, the next he was so close the attraction, or whatever it was between us, set my nerves tingling... and he'd still been yelling at me.

This wasn't the same Marcus Diaz who'd been my partner. He was more volatile now, more intense, and that turned a part of me on even more. Not that anything would or could ever come of that. It couldn't have happened before because we'd been partners and I'd almost gotten him killed. And it certainly couldn't happen now because he was fully immersed in all things supernatural, and I was going to get as far away from this as possible.

Once this thing with the wraith was dealt with.

If this thing with the wraith could ever be dealt with.

How the hell had things gone so wrong? One minute everything had been perfect, and now...

Now I was going to pull myself together and deal with the situation. Maybe if I focused on that, I'd be able to ignore the fear still whirling inside me. I couldn't do anything about what had happened. All I could do was try to fix it. And that meant I needed to clean up, put on proper clothes, and grab a bite to eat.

I didn't know how long Jacob would take getting my things, so I decided to have a shower first. If what Marcus had said was true, Gideon would want to head out soon and the angel didn't strike me as the kind of guy who'd wait for me to have a shower first.

The bathroom was decorated to match the bedroom with a mix of cream, gray, and blue tiles, plus chrome fixtures. The shower-tub combo took up one side, while the vanity and toilet took the other. It wasn't fancy, but it was better and fresher than the no-tub shower-stall-only bathroom in my one bedroom apartment.

Folded white towels in a variety of sizes sat on a rack on the back wall, between the toilet and the tub, and a full complement of toiletries were displayed on the vanity, including a toothbrush and toothpaste. Thank goodness, because while I'd been ignoring it, my mouth felt gross. In fact, my whole body felt gross.

And I looked gross. My long brown locks were disheveled and not in the sexy 'I just had sex' kind of disheveled. More in the 'I just went toe to toe with a wind storm and lost.' While pain didn't scream through me any more, I still looked like I'd lost a fight, except now it looked like I'd lost the fight a few days ago. A mottled purple and green bruise colored my cheek and jaw, and when I pulled off the hospital gown, I found more bruises. Most of the right side of my body where the wraith had slammed me into the alley wall was one giant bruise.

Bands of brighter purple wrapped around my chest and I shuddered. That was where the thing had squeezed me, so it could hold me while it poured into me.

Bile burned the back of my throat and my left inner biceps burned. It wanted me for something and I didn't doubt it knew I was a nephilim. How could it not when it had been inside me, flooding my cells with its essence? I didn't want to know what it wanted and I could only hope that this plan to win my freedom wouldn't expose my secret.

MARCUS

I STORMED DOWN THE HALL TO GIDEON'S OFFICE, MY WOLF HEAVING UNDER my skin fighting to gain control of my body. Essie Shaw had crashed back into my life with all her fierce determination and recklessness and fear, proving to me just how right I'd been to tell my wolf to shut the fuck up and leave her alone.

It'd been clear from the moment I'd met her almost five years ago that the supernatural world scared her. She'd put up a good front, but every time the topic came up she'd get a nervous look in her eyes and quickly change the conversation or grow quiet.

And after that night with the werewolves when I should have pulled rank and forced her to follow protocol despite knowing that kid would have died, I knew no matter what kind of chemistry sizzled between us — and there sure as hell had been chemistry — I could never see her again.

I'd become a super. The very thing that terrified her. And I sure as hell couldn't give in to my wolf's desires.

Besides, my wolf was crazy. He thought she was mine. Mine to hold and love and protect. But if I wanted to be with her, I couldn't protect her, not from myself or the world I now belonged in. And protecting her was more important than anything else.

Which was something my wolf and I both agreed on.

I had to do everything I could to keep her safe, even if that meant ensuring she kept as far away from me as possible by whatever means necessary.

It had been hard enough seeing her in that hospital bed, her beautiful face swollen and red, and knowing the rest of her was battered and broken as well. Hadn't she already learned facing off against a super was deadly?

I was sure she had scars from that night four and a half years ago to prove just how dangerous supers were, and even if she had tried to run from that wraith in the alley, she was now running straight at it.

Because she was fucking Essie Shaw and that's what she did.

Well, I sure as hell wasn't going to let her be bait to catch a serial killer that had already torn apart three supers and had branded her with a mark that could compel her to do its bidding.

There had to be a way to break the bond. There had to. I didn't care that Gideon thought there wasn't. There'd been a one in a million chance I'd be susceptible to lycanthropy and become a shifter. There had to be a chance, no matter how slim, that I could free her from that bond.

I yanked Gideon's office door open with so much force it slammed against the wall with a loud bang.

Gideon jerked his icy gaze to me, his expression colder and harder than I'd ever seen since I'd joined the team.

"She stays here," my wolf snarled as Gideon opened his mouth, most likely to reprimand me for losing control. "I don't care how many protections Zella can cast on her and I don't care if she's volunteered or not, we're not using her as bait."

The light in Gideon's eyes flared. "This isn't up for debate."

"No, it's not. She's not doing this." I couldn't keep her safe.

Mine to protect. Mine mine mine.

I gritted my teeth. *Shut the fuck up. She's not ours. She's never going to be ours. She's afraid of us.*

If I'd had any doubts about that, they were gone the second I'd stepped into her hospital room. Her pulse had picked up and her eyes had flashed wide with fear and then when the others had left she'd been so uncomfortable she could barely maintain eye contact with me.

She was terrified of me and supers, and Gideon had strong-armed her into agreeing to have her memories read because she was just a means to an end for him. And now he was serving her up as dinner to that monster.

"Come up with a better plan," I forced out.

"There isn't a better plan."

"She doesn't know how dangerous this is." *She doesn't know anything about the supernatural world and I'm not going to force her to learn.*

"From her reaction, I'm certain she does." He smoothed the page of the file in front of him. "She was your rookie when you were infected. Are you saying she's a liability?"

"She's human." *And mine! And I'm going to go insane trying to protect her.* "Of course she's a liability. Except for that incident, I doubt she's had any other experience with supers. She doesn't have a clue."

So show her.

No. She won't accept us. She belongs in the human world and we don't.

"She doesn't need a clue. She just needs to be present and know when to get out of the way," Gideon snapped.

"You're assuming she has a sense of self-preservation," I shot back. "She doesn't. You saw her in the hospital. She had the shit beaten out of her. The wraith is going to crush her or possess her first *then* crush her."

The light in Gideon's eyes flared brighter. "The decision has been made."

"She's going to challenge your authority," I pressed. Maybe he'd realize how insane this plan was if I pointed out that if she got a crazy idea in her head, she'd go off-script without asking permission. Even just taking her to Zella in the heart of the Quarter could end in disaster.

Hell. This was Essie and supers. She was two for two in completely fucking up a dangerous situation with them. Disaster was inevitable. And I'd rather never see her again and know she was safe than have her constantly in danger.

"Then keep her in line," Gideon ordered, his voice frigid. "This is the plan. The wraith is going to come for Miss Shaw whether we use her as bait or not."

"Officer Shaw," I ground out, correcting him.

The muscles in his jaw flexed, clearly not impressed with me pushing the issue. "*Officer* Shaw. Deciding the battleground will give us an advantage and we can capture this thing. This is her best bet for returning her to her normal life."

Yeah, if the wraith or any other super we encountered didn't kill her first.

ESSIE

I took a quick shower and avoided looking at my bruises in the misted mirror as I dried off. I pulled on the baggy T-shirt Kol had gotten for me, put the scrub pants back on, turned on the TV, and sat on the bed while I waited for the promised real clothes to arrive.

There was nothing on any of the all-day news channels about the wraith, not even on the news ticker at the bottom of the screen. That surprised me, but I suspected Gideon had made it clear to my captain that the attack in the alley needed to be kept under wraps. That was what I'd do. Having a super who crushed people beyond recognition and was roaming beyond the Supers' Quarter would cause panic and most of the human population still feared supers, or at least were extremely uncomfortable with them.

The rest were split into those who welcomed the supers for a variety of reasons, and those who welcomed the supers because the angels had told them to.

The news story changed to protests in Rome outside the Joined Parliament buildings. Like with all things, there was always a group that vehemently opposed those who were different even though, much to everyone's surprise — including myself — there wasn't a large difference in the crime statistics between humans and supers.

The current theory was that supers were so used to living in the shadows or hiding their true natures from humanity that they didn't want to screw this up — or were still really good at hiding their activities. I know many of the shifters loved that they didn't have to hide their packs. Vampires didn't have to hunt in the darkness for sustenance and cults had formed around most of the elder vampires made up of humans who were enthralled with the macabre or desperate for immortality and eternal youth. I couldn't see the appeal, but I wasn't going to judge. Not like the protestors on the TV.

Someone knocked on my door and I got up and answered it. Jacob stood in the hall holding my purse, a bulging bag — most likely the clothes he'd promised — and a sandwich on a plate.

"Gideon has contacted Zella and wants to be back before nightfall, so we're heading out as soon as you're ready." He held up his offerings. "You should probably eat before we go."

My stomach rumbled again and I stepped aside to let him enter. "Thanks."

"It would be best if you could eat while we head back to the garage." He set everything on the bed and stepped back into the hall.

"Copy that."

The door clicked shut and I opened the bag. Yep, clothes. A pair of black cargo pants that had an elastic waist and a stretchy black long-sleeve T-shirt that was going to fit a lot better than Kol's baggy one. There was also a pair of black socks, a sports bra with a small fit that didn't require a specific cup size, and a package of simple white undies.

Oh, thank God.

Everything was picked to be more or less flexible in its size and had only required Jacob to guess whether I had a small or medium build. Smart man.

I changed into the new clothes, shoved my feet into my runners, and grabbed my purse to get my wallet and my phone. I didn't want to take the bag with me, but I did want my ID, money for a taxi if I needed to get the hell out of there, and my phone.

Inside, at the top, was an unopened box of nicotine patches.

Thank you, Pam. She must have tossed it in my purse when it'd been found in the store. Thank you, thank you, thank you.

I took out a patch, pulled up my shirt, and stuck it to my side. It would take a few minutes for the nicotine to kick in, but it would kick in, and the buzz gnawing at my body would finally ease the hell up.

I shoved my phone, wallet, and room card into my pant pockets, grabbed the plate with the sandwich, and joined Jacob in the hall. His intense gaze swept over me and he gave a nod of approval. I was pretty sure the approval wasn't of me but of how well he'd picked my clothes.

"Tell me about Zella and where we're going. Is she the witch Marcus mentioned?" I asked, then bit into one half of the sandwich. Ham and cheese with tomato, lettuce, and mayo. Not my favorite but I wasn't going to complain.

Jacob hit the call button for the elevator. "Yes, and she's incredibly powerful. She fought with us during the war."

"Us?"

"Me and Gideon." He frowned. "Or is that Gideon and I? Gideon and me? I've been alive for well over a hundred years and I still can't remember which way is right."

I gasped and almost choked on my sandwich. "A hundred years?" I hadn't known shifters lived that long.

"I know. You'd think Gideon would have picked an older, more powerful vampire for his team. I'm still not sure why I was selected."

The elevator door opened and he stepped inside. He didn't look like a vampire at all. Of course, I hadn't seen many, only the few who made the news, and they were either young and had done something illegal, or very old and were a part of the Joined Parliament. Jacob, with his tanned skin, must have spent a lot of time outdoors before he was turned—

"If you're a vampire, how were you at the hospital in the daytime?"

The door started to slide shut and I realized I hadn't joined him. I scooted inside and the door shut, capturing me in the small space with his intense presence. It was like a physical thing with weight and thickness, pressing against my senses, but it didn't terrify me. No, the wraith had terrified me and nothing could compare to that. Jacob being a vampire who worked for the JP was almost reassuring, since I doubted uptight 'following the rules of good even if it hurt someone' Gideon would let anyone malicious onto his team.

"I'm a JP agent, so I've been given a charm that protects me." He held up his wrist, showing me a thick silver bracelet with prongs digging into his skin every eighth of an inch.

"That looks like it hurts."

"Not nearly as much as sunlight."

Yeah. There was that.

The elevator dinged, announcing the first floor, and the door slid open. Gideon, Marcus, and Kol waited in the hall.

"Good. You're eating," Gideon said. "Let's go."

He turned on his heel and marched away. Marcus followed without making eye contact with me, and Kol flashed me a grin that made my pulse stutter with desire, but it seemed like he'd intended it more for encouragement than anything else, since my thoughts didn't completely stall out.

"We're going to Rouge," Gideon said over his shoulder. "It's in the heart of the Quarter, about as far away from humans as it can get, and caters to the less than virtuous supers."

"And your witch is there?" I was surprised someone who'd fought with Gideon would live in a place like that, let alone that he'd continue his association with her.

"I would have preferred if she'd picked a different place to call home, but she has her reasons."

"She always did," Jacob said.

"It's mid-afternoon, so there shouldn't be a lot of supers at Rouge, but you're human so you might still draw attention," Marcus said. His glower darted to Gideon and darkened even more, and I got the impression heated words had been exchanged between them. Then his gaze jumped back to me. "So don't draw attention. Keep your head down and don't be stupid."

Gee, thanks for the vote of confidence. "Copy that."

We piled back into the SUV and drove deeper into the Quarter. The buildings still looked the same, a mix of late 19th century to modern, and only a few reaching taller than ten stories. Fewer buildings had store fronts on the first level, and those that did weren't as welcoming as the ones on the main strip. Many windows had a purple hue, indicating they were UV blocking, and others had the windows completely covered up.

We stopped at a red light. The street ahead as well as the crossroad were narrower than the one we were on. Four seven-story buildings, all in the same white modern architecture, stood sentinel on each corner, and each were joined with a walking bridge crossing the streets four stories up. UV-blocking glass shimmered in all the windows, and I could see people inside on the second floor of the building closest to me, sitting around a conference table.

The light turned green and Marcus drove around a corner and into the shelter of a UV-blocking canopy. The canopy was built down to the rooftops to prevent even a small band of light inside and stretched to the end of the street. It even carried over to a covered park where the plants were kept alive with angelic magic. This street had a little more activity on it than the previous one, but it was mostly delivery men and shop owners gearing up for the evening's business.

We turned at the last intersection before the park and stopped in front of a converted bank or courthouse or something. Here the canopy had been built tight to the side of the building, creating a wall of purple glass that reached across the street — leaving an enspelled opening for traffic — and carried on into the park. The building was set back from the street with a dozen wide, shallow steps leading up to a dozen glass doors, the whole thing framed by two towering Roman columns. A neon sign hung above the doors, proclaiming it was Rouge, and more signs glowed from behind the glass panels on either side of the doors, one saying 'Open 24 Hours.'

"Remember to keep your head down," Gideon said as he got out of the SUV, this time waiting — much to my surprise — for everyone to join him on the sidewalk before striding up the stairs.

Inside, past the vestibule, the place looked like any other nightclub, with the walls, floor, and vaulted ceiling painted in a red so dark it was almost black — I guess that was why it was called Rouge — and the inner doors had been blacked out, so it could look like a dance club all day. Booths lined the wall on both sides, while standing tables were scattered along the edge of the dance floor. A long bar sat against the far wall, manned by a single demon with leathery red skin and tall horns twisting from his temples.

On either side of the bar sat an archway, each opening into what looked like different rooms. One had more light and I could see the edge of a pool table, while the other was just as dimly lit as the main room. Dance music thumped from the speakers in the main room but at a modest volume and there were only half a dozen patrons, all of which were sitting in the booths.

Gideon led us into the room with the pool table and pointed to a table in a dark corner. "Jacob, Kol, stay here with Ms. Shaw. I need to check in with Bane first. Marcus, you're with me."

The room was bigger than I'd expected, its width going beyond that of the first room. It had the same vaulted ceiling, and a wide staircase in the back corner that curved up to a second floor landing. It reminded me of a local pub, complete with pub-like wood furniture, brass accents, five pool tables, three dart boards, a big TV playing a baseball game, and a dozen beer taps at the bar.

There were two dozen people scattered throughout the room, not including the bartender — who looked like she was human until the light caught in her eyes and it reflected back like a cat's. Two of the patrons played pool at the farthest table, while two more groups, sitting far enough apart that they clearly weren't together, watched the game. There were a few more patrons in booths, and all of them had drinks or plates of food.

"Do we know how long Gideon is going to be?" I asked, pulling out a chair from the designated table and sitting. "We're going to stick out soon if we don't get something to drink. Or do you come here on business often?"

"We don't," Jacob said, joining me. "Gideon usually goes by himself."

"But he didn't want to bring you without the whole team, just in case —" Kol snapped his mouth shut.

"You can say it. In case the wraith decides to come after me."

"He didn't while you were at the hospital," Jacob said. "That would have been the easiest time to grab you, which tells me he's waiting for something."

Yeah, and I'd rather not find out what.

Jacob offered me a smile but it didn't reach his eyes. "The brand manifested less than an hour ago, so I suspect he won't be able to use it to locate you just yet."

"So we're just a precaution." Kol pulled out a chair but didn't sit. "You're right, though. I'll go get us drinks."

"You know, I'm not some fragile woman who's going to faint the moment the wraith appears," I said to Jacob. I hadn't fainted when Marcus and I had ended up in that fight with those werewolves, and that had been before I'd had the advanced training for dealing with supers. "You don't need to pussyfoot around the truth with me. In fact, I'd rather have the whole truth then have to figure out what's not being said."

He cocked an eyebrow. "You sure? You had a meltdown when you found out about the brand."

"And then I volunteered to be bait." I met his raised eyebrow with my own. "Any normal person would have a freak out when they learned their soul was permanently bonded to a monster." And I really didn't want to think about that, because I was sure I was going to start freaking out again. "Now I'm dealing with it."

This time the smile did reach his eyes, softening the harsh intensity of his look and making him look more rugged instead of fierce. "That you are."

Movement out of the corner of my eye caught my attention, and a rake-thin man with sallow skin and stringy brown hair slid out of a six-person booth and headed toward us. Three more men of varying builds joined him. All moved like predators, their pace steady with the promise of powerful muscles ready to jump into action. Even rake-thin guy oozed danger. Just great.

The man reached our table and hooked his thumbs into the waist-band of his low-riding jeans. His gaze, filled with a hint of the same intensity that was in Jacob's but not nearly as powerful, slid over me, drawing an involuntary shiver that made my pulse pick up and not in a good way. Vampires. I wasn't sure how I knew which of the supers they were — they could have been shifters or one of the few demons who looked human — but I knew with that look exactly what they were and that they were dangerous.

"Jacob Lockwood," he said, "have you finally decided to bring Victoria her tribute?"

"Victoria knows I'll never pay her tribute." Jacob shifted, letting his duster open a bit, revealing the sidearm holstered at his hip.

The thin man didn't seem to notice. Neither did his friends who were inching closer around me.

"Every vampire needs to pay tribute," the thin man said.

"Even one living with the angels," one of the men behind me said. He had a stockier build than rake-thin guy and looked like he'd had a bath in the last few months.

"*Especially* one living with the angels," another said, the tallest of the group, and he slapped a meaty hand on my shoulder.

Jacob stood, and a sense of barely contained violence radiated from him. "No vampire has to pay tribute," he said, his voice low.

He was taller and broader than all of them, but the thin man sneered instead of backing down. "You're not strong enough to take all of us. I can see it in your essence. The angels have you convinced you don't have to drink from the vein, that you can survive on the stale blood they keep in their blood banks."

The guy gripping my shoulder snickered and his hold on me tightened. "If you're not going to pay tribute with the pretty human, maybe I should. Victoria is gonna like her."

"You're aware feeding on someone without their consent is illegal," I said. Not that I expected this group to just give up because of that, but I was obligated as an officer of the law to give them fair warning.

The thin guy sneered at me. "Oh, you'll give your consent. You'll be begging for it."

Jacob pushed his duster open all the way, looking every bit like a Wild West gunslinger. His hand settled on the grip of his sidearm, but he didn't draw. "It's not consent if it's coerced."

"And you're not going to open fire in your sire's establishment," the thin man said.

"Try me," Jacob growled.

"Hey, guys," Kol said, approaching the table with three full pint glasses, his posture casual but with a hint of hellfire in his eyes. "What's all the commotion?"

"Oh, and you brought a pretty boy, too," the thin man said, with a wicked smile that promised violence. "How did you know it's my birthday?"

ESSIE

One of the up-until-now silent vampires seized Kol and wrapped an arm around his neck. Kol dropped the glasses and wrenched against the guy's hold.

The guy squeezing my shoulder jerked me up. I twisted before he could choke me, but he grabbed my arm and yanked me toward him. I tripped on the chair, and he grabbed the front of my shirt and wrenched me off my feet.

Out of the corner of my eye, Jacob lunged at the thin man, who darted out of the way. Kol rammed his elbow into the guy holding him, and five more men from the back of the room hurried toward us.

The guy holding me shoved me chest first against the wall, capturing my body with his, and pressed his lips against my throat.

He sniffed and softly moaned in pleasure. "Victoria is going to enjoy you."

"Yeah, not going to happen." I bucked against him and hissed the spell that summoned a blast of divine light.

The guy shoved me back against the wall. "That's not going to work. I'm stronger than you, human."

I bucked again and finished the spell. "That was just a distraction." I slapped my hand against the side of his face, and white light burst from my palm.

The vampire howled and wrenched back, and I mule-kicked him in the gut, shoving him farther away. He snarled at me, my handprint red and oozing on his cheek, one eye cloudy and blinded. He lunged for me and I sidestepped his grab, seizing his wrist, twisting, and slamming him against the table.

Another guy rushed at me and I snapped a kick into his groin, making him stumble, and another kick into his knee making him fall. With all my pent-up anger and fear from the wraith's attack, I wrenched the arm of the vampire I still held, dislocated his shoulder, and shoved him off the table to the floor.

The guy I'd kicked was back on his feet. He grabbed my shoulder and yanked me to face him. I used the movement to strengthen my punch and rammed my fist into his throat. Something crunched, and he gasped and released me to grab his neck. It wasn't enough to stop him, but it was enough for me to summon another divine light strike and slap my hand on his face, catching both eyes.

I turned to block the punch from someone else when a gunshot roared through the room. Everyone froze, searching for the source of the shot. Jacob hadn't drawn and Kol had been fighting without a sidearm as well.

"That's better," a stunningly beautiful woman at the top of the stairs said in a sultry alto. She looked like a stereotypical vampire, dark locks hanging artfully past her shoulders to frame her narrow face and porcelain complexion. Her red dress plunged low in the front and hugged voluptuous curves, promising sinful sex, and her dark eyes were filled with the same intensity that I saw in Jacob's, only a hundred times more powerful.

Gideon stood beside her, his posture perfect and icy. Behind them, a sallow-skinned man shoved a gun into the waistband of his pants and sneered — I didn't know where he'd fired but no one looked like they had a bullet wound — while Marcus stood beside him with his arms crossed, glowering at me. Just great.

"It's been a long time, Jacob," she said. "You should visit more often."

Jacob bowed his head. "Of course, Victoria."

"Gus, did you try to take what belongs to Jacob?"

"I doubt she's his. I doubt any human is," the rake-thin vampire said, wiping blood from his upper lip and shoving his broken nose back into place.

Victoria's dark gaze leveled on the thin vampire, Gus, and he shrank back. "Is this true, Gideon? Is this human unclaimed?"

"No human should be claimed," Jacob said.

Victoria's eyes narrowed. "In my establishment they are. If she's not yours, Gus has the right to take her and you'll be confined to the box for a week."

"That isn't necessary," Gideon said. "They're here on my command."

"And you know the rules." Victoria turned to Gideon and traced her fingers over his sculpted chest. The temperature in the room warmed but I couldn't tell if it was with desire or anger. "Did you think you could just sneak her in?"

Wow, that was surprising. I thought angels abided by every rule, even when it didn't make sense.

"We're here to see Zella," Gideon said. "We won't be long."

"That doesn't make it better." Victoria raised a hand and made a fist.

Jacob gasped, grabbed his chest, and dropped to his knees, his face scrunched in pain, while Gus sneered in pleasure.

"That will be two weeks in the box for my offspring." Her fist tightened and Jacob screamed.

"Victoria, be reasonable," Gideon said.

"Reasonable?"

Jacob screamed again.

"You angels with your rules think you don't have to follow mine."

Another scream and the temperature turned sweltering.

"This is my house. My rules. The JP agreed to that." She glared at Gideon, and Jacob screamed a third time, collapsed on his side, and curled into a ball of agony. "You think you can disrespect me like that, angel? Think again."

She brought her other fist up and Jacob gasped and started gurgling.

For the love of God, just stop. I jerked a step forward. "I'm his."

"Essie—" Marcus barked.

"He's claimed me," I said, even knowing that my luck probably wasn't good enough for Victoria to just take my word for it.

Jeez, first an unwanted angel brand and now I was going to risk letting a vampire stake his claim to me. But I couldn't stand by and watch Victoria torture him. A vampire's claim entwined the vampire's essence with the human's in a way only vampires could sense. It signaled that the human had relinquished her free will and belonged to the vampire. I couldn't imagine why anyone would let someone else control them — and this control was complete, take-over-your-body-and-make-you-do-horrible-things-even-commit-suicide kind of control — but they did.

For whatever reason, some people didn't want control of their lives and some didn't care about that price tag to reap the benefits of being claimed, like enhanced senses and an extended lifespan. And there had been people willing to be claimed before the vampires had joined the cause and helped save humanity. It boggled the mind. Of course, maybe the rumors of sexual euphoria were true, that being claimed enhanced the already erotic sensations that came with a vampire feeding.

"She's lying," Gus said. "Give her to me."

"You can't just give her away," Marcus said. "There are laws."

"And there are laws in my house, too," Victoria said.

"She hasn't been claimed." Gus's tone sharpened. "His essence isn't in her."

"Well, either she's lying or it's been too long since he's fed and wrapped his essence in her." Victoria's eyes narrowed. "You should rectify that, Jacob."

Gideon shifted, the only indication he was anything but icy calm. "Zella is expecting us."

"You should have thought of that before trying to sneak an unclaimed human into my establishment," Victoria said, her tone sickeningly sweet.

"She said she was claimed." Marcus tensed and looked like he was going to attack, but Gideon put a hand up and stopped him.

"So she's already submitted." Victoria raised her chin, daring Gideon to defy her in her house. "Wrapping his essence in her again shouldn't be a problem."

Gus shoved me toward Jacob and I dropped to my knees at his side.

"You don't have to do this," he gasped, his voice low so only I could hear him.

"I'm not going to let her torture you," I said just as quietly, and helped him sit up.

He leaned close, pressing his forehead to mine. "You don't know what this will mean."

"If you have a better plan, I'm all ears."

"I'm waiting," Victoria said in a singsong. "On your feet, vampire, and repossess your human."

"I don't just have to bite you," he said. "I have to touch you, my palm over your heart, flesh to flesh to bind my essence with yours. It's... intimate."

A nervous tremor swept through me. I'd expected it would be something overly personal, but I had hoped just drinking my blood would have been personal enough. I didn't know this guy. I didn't know any of them other than Marcus, and now I was in a position where I needed them to protect me from the wraith. I still wasn't sure I trusted them — including Marcus — but I couldn't see any other option.

"Unless you'd prefer to take her on the bar floor." Victoria flashed a dark smile. "Or I could just keep killing you." She made a fist and Jacob tensed. He clenched his jaw but a strangled cry still slipped out.

"You do whatever it takes." I met his gaze, letting him know I meant what I said, then pushed away from him and stood.

Gasping, he grabbed the chair beside him to help him rise and joined me.

"Atta boy," Victoria said.

With an apologetic look, Jacob stepped close, with his chest at my back, and turned us to face away from Victoria and the others. But the master vampire tsked, and Jacob gasped again, tensing against me as if an electric shock had surged through him.

"You don't get to be ashamed of what you are, Jacob. Turn around." Her tone promised more pain if he didn't obey. "I want to watch."

"I'm sorry," Jacob whispered against my temple, then turned us.

"Very good," Victoria hissed, her smile deepening as Jacob wrapped a bulky arm across my waist.

He drew me tight against his broad chest and I was hyperaware of just how big he was, the broad muscular planes of his chest and his arms nearly the size of my thighs. He was probably double my weight if not more of pure muscle, and with my head tucked under his chin, his embrace nearly engulfed me.

I shivered but wasn't sure if it was fear or the fear that I wasn't afraid of him. His free hand tipped my head to the side and back and held me there with a light pressure. The hand at my waist slid along my stomach and dipped under my shirt. I expected his hand to be cold, being undead and all, but it wasn't, merely chilled, which meant he'd eaten recently.

My mind latched on to that. That was good. He wasn't starving. He could just take a quick sip, entwine his essence into mine, and we'd be done.

His hand moved up my chest, close to my skin but not touching, a whisper of movement that made me shiver, then his fingers dipped inside the sports bra, sliding over the top of my breast, and made my breath hitch. His palm settled over my heart, and I tried to detach myself from his touch, but it was so intimate it made my body thrum, desire flickering through me.

He dipped his head down, his lips against my throat, and murmured, "Just relax."

Sharp pain bit my neck and I tensed, the realization that his teeth had plunged into my neck making panic surge through me and my pulse pound.

Victoria licked her lips. Her canines extended and a hunger burned in her eyes. Beside her Gideon was rigid, his expression pure ice while Marcus's was pure rage. He looked like he was going to go on a rampage. To my left, Gus looked like he was going to throw a fit, and Kol had gone pale, hellfire burning in his eyes.

Jacob sucked, drinking my blood with a tug on my throat that pulled all the way down to my core. The tension that had seized me twisted into sudden aching need. My body grew limp, desperate to let him take me, overpower me, do whatever he wanted.

The boneless ecstasy seeped deeper, spreading over and into every nerve, making my breath shudder. Jacob held tight and his palm against my heart began to warm, adding a new pull, one that curled into me and made my head spin.

He took another pull, or was that his third or fourth? I couldn't tell, I couldn't feel his teeth in my neck anymore, only heat from his hand pressing against my heart and the aching pleasure coursing through me and gathering in my core.

I shuddered and Jacob groaned, the rumble in his chest vibrating through me, sending my cells into sympathetic vibration with his. The bliss swelled — I hadn't thought it could be possible, not without actually having sex — as if our aligned resonance allowed his essence to penetrate deeper into me, and every part of me turned its attention to him. There was no one else in the room, the city, the world. There was only Jacob and his desires. If he needed to drink me dry, I'd slit my throat for him. If he needed protection, finances, sex, whatever I had, it was his. I'd give it freely.

As soon as the thoughts rooted within me, a part of my mind started screaming. That wasn't right. He wasn't my everything. He couldn't be my everything. I barely knew him. A flicker of panic joined the screaming. He needed to let go. Release me. Stop. This wasn't right. It had to stop.

Please. Stop.

But if he stopped, Victoria would resume torturing him. I had the power to stop that so long as I let him finish his claim. That was the reason I'd become a cop: to have the power to help others.

He took another bone-melting pull on my neck that left me spinning and weak. His grip on me tightened and his body trembled, then with a growl he jerked his mouth away. A chill swept around me and the panic surged at his absence, while that other, small part of my mind screamed that feeling that way was wrong. Then his mouth was back again, his lips against the puncture wounds and a flicker of heat, the miniscule healing magic every vampire possessed, sealed the wounds shut. It would still be obvious for the next day or so that I'd let a vampire bite me, but at least I wouldn't bleed to death. The kiss was light, feathery, sending a shiver of desire down my spine, and he withdrew again, leaving me chilled even though I was still wrapped in his embrace.

"Satisfied?" he asked, his voice low, dark, and edged with hunger.

No, not even close.

"Until next time," Victoria said.

I tried to open my eyes to see her expression, tried to find strength in my legs to stand without help, but everything within me just kept whirling.

Jacob's hand slipped out from under my shirt and he hooked his arm under my legs, lifted me, and cradled me against his massive chest.

Just where I wanted to be...

Except I was pretty sure that wasn't right.

"It'll take you a minute to regain your bearings." He pressed his lips to my forehead and the part of me now connected to Jacob soared with pleasure at his attention.

"What the fuck is wrong with you?" Marcus growled, his voice suddenly close, not far away on the second-story landing.

I forced my eyes open. Marcus *was* close, they all were, but he was the only one glaring at me. Behind him, the room spun around and around and around and—

Marcus's glare jumped above me to Jacob. "What the fuck is wrong with *you*?"

"Zella is waiting," Gideon said, his body language so cold I wouldn't have been surprised if frost formed on his sculpted cheekbones.

"You should have told me I wasn't supposed to come here," I said, my lips numb with pleasure, my words muddling in my mouth. "I'm sorry I got you in trouble."

"That wouldn't have stopped us from bringing you here," Jacob said. His intense gaze had turned sad and the muscles in his jaw tightened. "It's been nearly a hundred years since I've claimed someone. I'd forgotten how... intense it can be."

"And the claim will fade, eventually," Kol said, the fire and hunger still burning in his eyes.

"If I don't feed from you again, it'll be gone in a few months."

My warring thoughts cheered and wailed at that, but I was too dizzy to try to figure out which side I wanted to win so I just leaned my cheek against Jacob's chest instead.

"The first claiming is always the hardest on the human." The angel glow in Gideon's eyes dimmed, more clouds passing over his summer sky. "We should get to Zella's apartment before anyone notices she's still stunned."

Marcus was hurrying toward a narrow door under the stairs before Gideon had finished talking. The others followed, with Jacob at the back still carrying me.

The room continued to spin and my muscles still felt like goo. At least this spinning was better than the concussion I'd had earlier. This time I didn't feel like throwing up.

"When will I stop being stunned?" I asked Jacob.

"Everyone reacts differently." His voice rumbled through me, making my essence vibrate again. "I tried to take as little as I could to keep the claim weak, but—" His grip on me tightened. "It's been a long time since I've fed from a human. The claim is stronger than I'd like."

Which meant he'd taken more than he'd intended. The sane part of me shuddered at that. The part that was possessed by him was thrilled.

And either way, there wasn't anything I could do about it.

"It's okay." I pressed my palm to his chest. The claim would pass, and there wasn't anything saying that once the wraith was apprehended I had to stick close to Gideon while I waited for Jacob's essence to work its way out of me. This was manageable. I could handle this. I *had* to handle this.

The door under the stairs led to a narrow, rickety set of stairs going into the basement. Marcus led the way into a narrow, dimly lit hall. Sparks of light flickered through the glow from the bare bulbs hanging at irregular intervals from the ceiling, but I had no idea what kind of magic was on them that made them do that. The walls were fitted field-stone, telling me the building was old, or that it sat on an old foundation.

Moisture glistened in the cracks between the stones and a runnel of water trickled along a shallow gutter on the floor into a small metal grate.

I couldn't imagine why anyone would want to live down here, but then I'd been assuming Zella was a human who'd made a demon-deal or had an ancestor who'd made a deal, and that was why she was a witch.

Perhaps she wasn't human at all and didn't want to live in areas frequented by humans. There were a few kinds of supers who could cast spells, primarily those who'd been born human and had been infected with lycanthropy or turned into a vampire. There were also a few angels who could cast spells beyond their one primary innate magical ability. But I couldn't imagine an angel wanting to live down here. Given that the bar above was a vampire den, I was guessing Zella was a vampire.

Except that didn't fully explain why she was in the basement when there was UV-blocking glass on the windows above as well as over the street outside.

We reached a wide, heavy wooden door at the end of the hall. Marcus knocked and the door creaked open an inch. He shot Gideon a wide-eyed, worried look and the temperature in the hall chilled.

Jacob set me on my feet and leaned me against the wall, my head still spinning. "Stay here," he said, and he drew his weapon.

Something twisted in my chest, but I didn't know what, and really, the unlocked door and the guys' fear was more important.

Marcus pushed the door open and froze. Frost rushed across my cheeks and a sense of powerful evil slammed into my chest. Gideon growled and Kol gasped.

The room was an underground chapel with a massive stained glass window against the back wall, impossibly illuminated — it had to be magic. An altar was positioned just before it and dead center above that was an angel, suspended in the air, her wings unfurled, mangled and bleeding, and her body ensnared in ice and wrapped in the wraith's writhing tentacles.

THE ANGEL GURGLED AND WRENCHED AGAINST THE WRAITH, BUT ITS SMOKE had poured into her while its tentacles crushed her chest and sliced shallow, torturous cuts into her body. An angry red scar disfigured three quarters of her face and twisted over her bare forearms. The tentacle around her chest had hiked up her shirt, revealing more scars across her belly, as if she'd been flayed or set on fire and hadn't been magically healed. Blood seeped down her body and pooled onto the floor, and ice encased her hands.

Except the ice wasn't capturing any other part of her body. Instead, it held three tentacles and poured down the wraith's side, anchoring it to the floor. More ice swelled around her hands, and spears of ice shot from her palms and shattered against the wraith's chest, tearing into the smoke until I could almost see through it.

Another barrage of ice shot from the angel's hands, but there were fewer spears and they hit with less force. None of them punctured the wraith this time. She was running out of strength.

The wraith's smoke shuddered and shrank, then billowed and the power radiating from it increased. The tentacle around her chest twisted tighter. Bones cracked and the angel screamed and convulsed with pain. The ice holding the other tentacles back started to crumble.

"Free Zella," Gideon said to his team and rushed into the room, his hands raised. A blast of divine light shot from each palm and slammed into the wraith, but didn't cut through it.

The wraith growled. Its form shuddered again, thinning and surging as if fighting a windstorm. One tentacle dissolved in a puff of smoke, but it wrenched another one free from the ice.

Kol unsheathed two daggers that he'd had hidden somewhere on his body and leaped into the room, while Jacob bolted around the corner faster than humanly possible and fired two rounds into a tentacle that was crushing the angel's leg. Marcus growled and barreled after them, claws extending from his fingertips.

My pulse tripped with horror.

He had claws.

I *had* ruined his life.

He dove for the wraith, jumping high, and dug his claws into its back. A tentacle snapped out, seized him, and tossed him against the wall. He hit the ground on his hands and knees but quickly stood. Kol sliced at the tentacles clutching Zella, but every time he cut one another would appear.

Light formed in Gideon's palms again as the ice anchoring the wraith to the floor snapped. It whirled around with a roar and hurled Zella into Gideon before he could get off his shot. She crashed into him and they skidded across the floor, Gideon trying to protect Zella's broken body with his.

Jacob fired another shot, the bullet slicing through a tentacle, but a flurry of more tentacles exploded from the wraith's body. They swatted at Jacob and he dove out of the way, then they flung Kol into Marcus and shot toward me.

Marcus's eyes flashed wide. "Essie, move!"

I jerked to get out of the way, but my muscles seized and I couldn't move.

Marcus scrambled toward me but he was going to be too late. "Essie, go."

I jerked again. Nothing. "I can't." *God, why can't I leave this spot—?*

Ah, shit. Jacob had said to stay there. He'd given me a command.

The tentacle reached for me and I cast a divine light strike as fast as I could. Light streaked from my palms and sliced into the tentacle as it tried to grab me.

"Jacob," Gideon said.

"Shit." Jacob fired at the tentacle that was already reforming to continue coming after me and severed it from the wraith's body. It turned to smoke and vanished. "Essie, defend yourself."

My body lurched away from the wall and I twisted out of reach of the reformed tentacle, my pulse pounding.

Gideon blasted the wraith with more light and Marcus tore into it. The wraith screeched and shuddered, its smoke shredding away. With another cry, it bolted past me and disappeared in the darkness at the end of the hall.

"Get the car," Gideon said, pulling Zella into his arms, her body limp, one mangled wing half on his shoulder, the other dragging on the floor.

Jacob rushed away, the fastest of the group with his vampiric enhanced speed.

Blood poured down the front of Gideon's pants and his grip on Zella tightened as if just by holding tight enough he could save her. Except if his angel magic didn't involve healing — and since Amiah had healed my broken bones my best guess was that it didn't — then there was nothing he could do.

Marcus ran ahead of us to clear the way, Gideon running after him, while Kol and I followed. The hall still threatened to turn into a vomit-inducing fun house from the effects of Jacob's claim, but I gritted my teeth and kept up. I was dizzy, but I was fine. Zella needed immediate medical attention and no way in hell was I going to slow the group down.

We barreled up the stairs, through the pub, across the dance floor, and out the doors. Jacob had the SUV turned around, the engine running, every door except the far middle one open, and his hands on the wheel ready to go.

Gideon climbed onto the middle bench, cradling Zella, blood oozing over the leather seats. Kol shut the door after him and jumped into the front passenger seat as Marcus and I piled into the back.

We peeled away from Rouge, our tires screeching around the first corner, gunned it down the stretch under the UV-blocking canopy, and ran every red light to get to Operations. Thank goodness we weren't far. Marcus called Amiah and told her to have a team waiting for us in the garage then glared out the window, pointedly refusing to look at me.

I, on the other hand, couldn't stop looking at him. I tried not to, but my gaze kept jumping back to his hands. His fingers had returned to normal, his claws gone, but the image of them filled my mind.

It was my fault. All my fault.

The SUV squealed to a stop in the parking garage where Amiah, two others — a man and a woman, I had no idea what kind of supers they were — and a gurney waited. Gideon set Zella on the gurney and they whisked her about twenty feet down the hall into whatever lay beyond the frosted-glass sliding door.

Marcus, Kol, and I got out and Jacob pulled into a parking spot.

Gideon stood rooted in the garage, staring through the glass doorway into the now empty hall. A blood trail, dark red against the pale gray floor, pointed the way they'd taken her.

Jacob placed a hand on Gideon's shoulder. "She's in good hands."

"I know," Gideon said.

Kol shoved his hands into his pockets, a hint of hellfire still in his eyes. "We didn't know the wraith was going to be there."

The muscles in Gideon's jaw flexed. "I know."

"And we couldn't have killed him without endangering Essie," Marcus said, his voice low and rough, as if he didn't like what he'd said.

The temperature in the garage ping-ponged between hot and cold and I hugged myself, keeping back from the group. If it wasn't for me, they could have stopped the wraith this afternoon.

Which was ridiculous. If it wasn't for me, we wouldn't have been at that bar and stumbled across the wraith.

Still, the guys looked angry and exhausted, and I didn't want to remind them that I was a complication they didn't want.

Gideon drew in a ragged breath. "Jacob, mind what you say to Officer Shaw until your vampire claim on her diminishes. We can't have her stuck in one spot again."

Jacob gave a tight nod.

"Marcus, take the coalescence snare we bought from Bane to Summer to ensure it's the real deal," Gideon said. "Without Zella's protection charm, we need it to work without a hitch because this plan just got more dangerous."

"So we're going ahead with using Essie as bait without the protection charm?" Kol asked.

Gideon glanced at me, his summer-sky eyes frosted and hard. Of course he was going ahead with the plan. I could see it in his eyes. The wraith had almost — please let it be almost and not actually — killed another angel. One measly human was worth it to end the slaughter.

I squared my shoulders. "You pick the time and place and I'll be there."

Marcus growled, shoved open the glass door, and stormed away.

The temperature in the garage continued to lurch between hot and cold, Marcus's departure not giving me any relief.

Gideon followed him, his stride tight, restrained, every inch of him radiating frozen control.

The heat eased up, but I was still cold. Uncertain what to do or where to go, I hugged myself and brushed the brand, sending a spike of pain through my arm. They'd given me a room. I should use it. I needed another shower and I needed a bigger meal than just a sandwich. Except I didn't want to leave Jacob.

Which had to be his claim on me.

That was going to become a serious problem if I needed his permission to do everyday things like eat, shower, or sleep.

"I should..." Kol glanced at Jacob then at me. The hellfire had vanished from his eyes, but there was still an edge there. Of course, we'd just witnessed the wraith tear into Zella. I'm sure there was an edge in my eyes, too.

"I should..." Kol jerked his thumb at the door. "I'll—" He rushed inside as well.

The door clicked shut and Jacob turned to me. "You need my permission to go back to your room, don't you."

"Yeah." And I didn't like the feeling one bit... even if a part of me seemed to love it. That had to be the part claimed by Jacob.

"I was afraid of that." His hand slid to the butt of his gun, but I didn't get the sense he wanted to threaten me. Instead, it felt as if this was an instinct, something his body returned to over and over again when he wasn't thinking about it. "I took too much and the claim is too strong."

"So what does that mean?" Was I going to be like this for the entire time that his essence was entwined with mine? Jacob had said that would be months. I couldn't live like that. I had to deal with this wraith and get away from Gideon before he learned the truth.

"It means I need to be more careful what I say to you."

I barked a bitter laugh. "You think?" I hadn't been able to move more than an inch from that wall.

His gaze shifted to the garage behind me and the grip on his sidearm tightened. "I don't have a lot of experience with this. I've only claimed someone once before." The air in the garage turned thick, foggy — at least for me, since I doubted Jacob saw it — his grief manifesting as water suspended in the air around me. "I don't want to have that kind of mastery over someone's life again."

"Does that have something to do with why you think an angel bond is unhealthy?"

His fog misted my cheeks and he frowned, drawing closer.

Shit. I turned my head to hide the moisture, but he captured my chin and urged me to look up at him.

The sadness in his eyes deepened. "It'll be okay." He cupped my face and traced a thumb across my cheek, wiping the mist away and drawing a shiver of need into my heart.

Please let him think I'm crying.

"We can protect you. We'll put the wraith in hibernation." He brushed more moisture from my cheek. "My claim will fade. You'll get your life back. I promise."

I pursed my lips. I wanted to run screaming from him, from all of it. Except it wasn't because I thought his claim on me was wrong, but because the longer I remained here, the greater the odds I'd be discovered. A part of me was in shock that entwining our essences and drinking my blood hadn't revealed my angelic nature to him. While another part, a part that didn't care about discovery or self-preservation, wanted to lean into his touch and beg for a command, anything to please him.

I resisted all of that and made myself just stand there, trying to ignore the fog billowing between us that he couldn't see.

"The need to be told what to do short of breathing will pass."

"How long will that be?" *Please say soon. Please don't let my kneejerk reaction to protect him have completely screwed up my life.*

"It's different for everyone. Could be a few hours, could be a few days."

Swell. No good deed goes unpunished. But even if I hadn't known the specifics about what I'd gotten myself into, I'd known enough. And if I could go back and do it again, I'd make the same choice and save Jacob.

And that wasn't the claim talking.

"Once it passes, you'll have more autonomy. There's still a danger of me commanding you if I don't watch what I say, but if I don't give you an order, you'll be able to do your own thing."

"Okay." I could handle this. Except the things I needed to handle were piling on and it hadn't even been a full day.

Jacob slid his other hand to my cheek, capturing my face between his palms, and met my gaze, the look in his eyes still intense and still sad. "I hate that I have to say this. Go take care of yourself. If I need you, I'll find you wherever you are."

A pressure in my chest released, and I let out a breath I hadn't realized I'd been holding. Two sentences and I'd been freed... a bit. I could do whatever I wanted and go where I wanted... although I sensed there were limits to how far I could actually go from him. But for now I was no longer obligated to stay by his side and wait for a command.

"Thank you."

"No. Thank you. Victoria wasn't supposed to be at Rouge. All our intelligence said she was out of town."

"Which is why you thought you could sneak me in." The fog thinned, Jacob releasing his grief. "I'm surprised Gideon went ahead with it. From what I've heard, it's not like an angel to break the rules."

"This is an unusual situation."

Yeah, and it wasn't because I was involved. If the wraith had killed three cops, the entire police force would be doing everything to catch him. With an attack on three angels, I could see why Gideon was willing to do almost anything to stop him.

Jacob slid his hands from my face and gestured to the door. "I don't know when Gideon will reassemble the team to work out the details of capturing the wraith. You should—"

The pressure returned around my heart.

"Sorry. Go take care of yourself. If I need you I'll find you wherever you are," he said.

I rushed into the hall before he could say anything else to me while he waited in the garage, probably with the same goal. A few feet away, a janitor mopped up the blood trail. I hurried past him, keeping my head down, afraid to make eye contact, and went straight to the elevator.

My stomach grumbled. I ignored it. Yes, Marcus had said the cafeteria was straight into the new section, but right now I just wanted to avoid any other super. I needed to figure out the best options for the plan to use me as bait so I wasn't strong-armed into a bad idea. Not that I thought Gideon would have a bad plan. He and everyone else on the team probably had more experience with these things than I did.

In honesty, my nerves were shot from the fear of being discovered, the wraith attack, and learning my soul was permanently bonded with that monster. And I really wanted to be in a room with a steady temperature for more than a few minutes.

The elevator door opened and I rode it to the fifth floor. With a ding, the door opened and I stepped into the hall. Marcus leaned against the wall beside my door. His gaze lifted and locked onto me and the temperature shot up.

His anger was still hot, the air thick with humidity. I'd never experienced anything quite like it before. His piercing green gaze froze me in place, and now I knew why. He was a predator, his human nature twisted with a wolf's, and I was prey.

My chest tightened. He was a predator because of me. God, how did someone atone for that?

A person couldn't atone for something that terrible and permanent.

But I also didn't have the emotional fortitude right now to take whatever he wanted to throw at me. Even if I did deserve it. And jeez, my arm was stinging and I was sweltering.

The elevator closed, blocking off my escape. Not that leaving wouldn't have been blatantly obvious that I was avoiding him. I shoved up my sleeves — doing nothing to alleviate the heat — and forced myself toward him. *Please just make it quick.*

"No Jacob?" he asked, his voice low.

I stopped just out of arm's reach. I needed to get past him to unlock my door, but I was afraid that if I got too close, the attraction sizzling within me would keep me there. "I have permission to do my own thing."

His eyes narrowed.

"I don't like it, either, but Victoria was going to keep torturing him."

"He's a big boy. He could have handled it."

"Sure. And she would have detained him to continue torturing him and you'd be down one team member. You needed everyone to save Zella, which means you'll need everyone to trap the wraith."

His hands clenched at his sides and he jerked a step forward. "Don't pretend this is about protecting yourself. We both know you have no sense of self-preservation. You'd sacrifice yourself in a heartbeat if it meant saving someone."

"Hardly." I forced a huff of disdain, his words hitting too close to home.

"The fight with those shifters was because a child was in danger. The fight with the wraith, you were protecting the pharmacist and cashier." Tension radiated from his body and the temperature rose. Sweat beaded on my forehead and between my breasts.

"I get it. You're pissed. You have every right to be pissed. But please —" My throat tightened and I fought back tears. God damn it, I was stronger than this. And I could be, if I just had a moment to steady my nerves.

"I'm not pissed," he growled, sounding even more furious. "I'm terrified."

"You're what?" My brain stuttered over his words. That didn't fit with the temperature or his body language or his tone or anything else about him.

He jerked closer, captured my face between his palms, and crashed his lips against mine, stunning me. The kiss was hungry and wild, his stubble rough against my skin. Sultry heat with humidity pasted my T-shirt to my body, my pulse roared, and heat spiraled through me.

A growl rumbled in his throat and my breath stalled, not from fear, but from the desire that had instantly struck the moment we'd first met and had never let up, even with four and a half years apart.

I slid my hands over his chest, savoring his sculpted pecs, and melted against him, needing to be closer, to feel his body pressed against mine.

His fingers tangled in my hair and tilted my head back to deepen the kiss, his tongue plunging inside. His passion was ferocious, consuming.

I moaned with pleasure, and he froze, his body trembling, his breath fast.

"Essie." He breathed my name against my lips and pressed his forehead to mine. "You're not supposed to be a part of this world. I know you don't want to be." He jerked away from me, his gaze piercing into my soul. "I left so you wouldn't have to be."

Then he stormed away, past the elevator and around the corner, taking his ferocious energy and the humid temperature with him.

What the hell?

I pressed my fingers to my lips, stunned, as the return-to-normal temperature chilled the sweat slicking my body.

He'd left to protect me?

And then he'd kissed me.

I had no idea what that meant.

JACOB

I watched Essie rush out of the garage into Operations, my awareness clinging to my connection with her essence with a desperate need to be close even as I forced myself to stay put and keep my mouth shut. Because with a single word — not even a single word, just clearing my throat — I could make her run back to me and that was terrifying.

It meant my claim on her was stronger than I liked. A lot stronger. And because I hadn't controlled my hunger, she'd almost been injured or worse, taken. The wraith had branded her and that meant it wanted her for something, something that could be worse than death.

My fangs ached with the need to sink them into her soft, sweet flesh and drink from her again, and I bit back a groan of frustration.

I'd taken more than I should have and yet I hadn't gotten nearly enough from her. She was intoxicating and not just the taste of her. All of her.

Whatever she'd experienced in that alley had to have been terrifying. Her broken body had been a testament to what she'd gone through. I hadn't needed the fight to save Zella to show me just how powerful this wraith was. But Essie had still agreed to have her memories read despite her obvious fear to relive the moment in the alley so we could get the wraith's essence and then volunteered to be bait to catch it.

She'd said she wasn't a fragile woman and she'd more than proven that by keeping her cool when my carelessness had almost gotten her hurt during the fight in Zella's apartment and by standing up to Victoria and letting me claim her.

But now we had another complication to deal with. I had control over her life, over everything she did. She'd needed my permission to go to her room and rest. She'd needed it just to look away from me.

I'd never wanted to have that kind of control over someone's life again and I swore, this time, it would end differently.

I just needed to ignore my hunger for her and let my claim fade. Then she'd never have to think of me again.

But that thought made the rest of me ache, not just my fangs. I wanted her so deeply, it scared me.

Except it wasn't really her I wanted, but fresh blood.

I'd denied myself for too long and this was the price. Victoria had sensed that, knew I was weak, and that was why she'd insisted on watching me claim Essie, not letting me turn my back on her and hide. She knew I battled with my vampiric nature, knew that while I'd come to terms with what I was, I didn't fully embrace it like other vampires did, and she took pleasure every time we met in reminding me of what I was. What she'd made me.

Now I had to live with that weakness and how it affected Essie and focus on the real problem. The wraith was targeting my squad mates, people who'd gone through hell with me facing Michael's nephilim army, who'd saved my and Gideon's lives more times than I could count and who didn't deserve such horrible deaths.

Essie stepped out of sight, heading toward the elevators that would take her up to her room, but I forced myself to stay where I was, waiting in the garage until I was sure she was gone before heading inside to look for Gideon... who was a whole other problem.

He was strong, stronger than me in a lot of ways, but if the death of one of our squad mates was going to break him it'd be Zella's.

She'd been a young, shy volunteer with only basic training when she'd been assigned to our squad as magical support — so timid, I was surprised she'd volunteered for the Angelic Defense in the first place — and it had taken Gideon almost a year to get her to open up to him.

But once she'd felt safe enough to share, we'd learned her convictions for life and justice were just as strong as any angel's and she, like the others, couldn't stand by while Michael destroyed the mortal realm.

My chest tightened at the memory of the horrors she'd survived — that we'd all survived — and at the nephilim and even angels we'd had to kill. I'd grown up in a harsher world where a man survived and protected those he loved with his revolver or rifle, and I'd given up my humanity and become a monster for vengeance.

I'd known what war would be like, but Zella hadn't had a clue and it hadn't mattered how hard Gideon had tried to protect her. He hadn't been able to protect her from that truth.

What she'd seen and been forced to do to survive had broken her. It broke a lot of angels. That was why most of them returned to the Realm of Celestial Light after the war.

Gideon had been hopeful when Zella had stayed in the mortal realm. His love for her had been obvious to everyone on the squad, and while he'd been heartbroken when she'd gone into self-imposed exile, I knew he still held out hope that one day she'd open up to him again and the budding relationship they'd developed during those horrible times would continue to grow.

I found him in the waiting area attached to Operations' small three-bed triage area, sitting on the tan leather couch. He still wore his blood-covered clothes and didn't seem to be aware that he was getting blood on the couch. He just stared at the wall, not even the TV, which hung a good three feet away from where he was looking. Not that the TV was on.

The matching two chairs that made up the rest of the waiting area were empty but that didn't surprise me. Marcus and Kol hadn't been part of our team during the war and hadn't known Zella. Marcus was too young to have fought with us and Kol, while also a little too young, had been one of Michael's victims, kidnapped from the Realm of Celestial Darkness and forced into slavery.

Gideon didn't glance up as I approached and I wasn't sure he knew I was there so I cleared my throat.

His attention jerked to me, his expression raw and exhausted, proving just how much Zella meant to him. I'd never seen him so emotionally exposed before, not even when his younger brother Dominic had been declared dead.

"No word yet," he said, his voice ragged.

My chest tightened at his grief. Knowing him, he hadn't told her how he felt and was looking at the possibility of never being able to tell her. He'd have given her time and space to figure herself out and heal before wanting to add the complication of love.

Of course, angels were immortal. He'd have thought he had all the time in the world.

"I'm going to call the others and warn them again," I said.

Gideon blinked at me, then the muscles in his jaw flexed and a hint of the commanding agent-in-charge and squad leader returned to his expression.

"I'll do that. Check in with Marcus and Summer about the coalescence snare spell," he replied.

"You're still going to go through with the plan?" Everything within me balked at putting Essie in danger — and not just because I'd woven my essence into hers and claimed her.

"The sooner the better. This monster has to be stopped," he replied, his expression returning to raw and exhausted. But his voice was also edged with a desperation that would compel him to do things that went against his angelic nature, and I couldn't help hearing what he didn't say, that the monster had to be stopped... whatever the cost.

Even if that cost was Essie's life.

ESSIE

For the next few hours I paced my room, trying to concentrate on devising a safe plan to use myself as bait to catch the wraith, finding a way out of this mess, or hell, just staying calm. But the pain in my biceps where I'd been branded was definitely growing stronger and my mind kept jumping back to Marcus's kiss.

God, he'd kissed me.

Sure, when we'd first been partnered together, I'd had fantasies about what that would be like. He was sexy and confident and there was a spark between us.

Boy, was there a spark.

My cheeks heated at the thought.

But I never thought it would actually happen. And that didn't mean it would happen again or that it should. He was right that I wanted nothing to do with the supernatural world. So why did it bother me that he'd disappeared from my life to protect me from it?

Maybe because he hadn't given me a choice? Or was it because he'd let me believe that I'd messed up his life? Although I had screwed it up, and we hadn't been anything to each other when he'd left. We'd been partners. Nothing more.

And did I want it to be more?

More meant staying in contact with the supernatural world when this was all over. More meant possible continued encounters with Gideon and the risk of revealing my angelic nature.

My stomach rumbled and I checked the time. A little after six. Dinnertime. I should eat. Take care of myself.

But I resisted the urge to rush out of my room. Going in search of the cafeteria now was a terrible idea, no matter how much my body thought it agreed with Jacob's command. Yes, Gideon could want to initiate the plan to capture the wraith at any moment, but facing that monster hungry was better than walking into a room filled with angels. Yes, there was only one investigative team stationed in Union City, but this was also a research facility. I didn't know how many other people were stationed here and I had no idea how many of them were angels. I was willing to bet, however, there were more than the two I'd already met.

I pulled out my phone for a distraction and checked my messages. Only two. Thanks to a childhood of fearing everyone and constantly moving, I wasn't close enough to anyone to be missed right away.

The first message was from my captain, telling me Gideon had demanded I be put on temporary medical leave and was taking me into protective custody, and the other was from my partner, Hank, telling me to get better soon. Hank's message sounded awkward, which didn't surprise me. We hadn't gotten close in the four and a half years we'd been partners. Everyone had heard what had happened with Marcus and no one had wanted to get stuck with me, including Hank, and the new-partner-tension had never eased between us. The middle-aged, slightly overweight cop was probably glad I was out of his hair.

I managed to kill another hour and a half flicking aimlessly through the TV channels and doodling on the notepad I kept in my purse instead of brainstorming solutions to my problems. There wasn't any safe way to use myself as bait, not with how powerful the wraith was. The guys had worn him down trying to free Zella, which was the only reason I could think of as to why it had fled, but I was pretty sure Zella's fight before we'd gotten there had helped. Without her and without being able to use lethal force, the guys were at a serious disadvantage.

My stomach growled. Again. After eight. Here was hoping enough people had visited and left the cafeteria that I'd be able to get food without being noticed, and that the unpredictability of a JP agent's job meant food would still be available.

I left the room, took the elevator to the first floor, and headed deeper into the new section of the facility — as instructed — to find the cafeteria. Ahead, the hall opened into an area sunk a few steps down. Tables ranging from two-person to eight-person with chairs neatly pushed in filled the space. Natural-feeling light — since it couldn't actually be sunlight because it was after dark — illuminated the front half of the cafeteria with a comforting glow, while the back half of the cafeteria was in shadow, closed down for the night.

The far wall was a bank of windows and a door leading to a patio, and to the left, creating a separation between the cafeteria and a sunroom-style glassed-in section with tables and chairs, stood a wall made of massive rocks. They were stacked to create nooks and crannies that held lush verdant plants and pathways for miniature waterfalls. The waterfalls trickled into a pool at the bottom that wrapped from the front around to the back. To the right were the standard cafeteria stations with metal counters and two fridges at the end, closest to the stairs, with glass doors.

Near the back, almost out of the light, Amiah and the woman from the team who'd whisked Zella away sat huddled around a table eating, their voices hushed.

I turned around before hitting the steps and darted into a dimly lit hall, hoping they hadn't seen me. I didn't want to deal with Amiah. She had to have known Marcus was a werewolf because of me and I had no doubt that her anger over that said she had strong feelings for him.

Great. I had no idea what I was going to do now. I could wait in the hall for her to leave, except she could easily see me when she passed by and with my luck she'd have business in this direction. My best option was to go back to my room and wait half an hour or so. Surely she'd be done by then.

Footsteps squeaked on the tiled floor, coming from the cafeteria. I hurried further down the hall and around the corner into a wide band of soft light emanating from a large window. Beyond the glass was a hospital room complete with high tech, beeping equipment. Zella lay on the bed, her tattered, bloody wings in metal braces extended and supported, holding them in place, and her complexion gray. The scar on her face was mostly covered with a bandage, while the other side of her face was puffy and red with the formation of a massive bruise. Both of her eyes were swollen shut so I couldn't tell if she was awake, but from the slow steady beep of the heart monitor, best guess was that she was heavily sedated.

Beside her, Gideon sat holding her hand, her knuckles pressed against his lips, his expression barren, not even icy, just stunned and aching, as if he'd been stripped raw and this was what remained. His clothes were still covered in blood, and a wide streak painted the side of his face into his hairline, as if at some point he'd swiped his hand through his hair without realizing it was covered in blood.

I shifted to sneak away, but his gaze lifted and locked on me, and I found myself going forward instead of back and opening the door.

"How is she?" I asked. The room was cold, but I suspected that was Gideon's worry and not the actual temperature.

"They've stabilized her, but she has to go back in for surgery." His attention swung back to Zella, and he lowered her hand to the bed but kept a hold of it. "She's resistant to magic. It's part of her unusual ability to create charms and what made her such an asset in the war. But it's not selective, so Amiah's healing magic barely works on her." He drew in a ragged breath. "She isn't certain if she can save Zella's right leg or her wings." His voice choked on the last word.

"Oh, Gideon. I'm so sorry." The horror of that made my throat tighten.

"She didn't deserve this. She was already in self-imposed exile, so ashamed of what she— of what *we'd* done. Of what we'd had to do." The muscles in his jaw tightened. "She's already paid too much. She'd paid it all back in the war." His thumb traced the raised flesh on the back of her hand.

"Her scars?" Duh, of course her scars, but the question slipped out and I couldn't take it back.

"A nephilim with a powerful fire magic," he said, and heat flickered across my senses. "The animal nearly burned her alive."

The heat flickered again, Gideon trying to control his rage. But I didn't need my empathy to see how upset he was. It was clear in the disgust and anger hardening his expression. "Those abominations murdered too many. Angels, supers, humans. I couldn't protect nearly enough and I couldn't protect her." His grip on Zella's hand tightened. "Be glad you're too young to remember those times and you never have to face one of those monsters."

I nodded, forcing myself to stay put and not flee in the face of his barely controlled rage. He didn't know what I was and running would only make me look suspicious. But God, I needed to get as far away from him as soon as possible. "So you think this has something to do with the war?"

"Three members of my squad are dead and Zella would have been next if we hadn't shown up," he said. "I wouldn't call that a coincidence."

Neither would I. "Who's left in your squad?"

"You mean should I warn them, Officer Shaw?" he asked, a hint of amusement in his tone.

"Sorry, I'm sure you did. I didn't mean to imply you didn't."

"I warned them after the first two and again while Amiah was working on Zella." His gaze lifted to mine and he studied me.

The hint of heat in the room vanished and ice returned to his eyes and posture. Not enough to eliminate the sense of soul-aching exhaustion radiating from him, but enough to make my nerves thrum with worry. Everything within me screamed to flee. Take care of myself. That's what Jacob had commanded. Risking discovery wasn't taking care of myself.

But neither was facing the wraith on my own.

The brand's burn was increasing and I knew that couldn't be good.

The immediate threat of the wraith's danger won out over the chance of discovery, and I stood my ground. I pressed a palm to the brand. God, would it just stop hurting for one minute?

Gideon's eyes narrowed, his attention on my biceps. "How bad is the pain?"

"Almost as bad as when it first appeared."

"He's using the unnatural connection to look for you. We don't have a lot of time." A hint of the ice melted in his eyes. "I'm sorry you're experiencing a perversion of an angelic brand. The connection is supposed to be pure, soul-deep."

"And compelling," I said, unable to keep the bitterness from my tone. How long would it take before the wraith found me? And how long after that before its brand made me do horrible things?

"Compelling because the bond is transformative for angels, attuning souls together in a connection closer than even a vampire's claim on a human. Mates, if they concentrate, can find each other, sometimes they can even communicate mentally with each other, on very rare occasions they can overhear each other's thoughts without trying," he said, with a hint of awe. "The bond is so strong, it even enhances an angel's magic."

I shuddered. Was that what the wraith was doing with me? Using me to somehow enhance his magic?

"The two souls belong together, have always been destined to be together, and the mating brand physically represents that knowing."

"I really hope I haven't always been fated to be mated with this wraith."

"If you were, your brand wouldn't hurt and it wouldn't look like it was infected."

I didn't want to check to see if the welt had gotten worse. It sure felt like it was worse.

"I have no doubt the brand was forced upon you."

"And that still doesn't mean you can get rid of it." A part of me hoped he'd correct me, say he'd been wrong when the mark had first been discovered, and tell me he could get rid of it.

But from his grim expression, I knew his answer hadn't changed.

"Which leaves us with catching him and putting him in hibernation."

Gideon's frown deepened and he pursed his lips. "Marcus thinks you'll be a liability."

Of course he does. "Marcus knew me when I was a rookie. I'm not a rookie any more." Although given the kiss, I was pretty sure me being a rookie had nothing to do with his fears. Regardless, we all knew, including Marcus, that using me as bait was the best, most expeditious plan.

"You're right, you're not a rookie, and you didn't have to step in and help Jacob, but you did."

"Yeah, about that—" I'd already gotten a dressing down from Marcus. I really didn't want another one.

"It was foolish but courageous," he said. "Still, you shouldn't have done it."

"I couldn't let Victoria torture him." Marcus hadn't really accepted that line, but I was still hoping Gideon might. Except his expression didn't change and I couldn't read it to tell what he was thinking. I shrugged, trying to look nonchalant. "I'm a cop. I serve and protect."

Still blank.

"We also need all hands on deck to capture the wraith."

He gave a tight nod that I took as agreement.

"We might need all hands just to kill it," I said.

The ice returned. "I told you killing it isn't an option."

"You saw what it did." I glanced at Zella, my body aching just looking at her. "Killing it might be our only option." And I knew he already knew that. "I know I'm not reading this situation wrong. I understand the consequences." Yes, I didn't want to die or go insane, but I wasn't a fool, either. Gideon's squad might be safe and in hiding, but what would that make the wraith do? Start killing innocent people indiscriminately? That wasn't a price I was willing to pay.

His gaze slid back to Zella. "I'd hoped I was done with horrible choices."

Marcus hurried around the corner at the end of the hall, stumbled when he saw me, then growled and picked up his pace heading toward me. Heat and humidity warmed the air. It wasn't sweltering like it had been before and I prayed it would stay that way. My pulse picked up and a strange mix of emotions churned in my chest. Desire, embarrassment, confusion, fear. None of which were going to help me, so I gritted my teeth and ignored them.

"Summer confirms the coalescence snare spell is the real deal," he said to Gideon, without looking at me. "It'll solidify the wraith into its humanoid form so we can cuff it."

"Good. Tell Kol and Jacob to meet us in the cafeteria in ten. We can make our plans there while I eat. But first I need a change of clothes." Gideon stood and brushed his lips against Zella's forehead.

"Come on," Marcus said, before Gideon had straightened. "I'll show you to the cafeteria." Without even a glance at me, he stormed away and I scrambled to catch up.

We returned to the main hall and down the steps into a thankfully empty cafeteria. Marcus pulled out a chair at a rectangular table with six chairs and sat, his arms crossed. I pulled out a chair opposite him.

He shifted, his gaze flickering to me, barely making eye contact before flickering away.

My lips tingled with the memory of our kiss. We should probably talk about what had happened. Except I had no idea what to say, and I had no idea what the kiss had meant.

He shifted again.

Come on. Just start a conversation. It couldn't be more awkward then sitting here. "So, ah—"

He jerked to his feet and paced to the rock wall.

So much for conversation. Fine. I still hadn't eaten anything and Jacob's compulsion to take care of myself was still gnawing at my insides. It was probably best anyway not to talk about what had happened. I'd screwed up his life, and he'd walked out on me without a word. Not that we'd had anything but a professional partnership to walk out on, so I had no right to be mad.

Jeez. Deal with the biggest problem at hand, then deal with Marcus.

If things didn't go well with the wraith, Marcus's kiss would be the least of my worries.

I headed to the closest of the two fridges with glass doors and peered inside. It had packaged sandwiches, wraps, salads, sliced fruit, and yogurt. The fridge beside it was filled with an assortment of beverages including... was that blood? Well, the Joined Parliament did employ vampires. I grabbed a sandwich labeled turkey club and a bottle of water and returned to my seat as Kol sauntered down the stairs.

A panty-melting smile curled his lips and lit his eyes, making my pulse stutter, and he slid into the chair across from me, where Marcus had been sitting.

"How you holding up?" he asked, his voice sliding across my senses. He had to know the affect he had on a woman just by talking to her. It didn't even look like he was trying. Without his focus on the business at hand, this was his natural, sensual self, lounging in a fold-up metal chair, exuding sexual invitation.

"Well enough to get the job done," I said, my voice breathy.

He straightened in his chair, frowned, and the sense of sexual invitation eased. "Sorry, it's been a day. I usually have better control than that."

"Have you eaten, Kol?" Marcus growled from close behind me, making me jump. He dropped into the chair beside me, crowding into my personal space but not touching me.

"I have," Kol said.

"Good." Marcus pushed my unopened sandwich closer to me. "Pick your jaw off the table, Shaw, and eat."

"And you back the hell off, Diaz," I snapped back. If I wanted to drool over the sexy incubus — which I wasn't — I had every right to. Yelling at me, kissing me, and then storming off didn't give him the right to be mean.

Marcus glared at me. I glared back. Finally! I was done with being afraid and tearful. Now I was pissed. Now I could get something done.

Marcus snarled.

I stood my ground. Probably the stupidest thing I could do with an angry werewolf, but I didn't care. He shouldn't have kissed and run.

"What the hell?" Gideon said. It sounded like he was near the stairs, but I wasn't going to look away from Marcus first.

Marcus snarled again, wrenched his gaze past my shoulder to the stairs, and shifted his chair away from mine.

"Oh, you made the angel swear," Kol said under his breath.

Gideon marched past our table to the fridge with the sandwiches. "I need you on this, Marcus. Don't make me bench you."

"By *this* you mean setting a human up as a sacrifice for a wraith?" Marcus asked.

For the love of—

"We've been over this." Gideon grabbed a sandwich and sat at the head of the table. "The decision has been made. You're either on board or off the team."

"Don't say I didn't warn you when that thing crushes her to death."

"Can we move on to actually coming up with a plan?" I didn't want to talk about my imminent death, because even if I survived, my soul was still bound to that monster. "He knows I'm with you, so it's going to be harder to lay a trap."

"I've been thinking about that," Jacob said as he hurried down the stairs and joined us, sitting beside Kol. "I know you want to keep as many civilians out of this as possible, but the best place to lay the trap is Essie's apartment."

I wasn't going to ask how Jacob knew I lived in an apartment. He'd probably read my file. They probably all had. Which meant they all knew I'd worked with Marcus before. Did all of them know I was the reason he was a shifter?

"Absolutely not," Gideon said. His attention jumped to my unopened sandwich. "You should eat that."

"The circle to cast the coalescence spell can only be about a five-foot radius," Jacob said. "If we set it in a room that's too big, that will give the wraith a chance to snag her with a tentacle without even getting close to the circle."

"And if the plan goes south, how many people in the building do you think it will kill?" Gideon asked.

I ripped open my sandwich's packaging and took a bite, but didn't really taste anything, trying to figure out whose argument was the best. That, and the pain from the brand was really becoming a distraction.

"Essie is right, it already knows she's with us," Kol said. "We won't get a second chance at this."

"Ensuring the circle encompasses as much space in the room as possible increases the likelihood of solidifying him," Marcus said.

Gideon shook his head. "It's bad enough we're endangering Officer Shaw's life. I can't endanger a whole building."

"Then force it up," I said. "It can fly and my unit is on the top floor. I have roof access and a skylight. If you can't capture or kill it, make it flee. If you block the way to the hall and the rest of the building, he'll take the path of least resistance."

I didn't like the idea of fighting this thing in my apartment, but Jacob's plan was good and no one had suggested anything better. This way, there wouldn't be any chance of it standing at the back of the room half a dozen feet away from the circle. The biggest problem would be close-quarter fighting.

That, and if we couldn't get it to solidify, all those tentacles were going to beat the shit out of the guys and it was going to take me.

ESSIE

THE GUYS TOLD ME TO MEET THEM IN THE GARAGE AND LEFT, RETURNING changed into presumably work clothes, although I couldn't tell what made these work clothes and the others not. Gideon was the only one who'd noticeably changed his style, but he'd done that when he'd changed from his bloody slacks and button-down into black cargo pants and a black T-shirt. Jacob was the only one who'd added a weapon, and now had a 92 FS Beretta holstered at each hip, although I suspected Kol had hidden his daggers back on his person — if he'd ever taken them off. Marcus looked the same. Sexy as hell in his T-shirt and jeans and without a doubt dangerous.

Gideon tossed a half-stuffed duffle bag into the back of a different SUV than before — guess our earlier one still needed to be cleaned — and we left the Supers' Quarter and drove to my apartment building. It was a four-story walkup in a neighborhood of four-story walkups. My building sat at the back of the three-building complex, creating a small green space between the sidewalk and the entrances, and the superintendent's wife did an amazing job planting flowers and making the space bright and friendly. At this hour, the flowers and shrubs farthest from the lit path were mostly in shadow, and the maple, just off center beside the walkway, filtered the streetlight's illumination into uneven, shifting bands of light.

Marcus dropped us off out front then drove around back to park in the alley. He'd take the fire escape up to my place, so no one had to wait by the building's locked front door to let him in. The rest of the team followed me inside and up to my unit.

My place wasn't big and I didn't have a lot of things, but with just me, I didn't need big or lots of stuff. What I loved about it was that it had twelve-foot ceilings, sat at the back corner of the building, and had two walls of windows as well as a skylight. The living room-kitchen combo wasn't much bigger than the five-foot radius needed for the spell, and my bedroom, to the left, was even smaller, barely big enough for my bed and dresser. Beside that was a narrow bathroom with almost no counter space and a stand-up shower. No tub — the unit's biggest problem in my opinion.

I had a second-hand couch that sagged on one side, a second-hand coffee table that was still perfectly good, and an old twenty-inch TV on an old cherry-wood stand that had seen better days. Nothing I owned was new, with the exception of my laptop, clothing, towels, and sheets. There wasn't any point in spending that kind of money on something I might need to abandon at a moment's notice.

Not that I'd had to flee since I was seventeen, but I wasn't willing to give up that particular old habit.

The back of the couch marked the invisible line between living room and kitchen, which was a counter with a sink in the center and the fridge and stove at either end. Beside the fridge and along the wall separating the apartment from the outside hall were the stairs leading up to the roof.

Gideon's gaze lifted to the ceiling and the pyramid skylight, dead center above my living room. If the night had been clear and I'd had my lights off, moonlight would have filled the room.

Kol mumbled something about a minimalistic look, took the duffle from Gideon, and set it on the floor beside my coffee table, while Jacob headed to one of the two windows against the back wall and pushed it open.

Marcus climbed inside from the fire escape, his gaze sweeping over the room before landing on me. His expression was hard, but I couldn't tell if that was because he was still furious with me or terrified for me or whatever his heated emotion had meant, because the room's temperature didn't change. Whatever he was feeling, he'd locked it down. This was Marcus the agent of the Joined Parliament, not whatever he'd been before.

"So." The pain from the brand now radiated up to my shoulder and down to my elbow, and I shifted, keenly aware that I was in imminent danger but uncertain what to do or where to go. That, and I'd never been so aware of how small my place really was. Although perhaps it wasn't just the room's size, but the guys'. They were all taller than me and I wasn't a slouch at five foot eight. Even Kol, the smallest of the group, had a few inches on me and a broader stature.

"Sit on the couch and stay out of the way," Marcus said.

Jacob pulled a compass from his pocket as Kol carefully withdrew four stone...? I had no idea what they were. They looked like squat miniature obelisks, about as big as both of my fists put together. Small glyphs were carved into each one, curling around and around from the bottom to the top, creating some kind of spell — I knew that from my enhanced supers training. The witches and spells session.

"Set the edge of the circle under the couch at the back, so we can catch most of the living room," Gideon said. "I don't think we can put it as far back as the cupboards, so we'll need to get smart about hiding the spell stones."

"You couldn't have had more stuff?" Kol asked. "It's not going to be easy hiding these."

Jacob turned to the couch, shifted, and pointed at an angle that hit the couch's back leg farthest from the door. "North is that way."

Kol placed the first stone. South required the TV stand to move a foot and a half, while the east stone was tucked behind the stairs. West was the hardest. I didn't have anything along the back wall. When I'd moved in, I'd fancied having a shelf with plants under the windows, but had never gotten around to setting that up.

"What are we going to do about this?" Kol stared at the stone on the floor, sitting in plain sight.

"We're going to pretend I'm a slob." I got off the couch, grabbed a pile of clothes from my dresser, and dropped them over the stone. "The pile might clue him in to something, but hopefully he'll be standing in the circle by the time he notices it."

Marcus rearranged the pile, shaking out folded shirts and pants. "It should work."

"Good." Gideon knelt on the floor, the coffee table between him and me. "Officer Shaw, wait until the wraith is in the circle — the closer to the center the better, because there's a second or two delay on the spell's activation — then say *vade*."

"*Vade*. Got it." A simple word, easy to remember. I had this.

"And be ready to get the hell out of the circle," Marcus said.

"If you can't," Kol said, "I'll grab you."

"If I can't?" I didn't like the sound of that.

"The spell shouldn't affect you. You're human," Gideon said.

I *really* didn't like the sound of that.

"But if it does," he continued, "you might feel numb or disoriented."

Wonderful.

"Once the wraith is solidified, I'll run in and slap on the containment cuffs," Jacob said. "Simple and straightforward."

I rolled my eyes at him. "In my experience, nothing is ever simple and straightforward."

Marcus snorted. "No shit."

"Do you see a problem with the plan?" Gideon asked Marcus.

"Only that Essie is involved." Marcus marched into my bedroom to lie in wait until the wraith showed up.

"He's normally not like this," Jacob said.

Kol shrugged. "Must be a super moon coming or something."

I forced myself to smile. "Or something."

Gideon cleared his throat, drawing my attention. "Repeat the activation word to me."

"*Vade*."

"Good. I'm going to awaken the spell." He pressed his palms against the floor and closed his eyes. A hint of light seeped from beneath his hands and through the cracks between his fingers. Then four strands of light shot out, each connecting to a stone, and the buzz in my body burst to life, overwhelming the calming effects of the nicotine patch.

What the hell? I hadn't even had it on for twelve hours.

Gideon sat back on his heels. "Now we wait."

"Great." I gritted my teeth against the buzz. "Wild guess on how long?"

"How does the brand feel?"

"My whole arm hurts." And I feared the thing was getting bigger. God, that would be just my luck.

"I can't imagine it will be long now." He motioned to the guys to take their positions, Jacob in the bathroom and Kol in the bedroom with Marcus. "I can't promise I can protect you now," he said, his voice low so the others couldn't hear.

"You do what you have to do."

He gave a tight nod, stood, and headed into the bedroom, leaving me alone in the living room while they watched me through partially open doors.

I turned my gaze to the skylight. I didn't know where the wraith would come from, but if it could see me before I could see it, I didn't want to give away the guys' locations. Not that staring up at the skylight wasn't odd with all the lights on.

This was the part I hated about stakeouts. The waiting. And I particularly hated it when my nicotine patch was running low, or out, or in this never-happened-before bizarre case where the buzz was stronger than the patch. I didn't like the idea that being in the center of this spell while it was awake but not activated set off the buzz. That was a new discovery I didn't need, not with an angel a few feet away in my bedroom. And I didn't want to think about what kind of effect the spell would have on me once it was turned on. At least Gideon had said it *shouldn't* affect me and not that it *wouldn't*. That still left the door open for them believing I was completely human.

I shifted, uncomfortable with the buzz and the growing burn from the brand. I contemplated turning on my TV. That would be a normal thing to do. More normal than the need to pace that was making me twitch.

Yeah, if I kept the volume low, I wouldn't look so obvious. I was professional enough to keep my attention on my surroundings. Why hadn't I thought of it in the first place?

But this was unlike anything I'd ever done before. I was a beat cop. I patrolled neighborhoods with my partner, answered calls for robberies, domestic disputes, shots fired, car accidents. I'd helped with a stakeout once when a witness needed twenty-four hour surveillance, and then I'd sat in an unmarked car with Hank watching the witness's house.

I grabbed the remote from the coffee table, turned the TV on, leaving it on the news channel I'd been watching when I'd had breakfast this morning, and set the volume low. They were no longer covering the protests in Rome. Now they were running a documentary on the Battle at Washington. The bloodiest fight between humans and nephilim during the war.

Grainy, shaking video from a body camera showed nephilim with brilliant white wings, just like angels, splattered with blood, tearing into a group of soldiers. All of the nephilim's eyes were wild, and many screamed or howled. They whipped bands of fire or shot bullets of ice or just pounded the soldiers to death with their fists. Fully automatic gunfire rattled over the TV's tinny speakers, nephilim staggered, some even went down, but it usually took a lot to kill a nephilim, more than just a regular angel. Weak flashes of light burst here and there as the soldiers who could cast combat spells, summoned divine light.

Then a flash of blazing white light blasted, the picture going blank for a second before returning to the horror. The camera panned away from the soldiers to the team of humans who had turned the battle in their favor. They each wore a ring imbued with divine light that could shoot multiple blasts, each blast as strong as the most powerful angels with combat light magic. So long as the human could cast a divine light strike, he could use a ring.

That had been one of the deciding factors in the war. We'd needed the supers to help fill out our ranks, but that hadn't been enough until angels had started filling rings with divine light.

The video jerked back to the fight as a nephilim lunged at the soldier wearing the camera and seized him. The camera caught the nephilim's face close up and there wasn't a hint of humanity in its eyes. It was a rabid beast, a monster, more horrific than the monsters who'd come out of hiding to help us.

The documentary paused for commercials, breaking the spell on me that had kept me watching even though I was horrified. It was like watching a car crash, except much much worse. It was no wonder everyone feared nephilim. Hell, I feared nephilim. They were the monsters Gideon had said they were.

Maybe it would be easy to convince everyone I wasn't that kind of nephilim. I didn't look insane. But I also knew from other videos taken during the war that when the nephilim hadn't been commanded into a fighting frenzy, they looked normal. If you couldn't sense essences and didn't get a good look in their eyes, you'd mistake them for a full angel.

I slid my gaze through my partially open bedroom door to the window beyond. Across the narrow side-street, light glowed from inside a few apartments, and work-out dude, as usual, had his blinds up — I wasn't sure he had blinds to cover his windows since they were never covered — and was shirtless, doing chin-ups on a bar secured on the frame of his bedroom door.

I turned my attention to the two tall windows on my back wall and the building across the alley. The light was on in the unit directly across from me, the shears drawn, but I could see the shadow of someone sitting close to them. Bookworm was in her window seat, staying up late reading again.

I sat up straighter to see to the unit two floors below Bookworm to see if the young couple with the newborn were awake. I hoped not. I'd come home late a few nights now after finishing an afternoon shift and grabbing a drink with a few fellow officers in an attempt to be social and not stick out by being a loner, and had seen them pacing back and forth with a red-faced, crying baby. The young couple's light was on, the curtains open. The guy paced into sight holding the infant as a billow of darkness swept past their window.

Was that the wraith?

My pulse picked up and I searched the darkness for confirmation that I'd seen the wraith.

Pain snapped through the brand on my arm and another billow of darkness swept past Bookworm's window. Was he heading for the roof? My mother had always said angels attack from above because most humans don't initially look up when searching for danger.

"Guys," I hissed. "We're on."

I drew in a steadying breath and concentrated on looking unaware. The trap only worked if he didn't think I was expecting him. I faced the TV but kept watch on the windows from the corner of my eye, but didn't see anything.

The buzz in my body made me jumpy, and the pain in the brand burned all the way to my wrist.

I glanced up. Nothing above the skylight.

Where the hell was he?

Darkness surged at the edge of my vision, and I jerked my attention down to the partially opened bedroom door as the wraith crashed through the bedroom window. The sense of malicious power filled the apartment, making my stomach churn.

"What the fuck?" That sounded like Marcus.

Blazing white light flashed — Gideon's divine light — and Kol dove into the living room and rolled to his feet, his daggers drawn.

Something crashed against the wall between the bedroom and the living room, drawing a grunt of pain. Someone growled — Marcus? — and the wraith howled.

Pain sliced into my arm, making my eyes water, and I jumped to my feet.

"Hey!" I shoved my coffee table toward the windows, hoping it was far enough out of the way that someone wouldn't trip over it.

Kol backed toward me, and I wasn't going to think too hard about what kind of effect the circle would have on him if he was caught inside it.

Another crash and the wall cracked. More light flashed.

Jacob glanced out the bathroom door but didn't rush out. He needed to be ready to secure the wraith with the magic containment cuffs as soon as it had solidified.

And I had to get that thing into the circle.

"I said hey!"

Someone roared. Another bone-crunching crash and Marcus smashed through the wall and hit the floor. Now visible through the hole in the wall, Gideon blasted more light at the wraith. It howled and a flurry of tentacles shot toward him. He twisted, trying to dodge the writhing mass of darkness. A dagger of light appeared in his hand, but the room was too small to avoid all the tentacles. There wasn't anywhere to go. The wraith seized his leg and hurled him at the hole in my wall. He crashed through, the throw so powerful that he flew over Marcus, slammed into the back of my couch, and knocked it over, revealing the spell stone.

Shit.

But the wraith either didn't care or didn't notice. It surged through the hole, its smoke smothering Marcus and flattening him to the floor, and shot a tentacle past me and seized Gideon's throat.

The angel gasped and slashed at it with his light dagger. Kol darted in with his blades, and Marcus thrashed on the floor, suffocating.

The activation word rushed to the tip of my tongue, but the wraith was at the edge of the circle and there was a chance it'd be able to escape.

"Come on." I hissed the combat spell at top speed and sent a small blast of light at it. My power was nothing compared to Gideon's but hopefully it was enough to get the wraith's attention. "Come on."

The smoke surged toward me and grew, the darkness fully obscuring Marcus. Tentacles seized Kol and Gideon.

It was a little closer, but was it close enough?

It was going to have to be.

"*Vade*," I yelled, as Kol was smashed against the ceiling with a sickening crunch and Gideon tossed out the window.

Magic exploded around and in me. The blaze from the brand seared through my body and the buzz kept the pain going as the world spun around me.

The wraith howled and the smoke whirled, caught in a tornado of power.

Marcus gasped and Kol shuddered. Both were prone, their eyes unfocused, but I didn't know if that was because of the spell or not.

Another surge of power made the two cry out and set my buzz into an inferno. The wraith screeched, and the darkness ripped from around him, revealing an angel with onyx devil's skin, fully extended black wings, and hellfire burning in its eyes.

Holy shit. It was an angel?

ESSIE

THE WRAITH-ANGEL JERKED TOWARD ME. JACOB BOLTED FROM THE bathroom, the magic containment cuffs in his hand, but the angel managed to yank his wrist up at the last minute and shoot darkness from his palms like a reverse divine light blast. Jacob twisted out of the way, but the blast clipped his shoulder and sent him tumbling back toward the bathroom.

Marcus staggered to his feet. The wraith-angel sent another blast at him and lunged at me.

I tried to leap out of the way, move, do anything, but my muscles had locked and I could feel, barely, beneath the inferno of the buzz, the brand seizing my body.

The wraith-angel grabbed my arm, shot a blast of darkness above him, cracking the skylight's heavy glass, and took off. We crashed through the skylight, tearing metal and shattering glass. Something sliced my cheek and my shoulder, ripping my shirt.

We flew past the roof, straight up into the darkness. I twisted against his grip. I had to get him to let go before we were too high and the fall would kill me. I cast a light strike and slapped my free palm against his hand around my biceps.

My light stuttered. Weak. Ineffective. Crap. Was I out of juice? There were only so many times a human — or even an angel, for that matter — could summon divine light before needing to recover.

Panic seized my chest. If I was out of juice, I was dead. Or not dead. God, that thought was worse. I didn't know what it wanted me for, and I didn't want to find out.

I clawed at his fingers. A tentacle of darkness swept from his body and wrapped around my chest, squeezing tight while another blocked my nose, forcing me to open my mouth to breathe, then poured down my throat when I did.

Oh shit oh shit oh shit.

I clawed at the smoke on my face, choking on it, my stomach heaving but unable to expel it or my dinner.

Wind whipped my hair, pulling strands loose from my ponytail and stinging my cheeks, and my head spun with the nauseating churn of fear, lack of oxygen, and the buzz.

It was not going to take me. It couldn't take me. *God, don't let it take me.*

The words of the light strike raced in my head over and over again and the buzz exploded from my body.

Blinding white light erupted around me.

The wraith-angel howled. His tentacles burst, releasing me and dissolving from inside me, and his grip on my arm disappeared. Gravity seized me and I plummeted back to earth.

The wraith-angel dove toward me, but a blast of divine light shot past my head and sent it reeling. It glared at me, hellfire burning in its eyes. The brand shot agony through me and I convulsed, a clear reminder that it still possessed me, and it flew away.

Then strong arms caught me, cradling me. The scent of spring wrapped around me, and the stinging wind rushing past me stilled. I twitched and gasped with another convulsion from the brand, and Gideon hugged me closer to his firm chest.

We landed on the roof and the guys came storming out the door.

"You're never doing that again. Never," Marcus growled before he'd fully stepped onto the roof. "And I don't give a fuck what you think. It's not happening."

"Was that actually an angel?" Kol gasped, his face tight with pain, hugging himself as if his ribs hurt.

Gideon's pulse thudded where my ear pressed against his chest and a churning mix of hot and cold flashed over me. I didn't know what it meant. I couldn't make my mind focus enough to figure it out.

"I have no idea what that was," Gideon said, thankfully saying nothing about how powerful my divine blast had been. There was a chance — a slim chance — that the guys inside hadn't seen it, but without a doubt Gideon had.

A whisper of a convulsion swept through me.

Marcus snarled. "It sure looked like a fucking angel."

The hot and cold grew stronger and my stomach churned.

"And a few minutes ago we thought it was a wraith," Jacob said.

Marcus jerked toward him, clenching his hands. "You guys are supposed to be the font of knowledge of this team. You're supposed to know what that was."

"Marcus, take a breath and calm down," Gideon said.

More hot and cold. More buzz burning my body, and my stomach heaved. "Put me down," I gasped.

"Calm down!" Marcus growled, claws extending from his fingers. "This is not the time for calm."

"Now more than ever," Gideon said, his tone frosty.

I pressed my palms against his chest, trying to get free from his hold, bile burning my throat. "Put me down."

His frozen gaze dropped to me and the fluctuating temperature made me dizzy. My stomach heaved again and I shoved out of his grip.

"Essie." Marcus reached for me, but I rushed past him. I had to get to the bathroom, hide until the world had stopped turning and burning. It was bad enough they were seeing me like this. If I couldn't pull my shit together fast, they'd agree with Marcus and I'd be locked in the Joined Parliament Operations Building until the wraith-angel was caught, or — and this was more likely — until I went insane and died.

I staggered down the stairs, barreled into the bathroom, and slammed the door shut. My stomach clenched and I threw up my measly dinner into the toilet.

Tremors raced through me and I sagged to the floor. The guys' nauseating mix of emotions still gave me hot and cold flashes, tears burned my eyes, and the buzz sliced into me stronger than ever before.

Come on, pull it together.

But I couldn't stop the shaking, or loosen the panic clutching my throat and chest. The tears released, streaming down my cheeks, and I bit back a sob, praying no one heard me.

It had almost had me. God. It had almost taken me. And there'd been nothing I could have done. The guys couldn't even protect me. There was no way out of this.

Someone knocked tentatively on the door.

"I'm fine. I just need a minute."

"Essie." Jacob's voice rumbled through the door.

"Don't you dare tell me to come out." I couldn't handle that. I wouldn't be able to resist his command and they'd all believe everything Marcus said about me if I came out looking like I was bawling my eyes out — even if I was.

Marcus said something, his voice dark, dangerous, but I couldn't make out what he said so he couldn't have been standing right outside the door with Jacob.

Gideon said something back.

"Do you need anything?" Jacob asked.

Yeah, for all of this to go away. A sob broke free.

"Essie?"

"A moment. I just need a moment," I said, my tone harsher than I'd intended. But what I really needed was a time machine so I could go back to this morning and... I don't know... wake early? Sleep in? Anything to change this horrible day.

Except if that had even been possible — which it wasn't — that would mean no one would have stopped the robbery and Abe could have been hurt or killed.

I sniffed and wiped at my tears.

So plan A hadn't worked. That didn't mean we couldn't come up with a plan B. We now knew more about the wraith. Knowledge was always good.

I spat a mouthful of bitter spit in the toilet, flushed, and used the edge of the sink to help me stand. My body still burned and shook, but at least my stomach had settled.

I gripped the counter and drew in a ragged breath, fighting to regain some control. The woman staring back at me in the mirror looked more stunned than she had when I'd caught glimpses of myself this afternoon, and I now had an ashen complexion and too-wide, puffy-red eyes. It was going to take more than a few minutes for that to clear up.

At least I could fix my ponytail. Maybe by then the shaking would have eased up enough so I could walk out of the bathroom without staggering.

Oh, wishful thinking.

I tugged the hair elastic from the mess, ran my comb through my dark locks, and retied it into a ponytail. I still looked like a disaster. I splashed water on my face and dried off with my bath towel. Nope, not any better. This was the best I was going to get.

My legs were still shaky, but I reached for the doorknob to leave anyway.

I grabbed for the knob and burning pain sliced through my arm. I gasped and clutched the counter, tears returning to my eyes. The agony seared like the wraith's brand, except it was now on the inside of my right forearm.

Another sob threatened to escape. It was making its claim on me stronger, adding another brand. It could find me with the first one. God, what would a second one do?

I shoved my sleeve up, revealing a complicated sigil made of delicate gold threads swirling through my skin.

Gideon's words jumped into my head. The wraith's brand wasn't a true mating brand because it wasn't gold.

My knees gave out and I crumpled to the floor.

Footsteps hurried to the door.

"Essie?" Jacob asked without opening it.

I couldn't tear my eyes away from the new brand. It was gold.

Gold. Real. Permanent.

This couldn't be happening. It was not happening. It was a night-mare. I'd wake up and everything would be back to normal. A real bond permanently tied me to an angel... or it revealed my angelic nature, if I wasn't bonded to another angel.

"What the—" Gideon said, his voice tight with pain.

Oh, no. Please, no.

"Dude, did you just get a mating brand?" Kol asked.

Not him. Anyone but him. He thinks I'm a monster, an animal, an abomi-nation. God, please. Don't permanently bind me to him. Please. Another sob broke free.

"Essie," Jacob said. The doorknob turned and I jerked my sleeve down and hugged myself, my shaking returning with a vengeance. The door opened all the way and Jacob's gaze dropped to me, his eyes widening in fear, the room's temperature settling on frigid.

Behind him, Gideon grimaced in pain and held his forearm just below where my mark had manifested. Divine light radiated from his eyes, accentuating his pain and shock.

"You said a real one was gold," Kol said. "Who is it?"

"I don't know," Gideon said with awe. His shifted and I caught a glimpse of his brand. I'd need a better look, but I'd bet it was identical to the one on my arm. Same spot. Same brand.

No, please. Another sob broke free.

Marcus hurried toward me as Jacob knelt to pick me up.

"I've got her," Marcus growled, pushing Jacob aside.

"How could you not know who it is?" Kol asked.

"The bond just happened. It needs to get stronger first. We don't have that kind of a connection yet, so it could be anyone. It could be Zella." He frowned, then hope flooded his expression and warmed his gaze into a perfect summer sky.

Heartache twisted in my chest. He thought his mate was Zella. He was going to be shattered when he learned the truth.

And then horrified when he learned the real truth.

ESSIE

Marcus pulled me into his arms and stood. "We need to get her back to Operations."

"It could be Zella," Gideon said. Now he looked even more stunned.

"Gideon," Marcus growled.

Gideon's attention jumped to us. "Right. I... I, ah..." Recognition of the situation flickered through his eyes, but it was like he couldn't think past the sudden appearance of the brand.

I couldn't blame him. I couldn't think past it either. My body shook so hard my teeth chattered with the shock of it. I hadn't had nearly as strong a reaction to the wraith's brand, and that only added to my horror that this one was the real deal.

His gaze landed on me, his eyes filled with apology, but it wasn't for binding my soul with his. It was because he needed to go to Zella, because he thought the brand was with her.

"Go," Jacob said to him. "We've got her."

"Thank you." Gideon extended his wings and flew out the shattered skylight.

Marcus growled again and hugged me closer. "You're freezing."

"Kol, go get the car," Jacob said.

"No." The muscles in Marcus's jaw twitched. "You've got the warmest body temperature. Have your broken ribs healed enough to take her?"

Kol gave a tight nod and Marcus handed me over to him, then hurried out the window to climb down to the SUV parked in the alley.

Kol's heat seeped into my skin, but my teeth kept chattering and my mind kept whirling. I was Gideon's destined mate. How the hell was I Gideon's destined mate?

Jacob and Kol hurried me out of my apartment, down the stairs, and out onto the street. Marcus drove the SUV up to the curb, and Jacob took the front passenger seat while Kol helped me onto the bench behind them, settled in beside me, and pulled me onto his lap.

I pressed my cheek against his shoulder and leaned my forehead against his neck, trying to get closer to him, desperate for more heat. This was a deeper cold than just my empathy. This went bone-deep, and I didn't know where it had come from.

A tear leaked from beneath my closed eyelids. I no longer had any control over my life. I couldn't even stop myself from crying.

"Hey," Kol murmured. "We can figure this out. We can fix this."

But they couldn't. There wasn't any fixing this.

My forearm ached with Gideon's brand, and my biceps with the wraith's. The buzz in my body was like a million bees stinging me over and over again, and I was clean out of emotional strength.

Please let me have seen it wrong. Let it be anyone else but Gideon.

Marcus drove us back to the Supers' Quarter and pulled up to the glass doors in the Operations Building's garage. He glanced back at me. "Is she still cold?"

"I can't get her to warm up," Kol said.

"We can't risk this being some kind of reaction to the wraith— angel — whatever the hell it is." His grip on the steering wheel tightened, turning his knuckles white. "Get her to her room and do whatever it takes to get her body temp up." He turned to Jacob. "We need a plan. There are wards on this building, but I have no idea if they will stop that thing."

"Agreed," Jacob said.

Kol climbed out of the SUV, still holding me, and carried me down the hall to the elevator and up to my room.

"Do you have your keycard?" he asked.

"Back pocket," I forced out.

He set me on my feet. The hall swayed and I was still shaking so hard I was having trouble standing. I pulled the card from my pocket and handed it over to him. No way was I going to be able to slide it into the reader.

He unlocked the door, carried me inside, and sat me on the bed. "Why don't I run you a bath," he said as he flicked on the bedside lamp and headed toward the bathroom, "see if we can't get your temperature to rise that way."

A bath? Panic seized me. There was no way he was going to let me bathe alone, not with how unsteady I was, but a bath equaled naked — or at least a lot less clothing. And while a part of me loved the idea of being scantily clothed with a drop-dead gorgeous man, scantily clothed risked revealing the new brand. And I just— I couldn't—

"No." I scrambled off the bed to stop him. My legs couldn't hold me and I dropped to the floor again, proving just how helpless I was right now.

Tears burned in my eyes. God, why couldn't I stop crying?

Kol knelt beside me, grabbed one of my hands, and rubbed it between his palms, his skin blazingly hot on my frozen fingers. "We need to get you warm."

"I know." I knew he wasn't going to leave me until I was, and honestly I didn't want him to. I didn't want to be alone with my thoughts, with the horror that I was mated with an angel. "Can you just hold me?"

His gaze captured mine and a hint of desire uncurled within me, then vanished as quickly as it formed — or at least some of it, but not all — and concentration pinched around his eyes. "I can do that."

He threw back the covers on my bed. I staggered into it, then he settled in behind me, both of us fully dressed, and pulled the covers back over top.

"It's going to be all right." He wrapped strong arms around me and tucked me tight against his body.

"Don't make promises you can't keep."

His warmth seeped deeper into my skin and for a second my brain stalled, as if he was enthralling me. That was probably for the best. I needed to get a hold of myself, break through the panic, and I couldn't seem to do it on my own.

"Gideon will do whatever it takes," he said, his warm breath caressing the back of my neck, drawing a shiver of desire.

"Now you're making promises for Gideon."

"He said he'd protect you and he's an angel of his word."

Another shiver slid through me and that hint of desire unfurled a little more, but a convulsion quickly followed and sliced through it, consuming it and drawing a gasp.

Kol's arms around me tightened and my brain stalled again, caught between thoughts. There was only glorious nothing and Kol's warmth and embrace.

He murmured something into my hair, his breath caressing my neck again, but the words muddled before reaching my brain. It didn't matter, though. All that mattered was his body wrapped around me, his heat melting away the cold, and the room's temperature thankfully rising.

I floated in that warmth, weightless and without pain. The buzz was gone, the burn of the brand was gone, and the sudden changes in temperature were gone. There was only heat and darkness.

And Kol. It was wrong to be attracted to him now that I was destined to be Gideon's mate, even if that attraction to Kol probably wasn't more than a human's normal response to an incubus. He and Gideon were co-workers. God, it was wrong to be mated with Gideon when it was clear he was in love with Zella and Marcus was attracted to me.

Except I didn't really know if Marcus was. Yeah, he'd kissed me, said he was terrified for me, but did that add up to a going-to-do-something-more-about-it attraction? Did I want it to?

And really, it didn't matter. Nothing was going to happen between me and Marcus, no matter what I'd fantasized about four and a half years ago, and nothing was going to happen with Kol.

And absolutely nothing was going to happen with Gideon. Whenever the brand's magic started to compel me to want to be with him, I would fight it. I would fight it with everything I had.

A laugh cut through the darkness. "You can't fight the brand," the darkness said, his voice low and sensual. A tendril of smoke slid across my belly and the buzz crackled under my skin. "I've marked you. You're mine. You will come when I call."

"If that was the case, you'd be calling me already."

The tendril broke apart, but another one slid up my leg, the buzz growing wherever it touched. "Give it time."

"Never going to happen."

The tendril broke apart again, and the darkness, or rather the wraith, growled. "They won't understand you."

"There's nothing to understand."

"Don't kid yourself. You're... complicated," the wraith said, and a tendril swept out of the darkness and curled over my wrist.

"Every woman is complicated." But I knew what he was talking about and my words didn't dispel the tendril this time. Somehow he knew I wasn't completely human and knew none of the guys would accept me when they learned the truth.

God, if they didn't kill me, they'd lock me up for life, or worse, use me as a lab rat to figure out why I existed and was different from the monsters Michael had created. It was my mother's greatest fear. She'd spent her whole life— *given* her whole life to protect me. She'd said no one, human, angel, or super, would understand me, and when I was old enough, she'd shown me video clips of the war and just how monstrous the nephilim had been.

"They won't understand," the wraith hissed again, and another tendril rushed from the darkness and curled around my thigh.

The buzz in my body increased. The tendrils thinned then thickened again, as if struggling to maintain substance.

"They'll fear you. They'll sentence you without due process. You're an animal. You don't deserve the same rights as them."

They would be my monsters, like I was theirs. Except there were more of them. They were more powerful than me. I was a nephilim without magic. I could barely summon a blast of divine light. Most humans who could cast a light strike were more powerful than me.

"But I don't fear you."

Another tendril curled around my waist.

"I don't think you're an animal."

His words slid across my senses and his tendrils tightened. I could sense the promise of desire from him, but also deep-burning rage.

"I crave you, Essie. With me, you'll have unimaginable power. Power enough to protect yourself and to wreak vengeance on all the hurt they've forced on you." The tendril around my wrist slid up my arm and curled around the wraith's brand, framing it and drawing my attention to the red sigil seared into my skin. "I understand you."

The buzz in my body increased, and my muscles twitched as if zapped with electricity. I gritted my teeth against the pressure of the tendrils and the lure of his words. There might be truth in what he said, that the world would never accept or desire me. That they would always fear me and because of that I'd always live in fear. But I didn't want the vengeance he promised. It didn't even hold a hint of allure. I just wanted to live a normal human life.

"But you don't," the wraith said. "I can feel your true soul struggling to break free. Your angelic nature has imprisoned you. Your fear has imprisoned you. I'm trying to set you free."

"By branding me and permanently bonding our souls together?"

"Because I love you."

"I doubt you do." I could feel it in the smoke and darkness. What he felt wasn't love, it was madness, a need for power, and for some reason he saw power within me that he could possess and control.

"I do love you. I *need* you."

"Yeah, to fulfill your need for vengeance." His reason for vengeance fluttered around in my head, but I couldn't grasp onto it. There was only his smoke and his hatred.

"You will give me what I want." More tendrils swept out of the darkness and wrapped around me. I jerked against them, but I couldn't break free. "We're the same," the wraith hissed. "You belong to me, your power belongs to me, and we will reap justice for the slaughter of our people."

A spear of smoke sliced into the ugly red brand on my arm, and the wraith's essence poured into me, flooding every cell, suffocating me from the inside out.

I screamed and thrashed. I had to get free. I couldn't let it control me, command me, possess me. I couldn't let it use me to do horrible things.

My elbow slammed into something solid and someone yelped, then a strong hand pinned my arm to my body.

"Essie," Kol gasped.

The darkness clung to my mind.

Get out. Get the fuck out, I screamed at the wraith, no— the nephilim.

"Essie, wake up."

I jerked into a sitting position and my eyes flew open. The darkness within me exploded into smoke and my mind swept it away with a ferocious wind. Nausea churned in my stomach and the buzz crackled under my skin at pre-nicotine levels. The wraith had been in my head, and I could feel its sickening darkness still clinging to me as if it had just poured down my throat.

"Essie."

I jerked my attention to Kol. He sat beside me, his arms around me, hugging mine tight to my body. A red welt marked his cheek. I must have elbowed him in the face. Behind him, sunlight streamed through the window, the curtains having never been closed for the night, and the sky was beautiful and clear, like Gideon's eyes.

"It's okay," he said.

I shuddered at the memory of the wraith in my head. Then the weight of yesterday's events slammed into me and panic squeezed my chest. I struggled to breathe. It wasn't just the wraith. It was so much worse than that. I was mated for life. To an angel. It wasn't going to be okay.

I shoved that thought aside before my panic took over. I'd deal with it later, after I'd dealt with the wraith — because I doubted I'd be able to avoid it completely.

Kol's eyes narrowed and he frowned.

Yeah, no one could maintain a positive attitude in the face of everything that had happened, but then I realized his attention wasn't on my face, it was lower.

"Is that—?" His frown deepened and he grabbed my wrist, turning it to expose the inside of my forearm. "Is that Gideon's brand?"

Oh, shit.

I tried to jerk my arm away, but he held tight and shoved my sleeve up higher, exposing the whole brand. It glimmered as if it were real gold reflecting bright sunlight. The lines were crisp and delicate — the complete opposite to the wraith's brand — and they swirled in a complicated design from mid-forearm to my elbow. It was beautiful, and it made my breath hitch in awe and fear. Gideon had said the connection between branded mates was deep and pure. That it grew stronger with time, transforming each angel's soul, bringing them closer together than even a vampire's claim. At the root of it all was an attunement, fitting souls perfectly together and creating a yearning that they had to be together. That they belonged together.

"It's a mistake."

"A mating brand is never a mistake."

"This one is." I tugged at Kol's grip but he still refused to let go, his gaze locked on my arm.

"It's destiny."

"It's a disaster."

His attention jumped up to me, surprise in his eyes. "How could this possibly be a disaster? This is fate, the universe bringing you together."

"And did you see the way he looked when he thought the bond was with Zella?"

Kol pursed his lips. I could see he wanted to argue with me, but knew I was right.

"He'll be heartbroken when he realizes fate has mated him with me."

"I don't think he will." Kol raised a hand to caress my cheek but stopped before making contact, as if suddenly realizing I belonged to someone else.

God, that thought made me want to scream. I didn't *belong* to anyone. I didn't *want* to belong to anyone. And I sure as hell didn't want that *someone* to be an angel.

"I want my life back." My words came out small and soft.

"Being mated doesn't mean your life is over."

I was pretty sure it did.

Realization flashed in his eyes. "In fact, if your bond with Gideon is stronger than the one with the wraith, I think it might actually save your life." He threw back the covers and hopped from the bed. "We have to tell Gideon, confirm if I'm right."

I scrambled from the bed and grabbed his hand, stopping him before he opened the door. "We're *not* telling Gideon."

"We have to tell him. He's going to find out soon enough. He said he'd know who his mate was as soon as the bond gets stronger."

"Kol, please." Yes, it was inevitable, but I wasn't going to be running around proclaiming it from the mountaintops just yet. Probably ever. "I need time to process this."

He pursed his lips.

"I need time to process everything." And make peace with how all of this was going to end. "It's all so complicated."

"It's your bond," he said, his tone soft, reluctant, then gave a tight nod. "It's your news to share."

I grabbed his hands and gently squeezed them. "Thank you."

He leaned toward me, as if he was going to hug me or kiss me or something, but pulled away before finishing the move. "We still need to figure out what to do about the wraith... angel... whatever it is. Are you up for that?"

"God, yes."

"Then let's go find the rest of the team."

I yanked my shirt sleeve down and opened the door. Marcus sat on the floor against the far wall, his knees up, arms across his knees, and forehead on his arms. His hair was tousled, making him look even sexier, and his clothes, the same as when we'd fought the wraith, were disheveled. He hadn't changed even though, unlike me, he'd had a chance to.

"Have you been here all night?" I asked.

His head jerked up. The agony in his eyes melted to complete, desperate relief, and he rushed to his feet and wrapped me in a tight embrace. "Oh, thank God."

His lean-muscled body pressed against mine, strong and sure and warm, and I melted into his hug. For a second I was going to pretend my life wasn't a complete mess.

"Thank God, thank God." His hands moved from my back to my head, his fingers tangled in my hair, and his lips captured mine in a fierce, possessive kiss, so intense it stole my breath.

Then he pulled back before it had really started and pressed his forehead to mine. "You're never doing that again. Please say you're never doing that again."

I cupped his cheeks in my palms and urged him to make eye contact. His fear licked cold across my skin and nearly broke my heart. "You know I can't make that promise."

A growl rumbled in his chest, but he swallowed it back. "I know. I just — God." He hugged me again, clutching me to him as if he was afraid to let me go.

Kol cleared his throat. "So I *am* into watching, but if I'm going to get a decent meal out of it, you guys need to be a little more... active."

"Shut up," Marcus growled without letting me go. "And thank you."

"Sure," Kol said. "Ask me to spend all night with a pretty lady—"

Marcus's head jerked up. He glared over my shoulder at Kol and for the first time I truly saw the wolf within him, feral, protective, ferocious.

I slid my hands to his chiseled chest and gently pressed, easing a step back. "And, fully clothed, he helped me raise my body temperature."

Marcus's piercing green gaze slid back to me and the wolf released a soft rumble. I was safe. It was happy.

And I was seriously confused.

Guess kissing me yesterday *had* meant something.

"Now let's find Jacob and Gideon and figure out plan B," I said.

"When we left Gideon last night, he was with Zella. He's probably still there. I'll call Jacob and tell him to meet us in her room. Gideon won't be wanting to leave his mate right now." Marcus pulled his phone from his pocket and turned slightly away from me.

Kol stared at me with wide eyes and he mouthed the word *compli-cated* to me.

No shit, I mouthed back.

Marcus's free arm snaked across the back of my waist and tugged me closer to him, as if he couldn't stand to be away from me.

Jeez. Complicated didn't begin to explain the mess I was in.

ESSIE

I slipped back into my room, using the excuse that I needed to visit the bathroom before heading down, and replaced my nicotine patch. I was going through them faster than I should, but these were extenuating circumstances. If I survived what was about to come and continued to burn through the nicotine at the same rate, then I'd start to worry.

The new patch brought the biting buzz back under control — or as under control as it ever got. I returned to the hall, and Marcus stepped close to me and stayed close as we got into the elevator and headed down to Zella's room.

If I was smart, I'd tell him right away about Gideon's brand. Letting him continue to hold me and kiss me like that could only lead to heartache for all of us. But if I was being honest with myself, I was thrilled at being held by him and the promise of satisfying the sizzling desire between us.

And maybe I was crazy. Fate said I belonged to Gideon. If I stayed in Marcus's world, I'd be Gideon's whether I wanted to be or not, and even if I wasn't, constantly being with supers guaranteed that someone would notice the truth about me. Hell, it was a miracle no one had noticed so far.

It didn't matter how comfortable and safe and turned on I was in Marcus's embrace. As soon as the wraith, or rather nephilim— Nope, I couldn't think of him as the same kind of super as me. We weren't the same. Not even close. As soon as the *wraith-angel* was taken care of, I had to leave — barring, of course, being insane or dead, and if I was either, then being a nephilim in the world of supers was the least of my worries.

The elevator door slid open, and Marcus's phone rang. We stepped into the hall as he answered it, and he stiffened at whatever was said.

"Change of plans. We're meeting Gideon and Jacob in the garage. Union City PD has found another body."

"Shit," Kol said. "And we're going to the scene? Can't forensics confirm it was the wraith?"

"I thought they could, but apparently not," Marcus said. "And I have no idea why, so we're going."

Kol frowned. "So who's staying here with Essie?"

"No one." Marcus shoved his phone back into his pocket, not sounding happy about that. "Gideon doesn't want to separate the team until the wraith is dealt with and she's safest with us, so she's coming along."

Given how we'd had our asses handed to us last night, I wasn't certain I was safe with anyone, but I had to agree that I had a better chance of not being captured by the wraith-angel if I was with all of the guys instead of just one of them.

That, and I wasn't going to argue with Marcus right now. I could still sense his wolf, barely contained within him — now that I knew what the fury radiating from him actually was — and didn't want to push him.

"Okay," I said, "then let's go. I'm sure Gideon has his reasons for wanting to go to the scene."

I motioned and Kol headed down the hall. I followed.

"I think he can't just sit here, even with Zella, waiting to find out who's dead now." Marcus fell into step beside me. "And if it's a squad member, he and Jacob are the ones who'll be able to make the identification."

"Yeah, but he's endangering Essie by leaving the protective wards on Operations," Kol said.

"If our wards could even keep that thing out." Marcus shifted closer to me.

Kol huffed. "I still think Gideon is starting to lose his shit."

"I do, too, but investigating crimes committed by supers is also our job," Marcus said. "Maybe we'll stumble across a miracle and there'll be something at the crime scene to help us deal with the wraith."

Gideon was already in the garage when we arrived, standing just outside the glass doors, his expression still raw and haggard like when I'd seen him earlier at Zella's bedside. It didn't look as if things were going well with Zella, and I could only imagine his pain at thinking he could lose his destined mate before the mating brand had fully formed.

Kol opened the door from the hall to the garage, and Gideon's attention jerked to us. Emotional ice swept over his face and through his posture, and the cold, emotionless angel I'd first met stared back at us. His attention jumped to the red mark on Kol's cheek — thankfully fading and it might not even bruise, so I mustn't have hit him that hard — and he frowned.

"Has forensics left for the scene already?" Marcus asked, still standing possessively close to me.

"Yes." Gideon's gaze slid to the space — or rather lack of space — between us. "The officer who called us said they hadn't managed to get an ID on the victim, but the scene looks like the other three. We're just waiting on—" His gaze shifted past my shoulder and Jacob stepped out of the hall into the garage.

His claim on my essence tugged in my chest, and I couldn't tear my gaze away from him. Every fiber of my being yearned to please him, begged for his touch and command.

I gritted my teeth and forced myself to stay where I was. Marcus bristled beside me, as if he could sense my need to go to Jacob. The tug squeezed tighter and I strained to draw a full breath. God, I couldn't wait for this compulsion to ease up, like he'd promised it would.

"As you were," Jacob said, his voice a low rumble, and the pressure in my chest evaporated.

Thank God.

"We good?" Gideon asked.

"Hardly," Marcus growled.

"Fine." It was as good as it was going to get.

Jacob gave a tight nod.

"All right," Gideon said. "Let's go. We're headed to Seventh and Foley." He tossed Marcus a set of keys.

Marcus caught them and glanced at me, as if trying to decide if he should decline driving to stay beside me, then squared his shoulders and hurried to one of the SUVs in the spot across from us. Thank goodness, because this whole situation was uncomfortable enough as it was.

Jacob fell into step beside me and pressed a hand to my back. "How are you feeling?" he asked in a low voice, his words just for me.

"I'm not going to start crying again, if that's what you're worried about." Although if something else monumental happened, I couldn't promise that I'd be able to keep holding it together.

"Given all that's happened, you have every right to still be crying."

"And what good would that do?" I climbed onto the middle bench with Kol, while Gideon took the front passenger seat and Jacob took the back. "We still need to figure out plan B."

"Ward you with everything we can find and keep you close," Marcus said, pulling out of the parking space.

"Unless I can wear those wards, no. I'm not spending the rest of my life trapped in a room somewhere."

Marcus shot a glare at me through the rearview mirror then drove onto the Quarter's main street and headed toward the human part of the city.

"I don't think we can try luring him again," Jacob said. "That didn't even work the first time."

"And what the hell is it?" Kol rubbed his face, suddenly looking exhausted. I might have passed out and slept last night, but how much sleep had *he* gotten? "Is it a wraith or an angel?"

"I think he's both." A part of me screamed that I was going to regret pointing out that this thing was a nephilim, but not telling them only prolonged the inevitable. One of them would figure it out eventually. There was no point in pussyfooting around it.

Gideon glanced over his shoulder, his gaze jumping past me to Jacob. "I think she's right. One of them survived."

"Michael destroyed them all when we raided his laboratory," Jacob said. "None of them hatched in that blaze. You double-checked yourself."

"I know." The muscles in Gideon's jaw flexed. "But I've spent all night thinking about it and there's no other explanation."

"What explanation?" Marcus asked.

"An archnephilim, specifically half archangel and half demon," Gideon said.

"Are you shitting me?" Kol asked. "Demon and angel DNA doesn't mix."

Gideon turned his attention back to the road. "Angel DNA doesn't mix with any species."

"Not true," Jacob said. "A regular angel's DNA is compatible with an angel-touched human's. That's how Michael and Lucifer managed to get their nephilim creation spell to work in the first place. Demon DNA has to be powerful enough to withstand combining with an archangel's. We saw the partially formed demon-archangel hybrids ourselves. We know it's possible."

"Our DNA is only compatible because of unnatural magic," Gideon said.

"So you're saying Michael was creating even more powerful nephilim when the war ended?" I asked. God, if anything like the wraith-angel had joined the war, humanity would have lost. I shuddered. And that was what had branded me as his. A nephilim with the power of a demon and an archangel.

My thoughts stuttered and jumped back to something Gideon had said. "You said Michael destroyed them before they'd hatched."

"So we couldn't take them into custody," Jacob said. "We lost more than half the squad trying to take that facility."

"Could this archnephilim think you were responsible for Michael destroying his lab? That could be why he's murdering your remaining squad members." The wraith-angel had said he wanted vengeance, that *I* should want vengeance, too, for the slaughter of our people.

"So we have a guess what its motivation is," Marcus said. "Doesn't help us deal with it."

He had a point, but I wasn't willing to give up on that train of thought. "Maybe we can use that to make him make a mistake or something. In the very least, does knowing he's an archnephilim help?"

"It doesn't help you," Gideon said, his voice suddenly void of emotion, as if he didn't want to say what he had to say. "It's nearly impossible to win a fight with an archangel if you're not trying to kill him, and we'd need help from more than one archangel to do that — which, with the toll of the war being so recent, is never going to happen. The only sure way to stop this archnephilim is to kill it."

Marcus slammed on the brakes, stopping in the middle of the busy two-lane street, and growled at Gideon. "We are not killing it."

"If it's an archnephilim, there isn't any choice." A hint of Gideon's ice melted, revealing soul-rending pain. His gaze slid to mine and I could see he'd come to the horrible realization that he couldn't save me as he'd promised, and it was tearing him apart.

"What happened to not killing the human?" Marcus's wolf rose to the surface and his pupils turned to slits. "We don't kill humans."

"It might not kill her." Kol's gaze jumped to my arm.

Please, don't say it. Please. I'm not ready and there wasn't any guarantee Gideon's brand would save me.

He must have seen the panic in my face, because he opened his mouth to say more then snapped it shut.

"Sure," Marcus said. "She'll just go insane instead."

The temperature in the SUV dropped with Marcus's fear, and the driver in the sedan behind us leaned on his horn.

Marcus ignored him. "That's not acceptable. Essie gets out of this. She gets her life back. Free and clear of all of this."

More horns blared and someone started shouting.

"We all know that isn't going to happen," Gideon said.

"It God damn is gonna happen," Marcus growled, the temperature dropping even more.

The driver behind us jerked his sedan into an opening in the oncoming traffic and drove around us.

"If magic can create the impossible, maybe magic can capture the impossible," Jacob said. "Or break it. We have an archive of ancient texts and a handful of journals that we managed to confiscate from Michael's laboratory before it burned down. There might be something in them that can help."

His claim tugged in my chest. He wanted what he said to be true and, even without saying it, the claim needed me to help him. Now.

I dug my fingernails into my palms, hoping no one would notice, praying the urge to jump out of the SUV and go back to Operations would pass. Jacob wasn't rushing back. He was headed to the crime scene with the rest of the team. That was where I should be. Really. A hint of pressure eased, but not all, as if the claim only half agreed with my argument to stay.

Gideon shot Jacob a dark look, the warning clear: don't give false hope.

Jacob raised an eyebrow in response, *his* message clear: stop being an ass. "I'm not willing to give up on Essie. We're going to this crime scene then to the archives to find an answer."

The pressure vanished, but the temperature continued to drop until it was a struggle to keep my teeth from chattering.

More cars jerked around us, and people rolled down their windows and yelled at us.

I rubbed my arms, trying to get myself to warm up before my breath misted and frost formed on my skin. Now I could tell without a doubt that Marcus was terrified and he needed hope more than I did, if only to raise the temperature in the SUV. "We still don't know what to do about this archnephilim," I said. "Seeing if there's anything in these texts might help us to form a plan that won't get our asses kicked the next time we face off with it."

"*You're* not facing off with it again," Marcus growled.

"We've already been over this. I can't make any promises."

"I can," Gideon said. "Whatever we do, Officer Shaw is going to stay behind Operations' wards. With luck, their protection against malicious intent should be enough to prevent the archnephilim from entering."

But would they be enough for me to resist the pull of his brand? Gideon had said the brand drew mates together, and the archnephilim had said I'd give him what he wanted, that I belonged to him.

"Fine," Marcus said, his voice low.

"Now, can we get to the crime scene like we're supposed to?" Gideon asked. "If this perp is an archnephilim, this is my mess to clean up. Not the humans'. And it needs to be soon. Like yesterday."

Yeah, yesterday would have been great. Preferably before I'd gotten involved.

We arrived at a two-story motel on the outskirts of town, with exterior corridors, faded blue siding, and peeling gray accent paint. The parking lot was riddled with weeds growing out of the asphalt and if there'd been lines marking parking spaces, they were long gone. The neon sign at the front of the property wasn't on, since it was just after eight in the morning, but I suspected not all of it lit up, if any of it actually did.

Half a dozen cruisers were parked near the back of the lot, along with a black SUV — presumably the JP forensics team. Two uniformed officers were scouring the parking lot for evidence, while four more were in the field behind the motel. Another two stood outside the open door of a room on the second floor.

A young man with a rumpled dress shirt and glasses stood at the front of the building near a sign labeled OFFICE, talking with a man in a suit — probably the detective who'd caught the case before the JP agents took over.

Marcus parked halfway down the lot, putting us between the young guy being interviewed and the crime scene, and we piled out of the SUV.

"Marcus, talk to the detective and find out what he's learned," Gideon said. "Kol, Officer Shaw, you can wait with the officers outside the door while Jacob and I check in with Summer and her team. Let's make this fast."

Marcus stormed away toward the detective, while the rest of us took the stairs and headed to the room in question.

The two officers at the door frowned as Gideon approached, but he showed them his ID, and they waved him and Jacob inside. A flash of heat swept over me. Anger from Gideon or Jacob that was quickly contained under tight control. I didn't know if that meant they recognized the latest victim or if there was something else.

Kol leaned against the faded siding beside the closest officer, a woman with flecks of silver in her hair and a slightly green complexion. Her gaze swept over Kol and heat colored her cheeks as he settled in. The officer on the other side of the door, a man with a clean-shaven baby face who was probably in his thirties, cleared his throat, but the woman was too distracted by the incubus to notice.

I pulled my attention away from them and searched the horizon. Not that the wraith couldn't come from the other side of the building, but I couldn't help keeping an eye out. It was coming for me. Unless, of course, what he had said in my dream was true and I'd end up going to him because I wouldn't be able to resist the brand.

A shiver swept over me and I rubbed the sore spot on my biceps. It didn't hurt like it had last night, but it was still painful. Did that mean this was a temporary reprieve? Or had I just gotten used to it?

Gideon's brand, not even a day old, didn't hurt at all. In fact, I could almost pretend it didn't exist. God, I desperately wanted it to not exist.

I shoved that thought away. If the wraith-angel was really this archnephilim, as Gideon had said, and the only sure way to stop him was to kill him, then I *had* to pretend Gideon's brand didn't exist. If the mating brand made angels do crazy things to protect their mates, then there was a risk Gideon wouldn't be able to kill the nephilim for fear of hurting me. And this archnephilim had to be stopped. Gideon's team was just the beginning. He was going to go after every angel and every super who'd ever had anything to do with the destruction of Michael's nephilim laboratory. His thirst for vengeance would never be quenched.

So that left me with what? Lying to Gideon and Marcus, and hell, everyone else on the team until I died or went crazy?

I glanced at Kol from the corner of my eye, hoping he wouldn't notice I was looking at him. I couldn't trust him to keep the brand a secret, not if he thought I was endangering myself, and not if he thought I was endangering Gideon. And if I died, Gideon would die or go insane.

Jeez, this was becoming a complicated mess. But I was pretty sure Gideon would be willing to sacrifice himself to protect everyone else.

Was that why fate had paired us together? We were both willing to do whatever it took to save lives?

Except if that was the case, then fate had royally screwed us both.

A Joined Parliament Medical Examiner's van pulled into the parking lot and two guys, one who looked human but could have been any number of supers, the other a demon with green skin, pulled a gurney out of the van and headed for the stairs.

I shifted to get out of the way, and the male officer across from me pushed the room's door open further, giving me a perfect view of the horror show inside.

The body of a demon with onyx skin lay on an unmade bed, like a discarded crushed doll. All of his limbs except one arm had been crushed and twisted, and half of his face had been smashed in. But what horrified me the most was the fist-sized hole in the middle of his chest.

Up until now, the archnephilim had crushed and sliced but not punctured. Now his smoke tentacles were powerful enough to stab straight through someone and I doubted that power had anything to do with natural development. Gideon had said the mating brand enhanced an angel's powers. I was enhancing the archnephilim's. That was why he'd wanted me.

I tore my gaze from the body, but my attention got stuck halfway up the wall, staring at a blood smear. Blood splattered everywhere, walls, floor, ceiling, but that smear looked like it had been done on purpose.

The medical examiner guys pushed the gurney inside, the demon going first and using his body to open the door even further.

That smear looked like a T and the smear beside it an H.

I stepped into the doorway to get a better look, and my pulse stuttered. The archnephilim had written in blood on the wall, 'thanks for the power,' confirming what I suspected. I was responsible for this new level of gore.

KOL

I couldn't stop sneaking glances at Essie even though I was supposed to be keeping an eye out for danger and any nasty spells the perp might have left behind. I could almost see her determination radiating from her essence with my heightened ability to sense magic, but I also couldn't stop seeing her as she'd been last night, ashen, shocked, and crying.

She'd clung to me as if I was a lifeline, someone who could keep her safe, and I hadn't had to use any of my magic to make her act that way. I didn't understand how she could trust me so completely. Even those who wanted to feel my seductive power where hesitant because of what I was and how I could manipulate them. And I knew exactly how horrible it was to misuse my magic.

I fought the sudden panic that still seized me when I thought of the things I'd done and craved and survived while trapped as Michael's slave. But despite my efforts, the fear gripped my body and it took everything I had not to scream. I didn't want to. Don't make me. Please. Stop.

Stop.

God damn it. Stop.

I'd survived. It had been years since Gideon and Jacob had saved me. I was no longer that teenaged incubus forced to use his magic so Michael's angels could—

I squeezed my eyes shut and strained to concentrate on the ridges in the siding at my back.

People thought incubi wouldn't have had a problem with what Michael had wanted, and a lot of incubi wouldn't have. They didn't have the same magical sensitivity I had. But coerced desire tasted foul to me and I couldn't survive on energy tainted with darkness and fear.

What I'd done—What Michael had made me do—

It was wrong. So horribly wrong and I couldn't— I didn't—

No.

Focus on the present. Stay grounded. Concentrate on the here and now. Don't slip back into the darkness.

I refocused on the uneven siding at my back, the uncomfortable ridges digging into my shoulder blades then pushed my awareness farther, searching for more details to keep me from falling back into those nightmare memories.

Desire radiated from the female cop beside me, strong enough to give me a candy-sized bite of sustenance, and a cool breeze whispered across my face. Inside the hotel room, I could hear the Medical Examiner's men packing up the body of yet another of my rescuers.

My throat tightened at the thought. My saviors were being slaughtered and our one plan to capture the wraith— or rather *the archnephilim* had failed.

Who was gone now? Was it another face that had been seared into my memory along with Gideon's, Jacob's, Paul's, and Zella's?

The panic flared again and my control on my magic slipped, making the female cop look at me with eager eyes. Even Essie, who'd gone pale after watching the Medical Examiner's men wheel their gurney into the room was starting to feel the effects of my power, her desire whispering inside me.

Crap. I was better than this. But these murders were dredging up memories I'd wanted to keep buried and it was harder than usual to pretend it had never happened.

"I've seen enough," Gideon said and he strode out of the room.

Essie's gaze jumped to Gideon, like it should because he was her mate, then it jumped to Jacob who followed behind him. More of her desire whispered across my senses and a mix of hope then frustration flickered across her expression as the pressure from Jacob's claim took over.

"As you were," Jacob murmured, making Essie sigh with relief and Gideon tense.

Except he wasn't tensing because Jacob could control his mate. He didn't know Essie was his yet. It had to be because he'd told Essie he could protect her and now she was Jacob's servant.

And that was just a small complication compared to what I'd seen in the hall outside her room.

Marcus's desire for her had been strong and the look of desperate relief when he realized she was okay was shocking. I'd never seen Marcus react that way.

Sure, the attraction between Marcus and Essie had been a constant stream of power teasing me from the moment he'd stepped into her hospital room, so it was obvious they desired each other. But for him to spend all night sitting in the hall, waiting to hear if she was all right spoke of a much deeper desire.

They'd worked together before he'd gone through his transition from a human into a shifter. Had there been more? From the way they'd kissed, both of them clearly wanted more. I hadn't thought he was in a relationship, but maybe he was with her.

I didn't ask about my coworkers' relationships. It was none of my business. If they wanted to tell me, I'd listen, but that was all I could do. Because of my nature, I didn't completely understand the kind of romantic relationships other people had, and even if I did want one, I couldn't have one. One lover wasn't enough to sustain me, so to survive I'd have to break what I'd gleaned was an important relationship rule: monogamy. It was either that or I'd end up draining my lover of too much life energy and kill them.

Except other than the kiss in the hall, Marcus had been aggressive and cold toward Essie, despite the desire I could feel from both of them. So the situation had to be more complicated than them being in a relationship.

And this was why I didn't understand love.

If they loved each other, they should just tell each other and give in to their desires. It really wasn't that complicated.

Except Essie was Gideon's mate, and from the brand on her forearm she'd always been fated to be his mate. Which, as she'd said, did make it complicated. She and Gideon didn't know each other and while I'd sensed a bit of desire from her over him, that could be attributed to his good looks. He was handsome and an angel and many women were attracted to him.

Added to that, the archnephilim had branded Essie and if we couldn't figure out a way to capture it, there was a chance she'd die or go crazy and that could kill Gideon.

Gideon strode back to the car with the rest of us following. Marcus, who stood at the front of the building talking to the detective, glanced our way and even from a distance I could feel his need for Essie. It was so strong, almost as if his wolf had picked Essie for his mate.

Shit. If that was the case and Essie died, Marcus would lose it as well. It didn't matter that they didn't have the same kind of bond she and Gideon had. A wolf's mating bond was still a powerful thing.

And to top it off, *I* couldn't stop looking at her. There was something about her, something that put me at ease, something about the feel of her body against mine while I held her that filled me with a feeling I couldn't figure out.

I got into the SUV beside her and forced my attention to my phone to search the JP's online archives for anything that might help capture this archnephilim and save Essie.

Complicated didn't begin to explain Officer Esther Shaw.

ESSIE

We returned to Operations, the mood in the SUV grim. Gideon and Jacob had identified the victim as another squad member, which only made Gideon more brooding because the rest of his squad was supposed to be in hiding. Frustration and fear radiated from Marcus in snaps of hot and cold, and his fingers had elongated and narrowed, not fully forming into claws, but on the verge, while Jacob and Kol were on their phones, accessing the JP archives catalogue and searching for any document or recording that might offer a hint to capturing an archnephilim or severing an angelic mating brand.

Marcus pulled into the garage and parked in a spot near the door, and we piled out of the SUV.

"Show me where this archive is," I said to Jacob, the claim urging me to please him thankfully agreeing with my need to find answers. I hoped we'd be able to find a way to free me, but I was enough of a realist to know I shouldn't hold my breath on that. Knowledge, however, was power, and I was painfully short on any kind of information about archnephilim and angel brands, so learning as much as I could on this mess wasn't wasted time.

Except Gideon didn't think there'd be answers, let alone a solution. Even Jacob seemed doubtful.

God, I was going to die or go crazy, and I was going to take Gideon with me.

That thought burned the most. I couldn't even contain the casualties to myself. I was going to ruin someone else's life, just like I'd ruined Marcus's. The only way to save Gideon would be to give myself to the archnephilim and let him use me, but that would mean the deaths of others, many more than just me and Gideon.

A part of me wanted to scream and cry at the injustice. It wasn't fair. All I wanted was a normal human life. Why was that too much to ask for? I'd spent my childhood on the run, always afraid. I'd finally found balance and a purpose in my job. That balance had been slow in forming, but I had it, and I had no doubt the next stage, friends, maybe even a family, would also be— *have been* slow in coming, but it would have eventually come.

If I hadn't screwed it up by getting involved in the supernatural world.

And I'd tried. So damn hard. I'd had that one scare with Marcus where I'd realized I couldn't just pretend supers didn't exist, but I'd also managed to have nothing to do with supers since.

Until now.

And there hadn't been anything I could have done to avoid it. If I went back in time, I would have done the same thing, interrupted the robbery then convinced the robber to go into the alley.

It was as if all those years I'd spent avoiding my supernatural nature had finally come crashing down on me in one horrible day, and fate had decided that even though I wasn't one of Michael's monstrous creations, my existence couldn't defy the natural order. Nephilim weren't supposed to exist.

I wasn't supposed to exist.

Perhaps this was why I'd been born. To help end this threat. Although why I also had to be mated to Gideon was beyond me.

And really, none of it mattered. Fate or not, it was what it was, and if I spent too much time thinking about how unfair and horrific the situation was, I'd curl into a ball and cry. That, and the part of me that knew being a cop was the only job for me wouldn't allow me to just give up.

If I was going to face my end, I was going to face it head on, and I was going to make sure the archnephilim didn't killed anyone else or any of the guys. That was the least I could do.

Which meant my main objective now was to join the guys in searching the archives to find a way to help kill the archnephilim and minimize casualties, since so far he'd kicked our asses.

And while I hoped the odds would be better now that lethal force was an option, the archnephilim was also now more powerful. Because of me.

"The archives is in the basement," Jacob said, and he headed toward the glass doors leading into the main hall, Kol close behind.

"A word first, Officer Shaw," Gideon said, making Jacob and Kol pause and my heart skip a beat. Did he know about the brand? Had it already solidified enough for him to tell I was his mate instead of Zella? If he did, that could stop him from planning to kill the archnephilim and that would mean more people would die. That would mean some or all of the guys on the team would die. I couldn't let that happen. I wouldn't be responsible for that.

"You can meet me in the archives if you'd like," Jacob said, the command blessedly open-ended.

Marcus came around the back of the SUV and stepped possessively close to me again.

Gideon leveled a frozen glance at Marcus. "Alone, please."

Marcus's claws extended a little more from his fingers.

I brushed his arm, drawing his attention to me. "Get started without me. The more eyes, the greater the chance we find something." That, and if Marcus stayed, my chances decreased of convincing Gideon to go against the nature of the mating brand and keep his original plan to sacrifice me. If it was just us, I might be able to convince him to hold firm. But with Marcus arguing against it, there was a chance Gideon would break and give in to him.

Marcus — or was that his wolf? — huffed with displeasure, but he turned and marched after Jacob and Kol.

We waited in the garage as Gideon watched the others leave, the temperature unnervingly steady as if the angel had managed to freeze over everything, expression, body language, and emotions, locking it all deep inside. That was good. That meant he'd hardened his heart to the inevitable.

Then a hint of mist unfurled in the air around me. Grief. Strong enough to manifest.

Shit. Where was the icy, hard angel when I needed him? I wouldn't be able to do this on my own, not against Marcus's ferocious protection.

"Can we talk at my mate's bedside? I—" He ran his hands through his hair. "I thought I could leave her and go to the crime scene, but the thought of her waking up alone is driving me crazy."

"Sure." Disappointment I wasn't supposed to have squeezed in my chest. He still thought Zella was his mate. That was supposed to be a good thing.

I shoved the emotion down deep, as far as it would go. It was an effect of the brand, nothing more. We didn't know each other, and he despised my species. Our joining wasn't wonderful, it was cruel.

He headed inside and I followed, giving my sleeve a tug even though the brand wasn't close to being revealed, unable to help myself. The mist followed me, growing stronger the closer we got to Zella's room.

"You said she's strong," I said, needing to say something, praying I could alleviate some of his grief before moisture collected on my cheeks. "She'll pull through this."

We reached the room's window and Gideon stopped, pressed his hands to the glass, and stared inside. Her tattered wings had been cleaned but were still in braces, and her face was one big ugly bruise, although it looked like maybe some of the swelling had gone down. The blanket over her body, however, didn't look right, and I realized it dropped off above her right knee and lay flat where the rest of her leg should have been.

"Amiah still doesn't know if she can save her wings. I don't know if she'll survive losing them," he said, his voice low, raw, and the mist thickened, clouding my vision. He pressed his palm to his brand and heat seeped up my arm. "And with the scars on her arms and in her soul, the brand isn't visible and might not be noticeable for a long time. I won't be able to use it to save her. Losing them will finish the job the nephilim started during the war. It'll destroy her spirit completely."

"It won't, because she has you." Even if they weren't mated, his love for her was strong. And I really didn't want to think about what was going to happen to him if killing the archnephilim killed me or drove me crazy. Perhaps if we did it before the bond fully formed, that would save him. Perhaps his love for Zella would save him. I was sure it could save her. If I had someone who loved me that much, I could pull through anything. Well, anything except this.

My mind jumped to Marcus's breathtaking, confusing kiss in the hall this morning. He was going to be... I had no idea. Furious? Shattered? Broken?... when the inevitable happened.

I swallowed at the lump forming in my throat. "I need to ask you a favor."

"As much as Jacob thinks there's a way to save you, there isn't."

Gideon pressed his forehead to the glass and the mist billowed around me. "I said I'd protect you, but I can't."

"I know you can't. What I need is for you to do whatever it takes to stay on mission."

Gideon glanced at me, clouds of grief and determination darkening his summer-sky eyes. "You don't have to ask that of me."

"Even when Marcus fights you over it." I met his gaze head on. "And he'll fight you over it." He'd been fighting to keep me out of this since he'd first yelled at me in the hospital. I just hadn't realized that was what he'd been doing until he'd kissed me.

"His file said you were partners about four and a half years ago. I didn't realize you two were still in touch."

I didn't ask if his file also said I was the reason he was a werewolf. "We aren't— weren't—" I didn't know how to explain it. "It's complicated."

"It didn't look that complicated when you met me in the garage this morning."

And if I wasn't Gideon's fated mate and about to die or go insane, it wouldn't have been.

"You two should talk about it." His attention slid back to Zella. "Soon. You have less time than I'd hoped. The archnephilim's brand isn't even a day old and the magic connecting you has already made it stronger. The longer we wait, the stronger it will get."

"And the harder it will be to kill him." Yeah, I'd already figured that out, too. Another thing I was trying not to think about.

"Have you tried sensing where it is?" he asked. "It found you last night, so the brand is strong enough. Even though you're human, your angel-touch is strong. I've only met a few other humans who could cast a light strike with as much power as you did last night."

Yeah, because I wasn't actually an angel-touched human.

"That's probably why the archnephilim branded you," Gideon said. "Which means there's a good chance you'll be able to use its brand to find it as well."

"How do I find him?"

"Close your eyes and concentrate on the brand and your connection to the archnephilim."

I closed my eyes and took a breath, hoping it would steady me and help me concentrate.

"Touching the brand might also help."

Without rolling my sleeves, I pressed my palm against the arch-nephilim's brand. It throbbed like a fresh burn. Not the searing pain when he'd been searching for me, but still painful.

"Flesh to flesh would be better."

I opened my eyes and gave him my driest look. "I'm not taking my shirt off."

"That's fair," Gideon said, his voice soft.

I closed my eyes again and concentrated on the pain in my biceps. The archnephilim had visited me in my dreams. He'd found me at my apartment. Whether I liked it or not, we were connected. I could sense his inky darkness, a noxious smoke under my skin, creeping thick tentacles out from the brand. My mind flinched away from it, but I forced it closer to the darkness, trying to find a way to connect to him, find him, but his essence wouldn't let me in.

"Just take a breath and relax," Gideon said, and heat from his brand curled up my other arm, drawing my essence like a moth to a flame. His brand was warmth and affection, determination and honor. I yearned to be wrapped in his confidence and take comfort in the heat of his spirit, but I knew if I let myself sink into our connection, it would solidify the bond and he'd know I was his mate. And that would make everything more complicated.

"Can you sense him?" he asked.

I pushed my concentration back to the darkness. It oozed between my mental fingers, making me shudder, twisted back around my mental hands, and tightened. Pain exploded from the brand, slicing into my mind and body, and a low, dark chuckle echoed in my head.

"*Changed your mind already?*" the archnephilim asked, his desire oozing through the pain. "*I thought you had more fight than that.*"

"*Isn't this what you want? Me?*" I strained to sense anything about where he was.

"*Except that isn't what you're doing.*" The archnephilim's desire spread across my chest, making my breath hitch. "*But it should be. Your wolf can't make you feel the way I can.*"

Aching heat gathered low within me, my nerves thrumming with sudden consuming need. I yearned for his touch—

No. I gritted my teeth. I didn't want his touch. This was him messing with my mind. Where was he? He seemed close, but I wasn't sure if that was because he was in my head or actually somewhere close by.

"*Not even your angel can make you feel like this.*"

More desire flooded me, drawing a gasp. If my eyes hadn't already been closed, I'm sure they would have rolled back, as the promise of a climax fluttered within me.

I jerked my hand from the brand and pressed my palms to the wall to keep standing. A foggy image fluttered across my vision. A concrete pillar with chunks chipped out of it. A band of weak hazy sunlight. A pool of murky water.

"Come to me." The archnephilim chuckled again, the sound racing through me. *"Come for me."*

The pain from the brand burned hotter, with a shocking mix of pain and pleasure. I struggled to fight it, to deny that his inky darkness and aching pain turned me on, and concentrate on where he was. The feelings weren't me. It was his connection to me, his control over my body. But my body didn't want to listen to my mind, and the image vanished, leaving me surrounded in a darkness that ratcheted up the sensations within me. My breath came fast, my need for release twisting tighter. Tears burned my eyes at the pain and pleasure and hopelessness.

"You're not hopeless, you're powerful. We're *powerful,"* he said. *"I can give you pleasure and power beyond your wildest dreams. You never have to fear again. They will fear you."*

"I don't want them to fear me." I just wanted to live my life.

But that wasn't going to be.

"It can be if you join me."

"I don't want vengeance."

"You should." The pain burned brighter, slicing into the pleasure. *"We're not animals. Our kind didn't deserve to be slaughtered before we were even born."*

"You were made. You're not natural."

"You're not better than me," he snarled. More pain flooded me, consuming the rest of the pleasure. *"And you're not as strong as me. You're mine. You belong to me. You'll give me your strength and power and do as I say until I'm done with you."*

My hand clenched and I punched out, the archnephilim controlling my body. I jerked my eyes open as Gideon blocked my attack, shock flashing through his eyes. My other hand clenched and punched.

Gideon blocked my other strike, grabbed my wrist, twisted, and jerked me around. He captured my hand behind my back, wrapped his arm across my chest and held me tight, my back against his chest. "Officer Shaw."

My body wrenched against his grip as my mind struggled for control against the archnephilim.

He howled with laughter. *"That's it, little nephilim. Struggle."*

He made me heave against Gideon's grip, forcing the angel to yank my hand higher up my back, drawing a whimper of pain. A new pleasure swept into me, one thick with malice and delight at my suffering.

"Get out." I mentally shoved at the archnephilim's essence in my body.

His laugher increased.

"I said get out."

"Make me," the archnephilim sneered.

I mentally twisted and clawed and shoved at his essence within me, but his sick pleasure kept growing. He was consuming me, his darkness oozing into my cells, clinging to my soul, and drowning me as if his smoke was pouring down my throat again, and there was nothing I could do.

ESSIE

Panic squeezed my chest and I fought to breathe against the archnephilim's control. I screamed at my body to stop writhing in Gideon's grasp, to stop obeying the archnephilim's commands, but it wouldn't listen. My body no longer belonged to me, nor did the sensation of dark pleasure and ferocious vengeance. I was trapped, a prisoner within myself, and his darkness was consuming me.

"Get out." *Please get out get out get out.*

The light strike spell flashed into my head, the words racing around and around, and tears burned my eyes.

The archnephilim's laugher increased, his certainty that he possessed me making my stomach churn. This was not supposed to happen. None of this was supposed to happen, and I wasn't going to die possessed by this monster.

"Get out!" The light strike released within me. Light flashed, turning the darkness inside my lids white, and the archnephilim screamed. The divine light seared through my being, consuming the darkness and driving him from my head.

My knees gave out and I sagged against Gideon.

"Officer Shaw?" He released my wrist and wrapped both arms around my waist, taking my weight and helping me stand. His scent and warmth enveloped me and all I wanted to do was stay in his embrace forever. It was where I belonged. Every fiber of my being thrummed with that knowledge while my mind screamed at the danger of even just being near him.

I pushed out of his hold — he let me go easily — and clung to the wall to keep standing. "When were you going to tell me he could use the brand to control me?"

"He can what?" He sounded genuinely surprised.

"He can control me." I shuddered at the memory of everything the archnephilim had made me feel, the need, the desire, and the terror.

"That's not possible—" Realization rushed across his expression. "It must be because he's also a wraith. The brand connects you, gives him access to your soul, which is what a wraith needs to possess someone. Do you know where he is?"

"No. If he hadn't—" The memory of his pleasure and the need he'd made me feel shuddered through me. "If he hadn't—" Another shudder and I gasped back a moan.

Gideon shifted to grab my shoulders, probably to steady me, but the thought of his hands on me made my pulse race faster.

God, what was wrong with me?

I jerked back and raised a hand, stopping him from holding me. "I'm all right. I started to get a sense of where he might be, then he took over."

A hint of mist billowed around me with Gideon's grief... or maybe this was regret, and I knew what he was going to say next.

"You want me to try again." If we were going to hunt down the archnephilim, it was the only way, but the thought of doing that again made my pulse race and not in a good way.

"Yes, but I'll need to arrange for some precautions first, so hopefully it won't be able to possess you again." The mist thickened. "Or you'll be contained when it does."

"Wonderful."

"In the meantime, you should say what you have to say to Marcus." He glanced through the window at Zella, his message clear: before it was too late. "Take the elevator to the basement. The archives is right there."

"Right." I couldn't tear my gaze away from him as he stared at Zella. My emotions were a mess, the desire from the archnephilim making me yearn for something I couldn't have and didn't want with Gideon.

"Right." I forced myself to turn and head away. I didn't know how much time I had left, but I wasn't sure I wanted to have a conversation with Marcus. What could I say when I couldn't tell him Gideon's plan was the only one that would work?

And even then, with the archnephilim able to possess me, that had the potential to make everything more complicated.

Except I had managed to break free. By the skin of my teeth, but I had. Perhaps there was an angle there I could use, a way to help the guys. Maybe if I could distract him, Gideon would be able to strike a killing blow? And maybe I could do more than just distract him, but I needed to learn a hell of a lot more about angelic mating brands to figure out if that was even a possibility.

I hit the call button for the elevator as Amiah came down the main hall toward me, and I prayed she'd just glare at me and head down the stairs to the cafeteria. But she joined me, waiting for the elevator, her hard gaze locked on the closed door.

The temperature around me rose.

I shifted, waiting for her to hit the up button. She didn't, which meant I was going to be trapped in the elevator with her and her hot fury. Wonderful.

"I think you're reckless," she said, her tone filled with ice and the temperature rising a few more degrees.

"You don't even know me."

She slid her icy gaze to me. "I know enough."

Right. One fuck-up before I knew what I was doing, and I was forever reckless. Except that wasn't true. Marcus was right. I was still taking chances, letting Jacob claim me to protect him and using myself as bait before we knew anything about the archnephilim.

"I also know if it wasn't for you, Zella would be dead."

The elevator dinged, the door opened, and I hit the only basement button.

"Gideon will eventually get past his shock and thank you," she said, her tone softening and a hint of the heat diminishing. "But until he does, on his behalf, thank you. You brought her back to us."

In the most horrific way possible. "I wish it had been under better circumstances."

"And I wish," she said, her voice icy again, "whatever happens next, you think before you act and don't do something that gets any of the guys killed."

The door opened and she strode out, heading down a narrow hall to the right, taking her heat with her. A chill settled around me, the actual temperature of the basement, filled with a hint of musty air and the smell of old books.

Ahead of me, Jacob sat at a wide wooden table that was piled with books, looking at me, while Kol sat behind him on a couch watching his phone, listening to the video flashing on his screen with earphones and not disturbing the quiet. Two fluorescent lights hung from the ceiling, offering stark illumination, and beyond stood shelves and shelves of books creating long passages. Across from the table, opposite the couch, was a metal door secured by a lock with a fingerprint scanner, and through the thick security glass I could see a neatly stacked row of rifles. The archives and the armory.

"Find anything?" I asked, not that I'd expected anything to be found in the fifteen minutes I'd been talking with Gideon... not that I expected them to find anything at all.

"Not yet. I'm going through the journals and records confiscated from Michael's facilities. Kol is watching the videos we recovered. If Michael was making archnephilim, he had to have a way to control them. He may have thought humanity was a parasite on the planet, but he wasn't a fool. An archnephilim is too powerful a weapon to create without having a guaranteed means of controlling it."

I sure hoped he was right, but I couldn't place all my bets on that one hope. Michael might not have had a plan to control the archnephilim. Perhaps he was just planning on letting them wreak havoc until the archnephilim were dead or the humans and the supers were.

"I should learn more about the mating brand. Maybe there's a way I can use it to influence the archnephilim, give you guys a chance to subdue him."

"Or weaken or sever the bond completely," Jacob said. "Gideon says it's not a true brand. There's still a chance we could find a way to remove it."

Except Gideon had been adamant from the beginning that once a brand formed, the bond could never be severed, and I really didn't want to get my hopes up because if there was a way to sever the bond between me and the archnephilim, then there was a way to sever the bond with Gideon. And then I could leave all this insanity behind.

"I really hope you're right. I would give just about anything to remove the brand."

Kol's gaze jumped to me then slid down my arm to where Gideon's brand was hidden beneath my shirtsleeve.

Both of the brands.

Except a part of me didn't want to sever the bond with Gideon. It was crazy. God, it had to be the influence of the true mating brand. Staying with Gideon, who didn't even know me let alone love me, was a disaster waiting to happen.

But even if I didn't stay for Gideon, there was still Marcus. Confusing, frustrating Marcus. I still had no idea what to make of him or his ferocious protectiveness, and I really wanted to kiss him again and let his wild passion make me forget everything that was happening.

Jeez. This was a mess. I was a mess.

"Marcus is in the stacks toward the back left corner of the archives, looking for books on the angelic mating brand. You can join him or he can point you in the direction of books on archangels," Jacob said. "Maybe there's a way to capture them and we can go back to plan A."

For a moment, I considered asking Jacob to point me in the direction of the books on archangels so I could avoid Marcus entirely, but I really needed to know if I could use the archnephilim's brand against him. Everything else — finding a way to control him or capture him — sounded lovely, but that wasn't anything I could control or probably even help with. Using the brand, though? That was something I could do.

I headed down a long aisle, the shelves reaching all the way to a ceiling with long fluorescent lights running down the center. The aisle ended in a T-intersection and between the uneven top of the books and the books of the closest shelf, I could see more shelves beyond. I couldn't tell if the library took up the entire basement, but I wouldn't have been surprised if it had.

I wove my way through the shelves, always going toward the back and the left, until I rounded a corner and found Marcus sitting on the floor, an open book in his lap, more books piled on the floor around him. His piercing green gaze, filled with a need more powerful than I'd ever seen from him before, rose to meet mine.

My pulse stuttered. Sultry heat fluttered around me, tentative and uncertain, but while I hoped it meant he desired me, I didn't know for sure. I didn't know what anything with Marcus meant. I didn't understand this man at all. He'd acted professionally when we'd been partners, even with the chemistry sizzling between us, and had never said he was interested in me, no matter what the temperature around him had told me.

And then I'd messed up.

"I thought you were mad at me."

"I was mad— *am* mad. You keep taking risks, putting your life in danger when you're not supposed to have anything to do with the super-natural world." The desire in his eyes hardened. "My world."

"That doesn't make any sense." He had no right to be mad at me now. This was my life, my decision, and this time it had nothing to do with him. "Why would you care? I'm the reason you're in this world in the first place. I'm the one who messed up and ruined your life. You have every right to be mad at me for that, but this—" I gestured to the library around me, meaning the supernatural world and not just the library. "—this has nothing to do with you."

"It has everything to do with me," he said, his voice low, and for a moment it seemed it wasn't him talking but his wolf.

"Bullshit. You haven't talked to me since that night. No call, no email, nothing. You didn't even clean out your locker. You just left. You made your point absolutely clear." My throat tightened with guilt that I'd never managed to get rid of, only gotten better at ignoring.

"And what point was that?" His grip on the sides of the book tightened.

"That you were furious. That you didn't even want to accidentally run into me when you emptied your locker. That I'd destroyed your life." And there wasn't any way I could make it up to him. The only thing I could do now was ensure my new mess didn't get him or any of the other guys hurt or killed — and with Gideon's brand on my arm now, at least one of them was going to get hurt.

"I didn't come back to clean out my locker because I started turning right away. I barely managed to get to the hospital in the Quarter in time." His gaze dropped to the book in his lap and he took in a breath that did little to ease the tension in his body. "And then I was angry."

A hint of mist curled around me, and I realized the flickering heat had vanished. His anger or whatever it was I'd felt before was gone, replaced with grief or regret.

"I was angry for a long time, but not at you. You were a rookie. You had less than six months on the job," he said. "I was angry at myself for letting you put yourself in danger. I should have done whatever it took to stop you."

"I shouldn't have rushed in. We should have waited for backup."

Marcus shrugged, but the action looked forced. "We should have. But every time I think about that night, I know Ariel Cromer would have died if we had."

"We don't know that." Except I knew he was right... or was it that I hoped he was right? I'd panicked. She'd been screaming and I'd rushed in to save her. And Marcus had been bitten. I had no idea how we hadn't been killed that night.

His gaze lifted back to me, stalling my pulse again with the desire in his eyes. God, with just one look he could control me, steal my breath, and he didn't need to use a mating brand. "But most of all I was angry because I couldn't stop thinking about you. There was something about you, Essie. There still is. I can't explain it. I'm drawn to you—" He huffed a sad laugh. "My wolf is really drawn to you. That's why I had to stay away."

"That still doesn't make sense." If he was drawn to me, why would he have had to stay away? Why say nothing about it for the six months we worked together? He had to know the attraction went both ways. You didn't have that kind of chemistry with someone when it only went one way.

"Come on, Essie. We'd had enough conversations while on patrol for me to know you wanted nothing to do with supers. Every time I brought the conversation up, you'd get this scared look in your eyes and change the topic." He flicked the tip of the pages with his thumb and the muscles in his jaw twitched. "It took me over a year to get through my transition, to feel right in my skin again. Thank God for Amiah. She was working at Mercy Memorial then. If it hadn't been for her, I wouldn't have gotten through it. But when I finally had my head on straight, I knew no matter what I'd felt about you, I had to stay away. You wouldn't have accepted my wolf and my wolf wouldn't have accepted that."

I opened my mouth to protest that, but couldn't say the words. Up until a day ago, everything he said about me had been true. I was afraid of supers and wanted nothing to do with their world. I still didn't want anything to do with them.

"So now what?"

"Now I tell my wolf to shut the fuck up, keep my distance from you, and get you your life back."

"Gee, when you put it that way it sounds so easy," I said, unable to keep the sarcasm from my tone. "How's that working for you?"

"Not well," he growled, the heat in his eyes making my pulse race. "I shouldn't have kissed you."

Pain flickered through the archnephilim's brand, reminding me that as much as Marcus wanted me to get my life back, it wasn't going to happen.

I pressed my palm to the brand — as if that would do something to ease the pain — and sat on the floor across from him. "I think you're also going to have to accept that this isn't going to turn out well."

His attention dipped to where I held my biceps and his expression darkened. "What happened to the rookie who thought she could run into a room with four werewolves and get out alive?"

"She learned a hard lesson that night." I picked up the book closest to me. "And I never thought about me. I always thought about the girl. Right now I'm in a position to save a lot of girls. Don't fight Gideon on this, help me end this."

"I'm not losing you."

"I don't think you have much of a choice in the matter." Because even if I survived, Gideon's brand said I belonged with him.

ESSIE

We read in awkward silence, a strange mix of attraction and regret and anger crackling between us that I didn't need my not-very-helpful empathy to sense, until Marcus's phone rang and he left. I wasn't sure what I thought about his revelation that he'd disappeared to protect me, that he wasn't angry at me for ruining his life, and I didn't want to think about it. It was complicated and I didn't want to spend my last days, hell, maybe even my last hours, worrying about that. I also didn't want to completely break his heart, so I didn't act on the desire to kiss him again, even if that would have been a much better way of spending my remaining time.

The first three books I flipped through were different texts of pretty much the same information, long-winded explanations of what Gideon had already told me about angelic mating brands. They were rare — sometimes centuries would pass between mated pairs — and they were unique to the angels involved. Not just the sigil etched into the angel's body, but how it connected their souls and how long it took to form. Sometimes it enhanced magic. Sometimes it didn't. Sometimes an angel developed new magic. A branded pair could almost always find each other, and the mating bond was never ignored — although I wasn't sure if anyone had ever tried. It was always seen as beautiful and sacred and couldn't be broken, even in death. The death of one killed the other or drove him or her insane, either raving mad, catatonic, or sobbing uncontrollably all the time. The soul-deep connection between mated angels was stronger than any other connection known to man or super and was seen with awe and respect among the angel community.

Yeah, because they'd never had an angel mated to a nephilim before. I was pretty sure all that *sacred brand* stuff would get thrown out the window the minute Gideon knew what I really was. He'd probably say it was a fake brand, like the one the archnephilim had given me. Except his brand didn't look anything like the archnephilim's and he wasn't behaving as if he even suspected it was fake — although that might be because he thought the bond was with Zella.

Of course none of that stopped him from changing his mind once all was revealed. And none of that really mattered. The hope I'd found in those books had been a paragraph in one of them about the bond not being completed if something happened to one of the angels before the brand had fully formed. That, at least, confirmed my theory that the sooner we dealt with the archnephilim, the better Gideon's chances were at surviving this mess.

The next book was more biographical than textbook, and I wasn't certain how much was truth and how much legend. The first few chapters were the histories of the first recorded mating brands with an account that matched everything I'd learned in the previous books. The next chapter was about a branded trio which surprised me and yet didn't surprise me.

When angels had first revealed themselves to humanity, they'd been clear that they were beings of energy who existed in the Realm of Celestial Light — while demons existed in the Realm of Celestial Darkness — and that while they claimed to be divine, they predated all human religions. Angels were the law to the demons' chaos. Or at least they were supposed to be, until Michael decided humans were a plague that wasn't just draining the life of our planet but the life of the Realm of Celestial Light as well.

No one human religion ruled angelic behavior, so while a lot of the human population felt polyamory was taboo, that didn't mean angels did — and I doubted anyone had tried asking them about it. Most angels didn't leave their celestial realm, and those who did didn't socialize with humans. Given Gideon's insistence that angel DNA wasn't compatible with any other DNA, I suspected very few if any angels dated outside of their species.

The three stories after that were back to the usual pattern of perfect soul bonds and all the unconditional love that went with it — heterosexual and homosexual bondings, so I guessed the brand didn't mean *mating* in the sense of species reproduction — but the story after that was different.

This one started the same as the others, but the man was captured during an assault into the Realm of Celestial Darkness in an attempt to correct an imbalance between the two energies. His soul had been damaged, allowing him to be infected with dark energy and driving him insane. Not even the mating brand had been able to help him, and with the combination of both light and dark energy, he was more powerful than before, killing indiscriminately: angel, demon, human, whoever stood in his way.

After many failed attempts to save him, his mate gathered all the divine power within her — and according to the record she was a powerhouse when it came to summoning divine light — and blasted it through their brand, using their connection to reach and destroy his soul unobstructed.

The record wasn't clear if the blast had burned away both of their souls, killing them, or if her heart had stopped killing her because they were bonded and he'd died.

I'd found my answer.

I sat back and cracked my neck, feeling the weight of everything that had happened since I'd walked into Pam and Abe's pharmacy yesterday. Even though I'd slept last night, I was back to being exhausted. Maybe I wasn't back to anything. Maybe I was *still* exhausted. I couldn't tell. Or maybe it was the story that made me feel like I was carrying an enormous weight.

There was a way to end this, but it meant I was going to have to ask Gideon for help, since there was no way I'd be able to summon enough divine light to burn into the archnephilim's soul. I wasn't a magical powerhouse — even if it seemed as if my blasts had grown stronger the last two times I'd used them. It hadn't been enough to kill the archnephilim then, and it wouldn't be enough now.

So long as Gideon didn't know about *his* brand, I was pretty sure I could convince him of the plan. I doubted I'd be able to convince any of the guys, not until all other avenues had been exhausted, and if I wanted any chance of saving Gideon, using the archnephilim's brand to kill him had to be done right away before our connection solidified.

I was about to stand when Kol rounded the corner, carrying a bottle of water and a sandwich on a plate.

My brain stalled. Just for a second. He really was breathtaking. Every step radiated power and sensuality, and a hint of desire darkened his eyes. I was pretty sure he wasn't even aware of his movement or expression. This was just Kol, a demon who survived on sexual energy with a body that ensured he never went hungry.

"How goes it?" he asked.

My stomach rumbled in response.

"Thought so," he said, a tired smile tugging on his lips and softening his demonic look to almost boy-next-door, if the boy next door had horns. "You strike me as the kind of person who works through meals, so I figured—" He sat across from me, where Marcus had sat, and passed me the plate and water bottle.

I set the book aside and accepted the food and water. "How long have I been down here?"

It hadn't occurred to me to check the time and even if I'd wanted to, I'd left my phone in my room.

"It's almost seven. You've missed lunch and dinner."

And breakfast. No wonder I was so hungry. The last time I'd eaten had been yesterday evening, before the disastrous attempt to capture the archnephilim.

"Have you and Jacob found anything?" I took a bite of the sandwich. Ham and cheese again, but I was too hungry to care.

The smile melted from Kol's face. "No. All I've learned is that Michael was a nasty piece of work. I mean, I knew he was nasty. I was manifested into the human realm by him and forced to enthrall his victims into complacency until they were used to conceive his nephilim, but the video of his actual laboratory—" He shuddered. "He documented his experiments and didn't use demons to conceive his angel-demon hybrids."

"How could he not—?" Horrified realization swept through me. "He used human women as surrogates for those, too?"

"Humans are easier to control than angels or supers. The hybrids were carried to term, if the surrogate survived — which according to his records didn't usually happen — then put in tanks to rapidly mature, just like his regular nephilim." The muscles in his jaw tightened. "The human body wasn't made to give birth to that kind of monster. I know because I've now watched more than enough of Michael's videos."

I started to take another bite of my sandwich but didn't know if it would stay down, and instead set it back on the plate. "And Jacob hasn't found anything in the journals or records about how to control one of these monsters?"

"No, but he's only a quarter of the way through."

Well, damn. I knew they wouldn't find anything, at least not in the time I needed, but a small part of me had hoped a miracle would show up. Sure, I knew what needed to be done, but that didn't mean I liked it. "I'm not sure how much longer we can spend searching."

"It hasn't even been a day."

"And by tomorrow, someone else from Gideon's old squad could be dead."

Kol rubbed his face, looking as exhausted as I felt. "Well, we can't do anything about that until the archnephilim attacks or we have a way to find it, so we might as well keep looking."

"Actually, we can." I pulled out the book that had mentioned the risks before a mating brand had fully formed and offered it to Kol. "I think I can locate the archnephilim through his brand, and there's a chance Gideon can get out of this mess unscathed if we deal with the archnephilim before my bond with him solidifies."

"That would have to happen soon." Kol didn't open the book I'd given him. "We wouldn't have a chance to get through all of Michael's journals."

"I know." I met Kol's gaze. There wasn't any hint of desire smoldering in his dark eyes now, only worry and exhaustion. "I'm not willing to sacrifice anyone else on the slim chance that there's a way to save me."

"I'm sure if Gideon knew the truth, he'd disagree." Kol broke eye contact and studied the cover of the book I'd given him. "You have to tell him. You have to tell both of them. It's going to come out whether you want it to or not. Who do you think Marcus would rather hear it from? You or Gideon?"

"You're assuming there's actually something between me and Marcus."

Kol's gaze rose back to me and a hint of seductive hellfire burned in his eyes. "I felt that kiss. I *know* there's something between you and Marcus."

"Jeez." I took a swig of water as heat flushed my face. "Can't hide anything from an incubus."

"Well, you can't hide *that*. Although next time, if you want to hold my hand or let me... I don't know, touch your back, flesh to flesh would be ideal if we're not talking actual sex..." He batted his eyelashes at me, doing nothing to look innocent, then dropped his act, his expression serious... and strained. "Honestly, though, I could use a meal too, but I don't want to waste time going out."

I had no idea what to say to that. There were probably rules about seducing co-workers and while it had looked like the cafeteria catered to those supers with human dietary needs as well as vampires, I doubt it catered to incubi. And it didn't sound like he was willing to order in. "How about hanging out near Gideon and Zella?"

He rolled his eyes at me. "Wrong emotion. I need sex, not love, and what they have isn't going to turn into sex. At least it won't until she's healed up, which is going to be days longer than I can hold out and even then it probably won't turn into anything because of... well..." He waved at my arm.

"Because of this." I moved to press my palm to Gideon's brand, but thought better of it and took another sip of water.

Kol pursed his lips, his expression tight, the strain even more obvious and, now that I knew what I was looking for, so was his hunger. When was the last time he'd eaten? I knew many demons who sustained them-selves on humans — be it memories or emotions or something else — didn't need three meals a day. Some could go days without *eating* unless they sustained injuries or expended more then their usual amount of energy.

Kol had been going since I'd met him in the hospital yesterday. There might have been a time after rescuing Zella and before trying to capture the archnephilim that he'd had an opportunity for a meal, but then he'd broken his ribs and healing that had probably expended a lot of the magic that sustained him.

"You should make time sooner rather than later to replenish your magic." He'd gotten up just fine after last night's fight, but if he didn't replenish his magical essence, another fight could seriously injure or kill him.

He flashed me a wicked grin that made my pulse stutter and heat flood me. "Are you making an offer?"

"I... ah..." He was low because of me, and if he could replenish some of his magic by riding along on someone else's kiss, then I could help him out by kissing him. I didn't actually need to have sex with him. And really, I doubted kissing him would be a serious hardship. "How hungry are you?"

Surprise flashed across his expression. "You can't be serious. I must have slipped with my enthrall and I'm influencing you. You don't mean that."

"I'm not talking sex." I really couldn't believe I was saying this, and I knew — if all the stories about incubi were true — that while in the moment I'd beg for sex and I'd have to trust him to keep his word. "But I can offer you a kiss."

"That's not a good idea."

"If the archnephilim attacks, will you survive the fight?" I asked. "How hungry are you?"

"Hungry." The hellfire in his eyes burned brighter and the muscles in his jaw twitched. "But you're Gideon's mate. So not *that* hungry."

"So you won't kiss me because of Gideon even though I'm offering, but you'd ride along if I wanted to make out with Marcus?"

"You and Marcus clearly had a thing before all this started. That could be forgiven," Kol said.

"And I don't get a say in any of this?" I really didn't like the implications of this *belonging to Gideon* thing. What if I'd wanted to have sex with Kol or Marcus or anyone else before the archnephilim killed me? I didn't ask to be mated with Gideon. I didn't even know him.

"I owe Gideon my life. I won't do something that I know will hurt him."

And that was the crux of it. I didn't really *belong* to Gideon. I probably could have sex with anyone I wanted except his teammates, because they were standup guys and didn't do that kind of thing to their friends.

"Then you should slip out now before Gideon assembles the team and asks me to find the archneph—"

Pain lanced through the archnephilim's brand. The plate slipped from my suddenly numb fingers, dumping the sandwich on the floor, and a fire alarm began to wail.

"He's here." I could feel his inky darkness sliding against my mind, trying to find a way into my soul.

Kol leaped to his feet. I scrambled to stand as well.

"Stay here."

"Do you really think leaving me alone in the archives is a good idea?" That, and I needed to get to Gideon to have him blast divine light into the archnephilim's brand.

"Fine," he said, and we darted down the aisle, back to the front of the archives where the table and couch were.

Books still covered the table but Jacob was gone. I didn't know if he'd been gone before the alarm had started or if he'd just left.

Kol ignored the elevator and headed to a door a little ways down and around a corner. He jerked it open, revealing a plain metal and concrete stairwell, and ran up the stairs, taking them three at a time with his long legs.

I followed, but with my slightly shorter legs I could only safely manage two at a time.

Kol wrenched open the door at the first floor landing and someone screamed. He drew his daggers, hidden in sheaths under his shirt and strapped to his back, and rushed out.

I reached the doorway and stopped. I didn't have a weapon, and while I was sure the archnephilim knew where I was, I wasn't going to make it easy to grab me by running headlong into danger.

The doorway opened into the cafeteria near the shallow steps. In the center of the room was the archnephilim in his wraith form. Zella writhed in his tentacled grip, gasping against the smoke crushing her chest. Her hospital gown had ridden high, exposing the bandaged stump of her right leg. One wing was still captured in a brace and stuck straight out, while the other hung limp at her side, bumping into a knocked-over table.

More knocked-over tables and chairs littered the area, along with two that had crashed into the fridges holding food and drinks for when the kitchen was closed. Dark liquid, thick like blood, oozed across the floor beneath them.

Gideon stood at least ten feet back, his expression desperate. He yelled for Zella, swinging a massive sword of divine light and slicing through tentacle after tentacle but not gaining any ground.

The archnephilim threw a table at him. He dove out of the way as it crashed to the floor, but another tentacle swept up and slammed him across the room. Gideon's temple cracked against the step and his sword vanished. His eyes rolled back for a second, then he gasped and his gaze locked onto me.

"Stay back." He shoved to his feet and his sword returned.

"I know how to stop him," I said.

His eyes widened, but Zella screamed, jerking his attention away from me.

The archnephilim slammed her against the ceiling, drawing a strangled cry. Kol dove in, slashing at the tentacles near her, but couldn't get close enough to free her.

Jacob and Marcus ran onto the half dozen shallow steps leading down to the cafeteria, and Gideon leaped back toward the nephilim.

"Get the hell out of here," Marcus said to me, his fingers extending into claws.

Jacob drew both of his sidearms and fired four shots as fast as the weapons would allow. The bullets slammed into what was probably the archnephilim's chest.

"Stop trying to kill Essie," Marcus growled, and he raced after Gideon.

The archnephilim swept a tentacle at Kol, who twisted out of the way and sliced it off, as more of its smoke wrapped around Zella.

"This blood is on your hands, angel," the archnephilim said, his voice booming more in my head than in the room, and he ripped off Zella's dangling wing.

ESSIE

ZELLA SCREAMED, HER BLOOD SPRAYING ACROSS THE ROOM AND RUSHING onto the floor. Gideon yelled her name and staggered, his face a mask of utter horror.

The world froze. I couldn't look away as the horrific image burned into my mind. Zella, bleeding, broken, her face locked in agony and eyes wide with terror, captured in the archnephilim's smoke. Her arms were wrenched taut and tentacles crushed her chest and choked her.

Then the world snapped back into action, and the archnephilim shot a tentacle at Gideon. He tried to twist out of the way, but wasn't fast enough. The tentacle swept around his neck and wrenched him up to Zella's level.

"This is for me and mine," the archnephilim said and speared a massive tentacle through Zella's chest.

I jerked my hand out, too late to do anything — not that I could stop him — and screamed. Gideon's grief and rage burst around me like a steamy sauna.

Zella sputtered and convulsed, and the archnephilim tossed her against the rock wall. She fell, tearing plants from their crannies and splashing into the water, her head and torso submerged.

Gideon howled and light exploded from his hands, consuming the tentacle around his neck. He hit the floor, barely kept his balance, and rushed to Zella as Marcus slashed through a tentacle and raced to her as well.

Marcus got to her first and dragged her out of the water, but she didn't move, her body limp. Gideon dropped to his knees, grabbed her from Marcus, and wrapped his arms around her. Blood pooled around them, but his gaze was frozen on Zella. His whole body was frozen, as if his whole essence had stalled, unable to get past holding Zella's lifeless form. His grief burned stronger than his rage and the steam thickened, obscuring the room, but his emotions also cut into me, squeezing my chest and making me gasp for breath.

"Now I'm taking what's mine," the archnephilim said. "Essie. Come."

Searing agony exploded in the archnephilim's brand and my body jerked forward a step.

Panic, my panic, sliced through Gideon's grief, giving me a jagged breath and evaporating the steam. I clenched every muscle within me, squeezing as tight as I could, and forced myself to not take another step.

"I said come," the archnephilim hissed, his voice in my head screeching across my nerves like nails on a chalkboard.

More agony blazed through the brand, and the buzz burst past the nicotine from the patch and snapped under my skin. I staggered forward two more steps.

No. Please, no. I gritted my teeth and mentally heaved at the archnephilim's command.

"Essie." Marcus jerked away from Gideon and Zella and barreled toward the archnephilim.

Jacob fired another four rounds, center of mass again.

"Jacob, please," Marcus begged, slashing at tentacle after tentacle.

Kol also dove in, ramming his blades into what was probably the archnephilim's shoulder. The archnephilim seized Kol and flung him out the cafeteria entrance, sending him tumbling into the hall near the elevator.

I took another staggering step forward.

Come on. No. This was my body. I had to be stronger than him. *Please, let me be stronger than him.*

The fire from the brand screamed through me, and my breath came in ragged gasps. I tried to drop to my knees but my muscles wouldn't obey. I tried to fall, to step back, to do anything, but I could only clench everything within me and force myself still. Except the buzz was chewing away at my concentration and I didn't know how long I could resist him.

"You're taking too long," the archnephilim growled, and an inferno, a hundred times more ferocious than anything I'd felt before, erupted from the brand and devoured every other sensation within me. It rushed up my arm, across my chest, and crushed around my heart. I was burning up, being consumed from the inside out. Every breath I took burned, every thought evaporated the moment I thought it. I shuddered and broke into a run. Toward the archnephilim.

My mind screamed at me, cold panic fighting through the fire, but I couldn't get my thoughts out of my head and into my body enough to just slow down. I hurdled over a fallen table and a flicker of control seized my muscles. I staggered, but caught my balance and kept running.

Jacob jerked toward me. "Essie." He locked gazes with me, the dark intensity in his eyes capturing my essence. "Stop."

I jerked to a stop, lost my balance, and fell, cracking my knees against the linoleum floor. Jacob's command flash-froze through the archnephilim's fire, and everything within me trembled with the need to obey both Jacob and the archnephilim. I pressed my palms to the floor and locked my gaze on the tile beneath them.

Just stay. All I have to do is stay where I am.

But the contrary commands ripped at my will, and the buzz had returned, threatening to steal my concentration.

The archnephilim's power jerked my head up as Marcus roared and dove at the archnephilim, his claws slicing through tentacles. Jacob fired at the center of the archnephilim's mass, making Marcus roar again, this time with desperation. But no matter what Marcus wanted, it was the right call. The guys were barely making a dent against the archnephilim. It would be a miracle if they managed to kill it. No way were they going to be able to capture it.

My trembling grew stronger, making my teeth chatter as I fought to keep my jaw locked.

"Marcus, you have to kill it," I gasped.

"I'm not killing you."

"Please." The warring commands ripped deeper, tearing into my soul, and then the fire from the archnephilim's brand exploded again, consuming Jacob's ice and the buzz.

I staggered to my feet, my attention locked on the archnephilim, and I couldn't look away as if I were a passenger in my own body.

Marcus barked my name, and Jacob commanded me to stop again, but his ice didn't blast through the archnephilim's fire and I heaved forward one step... two steps.

Someone swore. I didn't know who.

The archnephilim howled with pleasure, his satisfaction oozing inky darkness into the flames within me. My stomach heaved. He didn't have to pour a tentacle down my throat any more to control me. He was already inside me, ripping into my soul.

A sob tightened my throat and my eyes burned.

"Gideon, I can stop him," I said, but my words were a gasp, I wasn't even sure if they came out, and I couldn't look to see if Gideon was still locked in shock, holding Zella.

A tentacle swept toward me and out of the corner of my eye, Kol rushed forward and tackled me. We crashed to the floor, sliding into the side of a knocked-over table.

Thank God.

The archnephilim surged toward us, his tentacles tossed the table aside, and a massive tentacle grabbed for me. Kol seized the back of my shirt and wrenched me out of reach while Marcus tore through the tentacle with his claws. My body jerked, trying to break free from Kol's grip and stand.

The tentacle reformed and Marcus tore through that one, too, his lips curled in a snarl revealing his wolf's teeth. He swiped as the tentacle reformed again, and another one seized his leg. It jerked him off his feet and slammed him against the rock wall, then down onto the stairs.

I screamed. Blood rushed onto the steps around his head and he lay still, too still.

I heaved in Kol's grip, but I wasn't sure if it was to run to the archnephilim or Marcus. He was hurt because of me. Again. And this time I might have killed him.

A sob broke free. *Please don't let him be dead. Please, God.* If someone was supposed to die, it should have been me. Me. No one else. And certainly not Marcus.

"Gideon." This had to end now. He had to blast divine light into the archnephilim's brand and stop this. "Please, I can stop him."

Marcus moaned and his eyes fluttered open.

Relief flooded me, but the archnephilim surged toward him and a flurry of tentacles swarmed around the rock wall.

I screamed for him to get up, get out of the way, for Jacob, for anyone, to help him, but the archnephilim was too fast. He yanked the wall down, the stones crashing onto Marcus. Gideon dove out of the way, dragging Zella's body with him, and Jacob wrenched to the side, narrowly dodging another block.

"Marcus!" I twisted harder against Kol's grip. His hold slipped, and I scrambled to my feet and headed toward the archnephilim. *Shit. No.*

Kol snagged my shirt again, yanking me off my feet. My butt hit the floor, the impact jarring up my spine and making my teeth snap. The force sliced through some of the archnephilim's power and I seized control of my muscles and fought to stay with Kol. I wanted to go to Marcus, somehow find the strength to heave those stones away and save him, but there was no guarantee that if I got free, I'd head to him. All I could see beneath the pile on top of him that now blocked the entrance to the cafeteria was his arm and half of his head. His eyes were closed and I couldn't tell if he was breathing.

"Essie," the archnephilim said, and his fire consumed all but the smallest voice screaming about Marcus.

My body wrenched to face Kol, twisting my shirt in his grip and using that hold to slip out of it, leaving me in my sports bra, then stood. Kol seized my arm and jerked me close, capturing me in a bear hug.

"Keep her away," Gideon yelled at Kol, his gaze filled with an icy fury, and with a scream, he charged at the archnephilim, his sword of light forming in his hand as he ran.

The archnephilim tossed another table at Gideon. He sliced it in half with his sword, without losing stride, and swung at the middle of the archnephilim's form. The blade sank into the archnephilim's smoke and jerked to a stop. The smoke burst apart, revealing the archnephilim in his angel form, blocking Gideon's blade with one made of darkness.

"Your mate makes me stronger than you," the archnephilim said with a sneer.

"And you killed her." Gideon leaned in, his blade grinding against the archnephilim's until they were hilt to hilt.

"Not yet."

My body wrenched against Kol's grip but he held tight.

Jacob grabbed Kol's daggers, discarded on the floor by our feet, and lunged at the archnephilim. The archnephilim shoved Gideon's blade from his and blocked Jacob's attack, then swung back at Gideon before he could strike. Gideon blocked the attack and Jacob jabbed at the archnephilim's torso, but a tentacle seized Jacob's wrist and wrenched the blow off target.

More tentacles swept from the archnephilim like extra arms, working in conjunction with his sword strikes, yanking at wrists and ankles, forcing the guys to slice at the tentacles before they could strike his body.

I twisted and heaved against Kol, my mind screaming to go to the archnephilim and not to go, my insides burning and buzzing.

Gideon sliced through two tentacles and twisted his attack, slipping it past the archnephilim's blade. His sword of divine light sliced into the archnephilim's side, drawing a yell. The tentacles dipped and Jacob leaped close, jabbing both daggers into the archnephilim's other side.

The archnephilim howled and the agony of his brand burned hotter.

"Essie!" he roared and power, not just fire, exploded under my skin, fiery, dark, consuming. Divine light blazed from my hands without me summoning it, more powerful than anything I'd ever manifested before, and my body slapped my palms against Kol's thighs.

He screamed. His grip on me loosened and I wrenched free, but instead of rushing to the archnephilim, my body slammed a blast of divine light into Kol's chest, making him stagger, then grabbed his head between my hands and shot another searing blast into his face.

Time slowed and bile burned my throat at what I'd just done.

Kol screamed with heartrending agony, his face and neck horribly burned and bleeding, his skin blackened and red, his features almost unrecognizable, his eyes barely open, unfocused. He wrenched back, but his legs, also with bleeding burns, gave out and he dropped to the floor.

Get up. Please get up.

Blood oozed from his chest, his T-shirt seared away, and he clutched his head, his body shuddering, wracked with pain, his breath shallow and desperate.

My body jerked toward him, divine light blazing from my palms again, and my mind screamed. *Take control. Stop this. Save him.* One more blast and I could kill him. I'd already—

My throat tightened. God, I'd already horribly disfigured him, probably blinded him. *I couldn't. Please, God, don't let me.*

The archnephilim's power made my hand rise.

No.

I wouldn't. I. Would. Not.

I wrenched my hand even higher and sent the divine light into the ceiling, the blast ripping through the ceiling tiles and showering the bits down on me.

Surprise and fear swept cold around and through me. The archnephilim hadn't expected me to resist him. Bully for me. Except I had no idea if I could do it again.

"Enough," the archnephilim growled. "Essie."

My body started to step toward him. I wrenched my foot back. "No."

"Essie."

His fire squeezed tighter around my heart and I trembled with the effort to stay put.

"I said no."

Jacob rammed one of Kol's daggers into the archnephilim's back. Gideon swept his sword at the archnephilim's legs, and the archnephilim exploded into his wraith form of writhing smoke. He whipped a tentacle at Gideon, who sliced it in half, then surged toward Jacob.

Jacob sliced at the archnephilim, his hands a whirl of movement, but the archnephilim's flurry of tentacles slashed and twisted, and one shot past Jacob's guard and slammed into his body. He staggered, just for a second, but it was enough for the archnephilim to ram a massive tentacle through his chest.

The vampire screamed and the archnephilim tossed him at Gideon, who half caught him and half slowed his fall — his sword vanishing between one second and the next. Jacob sagged against Gideon, as lifeless as Zella had been. Gideon let him slide to the floor and leaped at the archnephilim, his sword reforming.

The archnephilim sent a barrage of tentacles at Gideon, jabbing and slicing into him. Nothing cut deep enough to stop him, but he was starting to slow down. Blood splattered the cafeteria floor, making the footing slick, sweat glistened on his face, and his breath was ragged.

He twisted, dodging a tentacle, took another one in his right shoulder, and lunged, driving his sword in the center of the archnephilim's form.

The archnephilim howled again and his fire within me shuddered, weakening, and I seized control of my body. I yelled the light strike spell and sent a blast of divine light at him, not nearly as powerful as what I'd hit Kol with, but it didn't matter. I had to do any little thing I could to help Gideon. The blast slammed into the archnephilim, drawing a grunt of pain.

His fire flickered, and for a moment he had control of me again, but I forced him out with another yell of the spell and sent another blast at him while Gideon sliced a huge chunk out of his smoke.

The archnephilim roared and a massive barrage of thin, spear-like tentacles shot toward Gideon.

Gideon wrenched his sword up, slicing through four or five, but seven more impaled him, drawing a scream and jerking him off his feet. He swept his sword down to cut the smoke impaling him, but the arch-nephilim surged around him, completely covering him.

The archnephilim's form writhed, the edges tearing free, forming and reforming as if caught in a ferocious wind. A hint of light sliced out of the top, and Gideon's head emerged from the smoke. He gasped a desperate breath and heaved against the archnephilim's grip.

I shot another blast of divine light at the archnephilim, but this one was weaker than all the others. I was running out of juice. Still, it hit him and his inky fire within me shuddered, weakening even more.

All I could hope was that I could find another blast within me and that it would be enough for Gideon to break free. I yelled the spell again, using the cry to strengthen my will against the archnephilim's fire and the buzz within me, but the archnephilim surged back and crashed through the bank of windows at the back of the cafeteria.

I scrambled after them, everything within me now screaming that I couldn't let him take Gideon, couldn't let him die. Energy like sizzling electricity raced up my right arm from Gideon's brand and light gathered in my palms, stronger than my last few blasts.

The archnephilim swept to the end of the small patio enclosed by the buildings behind the Joined Parliament Operations Building.

I let a blast fly. It sliced through the archnephilim, nicking Gideon's shoulder and drawing a scream of pain, and erupted out of the back of the archnephilim's smoke.

"Do that again," the archnephilim sneered, a hint of his fire making my body twitch. "Next time I'll make sure you hit your mate."

"He'd be willing to make the sacrifice," I said, fighting his power and concentrating on Gideon's electricity to strengthen my will.

"But are you?"

The archnephilim's smoke curled away from Gideon's head, revealing the angel twisting and heaving to break free. Smoke poured down his nose and throat, and he gasped and coughed, desperate for air. Hints of divine light sliced through the darkness, but were quickly devoured.

"If I just squeeze, he'll be dead."

"Go ahead and squeeze." My pulse pounded, fear clutching my chest. I was going to kill Gideon, my mate, the mate who'd hate me the moment he knew the truth about me, and every cell in my body howled that I had to save him.

If he died, the archnephilim would still be allowed to slaughter supers.

Really. That was the only reason I had to save him.

The archnephilim's smoke contracted around Gideon, making him moan in pain.

I flinched and jerked forward a step.

"Are you sure?" he said with a dark laugh.

No. Not at all. Please, don't.

"I'm in your head. I know what you're feeling."

A flicker of divine light burst from the middle of the archnephilim. He shuddered, physically and in my head, weakening for a moment, and his smoke peeled farther away from Gideon's head. Then the archnephilim regained strength and twisted a tentacle around Gideon's neck and squeezed, drawing another strangled moan from Gideon.

"Give yourself to me," the archnephilim said.

Gideon's pale eyes, bright with angel glow, locked on me. I could see his desperation and feel it in the brand. If I gave in, the archnephilim would win.

Black misty angel wings pulled out of the archnephilim's smoke and he rose a few feet off the ground.

"Give yourself to me and I'll let your mate live."

Confusion flickered over Gideon's expression. His attention dipped to my arm then shot back to my gaze, his eyes now filled with realization and horror.

"Tick tock, tick tock."

Gideon's struggles grew desperate. He thrashed against the smoke, and shot feeble blasts of divine light from his palms. The archnephilim's form shuddered, weakening even more.

With a snarl he swept into the air and bolted away. "You have one hour. You know where to find me." The image of a warehouse and the knowledge of its location flashed in my mind. "Come alone."

ESSIE

I RACED TO THE EDGE OF THE PATIO, FEAR RIPPING INTO MY SOUL, TEARING at my heart. "Come back. I'll trade."

"*Come alone,*" the archnephilim said in my head. "*I see anyone else and your mate dies. Slowly.*"

"You kill him and I die. I die and you die."

The archnephilim laughed. "Your essence isn't strong enough to shatter mine, but his is definitely strong enough to shatter yours."

Pain bled through the electricity of Gideon's brand and I gasped for breath. I couldn't let him die. It didn't make sense. I didn't know him, didn't love him, and we weren't anything to each other, but the bond between us twisted deep within me.

I clenched my jaw and fought to draw a breath deeper than a shallow gasp. I needed to think, but with the archnephilim's fire gone, the buzz had taken over, screaming through me and making it hard to focus. Rushing off without a plan would get both of us killed. I needed a way to make sure Gideon lived—

My thoughts stuttered.

Jacob. Kol. Marcus.

I scrambled back into the cafeteria. The massive rocks from the wall still crushed Marcus, Jacob lay, his eyes closed, in an alarmingly large pool of blood, and Kol lay a few feet away, drawing ragged gasps that were coming too far apart.

I didn't know if Marcus was alive—

My chest tightened at the thought. But if he was, I wasn't strong enough to uncover him. I needed Jacob, probably Kol as well.

Vampires could take deadly blows and lose massive amounts of blood and still live. So long as he had his heart and his head, I could save him. He just needed blood.

I glanced at the shattered fridge, where the blood had been stored. There was no guarantee any of the blood bags survived, and if I wanted to help Kol — who'd been magically depleted before the fight had even begun and was probably unable to heal himself — my best bet was to let Jacob bite me. I already knew the sexual euphoria that came with a vampire feeding was strong, and if rumor was true, it would be even stronger now that he'd claimed me. I just hoped it was enough to help Kol if I was only holding his hand.

That, and I had to hope that Jacob would break free of the feeding frenzy that came with such a serious injury and come to his senses before he killed me. Of course, if the archnephilim had completely destroyed his heart, there would be no coming back from that, but I couldn't think about that possibility because I didn't have a plan B.

I grabbed the closest of Kol's daggers, set it on Jacob's chest — because I needed both hands to move him — and hauled him to Kol's side. Then I dropped between them, praying that this would work.

Before I could lose my nerve, I sliced the dagger against my forearm. The blade was sharper than I expected and cut deep. Blood rushed from the wound and I pressed it to Jacob's parted lips.

My pulse pounded, but Jacob didn't move, didn't even draw breath.

Blood leaked over his lips and oozed down his cheeks, and the buzz set my nerves on edge, making me tremble.

"Come on." I pressed my arm harder against his lips. "Please." This had to work. It had to. If it didn't, I didn't know if I'd be able to help Kol, not with his face — and God, his hands, too — so badly burned.

Then Jacob snarled, his eyes still closed. He seized my arm in a vise-like grip and bit hard, tearing at my flesh. I screamed and jerked, my body instinctually trying to stop the pain, but he held tight and sucked, the pain excruciating.

A whimper escaped my clenched jaw, but I had to keep going. Even if the sexual euphoria didn't come and I couldn't help Kol, Jacob might still be able to uncover Marcus.

Please, God, let him be alive.

Jacob's teeth dug deeper, and I sobbed. Tears leaked from my eyes, the agony more than I could bear. I had made a mistake. A horrible mistake. He wasn't going to come to his senses before he killed me and if I died, the archnephilim was guaranteed to kill Gideon.

I tried to pry his fingers from my arm but couldn't make them budge. "Jacob, wake up." I wrenched against his grip, making the room spin, proving just how much blood I'd already lost. "Wake up."

His eyes flashed open and his dark, intense gaze locked with mine.

"Essie." He breathed my name against my skin, sending a shiver of desire sweeping through me. One little word, and it was as if a switch had flipped and the pain melted into yearning. Even the buzz was muted.

I shuddered and grabbed Kol's closest wrist, trying to avoid the bleeding, oozing burns on his hand.

Jacob glanced at the connection then recaptured my gaze with his. His grip on my arm, both hand and teeth, loosened a bit, and the heat from his lips threaded into the ragged wound, staunching most of the bleeding but not all of it with a whisper of his healing magic. He took a long pull on my vein and another shiver swept over me.

The desire low within me erupted, hot and needy and insistent, and I focused on that. Not the pain. My pulse sped up, my breath suddenly ragged, and my whole essence throbbed. Need teased, taunted, strained within my skin and across my lips, and my thoughts jumped to the kiss with Marcus and his ferocious passion. The ache swelled low within me, tightening, trembling. I concentrated on the memory of Marcus's hands capturing my face, his lips forceful, commanding, taking control of me, body and soul. Just like Gideon was doing with his brand. Just like every cell in me craved from Jacob, *right now, please, God.*

I let a moan of pleasure escape my lips, not trying to fight it, not that I could. I needed to embrace all of it and not hide from any of it if I wanted to help Kol, but I also didn't want to give myself fully over to Jacob. If I did, I knew I'd rip the clothes from my body and beg him to take me. I was barely resisting the urge as it was, but I knew neither of us would be happy once the moment was over... well, I had a feeling I'd be incredibly satisfied, but Jacob wasn't the one I wanted to have a relationship with.

My pulse stuttered. Did I actually want a relationship with Marcus?

Jacob sucked on my arm and all thoughts of relationships melted into a need for Jacob. I needed him inside me, needed to please him, needed—

No. Focus on Marcus. Just hold out. Think about his kiss. I shuddered. His kiss had been everything I'd thought it would be and so much more. I yearned to be back in his arms, to have his powerful body moving against mine. To hell with having Gideon's brand. The thing between Marcus and me had been sizzling long before Gideon, and time away hadn't changed it. Whatever lay between us, I wanted more, craved more. If he was alive—

I jerked, my eyes opening. A chill swept away my aching desire, and the buzz flared back to life. The room darkened and spun and I blinked, trying to get my eyes to focus.

Kol had broken free from my grip and now held my knuckles to his cracked lips. His face still looked burnt and painful, but his skin no longer bled or oozed, and his eyes were blazing with hellfire. Jacob had stopped feeding and stared at the partially healed wound he'd ripped through Gideon's brand, his expression stunned.

"Can you stand?" I asked him. He needed to touch me, satisfy me— Jeez. He needed to help Marcus... who had to be alive. He just had to be.

Jacob's piercing gaze shifted to me and my heart lurched.

Tell me what to do. Anything. Please.

"Essie." His low voice rumbled through me, sending my essence into sympathetic vibration with his.

"Yes," I said, my voice breathy. *Anything.*

Footsteps pounded behind me, and I was suddenly struck by the fact that someone had turned off the fire alarm because I could hear foot-steps. But I couldn't tear my gaze away from Jacob to see who'd arrived. Out of the corner of my eye, I saw Amiah kneel by Kol's head. She said something to him, and his grip on my hand tightened, keeping it pressed to his lips.

More people rushed past, heading toward the cafeteria steps and Marcus. I still couldn't tear my gaze from Jacob.

Someone called out, but the words muddled in my head.

Jacob groaned and sat up, his attention turning to the pile of massive rocks.

By looking away, the pressure of Jacob's claim squeezing in my chest eased just enough for me to notice the hint of desire curling from Kol's lips and trailing up my arm.

A panicked conversation with raised voices erupted from the rock pile. Was Marcus still alive? *Please let him be alive.* But the room kept spinning and my essence was trapped between Jacob and Kol and I couldn't concentrate on looking for Marcus.

"Save him," I gasped to Jacob. "Please." Except I wasn't sure if I was begging for Marcus or Gideon.

"I'll try." Jacob stood, my attention locked on him as he headed to the rock pile.

Then Amiah shifted in front of me and my mind stuttered before my gaze slid past her shoulder back to Jacob. Behind her, Jacob and another man — an angel by the glow of his eyes — heaved a stone aside, revealing more of Marcus's body.

"Is he dead?" I asked, my voice too small for Jacob to hear across the cafeteria. *Please don't be dead.* I couldn't handle it if he was dead.

"Essie." Amiah gripped my shoulders. "Where's Gideon?"

I couldn't tear my attention from Marcus and Jacob.

Please be alive. Please.

Jacob and the angel lifted the stone pinning Marcus's legs and another man and a woman pulled him free, smearing his blood, too much blood, on the floor.

"Essie!" Amiah shook me, making the room whirl. "Where's Gideon?"

"He's alive," one of them said.

The fear clutching me shot me to my feet to rush to him, but the world heaved and darkened and I stumbled.

Amiah grabbed me, sliding me back to the floor.

"Amiah, we need you," Jacob said, his tone urgent. My pulse pounded and the buzz burned through me. Jacob needed help. No, Marcus did. No—

Amiah captured my chin and forced me to look at her. "Where's Gideon?"

"Taken," I gasped.

Fear snapped frozen across my skin, but my thoughts were too muddled to figure out who it had come from. Best guess was Amiah.

"By that monster?" Amiah asked, the cold fear bleeding from her fingers onto my cheeks. "Why would he take him?"

"Torture," Kol said, his hand snaking out to capture mine again.

Horror widened Amiah's eyes and the cold deepened.

"But that means he's still alive," I said, and while the archnephilim might torture Gideon, his main target was me.

And it was torture. Even with the dizzying blood loss, the ache for Jacob, and the shiver of desire from Kol's enthrallment, my soul screamed to go to Gideon. Nothing else mattered.

"Amiah," Jacob barked.

Her expression hardened. "We're not done here."

"Amiah." Jacob sounded desperate.

My heart clenched and I fought to rise, but Amiah shoved me back onto my butt.

"Jacob, tell her to stay," Amiah said as she hurried to him and Marcus.

Jacob frowned. Guess someone had told her about Jacob's claim on me.

"How much blood did you take from her?" Amiah shot him a dark glare and knelt beside Marcus. "How much life force did Kol? She'll hurt herself if she moves."

"Fine." Jacob locked gazes with me and his claim sang with joy at the attention. "Stay there until someone helps you."

The compulsion swept through me and a part of me was grateful. There wasn't anything I could do to save Marcus, no matter how much I wanted to be by his side. That, and the need to save Gideon was twisting tighter and tighter within me. I didn't know how much longer I could hold out, not with the buzz tearing at my concentration. Jacob's command gave me time to pull myself together and think.

Except that was the hardest thing in the world to do at the moment. I was dizzy and exhausted. I didn't know if that was because of healing Jacob and Kol or something else. Maybe it was from resisting the arch-nephilim's possession. I was also cold with Amiah's fear.

"He'll be okay," Kol said, squeezing my hand and sending desire shivering through me. "Amiah is the best."

My throat tightened and I forced myself to look at him and at the damage I'd done. Hellfire still burned in his eyes, although the fire was banked to a low glow. He looked like he'd been set on fire and ugly red scars covered most of his face. But they looked like scars, not fresh or even partially healed wounds like they'd been moments before.

"Are you going to be okay?" I asked.

"It was smart of you to use Jacob's bite to help me."

"I can give you more if you need." I'd give him everything, but not even that would make up for what I'd done.

His gaze dipped to Gideon's brand on my arm and he release my hand. "I've got enough to get me through."

Light flared, dragging my attention back to the steps. Amiah sat at Marcus's head, her palms pressed to his temples, and the power of her healing magic radiated around her, growing brighter and brighter, forcing me to look away.

Then it vanished and Amiah sagged back onto her heels, her shoulders slumping forward.

Marcus groaned and his eyelids fluttered open. His face was still tight with pain and his breath a little too short, but he was alive. *Thank God, he was alive.*

"You have to finish the rest by shifting," Amiah said. "Cassey, help him undress so the shift doesn't destroy his clothes."

"Let's clear the room and give him some privacy," Jacob said. "Reassemble in the triage waiting room."

"We won't be long," Amiah said, sounding exhausted.

With the exception of a woman, who I recognized from the team that had taken care of Zella, the others headed back to the patio and around the side of the building.

Kol staggered to his feet and offered me a hand to help stand. I gingerly took it, afraid I'd hurt him, and rose. The room twisted, and he stepped close, wrapping his arms around me and holding me up. His body was almost too hot for comfort, but I leaned into his embrace anyway, hoping his heat would melt some of the cold. I still couldn't stop shaking, but most of that wasn't the chill. My legs were weak, and I throbbed with pain and unsatisfied sexual desire.

"Jeez, Essie. You're freezing." Kol's embrace tightened as if he could hug the cold out of me.

My throat constricted. How was I going to help Gideon when I could barely stand? Even if I was going to go to the warehouse to make the trade, I was too weak to walk. I'd need help getting there, certainly within my one-hour time limit, but if I asked, the guys would refuse to help me.

"I can take her," Jacob said as he approached.

Kol opened his arms, and Jacob swept me off my feet and cradled me against his chest. His shirt was sticky with blood, but there wasn't a hole in his chest any more. His claim soared through me. He was touching me. He wanted me. And I didn't try to fight it because it was stronger than the buzz and the pull to Gideon. The sensation was a lot stronger than before. Before I'd needed him to tell me what to do. Now I outright needed him, to think, to breathe, to live. I could only hope Jacob wouldn't take advantage of that and I could control myself long enough for the effects to ease off. Except I had no idea when that would be now that he'd bitten me twice.

"We need a plan," Jacob said, his voice rumbling through me, making the claim thrill at the sensation.

Have sex—

No, save Gideon.

That's right. I had to save Gideon. But that wasn't a plan, that was a desire born from a mating brand I didn't want to have.

Kol grabbed the vampire's shoulder to help keep his balance, and we left the cafeteria, stepping onto the patio and heading around the side to a plain metal door.

"We need to go down to the armory and grab that ring imbued with divine light from the war that still has its charge," Kol said.

"You said the archnephilim took Gideon," Jacob said, and I realized — thank God — he, Kol, and Marcus had probably been unconscious for the archnephilim's ultimatum. That meant if I could find the strength to move, I could go to Gideon and kill the archnephilim without having to fight the guys about it. "Why wouldn't it kill him outright like it had with the rest of the squad?"

I pressed my hand to Jacob's chest. His skin was cool, which meant we were far enough from Amiah's fear for me to warm up, but I couldn't feel a heartbeat. Of course, he was undead. He didn't have a heartbeat. But that didn't mean he wasn't alive in a magical sense or couldn't be killed. God, they all could have been killed. And now I had less than an hour to meet the archnephilim's demand.

"Gideon was the squad leader," Kol said. "The archnephilim also made a point of killing Zella in front of him. He wants Gideon to suffer."

We entered the side door and stepped into a narrow hall that looked like all the other halls in the building — white walls, gray floor — except this one was about two feet narrower and only had one door in the middle of the left-hand side.

"Except Zella wasn't his mate." Jacob's grip on me tightened.

"But he didn't know that at the time," I said.

Jacob shook his head and sighed. "He would have known once the bond had gained more strength. You wouldn't have been able to hide it forever. Why didn't you tell him?"

The compulsion to answer him twisted in my chest and the buzz ate away at my willpower, but I couldn't just tell Jacob it was because I didn't want the bond with Gideon to be real and I didn't want to break his heart. He loved Zella and knew her. She's been a member of his squad during the war, and she was an angel like him. I was, as far as everyone believed, just a powerless human he didn't know.

"Our wolf makes it complicated," Kol said.

Among other things.

The claim twisted tighter. I needed to say something but I couldn't tell the whole truth, that I was the thing Gideon and everyone else hated and feared the most.

And I needed to save Gideon. Save him.

"I'd hoped we could kill the archnephilim before my bond with Gideon fully formed," I said, the words blurting out, easing the compulsion from Jacob's claim. "If he didn't know the truth, my death might not have killed him or driven him insane."

Except it was too late now. The electricity from his bond tingled up my arm, told me he was alive, and that we were permanently connected.

Jacob led us around a corner into a wider hall with more doors, which I soon discovered was the main hall. We reached the sliding frosted-glass doors where Amiah and her team had taken Zella when we'd first brought her in and entered. To the right was a waiting area with a padded leather couch, two matching armchairs, and a TV — currently not on. To the left was a miniature version of a hospital emergency room, packed with equipment and three beds, while the hall continued straight ahead with more doorways leading to other areas of the miniature hospital.

The others who'd rushed into the cafeteria to help — one girl and four guys — sat on the couch and chairs. They'd been talking when we entered but had fallen silent.

"I've lifted the lockdown, sent the research team home, and called in Chris and Jasmine to help us with clean up," the angel who'd helped Jacob move the rocks said as he stood and offered his chair.

"Good." Jacob sat me in the chair and Kol perched on the wide arm. "Grab a body bag for Zella and go help Amiah."

The angel jerked his thumb. The three other guys stood and they left.

"Summer," Jacob said, and turned his attention to the petite woman with a hint of divine glow in her soft brown eyes. Her brown hair was cut into a short bob, accentuating her cherub-like face, but her expression was anything but innocent and childlike. "Call in a specialist to reinforce the wards, and then take stock of what we have in the armory that can kill a wraith or an archangel."

Summer's eyes widened, but she nodded and hurried out the door as well.

"So that leaves us with what?" Kol asked, still sitting beside me even though the rest of the seats had opened up.

Jacob eased onto the couch across from me, easily taking up half the space with his massive frame and making me lean forward, the claim urging me to move and join him.

He ran his hands over his face, looking exhausted. "I have no idea. Now if we kill the archnephilim, we not only kill Essie but Gideon as well."

Not if I kill him before—

Fear squeezed around my heart. The bond was fully formed. Jacob was right. How the hell was I supposed to save Gideon now?

"Can we please stop talking about killing the archnephilim?" Marcus said from the doorway. Blood stained his gray T-shirt and blue jeans, but other than that I wouldn't have known he'd almost been crushed to death. His gaze slid from Kol, sitting close to me, to Gideon's brand on my right forearm. His expression darkened and he took the seat beside Jacob on the couch, facing me but farther away than the armchair beside me. His churning mix of hot and cold emotions fluttered through me, adding nausea to my spinning head and grating buzz.

"You need to call in backup," Amiah said, entering after him. She dropped my shirt in my lap and sagged into the empty armchair, her complexion gray, the skin around her eyes pinched with tension.

"The closest team that's bigger than two people is over four hours away in Los Angeles," Kol said. "Do we think he'll let Gideon live that long?"

Jacob sighed. "We're going to have to hope he will, because we nearly got slaughtered."

Except Gideon didn't have four hours and time was slipping away. And if the archnephilim killed him, that would kill me and ruin any chance of using his unnatural bond with me to stop him. I already knew he was willing to give up the extra power I gave him. Killing Gideon was part of his vengeance. I'd only been a surprise bonus in all this. He didn't need me, hadn't wanted me, but was more than happy to use me to achieve his goals.

I had to trade myself for Gideon. I had no doubt the archnephilim would go against his word and try to kill Gideon, but if I could get him free long enough to blast the brand, we could finish this.

The other guys, however, couldn't come. The archnephilim had said to come alone and if they showed up, he'd kill them this time. I doubted Kol could fully recover all of his magical strength within the hour, especially if he wasn't going to go out and replenish it, and while Marcus looked fine, I could still see a hint of tightness in his jaw that said he wasn't completely healed. Even Jacob, while no longer physically hurt, looked exhausted. It was a miracle they were all alive, and I suspected that was exactly what the archnephilim had wanted.

I clenched my jaw to keep from saying something stupid. If Jacob even suspected I was going to face the archnephilim, he'd command me not to go, and with his claim on me strengthened, I wouldn't be able to resist him.

Going alone was the only answer. It was the only way to protect them. Too many people had already died, and I wasn't going to add the guys to the list.

That, and no matter what I wanted or how foolish it was, I couldn't ignore the twisting need to save Gideon.

ESSIE

"ALL RIGHT," MARCUS SAID, HIS VOICE LOW, DANGEROUS, HIS GAZE LOCKED on me as if daring me to argue with him. "We call in backup and capture the archnephilim."

Sadness crept into Jacob's eyes. He offered me a bitter smile and a hint of mist curled around me. "You've got to accept the truth, Marcus."

"My wolf is making that difficult," Marcus growled.

"Then you should sit this out," Kol said. "When we go out with the other team, stay here with Essie."

Amiah turned to me, making the leather creak. "How strong is your bond with Gideon?"

"I don't know. I know he's alive." But now that I thought about it, the electricity had shifted from a steady hum — kind of like the buzz, but at a gentler, lower vibration, and almost imperceptible against my grating buzz — to something more jagged, painful. He was in pain. Every fiber of my being knew it. The archnephilim might have said he'd let Gideon live, but he hadn't said in what condition.

Panic seized my heart as the image of the archnephilim ripping off Zella's wing flashed through me, making my throat burn with bile. I had to fight past my weakness and get to the archnephilim's warehouse before the damage done to Gideon was irrevocable.

Except my dying still meant Gideon would die. And yet I couldn't convince the need coming from the brand that my only plan was doomed, that it was impossible to save him.

"Can you sense anything else? His pain, his essence?" Amiah asked.

"I can't feel his pain like it's my own, but I know he's in pain." *God, so much pain.*

"We might be able to sustain him through Essie." Amiah eased from the chair and knelt beside me. The glow in her eyes was feeble, allowing me to see her exhaustion. "Right now you're weak, so the mating brand won't let him use your essence. You might even be draining him."

Marcus sat forward. "Amiah, don't hurt yourself. Gideon is strong. He can last at least an hour, long enough for you to partially recover your magic before you heal her."

Heal me? *She was going to heal me?* If she did, I'd be able to satisfy the compulsion from the brand and go ahead with my plan. And while Gideon could technically survive the archnephilim's torture for an hour, if I didn't show up, that would be all the time he'd get—

I forced a hint of a sob — I didn't want to overdo it — and dropped my gaze to my hands. I didn't want any of the guys to read my expression, for fear they'd be able to see the lie. "I don't know if he can survive an hour."

"Essie, he's strong," Kol said, brushing his hand across my shoulder, but not maintaining contact as if he wanted, but didn't want, to touch me.

"But he was hurt when the archnephilim took him." For all I knew, the archnephilim wasn't doing anything to him and he was just bleeding out from all the holes in his body. His pain could be the emotional agony from seeing Zella murdered. And finding out he was mated with me.

"She's low on blood and life essence. It's not like I'm fixing broken bones again," Amiah said, and she grabbed my hand.

I flinched, expecting the same agony from Amiah's healing as before, but instead a tingling warmth swept up my arm, mingling with Gideon's electric hum before spreading into my chest. I closed my eyes and let myself float on the sensation, wrapped in its warmth. There were no fears or worries, no heartache for Gideon's loss or my own. There was just peace and heat... and my God damned buzz. I could have stayed there forever, but that wouldn't save Gideon... not that I could actually save him... but I had to try.

Then the tingle vanished and Amiah sagged back onto her heels like she had when she'd healed Marcus, her eyes unfocused. My dizziness, exhaustion, and churning stomach were gone. Even the nasty, partially healed wound Jacob had gnawed into my arm was only a pale patch of pink over the top of the perfect golden swirls of Gideon's delicate mating brand. The buzz, however, remained.

Marcus left the couch and helped Amiah back into the armchair. "You shouldn't have done that," he said to her.

She brushed her fingers along his jaw, trailing them through his stubble, the tender move speaking of a familiarity between them that went deeper than just physician and patient.

"I bought Gideon time," she said. "Now go call in backup. He's mated with a human. There's a good chance he'll survive her death and a certainty he'll survive if she just goes insane."

The muscles in Marcus's jaw twitched and he shifted away from Amiah, closer to me.

"Is that true?" I asked her. Maybe Gideon *could* get out of this alive. Maybe only I had to be the archnephilim's last victim. Which sucked, but was the best of a lot of horrible choices.

"I've successfully treated the angel half of a broken angel-human bond."

"It wasn't in any of the books I read in the archives downstairs."

"Those books are older than the war," Amiah said. "A lot of things happened during the war, along with at least one human marked with an angelic mating brand."

Which meant there was hope. I had hope. I was half human. That had to be human enough to save him. Now I just needed to figure out how to get Gideon to blast light into my brand — since light magic was surprisingly rare among angels and I doubted there'd be another angel stationed here who could summon light. Would he even risk my life to do it? I was willing to do anything to save him. Was that because my human half wasn't strong enough to withstand the compulsion from the brand or was that just what the brand did? If Gideon felt what I felt, there was a chance he wouldn't be willing to kill me to stop the arch-nephilim. Better to not even go there. Kol had said there was a divine light ring in the armory. I needed to get my hands on that.

Yes, get the ring. That was a good plan. If I went soon, I might be able to catch Summer still doing inventory, so I wouldn't have to figure out how to get past the fingerprint scanner on the door. I'd either have to lie to her or steal it when she wasn't looking, but that was my best option. Then I'd go to the archnephilim. Sure, I could try to kill him from afar, but there was a risk he'd kill Gideon before the blast burned him up since I didn't know how long it would take. I needed to get him to let Gideon go, just long enough to kill him.

My stomach churned with hope and fear, all while my mind cheered that I could free Gideon. I could free my mate.

But I had to get away from everyone first. I could say I wanted to go to my room — and replacing my nicotine patch would be awesome — but I suspected someone would go and keep an eye on me.

"Okay." Amiah took in a deep breath and straightened. "Jacob, go into triage and grab a blood bag from the fridge, Kol, you need to eat."

"Can you get it done in thirty minutes?" Jacob asked, heading into the triage area and opening a small fridge under a stainless steel counter.

Kol shrugged. "I'm fine enough. I'd rather not leave you guys shorthanded."

Amiah huffed. "You're hardly fine. Every bit of magic you have is going to be diverted to healing your injuries and you know it. You're going to be weaker, slower, and less nimble. That makes you a liability and not an asset."

"She's right." Jacob pulled out a blood bag.

"Fine." Kol stood and marched out the sliding glass door.

"Marcus, can you be on Essie duty?" Jacob asked. "I should call the head office and request backup."

Shit. I wasn't going to be able to slip away, let alone snatch the divine light ring if I had Marcus shadowing me.

And I still needed a reason to go to the basement.

"I... I'm going to continue looking through Michael's research. Maybe there's a way to control the archnephilim and limit casualties the next time we— *you* go up against him."

"My phone call might take a bit," Jacob said, "but I'll join you when I'm done."

"And I need to change clothes." Marcus stood and tugged on his bloody T-shirt. "I'll meet you down there."

"Great." Fantastic! If I hurried, I could grab the ring and get out of there before Marcus returned.

Marcus held out his hand to help me stand, the action fast, easy, as if it was instinct, and I took it with the same thoughtless ease. But his attention jumped from our joined hands up my arm to Gideon's brand, and my chest squeezed. None of this was fair to Marcus. He'd said his wolf made it hard for him to stay away from me, but that he'd stayed away so I wouldn't get caught up in the supernatural world. Now I was, couldn't be his, and was probably going to die. All in a matter of days.

And above all that, I ached for Jacob to give me a command, and was terrified that Gideon would die.

"I'll meet you down there," I said, slipping my hand from his and pulling on my shirt.

This situation was impossible. No matter what I did I couldn't win, so I had to focus on what I could do. Get the ring, go to the warehouse, and kill the archnephilim.

I strode out the sliding doors as fast as I could without looking like I was running, and hurried to the elevator and hit the down button. It dinged immediately, the door slid open, and I got inside and took it to the basement.

The large reading table was still covered in books, some half open, others with scraps of paper sticking out of them marking a spot Jacob wanted to return to. Had it really only been a few hours? Hell, it probably had barely been an hour. Most fights didn't last long and the arch-nephilim had been ferocious in his attack.

The armory door was open and the light was on. Summer stood at a small standup desk just inside the door, staring at a computer screen.

"Any luck finding anything that can kill a wraith or an archangel?" I asked.

She jerked her thumb to a long narrow table in the center of the room. On it were two rings — not placed together — and an HK416 assault rifle beside three boxes of ammunition. "You tell me. We've got two divine light rings but only one that's charged, and Gideon is the only angel in town able to summon divine light to put in the ring. And we have the rifle with ammunition enchanted to take down a greater demon, but I have no idea if that would work on a wraith since wraiths are insubstantial."

I had no idea either. My education on demons from the advanced combat training involved those I'd most likely run into while walking the beat, and most of those could be taken down by a Taser on its highest setting — added special for supers — or a few of the department-issued enchanted bullets. But the highest Taser setting and the enchanted ammunition wouldn't take down anything like a master vampire or an alpha were-anything. We'd also been told it wouldn't affect the more powerful greater demons. I didn't know where a wraith stood on the scale of a lesser demon with almost no magic and a greater demon with lots of magic.

I did know the ring would work. Just not in the way everyone thought it would.

"Not surprising," Summer said, waving at the computer screen, "we have nothing in our inventory that can kill an archangel. The only weapon made to stop Michael and Rafael is with Gabriel in the Realm of Celestial Light, and no one has been able to contact him since he killed his brothers."

"Well," I said, trying to keep my tone even, "I'll take the ring up to Jacob so he's prepared for anything, and you keep looking."

Summer stared at me, her eyes a little too wide. "You honestly think the archnephilim will attack again so soon?"

"We're hurt and disorganized. That's a serious advantage for him. I wouldn't put it past him." Save for the fact that I knew he was waiting for me to come to him. Which meant perhaps the fight had taken almost as much out of him as it had out of the guys. They'd gotten in some good strikes and by the end, his power over me had weakened enough that I could resist him. Maybe he was licking his wounds just like we were. Hopefully that meant I was guaranteed to kill him by blasting divine light into his brand.

"It's the one closest to us," Summer said, and she turned back to the computer screen.

"Thanks." I picked up the ring. It was heavy and masculine, too big for any of my fingers, but would probably fit my thumb. Power radiated from it, crackling over my hand, so much like the electricity coming from Gideon's brand. The compulsion to save him twisted inside me, my soul chanting, *save him, save him, save him,* and I turned to leave.

"The guys will get Gideon back to you," she said, her voice soft, making me pause. "You should have told him about the brand."

Jeez, did everyone know I hadn't told Gideon that I was his fated mate? Of course, a mating brand was rare, and Gideon had been certain Zella had been his mate. With a workplace this small, I shouldn't be surprised if everyone knew about Gideon's brand. And yeah, the odds were good everyone also knew about my kiss with Marcus.

"Just keep looking," I said, and hurried back to the elevator. If my plan didn't work, the guys would need every advantage they had to stop the archnephilim.

I pressed the call button and shoved the ring in my pocket while I waited. I could have taken the stairs but they would have put me in the cafeteria with everyone cleaning up the mess from the fight.

Except each second waiting for the elevator felt like an eternity.

I had the means to save Gideon, to protect the guys, and to end this nightmare. I couldn't make myself see the situation as a good thing, but I could keep telling myself this was the best of many horrible options. If I died with the archnephilim and Gideon survived, he'd never have to find out what I really was. I wouldn't be imprisoned or sentenced to death or studied like a lab rat. I also wouldn't completely break Marcus's heart. He wouldn't have to live seeing me being Gideon's mate and not his. We wouldn't have to figure out how to deal with or ignore the sizzling attraction between us, because I knew Marcus was like Kol. A friend didn't get in the way of another friend's relationship, apparently even if that relationship was forced on both parties.

The elevator door slid open, revealing Marcus leaning against the back wall. He'd changed into a clean T-shirt that pulled tight over his deliciously muscled chest and jeans that hugged his hips and thighs.

He raised his piercing green gaze to mine and my pulse stuttered. Even with Gideon's brand fully formed, the attraction still burned between us. My heart raced and my breath came a little too fast just at the sight of him, while a hint of heat caressed my skin, telling me he felt the connection, too.

The door began to slide shut and we both jerked forward. Marcus caught it with his arm and it reopened, but now we stood so close his breath tickled my cheeks. If I took a deep breath, my breasts might brush his chest. God, how I wanted my breasts to brush his chest.

A hunger burned in his eyes and more warmth curled over and under my skin. I had to touch him, give in to the power between us, or I'd combust. But I couldn't be his. I wasn't going to survive past the next hour and that wasn't fair to him.

He must have seen something in my eyes, because the heat of his desire chilled with a hint of fear.

"Essie." He growled my name, tugging on something primal within me, and I leaned closer. Now barely a breath stood between us and I could feel the heat of his body, sense the power of his wolf, ferocious and passionate, curled tight within him.

I pressed my hand against his chest before I fully realized what I was doing, then jerked back when common sense kicked in a second later, but Marcus grabbed my wrist. The door started to shut, and he pulled me inside, turned, and backed me against the back of the elevator. He captured me with his body, his hands pressed to the wall on either side of me, and kissed me.

The kiss was soft, quick, tentative, as if Marcus was uncertain of his reception, but it sent a shudder sliding through me, making me moan with desire. Even just a brush of lips sent me trembling, aching for him.

I ran my fingers through his stubble, up into his hair, and pulled his lips back to me. He didn't need any more of an invitation. Heat swept around me and he claimed my mouth with his. The ferocity of the kiss left me breathless. His tongue invaded me, fueled the fire of my desire for him, and sent me spiraling.

His hands pushed under my shirt, a sizzling shock of flesh against flesh. One hand slid around my back, securing me — which was good, my mind was spinning and I wasn't sure if I'd be able to keep standing — and the other dipped into my sports bra and kneaded my breast. There wasn't anything delicate or slow or drawn out about it. This was ferocious, pent-up desire, released without control, and it made my blood sing, made me crave all of him. And it had nothing to do with being unsatisfied after Jacob's bite. It was all Marcus, all the desire between us that I thought was impossible, that I shouldn't be feeling, that I wanted to lose myself in.

He shoved my shirt and bra up, the heat of his desire building around me, and dropped his mouth to my breast, sucking my nipple into a tight bud and drawing a gasp. His hand that had been on my breast swept under the waistband of both my cargo pants and underwear. He found my slick heat, and plunged two fingers inside of me, sending a shock of pleasure zinging through me.

I gasped and he smiled against my breast.

"Mine," he growled, his voice low, dangerous, and so damned hot.

His lips returned to mine, capturing my ragged breaths, as his fingers worked inside me. The pleasure built fast, this whole moment fast and ferocious. The attraction between us couldn't be denied. It felt as fated, *more* fated than my brand with Gideon. Our desire for each other had nothing to do with a magical connection. It was pure, hot need.

The first tremor of a climax swept through me. I moaned, trying to keep my cry of pleasure in, but I couldn't, and cried out his name as ecstasy roared through me. He growled again, a noise of pure masculine satisfaction, and held me tight as I rode the wave, my legs wobbly, my whole body wobbly and satiated.

He pressed his forehead to mine, his breath fast and ragged like mine even though he hadn't come. "I don't care what marks your arm. You're mine."

ESSIE

I SHUDDERED WITH DESIRE AT HIS WORDS AND AN AFTERSHOCK OF MY climax rushed through me.

He hit the basement button and the elevator door slid open right away. We hadn't pressed a button when we entered and I guess no one had hit a button on another floor.

"You're mine," he said with a growl, "and I will move heaven and earth to get you your life back."

I didn't know what to say to that. A primal part of me thrilled at how much he wanted me, while the rest of me cried. There wasn't any way I could make this end well. "I... ah... I'll be back down in a minute."

He frowned. Yeah, not the response I'd expect either, but I couldn't stay no matter how much I wanted to.

"I was on my way to the bathroom when you... when we..." Desire flamed my cheeks, a mix of mine and his, inside and out.

He grabbed the door before it closed again and flashed me a heated smile. "When we...?"

"Yeah. When we." Another aftershock shook me, drawing a gasp. God, how I wanted to stay with him, satisfy him like he'd satisfied me, forget about everything.

But I couldn't forget. The buzz still crackled under my skin, reminding me that even if everything hadn't gone sideways, being with Marcus, living in the supernatural world, put me in danger. As well, the need to save Gideon twisted in my chest, reminding me destiny had shoved me to someone else, someone I didn't even know. Marcus had given me a temporary reprieve from the madness. Nothing more. Still, I was grateful for the gift.

"I really do need to go."

His smile softened. "There's a bathroom in the triage waiting room. You don't have to go all the way to your room."

He stepped away from the door and it slid closed.

God, this was a mess. Such a big, heartaching mess.

And there wasn't a damned thing I could do about it.

My shirt had fallen down, but the sports bra was still shoved above my breasts. I tugged it down and hit the button for the first floor. If I had the time, I'd go all the way back to my room and replace my nicotine patch, but I couldn't afford to run into anyone else. I had to leave now.

And please, God, don't let me run into Jacob and have him tell me to do something, whether he intended it as a command or not.

The door slid open to the first floor. No one was around, but I could hear people working in the cafeteria, the massive rocks still covering the entrance.

I hurried to the main hall and down to the garage. Raised voices, coming from behind the door to the building's emergency room, made me pause, my pulse racing. It sounded like Amiah and Jacob, her voice shrill with distress and Jacob's a firm rumble.

"There's nothing to think through," Amiah said.

Jacob said something back, but I couldn't make out his words.

"Well, that's not my problem," Amiah said.

I hurried past the door and into the garage. Jacob and Amiah arguing wasn't my problem, either. Saving Gideon. Stopping the archnephilim from murdering any more people in his mission for vengeance. That was all that mattered.

First up, I needed transportation. All of the JP vehicles were too modern to easily hotwire, but I was pretty sure I'd seen a late model minivan and a late model compact hatchback at the back of the garage, most likely personal vehicles of people who worked here.

The minivan was gone, but the tan hatchback was still there. I hurried to it and tried the door. No point in breaking a window if it was unlocked. And in an enclosed parking garage belonging to the JP, I was hoping the owner wasn't security-conscious.

The door was unlocked. I checked the middle console and the sun visor for a key, but didn't find one. Guess that was too much to ask for, so I leaned down under the steering column and pulled out the wires I needed.

When I was in my late-teens, just before my mom had died from cancer, she'd taught me how to hotwire a car in the event I had nothing on me and needed to flee. I don't think she'd ever expected me to use the knowledge to head straight to an angel instead of away from one. I know I hadn't.

Never in my wildest imagination or even my nightmares did I ever imagine I'd find myself in a situation like this. My entire goal in life had been to be unnoticed, fly under the radar, and nothing about this was flying under the radar.

I stripped the wires with my teeth, twisted the ends together with my fingers, and got the car to start. My pulse racing with a mix of fear I'd be caught and what I was headed to, I put the car in gear and pulled out of the garage.

The archnephilim's warehouse wasn't in the Supers' Quarter, but close on the outskirts of town. I didn't recognize it as anywhere I'd been before, but I *knew* exactly where it was. I could also feel the pull of both Gideon and the archnephilim drawing me in its direction. Even if the archnephilim hadn't slapped the warehouse's location in my mind, I probably would have been able to find him.

Which only made me more nervous. My connection with both of them was growing stronger. I could feel their essences, the arch-nephilim's fire and Gideon's electricity, under my skin. Gideon's pain hadn't increased, but it hadn't decreased either. His electricity was still jagged, and now I could feel a pull on my soul draining strength from me to him.

The archnephilim's fire, however, flared and banked without rhyme or reason, as if his fire was being battered within me by a ferocious wind. His brand also tore strength from me, ragged spurts cleaving chunks off my essence. I hoped that meant he was still weak from his fight with the guys and that I could manage to keep him from controlling me long enough to release Gideon and sear the brand with divine light. But I feared with both of them consuming my essence, I'd be too weak to withstand much of a mental assault from the archnephilim.

That only meant I needed to get to the warehouse as soon as possible.

I drove through the park ring separating the Supers' Quarter from the rest of the city, the need to hurry making my nerves thrum, but I managed to hold it together and not speed. Getting pulled over without a license and no key in the ignition was a surefire way to screw everything up.

I headed south toward the highway, but instead of getting on, I took a side road that, while it wasn't dirt, hadn't been maintained in a long time and only a third of the streetlights were working. The road headed into an old industrial section with the shells of factories and warehouses lining the street all the way to the end. It was a perfect spot for a business, close to the city for employees but also less than a mile from the interstate onramp. Most of the buildings, however, were barely standing and abandoned. Only a few had cars in their parking lots and half of those lots weren't full — although given that it was after suppertime, those businesses might be shut down for the night and not running twenty-four-hour shifts.

While Michael hadn't managed to exterminate all of humankind, he'd sure been determined to try, and even with the influx of supers coming out of hiding and those — mostly demons — coming from the realms of light and darkness, the world population of over seven and a half billion was now closer to five.

Europe had had a casualty rate higher than North America since the main passage to the Realm of Celestial Light was in Rome — the focus of all those centuries of worship from a religion that gave angels a prominent role thinning the veil between the human realm and the light realm. But countries with the densest populations and the densest cities took the worst of it. Easier to exterminate the humans if they were all bunched together. Thankfully Gabriel had stepped up after the first few brutal assaults, making it harder for Michael to target large cities and forcing him to be more strategic in his attacks.

There'd already been a weapons manufacturer on this side of town, and the federal government had confiscated most of the factories and warehouses in the area to increase production. But that had made the area a target, and during the height of the war, the nephilim had attacked, destroying or damaging beyond reasonable repair most of the buildings in the area.

As a result, when humanity and supers turned to rebuilding, they focused on city cores, creating areas for supers, hospitals, and schools. Buildings not in use, whether they could be useful in the future or not, weren't a priority. And in reality, the war had only been twenty-three years ago and the rebuild effort had barely begun.

The archnephilim's warehouse stood at the end of the road, which stopped with a metal barrier and a forest growing in and around the stumps and fallen trunks of the original forest, destroyed by powerful magic during the war. The small parking lot looked uneven, riddled with cracks and weeds, and had a massive wave of asphalt cutting through the middle of it, the top curled as if it had actually been liquid at some point. It hid the front half of the building from the road, and I had to pull into the lot and drive around it to get a full look at the structure.

The warehouse was a tall single-story building, with windows up high near the roof, backlit by a blazing red sunset that turned the clouds above ominous. The back half of the structure had collapsed, and parts of the roof had been ripped away. At the end closest to me, one of two wide bay doors hung precariously from broken hinges and creaked in the breeze, while the other one stood about ten feet away, partially embedded in the ground, and twisted into what people were now calling post-war urban art — anything damaged by the nephilim's magic that had yet to be cleared away.

I could sense both the archnephilim and Gideon inside. Their essences burned and vibrated through me. Gideon's jagged electricity was now stronger and made my buzz claw under my skin, while the flares in the archnephilim's came farther and farther apart because his overall fire had grown in strength.

This was the worst idea ever.

I shut off the car and got out.

But there wasn't a better plan. While there might be a way to capture the archnephilim, no one would find it before Gideon's hour was up. And even if I wanted to, I couldn't resist the need to go to Gideon and do whatever it took to save him.

I pulled the ring from my pocket and slid it onto my thumb. It was a tight fit, but better that than too loose on my finger and falling off. It would be awkward if I was going to shoot a blast at the archnephilim, but not a problem for pressing it against the brand burned into my biceps. Light flickered from it and power swelled around my hand for a moment then dimmed, ready, waiting. All I had to do was cast the spell summoning divine light to release the power from the ring.

I squared my shoulders and strode toward the creaking bay door, feeling naked without my department-issued sidearm. Funny how I'd gone two days now, talked down a robber and faced the archnephilim three times, without my Glock, and now I wanted the weapon when I knew it wouldn't do any good.

But the sense of self preservation that Marcus claimed I didn't have was screaming at me, proving that it wasn't that I didn't have it, it was that I was practical enough to ignore it to do what needed to be done. I'd grown up understanding that sometimes hard choices had to be made, and this was one hell of a hard choice.

Except it hadn't been my choice at all. I hadn't asked the archnephilim to brand me, or Gideon. The only choice I had left was how many people were going to die before I ended this.

"I knew you wouldn't be able to stay away," the archnephilim said in my head as I reached the bay door.

I hadn't expected the element of surprise since the archnephilim could probably sense me better than I could sense him, but his voice, suddenly within me, still made me jump.

"Myself for Gideon." I entered the gloomy darkness of the warehouse, the air cold and musty. "That was the deal."

Weak light shone through the holes in the roof, while the last of the sunset streaked through the cracks in the wall. Gideon hung from a metal rafter thirty feet from the floor, hands tied behind his back, noose tight around his neck, and hooks — the only thing actually holding him up — sliced into his wings, spreading them taut. Blood caked his wings, the side of his face, and his shirt. Light glimmered on his pants, tracing a thick trail of still-wet blood down his legs to a blood pool beneath him. His head lolled forward as if he were unconscious, and maybe he was, but his eyes were partially open, light radiating across a face swollen and bruised. His electricity was still jagged inside me, almost as painful as the buzz now, and the pull on my strength was now an urgent tug.

The archnephilim stood on the floor near him. He was mostly angel with onyx wings, hair, and even clothes. Hints of smoke curled around him, softening his edges, and half a dozen tentacles writhed around his torso.

The heat from his brand flared in my arm, and I stopped in the doorway, hoping it was far enough away that the archnephilim would have to come closer if he wanted to grab me — as well as to prove to myself that I actually could stop. "Release him and I'm all yours."

"Release him yourself," the archnephilim chuckled in my head.

Yeah, not going to happen. Getting closer was the last possible option. If the archnephilim grabbed me before I could activate the ring, all was lost. But if I couldn't get Gideon free, or at least the archnephilim away from Gideon, then he was dead, and the connection between us wasn't willing to accept that. "I don't see a ladder."

"Free your wings, little nephilim," he hissed, sending panic racing through me even though he was still in my head and Gideon hadn't heard him... I hoped. *"Or do you not want your mate to know what you are?"*

The archnephilim curled a tentacle up Gideon's leg, around his ankle, knee, and thigh, then yanked down. Gideon's wings bowed, and his head jerked up with a strangled cry of pain. Light blazed from his eyes then sputtered out, leaving him shuddering and gasping for breath.

"Wakey, wakey. Your mate has arrived," the archnephilim said aloud, his voice no longer in my head.

Gideon's unfocused gaze lifted slowly, dragging across the warehouse floor until he found me. For a second his eyes were filled with hope, then realization swept across his expression and his grief rushed around me in a thick mist. He'd thought Zella had come, and just my presence reminded him that she hadn't been his mate and was now dead. His disappointment tightened my throat with emotions I shouldn't have for a stranger and certainly not for an angel. But I couldn't resist the connection, and right now I had other things more important to resist, like the archnephilim's control over me.

The archnephilim chuckled. "Doesn't look like he's happy to see you."

I pushed back my hurt at Gideon's disappointment. "Doesn't matter if he is or not. The deal was him for me. I'm here. Let him go."

"And I said, get him yourself." The archnephilim burst into his wraith form, growing in size, massive tentacles writhing from his smoke, crushing around Gideon's chest.

Gideon cried out, his agony cutting through the mist and stealing my breath.

"Go on. Get him."

"I can't."

"Then let me help you." The archnephilim's power exploded from his brand and fire seared my back with such force I screamed and my knees gave out.

ESSIE

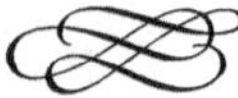

MY PULSE ROARED AND PANIC SWEPT THROUGH ME. I TRIED TO STAND, BUT the archnephilim's power heaved me forward. I caught myself, my palms scraping against the debris littering the concrete floor, but my muscles contracted, freezing me on my hands and knees.

No, please. The power tore through my back, slicing between my shoulder blades. I gasped, fighting to breathe past the pain. I didn't have wings. He couldn't just make them appear. But I convulsed and a new power, something different, not fire or electricity, something else and without a doubt mine, curled tight in my back.

Oh, God. Do I actually have wings?

The archnephilim howled with laugher, his inky darkness sliding from his brand around my heart, while his power ripped at my skin.

Gideon wrenched against the hooks, light blazing from his eyes. Whatever disappointment he'd had that I wasn't Zella was gone and now his electric hum crackled through my buzz with ferocious determination. It set my nerves on edge, my muscles contracting as if the low voltage electric fence of my buzz had been turned up to medium, zapping it through the fire.

The archnephilim's heat in my back shuddered, dimming for just a second, and I jerked myself up, sitting on my heels. The fire flared back with a vengeance, screaming not just through my back but every inch of my body.

I clenched every muscle I had and fought to stay upright. I couldn't let him win. And there wasn't any chance now to ensure Gideon's safety. I had to go ahead and burn the brand.

Except I couldn't move. It took everything I had just to stay up and not collapse on the floor, writhing in agony.

Come on. Just move your hand. That was all I needed to do. But another surge of the archnephilim's power screamed through me, stealing my breath.

Just move.

Come on. Move.

The muscles in my arm twitched, but not enough to raise it.

Come on. Come on.

But the archnephilim was too strong and all his power was focused on me.

He rushed toward me and whipped a tentacle around my neck. "Stop fighting. Become what you're supposed to be."

"No."

The tentacle tightened, choking me, and wrenched me up until my toes skimmed the floor. The fire in my back burned hotter, and I strained to breathe, my muscles still frozen, unable to raise my hands and grasp at the tentacle.

"We could rule this world. All would bow before us and our power."

"You honestly think you can do what Michael couldn't?"

"I control both light and dark power, and with my brand on you, I'm as powerful as Michael." Another tentacle caressed my cheek, and his tone turned low and dark. "And when you accept what you are, I'll be more powerful than him."

"But you'd give that up and still kill me just to kill Gideon?"

"Release your wings and you'll be more powerful than him." The archnephilim's face solidified in his smoke and he sneered at me. "I don't need you sane to reap the benefits of your essence."

The tentacle around my neck squeezed tighter, making me gasp, and the tentacle caressing my cheek plunged into my mouth.

"You might be strong enough to fight me through the brand, but you can't fight me inside you." His smoke poured down my throat, surging around my heart and up into my head.

Gideon yelled and wrenched one wing free, tearing feathers, the bits falling like oversized snowflakes and sticking in the blood pool beneath him. His weight yanked him down on his other wing and the noose jerked tight against his neck, making him gasp.

A red haze swept over my vision and all thought vanished, papers in a fire, leaving only searing heat, consuming power, and fear. Heart-stopping, utter terror as I helplessly felt myself burning away.

Gideon's electricity went first. Then the buzz.

Something flickered inside me. A hint of light? Electricity? My soul? The archnephilim's power devoured that as well. All that was left was a tiny, barely audible voice screaming in fear and agony and desperation.

Then a gunshot roared nearby and the archnephilim's power shuddered.

Another gunshot and the smoke pouring into me vanished.

Strong hands grabbed me as I collapsed. My mind and soul jerked back into my body as those hands yanked me away from the archnephilim.

A barrage of semi-automatic gunfire thundered through the empty warehouse. The archnephilim howled, his form shuddering, and Kol leaped past me. His face was still disfigured and his hands covered in angry red scars from my divine light, but he held both of his daggers as if that didn't affect him and slashed at the archnephilim, as fast and as powerful as I'd seen before.

"You're a God damned fool," Marcus growled, his voice close to my ear.

I glanced back at him and his hands on my shoulders tightened. His piercing green gaze was filled with fear and if my body wasn't still on fire, I was sure the temperature in the warehouse would have plummeted.

"You're not supposed to be here." I tried to pull out of his grip but he held tight. "How are you here?"

"I know you, Essie. I knew you'd do something stupid. So I planted a tracker on you."

"When did—? In the elevator, when we—?" That was the only time he could have done it. Had our moment in the elevator just been a ploy so I wouldn't notice? As much as I craved Marcus, I didn't really know him. Except that didn't make sense. Everything he'd done had been to protect me.

"You made it too easy," he said, and bolted toward the archnephilim. His body turned to liquid flesh, expanding and twisting, and within three quick steps, never missing a beat, he'd transformed into a massive black wolf, the magic of his lycanthropy permanently consuming his clothing. I'd only seen a shifter transform once before, and it was beautiful and horrific all at the same time. Marcus leaped at the archnephilim, snapping through tentacles, and Kol dove past to a concrete pillar supporting the roof and began to climb.

Behind me, Jacob, holding the HK416 assault rifle from the armory in Operations, fired another barrage of bullets. They sliced through the middle of the archnephilim, drawing a howl. Guess bullets enchanted to take down a greater demon did affect an archnephilim, but one shot, let alone four, still hadn't been enough to bring him down.

The only sure way to do it was my original plan.

I tried to raise my hand, but couldn't.

God damn it.

I gritted my teeth. The archnephilim's smoke wasn't in me any more, but the power from his brand was still strong, still threatening to rip me in half.

Kol reached the rafters and ran to Gideon, who flapped his free wing, trying to raise himself enough to unhook his other wing or, in the very least, not choke on the noose, but his flaps were uneven and yanked him against the hook and noose.

The archnephilim swept out a tentacle to hit Kol, but Jacob fired another short barrage, slicing through the smoke, making it vanish before it struck.

Kol cut the rope securing the noose to the rafters, and Gideon jerked up, above the rafter, and yanked his wing from the hook. He hit the ceiling with a boom and crashed, stomach first, onto the girder. My pulse stuttered with a fear for him that I shouldn't have. Kol grabbed him and steadied him then cut the rope binding his arms.

The archnephilim howled with a rage that made his fire within me burn brighter. He shot two more tentacles at them. Jacob hit one of the two tentacles but didn't completely sever the second one. It bashed Kol off the rafter. Gideon threw himself after Kol and grabbed his arm, but Gideon's wings couldn't get enough air or were too damaged and they crashed to the floor.

The electricity within me flared and yanked on my essence, pouring it into Gideon. I shuddered, my muscles weakening, and fought to maintain what little control I had on my body.

Jacob fired again into the center of the archnephilim's writhing form.

The smoke whirled, caught up in a wild wind I couldn't feel, and his fire within me stuttered. Marcus tore into him, and Kol scrambled to his feet his daggers ready, while Gideon groaned and pulled his wings into his body. The electricity from his brand flared again, jagged spikes under my skin, weakening me even more as he stood, swaying.

"Get Gideon out of here," I yelled. I didn't care who did it, just that it was done.

"You can't protect him," the archnephilim said, and a massive tentacle slammed Kol across the warehouse, sending him crashing through the debris littering the floor. "You can't protect any of them."

Dozens of tentacles shot at Marcus, who twisted and snapped at them, but two sliced deep into his side, making him howl. Gideon half lunged, half staggered toward the archnephilim, his sword of light forming in his hand. He slashed at the archnephilim, but a flurry of tentacles batted the blade aside.

Another barrage of bullets cut through where the archnephilim's head would have been, and Kol barreled toward him, daggers raised.

The guys slashed and tore and shot the archnephilim, but it was like the fight in the cafeteria, and for every hit they made on him, the archnephilim gave them two.

I mentally heaved against the archnephilim's control.

Marcus was speared again with another tentacle and his blood splattered on the floor. The archnephilim heaved him up and Gideon took that moment of distraction and rammed his blade into the archnephilim's side. The archnephilim slammed Marcus against the warehouse wall, and Gideon twisted and wrenched the blade through the archnephilim's smoke, drawing a howl of pain.

The fire within me weakened again and I jerked my hand up. My thumb with the divine light ring swept through a stream of weak sunset light and flashed brighter than it should have.

The archnephilim burst out laughing as he sent a tentacle through Kol's chest and tossed him at Marcus.

"You brought a toy," the archnephilim said. "How cute." He whipped a tentacle around Gideon's chest and squeezed what had to be already broken ribs. Gideon screamed and his electricity sliced through his brand. More power rushed out of me into him.

I staggered, trembling, my head whirling. I fought to keep standing, then realized there was no point. I could end this on my knees.

I sagged to the floor. My hand shook. I still had control, but barely. The words of the light strike raced through my head, over and over again, and the new power, the one I recognized as mine, built within me. I squared my shoulders and embraced that power.

"You're not powerful enough," the archnephilim sneered. "That won't kill me."

"Not directly." I rammed the ring against the archnephilim's brand and released my power. It poured into the ring, turned to divine light, and exploded into my arm with searing white agony.

Gideon jerked toward me. Marcus yelled my name.

The archnephilim howled. His smoke burst apart, revealing his angel form, and white light blazed out of his eyes.

His fire in my body surged, fighting the divine light, and my hand with the ring trembled. I gritted my teeth, keeping it in place while my body was trapped in the center of a sun, burning up from the inside out.

Tears filled my eyes, and the divine light overwhelmed the archnephilim's fire, consuming it and everything it touched.

"*He'll betray you,*" the archnephilim hissed in my head, dropping to his knees. I could feel him fighting to control me with our mental connection, using his words to dig himself deeper into me.

The agony in my arm was all-consuming. It was too much. I had to stop. Except I couldn't. If I survived, then the archnephilim did. The choice had been made for me the moment the archnephilim had branded me. I was already dead. And I hated that. I hated that I'd spent my childhood scared and hiding. I hated that my mother had given up the semblance of a normal life because of me. And I hated that the one thing I wanted, a normal life, would never be possible.

Even if I survived this, even if I wasn't Gideon's mate, I'd never have a normal life. I wasn't even sure if I could get close to having one. If I got too close to a friend, even a human one, they could become suspicious. Eventually someone would notice and question my temperature issues. And there wasn't any way I could have a romantic relationship. How could I let myself get close to someone when I had to lie to them about who I really was?

"*He'll kill you,*" the archnephilim said. "*That's what angels do to our kind.*"

"*You'd kill me, too, and then you'd kill others, innocents.*" At least if I couldn't have the life I yearned for, my death could mean something.

"I'm not killing the innocent. They slaughtered babies."

And that was the true horror of what Michael had done with his war. Forced good people to make the choice between themselves and unnaturally created babies that would, in a matter of months, be mindless, monstrous soldiers. *"So vengeance is the answer? Killing in kind without mercy?"*

"It's the only answer."

"No. It isn't." A seizure jerked me. The ring jumped away from my arm. The divine light dimmed and I yelled the light strike spell again and rammed it back in place.

The light in the nephilim's eyes burned brighter. He screamed and divine light poured out of his mouth and nose. I could feel his pain. It was my pain, consuming both of us down to our very essence. It would be over soon. *Please let it be over soon.* I needed to last just a little longer. *Please.*

But I was weakening and so was the light pouring from the ring. I wasn't going to hold out long enough. I was going to fail and then Marcus and Gideon and the others would be in danger. The archnephilim would torture and slaughter them. I could feel his rage through our connection. He despised Gideon, and all those who'd fought in the war, and he hated me with a consuming fury for turning my back on my own kind.

Except I wasn't anything like the archnephilim, I hadn't been made in a laboratory, and I didn't have his blood lust.

I threw what was left of my essence, the strange power within me, the gnawing buzz grating in my mind, always present, even what little of Gideon's electricity I could feel, into the ring. All of it. All of me. Every bit, every miniscule flicker of magic, every hope and fear and heartache. Everything I had. It went into the ring, and poured through me into the archnephilim in a ferocious inferno a thousand times stronger than the archnephilim's fire.

Cracks snapped through his body, blinding white light slicing out, slicing through me. I fought to see past the blaze, to hold on, and see it through to the end. One of the cracks erupted and the light roared out of him.

He howled and writhed as it consumed him, and collapsed in a smoldering black heap.

The weight of his brand, a weight I hadn't realized had been there before, shattered, and the divine light, with no place left to go, surged back into me.

I screamed as it devoured me, unable to move or stop the power flowing from me and the ring into my body, knowing I'd end up a smoldering black heap like the archnephilim.

But that had been the plan. To save the guys, to save everyone, and sacrifice myself.

GIDEON

I SAT IN THE TRIAGE WAITING ROOM, PAIN THROBBING THROUGH MY partially healed injuries despite the painkillers I'd been given. I couldn't stop staring at Officer Shaw lying limp on the triage bed, her face too pale, each shallow, ragged breath coming too far apart.

Amiah stood over her. White light, that had started off blindingly bright and was now barely visible, radiated around her hands, and her body trembled with the effort to heal the massive amount of internal damage Shaw had done to herself when she'd killed the archnephilim.

It had been over an hour since we'd called in the cleanup team, limped back to Operations, and the rest of the team had been patched back together. Jacob had been wheeled to a recovery room with an extra supply of blood, Kol had left to feed, and Marcus had gone to Operations' secure yard to shift and speed up his healing process, but Amiah was still working on Shaw.

Because she was human, Amiah couldn't just flood her body with power. She had to work slowly — agonizingly slowly — to heal the damage without damaging other parts of Shaw's body as well as her mind. Even then Amiah couldn't heal everything right away, not without risking brain damage, and there was still a chance Shaw wouldn't survive.

My pulse still raced with the overwhelming fear that had gripped me when she'd collapsed after killing the archnephilim, and I knew that was the effect of my brand on her.

Her. Officer Shaw... Essie. My destined mate.

The thought stole my breath, but not with the awe I thought I'd have at being one of the few angels blessed with having a sacred soul bond.

No, it filled me with a grief almost as deep as the grief I'd felt when I'd learned Michael had murdered my younger brother because it reminded me that Zella was dead. It reminded me the hope I'd been holding onto, that she'd come out of her self-imposed exile and return to me, be as in love with me as I was with her, was gone.

There wasn't even a small glimmer left. I couldn't continue to be patient. I'd thought I had all the time in the world, that eventually, with the gentle help I'd been carefully offering her over the years, the soft-spoken, shy, beautiful angel I'd fallen in love with during the worst years of my life would come back to me.

But fate was cruel. Zella had died in the most horrible way and I was stuck with a human I didn't know, didn't love, and didn't want to love because she was in love with Marcus and he loved her. I didn't want to get in the way of that.

Their attraction for each other had survived a four and a half year separation and — from the way Marcus reacted to her — a whole bunch of complicated, messed up emotions. But I bet if I asked Kol, he'd tell me that their desire was intoxicatingly strong, too strong to be ignored.

What was worse than having the one you love killed? Having them still alive and forced to be with someone else? I wasn't going to be the man who came between them. And if I gave into the mating brand, I would be.

On top of that, it was obvious Marcus's wolf had claimed Essie, something he might not even be aware of, and he wouldn't stand for her to be in a relationship with anyone else.

He hadn't been born a shifter and probably didn't understand the signs. He probably thought he could suppress his desire for her. That's what he had to have been doing for the last four and a half years, which spoke to his remarkable strength of will.

Maybe he'd be able to keep ignoring her. I didn't know. But as soon as he learned she was in a relationship with anyone else, his wolf would possess him and take her back. Wolves were notoriously possessive of their mates. They didn't share. She was his. He'd fight to the death to keep her and wouldn't be able to control himself, even if he was fighting me.

Which was what would happen if I gave in to the mating bond.

One of us wouldn't survive the battle and because Essie was human, if that was me, she'd die, too.

And if it was Marcus, she'd never forgive me.

Neither option was acceptable.

Marcus was too inexperienced a shifter to control his wolf after it had claimed a mate. Even those who'd been born shifters would struggle, so it was up to me to be the bigger man. It didn't matter that Essie—

No. I had to stop thinking of her in such a personal way.

It didn't matter that *Officer Shaw* was beautiful and brave and willing to sacrifice herself to save lives just like an angel would. It didn't matter that despite her recklessness, I could easily fall in love with her. Right now I wasn't in love with her and as long as I stayed strong and resisted the brand's compulsion to love her, I could ignore our bond.

Angels were immortal and my brand would give that immortality to Officer Shaw. If I didn't get in the way, she and Marcus could live a happy life together.

In the face of eternity with her, waiting another sixty or seventy years was nothing.

Of course, I'd thought I had forever with Zella, too.

No, Shaw would be different. She'd have Marcus to protect her.

As if thinking of him made him appear, he stepped through the frosted glass door into triage. He wore the shorts he kept in a locker in the secure yard, the clothes that Chris, the head of Operations' cleanup team, had brought him when he'd arrived at the warehouse were wadded in a ball under his arm, covered in blood. His body was still mottled with scratches and bruises and he still looked like he'd lost a fight, but at least he no longer looked like he was about to die.

His attention instantly locked on Essie and whatever tension that had left his body when he'd given his wolf a chance to take over, returned, his wolf's ferocity once again barely contained just under the surface of his skin.

But then his mate was still hurt.

I was actually shocked he hadn't refused Amiah's orders to go and shift so he could remain standing behind her, glowering as she worked.

"She's still going?" he growled thankfully stalking over to me instead of distracting Amiah.

"Just finished," she gasped, the light from her hands flickering then completely vanishing.

Marcus took a step across the invisible threshold between the waiting room and triage then jerked to a stop as if he was fighting his wolf's desire to be with Shaw. "Will she live?"

"Her body will live. We won't know about her mind until she wakes up." Amiah sagged against the bed, her head bowed with the exhaustion of having drained all her magic. "If she wakes up."

Cassey, a shifter and Amiah's second-in-command, who'd been nearby ready to offer non-magical assistance, helped steady her. "Let's get you to a bed. I'll come back for Essie."

Amiah mumbled something and Cassey nodded as she helped Amiah stagger down the hall to a recovery room.

The second they were out of sight, Marcus jerked around to face me and I opened my mouth to tell him I'd leave so he could be alone with Shaw — because now that I knew she would live, I had to leave or I never would.

"No," he snarled, cutting me off before I could say anything. "I don't give a fuck about your mating brand. She's walking out of here and going back to her life."

"Marcus—"

"I told her she'd get her life back, the same as it was before, and that's what's going to happen." His pupils slitted and his fingers extended into claws as his wolf strained to take over.

"That's not a reasonable expectation." He wouldn't be able to pretend that his wolf hadn't claimed Shaw.

He growled low in his throat and bared his canines. "It's the only expectation. Promise me."

"I can't promise that." Even if that would make it easier for me to ignore the mating brand. "She can't go back to how things were."

"She can and she will," he snarled. "I won't let you or anyone force her into a world that scares her, and I know for a fact supers scare her."

Hurt flickered in his gaze and realization hit me. He'd denied his wolf's claim on her *because* he loved her. He was the very thing she feared, so he— no, not just him. He *and* his wolf had decided he needed to protect her from himself and he wasn't ever going to be with her.

Which was insane. She knew he was a shifter and her body language said she wasn't afraid of him.

"She gets her very human life back," he said, his voice low and dangerous. "No supers. Not you. Not anyone. Ever." And from the tension in his body and the darkness in his eyes, he meant that. He'd kill for that. "Promise me."

"I promise," I forced out, despite everything inside me saying it was a mistake.

But he and his wolf had decided the only way to make her happy was to let her go, and with her near-death experience — along with the chance that she might never wake up or wake up insane because of her broken soul bond with the archnephilim — there was no point in arguing with him right now.

Wolves weren't just fiercely possessive, they were also fiercely protective, and he was going to protect Shaw with everything he had no matter how much that hurt him.

ESSIE

The buzz returned to my senses first, snapping under my skin at pre-nicotine levels and grating against nerves that had been burned raw with the archnephilim's power and divine light. The damp musty smell that had filled the warehouse was gone. So too was the chilly evening air.

I couldn't hear the guys and panic seized me. I must have failed, passed out before killing the archnephilim. Surely if they'd survived, they'd be talking, regrouping, trying to figure out what to do next. But I couldn't hear anything—

No, that wasn't true. I could hear the gentle whoosh of air, the kind of steady, low hum that came from the heating-cooling system of a big building. And the temperature was consistent with being indoors.

Recognizing those two details tripped a switch in my brain, and I realized I lay on my back on something soft, instead of being crumpled on a wet concrete floor, and was covered with a blanket.

I cracked my eyes open and stared up at a white ceiling cast in partial shadow. The fluorescent light above me was off, but, given the way the illumination and shadow painted the ceiling, a light to my left had to be on.

I let my head slowly fall to the side, afraid to discover just how injured I was underneath the biting buzz, not yet ready to take stock of the damage I'd taken from the archnephilim or the divine light ring, but nothing screamed in pain.

My gaze followed the light, stalling on an IV bag with a line trailing toward me. I didn't look to see if it was hooked up to my hand. If I was alive and in a hospital, I was hooked up to the IV. Beyond the bag was a small reading lamp turned away from me, shining on Kol.

He slouched in a chair, one leg up — ankle on thigh — his head bowed, reading whatever was in the folder in his lap. My pulse stalled, but I didn't know if it was desire because he exuded sexual grace — and a hint of danger — or fear for what I'd done to him.

His black hair had fallen forward, veiling most of his face, and I couldn't tell if he was still horribly scarred or not. His body language was loose, not tight with pain, suggesting that whatever had happened with the archnephilim, he'd managed to recover from his injuries. Had Marcus?

My pulse stuttered again and my right forearm ached, but not enough for me to know what that meant. Had Gideon survived?

Gideon didn't have the same kind of self-healing that Kol did, and I couldn't sense his electric power within his brand or the pull of strength from him to me. Of course that might have something to do with the strength of my personal, torturous buzz and that I was too weak to offer him any strength.

No, if I was in the Joined Parliament Operations Building, then I had no doubt Amiah would have taken care of Gideon and Marcus before she'd taken care of me... if they'd lived.

My throat tightened. They had to have lived. All of them. That had been the whole point.

I must have made a sound because Kol's head rose, his warm brown eyes capturing my soul, making my thoughts flicker — and not fully stutter like they had the last time. I wasn't sure what that meant, either.

He was still breathtakingly beautiful. His face was perfect, as if I hadn't badly burned him with divine light, but there was a tightness in his eyes as if he were worried, or holding back, or something.

God, it's bad news. It has to be bad news.

"Is he alive?" I asked, my voice rough, barely a whisper.

"The archnephilim, your mate, or your wolf?" he asked, the tightness melting into relief edged with a hint of wicked sensuality.

"All of them. And Jacob, too." *Please tell me everyone made it and it's over.* I didn't know if I could burn the archnephilim's brand again, especially if I needed to hold out longer to make it work.

"The archnephilim turned to ash when you passed out. He's well and truly dead. Everyone else is alive." The sensuality vanished, his relief the stronger emotion, but his eyes turned glassy.

"Thank God." *Thank God, thank God, thank God.*

"Tell me you're okay. Tell me Gideon's brand protected you and you're all right," he said. "We all hoped it would, but Amiah said we wouldn't know until you woke up. And you've been unconscious for days," he said.

"Days? How many?"

"Five."

"Five days?" No wonder the buzz was going insane. I'd been without nicotine for five days.

Kol grabbed my hand with both of his, holding it tentatively between his palms, careful not to touch the IV needle.

"Tell me you're okay." His gaze flickered to my left biceps and realization flashed through me.

The archnephilim was dead. I wasn't. That meant the outcome for me was insanity. Except I felt fine, or as fine as I could be with the God damned buzz in my body.

"I—" Would I even know if I was insane? Except I didn't feel as if my life had been shattered... I mean, I did and it had been. I had feelings I couldn't ignore for Marcus and wore Gideon's mating brand, both situations risked revealing my secret and endangering my life, but I wasn't heartbroken to hear about the archnephilim's death. I didn't *feel* any of the things the textbooks said I'd feel when someone I was bonded to died.

"I think I'm good. I still feel like I was lit on fire, though."

Kol winced and I regretted using that comparison.

"And probably torn apart from the inside out, too" he said. "That's what Amiah said it looked like the archnephilim tried to do to you. Burn you up and rip you apart."

I shuddered at the memory, making the buzz snap within me. "So Amiah healed me?"

"The physical damage, yes. But Amiah can't do anything for the mental. So—"

"So you're sitting at my bedside waiting to see if I'll wake up insane."

"Pretty much." He flashed a full-watt smile with hellfire flickering in his eyes that made my insides heat with desire. Then his eyes widened, as if he'd realized what he'd just done, and he jerked away, releasing my hand and leaning as far back into the chair as he could get. "That's me. On damsel duty again."

"Tell me you haven't been sitting here for five days."

"It hasn't been a problem. I've gotten caught up on a ton of paperwork."

"So just you." Perhaps that was a good thing. I had no idea what I'd say if I'd woken with Gideon or Marcus at my bedside. But it still stung that they were clearly avoiding me. Jacob, too.

"Jacob is staying away because of the power of his claim on you. He didn't want you to wake and be caught up in his compulsion, not if your mental state was fragile." Kol's expression turned somber. "The moment Amiah said you'd live, Marcus made Gideon promise you'd get your life back, no supers, nothing, then left."

Of course he did. I shouldn't have been surprised or disappointed. He'd promised he'd do everything to get me away from the supernatural world, and that meant getting away from him. He hadn't said goodbye the last time. Why would I think this time was different?

Except this time had been different. We'd given in to our desires, at least in part. I ached to kiss him again, even if he'd used my desire against me to put a tracker on me.

But what hadn't changed were my reasons for not being able to stay in the supernatural world.

"And Gideon?" I couldn't believe he'd agree to Marcus's demand to leave me alone, not with how much he'd said the mating brand was a beautiful fated thing.

Of course that was before he'd learned he was stuck with a human.

"He took Zella's body back to the Realm of Celestial Light."

And before he'd lost the woman he'd really loved.

Which left me where?

A part of me wanted to get out of Operations, grab my go bag, and get out of town. If I'd been a cat, I was sure I'd used up at least six, probably seven, of my nine lives just by being caught in this mess. Hell, I had to be down to one life left because somehow Gideon hadn't heard enough of my conversation with the archnephilim to figure out the truth. If he had, I was sure I would have woken up handcuffed to the hospital bed. The longer I stuck around, the greater the chance someone would discover my supernatural nature.

Except if I ran, Gideon would know. And really, there wasn't anywhere in the world I could go where Gideon wouldn't be able to find me.

My best bet was to carry on, life as usual, and hope I, as well as

Gideon, could ignore the compulsion from the mating brand to be with each other. The bond between us made that thought sting, but the rest of me knew it was the right call. Maybe if we cut ties now, before we really had any kind of a relationship and while he was still in love with Zella, our connection wouldn't grow stronger.

Maybe I'd be able to find a magical solution that, while it might not be able to break the bond between us, could mute its affects. I doubted angels with mating brands went to see witches or demons to diminish the strength of their bond.

It was a slim chance, but my best option. Besides, if I was going to risk everything for a relationship with a super, it was going to be with Marcus. Which I wasn't. So I needed to go back to flying under the radar.

Someone walked past the large glass window behind Kol, drawing my gaze up to the dimly lit hall, and I gasped at my reflection. My eyes were glowing. Why hadn't Kol questioned my glowing eyes?

Perhaps I wasn't really seeing the glow, or I was and no one else could, like how no one else could feel the temperature change when someone had strong emotions.

I squeezed my eyes shut, then opened them again.

Still glowing.

"Ah…" I didn't want to ask, but I had to know. If my eyes were glowing, I needed to figure out how to deal with that. "Are my eyes—?"

"Glowing?" Kol asked. "They have been since you passed out in the warehouse. Even with your eyes closed, it bleeds out under your lashes."

"And you're not worried about that?" He was acting the same as always, not like he knew I was a monstrous nephilim.

"You just blasted yourself with who knows how much divine light and you didn't die. I'm surprised your whole body isn't lit up like a Christmas tree."

"Well, thanks for small miracles." That no one knew, and that I wasn't fully lit up.

"Although it would make it easy to always find you," he said with a soft laugh that caressed my senses.

"But impossible to do my job."

"I don't know." He offered a sensual shrug, his mirth making his eyes shine. "You could be the new poster girl for the Union City PD, what with your new *glowing* personality."

I rolled my eyes at him. "Yeah, and I'll never be put on a boring stakeout again. Can you imagine? Me, at night, sitting in a car, trying to look inconspicuous while brilliant white light blazes around me?" I burst out laughing.

It was so utterly ridiculous and amazing and... hell, I was still alive. I'd faced an archnephilim, saved who-knew-how-many lives, and Kol didn't seem at all bothered that my eyes were glowing.

Kol snorted, his laughter growing. "What about trying to sneak up on a perp in the dark?"

"Would it mean I'd never get stuck on the graveyard shift?"

"Or would you always? I mean, you'd never need a flashlight."

I laughed so hard tears streamed down my cheeks. Really, it wasn't that funny, but I couldn't stop. All the worry and stress and fear and heartache that had built up over the last few days needed a release and this was how it was coming out. Which was fine with me.

Kol grinned at me, his smile slightly lopsided and boyish. There was a hint of sensuality to it — I didn't think he'd ever be able to dampen all of it — but it was warm, friendly, and genuine. "I'm so glad you're not crazy."

"Me, too."

I was going to be okay.

"And Amiah did say the glow in your eyes would go away, once all that divine light leaves your system."

Everything was going to be okay.

Marcus had said he'd get me my life back and for the most part, all things considered, he had.

Except did I really want to go back to that life?

It was the safest option for me, but it was also the loneliest. I'd had a taste of what it felt like to be part of a team, and an ache for the kind of physical contact I'd always been afraid to commit to.

I wasn't sure I could go back to the life I'd had before.

DESTINED SHADOWS

NEPHILIM'S DESTINY PREQUEL STORY

The night Marcus became a shifter...

ESSIE

FOUR AND A HALF YEARS EARLIER ON THE NIGHT OF A FULL MOON...

Even with my back turned, I could feel him watching me. His attention simmered in the air, warming it around me by a few degrees, manifested by my weird next-to-useless empathic magic.

It made my pulse thrum a little too fast and my cheeks a little too flushed. And it had been like that between us from the moment I'd walked into the bullpen at the precinct only a few months ago and met my new partner's gaze.

Marcus Diaz. He was sexy and edgy, with a hint of wild ferocity that tightened my nerves with anticipation, and a damn good cop on top of it all.

The attraction had been instant, breathtaking, sizzling. Just knowing he watched me through the coffee shop's large front window made me ache for something I knew was a terrible idea.

Partners didn't get involved with each other. Especially a more experienced officer and a rookie with less than six months on the job. Not to mention I wouldn't be able to grow my career if I was branded the rookie who slept with her partner.

And I wanted to grow my career. I'd been working toward being a cop since I was a teenager and had realized I couldn't stop myself from fighting injustice and protecting those who couldn't protect themselves. And yes, becoming a cop risked revealing the supernatural part of me that I'd been hiding my entire life, but the need to protect had kept growing. I'd originally ignored it and jumped from minimum wage job to minimum wage job, but in the end, I couldn't resist.

Now I feared if I let Marcus get too close, he'd discover the truth. Not just the truth that I was a nephilim, a half human half angel supernatural being that the entire world hated and feared, but the truth that I didn't really know how to have a relationship. Not a friendship and certainly not a romantic one.

The coffee shop girl, a teenager with bright pink streaks in her blond hair, set our coffees on the counter. I paid her and checked to make sure the lids were secure.

All my life I'd kept everyone at arm's length. If they didn't get too close, they'd never learn the truth.

I'd been fine with that. It made me feel safe. Alone — especially when my mother had died shortly after my seventeenth birthday — but safe. Sure, I'd had one-night stands and a few flings, but I never brought them home and never met their families. I'd never wanted to.

But with Marcus—

God, I wanted to take him home and explore the sizzling heat between us and so much more.

I grabbed our coffees and headed to the door.

Although maybe I wasn't craving a relationship. Maybe I just wanted human contact. Maybe I just wanted sex. And hell, even without the heat in his eyes and in the air, I'd think of sex every time I looked at him. He was gorgeous, with a lean-muscled body, rich skin tone, and a perpetual five o'clock shadow that I'm sure frustrated the hell out of the captain but made every woman in the precinct look at him just a little longer than the other guys.

He leaned against the cruiser's driver's side door in a parking spot on the other side of the street illuminated by the warm glow of a streetlight. He'd hooked his thumbs in his duty belt, and watched something on the sidewalk a few feet down from me. Then he turned his piercing green gaze, capturing mine through the shop's glass door, and the temperature around me flickered hotter for a second.

My pulse stuttered. If I was smart, I'd ask for a different partner. But I didn't want the captain to think I was difficult to work with, especially with only a few months on the job. Marcus was a great cop, and there were more than a few officers who were pissed I'd been partnered with him — and not all of them were women. I'd be an idiot to ask for someone else. Not to mention, I didn't really want a different partner.

He blinked, and the heat in his gaze vanished behind a mask of pleasant professionalism, but the heat in the air continued to warm me. If I hadn't been holding two cups of coffee, I would have rolled up my sleeves to cool off.

I'd yet to work a winter with Marcus, but I had a feeling I wasn't going to be feeling the cold no matter how snowy it got. I'd already learned not to bother wearing my light fall jacket, even if the cool fall temperatures made everyone else wear one, and so far Marcus hadn't commented on that. I could only hope it would stay that way.

I shouldered the coffee shop door open and stepped onto the sidewalk. A whisper of cool air — the actual temperature of the fall evening — swirled around me then was consumed by Marcus's heat.

Someone yelped, and Marcus's attention jumped back down the sidewalk toward the sound. I jerked toward the cry as well. A woman sat on the sidewalk, her expression stunned, as a thin man in a black hoodie and ripped jeans barreled toward me. He clutched a bright yellow purse, and his muddy brown eyes in his sallow thin face flashed wide as our gazes met. Yeah, big mistake snatching a purse right in front of a cop.

"Stop. UCPD," I said, hoping he'd just stop and I wouldn't have to drop my coffee.

He shoved a guy in a navy suit into me and bolted past us.

Shit. I stumbled, sloshing burning coffee out the tiny hole in the lids onto my hands.

"Go," Marcus yelled from across the street as he yanked open the driver's side door of our cruiser.

I dropped the cups and ran knowing Marcus would follow.

The guy in the hoodie ran past a group of teenagers and barreled down the street with a speed that made me wonder if he was just a good runner or if he possessed a bit of supernatural power — either because he was a super or because he wore a magical charm.

I really hoped it wasn't because he was a super. Yes, it was impossible to avoid all things supernatural in Union City — hell, pretty much anywhere in the world since the supers had come out of hiding to help the angels save humanity — but I'd worked hard to keep my exposure to a minimum. The more involved I was with supernatural people and things, the greater the chance someone would start asking questions about me and my unusual temperature issues.

Thank God that was all the power I had. The angelic half of my nature could have been a lot more obvious. My eyes could have glowed with angelic light, or I could have had an innate magical ability like a full angel, but one I couldn't hide. And while most angels could hide their innate magic, about a third of the nephilim Michael had created to destroy human and supernatural kind couldn't.

The radio chirped as Marcus called in our pursuit to dispatch. I pushed myself to run faster. In the very least, I needed to keep eyes on our thief.

The guy jerked into a dark alley, large shadowy mounds — garbage bins and garbage that hadn't made it into the bins — lining both sides. Halfway down, he stumbled, but it wasn't enough for me to catch up. A few seconds later, my foot hit something slick — wet cardboard? — and I jerked my arms out to catch my balance.

For a second I considered pulling out my flashlight, but the guy was almost at the end of the alley and beyond lay a bright, busy street. Not to mention that pulling out my flashlight could slow me down even for only a second, and that could be the second he needed to make it to the street before I got out of the alley and lose me.

Not going to happen. I put on a burst of speed. He reached the mouth of the alley and turned right. I hit the street a few seconds later.

"Stop. UCPD," I gasped, lunging for him. My fingers brushed the back of his hoodie, but he jerked between two parked cars into oncoming traffic, and I couldn't get a hold of him.

Horns blared and brakes squealed. The guy skidded over the hood of a cabbie and ran into the open bay door of a mechanic's garage. I ran around the front of the cabbie and chased after him.

Two burly mechanics glanced up as I followed the thief through the garage and out the back door into a fenced-in lot with a dozen rusted vehicles.

The guy ran to a narrow spot between the shell of a rusted sedan and a pile of barrels stacked three high. With the yellow purse slung over his shoulder catching the light of a bare bulb hanging at the top of a post, he leaped onto the chain link fence, his chest heaving with ragged gasps from our run.

I lunged in, seized the bottom of his hoodie, and wrenched. His foot slipped, and he jerked around and dove at me.

Oh, shit.

I still had no idea if this guy was a super or not, but from the hard look in his eyes, he was pissed, and even though he was skinny, he was still bigger and heavier than me. He tackled me to the ground, the force knocking the air from my lungs, and punched at my face.

I wrenched my head to the side, somehow dodging the blow, and his fist slammed into the broken asphalt. He yelped in pain, and I heaved him off me, determined to regain my footing and put some distance between us so I could draw my sidearm.

But he dove at me before I could fully stand. We crashed into the barrels, toppling the pile. The lid on one of them popped off and black oily liquid rushed out into a wide puddle.

The guy jerked to his feet and grabbed the neck of my vest, hauling me up with him. God, he must be a super with that kind of strength.

I rammed my fist into his throat before he could hit me, my pulse racing half from the exertion of the run and half with fear — because there was no way I was strong enough to deal with a super.

With a gasp, he staggered back. His foot hit the oil and he fell backwards, yanking me down on top of him.

I rammed my elbow into his chest as I fell, drawing an *oomph*, and seized his hand still clutching the neck of my vest. He bucked, throwing me off balance, and rolled us over into the oily spill, straddling me with one hand pressed against my chest and punching me in the ribs with the other.

My breath vanished and pain exploded in my chest. I fumbled to grab my cuffs and capture the wrist of the hand holding me down as he punched again. His fist flew toward my face. I jerked my arm up, blocking his punch as best I could, which meant pushing it aside enough that only his knuckles skimmed my temples before he hit the asphalt again.

"You bitch. You God damn fucking bitch." He yanked back his hurt hand.

Black specks danced across my vision and I heaved against him. His knee slipped in the puddle, and I shoved him off me, somehow managing to keep hold of his wrist. With a twist, I got to my feet and wrenched his arm behind his back and secured the cuff.

"Fucking bitch." He wrenched against my grip, but I jerked his hand higher up his back, making him cry in pain.

"UCPD," I gasped. "And I said stop."

ESSIE

THE THIEF STRUGGLED IN MY GRIP AS THE CRUISER ROARED INTO THE LOT from the narrow driveway at the side of the garage, and Marcus jumped out and drew his sidearm. His gaze swept over me, and he pressed his lips tight. The muscles in his jaw flexed, as if he was fighting to hold something back. Then his lips quirked up and his shoulders started to shake.

Jeez. He was laughing at me.

That wasn't the impression I wanted to make as a rookie or a woman. But given I was covered in oily goo to the point it made my uniform cling to my body and it oozed from my scalp down the back of my neck into my collar, the good-impression ship had already sailed.

Something rolled from my hair, across my temple to my jaw, and plopped onto my shoulder.

Yep, the ship was so far out of sight he was going to be laughing about this for days.

"Twice in one week," Marcus chuckled, unable to hold his laughter back. "That's a new record for you."

I gave him my driest smile. Three days ago I'd ended up in a mud puddle in the middle of a construction site. "You know I love to excel."

He rolled his eyes at me. "Come on. Don't just stand there. Finish cuffing him." His gaze lifted to the clear sky, its sparkling pinpricks of stars barely visible with all the city's lights and a full moon. "The crazy for the night has just started."

Up until I'd joined the force, I'd thought crazies coming out on a full moon was just a myth. And yes, I still thought it was a myth even knowing werewolves, and heck, were-just-about-every-predator existed.

Of course, there was still something about the full moon that made the lycanthropy woven into a shifter's DNA more powerful and virulent, but it wasn't as extreme as the pre-war movies had made it out to be. Shifters acted more like they were having a really bad period — both female and male shifters — and were uncomfortable and moody.

And while the full moon did make lycanthropy contagious, the chances of contracting it were so slim it was almost impossible. One of the shifter's bodily fluids had to enter the human's bloodstream, and then that human had to be the one in a million whose DNA was susceptible to being taken over.

Marcus's laughter broke through his control again as he marched toward me. "You don't even need the full moon for crazy. Crazy just finds you."

His green gaze captured me and the heat in the air billowed. My pulse skipped a beat and my mouth went dry.

He grabbed the yellow purse, which somehow hadn't ended up in the puddle. "Let's get this guy to booking."

I secured the thief's other hand, got him into the car, and reached to open the front passenger side door.

Marcus cocked an eyebrow and shook his head.

"I'm riding in the back again, aren't I?" The mud had banished me to the plastic seats in the back. I should have known the oil would, too.

"No way am I letting you ride up front." Marcus tossed the purse onto the passenger seat and settled in behind the wheel. "If you're good to your station trustee, rookie, they'll be good to you."

"What about being good to your rookie?" I jerked my chin at the thief, telling him to move over, and got in beside him.

"I am being good to you," Marcus said through the metal grate between the front and back seats. "I could make you walk back to the station."

"Pretty sure everyone would think you'd lost me if you did that."

"Nah." He pulled onto the street. "I'd call dispatch to warn the others not to pick up the oil demon slowly making her way to the station."

The thief snickered, and I glared at him. "Not sure you should be laughing. You grabbed a bright yellow purse in front of a cop. I might not have been able to notice you right away if it had been black or brown."

"But it was yellow," the guy said with a strange glimmer in his eyes.

"Yeah, and it was easy to spot."

He leaned forward and pressed his face against the grate, his gaze on the purse. "So yellow."

Marcus's gaze flickered to mine through the rearview mirror. "How much heat is he giving off?"

Shit. I should have been paying attention to that. With an appearance that didn't look supernatural, I'd assumed if he was a super, he was a shifter. And when he hadn't turned his fingers into claws, I was pretty sure he wasn't a shifter. Not to mention he hadn't used any supernatural abilities in the fight aside, perhaps, for strength, so I'd then assumed he was human and more or less magically safe.

But there were still a few demons who could pass as human as well as half demons — who, unlike a naturally born nephilim, were entirely possible — and I hadn't even thought about those... let alone knew much about them or any type of demon, for that matter.

I inched closer to the thief who, with his attention still locked on the yellow purse, didn't notice. The air around me didn't change, but I couldn't tell if that meant the thief wasn't a demon or if Marcus's attraction was too strong for me to tell if the guy was giving off heat.

"Sooooo yellow," the guy crooned.

"If you're that close and you can't feel the heat from him, then he isn't a full magpie." Marcus stopped at a red light.

"I'm magpie enough," the guy huffed. "And we prefer Demonica Corvidae Cissa."

"Looks like we're hunting for his stash after we book this guy," Marcus said as the light turned green.

"I won't tell you where it is," the thief said, and he snapped his mouth shut.

Marcus ignored him and scrunched his nose. "And after you shower and change."

We pulled into the station's garage. Marcus opened the back door to let me out, and we hauled the thief into booking.

Tia Jackson glanced up from her computer behind the booking counter and burst into laughter. "Looks like Sean won the pool," the sturdy war-vet said, her dark eyes filled with mirth.

"You guys were betting on me?" Ouch. I hadn't thought I'd ended up covered in gunk that often, but if I thought about it, Tuesday's mud puddle put my count past one hand… and I'd managed to go through my first two months on the job without incident. Which put me at… jeez, seven in less than four months.

"I figured you'd at least get through the week," she said.

Sean White, the other officer on booking duty, strode through the door. He was lanky to Tia's stocky build and was about a hundred shades paler. If I saw him at the beach in his swim shorts, I was sure I'd have to wear shades just to look at him. Of course, given his pale coloring, I doubted he ever went out in the sun. And no, he took the day shift as well as the night shift, so he wasn't a vampire.

He let out a whoop, his full lips curling into a wide smile. "Holy crap, I won!"

Marcus snickered and I slid my glare to him, which only made him laugh harder and made my pulse pick up with desire.

"How many days did *you* give me?" I forced out, determined not to let my attraction soften my tone.

"I apparently think too highly of you. I thought you'd at least finish the month." He turned to Tia and Sean and set the yellow purse on the counter. "Watch this one. He's half magpie."

"Demonica Corvidae Cissa." The thief leaned closer to the purse, that strange glimmer in his eyes again.

"And you don't have a drop of oil on you," Tia said to Marcus.

"Essie ran him down by herself," he said, his tone warm as he flashed me a proud smile.

"Well, score one for the rookie," Sean said, grabbing the thief by the arm and taking over. "You should sign up for the advanced combat training for dealing with supers."

Yeah, no way in hell. It was bad enough I couldn't resist the urge to help people and that I became a cop, risking encountering supers on a daily basis. But purposely taking the training to deal with supers meant all things super would be sent my way and then I'd be side by side with supers for others to compare me to.

"I'm sure they wouldn't take a rookie." Thankfully, there were only four slots for officers from our precinct in the class, so even if I were forced to sign up, the odds were good I wouldn't be selected.

"You ran down a half demon. That proves you won't freeze up when push comes to shove," Tia said.

"I didn't know he was a half demon." I shifted away from the counter. *Come on. Just take over booking him already, so we can stop talking about this.*

"It would look good on your resume," Sean said.

"If you want a good career, you want to stand out." Marcus's gaze swept over me and he chuckled again. "And for something other than always needing to shower mid-shift."

My cheeks burned. "Why don't *you* sign up for the advanced training."

"I just might. We could do it together." He flashed me another warm smile. The heat of his desire billowed a little, but it clearly wasn't the driving emotion behind his suggestion. "We could be the team everyone in the precinct goes to for dealing with supers."

My pulse fluttered, a mix of attraction and fear.

Yeah, terrible idea on so many levels. It was great knowing Marcus trusted me and wanted to continue working with me, but the closer he got while being constantly reminded about supers, the greater the chance he'd notice something strange about me.

Jeez, it always came down to that. Above everything else, hide in plain sight. Don't draw attention. Stay in the middle of the pack, helpful but forgotten.

"Sounds like a great plan," Sean said. "I'll go get the sign-up sheet for you."

Oh, shit. "I should clean up... and... ah... we should get back on patrol."

"See if you can get the location of this guy's stash," Marcus said.

"Will do," Tia said. "I'll also tell the trustee you need a quick clean."

"Thanks." Marcus headed to the locker rooms and I followed so that I, for the second time this week, could shower and change—

"Crap." This just wasn't my night... or my week, for that matter. Maybe I really should ask for a different partner, because it seemed the more I tried to do a good job and impress him, the more I screwed up. "I didn't replace my backup uniform. I'm going to have to go home to change."

"Shower here first and get out of that uniform." Marcus snapped his mouth shut, and the heat in the air around me jumped another ten degrees as if he'd just realized what he'd said and how he felt about it.

My gaze jumped to his. I wouldn't have been able to stop it if I'd wanted to. His desire had never been this strong before, and even though

I knew I wouldn't see it in his expression, I could still feel it burning around me.

But this time his desire darkened his eyes, his pupils fully dilated, making my thoughts stutter. I had no idea what to say. I knew he was attracted to me, but he'd never looked at me like this before.

ESSIE

THE TEMPERATURE TURNED SULTRY AND MARCUS'S GAZE DIPPED TO MY lips, making my breath hitch. *Oh, please, God, kiss me.*

Humidity joined his heat, turning it sweltering.

Please. I leaned closer to him, unable to help myself, but managed to stop before pressing my oil-soaked body against his... which would have been a terrible mistake... and not because that would get oil all over his uniform... even if that meant he'd have to get out of his clothes, too—

Snow. Frozen showers. Losing my job—

"Essie," he said, his voice raspy with need.

Come on, think of anything but him with his clothes off and step back. Just step back. But I couldn't pull my thoughts from what he'd look like naked or even make myself step back an inch.

"Got the location of his stash," Sean said from behind me, making me jump. "The basement of a tenement on the corner of Seventh and Lincoln."

Marcus's gaze jerked over my shoulder and the mask of professionalism snapped back over his expression as well as his emotions, banking the heat back to its normal levels and leaving me cold and aching.

"Thanks." He turned back to me, all the heat I'd just felt gone, although a flicker of it still simmered in his eyes. "Give me your duty belt. I'll clean it up while you shower, so we don't waste more time."

"Sure." I handed over my belt and hurried into the women's locker room, my pulse still thrumming with desire.

I couldn't believe he felt like *that* about me. Searing, breathtaking desire. I ached just thinking about it, and I'd only experienced it for a minute, probably less. No one had ever felt that way about me before. Not my flings or my few one-night stands, and I had no idea what to do about it.

Even just as partners, there was a chance he could learn my secret, but as lovers, like I wanted, learning the truth was guaranteed. Then I'd have to leave him and my life here in Union City. I didn't want to change my name and start over again. As much as everyone at the precinct teased me, I liked it here, liked who I was, and God, I liked being Marcus's partner.

I also couldn't just make it a one-night stand. That would make things weird between us — not that sleeping together repeatedly wouldn't — but I had a feeling sleeping only once with Marcus wouldn't be enough.

I scrubbed enough oil from my hands to unlock my locker, grab a towel, a shower pouf, and my body wash, then headed to a shower stall.

But God, all that heated desire focused on me.

I dropped my towel on the bench near the glass door of the individual stall and turned on the spray.

All that edgy sexiness.

I shivered at the thought of his scruff against my cheeks as he kissed me. His sexy scruff on other places. His lips on other places.

I pulled off my boots and set them aside, then peeled out of my uniform. The oil had soaked into my underwear, so I shimmied out of those too and added them to the pile.

The water turned hot and filled the stall with misty, sweltering air, just like Marcus's desire.

Biting back a groan, I stepped into the spray. This wasn't the first time I'd fantasized about my partner, but it was the first time I knew how much he wanted me.

I rubbed my soapy pouf across my breasts, the rough mesh brushing against my nipples. They tightened in anticipation, and my mind jumped straight to Marcus's fingers tweaking them into tight buds. Heat throbbed between my thighs, and I slid my soapy hand down my stomach into my curls. His hand would be bigger, stronger. There'd be a ferocity in his touch, a passion I'd glimpsed just moments ago in the hall outside the locker rooms.

He'd press his naked body against my back, his erection hard against me, and he'd knead one breast while teasing me down below with his other hand.

I clenched my jaw on another groan, and brushed my fingers over my clit. I'd beg for more, more than just a tease, more than just his hands, but he'd be deliciously cruel and draw it out, until I quivered on the edge of climax. Then, while panting and aching, he'd slide into me, hard and thick, filling me completely. His need would sear my skin with glorious heat, and he'd pump into me, driving me over the edge with a breathtaking release.

My finger brushed my clit again, and I shuddered with a miniature release. Now I ached even more for Marcus. My partner. What the hell was I going to do?

Nothing.

The smart thing was to do nothing, no matter what I yearned for. Getting into a relationship ruined everything.

But God, just thinking about the power of his desire made me ache on the edge of a climax again.

I turned off the hot water and scrubbed myself as fast as I could under a stinging cold spray that did nothing to ease my yearning.

This was going to be one hell of a problem if I didn't pull myself together.

I toweled off, changed in front of my locker into the street clothes I'd worn to work that afternoon — minus underwear because I hadn't brought extras — and grabbed a garbage bag from the janitor's closet for my oily uniform.

Marcus waited for me in the hall with my duty belt, and my pulse stuttered at the sight of him, at the memory of his searing need and my fantasy in the shower.

"Here." He handed me my belt, his tone and expression back to warm partner professional. "The worst of the oil was on the back where you didn't have many pouches."

I wrenched my attention away from him and took my belt. "Thanks."

"You didn't get much on your holster or sidearm, but since we have to stop at your place, I'd recommend switching to your off-duty weapon until you can give your Glock a thorough cleaning."

We turned to head down the hall to the back door to see if our cruiser was cleaned or if we'd need to take another one from the motor pool when Sergeant Faucher rounded the corner ahead of us.

He took one look at me in my civilian clothes and heaved an exasperated sigh. "Twice in the same week, Shaw?"

"Worth the mess, though. She ran down a half magpie," Marcus said. "We're off to retrieve his stash, see if we can reunite the treasures with their rightful owners."

"That'll have to wait. Michelle Cromer's daughter has been abducted, and I need all available bodies on this."

"The head of GVT Pharmaceutical?"

"Is there another Michelle Cromer in Union with a five-year-old daughter?" Faucher asked.

There could be, but that wasn't his point. Michelle Cromer was the wealthiest woman in town, with a multi-billion dollar pharmaceutical company. She'd been the first to partner with supers after the war and had taken a decisive hold on the market by developing drugs for supers where the human equivalent wasn't as effective. As well, she'd been the first to use supers' abilities to develop new drugs for everyone. Rumor had it she was working on a drug to help cancer patients that she'd unveil early next year.

"Do you know who?" Marcus asked.

"No."

"What about why?" My best guess was for money, but humankind advocates could have kidnapped the kid to demand Cromer stop working with supers, or super extremists could have done it for the same reason.

"We don't know why and that's not part of your job," Faucher said. "Getting into uniform, rookie, and canvassing your part of the search area, is."

"Yes, sir." I resisted the urge to argue. He was right. Knowing who or why wasn't my job. But *not* knowing bothered me. Human extremists could be well-armed and supers were just downright dangerous.

"Dispatch has sent the details to your phones," Faucher said. "Now get out of here."

We hurried to the lot where we parked the cruisers. The station trustee, a pudgy guy with a face full of freckles, tossed Marcus the keys.

"I can do a more detailed clean if you like." His gaze jumped to me and he frowned.

"Not tonight," Marcus said. "Officer Shaw and I need to get back out there."

"The kid?" the guy asked.

"Yeah." Marcus opened the driver's side door, and I hurried around to the other side.

"Takes a real special asshole to abduct a five year old." The guy's hands curled into fists.

"Couldn't agree more." Marcus shut the door and started the engine.

We drove to my apartment building at the edge of the precinct — in the opposite direction of where we'd been assigned to search. My building wasn't in the precinct's seediest neighborhood, but it wasn't the nicest, either. Most of the buildings were tired three-story tenements that had been tired before the war. And while there were many affordable buildings in town, the ones with absentee landlords and lazy superintendents were best for remaining unnoticed. That, and when I'd first moved to town, I'd been seventeen and unemployed. There were few landlords who'd been willing to rent to me, and while I could pass a credit check now, I couldn't bring myself to leave the safety of my nobody-really-notices-me neighborhood.

Marcus pulled up to the curb and I hopped out.

"I won't be long," I said, closing the cruiser door and racing to the unsecured front door, since every minute counted with a child abduction.

Marcus got out and followed me.

Crap. I'd expected him to wait in the car. It wasn't like my apartment was a mess — I didn't have enough stuff for a mess — but I'd never had anyone in my apartment before. It was my only safe space where I didn't have to worry about revealing my temperature fluctuations by sweating or freezing or hell, getting my face misted with someone's grief. That, and my building was a dump.

He raised his eyebrows at the building's front door. No lock and no buzzer system. A chunk of tile along the right side of the hall floor was missing and a large piece of cardboard had been duct-taped over a hole in the wall.

"Wow, they must have cut back on a rookie's pay."

I took the stairs to the basement where half the lights were out, throwing the narrow, dingy hall into perpetual shadows, and unlocked my door. The urge to insist Marcus remain in the hall clawed in my chest, but I recognized the feeling for the ridiculous emotion that it was.

I couldn't ask my partner to stand in the hall. That would just make him ask questions I didn't want to answer.

Gritting my teeth, I hurried into my one-bedroom unit, dropping my garbage bag of filthy clothes by the door and pulling off my boots so I didn't track in oil.

"They've *really* cut back." His gaze slid over my living room, with its grayish-beige walls, once-was-light-brown worn carpet, and secondhand couch and TV.

I could have painted when I'd moved in, and I could have bought a new couch. I could have bought tons of new things now that I had a secure job, but instead I put my money into an escape fund. My mom had done it for as long as I could remember, and when she'd died and I'd started working to pay my rent, I put every extra cent into the fund.

Besides, what was the point of having stuff if I had to abandon it at a moment's notice?

I already knew, and had already lost precious keepsakes because Mom and I had needed to flee the angels and Joined Parliament agents hunting Michael's remaining nephilim and fellow fallen angels. I wasn't going to become attached to anything else and lose it, too.

"No photos. Barely any furniture. You don't even have a plant."

"Sure, I'll get a plant." I jerked my thumb at the small, grimy window on the back wall before hurrying down the short hall to my bedroom.

"How am I supposed to learn anything about you if you don't have any pictures?"

"You've already learned lots of stuff about me. We've been patrolling together for months." I dropped my duty belt on the floor, yanked off my T-shirt, and shimmied out of my jeans — doing my damnedest to ignore the fact that I now only wore a bra and socks and Marcus stood a few feet away in my living room.

"You don't really share much personal information," he said. "I don't even know how you take your coffee."

I pulled on a clean pair of underwear. Plain and white, nothing sexy about them, but it didn't help me stop thinking about sex. "That's because you keep making me get our coffee."

"You never talk about your family."

I shrugged into my uniform shirt. "You never talk about yours."

"Yeah, but you know stuff about me."

"Sure, I know how you take your coffee," I said sarcastically. Except I did know a fair amount about him. He boxed with a few of the other officers and worked out on top of that — and God, I really wanted to see and run my hands all over the fruits of that labor. On his days off, he alternated between volunteering as a big brother to a kid who'd lost his dad due to PTSD from the war and visiting the veterans' wing at the hospital. Hot to look at and a nice guy. I bet he helped old ladies cross the street when he wasn't saving kittens from trees.

What I didn't know was if he had a girlfriend. I hadn't asked and he hadn't brought it up. It seemed like family and romantic life were taboo topics in our partnership... until now.

I finished dressing, secured my duty belt, and knelt at the back of my closet so I could unlock my gun safe and trade out my on-duty Glock for my off-duty one.

"If we're going to be partners, we should at least get to know each other."

"We've been partners for months. You've never wanted to share like this before." I shoved the magazine from my on-duty weapon into my off-duty one, holstered it, and turned around.

Marcus leaned against the doorframe with his arms crossed. The heat of his attraction wasn't strong, and there was something in his eyes I couldn't recognize. What the hell did that mean?

"I was afraid we wouldn't be a good match before."

"And now?" My pulse stuttered. Did he think we were a good match? As partners or something more? His attraction right now suggested just work partners, but the memory of the heat from before at the station made me flush.

"I think you're becoming a decent cop," he said.

"Decent. Gee, thanks." But that was high praise coming from him.

"I mean it. You should sign up for the advanced combat training with me."

Fear flash-froze my desire. No way in hell.

I pushed past him and headed to my boots by the front door. "I'm a rookie. They won't take me."

"You mean you're too afraid of supers to even try."

I was too afraid of being discovered. "I like walking the beat."

"You'll still walk the beat." He glared down at me as I crouched and tied my boots.

"But I'll also get put on special units." Units that might have to interact with JP agents, the very people I'd spent my whole life running from. Just the idea of being close to a JP agent, let alone an angel, made my pulse race.

"Not all supers are monsters." He crossed his arms as if daring me to argue with him. "The only true monsters are nephilim and the JP has captured all of them."

And by captured he meant killed. Unless the Joined Parliament had a secret prison filled with nephilim, there wasn't a single one in prison. They'd either died fighting or committed suicide before their magic could be contained. No way in hell was I going to become the only nephilim in captivity. Especially since I'd had nothing to do with the war. I was — for all intents and purposes — a powerless, naturally born nephilim. Impossible and defenseless.

I straightened and opened my front door so Marcus could leave and I could lock up. "We should search for this girl."

"You're going to end up dealing with supers whether you want to or not." He strode into the hall. "Why not be fully prepared?"

"You honestly think anything they could teach us would give us a fighting chance against a super?" I locked my front door and we took the stairs up to the first floor.

"Of course. The program was designed by the military based on their experience fighting nephilim."

He wasn't going to give up on this. Which, if I was being honest, thrilled me. Marcus liked working with me and wanted to stay partners.

God damn it. "Okay. I'll think about it."

He flashed me a brilliant smile that made my pulse trip. The temperature rose a few degrees, but it didn't feel as if it was because of his desire — more like his joy.

Maybe I could get through the training without being noticed.

Of course, that still didn't address the issue of being assigned to teams that worked directly with Union City's JP team. But maybe if the JP agents were focused on a supernatural criminal, they wouldn't give me a second glance. I really didn't want to give up being Marcus's partner, even if at times it was difficult not to fantasize about him.

We got in the cruiser and I looked at our assignment on my phone. "We're to start at the west end of Birch Hill."

"Birch Hill is a large area with a lot of abandoned buildings." Marcus started the engine and pulled onto the street. "Anyone else with us?"

"No. Ariel Cromer was abducted by two men in a black van that was last spotted on Monroe heading to the border between Birch Hill and Northvale."

"And Northvale has more abandoned buildings, most of them multi-story apartments that are in better shape. If I was the sergeant, I'd start at the border and fan out."

"Which means we're not going to get much help," I said, since our assignment started us on the far side of Birch Hill moving in toward Northvale. And while there were fewer squatters in Birch Hill, so fewer people to notice the kidnappers, that was because the buildings and the roads were in worse shape. More than one adventurous teen had ended up in the hospital after exploring the ruins of Birch Hill, and anyone who knew the city knew there were safer places to explore or squat.

Marcus crossed Foley, the unofficial border marking the livable part of town and the unlivable part. More than half the streetlights were without power and only one out of every six buildings still stood. He slowed at an intersection with a dead stoplight, glanced both ways down the abandoned cross street, and pulled through to park at the corner under a working streetlight.

"Ariel Cromer is five, straight black hair, last seen wearing a pink party dress with a pink bow in her hair." I showed Marcus the picture of the kid with her sweet, innocent smile. It made me want to scream. If she'd been taken for money or leverage, she had to be terrified. If she'd been taken for anything else, she was either suffering in ways I didn't want to think about or dead.

We got out of the cruiser. I pocketed my phone, drew my sidearm, and pulled out my flashlight. The first three streetlights down the street worked, but the next dozen were out, throwing the ruins ahead of us into deep shadow.

In daylight, it looked like a war zone, because it had been a war zone. I didn't know why Michael had chosen Birch Hill as a battleground, but he had and his army had killed hundreds and destroyed buildings, as if a tornado and dozens of bombs had been dropped on the neighborhood at once — which, given that nephilim possessed magic like angels, was entirely possible.

The three three-story apartment buildings beside me, those within the working streetlight radius, still stood. The ones across the street had been leveled. Marcus shone his flashlight into the lot between the first and second buildings, over the shells of cars that had long ago been stripped of anything of value.

No sign of a black van.

I shone my light through the building's missing front door onto the floor of the entranceway. Dirt and debris littered the area, but none of the scuffed footprints looked fresh. Which, of course, didn't mean anything. The kidnappers could have entered the building from a back door or one of the broken windows or even a fire escape at the side... if there was a fire escape at the side.

This was going to be a long night. And just that thought filled me with frustration. There wasn't a fast way to do this search, and yet I knew every second counted.

Down the street, something heavy thumped, and a wolf howled.

"Was that—?"

I jerked my gaze to Marcus's. Shifters weren't known to hang out in Birch Hill. They had a number of large forests in the Supers' Quarter that appealed to their feral natures more than urban ruins, but that had sounded close.

Another thump. Something crashed against something else with a loud boom, and someone started yelling... at someone? I couldn't tell. All I could tell was that they weren't yelling for help.

"It's this way," Marcus said.

I tightened my grip on my flashlight. I doubted it was the kidnappers, but that didn't mean it wasn't shifters who'd lost their common sense because of the full moon. And that worried me more.

"It's not like the movies," Marcus said, his voice low. "The odds of being infected are almost negligible."

"I know that." Except even knowing it didn't make me feel better. I'd never encountered a shifter during a full moon, but I'd talked to enough people and watched enough news reports to know that even if it wasn't like the movies, it wasn't pleasant.

We passed a small church, only the brick arch of the front door remained standing. The streetlight in front flickered on for a second then went out.

The wolf howled again, and the hair on the back of my neck stood up. *Not like the movies. Not like the movies.*

Whoever was yelling stopped, and the street fell into an eerie silence. My pulse pounded in my ears and I sucked in a steadying breath. This might be my first time in a situation like this, but I could handle it. I had my training and I had Marcus. We'd approach whoever was yelling, find out what the problem was, and move on.

"I think it came from there." Marcus jerked his chin toward a set of eight townhouses beside the church. The first two in the row were mostly destroyed, but the ones in the middle had somehow managed to avoid most of the destruction, kind of like that one house still in perfect condition in the middle of a tornado's path of destruction. From the weak glimmer of moonlight, it even looked like some of the middle townhouses still had a few intact windows.

The streetlight flickered back on for a second and my gaze jumped to a bright pink something in front of the doorless entranceway of the fifth townhouse down before everything plunged back into shadows.

"Is that—?"

I hurried toward the doorway, scanning the area around me, looking for the wolf or whoever had been yelling. This townhouse looked the best of the whole row, with its bay window still intact.

My flashlight hit the pink thing, and my stomach lurched. It was a pink bow hairclip. *We might have found Ariel.*

The streetlight flickered back on, and a massive man walked past the partially open curtains in the bay window. I didn't think I'd ever seen anyone so big before, and there was a ferocity in his expression that scared the crap out of me.

Marcus grabbed my arm and yanked me down. We pressed our bodies tight to the front of the house, and I flicked off my flashlight, my pulse pounding.

"Is he a shifter?" I asked. He couldn't have been the howling wolf because he was still in his human form, but that only meant there was at least one shifter still in the area.

"I didn't get a good enough look," Marcus replied.

The guy turned his back to the window and said something, his rough voice too quiet for me to make out the words.

"They're all over the neighborhood," a reedy masculine voice said in response, his volume rising with each word.

"Not this neighborhood," Rough Voice snapped, matching Reedy's volume. "So keep your shit together."

"Don't tell me what to do," Reedy snarled.

I inched closer to the window and peeked inside. Rough Voice still stood with his back to the window, barely visible with the streetlight the only source of illumination. His body was tense and his hands didn't look right, his fingers too long and pointy at the end. The guy he was talking to paced back and forth between two pale couches, raking his hands through dark hair that hung loose to his shoulders.

"We should just kill the brat and run," Reedy said.

"Not until we have our money." Rough flexed his hands and my pulse skipped a beat. His fingers extended into claws.

"Shifters," I gasped.

Then the biggest wolf I'd ever seen prowled in between Reedy and Rough and snarled at the both of them, and a young high-pitched voice started to cry. My pulse froze, and I jerked my attention past the guys to a small figure huddled in the corner at the back of the room, the street-light catching on her shiny pink clothes.

"Shut the kid up," Rough barked.

"Shut up," Reedy yelled.

The wolf snapped at Reedy, who punched it in the head. "Fuck off."

I glanced back at Marcus, my stomach churning. "They have Ariel."

"Are you sure?" he whispered.

"Even if they don't, there's a terrified kid in there." I wrenched my attention back to the window. My breath came too fast, and no matter what I did, I couldn't control it. There was a kid in there, and we were going to have to face at least two shifters. "We can't just leave her in there."

"You want to fuck with me?" Reedy growled and grabbed the wolf around the neck and punched it in the head.

The wolf dug its claws into his gut, making him howl with laughter, as a fourth guy slunk out of the shadows at the back of the room and grabbed the girl by the arm. Her screams turned to frantic shrieks and the temperature plummeted around me, her fear so strong it swept past the confines of the house.

"Shut that bitch up," Rough said. He jerked toward the window, and I wrenched back down against the rough brick wall beside Marcus. Rough's jaw was elongated, inhuman, his lips curled back revealing long canines, and a vicious wildness filled his eyes. He was barely holding onto his humanity.

We had to get the kid out of there. But there were at least two shifters, and it was a full moon. I couldn't catch my breath. Frost crept over the back of my hands, the kid's fear fueling my own. We didn't stand a chance, but I couldn't just watch them hurt her.

ESSIE

"WE HAVE TO DO SOMETHING," I SAID, MY VOICE CRACKING WITH desperation. I couldn't just sit there and watch them hurt her.

"Take a breath, Essie," Marcus said, his voice low and calm, but I could see the worry in his slightly too-wide eyes. "Two Charlie Eight requesting backup at—" He glanced at the house behind him.

I followed his gaze to the numbers beside the door.

"—Eighty-two Brosville Street. We have a juvenile being held by four men. At least two are shifters," Marcus finished.

The kid's screams grew louder, tearing at my nerves, at my whole being.

Do something. Do something. God, just do something. But protocol was clear. Two officers didn't confront more than one shifter, not unless we were trained to deal with multiple shifters at the same time. We were supposed to wait.

How the hell was I supposed to wait?

"Shut. Her. Up." Rough Voice jerked away from the window and stepped deeper into the room. "I don't care how."

Reedy jerked his head up, his wicked glee making bile burn my throat. "She's mine. Give her to me."

"Come and take her," the up-until-now silent guy said, his voice dark and dangerous.

I jerked up, but Marcus grabbed my arm and yanked me back down. "Wait for backup."

The wolf lunged at Reedy's back, while the no-longer-silent guy yanked the kid through a doorway and out of sight.

"We can't just sit here." My pulse roared, my emotions in churning turmoil. I couldn't let them hurt this kid because of protocol.

The kid shrieked, and I lurched to my feet.

"Essie, stop. We're no good to anyone if we're dead." Marcus grabbed for my arm, but I jerked out of the way and rushed through the doorway into a narrow hall.

My Glock shook because my hands shook, hell, my whole body shook. It didn't occur to me to turn my flashlight back on. If I'd been thinking straight, I would have. But I wasn't. All I could think about was the screaming need to save that little girl.

This was the dumbest thing I'd ever done and probably ever would do, since these shifters were going to kill me. But every fiber of my being howled at me. I couldn't just sit there and listen to them hurt and kill her. I had to do something. Even if it was to sacrifice myself to buy time for backup to arrive.

"Stop," Marcus hissed. "Wait for backup."

I reached the opening from the hall to the living room and three sets of wild eyes turned to me. I could only assume the quiet one was with the crying kid in the next room, and I could only hope my arrival was enough of a distraction to draw him away from her.

"UCPD," I said, pointing my Glock at Rough, the biggest guy in the room.

Reedy charged at me, and I wrenched my aim to him and fired.

Holy shit, I fired my gun. I'd never shot at anyone before. I'd had to change my clothes while on duty more times than I'd drawn my weapon on someone, let alone fired it.

The gunshot roared around me, making every muscle in my body clench. This wasn't like shooting in the target range at all. I shook with adrenaline and icy fear.

I hit Reedy twice in the chest.

He howled in pain but didn't drop.

Oh God oh God oh God.

He heaved closer, his fingers turning into claws, and swiped at me. I fired again. Two more shots. His body slammed into me, knocking me back into the hallway wall, but he sagged to the floor instead of clawing me to death.

My throat tightened, cutting off my air, and I couldn't rip my gaze away from him. His blood rushed into the thick dust on the floor, and he didn't move, didn't even draw breath. I'd killed him. *Oh, God, I killed him.*

The wolf snarled, and I wrenched my gaze up, but it wasn't the wolf who lunged at me, it was Rough. I yanked my weapon up to fire, but wasn't fast enough. His claws sliced into my forearm, drawing fiery agony, and he rammed his shoulder into me, his weight crushing me against the wall, stealing my breath.

"UCPD," Marcus yelled.

Rough jerked toward him. I squirmed against Rough's weight, trying to bring my weapon up to get any kind of shot.

"Release the officer," Marcus said.

Rough curled his lips back, baring his teeth. "Sure." He grabbed my vest and tossed me into the living room.

I tumbled across the floor and crashed into the couch, sending sparks dancing across my vision. My Glock flew out of my hand, and the wolf pounced at me. I flung myself out of the way, scrambling to grab my weapon.

Two gunshots exploded and blood and brains sprayed me and the couch. The wolf dropped onto my legs, pinning me with its massive weight, and I wrenched my gaze to Marcus, time frozen for a split second. He stood in the hall, his eyes wide, his breath fast. His fear swept frost up my arms and across my cheeks.

Then Rough swiped his sharp wolf claws at him, and Marcus wrenched out of the way and out of sight into the hall.

I shoved the wolf off me and turned to grab my gun, but strong hands seized my ankle and jerked me back.

"You killed Lars," the quiet dangerous one said, the look in his eyes pure animal ferocity. He drove his claws into my thigh and wrenched me closer, dragging my body through the dead wolf's blood.

I kicked at him with my free leg, but he twisted his claws in my thigh, sending agony screaming through me, and yanked me under him, pinning me with his body.

"You can scream better than that." He dug the claws of his free hand into my gut, drawing another scream that made him sneer with pleasure.

I bucked under him and scratched at his face, but that only made him dig his claws in deeper and grind his erection against me, showing me just how much he enjoyed my pain.

Marcus stumbled into the living room, holding his baton instead of his sidearm, and dodged a swipe of Rough's claws. His gaze locked on mine, his expression a mix of horror and rage.

Rough roared and leaped at Marcus, fur rushing over his body as it melted from human to wolf in one fluid, horrifying moment. It was so fast that if I'd closed my eyes for a second, I would have missed it. Rough, now a massive gray wolf, slammed into Marcus, who jerked to the side, somehow keeping his balance. But Rough wrenched his head around and snapped his teeth onto Marcus's biceps. Snarling, Rough wrenched on Marcus's arm and yanked him to the floor.

No. Please, God, no. I had to get my Glock. Save Marcus. Save the girl. *Where the hell was our backup?*

I heaved against Quiet Guy on top of me and punched him in the throat. He jerked back, and I scrambled for my Glock, but he drove his claws back into my thigh and yanked me toward him again. I kneed him in the head with my free leg, but that only made him dig his claws in deeper.

Marcus screamed, and my pulse lurched.

Blue and red light swept through the window, then a gunshot exploded in the room and Rough yelped. Officers McLellan and Herberling rushed into the living room, their flashlights jerking around the room as they yelled for the shifters to lie face down on the floor.

Officers Keels and Nishida rushed in as well and yanked Quiet off me, but Rough lunged for McLellan. Herberling shot him with one of the department's new Tasers, with a setting specifically for supers. Rough stiffened as electricity surged through his body, then his fur rolled off of him and he melted back into a naked man — his clothes destroyed by the magic that let a shifter shift.

Marcus glared at me, his breath quick gasps, his eyes wide. "What the fuck were you thinking?"

"They were going to kill her." Except I didn't know that for certain, and really, I hadn't been thinking at all. I'd panicked and rushed in.

"So instead they almost killed all of us." He hugged his arm to his chest.

Oh, shit. My stomach bottomed out. *Oh shit oh shit.* He'd been bitten. The odds were slim he'd be susceptible to lycanthropy, but there was still a chance, and it was my fault.

With the flashlights jerking around the room and the strobing lights from the cruisers outside, I couldn't see how badly he'd been hurt, but blood dripped from his elbow into a dark puddle on the floor, so it had to be significant.

"Marcus, I'm sorry."

"There's God damn protocol for a reason."

A paramedic hurried into the room, saw Marcus first, and knelt beside him.

"I'm fine," Marcus snarled.

"Officer—"

"I'm. Fine." Marcus glared at me, his expression dark with barely contained rage as the temperature skyrocketed. He shoved up to his feet and stormed out of the townhouse.

I scrambled up, my body screaming in pain.

The paramedic reached for me, but I pushed him away. "Go check on the kid," I said, and chased after Marcus. "Marcus—"

He shoved past another officer headed into the townhouse, the heat of his fury searing my skin, and stormed up the street to our cruiser.

"Marcus, please." God, I hurt. My arm and gut burned, and my legs were on fire. "Marcus."

He wrenched around. "I told you to wait. I told you to follow protocol." His expression tightened, his piercing green gaze dark and ferocious, terrifyingly similar to the shifters we'd just fought. "I told you!"

I stumbled back, the force of his emotion burning me up and making my stomach clench with guilt. He could have died. I hadn't known for certain the kid was in imminent danger, and even if she was, protocol said we weren't to confront that many shifters. And I'd just proven why. If backup had been a few seconds slower, we would have died.

The muscles in his jaw flexed and a strangled groan escaped. "I fucking told you," he snarled.

The ferocity of his words froze me in place. He stormed to our cruiser, got in, and drove away, taking his burning rage with him.

Cold rushed around me, and my throat tightened. I'd almost killed him because I hadn't followed protocol, and worse, I hadn't stopped to think. I had to make this right, prove to him I wasn't a fuck-up or a danger to him. I had to—

God, I had no idea what to do. There wasn't anything I could do that could make up for nearly getting him killed.

DESTINED BLOOD

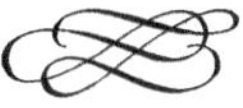

NEPHILIM'S DESTINY, BOOK 2

ESSIE

I COULD HEAR THE COUPLE YELLING AT EACH OTHER THE MOMENT I GOT OUT of the cruiser even though I was outside on the residential street and they were, from the muffled sound of it, still inside their apartment building. I could also hear the traffic on the busy street five blocks over, the buzz from the streetlight fifty feet away, and, if I concentrated, the calm steady breathing of Hank, my partner, who stood on the other side of the car from me.

The woman screamed something incomprehensible, but my partner's expression didn't change, which meant he couldn't hear it, proving that my senses had in fact been enhanced.

I hadn't been sure of it when Amiah — the head of the medical team at the Joined Parliament Operations Building — had released me from her mini hospital. Of course, it had been hard to think past anything with my painful, grating buzz clawing under my skin, but even after I'd managed to medicate that down to a manageable level — now requiring two nicotine patches at the same time — I hadn't been sure.

Yeah, there'd been moments when I'd suspected, but nothing quite as definitive as this. With its surprisingly subtle only-seeming-to-appear-when-I-concentrated manifestation, it had been easy to keep myself distracted and to pretend that life as I knew it hadn't completely changed two weeks ago.

In a way, it hadn't. I was back in my apartment — and the skylight and hole in the wall had been fixed — and I was back to my job in the Union City Police Department. And yet...

I couldn't deny that, core deep, everything had changed. And that scared me.

Yes, I'd survived having an unnatural angelic mating brand forced upon me by an archnephilim — a monster that was part archangel and part demonic wraith — and having his power tear through me as he'd tried to rip out wings I was sure... well, pretty sure I didn't have. But I hadn't gotten through that unscathed. My buzz was stronger than before, feeling more like I was in constant contact with a medium-voltage electric fence and not just a low-level one. Not to mention my eyes still glowed from blasting a massive amount of divine light into myself to stop him.

And it was my eyes that worried me the most. I couldn't pretend to just be a human if my eyes were glowing. I'd purchased enspelled contacts from a shady witch who'd promised discretion, and they were supposed to hide the glow until the divine light left my body.

But even after a week and a half the light hadn't faded, and I feared it was still around because I was a nephilim and blasting all that magic into me had somehow awakened the angelic part of my DNA. To make it worse, I was sure my essence — readable by those supernatural beings who could sense magical essences — still said I was human, which made the angelic glowy eye thing look really suspicious.

Add to that my enhanced hearing... oh, and the ability to see in the dark... and my goal to live as a nothing-to-see-here human just serving and protecting my city had become nearly impossible.

It was only a matter of time before someone started asking questions, and those questions could get me imprisoned, experimented on, or killed. Probably all of the above.

At least I could attribute my enhanced senses to Jacob's vampire claim on me. The claim, at least, would go away... eventually... I hoped. But I wasn't sure how long the effects would last, and I wasn't sure I wanted to ask.

At least none of the guys had tried to contact me in the week and a half I'd been gone from Operations, so the risk of being revealed wasn't as great. I hadn't expected Marcus to. He'd been adamant in respecting my wishes to have nothing to do with the supernatural world, and had been gone before I'd even woken in Amiah's hospital. Jacob and Kol hadn't contacted me either, and much to my surprise, neither had

Gideon, even with his angelic mating brand on my arm permanently bonding us together.

And I was going to ignore the empty ache in my chest over him—over all the guys. It had been growing within me from the moment I'd returned home.

It would go away.

Just like the effects of Jacob's vampiric claim.

Really.

"Dispatch said the call came in for unit one-o-seven," Hank said, adjusting his duty belt at his slightly paunchy waist as we headed for the apartment building's front door. "That must be at the back or maybe they've resolved their differences and have stopped yelling."

Glass shattered and the woman screeched something else, her voice still too muffled with the building between us for me to make out her words even with my enhanced hearing. Hank still didn't react, but I was sure as soon as we got inside, he'd be able to hear them as well.

The building was a tired six-story structure that had been built in the 60s or 70s. Its utilitarian construction hadn't aged well and the owner had done little upkeep. Through the filthy glass front door, the vinyl tiled floor was scuffed with at least a quarter of the tiles missing. Holes and graffiti scarred the walls and paint peeled from the ceiling.

Three homemade missing person flyers were taped to the window beside the door, two for guys who looked like they were teenagers or in their early twenties, and the other for a middle-aged woman. The number of missing persons — all over town, with the exception of the precinct in the downtown core — had spiked in the last month and a half, and no one in the department had a clue as to why. Although I suspected it was probably one of the many after-effects of the war. Michael's slaughter to exterminate all humans and supernatural beings had only ended twenty-three years ago and most of the world's population was still coming to terms with what had happened. Some people dealt with that by running away.

Hank opened the door, not bothering to buzz the superintendent to unlock it. Every few months or so we'd get a call to this building, and, for as long as I'd been with this precinct — just over five years, which was as long as I'd been a cop — the building's door had been broken.

A man's angry voice roared around me as we entered. If I hadn't known I had enhanced hearing, I would have sworn the guy was standing in the hall with us.

"Hunh, guess they're still at it," Hank said, and he headed down the hall, his walk quick but his body language calm. Thankfully, not much bothered the middle-aged cop, or he was able to keep his emotions in check, which was good given how my next-to-useless weird empathic magic reacted to strong feelings. He had almost nine years of experience on me, and while he hadn't been happy to be partnered with the rookie who'd gotten another cop seriously injured, he hadn't tried to make my life difficult.

Of course, he hadn't tried to become friends, either. Four and a half years together and our partnership was still awkward. Which, given that I was trying to stay under everyone's radar, was better than a partner who wanted to know everything about me and stick his nose in my business — like why I didn't have a social or dating life.

My nerves, however, thrummed with adrenaline and fear. This wasn't my first domestic call and it wouldn't be my last, but even with experience, I couldn't help but worry about how dangerous the situation could get.

The temperature rose as we drew closer to apartment 107, turning the early summer evening that was already unusually warm and muggy even warmer... at least it did for me because my empathic magic manifested as temperature changes and not something useful like being able to actually sense emotions.

Another glass something shattered, sounding like it had been thrown against the wall, and the man yelled obscenities at the woman. The woman screamed back.

Hank reached up to knock on the door, when a gunshot exploded inside the apartment.

My pulse leaped into a fast tattoo, and Hank's eyes flashed wide.

We drew our sidearms, and our gazes met for a split second, confirming we were good to go.

"Police," Hank yelled, and he kicked in the door.

Inside lay a living room filled with garbage — empty pizza boxes and beer bottles, food wrappers, and crumpled clothes — along with old, chipped, dented, and even broken furniture. We stood at the far end of the unit, which ran parallel to the hall, and while from my position I could see fully into the room, if both of us wanted a clear view of the entire room — and more importantly a clear shot — someone was going to have to enter.

I gritted my teeth and hurried inside. This situation was all human. There wasn't a super in sight. I had nothing to worry about.

At the back, near the closed patio door, stood a brawny man with swarthy skin in his twenties, wearing a black wife-beater and navy cotton-knit shorts with frayed ends. He pointed a Ruger 9mm at a short curvy woman, also in her twenties, with bleach-blond hair and a dingy yellow sundress. The guy had fingernail marks on his cheeks and arms — nothing supernatural looking about them — and the woman had a black eye and a fresh bruise in the shape of a handprint on her left biceps. She didn't look like she'd been shot, but both had ashen complexions and wild eyes.

They stared at us for a tense second and their expressions twisted with rage.

The room's temperature shot up another ten degrees, and sweat instantly slicked my body, making my uniform stick to my skin.

On the floor between them lay a spilled bag of little purple pills, and I inwardly groaned. Zip. Again? Jeez, this was twice in just over two weeks that I'd had to deal with someone high on zip. Except given their expressions, I was pretty sure they weren't high. They were starting to come down. And that meant aggressive mania and violent hallucinations enhanced by magic.

Just great. I pointed my Glock at the guy. "Police. Drop the weapon."

The guy snarled.

"Drop the weapon," Hank repeated.

The woman screamed and lunged at the guy. He fired two shots as she slipped on a half-empty pizza box and crashed to the floor. I dropped to the floor as well. The guy's rounds slammed into the wall above me, and my pulse jumped with the knowledge that I'd almost taken two in the vest.

"Drop the weapon," Hank yelled, not taking a shot because the woman was climbing to her feet and in the way.

The guy snarled and lunged toward the patio door. He wrenched it off its hinges with a burst of zip-enhanced strength and bolted outside, gun still in hand.

"Shit." I scrambled to my feet and gave chase. Hank followed close at my heels and called the change of situation in to dispatch on his radio.

The guy raced across the building's uneven parking lot and onto the street. This neighborhood had been old and tired before the war and had yet to see any revitalization money. Only half of the streetlights worked, making footing on the crumbling sidewalk dangerous, and the farther we went down the street, the fewer buildings had lighted vestibules or front doors that weren't boarded up.

I pumped my arms, trying to keep up with the guy. He ran with bursts of wild speed that came and went, making him jerk and stumble, but not enough to let me catch him.

Hank's footsteps pounded behind me, getting farther away. He was starting to trail, but I knew he wouldn't give up. He might not have the physique of any of the guys on Gideon's JP team, but he wasn't completely out of shape, either.

The guy stumbled, his arms windmilling to keep his balance, and he skidded into the narrow alley beside a seven-story building with a boarded front entrance.

My nerves thrummed stronger, more fear than adrenaline. The last time I'd run blindly into an alley, I'd gotten the shit beaten out of me and been branded by a serial killing archnephilim.

I gritted my teeth and pushed on. I couldn't let this guy get away. He'd already tried to kill his girlfriend, still had his weapon, and was in the middle of coming down from a magically induced high. He was a danger to others and himself, and I was pretty sure the violence-inducing hallucinations hadn't started yet.

The alley was narrow, not even wide enough for two people to walk side by side, and smelled of stale urine. A flashlight beam hit my shoulder and spilled against the alley walls on either side of me. If Hank had brought his light out, the alley was too dark for him to see properly, which meant it was supposed to be too dark for me.

Shit. I was supposed to be hiding my enhanced abilities. I could only pray that with the heat of the fight and the crazy zip addict with a gun, Hank wouldn't think much about my running down the alley without light.

Hank's light rose a little higher and caught the back of the guy we were chasing. The guy reached the end of the alley, crossed the street, and ran to a boarded-up entrance. With a roar, he ripped off one of the boards and darted inside.

I barreled out of the alley. Ahead of me stood a three-story partially-standing condemned school. The guy's footsteps pounded inside, drawing farther away. If he thought enough to slow down and hide, he might be able to slip past us while we searched the school.

I pulled out my flashlight, even though I didn't need it, waited a beat for Hank to get closer, and rushed inside. This had been a side entrance to the building and it opened into a gymnasium, the space vast and empty, smelling of mold, dust, and decay as if an animal, or more than one animal, had died there. The sound of the guy's footsteps headed straight away from me but didn't echo, so he was already through the door and into the hall across from me.

Then his steps changed to the rapid patter of going down a set of stairs.

"He's in the basement," I told Hank, and put on a burst of speed.

I ran into a hall lined with metal lockers, their doors a mix of closed, opened, and missing, all tagged with graffiti on top of graffiti, while electrical and lighting boxes hung precariously from the walls and ceiling, their wiring scavenged for reuse. The smell of dead animal had thickened and a heavy layer of dust, marked with dozens of different footprints, coated the floor.

I hurried down the stairs into a dark corridor running right and left and stopped, nearly choking on the reek, the smell of death clinging to my nose and the back of my throat. More footprints trailed in both directions, and I couldn't tell if any of them were fresh.

Crap.

I really didn't want to lose this guy.

Hank reached the top of the stairs and clattered down, but I ignored him and drew a steadying breath. If the guy was still running I should be able to hear him.

Nothing.

Hank stepped close, his nose crinkled in disgust, his sidearm raised, and his flashlight sweeping into the hall behind me.

"Did you see which way he went?" he asked.

"No idea." I squeezed my eyes shut, focusing on slowing my pounding heart and hearing past the rush of blood in my ears. Hank's breath came fast, and I could hear the faint thu-thump of his pulse.

Protocol said in a situation like this we had to stick together, even if that meant losing the perp. If the guy had been normal— or rather, if he'd *seemed* normal, we could have made a judgment call and separated, but no Union City officer faced anyone or anything magical alone. Ever. That was a policy only the dumbest or most desperate cops broke. And I was neither dumb nor desperate... not any more.

"Dispatch, two Charlie eleven in pursuit at Washington Park High

School on Glendower," Hank said into his radio, his voice soft. "Requesting backup."

The radio crackled and clicked. "Ten-four two Charlie eleven, backup is on its way."

"Do we honestly think backup will arrive in time to trap him in the school?" I asked, still straining to hear the guy's footsteps.

"No, but at least there'll be more of us in the area to answer a call when he loses it on someone." Hank glanced the other way down the hall, his expression grim. "So which way?"

"It's fifty-fifty. How about—"

The temperature plunged and a scream ripped through the air. My pulse, not even back to normal, shot back into a rapid beat.

"Left," Hank said, passing me to take point.

We hurried down the hall. The guy screamed again, a desperate, wild sound that made the hair on the back of my neck stand up.

A door jerked open, and I could see the guy racing to get back out into the hall. But something yanked him back, pulling the door partially closed after him. Cold stung my hands and cheeks, the guy's fear a sudden, deep-winter freeze.

Oh, shit. This is bad. The memory of running into the alley and finding the archnephilim flashed through my mind's eye. *Please let it be a hallucination making him terrified of whoever is in that room.*

"Second door down," I said. "Someone else is in there."

"I see it." Hank hurried to the entrance, but the crack wasn't big enough to see inside.

The guy screamed again, followed by a low growl, crunching, and the sound of something wet.

Shit shit shit. That really didn't sound human.

I opened my mouth to warn Hank, but he shoved the door open and rushed inside to make way for me in the doorway.

I jerked into the opening to cover him and my thoughts stuttered. Time froze and all I could do was stare at the horror in front of me and wish to God I couldn't see in the dark.

The room was large, with no windows, and filled with massive pieces of equipment. Large pipes ran along the low ceiling and up the walls, snaking deeper into the room and beyond my ability to see in the gloom even with my enhanced vision.

The temperature had snapped back to normal, and I knew our perp was dead or awfully damn close to it. Hank's flashlight shone on him, his throat ripped out, his body limp and held in the arms of a pale, almost translucent-skinned woman. Blood covered her face around her mouth and her lips were drawn back in a feral sneer, revealing vampire fangs. Her eyes were all black, but didn't hold any of the intensity I'd come to recognize as pure vampire. All I could see was animalistic fervor and hunger. Desperate, consuming hunger.

Behind them, piled in the corner between two big pieces of machinery, were more bodies. All were mangled in some way, missing limbs, throats ripped out, faces smashed, and all in various stages of decomposition, the worst at the bottom of the pile. So many bodies. I could count at least two dozen, but with the size of the pile there had to be a lot more.

Bile burned my throat and I couldn't make my mind fully accept the horror. Vampire dens like this, with piles of discarded bodies, only existed in horror movies. They weren't real. Even before supernatural beings had come out of hiding to save themselves from Michael's war, vampires had had laws governing their behavior. Sure, some disobeyed those laws, but vampire society had been swift in controlling them. They were swifter now since humans knew about them, and there were enough interested in becoming blood bunnies that they didn't have to kill anyone to keep their secret.

But this was more than just killing to keep a secret. This was primal, feral, inhuman in ways not even vampires or demons were inhuman.

The temperature plunged, this time with Hank's fear. Blood spurted from our perp's neck with his heart's last desperate beats to keep him alive. The viscous liquid oozed over the woman's arms and splattered to the concrete floor.

She hissed at us, her fangs extended and eyes filled with a wild hunger, and leaped at Hank.

ESSIE

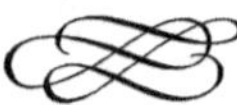

I FIRED TWO SHOTS AT THE VAMPIRE AND THE BULLETS SLAMMED INTO HER chest. Hank dropped his flashlight, drew his Taser, and shot from his hip. The barbs hit her square in the chest, the LEDs on them turning red, indicating Hank had pulled the trigger past the first and second catch to the device's highest voltage, intended to drop the average super.

She screamed but kept going, something I'd never seen before. Even without bullets enspelled to hurt supers, two shots to the chest and that much electricity should have made her at least stumble.

Hank scrambled back, but she grabbed his arm and tossed him deeper into the room. His Taser clattered to the concrete, and he slid across the blood-slicked floor into the pile of rotting bodies. Somehow he'd managed to keep hold of his gun, but without his light, he couldn't clearly see the woman leaping toward him as he scrambled to his feet.

My breath misted, Hank's fear growing stronger. I fired again at the woman, and hit. She wasn't using enhanced vampire speed, but I didn't know if that meant she wasn't using it or if she was too young to have it.

The shot made her jerk around and hiss at me, giving Hank a second to eject the magazine from his Glock and grab the magazine of enspelled ammunition. But a hand reached out from the pile of bodies, seized Hank's ankle, and yanked, toppling him to his hands and knees.

Oh, shit.

The magazine slipped from his fingers and skidded across the floor into the band of light from his discarded flashlight.

Frost swept over the back of my hands and across my cheeks, making my teeth chatter. I aimed to shoot at the hand, but the woman lunged for me, yanking my attention back to her, and my shots hit her, point blank in the chest. She staggered — bully for that, she only had to be shot six times — but kept moving forward. Which meant I had to change my ammunition, because regular bullets sure as hell weren't doing anything.

She slashed at my arm with her claws. They weren't nearly as big as a shifter's claws but I suspected they were just as sharp and I didn't want to find out if that was true.

I jerked back and hit the edge of the doorframe.

The woman seized my arm and yanked me close, her fangs headed for my neck.

I dropped my flashlight and shoved her with everything I had. I wasn't strong enough to get her to let go, but the push did put enough distance between us for me to rush through saying the combat spell and summon a divine light strike.

Light flickered from my palm. Weak and uneven. The power wasn't even close to what I'd been able to summon when fighting the arch-nephilim, and not even as strong as it had been before that whole mess had happened, but it was all I had.

The vampire jerked her fangs back toward my neck, and I slapped my palm against her face, releasing the light strike.

She hissed and wrenched back, letting me go, and I scrambled away. With fingers numb with cold, I ejected the magazine from my sidearm, letting it drop on the floor.

The vampire snarled at me. She had a handprint on her face that only looked as bad as a mild sunburn, not the first- or second-degree burn it should have been. My blast had barely done any damage.

Hank screamed, and the frost on my hands swept over my wrists and up my arms. The front of his vest was shredded and so too was the left shoulder of his uniform, revealing deep, bleeding gashes. He fought with a bulky man wearing tattered clothes and covered from head to toe in blood. The man's eyes were wild and filled with hunger like the woman's, and his fangs were fully extended. They were ten feet away from the pile of bodies, and farther away from Hank's magazine of enspelled ammunition. And Hank didn't have the ability to summon any divine light like I did.

I opened the pouch on my duty belt containing the enspelled ammunition. The woman slashed at me again, her claws slicing into my vest.

Shit. I scrambled back, grabbed the magazine, and a blast of lightning screamed through my right forearm from Gideon's brand and blazed through me.

My muscles seized, contracting tight as if I'd just been hit with a Taser. Panic raced through me, and my thoughts jerked to one thing: Gideon.

Gideon was in trouble. Gideon was hurt. Dying.

Every fiber of my being knew it.

For a week and a half, I'd been pretending I wasn't permanently bonded with the angel. With my increased personal buzz, even with two nicotine patches muting it, I'd been able to pretend the electric hum radiating from Gideon's angelic mating brand wasn't there. Now it was the only thing I could feel, and my soul was screaming.

The white lightening sliced through my buzz, my thoughts, everything. Even the burn of my empathically created frost was gone. There was only him. There'd only ever been him, and I couldn't lose him. I had to go to him, help him, protect him—

Hank screamed again. The male vampire had tackled him to the floor and straddled him. The sleeves of Hank's forearms were shredded, the skin beneath bloody as he fought to keep the vampire's claws from his face and neck. He bucked and twisted, but couldn't get the vampire off of him.

The woman snarled and grabbed the front of my vest with both hands. I fought to move an arm, a finger, anything to defend myself, but Gideon's electricity burned through every command my brain sent to my body, and I couldn't think past the desperate need to go to him. Now.

With a roar, the woman jerked me around and slammed me into the wall with her enhanced vampiric strength. Air burst from my lungs and my head cracked against the cinderblock wall. Darkness swam over my vision, but still my panic was for Gideon, not for Hank or even myself.

Save him. Save him. I had to save him.

The voltage surging through me suddenly stopped and all my muscles went limp. My gun and the magazine with enspelled ammunition clattered to the floor, and my knees gave out.

A rush of exhaustion swept through me as Gideon's brand stole strength from me to save him, and the woman yanked me forward and shoved me to the floor.

Hank howled in pain as the vampire gnawed on his forearm and the woman sank her teeth into my neck. I screamed the spell to summon divine light, praying the force of my summoning would somehow make my blasts stronger.

Somehow, the light hit with enough force to shove her off me, her teeth tearing my skin, and I dove for my sidearm and magazine. I managed to grab and slam the magazine into place, but the woman seized my ankle and jerked me toward her.

I twisted to face her and fired three times — because the bullet in the chamber wasn't enspelled — point blank into her head.

Blue lightning crackled around her body. She roared in pain and collapsed on top of me. I turned my aim to Hank, who was thrashing and screaming. The vampire had pinned him with his body and was now latched to his neck, feeding.

I fired two more shots, hitting the vampire in the chest, not wanting to risk hitting Hank by going for its head. The shots sent blue lightning crackling around the vampire, but the spell didn't drop him. It did, however, make him jerk away from Hank and rush toward me.

Another shot in the knee made him fall, and a final shot in the head — now that he was only a few feet away — killed him.

Hank gurgled and grasped at his neck, blood oozing between his fingers. The frost had thickened to ice on the backs of my hands, and my nose and throat burned with every frozen breath I gasped.

I scrambled to his side. My neck hurt. It was bleeding, but I didn't think I was bleeding out — just being magically drained by the soul mate I didn't want.

I dropped to my knees beside Hank, found the enspelled pip at his collar, and activated the distress beacon. The spell was for life-threatening injuries only, since it was ridiculously expensive. It immediately alerted paramedics to an officer's location, wherever he was. No need to call dispatch and try to explain where in the school we were. The spell would lead the EMTs right to us.

Hank gasped a weak wet breath, his eyes rolled back, and his hands slid away from his throat.

My pulse raced, and I slapped my hands over the ragged gaping wound on his neck, fighting to keep the blood from seeping between my fingers.

"Hold on, Hank. Just hold on. Help is coming." *Please, hold on.*

I shook with fear and adrenaline and jagged spikes of electricity from

Gideon's brand. And my skin hurt from the cold, even though the ice on the back of my hands was now cracking and falling off because Hank was losing consciousness.

I searched the room for signs of any more vampires, but nothing moved. Our flashlights shone with small stark bands across the floor, Hank's into the pile of decomposing bodies, mine under a hulking piece of equipment.

Hank jerked and his eyes opened and focused on me, his gaze desperate and afraid. A blast of cold swept around me and my breath misted, but I didn't care if Hank saw it. All I cared about was that he lived. *Please live.*

And I would God damn not leave his side to help Gideon. No matter what every cell in my body was screaming.

"I've got you. Just hold on."

He gasped another wet breath. His heart pounded, ragged beats pumping his blood through my fingers. *God, why couldn't healing magic be contained in a spell?* But for whatever reason, it didn't work that way. Spells could be created that enhanced immune systems, like the drug Divifend, or sped up healing for pulled muscles or the common cold, but no matter how hard every spellcaster tried, the innate magical ability to heal a life-threatening injury couldn't be replicated with a spell.

His body jerked again and his ragged pulse started to slow.

I fought back a sob. Hank and I hadn't been friends, but he'd been a decent partner and didn't deserve this.

Finally I heard footsteps racing toward us and saw beams of light dancing in the hall.

"In here," I gasped out, and an EMT team rushed into the room.

They took over, and I staggered back to the wall beside the door and sat. Gideon's jagged electricity had eased off a bit, and I couldn't tell any more if the dizzy exhaustion that numbed me came from him siphoning strength from me, shock, or blood loss.

I stuck my hands under my armpits to get them to warm up, my teeth chattering, my shivering spiking agony through my neck. I could only pray the EMTs would mistake it for shock and not actual cold.

And perhaps it was both. I'd had another horrible encounter in the world of the supernatural and another partner had been seriously injured. While there wasn't any chance he'd become a vampire, not even the one-in-a-million chance like there was with lycanthropy — the vampire had to perform a ritual to sire another vampire, not just bite someone — that didn't mean Hank's life wasn't in danger. *God, please don't let him die.*

Logically I knew this time wasn't my fault. I hadn't run headlong into this situation because I was naive. But that didn't ease the guilt churning inside me.

Fellow officer Brant Keels and his rookie — I still hadn't learned the guy's name — arrived, took one look at the scene, and the rookie promptly threw up in the hall. They called in the detectives, something I should have done the moment the EMTs took over. But it felt like I was thinking in slow motion and under water, every thought dragging and churning. Which wasn't like me at all. It had to be an effect of Gideon's brand draining me.

Hank was rushed away and another set of EMTs arrived. The bulky woman with a buzz cut checked out the dead zip addict, while the man, just as bulky but with a less severe haircut, knelt beside me and checked out my neck.

"You should probably get stitches, and you're going to have a nasty scar, but you must have a horseshoe up your ass," he said, his voice soft, calm, doing nothing to clear my muddled thoughts. "That vamp just missed your artery." He pressed a wad of gauze to my neck. "Hold this."

I obeyed.

"Any other injuries?" He shone a penlight in my eyes, making me wince.

"I don't think so." The back of my head hurt, but I didn't think I'd hit it as hard as I had two weeks ago when facing off with the arch-nephilim... although now that I thought about it, the blow could be another reason for my muddled thoughts.

"We should get you to the hospital anyway, just to check you out."

"Can that wait until we talk with her?" a firm feminine voice asked.

A set of practical shoes and gray slacks stepped into sight. I followed the legs up to Detective Abby McLellan's narrow face. Her already pale complexion was white, making the freckles dusting her cheeks and nose stand out.

"Are you up for answering questions, Essie?" she asked, crouching beside the EMT and brushing her strawberry blonde bangs across her forehead.

I glanced at the EMT. "Am I?"

"You're not emergent, so you should be fine," he said. "Get her to the hospital if anything changes, detective." He rummaged in his bag, pulled out a roll of thick medical tape, and taped the gauze to the side of my neck.

"Jeez, Shaw," Detective Tim Snyder, Abby's partner, said as he strode up to us. His rich complexion hadn't paled, but the hard line of his jaw said he was as shocked by the scene as Abby. "You have the shittiest luck."

"Funny. The EMT was pretty impressed with my luck," I said.

"Sure, you can survive some serious shit." He rolled his eyes at me. "But that shit keeps finding you. I'm glad I'm not your partner."

Abby shot him a dark look, and he shrugged and walked over to the pile of decomposing bodies.

"Do you want to give your statement now and then again when the agents of the Joined Parliament arrive, or wait and only have to do it once?" Abby asked.

And by agents of the Joined Parliament, she meant Gideon and his team, since they were the only agents stationed in Union City.

I leaned my head back against the cool cinderblock wall, agony slicing through my neck, and groaned. A part of me thrilled at the idea of seeing Marcus again... and Jacob... and Gideon... and jeez, Kol, too. The rest of me wanted to cry that no matter what I did, how good I was, fate just kept throwing me back into the supernatural world. Not to mention Marcus was going to read me the riot act — most likely yell it at me — about being in dangerous situations, and I wasn't sure I was up for the sweltering temperature that came with that.

Of course, if they showed up, then I could vent my frustration on Gideon for doing something equally stupid. Because he had to have done something stupid to get so seriously hurt. If it hadn't been for him, I might have gotten through the incident without a scratch and Hank might not have had his throat ripped open.

Regardless, I was going to have to face them, so I might as well wait for them to arrive to give my statement. No point in giving it to Abby and then again to the guys. That, and once Gideon and the team arrived, the case would no longer be Abby and Tim's.

Hank and I had been attacked by vampires and the pile of bodies strongly indicated we weren't their first victims. That meant this was a Joined Parliament case, and I was pretty sure both Abby and Tim would be happy to hand it over. This wasn't like the Feds coming in and taking over. Union City's cops weren't equipped to handle powerful supernatural criminals, and a major supernatural case was usually deadly for human officers. Case in point.

"I'll wait," I said, feeling even more exhausted at the thought. "They're going to take this mess off your hands anyway."

Abby glanced at the pile of bodies. "And I couldn't be happier about that."

I sat against the wall watching the detectives and officers come and go, my head still whirling and my neck throbbing in agony. No one came to tell me to move, and I didn't want to risk standing and passing out. I really didn't want to face the guys from a hospital bed this time, and if I collapsed, I was sure I'd be rushed away.

The jagged electricity in Gideon's brand eased completely, but the sense of bone-deep exhaustion dragging at my thoughts remained. At least that muted the stomach-churning temperature fluctuations coming from the strong mix of emotions and the increased number of people in the room.

Summer, the angel who handled forensics at the Joined Parliament Operations Building, arrived with another guy who looked familiar. I was pretty sure I'd seen him while I'd been at Operations, but I couldn't remember his name.

They started working the scene, looking at the zip addict and the two vampires first. A little while later, the Joined Parliament Medical Examiner showed up. I recognized both guys from the motel where the arch-nephilim had left me a message written in his victim's blood.

They waited until Summer released the bodies then worked on loading them into body bags and taking them away.

After a bit, the Medical Examiner guys returned, along with a contingent of officers to help deal with the pile of bodies.

The temperature fluctuations strengthened — because the number of people in my immediate vicinity had increased again — and I tried not to look like I was going to throw up like the rookie had.

The new officers stood across the room from me, waiting for Summer to say she was done taking pictures and samples and whatever else she needed from the pile as she worked it from the top down. I recognized all of them. It made sense that the extra hands would come from my precinct. And every one of them shot me dark looks.

Some hid it better than others, but once again I was the cop who'd endangered her partner. Even the cops who hadn't been part of the precinct when the incident with Marcus had happened and hadn't looked at me like that before looked at me like that now. The rumors had been confirmed. I was a deadly incident waiting to happen for anyone who worked with me. It didn't matter that Hank and I had worked together safely for four and a half years. This was my second strike and the captain was going to be hard pressed to find someone happy about being partnered with me.

Which left me with what?

Angry and sad at myself for ending up in situations like this again.

Sure, I'd been living just fine without a lot of close friends, but I hadn't been completely ostracized. I'd still been able to go out and have beers with the handful of officers who'd been warming up to me.

Yeah, that wasn't happening any more.

I hated to think it, but perhaps it was time I put in for a transfer. I wouldn't be able to leave town without drawing Gideon's attention, since the mating brand would make him aware of my location wherever I was, but maybe I wouldn't be a pariah at a different precinct.

The idea of giving up stung. But knowing when to retreat wasn't giving up. This was a fight I couldn't win no matter how much I wanted to keep fighting. Better to retreat and regroup than risk making the situation worse.

The gut-churning temperature fluctuations made bile burn the back of my throat, and I feared if I stayed in the room much longer I would throw up.

Using the wall to keep my balance, I struggled to stand. A wave of dizziness washed over me, hints of darkness creeping over the edges of my vision, and the throbbing in my neck turned to stabbing pain.

God damn Gideon and his brand.

I blinked the darkness back, and walked — trying not to look like I was staggering — to the door.

Abby noticed and hurried to my side as I stepped into the hall. "I'm sure the JP agents will be here soon."

Given how seriously Gideon must have been injured for the brand to pull so much strength from me, I wasn't so sure. And I wasn't at all sure how I felt about that. "I'm sure they will."

"Should I tell them to meet us at the hospital?"

"I just need some fresh air." And to get away from all those emotions.

I headed for the stairs, Abby at my side, her flashlight lighting the way. The temperature didn't even out until I was back in the gym. I didn't know if that was a testament to the strength of my empathy or the strength of all those emotions.

A flicker of electricity danced over Gideon's brand, making my heart lurch that he was in danger again, but this time strength didn't drain from me. Instead, a soft heat warmed my arm and seeped across my chest, muting everything, my empathy, my exhaustion, even my God damned buzz.

We stepped out the side door, and I leaned against the rough brick wall, unable to remain standing without help.

Abby stood beside me, her gaze on the sliver of moon peeking out from behind ominous clouds, her expression grim. "I don't like what that room is saying."

A hint of cold — her fear — shivered across my skin. "I don't either."

The soft heat in my arm grew and the ache in my chest, my yearning for a man— an angel I didn't really know, swelled fully, replacing my buzz that was always nipping under my skin.

"All those bodies?" Abby shivered and the temperature dropped a few degrees more. "The Joined Parliament claimed our vampire horror movies were pure fiction, but—"

"That was definitely a horror show." The yearning and heat increased, bleeding through Abby's fear.

Gideon was close and coming closer. A part of me thrilled at that, but the rest was pissed. And I needed to focus on pissed or I was going to lose my mind. Hank was fighting for his life because I'd been frozen by Gideon's brand.

Abby slid her gaze to mine, her brown eyes dark in the dim moon-light. "Do you think this is an anomaly or something the Joined Parliament has kept hidden from us?"

"Why don't you ask their agents?"

Abby frowned and a large gray SUV, the kind driven by the JP team, came around the corner. It pulled onto the curb and parked, half on the sidewalk, behind a cruiser.

The front passenger door opened, and Gideon got out.

My pulse stalled. All of me stalled and zeroed in on him, his strong, clean-shaven jaw, short blond hair, muscular shoulders and chest, narrow waist, and pale eyes. God, those eyes. They glowed with light, giving away his angelic nature, and I knew they were blue. The perfect blue of a cloudless summer sky. His soul called to me, and his brand heated my skin. All of me hungered for him, and I hated myself for that.

His gaze rose and locked with mine and even with the distance between us, I was falling into those pale depths and didn't care.

ESSIE

She mustn't have been on site at the archnephilim's attack two weeks ago when Gideon had shown up or she would have already known the head of Union City's JP team was an angel. And while Summer, who was already at the crime scene, was also an angel, she didn't have the same magnetic draw Gideon had.

"Wait until the incubus gets out," I said, not wanting to talk about Gideon.

Abby's eyebrows shot up. "There's an incubus, too?"

Marcus got out from the driver's seat and the yearning in my chest turned into a throbbing ache. He was just as stunning as Gideon, but where the angel was a perfect clean-cut poster boy, Marcus was dark and brooding with a swarthy complexion and perpetual five o'clock shadow that made him look wild and dangerous.

His gaze, the night stealing all the warmth from his green eyes, jumped to me as well, and the snap of sizzling attraction between us stole my breath.

It had always been like that, ever since the moment we'd first met in the squad room and I'd been assigned to be his partner.

I hadn't known until a few weeks ago just how combustible the desire between us was. And a few days after that, just like the first time we'd been partners, he'd left without saying goodbye, leaving me to return home to my normal human life empty and cold.

It had been for my own good.

Honestly.

I just needed to figure out how to believe that.

Except in the time since I'd left Operations, I hadn't been able to convince myself of that.

His expression hardened, and he said something. Gideon gave a tight nod, and Marcus stormed away, heading around the side of the school, making me ache with the knowledge that he didn't even want to talk to me. He hadn't even gotten close enough for me to pick up a hint of his emotions.

The rear passenger door opened, Jacob climbed out, and all thoughts of Marcus vanished. My attention snapped to the vampire, completely out of my control, and the compulsion of his claim made me shift forward. I needed to go to him, please him, have him command me. I wasn't complete until he commanded me to do something, anything.

Crap. I'd hoped with time and distance the need to have him tell me what to do would have faded.

I gritted my teeth and forced myself to stay put. Jacob's dark gaze — his was actually black — held me captive, and his frown made my soul weep. He wasn't happy. He needed to be happy. The intensity in his eyes that indicated he was a vampire — something I'd seen him hide better than what he was doing now — filled the air between us with an energy that was on the verge of physically manifesting.

Out of the corner of my eye, I saw Abby shift, icy fear flickering over me. Her hand dipped to the Glock at her hip then her posture suddenly relaxed, and Kol stepped into my line of sight.

My thoughts stuttered as he rushed up to me — I hadn't even seen him get out of the SUV.

"Essie, are you all right? You're covered in blood." Kol's body blocked Jacob from view, releasing me from the pull of the claim — at least it had weakened enough that him being partially out of sight freed me, and I didn't strain to see past Kol to find Jacob.

And really, it was easy to stay focused on the incubus. He was drop-dead gorgeous. All the guys were hot, but Kol always stole my breath when I looked at him — which I supposed was part and parcel for a demon who survived on sexual energy. His T-shirt was tight and left nothing to the imagination, revealing perfectly sculpted muscles, and he wore blue jeans ripped at one thigh that I didn't doubt showed off his amazing ass... if only he'd just stand up and turn around.

He gingerly took my blood-covered hands, sending heated desire sweeping up my arms as he examined them. His black hair veiled his eyes, and when he lifted his gaze to meet mine, a hint of hellfire simmering with sexual desire burned within their dark orbs. If it hadn't been for that, and the small horns poking out of hair that perpetually looked like he'd just woken from the most amazing sex, he'd have looked like a human. A heart-stopping twenty-something who exuded wicked sexual grace that made me think of hot nights and even hotter sex.

Abby stared at him with blatant desire, a blush bright against her pale cheeks, obvious even in the dim streetlight. I couldn't blame her. Even having worked with him, he was still breathtaking.

"Your vest is ripped," Kol said. "How bad is your neck?"

"Officer Shaw is fine," Gideon said, his voice icy and hard.

"This time," I mumbled, the words slipping out.

Kol's eyes narrowed, close enough to hear me, but I shot a glance at Abby, hoping Kol would understand the look. I didn't want this to be discussed, not while she was near. I didn't want her to know I was permanently bound to Gideon or that I had other connections with the team. I didn't want anyone to know, because then I'd have to accept the truth of my situation: that no matter how much safer it was for me to have nothing to do with the supernatural, it had pulled me in again.

Jacob stepped up beside Gideon, almost a head taller than him and twice as wide with his massive, muscular chest. With his black calf-length duster, one hand resting on his hip and the other on the grip of his Beretta, he looked every bit the part of a Wild West gunslinger. Given that he was older than a hundred, he very well could have been a gunslinger. His frown had deepened and his expression was tight with worry... or strain? I wasn't quite sure which.

Abby's gaze flickered back to Jacob, her fear cold on my skin. More sensual heat radiated from Kol's hands and slid up my arms, making me ache with desire, but I got the sense his enthrallment wasn't intended for me.

And just as I thought that, Abby's fear warmed and her attention turned back to Kol.

"Abby McLellan," she said, holding out her hand to Kol, her voice breathy. "Detective."

Gideon took her hand instead and gave it a firm shake. "Your precinct called in a vampire attack."

She shuddered. "More like a horror show."

"And Officer Shaw's involvement?" Gideon didn't even glance at me, which stung more than I wanted it to.

"Do you have time for Officer Shaw's statement?" Abby asked, pulling a notebook from her pocket.

"The JP M.E. and forensics are already on site." Gideon now turned a frosty glare at me, not even a hint of warmth in his eyes. Yeah, he wanted to be permanently bound to me for the rest of his life as much as I did to him. Of course, I couldn't blame him. He was in love with someone else and had just buried her, or whatever it was angels did with their dead.

His emotions were completely locked down so I wasn't getting a sense of anything from him, but that was probably a good thing. It meant I wouldn't be swamped with uncomfortable temperature changes from him or surrounded by mist from his grief for Zella's passing.

"Go ahead," he said to me.

I opened my mouth to speak—

Except I didn't. The thought didn't reach my body, because the command hadn't come from Jacob.

Jeez. I tried to fight through the compulsion to say anything, even just make a sound, but nothing came out, and all I managed to do was set off more agony in my neck with my straining.

Gideon's eyes narrowed. "Well, officer?"

"Your statement," Jacob said, his voice a low rumble, and the compulsion released me. Relief and joy and need swelled through me. And I hated a part of myself for having that reaction.

I gave a detailed statement, which included my observation that the female vampire hadn't been using enhanced speed, that a Taser at its highest setting and regular ammunition hadn't even made her stumble. The only thing I left out were the affects of Gideon's brand. That didn't need to go in anyone's report. As much as I was pissed that the brand had endangered my life and Hank's — and I really wanted to yell at Gideon for that — I had to accept that he had no control over it. Just like I didn't. And I couldn't tell him to stop getting hurt. His job was more dangerous than mine. Getting hurt was an inevitability in his line of work. I just had no idea how I was going to handle it if his job kept endangering me.

Which was just great. So much for venting all my frustrations on him.

Although if he kept up the frozen shoulder and the brand kept making me feel like my soul was breaking every time he talked to me in that icy tone, I might just snap anyway.

Thankfully Jacob didn't ask me if that was everything, because then I would've had to mention getting shocked by Gideon's brand and being unable to stop the vampire from biting me.

Abby was back to looking too pale and the guys were grim.

"So it's your case, right?" Abby asked, her voice shaky, her fear again cold on my skin.

"Without a doubt." But Gideon didn't sound happy about that. Which I couldn't blame him for, either. A pile of bodies and two crazed vampires looked bad for the supernatural community.

"Good." Abby shoved her notebook back into her pocket. "If you're done with Officer Shaw, I need to take her to the hospital to get stitches."

The muscles in Gideon's jaw tightened. "I'm done with her," he said, his tone so cold it made my throat tight.

Another bit of my soul fractured, and I couldn't help but feel there was more to his words than just a dismissal from this conversation.

I'd been told Marcus had demanded Gideon release me, let me return to my normal human life with no further involvement with the supernatural world. Now I was sure Gideon would have done that without Marcus's demand. The angelic mating brand wasn't a beautiful destined thing when you were stuck with someone you didn't love, and I was just a reminder to Gideon that his real love was dead. Not to mention, as far as he knew, I was a mostly powerless human, a detriment to any partnership.

And if he ever learned the truth, it would be even worse.

Abby stepped toward the street, but I didn't follow, Jacob's claim keeping me where I was even though I wanted to get the hell away from there and Gideon.

"Essie?" Abby asked.

The light from Gideon's eyes billowed. "Jacob, get her out of here."

Jacob shifted toward me. "Essie—"

My pulse leaped, and my essence zeroed in on him. *Give me an order. Tell me to do something. Anything.*

Please.

Release me from your claim.

But a vampire's claim didn't work that way. If he didn't bite me again, eventually his essence would work its way out of mine, but until then I was his to command whether either of us wanted that or not.

A silver sedan pulled onto the sidewalk behind the JP SUV, drawing everyone's attention, and an average-looking man in all respects, height and weight, with brown hair and brown eyes got out. Chief of Police Ken Fields.

I'd only met him once before and that had been at my graduation from the academy, but given that this was the second serious super incident in just over two weeks, it wasn't a surprise that he'd come to the scene himself to put whatever pressure he could on the JP agents to deal with this quickly and quietly.

Not that Gideon didn't already know the serious nature of this situation. Relations between humans and supernatural beings were still tentative, and while most humans were happy to abide by the law and let the supers be, many of them did that because the supers stuck to their Quarter and didn't mix with the human population.

"Done with the scene already?" Chief Fields asked as he marched toward us.

Abby straightened as the chief approached and my insides squirmed, desperate for Jacob to finish his command since there was also a chance the chief would want to have words with me for being involved in both of the recent supernatural incidents.

"We just arrived," Gideon said.

"You were called over two hours ago." Fields crossed his arms. "There's more to this city than the Quarter."

"And there's more supernatural crime than whatever your officers stumble across." The chill in Gideon's expression deepened — I hadn't thought it was possible for it to get any colder — but a hint of heat, which had to be anger, also started to dance through the air around me.

"Some are questioning if you have the safety of the human population in mind," Fields said. "Your JP team doesn't have a human agent and therefore doesn't have a human perspective."

The heat from the anger — best guess it came from Gideon — increased. "We don't deal with human perps."

"But you do deal with human civilians."

"What are you getting at, Chief?" Jacob asked.

"The LA news just ran an exposé on JP teams and their lack of human consideration. That's not the kind of press I or the mayor want for Union City. You may have managed to keep most of the details quiet from the case two weeks ago, but details still slipped out." Fields met Gideon's glare head on. "Namely the damage done to an apartment building and all the 911 calls that night when we received the report about a fight among supernatural beings."

"That couldn't be helped," Gideon said.

"I don't doubt that," Fields said. "But that's not the point. Policing isn't just about catching the bad guy any more. It's also about optics. Showing up to a crime scene two hours later doesn't look good. Destroying an apartment with civilian neighbors still in the other units isn't good, either. It looks like supers are taking over without any consideration to humans."

"I don't know how we could make it more obvious that we're protecting humans from supernatural perps," Gideon said.

"The mayor has told me to assign a human member to your team and I heartily agree."

Sweat trickled between my breasts and I tried not to squirm. *Come on, Jacob, just tell me to leave.* If Gideon and the chief wanted to go at it, fine, but I didn't have to be standing there, aching for Gideon and straining for Jacob, while they did.

"You can't just assign someone," Gideon said. "My team doesn't fall under your jurisdiction or the mayor's."

"The trial period for a human agent has already been approved by the Joined Parliament. I'm sure you'll receive notification soon," Fields said.

Gideon's eyes narrowed and the heat around me billowed, making my face flush as if I'd gone out running in August at noon. "Our work is dangerous, even for a super. I can't guarantee your officer's safety."

"I'm aware of that." Field's attention slid to me. "Officer Shaw has taken advanced combat training for supers."

My pulse stalled. Oh, shit. He was going to assign me to Gideon's team, immersing me in the supernatural world again, and worse, forcing me to spend time with Gideon.

"Sir, I—"

"And she has more experience with serious crimes by supers than any other officer," Field said, cutting me off.

I doubted I actually had more experience than the senior officers.

"I can't—" I could barely stand five minutes with the yearning from the mating brand and Gideon's icy demeanor. I couldn't work with him. Not even for one case.

"Congratulations on your new assignment." Fields turned to Gideon. "She's all yours, agent. Now, Detective McLellan, show me this scene."

"I won't accept Shaw on my team," Gideon said, his words stinging a part of me I desperately wanted to ignore.

I didn't want to be on his team, either. In fact, I was thrilled he was fighting to keep me off the team. His rejection shouldn't have bothered me.

"You don't have a choice. The mayor wants a human seen working in the field with your team, and I don't want to sacrifice any of my other officers."

Jeez, he wasn't even trying to keep his true intentions a secret.

Gideon's back straightened, and the temperature turned sweltering. Light flared from his eyes, and Jacob cleared his throat.

The light snapped back to normal and so did the temperature, as if Gideon had been reminded to control himself, something I'd never thought an angel would ever need.

"Feel free to complain to the Joined Parliament. I'm sure training more human agents will be in the works soon." Fields headed to the doorway into the school. "Remember, the mayor wants her seen working in the field with you. Now, show me the crime scene, Detective McLellan."

Abby shot me a worried glance but hurried after the chief.

"Just great," Gideon growled and marched after them as well.

The ache for him swelled as he left and so too did the buzz in my body, nipping under my skin almost at pre-nicotine levels. At least the temperature dropped back to normal, but the sweat slicking me from Gideon's anger made me shiver even though it wasn't close to being cold out.

"Well, that's a development," Kol said, his eyes wide with surprise. "Not it. No way am I telling Marcus the news."

ESSIE

I HUGGED MYSELF TO WARD OFF THE CHILL FROM MY SWEAT, NOT CARING IF it made me look weak. I didn't need to be strong in front of Kol or Jacob, just Gideon and Marcus. My mind whirled, but there wasn't a way out of this situation. At least not one that let me keep my job. If my new assignment had come from my captain, I might have been able to ask for a transfer, but the order had come from the chief. There wasn't anyone higher in the ranks to go to.

If I wanted out, I had to quit.

That thought stung. All I'd ever wanted to be was a cop. A life of running from an unjust danger had only strengthened my desire to help those who couldn't help themselves. If I wasn't a cop, then who was I? I had to be more than just a nephilim, more than the nightmare monster everyone believed nephilim to be. I—

I drew in a steadying breath and squared my shoulders. I needed to not make any rash decisions, not after the night I'd had and with Gideon's brand making me exhausted.

I glanced at my watch. 2:30 a.m. "My shift is almost done. Jacob, please tell me to go to the hospital to get stitches and check in on my partner— *former* partner." I fought to keep my gaze down and not meet his eyes. If I did, my request would change to something personal and desperate. *Take me. Command me. Let me ease the worry I see in your eyes.*

How the hell was I going to be a productive member of the team if I couldn't do anything without Jacob's say so? But then the chief didn't know about any of my supernatural *conditions* and that wasn't the point.

"I can take you to Amiah and then we can check in on your partner," Kol said.

The memory of the first time Amiah had healed me flashed through my mind. It had been painful, like an electric current scorching through me, because she knew I was responsible for turning Marcus into a werewolf and she had — still had? — a thing for Marcus. I didn't know if she'd forgiven me or if she'd be back to being angry at me because I was now stuck on the team, recklessly endangering the guys again.

"The regular human hospital will do." I'd already hit my quota of angelic searing agony for the day. I didn't want a repeat even if it meant I'd have a scar.

Come on. Let me go. Please. Don't fight me on this.

"All right," Jacob said, the rumble of his voice sliding over me, drawing my attention against my will back up to his face. The strain around his eyes twisted his claim tighter within me. "If this is what I think it is, we're working through the night—" He glanced at the moon, partially hidden behind the clouds. "Or rather morning. Kol, take her to get stitches, then cleaned up, and then to Operations. Make it quick. Gideon will want to get on this, fast."

My soul thrilled at the order. I needed to go now. It would make him happy. It would—

I clenched my jaw. "Can I check on my partner?" I asked between gritted teeth.

The strain around Jacob's eyes tightened. "Yes," he said, the word clipped, then he headed into the school, leaving me with Kol, the only member of the team I wasn't somehow bound to — and yes, what I had with Marcus was as strong— no, stronger than what I had with Gideon and Jacob.

"Is he all right?" I'd been given my orders so I couldn't follow him inside even if a part of me wanted to, but something wasn't right with Jacob. I couldn't put it into words. I just knew it with a knowing that was more certain than anything I sensed from Gideon through the brand.

"It's been a rough night." Kol pulled out his phone and sent a text. "Gideon was seriously injured tonight."

"I know."

"How—?" His gaze jumped to my right forearm, where Gideon's brand lay underneath the sleeve of my uniform. "The brand, of course."

His eyes widened. "Oh, jeez. No wonder you look like shit. The brand probably used your strength to stabilize him."

"Wow, way to make a girl feel pretty."

The expression in his eyes turned to horror. "No, I didn't mean— I— You look... fine? Hurt but fine?"

I rolled my eyes at him and winced as I started to shake my head, sending pain slicing into my neck. "Aren't you supposed to be the slick charmer?"

"Women don't usually tease me. Well, not in *that* way." A hint of hellfire flickered in his eyes.

Yeah, I imagined the teasing was a lot less innocent.

His expression turned somber. "I know Gideon said you were fine, but you really don't look fine."

"I hurt and I ache and I want to scream at the fact that two weeks later I still need Jacob's permission to do anything short of breathing." And now I had to work with the source of most of that pain. Unless I left the force. Which was the worse choice ever. "And my boss thinks I'm expendable. How was your night?"

"We raided a zip lab that had more security than we initially saw when we scouted, and Gideon took two in the gut just under his vest and one in the leg, severing his femoral artery."

No wonder the brand had gone crazy. Even with his angelic healing — which was better than a human's but not nearly as good as a vampire's or an incubus's — he wouldn't have been able to heal that. "Well, then, looks like it was a shitty night all around."

"You sure I can't convince you to go to Amiah?"

The claim twisted in my chest. Even if I wanted to risk her anger, I couldn't. "Jacob said stitches."

Another chunky medium gray SUV drove onto the street and stopped on the road across from us, not bothering to pull over.

"Then let's get you some stitches," Kol said, heading to the SUV.

An angel I also recognized from my brief stay at Operations got out, leaving the vehicle running.

"That was fast," Kol said.

"Summer had called for another set of hands, so I was already on my way." The guy pulled out a packed duffle bag from the back seat. "I'll grab a ride back with Summer, so it's all yours."

Kol got in behind the wheel and I settled into the front passenger seat. The buzz was getting stronger, but it was also nearing the eight-hour mark, when I needed to replace my nicotine patches. At least the exhaustion from Gideon's brand wasn't getting any worse.

We drove to the hospital, and Kol parked in an emergency-only short-term parking spot and flipped down the front visor, showing the SUV's JP credentials. But he hesitated before getting out of the vehicle.

"You should probably go in first," he said. "By yourself. Even if I do everything I can to suppress my nature, I tend to be... distracting."

"You were there the last time I was brought into emergency." A shiver of desire tickled along my spine and heated into embarrassment. He'd been there when I'd been on the verge of unconsciousness, in writhing agony, and the doctors had stripped me of all my clothes. Every last piece.

"You were in serious condition then. That's enough to make any doctor or nurse ignore me." He flashed me a wicked smile that made my skin heat, even though I suspected the smile was supposed to be encouraging and not sexual. "You're in much better shape this time."

Thank God for that. And while I hoped there wouldn't be a next time, the only way to guarantee that would be to leave my job. Which was looking like the only way out of this situation.

I bit back a sigh. "Are you going to wait in the SUV?"

"No, I'll give you a few minutes then join you." He frowned and for a second he looked uncertain of himself, the expression strange on the face of someone who exuded such sexual confidence. "Unless you don't want the company."

"I'd rather have the company while a doctor repeatedly pokes my neck with a needle."

"I'm sure he'll numb your skin first."

Not the point. "It's been a shitty night. Keep me company, Kol." Help me forget how much my heart hurts.

His smile brightened, sending a flood of sensual warmth through me. "See you in a few, then."

I got out of the SUV and walked through the emergency department's sliding doors. A nurse took one look at the uniform, the big piece of gauze taped to my neck, and all the blood covering me — it caked my hands and sleeves almost to my elbows, my shoulder and over my chest from the neck wound, and my knees — and hurried me to a bed.

Kol soon followed, sliding in the chair beside the bed with a sensual boneless grace, and shortly after, a doctor arrived.

"I'm doctor Ing," he said, sliding the privacy curtain aside to enter with his attention on a tablet, probably with my history already pulled up. "Officer Shaw—?" His gaze lifted and landed on me and my bloody mess. "The paramedic report says it's just your neck."

"Only about a quarter of this is mine."

"That's still a lot." He set the tablet on a nearby trolley and pulled on a pair of latex gloves. He was handsome in a very human, very comforting way, with warm eyes and short black hair. I pegged him at about my age, maybe a little older into his mid-thirties, and while the blood had made him pause, it hadn't been in horror, more in a professional assessment. "Are you light headed?"

I was, but not enough that I was going to tell him and risk getting held in the hospital for observation.

Although that at least would buy me some time to figure out what the hell I was going to do about my new assignment to Gideon's team.

The claim twisted tight in my chest, and I fought to keep my expression the same.

Jacob had said stitches, cleaned up, and then go to Operations. Quickly. A stay in the hospital wasn't quick.

"I'm good," I lied. "Nothing some stitches and a good sleep won't fix."

Ing's gaze jumped to Kol and back to me. "So long as you actually sleep."

Kol rolled his eyes and pulled out his identification. "JP agent assigned to Officer Shaw's case. How about we focus on those stitches."

Ing didn't look like he fully believed Kol, and I wondered if the incubus got that a lot. Was he always being judged when he was with a woman? God, I couldn't imagine trying to go on an innocent date with someone and having to deal with those assuming looks.

Of course, did an incubus ever go on an innocent date? Did Kol? How did someone who survived on sexual energy manage a relationship that was more than just sex?

"Let's get your shoulder out of your uniform so I can get a proper look," Ing said.

I undid the first button of my uniform and Kol shifted, a hint of hellfire flickering in his eyes. "I should wait outside."

"I'd rather have your company," I said, not wanting to be alone with my thoughts. Gideon and Marcus and Jacob were all problems I'd eventually have to deal with, but I didn't know how, and that scared me. Not to mention I couldn't think of a way out of this situation without losing my job. Besides, it wasn't as if Kol hadn't already seen me naked and at most I was barely going to show my bra. "Please. Distract me."

The hellfire dimmed in his eyes, replaced with worry, as if he could sense the whirl of emotions within me. "What do you want to talk about?"

"Did you manage to shut down the zip lab?" I undid the next button and Kol turned his back to me.

"Only in the sense that I'm sure the moment we dragged Gideon back to Operations, they packed up and moved locations."

"Just great. I'm getting tired of dealing with zip addicts." I shrugged my shoulder out of my uniform, clenching my jaw against the movement's pain.

"Me, too," Ing said, peeling the gauze from my neck, taking a quick peek, and pressing it back in place. "Lie down on your side."

I took off my duty belt and handed it to Kol, who took it without looking at me, then I eased back onto the bed. Ing grabbed a needle, a vial of something, and a suture kit from a drawer, set them on the trolley, and pulled it to my bedside.

"And it's not just the addicts we get in here. It's their victims, because the damn drug makes them violent and strong." Ing removed the gauze and numbed my neck.

"It's worse with supers," Kol said. "Zip can also enhance their strength and speed. Even with supers who have beyond-human abilities. Their reaction is almost always violent and the odds that they'll OD is higher."

"I wouldn't have thought supers would be interested in zip," I said.

Kol shrugged, his back still turned to me. "A high is a high."

Jeez, a human with enhanced abilities in the throes of a terrifying hallucination was hard enough to handle. I couldn't imagine trying to deal with a super thinking he was being attacked from all sides. Would I have to deal with that now that I was on Gideon's team?

Only if I stayed on the force.

Which if I was smart, I wouldn't.

My throat tightened at that thought. *Damn, think of something else. Anything else.*

But I couldn't make my mind think past it. "Will there be a lot of cases that are that dangerous?"

Kol shifted and glanced at me, the hellfire still burning, tiny pinpricks in his eyes. "Gideon made a promise. He doesn't break his promises. He'll find a way to get you off the team back to your normal life."

Except he'd broken a promise before. He'd said he'd be able to protect me from the archnephilim, before he'd known we were up against an archnephilim and he'd realized he wouldn't be able to.

"And until then, we've all got your back." He flashed a smile and sensual heat warmed my chest.

"Did you have her back tonight?" Ing asked.

"If we'd been there tonight, you wouldn't be stitching her up," Kol said, his tone fiercely protective, reminding me of Marcus, and an intensity filled his eyes, changing the hint of hunger to something else, something I couldn't quite recognize. Then the intensity vanished and he flashed another heart-pounding smile before turning his gaze away from me. "Are you done?"

I heard the snip of scissors, and Ing taped a fresh piece of gauze to the side of my neck. "You're free to go. Get this filled at the pharmacy." He peeled off his latex gloves, scrawled a prescription for painkillers and antibiotics on his pad, and handed it to me. "Don't get your stitches wet for twenty-four hours and make an appointment with your GP to have them removed in about a week."

I sat up and rebuttoned my shirt.

"Your file says this is your second super attack in just over two weeks," Ing said as he typed something into the tablet. "I hope it's your last."

"Me, too." But with my luck, I doubted it. "Can you tell me where my partner, Officer Hank Dacosta, is?"

Ing tapped on the tablet a few times. "He's still in surgery."

"Do you want to wait?" Kol asked, his gaze once again averted.

"Yes." But as soon as I said it, Jacob's claim twisted. There'd been nothing in his instructions about sticking around to ensure Hank got through surgery, only that I could check on him. God damn it. "But I need to get to Operations."

"We can wait."

"The waiting area for surgery is on the second floor, straight down that hall," Ing said, opening the curtain and pointing down the hall before he headed in the opposite direction to the nurse's stations.

"I can't wait. Jacob's command won't let me." I slid off the bed, too tired to generate any real anger at that. "Let's just go."

"Sure." He handed me back my duty belt.

We filled the prescription, left the hospital, and drove to my apartment, which sat in the top corner of a four-story walkup on a street of four-story walkups. When I'd returned home after being unconscious at the Joined Parliament Operations Building for five days, I'd found my place as good as new. Better than new, actually. The hole in the wall between my tiny bedroom and my slightly larger living room had been patched and all the walls were covered in a fresh coat of paint. And the skylight in the ceiling above my living room had been replaced, and so too had the bedroom window, where the archnephilim had crashed through to attack. Any furniture that had been broken during the fight had also been replaced and this was the first time I'd ever had a couch, TV, or bed that wasn't secondhand.

Because of the stitches, I couldn't take a shower like I desperately wanted, but I could certainly get out of my clothes — now tacky, and in places crunchy, with dried blood — and wipe most of the gore off.

Kol hadn't said anything on the ride over, and I wasn't sure what he was thinking. I, on the other hand, hadn't wanted to be thinking, but, like it had been all night — or rather morning — I just couldn't avoid my thoughts.

Stay or leave. That was what it came down to.

I grabbed a change of clothes from my brand new dresser and headed into the bathroom. Kol flopped on my couch, making even that look sexy, found the remote, and turned on the TV.

Stay or leave.

God, it was a horrible choice. I didn't want to do either.

I shrugged out of my shirt, my reflection in the bathroom mirror catching my attention. At least this time I didn't look as stunned as I had the last time something had happened, and I stared into the mirror. I had thought things had been bad when I had just been branded with a wraith's unnatural angelic mating brand, and then everything had changed. The wraith hadn't been just a wraith, and Gideon's brand had seared into my skin.

I turned my arm and looked at my left biceps, where the archnephilim's angry red mating brand had been. The brand was still thick and slightly raised, but it was now silvery like an old scar, with a spiderweb of silver threads around it. I turned to my other arm, where Gideon's brand marked my right forearm. If I didn't think about the sigil forever binding me to an angel, I could see its beauty. Gold threads wove a complex design from the middle of my forearm up to my elbow and shimmered with a hint of light. A gentle heat and a soft electric hum, both barely noticeable, pulsed around it and into my soul.

If I stayed, I'd be able to be with Gideon.

My heart squeezed. But not Marcus.

Jacob's claim gave a fierce twist. If I stayed, I'd be able to please Jacob.

Which wasn't at all what I wanted, God damn it.

If I quit the force, the chief would either have to accept that he couldn't have a human on Gideon's team or assign the next expendable officer.

That thought made my stomach churn. If a human officer was going to be an equal member of Gideon's team and not a dead man walking, he was going to need extensive training to deal with supers. Whoever was picked would be in just as much danger as I was, more so because they didn't have an angelic mating brand that could help save them. They'd also have a family, certainly they'd have friends. I didn't have either. I never knew my father, and my mother was dead. She had a sister somewhere in New Mexico, but I'd never met her and didn't know how to contact her.

Well, that just sucked.

If I quit, I'd put someone else in danger.

Which meant once again I didn't have a choice.

Well, I supposed I did. I could go against my every instinct and let someone else be seriously injured or killed. But then I wasn't sure how I'd be able to live with myself. I didn't purposefully hurt people. I protected them. To the expense of my well being.

I could only pray, like the last time I'd worked with the guys, that I'd be able to fly under the radar and protect my secret.

Except this time I also had to protect my heart.

GIDEON

I'D FOLLOWED CHIEF FIELDS AND DETECTIVE MCLELLAN INTO THE abandoned school, looked at what could only have been a feral vampire's nest and confirmed with the chief that yes the JP was taking over this case. Then I'd touched base with Summer to get an ETA on her preliminary forensic reports before marching back to the SUV to wait for Marcus to finish checking the school's perimeter.

It had taken everything I had to leave Shaw with Jacob and Kol and not rush her back to Operations so Amiah could heal her.

The mating brand told me she wasn't seriously injured despite her too-pale complexion, the large piece of gauze taped to her neck, and her blood-soaked uniform, but she was exhausted. The brand had drawn strength from her to save me yet again, like it had when I'd been captured by the archnephilim, and seeing her like that had made all the unwanted emotions I had for her threaten to break the tenuous hold I had on them.

I'd thought it would be easy to ignore the draw of the angelic mating brand, that I could hold out on claiming my destined mate until Marcus and Shaw had lived a full, happy life together. But I was already feeling the strain and it had only been a week and a half since she'd woken up, healthy and sane, and had left Operations.

And now she'd been foisted onto my team.

The only way I was going to get through this was not move an emotional inch. I had to stay firm, icy, detached, and figure out how to handle this new situation without succumbing to the brand's desires since I'd already tried to refuse her and been denied by the Chief.

He'd said the mayor wanted this and that it had been approved by head office, which meant I couldn't just ask for her to be reassigned. I had to come up with a good excuse.

I could probably get her reassigned by saying she was mine or Marcus's mate, but then one of us would have to step up and prove that was the case and Marcus was determined to have nothing to do with her so he could give her the normal human life he thought she wanted. He'd even convinced his wolf that keeping his distance was keeping her safe.

Although given how he'd barely looked at her then stormed off to check the perimeter without even confirming she was okay, it was clear he was struggling with ignoring his mating call as much as I was.

Getting her kicked off the team by saying she was mated to one of us also wouldn't keep her out of the supernatural world... even if it was starting to look like she was going to end up in our world whether any of us wanted that or not.

On top of all of that, Jacob's claim on her was still strong. She hadn't even been able to answer my question without getting his permission first.

I was grateful Marcus hadn't been around for that. It was hard enough for me to accept that someone else controlled my mate, and half of my soul wasn't a ferocious, possessive creature. It would have been impossible for Marcus.

How ironic that of the four of us, Shaw was safest with the sex demon. Not that Kol would use his magic inappropriately. In fact he was almost tentative about using his magic, still uncertain about where the boundary was between enhancing an experience or calming someone down and outright manipulating someone into doing something they didn't want to do... because Michael and his angels had done a number on the kid. It was actually a miracle he was as good natured as he was.

Now I stood by the SUV with Jacob, still a little sore from the three shots I'd taken earlier tonight even though Amiah had said I was safe to return to duty. Hopefully, she hadn't drained herself and had been smart enough to hold a little magic back because it wasn't looking like the team was done with trouble for the night.

Marcus strode around the far edge the school, radiating a tense fury

— like he had been since Shaw had been thrown back into his life two weeks ago — and stormed down the sidewalk toward me and Jacob.

"Where's Kol?" he growled.

"Taking Essie to the hospital to get stitches," Jacob replied, climbing into the back seat of the SUV.

Marcus yanked open the driver's side door with a little more force than necessary but thankfully not enough to damage the vehicle.

"We don't have time for him to be playing chauffeur." He jammed the key into the ignition. "Why would you let him take off like that?"

I got into the front passenger seat and shot Jacob a hard glare. "He should be taking her to Amiah."

"Essie wanted to check on her partner and Amiah nearly drained herself saving you," Jacob replied in his low western drawl, but even he, who was usually the calmest member of the team, looked tense. "It's only been an hour. Her magic is still low. We don't know where this investigation is headed and Essie may need Amiah to have all her magic back before this is done."

Marcus tensed and his fingers extended into claws, his wolf straining to break free. "Why would Essie need that?"

"Because the chief of police just put her on the team," I said, fighting to keep my tone even and not show the frustration or panic churning inside me. I could do this. I could work beside her, keep her safe, and let her and Marcus have their happily ever after.

I. Could. Be. Patient.

"Fields and the mayor want to see us working this case with a human. For good optics." The words left a bad taste in my mouth. Fields knew our cases were potentially deadly for a human and had made it clear that he thought Shaw was expendable. Something else I wasn't going to point out to Marcus.

"For optics?" Marcus snarled. "You're dragging Essie back into our world and putting her life in danger for optics?" Fur swept over the backs of Marcus's hands and his canines extended.

"I'm not. The chief is. Now get ahold of yourself," I commanded. "We need to get back to Operations and get on this case."

"Maybe they'll hold her in the hospital and we'll be able to call head office and fix this," Jacob added.

The mention of Shaw needing to be admitted to the hospital did nothing to help Marcus calm his wolf but did make me wonder if Jacob had other reasons for sending her to the humans for medical attention instead of Amiah.

I glanced back at Jacob who gave me an ever-so-slight nod, confirming my suspicions. He was hoping he'd bought us a little time by sending her to the hospital.

"I'll make the call as soon as we're back at Operations." But I wasn't going to hold my breath.

If head office had already agreed to having a human on the team and the chief had personally picked Shaw, we were going to be working with her... whether we wanted to or not.

ESSIE

I POPPED THE ANTIBIOTICS AND PAINKILLERS AS PRESCRIBED, CLEANED UP AS best I could without being able to shower, and stuck two new nicotine patches to my left side. Pain sliced through my neck as I tugged on a black T-shirt and it brushed the bandage, but I gritted my teeth and finished dressing into a pair of jeans.

From everything I'd seen, the guys' work clothes were casual and easy to move in. I'd stand out if I wore my uniform or a suit, and while I was sure the chief and mayor would love it if I stood out, I wasn't going to make myself any larger a target than I already was. And with my essence telling supers who could sense essences that I was a human and therefore the weakest member of the team, I was a pretty big target.

I packed a bag with an extra set of clothes, my box of patches, and my new prescriptions. Even if Jacob hadn't implied that the situation with the vampires was bad, I would have known it was. Which meant the team was going to work this case at top speed. Best case scenario, I'd find a few minutes here and there to return home and change, but I wasn't going to hold my breath on that.

After the clothes, I added the gear from my duty belt, then rummaged through my top dresser drawer to find the waistband holster for my off-duty sidearm that I never used, secured it to the waistband of my jeans, and holstered my service weapon — still loaded with the rounds of enspelled ammunition. My off-duty Glock, which was in my gun safe, could stay in my gun safe since I was still on duty.

Kol watched without saying a word and then held the door for me when it looked like I was ready to go.

"Got everything?" he asked, a hint of mirth in his eyes.

"Are you making fun of me?" I hadn't packed that much. The small duffle bag wasn't even bulging.

"Actually I was wondering if you packed enough. I didn't see any toiletries go into the bag."

"If I'm staying at Operations long enough to want my own toothbrush, things have gotten really bad."

The mirth vanished. "You want to avoid us that much."

A whisper of cold and mist breathed through the air around me. I'd hurt Kol's feelings.

"It's not that—" Well, actually it was. Except I wasn't trying to avoid Kol because of who he was but because he belonged in the supernatural world. "It's complicated."

I grabbed a fitted, stretchy — for free movement — jacket from the hook by the door, spiking more pain through my neck, and stepped into the hall.

"Marcus said you were afraid of supers." Kol closed my door and stepped back so I could lock it.

"He did, did he?" It wasn't a lie, but I wasn't thrilled at the idea of Marcus sharing personal details like that about me.

"Gideon wouldn't agree to his terms without an explanation, and I overheard them arguing."

Did that mean Gideon hadn't been happy when I left? No, his reaction had to have been because of the brand and not being able to control me. If I died, he'd die or go crazy. Except, since I was mostly human, my death might not affect him at all.

Kol shot me a wary look. "I know you had a... difficult experience with the archnephilim—"

I snorted and headed down the hall for the stairs. "Difficult is putting it mildly."

"But you're not afraid of us— the team, are you?" He fell into step beside me.

I was as much afraid of them as I'd been of the archnephilim.

But for entirely different reasons.

Nephilim were enemy number one, responsible for the slaughter of thousands upon thousands of humans and supers. Even though I'd been a child, not even seven during the war, according to angelkind a naturally born nephilim was impossible, which meant they'd think I was one of those monsters, and I didn't want to find out what they'd do with me. If they thought I was from the war, I'd be sentenced as a war criminal, imprisoned, or executed. If they believed I really was natural, I could be turned into a lab rat to find out why I existed.

And now I was going to work with the team and increase the risk of being discovered.

The chill and mist deepened as we headed down the stairs.

"You know I wouldn't hurt you," Kol said.

I'd been quiet too long, and now Kol feared I was actually afraid of him because of who he was and not what he represented.

"I know you wouldn't hurt me." Jacob wouldn't either, not until he learned the truth. But the jury was still out on Marcus and Gideon, regardless of whether they knew my secret or not.

I offered Kol the warmest smile I could muster given my thoughts, strode out my apartment building's front door, and headed to the SUV parked at the curb.

Kol unlocked the vehicle with the key fob and got into the driver's seat. "The rest of the guys wouldn't hurt you, either. You're officially part of the team now. Not that they'd have hurt you before."

"I'm the powerless human member on the team, and I just about had my throat ripped out by a crazed vampire tonight. I'm not sure any human belongs in the supernatural world." My throbbing neck was proof of that.

He started the SUV and pulled onto the street. "Lots of humans do just fine living in the Quarter."

"Lots of humans aren't part of a JP team. Are you trying to convince me to live in the Supers' Quarter?" I couldn't figure out his emotions or this train of conversation.

"Not live, just visit."

Hunh? "Okay, why are you trying to convince me to *just visit*?"

His grip on the steering wheel tightened and he stared out the windshield. The temperature grew colder, forcing me to fight my shivers and spiking agony through my neck.

Not the reaction I'd expected. "Kol? You wanna share?"

The muscles in his jaw clenched and his attention remained locked on the road.

"Kol?"

"I like your energy," he said, the words rushing out.

"You what?" I wasn't sure what I'd expected him to say, maybe that Marcus and Gideon were difficult to work with now that I was gone or something, but 'I like your energy' wasn't even close. "I thought I was off limits because of Gideon's brand?" Kol had made that clear when I'd offered to kiss him to help him restore his magic. Of course that had been before I'd burned his face with divine light and used the sexual euphoria of Jacob's bite to save him. Maybe things had changed.

"Not *that* energy," he said, still not looking at me. "I need *that* to survive, but some incubi have heightened attunement to essences and we feel essences more acutely than just about any other super and are drawn or repelled by certain energies."

My pulse skipped a beat. How much could he actually feel about my essence? Did he know I was a nephilim? He wasn't acting like I was, and he'd said he *liked* my energy. Would he still like it if he thought I was a monster?

"My attunement," he said, the words still rushing out as if this wasn't something he liked to share, "is ironically for essences on the light end of the spectrum."

"So divine light." Shit. He had to know I was a nephilim.

"Not just divine light. That's at the top of the spectrum, but there are varying degrees."

I resisted expelling a relieved breath. So he didn't know. Except— "You're a demon and you're drawn to the light and not darkness? Is that even possible?"

"I know. It's completely messed up. I'm completely messed up. I'm a being of celestial darkness and I feel better hanging out with an angel than my own kind. It's why I gave in and joined Gideon's JP team." His gaze finally jumped to mine and the temperature dipped a bit more with fear. He was terrified about what my reaction would be, and I sensed that he'd never told anyone else about this.

He jerked his gaze back to the road. "I hadn't realized how easy it was to be around you until everything was over with the archnephilim. Being around you is like hanging out with an angel without the attitude."

Gee, I wonder why that is? I struggled to keep my expression even. Out of all the guys on the team, I hadn't expected Kol to be the one best able to figure out I was a nephilim.

And what did I say to him? I liked his company. He was funny and charming, and his emotions were usually steadier than this. But now he was the one on the team I needed to avoid the most. He wasn't dumb. He'd eventually figure out why my energy was different.

"Jeez, it's not like I'm asking you out. Even if I dated, I wouldn't ask you out. You're Gideon's." The mist vanished with a snap and the cold turned bitter. His attention locked back on the road and his grip on the steering wheel tightened again. His expression hardened, but with my empathy I could see the hurt tightening around his eyes. And was that fear?

It couldn't be of me. It had to be of Gideon. But that didn't make any sense.

But then his reaction to me once he'd learned I wore Gideon's brand flashed through my mind's eye. He'd been quick to refuse me, adamant to keep his distance. I'd assumed that was because he was Gideon's friend and not wanting to hit on his friend's girl, but maybe there was more to it than just that.

He'd said he owed Gideon and Jacob his life and had been summoned by Michael to control the women who were being used to create the nephilim army. It hadn't sounded like he'd been a willing party to that, and because he was someone drawn to the light, Michael must have been confusing as hell. The archangel had been vicious and cruel to everyone but those angels who'd joined his cause. Everyone else, humans and supers particularly, were a virus that needed to be eliminated.

"I'm just asking you to stay with the team. I'd rather have you than some human who grates on my senses." The muscles in Kol's jaw tightened and for a second his fear was crystal clear. Fear of Gideon, or rather what Gideon represented. Even if Gideon had saved him, beings with light in their essences had still hurt him, and he was asking for something that he believed belonged to Gideon. I could only imagine his horror at being manifested in the human realm with the pure energy of an archangel only to find that angel's soul was blacker than night. And while lots of demons were older than their appearance, Kol might not be much older than his twenty-something years suggested.

How old had he been twenty-three years ago when Michael had held him captive using his magic against unwilling women? God, he could have been as young as sixteen, just when his ability to enthrall had strengthened enough to control multiple people at the same time. And while he'd said he'd joined Gideon's JP team, he'd also said he'd *given in* and joined. He *needed* to be around angels, but was still afraid of them. I was an opportunity to satisfy his need for light energy without reminding him of Michael.

And now I really had no idea what to say. I wanted to tell Kol it would be all right, he had every right to ask this of me and I wouldn't let Gideon hurt him because of his request. But that would be a lie. I didn't know if it would be all right, and if I had any sense of self-preservation, I'd keep my distance from him.

"Being part of the JP team is dangerous for me," I said.

"I get it," he replied, his voice flat, breaking my heart.

Shit.

"But right now I'm part of the JP team, which means I'm going to need someone to show me around the Supers' Quarter." Which was true, and I'd rather it be Kol than any of the other guys. Kol might have this deep emotional scar, but he hid it well enough that it usually didn't affect his emotions, and I wasn't bound to him like I was the others.

The freezing air warmed a bit. Was that hope? "I'm sure Marcus and Gideon would rather be the ones to show you."

Given my reception at the school, I doubted they would. "I asked you first."

"Then it's a date." The cold around me vanished, and he flashed me his breathtakingly wicked smile, the sultry incubus returning and hiding the fear and insecurity I'd just glimpsed.

I was still a little stunned by him as we drove through the park ringing the Supers' Quarter and reached the Joined Parliament Operations Building a few minutes later.

Kol hopped out of the driver's seat and checked his phone. "The guys are back from the crime scene and waiting for us in the cafeteria."

My stomach rumbled, reminding me I'd just gotten off a shift and needed to eat. Well, good thing the guys liked to meet in the cafeteria. At this hour, I suspected all I'd be able to find would be cold sandwiches and salads, but that was good enough. Given how the mess with the archnephilim had gone, eating when I could was a good idea.

We headed inside and down the long white institutional-looking hall with its pale gray floor and fluorescent lighting, and past the elevator sitting in the new five-story high rise section just past the edge of the original old two-story warehouse. It had only been a week and a half since the archnephilim had destroyed the cafeteria, killing Zella and nearly killing the guys, and the back section that had been a bank of glass windows and a door leading to the patio was cordoned off with large sheets of heavy plastic hanging from the ceiling.

The rock wall that the nephilim had pulled down, crushing Marcus and blocking the entrance, was standing again, creating a separation between the regular seating and a sunroom-style glassed-in section, but it was surrounded by scaffolding, the plants missing and the water not running.

Gideon, Marcus, and Jacob sat at a six-seater table in the center of the room, and everyone's gaze turned to me the moment I set foot on the first of the five shallow steps leading down into the room. Heat billowed around me, and I knew instantly it came from Marcus. The attraction between us zinged through me and my pulse sped up, but my gaze dragged past him to Jacob and his claim twisted in my chest.

I heaved my attention back to Marcus—

And I actually did this time. But it took everything I had to hold my gaze with his, and I was trembling by the time I'd gotten down the stairs, making the throbbing pain in my neck radiate into my chest and down my arm.

I let myself go back to Jacob. Fighting the claim right now just wasn't worth it. I needed to save my willpower for when it really mattered, and preferably when it wasn't going to cause me agony.

"So this is actually happening," Marcus growled.

ESSIE

THE LOOK MARCUS GAVE ME WAS TIGHT WITH ANGER AND THE
temperature in the room sweltering, and even then I could see and feel
the sizzling attraction between us in his eyes.

"This is God damn happening," he growled again.

"Unfortunately," Gideon said, his gaze stony and fixed on the
bandage taped to my neck.

His tone stung. He really didn't want me there.

Well, I didn't want to be there, either. "I could just quit and let you
have whatever yahoo the chief decides to send you next."

Kol stiffened and a flicker of cold snapped around me.

"That would be great," Marcus said, his heat bleeding through the
cold.

Jacob gave a slight tilt of his head to the chair between him and
Marcus, the order clear. *Sit.* "We at least know Essie can summon divine
light," he said.

I set my bag on the table behind the indicated chair and sat. Kol
slouched into the chair across from me beside Gideon, looking sexy as
hell, but now that I knew what I was looking for, I could see the hurt in
his eyes.

"And can you actually request to leave our team?" Jacob asked.

"I'd have to leave the force." Except now that I was there, as much as
a part of me was screaming this was dangerous, I didn't want to leave. I

wanted to stay beside Marcus, hell, be wrapped in his embrace and kissed breathless by him, but I also wanted to be near Jacob. Even Gideon called to me, the unwanted compulsion to draw closer to him oozing from his brand.

I gritted my teeth against all of that and focused on my throbbing neck. I'd get worse than that if they learned the truth. Why was that so hard to remember?

"So you'd lose your job," Kol said.

Marcus shifted beside me, his feral werewolf nature darkening his green eyes and sending a shiver of desire down my back.

And that was why it was so hard.

"The chief can't force this on you," he said.

"The chief can and has." Gideon glared at me, his summer-sky eyes filled with ice, but the chill didn't change the room's temperature. His emotions were back to being locked tight, only a fraction escaping through his gaze. "It is what it is. Are you staying, Officer Shaw?"

As much as I should say no, I'd already decided I couldn't risk another cop's life. "I'm staying."

The tension in Kol's body eased, but Marcus's and Gideon's tightened, and Marcus's heat burned hotter with his confusing ferocious fear. Jacob didn't move. It felt as if he was holding his breath, waiting for something or trying to come to a decision, but I couldn't figure out what that meant. All I could really tell about him was that he was tired and strained, the same sense I'd gotten about him back at the school.

"It'll be a while before the Medical Examiner has a report," Gideon said, his tone brusque, moving on to the business at hand, "but we all know that was a feral vampire nest, and we can't wait on a report to catch them."

I tightened my body, trying to suppress a shudder and spiking more pain through my neck. "How common is this? The JP assured humanity that vampires didn't do that sort of thing."

"The last time I saw one was about a hundred and fifty years ago," Jacob said. "I'd heard the previous one happened almost three hundred years before that."

"And what? The master vampires didn't say anything because you thought it would stop happening because humanity now knows about vampires?" Marcus asked.

Jacob sighed. "It's the same as when a shifter goes feral."

"Not really. Humanity knows we can go crazy." Marcus sat forward, his body drawing ever so slightly closer to me. "You assured us—" He cleared his throat. "You assured *humans* that horror movie vampire stuff was just fiction."

"So they lied," Kol said, matching Marcus's posture and drawing his attention. "That's not the point. The point is what we're going to do about it."

"We need to hunt down every last one of them, and fast. The longer this takes, the more people are going to die," Jacob said. "The sun will rise in a few hours and they'll go dormant, but as soon as the sun sets, they'll start hunting again."

"So we have about twelve hours before the body count rises," Marcus growled. "Jeez."

"And we need to figure out who's siring them," Gideon said. "This won't stop until the master vampire is arrested."

"Except—" Jacob pressed his palms to the table. His hands were wide, powerful, twice the size of mine, and yet I knew how tender he could be when he held me. "It doesn't have to be a master to create ferals."

"You mean any vampire can sire another vampire?" I hadn't thought that was possible. Everything I knew about vampires said only a master, someone who'd lived long enough to amass enough power in their essence, could make another vampire. And now there were laws about when and how a vampire could be created, laws the masters had helped create.

Jacob shook his head. "Not just any vampire, but more than just a master. I doubt a master would sire a feral in the first place. Ferals are hard to control and ruled by their hunger and base instincts, and not much else."

"So who are we looking for?" Marcus asked.

"A vampire who was a witch before he or she was turned," Jacob said, "or one who's claimed a witch."

"Well, that makes it easy," Marcus said, his tone dripping with sarcasm. "Any vampire who might be connected to a witch, and within twelve hours."

Gideon leveled a frosty glare at Marcus. "If it was easy, it wouldn't be our case."

"No shit," Marcus said.

"The nest looked fairly new, so this could be someone new to town." Gideon blew out a heavy breath. "Jacob and I will go to Rouge and talk with Victoria. She's the master in town. Even if the new vampire hasn't paid his or her respects, she's the only one who might be able to sense the newcomer."

"Are you sure it's worth the cost to see her?" Marcus asked. "It's always some kind of fucked up game with her. You probably won't even get a straight answer."

"We need to get on top of this before the ferals kill anyone else," Gideon said. "We don't have a lot of time and Victoria is the fastest way to our solution."

"What about the price?" Kol asked, his worried gaze jumping to Jacob. I couldn't blame him. The last time we'd encountered Victoria, she'd used her power over Jacob to fill him with agony and threatened to lock him up.

Gideon rubbed his face and for a second he looked exhausted, then his icy demeanor fell back into place. "If it's too high, we'll leave."

But I got the impression that if he were the one paying, no price would be too high to save lives.

"We need to move now and catch her before she retires for the day. Marcus, you go back to the school and see if you can pick up any more scents. See if you can figure out if these ferals have a second nest or a preferred hunting ground. Kol and Essie, go with him."

Marcus stiffened. "She shouldn't be in the field."

"Our orders are she has to be in the field." Gideon pushed his chair back and stood.

"I think she should come with us," Jacob said, shooting me an apologetic look.

The temperature in the room plummeted and my fear joined whoever was suddenly afraid. The last time I was in Rouge, I'd let Jacob claim me to stop Victoria from torturing him. I didn't want to go back and find out what other things the master vampire wanted from Jacob or me.

Except the part of me claimed by Jacob was doing a happy dance at the suggestion. He wanted me near, needed me. Jeez.

"We already know Victoria won't give something for nothing, not even information requested by the JP. Seeing Essie with my claim as strong as it is will... amuse her," Jacob said.

Marcus growled low in his throat. "I'd rather not amuse that sadistic bitch."

"Neither would I," Jacob said, his voice rumbling through me, making my essence vibrate and grate against the hum from Gideon's brand as well as my buzz. He wanted me to go with him. I had to go with him. "But I can guarantee that if I show up without Essie, she'll be furious."

"And it's less than fifty-fifty that she'll even talk to me without you present," Gideon said to Jacob. "Fine. Officer Shaw comes with us, but she's going to need to see Amiah. She can't walk into Rouge with a fresh vampire bite. Be in the garage in twenty." He stormed away, his emotions locked up so tightly the room's temperature didn't even shift.

Jacob stood as well. "Let's call Amiah down. We can meet her in triage."

Wonderful. For all the trouble I'd gone through to avoid Amiah, I was being ordered to let her heal me anyway — even if Gideon's argument did make perfect sense about walking into a vampire dance club with a fresh wound.

Jacob's compulsion took over, and I stood whether I wanted to or not.

"I'll take her," Marcus said, standing as well.

"But Jacob wants—" I snapped my mouth closed. I was not going to let the claim make me argue with Marcus. I couldn't even ask for a change in orders, could only think of Jacob's initial command. This was going to become a serious problem if it didn't ease up soon.

The words to agree with Jacob pressed against my lips. But Jacob said we could meet Amiah. *We.*

I clenched my jaw. God damn it. *We* could mean me, Jacob, *and* Marcus.

"I'll call Amiah." Jacob gave a tight nod. "You can take Essie to meet her," he said to Marcus.

Marcus cleared his throat and shot a glance at the fridge sitting near the cafeteria's metal serving counters. If its selection hadn't been changed when it'd been replaced after the fight with the archnephilim, it would have prepackaged sandwiches and salads.

Jacob pursed his lips, his expression strained. "Eat something, too," he said and hurried away.

I sagged back onto my chair, the pressure of Jacob's claim easing the farther away he got. I'd known working with the team was going to be hard, but this was a disaster.

"I'll—" Kol jerked his thumb to the stairs. "You know—" He shrugged, grabbed my bag from the table, and rushed after Jacob.

Marcus turned and towered over me, his eyes hard, his arms crossed.

His heat — my best guess was that it was a mixture of fear and desire, because fear wasn't usually hot — turned humid.

"What the fuck are you doing here? Didn't you listen to anything I said?"

Jeez, really? I shoved to my feet so he wouldn't be glaring down at me. "It's not like I volunteered for this."

"Yeah, but I bet you tried *so* hard to avoid it or protest the reassignment," he said, his tone mocking.

"You don't know what I did because you weren't there." And that hurt more than his anger. The desire between us might be combustible, but that didn't mean anything good could come from it. I ached for him and he still avoided me. "You ran the moment you saw me."

"I was respecting your God damn wishes." He jerked closer, and his lips pulled back in a snarl.

The memory of those lips on mine, his kiss ferocious and commanding, sent a shudder through me. I'd fantasized about kissing him since I'd returned home, replaying the moment in the elevator over and over again where he'd brought me to climax.

Jeez, I was still fantasizing about him.

"You wanted your life back, wanted nothing to do with me and my world," he said, his gaze boring into mine, daring me to deny it. "That was your choice. You made it perfectly clear."

"And you just gave up. You didn't even try to fight for me." Which was what had really eaten at me in the week and a half since I'd woken up after the fight with the archnephilim. I'd thought he'd given me a gift— Hell, he'd probably thought he'd given me a gift when he made sure I could go back to my normal human life, but the more I thought about it, the more it hurt that he'd just left. Again. "You could have at least said goodbye."

"If I had, my wolf wouldn't have been able to let you leave," he growled. His gaze dipped to my lips and his pupils dilated.

My pulse picked up, and my ache for him swelled.

"You *had* to leave. And now you're back." His expression hardened and he stepped back from me. "You're a liability on the team, and worse, you're fucking up my life. I had a perfectly good life before you crashed back into it." He raked his hands through his dark locks. "Stop being a fucking idiot and leave the team before you get one of us killed."

"And you think some other human cop would be better?"

"I know he would." He waved at my neck. "You got bit tonight because you can't handle a fight with supers."

I got bit because of Gideon's brand, not because I couldn't handle a fight with supers.

"I took down an archnephilim that handed you your ass. Twice. I'm not a complete pushover." And that was something I had to remember. I'd had the grit to stand toe to toe with the archnephilim, which meant I had the grit to handle this. "Stop being an asshole, and be a partner in this. I don't want to do this without you."

"I don't want you to do it at all. Guess neither of us gets what we want." He stormed up the cafeteria steps.

Jacob's claim jerked in my chest, stealing my breath. Shit. "You have to take me to Amiah."

"Take yourself to Amiah. You don't need me. You can handle anything, right?" He left, taking his heat and humidity with him.

"You want to know what's wrong with me, Marcus Diaz?" I yelled after him. "You." *God damn you and my desire for you.*

And that hurt all the more because I knew exactly what he was doing and I'd still taken the bait. He was pushing me away to protect me. That's what he'd done the last time. I'd just thought after everything that had happened with the archnephilim and in the elevator that he'd be different.

But everything he'd done had been to protect me and the life he'd thought I wanted, and now here I was back in the thick of the supernatural world, taking the world's most dangerous job for a human. He might still be trying to push me away to protect me, but it was clear by how hard he was pushing that he was also trying to protect himself.

And even knowing that, his words still hurt, adding to the ache of desire for him.

Jacob's claim twisted tighter in my chest, begging me to go after Marcus and fulfill Jacob's command.

I ground my teeth against it, grabbed a turkey club sandwich from the fridge, and took my God damn self to the miniature triage room and Amiah.

The angel, who could have been Gideon's sister with her brilliant blue eyes and blonde hair, sat on the tan padded-leather couch in the waiting area side of triage. She wore pale green scrubs and had her hair pulled back in a ponytail. She looked nothing like the slick, put-together angel I'd met before, but then it was after four in the morning and she'd already used a great deal of energy that day to save Gideon's life.

Her eyes narrowed when she saw me.

Swell. Looked like healing my neck was going to be as excruciating as the energy that had seized me and got me bitten in the first place.

"I've barely gotten a few hours' sleep, so I'm not at full," she said, pointing to the floor in front of her.

"I know."

Her gaze slid to my right forearm and a hint of the hardness in her gaze melted. "Which is why, in part, you're not at full."

"Yeah." I sat at her feet, facing perpendicular to her and giving her the best access to the wound.

She peeled the gauze away and frowned. "This is nasty. I won't be able to heal it completely. You'll have to come back once I've had time to rest."

"Can you do enough so it's not completely obvious to a master vampire?" That was the whole point in doing this.

"I can, and eliminate any possible infection, but you'll probably have a nasty scar."

I cocked my eyebrow at her.

"Which, if you keep the stitches, you'll have anyway." She brushed her fingers along my neck, close, not touching the wound, but somehow still making it sting. "Your lack of vanity doesn't make me feel better about you now being on the team. I still think you're reckless."

"What happened with Marcus was because I was an inexperienced rookie."

"That doesn't make me feel any better." Electricity snapped from her fingers into my skin, making me jolt. It sliced pain through my neck and sent my buzz into a wild frenzy. "Your other partner is in the ICU."

"The ICU?" Oh, thank God. A pressure in my chest that I'd being doing my hardest to ignore released. Hank had made it out of surgery.

Amiah's power flared and I tensed against the pain, the agony searing into every cell in my body even though it was just my neck she was supposed to be healing. My buzz roared, no longer controlled by the nicotine patches, stinging under my skin as if I were being bitten by a million bugs.

Then the blazing agony of Amiah's magic vanished. It happened so fast that I was still vibrating with the memory of it surging through me. It felt like this healing had happened even faster than the first time. Of course, maybe it had. This was just a stitched-up bite on my neck, not the broken ribs and collarbone and concussion I'd had before.

The buzz, however, didn't return to normal. It eased off a bit, but only to pre-nicotine levels even though I'd just applied two new patches. Whatever Amiah had done, her magic must have negated the patches' effect. Wonderful. Now I was going to have to figure out an excuse to find wherever Kol had taken my bag and replace my patches.

"That's the best I can do right now." Amiah sagged back into the couch, her breath a little too fast, as if she'd been physically as well as magically exerting herself. "Grab some tweezers from that trolley and pull out the stitches. They're just under your skin now."

I stood and crossed the small hall into the medical side of the triage area and found the tweezers on the indicated trolley. A small mirror hung on the wall over the sink, and I leaned in to get a better look. I hadn't seen the bite before so I didn't know how bad it had originally looked, but from the raised, dark pink, jagged scar, it looked as nasty as everyone had said it did.

The bite hadn't been clean or two simple punctures. It looked more like I'd been mauled by an animal than bitten by a vampire. And there was nothing I could do about it, especially since I didn't particularly want to go back to Amiah for another session to get rid of the scar.

I plucked the stitches free and was just about to go find my bag and replace my nicotine patches when the frosted-glass sliding door to the main hall opened and Gideon strode in.

<h1 style="text-align:center">ESSIE</h1>

GIDEON'S ICY GAZE JUMPED TO ME AND MY PULSE TREMBLED WITH yearning. The buzz in my body softened and the hum from his brand warmed my forearm. The connection between us made me want to cry and scream at the injustice of being forever bound to an angel, and yet beg him to hold me at the same time and ease my fears.

I squared my shoulders and tried to steady the whirl of emotions. If I was going to be an equal member on this team — or as equal as a human could get on a team of supers — I was going to need to deal with my unwanted emotions, or I'd end up proving Marcus and Amiah right and someone was going to get hurt.

"Officer Shaw," he said, his tone as icy as his gaze.

"I was just on my way to the garage." So much for replacing my patches. Although it seemed that if Gideon was close, my buzz wouldn't be so bad and I'd be able to think straight. Which only made me more frustrated at my situation.

"Where's Jacob?" Gideon asked.

"I don't know."

Amiah shifted on the couch, her scrubs sighing against the leather, but Gideon didn't look away from me, keeping me captive with his gaze.

"He said he'd meet you in the garage," she said.

"Good." Gideon's gaze dipped to my hip. "Do you have enspelled ammunition in that sidearm?"

"About two-thirds of a clip."

"Only use the gun as a last resort," he said. "Stick to your light strike. Things will get complicated if we kill one of Victoria's offspring." He turned on his heel and strode back out the door.

My buzz flared, and I hurried to follow.

"Your sandwich," Amiah said, reminding me of Jacob's command to eat.

The claim twisted tight. Crap. I rushed back to the couch, grabbed the sandwich where I'd left it on the floor, and hurried after Gideon.

"And don't you dare get any of my guys killed," Amiah said as I stepped into the hall and the sliding door closed behind me.

"It's not the guys I'd be worried about," I said under my breath.

"What was that?" Jacob asked. He stood in the hall between me and the door to the garage. The claim squeezed but the compulsion to answer him wasn't overwhelming, so I didn't.

No matter how much my insides squirmed.

I could do it.

Really.

Jacob frowned, the strain in his expression deepening.

"Are you okay?" I headed toward him, keeping my gait even and not rushing to his side like the claim wanted.

See, I could fight it. Maybe it was weakening and if fate had only waited a few more days before shoving us back together, it wouldn't have been such a struggle.

"Are you?" he asked.

"I've had better nights. But hey, it could be worse. We could be fighting the archnephilim again." Even with my emotions a complete mess, I had to admit the situation wasn't as bad as that. Sure, I was still magically bound to someone for the rest of my life, and from the looks of it he hated me, but at least he wasn't a homicidal maniac.

"The scale of difficult nights does change when you put it that way."

The door at the end of the hall slid open and we stepped into the cool musty air of the garage. Gideon waited for us beside one of the JP's SUVs, his posture perfect, his expression hard. He tossed Jacob the keys and got into the front passenger seat.

I climbed in behind him so it would be harder for him to make eye contact. The buzz dimmed ever so slightly again. Yep, being near him affected my buzz, and that made me nervous. It hadn't before and I hoped it was because I'd had Gideon's mating brand for two weeks now and not because something within me had changed when the arch-nephilim had flooded me with power.

Except I already knew something had changed. My eyes still glowed and the damned buzz was harder to mute with nicotine.

"When we get to Rouge, I'll find out where Victoria is and we'll get this over and done with," Gideon said without looking at me. "Jacob might have claimed you, but given how that whole... *situation* came about, there might still be trouble. So keep your eyes open, Officer Shaw."

"Copy that."

I ate my sandwich as we drove in uncomfortable silence, heading deeper into the Supers' Quarter and turning onto the street designed for vampires that was covered with UV-blocking glass. The purple canopy stretching from rooftop to rooftop reflected the street like a dark mirror, hid the stars, and muted the glow from the sliver of moon peeking out from the clouds. It was less than an hour before dawn, and while the street wasn't packed, it was busier than the last time I'd driven down it. Shops and restaurants were open and the sidewalk patios were full as diners enjoyed the warmer than normal summer's evening.

Most of the people looked human, although there were some demons present, and while many were vampires, since over ninety percent of the vampires in Union City lived in the Quarter, there were probably a lot of humans in the mix as well. Most of the humans were blood bunnies, happy to give blood and be in the presence of a vampire — and given the sexual euphoria that a vampire could induce during feeding, I wasn't as skeptical about why someone would want to be a blood bunny as I had been before. There were probably also a handful of claimed humans in the mix as well, those who'd gone even farther than a blood bunny and submitted their will to a vampire, giving up all control of his or her life.

Jacob's claim inside me twisted, reminding me that I'd submitted to his will. It might have been to save him from being tortured by Victoria and not because I wanted to give control of my life to someone else or because I wanted the benefits of being claimed — such as enhanced hearing and seeing in the dark — but I'd still done it.

We turned onto the last street branching off the UV-protected road before it ended in a UV-protected park, and stopped in front of Rouge. The dance club was a large building with wide front steps and two towering Roman columns that sat at the edge of the UV canopy, and from the sound thumping out of the building was still open for business.

Gideon got out, but didn't climb the stairs as I expected. He stared at the club's blacked-out glass doors and a whisper of mist — had to be his grief — curled around me.

My throat tightened in sympathy. Zella hadn't died in her basement apartment under Rouge, but that fight had started it all, and her injuries had been so severe she hadn't been able to fight the archnephilim when he attacked Operations and killed her. And now we were returning to where she used to live and reminding him of what had been taken from him.

I wanted to tell him how sorry I was, how I wished Zella had been his mate. Maybe the mating brand would have been enough to save her. But his shoulders squared before I could work up the nerve to say anything and the mist vanished.

He strode up the stairs without looking to see if Jacob or I were following.

Jacob shot me a worried look, but there wasn't anything either of us could do right now save watch his back.

Inside, past the vestibule and the bouncer who'd taken one look at Gideon and bristled but didn't say anything, was a writhing, pulsing mass of people dancing, standing, talking, or making out in the booths or shadows clinging to the edges of the room. Strobe lights flashed over the dark walls and ceiling, heavy music vibrated into my bones, and the room's sweltering temperature came from a mix of natural heat, along with the empathic heat of joy, desire, and need wrapping tightly around me.

Sweat slicked my forehead and pricked under my arms and between my breasts. I unzipped my jacket and shoved my sleeves up, but it did little to cool me down. And in all honesty, I'd either have to leave or strip to my underwear to alleviate the heat.

Gideon wove his way through the crowd to the archway leading into the pub-style room at the back of the club, and headed straight to the bar. Jacob and I followed and leaned against it, staying close, while Gideon asked the bartender about Victoria's location.

I slid my attention over the room. The temperature was still too hot and now my insides were churning with fear. This was where everything had gone sideways last time. The polished wood furniture and brass accents gleamed in the light, its cozy English pub feel doing little to ease my discomfort. People played at four of the five pool tables and one of the three dart boards. A group in a large booth cheered at a baseball game on one of the big screen TVs, while more groups of varying sizes, taking up about half of the tables and booths, chatted and drank and ate.

If I hadn't been put in the position to make Jacob claim me, threading his essence into mine and control me body and soul, the pub would have looked like any old pub. But I knew how dangerous its occupants were, and I could see the intensity in their gazes and the unnatural stillness in the bodies of almost everyone in the room. I was surrounded by vampires. More than the handful from last time. And that terrified me.

I hooked my thumbs into the waistband of my jeans. I really wanted to wrap my fingers around the grip of my sidearm, but someone could take that as a threat and the whole point of this was to get in and out without causing a fight.

Jacob shifted closer to me, but I didn't know if it was to reassure me or enforce his claim on me to the vampires staring at us.

"Victoria is in her suite." Gideon's gaze jumped to me.

"Shit," Jacob said, his voice low. "This isn't going to be pleasant."

"I'll pay her price. You don't have to worry about it," Gideon said. The mist returned for a second then vanished as he turned and headed for the stairs at the back of the pub.

Upstairs, we headed down a wide hall with gilded frescoes on the ceiling and a marble floor. At the very end stood a set of intricately carved wooden doors, and a bulky vampire who stood guard. He was as tall and as broad as Gideon — so not nearly as big as Jacob but still imposing. His body covered a third of the carving, but not enough for me to miss that the image depicted a woman and two men in the throes of a threesome.

The guard opened his mouth to say something, but his eyes flashed wide, and he reached for the door handle instead, his body jerking as if controlled by someone else — and given that Victoria had been able to squeeze her fist and make Jacob drop to his knees in agony, it was likely she was the one in control.

"Come in, Gideon," Victoria called in her sultry alto.

The guard finished opening the door, revealing Victoria lounging on a massive bed that sat in the middle of the room, completely naked, the red silk sheets only covering one leg and only up to her knee.

She was stunningly beautiful, everything I'd imagined a master vampire to be, with pale skin, dark hair, red lips, and curves that would make a man drool. If she'd had horns, I would have thought she was a succubus. But she didn't, and the intense energy radiating around her, along with the mesmerizing darkness in her eyes, told every cell in my being that she was an extremely powerful vampire.

Two men, naked as well, were in the bed with her, one behind her kissing her neck as if we hadn't just entered and interrupted, and the other sprawled face down beside her, bloody rents scored into his back, blood smeared on his neck, and his body limp, but his expression dreamy and satisfied.

The room was as opulent as the hall outside suggested, with four marble pillars at each point of the bed, and massive frescoes that covered the vaulted ceiling and poured down the walls. The floor, what could be seen beneath thick Persian rugs, was marble, and the furniture was heavy and dark and swirling with ornamentations and gold leaf. Floor-to-ceiling windows towered to my left and directly across from me, all with long gauzy curtains swaying in the early morning breeze, every one of them open.

"Have a drink, Gideon." She gestured to a sidebar against the right-hand wall, stocked with crystal decanters filled with liquids of various colors and glasses of all shapes and sizes.

Gideon met her gaze, no indication in his expression about what he thought about the master vampire receiving him without any clothes. "You know I don't drink on duty."

"Well, your other option is to join me." She ran her nails down the back of the guy beside her, drawing more blood and making him moan in pleasure. Her gaze drifted over Gideon's muscular body, pausing at his crotch before sliding back to his neck. She licked her lips. "I've always wondered what angel tasted like. Your choice."

"I'm just here to talk," Gideon said, his tone calm, casual. Which is exactly how I'd play the situation. Not react to the naked people and keep it relaxed. Without a doubt bad things would happen as soon as someone made demands from a woman like Victoria.

"Is that why you brought my offspring and his human?" A sensual smile lit her face. "They're your offering instead. How wonderful."

Her gaze locked with mine, capturing my soul and making my pulse pound. The sensual smile was now edged with a deep hunger, and I really didn't want to be desert. Her smile deepened, revealing her extended fangs.

"She's really very pretty, in a human kind of way," she said, her tone rich, sending an involuntary shiver of desire through me. "I can see why you picked her, Jacob. Is she as tasty as she looks?"

Her gaze trailed down my body, slowly, sensually, but stopped when it reached my right forearm and the exposed mating brand. The carnal hunger turned wicked, and she slid off the bed and glided toward us, every step exuding sex and danger.

"Oh, Gideon," she purred, grabbing his right wrist and dragging a nail through the mating brand on his arm that matched mine. "I didn't know you liked to share. If I'd known, I would have tried harder to entice you into my bed."

"Victoria." He captured her hand around his wrist, and a hint of light billowed from his eyes. "We really just want to talk."

"No." Her eyes narrowed and her sensuality turned dark, now filled with the promise of exquisite pain. "You're here to ask questions. Demand answers. That's what you angels do. Well, there's a price for answers. Did you think you could get away with asking without paying."

"This is for the benefit of both of us," Gideon said.

She leaned her naked body against him, her other hand pressing against his chest. "I don't see how giving you answers benefits me."

"Because the humans found a feral vampire nest," Jacob said.

"Oh, they did, did they?" Victoria raised a sculpted eyebrow and pursed her lips. "And you want to know if it's one of mine making them?"

"Or if there's a new player in town," Gideon said, his tone still soft, almost seductive, but the muscles in his jaw flexed, proving Victoria was getting under his skin.

Her lips brushed his jaw, and her tongue darted out and licked the flexed muscles. "Pay the price, angel, and I'll tell you."

He inched his head away from her. "Which liquor do you recommend?"

"That's not on the table any more." Her hand slid down to the waistband of his fatigues.

"You know I'm not having sex with you," he said, his voice low.

"No, you'd rather have it with my offspring's human." She turned her piercing gaze to me. "Do you think she's already fucked him, Gideon? Or is she still fantasizing about what it would be like for my offspring to fuck her while he drinks her dry?"

I shuddered, my breath picking up with desire, as Jacob's claim brought the fantasy to the forefront of my thoughts.

"Or do you share? He bites her while you fuck her? You know she's thinking of him, that it's him who's driving her mad with desire." Her hand slid past Gideon's waist toward his groin.

He jerked back and grabbed her wrist, his body stiff, his eyes icy. "People are dying."

"Only humans," she purred. "Besides, I said I'd tell you if you pay the price."

The ice in his gaze shifted, grew pained, and the mist of his grief returned, edged with a strange flickering heat. He was actually weighing the idea of letting Victoria use his body to save lives.

Jeez, I knew he'd do almost anything to save people, I'd seen that fierce determination when he'd promised to protect me from the archnephilim, but he shouldn't have to make that decision, especially not with his heart still mourning his one true love, Zella. That wasn't fair to him, and while the smartest option was to just walk away, that meant more people would die.

And *I* couldn't let that happen, either. "How about you find out how tasty I am instead?"

ESSIE

GIDEON'S EYES FLASHED WIDE, AND VICTORIA'S ATTENTION SNAPPED TO ME, freezing me in place with her vampiric intensity. My pulse pounded a wild tattoo but my offer was the right call. It was dumb, but the right call. I couldn't let others die at the hands of the feral vampires, but I couldn't let Gideon give in to Victoria's demands. Yes, using sex as a currency happened every day, but Gideon shouldn't be forced into it, not if I could help it.

"Shaw," Gideon said, his voice sharp with warning.

Jacob shifted closer to me. He opened his mouth to say something, but Victoria shot him a glare and his body jerked, his expression tightening with pain.

"You answer our questions and you get to find out how tasty I am."

"So you'd rather I feed from you than fuck your mate?" Victoria threw her head back and laughed a sultry laugh. "What if I want both?"

Gideon stiffened. "That's not—"

"On the table," I said, cutting Gideon off. I squared my shoulders and met Victoria's gaze. She was terrifyingly powerful, her intensity soul-consuming, but she wasn't an archnephilim, and I'd be damned if she forced my angel to sleep with her. "You either get to find out what's so interesting about me that your offspring and an angel want me, or we walk."

"I could crush you," she hissed.

"And then you'd have no hope in hell of getting into Gideon's pants."

"We're leaving." Gideon grabbed my arm and started to turn, but the room erupted into chaos.

Two vampires, their expressions filled with wild hunger, their fangs fully extended, rushed past the gauzy curtains into the room. They raced straight to the bed, one grabbing the dazed man before he could get up, the other vampire tackling Victoria's other man and sinking his fangs into his neck.

The men screamed. Victoria howled with rage and jerked a step toward them, but more feral vampires came through the open windows and threw themselves at us.

Gideon shoved me behind him and sent a blast of divine light at the closest vampire. She screamed, her face and hands burned, her skin red and oozing. Her body convulsed, but she didn't drop and instead jerked back toward Gideon, snarling. Jacob drew his Beretta, but his eyes widened at the non-effect of Gideon's blast, and he shoved the weapon back into his holster. With a snarl, he lunged at the vampire Gideon hadn't taken down, and ripped out her throat.

Victoria had taken out two ferals already with her bare hands and was moving, a blur of pale flesh and flying black hair, to the ones who'd killed her lovers, while her guard rushed into the room from the hall and joined the fight.

Gideon formed a sword of divine light in one hand and pushed me farther back with the other. "Stay back." Then he lunged into the fray.

I drew my Glock and fired at a vampire coming through one of the windows. The enspelled bullet slammed into his chest and blue lightning crackled over his body. He screamed and staggered, his arm tangling in the curtain and tearing it down, but the shot didn't kill him.

Shit. I still needed to make a kill-shot to take these things down. Head or heart. And while I was a good shot, I wasn't that good, certainly not when they were moving in a frenzy. There were over two dozen ferals still standing and I didn't know if more were coming. I only had ten of my sixteen shots left. I had to make them count, which meant I was going to need them to get closer to me to increase my odds of hitting my mark.

Victoria screamed, her vampiric speed slowing. Her chest rose and fell with wild gasps and blood rushed from gashes along her ribs. A chill tightened in my gut. These ferals could even hurt a master vampire.

Jacob ripped out the throat of another feral and lunged at a third when a gunshot roared into the room. It slammed through Jacob's chest, dangerously close to his heart, and likely would have hit it if he hadn't lurched forward a split second before to attack. It drew a strangled scream of pain, and he staggered. The vampire he'd been about to attack slashed at him with wicked claws, slicing his shirt and gouging deep rents in his chest.

I fired at that feral, aiming for the heart, hoping that even if I didn't hit, the enspelled ammunition would make it stumble long enough for Jacob to get away. Blue lightning snapped around the feral's body and it dropped to the floor, my shot striking true. But another gunshot roared into the room. Jacob wrenched to the side and the shot tore through the sleeve of his duster.

"Sniper," he yelled as he ripped out the throat of another feral. "Take cover."

Gideon decapitated a feral with his sword and glanced around the room, and in that second of taking stock, the sniper fired again. The bullet sliced through the right side of Gideon's upper chest near his collarbone with a spray of blood, drawing a scream of pain.

A hint of jagged electricity flickered in the mating brand, but it wasn't all-consuming like it had been before, which meant his injury wasn't fatal. Yet.

He twisted with the force of the blow and his light sword vanished. A feral vampire lunged at him, and he wrenched his hand up, his sword forming with the movement and impaling the vampire at the last second.

Two more gunshots roared into the room, one skimming Victoria's cheek. She stumbled, her enhanced vampiric speed making her lurch halfway across the room. The other hit Jacob's thigh. He staggered and the feral beside him raked her claws across his face.

Gideon ran his blade through that feral's chest and yanked Jacob to his feet.

I dove for the bed and ducked behind its meager cover. But all the shots had come through the one set of windows and there weren't a lot of other pieces of furniture in the room that I could hide behind. The body of one of Victoria's lovers hung over the side, a massive swath of blood darkening the sheets and pooling on the floor.

Four feral vampires remained, more than two dozen bodies lay bleeding on the floor, and another gunshot erupted. The sniper fired again. This time the bullet tore through a gauzy curtain and exploded out the back of the head of Victoria's guard. The guy dropped, his eyes vacant and dead.

Gideon hauled Jacob back toward the bed while Victoria made a dash for the door. The remaining ferals dove for Gideon and Jacob, and another flurry of shots erupted, drawing a scream from Victoria and forcing her to wrench away from the door. Blood slicked her body from killing the ferals with her bare hands, but also oozed from two bullet wounds in her chest.

She dove for the bed as another gunshot slammed into the wall behind her, and she crashed to a stop beside me, bumping me into the blood pool. I fired another shot at a feral on Jacob, giving him time to kill a different one before turning to the one I'd hit. He and Gideon were only a few feet away from the bed, but with the ferals not pulling back, there was no way they could take cover.

Gideon killed another one and turned to the last remaining one, but another gunshot slammed through that feral vampire, into Gideon's chest, closer to his heart than the last shot, and out his back. He screamed and lightning erupted from the brand.

My muscles seized, agony roaring through me. Everything within me howled to save Gideon, help him, do *anything*, but what I really needed to do was duck back behind the bed. My head and shoulders were still exposed from the shot I'd taken to help Jacob. I was a target, and if I got shot that wouldn't help Gideon. Except I couldn't move.

Another gunshot roared into the room.

Time stuttered into slow motion. Gideon clutched his chest, his sword of light gone, and staggered for the cover of the bed, Jacob close behind him, while Victoria's eyes flashed wide. Frost swept over my hands and cheeks from a sudden fear-induced temperature drop, and the master vampire seized my arm and yanked me to the floor.

Searing pain sliced across my cheek and into my hair. My head hit the marble floor and specks of light snapped across my vision.

Time jerked back to normal. Gideon scrambled around the foot of the bed and dropped down beside Victoria, while Jacob dove over it and landed with a heavy thump beside me. The jagged lightning released its hold on my muscles, but still burned agony through me, and now strength bled out of the brand from me to Gideon.

"We have to get you to Amiah," I gasped, struggling to sit up and making the room spin around me.

His gaze locked with mine and for a second all the ice was gone and I was immersed in a perfect summer sky. God, he couldn't die. I couldn't let him die. Please.

"We have to deal with that sniper first," Jacob growled, drawing Gideon's attention away from me.

"I commanded my lieutenants to search the buildings across the street and find the bastard," Victoria snarled.

"And yet they're not going to find me there," a raspy tenor said from the far side of the room by the windows.

The frost on my hands crept over my wrists and down my neck.

Victoria shot Jacob a terrified look. "You said you killed him."

"I did."

"You know I can hear you," the tenor said in a singsong. "You did kill me, Jacob, but my century and a half is up and I'm back to take what's mine."

"I'll stop you the same as I did last time." Jacob glanced over the edge of the bed. "And now you've lost the advantage of surprise."

"How's your chest, Jacob?" Raspy Tenor asked. "Half an inch to the right and I'd be done with you."

Gideon drew in a ragged wet breath, his hands pressed tight to *his* chest, and the lightning from his brand threatened to seize me again. We needed to get out of there, but the only other door in the room was farther away than the hall door. We'd be bigger targets if we ran towards it. Perhaps if I shot this guy with my enspelled ammunition, we'd be able to make a break for the door. Which was ridiculous, given how both Gideon and Jacob had been shot and couldn't run at full speed. We'd be shot before we made it halfway there.

I peeked over the edge of the bed to see who we were dealing with, then quickly dipped back down. Raspy Tenor looked like another Wild West gunslinger. He was lean, a complete opposite to Jacob's bulky build, but just as tall. His eyes were black, and he radiated the terrifying intensity I recognized as vampiric. The intensity, almost as strong as Victoria's, made my gut clench in fear.

He too wore a black duster that looked an awful lot like Jacob's, and a black hat, the wide brim pulled so low that if I hadn't been sitting on the floor looking up at him, it might have shaded his eyes from sight.

The only things that didn't say he'd just stepped out of history was the modern sniper rifle slung over his shoulder and the SIG Sauer P210 in his hands trained at the bed.

"Still with Mommy, I see. Has *she* hooked up with the angel or have you?" The soles of his boots shushed against the carpet. He was moving, drawing closer to the head of the bed. "And you've found yourself another human. How cute."

Jacob drew his Beretta and shifted his attention to the head of the bed as well. "Give up now and I'll make your death fast."

"But I've barely been back, and I'm having too much fun." Raspy Tenor rushed around the bed, his SIG raised to fire, but Jacob shot first. His bullets drove through Raspy's chest, making the other vampire jerk. It threw off his aim, and his shot hit the wall behind us. Blood rushed across his chest and splattered onto the rug.

"Run," Jacob barked, and I jumped to my feet.

I wrenched against his claim, staggered, the jagged electricity from Gideon's brand slicing through Jacob's command, and forced myself to grab Gideon's arm and help him stand. Victoria rose to her knees, glared at Raspy, and squeezed both of her hands into fists.

Raspy hissed in pain against Victoria's mental control, but didn't drop, and snarled back at Jacob as bullet after bullet slammed into him.

Jacob scrambled to his feet, grabbed Victoria under the arm, and hauled her up, still firing one-handed.

She wrenched out of his grip and stood her ground. "You're still my offspring. I still control you."

"Keep on trying, bitch."

Jacob's Beretta clicked. Out of ammo.

Raspy snarled, revealing his fangs, and fired his SIG.

Gideon wrenched me close and put his body between me and the danger. Victoria screamed and I shoved Gideon's arm aside and fired my gun, hitting Raspy in the chest. He didn't even bother getting out of the way. Blue lightning crackled around him. He dropped to one knee and his eyes widened.

I aimed to fire again, but the door crashed open. Five vampires — Victoria's lieutenants? — rushed inside, exuding dangerous ferocity, their fangs extended.

Raspy sneered. "Next time I won't miss, Lockwood." He bolted with his enhanced vampiric speed to one of the windows and leaped out.

Victoria's vampires rushed after him. A gunshot roared outside and someone screamed.

Victoria turned to Jacob and clenched her fist, making him groan in pain and sag to his knees.

"You said he was dead," she snarled. She was even more ferocious than her lieutenants. Blood gushed from another gunshot wound in her chest — Raspy's last shot — mixing with the blood splattered over her naked body.

Jacob gasped for breath. His blood oozed from the gashes on his face and chest, shallow enough that his vampiric healing was already starting to close them. But the gunshot in his thigh still bled profusely.

"I didn't know his soul was bound to the demon's seal," he said.

"Victoria," Gideon gasped, his breath wet and rattling. He pressed his palms to the wound in his chest, blood oozing between his fingers, and dropped to his knees before I could even try to ease his descent. His head dipped forward as if it was too hard to keep up. "Please."

I holstered my Glock, wrenched off my jacket, and pressed it as best I could to both the entrance and exit wounds near his collarbone. He was losing a lot of blood, and while an angel did heal faster than the average human, it wasn't anywhere fast enough to save him from bleeding out from the two gunshot wounds.

Strength rushed from me into him, and the room started to slowly spin and darken. This was worse than when the archnephilim had hurt him, his injuries were more severe, and I was still weak from earlier that night.

If we didn't get him to Amiah, he would die. And he just couldn't die. Please. He couldn't. My soul would shatter if he did. I wouldn't be able to keep living. It was because of his brand binding us together, and I didn't care. All that mattered right now was him.

I sank to my knees beside him into a growing pool of his blood, all my strength going into holding my jacket to his chest and into the brand to keep him alive. I had to stand, had to find the strength from some-where to get him out of there.

"Jacob, help me," I said, my throat so tight I could barely get the words out. Gideon wasn't going to die. I wouldn't let him die.

A flicker of power snapped beneath my skin. Like my buzz but more powerful, almost like the fire that had unfurled in my back when the archnephilim had tried to make the wings I didn't have manifest. I strained to stand, but the power turned into my stuttering angry buzz and the room twisted with exhaustion instead.

I couldn't do it without his help or Jacobs. "Come on, Gideon. Stand."

A burst of my strength swept into the brand and he shuddered, his head turning just enough to capture me with a single summer-sky eye.

He raised a bloody hand to my cheek. His fingers whispered over my skin and my pulse stuttered, every cell in my body yearning for him.

"The team needs you," I said. "You don't get to die on them." Or me.

"I'm trying not to," he said, each word a struggle, each breath getting harder. The muscles in his jaw clenched. "I just need a minute. I'll be fine."

"Not unless you get help, so stand up." I imagined more of my strength flooding into him.

He groaned, his muscles bunched, and he stood, the movement sending jagged electricity screaming through me. I rose with him, but we were both unsteady and started to tip.

Victoria swore and both she and Jacob rushed to help us, Jacob grabbing Gideon, Victoria grabbing me.

"You should be healing faster than this, angel," Victoria said, her tone concerned but her gaze filled with hunger and lingering on his bloody shoulder.

Gideon leaned into Jacob. "It's been a rough night. I'll be fine in a few minutes."

"Or you're going to end up dying in my suite. And I can't have a JP agent dying in my suite." She released me, jammed a finger into one of her already healing bullet wounds, and coated it in blood. Then she grabbed Gideon's jaw with her other hand, forced his mouth open, and wiped her bloody finger over his tongue.

He gagged, jerking away from her, and she let him go — with her strength she could have held him there, probably even crushed his jaw.

"That should be enough to keep you alive long enough to get back to the Joined Parliament Operations Building."

Light billowed from his eyes, and the jagged energy coming from the bond eased to the same level as my buzz. Thank God. While I still swayed, the room slowly spinning, it was now a little easier to stay upright. It was certainly less painful.

"That wasn't necessary." Gideon glared at Victoria, clinging to Jacob to keep standing. Blood still rushed from his wounds, but the brand told me whatever Victoria had done, it had helped.

"Yeah, I know, now your pure angelic essence is tainted by vampire blood." She turned on her heel, strode to her bar, and poured herself a drink. "You're welcome. Now get out. You're not one of mine, so the healing properties of my blood won't last long."

"I didn't even know you could do that for non-offspring," Jacob said.

"One of the perks of being as old as dirt," she snarled.

"Thank you." Jacob wrapped an arm behind Gideon's back.

"I didn't do it out of the kindness of my heart." She took a long drink and leveled her intense gaze on Jacob. "We're not done with our conversation. If Logan Dunn is back, so is the danger of his demon. I can't have you distracted because your human has died because her angel has died." She rolled her eyes. "And I know you'll be useless if that happens. You were useless the last time. Now clean up this fucking mess."

We staggered out of Victoria's suite, taking the back stairs — as instructed — and climbed back into the SUV. I didn't know where Raspy Tenor was or Victoria's lieutenants, but the master vampire had been right, the effects of her blood were already starting to wane, and the jagged spikes of electricity were back to slicing through me.

Jacob drove while Gideon sat in the back, his eyes closed and his hands pressed against his chest wound. I crouched on the bench beside him, keeping pressure on his shoulder.

"It's going to be okay," he said, his voice soft, his eyes still closed, his breath shuddering gasps.

"Until you get shot again." God, here I'd been afraid I wouldn't be able to survive my job when I should have been afraid I wouldn't survive his.

"I'd have been good enough to get to Amiah if I hadn't been shot earlier this evening."

"That doesn't make it better." A stronger zap of electricity sliced up my arm and across my chest. I jerked and swallowed back a moan of agony.

He opened his eyes, captured me with his gaze, and I was falling into a summer sky again. This was where I belonged, wrapped in his pure warmth, wrapped in his arms.

A hint of clouds passed over his summer sky, dimming his angelic light, and he turned his head away from me and closed his eyes again. A chill bled into my heart, filled with the empty ache of losing the momentary connection we'd had. The connection had been so quick, only a few seconds. Losing it shouldn't have felt like I was suddenly lost in a vast sea of ice.

Jacob pulled into Operations' garage, and Amiah and another woman in scrubs — I think her name was Cassey — rushed out the door with a gurney to greet us. I scrambled out of the SUV to get out of the way. The garage dimmed and twisted, and I clung to the side of the vehicle to keep standing. Jacob helped Gideon out and onto the gurney.

Amiah shot me a withering glare then hurried Gideon inside, down the hall, and through the frosted sliding glass doors into triage, taking my heart with them.

Jeez. What a complete mess.

"Come on," Jacob said. "You should get looked at, too."

Jacob's command rushed through me, and I stepped away from the SUV. The garage twisted, and I staggered. Jacob caught me before I fell to my knees and lifted me in his arms.

I leaned my head against his shoulder, mindful of the gashes across his chest — although they looked like they were mostly healed — and the bullet wound near his heart — not bleeding as profusely as it could have. I closed my eyes, not wanting to deal with the world whirling around me. In his massive arms, cradled close against his broad chest, I felt small, delicate, and safe. The vampiric intensity that terrified me in the other vampires comforted me, centered my soul, and I knew, without a doubt, I also belonged there, in Jacob's arms.

Because of his claim.

Except a part of me wasn't sure the rightness of being held by Jacob was completely because of the claim.

"How badly are you hurt?" he asked, his voice rumbling through me as he headed down the hall with uneven steps, his gait still affected by the gunshot wound in his leg.

"It's the brand making me dizzy." And sore and exhausted and heartbroken.

"He'll be okay."

A sliding door shushed open, and a jagged spike of electricity sliced through me. My eyes wrenched open and locked on Gideon as he convulsed and screamed. He lay on the gurney, his hands clutching the sides. Someone had cut off his shirt exposing his chiseled chest, the sculpted muscles smeared with blood. The shirt lay on the floor in a wet heap along with my jacket and an unnervingly large pool of blood. Light flared from Amiah's eyes with a sudden blast of her healing magic, surging through his body with an excruciating pain I was all too familiar with.

"Push the Midazolam," Amiah said. She captured Gideon's face with her gloved, bloody hands and met his gaze. "I've slowed the bleeding, but that's all I can do until my magic recovers. You'll heal faster if you're unconscious. Do you understand?"

"Essie," Gideon said, his voice so soft I wouldn't have been able to hear it if Jacob's claim hadn't enhanced my hearing.

"Gideon, do you understand?"

He gave a tight nod and gasped, his face tightening in pain. "No more than four hours. I can't be down longer than four." His eyes rolled back as the sedative took over, and the jagged electricity snapping from the brand eased, blending back in with my buzz.

"Hang a bag of O-neg and finish packing these," Amiah said to Cassey then turned to us, her expression exhausted and pained. "How bad is your face, Jacob?"

Jacob sat me on the bed beside Gideon's and pressed tentative fingers to the gashes in his face. "Mostly healed. The gunshot in my chest and leg are the worst."

"Can you get by without my magic and just a blood bag or two?"

"Yeah." He turned to the small fridge where they kept the blood, pulled out a bag, and shifted away from the gurney.

"And you?" Amiah asked me, peeling off her gloves, tossing them in the hazardous waste bin, and pulling on new ones.

My cheek was still bleeding, I could feel my blood oozing down my skin, hanging on my jaw before dripping onto my shoulder, but it wasn't gushing and I was just too tired to care. "I'm fine."

She rolled her eyes at me. "You're not fine, but you're clearly not going to die, either."

She doused a piece of gauze in saline, grabbed my chin, turning my head and angling it up to give her easier access to my face, and wiped at the blood.

"So much for your promise not to get my guys killed."

I didn't recall making that promise to her, even if I'd made it to myself, and I was just too tired to argue with her.

The other doctor grabbed a blood bag from the fridge, hung it on the pole by Gideon's head, and attached it to his IV. Then she wheeled his gurney down the hall, deeper into the building where I knew there were patient rooms.

Amiah turned my head even farther. The gauze rasped against the gash in my cheek and into my hairline with biting pain, and I ground my teeth, trying my best not to show it.

Out of the corner of my eye, I saw Jacob slip the blood bag back into the fridge and leave through the sliding glass door. Guess he needed more than just a bag or two. I'd heard that while a vampire could live just fine on bagged blood, drinking from the vein had better healing properties. He was probably off to find a blood bunny to recover faster, and I wasn't going to think too hard about that because even just acknowledging that made his claim twist inside me to volunteer my blood.

I squeezed my eyes shut and concentrated on just breathing. Everyone was still alive. It was going to be all right.

"I'm not going to bother with stitches," Amiah said. "Jacob's claim on you is helping speed up your healing and they're just going to get in the way when I have to heal you properly." She taped a piece of gauze to my face. "If you bleed through this, just replace it."

She peeled off her gloves, tossed them, and headed down the hall in the direction they'd taken Gideon, leaving me alone in the small triage room. The agony from Gideon's brand was gone, more or less, my buzz now the strongest biting sting between them, and I was exhausted.

I laid back on the gurney and closed my eyes, but without a pillow, it wasn't particularly comfortable, and all the bruises and strains from the last few hours throbbed even more. All I really wanted was to sleep— well, have a shower since I was once again covered in someone else's blood, and then sleep, but I had no idea where Kol had taken my clothes and had no idea who to ask to find out.

The whirr of air through the vents and the hum of equipment plugged in and ready for use wrapped around me, lulling me, but I still just couldn't get comfortable.

With a sigh, I climbed off the gurney and settled on the overstuffed leather couch in the waiting area. At least there I could get some support for my neck. A small part of me felt guilty for getting blood on the couch, but the rest of me was too tired to care.

The buzz gnawed at me, and even with my eyes closed it felt like the room was spinning. I tried to concentrate on just breathing. My face—hell, my whole head throbbed, radiating from the slice in my cheek, that, now that I thought about it, had been a near-miss with a bullet, thanks to Victoria yanking me out of the way.

Because once again the brand had locked me in place.

How the hell was I going to convince Gideon to be more careful? I was a liability on the team if I was out of commission every time Gideon was.

But the idea of benching myself made me want to scream in frustration. That, and the chief would be furious if I wasn't seen in the field working with the team, and he'd fire me. And damn it, I liked my job. I was a good cop. Another day, another time, and it would have been a different car answering that domestic and running into that vampire nest. It was just my shitty luck that it had been me.

But was it shitty luck? As much as I wanted to have a fully human life and live exclusively in the human world, I wasn't just human. My essence, while perceived as human by supers, couldn't possibly be wholly human and maybe supers were unconsciously drawn to that—

Or I was unconsciously drawn to them.

I'd thought I hadn't allowed myself to completely live in the human world because of the fear of being discovered, but maybe a part of that was because I didn't belong in their world.

Of course, I didn't belong in the supernatural world, either. I was still half human, and I was a nephilim with almost no magic, and certainly not any useful magic.

The sliding door to the hall shushed open.

"You're still here?" Jacob asked.

I peeled my eyes open. They were gritty and sore from my contacts enspelled to hide the glow in my eyes, but I managed to focus my blurry vision on him as he knelt beside me. He'd changed his clothes, and the gashes in his cheek were gone, not even a hint of a scar, but there was still a strain around his eyes.

"Is the brand keeping you here?"

"No." I struggled to sit up, and he captured my arm and helped me. "I didn't know where else to go."

"I'm sure you've been assigned a room."

"So am I. Kol took my bag somewhere, but we left for Rouge so fast I wasn't told a room number or given a key."

He pulled out his phone and sent a quick text. "If they're in the middle of a hunt, he might not get back to me right away." He sat on the couch beside me, his weight lowering his side of the cushion and sliding me against his side.

I leaned into him, unable to help myself and too tired to fight it.

"Do he and Marcus know about Gideon?" My pulse tripped, speeding up. "Do they know about that sniper vampire? It looked like he was in charge of those ferals. If he isn't the one making them, then he's in league with whoever it is."

"I'm pretty sure the ferals are Logan's." His gaze slid to my gauze-covered cheek, his vampiric intensity crackling in his eyes for a second, then he pulled his attention back to his phone. "They've been warned, but Gideon will want as much information about the situation as possible when he's back on the job."

"In four hours," I said.

"Just under three now."

Jeez. I'd slept for an hour and I still felt like crap. "So what *is* the situation?"

He glanced back at me, his gaze returning to my gauze-covered cheek before jerking away again. He shoved off of the couch, strode back into the triage area, and grabbed a package of gauze and a roll of tape. "Why don't you clean up in my room? I'm sure by the time you're done, Kol will have gotten back to me."

"Sure." I stood, my muscles aching with the movement, my body still heavy with exhaustion and the room still ever-so-slightly spinning. "You know I'm still going to find out who this Logan guy is."

"I wasn't trying to avoid the conversation." He watched me shuffle toward the sliding door, determined to keep my balance. "Let me carry you."

The part of me he'd claimed thrilled at the suggestion. "I'm just stiff."

"And it hurts just looking at you." He shoved the gauze and tape into his pockets and picked me up.

"At some point I'm going to have to stand on my own two feet." But I leaned into him, savoring the feel of his bulky muscles pressed against me. A hint of heat radiated from his body, but not as much as I would have expected if he'd just fed.

"Given how you looked when we met you at the ferals' nest and again after Logan's attack, I'm surprised you're conscious." He strode into the hall and headed toward the elevator. "Almost all of that was the mating brand, wasn't it?"

"I wish Gideon would stop getting shot."

He chuckled, the sound a low rumble that sent my cells vibrating in resonance with his essence and making the claim surge warm within me. "I'm pretty sure he'd like to stop getting shot, too." His expression turned grim. "I haven't seen him have such a rough night since the war. I also haven't seen him as brash since then. He's usually got a tighter control of his emotions."

"The love of his life is dead and he's permanently stuck with me. I doubt that's what he imagined for himself." Add in that his emotions had already been strained because the archnephilim had been murdering his squad members who'd survived the war with him, and that would be enough to break anyone's control. Even an angel's.

"It's not being stuck with you that makes the situation hard."

"It's because I'm not Zella." I fully understood that. I didn't want my soul forever bound to someone I didn't know or love.

"In part." Jacob reached the elevator and hit the call button with his elbow. "But you and Marcus are also a thing. He respects that."

Just thinking about Marcus made me want to scream in frustration, and given how cold Gideon had been toward me, I didn't believe for one second it was all about respecting whatever I had with Marcus. That, and no matter how much I ached for Marcus, he was determined to push me away. Which I had originally thought during the mess with the arch-nephilim was for the best, and now... not so much.

The elevator door slid open and Jacob carried me inside.

"Marcus and I aren't anything," I said.

"He's worried about you."

The door slid closed, reminding me of the last time I'd been in this elevator with Marcus and sending a shiver of desire sliding through me.

Jacob's grip on me tightened. "We all are."

"I'm determined not to be a liability on the team." Or to at least minimize my powerlessness against supers as much as possible.

"You're hardly a liability," he said, his rich voice sliding another sensual shiver through me. "You took down that archnephilim almost entirely by yourself."

"So, hey." I forced a laugh, determined to not acknowledge my growing desire for Jacob. "What's to worry about, then?"

Jacob's gaze locked with mine filled with—? Hunger? No, need? Longing? Desire? The emotions flitted across his expression, stealing my breath. His pupils dilated, and the temperature in the elevator shot up. It was desire in his eyes, one matching the desire sliding slow and sensual within me.

ESSIE

I DIPPED MY GAZE TO HIS LIPS, WONDERING WHAT THEY'D FEEL LIKE AGAINST mine. I already knew the bone-melting bliss of his bite and couldn't help but think back on Victoria's words. How would it feel to ride that bliss while he pushed inside me?

But I didn't know if I wanted to sleep with him because he was damn hot and because I felt safe in his arms, or because of his claim.

Except I couldn't feel the claim in my chest at all. Not even a hint of a twist. There was just the unfulfilled desire I'd been aching with since I'd left Operations a week and a half ago.

The elevator door slid open, and Jacob wrenched his gaze away from me.

He cleared his throat and strode down the fifth floor hall, lined with dark wood doors each with a card reader lock. "You're right. There's nothing to worry about."

But the raised temperature didn't decrease.

We passed the room I'd had last time, turned right at the end of the hall, and stopped at the first door. This one didn't have a card reader but a fingerprint pad. Jacob unlocked the door with his thumb and opened it without jostling me.

Inside was a small apartment with a kitchenette smaller than the one in my apartment — and mine was small. It sat along the left side of a living room area that had a huge dark brown couch, a floor-to-ceiling bookcase packed with paperbacks, and a mahogany desk in the back corner by the large bay window. The room was done in creams and yellows, with hints of oranges and reds, reminding me of a warm summer day with the sun high in the sky. Midday, something he wouldn't have seen for a long time until the JP had given him the enspelled silver bracelet that protected him from the sun.

He headed through the only other door in the apartment and stepped into a bedroom the complete opposite in coloring, in varying shades of gray. A California king bed with a dark gray comforter and black sheets took up most of the space, which didn't surprise me given how big he was, but the large clear-front gun case beside it, displaying a variety of antique pistols and rifles, did. A leather hat with a wide brim, similar to the one Logan wore, hung on the corner, and I couldn't shake the feeling that their connection was more than just being Victoria's offspring.

The bathroom, just off the bedroom, was similar to the one that had been in my assigned room, with creams, grays, and blue with chrome fixtures. It was probably the standard design for all the rooms. The only difference for Jacob's was instead of a tub-shower combo, he had a large standup shower.

He set me on my feet, leaning me against the glass shower wall, and shifted back, his arms crossed against his broad chest. "You good if I leave and figure out where Kol put your bag, or do you need me to stay?"

The claim returned with a vengeance, twisting in my chest. *Stay. Don't leave me. Tell me what to do. Let me please you.* Damn, for a second there I'd thought it was finally easing up.

Jacob frowned. "Essie?"

"Can you please tell me to clean up," I forced out.

"Do you think you'll pass out?"

I opened my mouth to say no but "I'm not sure" came out instead.

Why the hell had I said that? I was fine walking in triage—

Except I hadn't been fine. I was sore and exhausted and dizzy. I was still God damned dizzy.

He pursed his lips and frowned, his gaze boring into mine for an agonizing second as if he could see into my soul, then gave a tight nod, coming to a decision.

"Okay." He shrugged out of his duster and pulled off his T-shirt, exposing a muscular chest with a fine dusting of dark hair that trailed down his washboard abs and into his pants.

My pulse stalled and the desire I'd felt in the elevator flared hot and entwined with his claim.

He pulled off his boots and socks, started the shower, and turned back to me. The temperature in the bathroom increased and turned humid — too soon to be from the heat of the shower.

The need to touch him and be touched by him was overwhelming. I reached out and pressed a hand above his no-longer beating heart. His breath came up short, and the muscles in his jaw clenched.

This was a bad idea. I could shower myself. It would be fine.

I straightened to prove to him I was fine — no matter what the claim had made me say — and the bathroom twisted and darkened.

He grabbed me, wrapping an arm around my waist, and pulled me close to him, steadying me. "I got you."

God, he did, and I wanted more.

I needed a distraction.

"Tell me about Logan." Maybe talking about the reason I was dizzy and exhausted from Gideon's brand would cool me off.

"Good idea." He leaned me back against the wall, grabbed the bottom of my T-shirt, and tugged it off over my head.

I locked my gaze on the wall. If I looked in his eyes — or watched us in the mirror over the sink — I'd give in and kiss him, and that would just make a complicated situation more complicated. It was the claim. The claim. It had to be. Maybe if I said it enough times I'd completely believe it.

"Logan Dunn and I are blood brothers."

He knelt, his warm breath feathering down my chest and stomach, and helped me take off my runners and socks. Then he reached for the button on my jeans and my breath hitched.

I grabbed his hands before be could undo my pants, my gaze leaping back to his dark eyes.

"I know the affects of the claim," he said, his voice a low rumble.

And in that moment, with that look in his eye and the heat of his emotions, I wondered if the affects went both ways.

"But I'm not going to let you pass out in the shower." He pushed my hands away, undid my pants, and pulled them down. "We can keep this professional."

The claim tightened at his command, fighting my desire. He'd said to keep this professional. That would please him. Except my yearning still heated my skin.

I stepped out of my pants and turned my back to him to take off my bra and underwear. Perhaps if I wasn't looking at him, I could embrace the claim's command to keep it professional, except I could still sense his massive body close behind me.

"You and Logan were blood brothers?" I reached to unhook my bra, but his hands got there first, releasing the clasp and sliding the straps from my shoulders. "Is that because Victoria sired both of you?"

"We were blood brothers before we were turned." He tugged down my underwear and I resisted the urge to press my naked body against him. "His family took in my unwed mother when she had me and her father, my grandfather, disowned her."

"Because she had you out of wedlock?" I forced myself to move to the shower's entrance, still clinging to the shower wall to keep standing.

Jacob stayed close, his hands on my upper arms to steady me and catch me if I fell.

Darkness shuddered at the edge of my vision, but I managed to slide inside, shuffle to the other side, and lean against the white tiled wall.

"No, because she had a Cheyenne's baby out of wedlock." He leaned closer and reached past me to grab a shower pouf from the hook at the bottom of his shower caddy. His bare chest pressed against my shoulder, and I struggled to stand perfectly still. He filled the pouf with soap, handed it to me, and moved back to steady me, only his hands in contact with my skin, barely skimming my hips, making the claim thrill that we were managing to keep it professional. And yet my body continued to ache with desire for him.

"Logan and I did everything together." He blew out a heavy breath that rushed across the back of my neck.

I bit back a moan and concentrated on washing myself as fast as my dizzy head would let me.

"We were getting into trouble from the very beginning, and when his family was killed, we swore a blood oath to avenge them." His grip on my hips tightened. "That was the night we learned he was a witch. Magic had burst around us the moment we'd cut our palms and pressed them together. Scared the shit out of both of us."

"So he didn't know he was a witch?" I shuffled into the spray of water to rinse myself off. Jacob shuffled with me, drawing close enough that my back brushed his chest. I bit back another moan. Even with the compulsion from the claim to keep it professional, I wasn't going to be able to last, because in truth, my aching desire was a need to be held, to lose myself in the physical and release all my churning worries just for a moment. I wanted Marcus but he was pushing me away. I pushed away from Gideon, because I was afraid of what would happen with his mating brand if I actually got to know him.

And if I was smart, I'd keep my distance from Jacob, but even as I thought that, I leaned back, pressing my body against his. His hands slid across my skin, one wrapping across my belly, the other cupping my breast, and pulled me close. My head tipped back against his chest and this time I did release the moan. God, he felt so good. To hell if this was the claim making me desire him or not. I was going to shatter if I didn't release the pressure inside me. Right now I could live with having claim-induced sex with him.

"Essie," he murmured, his lips pressed to the back of my head.

"Kiss me."

"You don't mean that," he said, but his hands didn't move from my body.

The shower spray beat against my hypersensitive flesh, and I rubbed against him, savoring the feel of his hardened erection underneath his wet jeans rough against my skin. "Kiss me."

He groaned and his hand on my breast tightened as the one on my waist trailed lower. His fingers reached the crux between my hip and thigh, and his lips dipped to the sensitive spot just behind my ear.

I trembled with anticipation and tipped my head, offering him better access. A groan rumbled low in his chest and his lips grazed against my neck. My pulse picked up. The last time he'd bitten me there, I hadn't known how good it would feel. I hadn't wanted to give him control of me and my body, and a part of me had fought it. Now he already had control. There was no point in fighting, only in losing myself to the sensations and forgetting about everything else.

A shudder swept through him and he released my breast, yanked the soaking wet gauze from my cheek, and slowly, firmly, raked his tongue along the wound.

Sensual heat shot straight to my core, and I gasped. I was already wet and yearning, trembling with need. There should have been pain, that should have stung, but there was only bliss, curling tighter in my womb. And all he'd done was lick me. God! I squirmed in his grasp, rubbing myself harder against his erection. He needed to take those jeans off, but his hand returned to my breast and his embrace controlled me. I couldn't turn around to kiss him or unbutton those pants.

He raked his tongue across the wound again, and his fingers on my thigh brushed through my curls and skimmed my folds. The heat jerked taut within me.

"Oh, yes," I gasped. My thoughts whirled. *Take me, control me, satisfy me.* And I wasn't sure if it was the claim or not. All my aching heart and soul was gone, burned away in a blaze of pleasure.

He pressed his lips to my wound and sucked as he slid a finger inside me. My climax shuddered already on the edge from his magic. He added a second finger, filling me, and rubbed circles on my clit.

I moaned, my breath fast, and he took another pull on my cheek. His thumb pressed hard against my clit, the circles faster, matching the pace with my breath and pulse, and his fingers worked inside me building the heat into a tightly formed supernova that exploded with a cry of pleasure.

He held me tight as I rode the wave, his lips still pressed to my cheek, but instead of sucking, this time a wave of warmth seeped across it, his miniscule bit of healing magic closing my wound just enough to stop the bleeding.

"Thank you," he whispered against my cheek, then lifted me and carried me out of the shower. He set me on my feet long enough to wrap me in a towel, and carried me to his bed. Now I couldn't tell if I was dizzy because of Gideon getting shot or Jacob bringing me to climax.

He pulled back the covers and laid me on the bed. "I'll go find your clothes."

I grabbed his hand before he could leave and tugged him back to me. "I meant what I started in the shower."

His pupils dilated, his desire raw in his eyes, and the temperature, still hot and humid with need, spiked to sweltering for a heartbeat. "You won't know that until the power of my claim has eased enough for you to say no to it."

He tugged his hand free, grabbed a dry pair of pants and a T-shirt from his closet, and left.

I groaned. He was right, and yet I didn't want to fight my attraction to him. Just like I didn't want to fight my attraction to Marcus.

Jeez, and they weren't the ones I was supposedly destined to be with.

I tugged the sheet and comforter over me and curled up in Jacob's bed. It smelled like him, masculine, rich with a hint of freshness that I now knew came from his body wash. My skin still tingled from my climax, and I closed my eyes and embraced the sensation. There was nothing I could do until Jacob found me a clean set of clothes, and for just a few minutes, I didn't want to worry about Marcus and Gideon. So I focused on Jacob's arms around me, his wet body pressed against mine, and his hands on me.

I imagined him finishing what we'd started in the shower, his power sliding through me as he drove into me, bringing me to climax again, my name on his lips as he came.

JACOB

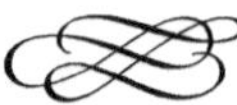

I HURRIED OUT OF MY BEDROOM BEFORE I LOST WHAT LITTLE CONTROL I'D managed to hold on to and went back to Essie lying naked in my bed.

The shower had been a huge mistake.

I should have found someone else to take care of her, but she'd already spent an hour in her bloody clothes on the waiting room couch and I'd been so sure with Gideon's brand on her and Marcus's claim, I'd be able to resist my own connection with her. Mine was temporary. If I didn't weave my essence with hers again it would eventually go away.

And yet after a week and a half of keeping my distance from her, I still hungered for her blood and body. My craving was stronger than even my craving for my first and only other claimed human and I'd been madly in love with Sarah. A part of me feared my hunger for Essie was as strong as my hunger when I'd been newly made a vampire — and that hunger had almost consumed me.

As it was, I couldn't stomach bagged blood anymore and blood bunnies — humans who sold their blood and body to vampires — could barely sustain me and couldn't hold my interest.

Every time I fed, I thought of Essie, of her sweet, rich taste and the enticing strength in her essence that I'd captured within mine. I heard that soft seductive groan of desire, the one she'd barely breathed when I'd first claimed her in Victoria's nightclub and again when she'd saved my life in the cafeteria, over and over again, and ached to hold her in my arms again.

And now I'd tortured myself with her taste and sounds and so much more. Now I knew just how beautiful she was when naked, how soft her skin, and how she responded to my touch. Now I knew exactly how she sounded when she came apart in my arms.

My hard cock grew harder and my gaze leaped to my closed bedroom door, the urge to go to her threatening my control.

She'd said she'd finish what we'd started in the shower. She wouldn't deny me if I said I wanted to sink my fangs and cock into her. She'd been the one who'd started it, begging me to kiss her and rubbing herself against me.

But I'd been the hungry fool who'd given in. The still bleeding gunshot wound on her cheek and her naked body in my arms had been too tempting even though I knew better, knew it wasn't really her choice. My claim was still too strong — she'd needed my permission to answer Gideon back at the feral vampire's nest — and a strong claim increased sexual desire in both the vampire and his human.

She'd have offered to feed and please me whether she wanted to or not, and I wasn't going to take advantage of that. No matter how much I wanted her.

Besides, I might have temporarily claimed her body, but Gideon had claimed her soul and Marcus her heart. My claim could never— *should* never be permanent.

It didn't matter that Marcus and Gideon were currently acting like idiots and not even bothering to figure out how to deal with each other's claim on her. That didn't give me permission to have sex with her, especially since I couldn't be sure she actually wanted to have sex with me.

And damn it. Now I really wanted sex. With Essie.

I had to get farther away from her, out of my apartment, and find where Kol had put her bag of clothes.

I undid the fly on my wet pants so I could change and my cock sprang free, hard and heavy, and in desperate need of attention.

Essie's attention.

I gritted my teeth. Not going to happen. I wasn't going to wake her so I could satisfy myself... no matter how much I wanted to hear her come apart again.

Except I wasn't going to be able to think straight with this raging hard on, and I sure as hell didn't want to show up to the team meeting in a few hours hard as hell for Gideon's and Marcus's mate. Gideon might not notice, but Marcus certainly would, and Kol—

God, I didn't want to think about Kol's reaction. He was still shaken up from dealing with the archnephilim. He put up a good front and I wasn't sure if Gideon or Marcus had figured out that the kid was still shaken, but it was clear to me he still was.

I couldn't let my desire for Essie create problems. Stability within the team helped him, which was funny in a grim, anger-inducing kind of way. He was a being from the Realm of Celestial Darkness, he was supposed to be the chaos to Gideon's order, but I knew sure and steady and predictable helped him keep the nightmares at bay. Twenty-three years and the kid — who wasn't really a kid anymore but still a hell of a lot younger than me — continued to be haunted by his time as Michael's slave.

Our job was chaotic enough. Chaos between the team members didn't help him.

Gideon and Marcus both claiming Essie created enough conflict as it was and adding me to the mix would just make things worse. It was bad enough I'd made her come in the shower — something Kol was sure to pick up on — showing up to the team meeting with unfulfilled desire would only complicate an already complicated situation.

Not to mention with Logan in town, now was the worst time to be divided.

I tried to shove that thought away. I didn't want to think about what I was going to have to do to stop him. He was my brother and it had been hard enough killing him the first time. I didn't want to have to do it again.

Except it looked like that was exactly what was going to happen. That, or he'd end up killing me, Essie, the team, and everyone else in Union City.

I needed to pull myself together, go find a bunny, and deal with my needs before I got anyone killed.

Except that thought had absolutely no appeal. I'd already tried to get blood and sex from a bunny tonight and hadn't been able to go through with it. Just like I'd tried for the last week and a half.

Which meant I was going to have to take care of this need myself and pray my claim on her would wear off soon.

I shoved my pants off, sagged onto my couch, and grabbed my cock.

The image of Essie, her naked body pressed against mine, her head tipped back, and her eyes closed in pleasure, flooded my mind's eye.

She'd melted into my embrace, her nipples had hardened under my touch, and she'd rocked her hips into my hand as I brought her to climax.

I pumped my hand down my length and imagined it was my cock and not my fingers that had filled her.

How would I take her? From behind like I had in the shower?

She'd pressed her hands against the slick tiles, the water sluicing over her hair and back. It would drip from nipples I'd worked into tight buds with my fingers and slide over her rear, showing me the way to paradise.

I'd nudge her legs apart and tease her entrance with my tip. She'd tremble like she had when I'd teased her with my fingers, then I'd slowly push inside her, drawing another delicious "oh yes."

Two small words and I'd almost lost all control. Two small words again and I would.

My balls tightened and I picked up my pace, jerking my hand up and down my length, my climax starting to build. The urge to go, yank open my bedroom door, and burry myself in her squeezed my chest, and I dug the fingers of my free hand into the couch cushion beside me, fighting to stay where I was.

The shower fantasy jumped to her in my bed and the heat in her eyes when she'd told me she'd meant what she'd started in the shower.

Now she lay beneath me, her head thrown back on my pillow, panting and moaning as I thrust inside her, building her up until she tensed and cried her pleasure.

Her imagined cry shot straight to my groin and I came hard in my hand with a long low groan of pleasure that I prayed she didn't hear. I couldn't afford for the claim to compel her out of the bedroom and offer to continue pleasuring me, and there was a chance that it would.

And right now, if she offered to have sex with me again, I wouldn't be able to refuse her, no matter how much I feared my claim was making her want me against her will.

ESSIE

"Essie." My dream-Jacob rumbled, his deep, resonant voice feeding his claim within me, as my dream spun my desires higher. We were in his bed, his teeth in my neck, his power building an earth-shattering climax while his essence sank deeper into mine, attuning me perfectly to him.

"Essie."

God, I felt so good.

A weight settled on my shoulder, and another, bigger one on the bed.

"Essie," Jacob said, his voice clearer, no longer soft and dreamy.

I opened my eyes and met Jacob's gaze. For a second I'd thought he'd returned to take me up on my offer and make my dream come true. There was a tenderness in his expression I hadn't seen before, one that warmed me to my core. But he drew his hand away from me and shifted back. He still sat on the edge of the bed beside me, but the distance between us was clear.

Which, as much as I was disappointed, was probably for the best. I'd had, if not a full reprieve, at least some reprieve from the emotional mess with Marcus and Gideon. But I wouldn't be able to ignore it. As much as I might want to at the moment.

"How do you feel?" he asked.

Still a little boneless and definitely satisfied. But that wasn't what he was really asking about.

I stretched, testing my aching muscles, which weren't nearly as achy as they had been before or should be after lying down for—?

I had no idea how long I'd been out. If Jacob had just contacted Kol and found my bag, it should have only been a few minutes, but my eyes felt gritty, as if I'd slept with my contacts in for at least an hour.

"How long have I been asleep?"

"Almost three hours." He shifted back even farther. "Try sitting up. See if you're still dizzy."

"You let me sleep for three hours." I held the comforter to my chest and eased into a sitting position. The room remained perfectly steady. There wasn't even a hint of exhaustion from the brand, only the gentle hum that I recognized as Gideon's magic felt between the skin-crawling bites from my buzz.

"Recovering was the best thing you could do. You should get dressed." He stood, headed to the doorway to the living room, and leaned against the frame with his back to me. "Kol and Marcus will be back in about ten minutes and Amiah is about to wake Gideon."

My duffle bag sat beside the bed with a keycard and my holstered Glock on top.

"You found out which room I was assigned?"

"Same as before."

"Well, that'll make it easy to remember the next time Gideon gets shot and I'm too exhausted to think straight." I set the Glock and the keycard on the nightstand beside a paperback with a planet and a spaceship on the cover, and opened my bag.

"If that happens, you don't honestly think anyone on the team is going to let you stagger up to your room by yourself?"

Probably not. It depended on what condition the rest of the team was in and if Marcus was still doing everything in his power to push me away.

Except I knew that wasn't true. If it really came down to keeping me safe, Marcus would step up in a heartbeat.

"So what's the plan?' I dressed in the only other set of clothes I had at Operations, and did a quick search for my shoes. They sat beside the bathroom door without a drop of blood on them. "You cleaned my shoes, too?" And I hadn't noticed him return to the room to grab my stuff from the bathroom.

"And sent your other clothes down to be laundered." He jerked his chin toward my shoes without fully looking into the room. "Come on. Let's get you to Amiah to take care of that gash on your cheek."

"Bathroom first, then I'm all yours." *Fully and completely.* I pushed back the claim's urgings, palmed two nicotine patches from my bag, and hurried into the bathroom.

I raked my fingers through my hair, trying to get some of the tangles out, and retied my ponytail, all the while trying to not think about being in the shower with Jacob. The gash in my cheek had stopped bleeding — thanks to Jacob's magic — but it still throbbed and stung.

At least I didn't look so exhausted. It had only been three hours, but it felt like eight. I was back to myself and ready to face my new terrifying job.

I could do this.

I'd squared off with the archnephilim and won. I just needed to be smart about how I worked and dealt with supers.

I peeled off the old patches — and I wasn't going to ask Jacob what he'd thought of them — and slapped on two new ones, then shoved my feet into my runners, pocketed the keycard, and clipped my holster to the waistband of my jeans.

We took the elevator back down to the main floor and strode into triage to find Amiah and Marcus in a tight embrace, the temperature in the room sweltering. Desire. But I didn't know whose. Amiah's cheek was against his shoulder, her hand over his heart, and her eyes closed. His arms were wrapped protectively around her and his lips pressed against the top of her head.

Marcus's gaze lifted and captured me, stealing my breath and making my chest ache for him. For not having him. For everything between us. His eyes were filled with the ferociousness I recognized as his wolf, but I didn't know what it wanted. Hell, I never knew what it or Marcus wanted. Maybe he'd been pushing me away because of what he had with Amiah. Maybe I was imagining the heat between us—

No, the attraction sizzling within me had been there from the moment I'd seen him, and I could see it simmering in his eyes right now. But that didn't mean anything. Just because you were attracted to someone didn't mean you had or even should have a relationship with him.

Except my soul hurt just thinking about him moving on. He'd said in the elevator that I was his. That he didn't care if I had Gideon's mating brand or not.

And then he'd given me up.

Because that was what I'd wanted.

If I cared for him, I'd give him up. But I didn't want to. I'd been dreaming of him for years, of the desire burning between us and his ferocious passion, and I didn't want him to focus that passion on anyone else. He was supposed to be mine.

"Is Gideon up?" Jacob asked.

"He's waiting in the cafeteria," Amiah said, not moving from Marcus's embrace. She sounded exhausted, and if I concentrated past my jealousy, she looked exhausted, too. Sure, she might have gotten as much sleep as I had this morning, but then she'd had to get up and heal Gideon again. I might not like her in Marcus's arms — which was really none of my business since Marcus and I weren't anything, honestly, really — but I did feel bad about her barely being able to recover before needing to use her magic again. "I'm just waiting on Officer Shaw."

"My cheek has stopped bleeding. I'll be fine." That, and I didn't want her to ruin the effects of my new nicotine patches.

"It doesn't look fine," Marcus growled.

"I didn't say it *looked* fine, only that I'll *be* fine."

"It has to still hurt, Essie," Jacob said.

"Jeez. Guys. On the scale of fine to dying, I'm fine."

Amiah pushed out of Marcus's embrace and sat on the arm of the couch. "Just come here."

Marcus glared at me as if he was daring me to refuse medical attention so he could let his wolf loose.

"Fine." I stepped up to Amiah. "I don't care if I have a scar."

"Good, because given how Gideon seems to be a bullet magnet at the moment, I'm doing the bare minimum with everyone else."

"Works for me."

She pressed a finger to my cheek and a flash of heat exploded across my face. I gasped and staggered back, bumping into Jacob's broad chest. He grabbed my upper arms and steadied me, then quickly stepped back as if he didn't want to stay too close to me.

"Let's go," Marcus growled, and he headed deeper into the hospital section of Operations, taking the smaller halls to get to the cafeteria.

Given that it was just after ten in the morning, the cafeteria was empty with the exception of two women — one with the glowing eyes of an angel, the other looking human — who sat at a table in the sunroom side. Gideon and Kol already sat at the six-person table, with three mugs in the center, along with a carafe that smelled like it contained coffee, and half a dozen tinfoil wrapped somethings that smelled like eggs and bacon.

Gideon was eating one of the wrapped somethings — best guess a breakfast burrito — looking as if he hadn't almost died last night. His gaze jumped to me.

Just like Marcus, he could stall my pulse with a glance. His summer-sky eyes were icy. Any warmth I'd glimpsed last night was gone. And just like Marcus, that made my chest ache with a yearning that could only be compelled by his mating brand etched onto my arm, because we didn't really know each other.

His attention slid to my cheek and his eyes narrowed. "You should get Amiah to heal that."

I brushed my fingers over the gash. I hadn't bothered to look in a mirror to see how much she'd healed it. I was just grateful her magic hadn't manifested as searing lightning and that my nicotine patches still kept my buzz manageable — and hey, now that I stood only a few feet from Gideon, my buzz had quieted even more. Besides, my cheek no longer throbbed and didn't sting when I touched it, so I considered it a win all around.

"It's fine."

"It's not fine," Gideon said.

"I've already had this argument with Marcus. I'm not having it with you." I sat in the chair beside Kol and across from Gideon, and grabbed one of the breakfast burritos from the pile at the center of the table.

Marcus and Jacob sat on either side of Gideon. Now all three of them could glare at me. Wonderful.

Kol shifted in his seat, his attention sliding from Jacob to me, his eyebrows raised.

And just great. The incubus had figured out something had happened between me and Jacob. I wondered if he'd felt the sexual energy of my climax when it happened, or if he was just now noticing the residual energy that probably still clung to me.

He jerked his gaze away from me and took a long sip of his coffee.

"Jacob, why don't you tell us what's going on?" Gideon said.

My pulse stuttered, my mind jumping to what we'd done in the shower, and Kol choked on his coffee.

ESSIE

GIDEON FROWNED AT KOL THEN TURNED HIS ATTENTION BACK TO JACOB. "I'm assuming that vampire at Victoria's is connected to the feral vampires."

"Logan Dunn." Jacob poured himself a cup of coffee, didn't add anything to it, and hunched forward over the table, the cup captured between his palms.

He still had the tightness around his eyes that I'd seen last night, and while I was sure he'd eaten — now that I was paying attention and not still fantasizing about how he'd made me feel — he still looked worn down.

"He's making them," Jacob said. "He was a witch before he was turned and afterwards he made a deal with a hellfire prince."

Kol's eyes widened and the room's temperature dropped. "Oh, shit."

"We'd know if one of the princes was free," Marcus said, reaching for a breakfast burrito and digging in.

"Ibizual isn't free. That was Logan's deal. A taste of the power promised by the prince for his freedom and then the rest of the promised power upon release." Jacob ran his thumb over the rim of the mug. "Logan is supposed to be dead."

"That's what Victoria said," Gideon said.

And was probably why Jacob hadn't mentioned him when we were last sitting around this table trying to figure out who was making the ferals.

"If the seal imprisoning Ibizual is weak enough," Kol said, "he would have the power to bring a vampire back."

Jacob raised his gaze to Kol, and a hint of misty grief curled around me. "Even if that vampire was burned to ash?"

Or the mist could be guilt. Probably a combination of the two. Jacob had said he and Logan were brothers, they'd grown up together, and in the end Jacob had killed him.

"If Ibizual had claimed that vampire's essence, then yeah, he could." Kol's hands trembled, and he gripped his mug tighter. "There's a reason demons imprisoned the princes two millennia ago, and why Lucifer didn't try to free them to escape the Realm of Celestial Darkness."

"So we have to assume Ibizual is attempting another escape," I said between bites of burrito, hoping Jacob's mist would ease up before it gathered on my cheeks and drew suspicion. "I can't imagine any other reason to bring Logan back."

"I agree," Gideon said. "Logan said his hundred and fifty years were up. Any idea what that meant?"

"I think it has something to do with the key to break the seal on Ibizual's cage. It's also why he came after me. We're magically connected. I felt where the key manifested the last time. He must believe I'll feel it this time, too."

"Does this magical connection allow you to find him?" Marcus asked.

"No. But he can't use it to find me, either." Jacob glanced at Gideon. "From my guess on the decay of the bodies we found in the nest, he's been back for about a month and a half. The new moon is tomorrow, which means the key will manifest in this realm tonight."

"Of course it will," Marcus said, finishing his burrito and taking another one. "Because a bunch of ferals and a witch-vampire-sniper just isn't enough."

Gideon shot him a dark look. "Is he as good a marksman as you, Jacob?"

"We were close in skill, but I was always better," Jacob said.

"That doesn't make me feel better," Marcus said around a mouthful of food. "You're the best marksman I've ever seen. Even if he has half of your skill, he'd still be damned good."

"Okay." Kol took a steadying breath, but his fear still dropped the temperature, mingling with Jacob's mist. At least it wasn't absolute terror, and I didn't have to hide the frost on my hands, although much more and the mist might start to freeze in the air around me. "You beat him before. You can beat him now."

"Except I didn't really beat him. He's still alive." Jacob pursed his lips, the tightness around his eyes deepening and his mist thickening. "We fought over the key until sun up. I got in a lucky strike and managed to get to cover before I burned up. Then I watched the sunrise turn him to ash and stared at that ash until the sun set."

I wanted to reach across the table and grab his hand, let him know it would be okay, and it wasn't just the claim tugging at my heart. But the horror of the situation was that he'd killed a man who'd been his brother and now he was going to have to do it again. I couldn't even begin to imagine what that felt like. That, and he hadn't mentioned that specific detail to the guys, and I didn't know if he wanted them to know.

His gaze lifted to mine as if he could hear my thoughts. "Am I going to have to kill him every hundred and fifty years?"

"We need a witch who knows about the cages," Gideon said. "I'll talk to—" Despair flashed across his expression, exploding in a mist so thick I couldn't see across the table, before it vanished and his expression hardened into an icy mask. He'd been about to say Zella. She'd been an angel able to cast spells and, from the fact that he'd instantly thought of her, must have had knowledge, or a way to find information, about the cages imprisoning the hellfire princes.

And now I wanted to hold *his* hand. But I was a reminder that no matter how much he'd loved Zella, they were never meant to be.

"Bane might know," Marcus said, his tone even, as if he hadn't noticed Gideon's reaction, even though I'm sure everyone at the table had.

Jacob shook his head. "We've already asked him to get us that coalescence snare at the last minute to deal with the archnephilim. He'll raise his price if we come to him again so soon with another rush job."

"Then he raises his price," Gideon said.

Jacob opened his mouth to argue, but Gideon stopped him with a sharp look before he could speak.

"Even if you weren't connected to this, we'd still need the information. We need to know everything we can about Ibizual and his cage, and most important, we need to find out if we can prevent Ibizual from bringing Logan back again. There were over two dozen bodies in that nest and at least a dozen ferals at Rouge. That's already thirty-six people he's murdered at a minimum. We need to permanently stop him before he kills more people."

"And Marcus and I think we've found another nest," Kol said.

Gideon gave him a questioning look.

"The place reeks of human decomp," Marcus said.

"We didn't go inside to confirm, just in case there were a lot of ferals, but if it's anything like the first one, there's another pile of bodies in there," Kol said.

Gideon turned his hard gaze to Marcus. "Call Bane and get him on this. And I don't care what the price is. The JP will understand the expense."

Marcus pulled out his phone and tapped out a text.

"We also need to clean out that nest," Jacob said.

"Do you think Logan will be there?" Kol asked.

Jacob shook his head. "I doubt it, but he's clearly making himself an army and it'd be better to deal with them now when they're at their weakest than tonight when they're stronger and the key is manifesting."

"Okay." Gideon folded his burrito wrapper into a perfect square and smoothed out the foil. "We clear out that nest now. With luck, there'll be a clue there pointing to Logan's location. Regardless, tonight we'll secure that key then wait it out until the new moon has passed."

"Any idea what kind of magic the hellfire prince gave Logan?" Kol asked. His fear had eased up a bit, but the coffee in his mug still quivered, revealing the tremor in his hands.

"He has power over the dead," Jacob said.

"Of course," Gideon said. "That's how he resisted Victoria's power over him."

"Does that power over the dead include you?" I asked.

Jacob met my gaze, and I knew instantly the answer was yes.

Gideon stiffened and Marcus swore.

The claim started screaming, but I shoved its voice to the back of my head. "Is there a way to protect yourself?"

"I don't know. It happened so fast last time, I didn't have to figure much out," he said. "And I'd thought I wouldn't need to think about it ever again."

"Get Bane on that, too." Gideon stood. "These ferals are hard to kill and blades are our best bet. Marcus, take Officer Shaw down to the armory and get her situated."

"Essie isn't coming," Marcus growled.

And after the fight at Rouge, a part of me wholeheartedly agreed with him. But another part knew they'd need all the help they could get.

The muscles in Gideon's jaw tightened. "Our orders say differently."

"Fuck our orders." Marcus stood and met Gideon eye to eye — or almost eye to eye since Gideon was a few inches taller than Marcus. "She's not running in there with a fucking sword decapitating ferals."

Put that way... Yeah, that seemed like a terrible idea. "Can any of the ferals be saved?" Maybe there was a way to prevent a bloodbath.

"No." Jacob downed his coffee and squared his shoulders. The grief and guilt he'd felt earlier had been shoved down and he was back to business. "The magic that makes a feral is incomplete. Their minds are gone, and they're driven only by the command of their sire and their base feral hunger."

"Like Michael's nephilim," Kol said.

"Michael's nephilim were worse." The light in Gideon's eyes darkened. "We say they were animals because of their merciless brutality, but when Michael didn't have full control of them, they could think for themselves. And when they could, they still slaughtered humankind. That's what truly made them monsters."

The room's temperature rose, Gideon's anger burning through Kol's fear, and my fear tightened within me.

This was why I had to resist the pull of the mating brand. I couldn't let myself forget that. It was bad enough I had to work with the team to keep my job. Letting myself get closer to Gideon would just increase the risk of him discovering the truth. At least my only magic was my screwed-up empathy and now my glowing eyes. The eyes I could say glowed from blasting all that divine light into my body, and because of the mating brand, it hadn't faded. As for the empathy... I might be able to pass that off as having a bit of supernatural DNA somewhere in my family tree.

It was a risk, but it let me keep my job, and it let me stay with the guys—

Holy shit. As terrifying as being a JP agent was, I didn't want to leave. I didn't want to go back to my old life. I couldn't go back. And while I could argue that was because I was magically connected to Gideon and Jacob, that didn't address my desire to face my fears and explore what could be between Marcus and me, or the friendship I wanted with Kol.

That, and a part of me, a small voice in the back of my mind, wondered if Gideon would really despise me if he knew the truth. Fate claimed we were soul mates. Was that enough for him to see me differently?

"—kindest option for a feral is a quick death," Jacob said, and I jerked my attention back to him.

He frowned at me. All the guys were staring at me. Did they know what I was thinking? Was my realization clear on my face?

A blush of embarrassment crept up my neck even though I had nothing to be embarrassed about. "If they can't be saved, load me up with an assault rifle with enspelled ammo and I'll cover your backs."

"Only a kill shot will take them out," Gideon said.

"A non-kill shot will make them stumble." I met his gaze. "I believe I saved your ass at least once in Rouge with that technique." *I also saved your ass by feeding my strength into your body when you were shot.*

"Marcus, take Officer Shaw to the armory and set her up with an M4 and a vest."

"One point for the human," Kol said under his breath.

Gideon shot him a fierce glare, then rolled his eyes and shook his head. "Be in the garage in ten minutes, and I better see everyone with a sword and a vest." His attention jerked to Marcus. "Even you. Your wolf isn't going to be an asset in this."

Gideon grabbed his empty burrito wrapper and coffee mug, set them on the stainless steel counter by the kitchen door, and marched out of the cafeteria.

Jacob shot me a worried glance and followed him as Marcus rolled his burrito wrappers into one ball and tossed it into the garbage can twenty feet away.

"Let's get this over with," he growled, standing and heading to the stairs.

I stood to follow, but Kol grabbed my wrist, his hand hot against my skin from his heightened demonic body temperature and the air still a bit chilly from his fear.

"What the hell are you doing?" he asked.

"My job?" Jeez, I hadn't thought Kol would fight me on this like Marcus.

"Jacob isn't your job." A hint of hellfire flickered in his gaze and a trickle of sensual heat slid up my arm before his eyes narrowed and it vanished with a flash. "You might have washed away the scent so Marcus can't smell it, but I can still feel the residual energy radiating off the both of you. If I'd been here when you guys had—" His gaze jumped to

Marcus, who was now at the top of the cafeteria steps. "Jeez, I could have been anywhere in the building and it probably would have brought me close to full."

"We didn't have sex," I said, keeping my voice low. It had been awfully darn close, but technically there had been no intercourse.

He raised his eyebrows, clearly not believing me. "The situation is complicated enough."

"No shit. And Jacob's part of that complication."

"He is now."

"He was before. You know what his bite feels like. I fed that into you when I was saving your life." That was when the archnephilim had nearly killed them and I'd been desperate to save them. I shuddered at the memory of that moment, along with the memory of being in the shower with Jacob.

Kol's breath hitched and the hellfire in his eyes flared. "Jesus."

"Stop making eyes at the incubus, Shaw, and get a move on," Marcus barked from the top of the cafeteria steps.

Kol's attention jerked to Marcus, but his volume didn't rise. "You have to stop. Marcus is going to lose his shit when he finds out."

"Well, I'm going to lose my shit if Jacob's claim doesn't ease up. If Jacob was any other kind of guy, I'm sure we would have finished what we'd started last night." Which was one of the reasons I was attracted to him and knew that wasn't because of the claim.

"I need this team," Kol said.

"For fuck's sake, Shaw," Marcus snarled.

"You have to work it out with Marcus."

And that was the truth. If I wanted to stay with the team, I'd be miserable if Marcus was constantly trying to push me away. Except how did I convince him I was there to stay, that I wanted to be a part of his world, when the brand on my arm said I belonged to Gideon?

ESSIE

I HURRIED UP THE CAFETERIA STEPS TO MARCUS, AND HE JAMMED HIS thumb against the elevator call button, the air around him searing with his frustration.

"This is the stupidest thing you've ever done," he said.

"I'm pretty sure shooting an enormous blast of divine light into myself to kill an archnephilim was the stupidest."

"Yeah, and how many lives are you down to now, kitty?"

The elevator door slid open and we got in.

Marcus hit the button for the basement and desire unfurled low within me at the memory of what we'd done in there only a few weeks ago. Add that to his emotional heat, and I was instantly covered in sweat.

"You'd rather I be fired from the force?" I asked, determined to ignore my attraction to him.

"I'd rather you be alive."

"I could be killed just as easily walking the beat."

The door slid open, revealing the study area straight ahead with a wide wooden table and a couch illuminated by two hanging fluorescent lights. Across from the couch stood a security door with a keypad lock, and through the safety glass window, I could see a long rack filled with different kinds of rifles.

"No, pretty sure chasing down supers is more dangerous than

walking the beat." Marcus headed to the security door and pressed his thumb to the fingerprint pad.

"It would be less dangerous if I knew you had my back."

"If I have your back, then I have all of you." He opened the door and stormed inside. "And I already know I can't have all of you."

"Marcus I—"

He wrenched around, his gaze jumping to Gideon's brand on my arm, his wolf darkening his green eyes, making him look dangerous.

I crossed my arms and glared back at him. "You said you didn't care about the brand."

"And you said you wanted your life back."

"What if I was wrong?"

Horror flashed through his expression and the room's temperature plummeted. "Don't ever say that. You don't belong here. You deserve a normal life, a normal husband, normal kids, normal friends, normal God damn everything."

I pressed my hand to the brand. "This says differently."

"You already know what I think about that." He jerked away from me, opened a wide locker beside him, and grabbed a bulletproof vest with the letters JP printed on the front and back in blocky white letters. He tossed it on the long narrow standup table that stood in the middle of the room, headed to the end of the rack with the rifles, and pulled down the M4 carbine.

And while I knew he didn't care that I wore Gideon's brand, he also knew, whether I wanted to be or not, I was always going to be bound to Gideon. "I—"

"We're not having this discussion," he said, setting the M4 on the table and heading to the shelves filled with boxes of ammunition and extra magazines. "Focus on not getting us killed."

"I'm not the one who's been shot twice in the last twelve hours." I drew my Glock and ejected the magazine.

Marcus set extra magazines, a box of enspelled 9mm, and a box of 5.56mm on the table. He grabbed one of the magazines for the M4 and started loading it. His frustration simmered around me as he filled the first magazine then started on the second one.

I reloaded my magazine, my fingers slippery with sweat, slid it back into my Glock, and reholstered my weapon.

The heat in the cramped armory kept growing. Marcus and I needed to clear the air, but I knew if I opened my mouth, he'd stare me down, so

I started on filling the second 9mm magazine, my lips pressed firmly together.

I tried to concentrate on something else. Anything else. I didn't have deep enough pockets in my jeans for the extra magazines and was going to need to run up to my room to grab my duty belt. At least I wouldn't also have to bring along my Taser or flashlight. All the guys knew the effects of Jacob's claim, and if we ended up in a location with low light, I wouldn't need to hide my enhanced night vision. And if we ended up someplace with no light, the light on the M4's scope would do.

But Marcus's heat made staying focused on the task at hand impossible.

He popped round after round into the magazine, the muscles in his jaw getting tighter with each passing second.

"If things go south," he said, his voice low, "you get the hell out of there."

I couldn't tell if this was him compromising or not.

"Promise me," he growled.

"I'll promise if you promise."

He set the magazine on the table and captured me with his gaze. "I'm smart enough to know when to leave."

"You leave because you're afraid."

His eyes narrowed, his expression clear that he knew I wasn't talking about leaving a fight but leaving me. "I leave for you because you're too stupid to know you're supposed to be afraid." He stormed past me and out the door. "Put the ammo boxes away before you go," he growled over his shoulder and headed for the stairs instead of taking the elevator.

I bit my lip, stopping myself from yelling after him again and reminding myself that he was just trying to protect himself.

And I wasn't too stupid to know I should be afraid. I was afraid. But some things shouldn't be avoided even if they were terrifying. Fate was determined to keep me in this world. And foolish as it was, *I* was now determined to stay, too. I wasn't going to fight it any more.

When this situation was over, I was going to need more training. Whatever it took to not be a liability to the team.

I shrugged into the vest, put the ammunition boxes back, and with the M4 in hand, headed to my assigned room. It hadn't changed since I'd last been there — not that I'd expected it would. It had looked like a hotel room then and it still did now, decorated in blue-grays and creams, with a queen-sized bed, a panel TV on the wall, and a couch near the large window that took up most of the back wall. My duffle bag sat on the floor at the foot of the bed and the clothes I'd been wearing last night were clean and folded on top — including my bra and undies.

I grabbed my duty belt from my bag, took off everything but my holster and two pouches for my extra magazines, and headed down to the garage.

MARCUS

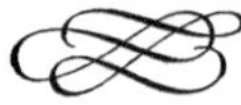

She was going to kill herself! She was God damn going to blindly run into danger — again! — and this time kill herself.

How could she possibly think being in my world was a good idea? It didn't matter that she had Gideon's brand or that my wolf was snarling at me to fully claim her. It was too damn dangerous. And for her to say that she'd been wrong, that maybe she did belong in the supernatural world—

I slammed my fist into the cinderblock wall of the stairwell and roared my frustration as I barreled up the stairs to my room.

She was human and fragile and deserved a long, happy, *normal* life.

With me.

Not. With. Me. Why won't you accept that?

Because she's mine.

It was as straight forward and messed up as that.

Essie was mine. It didn't matter that she had Gideon's brand or that just being near me endangered her life. It didn't matter if I dated other women or swore off them completely. Essie was my mate. *Mine mine mine.*

And I had to get her to leave the team. Even if I broke her heart or destroyed her career, I had to get her away from my world. It was the only way I could protect her, since she seemed determined to throw herself into every dangerous supernatural situation she stumbled across.

She already had an ugly scar on her neck from last night and now she had one on her cheek from a barely missed gunshot. I had no doubt the archnephilim's brand was still on her body. How many more scars would she get? How many more injuries? How many more near misses could she survive?

I'd tried to avoid her to keep her safe — hell, I'd spent the last week and a half barely holding my wolf back from going to her apartment and claiming her — and when I'd seen her on the sidewalk outside of the abandoned school, I'd had to force myself to walk away. I couldn't look at her, couldn't even glimpse her. My wolf had been howling at me with a gut-churning mix of need and fear, its desires as fucked up as mine. He wanted her but he also wanted her safe.

Seeing her walk into the cafeteria and learning that she'd been forced onto the team, not to mention finding out that Jacob's claim on her was still strong, had been too much.

It was all too much.

I needed her gone. I was going to lose my mind being near her but not being able to have her, not to mention watching her run headlong into danger with Gideon's blessing no less!

I had to protect what was mine.

Hold her. Claim her. Mine mine mine.

No. Get her back to her safe — or rather safer — human world.

But yelling at her hadn't worked, and yelling at Gideon never worked. He didn't seem to care that she was supposed to be his mate. The icy bastard was treating her like any old disposable soldier and that pissed me off more than knowing she was his destined mate.

The only thing that had seemed to make the fire in Essie's eyes dim was seeing me hugging Amiah. Of course then that fire flared even stronger with a jealousy that made my wolf mentally roll on its back and happily beg for belly rubs. Jealousy meant she recognized our claim on her. Jealousy meant she wanted us as much as we wanted her.

But then we'd already known that. Even before I'd kissed her or made her come in the elevator, the attraction between us had been explosive.

What I had with Amiah was nothing compared to what I had with Essie.

Sure, Amiah and I had gotten close during those months four and a half years ago when I'd been in the hospital, and we'd flirted a bit over the years — and I still wasn't sure if she was attracted to me or not — but my wolf only ever had eyes for Essie.

Amiah was a good friend, the kind you hung out with and hugged when they were feeling down and exhausted. The kind who protected you when they thought you were acting like an idiot... which was what Amiah was doing now with Essie.

She blamed Essie for my transition into a werewolf, a transition that had been a week straight of blinding agony that couldn't be eased with sedatives or painkillers, and it didn't matter that I'd tried to tell Amiah it wasn't Essie's fault. Amiah knew my wolf wanted Essie and she'd decided that I wasn't thinking straight — which I wasn't — and wasn't going to change her mind.

The only way Amiah would accept Essie was for Essie to prove herself, and she wasn't off to a good start. She'd acted recklessly to save that little girl and I got infected with lycanthropy, and then she'd snuck off to face the archnephilim alone, forcing the rest of the team to scramble to protect her and Gideon.

Given how Essie thought, I had no doubt she was going to continue to be reckless in an attempt to save lives which would only put her in a deeper hole in Amiah's eyes.

And that didn't solve my problem. Amiah's animosity and Essie's jealousy over our friendship wouldn't push her away, and it was getting harder and harder to push her away myself. Every time I said something nasty, my wolf tried to take over and hold her closer.

God, it had been so much easier when I didn't have to look at her, and I had no idea how I was going to hold my shit together while working with her, especially when we were about to walk headlong into a feral vampire nest.

Our mate is strong. She fights like a wolf.

But she's not a wolf. She'll get herself killed.

Not if she fights at our side. We can protect her.

No. We can't and you know it.

We can. She's mine. Forever.

Gideon's brand says differently. She's destined to be his. And from the continued strength of Jacob's claim, not to mention the fact that he'd started to smell different, suggesting his hunger had become focused on Essie, she was also Jacob's.

And mine, my wolf snarled, furious at the reminder of how strong Jacob's claim was.

She can't be ours. She's theirs.

And ours.

I punched the stairwell wall again and screamed.

Why couldn't my damned wolf understand? Destiny said she belonged with Gideon and the only way we could possibly fight destiny was to force her away from him and us and everything supernatural. It was the only way to keep her safe and I was God damned going to make it happen if it was the last thing I did.

ESSIE

All the guys were waiting for me, even Marcus, who'd only left to go up to his room a minute before me. They all wore vests, even Gideon — thank God — and Marcus and Jacob wore sheathed swords at their hips. Gideon didn't need one since he could make one out of pure light, and Kol had a pair of long daggers in sheaths strapped to his back and hidden beneath his shirt. Jacob also had his pair of 92 FS Berettas holstered at his hips, but had left off his duster, making him look a little less like a Wild West gunslinger, but not by much.

Jacob handed me an earpiece, his fingers brushing mine, making the claim sing and Kol scowl. We piled into a JP SUV, Marcus driving, Gideon beside him, Jacob in the back, and Kol and I in the middle, and headed to the second nest.

The tension and whirl of emotions from the guys made the air thick and hot, and I scrambled out of the vehicle the moment Marcus parked in front of a squat brown-brick subway station entrance. Three of the four doors were boarded up, along with a wide window that belonged to the attached variety store. This had been the last stop for the red line before explosive magic from Michael's nephilim army had destroyed the tunnels halfway between there and downtown. And while it was beyond the borders of my precinct, it was still less than three miles from the abandoned school.

All of the buildings on the street, two-story storefronts with a smattering of three- and four-story office buildings, were boarded up. Redevelopment hadn't reached this far from the downtown core and until the city's human population rebounded, it probably wouldn't.

Gideon got out of the SUV and strode past me to the door that wasn't boarded up. The glass had been broken and lay in chunks, half on the concrete outside and half on the gray tiles inside. He glanced into the darkness, the glow in his eyes billowing. "I can't smell anything."

"Trust me, there are a lot of dead things in there." Marcus joined him, his nose scrunched in disgust.

"I don't doubt you," Gideon said. "You take point with Kol and get us to that nest. Jacob, you and Essie have the rear."

Marcus drew his sword, dipped under the handrail, and stepped inside, his boots crunching on glass. Kol followed, drawing his matching daggers, then Gideon, then me with Jacob close behind.

Inside the air was cool and musty and clashed with the flickering heat of the guys' emotions. I couldn't smell the decomp Marcus had mentioned, but I also didn't have the senses of a wolf. To my right, the metal grating in front of the wide entrance to the variety store had been forced open wide enough for a large person to get through. The space had already been picked clean by scavengers, anything metal that could be melted down and reused — including shelves and racks — had been taken, and most of the ceiling panels had been pulled down and the wires ripped out.

I swept my gaze over the empty storefront, pausing at the open door at the back — likely leading to the stock room — then along the wall to the front beyond Gideon's arm and the wide stairs leading down. There wasn't anywhere else to go.

We crept down the stairs. Someone had cut off the metal handrail and many someones had covered the tiled walls with graffiti. The air grew cooler, but it did nothing to ease the emotional heat from the guys. I didn't know if it was better or worse that the heat wasn't steady. I wasn't boiling, but the fluctuations made it harder to ignore.

The stairs led down to a wide platform with sunken subway tracks on either side. A colorful abstract tile mosaic covered the walls and the arched ceiling in a drastic difference to the austere brown exterior.

I scanned left and right, searching for any hint of movement. There was almost no light down there — the only illumination came from the stairs behind us and somewhere far ahead down the right-hand line — and while my vision wasn't perfect, it was still pretty good.

Jacob shifted closer to me. "You should switch on your light."

Marcus swore. "That'll fuck up my night vision."

"All of our night vision, and I don't want to waste power to make a light," Gideon said. "Switch the scope on your M4 to thermal, and I'll order gear for agents without night vision when we get back."

"How about not ordering the gear and not bringing Essie into near-blackout feral vampire nests," Marcus said.

"Let it be," Gideon said, his voice more low and dangerous than I'd ever heard before. "Officer Shaw is staying. Those are our orders."

"I'll be fine." I thumbed the switch on my scope to thermal. "Thanks to Jacob's claim, I can see as well now in this almost-no-light as I could before at night with a streetlight and no flashlight."

Gideon's back stiffened. If I hadn't been close and right behind him, I might not have noticed. "The claim is that strong?"

The emotional heat around me flashed hotter. I glanced at Jacob, who frowned, but I didn't know if the frown meant he was worried about how strong his claim was or if my night vision was better than it was supposed to be — which might give away my partial angelic nature.

A thread of fear curled small and tight in my gut, and I vowed to ignore it. It was Jacob's claim, not another side effect of having the arch-nephilim trying to awaken any nephilim magic I didn't possess.

If asked, I'd chalk it up to an unexpected effect of the brand and blasting all that divine light into myself.

But a part of me feared that excuse would only go so far and last so long. Being here with them was playing with fire, and yet just the thought of changing my mind made my chest ache with loss.

And now wasn't the time to deal with it.

I ground my teeth against my whirling emotions — and the heat from theirs and my God damned buzz — brought my scope to my eye, and glanced into the dark tunnel behind us.

Marcus led us forward and to the tunnel on the right toward the only other light source. We hopped off the platform, Marcus and Kol landing without a sound. Gideon's feet crunched slightly in the gravel, mine definitely crunched — even though I was the lightest in the group — while Jacob's didn't make a sound.

I was beginning to have a good idea why humans weren't on JP teams. Aside from the fact that they barely stood a chance against the more powerful supers, a lack of night vision and the inability to move silently over noisy terrain made the human the weakest link. Which stung my pride. I might have made one error in judgment when I was a rookie and turned Marcus into a werewolf, but I'd never before been the weakest link. Even when my buzz had first manifested and been out of control, I'd still managed to hold myself together and do my job.

I scanned the tunnel behind us. No sign of movement or heat signatures — and the scope would still pick up the ferals even if they hadn't recently fed and had low body temperatures.

The tunnel gently turned and ended fifty feet down at a cave-in, the pile of concrete and earth from the ceiling scorched black from some kind of magical attack. Sunlight streamed through a hole edged with the ragged ends of a wide broken pipe and twisted tree roots. A narrow doorway, the metal door ripped from its hinges and lying on the ground a few feet away, stood to the right.

"The nest is probably less than a hundred feet this way," Marcus said, and he headed into the narrow access hall.

Ten feet down the hall, I could smell the bodies. The reek of decomposition thickened the air and clung to the inside of my nose. The temperature in the hall was even cooler than the subway tunnel and a starker contrast to the heat coming from the guys. Moisture clung to the walls, dripped from the seams in a pipe running along the ceiling, and pooled on the concrete floor.

We hit a T-intersection, turned right, and reached a narrow set of concrete stairs, its metal railing still intact. The stairs led down into a wide area, three stories tall, with a bright band of sunlight slicing from one of a dozen grates close to the ceiling into the mouth of a large sewage pipe on the third story. More pipe mouths peppered the walls, some caved in and shallow, but most black maws that I could only see a foot or two inside. They were all big enough for a human or bigger, and more than I could keep an eye on at any given time.

The floor was tiered, as if the area had been built in a patchwork. A few of the highest ones looked like landings, while the rest had slopes, all directing to the lowest level and the widest, floor-level tunnel. Water pooled on the lower levels, and the reek of decomposition was nearly suffocating. Bodies littered half the landings, the piles more haphazard than the one in the school. There were easily three times as many victims here than there had been at the first nest.

"Eyes open," Gideon said, his voice low as he followed Marcus down the stairs.

I swept my scope to a pipe mouth on the other side of the stairs.

Three heat signatures. Two more in the tunnel beside it. Another one in the tunnel beside that.

"They're in the tunnels," I said. "I've got six—" Four more in the next tunnel and two in the one above. "At least twelve."

"Jeez, Logan's been busy," Marcus growled, reaching the bottom and scanning the tunnels closest to the stairs.

Kol hopped over the railing, skipping the last five steps, and landed beside Marcus. "How the hell did no one notice this many missing humans?"

"Since the war, more people are living off the grid," Gideon said.

"And we did notice," I said. "Missing persons has seriously spiked in the last month or so."

A low growl rumbled around the chamber, echoing off the concrete walls and growing in volume until it felt as if it came from all around us. Then someone screamed a high-pitched howl and a woman, covered in blood and filth, with matted hair and a ripped T-shirt, barreled out of the tunnel across from the stairs. Her eyes were wild, her fangs extended, and her nails sharpened claws.

She rushed toward Kol, throwing herself at him, and he deftly side-stepped her attack, sliced her arm with one dagger, and rammed the other into the base of her neck.

With a gurgled scream, she collapsed to the ground, but more ferals started howling and the dozen I'd counted ran from their tunnels toward the guys.

Kol rushed to the center of the room to meet them, making space for Gideon, who summoned his sword of divine light and decapitated a feral as he marched to meet a group of three coming from a pipe only a few feet from the stairs.

Marcus snarled and stabbed at a feral rushing toward Kol. He sliced open the feral's side. The creature stumbled but didn't drop and changed targets, lunging at Marcus.

Jacob drew his Berettas and fired at a feral coming from a tunnel on the other side of the room. His shot hit right between the eyes. Blue lightning crackled around the feral's body. The creature screamed and died, his body crumpling to the floor, but two more jumped over it and rushed into the fight.

I kept scanning the tunnels, but there were heat signatures in all of them. I fired a three-round burst at a feral dashing toward Marcus. Lightning crackled around it as it stumbled but didn't drop, and Marcus swept his sword out and decapitated it.

Jacob fired again and dropped another one with a flash of blue lightning.

Someone above me howled, and a bulky feral dropped from the third-story tunnel and crashed down on Jacob.

My pulse leaped. They weren't just on the ground level.

Jacob jerked out of the way, but the feral's razor sharp claws still slashed his hand and ripped the Beretta from his grip. He grabbed the feral by its leather sports jacket, pressed the muzzle of his other Beretta to its heart, and fired.

Lightning swept around the feral, and Jacob tossed his body into another feral who was moving faster than humanly possible. Many of them were, actually, which meant they were older than the ones I'd come across in the school, or Logan had figured out how to make stronger ferals.

I jerked my attention to the second- and third-story tunnels and counted more heat signatures. "Heads up. There are more in the second- and third-story tunnels."

"How many more?" Gideon asked.

"Two dozen— Three—" And those were only the ones close enough to see. Whatever Logan's plan, he'd definitely made an army of vicious creatures that were hard to kill. And while the guys were deadly efficient, more ferals kept coming. We were already outnumbered and our odds were getting worse.

ESSIE

I SHOT A THREE-ROUND BURST AT A FERAL ABOUT TO JUMP FROM A SECOND-story pipe onto Kol. The feral fell out of the tunnel and hit the concrete with a sickening crunch, but still staggered to his feet.

Jacob grabbed for his dropped Beretta but it was kicked down a ramp in the scuffle, while Gideon impaled a feral rushing toward Jacob.

The feral I shot lunged at Kol. He twisted out of the way but into the reach of a petite female feral. She grabbed his arm and wrenched him around with her enhanced vampiric strength. He rammed his dagger into her gut, but she didn't even flinch and slashed her claws across his face.

With a roar, Jacob shoved out of the grip of a feral clinging to him and shot Kol's feral in the head before turning back to the group surrounding him. His eyes were black and his vampiric intensity radiated around him, a palpable energy that sang to his claim entwined with my essence.

I wrenched my attention away from him and fired again at the ferals jumping from the pipes. Lightning crackled around all of them, but I wasn't the marksman Jacob was and only managed to drop one out of the five. More rushed from a tunnel on the other side of the stairs. I stepped away from the wall to get a better shot and sent a barrage into the group as they barreled toward Marcus, who snarled, his wolf still captured within his human skin, but barely. Blood splattered him from the ferals he'd killed and oozed from deep gashes on his arms and legs.

Out of the corner of my eye, I watched as Gideon's blazing sword swept through the dim light, leaving a trail in the air. He too was covered in blood, his expression hard and icy, as he moved with powerful precision, each strike meant to kill or maim then kill. He decapitated a feral, twisted and impaled another through the heart, then ducked low, twisting again, as a feral swiped at his back. His blade slashed through one of the feral's legs, drawing a scream and toppling it to its knees.

Another feral lunged for Gideon's back, but he was engaged with two others. I fired a quick burst, making the feral behind him stumble. His gaze leaped up to mine, and the heated electricity from his brand swept up my arm, then he wrenched his attention back to the ferals he was fighting.

Marcus roared and killed another. The bodies were piling up and blood slicked the concrete, making the footing dangerous. I scanned the tunnels for heat signatures.

Nothing.

I did another sweep.

Still nothing.

"I think we're at the end of it."

"Thank God," Marcus growled.

"God has nothing to do with this," a raspy tenor said, his voice carrying over the growls and screams of the fight.

"Take cover," Gideon barked.

Jacob tossed the feral he'd just killed and jerked his attention up, his gaze jumping around the chamber. "Too afraid to come out and fight me?"

"You don't scare me, Lockwood," Logan said.

Marcus shoved past a feral and headed to the closest tunnel's mouth. Kol did the same.

I bolted to the closest cover, an alcove with a pile of bodies, pressed my back tight against the damp wall, and searched the chamber for Logan's heat signature. Still nothing.

Gideon impaled a feral as he ran for the tunnel across from him, and a rifle blast roared through the chamber.

My heart seized and Jacob tackled Gideon, moving with his enhanced vampiric speed. Blood blossomed across the top of Jacob's shoulder. He wrenched Gideon to his feet, and they bolted the rest of the way to the tunnel.

I yanked my scope back to the tunnels where I guessed Logan would be. Still nothing. I had no idea how he was hiding his heat signature, but in the world of supers, anything was possible.

"Jacob, can you find him?" Gideon asked over the coms. "Shoot him?"

"No," Jacob said.

"We can't just wait around," Marcus snarled.

"I'll draw his fire," Jacob said. "I have the best chance of surviving."

"Not a headshot, you won't," Kol said.

"Then I'll have to move fast enough he can't hit me."

Jacob darted from the tunnel mouth.

"Son of a—" Marcus snarled.

Another rifle shot roared through the chamber, and I caught a flicker of muzzle fire from a floor-level tunnel — not at all where I expected a sniper to hide. Another shot and another flare of muzzle fire.

Got you. I aimed just behind the muzzle flare and fired. Lightning exploded around Logan, illuminating him in the tunnel, and he screamed.

"You damn bitch," he howled and jerked his rifle toward me, the temperature spiking.

I wrenched back against the alcove arch as he fired. The shot roared and concrete shrapnel exploded from the edge of the arch.

"Get on out here," he snarled, and a low growl rumbled through the cavern.

"Holy shit," Kol said.

Cold sliced through the heat.

"Essie, watch your back," Jacob yelled.

His claim twisted in my chest, and I wrenched around. The bodies in the pile were moving. A hand, the skin bloated and oozing, reached out from the bottom of the pile and grabbed for my ankle.

I jerked out of the way and shot at it as all the bodies on top rose and heaved toward me.

I fired again, then wrenched back around to face the chamber even though the animated corpses were the biggest threat. All of the bodies with the exception of those the team had decapitated were rising up and rushing toward the tunnels where the guys hid.

Jacob's claim twisted tighter, and my body heaved around again. I scrambled out of reach of an ashen-skinned guy with cloudy dead eyes who wasn't decomposing yet. I fired again, scrambling to get out of the way, only to wrench back around.

God damn it.

"Jacob. Command," I yelled, straining against the claim. It wrenched me around again, and I stumbled to the side, losing my balance as I fought it. A rifle blast sliced across the side of my shoulder, and the claim wrenched me back to face the chamber.

I emptied the rest of my magazine into Logan's tunnel but didn't hit him.

"Essie, protect yourself," Jacob said as he bolted across the chamber toward Logan.

"Stay with the team, Jacob," Gideon said, but Jacob kept running.

Logan fired again, and Jacob twisted, the bullet slicing across the front of his vest.

"Marcus, cover him." The light from Gideon's blade blazed from the mouth of his tunnel.

Marcus surged into sight, but the animated corpses pressed close and clung to him.

The woman with bloated skin broke free of the pile and lunged at me. I jerked out of the way, but another corpse swiped at me. His claws sliced into my arm with burning agony, while another woman wrenched the M4 out of my hands.

"Marcus," Gideon snapped. "To Jacob."

"Trying," Marcus growled back, but he couldn't break through the press of bodies.

Jacob fired into the tunnel where Logan was, didn't hit, holstered his Beretta, and drew his sword without missing a step.

"Kol?" Gideon asked.

"Almost. There—" Kol dove through the press of corpses at the mouth of his tunnel, and they wrenched around and grabbed at him. One snagged his ankle, tripping him just long enough for another to tackle him.

I scrambled out of reach of another body, my mind whirling. Of the team, I was the closest to Logan's tunnel and the only one not completely surrounded by animated corpses, but what kind of backup would I be for Jacob?

Jacob rushed into the tunnel and half a dozen corpses followed him.

I drew my Glock and bolted after him, instinct propelling me forward. I might not be able to help with Logan, and certainly wasn't fast enough to catch a vampire running at full speed, but I could hopefully stop the corpses so they didn't slow Jacob down, making him lose Logan. I'd need to be close enough to get a good shot, but I could handle them long enough for one of the other guys to break free.

"God damn, Essie," Marcus growled over the coms.

"Officer Shaw," Gideon yelled.

"We can't let Logan get away." I barreled after Jacob and the corpses.

The one at the end, slower than the others because of the rotting state of its body, jerked around and rushed at me. I fought my panic and kept running forward. I didn't know if I needed a head shot to stop any of the feral vampire's now animated victims, but I wasn't going to take the chance that I didn't. *And please, God, let a head shot work.*

The corpse snarled at me. I shot it in the chest. It stumbled, and I shoved it against the wall and shot it in the head.

I raced away as the spell's lightning enveloped it, destroying whatever magic animated it. My feet splashed through water and my lungs burned as I strained to run faster.

I reached another corpse with a gaping wound in its chest — this one had been a feral that one of the guys had killed. I shot it in the chest and shoved it against the wall. It raked its claws at my face and I jerked back, but not fast enough. Fire blazed along my jaw. I finished it off and kept running.

"Essie, I'm on your six," Marcus said over the coms.

I bolted around a corner, and Jacob roared. My pulse seized in fear. He stood at the mouth of another chamber, fighting the four remaining corpses, and Logan had his rifle aimed at him.

I fired at Logan, hitting his shoulder with a flash of lightning, and his shot went into the tunnel's ceiling. Jacob slammed an animated corpse at another one, crashing them against the wall, and lunged for Logan.

"Essie, get out of here," Jacob yelled, swinging his sword at Logan, keeping close so the vampire couldn't use his rifle.

The claim twisted, but I clung to my willpower, fighting it. Marcus was close. I could handle these corpses until then. Just a few seconds. That was all I needed to last, because Jacob had to deal with Logan.

I reached the first of the still-standing corpses, shot it in the chest, but I had to wrench out of the way of a slash from another one before finishing it off. The new one, a bulky man with fangs, seized the front of my vest and jerked me close to bite my neck. I shoved the muzzle of my gun to his chest and fired. He screamed and collapsed in a blast of lightning, but the first one was back on me.

I scrambled aside as it swiped at me. Jacob's claim twisted tighter. I had to run, to leave, to get out of there—

God. Damn. No.

I could hear Marcus's footsteps pounding against the water-slick concrete. I just needed to stay a few seconds longer.

"Essie," Jacob barked.

"No." I fired two shots into the reanimated feral in front of me, making it stumble, and shot at its head, killing it.

Marcus rushed around the corner as Logan howled. The animated corpse closest to me lunged. I leaped back but my heel caught on a lip in the floor as an explosion erupted from the chamber's entranceway. I hit the floor, and massive chunks of concrete rained down on me, slamming against my chest and legs and pinning me to the floor.

"Essie," Marcus said over the coms. "Talk to me."

"I'm here."

"What happened?" Gideon asked.

"Cave-in," I said. Jacob, Logan, and I were in another chamber, this one only about thirty by thirty, with only one tunnel leading out. A hint of light came from a grate high above, but no light came directly into the chamber.

Logan laughed, the sound filled with dark glee. "This is wonderful." He blocked Jacob's sword swing with his rifle, and turned so I was in Jacob's line of sight. "Your human is here to watch you die."

"I don't think so." I fought to move under the press of rubble. My left arm was buried, but my right arm and head were clear. Except I couldn't get anything to budge and could barely breathe against the pressure.

"You think you're that much more powerful than me?" Jacob snarled.

"I know so." Logan leaped back, dropped his rifle, and raised both his hands, palms up. "I have Ibizual's power rushing through my veins."

Jacob froze, his arms raised mid-swing, and groaned in agony, his eyes wide.

Logan clenched his hands. Jacob groaned again and collapsed forward, his palms pressed to the concrete, his chest heaving with desperate gasps.

I searched the ground for my Glock. The gun lay a few inches from my outstretched hand.

"And with a touch—" He laid a hand on the back of Jacob's head. "—I can take your unnatural life."

Red energy swept around Jacob, and he screamed. His body went stiff, and Logan howled with glee.

I heaved against the rubble and strained to reach my gun. I was close. So close. My fingers grazed the butt and pushed it a fraction farther.

Shit.

"What the hell is going on in there?" Gideon asked.

"Essie," Marcus said, his voice clipped, "I'm coming. Hold on."

Logan leaned close to Jacob's ear. "I'll take every last drop of your essence," he snarled, "and then I'll take your human's."

Jacob's screams turned desperate.

My soul howled, frantic to stop this, to save him, and it had nothing to do with his claim.

There was no way in hell I was going to reach my gun. My only choice was to pray I could find enough juice for a light strike to break the spell on Jacob so he could fight back.

I flexed my hand back, pointing my palm at Logan, and screamed the divine light strike spell, hoping the force of my words would aid the force of my spell. A blast of light shot from my palm with almost as much power as I'd had when I'd fought the archnephilim.

The blast hit Logan and he jerked toward me, barely a hint of a burn on his neck and face, and that healing before my eyes.

He sneered, and my pulse froze.

"Wait your turn," he growled, and he seized Jacob's head and sank his fangs into Jacob's neck.

ESSIE

FEAR CLENCHED COLD IN MY CHEST. THE RED ENERGY BLAZED BRIGHTER around Jacob and he convulsed as Logan fed on him.

I had to stop him, except my light strike wasn't powerful enough. I couldn't do this alone. Hell, I couldn't do this at all. "Marcus, help."

"I'm trying."

Rubble shifted behind me, but everything within me screamed he wasn't going to get through fast enough.

My mind whirled. There had to be something. All I had was the light strike, but I needed more power. The gold in Gideon's brand on my arm flickered. I'd given him strength to save his life. *Please, God, let him be able to give me power to save Jacob's.*

"Gideon, give me power."

"What?" he asked.

"I need power."

"How can I give you power?" he asked.

"You can—" Shit. There wasn't time to explain this. It had to happen now or Jacob was going to die.

I shoved back all my racing thoughts and concentrated on my connection to Gideon. I imagined drawing every ounce of magic I could get from him into my body and focusing it in my palm.

The electric hum from his brand grew stronger, but it wasn't enough. I needed more.

Come on. Come on. Give me your God damn power.

I mentally yanked with everything I had, and Gideon's power exploded into searing white lightning in my hand. I clung to it, forcing the pressure to build into a blinding agony until I couldn't hold it any longer and then blasted it at Logan.

It slammed into the vampire and smashed him against the chamber wall. He sagged to the floor, his face, neck, and shoulders blackened and bleeding. One eye was completely gone and the skin on his cheek burned down to the bone.

He stared at me, what remained of his face a mask of shock and horror. My whole body shook with electric tremors, and my buzz screamed to life, burning past the nicotine patches.

Rubble tumbled past my head and Marcus scrambled into the chamber.

Logan wrenched to his feet and bolted down the tunnel. Jacob collapsed, blood rushing from the gaping tear in his neck, and didn't move. *Please, God, don't let him be dead.*

Marcus rushed to me, splattered in blood, his body covered with bleeding gashes.

I waved him off. "I'm fine. Check Jacob."

He glared at me but hurried to Jacob, who, thank God, was now groaning, which meant he was still alive.

Kol bounded in next, looking as beat-up as Marcus. He heaved the piece of concrete off my back and left arm, and I gasped in a full breath, my chest aching but not enough to suggest I had broken or cracked ribs.

Gideon staggered in last, also covered in blood and gashes, but his complexion was gray and he clutched his brand. The light radiating from his icy glare flickered and heat from an emotion — I'd place money on anger — surged around me.

"What the hell was that?" he asked.

"One massive light strike, at least as powerful as a blast from a divine light ring," Marcus said. "I didn't think a human could cast a combat spell with that much power."

Kol pushed aside the concrete pinning my legs and helped me shift into a sitting position, my body throbbing and on fire with the buzz.

"They can't. She stole mine." The muscles in Gideon's jaw tightened. "Don't ever do that again," he said, his voice low.

"He was going to kill Jacob. I had to do something." Blood wept from a wide gash in my right leg and I could also feel it trickling down my neck from the slices in my jaw.

"I could have been in the middle of fighting ferals," Gideon snapped. The temperature rose even more, the heat making sweat bead on my forehead and flush my cheeks. "Marcus was almost through the cave-in. Taking all my magic without warning was reckless."

"Marcus wasn't going to be fast enough." I wasn't going to justify my decision to him. Okay, maybe I'd taken more than I should have, but I hadn't even known I could and I'd been desperate.

"You didn't know that. You couldn't see him. Marcus was right. You are a liability." The frustration and disgust in his tone stung. I saw that same look in his eyes that I'd seen in the cops gathered in the basement of the abandoned school. I was dangerous, a death sentence to anyone who worked with me.

I shoved myself to my feet and wobbled, my legs aching. Kol reached to steady me, but I gritted my teeth, fought for my balance, and shoved his hands away. "I made the right call."

"You made a bad call. I'm calling the chief when we get back to Operations and having you replaced."

If he had me replaced, the chief would fire me. Everything I'd worked for, everything I wanted, would be taken away. I'd be a pariah. Even if Gideon's brand did let me leave town, no police force would ever hire me again. God, and here I'd thought Gideon learning I was a nephilim was what would ruin my life.

"It wasn't a bad call," Jacob said, his voice weak, his hands clamped to his neck to staunch the bleeding. But blood still oozed between his fingers.

The fury in Gideon's eyes didn't soften. "She abused the connection of the brand."

"And you're going to destroy my career because of it?" I said.

"You're a danger to everyone you work with." He jerked toward me, using his taller, bigger stature to glare down at me.

"I'm not the one who keeps getting shot," I said.

"My problem. Not yours. Taking all my magic without warning could have killed me."

"And you getting shot almost *did* kill me. I just about had my throat ripped out by a feral because of you. Consider us even." The color drained from his face, and I jerked away and staggered to Jacob's side. "Let's get out of here."

Marcus stared at me with his piercing green gaze, his expression just as hard as Gideon's.

Well, fuck you, too. I'd reached the end of my emotional rope and just couldn't handle them any more. I hurt, inside and out, and the buzz—

God. It was so hard just to think straight.

Marcus shoved between me and Jacob and helped the vampire stand. Kol drew close to me, but didn't try to help me walk. Thank goodness, because I was just as likely to start yelling at him as I was Marcus and Gideon, because I was barely holding my frustration and anger at bay.

I grabbed my Glock, climbed over the rubble now partially blocking the doorway, and marched as best I could back to the SUV. Kol and Gideon gathered the rest of the discarded weapons, and without a word, we piled in and headed back to Operations.

If I'd thought the tension in the vehicle had been tight before, it was practically suffocating now, with drastic temperature fluctuations that made me sweat and shiver at the same time.

Gideon called ahead to alert medical of our situation and have a clean-up team head back to the abandoned subway station to deal with the remaining bodies. When we arrived, Amiah was waiting for us with a gurney and a scowl, and Marcus jerked the SUV to a stop just outside the garage's glass door. He climbed out, leaving the keys in the ignition.

"I'm shifting out the rest of my injuries. Kol, park this," he growled, and stormed to the far end of the garage and out the heavy metal door at the back to the rest of Operations' property.

Gideon and Kol helped Jacob out of the back of the SUV. The vampire was ashen. His hands were still clamped to his neck, blood still seeping between his fingers and soaking into his T-shirt. What the hell had Logan done to him? His neck should have at least stopped bleeding by now. The gashes on his hand from a feral's swipe hadn't healed either, and they were much shallower than the tear in his neck.

"I'm fine," he said.

Amiah huffed. "Get on the gurney so they don't have to carry you." Her attention jumped to Kol. "Can you manage?"

He wiped the blood off his cheek, revealing mostly healed gashes. "I'm good."

"Good." She turned to Gideon, raked her gaze over him, then turned to me, her scowl deepening. "Let's go, you two."

Gideon helped her push Jacob into the triage room and I hobbled along behind. I was going to lose my job, and I hadn't even screwed up this time. Jacob would have died. I didn't understand why Gideon was so angry.

Of course, maybe it wasn't anger that was driving him. Having all his magic stolen for the time it took me to cast that light strike could have been terrifying. He was Mr. Icy-In-Control-Angel, and I'd made him helpless. That must have been terrifying.

And I was the target he could take that fear out on. I wasn't really a team member, I was just the human fate had bound to him, reminding him that the woman he loved was dead.

Well, I didn't want to be bound to him either. God, I wanted to scream out all my rage and frustration and heartache.

Amiah grabbed two blood bags from the fridge and shoved them into Jacob's hands. "Drink both of those."

"Sure." He moved to hop off the gurney.

"Here. Now. You don't get to leave until both those bags are empty." She wrenched around to me, grabbed my wrist, and agonizing lightning screamed through me then vanished so fast it left me dizzy. I had no doubt this was the barest minimum healing Amiah could do and my bleeding had been stopped and nothing more.

"Get out of here," she snarled at me.

Absolutely. The best idea ever. I needed to figure out how to save my job, and I couldn't do that with Gideon's fiery emotions and icy glare drilling into me.

I marched out of triage and down the hall to the elevator. My buzz gnawed at my senses, growing stronger the farther I got from Gideon, but the heat of his emotions didn't cool.

God damn. How was I going to fix this?

An achy cold thread seeped into my chest.

Could I even fix this?

I took the elevator up to my room, pulled off my bloody and filthy borrowed vest and clothes, and turned to take a shower, but stopped before turning on the water. I didn't want to stay there long enough to have a shower. I wanted to go home, get away from Gideon and Amiah and everyone. If I had a moment of calm, maybe I'd be able to figure a way out of this mess.

I scrubbed the blood and dirt from my face, neck, and arms with a washcloth, changed into my only set of clean clothes, reapplied two new nicotine patches, and shoved my dirty clothes into my duffle bag. I left the vest, the extra magazines, and the room's keycard on the bed.

I wasn't coming back. The only person on the team who wanted me there was Kol, and quite frankly he could spend time with me without me being on the team. In fact, me leaving would be better for him. He wouldn't have to worry about me fucking up the team dynamics.

Marcus might have been right that I didn't fit on the team, but he'd been wrong about me and the world of the supernatural. I hadn't been terrified like I thought I'd be facing those feral vampires as part of the team. I hadn't frozen, hadn't broken down, hadn't done anything but stand my ground and do my job. Physically I might have been the weakest link on the team, but I'd still managed to hold my own.

I took the elevator back to the first floor and headed to the garage, my buzz easing just a bit as I drew closer to the sliding glass triage doors.

"Good, now the second bag," Amiah said, her voice sharp.

"I'm fine," Jacob growled.

"The second bag."

And Jacob was alive because of me. They were *all* alive because of me, because I'd faced down that archnephilim and killed him. Of course, I'd thought I was going to die, too, but that was beside the point.

I strode out into the garage and headed to the door, my buzz growing with each step that I took away from Gideon.

God damn buzz. God damn Gideon.

I jerked back toward the glass door to the building.

This was giving up, and I hated giving up, especially when there was no victory in it. I was more than willing to do what was necessary and sacrifice myself for the good of the many, but this wasn't anything. It was just losing. The team might not be worse for my departure, but it wasn't necessarily better. They were still going to be stuck with a human officer and that human wouldn't have the few supernatural advantages that I had.

Except leaving protected my secret. The longer I stayed with the team, the better the chance that someone would discover the truth. And I needed to protect my secret. Didn't I?

I stormed back to the big garage door and the way out of Operations.

Gideon clearly despised nephilim. They were responsible for horribly disfiguring Zella and the archnephilim had been responsible for murdering her. His hate for me would turn into outright loathing if he learned the truth.

And Marcus would be furious. I'd been so adamant about protecting my perfectly human life, afraid to have anything to do with the supernatural world, and he'd sacrificed his feelings for me to give me that. Of course, he had also been an asshole about ensuring I kept my human life, but I knew that was to protect himself.

Except a part of me didn't want to be protected any more. For the last week and a half my soul had hurt. The man I yearned for had given me everything I thought I wanted, and it had been horrible.

I jerked back to the glass doors leading into the building.

God, Marcus. The look on his face when I'd said I'd been wrong about leaving. He'd been so angry, so horrified, that I'd changed my mind and wanted to be in his world. He thought I was weak. Maybe I was weak.

I wrenched back toward the way out.

I was not weak. I'd struck a serious blow to Logan when even Jacob couldn't. Another blast like that, and I might have taken him out and ended this whole mess.

I was not God damned weak. I spent my life in hiding, being afraid because I was a nephilim without magic, unable to defend myself against any supernatural beings but the weakest ones. I was practically human with the exception of my father, an angel I'd never met, who my mother had never mentioned by name. And I had just stood up against a vampire possessing magic from a hellfire prince and struck a damaging blow.

Take that, Gideon and Marcus, and your Essie is too weak, a liability to the team. God, I wanted to scream that at them. I, a human, took out an archnephilim. I, a human, seriously hurt Logan when no one else could.

I stormed back to the inside door.

I was God damn strong. And I belonged.

God, why the hell did I want to belong so much? Why did I care? Why couldn't I just leave? I *needed* to leave. Now. It was for the best.

I screamed. Jerked to face the way out. Jerked back to face the way in.

The brand filled me with yearning for a man who hated me. My heart ached for another man who was determined to push me away for my own God damned good, as if I didn't know what was best for me.

And I was stupid. So fucking stupid. I *wanted* to stay. I finally knew where I belonged, knew what my purpose was. Even at the expense of my own safety, this was where fate said I belonged.

And Gideon was going to end it all. Hell, he'd probably already made the call. There was probably a message on my phone from the chief, firing me. Don't bother cleaning out your locker. Don't bother showing your face at your precinct. Disappear, Essie Shaw. Disappear like you always did when things got dangerous or scary.

I screamed again, and my eyes burned with tears.

Except even if I could disappear with Gideon's brand on my arm, I didn't want to.

My throat tightened and my threatening tears made my legs tremble. What the hell was wrong with me?

Just leave. Just God damn leave.

I took a step closer to the inside door.

I couldn't go back inside. And yet I couldn't leave. I couldn't do anything, and even when I did everything right, it was wrong.

I jerked past the door, storming deeper into the garage.

Fuck Gideon. Fuck Marcus. And fuck my father for falling in love with a human.

Shaking with rage and heartache, I ducked into the hidden alcove made by the door leading into the building. It hid a black metal locker recessed into the wall, secured with a fingerprint scanner. I pressed my back against the concrete wall beside it and slid to the asphalt.

Fuck all of this. This was no way to fix any of it.

Tears streamed down my cheeks, and I didn't care. I had to release my frustration and heartache and fear or I was going to shatter. My throat and chest and heart hurt, squeezed tight with too much emotion that I couldn't release fast enough.

The door to the hall shushed open, and I clamped my hand over my mouth, trying to muffle my sobs. Any of the guys but Kol would see me crying in the garage as proof of how weak I was.

Jacob hurried into sight, and his claim twisted, ever so slightly, in my chest. He might have drunk Amiah's bags of blood and his stride had evened out, but there was something still wrong with him. I didn't know what. That tightness around his eyes that had been there all day? His still slightly ashen complexion?

He glanced back to the glass door, then rushed deeper into the garage and not out the door to the street like I'd expected.

I pressed tight against the concrete wall, even though I knew he'd see me regardless if he glanced my way.

But he didn't look. Instead he rushed to the sewer grate a few feet away, dropped to his hands and knees, and threw up blood.

My essence locked onto Jacob, fear rushing frozen through me as his back heaved and his body shook. He threw up more blood, again and again, until he was trembling and gasping and dry heaving. My breath caught in my throat, an almost inaudible gasp, and his gaze jerked toward me, capturing me with his vampiric intensity.

"Essie," he said, his voice a low rumble, making the claim vibrate with joy. "You shouldn't be here."

Him too? Of course he'd want me gone, too. He'd been forced to bind his essence to mine to protect himself from Victoria. I was a reminder of his weaknesses, and now I'd witnessed another one.

And yet I couldn't make myself stand up and leave him. Something was horribly wrong. He shouldn't have been throwing up blood. He needed it to survive. Amiah had told him to drink the blood to heal from whatever Logan had done to him.

Except he'd also snuck the blood bag he was supposed to have taken after the first fight with Logan at Rouge back into the fridge without drinking it.

"You can't consume bagged blood," I said, the realization hitting me. "I thought vampires could."

"They can. I could—" His body stiffened with another dry heave, and he gasped for breath. "I could until I claimed you."

Oh, shit. "Is this something else I did?" I'd barely known anything about how a vampire's claim worked, only the effects it had on the human being claimed. Had I unknowingly screwed up his life by trying to save him then returning to my normal human existence? "Why didn't you tell me? Have you been starving for a week and a half?"

"Essie, it's all right." A tremor swept through him, drawing a ragged gasp.

I scrambled to his side, not caring if it was his claim compelling me or not, and rubbed slow circles on his broad back. "It's not all right. I made you claim me."

"You didn't make me do anything." He shuddered again and groaned. "I just didn't expect this. I knew my claim was strong, but I didn't think it was this strong. It doesn't feel like it is."

"So this is what happens when the claim is too strong?"

"I've only ever heard of it happening when a vampire has a strong claim on a super," he gasped. "But yes. I can't keep down bagged blood, and blood from a bunny isn't nearly as effective as it used to be." He groaned again, squeezing his eyes shut, his face etched in pain. "I need you, Essie. My essence has locked onto yours as yours has onto mine."

"You should have asked." If he needed me, I'd be there.

He captured me with his dark gaze, stealing my breath.

"Because it's rarely just blood with a claimed one," he said, his voice husky, the strain around his eyes so tight it hurt my soul. "And I won't put you in that situation." He jerked his gaze back to his hands, still pressed against the asphalt beside the grate. "I can wait it out."

"How long will that be?"

"I don't know. My essence has to work its way out of yours."

"You've bitten me twice now. That could be months." Could he survive without bagged blood for that long? I raked my gaze over his body. He looked like shit, and the tear on his neck was still weeping blood. He'd said the key that would break the seal to Ibizual's prison was going to manifest tonight. That meant he was going up against Logan again. He wouldn't survive another encounter like this.

I grabbed his arm to pull him to his feet. "We need to get you to a bunny."

"It won't help."

"You said a bunny's blood isn't nearly as effective, but it still does something."

"Whatever Logan did, it was powerful. A bunny won't help this time. If I'm going to recover, then I need your blood."

"Then take it."

The muscles in his jaw tightened and his gaze locked back onto mine, filled with not a physical hunger but a sexual one as well. "I can't. I won't be able to control myself this time."

A shiver of desire swept through me. Was I willing to have sex with Jacob to help him? A part of me screamed 'Yes!' I'd been willing to sleep with him earlier that morning in the shower before I knew it would help him, and my reasons then hadn't changed now. I still ached with unfulfilled desire for men who either wanted to push me away to protect me or hated me. Jacob could satisfy that need, and I could help him out at the same time.

"Do you expect a relationship out of this?" I asked. I didn't want another complication. I just needed a release or I'd shatter.

"No. Your heart belongs to Marcus and your soul to Gideon."

"I don't *belong* to anyone." Why was that the given in this mess? They didn't want me, and all they'd done was hurt me. God! I wanted to go back to screaming. "I'm so sick and tired of everyone acting as if I'm not an adult able to make my own choices. This whole situation is completely fucked up. At least let me help you. You say I'm the only one who can."

"Yes." He didn't sound happy about that.

"I'm not going to let you suffer. If Marcus and Gideon can't understand that, then I don't care what fate says, I don't belong with either of them." And they didn't want me anyway. I'd release the emotional pressure threatening to shatter me, and Jacob would be well enough to face Logan. In the long run, it might be a disaster, but in the short term it was a win-win. Once the situation with Logan was done, we'd figure out what to do about his need for my blood after that.

"I'm not going to let you make a decision influenced by my claim," he said. "You don't really want to do this."

"I'm volunteering, and your claim has nothing to do with it." Even if it was thrilling with ecstasy at the idea.

"The claim is making you say that. My control of you is too strong. You can't resist it."

Except I'd resisted it in the tunnel when he'd told me to leave and I hadn't. "Tell me to do something."

"Get away from me," he said.

The claim twisted. I jerked to my feet, but squeezed my muscles tight before I could walk away, crossed my arms, and glared down at him. "I can resist you."

"Give me your blood."

"Only if you ask nicely."

He jerked to his feet, his gaze capturing me, locking my soul in those black depths. "Feed. Me."

The claim clenched, stealing my breath and screaming through me. Help him. Feed him. Satisfy him. There was only him. There would only ever be him. And I had to please him.

"No." This was my choice. My decision. And magic wasn't going to coerce me. A part of me feared that the other guys would think Jacob had taken advantage of me because of the claim, but if I had to deal with that to save his life before he faced Logan that night, so be it.

He pulled out a switchblade, flipped it open, and held it out to me. "Cut your wrist and feed me," he growled. His claim tightened until I couldn't breathe.

"You can't make me do something I don't want to do," I hissed back. "If you don't feed now, Logan will kill you tonight and Ibizual will be set free."

"So you're making yet another sacrifice." He closed the knife, shoved it back into his pocket, and captured my face with his hands. "Essie, you have to stop doing that. You don't have to kill yourself to prove yourself."

"I'm not trying to prove myself. I'm doing what needs to be done." I pressed my hands over his. "I make this choice freely. Let me help you." And help me release my desire for men who don't want me.

He pursed his lips together, but his gaze had shifted from soul-capturing concern to hungry.

My pulse pounded with hope and yearning and fear. *Say yes. Please say yes and save yourself tonight.*

"Okay, but not here." He released my face and grabbed my hand. "The feeding could make you dizzy. You'll need time to recover."

I grabbed my duffle bag and we hurried back inside as fast as Jacob's weakened body would let us, thankfully not running into anyone since I didn't want to have to explain why I was holding Jacob's hand or why my eyes were red and puffy. And I was grateful he hadn't mentioned them.

We took the elevator up to the fifth floor and headed to his room. His grip tightened on my hand the closer we got, and his stride became uneven. His breath came fast and his complexion was even paler than before.

Gasping, he unlocked the door and dragged me inside. His arm wrapped around my waist and jerked me close, my back against his chest, as he braced himself against the door. The temperature snapped to sultry, hot and humid and sensual. I didn't know if it came from his desire for me or my blood, and right now I didn't care. We were both going to satisfy a need, and I was good with that.

His other hand combed into my hair, capturing my head and tugging it to the side to expose my neck.

I dropped my duffle bag. My pulse leaped in anticipation and instant desire surged hot within me. With a growl, a low rumble that vibrated through his massive chest into my back, he sank his teeth into my neck.

Pain sliced through me, followed by a rush of sudden, bone-melting pleasure. My breath hitched, and I moaned. There was no need to keep it in or hide how he made me feel. The whole point of this was to help him and help myself.

His hand on my stomach dipped under my shirt and slid up my chest to my breast, putting us back in the same position as when he'd magically entwined his essence into mine.

He took a long pull on my neck, and the sensation seeped hot across my chest and into my core, drawing another moan. I slid my hands down his thighs and rubbed my body against his. His erection, huge and firm, pressed against me, and my pulse quickened.

His hand slipped beneath my bra and he kneaded my breast, drawing a searing line of desire from neck to heart. I arched my back, needing more, needing all of him. The desire that had wound tight within me from the moment Marcus had stormed back into my life clenched my heart and my core, and I ached for release.

Jacob took another pull on my neck. The ache curled tighter. My head spun, and I reveled in the sensation. There was only him, his need for me, and my burning desire to have him in me, filling me.

With a moan, he drew his fangs from my neck, and a flicker of heat, his vampiric healing magic, sealed the wounds shut. My soul throbbed with unfulfilled desire, disappointed that this was it. But with a growl, he picked me up, carried me into the bedroom, and laid me on the bed.

The hunger in his eyes, for me and not just my blood, stole my breath. He yanked his T-shirt off, exposing the vast expanse of his muscular chest and making my mouth water. I flicked open the button on my jeans. He hooked his fingers under the waistband and slid them and my underwear off, then crawled up the bed toward me, his gaze never leaving mine, his desire for me making my pulse pound. He pressed his hands against the insides of my knees, urging me to open for him, then licked his way up my thigh and blew a feathery breath against me.

I bucked as the sensation jolted through me, drawing a low sensual laugh from him.

"God, Essie, you're so beautiful." He brushed my folds with his fingers and licked the inside of my thigh, sending another jolt through me. "You have a vein here—"

"Yes," I said before he could finish, the thought of his erotic bite rushing through me so close to my core making me tremble on the edge of climax. "Jacob, yes."

He teased his finger through my folds again, building the anticipation of his bite, spiraling my desire tighter. His powerful shoulder muscles bunched as his body settled between my legs.

"So here?" he teased, flicking his tongue against my thigh as he flicked his thumb against my clit.

I bucked again, another rush of pleasure shooting through me. "Yes, Jacob. Yes." Please. Yes.

His thumb circled my clit and his fangs sank slowly, agonizingly slowly into my thigh with a surge of need. I gasped, the sensation stealing my breath and thoughts. There was only the desire squeezing tight within me, hot and hard, building and building, and nothing else. No worry about what I was, no heartache over Marcus pushing me away or Gideon ruining my career. Right now there was only Jacob and my aching need, and it was perfect.

He sucked on my vein and slid a finger inside me, his thumb circling my clit, pressing harder and harder with each rotation. I writhed against him, craving release, and yet clinging to the pressure, waiting until I couldn't hold it back any longer, knowing I would come screaming.

Another suck and he added another finger, sliding them in and out of me. I ground into him, matching speed with his hands, driving him deeper into me, the pressure growing, squeezing, clenching—

Suddenly he froze, his hand, his mouth, everything absolutely still, and he squeezed his eyes shut. The ecstasy of his bite flickered, and a whisper of pain crawled up my leg.

My pulse stalled. Something was wrong. "Jacob?"

"No. Not now," he hissed.

"What?"

He groaned, but it didn't sound as if it was in pleasure. "Please, no."

"Jacob?" Was he regretting what we'd started? Every fiber of my being thrummed on the edge of climax, threatening to tear me apart. "I said yes. I meant it."

"Shit." He released his teeth from my thigh and a hint of healing magic sealed his bite shut. The room's temperature suddenly dropped, his desire vanishing between one heartbeat and the next.

"You're stopping?" The ecstasy his bite had induced twisted into loss. It still pulsed, close, so close to climax, but now the feeling was cruel, an unfulfilled tease. "Please." I needed him to finish what we'd started.

"God, I want you. I want to give you what you deserve." His body shook, and he jerked out of the bed. "But I have to go. Now."

"Go?" I sat up, the movement sending a shudder of desire through me, and I moaned.

The hunger in his eyes deepened, but his body wrenched toward the bedroom door. "Fuck." He grasped the doorframe, as if his body had a mind of its own and he was trying to keep himself in the room.

"Jacob?"

"Victoria's summoning me and I can't—" The muscles in his neck strained as he fought to keep hold of the frame. "I can't resist her. I'm sorry, Essie. We'll finish this. I promise."

His grip broke free of the doorframe, and he hurried out of his apartment, still shirtless, leaving me aching with want.

I squirmed, sliding my legs against his comforter, the movement ratcheting up my need, curled so tight that it was painful. Collapsing back on his bed, I rubbed my finger over my clit, desperate to relieve the pressure, but it was as if Jacob's magic had frozen within me, trapping me on the precipice and unable to crash over the edge.

The pain spread across my abdomen and into my chest, and I couldn't draw a deep enough breath, could only gasp. And each gasp made me quiver, ratcheting up my pain and need.

I ground my teeth and forced myself out of his bed. His magic would pass. I just had to ride it out. I didn't know how long he was going to be, but I knew if I stayed, surrounded by his rich, masculine scent, I'd go mad.

I dragged on my underwear and pants, the fabric sliding up my body drawing a moan, left Jacob a note to find me at home, and grabbed my duffle bag. I had to go back to plan A. Go home and then figure out what to do about my life once I was away from the guys. I could barely think straight right now and with Jacob gone, my thoughts were jumping to who was in the building that I could convince to help satisfy me. Which was a terrible idea.

Each step down the hall to the elevator sent tremors through me, but none of them strong enough to release me, and my head spun from the blood loss. I had no idea how I was going to make it out of the building, let alone down the street to wait for a taxi — since I wasn't going to wait for one here — but there wasn't any other choice.

The elevator dinged and the doors slid open, revealing Marcus, holding his vest, sheathed sword with belt attached, and boots. He wore baggy workout shorts and nothing else, and looked sexy as hell.

ESSIE

MY BREATH VANISHED, BOTH WITH MY DROWNING NEED FROM JACOB AND the attraction that always sizzled between me and Marcus. Every time I saw him, I thought he was hot, and right now, wearing only shorts because the magic to shift into his wolf consumed his clothing, he was mouthwateringly sexy. He wasn't anywhere near as bulky as Jacob, but his chest and arms were ripped, each muscle defined, making me yearn to run my hands over them and scratch my nails across his washboard abs.

His piercing green eyes captured me, and a feral hint of his wolf stared back at me. The air around me ignited into a heat stronger and more humid than the heat of Jacob's desire. Marcus's gaze raked over my body, amping up my need with just a look, making me yearn for him to touch me, then it settled on my neck. Jacob's magic was only strong enough to seal his bite shut, not enough to hide the evidence.

"Of course," he said as he stepped out of the elevator, his voice so soft I couldn't get a good sense of his inflection. "You let him feed on you."

No point in denying it. "Of my own free will. His claim had nothing to do with it."

The temperature didn't change from sweltering, but I still couldn't read his expression, as if he was trying to hold his emotions at bay but couldn't contain his desire— no, with him, it was more likely anger and I just desperately wanted it to be desire.

"I saw you resist him in the tunnel. I know you could have said no if you wanted to."

"I didn't want to."

"I know you didn't." His expression... still so strange and impossible to read. "You willingly give of yourself to save people, Essie. It's just who you are, and Jacob needs you."

"What?" My already struggling thoughts tripped. I mustn't have heard that right.

"He's starving." Marcus stepped closer, and I shifted back. If he got too close I was going to beg him to take me, and I wouldn't be able to handle the rejection.

"It's his claim, isn't it?" he said. "It's stuck on you."

"Does everyone know? I got the impression Jacob was trying to hide it." I clung to my duffle bag, praying that would stop me from throwing myself at Marcus.

"I doubt anyone else has figured it out. He's certainly hiding it. But after the archnephilim, his scent changed. I couldn't smell the blood in him like I should."

"So this... *situation* is common?"

"No. I only read up on it when I saw a vampire starving to death at Mercy Memorial during my transition," he said. "There wasn't much else for me to do during that time. The vampire's werewolf had been killed in the war, and she was unable to feed from anyone but the one she'd claimed. It's a terrible way for a vampire to go. Very very slow, and I suspect she's still in the hospital starving if she hasn't managed to make another claim."

"How come Amiah doesn't know about Jacob?" She'd been the one to help Marcus through his transition. She'd been at the hospital at the same time he had. She had to have seen that vampire, too.

"She's not looking for the signs and the claim on you is so new, if he can hold out, his body's singular focus on you will pass. We just needed to wait it out."

"But he keeps getting hurt and needing more blood than normal."

"Yeah." His gaze raked over my body again and his eyes narrowed.

I bit back a moan. *I will not beg. I will not beg.* He was determined to keep his distance, and I had to respect that, no matter how stupid it was. And I didn't think how well I'd handled myself in the ferals' nest would convince him I could be in his world. It probably had just made him more terrified for me.

"Tell me the truth, Essie. Did you finish?"

My desire twisted so tight I wanted to scream with frustration. "I think he got enough."

"But did you?" He raked his hand through his hair, mussing his dark curly locks, making me yearn to touch them, and looking uncomfortable. "Did you come?"

"I don't think that's any of your business."

"I can smell the sex on you," he said. "Stop trying to hide it. It goes hand in fist with the claim and bite — that's just a given. But you look as jacked up as a zip addict."

I probably felt as desperate as one, too. Which was my own God damn business, and I would not beg him to help me. "Victoria summoned him."

"Shit," he said, taking my omission as a negative to his question. He stepped closer to me, and I lurched back, hitting the hall wall, making him stop, his empty hand raised, palm out, as if he was trying to keep me calm. "He mustn't know just how much the claim has changed the power of his bite for you. He wouldn't leave you hanging if he did. That's just not his style."

"What do you mean?"

"It's a side effect of a strong claim," he said. "Most consider it a bonus. The magic of his bite keeps building until released by a climax."

I trembled, throbbing at the word *climax*, desperate for release.

Then horror flooded me. I'd tried for an orgasm myself and it hadn't worked. "I have to wait for him to come back? If Victoria's pissed, she could hold him for days." She'd threatened to do that before.

Marcus shifted closer to me, and I gritted my teeth, fighting the need to throw myself at him.

"It doesn't have to be him, just someone to unlock your hold on it. It'll be okay."

"Okay?" I said, my voice rising with panic. "It's not okay. And how the hell are *you* okay with this? Why aren't you furious and pushing me away?" And making me cry with heartache. Wolves were notorious for their possessiveness.

Except the temperature around me was still hot, so he had to be feeling something. I just couldn't understand the powerful emotion combined with his calm understanding.

"Oh, my wolf fucking hates this, and I don't like it, either, but nothing

Amiah is going to do for Jacob is going to help him. You had to let him bite you or he was going to die."

"So you've just changed your mind?" Now his calm was making me furious. And God damn, I needed a fucking orgasm. "What about a normal life and normal babies and normal fucking everything?"

"I was wrong, okay" he said, the ferocity of his wolf suddenly darkening his eyes. "You're neck deep in the supernatural world whether I like it or not. You won't listen to reason and you won't leave. There's no getting out for you now, and my wolf gave me a whole lot of shit while we were running off that mess with the ferals' nest. He doesn't give a shit that you belong to Gideon—"

"I don't *belong* to anyone."

"You keep telling yourself that."

"You God damn listen to it."

"My wolf doesn't care. He wants you— *I* want you. However I can get you. I can't let you go again, Essie. If you leave, I'll follow. If I have to share you with Gideon— and shit, I guess Jacob too now, so be it."

"Whoa, wait a minute." Except my straining-to-explode need thought that was a fantastic idea. All of them. Now.

I shuddered and hugged myself tighter. All that testosterone in one bed was a terrible idea, and I didn't think that was what Marcus meant.

"Life with supers is always a mess whether we like it or not, and Essie —" He captured me with his gaze, and a surge of emotion, true, honest to goodness actual emotion, not wild temperature fluctuations, swept through me: sincerity, awe, determination, fear, and love. "You weren't a weak link in that fight in the ferals' nest. Hell, you almost killed that vampire, and I can't argue with my wolf any more that you can't hold your own in this world."

Marcus's fear deepened, and my soul cried that ferocious, powerful Marcus felt it so deeply.

"I need you, Essie. I'm done pushing if you're done running."

"I already tried to tell you I was done running in the armory, you jerk."

He gave me a rueful smile. "You did and I freaked out." His expression turned fierce, hungry, and he offered me his hand. "Let me help you release Jacob's magic."

I stared at his hand, aching, burning to take it. "I don't belong to you."

"No, I belong to you," he growled.

Jacob's magic swelled, teasing me, God, driving me insane. I gasped, and my knees grew weak.

Marcus dropped his gear and grabbed me by the hips, steadying me against the wall. My breath stalled, and the attraction that had been between us the moment we'd first locked eyes across the squad room in the precinct seared through me. "Fuck, Marcus."

"That's the offer."

I dropped my duffle bag and crashed my mouth against his, unable to resist any longer. I'd dreamed of having sex with Marcus for so long. I was sure he was going to change his mind about sharing and me being part of his world and everything, and I was terrified for that moment. But right now, he was offering me a release and there wasn't anyone else I'd rather be with.

He met my kiss with a hunger of his own, one hand tangling in my hair capturing my head, the other wrapping around my back and pulling me close to his body. His tongue swept into my mouth, plundering me.

I couldn't get enough of him. His desire, back to being felt as a change in temperature, seared me inside and out, and I clung to him, pressing against him.

His lips left my mouth and trailed down my neck — the opposite side of Jacob's bite — his stubble scraping my hypersensitive skin and sending a shudder through me, twisting my need to release tighter.

"Your room is closest," he growled into my neck, and he kissed his way down my body, setting every nerve within me on fire even though his lips were on my clothing and not my skin.

"I was leaving." My breath heaved, quick gasps making my head spin and ratcheting up my need. "Left my key in the room."

"Of course you did," he growled, grabbing his gear and my duffle bag in one hand. "You never make anything easy."

"Don't blame this on me." I captured his face and tipped his gaze back up to mine, groaning at the ferocity in his eyes, the need to have me, and the sight of his erection tenting his gym shorts. "You didn't want me here."

He rose, exuding lithe, dangerous power, and pinned me against the wall with his body. "And I was a fucking idiot."

I wrapped a leg around him and rubbed myself against him.

He groaned. "A real idiot. Come on, I'm not taking you in the hall."

"Don't want the others to watch?" I teased. I wasn't into voyeurism, and I was sure Marcus wasn't, either... of course he had said he was willing to share...

He brushed his lips against my ear, his breath teasing me with rushing pleasure. "First time is just for me."

I stared at him. "You *are* a voyeur?"

He grabbed my butt with his hand and nudged me. "Up you go."

I hopped up, wrapping both my legs around him, still amazed he could easily support my weight with one hand and walk, even though I knew werewolves were stronger than the average guy.

"Marcus?" I asked, clinging close to him and brushing my lips against his jaw, just below his ear. "Are you into having people watch?"

He groaned and picked up his pace. "No. I just wanted to see your reaction."

"And?" I flicked my tongue against that tender spot again.

"If I could think straight, I'd have thoughts about it." He unlocked his door with his thumb, and dropped his gear and my bag the moment we were inside.

His room was set up the same as Jacob's, living area with kitchenette and bedroom with en suite bathroom. His color palette was more toward greens and browns and his furniture different with a different set up, but that was all the impression I took in before my desire jerked me back to Marcus and his body and how he made me feel.

He shoved a pile of papers off his desk and set me on the edge. I kicked off my shoes, and he grabbed the bottom of my T-shirt and yanked it off over my head. His mouth captured mine again, one hand on the back of my head to control me, the other sliding inside my bra and teasing my nipple into a taut, painful bud.

I needed a release so much I was certain I'd explode if it didn't come soon. My nerves, my soul, every cell in my body was wound tight, pulsing with desperate, hungry need.

He pushed the cups of my bra down and sucked my breast while kneading the other one. I arched my back, moaning. I needed more. God, please. I had to have more. Now.

"Marcus. Please," I gasped. "Don't play with me."

I grabbed for the waistband of his shorts, but he pushed my hand away.

"Not yet."

"Not yet? Do you have any idea how Jacob's bite is making me feel?"

He smiled against my breast. "I have a good guess."

"Then please…"

He undid the button on my jeans and grabbed the waistband. I raised my hips and he yanked the fabric, underwear included, down my legs. The material sliding against my skin made me buck, heat flooding my core, but still no climax. I needed him now. Had to have him filling me. God, I never thought this was what our first time together would be like. I thought we'd take our time, enjoy each other's bodies, not rush into it filled with desperate need.

He grabbed my knees and shoved my legs apart, spreading me wide for him, and the feralness in his gaze, the one that was all wolf, darkened his eyes. Then his attention jumped to Jacob's bite on my thigh and he growled.

My pulse stuttered. "You said you didn't care." This was a bad idea. Marcus ran hot and cold toward me at the best of times. Knowing I'd had Jacob between my legs—

"I don't." He leaned in and licked the bite. "I'm pissed he had the opportunity to give you what you needed, what you deserved, and didn't."

I shuddered, remembering the feel of Jacob's bite and his fingers pumping into me, then the image shifted to Marcus, sliding inside me, driving me to climax.

"Victoria didn't give him a chance," I said. "Literally forced him away half dressed."

"Serves him right," he said, his voice low, dangerous.

My breath hitched, and I fought to think past the pain and lust and need. I dug my hands into his scalp, grabbing his hair, and pulled his head up to look at me.

His piercing green gaze stole my breath. So too did his hunger.

"I want you in me. Now."

"I don't want you riding Jacob's magic when you come for me," he snarled, and he jerked my butt right to the edge of the desk and raked his tongue over my clit.

I gasped, my breath completely gone, the promise of a climax sparking within me, close, so God damn close, but not there.

He pushed my legs open as wide as they would go, opening me completely to him, and growled against my folds, the sound pure masculine desire.

I tightened my grip in his hair, writhing against him. "Yes, please, yes."

His tongue tormented me, his stubble rasping against my sensitive skin as his fingers dug into my thighs. My need was so tight I couldn't breathe, then he sucked hard on my clit and fireworks exploded behind my eyelids. Pleasure roared through me, making every muscle contract, and Jacob's magic flooded every cell in my body.

Marcus groaned, his nails biting into my flesh, his mouth grinding against my clit, his breath fast and hot against my skin.

Tremors raced through me, bolts of electricity that kept zapping me, making me twitch and gasp. I fell back on the desk, unable to keep my body up, unable to catch my breath or think straight.

"Holy fuck." Marcus sagged to his knees, his expression stunned. "I didn't think it felt like that."

I managed to rise up on my elbow to meet his gaze. "Regretting not coming with me?" I flashed him a wicked smile, teasing him, but the moment the words came out, I realized I wasn't done. Jacob's magic was gone, but I still wanted Marcus. Again and again if he'd have me.

His pupils dilated, seeing my desire for him. "I have protection in the bedroom."

He stood, wrapped an arm around my back, and pulled me close to lift me, but his erection, still tenting his shorts, brushing against me, drawing a gasp and a sudden, desperate need.

I scratched my nails down his chest, making him moan.

"I trust you're clean, and I'm on birth control." I didn't want to wait. Jacob's magic might be gone, but I still burned for Marcus. There was a different kind of magic between us that was just as powerful as Jacob's, and I'd been aching for Marcus for years.

He growled at that, leaned into me, and slid his hands up my thighs, the movement tender and so fucking sensual. His wolf darkened his eyes and his body trembled. I could tell he was trying to hold it back, keep it controlled. But I didn't want control. I wanted all the ferocious passion the sexual tension between us had been promising since the mess with the archnephilim had brought him back into my life.

I slid my hands over his and up his arms. "Marcus, let go."

The muscles in his jaw clenched.

"Marcus—" Screw words. Actions were better. I slipped my hands down the front of his shorts and shoved them off his hips, freeing his thick, straining erection.

My pulse tripped at the sight of it, and I wrapped my hand around the base. His eyes rolled back, and he moaned my name.

"Let go, Marcus." I drew my hand along his length then pumped back down. "Please."

He shifted closer, aligning with my core, and I slid his tip through my wet folds, proving how ready I was for him, how much I wanted him inside me.

With a groan, he pushed his hips forward, sliding himself inch by agonizingly sensual inch into me. My heart pounded, my yearning ratcheted back up, as intense and aching as it had been with Jacob's magic.

His breath came fast, and his body shook. His control was astounding and driving me insane.

"You feel so good," he said, the muscles in his jaw and neck straining. He slowly drew out. I shuddered, my head dropping back, and closed my eyes, every nerve focused on the sensations.

He pushed back again. So. God. Damn. Slowly.

"Marcus, let go."

"I don't want to hurt you," he growled, his wolf right at the surface.

"You won't hurt me."

"Not me—"

I moaned and met his gaze. "He won't, either."

The struggle in his eyes deepened.

"I trust you. All of you. Please, Marcus." I was back again to feeling like I was going to burn up with desire. He was driving me mad. "Fuck me," I snarled.

His wolf snarled back, and he plunged into me with a fierce push. I gasped, and his eyes blazed with hunger. He shifted a nail into a claw long enough to slice through the front of my bra, exposing my breasts, and shoved me back against the desk. I clung to the edges as he drew out and plunged back in, each stroke adding more fuel to the already blazing fire within me.

He squeezed my breasts, and drew back out. Growled, then plunged back in, each stroke faster and more forceful than the last. His breath turned into quick needy gasps. So did mine. The pleasure was consuming. There was only him and his body driving into me and it was perfect.

His hand left my breast and he clutched my hips, his thumb finding my clit.

I cried out, pleasure zinging through me, twisting my need higher. He pounded faster and harder, grinding his thumb against my clit until my climax once again seized every muscle, this one more powerful than the last. I screamed his name as a wave of pleasure crashed into me. I rode it, clinging to it, as I ground against him, straining to hold on until he came. And then his body jerked hard against me, all his muscles contracting as his orgasm seized him. Mine surged, my hold on it shattering, and the sensation consumed me, lightning crackling through every cell with glorious, mind-blowing bliss.

"God, Essie, you're amazing." He collapsed forward, resting his head on my belly, his breath ragged.

I slid my hand through his hair. My breath was just as ragged, my muscle still twitching with aftershocks. My heart pounded, filled with joy, every cell in my body reveling in the rightness of being with Marcus.

This was where I was supposed to be. I knew it in my soul.

To hell with what fate said about Gideon and me. Marcus was who I belonged with.

"Marcus, I—"

Blazing white agony erupted in my head. All the muscles in my body jerked so tight I couldn't scream, couldn't draw breath, and could barely think.

ESSIE

THE AGONY RIPPED EVERY OTHER SENSATION AWAY UNTIL THERE WAS ONLY it, screaming through my head, threatening to consume my vision in darkness and suffocate me with pressure. It was coming. *He* was coming. With his massive power and devouring darkness.

Marcus jerked off me, captured my cheeks, and locked gazes with me. Worry filled his eyes and cold swept over my skin. "Talk to me, Essie."

But I couldn't draw enough breath to speak. I wasn't sure I could get my jaw to unlock to say anything even if I could.

The sense of black malevolence, pure evil, flooded me. The walls of his prison were weakening, and now he could slip a thread of magic beyond its confines. The seal holding it altogether, bouncing for eternity among all the realms of existence, was going to manifest in the weakest magical realm, the realm of mortals, and once again he had a chance to empower the spell he'd set over a millennia ago to free himself.

"We have to get you to Amiah." He pulled up his shorts and grabbed a throw blanket off the back of his couch.

God, I didn't want to go back to Amiah, and certainly not naked in Marcus's arms. Tears leaked from my eyes and I convulsed.

Marcus grabbed me before I fell off the desk and sat me up, leaning me against his chest.

"It'll be okay," he said, but his fear swept frost across my cheeks and up my arms.

Find it. The key was going to manifest. I had to get ready— No, Logan had to get ready.

I shuddered with cold and fear. Marcus wrapped the blanket around my shoulders.

Free me.

"No," I gasped. But somehow I knew *he* couldn't hear me. It was the compulsion from his spell, set into the magic *he*, Ibizual, had given to Logan. That had been his demon-deal to gain more power.

Secure the key tonight. Break the seal tomorrow.

"Essie, you need help." Marcus lifted me, cradling me against his chest, and headed to the door.

The agony released my muscles but still burned in my head. I sagged into his embrace, my skin stinging with the frost of Marcus's fear. "The key is starting to manifest."

Marcus froze, his hand on the door about to open it. "What?"

"I can feel the spell." I shuddered, sending agony slicing through my head. "I can feel *him*."

"I'm still taking you to Amiah."

"She won't be able to do anything." This wasn't the kind of injury Amiah could heal. It wasn't actually an injury. I pressed my palm over Marcus's heart, feeling his pulse race. "We—" I stopped myself. I wasn't part of the team any more. "The *team* needs to get ready."

Marcus's grip on me tightened, conflict pinching the corners of his eyes. He had a job to do, and yet he didn't want to let me go.

"You were convulsing," he growled. "You have frost on your cheeks."

"And you guys are going to get slaughtered if you don't come up with a plan," I snarled back and pushed against his hold on me, trying to break free. My throat tightened as my fear clenched my chest. I couldn't lose him—

No, I couldn't lose Gideon—

Jeez, I couldn't lose either of them.

Shit.

"Ibizual can't be allowed to escape." He'd consume everything and everyone.

"Fine." He set me on my feet, and I clutched the blanket to my chest, unable to get warm. "Can you tell where it's going to be?"

I sucked in a ragged breath and concentrated on the sensation inside my head. Thick, consuming darkness. It was a lot like the clinging, suffocating smoke from the archnephilim, but a thousand times stronger. It enveloped me, pressing against my senses, but there was no sense of location, or direction or anything. Only the knowledge that the key was coming. *Prepare. Find me. Free me.* The darkness squeezed tight. Agony sliced across my skull, and I convulsed.

Marcus pulled me back into his arms before I collapsed. The frost from his fear thickened on my face. His expression pinched tighter, and his wolf darkened his eyes. "Anything?"

"No. Maybe Jacob knows. This is supposed to be his connection with Logan." And I could only assume the strength of his claim was the reason I could feel the power building to manifest the key.

Marcus leaned me against the door and grabbed his phone from inside his boot in the pile of gear he'd dropped the moment we'd entered his apartment.

I pulled the blanket tighter around my shoulders, my teeth chattering, and focused my attention on my clothes a few feet away by his desk. His gaze followed mine as he dialed Jacob's number.

"Marcus," Jacob said after the third ring, his voice clear thanks to the enhanced hearing from his claim. Question and uncertainty filled his tone as if he didn't know what kind of reception he was going to get.

"Do you know where the key is going to form?"

"No, I—"

Marcus retrieved my clothes and dropped them in a pile beside me. "Are you sure?"

"Shit. It's less than eight hours until dusk. I should be feeling something now." Tension tightened his tone. "I'm coming in. We need to figure out how to get eyes on Logan so we can stop him from getting the key."

Marcus's gaze locked with mine. "Essie can feel the key."

I sank to the floor and opened my duffle bag to grab my dirty bra, which was now better than my sliced-in-half bra.

"You heard me, right?" Marcus growled. "Essie can feel the key."

More like it was tearing into my brain. I dropped the blanket from my shoulders and shrugged out of my ruined bra.

"How can she—?"

"Jeez, Jacob. It's your claim on her. It so fucking strong she's bitelocked." He clenched his jaw, his wolf now more than just darkening his eyes but pushing through into his expression and body language with dangerous ferocity.

A blast of agony sliced into my brain, seizing my muscles as I tried to secure my bra clasp behind my back.

"I know the claim is strong, but she can't be bite-locked," Jacob said. "That only happens when a super is claimed or—"

"Or when your claim on the human is unnaturally strong. I know, it's rare, but she's bite-locked and you left her hanging." He jerked away from me and stormed to the far side of his living room to glare out the window. His frost vanished, replaced with sudden blazing rage.

"Marcus, I didn't know."

"How can you not know how strong your claim is? How could you do that to her?"

But Jacob didn't know I was half super, and I hadn't known there was a difference between claiming a human and a super. This was my fault, and now Jacob wasn't going to survive without me.

"I swear, I thought the strength of the claim was just a problem for me. I know your wolf has claimed her."

"He has," Marcus growled.

"My claim isn't an emotional bond. I'll keep my distance from her. I'll—"

"You'll fucking starve to death. Don't be an idiot."

"Marcus—"

"But if you leave her like that again," Marcus said, his voice low, dangerous, his wolf barely contained, "I'll rip your fucking throat out."

I managed to clasp my bra and pull on my T-shirt.

Marcus wrenched back to face me. "Now, what do we do about this key?"

"We have to wait until dusk to know which direction to head."

"Until dusk?" I had to deal with this agony until dusk? Realization made my stomach drop. Just because the key manifested didn't mean the pain would go away.

"How the hell did you function enough to find that key the first time?" Marcus asked, helping me stand so I could put on my pants.

"What do you mean?"

"Essie is in so much pain she can barely stand."

"Last time it hurt, but it didn't hurt that much. It's either because she's human, something to do with the claim, or something about the key manifesting that's different this time."

"So you have no fucking clue." Marcus blew out a heavy breath. "Wonderful."

"I'll call Gideon and Kol, and we'll meet in the lounge."

"Good. *You* can explain to Gideon why Essie is still involved."

Jacob groaned. "If she's the one who can feel the key, we need her. Are you going to fight me on this?"

I slid back to the floor to put on my runners.

"Essie handled her own in the nest." Marcus knelt and helped me with my shoes, his piercing green gaze capturing mine, the heat of his anger turning sultry. "And I've been reminded that I'm an idiot."

"Okay. I'll be there in ten."

Marcus hung up as another blast of agony seized me, making me convulse.

Find it. Free me.

I had no idea how I was going to last until dusk, or God, even longer. Gasping, I tried to stand.

"Stay there while I change." He stood and glared down at me. "You don't need to prove how tough you are right now."

I raised my hands in defeat. "Fine." Besides, I wasn't sure if I could stand.

He hurried into his bedroom, changed into jeans and a T-shirt, and returned to the door to pull on his boots. Then he picked me up, and he stepped out into the hall.

A few doors down, Kol stepped out of his apartment, and his attention jumped to us. A sultry smile lit his face, billowed desire through my chest, and stole my breath. God, he was so beautiful. He hurried to catch us, his gate not nearly as smooth as usual, as if he were trying too hard to be steady, and his eyes were glassy. If I hadn't known better, I'd guess he was drunk or high.

"Really? We're in the middle of a crisis and you over-indulged?" Marcus said as we headed to the elevator.

Kol glared back at him. "Well, the next time you and Essie have magically enhanced sex, warn me. The first round burned through all my shields and I had no defenses for round two."

"We didn't have magically enhanced sex, we—" Marcus frowned.

Heat rose to my cheeks. "Would Jacob's bite count?"

Kol's eyebrows rose.

"Well, shit," Marcus said. "Releasing Jacob's bite-lock does count. But round two wasn't magical."

"I would beg to differ," Kol said.

I playfully slapped Marcus's chest, feigning anger. "So you're saying it wasn't magical for you?"

He rolled his eyes at me. "That's not what I meant."

"Then what *did* you mean?" I pressed, making Kol snicker.

"Essie," Marcus growled.

"Marcus," I growled back, and a blast of agony slammed into me.

I managed to gasp in a quick breath before all my muscles clenched, but the first convulsion pushed it out of me, and I was suffocating with agony and darkness, all of it threatening my consciousness.

"Holy shit." Kol's eyes grew wide, all playfulness gone. "What the hell is that?"

The pain released my muscles but continued to throb in my skull. I clung to Marcus, fighting to get my breath back. "The key is starting to form."

And every cell in my body was screaming that I had to get to it first. I couldn't let Logan release all that evil.

MARCUS

 down the hall to the elevator.

"That's the key starting to form?" Kol asked, his slightly unfocused eyes wide. He staggered into the wall, grunted, and slid his shoulder against it to keep up with me while fighting to regain his balance. "How did Jacob stop Logan the last time?"

"He wasn't this bad and no, he has no fucking clue why it's affecting Essie like this," I snapped, my wolf growling inside me at that.

Kol frowned, heaved away from the wall and almost staggered into me before recatching his balance. "You said she's bite-locked?"

"Yeah." And it pissed both of us off that Jacob had no clue how strong his claim on Essie was. Of course if he hadn't claimed someone before — and given what I knew about the vampire, there was a good chance he hadn't — then he might not know what a strong claim felt like.

"Maybe the strength of the claim is why it's affected her like this," Kol said.

"The why isn't what we should be focusing on," Essie forced out. "You guys need a plan to fight Logan."

"And you—" I shot a glare at Kol "—need to burn that excess energy off." And I didn't care how he did it. He couldn't be high when we faced Logan. We'd barely made it out of the sewers the last time and we'd all been perfectly sober.

And I didn't want to think about why he was high... well, I did, certainly the part where I'd taken my mate.

God, she was ours. Finally. She was ours and she *wanted* us.

Despite her current agony, we couldn't help but be thrilled that our mating claim had finally been recognized. I was still terrified that if I let my wolf truly take her I'd hurt her, but for now my wolf was satisfied that my human half had finally seen reason and accepted our mate.

Of course with Gideon's brand and Jacob's claim, our mate was destined to have a completely fucked up love life, and my wolf was a confusing mess of pissed off that she wasn't just ours.

But at least he grudgingly accepted that it couldn't do anything about the others. Gideon's brand was permanent, and from what I'd read about vampire claims, the chances that Jacob would be able to release his claim now that his hunger was solely focused on her were slim to none. And no matter how much Essie feared supers and the supernatural world, she'd never let Jacob starve.

I doubted she'd leave Gideon to suffer whatever dire consequences there were to ignoring his brand, either, because that was just who Essie was.

The elevator door slid open and we hurried inside as Essie convulsed in my arms again.

How the hell was I going to protect her? Sure, she hadn't been the weak link in the sewers and she was strong and determined and could handle herself in a fight, but that didn't diminish the fear howling through me that I needed to keep her safe.

It didn't matter that my wolf saw her as an equal, as powerful as any wolf in her own right. I was still scared shitless. She could die and I'd be shattered. Everything I'd heard, said a wolf's mating claim wasn't like an angel's, but my soul said differently.

She was mine. *Mine!* And I wasn't going to deny myself or hurt her any longer in a ridiculous attempt to protect her.

I'd share her with Gideon and Jacob and I'd fight at her side, and I wasn't going to hold her back to protect her.

I. Would. Not.

But my determination to let her be an equal didn't lessen my primal instincts to keep her safe, especially knowing she'd throw herself into the line of fire if it meant protecting someone.

Fuck.

Fuck fuck fuck.

I was just going to have to throw myself into danger and be right there beside her to save her ass when things went sideways... just like she would for me.

Because that's what a good mate did.

ESSIE

WE HEADED DOWN TO THE FIRST FLOOR TO A LOUNGE NEAR THE BACK OF the building. It was a comfortable space, decorated in tans and creams with two over-stuffed couches and six matching armchairs. An enormous panel TV hung on the wall and past that, deeper into the room, stood a floor-to-ceiling shelf filled with books and puzzles and games near a large pale-wood table with half a dozen matching chairs. At the back wall, patio doors opened to a small patio enclosed with a tall privacy fence and two small wrought-iron cafe tables and chairs.

"This place has everything," I said, trying to distract myself from the agony pounding in my head.

"All essential JP team members live here, along with the almost dozen angels living in Union," Kol said. "We have a variety of amenities since we can't spend all our free time working out in the gym." He shot a hard look at Marcus.

"Says the demon whose body will never change." Marcus set me on the couch. "How about you put your extra juice to good use so Essie can concentrate?"

"It is yours." Kol flashed a wicked smile, making Marcus stiffen.

His wolf darkened his eyes until he clenched his jaw and forced his beast back down.

"Well, mostly." Kol shrugged. "I guess round one is partially Jacob's and round two... whoever cast the spell you two used."

Kol settled in beside me, within reaching distance and not closer.

"There was no spell," Marcus said, sitting on my other side, also not touching me. Which was good, because if I understood what Marcus was asking, Kol was going to use his magical enthrallment to help me think past the pain by making me focus on other sensations. And I had no idea how I'd feel while turned on again by the incubus with Marcus's body brushing against me.

"You need to be careful with that. Sex magic can be dangerous."

"There was no spell." Marcus glared at Kol.

"What spell?" Gideon asked as he entered the lounge. His attention jumped to me and the icy look in his eyes grew harder.

"Nothing." Kol grabbed my hand and a hint of heat swept up my arm, muting but not eliminating the pain and making my mind jerk back to the memory of climaxing with Marcus inside me.

My pulse picked up, and I shuddered. So did Kol. Marcus's glare deepened.

"Sorry," Kol mumbled, and the heat dimmed until I almost couldn't feel it.

Gideon leaned against the side of an armchair and frowned, his attention on Kol. "What's wrong with you?"

"Nothing." But Kol's grip on my hand tightened. "What's the plan?"

"We have to wait until Officer Shaw can tell us where the key is," Gideon said, not sounding happy about that at all. "Then we go get it. We should be prepared for more ferals."

"We've killed a fair number already. How many more do you think Logan made?" Marcus asked.

"Assume there's more," Jacob said, striding into the lounge. He still wore his dirty pants from the fight with the ferals, one leg with a wide blood-encrusted gash mid-thigh, but he'd put on a shirt. I could see the question, the need to talk in his eyes, but his glance at Marcus beside me told me he wanted to talk in private.

And yeah, we had a lot to figure out, now that everything was completely complicated.

"There's always more." Jacob sat in an armchair and turned his attention to Gideon. "And Essie won't be able to tell us where the key is. It doesn't work that way. She has to lead us to it."

"Of course she does." Gideon pinched the bridge of his nose. "So we know the key won't form until dusk, we know Logan will have more ferals, but we have no idea how many or where they are. Do we know *anything*? What about Bane and information on hellfire princes and their cages?"

"I haven't heard from him yet," Marcus said.

"Victoria said she can't sense Logan, but she did gift me with a little extra magic, so hopefully it will be harder for him to control me."

"Do I want to know what that cost you?" Gideon asked.

"The terms are reasonable," Jacob said. "I'm to pay it when this is over."

"How long will I lose you for?"

Jacob glanced at me then jerked his attention back to Gideon, the movement so fast I would have missed it if his claim hadn't attuned me to him. "Just one full twenty-four-hour period."

"I see." Gideon gave a tight nod. "I'll make sure the kitchen is stocked up so you can recover quickly."

That meant Jacob was going to get hurt. I jerked forward, and the throbbing in my head swelled, overcoming Kol's enthrallment, making me wince. "We're not letting her torture you. We'll find another way to protect you from Logan's magic."

"It's not intended as torture," Jacob said.

"Not intended as torture? What's that supposed to mean?" Perhaps I couldn't understand because of the pain in my head.

"Sex, Essie," Kol said, sending a shiver of need through me. "Victoria likes a lot of blood with her sex."

"Jeez, Jacob—"

"The deal's been made. Don't worry about it," he said, emphasizing the command.

The claim twisted, and I fought the compulsion and managed to resist it. I gave him my driest look, letting him know he couldn't command me any more.

"The decisions of my team are no longer your concern, Officer Shaw." Gideon crossed his arms, and a hint of heat whispered around me. "They never were. Do you understand?"

"I—" The agony exploded in my head again, stronger than before, as if avoiding it with Kol's magic only made it more powerful. Whatever I'd been about to say vanished as the pain blazed through my skull and down my neck, searing into my heart. I fought to draw breath, fought to relax my muscles, but I was locked tight, worse than being hit with a Taser, worse than Gideon's brand shooting lightning through me.

Marcus and Kol grabbed my shoulders as I convulsed. Jacob jerked forward and knelt before me, bringing a bracing cold with him, while Gideon looked frozen, trapped, horror in his eyes.

The agony released me and my muscles went limp. Marcus and Kol caught me, and Kol pulled me into his arms, wrapping them around my waist and pushing soothing heat into my freezing body.

The frost was back on my cheeks, and Marcus scraped it away with his thumbs, making my pulse pound in fear. They were going to learn the truth. They were going to discover what I was.

I fought to focus on the bone-melting thread of desire curling from Kol's hands. I couldn't let my fear or the pain consume me. *Please, God, let them think the frost is because of the key. Please.*

"Tell me it goes away or eases up or anything," Marcus said to Jacob. "That it won't be like this once the key forms."

"I don't know." Jacob's fear was clear in his eyes. "It was never like this for me."

"We can't let this distract us," Gideon said.

Marcus glared at him and growled.

I grabbed Marcus's hand to keep him by me. "Gideon's right." Jeez, it even hurt to breathe now. "You need to figure out if there's a better way to deal with ferals and zombies, or whatever it was Logan made in that nest, and if there's anything you can learn about Ibizual, the key, and his cage."

"Marcus, get a hold of Bane again and anyone else who might know anything about hellfire princes. Jacob, Kol—"

"I'll stay with Essie," Kol said, his arms tightening around my waist. "I can search the JP's online records and let you know as soon as she can sense the key."

"Fine. Jacob and I will head to the archives and search the books." Gideon shoved away from the chair. "Come on. Maybe we'll get lucky and stumble across something useful."

He marched out of the lounge. Jacob gave my knee a squeeze then followed. Marcus grabbed my hand, his gaze capturing me and stealing my breath, and brushed his lips across my knuckles.

I shivered with desire.

"Hey," Kol groaned. "At least give me time to bleed off the excess first."

Marcus ignored Kol, flashed me a hungry smile, then left.

"I see you've worked things out with Marcus." Kol pulled his phone from his pocket while keeping one arm around me.

"Until he realizes this is a terrible idea and changes his mind again." I leaned into his side and concentrated on his soft sensual heat pulsing into me. I knew it was a whisper of what his magic was really like. I'd gotten a glimpse of what it would feel like when he'd released it when I'd saved him from the archnephilim, and I struggled not to think about that.

"I don't think he's going to change his mind." Kol's magic seeped deeper and with that, and the heat from his raised body temperature — because of his demonic nature — I was starting to feel like I was drifting.

"I wouldn't put money on that," I said, so relaxed my words slurred. I prayed Marcus had made his final decision, but once this crisis and the glow of sex passed, he was going to realize what a complete and utter mess this was. "It's all so complicated."

I shifted, trying to get more comfortable against Kol's side, our current position straining my neck when I leaned my head back.

Kol sighed, and turned so his back was against the arm of the couch. He slid a leg on the other side of me, boxing me in, and drew me back against his chest.

I leaned in, one hand pressed over his heart, feeling the steady, soothing thump beneath my palm. The pain from the key remained, a far-off stinging in my head, but the overall sensation within me was enveloping warmth and safety. I could do anything in Kol's arms, ask for anything, and he wouldn't judge. His pleasure was my pleasure.

Except it wasn't his pleasure I craved. Well, right now it kind of was, but the need wasn't overwhelming. It was just enough to ease the pain and relax me. Who I really wanted was Marcus. He was all I'd ever wanted. "Why does it have to be so complicated?"

"I hear that's the defining feature of relationships."

"You hear?" I closed my eyes.

"Incubi don't fall in love. We don't have relationships like everyone else because of the nature of our magic." He shrugged, the movement rubbing his body against mine, drawing a curl of desire. "It is what it is."

A hint of mist whispered around me, telling me he wasn't as nonchalant about the situation as he pretended to be.

"Are you really bite-locked with Jacob?" he asked, his tone too bright, forcing the topic change.

Sudden hot need rushed through me at the memory of Jacob's bite and Marcus releasing it.

Kol hissed out a sharp breath, and his pulse picked up. The heat from his magic billowed, swelling from comforting to needy, and made me ache with yearning.

"Shit. Sorry." He wrenched back on his magic, the sudden absence leaving me cold and spiking agony through my head.

I gasped in pain and my muscles contracted, threatening to wrench me into convulsions again.

"Crap." His arm around my waist tightened, and he pressed his lips to the top of my head. A hint of his power returned, steadying me out then dragging me back to the sensual sleepy state. "I've never felt anything like the power of your release before."

"Blame Jacob," I said, my lips heavy. "I've never felt anything like it before, either."

"You know sex magic is dangerous, right?" He tensed beneath me, as if preparing for another surge of my desire, and the heat from his magic grew strained, edging back toward sexual. "You can't do that again."

"There was only Jacob's bite. I swear." Why wouldn't he believe me? Yes, both climaxes with Marcus had been amazing, the second as powerful as the one induced by Jacob's bite, but magic hadn't been involved. It had just been the result of years of pent-up anticipation.

Years of fantasizing, dreaming, aching. Perhaps there was magic involved, because Marcus's wolf had claimed me. I hadn't heard of anything like that in the shifter community, but maybe it was rare, like a vampire's bite-lock, and shifters didn't talk about it.

I'd have to ask Marcus about that.

I wondered if he knew. He hadn't been a shifter for very long, hadn't been born one. He'd been that one in a million susceptible to the lycanthropy infection.

God, I really didn't know anything about him. Did he belong to a pack? Did his family know? Hell, even before he'd been bitten and we'd been partners, I hadn't known much about him, like how big his family was and if they lived in town.

But did any of that change the way I felt about him?

Not really. It just meant we were going to have to learn about each other, figure out how things were going to work—

If he didn't change his mind.

And if Gideon didn't get in the way. He'd known Marcus and I had feelings for each other before fate had branded me with his mark, but would knowing we were together change things? Would he free me of the obligation neither of us wanted as mates?

He would free me.

He had to free me.

Free me.

Find it and free me. I can give you power beyond your wildest imagination.

No. But a part of me yearned to say yes. I needed power, needed to protect myself.

I know the darkness within you, the thin thread wrapped around your soul. Ibizual's dark laugher grated against my senses and sliced agony through my head. *You've been touched by my kin. You'll never be able to burn it all away, no matter how hard you try.*

His malevolence swept around me, crushing me just as the arch-nephilim's had, and I fought to break free, but couldn't move, couldn't breathe, could only think and feel. And I was drowning in fear and helplessness.

Never, I gasped at him.

KOL

magic soothed her into sleep. Even unconscious, she radiated sexual power, filling me almost as fast as I was using it to ease her pain, since I couldn't just flood her with power and get rid of my excess. That would only add to the loop of desire we were struggling with, turning her on even more and drowning me with power until I was drunk on her desire — or rather, drunker.

As it was, the lounge was happily spinning around me and my body was heavy and relaxed. I hadn't had this much desire coursing through me since Jacob had taken me to a blood house shortly after I'd been rescued and released from the hospital. He'd been trying to show me that desire wasn't foul, that it could be freely given and I didn't have to starve myself for fear of hurting someone.

But it had been too much, too soon. I hadn't known how to control how much sexual energy I absorbed. I'd never had to learn that. I'd matured into my incubus nature in captivity, and the desire in Michael's laboratory of horrors had been thin and tainted. I'd never been able to get enough to properly sustain me, so I'd never learned to properly shield myself from taking in too much.

At least the sexual energy from Essie and Marcus had been pure. Even with whatever magic they'd used to enhance their experience — and they had to have used something else on top of Jacob's bite-lock —

the power had been filled with Essie's light. And God did it feel good to absorb light energy with genuine desire and love, not soured by anger, disgust, or fear.

Essie groaned, the convulsions from the manifesting key affecting her even while unconscious, and I strengthened the stream of magic I was pouring into her, even as I resisted the urge to wrap my free arm around her.

I wanted to hold her like I'd held her after our first failed attempt to capture the archnephilim. I hadn't realized how good it felt to be with her, how safe and comfortable I was with her until she'd left. I wanted to be near her, to keep holding her, to ride her desire.

As much as it was awful seeing her in pain and bloody at that first feral vampire's nest, a part of me had been thrilled that fate had thrown her back into my life and hadn't cared that she brought far too many complications to the team.

Maybe being around her light would be enough to keep the nightmares at bay.

Except that was just wishful thinking. Being around beings on the light end of the spectrum hadn't helped before, I doubted they would now. It hadn't been Gideon and living surrounded by angels that had helped, it had been the job and the stability of the team — something that was currently in flux thanks to Essie.

But I wouldn't give her up just to get my nightmares to go away again. As chaotic and complicated as she was for the team what with Marcus's wolf claiming her, destiny saying she belong to Gideon, and her and Jacob being unable to resist his vampiric claim on her, she steadied me.

Holding her like this, focusing my magic on her and feeling the brightness of her power steadied me, made me feel safe. It was like her life was a hurricane and she was the eye of the storm. The closer I got to her, the calmer everything became.

No, I just needed to suck it up and wait for the nightmares to pass. After years of working with empaths to ease the emotions and lethe demons to dampen the memories of what I'd survived, the memories were as healed as they were ever going to be. I was always going to have nightmares. That was just the way things were. They would ease up. Eventually. Even with the team in chaos.

In fact, Essie was probably helping. My nightmares would have returned whether she'd been around or not. The archnephilim had been murdering the men and women who'd saved me, bringing back all those horrible memories. At least with her around, I had contact with an energy that didn't grate on my senses and didn't belong to someone who had the emotional capability of an ice cube.

At least she and Marcus had finally worked things out and he hadn't lost his shit on Jacob even after learning that Essie was bite-locked. Wolves were notorious for being possessive — especially an alpha like Marcus — but he hadn't snarled at Jacob or attacked when Essie had convulsed and Jacob had drawn near.

Marcus had to know that Essie had let Jacob bite her and probably more given the sexual energy that had radiated off of them this morning. She hadn't made an attempt to hide the marks on her neck and they'd openly talked about her being bite-locked.

I didn't know how he was managing to keep his wolf controlled, but it gave me hope that he and Gideon — and I guess Jacob, too, until his essence faded from hers — could work out their complicated relationship with Essie.

Of course, that would mean that Gideon would have to accept that Essie was his mate, and from the way he'd kicked her off the team, not caring that he destroyed her career, it didn't look like he was going to acknowledge their connection any time soon... if at all.

ESSIE

Lightning exploded through me, and I jerked forward. The silvery remains of the archnephilim's brand burned while Gideon's brand pulsed with snaps of electricity, both grating against the burning crackle of my buzz. My entire body was alight with battling energy and my stomach churned with the memory of the dream... not dream?

I'd thought the horror of the archnephilim was behind me, thought I could move on from the darkness that had threatened to consume my soul. I'd thought I was free. But I wasn't. I'd never be free. I had to leave, had to escape before everyone knew the truth, had to—

"Essie, it's okay." Kol sat forward and hugged me, his body and heat wrapping around me. "It's just a dream."

But the second he said it I knew it hadn't been a dream. Once again a demon was in my head and knew exactly what I was.

The pain in my head swept down into my chest, squeezed tight, and yanked me out of Kol's embrace to my feet. I had to go. Now.

Free me.

My body jerked toward the door.

"Essie?" Kol grabbed my wrist, stopping me from leaving.

"I have to go."

"Where?"

Good question. "I don't know."

He frowned, and my gaze jumped past his shoulder and out the patio door. The sky was dark, only a hint of light remaining. It was dusk. The key was calling me.

Kol called Gideon and Marcus, and we hurried to the garage to wait for them. Thankfully the pain in my head was mostly gone, and while the pull in my chest was fierce, it wasn't agonizing.

Except now that the agony in my head was gone, I was painfully aware of my buzz biting under my skin. If I was smart, I'd run up to my room and change my nicotine patches, but the compulsion to go to the key wouldn't let me head back inside.

Jacob arrived first, in clean clothes and with his bulletproof vest back on, and his matching Berettas and a sword on his belt. He handed Kol a vest, his gaze once again jumping to me, dark, intense, and filled with the need to talk. In private.

Gideon arrived next, decked out like he'd been before to clean out the ferals' nest. He handed me an M4, and I checked the magazine to ensure it was full in hopes that the movement would distract me from the need to move.

Get the key. Now now now.

Marcus rushed out the door last. He also wore the same gear as before, and had brought down my borrowed vest, duty belt, Glock, and extra magazines for both the Glock and the M4. He also handed me a sheathed sword. It wasn't as long as his or Jacob's, but then I doubted I'd be able to handle anything bigger.

"She's not going to need that," Gideon said as Marcus helped me secure it to my duty belt. "She's staying in the SUV."

"I'm not taking any chances," Marcus growled. He finished with the belt and slipped my room keycard into my hand.

Gideon glared at me. "Do you even know how to use that?"

Not really, but I wasn't going to admit that to him. If it came down to me needing the sword, we were in dire straights.

"We need to get going," I said instead, unable to stop myself from shifting from side to side.

Gideon didn't move and his gaze bore into me. "My magic is off limits."

I struggled to hold his gaze, and the electricity from his brand burned up my forearm.

Now. Go now.

"Is that clear?" he said.

"Copy that."

"Let's go." Jacob hurried to the SUV.

Gideon tossed the keys to Marcus, who grabbed them one-handed and ran past Jacob to the driver's door.

We all got in, taking our usual seats. The pull was yanking me to the back of the garage and, since that direction led out of the Supers' Quarter, I had to assume the key was going to manifest somewhere in town.

"We're going into the city," I said as Marcus pulled out of the garage.

"How's the pain?" he asked.

"Mostly gone." If I didn't take into account my God damn buzz, which, if I leaned against the back of Gideon's seat, was almost at new-patch levels.

"Thank God," he breathed.

"Focus on the job," Gideon said, his voice low as he turned on the SUV's GPS then handed out coms to everyone in the group but me. "Where in town are we going?"

I pointed down the road leading through the park and ringing the Supers' Quarter, squirming in my seat. "That way and a little to the right." It was as specific as I could get.

We left the Quarter, and the pull to the right got stronger. Gideon studied the streets, directing Marcus as I gave vague directions and trying to keep us from getting stopped at a dead end.

The pull kept getting stronger. A part of me feared the agony was going to explode through me again, and I would go back to convulsing and being at best useless and at worst a dangerous distraction. It was getting harder to breathe, and I was getting hot — and I wasn't sure if it was because of the key manifesting or someone's emotions.

We worked our way through town, breaking the speed limit and running through red lights, until I knew we were almost on top of it.

"Here," I gasped.

Now. Free me now.

Marcus jerked the SUV to the curb, narrowly missing the front of a car already parked there, and swore. We were on a busy street near the heart of downtown. The driver who'd been on the road behind us yelled as he passed us.

"You're sure it's here?" Marcus asked.

Now.

High rises towered to our right, half of the buildings rebuilt from the war, all shiny glass and steel. They sat interspersed among the older, original city buildings, constructed of brick with sculpted concrete ledges — the same turn-of-the-century architecture found in the Supers' Quarter. Most of the main floors were vast lobbies for whatever business resided inside, but a few had cafes or restaurant or stores. Even now, well past regular business hours, there were people on the street. Not nearly as many as there would have been if it hadn't been almost nine at night, but still too many for my liking, given how vicious Logan's ferals had been.

The pressure in my chest was fierce, and I strained to breathe, but the certainty in my soul was also fierce. The key was going to manifest here—

To my left. Across the street. In the park.

Gideon pulled out his phone and hit a pre-programmed number as he climbed out of the SUV. My buzz roared back to life, and I gritted my teeth.

"JP agent o-seven-one-four," he said. "I need a full lockdown on Seventh and Bell by Unity Park and a four-block radius around it. Equip for feral vampires."

"Copy that," a voice said on the other end of the line and hung up.

"The local PD isn't going to deploy in time," Jacob said, getting out of the SUV.

"It's still protocol." Gideon pocketed his phone.

Kol and Marcus got out. I opened my door to get out but Gideon froze me with his icy glare and grabbed the door, blocking my way. "Can you pinpoint where the key will form?"

"In the park. Maybe a hundred feet that way." I pointed directly across from me down a winding gravel path that twisted along the gently sloping lawn, sheltered by tall trees — many magically aged since they'd only been planted in the last twenty-five years. The pressure squeezed with the certainty of my words, and I fought to have enough breath to speak. "Yes, a hundred feet that way."

"Good. Stay here." He moved to close the door but stopped. "Better yet, wait here until Chris can pick you up."

No. I had to go to the key. Now. Everything in my being said I couldn't wait, couldn't leave. I had to go.

Gideon pulled out his phone again as a woman down the street screamed.

We all jerked our attention toward the scream. A woman scrambled into the lobby of an office tower as a pack of ferals barreled down the street toward us. One of them snarled at her but didn't stop to attack, their aim fully on us.

"Essie, get out of here." Marcus tossed me the keys, shoved Gideon out of the way, and slammed my door shut.

The first feral leaped at the guys, and Gideon lunged into its attack, his sword of pure light forming in his hands and plunging into the feral's chest.

Marcus drew his sword and met the next one, while Kol slid over the front of the SUV's hood to meet another.

"Essie, please," Marcus said, frost sweeping over my arms.

I wanted to stay. Fight. But we were already overwhelmed, and I was cop enough to know that even if I could draw a full breath, I was still a liability right now. If I could get some distance, I could use the M4 to slow the ferals down like I'd done in the nest.

Clenching my jaw against the call from the key, I scrambled into the driver's seat and hit the power locks. I fumbled to get the key into the ignition, but a feral shoved past Gideon and Kol and jumped onto the SUV's hood. It slammed its fist into the front windshield, cracking it, then smashed through with the next punch, spraying me with safety glass pebbles.

It shoved its arm up to its shoulder through the hole and clawed for my neck. I grabbed the seat recline and wrenched back out of reach. The feral snarled and smashed its other fist through the windshield. I dropped the keys in my lap, drew my Glock, and shot it point blank in the forehead. Blue lightning crackled around its body and with a howl, it collapsed, dead.

Outside the SUV, the guys were surrounded, at least a dozen ferals clawing and biting and snarling, and more ferals — I wasn't sure if they were ferals or reanimated ferals — rushed down the street toward us. Jacob, the combat too close quarters for his Berettas, was using his sword with deadly efficiency, and Kol's blades were a whirl as he danced and ducked the ferals' attacks.

"We have to get to the key," Gideon said.

Yes. Get the key. It's coming. Now now now.

"Go. I've got Essie," Marcus growled.

Gideon shot a hard glare at me. "Get out of here."

And he was right. They were going to need everyone to fight the ferals and get to the key before Logan. I couldn't let Marcus stay to protect me. But God, I had to get that key. The compulsion was almost as bad as Jacob's claim when it had been new.

I grabbed the keys from my lap to shove them into the ignition, but a feral slammed its shoulder against my door, heaving the SUV off the driver's side wheels.

The wheels crashed back to the asphalt, jarring me, and I missed the ignition. In the rearview mirror, I could see more ferals racing toward us.

Jeez, how many people had Logan turned? There were just so many.

"Officer Shaw, go!" Gideon snapped. He slashed at a feral's neck, but it jerked to the side. The strike didn't decapitate it, only sent a wild spray of blood into his face. He flinched, the action less than a second, but long enough for the feral to grab the front of his vest and wrench him close.

The feral at my door smashed its fist through the window, sending glass flying toward me, nicking my cheek and neck, and clawed at me as I shoved the key into the ignition. I wrenched to the side, its claws raking over my shoulder with fiery agony, and tried to keep a hand on the key and start the SUV.

For a heartbeat, the idea of glancing into the backseat to grab the M4 flashed through my mind, but I only had time for one thing and getting away would be better for the guys.

Jacob shoved the feral closest to him to the side and rushed to the feral on me. He yanked the feral away from the door, but two more slammed against the driver's side of the SUV before he could stop them.

The vehicle heaved up, and with a roar from the ferals, they tossed it onto its side. My shoulder and head slammed into the passenger side door, and what little breath I had burst from my lungs.

Marcus yelled, his fear frosting over my cheeks, but he was caught five feet from the front of the SUV between two ferals and couldn't get to me.

One of the ferals who'd shoved the SUV over, a guy about Marcus's size and build, dove through the broken driver's side window, showering me with more glass.

He swiped at me, and I yanked my Glock up and fired two shots into his forehead as his claws dug into my forearm. Blood sprayed my face, and he collapsed on top of me, pinning me with his one hundred and fifty plus pounds. I fought to draw breath against his weight and the pressure of the soon-to-be materializing key, and my muscles twitched with the force of my buzz biting under my skin.

Now. Go now.

The other feral leaned into the window, snarling, but someone yanked it away. I gasped in a shallow breath and shoved at the feral's dead weight pinning me, but couldn't move him one-handed. I really didn't want to put my Glock down, but if I was going to get out of the SUV, I had to move the feral.

Out the front windshield, I could only see Marcus and hoped that meant the guys were moving the fight closer to the key. Somehow I knew it hadn't manifested yet, but that didn't mean Logan wasn't already set and waiting, ready to grab it the moment it did while the guys were still fighting his ferals.

Something crashed against the bottom — now side — of the SUV, making it rock. Shit.

Gasping, I set down my Glock, heaved the feral's head and shoulder into the space between the seats, and retrieved my sidearm. I shot at the windshield six times, trying to make enough of a hole to get me started, since windshield safety glass was hard to kick through and even harder if it hadn't already been broken.

I kicked again and again as fast as I could, fighting to get the glass to peel away and create an opening large enough to crawl through.

A feral rushed toward the front of the SUV, its gaze locked on me. Marcus grabbed it by the back of its torn and filthy shirt and yanked it off its feet. Again I consider the M4 in the back seat. I didn't want to leave it behind, but there was no way I'd have time to search for it.

Still fighting for breath, I half crawled, half squirmed out the windshield, the hole barely big enough for my body, the glass pebbles biting into my palms.

Marcus had decapitated the feral who'd been about to attack me, but another one had tackled him to the road.

"You were supposed to leave," Gideon yelled at me. He stood in the middle of the road, light blazing from his eyes, a match to the light making up his sword. None of the guys had gotten far from the SUV, with Kol the farthest, at the mouth of the path leading into the park.

"Don't think I didn't try. I know I'm best suited to fight this fight from a distance." I drew in a strained breath and fired at a feral lunging for Jacob's back. The buzz made me twitch, and I hit the feral's shoulder and not its chest. Thankfully it still stumbled long enough for Jacob to wrench around and decapitate it.

"So you were going to disobey an order and not leave?" Gideon impaled a feral and grabbed the arm of another about to slash at Marcus.

"Are you really having this fight now?" Kol asked, dodging the claws of one, then another.

Free me. Now.

The pressure of the key billowed, and I gasped, clutching my chest. It still wasn't the agony of before, but it wasn't much of an improvement. "We have to get to the key."

"Officer Shaw, take cover in one of the buildings." Gideon jerked his chin toward the closest high rise lobby door. "The rest of us, in the park."

I bolted toward the lobby door, my chest burning from the pressure and lack of air, but half a dozen ferals broke away from the guys and chased after me.

Crap. I was as much of a target as the guys.

Marcus swore and ran toward the group going after me. Gideon barreled toward me as well, shooting a light strike at the feral closest to me as he ran. It wasn't enough to kill it, but the blast made it stagger long enough for me to jerk close enough to guarantee my aim and shoot it in the heart. And I had no choice but to stand and fight. All the ferals were faster than me, and with almost no distance between us, there was no point in running away.

The feral I'd shot dropped with a flash of blue lightning, but now I was surrounded by the remaining four.

One slashed at me. I jerked away from it into the claws of another, who sliced rents into the back of my vest.

Marcus yanked that feral out of reach and killed it.

Almost time. Find me. Free me.

"New plan." Gideon reached the pack and impaled another feral. "Officer Shaw in the center." His tone was all business, but I could tell by the waves of searing heat sweeping through the air that he was pissed.

Yeah, well, this wasn't how I'd planned for my evening to go, either. My shoulder and forearm burned from the wounds I'd already received, and blood once again oozed from shallow cuts on my cheek and neck. And God damn it, I could barely breathe.

I shot another feral in the chest to slow it down and bolted toward the park as Marcus and Gideon finished off the other two who'd attacked me. Jacob and Kol fought to clear a path for me, but there were still too many. Jeez, how the hell were there so many?

I jumped over the body of a dead feral, lying in a pool of blood on the asphalt, and its hand jerked out and seized my ankle.

Ah, shit. The damned thing wasn't dead.

ESSIE

I crashed to the road, the feral's grip a vise around my ankle, and somehow managed to not smash my face against the asphalt or lose my Glock with the impact. I wrenched around and the feral snarled at me. It grabbed my leg with its other hand and sank its teeth into my calf.

Pain screamed through my leg. I kicked it in the head, and its teeth ripped from my flesh and shredded my jeans.

Shit shit shit.

I shot the feral in the head before it could bite me again. Blue lightning exploded around it, but I scrambled to my feet, not waiting to see if the enspelled ammunition had actually killed it.

Around us, all the ferals who hadn't been decapitated or shot in the head groaned and hissed and climbed to their feet.

"I'm beginning to really hate this guy," Marcus snarled.

Gideon decapitated the feral closest to him, but another at his feet dug its claws into his thigh. "Just get to the key." He shoved the feral off him, the creature's claws ripping his fatigues and drawing blood.

Now. Now.

I fought to run down the path. The pressure in my chest was so heavy I couldn't catch my breath, barely managing shallow gasps.

Trees crowded close, casting heavy shadows, and even if there had been more than a barely seen sliver of moon in the sky, the path still would have been dark.

A few feet down the path a streetlight, made to look like an early 19th century wrought-iron street lamp, flickered on then went out.

The pressure squeezed tighter, and the whole row of streetlights flickered on and went out.

Now. Free me. Join me. Kin.

"I'm not your kin," I hissed at Ibizual. "Your kin tried to claim me, and I killed him."

Ahead, the path ended in a T-intersection, and the trees opened up to a grassy embankment with a steep incline down to Unity Lake — a crater formed from an eruption of powerful nephilim and angelic magic during the war that had been turned into the lake.

Light shimmered at the top of the embankment, red and pulsing and radiating evil, dispelling any doubt I might have had that the arch-nephilim and Ibizual were kin. The power felt the same, an inky, consuming darkness that made the remnants of the archnephilim's brand pulse on my biceps.

More ferals crashed through the bushes, the stream of monsters never ending. They all rushed toward the shimmering light, a pinprick at chest height.

Jacob grabbed two and yanked them into a fight. Kol tackled another, and Gideon cut down two more. Marcus barreled into the bushes, blocking the way for four more.

I scanned the area for Logan. He had to be close by, waiting for the last minute to rush out with his enhanced vampiric speed and grab the key.

A feral broke free from Jacob. I shot at it, missed, and the Glock's slide clicked back. Out of ammo. My thoughts whirled, taking a split second to figure the possibilities. All the guys were caught in fights with multiple ferals, and I wasn't going to have enough time to eject the Glock's magazine and replace it.

I dropped my Glock and drew my sword, sweeping it at the feral at the last minute. The blade dug into the creature's shoulder, drawing a howl, and it batted the weapon aside and dug its claws into the front of my vest.

The pressure in my chest exploded with ferocious power, stealing my breath. My knees buckled, dropping me to the ground. The movement ripped off my vest, still caught in the feral's claws, but saved my neck from a slash by the feral's other hand.

My attention jerked toward the manifesting key of its own volition, and my pulse sped up.

The key had fully formed, now a small red jewel, pulsing with so much power it made my buzz scream in defiance.

"Shaw. Get the key," Gideon yelled. He blasted a light strike at the feral attacking me, the force of the blast tossing it back into a tree trunk.

I scrambled to my feet. Another feral rushed toward me. I was going to get there first, but just barely, and I had no weapon to defend myself with once I had the key—

No, not true. I had a light strike that might be powerful enough — if, God, it was working again — to slow it down long enough for the guys to help me.

I thought the words of the combat spell, unable to draw enough breath to even hiss them as I dashed out of the trees onto the embankment. The power and evil from the key churned my stomach. I didn't want to grab it, didn't want Ibizual's power touching my skin. But I couldn't let the feral get it.

And where the hell was Logan?

With gritted teeth, I seized the key. Its magic burned into my palm, drawing a scream and making my stomach churn. I wrenched up my other hand to shoot the light strike at the feral leaping toward me, but blinding agony exploded in my chest, and the key tumbled from my hand, my fingers suddenly numb.

Gideon screamed, and a blaze of white light flashed through the park.

The muscles in my legs gave out, and my momentum from running heaved me forward. I tumbled down the embankment and crashed into the gravel path skirting the edge of the lake.

Now I really couldn't catch my breath. The pressure was replaced with an agony that leached the strength from every cell in my body.

I strained to get up, to move, to, hell, look at the top of the embankment to see if one of the guys had gotten the key. But I could barely move, barely breathe.

Somewhere in the back of my mind a voice screamed that I'd been shot, that I needed to apply pressure, get help, but I couldn't get my thoughts to focus enough to take action.

Gideon scrambled down the embankment and frost instantly formed on all my exposed skin. His expression was filled with horror and panic, illuminated by the glow from his eyes.

"No. God, no." He slammed his hands against my chest and pressed down hard, shooting white lightning through me. "Jacob! Marcus!" His voice cracked with desperation. "Kol!"

"The key," I gasped. *Did you get the key? I lost the key.*

"Jacob!" Gideon's body shook, and he panted with frantic gasps as a hint of heat whispered through his brand.

"Essie, no." That was Jacob, but I couldn't turn my head to see him.

Marcus tumbled down the embankment. "We have to get her to Amiah." But his gaze jumped to the ground around me, and he collapsed to his knees beside me.

Every breath was agony, gurgling in my lungs.

"No time, there's no time." Gideon yanked me into his lap, clutching me to his chest. "I can't lose her, please, God, not her, too."

"Fly. Now," Kol said from somewhere above me.

"She's bleeding too fast," Jacob growled.

A chill shuddered through me, making me colder even with Gideon's fear already frosting my skin. It sliced agony through my chest, and danced darkness at the edge of my vision.

"The key—" I couldn't get my mind past losing the key. I coughed, and the metallic tang of blood filled my mouth.

Gideon's gaze jumped to Jacob. "Turn her into a vampire. You have to turn her."

"I'm not a master." Jacob grabbed my hand, his expression just as desperate as Gideon's. "Can the brand sustain her?"

"No, not enough. It won't be enough to get her to Amiah. Marcus, please," Gideon begged. His grip on me tightened, and the pain started to bleed into a frozen numbness, the darkness creeping further across my vision. "I can't lose her. I can't."

"Even if she's that one in a million susceptible to lycanthropy, she'll die before the change hits her."

"No," Gideon gasped, a sound too quiet, too broken. "Please, no."

I coughed, more blood slicing agony through the numbness. The darkness filled most of my vision, and all I could see was Gideon, panting, desperate, tears streaming down his cheeks. He clung to me and crumpled forward, his forehead pressing to mine and enveloping me in the brilliant white blaze from his eyes. His scent of springtime, fresh and green and warm, swept around me and entwined with the darkness, dragging me toward it.

"Essie, please. Don't die. Please."

"I can heal her enough to get her to Amiah." Kol shoved Marcus aside and dropped to the gravel beside me.

"Incubi don't have healing magic," Marcus growled.

"Not that we like to tell anyone, but just like I can take energy, I can give it." Kol reached for me, but his gaze was locked with Gideon's, asking permission. "I'm willing to pay the cost."

"Whatever it takes," Gideon said.

I coughed again, slicing more pain through me, and more blood filled my mouth. The darkness swelled over my vision, and I was floating in a heavy, black, numb nothingness.

Kol's warm hands captured my face. The frost instantly melted at his heightened body temperature and my eyes jerked open. Suddenly I was drowning not in black nothingness, but black warmth with a flicker of hellfire.

His lips brushed mine, and a whisper of heat slid into my mouth, cutting through the heavy numbness. Agony roared through my chest, and my muscles convulsed. Kol's grip on my face tightened, forcing me still, and his kiss grew fierce, crushing against my lips.

The whisper of heat flared into a thick thread. He shoved his tongue into my mouth, forcing it open, and dug his fingers into the hinge of my jaw to keep it open. His heat turned into a flood, and I thrashed against the agony, desperate to escape the pain. But it kept growing until my entire body was on fire, burning and wailing.

"You're killing her," Marcus growled.

"He's not," Gideon said, his voice tight. Light snapped from his eyes and lightning from his magic cut through his brand.

The flood turned into an ocean, and I was choking, drowning on Kol's power just like I'd been drowning on the archnephilim's power when it had tried to possess me. Fear clenched tight around my heart. This was too much like the attack from the archnephilim. I had to get away. Had to stop this. I couldn't breathe, couldn't let him take me, couldn't let him possess me—

"Don't fight me, Essie," Kol gasped against my lips.

I fought my panic to accept his magic, but I couldn't concentrate past the pain to do anything other than try to breathe.

He groaned, the sound tight and pained, and his fingers dug into my cheeks. The heat snapped from drowning to sensual and the agony swept into bone-melting desire. I gasped, and his magic poured down my throat without resistance. My muscles went limp and my head spun.

I ached with need, with the promise of Kol's magic, knowing that this was just a glimpse of his power, just enough to get me to relax.

It lit up every nerve, and I was suddenly hyper aware of his lips, firm and demanding on mine, his tongue fueling a need within me, and the heat from his hands on my cheeks, seeping into my skin. I also thrummed with awareness of Gideon, every frantic breath that shook his body against mine, and his strong arms clinging to me, desperate to protect me. I ached with a yearning for Gideon that I'd been trying to ignore since his brand had formed on my arm. I had to know him, to be with him. I knew in my soul I belonged with him.

The brand said so.

Fate had decided and permanently bound us together.

Of course my body right now also said I belonged with Kol. God. I needed him, needed his hands on more than just my face, needed his lips on more than just my lips. My pulse raced with desire and anticipation, and his heat swelled low within me.

I opened my eyes, not realizing I'd closed them, and stared into a hungry darkness filled with hellfire. His gaze captured me completely and held me hostage, promising me satisfaction. Then his eyes rolled back, the power of his magic vanished with a gasp, and he collapsed onto the gravel path beside me.

"Kol—" I tried to reach for him, but my body wouldn't obey my commands and my head was spinning too fast. The darkness now threatening my vision was warm and heavy and comforting, and the agony in my chest was still there, but half of what it had been... maybe. I couldn't tell, because my body was so focused on the aching need brought to life by Kol's magic.

Marcus grabbed him and rolled him over. He was pale and sweat slicked his face and neck, but he was still breathing. Thank God.

Gideon tightened his grip on me and stood, cradling me against his chest. His wings swept out with a flash of white light and he leaped up, caught the air, and pulled us into the sky. Kol's soft sensual darkness blanketed me, and I drifted, only half aware of the wind in my face, Gideon's strong arms around me, and his soothing scent.

My thoughts slid from flying to the archnephilim trying to pull wings I didn't have from my body. A part of me, I guess the angelic part, ached knowing I didn't have wings and I'd never be able to fly like this, while the human part was relieved. It would kill me to know I had the ability to fly but couldn't without endangering my life.

Between one blink and the next we landed in front of the garage, and Gideon ran inside screaming for Amiah, his fear and heartache making me cold and fogging my vision.

I knew it had taken longer than a few seconds to cross town, that I'd passed out, but even just coming to that conclusion was like thinking through water.

Amiah and her assistant met us in triage. Gideon set me on the closest bed, his clothes soaked with my blood, and Amiah shoved him out of the way. The assistant — Cassey? — inserted an IV into my arm, while Amiah cut open my shirt and grabbed something from the tray beside me. Her mouth moved, but I couldn't understand her words. Her tone was sharp, and I couldn't figure out if she was angry with me or not.

Gideon was still hyperventilating, and the chill deepened, thickening the fog. I wanted to tell him it was all right, that it didn't hurt any more, or at least not that much. But I couldn't get my mouth to move, and then I was floating, half hearing, half feeling, riding the heat of Kol's magic.

I blinked, my lids moving in slow motion, the darkness clinging to me, and when I opened my eyes, Gideon, Amiah, and Cassey were gone. So, too, was triage. I lay in one of Operations' hospital rooms, hooked up to a softly beeping monitor and an IV, dressed in a hospital gown. My chest throbbed with the promise of searing pain tickling at the edge of what I could only assume were drug-muted senses.

The lights in the room were low, which meant the lights in the hall were low, too. Unless I wasn't in a room with an observation window. I turned my head just enough to see. Yep, a window, with the blinds up. Did the low lights mean it was still night and I hadn't been out for that long?

I had no idea.

"I can't do this, Amiah," Gideon said, his voice low and still breaking with pain and fear. "I can't. How the hell do I do this?"

I searched the hall — since his voice was too far away to be in the room — and caught a glimpse of him almost out of sight of the window. He stood shaking, his forehead against the wall opposite the window, and everything within me said I had to go to him, comfort him, tell him I was alive and okay.

"I don't even know her. I don't even want to know her, and yet when I knew she was dying—" He drew in a choked breath and looked at someone out of sight. "It was worse than watching Zella die. I couldn't think of anything else and my soul—" He shuddered. "If she dies, I'm going to lose my mind."

"No," Amiah said, her tone firm. "She's human and you're stronger than her."

He pressed his hand to the wall, and his fear deepened, stinging my cheeks with frost and digging into my chest as a genuine emotion. "She can take my magic and use it."

Amiah gasped, her surprise zinging through me before it twisted into anger. "You can deal with that."

"I don't want to deal with it. I don't want any of this."

And he didn't. I could feel it in my soul. He didn't want me, didn't want our bond, and didn't want a repeat of the terror he'd just experienced.

"Well, you can't fight it," Amiah said, her tone now tender, surprising me. "She has your brand. She's your mate."

Gideon's desperation deepened, and he drew in another ragged breath. "She might have my brand, but she's not my mate. She's Marcus's. And she was his before she was mine." The hand I could see clenched, and he punched the wall, cracking the drywall. "But everything within me says Essie, a complete stranger, is mine. Mine. What am I supposed to do with that? I'm not fighting Marcus for his mate. I'd have to kill him. He'd never submit and give her up."

Amiah huffed and a flicker of something dark and hard, I wasn't sure what, whispered through all the other emotions. "Marcus's wolf will just have to pick someone else."

My thoughts stuttered, stuck on Amiah's strange emotion, then jerked to her words. Marcus would pick someone else? But I didn't want Marcus to pick someone else.

"Easier said than done," Gideon said.

"He at least can do it. You can't." She sounded so certain, so determined.

Except didn't I have a say in this? It was my life, too. Marcus and I had been destined long before Gideon and me. I knew that in the core of my soul.

Amiah's hand slipped into view, rubbing slow circles over Gideon's back, and her emotions turned to pity. "Fate says she belongs to you and you to her."

"Fate also said this is supposed to be beautiful, magical, perfect destiny," he said, his tone and emotions turning bitter and squeezing in my chest. "Nothing about this is beautiful or magical. It's a nightmare."

"Gideon—"

"I can't love her. I never want to." He spat out the words, his fear and grief and frustration battering me and stealing my breath.

My throat tightened and my eyes burned. I wrenched my face away from the window and pressed my mouth into the pillow to hide my sobs.

His words shouldn't have hurt. God, why did they hurt so much? I didn't want this, either. I wasn't in love with him. I was in love with Marcus. And Gideon was an angel who despised nephilim. I should be terrified of him. Which I was, both because of what he'd do if he found out the truth and of how much his words hurt me. God, those word and the dark storm of his emotions—

They sliced into my soul and shattered me.

GIDEON

I forced myself away from Shaw's room instead of going in like my screaming soul wanted and headed to my suite. I was still covered in Shaw's blood and wouldn't be able to focus on stopping Logan while wearing the proof of the night's disaster.

Except it had been more than just a disaster. It had been a horror show. Every time I closed my eyes, I saw Shaw gasping, too shocked to even try to put pressure on the wound just above her heart that gushed blood, so much blood.

I'd almost lost her.

No, I'd almost *killed* her.

I'd told her to get the key, and for some crazy reason she'd taken off her vest. Not that it would have protected her. Vests couldn't stop a shot from a high-powered rifle, but still. She should have kept it on. Except she'd probably had a good reason to take it off because even if she was reckless, she wasn't foolish. She'd proven that time and again. And she was only reckless when she was saving someone else's life. Just like an angel.

At the thought, the panic that had seized me when she'd fallen threatened to overwhelm me again. I had to be by her side. I needed to turn around and go back to her. Now.

But that was the mating brand. It wasn't how I really felt. I didn't want to be with her. I couldn't. She was Marcus's mate first.

I couldn't love her.

I can't. Ever.

Maybe if I convinced myself of that, I could hold it together. Maybe if I believed with everything I had that I'd never be allowed to love her, I could give her and Marcus what they deserved.

Because if I couldn't convince myself of that, I wouldn't be able to resist the urge from my brand that said I had to be with her.

God, it would be so easy to fall for her. She was beautiful and strong and brave, and she cared so deeply for the people who couldn't protect themselves. She'd been willing to sacrifice herself to save the lives of the city against the archnephilim and had faced that certainty head on. If her essence hadn't clearly said she was human, I would have sworn she was an angel. An angel who liked to bend or ignore the rules like a demon, but still an angel.

No. I had to keep my distance, convince myself I didn't want her. It was the only way. She and Marcus were getting their happily ever after. I was God damned going to make sure that happened, no matter the cost to me.

That said, Shaw was going to have to pay a cost as well. As much as I hated it, I had to get her off my team even if it meant her losing her job. I couldn't afford to freeze up like that again. Ever.

Nothing and no one had mattered. Lightning had shot through our brand, seized me, and all I could think of was her. Protecting her. Saving her. Our bond was so strong I knew without a doubt her death would kill me. But I wouldn't have wanted to go on without her. Watching Shaw fall had been a hundred times worse than watching the archnephilim kill Zella and I'd been in love with Zella for decades.

My throat tightened with anger and fear and grief. There were too many emotions raging inside me, threatening to drown me, and I couldn't seem to find the surface to catch my breath.

Everything would have been so much easier if Zella actually had been my mate.

But the more I thought about it, the more I knew Zella would never have been destined for me, even if I had gotten her to forgive herself and open up to me. She was too timid, too submissive. The only thing she'd ever decided for herself and stood firm on was her self-imposed exile. Even joining the Angelic Defense had been her mother's idea.

Shaw, on the other hand, challenged me, questioned my orders, and made me consider different perspectives just like the rest of the team.

We'd only really been working together for a handful of days and I already knew she'd be a better match for me than Zella. I'd never have been happy with the timid angel, no matter what my mind wanted to believe. Not completely.

Of course, I wasn't happy with Shaw, either... because as much as she was destined to be mine, right now she belonged to Marcus. And as much as Amiah believed Marcus was capable of picking another mate, he wasn't.

Everyone believed angels were the only ones who mate-bonded like I had with Shaw because we wore the proof of our bond etched in our skin, but it was obvious — perhaps because I was trapped in a bond and could see it in others — that Marcus was just as bound to her as I was. More so because he'd actually fallen in love with her and *wanted* the bond.

It didn't matter that he was fighting it to keep her safe. His wolf would never give Shaw up and I could only imagine the nightmare he was going through knowing she wore my brand and was claimed by Jacob.

I had no idea how he hadn't lost it on Jacob since it was obvious she'd let him feed on her. The marks on her neck had been fresh when he'd carried her to the lounge, but he hadn't even growled at Jacob when he'd gotten close to her.

It had to be because he knew Jacob's claim was temporary and knew he wouldn't have been able to stop Shaw from helping Jacob. Even Shaw, who knew next to nothing about supers, knew blood from the vein was the most potent, and Jacob had been seriously wounded after the fight in the sewers.

Shaw had probably insisted, and Jacob, in his weakened condition, hadn't been able to resist his claim on her. Except letting him feed again only strengthened his claim which Marcus should have been furious about.

I ran my hands over my face, fighting my exhaustion, and looked up to—

I thought it was to push the button to call the elevator and go to my suite, but I'd walked a circle without realizing it. I was back in the hall outside Shaw's hospital room, drawn to her despite what I wanted and despite what was best for her and Marcus.

She had to go. It was too dangerous for her and everyone else. For the sake of the team, for my sanity and Marcus's, I had to stand firm with kicking her off the team.

That should make his wolf happy. It should make me happy, too.

But it didn't.

ESSIE

I MUST HAVE FALLEN ASLEEP, BECAUSE WHEN I OPENED MY EYES AGAIN THEY were raw, my enspelled contacts scratchy and irritated. Technically I was supposed to be able to have a full night's sleep with them in, but I hadn't taken them out and cleaned them in over twenty-four hours, and I was paying the price. My buzz now screamed at me, grating on my nerves even though I still floated on a hazy cloud of painkillers, and the room's temperature flashed from hot to cold. Agony still throbbed, far away, still at the edge of my senses, and I couldn't focus long enough on that to figure out if that was because Amiah hadn't fully healed me, or if it was some kind of side effect of the massive amount of magic Amiah would have needed to use to save me.

"—need to see her," Marcus said from somewhere in the hall outside my door.

Ah, the source of the temperature fluctuations.

"Let her sleep," Gideon said, his tone flat. But his emotions, real, inside me and not just the air temperature, twisted, a nauseating whirl in my chest.

"You can't stop me." Marcus's tone darkened and the air grew hotter.

"I'm not, just give her time to rest," Gideon snapped, his anger growing. "Amiah didn't want to risk killing her or giving her brain damage by flooding her with the magic necessary to completely heal her."

"She isn't fully healed?" Jacob asked, his voice a low rumble, drawing a small twist in my chest from his claim.

Well, that explained why my chest still hurt and why I was still doped up on painkillers.

"We can't take her in the field if she's still hurt," Marcus said.

"We're not taking her in the field." Fear from Gideon flashed through me, and my buzz spiked.

"We may not have a choice," Jacob said. "If I couldn't feel the key manifesting, I might not be able to feel where the seal is manifesting."

"I'm not putting her in Logan's sights again," Gideon said. "She's human. She doesn't belong on a JP team."

"That shot would have killed any of us," Marcus growled, "except for maybe Kol, but only if he was at full power."

"That doesn't make it any better." Guilt twisted into Gideon's fear.

"You can't blame yourself." Jacob's back and shoulder shifted into sight at the edge of the window. "She was the best one to grab the key."

"I don't blame myself," Gideon said, but his guilt twisted tighter. "She's a liability. We lost the key, the remaining ferals, and Logan because she was shot. That wouldn't have happened if it had been anyone else on the team."

"You can't just kick her off," Marcus said, heat flashing through the air.

"How are you not on board with this?" Gideon asked. "I know your wolf has claimed her. Stop pretending you don't care."

"I'm not going to let you destroy her life," Marcus growled. "She's always wanted to be a cop, and she's a damn good one, too. You kick her off the team, and she's lost her job, her identity."

"At least she'd be alive." A hint of fear swept through Gideon's guilt.

"If you actually cared for her, you'd know she wouldn't be, not really," Marcus said, the air jumping and staying at sweltering. "And then what? She's fucking stuck with you. Would your brand let her leave town?"

Gideon's fear exploded within me, and the buzz went crazy. I gritted my teeth against the pain and tried to concentrate on their conversation.

"Of course I would," Gideon said.

But I could tell that was a lie even without his emotions raging through me. My throat tightened with tears again. He didn't want me, but he'd never let me go. And why did that hurt? It should make me furious.

"You could try," Jacob said, "but an angelic mating brand is powerful."

"She's a danger to the team," Gideon said.

"She killed the archnephilim, and saved me in the ferals' nest by nearly killing Logan." Jacob crossed his arms, making his T-shirt strain against his broad, muscular back. "We have to have a human on the team. She's a good candidate. Imagine the kind of asset she'd be if she was properly trained."

"You, too?" White light flickering in the hall had to be the magic in Gideon's eyes flaring.

Jacob's support surprised me, too, since if I died, he'd starve to death.

But then if I was kicked off the team and off the police force, what would I do? Gideon wouldn't let me leave town. Would I be happy holding down some office job? The thought made my stomach churn. I didn't want to even think about that. I supposed I could get my P.I.'s license, or do private security or something.

"I've tried letting her go, sending her back to her normal human life," Marcus said, his tone sharp and dark, as if his wolf was fighting to break free. "She keeps ending up in our world. If we push her away, she's going to end up caught in some kind of mess she can't get out of without us. Do you want to freeze up like that for no apparent reason in the middle of a fight? Do you want Essie to? You were shot and a feral almost killed her. At least if you're together, you'll be able to see it coming."

"We're not going to be together. Ever," Gideon said, his tone dark, his fear and guilt and anger choking me as my buzz sliced under my skin.

"Good," Marcus snarled, "because she's fucking mine, and I'm not letting her out of my sight again."

"So if I send her packing—?" Gideon asked.

"I go with her." Marcus shoved past Jacob and stormed down the hall, his footsteps getting farther and farther away, taking his heat with him.

My heart soared at his words, but also cried at Gideon's. I wanted to scream and sob with frustration but didn't want to face Gideon or Jacob right now, and strained to keep quiet.

"You've had a scare," Jacob said, his voice a low rumble, barely audible even with my enhanced hearing.

"Don't talk to me like I'm a soldier after my first fight."

Jacob shifted back, coming into full view, and now I could see half of

Gideon's profile. His expression was hard, with more ice in his eyes than before. His gaze leaped to mine and captured me, stealing my breath.

His anger swelled, and tears filled my eyes and tightened my throat.

God damn, I didn't want to be upset that he hated me.

"I'm going to check on Kol, see if he's awake." He too shoved past Jacob and stormed down the hall, taking his gut-churning emotions and the rest of the flickering heat.

Jacob turned to watch him go, noticed I was awake, and opened my room's door instead of leaving.

"Hey," he said, soft, low, and making my essence vibrate in perfect resonance with the part of his essence entwined with mine. "How are you doing?"

"My chest hurts." And my heart. And my soul.

And my skin. Jeez, my God damn buzz felt like fire ants were chewing me up, one tiny painful bite at a time.

His expression grew grim, and a hint of misty grief whispered around me. "Yeah."

"How badly were you hurt?" I forced out. "Do you need to feed?"

"The extra power Victoria gave me is dealing with my injuries." The mist thickened. "About that—"

"I'm not going to let you starve," I blurted out before he could say anything. I wasn't going to let him argue with me about that. He was in this mess because of me, because I couldn't tell him I was part super and hadn't known the consequences when I'd tried to protect him from Victoria's temper.

He sat on the edge of the chair beside the bed, the strain around his eyes not as tight as it had been before he'd fed on me, but not completely gone, either. He reached to grab my hand but thought better of it and drew back instead, making his claim ache within me. "I'll find a way to fix this. I promise."

A part of me didn't want him to fix this. Which was ridiculous. I didn't want to be Jacob's only means of survival. That was dangerous for the both of us. But that part of me, the part that could only be because of his claim, wanted him near. Just like I wanted Gideon and Marcus near.

"I didn't even know I was old enough to make a claim so strong." He rubbed his face and the mist swelled, obscuring my view of him. "We need to figure out what to do about the bite-lock. I can feed without using my magic, but it'll hurt, and I'd rather not do that to you."

"I'd rather not, either." I'd had a glimpse of what a vampire feeding felt like without the erotic magic seeping into me, and I didn't want to repeat that.

A shiver swept over me, and the buzz bit deeper. "Does the bite-lock cause problems for you, too? Do we need to... you know?" I asked, uncertain how I felt about that. I didn't love him like I loved Marcus, but I was still drawn to him, and I wasn't entirely sure that came only from his claim.

"No," he said, but the mist turned cold and I got the sense he didn't really know. "The best way to manage this is to make sure Marcus is around when I need to feed."

"So you bite me and Marcus releases it?" Poor Kol was going to be high all the time if we kept getting into fights and Jacob kept getting hurt. Except I was off the team, which meant all of it would have to happen someplace else, probably my apartment, and not at Operations.

"It's better than me releasing my bite-lock." Jacob's dark gaze captured mine and filled with a hungry intensity. The room's temperature rose, but I couldn't tell if he was hungry for my blood or my blood *and* my body. "I'm surprised Marcus hasn't lost it on Gideon. Wolves are ferociously territorial, and it's clear now he's claimed you as his mate."

"Marcus recognizes this is a complicated situation." Which was the understatement of the century.

"I'll talk to Marcus about our... necessary arrangement." He looked like he was going to hold my hand again, but rose instead. "You should sleep. If you're still connected to the key and the seal, you're going to need your energy this evening."

"Is Kol okay?" I asked as he headed to the door. While I knew he was alive, I didn't know anything else and my gut twisted with guilt that he might have seriously hurt himself to save me.

"Amiah can't sense anything wrong with him, but we won't know until he wakes up."

God, I hoped that meant he was all right. He'd said there was a cost. Please let that cost only be falling unconscious in the middle of a potentially dangerous situation.

Jacob left, and I stared at the ceiling, trying to think past my buzz. How did everything get so complicated so quickly? And why couldn't I just thrill at the knowledge that Marcus and I were finally figuring out the searing attraction between us? God, and why did Gideon's words have to hurt so much?

My eyelids grew heavy, and I rolled to my side to get more comfortable.

I also needed to figure out if I wanted to stay on the team when Gideon clearly didn't want me around. It would be best if I got as far away from him as possible, except—

Jeez. My mother would be so upset with me. She'd worked so hard, sacrificed so much to protect me from the angels and the Joined Parliament, and here I was, my heart aching because an angel hated me and because I was hoping to become part of a JP team.

Nothing good could come of it, even if I had figured out an explanation for my eyes and next-to-useless empathy. Why couldn't I remember that? I was playing with fire, and it wasn't just Gideon and the Joined Parliament I should be afraid of. I'd been shot and nearly killed. While I suspected this wasn't a typical JP case, I didn't doubt any others would be less dangerous for a powerless human.

But I also knew in my soul that this was where I belonged. God, it was crazy. But I was more certain that I was supposed to be a JP agent helping humans caught up in the world of supers, with these men, than I was of anything else in my completely messed-up life.

My mind drifted, and I yearned for Marcus and the others and the sense of belonging that I'd never had on the force with the other cops. I wanted to be part of a team, respected, not despised. I wanted to have a family, a group of people who cared about me, something I'd gotten a small glimpse of when it had just been me and my mom. But then I'd lost it all when she'd died. I hadn't realized how alone I was, how much of an outsider I was— how much of an outsider I'd made myself to be.

The door opened with a soft *shush* of movement, and Marcus's emotional heat seeped over my skin. At least I thought it was Marcus, but I was still half asleep, floating on fear and warmth and heartache.

"Marcus?" I breathed, needing to know if he was real or just a dream.

"Go back to sleep." His weight settled on the bed behind me and his arms wrapped around me. He drew me close, my back to his chest, his lips pressed to the back of my neck. His perpetual five o'clock shadow tickled my skin while his breath heated it. A hint of desire unfurled low within me, but more of me was warm and secure than turned on.

"I've got you," he said. "Go back to sleep."

Yes, this was definitely where I belonged. Everything else was complicated, but I knew with certainty I belonged with Marcus.

ESSIE

At some point Marcus left the bed. I didn't feel him go, but when I woke next, I was alone and the spot where he'd been wasn't warm, so he'd been gone long enough for it to cool down.

A hint of an ache squeezed my chest, one part missing Marcus, another part gunshot wound, and the rest Ibizual's seal. Thankfully the seal wasn't calling to me like the key had, not yet at least, but the pressure *was* starting and I knew something would happen soon. Whether I was fully healed or not, I was going to have to get ready, and that started with getting out of the hospital gown and eating something, since I couldn't remember the last time I'd actually had a meal. Oh, and nicotine. I needed to replace my patches before I started scratching my skin off and sobbing.

My clothes weren't in the hospital room, neither were my shoes, and most definitely not the keycard for the room upstairs. I turned off the vitals monitor, peeled away the leads taped to my chest, and carefully pulled out the IV so I could look in the attached bathroom.

No clothes there, either.

Well, shit. I didn't particularly want to be wandering around Operations barefoot in a hospital gown, but I also wasn't going to wait around for someone to check on me since I had no idea when the seal would start calling me. At least the gown wasn't backless, it was the kind with three arm holes that wrap around one and a bit times.

Unfortunately, I had no idea where anyone would be. I was sure Amiah didn't usually hang out in triage and while I'd been to her office once, I'd been doped up on painkillers and Kol's enthrallment at the time and wasn't sure I'd be able to find it again. As for the guys, they could also be anywhere, but I doubted, given the severity of the situation, that they'd be in their rooms waiting for something to happen. They were probably planning or scouting or researching.

Food, however, was something I could immediately fix. Perhaps once I'd had something to eat, my head would clear enough so I could think past the buzz and figure out what to do next.

Like dealing with Gideon.

How the hell was I going to convince him I wasn't a liability to the team? Especially since I was pretty sure I was, no matter what Marcus and Jacob said. But I also had no idea how to make myself accept that I shouldn't be part of the team, not with the certainty that I belonged growing stronger within me.

Jeez. What a mess.

I took the smaller hall away from triage to the hall that exited by the elevator and the cafeteria. I could hear the guys talking before I reached the end of the hall, and hesitated long enough to consider returning to the hospital room, then to dismiss that idea as stupid. I was going to have to face Gideon eventually and, God damn it, I was hungry.

"—can't afford another mess like downtown," Gideon said. "Both the mayor and the chief of police called head office to complain."

"As if we had any control over where the key manifested," Kol said, his voice lifting a weight from my chest that I hadn't realized was there. He was okay. Thank God he was okay— or at least okay enough to be up and talking.

"We— *I*—" Gideon said. "*I* left a street and park full of bodies."

"I would have loved to have seen that," a smooth tenor said with a laugh, someone I didn't recognize. "You—"

I reached the cafeteria stairs and all eyes turned on me. The guys sat in the middle of the otherwise empty room at their usual six-seater table, all of them strikingly handsome, each in their own way. Even Gideon with his stiff, hard, expression. That merely accentuated his sculpted cheeks and jaw.

Jacob, as always, drew me with his intensity — and the more I thought about it, the more I was certain it wasn't just his claim. With his broad shoulders and massive arms straining his T-shirt, he dwarfed lean-muscled Kol sitting beside him even though Kol wasn't that small. Stunningly handsome Kol always stole my breath and made my thoughts stall, just for a second. God, he was so beautiful. And thank God, he didn't look as if anything had happened to him, not a fight with dozens of ferals or pouring his life force into me. The thought of that sent heat swelling within me and even from the cafeteria steps I could see hellfire flickering in his eyes.

Then Marcus shifted, and my attention jumped to him, my pulse picking up with need and certainty. He did look like he'd had a bad night, but it wasn't anything to do with his physical appearance. His clothes were fresh and there wasn't a hint of a scratch on any visible skin — he must have shifted and healed — but he looked exhausted, with his hair mussed and dark circles under his eyes. He'd said he wanted me on the team, wanted me close, but I had a feeling he was going to regret that decision and change his mind. How many times could I end up in danger just doing my job before he'd had enough?

I pulled my gaze away from him and the panic those thoughts were stirring to look at the new guy. He was also shockingly handsome, almost on the same level as Kol, but where Kol exuded a sense of darkness and fire, this guy was light and cold. His skin was so pale it seemed translucent, which I knew wasn't true because I couldn't see his bones or veins. A hint of a glow, as cold as the glow in Gideon's eyes but barely there, only really noticeable from the corner of my eye, radiated from all skin not covered by his clothes with a hint of icy blue. His eyes were so pale blue they were almost clear, and his hair was a mix of white and silver cut short and spiked.

But what really stole my breath about him were his pointed ears. He was faekin, half human and half fae. I'd never seen one before. Hell, I'd never seen a fae before. They'd stayed in their realm during the war, only sending a few sorcerers to help, and those sorcerers had remained hidden the entire time then returned to the fairy realm once the war was done. Some humans still didn't believe fae existed.

"You're the human," he said, crossing his arms, drawing my attention to the swirl of black tattoo curling out of the V of his blue button-down, over his collarbone, and up his neck. His gaze raked over my body with a slow, sensual perusal, adding fuel to the heat within me that had come from seeing Marcus and thinking about Kol's magic.

His lips curled up just enough for a wicked, inviting smile, which surprised the hell out of me because I was sure I looked like a hot mess in only a hospital gown. I hadn't even thought to pull my — without a doubt wild — locks into a ponytail.

Gideon stood, his expression frigid. "You should be in bed."

"Don't start." I was tired and achy and my skin was on fire with my buzz. "The seal is starting to form, and I'm having a meal before it compels me to wherever the hell it's going to manifest." I headed to the fridge with the pre-made sandwiches and salads. Out the back windows, the sky was starting to darken, and the one cloud I could see was pink. It was nearly dusk, and round two would be beginning any time now.

Gideon's attention jumped to Jacob. "Can *you* sense it?"

Jacob shook his head. "No."

"Shit." Gideon sank back into the chair.

I grabbed a turkey club and a bottle of water and took the last chair at the table between Kol and the new guy.

"Sebastian Bane." He held out his hand. I half expected cold to radiate from him, but I didn't feel anything. Of course, that could be because of my damned distracting buzz.

"Officer Esther Shaw," Gideon said before I could reply.

I sighed and reached to shake Sebastian's hand, but a snap of frozen magic sliced up my arm before we even touched.

Gasping, I jerked back, and Marcus shot up from his seat and growled low in his throat.

Sebastian's wicked smile deepened for just a second before he shoved away from me. His chair screeched against the floor, and he raised his hands palms out, but I didn't buy his no-harm, just-innocent posture. He'd meant to do that.

"Switch seats," Marcus said. "Now."

"Sure," Sebastian said with a laugh as he rose and traded seats with Marcus, who pulled his chair close to me. His hand found my knee under the table and settled there, the action neither sexual nor possessive— well, maybe a little possessive, but also comforting and protective. I'd have loved this new Marcus, if I wasn't certain he was going to have a complete change of mind after we'd dealt with the seal.

"So you can sense the key and seal," Sebastian said, his gaze locking on me. "Fascinating."

The muscles in Gideon's jaw twitched. "And not what we were talking about."

"No, we were talking about messes." Sebastian continued to stare, his gaze boring into me as if he could see something, or was looking for something, hidden within me, which made my pulse pound. *Please, God, don't let it be my angelic nature.*

His eyes narrowed. "Unless the seal manifests in the Supers' Quarter, I have no doubt the mayor will be complaining about another dangerous mess."

"So there's no spell that will stop this?" Jacob asked. Now that I was sitting across from him, his posture was almost as rigid as Gideon's. I couldn't begin to imagine how difficult this whole situation was for him, needing to stop, most likely kill, his blood brother all over again.

"There's nothing you can do at a distance," Sebastian said, still not looking away from me.

Marcus's hand on my knee tightened. "She's taken."

Sebastian's gaze dipped to Gideon's brand on my forearm. "I can see that. Can you feel the key right now, Esther?"

I opened my mouth to say no, that the ache in my chest was definitely the seal, but—

I closed my eyes and concentrated on everything churning and biting and throbbing in my body. The buzz stung and urged me to get closer to Gideon even though we only sat across the table from each other. I slid the foot of my Marcus-free leg as close to Gideon's as I could without touching him, and the buzz softened enough for me to really feel the ache of the seal. But it also made me aware of the wildly fluctuating emotional temperatures.

Which was just something I was going to have to learn to deal with if I could convince Gideon to keep me on the team.

I shoved that thought aside and concentrated on the key, searching for any kind of pain or pressure that would tell me I could still feel it.

"Nothing."

Sebastian pursed his lips. And God damn it, he still stared at me— No, actually his eyes were unfocused, but without a doubt all his senses were focused on me, still searching for something. I shivered at the intensity of his scrutiny. It wasn't like the soul-capturing look I got from Jacob and pretty much every other vampire I'd encountered. My soul wasn't being held. It was being dissected.

"She's telling the truth," he said.

Marcus's eyes darkened, his wolf barely contained, and Jacob sat forward and squared his shoulders.

"She has no reason to lie," Jacob said, his voice soft and low but edged with warning.

Sebastian shrugged and finally turned his attention away from me. Thank God! Now his unnerving gaze was on Gideon, and I dug into my sandwich to hide my relief. Somehow he'd known I wasn't lying about the key — and none of the guys called him out on that, so he must have that magical ability — but did he know I was lying about other things? Would he reveal my secret to Gideon? I didn't get the sense he'd care if I was a nephilim or not, more that he'd do it just to see what would happen, see if Gideon would turn on his mate. Which he would, because while I might have his brand, I wasn't really his mate.

"The only way to stop the spell is to destroy the key," Sebastian said. "How strong is your divine light?"

The muscles in Gideon's jaw flexed. "How powerful does the blast need to be?"

"At the level of divine light ring or stronger."

"That strong?" Kol asked.

"There aren't a lot of angels who can summon a blast that strong," Jacob said.

"You could try less, but I suspect you'll only get one chance on this." Sebastian leaned back in his chair. "Probably not worth the risk."

Gideon's gaze flickered to mine then back.

Sebastian's eyes flashed wide, and his wicked smile returned. "And she can summon divine light, too?" he asked, his unnerving attention back on me. "Gideon, where have you been hiding her?"

Gideon's posture tightened even more. Now the muscles down his neck and across his shoulders joined his jaw. "Her services are not for sale."

Marcus shifted closer to me, heated emotion radiating from his body, and glared at Sebastian.

"I think that's for the lovely Esther to decide." Sebastian leaned toward me. "I know some witches who'd love to buy light magic from you. The salary for one year would make your head spin."

"Yeah, but what would it cost me?" Even if I hadn't known that the team bought information and hard-to-get items from Sebastian, I'd know he was the kind of guy who exacted a price for everything.

Mock surprise filled his expression. "Would I make an offer with a catch to it?"

"Yes," Marcus growled.

"There's a reason angels with light magic don't sell their light to witches," Jacob said.

"Because they're all control freaks with sticks up their asses." Sebastian's smile deepened. "If you ever get tired of Mister Always-in-Control —" He jerked his thumb toward Gideon, his tone filled with sexual invitation.

"I've got better offers on the table," I said before Marcus leaped over the table and ripped out Sebastian's throat.

"Honey, there are no better offers than me."

Kol huffed a soft breath and rolled his eyes.

"The incubus's company excluded, of course," Sebastian said, "but I'd bet that year's wage of light magic *his* offer isn't on *your* table."

A hint of a blush crept across my cheeks at the thought of Kol's magic—

Yep, not going there.

"So we think Gideon's magic might not be enough to destroy the key?" I forced out.

Delight flared in Sebastian's eyes at my obvious change of topic.

"And we won't know where the key is until the seal manifests and Logan arrives to break it." I opened my bottle of water and took a long sip, struggling to keep my hand steady with my buzz making me twitch.

"So other than we need to find enough light magic to end this, this is a repeat of the key," Kol said.

Marcus's grip on my knee relaxed a bit — thank God, because it was starting to get painful. "Hopefully not a repeat."

Hellfire danced in Kol's eyes. "Well, yes."

"Any other information our money purchased?" Gideon asked.

Sebastian huffed. "You have no idea how hard it was to find that, let alone anything else on short notice."

"Then thank you for your time," Jacob said, standing and gesturing to the stairs for Sebastian to leave.

Sebastian stood. "You really should make an effort to stop this. Ibizual is the prince of death."

"We already know that," Gideon said.

"So imagine the kind of terror he'd wreak in this realm if he got loose." A shudder swept over Sebastian and cold rushed around me, revealing a deeper fear than his nonchalant posture and tone implied. "I don't know about you, but there are corpses out there I'd rather stayed in the ground."

Gideon and Jacob shared at glance that then moved to Kol. The incubus's eyes had gone hard, and I could only imagine who they were thinking of. A lot of people, humans and supers, had been killed during the war, but I doubted, considering the nauseating sense of evil that had come from Ibizual, that he would raise any of the good ones from the dead.

Sebastian strode around the table toward me. "It was a pleasure meeting you, Officer Esther Shaw." *And be mindful. Whatever you're hiding under those contact lenses, it's burning up the spell a lot faster than it should. You've got a week left, at best.*

I frowned, fighting to hide my surprise, both at his voice in my head and his warning.

He flashed his wicked smile. "It's been… intriguing."

"It's—" A blast of agony exploded through my chest, then snapped into a crushing pressure that stole my breath and set my buzz screaming under my skin. The mostly full water bottle tumbled from my hand and hit the floor, spraying water up mine, Marcus's, and Sebastian's legs.

Gideon, Jacob, and Kol jerked to their feet.

Marcus grabbed my shoulders and met my gaze, panic in his eyes. "Bane?" he growled. "What did you do?"

Sebastian's eyes were wide with surprise. "Not me."

Find me. Free me. Kin.

"The seal," I gasped.

Deny me and die.

ESSIE

IBIZUAL'S VOICE ROARED IN MY HEAD WITH A FORCE STRONGER THAN WHEN the key had manifested. It came with a pressure that threatened to tear me apart from the inside out and stole my breath. His inky darkness swelled within me, too much like the archnephilim's darkness, and my pulse raced, my panic a biting thread slicing into the pressure.

I will be free.

I will stop you, I thought back at him, shoving all of my will and determination into my words.

He laughed at me, a dark grating sound that billowed the pressure in my body. *With what power?*

The force of his magic crashed into me, drowning me, more powerful than the archnephilim's. I gasped, my terror making me shake and my buzz searing through my skin in defiance.

"Essie." Marcus's grip on my shoulders tightened, his gaze filled with concern.

Beside him, Sebastian stared at me, the fear deepening in his gaze and — along with everyone else's fear — dropping the room temperature.

"The payment will be in your account," Gideon said then turned to Marcus, clearly dismissing Sebastian. "Clothes and gear for Officer Shaw."

"What about the light blast?" Jacob asked.

Gideon's expression hardened and frustration swept through me. "Officer Shaw has already demonstrated our powers together can be as strong as a blast from a divine light ring. We don't have time to call in anyone from another JP team or get a loaded ring."

"Absolutely fascinating," Sebastian said to me, his tone edged with awe that only added to my terror.

"What are you still doing here, Bane?" Marcus growled.

"Just leaving." He headed to the stairs. "Don't get killed, Gideon. You're not by far my best customer, but you're the most entertaining."

"Why do I always want to strangle him every time I see him?" Jacob asked.

Another explosion tore through me, and the pressure contracted even more, making my buzz blaze stronger. I wasn't sure I'd be able to rise let alone walk, but as much as I wanted Marcus's arms around me, I also wanted to stand on my own two feet. I needed to prove as much to myself as to Gideon that I could handle this job.

Free me and you'll have more power than all of them combined.

I don't want your power. I shoved up to my feet, using the table to keep my balance. "We need to get moving. We can plan in the SUV. Hell, I should probably change in it, too, and not waste time going to wherever my clothes are." I turned to Jacob. "You can grab my clothes and gear faster than I can."

Gideon gave a tight nod to Jacob. "Go."

Jacob ran out of the cafeteria. While he wasn't nearly as fast as a master vampire, he was still faster than a human.

But you do want power. Ibizual laughed again, and I gritted my teeth against the pain. *You've accepted you can't be human, but you're too weak to be anything else.*

"I restocked the locker in the garage and added enough swords for the team," Marcus said, picking me up while I was distracted by Ibizual and couldn't argue with him.

"Good." Gideon pulled his phone from his pocket, dialed a number, and headed toward the steps. "Meet us in the garage."

You're weak, Esther.

I'm strong enough. I had to be strong enough. I couldn't go back to life as normal. Whether I wanted to be or not, I was a super and couldn't avoid the world of the supernatural any more.

We hurried out of the cafeteria and down the hall to the garage. Amiah rushed out triage's frosted-glass door and met us just before we left the building. Her attention jumped to me in Marcus's arms and her expression darkened, then she turned to Gideon.

"She has to go?" she asked.

"Yes." Gideon's tone was flat. Whatever emotion he might have been feeling was locked down tight. I couldn't feel anything from him inside me, and the temperature right now was hot, most likely from Marcus, whose fear seemed to manifest more like hot rage.

"Fine." She pressed her hand over my heart, and a searing blast of magic sliced through me.

All my muscles contracted, and Marcus's grip on me tightened. Then it was over in a flash, and I was left trying to pant past the pressure in my chest and think past the buzz.

"Hunh," she said. "You're farther along than I would have thought, even with Jacob's claim."

Jeez, I just couldn't catch a break. Yet another thing I was going to have to come up with an explanation for. My eyes, my weird empathy, and now my faster-than-average healing.

They'll learn the truth, and you'll be powerless to defend yourself, Ibizual said in my head.

Still not freeing you. The archnephilim had told me that as well, threatened me with my greatest fear. I hadn't listened then and I wasn't going to listen now.

"Jacob's claim is a little stronger than expected," I said.

Kol rolled his eyes. "You could say that."

Marcus shot a quick glare at him, the look clear — *shut up.* And I could fully understand why. The situation was complicated and without a doubt others — chiefly among them Amiah, with her feelings for Marcus — wouldn't understand or approve of my arrangement with Jacob and Marcus, even if it was the best solution for this mess. The less attention that was brought to our situation, the better.

They won't understand.

Just shut the fuck up.

"Is she good to go?" Gideon asked.

Amiah shrugged. "Yes." She didn't sound happy about that at all.

"Good." Gideon strode out the door to the garage and we followed.

He headed around the corner to the black metal locker recessed into the wall, and unlocked it with his thumbprint.

Another blast of agony swept through me, drawing a gasp, and Gideon's eyes narrowed, while Marcus's grip on me tightened.

Only a matter of time before I'm free.

"Get Officer Shaw in the SUV," Gideon said, handing me the keys.

I hit the unlock button on the key fob, and Marcus set me in the SUV then returned to the locker to get his gear. The guys loaded up with sidearms, vests, and swords, while I fought to breathe. The pain wasn't as bad as when the key had formed, but the pressure was worse and filled with Ibizual's malicious darkness. That and my buzz was going wild, the bites so forceful they now felt more like miniature explosions under my skin, and I couldn't hide my twitching.

Jacob rushed through the glass door as the guys were closing up the locker. Marcus tossed a vest and sword into the back for Jacob and handed me a Glock, M4, and vest.

"Keep that on this time," he said as he climbed into the driver's seat.

"We both know Logan's shot would have gone right through the vest." I checked the magazine in the M4, fighting to keep my hands steady and failing. Full, but no spare. It was just going to have to be enough.

Kol climbed onto the bench beside me, setting his gear on the floor, and took my clothes and duty belt from Jacob, who then climbed into the back.

"Where to this time, Officer Shaw?" Gideon asked, his tone still flat and hard, breaking my heart, as he settled into the front passenger seat, turned on the GPS, and put his com in his ear.

I drew in a steadying breath and tried to concentrate past my emotional hurt and physical agony. This time the pull wasn't as obvious, and I wasn't sure if that was because the seal wasn't fully calling me yet or because of something else. I did, however, sense a slight pull to the back of the garage.

Join me, and I'll tell you where the seal is manifesting.

Sure, I lied.

Ibizual's pressure snapped, jerking every muscle taut for an agonizing second. *Try again.*

Yeah, I hadn't thought it would work, but I didn't want to actually commit to my lie for fear he'd be able to control me like the archnephilim had. Sure, the archnephilim had needed a false angelic mating brand on my arm to possess me, but Ibizual, even trapped in a cage, was more powerful.

"Head out of the Quarter," I told Marcus.

"Swell." Marcus inserted his com and pulled the SUV out of its parking space.

Kol handed me my jeans, his expression worried, and I leaned back on the seat and pulled them on.

"So you think if we combine our magic, we'll have enough power to destroy the key?" I asked Gideon.

No, Ibizual hissed. *You're weak.*

But just like he could sense I was lying, I could sense he was, too.

"Marcus?" Gideon asked, his attention locked on the road out the front windshield. "You said her blast on Logan was as strong as a blast from a divine light ring."

"It was," Marcus said, swerving around a vehicle pulling out of a driveway.

Gideon gave a tight nod. "Then that's the plan."

"So we what? Fight who knows how many ferals so you and Essie can get the key away from Logan?" Marcus asked. "That's a terrible plan."

Gideon shot him a frozen glare. "If you can think of something better, I'm all ears."

"I agree it's a terrible plan," I gasped, fighting the pressure and pain drowning me.

It'll never work. My servant will kill you unless you join me.

I ignored Ibizual and shrugged out of the first of the three sleeve holes in the hospital gown, trying to figure out how to pull on my T-shirt without flashing the guys and everyone on the street since I wasn't wearing a bra. We were nearing the center of town again and on this warm early summer evening, people were on the streets shopping and dining, while the roads had a steady stream of traffic. "But there isn't any other option."

And crap. There was no good way to remove the hospital gown without baring my breasts. Well, at this point the only one in the SUV who hadn't seen them was Gideon, and his attention was rigidly focused on the road as if he were making a point of offering me privacy. As for the street and other motorists... well, maybe if I did it fast enough, not too many would notice.

The pressure jerked me to the left. "Turn left."

Are you sure? Ibizual asked. *Maybe I'm sending you in the wrong direction.*

Try again, I said back to him.

Marcus wrenched the wheel to take the next left, throwing me into the door and squealing the tires. Then he gunned it through a just-turned-red light, and swerved around a slower-moving cargo van.

You'll die this time.

My buzz burned hotter. *So be it.*

I slipped my arm out of the next armhole and moved to take off the gown completely, when Kol leaned forward. He grabbed the gown by the shoulders and held it up to offer me privacy.

"Any idea how we're going to deal with Logan?" he asked.

"If you and Marcus can hold off the ferals, I can deal with Logan," Jacob said.

They will all die.

The pressure tugged forward and to the right. "We need to head more right."

I pulled on my T-shirt and Kol shoved the hospital gown under the seat to get it out of the way.

"Did Victoria give you enough power for that?" Gideon asked.

She didn't. Not to defeat my servant. I'm going to keep you alive long enough to watch them all die.

"Not to kill him," Jacob said. "With Ibizual's magic empowering him, I'm not sure even Victoria could kill him. But I have enough to hold out until you destroy the key."

Ibizual roared with laughter, making the pressure surge, and I fought to gasp in any small amount of air. Kol pressed his hand to my knee. A whisper of sensual heat swept through me, muting some of the pain, pressure, and buzz.

Oh, thank God. I drew in an almost full breath. "Thank you."

He handed me an earpiece and gave a half shrug, a hint of hellfire dancing in his eyes before he looked away.

I'll make the demon suffer the most. Slowly rip the life from him, Ibizual snarled.

"Do we know what will happen with Logan once we destroy the key?" I asked through gritted teeth as I shrugged into my vest and buckled on my duty belt. "Stopping him from breaking the seal might not be the end of it."

There will never be an end for me.

I secured my seatbelt and pulled on my runners.

We sped past Unity Park, and a flash of hot and cold swept through the air with a churning mix of the guys' emotions.

This time my servant will kill you. Your demon won't be around to save you.

Promises, promises, I thought at him, feigning bravado more for myself than him since he knew it was an act.

"I hope to God it's the end of it," Marcus said.

"We can't count on that," Kol said.

You won't stop me.

The pressure squeezed tighter, drawing a groan. I clutched my chest, not that it would ease anything, and curled forward, unable to help myself. Kol's magic swelled, turning my pain into sensual, dreamy need, and making Ibizual howl with laughter.

So weak. Powerless.

Gideon twisted in his seat, capturing me with his icy gaze. God, I ached for it to return to its warm summer sky, like it had been when I'd first met him, but that yearning had to be Kol's magic and the brand influencing me. That, and no matter what I wanted, it was clear that he was going to be forever angry that I was his destined mate.

"If destroying Ibizual's connection with this realm doesn't end the unnatural magic that brought Logan back, you get to the SUV and get out of there," he said to me.

I glared back at him, still bent forward, clutching my chest. "If I still have the M4, I'm staying at a distance and supporting the team."

"You're not part of this team."

"Right now I am. You can't do this job without me." The pressure erupted into a blazing, consuming fire. Holy fuck.

I bit back a scream. "Straight ahead," I gasped. "We're close. Directly ahead of us."

Marcus slammed on the brakes, jerking us forward and making the seatbelt dig into my gut. "Are you shitting me?"

I looked out the front windshield. We were at a T-intersection and straight ahead lay a winding road into Union City's largest cemetery.

The road curved around a small fountain then disappeared over a gentle, grassy rise. Rows upon rows of headstones stretched ahead of us, intermixed with mausoleums and towering trees. Statues of weeping and guardian angels stood sentinel, and off to the left sat the massive memorials for those from Union City and the surrounding area who'd served and died in the war, as well as those who Michael and his nephilim had slaughtered. The two-story twin walls of white marble, facing each other, curved in a symbolic embrace to those who visited.

Come find me, Ibizual taunted with another roaring laugh.

"Stay here. I'll scout for Logan." Gideon jumped out of the SUV, his wings sweeping from his back with a blaze of white light. He was the epitome of the perfect, gorgeous angel, fully illuminated with blond hair, blue eyes, and a face and body sculpted by a master. Just looking at him stole my breath and made my heart ache. Then with a sweep of his wings, he took off into the air.

"Be careful," I said before I could stop myself.

"I'm not going to get shot," he said, his voice coming through the coms, his tone exasperated.

"You better not," I said, trying to hide my genuine worry and hurt at his tone, "because I've got enough going on without also needing to keep you alive through the brand."

He huffed and soared up into the darkening sky until I could only see him because I was watching him go.

"Gideon is right," Marcus said. "If destroying the key doesn't end Logan, you get out of here. Completely. No hanging back." He pulled out his com, muffling it in his fist, and looked past me to Jacob. "We're agreed?"

"Agreed," Jacob said, his voice low.

So much for being competent enough to be on the team. But I couldn't voice that thought out loud without alerting Gideon that the guys were having a conversation without him.

Kol gave a tight nod.

Jeez, you, too?

They know you're weak. Ibizual laughed, and I shook with the swelling pressure. *They think they can protect you, but they can't. And when they learn what you really are, they'll turn on you, kill you like they killed our kin.*

I'm not *your kin.*

Marcus slid the earpiece back into his ear. "What's the word, Gideon?"

Accept the truth, Esther. Ibizual's darkness surged inside me.

My buzz flared, burning some of it away, but not all.

"There's a flicker of magic forming in the center of the large fountain on the other side of the hill," Gideon said. "I don't see any ferals, but there's a significant area with trees beyond the rise. They could be hiding there."

Accept it, Ibizual snarled. *Accept the truth that you're kin.*

I'm a nephilim. That's the truth. I gritted my teeth against the pain. *A naturally born nephilim.*

"Do you see Logan?" Jacob scanned the surrounding buildings. We were in a mostly residential area with single detached homes and a few three-story low-rises, which thankfully meant there weren't a lot of good perches for a sniper to lie in wait for someone to approach the seal manifesting beyond the rise. In fact, the best shots from the surrounding buildings were for right there, and I had no doubt Logan would have tried to pick at least one of us off while we'd been sitting there if he'd been lying in wait.

"I don't— No, he's— Marcus, go. Straight ahead," Gideon said. "Logan is making a beeline for the fountain."

"Hang on," Marcus said and gunned the SUV into the cemetery, throwing us back into our seats.

Last chance to join me, Ibizual said.

"Never," I hissed.

"Essie?" Kol asked.

Shit. I'd said that out loud.

Join me.

The SUV screeched around the small fountain just inside the gates. The passenger-side wheels hit grass, jerking and bumping us, then hit asphalt again.

White light shot from the sky ahead of us down to the ground somewhere beyond the rise, and I caught a glimpse of Gideon, pulling his wings back and diving down after it.

"Gideon, we need you alive to end this," Jacob said. "Don't fight Logan."

"We won't be able to do anything if he breaks the seal," Gideon said. Another blast of light exploded behind the rise.

We careened up the road, hit the top of the rise, and I gasped in horror.

Sickly red magic seeped from the ground in pulsing thick strands. "Holy shit."

"Jesus," Kol said beside me.

"What?" Marcus asked.

"What do you mean what? The ground— The magic—" Perhaps this was just something that happened all the time on this job and Marcus was used to seeing massive amounts of magic, but Kol had sounded as surprised as I had.

"It's demonic," Kol said. "He can't see it yet, not until it gets more powerful."

"More powerful?" I could already feel the massive power pulsing from it.

"Can I avoid it?" Marcus asked as we hurtled down the road.

"No," I said. "It's everywhere." The whole ground all the way into the group of trees on the left and where the rise dropped away to the right was filled with magic. And it grew brighter and thicker the closer it got to the fountain straight ahead of us.

Agony and seething darkness exploded inside me as we drove into it. Red tendrils rushed into the SUV right through the floor, twisting around my legs and burning my skin. Kol groaned, the magic flooding into his body and not just wrapping around him, while Jacob hissed and clenched his jaw.

My buzz blazed through me, devouring the darkness, burning so hot it radiated from my skin and consumed the magic around me.

Ahead, Gideon jerked into the air to avoid Logan's grasp and shot another light strike at him. They'd drawn even closer to the fountain and the blazing sphere of the seal's manifesting magic.

The demonic magic grew stronger, and more strands, thick as rope, shot up from the ground.

"Shit." Marcus swerved, avoiding a red pillar of power shooting out from the middle of the road.

I slammed into the door and Kol slid into me, the touch of his skin against mine burning, all that demonic magic raising his body temperature.

My buzz blazed hotter, suddenly turning his body heat from searing to freezing. He gasped, his wide eyes, filled with hellfire, locking with mine, and my buzz started to consume the magic within him.

Marcus swerved again. The sudden movement jerked Kol off me, and I grabbed the door handle to stay in my seat. My buzz released him, but I couldn't help fearing that it would have consumed all of his magic, not just Ibizual's excess.

And from the look in Kol's eyes, he feared that, too.

The SUV fishtailed off the road, rattled over the uneven grass, and scraped against a squat tombstone. Marcus growled, yanked us back on the road, and floored it. Ahead, the magic of the manifesting seal blazed like a miniature sun.

We were almost there. Gideon just had to hold on a little longer.

More pillars of magic exploded from the road, and a massive one slammed into the bottom front of the SUV instead of passing through.

The impact tossed us into the air. My head hit the side airbag, and Kol crashed into me. Then he smashed into the ceiling, and I was jerked hard against the seatbelt before being wrenched around and around and around.

ESSIE

THE WORLD WHIRLED AND JERKED, BLURRY, DARK, AND EDGED WITH burning red magic. The windows shattered and showered us with glass. Agony screamed through my neck, chest, and gut, and I couldn't catch my breath. We smashed through tombstones, careened off a statue, and crashed to a jarring halt.

Everything was muffled and spinning, and my buzz was burning me up.

"Guys," Gideon said through the earpiece. "Status."

I tried to respond but couldn't make my thoughts turn into action.

Someone groaned, and I struggled to focus my eyes to see who it was — Hell, just to see anything clearly.

The SUV lay upside down on an angle, with the driver's side edge of the roof dug into the ground. My head pressed against an airbag, and red magic pooled around me, the source of my burning and the reason I couldn't tell if I had any serious injuries, since its fire was all I could feel.

Kol was gone and panic clenched around my heart. *Please, God, be alive.* The idiot hadn't put on his seatbelt after helping me dress. Ahead of me, Marcus hissed, and I dragged my attention to him, struggling to make my sluggish thoughts speed up.

"Sit. rep. Now," Gideon said with a gasp, and blinding white light flared somewhere ahead of us, his fight obscured by the spiderweb of cracks in the front windshield, the airbags, and a toppled-over angel statue.

"Here," Jacob said. "Essie? Marcus? Kol?"

"Here," Marcus groaned.

"Kol got ejected." I fumbled with the seatbelt release.

"I'm here," Kol gasped through the earpiece.

Jacob shifted in the seat behind me, and the SUV shuddered, showering gravel—? No, stone and concrete from the crumbling mausoleum wall we were wedged against.

"Essie, you're bleeding," he said.

"I am?" I couldn't feel anything but my buzz, the fire as powerful as when the archnephilim had been trying to pull wings I didn't have from my body.

"How bad?" Marcus asked. He fought with his seatbelt then gave up and sliced through the belt with a claw. "I can't smell anything other than the reek of the demonic magic."

My seatbelt catch released, and I slid, head and shoulder, into a chunk of broken tombstone.

"The brand isn't draining me," Gideon said. "She'll live. Now get out. All of you out. Now."

Ibizual's magic surged, and the ground shuddered. Someone moaned, but it didn't come through the coms.

"Get out!" Kol cried.

The SUV crashed back into its wheels, jerking me onto the bench, and a skeletal hand clawed through the broken window.

"Oh, shit." Marcus kicked open the driver's side door, snapping it off its hinges and sending it flying to the crumbling mausoleum wall.

I scrambled back and wrenched on my door but couldn't get it to open. The skeletal hand ripped out the airbag blocking most of the window across from me, and my pulse stuttered. There were dozens of animated skeletons—? Zombies—? They moved too fast to be real zombies— God, I had no idea what they were! They pressed against the SUV, their claws screeching against the metal and tearing into the airbags. While hundreds more rushed toward us and more climbed out of their graves. Ibizual's magic bathed them in a sickly red aura and glowed from their eyes. They moaned and screamed and hissed, in varying stages of decay, some only skeletons, some skeletons with filthy tattered clothes, and some with rotting flesh.

Kol stood about thirty yards away surrounded by them. He sliced and jabbed, but his movement was stiff and slower than usual, and his expression was strained. Without a doubt he'd broken something, probably many somethings, when he'd been ejected from the SUV, and all his magic was focused on healing him.

You really think you can stop me? Ibizual asked in my head, and he howled with laughter. *I'm a prince of celestial darkness.*

The zombie-skeleton across from me lunged through the window, clawing at me. I wrenched back but its claws sliced into my thigh. I drew my Glock, and fired into its head. It howled and blue lightning swept around its body.

With a growl Marcus ripped off my door, and I tumbled out of the SUV.

How much ammunition do you have? Ibizual taunted. *You should have accepted my offer.*

Marcus grabbed my arm and jerked me to my feet, and I pressed my back to the mausoleum wall to get my bearings. My body burned, my buzz slicing out of my back, enveloping me and still devouring Ibizual's demonic magic. The inferno threatened to consume me, and no matter how hard I concentrated, it was still the only thing I could feel. Blood stained my jeans where the creature had clawed me, but I couldn't feel the wound and I couldn't feel the other injury Jacob had mentioned.

Jacob kicked open the rear door and dove into the closest group of zombies, punching one into another behind it while drawing his sword with his other hand.

"Go," he said. "Get her to the seal. I've got your back."

I fired at a zombie lunging for Jacob, making it stagger long enough for Jacob to decapitate it. He wrenched back to face me, his vampiric intensity capturing me and making time stutter in my head.

"Go," he snarled, and the claim seized my muscles and jerked me toward the manifesting seal despite the press of creatures between me and it.

"Shit, Essie." Marcus shoved ahead of me and drew his sword. He barreled into the closest zombie, ramming it into the two behind it, and gutted the one beside him. But more pressed in, replacing the ones he'd knocked over.

A zombie leaped onto Marcus's back, more skeleton than zombie. I grabbed it around the neck, wrenching its head back before it sank a mouthful of sharp teeth into his neck. It snarled and dug its claws into Marcus's shoulders.

My buzz surged and the magic around the creature swept into my hands. The creature thrashed and screamed, then Jacob jerked close, grabbed the creature's head, and ripped it from its body. It went limp, and I yanked it off Marcus's back.

How much more of my magic can you consume before you burn up? Ibizual laughed. *And you can't control it, can you? Your very nature will destroy you.*

I twisted out of the way of a zombie's claws and aimed for the head of another one, but the bullet grazed its skull. Jacob decapitated one beside me, then wrenched around to face the horde surging in behind us.

"Kol, we need you," Marcus said, shouldering a zombie back and impaling another.

"Trying," Kol gasped. He rose above the group surrounding him — he must have jumped onto a tombstone or something — and somersaulted over the zombies' heads onto the back of a weeping angel statue. The zombies closest to the statue wrenched around and clawed at him and he was back again trying to slice his way through the group.

Marcus snarled and hacked another two in front of us. "This isn't working."

Blood seeped from a deep gash on his biceps and another on his thigh. His chest heaved from the exertion of fighting so many zombies. The fountain stood less than a hundred yards away, but it could have been miles for all the progress we were making. We were barely holding our own, let alone moving forward.

Then the pressure within me pulsed with such force it made me gasp. I stumbled over a toppled tombstone and fell to my hands and knees.

The seal had formed.

Red magic undulated around me and surged under my skin. I fought to stand, to stop my buzz from consuming Ibizual's magic, but the fire within me just burned hotter. I had to get to the key, get it out of Logan's possession, and join my magic with Gideon's. It was the only way to stop this.

You can't stop this, Ibizual hissed. *You won't even live long enough to see me free.*

Jacob grabbed the back of my vest and wrenched me to my feet. "Gideon, fly in. We have to get Essie to join you."

"No." I shot a zombie in the chest as another one tore its claws through the back of my vest. "Protect the seal."

"Fuck," Marcus growled. "Jacob, you have to grab her and run. We have no choice."

Jacob flipped the grip on his sword so the flat rested against the underside of his arm then grabbed me and threw me against his shoulder with an arm under my butt. "Grab my neck and protect your face."

Marcus roared and dove into the group ahead of us, crashing through the press of zombies. I holstered my Glock and grabbed Jacob's neck as he barreled after Marcus. The zombies howled and clawed and threw themselves at us. A set of wickedly sharp claws swiped at my head, too close for comfort, and I buried my face into Jacob's neck to protect my eyes.

Pinpricks of pain bit through the fire consuming me, and the zombies' howling grew stronger. Jacob's muscles bunched and released beneath me as he ran and dodged and heaved them out of the way.

He grunted, his muscles contracting, then he stumbled. His grip on me tightened and he wrenched to the side. My foot bashed against something solid — likely a statue or a tombstone — and Jacob heaved to the side again, loosening my hold around his neck.

Claws dug into my vest and yanked me out of Jacob's grip. My shoulder crashed against something hard and I tumbled to the ground. A zombie lunged on top of me and sank its teeth into my neck with a pain that sliced through the fire and the pressure. But that fire, my buzz, raced through the magic animating the corpse, consuming it, and the zombie collapsed on top of me.

Jacob yanked it off me — hopefully not realizing I'd already killed it with magic I shouldn't possess — and killed another zombie as it swiped at my legs. He grabbed the neck of my vest and wrenched me up to my feet and shoved me behind him in the direction of the fountain.

I stumbled but managed to catch my balance. We stood at the edge of the fountain's wide concrete deck, beside one of the many stone benches placed around its perimeter — what my shoulder had struck when I'd fallen. The whole thing was enormous, with a vast space to stroll around, a large bottom basin, and a smaller second one above it. Water sprayed from the center in gentle arcs, filling the top basin then pouring over the edges into the shallower bottom bowl.

The seal, a complicated glyph of pulsing magic, floated in the air at waist height, almost hidden by the edge of the fountain from where I stood. It sat a few inches from the lip of the upper basin and blazed blood red, a deadly star in the dimming light reflected in the fountain's undulating water. And between me and it were Gideon and Logan, which didn't really matter since it wasn't the seal I needed to get to, but the key in Logan's possession.

Blood splattered the white concrete around their feet and an automatic pistol lay a few feet away under one of the benches. With a roar, Logan smashed his fist into Gideon's gut, grabbed his arm, and flung him, one handed, at the fountain. His wing and shoulder smashed against the lip of the upper basin, and spinning, he crashed into the water and lay still.

My pulse stuttered. Gideon wasn't getting up. He had to get up. But I wasn't frozen in agony and his brand wasn't draining me, so he had to be all right... unless of course I couldn't feel the drain through my burning buzz.

Which didn't matter.

No matter how much everything within me screamed that it did.

Ibizual had to be stopped at all costs, even if that cost were the lives of me and all my guys.

I'll still be free, and you'll still pay that price, Ibizual said. *Come. Now.* And I knew the command wasn't for me.

"Yes," Logan hissed. He yanked the key, a small red pulsing jewel, from his pocket and ran toward the seal.

I drew my gun and prayed I could make a good enough shot to seriously slow him down. I was too far away to catch him before he reached the seal, and I couldn't afford to cast the light strike spell to slow him down and risk not having enough juice to destroy the key.

Gideon staggered to his feet, and my heart soared. Water dripped from his wings and clothes, and his face was battered, one eye almost completely swollen shut. I couldn't sense his exhaustion through the brand or with my empathy because of the fire burning me up, but I could see it in the tight line of his jaw and the heave of his chest with each heavy breath. With a guttural yell, he dove at Logan, but the vampire was still going to get to the seal first.

I fired — *please let it be enough for Gideon to reach him first* — and hit Logan in the center of his back. Blue lightning swept around him, and he staggered.

Gideon crashed into him, tackling him to the ground, and the key flew from his hand and tumbled over the concrete.

Ibizual roared with fury, and the agony threatened to bring me to my knees, but I screamed back at him, a sound of desperate, primal rage, and ran toward the key. No way in hell would I let him win.

The key hit the edge of the bottom basin, stopping in a thick pool of red magic, and began to pulse with rapid, fluttering beats like an unsteady heart.

Logan rammed an elbow into Gideon's face. He lurched back, then rammed a spear of light into the vampire's chest, drawing a howl of pain.

A zombie dashed past Marcus and dove for me. I twisted out of the way, fired at it, but kept running. My shot missed the creature, and it seized my ankle. I slammed to the ground, catching myself on my left arm — the one with the already injured shoulder so I wouldn't drop my Glock. Agony tore through me, screaming up my neck and across my chest. My arm gave out, the entire limb numb, and I knew I'd broken something, probably my collarbone.

"Essie," Gideon gasped, and Logan shoved Gideon off him, sending the angel crashing into a bench in the opposite direction of the key.

The zombie sank its claws into my thigh, and my buzz devoured more of Ibizual's magic, the fire blazing through the pain. With a screech the zombie convulsed and collapsed, and I kicked it off me and scrambled to my feet.

A little more and you'll burn up, Ibizual said, and a rope of magic swept around my legs and sank into my skin, fueling the inferno.

Another rope disappeared into me. I screamed and pushed forward. Get the key. Only a few feet more. Stop this.

More zombies rushed for me, and Jacob ran into their midst to hold them off, while another group boxed Gideon in.

Logan jumped to his feet and bolted to the key. I dove to grab it before he could. But he didn't lunge for it and kicked at my head instead.

I twisted, slamming my broken shoulder against the ground, sending more agony screaming through me.

Shit. I dropped my Glock and grabbed the key with my good hand.

Logan seized my arm and wrenched me up, but Gideon barreled into him, and we crashed into the bottom basin. My head hit the wall of the second basin and darkness fluttered across my vision. Logan shoved my head under the water. It was only a foot deep, but that was more than enough to drown me.

I thrashed against his grip and clutched the key underneath me, desperate to keep it out of reach. He snarled, his face distorted by the churning water, and his fingers tightened around my skull. My lungs screamed for air, and the fire within me shuddered with a heavy pulse, a precursor to its final eruption.

A light strike flared and slammed into his back. His grip on my head loosened, and Gideon appeared behind his shoulder, his eyes blazing white, his face battered, ferocious, and terrifying. He wrenched Logan off me and I jerked up, gasping for breath.

"Essie, end this." Gideon heaved Logan out of the fountain and slammed him to the ground, as zombies surged around him and slashed at his arms and face. "Take my magic and end this."

My thoughts stuttered over the command. He'd been so adamant about me never using his magic again.

"Essie. Take it!" His magic exploded through the brand, crackling lightning that entwined with the fire of my buzz.

Logan kicked Gideon off him, and the zombies piled on top of him as Logan leaped for me. I scrambled out of the way, but all the power rushing through me made my muscles seize, and I couldn't get up to my feet.

"Essie." Jacob dove onto Logan, capturing him in a headlock, and wrenched him back.

The spell to cast the light strike leaped into my mind, and the combined magic within me roared into a hurricane, threatening to tear me to pieces and turn me to ash.

You should have joined me, Ibizual said. *I could have saved you, made you powerful, made you a god.*

I clenched my teeth and pressed the key between my palms. Gideon yelled something, so did Jacob, but all my concentration was on the spell, on blasting all the magic within me into the key and ending this.

You'll burn up. There won't be anything left, Ibizual sneered. *Not even your soul.*

"So be it," I said to him, then yelled the light strike spell and released all the magic within me out through my palms and into the key.

The fire and lightning scorched every nerve in my body, just like the blast from the light ring when I'd released its power into the arch-nephilim's brand on my arm. Except this time, the agony was worse, edged with all the bloody dark magic my buzz had consumed. It rushed from my back and my heart and my soul, taking all of me with it.

Ibizual screeched. His magic surged, flooding me, burning me up, and with a scream, I forced all of it back out my hands and into the key.

The key exploded with a blaze of light that left darkness clouding my vision and my head spinning.

Logan howled behind me, and I jerked around as he dove for me. Time stuttered. I wasn't going to be fast enough to stop him, hell, even if I was, I wasn't powerful enough. Gideon and Jacob were too far away to reach me in time. Logan was going to kill me.

Time lurched back to regular speed, and I wrenched my good hand up on instinct, knowing it was futile but unable to stop myself. Fire and lightning — God, I hadn't thought I had any more magic in me — screamed down my arm and a sword of light surged into my hand. Logan was too close to pull back before the blade plunged into his chest.

His eyes flashed wide with surprise then darkened. With a snarl, he shoved his body down the blade and slashed his short, deadly vampire claws at my face.

I jerked back and down, and Jacob rushed into sight and slashed his sword through Logan's neck, decapitating him.

Logan's blood sprayed me in the face, mixing with the fountain's water and oozing down my cheeks and neck. Then his body burst into a thick dust that filled the air and coated me in grime — and I wasn't going to think too hard about the fact that I was covered in corpse dust.

All the zombies lay on the ground not moving, and Ibizual's magic sparked and fluttered around them like embers caught in a breeze. The seal flared with a blinding burst of light and then vanished, and Ibizual's screams in my head stopped, the sudden silence making my ears ring.

I sagged onto my butt, not caring that I was still in the fountain. It was over.

Jacob dropped to his knees in the fountain beside me, but Gideon stayed lying on the ground, gasping for breath. Marcus and Kol, looking like they'd tumbled through a mess of whirling knives — which they pretty much had — staggered toward us. The guys were all bleeding, their clothes torn and filthy, but they were all alive.

Relief flooded me, and the tears of pain and terror that I'd been holding back leaked from my eyes. *They're alive. I haven't lost one of them. Thank God. Oh, thank God.*

I didn't even try to stop crying. I was too numb and raw to fight myself. The pressure from the manifesting seal was gone. So too was the snap of Gideon's magic and the burn of Ibizual's, but that had left an achy void within me.

My buzz, however, still remained, although it was now back to just painful bites under my skin and not a blazing inferno. Except those bites accentuated the fact that every nerve within me had been burned raw. I was still alight with pain, just not the kind that threatened to erupt and turn me into a human bonfire.

"Essie," Marcus said as he sagged into the edge of the basin, his expression a mix of emotions like mine: relief, pain, exhaustion. "Your hands."

I dropped my gaze, my body and thoughts sluggish. My hands were raw, bleeding, and charred. "At least I'm still conscious this time."

Kol snorted and wrapped his arms across his chest, as if his ribs were broken, his face twisting in agony. "I'm not sure this counts as an improvement from the fight with the archnephilim."

"Baby steps," Marcus said. "Next time we'll get her through without the serious burns."

If there was a next time.

Which, even exhausted and in pain, my soul prayed there would be. This was where I belonged, where I made the biggest difference in peoples' lives. I didn't know how I was going to convince Gideon that I belonged on the team, but everything within me said I had to.

Gideon made a call, and Chris and a JP clean-up team arrived at the cemetery. We returned to Operations, where Amiah greeted us in the garage with a gurney which Jacob insisted I take, while Gideon leaned heavily against it to keep standing.

The healing angel gave Marcus a quick blast of magic, enough so that when he shifted he'd be able to finish the job himself, then she turned to Gideon, gently angling his head to get a better look at the mess Logan had made of his face.

"Essie," Marcus said, his voice soft.

I dragged my attention to him. I hadn't even realized I'd zoned out. He jerked his gaze to Jacob then back to me, and even with my sluggish thoughts the message was clear. Jacob needed to feed, his injuries were as severe or worse than the fight with Logan in the tunnels, so blood from a bunny wasn't going to heal him fast enough. It was time to test our new arrangement.

"Yeah." I tried to nod, but moving even just a little bit made my head hurt.

"Amiah first, Essie," Jacob said.

"Yes." Marcus glanced at Gideon, who thankfully looked as stunned as I felt and was focusing on Amiah and not our conversation. "Give me five."

Jacob nodded.

Kol frowned, his gaze darting between the three of us.

"Consider this your phone call," Marcus said to him, and he strode to the back of the garage to shift in private.

"My what—?" Realization flashed through Kol's eyes. He'd asked for a call the next time Marcus and I had sex so he could prepare himself. At least this way he wouldn't need to leave Operations to replenish his magic. In a way it was perfect. I could be with Marcus and help heal both Jacob and Kol at the same time.

The guys helped push the gurney to triage than slipped away, Jacob mumbling something about having bagged blood in his suite, and Kol not saying anything at all.

Amiah, with her usual scowl, gave me a blast of healing magic that hurt. It healed all my physical injuries, but not my magical ones. Whatever veins or passages or whatever they were called that were inside me channeling all that magic had been burned raw, and still hurt. Not as much as before, but I sensed that Amiah's magic couldn't fully heal them.

Still exhausted, I pushed any fear about that aside. I'd worry about what all of it meant later, after I'd had time to clear my head.

I left her with Gideon, took the elevator to the fifth floor, and met Jacob outside Marcus's door. A few minutes later, Marcus joined us, dressed once again in a pair of baggy workout shorts and carrying his gear.

He let us in and there was an awkward moment with us just standing at the doorway, that would have been more awkward if we all hadn't been so tired. As instructed, I cleaned off a wrist so Jacob could feed at a modest location on my body. Then Marcus and I — starting in the shower and cleaning off the rest of the blood and grime before moving to the bedroom — both rode the powerful pleasure of Jacob's magic to a screaming, satisfying climax.

I fell asleep in Marcus's arms, snuggled in his bed, warm and content — if still a little internally sore — and woke a few hours later still in his arms. Warmth seeped from his body into mine, and his breath, steady with sleep, caressed the back of my neck. He was so still, so peaceful, all his ferocious energy, an energy that made my pulse race and my heart thrill, hidden within him. I could sense his contentment, not as a temperature but as an honest to goodness emotion, and it mirrored a contentment within me. This was exactly where I belonged, and who I belonged with.

But a sliver of doubt seeped in, and I slipped out of his bed before I became too restless and woke him.

Everything would become more difficult if I couldn't stay on the team, and yet everything would be difficult if I stayed.

I left my shredded and bloody clothes on the bathroom floor and dressed in Marcus's workout shorts — tying the drawstrings as tight as I could to keep them up — and pulled on one of his T-shirts. Once I left his suite, I wouldn't be able to get back in, so I wrote him a note saying I'd be in the lounge then slipped out into the hall. I needed air. I needed to think.

I didn't believe that our arrangement with Jacob would change if I wasn't on the team. The guys would just find me at my apartment whenever Jacob needed me. But it still was more complicated than if I stayed. And I still didn't know, if Gideon did send me packing, what I'd do if I couldn't be a cop any more.

God, I didn't know what I'd do if Marcus changed his mind about us. He didn't seem freaked out about the aftermath of the battle with Logan, but that could have been shock and then the glow of amazing sex. Once he'd had time to really think about it, there was a good chance he'd lock me in his suite and never let me out, or worse, he'd push me away again.

I wandered down the hall to the elevator and hit the call button. The door slid open, but instead of pushing the button for the main floor, I decided to hit the top unlabeled button. The elevator took me up one floor and the door opened, revealing a helicopter pad and a small rooftop patio.

Before me stretched the Supers' Quarter, the thick canopy of the ring park to my left and the UV-filtering glass canopy protecting the vampire part of the Quarter to my right. Streetlights illuminated the roads and buildings, and lights glimmered in a few windows, while a hint of light glowed on the eastern horizon. Dawn wasn't far off.

I wandered to a wrought-iron patio chair — secured to the roof with a length of chain so it wouldn't fly away in a strong wind but could also be moved around a bit — drew it out from the matching patio table, and sat. A cool breeze swept through my loose locks, and I shifted so it blew the strands away from my face. I should have put on a jacket, but I didn't have one. In fact I didn't have any clean or unshredded clothes at Operations, and didn't want to go back downstairs to search for something heavier — even if I could figure out where to look. That, and now that I'd shaken the lull of sleep and sex, I was too aware that the magical channels in my body still hurt and my buzz still wasn't back down to its new — after battling the archnephilim — normal, and I didn't want to move too much.

A crackle of electricity, nothing strong, just enough for me to notice, danced through Gideon's brand, and a flicker of shadow against the low-hanging clouds caught my attention. It drew closer and fear squeezed my chest. The archnephilim had flown through the air, a dense, deadly shadow.

I pushed my fear away. The archnephilim was dead. I'd killed him. I had nothing to fear from him any more.

Gideon's magic danced up my arm again, and I caught a flash of white with my Jacob-enhanced vision. Gideon's wings catching the streetlight.

My fear shifted from the terror of the archnephilim to the fear of facing Gideon and losing my job. But that fear was soon also edged with awe as he soared closer. He was majestic. He made my chest ache with yearning for him, for the wings I didn't have, for the freedom I couldn't allow myself to have to just be myself.

He landed on the roof on the other side of the table from me, his attention on something behind and to my right, and he drew his wings back into his body with a flare of the magic that made an angel an angel and allowed him to release his wings from his body and return them back again without destroying his clothes. He was back to being his handsome self, not a hint of a scratch or bruise on his face, and that only made my ache stronger.

I didn't understand how he could have such an effect on me. He didn't want me as his mate— *I* didn't want me to be his mate, and yet just thinking about overhearing his rejection hurt something deep within me.

Then he turned his glowing gaze on me, and I was falling into a summer sky. All the things that hurt within me stilled and everything else fell away. There was only him and the angel brand that bound our souls together.

His gaze travelled over me and my borrowed clothes, and a hint of ice chilled his summer sky. Wonderful. Just by being me, I'd reminded him that Marcus and I were a thing and Marcus would leave the team if

Gideon fired me. Staying on the team because Gideon didn't want to lose Marcus was not the way I wanted it. I wanted him to realize I wasn't a liability, that even if I was a powerless human I could offer them something.

Another crackle of his electricity snapped through the brand, making me wince.

His eyes narrowed, and he pulled his phone from his pocket. "You're still hurt. I'll wake Amiah."

"It's okay," I said before he could call, surprised he cared that I was still sore. Even if I was in agony right now, I still wouldn't want to piss off Amiah any more than I already had. "I don't think this is something she can heal. I've channeled massive amounts of power twice now in as many weeks. There's got to be a cost to that."

"You shouldn't have had to pay it."

A hint of heat whispered around me, and my stomach bottomed out with fear. Here it came, the moment where he said I didn't belong and I lost my job.

"Essie—" Pain flashed through the ice in his eyes, making my pulse stall. But he jerked his gaze away from me before I could figure out what that pain meant.

The temperature around me warmed a bit more, giving me even less of a clue about his emotions. Was he angry? The pain in his eyes should have turned the air humid or misty, but there was nothing.

"Just say it." I couldn't fight my worry, heartache, and buzz all at the same time right now. I was just too tired.

He ran a hand through his hair. "Officer Shaw."

"Joined Parliament Senior Agent Gideon." I stood and squared my shoulders. If he was going to ruin my career, end the only job I'd ever wanted, I was damn well going to make him say it to my face.

"I don't like the emotional complications you bring to the team." Ice flickered through the heat. "But we couldn't have stopped Logan without you."

So was this thank you and goodbye?

The muscles in his jaw flexed. "Do I need to arrange for a suite, or will you be sharing with Marcus?"

"Arrange for a suite?" For a second his words didn't make sense, then realization caught up to me. I was moving into Operations. I was on the team.

Oh, God. I was *moving* into Operations, angel central, living with all the angels in Union City. Working with Gideon was one thing, but living and eating and socializing with *all* the angels multiplied the risk of someone noticing something different about me.

"I, ah..."

"You're wearing his clothes. I've figured it out already," he said.

"That's because I don't have any more clothes fit to wear here."

"Then you should fix that, *Agent* Shaw." He strode past me toward the elevator, his hand pressing at the brand on his forearm that matched the one on mine before jerking away, as if the touch had been unconscious and undesired. "Report with the rest of the team in my office at o'eight hundred with your answer."

With the *rest* of the team. A whirl of emotions churned through me. This was what I wanted and where I belonged. I knew it in my soul. I couldn't resist it. But a part of me, a small voice whispering against all that certainty, said it would also be my doom.

DESTINED FIRE

NEPHILIM'S DESTINY, BOOK 3

ESSIE

Inky, malicious darkness poured down my throat, drowning me and burning into the core of my being. I fought to breathe, to resist, to do anything, but the nightmare froze my muscles and will, leaving only my helpless thoughts screaming. It was the archnephilim, suffocating me with his writhing essence— No, the hellfire prince Ibizual flooding me with his demonic magic, howling with laughter at the thought that I'd erupt into flames and burn up—

No, it was Gideon's mating brand etched into my body, somehow twisted and evil.

Yes, it was the brand, and my soul had warped it, tainted it, because I was a nephilim, I was lying to him, and I wasn't the woman he loved.

There had to be a toll, a price demanded by fate for what I was doing. I had denied my supernatural nature, and now I was neck-deep in the supernatural world. I couldn't escape and couldn't break free. Not from the power now pouring into me, or from my destiny binding me to an angel who hated nephilim. I needed to scream my frustration and fear, but the nightmare wouldn't let me.

For a moment, my thoughts cleared, and I fought to keep calm. It was just a dream. Nothing more. But no matter how hard I thought that, I couldn't push back the terror of being discovered, or of being truly evil. And I couldn't just make myself wake up.

In the last few weeks, I'd had nightmares that hadn't been nightmares, since I'd been fully awake for the horror, where both the arch-nephilim and Ibizual had invaded my mind. I couldn't shake the fear that they were at it again, determined to have me, determined to possess me. Were they still alive? Had I failed in stopping them? I'd barely managed to live through facing them the first time.

They'd tried to take over my body, tried to cajole me, convince me, threaten me. I was like them. No matter how hard I wanted to believe I wasn't, I couldn't deny it. Good people didn't lie. How could I even claim an ounce of goodness? I'd been lying to everyone my entire life, and dedicating my life to helping others didn't make up for it.

They won't understand you.

They'll kill you.

You're powerless.

Your mate despises you.

Yes, Gideon hated me.

My thoughts tripped over that. I might have Gideon's brand on my arm, but he wasn't my mate. Marcus was. I knew that in the core of my being—

Except a part of me felt that wasn't everything. Marcus wasn't my only mate. I was still bound to Gideon, and his rejection made my soul cry. I was also connected to Jacob, and here, in the drowning, burning horror of my nightmare, I could see his essence entwined with mine. Just like my soul sobbed over Gideon, it thrilled at Jacob, and in my heart I knew it had nothing to do with the power of his vampiric claim on me. I was bound to all three men. They were mine—

And me? What about me?

The voice was soft, sensual, and turned the inferno burning me into bone-melting desire.

Are we not also connected?

Strong hands captured my cheeks, and Kol brushed his lips against mine. A whisper of his seductive power slipped into my mouth, drawing a moan, and his face came into focus. Hellfire and need blazed in his eyes, fueling my own. I'd already had a glimpse of the ecstasy of his power, the breathtaking desire, and the promise of screaming, shattering climaxes when he'd saved my life, pouring the magic that sustained him into me.

You belong to Gideon, he said as his hands trailed down my neck.

More whispers of delicious power unfurled under my skin at his touch.

You belong to Marcus.

His palms skimmed the sides of my breasts, teasing me, making me ache with want.

You belong to Jacob.

He pressed his perfect, naked, lean-muscled body against mine, and his magic rushed through me everywhere our skin touched.

Belong to me, too.

Yes, I breathed... thought... begged.

I ached for him as much as I ached for Marcus and Gideon and Jacob. I needed his hands on me, his power engulfing me, his body inside me.

His lips captured mine, the kiss this time hungry and demanding. His magic surged down my throat like the archnephilim's had, but instead of drowning me, it filled me with breath and life. It infused with my essence, not just entwining through it like Jacob's. We were one, one breath, one soul, one aching desire.

I crave you, Essie. I'm tired of waiting. I don't want to ride your climax with Marcus, I want your climax with me.

His tongue plunged into my mouth. One hand found my naked breast and kneaded it while his other slid down my stomach, ratcheting up my desire with anticipation of where it was going.

I was alight with heated, liquid bliss, his power already teasing me to the edge, then his hand on my stomach dipped lower, fingers inching closer, and—

I jerked awake, my breath fast, my body thrumming with the promise of a mind-blowing climax while my skin burned with my out-of-control buzz and my insides ached, still raw from channeling the magic to stop Ibizual.

It had only been a dream. A part of me sobbed at that, aching to fully know Kol's touch, while another part was relieved. The archnephilim was dead and Ibizual still imprisoned. I was safe. Or as safe as I could get, being a nephilim pretending to be a human.

I stared at the lounge's ceiling, my eyes sore and gritty from having slept with my magic contacts in, and struggled to think past my headache and buzz to get my thoughts straight. We'd just defeated Ibizual, Marcus and I had ridden the ecstasy of Jacob's bite, and Gideon had just told me I was officially on the Joined Parliament team. I hadn't been able to return to Marcus's room because I didn't have a key, so I'd gone down to the lounge and curled up on the over-stuffed leather couch.

I must have fallen asleep.

A shudder of desire swept through me. I wasn't sure what was worse, the nightmare of being consumed by the archnephilim and Ibizual, or hot sex with Kol. Not that the sex part was a nightmare, but the idea that I was fantasizing about Kol when I was sleeping with Marcus. That wasn't fair to him, or Marcus, or any of the guys, no matter what Marcus had said about sharing.

If I was going to be on the team, I was going to have to figure out how to not think about Kol in that way, which, given that the incubus was made for sex and I'd already had a glimpse of his heart-pounding power, was going to be a challenge.

But I had no doubt Marcus's good will was already stretched thin. Wolves were notorious for their possessiveness, and I already had emotional connections — whether I wanted them or not — to Gideon and Jacob. Of course, it was a new day and there was a good chance Marcus now regretted his decision to be with me, that his fear for my safety would make him push me away again.

I rubbed my face and drew in a ragged breath, trying to dispel the yearning from the dream and the ache at the idea that Marcus might go back to avoiding me.

Outside, through the patio door at the back of the lounge, the sun shone bright and clear. It was going to be a beautiful day for my first day as a JP agent.

Yep, working for the agency I'd spent my life hiding from and being afraid of.

Fear seeped through the dream-Kol's sensual magic, and I shoved it back. No matter how dangerous it was for me to be mostly powerless and fighting supernatural criminals — not to mention living with all the angels in Union City — this was where I belonged.

This was who I belonged with.

All of them.

I pushed that thought back to join my fear. Wanting all of them was the dream talking. Nothing more. I didn't want all of them. I just wanted Marcus... didn't I?

I refocused on the light outside. There was something I was supposed to remember... something I needed to do this morning—

Shit. The team debriefing at o'eight hundred in Gideon's office.

I sat up so fast that my head spun and my buzz flared, the painful burning bites under my skin turning into an inferno. It joined with the pain from my raw magical channels, setting all of me on fire for an agonizing second before it calmed down. My phone, a room keycard, and a note lay on the coffee table beside me.

Have a debriefing this morning. Will make Gideon put you on the team and will meet you in your room after the meeting. Marcus.

He hadn't changed his mind. He was still going to fight to save my job and embrace the attraction between us, even though everything was complicated. What he didn't know was that Gideon had already offered me the position, and he didn't have to fight for anything... well, depending on what time it was, he might be figuring all of that out right now. Of course, if that was the case, Gideon was going to be pissed at me for being late for my first meeting.

I woke up my phone. 7:45 a.m. Thank God. I wasn't late. If I hurried, I'd be able to freshen up first. I wouldn't be able to change out of Marcus's T-shirt and workout shorts because I didn't have any more changes of clean clothes at Operations, but I could at least look like I'd washed my face and combed my hair.

For a second, I contemplated running to the bathroom in the triage waiting area to freshen up. It was closer, but I really didn't want to run into Amiah while wearing Marcus's clothes. Without a doubt the angel would be upset that I was still around. She hadn't wanted me anywhere near the guys, and she'd be furious to see me in my current state of dress. Better to spend the extra time to go up to my room to freshen up and not remind the team's physician of why she hated me.

Yes, I was going to have to face her at some point, but with luck the next few days would be uneventful, and I'd be able to convince her I wasn't a liability. As for dealing with her possible feelings for Marcus...? I had no idea. She knew Marcus and I were a thing. I'd overheard her saying to Gideon that Marcus had to give me up for the sake of the angelic mating brand. Something — if he'd well and truly decided we were a thing — his wolf would never let him do.

I hurried to the elevator, took it up to the fifth floor, and rushed into my assigned room. It looked like a hotel room, consisting of a bedroom with a small seating area and an attached bathroom, and was just as empty as a hotel room. I didn't have anything there any more. The day before yesterday, Gideon had kicked me off the team, and I'd packed my bag to leave. Then I'd been shot — and only survived because Kol had given me some of his magic — we'd stopped Jacob's vampire brother from releasing the hellfire prince Ibizual from his prison, and Gideon had changed his mind about me being on the team. My bag had ended up in Marcus's suite, and since I'd gone straight to his suite after last night's fight, my clothes — too bloody and shredded to be worn again — and shoes had ended up there.

A shiver of desire whispered through me and this time it wasn't from the dream, but the memory of Jacob's bite inflaming my need and Marcus taking over and bringing me to climax... a couple of times before we'd fallen asleep in his bed.

A part of me feared that what we had wouldn't last in the face of all my other romantic complications, but God, sex with Marcus was everything I'd imagined and more.

So far the first attempt at our strange arrangement, with Jacob feeding from me because his claim was so strong he could no longer effectively feed from anyone else, and Marcus having sex with me because I couldn't release the sensual magic of Jacob's bite without an orgasm, had gone well. Although that could have been because we'd been exhausted from our fight.

A part of me also wondered if Jacob was really onboard with the arrangement. He knew Marcus and I were involved and that fate had bound me to Gideon. He'd told Marcus our connection wasn't emotional, that he didn't have romantic feelings for me, but when he'd bitten me last night, there'd been a pain in his eyes, and with my weird empathic magic that pain had manifested as a barely-there mist, revealing his sorrow.

He'd said his claim didn't affect him like it did me, that he didn't have to have sex with his feeding, but I'd sensed he wanted to. And a part of me, a part that I was pretty sure now wasn't his claim, wanted him, too.

I splashed water on my face in the hope it would help me focus. I couldn't think about my feelings right now. I had to get to my first meeting and show Gideon that he hadn't made a mistake by keeping me on the team.

At least my reflection looked almost normal. The last handful of times I'd stared at myself in the mirror, I'd looked shocked and desperate. Now I appeared a little low on sleep, but not by much. The gash in my cheek had become a thin silvery scar, and while the ragged one from the feral vampire was now a pale pink, it still looked ugly. It probably always would. There were also still a few hints of bruises on my face, arms, and legs, since Amiah hadn't healed me completely last night. But the bit of better-than-human healing I had because I was half angel and the added enhancement from Jacob's claim meant I looked like I'd been in a car crash a few days ago and not last night — which I had been.

My gaze, like it always did when I looked at myself in a big mirror, jumped to the delicate gold lines of Gideon's brand etched into my forearm. It glowed, ever so slightly, but with my buzz blazing at pre-nicotine-numbing levels, I couldn't feel the hint of Gideon's electric magic that I usually did.

Just the thought of Gideon made my chest ache. I really hoped accepting me on the team meant he wouldn't be acting as coldly toward me. Just the memory of overhearing his rejection of me to Amiah, of never wanting to even know me, broke my heart. And it didn't matter how many times I told myself that I didn't know him and couldn't possibly love him, it still hurt.

Maybe fighting to stay with the team had been a bad idea. Leaving would offer some emotional relief. Except I knew it wouldn't. I'd already tried to keep my distance. After defeating the archnephilim, Marcus had let me return to my normal human life, and I'd been miserable. I couldn't go back to that, no matter how much staying risked exposing my secret.

I combed my fingers through my long light brown hair, but since I didn't have a hair elastic, I couldn't pull it back into a ponytail. And I wasn't going to think about the reaction I'd get from the team with me looking unprofessional in Marcus's clothes, no shoes, and my hair loose and feminine. It was 7:55 a.m. and I had to get a move on if I didn't want to be noticeably late.

Phone and keycard in hand, I rushed into the hall, tripped on a carry-on sized rolling suitcase, and slammed into a hard muscular body. We both lost our balance and crashed to the floor with me landing on top of him, the air knocked out of me — perhaps I wasn't as healed as I'd thought I was.

I pressed my palms to his shoulders to heave myself off, but froze when I met his gaze. Summer-sky blue eyes radiating angelic light. Gideon. And there wasn't a hint of hardness or ice in his gaze. It stole my breath and broke my heart. This was how it was supposed to be between us all the time.

I wanted to pretend the warmth from his eyes meant I was wrong about his feelings for me, but he'd made himself perfectly clear when I'd overheard him talking with Amiah and then again with his cold-shoulder every time we interacted. He didn't want me.

Well, God damn it. I didn't want him!

And yet I was forever connected to him. We were going to have to work something out. I wouldn't be able to spend my entire life with even a small part of me constantly grieving.

Except the look in his eyes didn't hold any hardness. Maybe there was a chance, not for a romantic relationship or even a friendship, but in the very least a truce.

I sat back and my mind stuttered. His perfect blond hair had been buzzed close to his scalp.

"What did you do to your hair?" And as soon as the words leaped out, my brain caught up. This wasn't Gideon. This angel's eyes were the same, and he had the same chiseled jaw, but his cheeks and nose were narrower and his eyes slightly farther apart. "You're his brother?"

Those beautiful summer-sky eyes locked on Gideon's brand on my right forearm, narrowed, and turned icy.

Yep, definitely his brother.

"You're his human." His gaze raked over my body, his expression hardening into disgust, and the temperature in the hall rose. "I can see why Gideon was so upset. At least you've come to your senses and you're here and accepted your fate." He grabbed the handle of his suitcase and stood. "I told him a human wouldn't be able to resist the brand. Your wills just aren't strong enough."

He turned and strode down the hall, deeper into the building toward the suites where the team members lived.

Jeez, what an asshole. I wanted to tell him off, but if he lived here — like his suitcase and the direction he was walking implied — it would be best not to make him any more of an enemy. It was going to be bad enough when he figured out Gideon and I weren't a thing and I was sleeping with Marcus.

Maybe if I didn't draw too much attention to the situation for the next couple of days, Gideon would have a chance to talk with him and explain everything. Like how he didn't want me. Ever.

I hurried to the elevator, realizing as I travelled to the first floor that Gideon had said to meet in his office and I had no idea where that was. With the buzz driving me crazy and the inside of my head being raw and making it hard to concentrate, I still hadn't managed to figure out what to do about that when the doors opened at the first floor.

Kol stood in the hall before me, and my breath hitched at the sight of him. God, he was so beautiful. His black hair, a little too long, curled around his ears and horns and was always slightly disheveled, making me think of sinful sex, while his T-shirt stretched taut across sculpted muscles and his jeans hugged lean-muscled thighs, making me want to join that sinful sex in whatever way he wanted.

Heat rose to my face, and the memory of the dream flooded me. His hands and mouth on my body, his power unfurling within me.

Hellfire flared in his dark eyes, and a shiver of desire swept through me. I bit back a moan, and the muscles in his jaw tightened.

"Gideon was wondering where you were," he said, his voice husky, sensual, turning my insides to liquid desire. "Marcus showed up for the meeting and you didn't."

It was just a dream. It wasn't him. But I couldn't convince my body that nothing had happened between us.

The elevator door started to close, and he stepped forward and stopped it with his hand.

"I—" My thoughts stalled, caught between aching need and my agonizing buzz. Holy crap, this was going to be a challenge. I hadn't had this reaction to Kol since our first meeting. How the hell was I going to be able to work on the team if I couldn't think straight around him?

He drew in a sharp breath, and the hellfire vanished from his eyes. The panty-melting desire within me softened to just sensual craving, and my buzz quickly consumed it.

Jeez, I never thought I'd be grateful for my buzz.

Focus on the pain. That at least wouldn't be embarrassing, since I had no doubt Kol knew exactly how I'd just been feeling about him.

"So does everyone know I'm on the team now?" I asked, making myself step out of the elevator without brushing up against Kol like I wanted to.

"I don't know." He headed down the hall, and I fell into step beside him. "I was running late because I still haven't figured out how to properly shield myself from you and Marcus. You've got to stop with the sex magic. It's too dangerous for a human."

"Kol, I swear. There's no sex magic. Just Jacob's bite." He hadn't believed Marcus and me the first time we'd denied it, and from his narrowed eyes, it didn't look like he believed me now.

But before I could continue trying to convince him, he stopped at an open office door. Inside, Gideon sat behind a perfectly organized desk, his expression hard, closed off, and not even a hint of a temperature change to reveal his emotions. He wore a pale blue button-down that accentuated his summer-sky eyes, and for a moment it was strange seeing him in something other than the T-shirt and fatigues he wore when he knew we were headed into a combat situation.

Behind him, framing the narrow window, stood two floor-to-ceiling bookcases with everything in place. The whole office looked like it had just been cleaned by a professional organizer, except I was pretty sure this was how the office always looked.

Jacob, looking like the Wild West gunslinger that he'd been before he'd become a vampire — even though he wasn't wearing his usual calf-length duster — sat on a stiff beige couch. His claim within me gave a slight tug, but not enough to make me fear he could control me. He'd pulled his shoulder-length hair into a ponytail at the back of his neck, his tanned face unblemished even after last night's fight, but strain still tightened his massive body and pinched at the edges of his intense black eyes.

He hadn't gotten enough blood from me last night to fully recover, since he'd needed more than I could give in one feeding, which meant the three of us were going to have to test our arrangement again, and soon, to bring him up to full.

Marcus sat beside him, his piercing green eyes bright with pleasure and affection. An affection that filled my chest with honest-to-goodness real emotion. It was the morning after — of a major fight and of having mind-blowing sex with Marcus. I was on the team, and he still wanted me.

"Agent Shaw." Gideon pointed to a chair across from Marcus, and I sat.

My buzz did a strange flicker, easing off for a moment before flaring back to life, and I resisted the urge to pull my chair closer to Gideon. I really needed to get to my bag and replace my nicotine patches, and I could only hope this meeting wouldn't take long, because it was getting hard to concentrate.

"—newest member of the team," Gideon said. "Agent Shaw?"

And crap, I'd already missed part of the conversation and everyone was looking at me.

"Do I need to arrange for you to have a suite?" Gideon asked, the rest of the question clear in his eyes: *or are you moving in with Marcus?*

Marcus and I hadn't had a chance to talk about it, but my immediate instinct was for my own space. I'd been living on my own since I was seventeen and moving into Marcus's suite while also working with him made a part of me panic. I'd be with him all the time. I wouldn't have a moment or a space to myself. That and maybe Marcus didn't want to suddenly share his suite. I couldn't make this decision without talking with him first.

"I don't know. Can I keep my assigned room and think about it?"

Marcus didn't move and his expression didn't change, but a strange mix of emotions swept through me and vanished before I could figure out what they were or what they meant.

"You can," Gideon said, his expression and tone flat. "I'd love to give everyone the day off, but we're still in the middle of the operation to shut down the zip trafficker in town."

"Is there anything we can do about that?" Jacob asked. "We tried to raid the lab two days ago, but..."

But Gideon had taken a life-threatening gunshot wound, and they'd had to race back to Operations to save him without completing the raid.

Jacob rubbed his face, looking tired when he should have been looking rested. "I'm sure they've already packed up and moved."

"Which means you're back to starting at the beginning again," a rich masculine voice said from behind me.

Gideon stiffened, and we all turned to look at the doorway to stare at his brother — and now that I could see them together, I was more certain than ever that they were related.

"You know why I'm here," he said, his gaze never leaving Gideon.

"Of course, Cassius," Gideon said. "The team is yours."

The room's temperature dropped, but I couldn't tell which of the guys were afraid. No one said a word as Gideon and Cassius stared at each other, their expressions hard. My buzz chewed under my skin, and I fought not to squirm.

"Taking down the zip trafficker and his operation is still the team's top priority." Cassius glanced at his phone. "Since you failed to shut down the lab, we need to go back to the initial intel. Jacob and Marcus, I need you to run down one of the low-level sellers and bring him or her in for questioning."

"That will alert anyone higher up that we're looking to make a move," Gideon said.

Cassius lifted his gaze back to Gideon. "They already know we're making a move. They're just lucky we're not coming after them for killing an angel."

So he knew about Gideon getting shot. I wondered if he also knew it was the mating brand that had saved him. I shuddered at the memory of that. I'd almost had my throat ripped out by a feral vampire because of the brand. But I also knew I wouldn't be alive, even with Kol's lifesaving magical transfer, without it, and we certainly wouldn't have been able to destroy Ibizual's key. The advantages and disadvantages of the brand went both ways.

Cassius's gaze dropped back to his phone, and he frowned. "You're missing your new human officer. An E. Shaw. We should report his absence to the chief of police and have him replaced."

"Shaw is here," Marcus said, jerking his chin toward me.

"You're Shaw?" The angel glow in Cassius's eyes flared. "You need to be reassigned."

"Officer Shaw isn't being reassigned," Marcus growled.

"Agent," Gideon corrected. "It's now *Agent* Esther Shaw, assigned by the Union City Chief of Police himself and approved by JP Head Office."

"Because they didn't know about—" Cassius gestured at me. "There are rules."

"Actually, there aren't any rules about branded mates or even just mates working together," Gideon said, his tone unreadable, making it impossible to tell how he felt about that.

"You risk your team thinking you're giving her preferential treatment."

I snorted at that. Yeah, no risk of that happening.

"Agent Shaw has already proven herself to be a valuable asset to the team," Jacob said.

Kol shifted forward from his spot by the door. "I'd rather work with Gideon's mate, too. We already know she can handle herself in a crisis. We don't know that about some other human UCPD might assign us."

Cassius turned his attention to Marcus, who was sitting too still, his body tense, a hint of his wolf darkening his eyes. "Agent Diaz?"

"Gideon knows where I stand with Essie," he said, his voice low as if daring Cassius to start a fight. "We'd be dead, twice now, if it wasn't for her."

"I see." Cassius's gaze shifted to me, and the pain from my buzz increased. He looked even less pleased than before that I was who I was. "All right. I suggest you change into something more appropriate and return here to fill out the paperwork to begin your reassignment from UCPD."

Marcus's phone chimed, and he pulled it from his pocket as Cassius stared him down.

"The Union City wolf pack alpha is requesting a meeting," Marcus said. "Right now. Says it's serious."

"You're the pack liaison," Gideon said. "Kol can take your spot with Jacob running down zip dealers."

"Actually, it's Kol's day off," Cassius said.

Kol shrugged. "I don't mind."

"I do. JP team members have assigned days off for a reason. You're always on call, and you'll burn yourself out if you don't take time off." Cassius shoved his phone into his pants pocket. "If things escalate, I'll call you back in. Until then, I won't expect your reports for the last two days on my desk until tomorrow afternoon. You're dismissed."

Kol glanced at Gideon, who gave a tight nod. The incubus slid his gaze to me, a mix of emotions flashing across his expression, and he left. His emotions were just as confusing as Marcus's had been over me not moving in with him, and for a messed-up moment, I missed the clear-as-mud temperature fluctuations instead of whatever the hell I'd just seen.

Cassius turned his attention to me.

Another snap from my buzz, and I clenched my jaw against reacting and revealing a weakness in front of this angel.

"Officer Shaw—"

"Agent," Gideon corrected.

"Agent." Cassius looked like he was trying to not roll his eyes at that. "Looks like you're starting early. Jacob, show her the ropes until Marcus is done meeting with the pack alpha and can replace her." He turned his glare to Gideon. "We need to talk about how you've handled the last couple of weeks. Head office is unsatisfied with your latest performance."

The temperature in the room dropped a few more degrees, but I still couldn't tell who the fear came from. Gideon's expression remained hard, but both Marcus and Jacob looked concerned.

"You have your assignments, agents," Cassius said, his words a sharp dismissal.

We stood and hurried into the hall where Kol leaned against the wall radiating a sexual intensity that I doubted he was even aware of.

Cassius closed the door behind us.

"Your mate?" he said, his voice low, only audible because Jacob's vampiric claim enhanced my hearing. "You've put your *human* mate on the team?"

"I didn't *put* her anywhere," Gideon said.

"And right on cue, big brother storms in to fuck things up," Marcus growled, drowning out the rest of the conversation behind the closed door.

"After the fight with the archnephilim at Essie's apartment and then the mess in the park and the cemetery, head office was going to send someone." Jacob rubbed his face again. Gideon and I might have gotten shot in the last two days, but Jacob had been slowly starving for the last two weeks. And while Amiah could probably heal the gunshot wounds, even if she'd known about Jacob's condition, she wouldn't have been able to do anything about it.

"You need to feed again," I said.

He captured me with his intense gaze, stealing my breath for a second. "You need more recovery time first."

"I agree with Jacob," Kol said.

"Me, too." Marcus shifted possessively close to me, his arm brushing my shoulder, but didn't reach to hold my hand or embrace me. I wasn't sure what that meant, if he was being professional while we were at work — or as professional as his wolf would allow him — or if he was upset that I hadn't wanted to move in with him.

I took his hand and threaded my fingers between his, a silent attempt to reassure him I was still his just in case he was upset — as well as to satisfy my own need just to touch him. "Fine. How worried should I be about Cassius?"

"Depends on how much he thinks Gideon has fucked up," Marcus said, tightening his grip on my hand.

"It's protocol for a team evaluation." Jacob jerked his thumb to the end of the hall. "Come on, let's get back to your suite so Essie can get her gear and shoes before you head out," he said to Marcus.

"Just because head office needs to send someone doesn't mean I have to like it," Marcus said.

We headed down the hall to the elevator.

"It is what it is," Jacob said.

"He won't understand the team." Marcus's voice darkened into a low growl, and his canines sharpened, his wolf threatening to break free. "And he won't give us time to figure out our new situation."

"Haven't you already figured the situation out?" Kol asked.

"Essie is still Gideon's mate. He won't be able to avoid that forever." Marcus glanced at me. "*You* won't be able to avoid it, either."

Given how adamant Gideon had been about never wanting to get to know me, I was sure he was going to avoid our branded-mates situation for a long, long time.

"And your wolf?" Jacob hit the elevator call button. "What will your wolf do about that?"

"You mean am I going to lose my shit on Gideon?"

"That's the worry," Jacob said.

A whisper of mist curled around me, and somehow I knew the grief came from Jacob. Both Marcus and Gideon had a legitimate, permanent claim on me, while Jacob's would eventually fade.

"Everyone shares," I said. And I meant all of them. I *hoped* for all of them. Which had to be because of my dream this morning and not because that was the way I really wanted it. How could I feel affection for all of them in so short a time? Except I did. They were mine. I belonged with them. This, with them, was the home I'd never allowed myself to have. My soul had recognized it already and now my mind was starting to catch up.

"Those are Essie's terms," Marcus said. "My wolf fully accepts them."

"Sharing. With everyone? At the same time?" Kol asked, his tone thick with innuendo but his expression playful.

"I didn't say *that*," Marcus growled, not noticing he was being teased.

"The terms are pretty open-ended." The elevator door opened and Kol slipped in first, hiding his wicked smile from Marcus. "You have a threesome going already with Jacob?"

"It's not a threesome," Marcus snarled.

Jacob's mist deepened.

"I'm already riding that high," Kol said. "I think I should join in."

"You're not joining in." Marcus released my hand, shoved Kol against the back of the elevator, and pinned him there with his forearm.

"Stop teasing him," Jacob said, his voice a dangerous rumble, his mist thickening and obscuring my vision. "I'm sure his wolf is already struggling with sharing Essie with Gideon."

And now I was certain Jacob was struggling as well.

ESSIE

WE ALL GOT INTO THE ELEVATOR, JACOB'S MIST GATHERING ON MY CHEEKS. It would soon look like I was crying if I didn't change his mood, but I wasn't sure how to deal with it, and I didn't want to bring it up in front of Marcus and Kol. When Marcus had first told me he'd share my affection, he'd included Jacob as part of the agreement because sex went hand in hand with a strong vampiric claim. But then Jacob had denied an emotional attraction to me and we'd come up with our arrangement. I knew if I broached the subject now, Jacob would continue to deny that there was anything more to our connection than a blood exchange, no matter how much his misty emotions said otherwise.

We headed to Marcus's suite, and he pressed his thumb to the fingerprint reader on the door, unlocking it for us. With a growl and a whisper of heated frustration sweeping over me, he marched back to the elevator to make his meeting with the alpha of Union City wolf pack.

"If you keep that up," Jacob said to Kol, "he's going to seriously hurt you."

"Yeah, but then he'll go to Essie to tame his savage beast, and I'll be back up to normal." Kol leaned against the doorframe, a pinprick of hellfire in his eyes. "Possessive shifter sex always comes with a little extra juice."

Jacob rolled his eyes at him.

Kol flashed a wicked grin that made my pulse skip and my body ache with need. Horror flashed over his expression, as if he'd just realized what he was doing to me, and all playfulness and hellfire vanished.

"Hand me your phone, Essie, and I'll give you my number." He held out his hand and my pulse skipped again, even though he wasn't radiating any sexual energy. All I could think about was the dream, and his dream-hands on my body. "So I can... ah..." The hellfire flickered back into his eyes. "You know... when..." He cleared his throat. "When Marcus takes over with Jacob and relieves you, I can help you get settled in, show you around... like I said I would."

If I wasn't so turned on, I would have burst out laughing. Twice in almost as many days, I'd managed to make Kol tongue-tied.

"Sure." I handed him my phone and grabbed my duffle bag from the bedroom. I desperately wanted to apply two nicotine patches right now, but I didn't want Jacob or Kol to see me doing it. I certainly didn't want to remind them that there was something not quite right about me. I was sure eventually I'd have to figure out an explanation — Marcus had seen me naked enough times now that he'd probably noticed the patches. But until I could come up with a reasonable explanation, I wasn't going to draw attention to it, so I decided to wait until I was back in my apartment and changing my clothes to reapply my patches.

Kol returned my phone and rushed down the hall to his suite a few doors down, leaving me alone with Jacob.

"Let's get you to your apartment so you can change," he said, his tone brusque and not leaving a good opportunity to broach the subject of our possible feelings for each other. And really, how could I bring it up? I couldn't say that I knew he felt bad about the arrangement with me and Marcus, because I couldn't explain how I knew that. While I *had* come up with an excuse to explain my empathy, it was another thing I wasn't going to voluntarily bring up. I might be stupid enough to believe this was where I belonged, but I was still keenly aware how dangerous it was to be here.

I shoved my feet into my runners, and we returned to the first floor, taking a detour to the cafeteria so I could pick up a breakfast burrito before heading to the garage. Instead of taking one of the JP's gray SUVs, we got into a silver four-door sedan. Given that there was a chance we might be sitting around in the car waiting to catch a low-level drug dealer, the nondescript vehicle was the better choice than the SUV.

The back windows were tinted, hiding the metal screen separating the back seats from the front like a cruiser — which thankfully meant if we did manage to pick up someone, they'd be contained for the ride back to Operations.

I climbed into the passenger seat and dropped my duffle bag at my feet. "Any idea who we might be looking for?"

Jacob pulled out of Operations' secure garage and headed out of the Supers' Quarter.

My buzz grew stronger the farther we went, as if even being in the same building as Gideon had eased it.

"There are two on the list who probably don't know we know about them."

"Any idea where we might find them?" A painful nip sliced into my neck, and I pressed my palm against it, as if that would somehow help... which it never did.

"One might be at Rouge."

My stomach clenched at the name of the nightclub owned by Jacob's sire. I didn't want to run into Victoria again... ever, if I could help it. She scared the shit out of me, and it had everything to do with the enormous vampiric power radiating from her and her willingness to hurt someone to get what she wanted. Not to mention the fact that Jacob owed her a full twenty-four hours of time with her for her help with stopping Ibizual. Which I'd been told would involve blood loss. Because that was the way Victoria liked her sex. And I wasn't going to think about how much it bothered me that Jacob had freely agreed to the price. He wasn't mine, no matter how much a part of me said he was. He could have sex with anyone he liked, even if that meant he'd need my blood to recover afterward.

"What about the other one? I'd like to avoid running into Victoria any time soon."

Jacob shot me a dark glance. "She's seen how strong my claim is on you. That should keep her happy for a good couple of decades."

"One can hope." Except I wasn't so sure about that. Victoria also knew I had Gideon's mating brand, and I had no doubt that complication amused her.

We drove through the park ringing the Quarter that separated the supers' part of the city from the rest of the city and headed to my very plain, very human neighborhood. Jacob's mist was gone and the temperature in the car didn't fluctuate, but there was a tension between us that made me want to squirm. I hadn't thought we'd gotten close in the last two and a bit weeks, especially with a week and a half with no contact, but the awkwardness now between us hurt.

Jacob parked on the street in front of my apartment building, a plain four-story walkup at the back of a three-building complex of four-story walkups. My landlord's wife knelt in the garden by my building's front door and started to wave as we walked toward her, but she stopped when she realized it was me.

Yeah, I was no longer in her good graces. I might have been a reliable tenant who kept quiet and paid the rent on time, but I'd also just hosted a fight with five powerful supers that had scared the crap out of my neighbors and required the Joined Parliament to repair the damages.

Her attention jumped to Jacob, and she grabbed her gardening caddy and moved to the flowerbed on the far side of the courtyard.

I glanced at Jacob. He was hiding his vampiric intensity, just like he had the first time I'd met him. If I hadn't known what he was, given that he was walking around in the daylight — thanks to a magical bracelet from the JP that protected him — I would never have known he was a vampire. Of course he was still huge, about six and a half feet tall with a massive muscular body. That was still enough to scare anyone.

My apartment was on the top floor in the corner. I'd fallen in love with it the moment I'd seen it, with its vaulted ceiling, two walls of tall windows, the skylight above the living room, and access to the roof.

The memory of being in Gideon's arms while flying made me shiver, and my buzz blazed, stealing my breath for a moment. A part of me ached at the thought of flying. I might be half angel, but I didn't have wings, and I would never fly.

I hadn't thought that was a problem. Except now that I was back here, I couldn't help but wonder if I'd subconsciously picked this apartment two years ago because I could sit in my living room or stand on the roof and stare at the sky.

"You okay?" Jacob asked.

And I realized I'd gotten lost in thought with my key in the lock, thinking about not having wings and never being able to fly.

"Yeah." I opened the door. "Sure."

"It's been a difficult couple of days." He followed me inside, his attention sliding over the room. I wasn't sure if he was looking for danger or checking if the JP had actually fixed my apartment from the fight with the archnephilim. "I'm sure if you talk with Gideon and Cassius, they'll give you a couple of days to adjust to your new position."

"Cassius already thinks I'm getting special treatment from Gideon." I headed into my bedroom and pulled out a change of clothes.

Jacob leaned against the doorframe with his back to me.

"Cassius also knows you're human. Once Gideon tells him what we went through last night, he'll know you're not fully recovered."

"And that will just give him another excuse to kick me off the team." Jeez, I'd been worried it would be Gideon who'd send me packing and give the chief of police reason to fire me from the force, since none of the other officers wanted to work with me. And really, I couldn't blame them. Dangerous situations with supers kept finding me, and my partners kept getting hurt. If the JP team refused me, I was sure I would be unemployed. And I had no idea what I'd do with myself if I couldn't be a cop.

"Essie." Jacob's voice was sharp, jerking my attention to him. His back was still to me, but it felt like he was focused on me and only me. It probably had something to do with his claim. I might be able to resist the compulsion to obey him now, but it didn't mean our essences were any less entwined. "You were shot yesterday and then barely got through last night's battle alive. I doubt Amiah healed you to full. You're allowed to recover."

A hint of mist curled around me, and what he didn't say squeezed my chest. If I died, he died. Not to mention if I died, Gideon would go insane because of the mating brand. And, given that Marcus's wolf had claimed me as his mate, I didn't doubt Marcus would suffer as well.

And yet I couldn't hide myself away to protect them. I needed to stand with them as an equal.

"Your claim has helped me heal." I changed out of Marcus's clothes into jeans and a T-shirt. "I can handle a little surveillance until Marcus relieves me."

"Cassius still should have given you Kol's day off."

"I'm pretty sure Cassius did what he did to see what I'd do about it." I shoved Marcus's clothes and three more changes of clothes into my duffle bag. "He wanted to see if I'd use my connection with Gideon to get special treatment. He hasn't figured out that Gideon wants nothing to do with me."

"Gideon—"

"Don't tell me that isn't true. I know Marcus threatened to quit if Gideon didn't keep me on the team. I know Gideon hates that I'm his mate."

"He doesn't hate that you're his mate."

I replaced my two used-up nicotine patches with new ones, sticking them on the back of my hip — I'd changed them so frequently in the last little while, I was running out of different places to stick them to avoid irritating my skin. "I'm not what he wanted or even expected. I get it. I'm okay with it."

Jacob snorted. "Doesn't sound like it."

"I'm okay with him not wanting me to be his mate." I was. Honestly. I didn't want to be permanently bound to an angel who hated what I was. "It's him acting like I can't do my job that bothers me. That he doesn't even want to try to work with me."

"And yet here you are on the team."

"Because Marcus gave him an ultimatum." I checked my sidearm and holstered it in my waistband holster. I hadn't reloaded since last night, so I was still down to half a magazine of enspelled ammunition.

"Actually, we all did."

I turned to him. He was looking at me now, his vampiric intensity darkening his eyes and stealing my breath.

"We don't want a different human on the team. We want you." He shifted, as if he wanted to move to me, but the muscles in his jaw tightened, and he stayed put.

My pulse stuttered, and my buzz blazed stronger, searing through the still enflamed magical channels in my body. I ached for Jacob, just like I ached for Marcus and Gideon and even Kol. We were stronger together. *I* was stronger with all of them.

Which was crazy. I didn't know them. How could I know with such certainty that we belonged together?

"You belong on the team," Jacob said, his voice a low, sensual rumble.

"I also complicate the team." I couldn't forget that. Jacob wasn't happy with our arrangement with Marcus and the jury was still out if Marcus's wolf would accept me having something with Gideon... or anyone else.

"Stop arguing against yourself. We both know you want to be on the team, and we both know you belong here." Jacob jerked away from the door, stepping into my living room. "Now, come on. You're clearly not going to take the day off, so let's go find a zip dealer."

"But not at Rouge." I hurried past him to my bathroom, loaded some toiletries into my bag, and tied my hair back into a ponytail.

"I know someone in Squatters' Row. She might know where to score some zip. We'll try her first." Jacob pulled up a picture on his phone and handed it to me as we headed back to the car. "This is who we're most likely to find. Floyd Webb."

The guy was handsome, not breathtaking like all my guys, but then very few men could be.

My heart thrummed at that. My guys. All of them.

I pushed that back as deep as it would go, concentrating on my blazing buzz to help distract me. Only Marcus was actually mine. It wasn't right to claim all of them.

I refocused on Jacob's phone. Floyd had a build similar to Marcus's with powerful compact muscles, and his sandy blond hair hung in waves to his shoulders that any woman would envy. His brown eyes though were hard, as if he wanted to kill whoever was taking his picture.

"He's a weretiger, was originally muscle for the Claws but sources say he's graduated to drug dealer. Zip for the humans and fentanyl for the supers. Apparently his good looks make him a good salesman."

"Yeah, and that death look probably means they always pay up front." I handed the phone back to Jacob.

"We'll see if we can get a line on his location, and keep eyes on him until Marcus can take over."

I opened my mouth to argue about that.

"Shot and almost died, remember?" Jacob said.

Right. Not at full. And my not at full was worse than his not at full. If I didn't take it easy now, I'd pay for it later. As much as I wanted to prove myself and not be a burden, Jacob was right. I needed to be smart about this. The team was under scrutiny and me being reckless put all of us in danger.

ESSIE

WE RETURNED TO THE CAR. I THREW MY BAG INTO THE TRUNK, AND WE headed back to the Quarter. Hopefully I'd packed enough clothes to get me through the next couple of days and wouldn't end up in Marcus's workout clothes again. I could just imagine Cassius's face the next time he saw Marcus wearing the shorts and T-shirt I'd been wearing this morning. Hopefully that wouldn't happen until after Gideon had explained the situation. But a part of me feared that even if Gideon did explain, Cassius wouldn't understand, not because angels believed only in monogamy — I had no idea if they did or not — but because their beautiful, sacred mating brand said Gideon and I were destined for each other and Marcus wasn't a part of that destiny.

Squatters' Row was a small neighborhood on the far side of the Quarter within the park ring. Only half of the area that had been expropriated by the Joined Parliament to create the Supers' Quarter had been repaired or redeveloped. The supers' population wasn't particularly big, but no one really knew how long it would take — if ever — for the majority of humans and supers to feel comfortable living side by side, so the city planners had set aside space within the Quarter for population growth.

Most of the buildings in the Row were in decent shape. Michael's war hadn't spent much time in this part of the city — which was one of the reasons it had been picked to become the Quarter. But the buildings were owned by absentee developers, or by developers who'd gone bank-rupt, and the city had other things to worry about than buildings it had no money to fix or fill with tenants. And just like many of the abandoned parts of the city, those who didn't care about — or had no other choice to —live without power or running water took shelter in the abandoned buildings.

These areas of town often bred violence and crime and every couple of months, my partner and I were part of a task force to clean up the abandoned neighborhoods in our precinct. It was pretty much an act of futility, since the residents just relocated to another abandoned neigh-borhood, but we usually picked up a few gang leaders and drug dealers in the sweep and criminal activity always settled down for a bit.

I'd only been to Squatters' Row once, and only recently. Because it was in the Quarter, it fell under the Quarter's policing jurisdiction, which was part JP team and part teams from the three supernatural heads of the community: vampire, shifter, and demon. That meant the Row was rarely cleaned out and housed many of the shadier supers — the threshold for criminal activities that required policing in the super-natural world was higher than in the human world.

The Row was where I'd found the witch who'd sold me the contacts that hid my glowing eyes... the glow that had manifested after my fight with the archnephilim and was supposed to have faded weeks ago.

I'd paid a lot of money for the witch's discretion, and she hadn't asked any questions as to why my essence said I was human but my eyes glowed with angelic light. In turn, I didn't ask her about her less-than-legal services. Better one shady witch suspecting I was a nephilim than everyone I worked with or met on the street.

Still, I'd taken a serious risk going to her. She could have easily gone to the authorities and told them she knew I was a nephilim. And while I hadn't outright told her I was one, just about everyone in the world could put two and two together. But I'd had no choice, and I'd hoped — which seemed to be the case — that me continuing to be a paying customer would trump reporting a possible nephilim.

Except I was going to need to deal with my glowing eyes a lot sooner than I'd expected. Yesterday, Sebastian Bane had said I had less than a week left before the spell on the contacts failed. They were supposed to have lasted months, and the fact that they were going to last less than three weeks worried me.

Scared the shit out of me, actually.

Things within me were changing. I really wanted to pretend it wasn't true, but I couldn't. It wasn't just my glowing eyes, but my buzz—

And speaking of buzz, we were back in the Quarter, at least a fifteen-minute drive from my apartment. My patches should have kicked in by now, easing the biting agony under my skin to manageable levels, but it was still just as powerful as before.

Jacob turned onto a narrow street lined with six-story apartment buildings and stopped halfway down. All the buildings looked rundown, but only half were completely boarded up. Most of those that weren't boarded up — and didn't look like they were going to collapse — had thugs hanging on the front steps enjoying the early summer heat. Only about a third of the thugs looked human — and while they could have actually been human, the better guess was that they were packless shifters or a type of demon who could pass as human.

I got out of the car and every eye turned to me. Half the gazes looked hungry, the other half slid to the Glock holstered at my hip and recognized me for what I was — a cop — and their looks turned angry. My buzz clawed through my body, and I gritted my teeth. The patches would kick in soon. They had to.

Jacob got out, and all but a few gazes looked away, anywhere but at Jacob. They'd all become suddenly interested in the windows across the street or the crossroad ahead of us. He released a hint of his vampiric intensity and the remaining gazes vanished. His claim gave a gentle tug in my chest, drawing a shiver, yearning for all the intensity to be turned on me. Funny how everyone else wanted to shrink away from it, knew it meant Jacob was the most dangerous super on the block, and I craved it.

We climbed the steep steps of the closest building, making the three green-skinned demons perched there scurry inside. Jacob ignored them, and we headed up to the second floor, stopping at a scarred door in a garbage-strewn hall of scarred doors.

He raised his hand to knock, but slid his gaze to me instead. "We're here to talk to Fawn. Not save her."

I didn't like the sound of that. "What's that supposed to mean?"

"Things are different in the Quarter than the rest of Union City," he said, his voice a low rumble. "You're not going to like Fawn's situation. Most humans don't understand it."

"What do you mean by that?" A painful nip sliced through my shoulder, and I dug my nails into my skin, trying to grind the buzz away before that muscle started twitching.

"Just know that this is her choice." He knocked.

Footsteps shuffled to the door. The deadbolt clicked open, and Jacob tensed, but it didn't feel like he was tensing for danger, more like my reaction.

The door cracked open, still secured by the chain, revealing the face of a pretty demon with small delicate horns poking through long blond locks. If she'd been giving off any kind of sexual vibe, I would have thought she was a succubus, but she wasn't. In fact, she was barely giving off any demonic vibe at all. No hellfire in her eyes and no radiating heat from a raised body temperature. Save for the horns, I would have thought she was human.

My brain tripped on that, then realization kicked in. She was a half breed. Half human half demon. Something that, unlike me being half human and half angel, was entirely possible. The demonic half breed community was tiny, but there were enough of them worldwide for them to claim a community and have representation in parliament.

"Jacob," she said, her voice soft and dreamy. "Have you changed your mind about bagged blood?"

She shut the door, and the chain rattled.

"Your blood bunny?" I asked in a voice so quiet only Jacob could hear it and only because of his enhanced hearing. I had no idea how I felt about that. He was a vampire. I couldn't pretend he didn't use a blood bunny's service. Most did. And while most humans saw the job as prostitution with blood donation, bunnies had more protection and rights than a normal human because of the nature of their occupation. Not to mention they were paid very well.

"She used to be my bunny," Jacob replied, just as quietly, "but she started liking it rougher than I do, so I moved on. Victoria had to let her go a few years ago so she wouldn't lose her license to house bunnies."

"That rough?" That said a lot. There were only a few things bunnies weren't allowed to do and they were pretty extreme.

The door reopened in full this time, and I fought to keep a straight face. The half demon wore a pink slip that barely covered her, exposing a body covered in vampire bites. They were everywhere, some clean, some ragged, all in various stages of healing. Pink and silvery scars thickened her neck and wrists, and it didn't look like there was a single spot on her that hadn't been bitten. And because I could tell that, it meant the vampires feeding on her weren't properly healing her. Yes, their magic didn't completely heal the wound right away, but it continued to work over time, eliminating even the scar.

I tensed, and Jacob pressed his hand against my back, as if hoping the physical contact would remind me of his warning.

"I don't do couples any more. Too dangerous." She leaned toward Jacob, her voice breathy. The need of an addict filled her eyes, and the temperature around me skyrocketed with lust. "But I know you're safe. I'll make an exception for you."

"We need information," Jacob said. "I'll pay and you don't have to bleed."

"Make me bleed, and I'll say you've paid." She ran her finger over a ragged bite just below her collar bone. The temperature turned sweltering, and her pupils dilated, her desire growing stronger.

Jacob was right. I wanted to save Fawn. She was a perfect example of the greatest risk for a bunny. Most would think it would be blood loss, or serious injury at the hands of a vampire, but it was really becoming addicted to the magic of a vampire's bite. There were successful forms of treatment, and the terms of a bunny's contract with a blood house ensured a comfortable retirement if he or she did become addicted. But Fawn had been fired from Victoria's club and must have kept working as a bunny on her own. Which meant she didn't have a contract to protect her from her addiction.

Except Jacob had made a point to warn me that this was Fawn's choice. It was a terrible choice, but it was hers.

"I won't tell you anything unless you bite me," she said, shifting closer to Jacob.

"You won't be able to tell us anything after I bite you."

Fawn pressed her hands to Jacob's chest and looked up into his dark eyes, her body trembling with her desire. "Please, Jacob."

A hint of mist crept through Fawn's heat, but I couldn't tell if it was because Jacob was sad for Fawn or something else.

"A bite," he said. "Nothing more."

"Jacob," she begged.

Another snap in my shoulder and the muscle spasmed.

"Nothing more." His tone was gentle yet firm. I wasn't sure how he felt about this kind of payment, but I was beginning to learn that some supers negotiated with non-monetary currency. Victoria traded in sex. Looked like Fawn traded with being bitten. There was a lot I was going to need to learn if I was going to work on the JP team, a whole lifetime of catching up, because I'd made a point of avoiding all things supernatural.

"What do you want to know?" She ran her hands down his chest, as if that might change his mind about biting her right away.

I ground my thumb into my shoulder, trying to stop the spasm.

Jeez. Why weren't the nicotine patches working?

"Where are the best places in town to score zip?" He grabbed her wrists as they reached the waistband of his pants.

Her desire flared, and sweat slicked my skin. "That shit will kill you. It's not worth the risk. Leave it to the humans and us half breeds. They say less than a quarter of supers who take it survive."

"It's not for me," Jacob said.

Fawn's attention slid to me. "No matter what powers the zip gives humans, you can't make your bunny into a super even just for a feeding. She won't be able to give you what you want," she said, her tone clear that she could.

More of Jacob's mist swept around me.

"Of course she can't," he said, his gaze darting to mine. "But she's new in town and still looking to score."

"So do you know where I can?" I asked, playing along.

"I've heard the guys a few doors down talk about scoring at the Third Street bridge as well as an apartment above the bodega on the corner of Morris and West, but I don't know if their dealers sells zip." Fawn pressed her body against Jacob's and tilted her head, exposing her neck.

"Do you know who their dealer is?" Jacob asked.

"You said you'd bite me." Her breath picked up with need and desperation.

"I want to make sure the guy is the real deal."

"Lloyd or something. Something about a spider for his last name maybe?" She clawed at a barely healed bite near her ear, breaking the scab and smearing the trickle of blood on her neck. "We made a deal."

Jacob didn't react to the blood. His pupils didn't dilate, and his fangs didn't extend, not like they did when I offered myself.

The air in the hall was sweltering, filled with mist, and my body stung.

"Should we step inside?" I asked, uncertain if Jacob wanted to bite her while standing in the hall.

"Yes," Fawn breathed, her eyes half closed in anticipation.

"Here's fine." With his expression tight, he pushed Fawn back a step, putting some distance between them.

Fawn's gaze shot up to his, filled with hurt and anger. "We had a deal."

"We did." He brought her wrist to his lips and sank his fangs into her scarred flesh.

She moaned and grabbed the doorframe to steady herself. Her need blazed in the air around me even though the first few seconds of a vampire's bite were painful, and I wondered if she preferred her bite without a vampire's intoxicating magic.

Then he sucked, a gentle pull on her vein that I knew flooded his magic into her body. She moaned again, the sound deeper, filled with euphoria.

A shiver swept through me, not at the sight of Jacob feeding from her, but at the memory of his magic rushing into me. Pure spiraling desire with a climax that exploded in every cell, and I couldn't help but wonder if this was my fate, addicted to the magic of his bite

He withdrew his fangs without taking a second sip, his magic sealing the wound shut, but Fawn didn't seem to notice. Just a few seconds, and she was riding the high of his magic. Gripping her shoulders, he walked her backwards to a bare, beat-up mattress on the floor a few feet inside the door, and left her with her hands roaming her body. He rejoined me in the hall, shutting the door behind him, radiating dark vampiric intensity and surrounding me with a thick mist.

"I suppose these are the ropes Cassius wanted me to show you." He didn't sound happy about that and it broke my heart, consuming my fear that I was walking a dangerous line with Jacob and reminding me that regardless of my fate, I would do anything to protect him.

Which was another thought that terrified me.

I pressed a hand to his biceps — the muscle so big I wouldn't have been able to encircle it with both hands — needing to reassure him, and myself, with physical contact. "Are *you* okay?"

"I only have a problem drinking bagged blood." Which was why we had our arrangement with Marcus.

But his mist wasn't clearing up. He was upset about something. "I wasn't talking about that."

He pressed his hand over mine. What remained of his claim thrilled at his touch, while another part of me warmed at the rightness of it.

"There are a lot of ugly things about the supernatural world that we keep from humans. It bothers me that you had to see me do that."

"I don't judge you for using alternative currency, like your bite for information."

He raised an eyebrow at that, his expression clear he didn't believe me.

"At some point, you're going to have to start taking me at my word. I might not know everything about you, but I know who you are."

Mine.

I shoved that thought back.

"The team wouldn't work together as well as it does if your moral codes didn't align, and I doubt destiny would have said Gideon and I were soul mates if we didn't share a similar moral center." I rose on my tiptoes and brushed my lips across his cheek with a need to show him that I wasn't afraid of him or found him disgusting.

The mist vanished, replaced with a sudden wild heat.

"Essie," he rumbled.

My breath caught, my heart pounding. "Yes, Jacob."

Jacob's gaze captured my soul, and my pulse pounded faster. The wild heat of his emotions blazed through me, consuming my buzz. But a second later the muscles in his jaw clenched and his expression tightened. The heat vanished, leaving me cold and stinging.

"Let's see if we can find a zip dealer." He squeezed my hand then realized what he was doing, released me, and shifted away.

The distance — emotional and physical — hurt. Almost as much as the distance Gideon put between us. "Yeah. Sure."

A sharp snap from the buzz cut down my neck, making me flinch.

Jacob's eyes narrowed, and I fought the urge to rub the twitching muscle and draw more attention to it.

"It sounded like Fawn might have been talking about Floyd Webb. The Third Street bridge is closest. We should check there first." I headed toward the stairs and Jacob joined me. We were definitely going to have a conversation, just not while we were working and after I'd gotten my buzz under control.

A masculine laugh echoed from the stairwell.

"The look on his face," a rich baritone said in response as footsteps clomped up the stairs.

I wasn't sure how many people there were, but definitely more than two, and most of the steps were heavy, suggesting they were all male.

I tensed, and my buzz sliced up my neck again.

"The look on *all* their faces," another guy chuckled.

I rolled my shoulders. This was just a bunch of guys — most likely supers, but still guys. Yes, I was a cop in their territory, but maybe they wouldn't see the aura of 'cop' radiating around me. Half the guys on the street hadn't.

The group reached the top of the stairs and were so caught up in laughing about whatever they'd been talking about that they made it almost ten feet down the hall before noticing us.

There were three of them. The guy in front, a bulky demon with onyx skin, milky white eyes, and almost as big as Jacob, stopped and met the vampire's gaze and held it. Whatever type of demon he was, he clearly thought he could challenge Jacob for dominance.

The guy beside him, a demon with red scales all over his body, a thin prehensile tail, and slitted pupils, glanced at my sidearm then sneered, revealing a mouth full of pointed teeth.

Crap. Smart enough to recognize me as a cop.

"You thought bringing a vampire to the Row would protect you, cop?" Scales said.

"Actually she brought a JP agent." Jacob released more of his hold on his vampiric intensity, and a whisper of cold swept across my cheeks — fear from the guys. I shivered with the chill, and my buzz sliced through my neck again. Jeez. This was getting bad.

"Still, two of you and three of us," Onyx guy said.

"We're not here for you." Perhaps I could deescalate the situation, although I had a bad feeling these guys were just looking for a fight.

The guy in the back shifted into the space between Scales and Onyx. He was average height, well-built, handsome, blond, and the zip dealer we were looking for, Floyd Webb.

Well, shit. I guess we were there for them.

So much for just doing surveillance until Marcus relieved me.

"I've got the demons," Jacob said, his voice low and dangerous.

Which left me with Floyd, the weretiger. How the hell was I supposed to apprehend a shifter by myself? The chief of police really hadn't thought things through when he'd demanded the JP include a human member on the team. Jeez, I hadn't, either. I'd wanted the job, fought to be where I was, and now I was faced with the truth. I wasn't strong enough to overpower a super like I could a human and arrest him.

But Jacob wouldn't be able to deal with all three of them by himself.

"Shot, remember?" I said, reminding him of his own words that I wasn't perfectly fit.

"Archnephilim," he replied, pointing out I'd dealt with much worse than a shifter.

Well, fine. Maybe my light strike spell would be enough to stun Floyd long enough for Jacob to deal with the demons.

Of course, my ability to summon divine light had been on the fritz, and then I'd channeled Gideon's power twice in as many days and my inner magical channels were still raw. Casting a light strike spell now was just as likely to fail or incapacitate me as it was Floyd.

Which left shooting him as my only other way to slow the weretiger down. Good thing Operations had a magical healer on staff.

I drew my sidearm to shoot, but Scales leaped forward and slapped my Glock with his tail. Somehow I managed to keep hold of my weapon, but in that split second the hall erupted into chaos.

Jacob bolted past me and shouldered Scales into Onyx, while Floyd shoved past them to lunge at me, his nails extended into wickedly sharp claws.

He swiped at me. I jerked back, his claws narrowly missing my chest, and brought my Glock up to shoot him. But he swiped again, forcing me to wrench my weapon away or be disarmed.

Behind him, Jacob punched Onyx in the gut, but Scales wrapped his tail around Jacob's neck. For a split second, I feared Jacob wouldn't be able to handle them — which was ridiculous, given what we'd dealt with in the last couple of weeks. He rammed his elbow into Scales's face and ducked under a swing from Onyx.

Floyd snarled at me and swiped again, lunging closer than before. I twisted to the side instead of wrenching back. His claws skimmed my shoulder, tearing my T-shirt and slicing into my skin with fiery agony, but it was worth it. Now I was positioned right next to him. I rammed my heel into his knee and my fist into his head. I didn't really want to shoot him, and I wasn't stupid enough to try to hold him at gunpoint when we were so close, so I needed him down so I could put distance between us and gain control of the situation.

He dropped to his knees, and I hopped back and aimed my weapon at him. "Hands on your head."

His eyes were wide and a nauseating mix of hot and cold washed over me. Anger and fear at me. Yeah, somehow this puny human had gotten the upper hand on him.

"Hands on your head."

Scales hissed and darted past Jacob, who had Onyx in a headlock. The scaled demon dove for me. I fired at him, but he twisted and the shot skimmed his ribs. Jacob heaved Onyx toward us and seized Scales's tail, but Floyd took my second of distraction, leaped to his feet, and bolted for the stairs.

I raced after him, praying Jacob could deal with Scales and Onyx quickly then help me. If he could, all I needed to do was keep Floyd in the area.

Floyd reached the stairs. I fired and skimmed his shoulder, making him stagger. It wasn't enough to stop him, but it did slow him down. Except instead of continuing down the stairs, he lunged at me.

I tried to stop my forward momentum, but I was running all out to catch him. My buzz snapped, making my neck and shoulder muscles spasm, and he grabbed the front of my T-shirt, his claws slicing into my chest.

With a roar, he tossed me toward the stairs. I dropped my Glock and seized his wrists before I could fall, but he was off balance and my weight yanked him down with me.

He slammed onto me, stealing my breath, then tumbled off. I fell after him, crashing down the stairs and careening off the wall. Pain exploded through my chest, head, shoulders. The world spun and flickered into darkness.

I landed in a heap on top of him, dizzy and filled with agony.

"Get off me, bitch." He shoved me aside, heaved himself up, and staggered out the front door.

I lurched after him even though I had no idea where my sidearm was. I didn't know why he didn't stick around to finish me off, but I couldn't let him get away. He might not have figured out that the JP was specifically looking for him, but there was a chance he'd tell his boss about the incident and then it would become harder to bring down the zip operation.

He was already at the bottom of the stairs when I reached the doorway.

"Floyd Webb," I gasped.

He turned and snarled at me, baring his extended canines. "You really want to fight?"

"I want you to get on your knees and put your hands on your head." It was the stupidest thing I could have said. I had no weapon, I was a weak human — more or less — and the world was still spinning.

Please don't let him notice that I don't have a gun. And please, Jacob, show up behind me and scare him into compliance.

But Floyd's sneer deepened. "I want to see you make me."

He rushed up the stairs, death in his eyes and his rage searing the air around me.

Oh, shit.

I jerked back and raised my hands in a useless defense. Agony exploded in my palms, and a massive blast of divine light, summoned without even thinking the words of the spell, slammed into Floyd's chest. It tossed him off the stairs and across the street. He crashed into the building across from us, the force of my light strike so powerful it cracked the bricks.

Holy shit!

I sagged to my knees, my body on fire from channeling too much magical power too soon after the fight to stop Ibizual. Gideon was going to kill me. There was no way I could have summoned that much divine light on my own. Even though it hadn't felt like I had taken his power, I must have to have made that shot.

Jacob barreled down the stairs, holding my sidearm. "Essie."

"He's over there." I pointed to Floyd, lying unconscious in the sidewalk. I really hoped I hadn't killed him. That would just suck. Yeah, it had clearly been my life or his, but I had no doubt this situation would bring out the JP's version of internal affairs to investigate. And I was pretty sure that was Cassius... who was already here and hated me.

Jacob returned my gun, called Gideon for support, and hauled an unconscious Onyx and a dazed Scales down the stairs and into the back of the car.

I sat in the doorway.

I knew if I stood, I'd throw up... if I could stand.

If I was smart, I'd really rethink the being part of a JP team thing. Except just the thought of leaving made my pulse race. This was where I belonged. With the guys. They were mine. And if I wasn't strong enough to deal with the situation, I'd just have to become stronger.

Gideon, Marcus, and Cassius arrived as Jacob shut the door on the demons. He headed across the street to the still-unconscious — please don't be dead — Floyd, and the guys piled out of the gray SUV.

"A little excessive even for you, Jacob," Cassius said, crossing the street to him and standing on the sidewalk in front of Floyd, while Gideon and Marcus hurried up the stairs to me.

Light blazed from Gideon's eyes. God, he was furious.

The air temperature didn't change, but that had to be because of the buzz burning me from the inside out. The pain was so powerful, I couldn't even feel a hint of Gideon's electric magic in his brand, and that had been an ever-present sensation since I'd returned to Operations two days ago.

"I didn't know I'd taken it until the blast came out," I said. Maybe if I apologized right away, Marcus would clue in and try to calm Gideon down before he reamed me out in public, not to mention in front of his brother.

"Taken what?" Gideon asked, standing over me as Marcus knelt and gingerly took my hands.

My palms were burned. Again. Although not as badly as they had been when I'd destroyed the key that could unlock Ibizual's prison.

"What did you—?" Marcus's gaze jumped across the street, where Jacob had hauled Floyd to his feet. The whole front of the weretiger's shirt had been scorched away, and an ugly red burn covered most of his chest.

"Why didn't you tell me your human could produce a powerful light strike?" Cassius asked as he marched across the street to us. His gaze jumped from Gideon to Marcus, who knelt too close to me, and he cocked an eyebrow.

"It's a new development," Gideon said, ignoring the eyebrow, "and dangerous." He gestured to my burned hands and glared at me. "You really shouldn't have summoned it. Not after last night."

Oh, yeah, he was pissed and didn't want Cassius to know. And for some reason that made me pissed in return. It might have been dumb to cast it today — not that I'd cast it on purpose — but it did mean I wasn't completely powerless and therefore not a liability for the team. I'd thought we'd gotten past that when Gideon had accepted me on the team. Maybe, with his brother in town, he was changing his mind.

"Well, the next time I fall down a flight of stairs, lose my sidearm, and am about to have my throat ripped out by a shifter, I'll take a minute and think about the last time I cast a light strike spell."

"And that's why she can't be on the team," Cassius said. "You're playing with fire, Gideon. If something happens to her..." He didn't say the rest because we already knew it.

"This isn't the time or place for this discussion," Gideon said.

"There shouldn't be a discussion." Cassius glared at me. "Lock her in your suite until she sees reason."

Gideon's expression turned icy, but the fire in my body wouldn't let me sense any temperature changes. He was definitely rethinking about me being on the team. He could use this incident to prove to the other guys that the job was just too dangerous for me. And a part of me couldn't disagree.

Marcus growled, the sounds low and dangerous, and his wolf darkened his eyes. "It was stupid to just pair her up. Given the situation, any human on the team would have ended up like this or worse. She should always be support for the full team. Any human agent should be."

"Agent Shaw isn't just any human," Cassius said. "She's mated with an angel. Her life is not her own any more."

Marcus's canines lengthened and his nails sharpened into claws. "Her life is always hers."

"Back off, wolf. This isn't your business." A flicker of real flames danced around Cassius's fists.

Marcus jerked to his feet, and Gideon shoved himself in front of him before he could attack Cassius.

"Agent Shaw needs medical attention, and we need to get Floyd and his demons to Operations." Gideon held Marcus's gaze as if daring him to try something. Or was he trying to will him into seeing reason? Fighting Cassius in the middle of the street was a terrible idea.

"Fine," Marcus snarled.

He bent to pick me up, but Gideon grabbed his shoulder and ever so slightly jerked his chin toward Cassius.

"Fine. I'll help Jacob." Marcus shoved past Gideon and Cassius.

"You need to get your wolf under control," Cassius said over his shoulder to Gideon as he headed back to the SUV.

Gideon knelt beside me, his expression still frozen.

I was in so much shit.

"Can you walk?" he asked.

"I have no idea." I hadn't tried to stand since blasting Floyd and with my buzz biting and burning me up, I couldn't tell if I'd broken anything. With the fall I'd taken, it was a miracle I hadn't broken my neck.

I reached for the wall to pull myself to my feet, but Gideon swept his arms around me and picked me up before I could fully rise.

The buzz vanished, and I almost sobbed with relief. One moment it was there, the next Gideon touched me and it was gone. Agony now sliced through me from the beating I'd taken falling down the stairs, but the biting, burning, every-inch-of-flesh-on-fire was gone. And all I had to do was get the man who wanted nothing to do with me to hold me.

I leaned my cheek against his chest and let his soft scent of spring-time envelop me. It broke my heart and made me angry at the same time. I didn't want to feel the things I did for Gideon, but my soul seemed to think he was as much mine as the rest of the guys. And every time he looked at me with ice in his summer-sky eyes, the brand made my soul cry.

I couldn't work with him if we didn't come to some kind of a truce. Which meant he had to know that I hadn't taken his power on purpose.

"I really didn't mean to take your power this time."

He headed to the SUV, the movement making my head spin. "You didn't."

"I must have." I closed my eyes before I threw up. Add concussion to my list of injuries. "I blasted him across the street, and my hands are burned. If it was my power, it wouldn't burn me."

"I don't know. It shouldn't have. But you're a human with an angelic mating brand. Brands enhance an angel's power. It might be affecting yours." He opened the back door to the SUV and set me on the seat, then turned to close the door.

My buzz reignited the moment he let go, blazing through me with blinding agony. I bit back a whimper and, without thinking, seized his wrist to stop the pain.

"Agent." His summer-sky gaze met mine, filled with worry and questions and tight discomfort.

Yeah, I know. He didn't want any extra physical contact. But I just couldn't deal with my buzz right now. It was so strong. Stronger than it had ever been before, and with my magical channels burned raw and my gut-churning concussion, I just couldn't stand it.

Except I had no idea how to tell him that, no idea how to tell him I needed him and still understood that he didn't want a relationship with me.

Especially with Cassius sitting in the driver's seat watching us through the rearview mirror.

ESSIE

I OPENED MY MOUTH TO SAY SOMETHING, ANYTHING, HELL, JUST BEG Gideon to let me touch him. While I'd come up with an explanation for my buzz — like with all my unusual abilities — I'd only wanted to use it as a last resort. Maybe this was my last resort. Could it get worse? But it would be safer if I mentioned the buzz when Cassius wasn't around.

Gideon must have seen something in my expression — most likely my fear and desperation — because the ice in his eyes softened. His expression, however, grew pained, and he climbed in beside me, helping me shift over just enough to make room for him. He carefully wrapped an arm across my shoulders and let me lean against him.

I closed my eyes, fighting my nausea, my soul crying. Even just sitting beside me upset him. And while I was sure I was a big part of that pain, I couldn't forget the angel he'd loved had only been killed a few weeks ago. That was a pain that didn't heal quickly, or at all, and I wished with all my heart that even if we never accepted the mating bond, I could ease his grief. Not enough to take it away. That would be a different form of torture. But just enough to take the edge off.

The SUV stopped, and I cracked my eyes open. We were in Operations' secure garage, parked in front of the sliding glass door instead of a parking space.

Gideon carried me inside while Cassius parked the SUV. Still without a word, we entered Operations' small triage area, where Amiah waited beside one of the three gurneys, glaring at me as we approached.

"Why are you still here?"

"Because head office approved her reassignment to the team," Gideon said, setting me on the gurney and stepping back.

My buzz screamed back to life. I gasped, unable to hold it back.

"What idiot thought that was a good idea?" Amiah grabbed a pair of scissors and cut away the front of my ruined T-shirt.

"The Union City chief of police," Cassius said as he entered. His gaze jumped to the ragged pink scar above my heart where I'd been shot.

Amiah's face lit up with joy and all her attention turned to Cassius. "When did you get back in town?"

"The human." Cassius jerked his chin toward me and returned her smile. "And I got in this morning."

"You should have called." Amiah cut off the rest of my shirt, leaving me in my bra. And if I hadn't been in so much pain, I might have been embarrassed to be topless in front of Gideon and his brother. One day. That was all I wanted. One day where I wasn't hurt and my buzz was manageable. Was that too much to ask for?

"She took on a weretiger and fell down a flight of stairs," Gideon said.

Amiah rolled her eyes. "Of course she did." Her attention fell on my hands. "Looks like she took your power again, too."

Gideon stiffened. Oh, yeah, that was something he hadn't wanted Cassius to know.

"She can take your power?" I couldn't tell if Cassius was shocked or mad. Probably a combination of both. "That's how she can cast such a powerful light strike?"

"It's how we managed to stop Ibizual from breaking out of his prison." The muscles in Gideon's jaw tensed.

"You have to pull her from the team," Cassius said, his expression darkening. If he hadn't been mad before, he was now. "If your connection is that strong, her death will kill you. I'm not losing my little brother because of some human."

Amiah sent a blast of her healing magic into me. It wasn't her usual blazing lightning, but it set off my buzz, snapping and slicing under my skin. I clenched my jaw and squeezed my eyes shut, desperate not to cry. That would just prove to Cassius what a disaster I was.

"Amiah, be careful with her," Cassius snapped. "That's Gideon's life you're endangering."

"I'm not flooding her with enough magic to cause brain damage." Her magic vanished and the buzz eased back to a searing agony. "It shouldn't have been enough to hurt her."

"Her magical channels are burned," Gideon said.

"Well, I can't heal those, and I can't heal her without pushing my magic into those channels." Amiah doused a piece of gauze in saline and wiped the blood from the gashes on my chest. "Her concussion, cracked ribs, and fractured vertebra are healed. Do you want me to finish the gashes?"

"Will they need stitches?" I gasped before either of the guys could respond.

"Not with Jacob's claim on you." Amiah tossed the gauze into a stainless steel tray on a trolley beside her, doused another piece, and went to work on my shoulder.

"And you let Jacob claim her?" Cassius's hands clenched and unclenched as if he wanted to hit something.

"She was claimed before the brand appeared," Gideon said. "It'll work its way out of her system eventually."

Cassius glared at me. "How eventually?"

The buzz flared, and I bit back a gasp. I really needed to replace my patches. Even if they'd been working before — which I seriously doubted — Amiah's magic would have ruined their effects. *Please, just slap some bandages on my cuts and let me go.*

"It's under control," Gideon said.

Amiah snorted.

"It's under control," he said again, light flaring from his eyes. "My mate. My business."

"Not if it gets you killed," Cassius growled.

"Agent Shaw is a member of the team who's proven multiple times that she's a valuable asset. Like with any human who might be assigned to a JP team, we'll need to pay closer attention to her assignments."

The frosted glass door slid open and Marcus marched in. His gaze jumped to me sitting on the gurney in my jeans and bra, and his breath picked up.

"Marcus." Gideon shifted in front of him, blocking his view of me. Yeah, telling Cassius that I was Marcus's mate would only add more fuel to the bonfire that already involved taking Gideon's power and being claimed by Jacob. "Are the demons and Floyd locked up?"

"The demons are in holding, and Floyd is in interrogation."

"Good." Gideon gestured to the door. "Cassius, would you like the honor of digging into Floyd?"

"I think we should make him sweat," Cassius said.

"You said we need to get a jump on shutting down this operation. If you won't interrogate him, I will." Gideon strode out the door.

Cassius growled and rushed out after him.

"The brand won't let Gideon let her go," Amiah said as she taped a thick wad of gauze to my chest. "He has no choice, Marcus."

"And you think I do?" His wolf darkened his expression with a sudden feral intensity.

I shivered with the memory of all his ferocity focused on me, which made my buzz snap again.

Amiah held his gaze without any fear of his beast. "I think you don't want to."

"If you think that, you know nothing about wolves," he said, but a wave of uncertainty — real honest to goodness emotion — rushed through me.

"The brand will make her choose him."

The uncertainty bled into fear. He might be okay with sharing, but that didn't mean he wasn't afraid the brand wouldn't force us apart.

Amiah cut more tape and stuck another piece of gauze to my shoulder. "These'll scar."

"That's fine." What was a few more scars added to the ones I already had?

She peeled off her gloves, shot Marcus an angry, sad look, and left down the hall, heading deeper into Operations' mini hospital.

"Jeez, Essie," Marcus said as soon as Amiah was out of sight. He cupped my face with his hands and captured my mouth in a quick fierce kiss that stole my breath. "You were supposed to wait for me to take over."

"It wasn't like we were looking for a fight." I slid my fingers into his hair and pulled his mouth back to mine. I needed his passion to burn away my fear and heartache, reassure me that being on the team wasn't a horrible mistake. Not to mention reassure myself that he wasn't going to change his mind about us now that the crisis with Ibizual was over.

He kissed me like a starving man, his tongue plunging into my mouth and fueling my desire as if we hadn't had sex earlier that morning. I couldn't get enough of him. He, like Gideon and Jacob, was a part of my soul.

His hands skimmed my shoulders, brushed the gauze, and he froze. "You could have been killed," he murmured against my lips.

"We knew that when we decided I should be a part of the team." *Please don't change your mind. Please don't push me away again.*

"I know. I just hadn't expected it to happen so soon." He eased back and sat on the edge of the gurney. "I should have known it would happen. You're a trouble magnet."

"I'm really not."

"What have the last two weeks been?" he asked with a wry smile.

"Terrifying." I leaned in and kissed him, slowly and sensually, showing him how I felt about him. "And amazing."

"I'm barely holding it together as it is, Essie. If you keep that up, I'll take you right here in triage," he said, his voice deliciously dark.

My pulse stuttered, and my focus shifted from my God-damn-annoying buzz to him and my need for him.

His pupils dilated with desire, but his fear seeped into me again. "My suite. Now," he growled.

He reached to pick me up as the frosted glass door opened and Cassius stormed back in. The angel froze mid-step, the light in his eyes flaring. Guess all the secrets were coming out right now.

"Agent Shaw," he said, his tone frigid.

Marcus snarled, and I squeezed his hand to stop him from doing something he'd regret. Cassius was his boss, and while I knew Marcus would do anything to protect me, I didn't want him to destroy his career.

"Cassius." I met his glare head on. *Yeah, you saw what you saw, and it's none of your God-damned business.* "Does Gideon need us?"

The room's temperature dropped. Not with fear but cold seething anger. His gaze darted to Marcus, and a flicker of fire danced over his hands then vanished. "If you're going to be a part of this team, Shaw, you should observe everything. That includes this interrogation."

"Do I get to put a shirt on first?" I asked.

The ice in his eyes deepened. Very soon he was going to get me alone and tell me what he really thought of me. He couldn't hurt me physically because of Gideon, but I couldn't help wondering if he'd hurt my other guys to get to me. How much did Cassius love his brother and how far was he willing to go to protect him?

"I have a bag in the trunk of the car."

"Jacob put it in your room. I'll let you in then show you to interrogation," Marcus said. He tugged my hand, urging me to hop off the gurney.

I wasn't sure why he'd lied to Cassius — Marcus had given me my keycard earlier — but I was grateful neither of us were going to end up alone with Cassius. I didn't know if he'd ever accept our weird situation or believe Gideon when he got around to telling his brother how much he didn't want a relationship with me, but Cassius had been hit with a lot of complicated information in the last ten minutes. He'd need time to process that, and I was more than happy to give it to him.

We hurried into the hall before Cassius could argue and rushed to the elevator.

"Do you have your phone on you?" I asked.

Marcus frowned. "Of course."

"I don't have Gideon's number yet, and we should give him a heads-up that Cassius knows about us. I don't want him blindsided by all the rage we just saw."

"Yeah." He sent Gideon a text as another wave of his fear and uncertainty seeped past my buzz.

God, I wanted to confront this head on, tell him that just because I was being nice to Gideon didn't mean I was going to leave him. But then I'd have to explain how I knew what he was feeling. Besides, words were just words. I needed to show him that no matter what, I was still his. Even if we didn't have a brand tying us together, I would always be his.

We reached my room. I slid my keycard into the reader, tugged him inside, closed the door, and shoved him against it.

His eyes widened for a split second then darkened with desire. I captured his lips with mine and kissed him, willing him to feel all the desire and passion I felt for him. There'd always been something between us, and there always would be. I didn't know what was happening with me and the team, but I did know what was happening with me and Marcus. I'd known it the moment I'd seen him. I just hadn't wanted to accept it.

"You're mine," I growled against his lips.

He growled back, wrapped an arm around my back, and jerked me tight against his body. "And you're mine."

His other hand slid into my hair, capturing my head, and he took control of the kiss. Even before Marcus had become a werewolf, there'd been a ferociousness about him, a sense that something powerful and wild was curled deep within him. Now he released that ferocity with his passion. He jerked me around, pinning me to the door with his hips and grinding his erection against me.

I moaned, and he stole it with his kiss. The room spun, not from my fall down the stairs but from the whirling need spiraling tight within me. He was mine. Mine. I knew it with the certainty that I knew myself.

His hold in my hair tightened, forcing my head back. With a snarl, his canines pressed against my neck, not with enough pressure to break flesh but enough to tell me he was in charge.

I dug my nails into his scalp and snarled back.

He shuddered, his grip on me tightening, but he jerked his teeth from my neck and pressed his forehead to mine. "Essie, please," he gasped, his breath ragged. "Don't challenge my wolf. You know I have trouble controlling him when I'm with you."

"And I know he won't hurt me." He'd released his wolf the first time we'd had sex, and it didn't frighten me.

I shoved him with all my might — since I knew that was what I'd need if I had a hope of moving him — and caught him off guard. He stumbled back. His legs hit the bed, and he fell back on it.

"I could see him in your eyes last night. If you don't let him loose now, he'll take over later and you'll have no control." Then he might actually hurt me.

I stepped on my heels and pulled off my runners then reached for the button on my jeans.

"God, Essie," he groaned. "We can't. Cassius is waiting."

"He can wait." This was too important. Marcus and his wolf needed the reassurance that he was mine. The whole team needed Marcus and his wolf to be certain of that. If Marcus was worrying about us, he might miss something, and that could be dangerous for everyone. "We can make it quick."

"I don't want quick." He started to stand, and I pushed him back onto the mattress.

"Consider this your appetizer for later."

His expression grew hungry, his wolf turning it fierce. "Mine or my wolf's?"

I shimmied out of my jeans, leaving myself in my bra and undies. "This one is for your wolf."

"Then if you don't want to buy new underwear, you should take them off." His canines extended, and he dug his fingers into the comforter. "Now."

I unhooked my bra, but his wolf took over before I could step out of my undies. He grabbed me, yanked me to the bed, and leaned over me, taking the dominant position. His lips found mine and his hands roughly kneaded my breasts. I gasped at his ferocity and blazing passion.

The gasp made him growl low in his throat, and he plunged his hand down the front of my underwear and pushed two fingers into me without warning.

I bucked against him, my body reacting to his sudden invasion. My desire was as wild as his wolf's, and I was already wet and ready for him, already needing him inside me. I grabbed his T-shirt and dragged it over his head. He released me and pulled it off as I reached for the button on his jeans. He pushed my hands away, took off his boots and jeans, and stared down at me, gloriously naked.

He was stunning, a powerful specimen with ripped sleek muscles and a thick erection. He'd brought me to climax many times yesterday, knew how to work my body into a frenzy and send me crashing into bliss.

His gaze raked over me, heating my skin, and I bit my lip in anticipation of what was coming.

His attention landed on my undies. "Take those off," his wolf said.

I slid them off.

He squeezed his eyes shut. His chest rose and fell with rapid breaths, as if he was trying to regain control. Which I couldn't have. His wolf needed to be released. It needed to know I recognized it as my mate.

"Marcus," I breathed.

His eyes opened, and I skimmed my hand down my belly and dipped my fingers into my folds. The hunger in his eyes deepened, and I spread my legs so he could see better.

"This one is for your wolf." I locked gazes with him. "My mate."

His breath hitched, and for a second I had no idea how he felt about that.

Then he snarled, grabbed me, and flipped me onto my stomach. "Mine."

He jerked my hips back against his, and ground his hard length against me. My pulse thrummed faster with desire. A heat swelled in my chest, my need for him, my certainty that we belonged together.

"Mine," he said.

I shuddered with the possessive ferocity of that one word, and he drove into me with a fierce thrust. Another snarl, and he thrust again, pressing one hand against my back, holding me down. His other hand slid over my belly, and his thumb rubbed over my clit. I clung to the comforter, my head spinning with sensation, the promise of my climax twisting tighter.

He worked me into a frenzy, driving into me again and again, and when I was trembling on the edge, he grabbed my hips and picked up the pace. His nails dug into my skin, a glorious mix of pain and pleasure, until I fell over the edge, gasping with satisfaction.

With a roar, his climax seized him, and he tensed, his body tight against mine. His ferocious desire for me seared the air around me and flooded every cell with true emotion. He was a part of my soul. Now and forever.

"Mine," I gasped, and his desire within me turned to satisfied masculine pride.

GIDEON

CASSIUS STRODE THROUGH THE HEAVY METAL SECURITY DOORS INTO THE secure section of Operations, smoke from his barely contained fire magic curling around his hands.

"My mate. My business," I said before he could speak. It was bad enough he knew Shaw could take my magic and that Jacob had claimed her. Now he knew there was something between her and Marcus — and I didn't know if I was grateful Marcus had texted me a heads up or not about Cassius catching him and Essie together.

Although if I really thought about it, Marcus had been barely holding it together knowing his mate had been hurt and he'd been unable to comfort her. Which meant it had probably been Shaw who'd made sure I was prepared for Cassius's new ammunition against why having her on the team was a terrible idea.

"I'm not going to lose another brother because of sheer stupidity," he shot back. "If you won't take her off your team, I will."

"If she hadn't been a part of our team, Ibizual would be free." And the archnephilim would still be murdering my old squad members.

She'd more than proven she belonged and the others all agreed. As much as it would be easier to me to ignore the call of our mating brand until she and Marcus had lived a long happy life together, forcing her off the team wasn't the solution I'd initially hoped it would be.

If I kicked her off the team, it would fall apart. Marcus would follow her and Jacob probably would as well, and without Jacob, I doubted Kol would stay. Not to mention the idea of some other human on the team didn't sit right with me. Which was crazy since I should be trying to stay as far away from Shaw as possible.

But no one, not even Cassius, could deny that she couldn't pull her own weight. She'd proven she could hold her own in a fight and did what had to be done, even when Marcus was in danger.

Not to mention, relationship complications aside, she fit. Kol didn't bother or distract her— well, not too much. She certainly faired better than some of other female agents we'd worked with and they'd been supers, fully aware of Kol's powers. He even seemed comfortable around her, which was telling in and of itself. He wasn't always comfortable around women. He hid it well behind jokes and smiles, but there were times I could see the shadow of what he'd gone through in his eyes, knew he didn't trust himself and his magic and, given how much time had passed since his capture, he probably never would fully trust himself.

"We need a human on the team and she's more than qualified," I added. "Any human would have had trouble facing off against a shifter by herself. The fact that she managed to subdue Webb is proof that she's the best human for the job."

"She's your mate," Cassius replied.

Not for another sixty or seventy years.

"That shifter could have killed her," he pressed, "and if your bond really is so strong that she can take your magic that would have killed you too."

"I'm well aware of the danger."

"Doesn't look like it to me." Sparks erupted from Cassius's hands and he sucked in a sharp breath, pulling his magic back under his skin. I'd never seen him so out of control before, not since we'd been told of our brother's death. He'd seemed fine when I'd taken Zella's body back to the Realm of Celestial Light, sympathetic and upset to my plight, but not furious and determined to lock her up in my suite.

Of course, seeing Shaw injured — and on her first day — had been a sudden, brutal reminder to him of how fragile humans were and how precarious my life now was. Our youngest brother, Dominic, hadn't been bound to a weak human, but he'd thrown himself into a dangerous situation, going undercover into Michael's army, and had paid the ultimate price. I wouldn't be surprised if in Cassius's eyes, the risk I was taking by keeping Shaw on the team was worse than the risk Dominic had taken.

On top of that, Cassius knew how I felt about the whole mess. Well, not the *whole* mess. I hadn't told him about Marcus and Shaw. But I had bared my soul to him, revealed how angry and frustrated and heartbroken I was that I was bonded to a human and not to Zella.

I shouldn't have said anything. But I'd been upset and there was no way I'd have been able to hide the fact that I had a mate. Everyone at Operations knew and the second he'd returned from his assignment in Rome Cassius would have found out as well.

That, and the shock of learning destiny had bound me to a human who was in love with Marcus, along with Zella's murder, had been too much. I'd needed to tell someone. Usually I turned to Jacob. I'd picked him to be my second in command because of how well we worked together and his calming presence, but he was also bound to Shaw and it didn't feel right to dump my feelings on him.

Why couldn't Shaw have just done what she'd been told? Stick to surveillance until Marcus could take over. Had that been too much to ask for? A few days of her not ending up in triage — and not drawing unwanted attention to herself — would have shown Cassius that she fit on the team, wasn't endangering my life, and that everything was fine.

But no. She just had to pick a fight with a weretiger, had to fall down a flight of stairs, and had to end up bleeding and weak and everything she wasn't in front of my brother who not only had a vested interest in kicking her off the team but had also been commanded by head office to figure out if our team needed to be broken up and reassigned.

"If you can't think straight around her, I will," Cassius said.

"I'm thinking just fine." Except I wasn't and I knew it.

"I've been given command of your team—"

"You can't just dismantle it," I said, fighting to keep my voice even. If I showed too much emotion he'd think I was losing control — because *I* was the in-control brother. "She was recommended by the UCPD's Chief and has been approved as an agent. There's protocols for dismissing an agent."

"I'm well aware." The muscles in Cassius's jaw flexed. "She has one strike against her. Three if you count the other two messes she was involved in as a UCPD officer. If she's screwing up your team, I will dismiss her. I'll dismiss the whole team if I have to."

"Cassius—"

"You don't get to argue with me on this. I've been given a direct order from head office. Your team is mine. This op is mine. I out rank you, agent," he snapped. "One more screw up and she's gone. Don't make me reassign everyone."

I opened my mouth to argue and sparks burst from his hands, hissing as they hit the floor.

"You, Jacob, *and* Marcus all have emotional entanglements with her," he pressed. "If she goes down, you won't be able to hold it together and get the job done."

"Of course we will." The lie twisted in my chest and my angelic soul screamed for me to correct myself but I clamped my mouth shut. I'd lost it when she'd been shot. I hadn't been able to think of anything else, had let Logan get the key, and had left a park full of bodies to race her back to Operations. If she was critically wounded again, without a doubt I'd lose it again.

Cassius's eyes narrowed.

"Shaw values the lives of the innocent as much as you and I do," I forced out. Not a lie... but not addressing his disbelief either. "She's a good officer and she'll make a good agent." And a good mate.

I shoved that thought down deep. I couldn't admit that. Not even to myself. Not yet. I had to stay strong, my emotions frozen. I had to.

The memory of her in my arms, the heat and warmth and rightness of holding her, squeezed my chest. Without her in critical condition — like the last time I'd held her — I'd been unable to ignore how it felt to hold her, how my heart sang when she leaned into me for comfort, how I wanted— *needed* to give her more.

I hadn't wanted to let go and put her in the car, and when she'd grabbed my wrist and her eyes had begged me to stay with her while she was in pain, I'd almost broken. Everything within me said she was mine. Mine to protect and love and worship. It didn't matter that I didn't know her and couldn't afford to until she'd had her happy full life with Marcus. Destiny said we belonged together.

Pushing her away, telling myself over and over again that I didn't want her, and keeping a frigid hold on my emotions so she could be with Marcus was killing me, and working with her, learning more about her would only make things worse. But kicking her off the team wasn't an option as much as Cassius thought it was. The only thing that was keeping me strong right now was knowing Marcus was her true heart's desire and that I would get my turn.

And I would, damn it. I would! But not yet. I wasn't going to break her heart by succumbing to something neither of us wanted. I couldn't do that to her.

ESSIE

MARCUS AND I QUICKLY CLEANED UP AND I APPLIED FOUR NEW NICOTINE patches in the hope it would control my buzz, then we headed down to the secure section of Operations. I wished we'd had time to cuddle so I could cement the certainty with him and his wolf that we were well and truly mates, but keeping Cassius waiting longer than necessary was a bad idea.

I'd never understood this mate thing before. Especially with shifters. It had always seemed overly possessive and, being on the outside looking in, sometimes without reason. The attraction was often instant, the shifter's instinct recognizing his soul's mate before the human side of him did.

Now I understood. I'd fully accepted our bond and that knowledge thrummed within me. He was mine. Just like Gideon was mine. And Jacob. And Kol.

I pushed those thoughts back. Fate said Gideon was also my soul mate and something in the core of my being said Jacob was as well. But Kol? We didn't even have a whisper of a connection. Not like the connection I had with the others. My attraction to him had to be because he was an incubus and radiated sexual desire without even thinking about it.

And what I really needed to be thinking about instead was how to manage the situation with Cassius. My complicated relationships were still so new and fragile, and while I'd secured Marcus's certainty, I still needed to work out a truce with Gideon, and have a heart-to-heart with Jacob.

The secure section of Operations lay at the back of the converted 19ᵗʰ century warehouse. It sat on the first floor beyond two sets of heavy metal security doors that were locked on both sides with fingerprint scanners.

Cassius stood in the hall a few feet inside the second security door, holding a blue file folder and glaring at us as we approached. Gideon stood beside him, his expression hard and icy, while Jacob leaned against the wall opposite them. He appeared relaxed, but he radiated more vampiric intensity than he usually did, and a hint of heat in the air around me suggested someone was upset.

The heat could have been coming from Cassius, but I suspected if I was going to feel his emotions, they would be icy fury again. For now, he was emotionally locked down. Which meant the heat was most likely coming from Gideon. Just great.

My buzz softened the closer I got to Gideon. It wasn't enough to ease all of the biting agony, but enough to help me think straight, and now the gentle electric hum of his magic in our brand tingled over my forearm. Relief filled me. I hadn't realized how much I'd needed to feel that, how much not being able to feel it through the burn of my buzz had worried me.

"Agents," Cassius said, the word clipped and hard. He turned on his heel, unlocked a door with his thumbprint, and stormed inside.

"He can disband the team," Gideon said, his tone just as clipped as his brother's. "Play by the God damned rules." He unlocked the same door with his thumbprint and left the three of us in the hall.

"I take it Cassius knows about the whole mess of our situation." Jacob pushed away from the wall and entered the room beside the one with Cassius and Gideon, this one not locked by a fingerprint reader.

I followed him into an observation room with low lighting and a large one-way glass window looking into an interrogation room. Floyd sat facing us, handcuffed to a stainless steel table that was bolted into the floor, and Cassius sat across from him, the closed file folder on the table between them. Gideon stood by the door, his arms crossed, angelic light radiating from his eyes.

"Amiah spilled most of it," I said.

"Then Cassius caught me being an idiot." Marcus shut the door behind us and stepped possessively close to me. "I should have controlled my wolf better. But it's having issues, and Essie was hurt. I'd thought Cassius was with Gideon."

"Does Gideon know how serious my claim is and about our arrangement?" Jacob asked.

"No, but we should tell him about it sooner rather than later." I didn't want to complicate the situation between me and Gideon any more than it already was. And if Cassius learned about the deal I had with Marcus and Jacob before Gideon did, there'd be no hope of a truce between us.

Jacob glanced at Marcus. Both had hesitation in their eyes, and I couldn't disagree. Telling Gideon needed to be handled carefully.

"I should do it." I didn't know when, but it had to be soon. Victoria could summon Jacob at any time to pay his debt to her for helping us with Ibizual, and twenty-four hours after that, I'd need to help Jacob recover. And then, because Jacob's claim on me was so strong and I was bite locked, I'd need Marcus to help me release Jacob's magic. There was just too much that needed to happen for Gideon or Cassius not to notice something was up.

In the interrogation room, Cassius drummed his fingers on the closed folder. "We have you on assault of a JP agent."

Floyd huffed. "I didn't touch the vamp, just the bitch cop he was with."

"That bitch cop is a JP agent." Cassius's tone remained even, but sharp icy fury flickered around me, telling me how he really felt.

Then Floyd's fear, colder than Cassius's rage but not as sharp, enveloped me. The weretiger leaned as far back in the chair as his handcuffed hands would allow in an obvious attempt to look unconcerned. "Everyone knows there ain't no humans on a JP team."

"There is now." Cassius opened the folder. "You've done time for assault before. This isn't a third strike, but I doubt the judge will care."

"Hey, I barely touched her." He pointed to his charred shirt and the now half-healed burn covering his chest. "She almost killed me."

"You threw her down a set of stairs," Gideon said.

"Dude, she tripped."

Cassius's sharp cold blasted around me again, and his back and shoulders tensed. "Her life is valuable."

Yeah, valuable because I was permanently connected to his brother, not because I was me.

"I will personally tell the judge how valuable her life is."

Floyd's eyes flashed wide, and the temperature plummeted to a teeth-chattering freeze. He didn't know the extent of Cassius's threat, but the rage in the angel's voice said it all. Vengeance would be his. Funny how when I'd first met Gideon, I'd thought he was overly emotional for an angel. They were known to be emotionally frigid. But clearly Cassius was the hot-head of the family.

"I could also tell the judge how helpful you were." Cassius's tone remained dark and dangerous, as if daring Floyd to reject the offer.

"What kind of help do you want?" Floyd asked, his voice small, all sense of bravado gone.

Frost gathered on the backs of my hands, and I shoved them into my pockets to hide it. Jeez. I wished Cassius wasn't being so aggressive with Floyd. Except I suspected the angel needed to vent, and it was better Floyd than me.

"We know you deal zip." Cassius turned to another page in the folder.

I had no idea how long the team had known about Floyd, but it didn't surprise me that they hadn't picked him up until now. They'd probably spent a lot of time watching him, seeing who he met with in an attempt to identify those higher up the ranks of the organization.

Floyd's gaze darted to whatever was on the page then back to Cassius. "I'm not a snitch."

Marcus snaked a hand across my belly and drew me back against his body. A hint of mist joined Floyd's chill, and Jacob shifted beside us.

"There's only one deal on the table, and it's a limited time offer." Cassius closed the folder, stood, and turned to Gideon. "Looks like we should talk to the demons."

"They won't tell you anything," Floyd sneered.

"You sure about that?" Cassius asked. "They haven't been with you when you picked up a new supply or handed off your earnings?"

The frost swept up my forearms. I shivered, but I couldn't tell if Floyd's fear was because of Cassius or his employers.

Marcus wrapped his other arm around me, and I leaned into his warmth, hoping it would melt the frost before he noticed, since I couldn't just leave the room. Not without drawing suspicion.

Cassius raised an eyebrow at Floyd, who pinched his lips tight.

"Guess they haven't overheard you talking on the phone, either." Gideon pressed his thumb to the fingerprint scanner and unlocked the door. "Pretty sure one of the demons will want to cooperate."

Cassius strode toward the door and Gideon opened it for him.

"Doubt we'll even have to remind them of the penalty for trying to kill a JP agent."

"Pretty sure it'll be increased," Gideon said, following him out. "Everyone knows humans are fragile."

Floyd jerked forward, his fear blasting around me, and my breath misted.

Shit. My pulse stalled and panic — my panic — seized me. I couldn't stay here. I had to get away from Marcus and Jacob before they noticed something was weird with me—

No. I had to face this. That was the plan.

I'd known that if I stayed, they'd learn about my magic. I just never thought I'd be discovered on my very first day on the job. All I could do was stick to the lie, since there was no way out of this situation. There wasn't anywhere I could hide where Gideon wouldn't find me. And now that I'd completed the mating bond with Marcus, he'd turn over heaven and earth to find me as well. Running wouldn't work. *Please, God. Don't let this be the worst decision of my life.*

"Wait." Floyd jerked to his feet, rattling the cuffs against the metal bar.

Gideon glanced back at him, ice in his eyes. Floyd shivered. So did I.

"Why are you cold?" Marcus whispered, his breath hot against the side of my cheek.

A swell of warmth, his affection for me, bled into the cold. But my mother's words, words she'd told me again and again, rushed through me. *They can never know the truth. No one will understand. They'll think you're one of Michael's monsters, even though you aren't. You were born. Not made.*

Except I couldn't run forever, not with my soul saying this was where I belonged, working with these guys.

Marcus's grip on me tightened. "Essie, you're shivering."

"It's just a chill," I said, unable to force out the lie, years of fear screaming I had to keep my magic a secret.

"I know when they're getting their next shipment of stolen Divifend," Floyd said.

"It's more than a chill." More of Marcus's warmth seeped into me. I clung to it, trying to push out Cassius's anger and Floyd's fear. If I could get it to ease up, Marcus would relax and this conversation could happen another time. When I was ready.

But Jacob brushed the back of his hand across my cheek, his flesh hot against mine, and frowned. More ice whispered through Marcus's warmth.

Great. Now I was feeling Jacob's worry.

"We should call Kol," he said. "His increased body temperature might help."

"I'm okay." I was such a fool. I shouldn't have allowed myself to get close to Marcus. I shouldn't have given into the need for him or the need to belong. I knew joining the team was dangerous, and I'd still gone ahead with it.

But God, I wanted him. Wanted *them*. Wanted to belong, be missed by someone, thought of, cared for. And now I was terrified of losing the guys.

The plan. Remember the God damned plan. It will work. It has to work.

"You're not okay," Marcus growled. "Is it Gideon's brand? It's not our mating. Shifters and humans are supposed to be compatible."

"Could be a delayed reaction to her light strike," Jacob said.

"But she wasn't this cold last night."

"You know, I'm still in the room." I tried to push out of Marcus's arms to put some space between us on the slim chance I'd be able to think straight, but his grip tightened.

"We need to get you to Amiah." His fear joined the others' and the frost swept up to my elbows and my breath misted again. "What the hell is that?"

Stick to the plan.

"Is that your breath?" Jacob's vampiric intensity turned his eyes fully black.

Marcus's fear grew stronger and frost formed on my cheeks.

"Essie," he growled. "There's frost on your cheeks again. I thought that was from the magic of Ibizual's key manifesting."

"It's—" *Remember the lie. It's logical. You could have a super somewhere deep in your family tree. The mating brand could be affecting you.* "I'm not sure what it is. It started after the archnephilim. But it always goes away. Best guess is that it's your fear or worry."

Please believe me. Please work. I need this team. I need them.

"His fear?" Jacob asked.

"Yours, too. And Gideon's, Cassius's, and Floyd's." The frost slipped down my neck and my teeth chattered. "I think."

"How many times has this happened?" Marcus asked.

"Not many." My soul twisted at the lie. But it would be worse if they knew the truth. Gideon's brand wouldn't be enough to protect me from the fury the world still held toward nephilim. Hell, it probably wouldn't be enough to protect me from Gideon. And Marcus— I didn't want to think about Marcus's reaction, how angry he'd be because I'd been so adamant to avoid the supernatural world.

Please. Believe me.

"It's got to have something to do with Gideon's brand," Jacob said.

"But she's human. Would the angelic mating brand really give her magic?" Marcus's fear shifted, and a strange hope whispered across my senses.

I tried not to hold my breath, waiting for them to come to the obvious conclusion. That I was a nephilim pretending to be human.

"Who knows." Jacob rubbed my forearms, melting some of the frost. "The archnephilim's magic could have affected you, as well. Not to mention blasting all that divine light into your body and channeling Gideon's magic. Who knows what could have changed in you."

My thoughts tripped at his words, and the fear churning in my gut eased. A bit. Did they actually believe me? I couldn't hear any suspicion in their voices. Not that they'd voice it in front of me if they thought I was a nephilim, but given how I was reacting to everyone's fear, the temperature would have changed if they were hiding such serious concerns.

"And who knows what's going to change," Jacob said.

Marcus's fear and hope flared with a nauseating snap from cold to hot. "She could have more magic?"

"Gideon's brand is only a few weeks old. It could take years before we know the full effects of it." Jacob's hands tightened on my arms, his body tensed, and his gaze grew unfocused. "Shit."

My pulse stuttered. "What is it?" I didn't think he'd realized I was a nephilim since his gaze wasn't focused on me, but something was wrong.

"Victoria's calling me." He pulled his phone from his pocket.

"She isn't even giving you a day to recover?" Marcus asked.

"Doesn't look like it." Jacob sent a text and took a jerky step toward the door.

"And she's compelling you to go to her?" Marcus growled.

Jacob staggered into the hall and pressed his hands to the wall across from the door, as if that would keep him from moving farther. "She's never been patient."

In the observation room, Gideon pulled out his phone, frowned, and glanced at the one-way window.

Cassius glanced at him, an eyebrow raised in question.

"I told you first," Floyd said, his voice sharp with panic. "The deal is mine. The courier is going to deliver the Divifend today."

Gideon jerked his chin to the door, and Cassius stood.

"We have a deal." Floyd's fear swept more frost over my cheeks.

"We have a deal if your intel checks out." Cassius strode to the door. "And not before then."

Gideon unlocked the door, and they stepped into the hall. Marcus and I hurried to join them.

"She's summoning you already?" Gideon asked.

"Can she wait until we've stopped the handoff of the Divifend?" Cassius asked. Guess he'd been brought up to speed on Jacob's deal with Victoria.

"You've met my sire." Jacob shot Cassius a dark look. "What do you think?"

"We've got this," Gideon said. "See you back here in twenty-four."

"Vampires still have to abide by consent laws with other vampires," Cassius said.

"Not my first rodeo with Victoria." Jacob shifted toward the doors leading out of Operations' secured section.

"Still," Cassius said.

"She plays harder than I like, but she's actually a very giving lover." Jacob's gaze jumped to me for a second, and a whisper of mist curled around me. "We couldn't have stopped Ibizual without her help, and given the stresses of the last few days— This isn't a hardship."

His claim — no, that thing within me that said our connection was deeper than just his claim — twisted in my chest. I wanted to be the one to release his stress, ease his misty sadness hanging in the air, not because I was jealous of Victoria — although I was, a little bit — but because my soul ached at his pain, at something I could mend just by embracing whatever it was that lay between us. Just like I'd done with Marcus and his wolf.

"Go," Gideon said. "We've got this."

Jacob hurried out the security doors, then rushed down the hall and out of sight with his vampiric speed.

"More Divifend means more zip on the streets, and that means more humans and supers will die," Cassius said. "We need to move on this handoff and track the Divifend back to the new lab."

"Agreed." Marcus shifted as if he wanted to step closer to me, but managed to stay at arm's length. "My meeting with the wolf pack alpha wasn't good. They have ten new zip deaths. Found a group of eight teens dead in the wolves' forest last night and two more in their apartment."

"Marcus—" Gideon said

"This isn't your op." Light flared from Cassius's eyes. "The mayor is breathing down the JP's neck about the human deaths and attacks from addicts suffering violent hallucinations. I won't let you turn this into another mess. Grab some lunch. We meet in Summer's lab in twenty to go over the op's details."

He marched away, taking the rest of the chill with him.

"I know he's your brother and all, but—" Marcus ran a hand through his dark locks. "How long is he supposed to be here?"

"Longer now because of you two." Gideon glared at me, the ice in his eyes breaking my heart.

"We should talk," I said. Now wasn't the best time to have a conversation about my arrangement with Marcus and Jacob, but I didn't think any time would be good.

"Is this about the upcoming operation, Agent Shaw?"

"You know it isn't."

"Jeez, Gideon." Marcus stepped possessively close to me. "Stop being a dick."

"If you want her here so badly, stop thinking with yours. Your wolf doesn't have to worry." Gideon's gaze captured mine. "The brand hasn't changed how I feel about you and it never will."

The truth in his words and accompanying emotion shook me to my core. He didn't want me, and he'd only let me stay on the team because the guys had threatened to leave if I did.

"Don't give Cassius a reason to disband the team." He stormed away, his desperation flickering in my heart, a mirror to my own need to be a part of this team. He needed this team so much that he was willing to let me stay even though just looking at me hurt. I reminded him of what he'd lost, what he'd wanted with Zella. Not talking to him was probably the best truce we were going to get, except I still needed to tell him about my arrangement with Marcus and Jacob.

Now, however, with his hurt and need still tightening my chest, wasn't the time. I had twenty-four hours. Maybe Cassius would be gone by then and the team could actually start figuring out our new normal.

ESSIE

"Come on," Marcus said. "Cassius works like Gideon. We should grab food while we can."

I followed him out of the secured section and down the hall, heading toward the cafeteria and — if my growing buzz was any indication — away from Gideon. "If we're going to make this work, we should be more careful while he's here."

"I keep trying to tell my wolf that." Marcus's fingers closest to me twitched, as if he wanted to hold my hand but was resisting the urge. "I've fought him for four and half years over you and he doesn't give a shit about what Cassius thinks."

"Then tell him to care about what I think." Gideon needed this team, and so did I. "Let's not give Cassius more reason to stay."

"Yeah. He might have been sent here to review the team, but he won't leave until he believes Gideon is safe." Marcus glanced at me, his wolf, a feral energy radiating from his expression, threatening to break through. "That means ensuring your bond is safe, but, given that he already knows we're in a relationship, I'm not sure how we can convince him of that."

We rounded the corner and crossed from the old section to the new one, a five-story high rise added to the back of the 19th century warehouse. Ahead, I could hear the rumble of voices in the cafeteria.

"The best we can do with that is not constantly remind him of it." We could get more elaborate by staging a fight and pretending we'd broken up, but that might cause other problems, like Cassius thinking one of us needed to be transferred to another unit for the health of the team.

Marcus huffed a soft laugh. "Good thing you didn't decide to move into my suite."

The temperature didn't change. I couldn't tell how he felt about that. Of course, maybe the emotion was subtle, and I couldn't feel it past my buzz. "I thought we should talk about that first."

"You know you're welcome to move in. Even before we completed our bond, you were welcome."

We reached the top of the shallow steps leading down to the cafeteria, and my pulse stuttered with fear. It was close to lunchtime, more than half of the tables were occupied, and at least a dozen of those occupants were angels.

I forced myself to keep moving down the stairs and past the still-under-repair rock wall water-feature that had been damaged during the fight with the archnephilim. They didn't know I was a nephilim, and Marcus and Jacob had believed my lie about my magic. They had no reason to suspect me. *Just stay calm.*

But there was a lull in the conversation and all eyes turned to me. My stomach churned and my buzz snapped through my chest. I gritted my teeth, trying not to react. I wanted this. I wanted to live and work in the one building where all the angels in Union City lived because I wanted to be with my guys.

"You do know you're welcome, right?" Marcus asked.

I dragged my attention back to him. "I know. I just—"

He headed toward the hot-food serving stations manned by a squat man who could have been human or any number of supernatural beings. Thankfully, his eyes didn't glow like an angel's, and I managed to grab a tray and keep it from shaking. So long as I didn't look at the angels behind me, I'd be fine. Really.

"This is just a big adjustment. I've been living on my own since I was seventeen."

"Yeah, and I have a lot of furniture and stuff," he said, referring to my nearly-empty apartment with my second-hand furniture — because what was the point in having a lot of stuff if you had to drop everything and flee on a moment's notice? "I'd embrace a minimalistic lifestyle for you."

"You know that's not why I kept my room."

"Essie." His voice softened and warmth fluttered around me for a second before my buzz consumed it. "Whatever you need. Always."

"The usual?" the man behind the counter asked Marcus with a smile, then his attention jumped to me and my right forearm where Gideon's brand glimmered as if it were real gold embedded in my skin and reflecting the sunlight. His eyes widened with surprise. "You're Gideon's human mate."

Those at the tables closest to us sat forward.

"The mated human."

"Have you seen a brand before?"

"—hundred years."

"Longer."

"No, I heard there was a pair during the war."

"—shouldn't be here. It's too dangerous for Gideon."

"Only here because of that brand."

The murmurs swept through the cafeteria, and I clenched my tray, desperate to keep my hands from shaking. This kind of attention— *any* kind of attention was bad.

And jeez, four patches and my buzz still wasn't under control!

Chris, a guy in his mid-twenties who'd helped with the cleanup at the cemetery last night, tipped his chair back and leaned closer. From the hint of feral intensity in his pale blue eyes, my best guess was that he was a shifter of some kind, but I didn't know for sure. He looked exhausted, as if he hadn't slept last night, and given the mess we'd left, that wouldn't have surprised me.

"I hear they've finally given in and put you on the team," he said.

"Un hunh." I didn't know what to say to that. From everyone's reaction, it seemed they all thought like Cassius, that I was a liability endangering Gideon's life.

"It's about time." He flashed me a warm smile. "Get the chicken. It's really good today."

"Ah... sure." My buzz snapped up my neck, making the muscles twitch.

He turned back to his lunch partner, a broad-shouldered angel in black fatigues. "Gideon lucked the hell out. The whole team did. That human can kick some serious ass."

The angel looked surprised, and Chris started recounting my *incidents* with the team as if they were major successes and not just a desperate fight to stay alive.

"She'll have the chicken to go," Marcus said, nudging my arm with his elbow.

I jerked my attention back to the server. "Yeah. The chicken."

"Make that two," Marcus said.

The guy filled two takeout boxes with a chicken, broccoli, and rice mixture, and handed it to us. It smelled amazing, and my stomach growled, reminding me I hadn't had much to eat lately. Most of my meals in the last little while had been eaten on the go or missed completely.

Marcus turned to head to an empty table deeper into the cafeteria when Chris shoved the empty chair beside him into Marcus's path.

"Come on, don't keep her all to yourself," Chris said. "Introduce the new hire."

Marcus glanced at me, his expression questioning. Did I want to join them?

"Sure." I sat in the offered chair. As much as I didn't want to sit with the angel — who was looking at me with awe — I needed to make an effort to fit in. I now worked and lived here. I needed to not look like an outsider any more than I already was.

"We don't have a lot of time." Marcus took the chair across from me and dug into his lunch.

Chris's expression turned grim. "I saw Cassius in the hall. He didn't look happy."

"Is Cassius ever happy?" Marcus asked.

"I think I saw him happy once," the angel said with a chuckle. He held his hand out to me. "Nathaniel. Did you really take on two feral vampires with just another human?" His warm brown gaze dipped to the ragged scar on my neck.

"Essie Shaw. I wasn't given much of a choice." I took a bite of the chicken and savored the rich juicy flavor. Wow. Chris hadn't lied. It really was good.

"And the ferals' nest? Did they really come back to life?"

"I hope I never run into that again," Marcus said between mouthfuls. He glanced at his phone. "Two more minutes. Then we need to run."

Nathaniel shook his head, his expression still awed. "We all thought it was trouble, a human mated to an angel. But if half of what Chris says is true— Wow, Gideon is lucky."

I glanced at Marcus, afraid the comment would rile his wolf, but instead he met my gaze with a satisfied, heated look. "Lucky indeed," he said. "Let's go."

I shoveled in two more mouthfuls and decided not to take the food up to Summer's lab. Chris said he'd return our trays, and we hurried to the second floor, my emotions a strange mix of fear and hope.

Nathaniel hadn't been angry or disgusted by me, and Chris seemed to think I could more than hold my own on the team. I could make this work. I could do this job, a job I knew in my heart I was supposed to be doing, and be with my guys.

My buzz was even easing off a bit, but that was because I was getting closer to Gideon, not because of the patches. If they were working, they'd have kicked in while Cassius and Gideon had been interrogating Floyd... which worried me, but not enough to dampen the joy of being exactly where I belonged.

Summer's lab was a large room filled with gleaming stainless steel tables and shelves, and a white spotless floor. Machines hummed at various stations, one of the many computers was running something with images and pictures flickering in rapid succession on the screen, and one whole wall was lined with locked cabinets.

The petite angel stood near a keyboard, looking at a satellite image on a large screen that hung on the wall beside her. Gideon and Cassius were staring at it as well. Both had their arms crossed, their hard expressions identical, which accentuated the family resemblance. Both could have been poster boys for angelkind with the same chiseled jaw, straight nose, and broad shoulders. Clean cut and handsome, radiating divine light from their summer-sky eyes. But only Gideon made my pulse pick up with a yearning and heartache I didn't fully understand and didn't want.

Kol stood a few feet behind them, leaning against an empty table, looking sexy as hell, his thick black hair hanging low, nearly veiling his eyes, adding to his bad boy aura. God, he was just standing there. He wasn't even looking at me.

The memory of my dream swept through me and drew a shiver of need.

His attention jumped to me, and liquid desire swelled in my chest and sank low. My breath stalled and I was captured for a long, sensual second, then he rolled his eyes at me, and the swell of desire — that had to have been his magic affecting me — eased.

"You were supposed to call me," Kol said as Marcus stepped past him to stand beside Gideon.

I hung back with Kol to keep a professional distance between me and Marcus. "Not until I got off work."

"Not what I was talking about," he whispered as he shot a glare at Marcus's back then gave me a knowing look.

Crap. Right. He needed a warning when Marcus and I were going to have sex to shield himself against our sexual energy. Even when we weren't releasing Jacob's magic, Kol had said our energy was too powerful and the last time that had happened, he'd ended up high.

"Are you okay?" I tried to read his expression. He didn't look high, but an hour had almost passed since I'd reassured Marcus's wolf. Kol might have found a way to release the excess magic.

He leaned toward me and hellfire danced in his eyes. "I felt it coming this time so I could prepare. But jeez, Essie—"

Gideon scowled at us, and Kol snapped his mouth shut and straightened, shifting away from me.

"We have less than an hour before the courier delivers the Divifend." Cassius pointed to a squat rectangular building with a gravel parking lot along one side and the back. It sat on a tired block of mixed commercial and residential buildings with a tree-filled ravine running behind it. "Floyd says the courier will make the drop at this bar, Hacksaw."

Not a surprise. There were a lot of potential places where an exchange like this could happen, abandoned areas of town, parts of the Supers' Quarter, and other bars that attracted a seedy clientele, but Hacksaw was one of the seediest and sat right at the edge of the still-occupied parts of Union City. If you were coming or going anywhere east, like New York or Washington, you ended up on Hacksaw's road. No one would notice guys coming or going from the place and a courier could make a quick hand-off then get back on the expressway. Most of Hacksaw's clientele were human members of the Nephilim Purge, a biker gang that had formed after the war and had hunted the remaining nephilim, often killing them gruesomely and posting it on social media.

"Do we know who's making the pickup?" Kol asked.

"No," Gideon said. "All we know is one of the bodyguards is a pit fiend and the pickup man usually has two guys with him."

"Let me guess." Kol hopped up and sat on the table. "We don't know who's making the drop, either."

"Or how many guys he'll have with him," Cassius said.

Kol flashed a wicked grin. "This sounds like fun."

"Fun?" Marcus growled.

"Yeah, you know, like the jobs we used to do before we started fighting feral vampire zombies and archnephilim," Kol said. "Anything's got to be easier than that."

"True." Marcus turned back to Gideon and Cassius. "So what's the plan?"

"Since we don't know any of the players, we need to identify the bag of Divifend." Cassius's gaze met Kol's. "You're magically sensitive. Do you think you can sense a bag of Divifend?"

"Depends on how big the bag is," Kol said. "I'd still need to be within the room and concentrating. Divifend isn't powerful, so I won't be able to sense it from a distance."

Cassius gave a tight nod. "Then we send you in, you identify the pickup man, and we trail him back to the zip lab."

"If that's the plan, Essie should come in with me," Kol said.

Light flared from Cassius's eyes. "No. We—"

"Trust me. If I go in alone, I'll be noticed." Kol's expression turned apologetic. "Unless I'm walking into a demon bar, I get noticed. If I go in with Essie, everyone will jump to conclusions and won't think twice about me."

Which was true. I'd seen him walk into a hospital emergency department and every female eye, along with a few male ones, had turned toward him regardless of what they were doing. And as soon as he'd sat with me, the doctor had immediately assumed we were having sex, even after Kol had said he was a JP agent.

"Absolutely not," Cassius said. "I'm not putting Agent Shaw in the line of fire."

"Identifying a pickup man isn't being in the line of fire," Marcus said, his tone calm with no hint of his wolf in his voice, making his statement sound entirely reasonable... which it was. "Besides, Kol is useful for a lot of things, but being unnoticed in a public place isn't one of them. If he's the only one who can sense the Divifend, then sending him in there with Essie is the best plan."

The muscles in Gideon's jaw flexed. He looked like he wanted to say something, but he kept his mouth shut. I didn't know what Cassius had said to him while Marcus and I were having lunch, but it was clear words had been exchanged.

I kept my mouth shut as well. While I wanted to be useful to the team, speaking up would only draw Cassius's attention.

"If she's a member of the team, then we need to use her skills like the rest of us," Kol said.

Cassius's glare deepened, and the room's temperature dropped. "Being your arm candy isn't a skill."

"No, but being dismissed as harmless while also being excellent backup is." Kol cocked an eyebrow. "You'd be wasting an opportunity to ensure this op's success by keeping her on the sidelines."

"She did apprehend Floyd," Gideon said.

"And was tossed down a flight of stairs." Cassius's cold deepened.

Kol jerked his chin to the screen. "Then it's a good thing the bar is one story."

Ice filled Cassius's eyes. He opened his mouth then snapped it shut. His cold shuddered but I couldn't tell what that meant.

"Fine," he growled. "But if she gets hurt, I'm pulling her from the team."

Marcus's wolf snapped across his expression, sharpening his cheeks and darkening his eyes. "You pull her from the team, you destroy her career."

"She doesn't need a career. She's Gideon's mate." Fire danced over Cassius's hands.

The guys glared at each other in an obvious attempt for dominance without actually fighting. Hot and cold snapped around me, Cassius's hate and Marcus's protective fury. This wasn't getting us anywhere, and it certainly didn't give Cassius reason to believe everything was fine and he could leave.

"We have an hour." No one looked at me. "Cassius," I snapped, using my command-the-perp voice and drawing his attention. "You're in command. What's the plan?"

He held my gaze, his cold forcing me to clench my teeth to prevent them from chattering.

"Go in with Kol," he said, his tone sounding more like a dare then a command, making me wonder what his threshold for "hurt" was. If I got something as small as a black eye, was I off the team? Probably.

ESSIE

WITH NO TIME TO GO HOME AND FIND GANG-BAR APPROPRIATE CLOTHING that covered Gideon's brand, I accept a loan from Summer. We agreed my jeans and runners would do — since I didn't want to wear a dress and be flashing the world if I got into a fight — and I changed from my T-shirt to a form-fitting top that revealed an obscene amount of cleavage. I used some of her makeup to look like I was actually Kol's arm candy, but kept my hair in a ponytail to keep it out of my face, then I hurried down to the garage to meet the guys.

Kol was the first one I saw. He stood on the other side of the glass door in the garage with his back to me, wearing a pair of tight leather pants that made his ass look amazing and holding a motorcycle helmet and a leather jacket. He turned to face me, and my thoughts stuttered. I thought he'd looked stunning before just hanging out in Summer's lab, but now he was breathtaking.

He exuded dangerous sexual need. His black T-shirt clung to his perfectly sculpted chest and arms, and all I could think about was running my hands across all that hard muscle. Hellfire danced in his eyes, flaring as his gaze landed on me, and I staggered to a stop, too stunned to make it out the door.

"If I'd known leather pants were your thing, I would have bought a pair," Marcus whispered in my ear, making me jump as his hot breath filled me with more yearning. I hadn't even heard him approach.

"So I'm allowed to drool over the incubus now?" I asked, breathless.

"Drool over anyone you want." The temperature rose with his desire, and he brushed his knuckles across the small of my back, the whisper of contact making my breath hitch even with my burning buzz. "You know I said that because I was afraid."

"And now?"

"I know you won't dump me for Gideon, or Jacob, or even pretty boy over there."

"Even with pretty boy's sex magic?" I didn't know why I pressed the issue. Kol and I didn't have that kind of a relationship, no matter what my dreams yearned for.

"You still want me after the magic of Jacob's bite is released. You'll still want me after Kol's."

Kol's expression turned wicked, the hellfire fully consuming his eyes. I knew he couldn't hear us through the door, but he could sense the desire rising within me. And God help me, I wanted both of them.

Marcus stepped past me, brushing his arm against mine and drawing a shudder of need, and opened the door. "You look hot, by the way," he said over his shoulder.

"Yeah," Kol said, his gaze never leaving mine. Then realization flashed over his expression as if he'd just remembered who he was looking at and who he was agreeing with. The hellfire vanished, turning into a wicked teasing gleam. "My threesome offer still stands."

"You'd have to talk to Essie about that," Marcus said.

Kol's eyes widened in shock. "Seriously?"

Marcus burst out laughing. "You should see the look on your face." But I got the impression his offer wasn't just to surprise Kol. Which surprised me.

My buzz suddenly softened. Gideon was near.

"Are we ready?" Cassius asked from behind me as he and Gideon headed toward us. Both wore bulletproof vests but neither had a sidearm. Gideon didn't need one because he could summon a sword of divine light, and I could only assume Cassius's magic was just as powerful.

Cassius's gaze swept over me, pausing at my exposed cleavage and drawing a frown.

"Remember we're looking for a pit fiend." Gideon handed out the coms. "You're taking your bike?"

"Thought it would work best with our cover." Kol handed me the helmet and leather jacket.

"Marcus, take the sedan," Cassius said. "Gideon and I will follow in the SUV."

The guys piled into their various vehicles and left. My buzz flared with Gideon's departure, clawing under my skin and making my muscles twitch. I held up Kol's jacket to return it to him. "This is too big. It might be in my way in a fight."

"I know, but Gideon would kill me if I let you ride without it. I also figured you'd need someplace to put your sidearm." His gaze swept over me like Cassius's had a moment ago but there wasn't a hint of disapproval in his eyes. "I guessed right. You can take it off when you get into the bar."

I pulled on the jacket and slipped my hands into the pockets. My fingers brushed against the metal grip of a gun, and I drew out my Glock and checked the magazine — full, although the ammunition looked strange.

"Enspelled stun ammo specially made for Supers." He led me deeper into the garage and stopped at a motorcycle that was black and sleek and sexy, just like Kol.

"This yours?"

"Oh, yeah." He grinned at me and straddled the bike. "Let me take you for a ride."

Heat swept through me, and all I could think about was a different kind of riding. Wow, have a few days of amazing sex and that was all I could think about.

He cleared his throat and yanked his attention away from me. "Not that kind of ride."

"Sorry. I've got—" I bit the inside of my cheek. I'd been about to lie and say I had Marcus on the mind, but remembered we had coms in and they were live. "I've got our roles for this op on the mind."

"See," Kol said with a laugh. "I told you guys, chicks like bikes."

"I'm beginning to hate this plan already," Cassius said over the coms.

I pulled on the helmet and settled in behind him, wrapping my arms around his waist and tucking myself tight against him. He hadn't put on a helmet or a jacket and his increased demonic body heat instantly enveloped me. I tried not to think about my hands against his sculpted muscles. But I couldn't stop thinking about my dream and *his* hands and lips on my body.

Jeez, if I didn't do something, I was going to be a quivering mess by the time we reached Hacksaw and then Cassius would have more reason to hate me.

We headed out, and I squeezed my eyes shut and concentrated on my buzz. It was easy enough. My patches weren't working and every inch of me stung. If I didn't get it under control soon, by the end of the day it would be all I could think about. And a week after that I wouldn't be able to control myself and I'd start clawing at my skin. Hell, who was I kidding. My buzz was stronger than it had been before. I wouldn't last a week.

God, I didn't want to go back to the time when I'd had no idea how to control it. I'd spent days sobbing. And that had been when the sensation had maxed out at the level of a low voltage electric fence. This was worse. The only thing that had worked to ease it had been nicotine. Now it was Gideon, and even if he wasn't trying to avoid me, I couldn't be near him night and day.

We arrived at Hacksaw and parked at the far end of the lot. Half a dozen vehicles — mostly trucks — and two dozen motorcycles filled the lot. On the one hand this was good. Kol and I could blend in with the crowd, but on the other hand so could the pickup man. Not to mention if things went sideways, there were a lot of bodies who could get caught in the crossfire or join the brawl.

The place didn't look welcoming with its two overflowing garbage bins around the back, weeds growing from the foundation, and boarded-up windows. If it hadn't been for all the vehicles in the lot, I would have assumed the place was abandoned.

I pulled off the helmet and unzipped the jacket. It was too warm to be wearing leather, let alone wearing it while snuggled up to a natural furnace. I scanned the street, jamming a knuckle into my thigh to stop the muscle from twitching. The neighborhood looked like a lot of neighborhoods in Union City. Old and tired. About a quarter of the buildings were boarded up. The rest had murky windows, peeling paint, and broken signs. Pot holes made the asphalt uneven and weeds grew in every possible crack on the road and the sidewalk.

From the lack of destroyed buildings, it didn't look as if this part of the city had been hit by Michael's war, so the area hadn't been partially abandoned because of damage. Most likely the majority of residents had left because, with there being more places to live than people, the middle-class parts of town where the war hadn't touched had been dirt cheap in the first few years afterward.

I spotted Marcus's sedan, parked close enough to have a good view of the front door and the parking lot, but not close enough to be obvious to anyone coming or going from the bar that he was watching them. I didn't see the SUV and my buzz hadn't changed, so Gideon wasn't close, but I didn't doubt he and Cassius had eyes on us.

"The courier is supposed to arrive in less than thirty minutes," Cassius said in my ear.

Kol hung my helmet on the bike's handle and wrapped an arm across my shoulders. He drew me close, hellfire whispering in eyes filled with wicked excitement, and released a panty-melting smile — something I'm sure he couldn't help. "Let's do this."

My buzz snapped in my chest, slicing through my desire. "Ready to be arm candy."

We sauntered across the gravel lot to the scarred metal front door and entered a dark smoky room that smelled of stale beer, sweat, and marijuana. Half the lights were out, mostly those at the edges, throwing those tables into a deep shadow that would have hidden the occupants if my vision hadn't been enhanced by Jacob's claim.

Blue and red neon lights illuminated the bar, catching in a mirrored back wall broken up by shelves of liquor bottles, while casting the bartender — a burly man with a craggy face — in a sickly light. None of the furniture matched, and the floor was sticky. I really hoped we weren't here long enough for me to see the bathrooms.

All eyes turned to us — close to thirty sets — and everyone, male and female, looked like they could handle themselves in a fight. Kol flashed a wicked grin at them, releasing a simmering flare of hellfire that thankfully felt focused away from me and didn't instantly turn me into a hot mess. He led me to a table halfway between the front door and the hall to the bathrooms, sank with a boneless grace into a chair, and pulled out a twenty.

"Why don't you get us some beers, babe."

"Sure." I reached for the bill, but he jerked his hand back, forcing me to lean forward to grab for it. As I did, his jacket fell open, flashing my ample cleavage and drawing a smirk, but the tease in his eyes was clear. This was the cover, the game, and he was finally getting to be himself.

Well, it was the plan. I might as well commit. Fighting my buzz to stay in the moment, I released my own smirk, slowly shrugged out of his jacket, making sure he and anyone able to see in the shadows got a good show, and set it on the table with the pocket holding my Glock facing up.

He cocked an eyebrow, not looking impressed. Yeah, not really a point for me. After a life of not letting myself get close to anyone, I didn't have a lot of experience flirting and pretty much sucked at it. But he didn't press it and handed over the bill.

Swishing my hips, I turned to head to the bar, but he jerked forward and slapped my ass with a loud hard crack.

Holy shit. I yelped in surprise. My butt stung, but a whisper of his magic swept through me, turning it into an exquisite need that shocked the hell out of me.

Someone at a nearby table snickered, and I managed to shoot Kol my sexiest smile instead of looking as shocked as I felt. An apology flickered in his gaze before the tease returned, and he jerked his chin to the bar, sending me on my way.

"What the hell was that?" Marcus asked.

"Just cementing our cover," Kol whispered. "We're fine."

"That didn't sound fine." Marcus's wolf turned his tone dark and edgy.

The bartender scowled at me as I ordered two bottles of beer. No way in hell was I trusting anything in a glass in this place.

"We're fine," Kol insisted.

"Someone's just really getting into his role," I said, trying to subtly hide my lips by looking down, pulling on my shirt, and adjusting my breasts for maximum cleavage.

"Hey, I'm supposed to be an asshole incubus. Gotta play the part," Kol drawled. "We've got just under a dozen supers here who can see in the dark. Six shifters, three lesser demons, and a lethe demon."

"No pit fiend?" Marcus asked.

I leaned my back against the bar while I waited for the beers and scanned the room before returning my gaze to Kol's like a good enthralled woman.

"No," Kol said. "Did we just get sent on a wild goose chase?"

"There's still time." But Cassius's tone said he thought Floyd had lied as well.

Movement in the hall to the bathrooms caught my eye. I turned back to the bartender as a burly demon, larger in height and bulk than Jacob, lumbered the few feet from the hall to a table in the corner. The guy had mottled black and white skin, a mouth that was too wide to be human, and leathery black wings tucked behind him. He sat backwards in his chair to avoid catching his wings, and laughed at something said by the other guy at his table, revealing a mouth full of shark-like teeth.

"Looks like the pit fiend was in the can," Kol said. "But there's only two of them at the table. Not three."

"What are the odds that two pit fiends would be here?" Marcus asked.

"There are less than twenty in Union City," Cassius said. "You do the math. Keep your eyes on that table."

Kol grunted his agreement as the bartender handed over our drinks. I paid, left the coins, and sashayed back to Kol. He took both of the beers and set them on the table, but before I could sit in the chair beside him, he grabbed my wrist and jerked me into his lap.

Heat surged through me, making my breath hitch and my nerves thrum with sudden aching need. I swallowed a gasp to avoid another comment from Marcus.

My gaze leaped to Kol's and stalled there. All hint of playfulness was gone, consumed by hellfire and surprise, as if he hadn't expected my instant desire— No, his body trembled beneath me and his shoulders were taut under my hands. Whatever this sensation was, it had struck both of us.

He drew in a shuddering breath and captured the back of my head with his hand. My pulse raced as he urged me close, brushing his cheek against mine. "Both of those guys can see in the dark."

Which meant we couldn't just stare at them. Not that we were going to.

"I've got the rest of the room." He nuzzled my neck, his body still tense beneath me.

I slid my fingers in his hair and concentrated on my buzz.

The pit fiend laughed again at something his friend said. The guy was small compared to the pit fiend and while he looked human, he had the same dark feralness Marcus had when his wolf was coming out.

"Do we know what kind of shifter he is?" I asked.

"Hyena." Kol's breath caressed my neck.

I clenched my teeth. *Focus on the buzz.*

Marcus growled, the sound rumbling through the coms. "What are the other shifters?"

"A wolf, three tigers, and a fox. And none of them are sitting together."

"Heads up," Cassius said. "You've got a group of three heading to the front door. Looks like the wolf is carrying a bag."

Daylight sliced into the bar, and I glanced over my shoulder to look at the new arrivals. All of the guys looked human… except not. The short one with the duffle bag had a shifter's feral intensity, but the others I couldn't figure out how they weren't human. Something about the way they walked? Or carried themselves? Or… hell, I had no idea, but I knew without a doubt that they were supers of some kind.

"Whoa." Kol let out a soft breath. "That's a whole lot of Divifend."

"Good," Cassius said. "Now let's follow it to the lab's new location."

The two non-humans sat at the table closest to the door, not bothering to order drinks, while the wolf with the bag walked past us.

"He's making the drop right away?" Kol asked, not turning to watch him.

The pit fiend and his friend didn't look up as the wolf approached and walked right on by, heading into the hall with the bathrooms.

"He's gone into the back hall," I said. "Not even a glance at the guys at the table."

"Stay with the bag," Cassius said. "Both of you. I don't want Shaw left alone for a second."

Great. How were we going to make it look natural for both of us to go to the bathroom at the same time?

Well, they already thought we were here for sex—

I captured Kol's head before I could rethink the plan and kissed him. He tensed with surprise, then leaned into me, a whisper of his heated magic slipping between my lips. I concentrated on my buzz, on the biting stinging my skin and my twitching muscles. My right thigh was the worst right now. If I didn't do something about it soon, it would cramp.

His hands slid down my back and grasped my hips, and the air around me heated.

Focus on the buzz. On the buzz. Just make this look real.

I sucked in his bottom lip, catching it with my teeth, and slowly drew back. Hellfire consumed his eyes, but this close, almost nose to nose with him, I could also see the tension there.

"Come on," I said, not needing to work at making my tone sound like I wanted him. I slid from his lap, grabbed his leather coat and his hand, and pulled him toward the bathrooms. Hopefully everyone in the bar would think we were off to have sleazy sex in a bathroom stall.

"Damn it, Kol," Cassius said, his tone dark. "Stop seducing Gideon's mate. You're working."

"You wanted us to both follow the bag," I whispered as we stepped into the back hall, lit by a naked bulb that barely gave off any illumination, in an unfinished light fixture between two unmarked doors — presumably the bathrooms. "We've barely arrived and there's only one logical reason for us to head to the back hall together."

The wolf with the bag, an average looking guy with stringy brown hair wearing a stained gray T-shirt and ripped jeans, stood at the far end beside a scarred metal security door. His eyes narrowed the moment we entered the hall.

Kol stopped a few feet in, tugged me close, and pinned me to the wall with his body. Glorious heat swept through me, along with the memory of his lips on mine two nights ago when he saved my life. Just the thought of his magic pouring powerful liquid bliss into my body stole my breath.

Focus on the buzz, not how close he is or the dream. I clenched my jaw against a shudder. My thigh cramped, and I embraced the pain.

"Trust me." Kol nuzzled my neck again, forcing me to turn my head toward the wolf. "This wasn't my plan."

"It fits your cover," Gideon said, his voice devoid of emotion, making my soul sob. "Just keep Shaw's head clear."

"Top priority." Kol glanced toward the bar. "The pit fiend and the hyena are here."

"Fucking incubus," the hyena said, as he and the pit fiend approached.

"Oh, man. You don't know what you're missing." The pit fiend's lips curled back, his expression hungry, sending a shiver of fear through me. "Hey," he said to Kol, "if you want a bigger meal, we'll fuck her, too."

"You honestly think I need your help?" Kol flashed the pit fiend a wicked grin and sent a surge of power through me that was a lot stronger than the whisper he'd used to ease my stinging ass.

I gasped at the sudden swell of power and a low throaty moan escaped my lips. Unable to stop myself, I arched against the wall, pressing my breasts against Kol's chest, and fisted my hands in the hem of his T-shirt. Too much clothing. Not enough kissing. Not enough—

Shit. Focus on the buzz.

I fought to catch my breath but couldn't stop panting. All I could think about was our kiss and my dream and how I wanted to ride his magic to its glorious, screaming end.

"What the hell, Kol?" Marcus growled in my ear.

"Told you they're all assholes," the hyena said.

"No shit." The pit fiend shouldered Kol into me — drawing another moan as our bodies pressed together — and headed to the wolf at the end of the hall.

Oh, my God. I was going to lose my mind and start ripping off our clothes. This was bad. Cassius was going to kick me off the team the moment this op was done. And really, it was only logical. How could I effectively work on the team when all I could think about was having sex with all the guys.

Except I'd managed to work just fine with Jacob that morning, and I knew, deep down, past all my aching desire, that I could work with the rest of the team as well. I just couldn't do it with Kol's magic flooding me.

Kol leaned close, the hellfire in his eyes gone, and I fought the urge to rub against him again. "Just take a breath, Essie."

I drew in a ragged breath.

The guys at the end of the hall said something, but I couldn't concentrate past my consuming need to listen.

"Another one." The muscles in Kol's jaw flexed, and the heat of his magic rose to the surface of my skin then seeped out, evaporating in a swirl of red smoke.

My desire turned into an aching emptiness for an agonizing second before my buzz surged, setting off my cramping thigh. "How did you do that?"

"With a lot of concentration," he said, his expression pained. He glanced to the end of the hall.

The wolf handed the bag to the pit fiend and, with the hyena, headed back into the bar, while the pit fiend shoved open the back door and stepped out into the blinding afternoon sunlight.

"The pit fiend has the bag," Kol said. "He just went out the back door by himself."

I rubbed my thigh, trying to get the muscle to relax. "I thought he was supposed to be the bodyguard."

"I don't see him coming around into the parking lot," Marcus said.

My thigh clenched tighter. Jeez, that hurt—

Wait. "What if the real handoff is happening in the ravine?"

"Marcus," Cassius said, "get eyes on that bag now."

"I'm too far away to catch him before he gets out of sight in the ravine."

"We'll stall him." Kol grabbed my hand and urged me to the end of the hall.

I stumbled, my thigh screaming. God damn buzz. Kol's eyes flashed wide, but I managed to catch my balance, and opened the door.

The pit fiend stood a few feet away, his expression jumping from surprise to realization to anger. "You're JP agents."

Something roared, blocked from view because of the open door, then something crashed into the door. Kol shoved me out of the way as it slammed him into the metal doorframe and concrete wall, drawing a grunt of pain.

A massive demon with red scales, a prehensile tail, and slitted pupils, like the one Jacob and I had faced picking up Floyd but twice as big, snarled at us. Behind him stood a man with a ragged scar running down the side of his face and the feralness of a shifter in his eyes, and a tiger. An honest to goodness giant tiger.

The scaled snake-like demon wrenched the door open and swung it back toward Kol with a force that was sure to break his ribs, while the tiger pounced at me.

KOL JERKED OUT OF THE WAY OF THE DOOR, CRASHING INTO ME AND MAKING me stumble. But instead of catching my arm to steady me, he shoved me again. Hard. I lurched to the side and fell to my knees, narrowly missing a swipe of the tiger's claws.

"Follow the pit fiend," Kol said, grabbing the tiger's neck and wrenching it away from me.

I scrambled to my feet as Snake drove his fist into Kol's ribs. The pit fiend sneered and ran across the parking lot to a break in the trees, but the shifter, Scar Guy, sneered at me and slunk around Kol and the tiger, his expression clear. He was going to kill me, and he was going to enjoy it.

"Go. I've got them." Kol heaved the tiger into the bar's cinderblock wall and turned to punch Snake in the gut, but Snake's tail wrapped around his neck, shoved him out of reach, and choked him.

It didn't look like he had them at all. Except the mission was to follow the Divifend to the new zip lab, or, in the very least, reclaim the stolen Divifend so they couldn't immediately make more zip.

"On my way," Marcus said over the coms.

The tiger lunged again at Kol, and I pulled my Glock from the jacket pocket and shot it. It roared, its claws grazing Kol's back, tearing his T-shirt but not digging deep into his flesh. For a second I was sure I'd missed because it didn't look like it was bleeding or even in pain.

But then red lightning exploded around it, and it tensed as if hit by a Taser.

With another roar, its fur melted into flesh and its body contracted into a man's. The guy panted on his hands and knees, completely naked — because a shifter's magic consumed whatever he was wearing when he transformed — and glared at me, feral fury in his eyes.

Oh, shit. One round wasn't enough to drop them.

Scar swiped at me, his fingers extended into claws. I heaved back, my buzz seizing muscles in both of my thighs, and hit the garbage bin. At the last second, I wrenched up Kol's jacket, catching Scar's claws. He tore the leather from my hand as Tiger leaped to tackle me. Kol, down on one knee and still being choked by Snake, snagged Tiger's ankle, crashing him to the ground. Then Kol grabbed a knife sheathed in his boot — I'd been wondering if he was armed, since I hadn't felt the sheaths he usually wore on his back — and sliced at Snake's tail, who released him before the blade cut too deep.

"Essie, the Divifend," he said. "I can handle them until Marcus comes."

"Not happening soon. I'm surrounded," Marcus growled. I glanced around the garbage bin but couldn't see him. He must have been ambushed at the side of the building by guys coming out the front door.

"Shaw, go," Cassius said. "We're on our way."

I shot Scar before he could lunge at me again and bolted past him to the break in the trees where the pit fiend had gone without looking to see if the shot had even hit.

A rutted narrow path led down a steep incline and disappeared around a man-sized rock and a thick pine tree. Dappled sunlight shone among the branches, dancing with the breeze on the thick shrubs and weeds lining the path. Too many places to hide.

Someone screamed. It didn't sound like Kol, but I didn't look back to check.

I gritted my teeth against my buzz and listened for sounds of the pit fiend, to determine if he'd stayed on the path or plunged into the thick underbrush. But all I could hear were the guys yelling and grunting and breathing in my ear. Marcus was still stuck at the side of the bar. Something boomed over the coms and behind me. Kol slid down the side of the garbage bin then lunged at Tiger, who'd shifted back into his feline form. Gideon was almost to Marcus, and Cassius was off to help Kol.

There was no way I was going to be able to hear anything like this.

I shoved the ear piece into my pocket and squeezed my eyes shut. No footsteps, and no heavy breathing. Not that I expected the pit fiend to be close enough for me to hear his breathing.

A twig snapped in the direction of the path. *Thank you, Jacob, for enhancing my hearing.*

I skidded down the dirt incline and hurried, but didn't outright run. The point was to follow him. Which meant I needed to hang back, and he needed to think he'd lost me.

My buzz increased, turning from stinging bites to a full, constant electric shock. I didn't know if that was because I was getting farther from Gideon, or if it was reacting to my adrenaline.

The path curled around the rock, the ground a steep tumble to the bottom of the ravine on one side and a hard climb on the other, then disappeared around a cluster of trees and shrubs.

Another twig snapped. I was getting closer... but was that breathing?

It was hard to tell with my buzz. The twig's sound had been sharp, but it was blended with the yells of the fight in the parking lot, the rustle of leaves, and the rumble of cars on a nearby road.

I glanced around the cluster of trees.

No sign of the pit fiend.

I had to be wrong. It wasn't someone breathing.

The path carried on for about twenty feet then switched back, dipping out of sight, and I hurried toward it.

A branch snapped, right beside me, and the pit fiend crashed out of the underbrush, lunging for me. I jerked out of the way and aimed my Glock, but the demon flapped his wings, sending dust and debris into my face.

Grit stung my eyes, and he leaped the distance between us and seized my gun. I fired before he wrenched it away, the bullet grazing his ribs, sending a crackle of red lightning lancing up his side, but not nearly as powerful as what had hit Tiger.

He tossed my Glock behind him, his gaze never leaving me, his expression hungry. My sidearm clattered against a stone on the side of the path and stopped half under a large tree root.

"I'm surprised the demon-whore didn't leave you to my guys." He sneered, flashing his shark-teeth. "Remind me to thank his corpse when I'm done with you."

With a snarl, he flapped his wings again. I turned my head and squinted to avoid the grit. He was going to jump at me. I had a second at best.

I hissed the spell to cast a divine light strike, and my buzz burst into wild lightning slicing under my skin. The pit fiend jerked close, and I released the spell.

Nothing.

Not a flicker of light or heat in my hands. Not a God damned fucking thing.

Are you shitting me?

Where the hell had the blast from this morning gone? Or did I only have one of those inside me per day?

The pit fiend grabbed my neck and squeezed. "I'm going to fuck you 'til you're torn in two then eat your heart."

My pulse stuttered. This was bad, and I had no way of getting out of it. I needed backup. Now.

He wrenched me close and licked my cheek with a long thin tongue. The temperature rose with his wild desire and the demonic heat radiating from his body. "You're going to be delicious."

I clawed at his hand and kicked him in the gut.

He grunted and squeezed, cutting off my air.

How could I have possibly thought I belonged on this team? Cassius was going to be so smug when he fired me. I shoved my hand into my pocket to grab my com and call for help, but the pit fiend grabbed my wrist and twisted, forcing me to drop the ear piece.

"I don't think so. Now be a good human and freeze." Red smoke, like the demonic magic that had flooded the cemetery during the fight to stop Ibizual, swept up my arm, immobilizing my muscles. My buzz burned, but the twitching was gone, along with all control of my body.

The magic swept across my chest and down my legs, immobilizing them as well. I couldn't let it cover me. I was dead if it did.

The light strike spell roared through my head and divine light shot from my hand, which was clawing at his around my throat. It didn't hit with nearly as much force as the blast that had sent Floyd flying, but it did make the pit fiend yelp in pain and release me.

My feet hit the ground, but only one of my legs held me. I staggered, but managed to regain enough muscle control of both legs to fall toward my gun. The pit fiend seized my ankle before I reached it and yanked me under him, pinning me to the ground with his hips, his huge palm crushing my chest.

"That fucking hurt," he snarled, and a blast of red smoke erupted from his hand and swept around my chest. My heart strained to beat, and I fought to draw breath. Every muscle within me went limp. With a growl, he ground his erection against me. "So I'll make you hurt."

Frozen panic stole my breath. I had to get free. Somehow. *Please, God.* I couldn't be helpless, not now, not when he was going to—

Another blast of smoke enveloped me, and my buzz roared into an inferno. My muscles went from limp to suddenly contracted, all of them in one agonizing instant. The pit fiend's eyes widened, and the temperature around me plummeted as the smoke billowed out from my body then rushed into me. Just like the demon magic when fighting Ibizual. My skin sucked it up, devoured it, and the fire within me blazed hotter.

"What the fuck." The pit fiend scrambled off me.

I crawled to my knees, my body back in my control. The demonic magic twisted tight in my chest then flooded into my palms like a light strike spell, except hotter, so much hotter.

The pit fiend lurched toward me and punched at my head, and I wrenched my hands up. A blast of red light, not the smoke I'd consumed, shot from my palms and slammed into his chest. He howled with pain and dropped, his entire body limp.

I seized my sidearm, aimed it at him, and scrambled to my feet to put some distance between us so he couldn't easily grab me. My hands stung, but they didn't look as if they were burned. Thank God for that.

"What the fuck are you?" he gasped before passing out.

I shuddered. That was a very good question. I'd thought absorbing Ibizual's magic had been because of my connection to his key, but now I wasn't sure.

Someone crashed through the underbrush behind me. I jerked around as Cassius tackled a guy with the feral intensity of a shifter, but another guy was close behind them with a revolver. He stopped to aim at Cassius, who was wrestling to pin the shifter to the ground.

Instinct kicked in and I shot twice at the guy's chest before he could fire. Red lightning swept around him. His muscles seized, he dropped the gun, and he collapsed, unconscious. Looked like two shots did the trick.

Cassius glanced at the unconscious man behind him then turned a frozen glare at me.

And here it came, the dressing down and being fired — with the rest of the guys listening in on their coms. But the truth was, I'd made it through another fight by the skin of my teeth, and the next time I might not make it. I couldn't argue any more that being on the team was a good idea, especially if I couldn't count on my light strike spell.

"Thanks," Cassius said, his voice gruff.

My thoughts stuttered. Not what I'd been expecting him to say.

He jerked his thumb to the unconscious guy. "For dropping him."

I must have looked as confused as I felt.

Kol hurried down the path, his T-shirt shiny with blood, although most of it didn't look like his. His attention jumped to the pit fiend, and his face lit up in a smile. "You took out a pit fiend all by yourself. How did you manage that?"

"Barely." I dropped my gaze to my hands. They were shaking and it was obvious, because I had my weapon aimed at the pit fiend again.

"Yeah, but you did it." Kol's gaze dipped to my neck, and his eyes narrowed. Yeah, I bet I had a hand-sized bruise forming there. But he waded into the underbrush beside me and pulled out the bag of Divifend.

Gideon stormed down the path, light flaring from his eyes, his hard gaze locked on me. "You went off coms."

Here was the dressing down I deserved.

And my God damned buzz wasn't easing off this time. I still felt like part of the demonic magic was vibrating inside me and amping up my regular agony.

"You're supposed to let the team know when you go off coms," he said. "Didn't you work with coms at all in the UCPD?"

"I'm a beat cop."

"Means radios only," Kol said.

"I know what that means," Gideon snapped.

"I'm sure she had a good reason." Kol jerked his thumb at the pit fiend. "Come on, enjoy the fact that Essie took out a pit fiend."

Gideon pointed to the com in his ear. "I heard. So much for following him back to the zip lab."

Cassius cuffed his guy and hauled him to his feet. I couldn't read his expression. It was weird, not quite angry but certainly not happy. And why the hell hadn't he kicked me off the team yet?

"He tried to ambush me. Thought I was Kol." My buzz snapped a muscle in my neck, and I flinched with all of them looking at me.

Gideon frowned. But just like his brother, I had no idea what his expression meant.

"Let's get these guys back to Operations." Cassius pulled out his phone. "Maybe we'll get something out of them."

He sent a quick text, and we gathered the thugs and took them up to the parking lot. Tiger was nowhere to be found, but Snake and Scar were both unconscious, bleeding, and cuffed together. Beside them were three more shifters — one naked — along with an unconscious demon with green skin. They were all handcuffed together, and Marcus glowered at those who were awake, his Glock pointed in their direction.

My guys — and Cassius — put our three criminals with the rest of the pack while I hung back with the bag of Divifend. Kol beamed and said something to Marcus, who rolled his eyes and half laughed. Even Gideon shook his head in amusement at what had been said.

My heart filled with a mix of joy and sadness. These were my guys, in their element, kicking ass and, each in his own way, looking sexy as hell. And I didn't belong. This was the second time today I'd almost been killed. I had to accept the truth. This job was far too dangerous for any human.

Of course, my argument from before still hadn't changed. If I left, some other human would be assigned to the team, and he or she wouldn't have the magical advantages I had. Even if I couldn't always count on my light strike, casting it was still a possibility. Most humans couldn't cast the spell. Not to mention my new unnerving ability to absorb demonic magic and shoot it like a light strike.

The pit fiend had asked what the hell I was, and a part of me wondered that as well. I didn't think angels could manipulate demonic magic. Could a nephilim, because I wasn't fully angelic?

Cassius said something to Kol and they headed my way.

"A word, Agent Shaw." I still couldn't read Cassius's expression, and the temperature around me didn't change. "How badly are you hurt?"

I gingerly touched my neck, but couldn't tell how bad the bruise was with my buzz still blazing from absorbing the demon's magic.

"I'm sure all of us got a little hurt." Kol shifted closer to me, the temperature cooling. Fear. "This op didn't go as planned."

"They usually don't," Cassius said. "How badly are you hurt?"

"I'm a little banged up."

He didn't look as if he believed me, which made me wonder how bad my neck looked.

"Take Shaw to Amiah and have her checked out," he said to Kol. "Then both of you are on call for the rest of the day."

"On call? You've got a parking lot full of supers you need to move." Kol jerked his thumb to the group we'd arrested.

"Chris and Nathaniel are bringing the transport. If three angels and two shifters can't handle this group, we don't deserve to call ourselves JP agents." Cassius held out his hand. "Your sidearm, Agent Shaw. We'll discuss this op after we've got this group booked. Don't turn off your phones."

Well, that didn't sound good. I handed over my Glock, and he shot me another strange look. It wasn't icy, but it wasn't pleasant. God, what I wouldn't give for a little telepathy, or hell, even an empathic magic that actually let me sense emotions.

He strode back to the group, but the chilly air didn't change, which meant the cold had to be coming from Kol.

"We won't let him kick you off the team." Hellfire blazed in his eyes.

"I don't want any of you to jeopardize your career for me." Especially since it was getting harder to disagree with Cassius's argument. I hadn't even had one full day on the job, and I'd already risked my life twice.

But jeez, everything within me said this was where I was supposed to be. Could I *be* with the guys without being a JP agent? What the hell would I do? I couldn't just sit around, watching them work, waiting for them to come home. That would drive me crazy. But did I really have any other choice? Staying on the team was selfish. Gideon, Jacob, and Marcus all needed me. If I died, they went insane or worse, and I couldn't do that to them.

ESSIE

I followed Kol to the bar's back door, where he grabbed his jacket from the ground and handed it to me. "Not being able to follow the Divifend back to the lab isn't your fault. Everyone but Cassius knows that."

I brushed the gravel dust off the jacket, cringing at the claw slices where I'd used it as a shield. "I barely got out of this fight alive. Again. I want to be on the team." God, I desperately wanted to be a part of the team. "But at this rate, I'd be surprised if I survived a week."

"That's because no one has really thought this through."

We headed around the building. Cassius watched us, his expression icy, while Gideon didn't even glance away from the thugs. Marcus and Kol shared a nod then Marcus's gaze slid to mine for a long second, filling me with heat, before he turned away.

The muscles in Kol's jaw clenched, but we kept heading toward his bike. "We're still treating you like you're a super."

"I won't be a useful member of the team if I can't risk being separated from one of you." I shrugged into his leather jacket and pulled on the helmet. "There will always be situations like today where we have to break up to deal with multiple perps."

"I'm not saying you have to be with one of us all the time. I'm saying you have no training for dealing with supers. I bet you have no idea what powers a pit fiend has." He straddled his bike and started it.

I climbed on and wrapped my arms around him. He tensed at the contact and didn't relax.

"I didn't even know a pit fiend existed or what it looked like until today."

"My point exactly."

We drove back to Operations. Amiah met us in triage, sent a slice of magic into me to find out just how hurt I was, then proclaimed I wasn't injured enough to waste her power. "Jacob's claim will fix that soon enough."

Which was fine with me.

Kol, from his perch on the arm of the couch in the waiting area, frowned at that, but thankfully didn't argue with her. My buzz still burned, the nicotine patches hadn't done a damned thing, and I didn't want another painful session with her.

"How about I show you around the Quarter and we get a bite to eat?" He flashed me his panty-melting smile, sending a shiver of desire strong enough to overcome my buzz sweeping through me. His eyes widened and the smile vanished. "Sorry. Forgot I hit you with a lot of magic at the bar."

"Do we need to talk about that?" I hadn't thought there was something between us, but now, after that moment in his lap, I wasn't so sure. There'd been a connection, something deeper than me just being attracted to an incubus.

"I didn't have much choice. If I hadn't made my position clear, the pit fiend would have tried to take you."

A strange heat filled the air. Humid but not sultry, warm, not searing. It didn't feel like desire but it didn't feel like anger, either. It was complicated. Just like everything else at the moment.

"And before then?"

"You mean the ass slap?" A playful glimmer lit his eye and all sense of the strange heat vanished.

Perhaps I was only seeing what I wanted because my base human instinct was drawn to him. A part of me would always desire him, just like a part of every other straight woman and gay man.

"Yeah, the ass slap." I hopped off the gurney, and we headed down the hall to the elevator.

"Really wished I could have seen Marcus's face," he said.

"What about Cassius?"

We reached the elevator, and I hit the call button.

"Him, too, but Marcus always gives such a good reaction." His grin turned wicked, still sexually charged, but I got the sense that wasn't his intention. Guess I really had been mistaken about there being something between us. "We should take him up on that threesome offer, so I can watch him back out of it."

The elevator door opened. I got in and hit the button for the fifth floor. "What makes you think he'll back out?" I asked Kol as he stepped in beside me.

"Come on, you don't honestly think he'd go through with it?" Kol frowned. "Okay, he might. But probably with Gideon, not me. He's your other mate. Marcus's wolf might see him as a part of you, which is why he hasn't lost his shit over this situation."

The elevator dinged, the door opened, and we headed down the hall.

"Oh, I'd love to see that." Kol chuckled. "You two propositioning Gideon."

"Yeah, that's never going to happen." Because Gideon didn't want me. Not that the idea didn't appeal—

Oh, wow! I just thought that, and... jeez... wow... had no idea how I felt or what I thought about that.

"Can you do it in front of Cassius?" The sinful gleam in Kol's eyes blazed, reminding me that he was still a demon, the chaos to the angels' order. "Pretty please?"

I bit back a laugh, imagining the look on Cassius's face.

Kol batted his eyelashes at me. "Pretty pretty please?"

"I'm going to get changed now." I unlocked my door.

"So that means you'll think about it?" Kol said as he headed down the hall to his suite.

"Depends on what you show me in the Quarter and where you take me for dinner."

He turned to face me, now walking backwards. "Oh, I'll show you such a good time, sweetheart, you'll do anything to make me happy." His eyes widened. "I didn't mean— You know what I—"

"Go get changed, Kol," I said with a laugh and stepped into my room.

I washed off my makeup, peeled off my four nicotine patches and didn't replace them. The level of my buzz didn't change, so it was clear the patches weren't doing anything. Not that I really had any doubts. I had red patches that I'd scratched on both thighs that weren't from my fight with the pit fiend, and another patch with fresh scabs along my ribs. I was already scratching and hadn't noticed. This wasn't good, and there wasn't anyone I could ask for help. I didn't know how much anyone at Operations knew about nephilim, but I couldn't confess that I was one in hopes that someone might know something that would help. And even if I didn't mention my half angelic nature, whoever I went to could still ask too many questions and stumble across the truth.

I changed into a fresh T-shirt. I only had one left from my hasty packing job that morning, but I didn't know if I should spend the afternoon packing so I could move in to Operations or not. Given Cassius's reaction to the op at Hacksaw, my money was on not.

Kol met me in the hall. He'd traded in his leather pants for jeans and his ripped and bloody T-shirt for another T-shirt. All hint of the hellfire in his eyes was banked, and his wicked playfulness was gone, replaced with the man who'd asked me three nights ago to stay on the team. He'd confessed that even though he was a demon, his heightened magical attunement meant he was repelled by and attracted to certain essences. Unfortunately he wasn't attracted to his own kind, but instead to essences on the light end of the spectrum. Angels, however, didn't usually like to hang out with demons, which made me the perfect find. I didn't look down on him like an angel, but my essence made him as comfortable as if I were one.

And I wasn't going to tell him that was because I was half angel.

We took a JP SUV and drove around the Supers' Quarter with the windows rolled down, enjoying the early summer warmth, while I tried not to claw at my body.

I'd already seen the vampire section of the Quarter with its UV-blocking glass canopy protecting a whole street and the park at the end, so we did a drive-by of the demon area, which looked a lot like the rest of the Quarter except that there were more demons on the streets and more businesses catering to demonic needs.

Next was Mercy Memorial, the JP hospital, a series of 19th century office buildings, converted and joined into a complex that catered to every supers' medical needs. It sat only a block off the main road near the ring park separating the Quarter from the rest of the city, so supers outside of the Quarter could reach it quickly, since supers couldn't go to just any hospital. Most human facilities — and all of those in Union City — weren't capable of handling a super in medical distress. And, depending on the super or the injury, it wasn't safe for humans to treat them.

This was where Marcus had suffered through his transformation into a werewolf after my horrible rookie mistake, and where he'd met Amiah. I still wasn't sure if there was anything between them. Marcus's wolf had clearly picked me, but that didn't mean there still weren't complicated feelings between them.

After the hospital was the shiny new UV-blocking glass and steel JP council chambers where the day-to-day running of the Quarter happened. The Quarter didn't have a mayor, but it still ran pretty much like a city inside the city. And while the community heads pretty much policed their own, there was an effort made to work together and uphold the laws they'd all helped make when supers had been given the right to representation in the world's governance. That, and supers paid taxes, got parking tickets, needed dog licenses, and everything else every other human citizen needed.

Kol shared entertaining bits of information as we drove, usually about this op or that, as if his whole life revolved around the team, and I couldn't help wondering if he had any family in the human realm or even in the Realm of Celestial Darkness. I didn't want to pry, so I didn't ask. I was sure it'd come up again at some point.

We ended up on the edge of the Quarter at the park entrance to one of the shifters' forests and stopped near a food truck.

"These are the best tacos in the city," he said, shutting off the engine and getting out.

I joined him, caught myself scratching my shoulder and digging in to get the muscle to relax, and forced my hand to my side.

We'd parked in a gravel lot beside a baseball diamond, a jungle gym, and a public bathroom. Three wolf cubs wrestled with each other in the grass a few feet away, while an adult wolf lounged on a blanket beside a shirtless man. At their feet sat an open picnic basket and a pile of dirty paper plates and plastic cups.

"There are usually more trucks here on the weekend when the ball diamond is in use, but Tasty Tacos is here all the time."

The middle-aged woman in the truck waved at us as we approached. Silver streaked her black hair, and laugh lines crinkled around her eyes. She had the feral intensity of a shifter, but I didn't know which kind. Best guess was wolf and that this was the wolves' forest.

"I was beginning to think you'd forgotten about me," the woman said.

"You know I could never forget you, Bonnie." He flashed her a friendly-for-an-incubus smile that still made my pulse trip with desire.

She clicked her tongue at him and blushed. "You mean you could never forget my cooking."

"Only because I know you're taken."

"By the most handsome wolf in Union City," she said with a laugh. The air around me warmed, and I knew her affection for her guy was genuine. "Who's your friend?"

"Bonnie, this is Essie. Essie, Bonnie. She's new in the Quarter."

"And you just thought you'd show her around?" Bonnie winked at me.

"It's not like that," Kol said.

"Un hunh," she said, clearly not believing him. "What'll it be?"

Kol glanced at me. "Anything you want. On me."

"Anything?" I studied the menu. There were over a dozen options, all of which sounded delicious. "I should order one of everything to get back at you for slapping my ass."

Bonnie laughed. "Yeah, not like that at all."

"I can see introducing you two was a mistake," Kol said, but mirth filled his eyes. In fact, he looked more relaxed than I'd ever seen him. "We'll each have the brisket taco combo."

"Hey! I thought I got to choose."

"Too slow."

He paid for the food, and we sat at a nearby picnic table, side by side, facing out, to wait for our order.

I leaned back against the tabletop and stretched out my legs. My skin burned and my shoulder was driving me crazy. "You must come here a lot."

"I like Bonnie's food." He matched my posture and stared up at the cloudless sky, a perfect summer blue. The same color as Gideon's eyes. "And I like her essence. Sometimes the angels are hard to take."

"Because of their... attitude toward beings of celestial darkness?"

"Yeah." The word came out soft, weighted with so much more emotion than just frustration at how people at work looked at him, and the temperature dipped with a hint of mist. "And sometimes they remind me of things I'd rather forget."

"The war?"

"Just over twenty years and I still—"

The mist thickened, the droplets of water catching the afternoon sunlight like miniscule diamonds only I could see.

He ran his hands through his hair. "I can't make up for the things I did."

"You mean the things Michael *made* you do."

"It was still me enthralling those women." He squeezed his eyes shut, and I didn't need the mist or chill to tell me how much it still hurt. During the war, Michael had manifested him in the human realm to keep the women he'd imprisoned and used to conceive his nephilim army compliant. "I picked me over them. And the things he and his nephilim did to them... to us."

The mist swept around me, obscuring my vision and blocking out the sun. I didn't know what to say to him. There wasn't anything I could say that would heal this. All I could do was listen to whatever he wanted to reveal without judgment.

I shifted closer to him, brushing my shoulder against his, and took his hand. He laced his fingers between mine, his face still turned up to the sky, eyes still closed.

Mist gathered on my cheeks. Soon it would look like I was crying. Kol drew in a ragged breath, and his grip on my hand tightened.

"We need to figure out a plan for Cassius," he said, his voice raw.

"We need for him not to be right." My buzz snapped the muscles in my neck, making me twitch.

Kol glanced at me and frowned. "Are you all right?"

"I'm fine now, but if I wasn't, Gideon and Jacob would be in trouble. Marcus might be as well, but I don't know enough about shifter mating bonds to know for sure."

Bonnie stepped out of her food truck with our order and headed our way.

"How deep is a shifter's mating bond?" he asked her as she set the tray of food on the picnic table.

She propped her hands on her hips. "A true bond, not just being in love?"

Kol glanced at me, the look quick, but Bonnie's eyes narrowed. She'd seen it.

"I'd say true," he said.

"Throw yourself on your mate's funeral pyre deep." She heaved a heavy sigh. "If he catches you holding her hand, he's going to tear you a new one. Especially if he's a wolf."

"Doesn't she get a say in it?" Kol asked.

Bonnie met my gaze. "Your brain just hasn't caught up with your soul. If you're not in love with him now, you will be."

"Oh, I'm pretty sure I'm in love with him." God, I really was. I had been from the moment I saw him.

"Then leave my boy out of this." Feral intensity radiated from Bonnie's eyes, and her canines sharpened as her wolf came to the surface. Heat swept around me, and Kol's mist vanished.

"Whoa." Kol stood, grabbed Bonnie's hands, and met her gaze. "I'm fine. It's all good. Marcus isn't going to kill me."

Surprise flashed across her expression. "Marcus is mated? But he's hung up on a— Oh." She huffed and cuffed Kol on the head. "You still know better than to hold her hand."

He took the blow. It wasn't very hard, but I was sure he could have dodged it if he'd wanted to. "Yes, ma'am."

"Don't yes ma'am me." She rolled her eyes at him. "I'm too young to be a ma'am."

"Yes—"

She glared at him, cutting him off, but the edges of her lips curled into a smile for a second before she sobered and looked at me. "You hurt Marcus or Kol and I'll rip your heart out."

She headed back to her truck, and Kol dropped to the bench beside me with his usual boneless sexual grace.

"She really likes you," he said, nudging the tray closer to me.

"That's what that was."

He shrugged, his eyes gleaming, all hint of grief over the war hidden. "Wolves tend to be overprotective."

"Gee, I hadn't noticed." I picked up a taco and took a bite. Oh, wow. This really was the best taco in town. Just the right mix of hard and soft, salty and sweet. "We still need to figure out how to make this job safer for me or three quarters of your team is going to be in trouble."

"Three fifths. You're part of the team, too."

"I really want to be." I really did. "But I'm also not an idiot."

"The first thing we need to do is get you off active duty and get you proper training."

"Except the mayor and chief of police want me seen on the job with the team." I was pretty sure they were hoping I'd be kicked off the team and sent back to UCPD so they'd have cause to fire me.

"Then I guess we have to use your time off to bring you up to speed."

"You make it sound so easy." And it still wasn't a guarantee that any of it would increase my odds of survival or that it would be good enough soon enough to convince Cassius everything was fine.

"I'm all ears if you have a better idea."

But there wasn't one. I was staying, and I had to protect my guys, which meant I had to do everything in my power to make this job safer for me.

"Okay. Hit me with your knowledge, oh wise incubus."

He grinned at me. "I like the sound of that."

We ate and talked, mostly discussing the afternoon's op and the various demons and shifters we'd encountered. The breeze rustled the leaves and the sun warmed me as it slowly moved in the sky. The couple with the pups packed up and left, and about an hour later a beat-up hatchback pulled into the lot. Five teenaged boys piled out and stripped, tossing their clothes into the car. They raced toward the forest entrance, their bodies transforming as they ran with breathtaking ease, as if they'd turned to liquid, melting from one shape to the other. Even after seeing it twice now, I still always thought that kind of transformation would be painful — and if you weren't born a shifter, the first one always was, as the lycanthropic disease rewrote your DNA — but after that, I'd heard most transformations were mostly painless.

More cars arrived in the lot and kids in baseball uniforms and their parents gathered at the ball diamond. My head was full of information about pit fiends which, as far as I could tell, weren't supposed to be able to cast a paralyzing spell — and I didn't push for more information on that for fear of revealing that I could still absorb demonic magic — as well as the scaled demons, called nagas, and werehyenas.

"We should head back to Operations," Kol said, gathering our garbage and standing.

"Yeah." Except I didn't want to deal with Cassius or Gideon. Neither had called us, and I didn't know if that was a good thing or not.

Kol frowned. He must have heard my not-so-overwhelming excitement at his suggestion. "Okay, what would you like?"

"I want—" A moment, a breath, two seconds where things weren't a hundred percent crazy in a supernatural world. This afternoon with Kol had been good, but I'd still been neck deep in all of it. I'd spent my whole life avoiding all things supernatural, and while I was committed to Marcus, the last three days, let alone the last few weeks, had been overwhelming. "I want to go home. My home."

His expression softened. "Sure."

We drove across town to my apartment, settled on my beat-up second-hand couch with a bowl of popcorn, and found a light romantic comedy playing on the TV. It felt strange and yet comfortable. I'd never done anything like this before, never had anyone over to just hang out. And yet it felt as if I'd always been doing this with Kol. The weight of the last few days sank into me with bone-weary exhaustion. Except I was pretty sure it wasn't sinking in but being revealed now that I wasn't constantly on the go. Two nights ago I'd been shot. The night before that I'd almost had my throat ripped out by a feral vampire.

My buzz burned, and I didn't care if I was scratching myself raw. I was just too exhausted to care. Amiah might have healed my injuries from the last few battles, but I'd been foolish to think everything was all right.

The rom com ended and turned into another one, and my living room started to darken with the setting sun. Kol's warmth seeped into me even though we were sitting side by side, and I couldn't keep my eyes open. Everything turned into a warm, soft hum, even my buzz — which, if I hadn't been so tired, would have shocked the hell out of me...

KOL

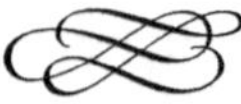

Essie's body relaxed, slumping against me, and her breathing deepened. She'd fallen asleep with me. Again.

A part of me loved the fact that she felt so comfortable with me. She hadn't even needed me to raise her body temperature or ease her pain this time, which meant she really did feel safe with me.

Except she probably shouldn't. I was still an incubus and I didn't have perfect control of my magic.

In fact, I seemed to have slipped more lately around her than I ever had.

It had to have been the stress of the last few weeks. My nightmares had returned with a vengeance and I hadn't been sleeping well, not even after we'd killed the archnephilim. If I was smart, I'd keep my distance from Essie, but this afternoon had been one of the best afternoons of my life. It felt good just talking with her. Even when I talked about the war and my fears and the guilt that I couldn't get rid of had risen to the surface within me, I'd still felt... okay. Like I could confess anything to Essie and she'd still love me—

My thoughts stuttered at that. I hadn't meant love. That was the wrong word.

Love like a sister?

Yeah... maybe?

Except I wasn't sure. I didn't have a sister, and on top of that I wasn't close to my family and didn't want to be. They didn't understand me or why I'd joined the JP and their energy made me nauseated. I'd been relieved — for a split-second — when Michael had pulled me out of the Realm of Celestial Darkness into the human realm. A churning pressure that I hadn't realized had been suffocating me had suddenly released and I'd felt for the first time that I could breathe. But then—

Then.

I shoved at the darkness inside me. I wasn't going to think about it. I was safe and, hell, with Essie and Marcus having figured themselves out, I'd never be starving again. I wouldn't spend days and weeks and months hungry and in pain without enough sustenance to heal myself and no one would force me to use my power against an unwilling victim ever again.

Essie murmured in her sleep and scratched an already raw patch on her arm that she'd been hiding under her sleeve. She was itchy even in her sleep. She'd been scratching a lot lately and a part of me feared this was a side effect of the sex magic she and Marcus were using. If it just stayed to an allergic skin reaction she was fine, but there were other, more deadly things that could happen depending on who'd made the spell.

With another soft murmur, she snuggled closer. Her hand slid across my chest to rest over my heart and her warm breath feathered across my neck.

That strange feeling that I'd felt in the bar when she'd straddled me flooded me again. It was warm and soft and aching. A little like my incubus hunger but... different. I wasn't sure how to describe it. I didn't need to feed and yet I wanted her. I wanted her to touch me, to talk with me, to see me. I wanted to feel her desire seeping through me, seductive and sweet, shimmering with light.

I wanted to just *be* with her. Not to fuck her — although I wanted that too — but I yearned for another day like today. Another day that ended with us on the couch, comfortable in each other's presence, just *being*.

It was the weirdest sensation. I'd never felt anything like it before. Did I want a friend? Was that what the feeling was? Friendship?

I'd never desired friends outside of the team and I hadn't actively gone looking to make friends with them, that had just happened. Gideon had invited me onto the team and I'd been so stuck in the darkness and emptiness inside me that I'd been willing to try anything.

Except as soon as I thought the sensation might be a desire for friendship I knew I was wrong. The heat I'd felt, the sudden roaring in my ears, and the stuttering thud of my heart when she'd straddled me and we'd made eye contact was more than friendship. I craved her, craved the feel of her desire and her release, and ached to feel more of her desire for me.

Which was ridiculous. I was an incubus. We couldn't feel anything more than friendship to anyone — and given how I didn't seek out friends, I wasn't sure I could feel that. We certainly weren't capable of the L-word. It wasn't in our genetic makeup.

Love was akin to a serious mental illness in incubi and succubi. We needed more life energy to sustain ourselves than one person could give and loving a single someone meant we'd either starve to death or kill our lover.

Besides, Essie was mated to Marcus *and* Gideon and even if they weren't my friends, I didn't seduce people who were in relationships. Hell, I didn't seduce people. I couldn't. I wouldn't ever go back to using my magic to hurt people. My lovers were willing before I released my magic and usually professionals because they knew I wouldn't be able to give them any kind of relationship.

No. I was a little lonely and a lot haunted and Essie made me feel safe. That was what I was feeling.

She made me feel like she saw beyond how I looked and the seductive promise of my magic, saw me for who I truly was and still wanted to spend time with me. That could easily be mistaken for a stronger-than-friendship feeling.

I rolled my eyes at myself. I was being ridiculous. What I felt was friendship. Honest to goodness friendship. I didn't feel the same way about the guys because they didn't let people in like Essie did. Even Jacob, who was the most emotionally open with me, had walls. They could have been a product of the era in which he'd been a human or because of the things he'd done as a vampire and then as a soldier in the war, but he still had walls.

The ache in my chest grew stronger. Was that why Gideon was being so cold toward her? He was broken just like Jacob and me, and he knew she'd see all his broken pieces.

A part of me wanted to yell at him, but it wasn't my place to tell him that she wouldn't care that he was broken, that she'd still see him for who he really was. Hell, she loved Marcus and he was grouchy and temperamental and way too easy to rile up.

But even if I did work up the nerve to say something, Gideon wouldn't believe me. What did I know about love and relationships? Nothing. And I never would.

ESSIE

SHARP POUNDING JERKED ME AWAKE. I MUST HAVE FALLEN ASLEEP FOR A good couple of hours since my eyes were gritty from my contacts. I lay against Kol, his legs on either side of me, my cheek pressed against his chest, and his arms wrapped around me. My living room was dark, even the TV was off, and through the skylight, stars sparkled in a cloudless night sky.

The pounding came again. From the door. Hard, insistent. "We know you're in there," a guy with a raspy voice yelled from the hall. "Don't make me break the door down."

I sat up and met Kol's gaze. Hellfire burned in his eyes, casting his face in a flickering light that made him look dangerous.

"Do you have a weapon?" he asked, drawing a knife from his boot and flipping the grip so the blade was hidden against his forearm.

"My off-duty Glock is in the gun safe in my bedroom."

"Get it." He stood and headed to the door.

"Victoria is summoning you, human." The guy pounded again. "Open up."

Kol glanced back at me. "Why the hell would Victoria summon—" Realization flashed across his expression at the same time it hit me.

"Jacob." I glanced at the clock on the microwave. It was a little after one, barely halfway through Jacob's agreed-upon twenty-four hours with her. "Something's wrong with Jacob."

And the moment I said it, I knew it was true. I couldn't tell what, and didn't know how — probably something to do with his claim on me — but without a doubt, something was wrong. The sensation sat hard and heavy in my chest, radiating dread.

I reached for the door, and Kol slapped his palm against it before I could open it.

"Or it's a trap," he said. "She's going to use you as leverage to get Jacob to go along with something else."

"Do you think she'd risk pissing off Gideon?" Last time I'd seen her, she'd been angry at Gideon and had tried to get him in her bed, but it didn't seem as if she'd been willing to make him furious to get what she wanted. And while Gideon didn't want a relationship with me, threatening my life threatened his, which Victoria knew, and that was sure to piss him off.

"You're right," Kol said, but he didn't sound happy about it.

He opened the door. Two vampires stood in the hall, both big and burly. The guy in front with his hand raised to pound again looked familiar. Best guess was that he was one of Victoria's lieutenants who'd helped with the fight at Rouge the other night.

His gaze landed on Kol, and his lips curled back in a sneer, revealing his fangs, before he turned to me. "You're coming with us."

"Lead the way," Kol said.

"Just the human."

The guy behind him clenched his hands and snarled.

The hellfire flared brighter in Kol's eyes. "Do you really want to make this a fight?"

The guy in front opened his mouth to say something, but his friend stiffened and his expression went blank.

"My offspring won't harm the human, but only if she comes alone," the guy in the back said, his voice flat. "Swear by it, Horatio."

The guy in front, Horatio, turned a wide-eyed stare at his friend. "Master, I—"

"Swear by it," his possessed friend said.

"Of course, Master." He turned to Kol. "As my master commands, we won't harm the human."

"I don't like this," Kol said, his voice low.

Neither did I. Especially since Victoria hadn't included herself in that promise.

I squeezed his arm, drawing his gaze to mine. "It'll be okay." At least I hoped it would. Not for myself, but for Jacob. The only reason he'd need me was if he hadn't been able to feed properly from a blood bunny or if Victoria, in her enthusiasm, had hurt him more than he could reasonably heal with a bunny's blood.

"Come on." Horatio grabbed my arm and tugged me into the hall.

"If I don't call you in an hour, tell Gideon."

We hurried down the stairs and out the door to a sedan parked on the street, the windows tinted and the engine running.

Horatio opened the door for me then got in beside me while his friend took the front passenger seat. My pulse picked up as we drove to the Quarter. If Victoria had been lying, I was dead. There was no way I could defend myself from three vampires. Even if I managed to get out of the car, I wouldn't be able to run fast enough to escape them.

I pulled out my phone. Horatio watched me with the same unnerving intensity I saw in Jacob when he revealed the full power of his vampiric nature.

A shudder swept through me, and I tried to stay calm as I sent a text to Marcus letting him know something might be up with Jacob.

"My sire made me swear. You have nothing to fear, human," Horatio said.

"I want to know what's so hot about you?" the guy who'd been possessed by Victoria asked. He leaned around and swept his gaze over me, his attention stopping at my neck. I couldn't tell if he was looking at the bruise or the scar. "That's one heck of a scar. Is that why Jacob claimed you? You like it rough?"

"That's from one of the ferals, you idiot," the woman driving said. "Everyone knows that. Do you really think Mr. Humans Are Delicate Flowers would want a screamer?"

"You never know," the guy in the front said with a shrug.

My phone chimed with Marcus's reply. He was tied up in another emergency meeting with the wolf pack alpha that could last for hours, but he'd drop it all if I needed him.

I texted back that I'd let him know. Maybe, if I could get Jacob away from Victoria, the situation could wait.

We arrived at Rouge, my pulse thrumming. The closer I got to Jacob, the more my dread grew. Horatio took me up the backstairs to Victoria's suite, avoiding the nightclub part of the building entirely, while the other two stayed with the car.

Light from the crystal chandeliers in the hall glimmered in the polished marble floor and gilded frescoes on the ceiling. It had only been three nights since I was last here with Gideon and Jacob, and all hell had broken loose with feral vampires and Gideon nearly dying. That had been terrifying. A horrible second act to what had already started as a bad night.

Surely whatever awaited me now couldn't be as bad as that. Except the temperature kept dropping the closer we got to the end of the hall and Victoria's suite.

The lanky female vampire standing guard at the door watched us as we approached, statue still, radiating powerful vampiric intensity. It wasn't as strong as Victoria's, indicating she wasn't as old, but it was more powerful than Jacob. She gave Horatio a tight nod and opened one of the intricately carved wooden doors which depicted an enthusiastic threesome.

The cold turned frigid before I'd even stepped into the room, the fear so deep frost swept over my hands, making my pulse lurch. Someone inside was terrified.

Fury boiled inside me at the thought that it was Jacob's fear, but that flash froze into an arctic wasteland at the thought it was Victoria's. If it was bad enough to scare Victoria, it had to be terrifying.

I drew in a ragged breath and stepped inside. Horatio didn't join me, and the guard at the door closed it with a heavy thump, trapping me with all that frozen fear. I didn't even look to see if Victoria had completely cleaned her suite from the carnage of the other night. My gaze jumped instantly to the horrific frieze around her bed.

Victoria, Jacob's sire and Union City's master vampire, stood over him wearing a white gauzy negligee that did nothing to hide her voluptuous curves, her hair disheveled, her eyes big, and her complexion pale even for a vampire. Sebastian Bane, the only faekin I'd ever seen, with his pointed ears and his glowing translucent skin, sat on the edge of the bed beside a gasping, bleeding Jacob. He had one hand on Jacob's forehead, the other over his heart. A glyph between Sebastian's shoulders glowed through his white button-down, making the fabric as see-through as Victoria's, revealing a swirling, intricate black tattoo covering his entire back.

Only Jacob's hips and thighs had been covered by a red silk sheet, exposing the rest of his bulky muscular body and all the bleeding gashes covering him. He gasped as if he couldn't catch his breath and sweat slicked his skin, shimmering in the candlelight from the lit candelabras placed around the room.

He was dying. Every fiber of my being screamed that truth. I could feel it in his essence entwined with mine, and my soul wailed at that. That was the dread I'd felt.

And this was Victoria's idea of a good time? How much had all those gashes hurt? I didn't want to believe Jacob enjoyed that kind of violence, but I really didn't know him, just like I really didn't know Marcus or Gideon or Kol.

Except I was certain this hadn't been what he'd signed up for.

Jacob's eyes squeezed tight and every muscle in his body convulsed, arching his back off the bed and making the veins in his neck and arms bulge. He screamed, the agony wrenching at my soul, making my pulse stop completely in horror and fear, and I rushed to him.

"What did you do?"

Victoria seized my arm before I reached the bed, yanked me close, and grabbed my throat, squeezing. "What did *I* do?"

I gasped for breath, and her nails dug into my throat.

"What did *I* do, human?" she snarled. "What did *you* do? He won't take bagged blood, a bunny barely heals him, and my blood does that to him."

Jacob screamed and convulsed again. I heaved against Victoria's grip even though there was no way I could break free against her enhanced vampiric strength.

Sebastian slapped his own shoulder and another glyph burst to life with a blazing white light, joining the first one, revealing that Sebastian's tattoo also completely covered his arm as well. He pressed both hands over Jacob's heart, and with a groan, Jacob sagged back onto the bed, still unconscious, still gasping, and now twitching, as if even unconscious his body continued to convulse.

"I can't keep casting my sleep spell." He captured me with his icy gaze, pure frost, and not because he was upset with me — he barely knew me — but because his eyes were just that pale. "Whatever you're going to do, do it now."

Victoria shoved me onto the bed. I fell onto my hands and knees, one hand landing on Jacob's exposed calf. Even with the fear frosting my hands, his skin was freezing, proving just how close he was to death.

"Fix him," Victoria said, her voice low and dangerous.

Jeez. She hadn't even said *save* him. "He's not some toy. You can't do

—" I pointed at his broad chest, my throat tight as I imagined how much all of that must have hurt. "You can't do that to him and expect it to be all right."

"I've been fucking your master for a lot longer than you've been alive. I'm more than familiar with what he can and can't take." Victoria grabbed my chin and dug her nails into my cheeks, her dark eyes capturing my soul.

I shuddered at the enormity of her power as hard and icy fear churned in my gut.

"I don't know what you did to him or how you did it, but he's mine," she said. "My offspring, my *toy*, and mine to do with as I please. Now *fix* him. His debt isn't fully paid."

God, she was going to keep going? A fury sparked in my chest. "No."

"No?" She wrenched me close. My feet tangled in the sheets and I couldn't get them under me to support my weight, forcing me to clutch her forearm to ease the strain on my neck. Her nails bit deeper, and blood seeped down to my jaw. She laughed, a low, dangerous chuckle, and turned to Sebastian. "She said no."

"No," I gasped. "Not until you release him from his debt."

Her laugh deepened, and her enormous power swelled and gained physical mass, enveloping me and squeezing tight. "You're not in a position to make demands. You're his human and he's my offspring." She flashed her fangs with a wicked smile that made my fear churn stronger. "Didn't Jacob tell you I can use his claim to control you, just like he can? You're going to feed him and then you'll keep feeding him until his debt is paid."

"There are laws."

"You let yourself be claimed. You've given your consent."

Her power squeezed tighter, and pressure exploded inside my skull. It sliced through my buzz, making it twist into a sudden inferno coiled tight in my chest.

"The law doesn't work that way," I gasped.

"You will fix him, and you will like it," she said.

The compulsion contracted my muscles, straining to follow her command. I gritted my teeth against it. "Not until you release him from his debt."

"Fix. Him."

Her power crushed me, inside and out, and my buzz roared through every cell in my body into a whirling firestorm. It raced over my skin, crackling with the lightning I'd come to recognize as Gideon's magic, except it didn't feel like his. It felt different. It felt like mine.

It rushed into my palms, twisting tighter and tighter into a blazing supernova that threatened to explode.

Victoria jerked back, her eyes wide.

I met her gaze, fighting to not flinch away from the enormous power I still saw there. "His debt is paid."

A deadly fury darkened Victoria's expression and her fangs extended in full, revealing her monstrous supernatural nature. "You don't want to make an enemy of me."

"No, I don't."

Jacob screamed and convulsed again, fueling my rage. He wasn't her toy, and I wouldn't let her hurt him again.

"Fix what's mine," she snarled.

"He's not yours," I snarled back, matching her intensity. "He's mine." The certainty of my words rushed into my soul. He was mine. Just like Marcus and Gideon were mine.

My power flared in response, as if it had a mind of its own, turning Victoria's expression back to shock.

"His debt is paid," I said, my voice low, my rage barely contained. "Get out."

I didn't care if this was her suite or not. Jacob needed to feed and I wasn't going to wait even a minute for Marcus to get out of his meeting.

Victoria glanced at Sebastian as if looking to him for help. He was wide-eyed with surprise, but I got the sense half of that was an act and he was searching my soul for answers. I could only pray he didn't figure out the truth. But if he did... God, it would be worth it to save Jacob.

"Out." The power around my hands turned into a brilliant, crackling nimbus.

"She's mated with an angel." Sebastian jerked to his feet and grabbed Victoria's arm. "She's sacred. You don't want a fight with the entire angelic race."

Victoria hissed, wrenched her arm out of Sebastian's grip, and stormed to the door.

Watch yourself, Esther. You've made a dangerous enemy and burned through most of the spell on your contacts, Sebastian said in my head.

I glared back at him, unable to contain my rage at Victoria and this whole situation. If I'd made an enemy, so be it. I'd do whatever it took to save Jacob, and everything else could be damned.

ESSIE

THE MOMENT THE DOOR SHUT, I DROPPED TO MY KNEES BESIDE JACOB, THE crackling power vanishing from my palms. I cupped his face, my pulse racing, fear consuming my rage. God, his skin was so cold, colder now because Victoria or Sebastian's icy fear had left the room, and his eyes were squeezed tight in agony. Blood wept from the gashes on his chest, and his body shook as he drew desperate ragged breaths that were too far apart.

"Jacob." *Come on. Wake up.* I didn't know how powerful Sebastian's sleep spell was, but I knew if Jacob didn't feed now, he was going to die. "Please, Jacob. Wake up."

I didn't want a repeat of the pain I'd experienced when I'd saved Jacob after the archnephilim had nearly killed him and he'd bitten me without his magic, but it didn't look as if I had much choice.

Jacob convulsed, his back arching off the bed, and screamed again, the agony tearing at my soul. The veins in his neck bulged and his face turned red. He gasped in a breath, then went limp, his chest still.

No. "Jacob."

He wasn't breathing.

No no no. He wasn't going to die. He couldn't. Everything within me howled at the idea of losing him. Just like when Gideon had been dying, my soul was shattering. I couldn't lose him. I couldn't.

"Just hold on. Please. Hold on."

I entwined my fingers to do CPR — which, if I'd actually thought about it, was ridiculous because he'd never had a heartbeat to begin with — but he sucked in a strangled breath before I could do the first compression or figure out what else I could do to save him.

I wrenched my gaze away from him to search the opulent room for something I could use to slit my wrist. There wasn't time to wait for him to fully wake up. I didn't know *if* he'd wake up.

Victoria didn't just happen to have knives sitting out — although it wouldn't have surprised me if she had some somewhere — which meant I was going to have to break one of the glasses on her sidebar.

I jerked to my feet, but Jacob seized my wrist and wrenched me back. I fell onto my butt beside him. His dark gaze locked with mine, filled with wild, powerful intensity. Its weight crushed inside me like Victoria's had, except his didn't scare me, his filled me with determination and yearning and heartache.

"You shouldn't be here," he gasped.

"Neither should you."

His attention jumped to my cheeks, where Victoria had dug in her nails and blood still dampened my skin. The intensity turned hungry, the monstrous nature, akin to Victoria's, that he'd always kept hidden now fully revealed, and his lips curled back revealing his fangs.

"Essie." A convulsion seized him, and he dug his claws — not nearly as big as a shifter's but just as sharp — into my wrist. "Essie, please."

Agony and fear swept through me, and a cold mist enveloped me. He was in such pain, his heart broken, his body breaking.

I cupped his cheeks again and leaned close. "You have to feed."

"I'll have no control."

"If you take too much, Gideon's brand will keep me alive."

His heartache ripped into my soul and tears welled in my eyes.

"That's not all I won't be able to control," he gasped.

"I know."

"I told Marcus—" Another convulsion tore through him, turning whatever he'd been about to say into a scream and then desperate, ragged pants. "God, Essie. I lied. I said our connection wasn't emotional, that I'd keep my distance, but—"

"I know." His mist gathered on my cheeks and a tear broke free. "There's something more between us than just your claim."

"There can't be. Vampires don't have mates like shifters and angels."

He wiped my tear away with his thumb. "It can't be anything other than my claim. We've just met. We don't know each other."

"And I don't know Gideon and we're supposed to be soul mates." I held his gaze, fighting back more tears. He couldn't die. Not when I'd just found him. "This is real. I feel this more deeply than I feel a connection to Gideon, and I know you feel it, too."

Another convulsion seized his body, and he let out a strangled scream.

Please. Please don't die.

He was losing strength, his breaths farther and father apart again. "You have to feed."

"Essie—"

"I won't let you die." I dipped in and kissed him, letting him feel my need and desperation and sorrow at his heartache. I wasn't crazy. There was something between us. It wasn't the instant sizzling attraction I'd had with Marcus. It was quiet, certain, intense, just like his vampiric power. It sang in my heart and soul, coursing through my veins with every beat of my heart. Our essences were more than just entwined. Whatever magic bound us together, it wouldn't fade like his claim on me. It was more powerful than that.

With a groan, he tangled his fingers in my hair and took command of the kiss with a desperate, hungry need. His sorrow deepened, as if he believed that when this moment was over we'd go back to the way things were.

But there was no going back. I couldn't go back. Not to my normal mostly human life, and not to a time without him, or Marcus, or any of them.

"Feed," I whispered against his lips and kissed my way across his cheek to give him access to my neck.

He groaned, his breath hot against my throat.

My pulse picked up in anticipation of his bite, of the moment of pain and then the glorious swell of his magic.

His grip in my hair tightened and slowly, with a slice of pain and a whisper of sultry need, he sank his teeth into my neck. But another convulsion seized him, and he clenched down, shooting agony into my neck and digging his fingers into my scalp. A terrifying mix of my pain and his grief sliced into me, and every nerve burned as if I— no, *he* had been lit on fire.

I screamed, crushed by Jacob's enormous power, unable to breathe or think. His back arched and his claws dug deeper. Darkness swarmed my vision for a second... for eternity. I had no idea how long his body and soul possessed me, only that my every cell was attuned to him with a connection a hundred times stronger than his claim.

The convulsion released him. He sagged back to the bed, his teeth still deep and painful in my neck, his breath ragged. His body trembled beneath mine, and the chill of his skin had deepened. I didn't know how much more of this he could take.

Then, with a groan, he took a weak pull on my vein, and relief flooded me. His bite was still painful, but he was feeding. *Please let this stop the convulsions, let this fix whatever Victoria did to him.*

A small spark of his magic curled around my throat, easing the pain, and he took a deeper, stronger pull. His hand on my head relaxed a bit, and he wrapped his other arm around me and pulled me tight to his massive chest.

Another, deeper pull, and heat and desire exploded within me with sudden, bone-melting need. The temperature in the room jumped to sultry, and my breath caught in my throat. My whole essence throbbed with my desire and my certainty of us.

A moan of pleasure slipped out, and he moaned back, the sound low and deep in his throat, vibrating against my skin and into the center of my being. It was like the first time he'd claimed me, except so much more. This connection was deeper, consuming, blazing, and right.

With a growl, he rolled us over, pinning me to the bed with his massive body. His erection pressed into my thigh, oh so close and yet oh so far from where I needed him. That, and I was wearing far too much clothing. I needed to feel his body brushing against mine, sliding into me.

I clutched his back, savoring all that hard muscle relaxing and contracting as he shifted and breathed and moved against me.

His magic sank deep into my core, twisting my need tighter, and he took another long pull on my neck. The room spun and darkened. I didn't know how much blood he was taking, and I didn't care, so long as he lived. He had to live. He could drink me dry, and I'd die happy if he lived. And that wasn't his claim talking, it was something else, something deeper within me. The same something I felt for Marcus. I knew I could live without them if I had to, but I'd be broken, a shell of who I was supposed to be. These men were a part of my soul, and I would do anything to ensure they were safe.

My breath came fast, pressing my breasts against his chest again and again, my nipples growing more sensitive with every second his magic grew within me. He trailed his hand down my side, not even coming close to the edge of my breast and still making my breath hitch. His magic contracted, so much stronger than anything I'd felt before. All the other times he'd been holding back. Now, he had no control, and with his bite lock, it didn't dissipate, just kept growing, filling me, until I was wound painfully tight with need.

I squirmed underneath him, the slide of my T-shirt against my hypersensitive skin ratcheting up my desire.

Jacob rumbled his pleasure, and my essence jerked with a tremble of a climax at just the vibration from his body.

"Jacob—" I gasped.

His hand slipped under my T-shirt, his fingers blazing a trail of need to my breasts. I arched into him, crying when he pushed aside my bra and pinched my nipple.

He growled and sucked harder on my neck, sending more magic flooding into my aching core. I needed him now. Please, God. I was going to combust if his power wasn't released.

I grabbed his hair and pulled him away from my neck. The intensity in his gaze stalled my pulse and made me shudder, teasing the throbbing climax within me. I couldn't catch my breath. His breath was just as fast.

"I'm taking my clothes off," I gasped.

His pupils dilated. "Yes."

I grabbed the hem of my T-shirt, and he sat back, giving me a breathtaking view of his naked body, the gashes sealed shut, his skin smeared with blood and absolutely perfect. Perfect powerful muscles, bulky chest and arms, taut abs, and huge erection. My mouth went dry with anticipation, and I yanked off my shirt and bra.

He flicked open the button on my jeans and pulled them and my underwear down to my ankles where they caught on my runners. With a snarl, he yanked it all off, tossing it to the floor beside the bed, and stared at me with hunger and desire.

"You're so beautiful." His heartache swelled in my chest again, bringing tears to my eyes and swirling mist around me.

I met his gaze, letting my desire for him fill my expression. How I felt for him wasn't just the throbbing need of his bite, but a truth I recognized in my soul. We were mates.

I reached for him, and he met me halfway, sliding his cheek against my hand, savoring my touch, before dipping forward and capturing my lips with his.

The kiss was ferocious, intense, and stole my breath. The throb of his magic clenched in my core, teasing the promise of my climax, releasing, teasing, releasing, teasing, until I was dizzy and aching. I raked my fingers down his chest, through the dusting of pale hair along his abs, and wrapped my hand around him.

"Essie," he groaned.

I pumped my hand down his erection, drawing a shudder and a rumble of pleasure. His eyes rolled back, and I slid my hand up his shaft and rubbed my thumb over his tip.

"God, Essie." His lips curled back, revealing his fangs, his expression hungry for more than just blood.

I pumped again. His breath hitched. He pushed my thighs apart and, with trembling restraint, settled between my legs. His erection brushed my folds, sending a shock of desire exploding through me. I bucked and ground against him, urging his tip into me. I was already wet and ready for him. I needed him inside me, needed to release his throbbing magic and cement the truth of what we were.

He grabbed my hips and slowly, oh so slowly, pushed inside, stretching me. My muscles clamped in anticipation, teetering already on the edge. I tried to move, drive him deeper and faster, but he held me tight, and kept the slow slide until I was panting and desperate and he was buried to the hilt inside me.

With a groan, he drew out and just as torturously slowly pushed back in. I dug my nails into his forearms, the promise of a mind-blowing, screaming climax burning in my core. His magic twisted and spun. I didn't think it could build stronger and yet now my entire body blazed with its promise.

"Please, Jacob. I need you."

He squeezed his eyes shut and shuddered.

"Please. Release me."

"Not yet," he said, his voice strained. And he drew back out, twisting his power tighter. "If you're going to be bite locked, you might as well enjoy it."

The memory of the mind-blowing climaxes I'd had with Marcus made my muscles clench, making him moan. "Pretty sure I have been enjoying it."

He locked gazes with me and ran his hands up my belly to my

breasts. Sensation snapped, stealing my breath, making my whole body clench in anticipation, starting my climax and yet not crashing me over the edge. "You haven't been getting the full effect."

He pushed back into me. My hips now free, I ground against him, my mind and senses on overload. His hands raked over me, tweaking my nipples, scraping against my too-sensitive skin, until I was one heightened, aching nerve. *Oh, yes. God, yes.*

Then he leaned forward, stretched me further, and sank his teeth into my neck. Ecstasy exploded through me. He sucked, the sensation blazing straight to my core and making the room spin. I was pure bliss and blazing magic. There wasn't anything else but the feel of him filling me completely and his power racing through every cell of my being.

Shuddering, his climax on the verge as well, he rolled us over. I ground into him, taking him deep, and he grabbed my hips to steady me, urging me to sit back and ride him. When I did, he slid a thumb to my clit and rubbed rough circles, spiking explosive ecstasy through me.

His hips rolled with mine, finding my rhythm, and with a moan, he tipped his head back, his expression filled with a need and joy that matched my own.

I closed my eyes and gave myself over to the feel of him, large and hard inside me, rubbing all the right spots. The climax, which had been teasing me from the moment we'd started, trembled, tightened, stole all breath and thought, and then exploded.

It roared through me, a blaze of light and sensation, and I screamed, the only way I could release all the pleasure. Jacob tensed beneath me, his fingers digging into my flesh as his own climax took him.

Heat and power erupted through every cell in my body with the full force of his magic. I screamed again, a second wave taking me, and then I was on fire, my skin burning up. The inferno contracted around my heart, Gideon's brand, and then seared up my arm with blinding agony.

ESSIE

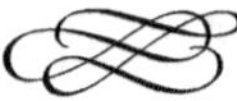

THE PAIN TORE ANOTHER SCREAM FROM ME. EVERY MUSCLE IN MY BODY seized, ablaze for an agonizing moment, then I lost all control, my muscles giving way. I collapsed on top of Jacob, unable to catch my breath, the room spinning.

Jacob's chest, warm against my cheek, rose and fell with deep quick breaths, and all I could think past the agony was that he wasn't cold. *He's going to live, and I'm cold.* It was as if I had taken his chill, a teeth-chattering freeze that reached deep into my soul.

In contrast, Gideon's brand on my right forearm burned, radiating beyond the edges of the sigil all the way to my shoulder, and my buzz stung like a million bees.

"Essie." Jacob rolled me off him.

I slid to the mattress, twitching and shivering. Tears welled in my eyes. What the hell was wrong now? But I couldn't get my mind to work and figure anything out. I was so dizzy, so weak, and so cold. *He's going to live. Thank God.*

At the edge of my vision, the door flew open, and a blur of blue-white light rushed in. No, not light, Sebastian, with his semi-translucent glowing faekin skin.

Jacob jerked up, putting himself between me and the door, and snarled.

"You have to get out of here," Sebastian said, hurrying toward us as if he didn't care that a massive vampire was threatening him.

Jacob's snarl deepened, and this time Sebastian stopped, his hands raised. "You just severed your link with Victoria. She doesn't know it yet, but when she does, she's going to be pissed."

"How do you know?" Jacob's vampiric intensity radiated off him in palpable waves, adding to the cold and spinning room and making my stomach churn.

"I don't know how you did it—"

"How do you know it's broken, faekin?"

"I watched it break. Explode is more like it."

I struggled to sit up, to move, to do anything other than hug myself, shaking with the cold and on the verge of passing out.

"You have to go." Sebastian frowned. "Is that an angelic mating brand on your arm? Did you just get added to Esther and Gideon's bond?"

Jacob's attention dropped to his arm, but from my angle I couldn't see what he was looking at. "I don't—" He turned to me and I strained to read his expression. Had he really just been branded?

He grabbed my hand, slicing agony up my arm. Tears welled in my eyes, and the cold sank deeper into me.

Sebastian drew closer. "No wonder she made an enemy of Victoria over you. You're her soul mate... her other soul mate."

"Her other *other* soul mate," Jacob said.

"There's another one in the bond?"

"Not exactly." Jacob squeezed my hand. "We have to go."

I nodded. Or at least I thought I nodded.

Jacob's expression darkened, and his fear frosted over my cheeks and belly. "Essie?"

I opened my mouth to say something, but couldn't get the words past my chattering teeth. A tear leaked down my cheek and my buzz flared.

"Come on, Essie." Jacob helped me sit. The world lurched with the movement, and I sagged into his embrace. "What the hell is wrong with her?"

"She's in shock. Very few supers can channel the amount of magic needed to sever a link between a sire and her offspring. Add the formation of an angelic mating brand and the blood loss—" He grabbed my T-shirt from the floor, handed it to Jacob, then untangled my feet from the blanket. "You can't stay here."

Jacob pulled me close, his arms protectively tight, and snarled at Sebastian. "Don't touch her."

"I'm trying to help."

"Why?" I forced out.

He flashed me a wicked smile filled with sexual invitation, the look shockingly similar to Kol's, as if he were Kol's icy twin, but it felt more like an act than anything else. "Victoria will kill you for taking Jacob from her, and you're just too interesting to die."

"She can't kill me. Laws... Gideon..." My lips went numb and the room darkened. "Marcus."

"Ah, so the wolf is the other part of the mix. Would have thought it was the incubus."

"Bane," Jacob growled, the deep sound rumbling in his chest and making me tremble. He shifted me and tried to pull my T-shirt over my head. I struggled to help, but couldn't stop shaking.

I should have been embarrassed as hell that I was naked in front of Sebastian, but I couldn't make my mind work past the pain and the cold and the holy hell Jacob was a part of my bond with Gideon.

"No time." Sebastian ran a hand through his spiky white and silver hair. "Wrap her in the sheet."

Jacob bundled me up in Victoria's red silk sheet, then pulled on his pants — which had been on the other side of the massive bed — and picked me up. Sebastian piled my clothes on top of me, and Jacob carried me out the door, cradling me in his arms. I pressed my cheek against his chest and savored the warmth of his skin.

He's alive.

I couldn't think past that, couldn't get warm, couldn't get my teeth to stop chattering, and couldn't get the tears to stop leaking from my eyes. It didn't matter that an angelic mating brand was supposed to be a beautiful wondrous thing, that my soul knew this was exactly the way it was supposed to be. The shock was overwhelming, and I didn't have the strength to fight it.

Bane left us at the door to the back stairs. I wasn't sure if he said anything to me in my head or not, but he had a strange expression. We hurried out of Rouge, Jacob's fear deepening as we went and fully frosting my cheeks by the time we reached the JP SUV Jacob had parked in a side lot near the bar.

"I'll be okay," I gasped as he set me in the front passenger seat and buckled me in.

He didn't look convinced, and the frost crept up to my elbows and down my neck.

"We need to get you to Operations."

"No. Not Cassius." I didn't want to deal with him. Especially since the first thing he'd see would be me naked, wrapped in a sheet, with Jacob's bite on my neck. Unless Gideon had already realized Jacob had joined our bond. Would Gideon know? I had no idea how it worked, and would the brand also make Gideon and Jacob fall in love like I was supposed to fall in love with Gideon? I couldn't deal with that now. I couldn't deal with any of it. More tears ran down my cheeks and I hugged myself, desperate to stop shaking.

"Essie—"

"Please. Not Cassius," I begged. "Take me home."

"You need medical attention."

"I was like this with Gideon's brand." I'd thought I'd been in shock over the attack from the archnephilim, and I might have been, but I guess I'd also been in shock by being branded with a true angelic mating brand. "Please, Jacob. I just—" More tears leaked down my cheeks. "I just need you." And Marcus and, God help me, Gideon, and—

Shit, Kol. I'd told him to tell Gideon about Jacob if I didn't call back. I found my phone — which by some miracle had stayed in my pants pocket — and shoved it toward Jacob, my fingers shaking too much to make a call. "Call Kol."

"Good idea. He'll be able to warm you better than I can."

My buzz flared, stealing my breath and making the world spin and darken.

"It's about time," Kol said.

I blinked. I'd completely missed Jacob dialing... or the SUV starting... or driving down the street beyond the UV-blocking canopy of the vampires' part of the Quarter.

"Meet us at Essie's," Jacob said, pulling onto the Quarter's main street and heading toward the ring park.

"Jacob? What happened? Where's Essie?"

"Just meet us," Jacob growled.

"I'm already there."

"Good." He hung up as Kol started to ask another question, and gunned it.

The trees and buildings and streetlights whipped by, a twisting, nauseating blur. I must have passed out because the next thing I knew,

Kol opened my apartment door and Jacob strode past him straight to my bedroom.

"What happened— Your arm!" Kol said, following us.

Jacob threw back the covers on my bed, set me on the mattress, and tossed my clothes and runners to the floor. I curled into a shivering, weeping ball. I just couldn't get warm, and Jacob's fear wasn't helping.

"What happened? She's so pale." Kol sat beside me, and I shifted closer to his warmth. "And cold."

"She severed my link with Victoria and—" Jacob ran a hand over the complicated, delicate gold threads of his sigil. It wrapped from his elbow, where Gideon's brand ended on me, and up and around to his shoulder.

"Holy shit," Kol breathed. He brushed his fingers across my shoulder. God. They were so warm. So so warm. I grabbed his hand and pressed my cheek against it, clinging to his heat.

"It's okay, Essie," he said, but his attention was on Jacob. "I'll take care of you."

"Please," Jacob said, his voice soft and heartbreakingly desperate.

Kol climbed in under the covers, wrapped his arms around me, and tucked my back tight to his chest. A whisper of his magic seeped across my neck with each of his gentle breaths, and a warm darkness enveloped me.

The cold vanished. My buzz vanished. So too did the ache in my arm, Jacob's heartache, and his fear. There was only peace and warmth and love. Marcus's love and now Jacob's. It filled my soul, and yet it didn't reach the fragile fractured part where Gideon should have been. God, I didn't know how he'd take this new development.

The thought of his rejection or his anger was crushing. It didn't make sense. I didn't love him. But that was the terrifying inexorable power of our angelic mating brand. At least I had Marcus. Thank God for Marcus and being so clear in his agreement of the situation. I could deal with Gideon and Cassius and anyone else because I was certain of Marcus and Jacob. They were mine. And I was theirs.

JACOB

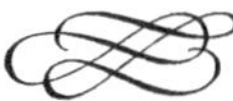

I forced myself to turn away from Essie, unconscious and trembling in Kol's embrace, and step out of her bedroom. My chest tightened at even that small distance between us, but I wasn't going to climb into bed with her while I was covered in blood and I had to call Marcus. He was her mate— or rather, he was her mate *as well*, and he needed to know what had happened.

I should also probably call Gideon. But telling him that Essie and I now shared an angelic mating brand was a complication I didn't have the energy to deal with, not with my body still weak from reacting so violently to Victoria's blood.

Funny how out of the two of them it was Marcus who I thought would be the calmest, most rational about the situation. And while Gideon wouldn't lose his temper, he'd add ice to the wall he'd already erected around his heart, and that would only hurt Essie even more.

I pulled Essie's phone from my pocket, found Marcus's number, but hesitated. Yes, he needed to know, but I'd also lied to him. I'd said my connection to Essie wasn't emotional, but it had been emotional from the start, and the soul bond that had formed between us was proof of that. The moment I'd held her in Rouge and been commanded to wrap my essence into hers, I knew I hungered for her, and not just for her blood but for all of her.

Because we were meant for each other. Just like she and Gideon, and she and Marcus.

My gaze slid to the delicate golden lines shimmering on my shoulder and biceps. Would Marcus really understand? I'd just claimed his mate in a very permanent way... and we'd had sex before that had happened. She'd been his and Gideon's when I sank my teeth and cock into her. Not mine.

I shoved that fear aside. Of course he'd understand. He'd known how strong my claim was and before we'd come to our unusual agreement with me biting Essie and Marcus releasing my bite-lock, he'd implied that he understood sex went along with a vampire's feeding and that he could handle that.

And really, my fears didn't matter. My soul was permanently bound to Essie's. What was done was done and I wouldn't change it for the world. My soul sang with the rightness of it, with the certainty that Essie and I were meant to be together.

A part of me was still stunned. She was an incredible woman, determined and kind, and she was already bound to two men who — once Gideon got his head out of his ass — would treat her like a goddess.

She didn't need another mate, but our souls had linked together in a bond so much deeper than just my vampiric claim. I could already sense a trickle of her life energy, made from light and warmth, teasing through the brand even though it had just formed, and I could only assume that was because we'd already been connected.

God, the bond was so powerful it had broken my sire bond with Victoria. I hadn't thought that was possible, that I'd ever be free of the woman who'd turned me into a vampire and her plaything, but somehow Essie had freed me.

The cost, however, had been great. Essie was a frozen shivering mess, and I was afraid it would take more than a few hours of sleep and Kol's warmth for her to recover this time, not to mention even after she did recover, her life might be in danger. Once Victoria figured out what had happened, she was going to be furious and I could only hope Essie's bond with Gideon would protect her from the master vampire's wrath.

The urge to go back to Essie swelled. I needed to protect her, comfort her, hold her, reassure my soul that she was okay and that I could keep her safe. But me holding her was the last thing she needed. My body temperature was still too low and I'd ruin Kol's work of warming her up.

Still, I could lie in bed and not touch her or I could sit on the floor. I *had* to be near her.

God, I had no idea how Gideon was managing to hold her at arm's length. Although maybe the need to be in constant contact with her faded after the initial binding. Our bond wasn't even an hour old and, unlike Gideon when his brand had formed, I knew without a doubt who my destined mate was.

That thought didn't ease the pressure and I didn't really want to fight it. I just wanted to clean up first... and I should call Marcus.

I dragged my attention back to Essie's phone, hit dial, and Marcus answered after the first ring.

"Essie," he said, his voice tight with tension, his wolf darkening his tone.

"It's Jacob. Marcus—"

"Is she all right?" he demanded before I could say anything else.

"Yes— She will be," I corrected, knowing he'd want the whole truth. "You should come over. We're at her apartment."

"I'll be there in ten."

I didn't know where he was in Union, but I doubted he was ten minutes away, which meant he was going to break the law getting here. Of course, if it was Marcus calling me, I'd speed to wherever she was, too.

"Marcus," I said, catching him before he hung up. "We're bonded. We share a mating brand." I should have waited until he was here, but I didn't want to blindside him. I doubted Essie had a shirt big enough to fit me, so he was going to see the brand on my shoulder the second I answered the door.

"The three of you?" he growled.

"No. Just me and Essie. I didn't get Gideon's part of the brand." And I had no idea how. Essie wasn't an angel and only angels created mating brands when they formed a soul bond.

Of course, she was already mated to Gideon and demonstrating magical abilities beyond that of a normal human. That and she'd blasted herself with so much divine light it was a miracle she was still alive. With those two things combined, maybe her soul was closer to an angel's now. Her essence hadn't changed. She still felt like a human to me, but that didn't mean the ability to create mating brands hadn't been awakened within her.

MARCUS

I FLIPPED DOWN THE JP CREDENTIALS ON THE SEDAN I'D TAKEN FROM Operations, turned on the lights, and sped out of the Quarter. Thank God it was almost two thirty in the morning because there was no way me or my wolf were going to be able to handle any traffic.

Our mate wasn't okay.

I didn't know how bad "not okay" was and I didn't care. Jacob wouldn't have mentioned anything if she'd had a papercut, which meant I needed to be by her side — even if she would eventually be okay.

I'd been scared as hell when she'd texted me to tell me something was up with Jacob and she was being taken to Rouge. But she didn't want me to abandon my job and give Cassius more ammunition against the team and thought it would be best to figure out what was going on first. It would have looked really bad if I'd dropped everything for something a single agent could have handled by herself, and Essie had already proven she was more than capable of handling things by herself.

On top of that, Victoria wouldn't risk pissing off all of angel kind by attacking a bonded mate. Angelic bonded mates were sacred and even if Gideon was being an asshole, she still had his brand. And while compelling someone wasn't necessarily a direct attack, I had confidence that Essie was strong enough to resist Victoria's mental control. If Jacob's claim on Essie was so powerful she was bite-locked and his hunger was stuck on her and she could resist him, she could resist Victoria... because she and Jacob were destined mates, which explained why Jacob's claim on her had been so strong.

And much to my surprise, my wolf was okay with that.

We knew when Essie had gone to Rouge she'd probably have to feed Jacob and there was a good chance neither of them would be able to resist the pull of desire that came from a vampire's feeding. I knew Jacob needed Essie and me not being near to release his bite-lock was bound to have happened at some point. My wolf and I had made peace with that. Letting her and Jacob have sex *was* protecting her.

That they were soul mates just seemed... natural. The next logical step.

I parked on the curb in front of Essie's four-story walkup, turned off the lights but left the JP credentials down so no one would bother to write me a ticket I wasn't going to pay, and raced up the stairs to Essie's apartment.

Jacob opened the door before I reached it and I barreled in, sweeping my gaze over the small living room-kitchen searching for her, but she wasn't there. She had to be in the bedroom.

"Marcus—"

"See her first," my wolf snarled, its need propelling me to the open bedroom door.

Inside was a sight I'd hoped to never see again, not because my mate was wrapped in Kol's arms, but because she was pale and shivering and needed his body heat. Just like the last time she'd formed a soul bond.

Kol tensed at my glare. "I can explain—" he whispered.

"You're good." And I wasn't going to think about the pile of her clothes on the floor by the bed, indicating that she was naked under that red silk sheet... that didn't look like it belonged to her. "She needs you."

"She needs you more. You should take over."

He started to move but I held up a hand, stopping him.

"Nope. You're hotter than I am and that's what she needs right now."

"Can you say that again with witnesses?" Kol asked, his hellfire sparking in his eyes. "You think I'm hot." He purred the word, his tone filled with sexual innuendo. "So that threesome—?"

"You know what I meant, pretty boy," I said, rolling my eyes at him then tearing my gaze away and turning back to Jacob standing in the middle of the living room.

He looked like shit, pale, covered in blood, with dozens of barely healed wounds on his chest — and if I were to guess — on his back as well. The delicate gold lines of an angelic mating brand swirled over his right shoulder and biceps, ending at his elbow where Gideon's brand began and a part of me howled that he now had a stronger connection with Essie than me. Except the frustration wasn't because I wanted to take his connection, but to have a similar one.

My wolf snarled and I told that part of me to shut the fuck up. Our mate bond, even if it wasn't branded on her skin, was still branded on her soul. It was just as powerful as any angel's bond and Essie had shown us that this morning.

"Jesus, Jacob," I said, refocusing my attention on him. He might not be shivering and unconscious, but that was about all he had on Essie. "Tell me you don't have to go back to that bitch."

He stared at me, his expression dazed, as if he didn't understand what I was saying. Then realization kicked in and he frowned.

"You're okay with this?"

"Essie needing to save you from your crazy sire. Fuck no."

"But the brand—"

"The brand makes your strong claim on her make sense. You're a part of Essie," I said, cutting him off. "My wolf and I accept everything that she is." Even if that seemed to go against everything everyone knew about wolves.

Jacob opened his mouth. I could see he didn't fully believe me so I glared at him, willing him to understand.

"Everything," I insisted. She was my world, the only woman I'd ever love, and I knew in my soul that we were mates. Just as I knew in my soul that she was also mates with Gideon and Jacob. Her soul was complicated. She didn't have any control over that just like neither of us had control over who our destined mate was.

Sure, we still needed to work a lot of stuff out — and Gideon needed to stop being a complete asshole — but this was the way it was supposed to be. And now that I'd stopped fighting my wolf and pushing Essie away, I understood that.

She was mine, they were hers... so that meant they were mine as well. It was just that simple.

MY buzz returned first, biting and crackling under my skin at its new uncomfortable normal. With a groan, I cracked open gritty, sore eyes to brilliant morning sunlight streaming through my bedroom windows. Kol still held me close, his body warm and soothing, but Victoria's sheet had shifted and now his one arm lay, flesh on flesh, between my breasts, his hand pressed against my heart, while his other hand cupped my naked butt.

My pulse picked up. The fuzz rushed from my head and vision, but before I could panic that I was in bed and naked with Kol, my gaze locked with Jacob's. He lay on top of the covers, close — because with his bulk the queen bed was barely big enough for the three of us — but not touching me. He still only wore his jeans, giving me a stunning view of his muscular, gash-free chest. He also wasn't bloody any more, which meant he must have cleaned up while I slept.

"Hey," he said, his voice low, making me shiver with desire. Magical shock aside, last night had been amazing — terrifying because of what Victoria had done to Jacob and amazing — and now I was naked in bed with him and my smoking hot incubus—

Who, jeez, wasn't mine.

"Are you warmer?" he asked.

"Yeah."

"Thank God." He brushed a lock of hair out of my eyes, his cool fingers lingering on my skin and yet heating my heart. "I've been dying to touch you all night, but you needed warmth and even after I feed I don't reach human body temperature."

"You've been watching me sleep?"

Kol murmured something unintelligible and his lips brushed the back of my neck, sending another shiver of desire through me.

"And Kol," Jacob said with a soft smile. "I don't think I've ever seen him this peaceful. He hides it well, you'd have to really know him to see it, but he still carries a whole lot of pain from what those animals did to him."

And by animals, he meant nephilim.

"How often do you watch me sleep?" Kol asked, his voice thick and drowsy. He nuzzled my neck, heating my desire even more, and sighed with contentment. "Is there something you want to tell me, Jacob?"

Jacob's lips quirked. "Sorry, man. Don't mean to break your heart, but I'm taken." His gaze, filled with absolute joy, held mine, warming me with a different heat. The ache of uncertainty and regret from yesterday was gone. We'd fully awakened that thing between us, and he had nothing but love for me. I felt it in the slightly raised room temperature and as an honest to goodness emotion in my chest.

Kol shifted behind me and lifted his head above mine. His hand left my ass to prop up his head, and he groaned. "There's something really wrong with a vampire making googly eyes."

"I could make vampire eyes at you instead," Jacob said, letting the full intensity of his power bleed into his gaze.

Kol snorted and brushed his lips over my shoulder, a whisper of his power leaking into my skin and thrumming through me. "I'm glad you're awake and warm." He slid out of the bed, still fully dressed. "I'll leave you two to it," he said as he left, closing the bedroom door behind him.

The intensity in Jacob's gaze vanished, or rather changed back to awe and joy, and it settled back on me.

My buzz crackled, and I clenched my jaw to keep from twitching. Just one moment. That was all I wanted. One moment of peace. But that wasn't going to happen until I figured out how to deal with the damned buzz.

Jacob frowned. "How are you feeling?"

"I'm okay. Just—" What could I say? On fire and wanting to scratch off my skin? Shocked and amazed at us, at last night? Terrified of it, too? "Overwhelmed."

"Yeah. Me, too." He traced his fingers over my shoulder, drawing my attention to the new delicate gold lines etched in my skin. They curled from the top of my shoulder, around my biceps to my elbow, and joined Gideon's brand on my forearm with no indication where one complicated sigil started and the other began. "I'd been wondering if our brands were identical, but didn't want to uncover you and look."

"Are they?" I was pretty sure my brand and Gideon's were identical.

Jacob sat up and turned his right shoulder to me. Delicate gold lines traced from his shoulder to his elbow in an identical pattern to mine.

"You don't have Gideon's half," I said. "Does this mean he doesn't have your half?"

"I don't know."

I tried to recall if I'd read anything about that in the many texts I'd pored through when trying to find a way to remove the archnephilim's false brand. There might have been something about an angel with two mates who were only connected to that angel and not each other, but I'd only skimmed that story because that hadn't been what I was looking for at the time.

"If he doesn't have your half, do you think he knows about us?" A new horrible thought struck me. If Gideon wasn't part of my bond with Jacob, how did I explain a human and vampire sharing an angelic mating brand?

My buzz snapped through my back, and I gritted my teeth.

Worry clouded Jacob's expression. "It'll be all right," he said, probably taking my clenched jaw as fear over Gideon's reaction. "We'll all work this out. Even if I have to beat it into Gideon."

"You can't make him love or even like someone he doesn't want to. I'm not Zella." Even if he did eventually accept our bond and love me, it was going to take time. You didn't just get over someone in a couple of weeks. Certainly not someone you loved with the kind of love I'd seen when he'd been sitting at her bedside.

And just thinking about that made my soul ache. I didn't expect him to stop loving or mourning Zella, but I needed him to not hate me.

I pushed back the grief that always welled within me when I thought of Gideon and sat up, pulling Victoria's silk sheet up with me. Not that Jacob hadn't already seen my breasts... a couple times, but... I didn't know. I suddenly felt awkward and exposed. The room tilted ever so slightly, and I drew in a quick breath to steady myself.

"Hey, take it slow." Jacob grabbed my shoulders to steady me. "You're still really pale. I took a lot from you last night."

"Because Victoria almost killed you," I said, unable to keep my anger from my voice.

"She didn't know the extent of our situation." Jacob ran a hand through his shoulder-length hair. It wasn't in its usual ponytail and hung loose around his face, making him more deliciously rugged. "*I* didn't know the extent of it. The bunny's blood was almost ineffective, and Victoria's blood should have healed me, not send me into convulsions."

"Why did that happen?" I wasn't going to talk about how they'd gotten to that point. His relationship with Victoria was over a hundred and fifty years old, complicated, and something that was going to take a long time for us to work out. "Her blood helped stabilize Gideon when he was shot. Why didn't it help you?"

"I don't know."

"Did I really sever your link to her?"

"Yes. I looked for it last night and can't sense it." Jacob's expression turned grim. "I don't know what she's going to do about that."

My buzz snapped in my lower back again, and I dug my knuckle into the muscle to get it to stop spasming.

"We'll figure it out." He captured my cheeks between his large hands and pressed his lips to mine in a tender kiss.

A warmth seeped low within me, my desire for him flaring. I shifted to deepen the kiss and embrace another hot sensual round of sex with Jacob but caught sight of my bedside clock. 7:32.

"What time is the morning meeting?" I asked against his lips.

Jacob cut off our kiss and pressed his forehead to mine. "You're not going to work today."

"Given how yesterday's op went, Cassius is going to fire me today. I want to get that done and grab my stuff in one fell swoop."

"He's not—"

I pressed a finger to Jacob's lips. "And if he's not, I should at least try to show up on time for my second day on the job."

Jacob held my gaze, all that intensity making my heart flutter and my desire burn hotter.

"Unless you need more," I said, suddenly breathless.

"Yes, but you're too weak. I'll visit a bunny. Hopefully it'll be enough to tide me over."

Disappointment swept through me, and I tried to hide it. The decision was practical, not emotional. He'd been on death's door, and I only had so much blood. I didn't have enough to give what he needed right now, not without dying. Besides, it wasn't as if he had to have sex with the bunny.

"I'm yours, Essie." He captured my lips with a fierce kiss, stealing my breath with his passion. "I have been from the moment I entwined my essence with yours."

"I know. Just still trying to wrap my head around all of this."

"Me, too," he said. "And if you really want to go to work, you should get dressed."

"Yeah. Might as well face my firing head on."

ESSIE

Jacob left to give me privacy to change, and I quickly pulled on jeans, a T-shirt, and my second — and last remaining — stretchy jacket. Even though it was early summer and we were in the middle of an unusual heat wave, last night's chill hadn't fully left me. I could only hope moving around and thinking about something else would shake off the rest of my shock — a shock that had been stronger with the formation of Jacob's brand than with Gideon's. I didn't know if that meant my bond with Jacob was stronger or if my bond had needed extra juice to sever his link with Victoria.

"We don't have time for breakfast," I said, hurrying into the living room.

"We have time for whatever you need," Marcus said, folding a blanket and setting it on my couch.

My thoughts stuttered over him being there quickly followed by a sense of immense relief and joy. "Did you sleep on my couch?"

"Your bed isn't big enough for the four of us."

Kol, who was looking in my fridge, snickered.

Marcus glared at him. "Don't you have something better to do?"

"Just waiting on Essie."

"I called Marcus," Jacob said, "figured he'd want to be here."

"But Jacob needed you more than I did and you needed Kol, so I got the couch." Marcus pulled me into a firm embrace, clutching me to his hard muscular chest and pressed his lips to my forehead. "You looked so pale."

"I'm okay." I clutched him back, savoring the feel of his body against mine and his ferocious love for me. It filled my chest with emotion and heated the room.

"You still look pale."

"Victoria almost killed Jacob." My throat tightened. I'd almost lost him before I'd even realized what he meant to me.

Marcus raised his head. "You didn't tell me that."

"Pretty sure Victoria didn't mean to," Jacob said, his voice a low rumble. "Now I need to see a bunny to see if I can get a little stronger, and you need to get Essie to work."

Marcus stiffened. "You're not seeing a bunny. You said the angelic brand severed your link with Victoria. Until we know how she's going to react to that, no one goes anywhere alone."

"I can't feed from Essie. She's too weak. I'll kill her."

"You'll also kill her if Victoria kills you." Marcus released me and turned to Jacob. "You can feed from me."

"We're *so* going to be late for work," Kol said with a gleeful smile.

Marcus rolled his eyes at him. "I'm not bite locked like Essie."

"But your mate is standing right there and you'll be hopped up on Jacob's magic. Twenty bucks says your wolf won't be able to resist her."

"I have more control than that," Marcus growled. "Besides, Essie gets a say in it, too."

"Hey." Kol raised his hands in defense. "I'm not saying it's a bad thing. Just that your bonds are all very new and you're all barely holding back your urges." Hellfire flared in his eyes and his smile turned wicked. "I'm getting high on your sexual energy just standing in the room with you."

Marcus raked his hand through his wild dark locks. "Fine. Bite but no magic."

"It'll hurt," Jacob said.

"Then make it fast." Marcus turned his pale green gaze to mine, his wolf turning his expression ferocious. "Why don't you freshen up while we take care of this?"

Meaning what? Get out of the room so I didn't have to watch?

The memory of Jacob's bite swept through me, drawing a shiver of desire for both of my guys.

Kol hummed low in the back of his throat before jerking his attention back to my fridge.

Right. Giving them some privacy was probably a good idea. Especially if I wanted to get to work on time.

I retreated to the bathroom, retied my ponytail, and splashed water on my face. I really wished I had time for a shower but it was at least a fifteen-minute drive from my apartment to Operations, and I just didn't have the time. Not that I supposed being late really mattered. Without a doubt, Cassius was going to fire me.

I yanked my attention from those thoughts to the mirror. Once again, the woman staring back at me was too pale, her eyes still a little too wide and—

I frowned and leaned closer to the mirror. A whisper of angel glow flickered in my eyes.

Oh, shit. The spell on my contacts was failing.

Sebastian had warned me. I'd just thought—

Hell, I hadn't been thinking at all. So much had happened last night that I hadn't given any thought to my contacts. All I'd been able to think about was saving Jacob.

But if I didn't deal with the contacts right away, Cassius would do more than just fire me. Everyone knew a being with a human's essence and glowing eyes was a nephilim, and while the team had seen my new glowy eyes, they'd thought it was an aftereffect of fighting the archnephilim and it was supposed to have disappeared over a week ago.

I could explain it away like I had with my weird empathy, but too many revelations too soon would certainly draw suspicion. Especially since Cassius was looking for reasons to lock me away to ensure Gideon's safety.

And what would the other guys think? Was my bond with Marcus and Jacob strong enough to survive that kind of revelation? *Hey, guys, I'm that monstrous, mindless animal you hate. No, Michael didn't create me, but—*

God, they'd think I'd falsely branded them like the archnephilim had branded me. A naturally born nephilim was supposed to be impossible, and I'd been lying to them from the start. They wouldn't believe anything I told them, not this early in the relationship.

A small voice inside me said they'd stand by me, that our bond was true.

But the voice of fear that I'd lived with my entire life was stronger. No one would believe the truth. No one would want to take the risk of letting one of Michael's nephilim roam free.

Someone knocked on the bathroom door, making me jump.

"You ready?" Kol asked.

No, I wasn't. Without a doubt, the truth would come out. There wasn't any way I could hide it forever from my guys.

My throat tightened.

I wasn't ready to say goodbye, and certainly wasn't ready to see the looks on their faces when the truth came out.

I squared my shoulders. If I could just buy myself a couple more weeks, Cassius would be gone, and I'd have more time to show Marcus and Jacob how much I cared for them, as well as what kind of person I really was. Gideon might even agree to a truce.

"Essie?" Kol asked.

"I'm coming."

The glow wasn't obvious — if it had been, Jacob would have seen it while we were staring at each other in bed — so I could deal with the morning's meeting, but then I had to find a way to slip out to Squatters' Row and get my contacts re-spelled.

I rinsed my mouth with mouthwash and opened the door, my gaze instantly jumping to Marcus and Jacob by the front door. Jacob, still without a shirt since his had been left at Victoria's, looked a little less pale. I was surprised at how fast he'd healed, since Marcus was essentially a bunny and his blood shouldn't have had an immediate effect. Marcus looked good, too. He was tying up his combat boots, and I couldn't see a bite on his neck or either of his wrists, which meant he must have shifted and healed the wound, hiding the evidence. It also meant I'd spent longer in the bathroom staring at myself than I should have if he'd had time to donate and shift.

We piled into our vehicles, Marcus in the sedan, Kol in the SUV we'd taken yesterday afternoon, and Jacob and I in the SUV he'd driven to Rouge. I'd expected an argument from Marcus about who I rode with, but he just brushed my cheek with a quick kiss and told me to go with Jacob.

"You're looking better," I said as we drove to the Quarter.

"I can put to rest any doubt you might have about your connection with Marcus." He squeezed my knee, sending warmth fluttering through me. "His blood doesn't heal me as quickly as yours, but my essence recognizes your essence is bonded to his. He's more effective than a bunny."

"That means Gideon's blood probably would be, as well."

"I'm not asking Gideon for a donation," Jacob said. "I'm not asking Marcus again, either. Not unless he lets me use my magic."

"If we had the time, I'm sure he would have."

The temperature in the SUV rose and Jacob glanced at me. "We'll figure this out, but things are... well, complicated."

"Now that I'm mated to three of you?"

"That, and keeping ourselves controlled while on the job. Certainly while Cassius is reviewing the team." He stopped at a red light. "Kol was right about our bonds being too new. All I want to do is take you back to bed. It wouldn't surprise me if Marcus wants that, too."

And all I wanted was to go back to bed with all of them.

"We're just going to have to be adults about this. We have a lifetime to figure this out." If they didn't learn the truth about me. "We don't have to rush."

Jacob's expression darkened, and I realized I had a lifetime, but Jacob and Gideon would outlive me.

Except I had no idea how long I'd live. The nephilim during the war hadn't allowed themselves to be captured. The only way to stop them was to kill them, and if by chance the Angelic Defense did get ahold of one, it was said they always turned their magic on themselves and committed suicide. Which meant I had no idea what the life expectancy of a nephilim was. For all I knew, I could be as long-lived as an angel—

And then I'd be alive and well with Jacob and Gideon, mourning Marcus when old age took him.

Jeez, I hadn't realized how complicated this whole situation really was.

"We'll figure it out," Jacob said. Again.

"Is that your new mantra? You've said it three times this morning and we've been awake for less than an hour."

"Because you keep looking like you're about to panic. I'm not saying it'll be easy, but the brand on my arm says we're soul mates. The bond between you and Marcus says the same. We *will* make it work," he said, with such conviction my soul sang.

The light turned green and we continued to the Quarter, my buzz easing the closer we got to Operations. It was still painfully distracting, but clearly better. Which made me nervous. If Cassius did fire me and

Gideon didn't want me around, was I going to spend the rest of my life feeling like I was hanging onto an electric fence?

Jacob followed Kol and Marcus into the garage and as their vehicles ahead of us turned and parked in their usual spots, my gaze locked on Gideon, standing straight ahead, without his shirt on. My thoughts stalled. He wore shorts and runners and held his shirt wadded in his hand. Sweat slicked his gorgeous muscular body and his breath came just a little too fast, as if he'd just finished running and had really pushed himself.

His brand hadn't changed, confirming I was the link between the three of us, and I was going to have to figure out how to answer the obvious question when it arose about a human and a vampire sharing an angelic mating brand.

Jacob parked, and I got out of the SUV. Gideon's gaze instantly landed on me, icy and hard, making my chest ache for even the possibility of a friendship.

He turned his back on me and glared at Marcus and Kol as they got out of their vehicles. "You all show up with Agent Shaw. Are you trying to get Cassius to disband—" Light flared from his eyes as Jacob came around the back of the SUV. "What. Is. That?"

"Guess what?" Kol said brightly. "Essie and Jacob are soul mates, too."

Gideon's expression jumped from shock to horror, and the temperature fluctuated so fast it made my stomach lurch. My buzz sliced through my neck, making me twitch, and still, even though it was clear the situation appalled him, I yearned for him.

"We'll deal with this later," he said, his tone sharp and cold. "Cover that up before Cassius sees it."

"Yeah," Jacob said, heading toward the door. "I'll be in your office in five for the morning meeting."

"Don't bother. It got postponed to eleven because you were supposed to be with Victoria. Didn't any of you look at your phones?" Gideon's eyes narrowed. The temperature lurched again, then he squared his shoulders and I was surrounded by a mild chill — probably the actual temperature of the garage. He'd locked his emotions down and become the emotionless angel he was supposed to be. But I didn't need to feel anything more from him. I already knew how he felt about me.

"Your text didn't indicate it was urgent and last night got—" Jacob glanced at me, and I could see the question in his eyes: did we tell Gideon everything?

He was going to find out eventually, if he hadn't already figured it out. Might as well tell him now.

"The short version is," I said, "Jacob's debt is paid but Victoria is one pissed master vampire." My buzz snapped through my neck again, and Jacob shifted toward me.

The muscles in Gideon's jaw clenched. "My office in three hours," he said and stormed to the door. "And eat something, Agent Shaw, before you pass out."

"Well, that went as well as expected," Kol said.

My throat tightened as Gideon left. Why the hell did it hurt so much? I had Marcus and now Jacob. I didn't need Gideon. But my God damned soul disagreed.

"I should—" I wasn't sure what I should do—

No, I *was*. I needed an excuse to get to Squatters' Row. It was about a twenty-minute walk from Operations, and I had more than enough time to get my contacts fixed right now.

"I should grab something from the cafeteria then lie down. It's been an exhausting couple of nights."

"I'll join you," Marcus said.

Of course he'd offer that, and I ached to say yes.

I grabbed his hands and met his piercing green gaze. I could see his wolf in his eyes, but it didn't darken his expression. It was content.

"If you join me, I'm not going to get the sleep I really need."

"I can be good."

Kol snorted.

Marcus glared at him. "What? I can."

"Bet you another twenty on that," Kol said. "I'm getting the hell out of here, because I can't keep my shields up to the level needed to protect against you two— you *three* for the next three hours." He shrugged and sauntered from the garage.

"Come on, Marcus," Jacob said, jerking his chin to the door. "We can keep it together without her for three hours."

"I know, but I don't want to." He tangled his hands in my hair and captured my mouth in a fierce kiss. "But I will because you do need the rest."

He turned me to face Jacob, who cupped my cheeks and kissed me tenderly, steadying me from Marcus's ferocious passion and filling me with warm certainty.

"Call if you need us," he said, and they headed inside.

God, I needed them right now. Always.

But I resisted calling them back as my guilt that I'd lied to them twisted in my gut.

This was for the best. Maybe by the time the second spell on the contacts had worn off, the glow would finally be gone from my eyes.

I doubted it, and eventually the truth would come out. But not now. I wasn't ready. I'd just found them, just realized what it was to have someone who cared about me and to be a part of a... hell, of a family. God, I wouldn't ever be ready to lose everything.

ESSIE

I HURRIED OUT OF THE GARAGE BEFORE I COULD CHANGE MY MIND. WITH luck I could sneak back in, grab something from the cafeteria, and get at least an hour's sleep before the morning's meeting. The sun warmed my skin and by the time I'd reached the edge of Squatters' Row I'd managed to work off most the night's bone-deep chill. In fact I felt better than I had in a long time. I'd thought my life before the archnephilim had been fine, but it had been empty. It had been empty since cancer had taken my mom from me just after my seventeenth birthday and I'd been forced to live my life under the radar alone.

Now it was full and amazing and perilous.

God, if my mom could see me now, she'd be horrified. I was a JP agent. And I *wanted* to be one. I was mated to an angel and lived in angel central. She'd say I was asking for trouble and demand to know how I could have been so foolish.

But it was fate. And as much as I didn't believe in fate, that a person made their own fate with their decisions and actions, I couldn't deny it had nothing to do with my situation. I hadn't chosen to have Gideon's brand, and I'd tried to go back to life-as-normal after the archnephilim, but the world of the supernatural had sucked me back in.

I couldn't fight this even if I wanted to. Which I didn't. I might have to accept it was too dangerous to be a part of the team — and God, just thinking that made my stomach churn with frustration — but I couldn't leave my guys. Something deep inside me knew they needed me as much as I needed them. Even Gideon.

I reached the witch's shop in the heart of Squatters' Row. It sat in the back of an abandoned building that used to have a restaurant on the main floor and apartments on the two stories above. The entrance lay around back, off the alley where the restaurant would have accepted deliveries.

A small Eye of Horus drawn in black marker near the top of the solid metal security door was the only indication I was at the right place. I'd found Mystic Mavis by doing an online search on the dark web. I was supposed to only use my dark web connections in an emergency, to change my identity and relocate if JP agents were closing in on me, but given my situation, there wasn't any way I'd be able to go to a registered witch to hide my glowy eyes — at least not without him or her alerting the authorities.

I opened the door, my buzz blazing, setting my skin on fire, and stepped into the long hall between the storage room and the walk-in fridge and freezer. Incense thickened the air with a purple haze that clung in my nose and the back of my throat. Large black glyphs decorated the walls, and low lighting gave the place a creepy ambiance. I hadn't enjoyed visiting Mavis the first time, and so far this time didn't feel any different.

"Changed your mind about a love charm?" a raspy alto said from the end of the hall.

"No." I gritted my teeth against my twitching muscles and stepped into what had once been the restaurant's kitchen. Most of the stainless steel counters had been taken out, replaced by dark-wood bookcases crammed with books and trinkets and boxes and other strange, twisted things. What remained of the counters lay between the sink and stove along the right-hand wall, cluttered with bowls, vials, and jars. One side of the two-compartment sink was filled with dirty dishes, and a pot of something foul-smelling simmered on the stove — and I could only presume the stove was heated by magic, since the building had neither gas, oil, nor electricity.

"I'm sure you've changed your mind," Mavis said.

She sat in the middle of the kitchen in a high-backed wooden chair, behind an intricately carved table. She was bedecked like a gypsy from an old movie with a billowy blouse cinched tight by a black corset that accentuated her ample breasts, and a skirt made of many layers of gauzy material. A multi-strand chain headpiece barely held back her wild black locks, the decorative glass...? or were they actually diamonds...? inset in the delicate gold chains catching the light of the three dozen candles placed around the room.

"I'm not interested in a love charm. Your contacts are failing."

"My spells don't fail." She leaned forward, making her dozens of bracelets and three necklaces tinkle together, and her large hoop earrings sway.

"Take a look for yourself," I said, keeping my voice even. I needed to approach Mavis from a position of confidence but not confrontation. The witch might look like a pre-war cliché and sell illegal love charms, but she possessed powerful magic. If I hadn't been able to tell by the way my skin crawled the closer I got to her, I still would have known by the reactions she received on the dark web.

Mavis pointed to the stool across from her, and I forced myself to walk the fifteen feet and sit. My buzz snapped and bit and even the magical channels in my head throbbed. Jeez, I hadn't noticed that pain for a while and had hoped that was on the mend.

The purple haze swirled, thickening around Mavis, and her power slid over me, curling against my skin, seeking entrance.

I gritted my teeth. She hadn't done this before—

No, she had. I just hadn't been able to feel it with such clarity before. Which either meant she was using more power or more of me was changing, becoming more sensitive to magic. I really hoped it was the former and not the latter.

She frowned, pursed her small, blood-red lips, and narrowed eyes almost as dark as Jacob's when he revealed his full vampiric nature. Her power tightened, no longer a caress seeking entrance but a slice, cutting into me, drilling into my core to expose the truth.

I held my breath, trying not to fight her. I needed her spell. I couldn't afford to accidentally force her out. But God, the invasion made my buzz blaze and my heart race.

Please finish. I didn't know how much longer I could resist the pressure building within me. *And please don't let her decide I'm too dangerous to be a customer and tell the JP I'm a nephilim.* Especially since the JP representatives in town were Gideon and the team and the whole point of the visit was to avoid them knowing the truth for just a little longer.

"You're going to need something stronger than just the contacts," she said.

Which of course would cost me more money. A lot of it, probably. "How long will that last?"

"Not forever, if that's what you're asking."

"That's not an answer."

"Feel free to ask around for a better deal." Mavis flashed me perfect teeth with one gold canine. "Oh right, you can't. None of my colleagues are powerful enough to cast what you need. None of my illegal ones, that is."

"I wasn't asking for a better deal, just better details." My buzz snapped in my thigh, and I ground my knuckle into the muscle. I was trapped, and I hated being trapped. If I wanted to keep my secret a little longer, I had to buy whatever Mavis was selling for whatever price she demanded. The only thing I could hope for now was that her spell would last long enough for me to solidify my bond with my guys so they'd be able to come to terms with what I really was.

Except a tiny voice inside me wondered if they ever would. Would I accept one of them if it came out that they were lying to me and had been from the start?

Mavis leaned back, her power slicing into my skin again. "Let's just say I wouldn't make plans more than a year out."

I bit back my relief. I could handle a year. Cassius would be gone — surely he'd be gone — and I'd have time to show my guys who I really was, prove to them I wasn't the monster they thought all nephilim were. Seeing my actions for a whole year would be enough time for them to know me, my soul, and see beyond what I was.

"How much?"

"Two hundred and fifty grand."

"For one year?" That would put a serious dent in my secret offshore bank account and then I wouldn't have much left if I needed to run — not that I could because of the brand — but I also wouldn't have much left for the next year or the year after that.

Except I wasn't going to have the spell recast... right? I only needed it for a year.

But the panic racing through me screamed I'd want more time, I wanted all the time I could get. No one would understand what I was. God, if Gideon hated me now, he'd despise me when he learned the truth.

"Don't try and barter, the cost is non-negotiable," Mavis said.

"I don't have that kind of money," I lied, testing to see if she would just kick me out or if her greed would make her suggest a different price.

"Then you're going to have to find it." A wicked smile pulled at her red lips. "Unless you'd like to give me some of that glow."

"My glow?" I asked, pretending I didn't know what she was talking about. Sebastian had said some witches paid a lot of money for angelic light magic, but I hadn't had time to learn more about that. Jacob had said angels didn't sell their magic but hadn't mentioned the reason, and I suspected I wouldn't like the answer. But if it kept my secret…

"Your glow. Your light magic. I can feel it in the core of your power." She flicked her fingers and a glass orb rose from a wooden shelf behind her and floated to the table. Light flickered like weak miniature lightning in the churning clouds captured in the orb. "Fill this every year, and I'll keep casting the spell."

Except what was the actual cost? I didn't know enough about what would happen to give her my light. Would I lose the ability to cast the light strike spell? At the moment that was the one thing keeping me alive on the job. Would Gideon or Jacob notice? That would make them ask questions I was trying to avoid. Giving Mavis my light magic could make my situation worse. I needed more information.

"I need to think about it."

"What's there to think about?" Mavis asked, her tone sickeningly sweet. "I could throw in a love charm."

"I don't need a love charm." She really wanted my light, which only made me more reluctant to give it to her.

"Everyone needs a love charm."

"No. Thank you."

"You need my spell. There won't be any place you can hide." Her tone jumped from sweet to dangerous, and she grabbed my wrist with her magic.

My buzz flared, and I jerked to my feet, ripping free of her power. "I need to think about it."

"I wouldn't think too long. My spell on your contacts will fail within twenty-four hours."

"Then I guess I have twenty-four hours."

"Two hundred and fifty grand or your light, little nephilim," she called as I hurried from the kitchen.

I hit the crash bar and stumbled into the alley, my gut churning. There had to be another way. Even if I paid her now, there was no guarantee she wouldn't turn me in, especially if she thought I wouldn't keep paying.

Someone hiding behind the door seized my wrist and wrenched me off balance.

My fear lurched from Mavis to the new danger. I jerked to face my assailant, the palm of my free hand blazing with divine light without me even thinking of the light strike spell, and I came face to face with Kol.

Shit.

The light exploded from my hand, and I wrenched my aim down, blasting a deep gouge in the asphalt at our feet.

He shoved me against the restaurant's concrete wall without even blinking an eye at my blast, his forearm pressed against my chest. Hellfire blazed from his eyes, but with anger not desire. "What the hell are you doing?"

"What are *you* doing?" I shot back as my pulse skyrocketed. He'd figured it out. Of course he'd figured it out. He was the most magically sensitive of the guys, and he wasn't influenced by any kind of bond. He already knew my essence was more light than dark. Hanging out with me was like being with an angel without me being an angel. And God! He'd been able to sense the Divifend. He'd probably noticed the enspelled contacts.

"I'm following an idiot," he said. "That's what I'm doing. What part of no one goes anywhere alone didn't you understand?"

"Kol—" My thoughts raced. What did I tell him? The truth. I had to tell him the truth and pray he didn't arrest me or—

But panic clenched my jaw and made my pulse race. He, out of everyone in the group, had the most reason to fear and hate nephilim. I had to do this delicately, find the right words. I didn't want him reliving whatever horror he'd experienced during the war.

"And don't tell me you didn't think about not sneaking here alone. You're smarter than that." He shoved away from me and ran his hands through his dark locks, mussing them even more and making me heat with desire.

Tell the truth. Come on, Essie. Just do it. It was the only way to salvage this. Perhaps we had a strong enough connection that he wouldn't freak out. Perhaps if he understood why I was so afraid, he'd forgive my lies. *Please, God, he had to understand. They all did.*

"You don't need sex magic to keep Marcus, Essie. Trust me, you're all he needs."

Really? That again? "That's not why I'm here."

"Stop lying. I know what I feel every time you have sex. I can find the charm on you easily enough."

"I swear. I'm not using sex magic. Kol, I—"

"For fuck's sake." He raked his gaze up my body.

My pulse quickened, and the memory of yesterday's dream flooded me with need. I ached for his touch, his lips, the full force of his power sliding into me. All of him in me, driving me to—

Jeez, if he didn't pull his magic back, I was going to rip my clothes off and beg him to take me.

"Kol, please," I gasped.

His gaze reached mine, his expression hard, making me think of angry, ferocious sex. With his power, he could make pain pleasurable. I'd never wanted that before, but right now if he asked, I'd say yes.

"How the hell do you not have a love spell on you? The power of your energy with Marcus has to be enhanced."

I shuddered, trying to tamp down my desire and draw breath to answer him.

He leaned closer, almost nose to nose. If I shifted forward, I'd be able to kiss him.

Which, God, I didn't want to do. Because he wasn't mine. This was just his power influencing me. That was all. Really.

"What's on your eyes? The spell is so subtle. You're clearly trying to hide something." His breath feathered across my cheeks.

My buzz snapped, slicing through my desire.

He jerked back with a gasp. "Are your eyes glowing?"

"Yes." This was it. Imprisonment or lab rat. Everything my mother had feared for me. "They never stopped glowing after the archnephilim."

"So you decided to visit the shadiest witch in the Quarter? Jeez, Essie. Why didn't you come to us?"

"Why didn't I go to you?" Didn't he realize the truth? And if he didn't, should I keep lying?

"Essie, you can trust us," he said, his tone soft, his eyes sad, heartbroken at the thought that I didn't trust him.

"No, Kol, that's not—"

"I might be able to understand you visiting Mavis after the archnephilim. You were trying to avoid us, but now? After you and Marcus have clearly worked things out, and now you and Jacob—" Kol frowned and pulled his buzzing, lit-up phone from his pocket. The call display only showed a number, but Kol's expression darkened as he accepted the call. "Yeah?"

"Jacob is back early," Cassius said, only audible because of my enhanced hearing. "Summer's lab in ten."

"I'm twenty minutes out."

"Fine," Cassius snapped, and the line went dead.

"Okay, I take it back." Kol shoved his phone back into his pocket. "I completely get why you snuck back to Mavis to respell your eyes."

Except I hadn't paid for the respell and within twenty-four hours I was either going to have to agree to Mavis's demands or risk everyone seeing me for what I really was.

ESSIE

"WE'LL GET RID OF CASSIUS THEN DEAL WITH YOUR EYES," KOL SAID AS WE hurried back to Operations. "It shouldn't surprise anyone that you're developing some magic, not with two angelic mating brands, but you're right. Cassius is a complication that's best avoided."

"Why shouldn't it be a surprise?" I asked.

"Angelic mating brands are powerful. They change both—" He flashed me a wicked grin. "—or rather, *all* of those involved. There weren't a lot of recorded bonds with non-angels and only one with a human, but the non-angels always developed or grew their magic. Sometimes in significant ways."

"When did you become an expert on angelic mating brands?"

"I did some reading after you left us."

"Really?" I raised my eyebrows at him. I didn't know why that surprised me, but it did. "After I left you?"

"Fine," he said, "after I realized I missed your energy. I wanted to know if you'd come back."

"According to what everyone tells me, I won't be able to resist Gideon." And the ache in my soul said that was true. Except Gideon was doing a perfectly good job at resisting me.

"You're soul mates, destined to be together."

"But I'm also soul mates with Jacob and Marcus."

"Who says there's only ever one?" Hellfire flickered in his eyes, making me shudder with desire, then his expression turned strange — worried? sad? I wasn't sure — and he yanked his attention back to the street ahead of us. "You humans can be so weird. If incubi could have soul mates, it would have to be more than one. We wouldn't be able to get enough sexual energy from just one person. We'd either starve to death or end up killing our mate."

I had no idea what to say to that, nor to his strange expression, but my phone rang before I could figure out a response. It was the same number that had flashed on Kol's phone a few minutes ago.

"Shaw," I said.

"Summer's lab in ten," Cassius snapped over the line.

"Copy that."

He hung up. Guess I was getting fired in front of the whole team. But hey, at least I had a reasonable explanation for all my weird magic. Everyone would think it was because of the mating brands and no one ever needed to know what I really was.

We made it to Summer's lab barely within my ten-minute deadline. Cassius stood at Summer's keyboard looking at the big screen on the wall, now showing the satellite image of a different, fully abandoned, mostly leveled section of town, while Gideon stood a few feet away, his arms crossed, his expression hard. He'd changed into a dress shirt and slacks, but now that I'd seen his hard, sculpted chest and abs, I couldn't think of anything else.

I resisted the urge to step close to him and fully mute my buzz. It was at the dimmest level it had been all day, almost post-nicotine levels from before the whole archnephilim incident, and I needed to just be happy about that.

Marcus and Jacob stood a few feet from Gideon, and I also felt a call to go to them, but for a different reason. Standing with them would make me feel strong when Cassius fired me. And I wasn't going to resist that. To hell with telling Cassius with our body language that there was something going on between us.

I drew up close to them, Marcus in his T-shirt, jeans, and perpetual sexy scruff, and Jacob in an out-of-character long sleeve shirt, the sleeves drawn down hiding the mating brand. They shifted so they stood behind me, showing their support and making Cassius glare at me.

Kol stopped close enough to look like part of the group but didn't actually stand behind me. Instead, he leaned against the same still-empty table from yesterday and crossed his arms, radiating relaxed sexual confidence. I didn't see Summer, but she could have been in one of the other labs attached to hers, or taking a quick break. I didn't know her well enough to know if she was purposefully avoiding the could-cut-it-with-a-knife tension between Cassius, the guys, and Gideon, but it wouldn't have surprised me.

"Marcus, you had another meeting last night with the wolf pack alpha," Cassius said.

"Another five teenagers dead from zip, and one of the wolves who found them accidentally picked up a pill without gloves and is in the hospital."

"Just by touching a pill?" The words blurted out before I could stop them. That put zip in the same dangerous category for supers as fentanyl was for humans.

"The mortality rate is high," Marcus said. "Four times higher than humans. I don't know why supers are even trying the stuff."

"And who's selling it to the pack?" Jacob asked.

"That's too many deaths in a forty-eight hour period." Light flared from Gideon's eyes. "We have to stop this. We should set up a sting, see if we can nab the dealer."

"No," Cassius said, making Gideon stiffen. "We need to stop this at its source. Summer cracked the lock on the pit fiend's phone. It pings the most from a cell tower in the Quarter and this neighborhood." Cassius pointed to the screen. "The last number the pit fiend called is in this warehouse, right now."

"So we're what? Going to blindly run in there?" Marcus asked. "We don't know what's there, if anything, and we don't know how many are inside. The last time we assaulted one of this operation's locations, Gideon almost died. And we'd *known* roughly what to expect."

"I didn't say anything about blindly running in, Agent Diaz." Cassius glared at Marcus. "I'm here to remind your team to exercise caution and not cause another incident with the humans. This is a recon mission. We check out who and what is in this building and the surrounding area." He swept his gaze over the rest of the team. "And yes, this is a part of your evaluation."

"In the garage in five," Gideon said, his tone void of emotion. "Everyone wears a vest."

Jacob, Marcus, and Kol shared a look then glanced at me. So far

Cassius hadn't said anything to or about me. He'd barely looked at me, and his emotions were locked down tight. Actually, everyone's were. The room temperature was normal, if a little warm because of my jacket — which I wasn't taking off because that would reveal Jacob's still-healing bite on my neck and the addition to my angelic mating brand.

"Come, Essie," Jacob said. "I'll meet you in the armory and get you set up."

"No. Agent Shaw, you're with me." Cassius strode toward the door, not looking to see if I followed.

Marcus stepped toward me, but I shook my head, stopping him, and hurried after Cassius. My stomach churned and my buzz grew stronger the farther I got from Gideon. I was going to have to face my firing without my guys. Which, as much as I wanted the support of just being near them, was probably for the best. I couldn't afford to make an enemy of Cassius, not when I was permanently bound to his brother, and I didn't want Marcus to lose his temper and ruin his career.

We got into the elevator, but instead of hitting the main floor button to escort me out the door, Cassius selected the basement.

I bit the inside of my cheek to stop myself from speaking. The best plan was to let him make the first move. There were any number of reasons to take me down to the basement. Perhaps he wanted to fire me as he got ready. Perhaps there were more cells, in the back, beyond the library stacks, where he was going to lock me up to protect Gideon.

The door slid open, and Cassius headed straight to the armory and pressed his thumb to the fingerprint scanner, unlocking the door.

"Gideon's report on the feral vampire nest in the subway tunnel says you're familiar with an M4 carbine." Cassius headed straight to the M4s, pulled one from the rack, and set it on the narrow table in the center of the room, then he grabbed a box of ammo and a magazine from the ammunition shelves. "Ammunition enspelled with a stun spell. Be mindful of your shots. It's expensive. But also don't forget the op from the bar yesterday. The rounds are too small for a strong stun spell, so most supers require two shots."

Now I was confused as hell. It sounded like I was going on this mission. "So you're not firing me?"

He captured me with his icy pale gaze, so much like Gideon's it made me ache. "It's been made clear to me that I have to have a human working actively on the team, even if she is a liability. We need to move on this intel and shut this zip operation down before more supers die, and I don't have time to wait for your replacement to show up."

Ah. So he wanted to fire me but couldn't. Not yet, at least.

He drew my service weapon from the ammunition cabinet and set it beside the M4. "You do what I say, when I say it, and always stay with a team member." The temperature rose, revealing how much he hated this plan.

I wasn't sure I disagreed with him. I still had no good answer to how I could be a part of the team while ensuring the guys didn't end up hurt.

"Is that clear, Agent Shaw?"

"Yes, sir."

"Your file indicates you'll have trouble with that."

Jeez. I just couldn't get away from that one rookie mistake.

"You stole a divine light ring and snuck out to face an archnephilim alone, and disobeyed a command from a senior agent and left the team while clearing out that feral vampire nest."

"I was the only one free to back up Jacob."

"That's not the point." Light flared in Cassius's eyes, and the temperature rose a few more degrees. "Every time you do something like that, you endanger Gideon."

Not myself and Gideon. Just Gideon.

My buzz flared, and the muscles between my shoulder blades spasmed. I clenched my jaw, putting up with the pain since there was no way to rub it out without contortions.

"Fill that magazine." He jerked his chin to the M4's magazine before turning to the locker with the bulletproof vests.

I started filling the magazine.

"Your file also indicates Jacob's claim on you is strong enough to enhance your vision." He didn't sound happy about that, and there was no point in denying it.

"Correct."

"At least you won't mess up the team's night vision." He pulled out two vests, set one on the table, and shrugged into the other one.

I finished filling the M4's magazine, inserted it into the carbine's well, and pulled back the charging handle to chamber a round.

"Amiah also says Jacob's claim has enhanced your healing." He set a waistband holster with my Glock on the table.

"Also correct." I checked my Glock's magazine. It had been reloaded since I'd handed it over to Cassius in Hacksaw's parking lot. I chambered a round in my sidearm and holstered it. "Anything else, sir?"

The muscles in his jaw flexed and the temperature flashed to normal. He was locking his emotions down. Not a good sign.

My buzz snapped again, cramping my thigh. Shit.

"Put on your vest." He grabbed a package of red zip ties, then strode to the door and waited for me to pull on the vest and leave the armory before making sure the door was secure.

We took the elevator back to the first floor and met the rest of the guys in the garage. Gideon had changed into a black T-shirt, bulletproof vest, and fatigues. The other guys had just added vests and weapons.

My buzz eased, but the grating tension grew. This was going to be a problem if we didn't get this solved soon.

Cassius handed Marcus the keys to an SUV and we piled in, with Cassius in the front passenger seat. Gideon got in next and there was an awkward moment between Kol and I about who'd get in with him.

"I'm the smallest, I'll fit better with Jacob," I said, my voice low so Cassius and Gideon couldn't hear us.

"You're not going to be able to avoid him forever," Kol said.

"Just as soon as he stops looking at me like I'm his worst nightmare."

"Whenever you're ready, Agent Shaw," Cassius said, his voice thick with sarcasm.

I headed to the back to join Jacob, forcing Kol to get in beside Gideon.

Marcus pulled out of the garage, and we headed out of the Quarter. The satellite image hadn't been wide enough for me to tell which abandoned part of town we were going to, it could have been any number of areas, but the moment we passed through the park ring, we turned south. Guess we were headed toward the industrial area where I'd fought the archnephilim.

My pulse thrummed the closer we got, and even my buzz crackled stronger, as if just drawing close to the spot where I'd blasted myself with massive amounts of divine light set it off.

I gritted my teeth. I was only a few feet from Gideon. That should have been enough to ease it. But it wasn't, and I liked the idea of me participating on this mission less and less. It was dangerous if I couldn't focus.

Jacob squeezed my knee, leaving his hand there, heavy and comforting. "You've got this," he mouthed.

I offered him a weak smile and pressed my hand on top of his. I wasn't sure I had this at all, but I was glad he had my back.

We turned away from the industrial area where everything had changed for me and drove into the old warehouse district near the now-abandoned rail yards. The pain from my buzz didn't diminish, but if I wanted to prove I could handle this job, I couldn't ask to sit this op out. I had taken out an archnephilim and stopped a hellfire prince from escaping. I could handle a little recon while surrounded by my guys.

The bright morning sun shone on the destruction around us. The buildings had been packed together, sitting side by side with narrow alleys between them or sharing walls, and had been easy targets for Michael's nephilim. One blast had taken out multiple buildings and destroyed goods and supplies that had been unloaded from the trains.

"Jacob and Kol, you've got the rear," Cassius said, turning in his seat and passing a handful of communication ear pieces to Gideon. "Marcus and I will take the front."

We stopped a block from a cluster of still mostly-standing buildings and got out. Birds chirped and something creaked in the gentle breeze. I slipped the sling of my M4 over my head and pushed my sleeves up to my elbows, hoping Cassius wouldn't notice the little bit of exposed extended mating brand. It was just too warm for the jacket and with the physical exertion and adrenalin of doing recon, it was only going to get warmer.

Gideon glanced at my arm, his back stiff, and turned away from me.

"Com test," Cassius said as he handed out handfuls of the red zip ties.

I slipped the ear piece into my ear as Jacob responded, pocketed a handful of ties, and drew one of his two Berettas.

"Marcus. Check." He drew his sidearm as well and accepted a handful of ties.

Kol took his ties, and drew one of his long daggers from the sheaths hidden on his back beneath his shirt. "Kol. Check."

"Essie. Check."

The muscles in Cassius's jaw flexed, followed by a flicker of heat, and he held out half a dozen ties to me. "They have a magic containment spell that will last an hour."

I shoved the ties into my pocket, surprised that Cassius would include me. Of course, if we needed the ties, that meant the recon mission had turned into a raid, and everyone having the means to contain a super's powers was probably a good idea.

"Eyes open," he said, his voice coming from my left and yet in my ear at the same time.

I raised my M4 and scanned the surrounding rubble through the scope. No sign of movement, but given that I couldn't use the thermal setting on the scope in the bright sunlight, anyone could have been hiding in the shadows.

We hustled as quietly as we could to the closest still-standing ware-house, a three-story red brick structure with a faded black and white logo painted on the side. There wasn't a single sign of activity, no people, no vehicles, nothing, which didn't surprise me. Lots of areas had been destroyed and abandoned, and there were abandoned places closer to the center of town with actual apartments and houses where it was more convenient to squat. I couldn't decide if that meant this was an ideal place for criminal activity or not because no one was around. No one to notice someone coming or going, but also no one to hide among.

"Second building down," Cassius whispered.

Marcus sniffed. "I've got more than five supers, but their scents are old."

"There has to be a fresh one," Cassius said. "We know someone is in the building."

"Could have come from the other direction." Marcus glanced past the open bay door into the abandoned warehouse, then hurried past to the next building, our main objective.

This one didn't have a big bay door, but it also didn't have a door blocking the front so Marcus could easily peek inside. It stood three stories with tall windows, some with large shards of glass still stuck in the frames. The far corner of the top story had collapsed, taking the weight of the four-story warehouse leaning against it.

"Jacob, Marcus, scout around back. Kol, Shaw, stay here." Cassius glanced at Gideon. "You're with me."

Cassius and Gideon hurried down the street ahead of us, while Marcus and Jacob doubled back and disappeared around the side of the red-brick warehouse.

I rescanned the area. Five warehouses stood on the other side of the wide road that was mostly massive potholes. All were missing their windows, and none of them had been boarded up like buildings in the neighborhoods closer to the center of town. A tattered gray tarp fluttered half out of a third-story window, and every time it went limp I could see streaming sunlight from a hole in the roof. I turned my attention to the building beside it and the darkness beyond the second-story windows. No sign of anyone.

"All clear around back," Marcus said over the coms.

"Clear to the end of the street," Cassius said as he and Gideon hurried back, stopping on the other side of the doorway of our target building.

We waited for the others to return, then resumed our previous search order with Marcus and Cassius slipping inside first. I glanced again at the buildings across the street as Gideon entered, then followed him.

For a terrifying moment, going from sunlight to shadow, I couldn't see anything. But I sucked in a steadying breath, and stepped to the side of the doorway to let Jacob and Kol enter, blinking several times to get my eyes to adjust as quickly as possible.

We stood in a thirty-by-thirty square and the only clear area in the warehouse. Ahead of us stood a mess of towering machinery and a narrow hall with at least five doorways. The musty smell of decay filled the air, and dust and debris covered a floor marked with hundreds of footprints, some that looked recent... or at least recentish.

I thumbed the switch on my scope to thermal and searched the darkness among the machinery as we headed to the hall. Still no sign of anyone. My buzz snapped over my arms, and the magic in Gideon's brand softly crackled in response. I couldn't shake the feeling that we weren't alone despite the fact that all evidence said we were.

Marcus and Cassius cleared the first five doorways. They all led into small rooms, one with a large desk, three that were completely empty, and the fifth filled with rotting cardboard boxes. Then the hall turned and opened into a long narrow room with a maze of interconnected rooms and halls stretching out on both sides. Footprints were everywhere, and the air grew thicker with dust. A weak band of sunlight cut across the ceiling from a crack in the outside wall, giving me enough illumination to see, but still allowing me to use my scope's thermal setting.

The sense that we weren't alone, and yet completely alone, made the hair on the back of my neck stand up. It had to be my nerves. We were expecting at least someone to be here, and yet this place was completely abandoned.

I slid my scope from one doorway to the other. No heat signatures. Nothing—

No, something had glimmered. Something taller than even a super. I moved my scope back to the wall between the last two doorways, and slowly scanned up. There, just where the wall met the ceiling, was a flicker of red... maybe. Now there wasn't anything on the wall.

"Shaw," Cassius whispered, his tone sharp.

I jerked my attention away from the—

There it was again! Definitely something giving off an intermittent heat signature.

"Shaw!"

Marcus, Cassius, and Gideon were almost ten feet down the hall from me, and Jacob and Kol were standing close, waiting for me to continue forward.

"There's no one here," Cassius said. "Don't get distracted."

"Right." Except while I felt certain — too certain — the building was deserted, I couldn't shake the feeling I was wrong.

"Essie doesn't get distracted," Marcus growled.

I would beg to differ with him on that. My buzz was really starting to drive me crazy, and it was taking everything I had not to take a hand off my M4 and scratch my stinging ribs.

"There's no one and nothing here connected to the zip dealers," Cassius said.

"But you saw something," Marcus said to me. "Didn't you?"

"I don't know." I looked through my scope at the wall again. Nothing—

No, there, a flicker of heat. "There's something small, giving off a heat signature, near the ceiling."

Someone blew out a heavy breath, the sound hissing over the coms, but I didn't glance away from the spot to see who.

"Kol?" Gideon asked.

"I don't—" Kol shifted closer to me, heat radiating from his body making me even warmer. "Shit. That's a concealment spell."

"Can you break it?" Cassius asked.

"If a weak amateur had cast it. But I'm not a witch. I didn't even notice the spell on the building walking in."

I turned my attention back to the doorways, my stomach churning with the conflicting sense that we were alone and not alone. "Any idea what it's concealing?"

"Doesn't matter. Back out," Cassius said. "Now."

I turned to leave the way we'd come as a bulky guy with the feral intensity of a shifter rounded the corner and stepped into the hall. He jerked to a stop and stared at us, eyes wide with surprise.

Jacob lunged for him with his enhanced vampiric speed, clamped a hand over the shifter's mouth, and tackled him to the ground.

"What the—" someone said just around the corner.

"JP agents!" someone else yelled, and more guys rushed toward us from every opening.

I jerked my attention from Jacob, wrestling with the shifter and his two friends who were blocking our escape, to Marcus and Cassius, at the front of our line. If we couldn't go back, maybe we could go forward. But a massive demon who looked like he was made entirely of stone was barreling toward Marcus, while another, smaller demon — actually about my size — with onyx skin bounded from floor to wall and punched at Cassius's head.

"On the ground. JP agents," Cassius barked, but as expected the guys didn't stop fighting.

Kol yanked one of the guys off Jacob, while a vampire with pale skin and hair lunged at Gideon. I fired and somehow managed to hit her shoulder even with her enhanced speed. Red lightning flashed around her. She stumbled, didn't drop, and I aimed to fire again, but something behind me wrapped around my neck and yanked me off my feet.

My assailant wrenched me through a doorway, and my butt slammed onto the concrete floor, but whatever had my neck yanked up, choking me. I grabbed it with one hand, trying to keep hold of my M4, and my fingers grasped something hard and scaly—

Shit. A naga's tail.

The naga wrenched me up and rammed me against the wall, lunging in fast and punching me in the gut. What little breath I had left burst from my lungs. He tightened his grip around my throat and seized the barrel of my M4, but that still left one hand free to punch me in the gut again.

Black specks danced across my vision and my body screamed for air. Kol had said this type of demon wasn't particularly dangerous. They didn't have any special magic, couldn't cast any spells. They were just quick and strong, and could grab you with their tail. And if I didn't do something soon, I was going to suffocate.

He sneered at me, flashing wickedly sharp teeth. I wrenched at my M4. If I could just nick him, the stun spell on the ammo might be enough for me to break free. But he held tight, so I grabbed my Glock instead.

With a snarl, he batted the gun out of my hand and slammed me against the wall again.

The specks turned into a veil, growing from the edge of my vision, darkening everything. My buzz blazed, biting my skin. Behind him, one of our assailants tumbled past the doorway, and white light flared with Gideon's divine light. A gunshot exploded — Jacob? — and Marcus roared. The guys gasped and grunted and growled over the coms, their voices a strange mix of being in my ear as well as just across the room.

I didn't know how many guys we were fighting, but it sounded like there were enough, or they were powerful enough, to challenge the team. I couldn't count on any of them noticing me in time. It was up to me to break free before I passed out.

The naga jerked his hand back to punch me in the ribs again, and I wrenched my hand up, ramming my thumb into his throat. It wasn't a strong hit, but it made him loosen his hold on me enough for a ragged breath.

"Bitch," he hissed. His tail yanked tight as I twisted the M4 in his grip and fired.

The bullet skimmed his thigh. A flicker of red lightning crackled around his leg, and a zap of magic sliced into me. My buzz screamed in response and divine light stuttered from my hands.

"What the fuck—?" He jerked away and I fired again, point blank into his gut, the bullet exploding into the stun spell instead of driving into him.

This time the lightning burst around him in full, swept to the end of his tail, and zapped into me as well. All my muscles spasmed as if I'd been hit with a Taser, but so did his.

We crumpled to the floor, my buzz blazing through the muscle-contracting magic enough for me to shove away from him and shoot him again.

His body arched off the floor, lightning encasing him, and he went limp, his eyes closed, still breathing but unconscious.

I didn't bother securing him with a zip tie. He didn't have any magic to suppress, and if I didn't secure him to something, he'd just be able to run away or rejoin the fight.

I reholstered my Glock and rushed back into the hall. Three perps lay unconscious, their hands zip tied together. Jacob fought with a big guy in the room across from me, and Marcus still battled the rock demon at the end of the hall.

"Anyone have eyes on Shaw?" Cassius called over the coms. He sounded like he was deeper into the maze.

"I'm in the hall," I said.

Jacob tossed the big guy into the hall, and I shot him. Red lightning raced around him. It didn't drop him, but it was enough for Jacob to grab his wrists and secure a zip tie.

I turned my attention to the rock demon, fired, and missed. The monster punched at Marcus, who bounded out of the way, grabbed it around the neck, and swung in behind, giving me a clear shot of its chest.

"Marcus, let go." I fired, praying he'd let go before the bullet hit, and he wouldn't get zapped with the stun spell.

He let go just as red lightning swept around the rock demon, and I fired two more times. If most shifters took two shots, then I was going to play it safe and hit this rock thing with three.

It staggered, dropped to one knee, and roared.

"Really? More than three?" I fired two more times, and it crashed to the floor.

Something moved at the edge of my vision, and I jerked to face it. Cassius fought, flames blazing from his fists, with a vampire and a woman who could have been any of a number of supers, while a naga rushed toward them.

I thumbed the switch on my M4 to a three-round burst and shot the snake demon in the chest. It dropped with a flash of red lightning, making the vampire, a muscular man about Cassius's size and build, jerk toward me.

Shit.

He bolted toward me. I had a split-second to decide if I should fire, but Cassius was in my line of sight and the odds were that I'd hit him instead.

The vampire grabbed the barrel of my M4 and yanked. I heaved forward, attached to the weapon by the sling, and the vampire grabbed my ponytail and wrenched my head back. He flashed his fangs, his vampiric intensity more powerful than Jacob's, indicating he was older.

My divine light rushed to my palms without me even thinking the words to the spell and before I could give that a second thought, I rammed my palm into his gut.

The blast slammed into him with almost as much force as the blast that had sent Floyd flying. The vampire screamed, but didn't let go of my hair. We crashed into a heavy metal shelf leaning against the wall. Dust and debris and plastic bits of something showered us.

Dazed, I wrenched my hair from his grip and scrambled back. The vampire's side was scorched and bleeding. He snarled and dove at me, and I shoved the muzzle of my M4 between us and fired.

Red lightning swept around him, and he collapsed on top of me, unconscious and twitching.

Marcus heaved the vampire off me and secured his hands with a zip tie. "You okay?"

"Yeah—" A woman with the ferocity of a shifter in her eyes leaped at Marcus's back. I yanked up my M4 and dropped her with another burst of gunfire. "Just fine."

"Yeah, you are," he said, pride and desire heating his gaze.

Cassius secured his guy, but two tigers bounded through the doorway, followed by another rock demon.

"I'm getting the impression there's more here than just a guy with a cell phone." I fired at one of the tigers, but it lunged to the side, and only one bullet skimmed its flank. Red lightning flickered around it, but not enough to even make it stumble.

Marcus dove for the tiger I missed, his fingers extending into claws, while Cassius sent a whip of pure fire to the other one. Kol rushed in behind the rock demon, slicing at its thigh as he darted past.

"Trade you," he said to Cassius, slashing at the tiger and making it twist out of the way. "My blades are useless on the rock demon."

The guys had all three assailants in the room, and while Jacob snarled over the coms, it didn't sound as if he was in trouble, so I took a second to catch my breath and check my M4's magazine. Seven rounds left and no spare magazine. Just great.

I thumbed the switch back to single shots. How many more of these thugs were in there? Although we probably needed to count our lucky stars that none of them had firearms.

"Jacob. Gideon. What's your head count?" I asked.

"I've got three shifters," Jacob said.

"I'm free," Gideon responded. "I'll— Cassius, I need backup. Two shifters just ran down a set of stairs."

Cassius twisted his fire whip around the wrist of the rock demon, but it wrenched its arm back, yanking him forward, while Kol and Marcus both wrestled with their tigers.

"Shit, another rock demon," Jacob said.

Semi-automatic rifle fire roared from somewhere.

"And they've got AK-103s," Jacob said.

So much for thinking we'd gotten lucky.

I aimed at Cassius's rock demon, but couldn't get a clear shot.

"Cassius," Gideon said.

"Marcus? Kol?" Cassius glanced at the two of them.

The rock demon roared and punched at Cassius's head. His fire whip vanished and he rolled out of the way. I fired and hit the demon in the shoulder twice, and Cassius's gaze leaped to mine.

"Cassius!" Gideon said.

"Could use a little help," Jacob called.

"Shaw, back up Gideon," Cassius said.

"I should back up Jacob. He's in the most immediate danger," I said.

Cassius glared a me, white light blazing from his eyes. "We don't know that. Anything could be at the bottom of those stairs and I want this building cleared."

I bit my cheek against my immediate response. He was right. All of my training said so.

Another burst of gunfire exploded from somewhere across the hall.

"Do your job, Shaw. Jacob can handle this." Cassius slammed a blast of fire into the rock demon, crashing him through the rotting drywall into the next room. "Back up Gideon. Kol, Marcus, stop playing around."

My buzz flared. I wanted to scream at all the conflicting feelings pulling me in different directions, but this was what it meant to be a member of a team where I was emotionally involved with the guys. And they were trusting me to trust them and stay focused. "Copy that. Gideon, what's your location?" I asked.

"Two rights from the end of the original room."

I rushed back into the original room and scrambled past the still unconscious rock demon I'd helped Marcus take down. Someone grunted in pain over the coms. Jacob screamed, and my heart lurched, everything within me saying I had to go to him. I gritted my teeth against the need, the pressure building in my chest, my buzz blazing as if my skin were about to burst into flames.

"On my way, Jacob," Marcus said.

With just those four words, the pressure vanished. I shouldn't have doubted that my mates would have each other's backs. I didn't have to do it all, and I didn't have to do it alone.

I ran through a cramped room with toppled shelves and rotting cardboard boxes. Gideon's divine light shimmered through the doorway ahead of me. Now my chest ached with what lay between us. I shoved that back as well. I could worry about it later when we were out of this mess.

He stood at the mouth of a dark stairwell, holding his blazing sword of divine light. His pale gaze, hard and icy, met mine, and he gave a tight nod then turned his attention back to the stairs.

I scanned the room, but there was nothing in it except for a well-worn trail of footprints leading down to the basement.

The wooden stairs creaked as we quickly snuck down, and the air turned musty and cool. I couldn't hear anything beyond the gasping, grunting, and yelling of the guys still fighting and the gunfire. I also couldn't see any heat signatures through my scope.

The stairs led to a long, narrow hall with a single door at the far end. Light illuminated it, bright in the hall's pitch darkness.

"You open the door. I'll enter first," Gideon said, his voice low as we hurried to the end of the hall.

"Give me a sec to listen." I wasn't sure how good an angel's hearing was, but I was willing to bet Jacob's claim had made mine better.

With no questions asked or any hesitation, he let me hurry past him. I leaned close to the door, slipped my com from my ear, and listened. No voices. No footsteps. Only a strange, low hum—

No, a hum with a faint rattle. "I don't hear anyone, but there's some kind of machinery or something on the other side." I put my com back in and grabbed the doorknob.

"Have we stumbled onto the new lab?" Kol asked.

"There are only two guys with AK-103s," Marcus said. "You'd think this lab would be as secure as the last one."

"Even with only two, this is pretty secure," Jacob gasped. "There weren't any rock demons at the other lab."

I met Gideon's gaze. The glow in his eyes was muted by the stark light of his sword. For a second, he looked haggard and raw, like how he'd looked when we'd rescued Zella from the archnephilim. Then the muscles in his jaw flexed, and his icy mask reformed over his expression.

He pressed his back against the wall to give him the fastest view into the room when the door opened, and nodded.

I yanked the door open. Gideon rushed in, and I followed and froze. A mass of writhing, dark, man-shaped smoke floated twenty feet away. Every muscle within me clenched, and I forgot to breathe. I forgot to do anything. I didn't know if there was anyone else in the room, had no idea how big it was, or what was in it. All I could think was one horrifying word: wraith.

"He's not dead?" The words came out choked and desperate. He had to be dead. I'd killed him. The guys said he'd turned to ash. His brand had become a silvery scar, but it hadn't gone away. Did that mean he could still possess me?

No way in hell was I going to let him or anyone else make me hurt my guys again.

Gideon bolted toward him as I shot two quick rounds. They tore through the wraith's smoke, drawing a howl of pain, but not a flicker of red lightning.

"It's a wraith. The ammo won't work," Gideon said.

"A wraith?" Marcus barked over the coms. "Fuck. Essie—"

"It's not him," Gideon said back. "It's just a wraith. Shaw is fine."

I wasn't fine, but I wasn't immobilized with fear, either. Sure, I'd had a moment — and a part of me was still in that terrified moment, afraid the archnephilim had returned from the dead to take control of me again — but I was fighting through it.

"There's no such thing as *just* a wraith," a masculine voice hissed. The wraith swept a flurry of tentacles at Gideon.

He slashed his sword through them, and drove his blade into the center of the wraith's mass. "Three weeks ago, I would have agreed with you."

I forced my attention away from Gideon to secure the room, something I should have done the moment I'd entered, since we'd originally followed a pair of shifters down the stairs. Harsh fluorescent lights hung from exposed wires on the ceiling, gleaming on two dozen stainless steel tables set up in rows to my left. Crates and boxes were piled on and underneath the tables, and only two of them had beakers, hot plates, rubber tubing, and gloves. The one on the left also had half a dozen sealed jars filled with bright purple liquid. Zip.

The hum with the rattle came from a generator powering the lights, its exhaust vented out a narrow window on the back wall. Beside it were four more generators with the same exhaust setup. They weren't running, but they added to the evidence that this was the new zip lab and it was in the process of being set up.

The shifters stood beyond the tables, about sixty feet away, at the mouth of a dark hall, with a green-skinned demon and a woman with long, wild bright red hair and a complex, colorful tattoo covering her right arm. She didn't have the intensity of a vampire or the ferocity of a shifter, but I could sense a power radiating from her that was so strong it made my buzz snap and crackle, burning through my skin. Even with the wraith in the room, I knew she was the most dangerous super there.

She met my gaze, and I fired at her. One of the shifters, a small stocky guy, lunged in front of her as she ducked into the stairwell. My bullet hit him. Red lightning crackled around him. He staggered, but didn't go down, and the other shifter — a woman about my size — and the demon — also a woman, but bulkier and taller than me — barreled toward me.

Crap. I fired again at the guy. I only had two shots left with the M4 and I wasn't going to waste them by not dropping at least one of the three, especially since I needed to hit them at least twice.

The second shot dropped the guy with a flash of lightning, and I aimed my last shot at the female shifter, who was closer to me than the demon.

She stumbled, her hip hitting the table, giving me the time to flick the quick release catch on my M4's sling, drop the weapon, and draw my Glock. But she was on me before I could fire, swiping at me with long claws.

I wrenched out of the way and tried to shoot her. It didn't need to be a good shot. It just needed to be enough to slow her down for a second.

I missed and the bullet slammed into the far wall. The shifter swiped again, her claws catching my shoulder with fiery agony and wrenching me off balance. My buzz blazed, stronger. I dropped and rolled away to avoid a swipe at my neck, and fired again.

The bullet skimmed her ribs and didn't even make her pause. She lunged at me and I scrambled back, desperate to put any kind of distance between us.

Behind her, the wraith tossed Gideon into a table piled with boxes. One crashed onto him before tumbling to the floor in a mess of empty mini baggies, broken glass, and white powder.

The wraith surged toward him and seized his sword arm with a thick smoke tentacle. He heaved Gideon up, off his feet, but between one blink and the next, his sword vanished and divine light blazed up his arm, searing through the wraith's smoke. The wraith howled and heaved back. Gideon lunged in, his sword forming as he moved, but the green-skinned demon leaped on him and wrenched his sword arm to the side.

Crap. I aimed to shoot the demon, but the shifter swung at me again, reminding me to keep my eyes on my own damned fight.

Her claws caught in my vest, and she jerked me forward. I aimed to shoot her, but she smashed my Glock from my hand before I could pull the trigger. Divine light blazed from my palms, and my buzz set my skin on fire. Her eyes widened with surprise, and she threw me into the table Gideon had just toppled over.

My divine light stuttered and vanished, making the shifter sneer.

The green demon tumbled beside me, clipping my table and sprawling into a pile of boxes. She leaped to her feet and grabbed a jar of the bright purple zip, her furious gaze locked on Gideon.

My pulse froze as she brought her arm back to throw it. If any of that hit Gideon, it could kill him. It could kill me, too, but odds were better, even if I was half super, that I'd survive.

I scrambled to my feet and dove for the demon. The green demon jerked toward me, eyes wide, and she smashed the jar against my head as I slammed into her.

ESSIE

An inferno blazed across my skin everywhere the zip touched and my buzz screamed, filling me with agony. We crashed to the floor, the liquid zip spraying her in the face as well.

Shock raced across her expression, and the liquid seeped into her skin, completely absorbed, not even leaving a trace of moisture.

"Time," the shifter barked, and the green demon shoved me off her and bolted to the hall.

What the hell?

The wraith blasted Gideon with a pillar of smoke, shoving him into me, and swept toward the hall as well.

A thunderous boom exploded. Part of the ceiling crashed toward me, and Gideon grabbed my vest's shoulder strap and yanked me away from a tumbling beam.

Another explosion roared around us. Gideon hauled me toward the hall where we'd entered as the rest of the ceiling fell. Something heavy smashed onto me, dropping me to my knees. I jerked to the side, slammed into something else— or did it slam into me? I wasn't sure. My head spun, and I couldn't breathe or see. All light was gone, dust thickened the air, and my ears rang.

The roar of chaos snapped to silence and for a moment there was nothing. No dust, no pain, no noise. Then fire blazed through me, and I gasped in a lungful of dust. My ears still rang, and I could hear the guys yelling, but couldn't understand what they were saying.

Light flickered above me and to my left, and I craned my neck and glanced up at it. Gideon stared at me through narrowed eyes, his divine light the flickering illumination. I lay half on his chest with one of his arms wrapped around me.

"—blew up the building," a gruff voice said over the coms.

Gideon closed his eyes, plunging me back into darkness, and panic seized me. I hadn't gotten a good look at him. I didn't know how hurt he was. But I couldn't make my mind work past that to figure out what to do if he was.

"Everyone check in," the gruff voice said.

Recognition swam to the front of my mind. Cassius. That was Cassius.

"I got out," Kol said. "Barely."

"—is trapped under a pile of concrete."

My thoughts tripped and spun. Who'd just spoken? Who was trapped?

"Gideon? Shaw?" Cassius asked.

Gideon's eyes fluttered open, bathing me in light again, but I wasn't filled with relief. His wings were fully extended above us, and they were tattered with one hanging at an odd angle, and a heavy beam sliced deep into his side, pinning him to the rubble behind him and squeezing him against a pile of massive concrete chunks on his other side.

I choked on dust and coughed to catch my breath, setting my whole body on fire, making it impossible to tell where or how I'd been injured. I tried to shift. Lightning cut through my chest, and I couldn't move my leg.

I dragged my attention to my leg. It was like I was thinking in slow motion. A chunk of concrete pinned me to the floor. If I was strong enough, I'd be able to move it. Maybe I could shift it enough to slide free.

"Gideon? Shaw?" Cassius asked again.

"Come on, Essie," Marcus said, his voice tight with fear. "Check in."

"She's here," Gideon said, his breath shallow, ragged gasps. "Alive."

"Status and location, everyone," Cassius said.

"Mostly scrapes and bruises. East side of the building," Marcus said. "Actually, in the building next door. If I have help, I can get Jacob free."

"If I could get the leverage, I could get myself free," Jacob said.

"Shaw and I... are on the west side... near the back." Gideon fought to draw every breath and his wings twitched. It didn't look like he was holding anything up, but he wasn't absorbing them back into his body to heal them, either.

"Can you get out?" Cassius asked.

"We didn't make it out of the basement," I said, the words coming out on a rush of air.

"You're under all that?" Kol gasped.

"Hang tight," Cassius said. "We'll get you out." There was a rustling noise and my best guess was that Cassius was taking out his com to call in backup.

"Can you see any way out?" Marcus asked.

"No, and Gideon is pinned between a beam and concrete." Again, my words came out too fast. What the hell was wrong with me?

Gideon's wings twitched, and he hissed in pain, drawing my attention to the growing pool of blood at his hip. I couldn't feel a pull of strength from me to him through our brand, but I couldn't feel anything but the fire burning through my body.

Which didn't make any sense. I was on top of Gideon. My buzz should be gone.

Except my buzz *was* gone. The biting, stinging inferno had been replaced with a deeper, fiercer blaze that was creeping into my cells and igniting every part of me. It was terrifying, painful. And exhilarating.

Oh, shit. I'd taken a face full of zip before the building had collapsed. Onset was supposed to be twenty to thirty minutes. But that was for an ingested pill, one cut with flour or baking soda. This had been a whole jar of pure zip, and it had probably absorbed into my skin just like it had on the green demon.

"You have to get us out of here," I said, sudden panic raising my voice. I shoved off Gideon and leaned as far away from him as I could in our cramped quarters, shooting agony through my chest and leg. If onset was accelerated, would the violent paranoid delusions come faster, too? "Gideon has to get out."

"We're working on it, Shaw," Cassius said.

"No. He has to get out. You have to get him out of here." It was all I could think of. I was going to hurt him. I might not have a gun, but I had my light strike and at this distance, already injured, I would kill him.

If the zip didn't kill me first... because I'd taken more than enough to OD an elephant.

"Essie, we're working on it. Stay calm," Marcus said.

"I can't be trapped in here with him." I met his gaze. "I can't. I can't—"
I couldn't catch my breath, my pulse raced, and the fire within me blazed
hotter.

"Work faster," Gideon gasped. "Shaw's... going to OD on zip."

"She's what?" Marcus barked.

"And you're going to bleed out if I don't get violent and kill you first."
I had to get him out of there. *He couldn't die. Please, God, don't let him die.
And don't let me kill him.*

"Gideon, how badly are you bleeding?" Cassius asked.

My thoughts jerked to Cassius. Of course he wouldn't ask about me.
He didn't care what state I was in so long as I lived.

"The beam is holding most of it back—"

"Not all of it." Every minute trapped was a minute where Gideon
bled out, or I could lose control and blast him.

"The beam will hold it back long enough. I'm not drawing strength
from Shaw, so I'm good." His eyes tightened, dimming the light. "You'll
want to have paramedics or better yet Amiah standing by."

"You have to get him out. Now. Please." I shoved my hands into my
armpits, desperate to keep my palms away from him. I could control this.
I wasn't going to lose my mind. In fact, I was powerful. I could feel my
power blazing inside me. I could move this pile of concrete, I could free
my leg, I could—

I gritted my teeth. That was the zip talking. I couldn't let it control
me, couldn't let it make me do something stupid like shift the rubble
around us. That could make everything worse.

"Just focus on something else," Gideon gasped.

"I'm going to kill you and you want me to focus on something else?"
My words rushed out and my pulse pounded faster.

The muscles in Gideon's jaw tightened. "Odds are you'll OD first."

"Not helpful," Marcus growled.

Except, strangely enough, it was helpful. I wasn't going to kill him—

Except I still was. If I died, he died or went insane. That was what
having his mating brand meant. We were destined to be together. Soul
mates. Although no one had said anything about one soul mate hating
the other.

I ached with that, the hurt sharp and sudden and reaching deep into
my soul. He didn't want me. Logically I knew I shouldn't care. I had
Marcus and Jacob. But whatever magic bound us together defied logic. It
just couldn't defy his true feelings for me.

He was staring at me like that now with his icy expression, his eyes narrowed as if it pained him just to look at me. And why wouldn't it? I wasn't the angel he was in love with. I was responsible for her death. I was a weak, powerless human who he didn't know and didn't want to know.

My throat tightened and tears filled my eyes. I couldn't keep doing this. No matter what I wanted or where I belonged, his frozen demeanor was shattering me.

"You win," I said. "I'll leave."

Maybe if I didn't have to see him, didn't keep seeing that look in his eyes, I'd be okay. Marcus and Jacob and I would need to figure something out, but I wasn't going to let any of them throw away their careers for me. I'd have to lose my career, but right now, with grief crushing me, living like I was missing a part of myself was better than knowing that part of myself hated me.

"I know I remind you of what you should have had with her, so I'll leave. It'll be better for everyone." I huffed with bitter mirth, sending agony screaming through my chest. "It'll be great for your brother."

Gideon's wings shuddered, blazed with light, but didn't sink back into his body. Gasping, he leaned his head back. "It's only great for Cassius... because he doesn't understand... the situation."

"Yeah, right," I said, unable to keep the sarcasm from my voice. "You didn't tell him how much you loved Zella? How happy you were when you thought the mating brand was with her?" My tears broke free and slid down my cheeks. He wanted her. Not me. He always had. "I know you told him how much you hate that you're mated with me."

"I didn't tell him I hated being... mated with you."

"But you do, don't you? This is your worst nightmare."

His head jerked up, light flaring from eyes filled with heated desire and agony. "It's my worst nightmare because you're Marcus's mate. All I want when I look at you... is to touch you, hold you... tell you how much the distance between us hurts."

"Then why didn't you?" More tears rolled down my cheeks, but the fire in my cells was burning through the heavy grief, turning it into something darker, fiercer. I was pissed that he made me feel this way, pissed that the brand I didn't want made me feel this way. Just plain pissed. I tugged at the collar of my vest, trying to cool my blazing skin. "Why the hell didn't you?"

"Because you're in love with Marcus," he snapped. "It's been obvious... since before our brand appeared." The pain in Gideon's eyes deepened, but that only made me more angry. "The best thing I could do for you was let you... be happy. If I gave into the brand's compulsion... Marcus and I would have fought... over you, and that wouldn't have turned out good for anyone."

What a load of shit. "I heard you," I said, jabbing a finger at him. "I heard you talking to Amiah. You don't care about me. You don't even want to know me."

"I *can't* know you." His wings blazed and shuddered again, leaving him panting in pain. "I can't. I was... already... falling in love with you. If I let you get closer... I wouldn't be able to ignore our bond."

My pulse stuttered at those words. He was in love with me? He couldn't be in love with me. He hated me. It was clear every time he looked at me.

"You're fearless and self-sacrificing. You'd do... anything to save an innocent. I knew fate had picked... the right soul mate... for me the moment you came to face the archnephilim alone. I knew... why you'd made that choice. Because you didn't want anyone else to get hurt." He pressed a hand to his ribs, as if that would ease his pain. His breath came too fast and too shallow. "If I got to know you better... I wouldn't be able... to do... the right thing and let you be happy with Marcus."

More tears rolled down my cheeks. "Do you know how much that hurt?" I raised my arm with his brand. "You're always here. I can't get away from you, from our connection. And when you look at me—"

"I know you don't want... a bond with me."

"I don't want to feel like a part of me is broken. You look at me with all that ice in your beautiful eyes and I want to scream."

"You have Marcus."

"And Jacob, and I know I'm supposed to." I knew that with certainty in the core of my being. I didn't know why, and maybe there wasn't a reason, but I was destined to belong with these men and they to me. "I'm also supposed to be with you. I don't understand it, but I can't keep going on like this, feeling like this."

"But Marcus—"

"Marcus is an adult," Marcus said over the coms, "and if you'd bothered to ask him, he'd tell you he fully accepts this unusual situation."

"But your wolf."

"Is fine with it," Marcus growled. "You're the only one with issues."

"I don't have a problem... Werewolves... aren't polyamorous. Not with their... destined mates." Gideon's face tightened. "I'm trying to give Essie... what she wants."

"What you *think* she wants," Marcus said. "I tried that once. Worst decision I ever made."

"You did it twice, actually," I said, ripping open the Velcro straps on my vest, desperate to relieve the heat.

"I'm a slow learner."

The light from Gideon's wings blazed brighter, and with a scream that made my pulse stutter with fear, he pulled them back into his body.

"What was that?" Cassius demanded.

"Couldn't get... my wings... in," Gideon gasped. "Too injured." Sweat slicked his brow, and his breath was even more ragged.

My pulse leaped back into a rapid tattoo. "Gideon doesn't look good." *Please, get-us-out get-us-out get-us-out.* I needed to move, to cool off. It was so damned hot in there.

I yanked off my vest, shooting agony through my chest, tearing the shoulder straps instead of releasing the Velcro or pulling it off over my head. What the hell? I stared at the rip, my mind tripping over it as my hands shook, the bright white letters on the front vibrating.

No, *I* was vibrating.

Every cell in my being thrummed with power and strength. Then a wave of pure bliss and power slammed into me as the zip's high roared through me.

ANOTHER WAVE OF BLISS SWEPT THROUGH ME, STEALING MY BREATH. I WAS alight with power, every cell awakened to its full potential and beyond. It was the most amazing feeling in the world. I could do anything, face anyone. I was powerful.

"Essie?" Marcus asked, his voice filled with fear and booming in my ear. It made the darkness shudder around me like a massive stone dropped into a still, black lake.

"Focus on me, Essie," Gideon said.

I dragged my attention to Gideon. Pinprick flashes of light sparkled in the glow radiating from his eyes, fireflies dancing from those beautiful blue orbs.

"What's going on?" Cassius asked, his voice another radiating boom.

I could hear everything. Cassius and Marcus breathing over the coms. Kol talking to someone. I was pretty sure he'd taken his com out and was on the phone, but then how could I hear him?

"Zip is kicking in," Gideon said, the flashes in his eyes dancing across the distance between us.

I reached out and one landed on my finger and sank into my skin. It ignited his brand, making it crackle with exhilarating electricity. The power rushed up my arm into Jacob's brand, and entwined with his deep intensity.

"So that's what you feel like," I gasped. So powerful, so quiet and still and certain. I should have expected that. Jacob might look like a wild brawler with his massive build, broad chest, and bulky muscles, but he was still a vampire. The power that had brought him back to life wrapped him in stillness.

"Come on, Essie, look at me," Gideon said.

I dragged my gaze back to Gideon... again. He panted, his complexion gray, and his head lolled to the side as if it were too heavy to hold up. The blood pool at his hip just kept growing, and while I still couldn't feel the pull of strength from the brand, I couldn't just sit there and watch him fade. I had extra strength. I was brimming with it, over-flowing. It blazed from my hands and heart, my whole body.

"Here," I said, and I imagined that power rushing through our bond.

He gasped and his head jerked up. "Don't do that. Save your power."

"I have lots. I have so much." Hell, I'd ripped a Kevlar vest. Hey! I could free my leg.

I grabbed the edge of the concrete chunk pinning me to the floor and yanked it up with so much force it shattered into pieces. The rubble around us shifted, debris showered us, and metal groaned. I was so strong, I could dig us out of there. No problem. The truth of the thought stunned me. This was the power of zip. It was amazing. I could save Gideon.

"Is this what you feel like?" I asked him. "All the time?" I shoved at the edge of a metal beam near my head, and with a boom that side of our pocket in the rubble collapsed.

Oh, shit.

I jerked out of the way, cramming up against Gideon, before I got pinned again. My euphoria snapped into panic. Even with enhanced strength I was a fuck-up. I would always be a fuck-up.

"No wonder you don't want me." My throat tightened again with tears. "I'm so weak. Nothing compared to a super. How could I have possibly thought I belonged on the team, belonged with you or Marcus or Jacob or Kol or anyone?"

"That's the zip talking," Gideon said, wrapping his free arm around me and pulling me to his chest, even though it had to hurt him.

"If how I feel now is how you feel all the time, I'm useless." I pulled out of his embrace, squishing myself against the rubble, embracing the agony in my body. It was the only thing that was real. Pain. Disappoint-ment. Fear.

The fireflies in Gideon's glow turned to stinging embers, biting my skin. He was an angel. He was going to kill me. Marcus and Jacob wouldn't protect me when they learned the truth. I was a naturally born nephilim. That was supposed to be impossible, and my mother told me over and over again that no one would believe me. No one could ever know the truth.

My pulse beat so fast and hard it felt as if my heart were trying to pound out of my chest.

And why wouldn't it? It didn't belong in my chest.

I clawed at my fitted jacket. I couldn't keep holding my heart hostage. It was fated to be with powerful beings like Gideon and Marcus. My heart didn't belong in a weak human chest.

My pathetic human fingers couldn't dig through the jacket's fabric, so I yanked it off, tearing the seam at the back and shoving it off my arms.

I had to get my heart out. I was killing it, just like I was killing Gideon and Marcus and Jacob and Kol.

"Essie, stop."

But if I stopped, my heart would die.

I dug my fingers into my chest. Surely with my zip-enhanced strength I could dig through my T-shirt. But I was a powerless nephilim, worse than a human. I was half super, and I still didn't have any powers. And my stupid empathy didn't count. It was useless. I was useless.

"Essie." Gideon tried to grab my hand, but couldn't reach me. "Stop."

Blood oozed around my fingers, staining my T-shirt. At least I could do this. At least my heart could be free.

"No. Essie." Gideon flexed his hand and a blast of divine light slammed me into the rubble. My head snapped back, cracking against the concrete, and the rubble shifted, showering us with debris and dust. The beam cutting into Gideon's side dug deeper, drawing a strangled cry of pain.

"What's happening?" Cassius asked, his voice far away, no longer a boom, barely a whisper.

"Get us out of here," Gideon gasped. "Essie, look at me."

I tried to focus on him through the black specks dancing across my vision. My chest hurt every time I took a breath and that was a lot. Blood covered my fingers and the front of my T-shirt, but I couldn't figure out why.

"Tell me something," Gideon said.

His words muddled in my head. "Tell you what?"

"I don't know. Where did you grow up?"

Everywhere and nowhere.

This had to be a trick question. He was going to get me to slip up, reveal the truth, and then kill me.

"Where did you grow up?" he asked again.

"My mom and I moved around a lot."

"Europe? Asia?"

I rolled my eyes at him. "Don't be ridiculous. America."

"Why is that ridiculous?"

"Because—" This had to be part of the trick. "It just is."

I clawed at my arms. My buzz was back with a vengeance, even with Gideon's foot against my calf. I just couldn't get rid of it. Why the hell wouldn't it just go away?

"Just you and your mom?"

"Yeah." I dug my nails into my skin even though I knew it wouldn't stop the buzz.

"Essie," Gideon snapped.

My gaze jerked up to him. I hadn't realized I'd looked away. He was so pale. His breath was shallow and slow. Why couldn't I feel my strength pouring into him? He needed my strength. But my God damn buzz wasn't letting me give it to him—

Even though he was trying to trip me up and learn the truth.

"You and your mom?" he pressed.

My thoughts splintered and whirled. He couldn't know the truth. He couldn't die.

"Essie."

"Yes," I gasped. "Me and my mom." My mom, who'd fallen in love with an angel before the war had even started. My mom, who'd given up everything to keep me safe. My mom, who'd died from fucking cancer because she refused to dip into my escape money to save herself.

She would be so mad and ashamed of me. I was in love with an angel... and a werewolf... and a vampire... and an incubus. I was a JP agent.

"Focus on... me, Essie."

"Why? You don't want me."

"I've already said I do."

"You're just saying that. The brand is making you say that." This was how it ended. Trapped with an angel and being stupid enough to think that love could conquer everything. The archnephilim and Ibizual had said my guys wouldn't understand me. That no one but them would. The other monsters wanted me. They were coming for me, and Gideon was going to hand me over, because they were who I belonged with. "No. No no no. I won't go back to him. I won't let him control me."

"Who, Essie?" Gideon asked.

"He'll make me hurt you. *I'll* make me hurt you." Wasn't that the nature of a nephilim? We didn't serve and protect. We slaughtered. Billions of people.

"Who the hell is she talking about?" Cassius asked.

"The archnephilim," Marcus growled.

"I won't let you keep me."

"She's not making sense," Cassius said.

"I don't make sense. I shouldn't be here."

"Neither of us should be here." Gideon gasped a ragged breath, his face pinched with agony.

"No, here here." They were going to learn the truth. I met Gideon's gaze. He was going to lock me away forever. Wouldn't that be for the best? I was a monster. My true nature would come out eventually. It would be better for all of them if I ended it now.

Divine light rushed to my palms. It didn't matter that I was naturally born. Everyone knew the heart of a nephilim was black, tainted by her unnatural existence.

I pressed my palms to my chest and pushed all the power within me, my God damn buzz, the lightning from Gideon's brand, and the intensity from Jacob's brand, into my hands. I would burn the abomination and everyone would be safe.

"No, Essie." Gideon wrenched against the beam, trying to grab me. "Stop. You have to stop."

"I won't become like him."

"You're not like him. Please, Essie." Blood rushed down Gideon's side. Light flickered in his palms, but I sucked that up through the brand.

"And I'll never be." My T-shirt blackened and curled away from my hands, and my power seared my skin. I focused my resolve, concentrating on squeezing everything into a final blast. This was how it had to end. I couldn't run from them and I wasn't going to hurt them. I wasn't going to become a monster.

The guys yelled over the coms, demanding to know what was going on.

"This isn't the answer. It's the zip making you think this," Gideon said.

"It's the only answer."

I released the power. It seared into my skin, then swept out of me with sudden shocking cold. Gideon screamed. Power — my power — erupted from him and blazed across his skin, burning him and blackening the concrete around us.

I screamed. He wasn't supposed to die. I was. I couldn't let him do this. I jerked toward him so fast I overshot the distance and slammed my forehead against the concrete above him. Light snapped across my vision and agony seized me. Every muscle, every nerve, every cell blazed with pain, and darkness devoured me.

But the pain kept burning and burning, threatening to consume me. Wasn't this what I wanted? To free Gideon and Marcus and Jacob from me, the monster?

How can you say that? Marcus growled.

I jerked toward his voice but couldn't see anything in the darkness.

You're my soul mate. His fingers slid into my hair and his breath feathered across my cheeks. *My soul wouldn't choose a monster.*

But I am a monster. The archnephilim was right. Ibizual was right.

His lips brushed mine, a whisper of contact that made me flush with need. *They don't know you.*

They know me better than you do. They know the truth.

The truth is that you're mine. His lips smashed on mine. I gasped, and he devoured my breath, stealing it with his passion. *You'll always be mine.*

And mine, Jacob said, his voice that low rumble that always made my soul vibrate until it attuned with his.

A second set of hands slipped under my shirt and skimmed up my ribs. Just that gentle touch, a whisper like Marcus's first kiss that sent a shiver of pleasure rushing through me. Marcus's kiss deepened, and Jacob's fingers brushed my nipples.

I ached for these men, and while I didn't need them, I wanted them. Desperately. But that didn't change what I was.

Which is also mine, Gideon said. A third set of hands pressed against the inside of my thighs, urging me to open to him, to join with him like I'd joined with Marcus and Jacob. Our bond needed to be solidified. Pieces of my soul were breaking away because I hadn't accepted my destiny.

But I couldn't.

Because of what I was.

Essie, accept me. Gideon's hands brushed close to my core and trailed over my abdomen to the waistband of my jeans. *Let me in. You let my power in. Let my body in as well.*

Yes, Kol whispered, his sensual voice sliding like silk over my skin. *Let me in, too.*

His power oozed, molten seduction through my veins, and my senses spun with Marcus's mouth plundering mine, Jacob teasing my nipples, and Gideon undoing my jeans.

Yes, I gasped. *I want you all. I belong to you all. I—*

Sudden cold swept around me, followed by searing agony.

"No, Essie," Gideon said, his voice ragged.

Light cut across my vision. People yelled. A burned leg with bits of fabric charred into raw oozing skin slid past me.

"Get them on a gurney," someone yelled. Loud. Too loud.

I winced, and blessed darkness rushed around me.

Accept me, Essie, Jacob said, his mouth teasing my nipple.

No, me. The pressure on my nipple grew fierce as Marcus sucked on it, drawing it into a tight bud.

The pressure vanished, replaced with a tongue tracing sensual circles. *Essie,* Gideon said, snaps of his electric power dancing over my skin.

Cold swept over me again, and the fiery pain seized me. I screamed and sobbed. I just wanted to go back to my guys, wanted the pain to end.

"Hold on, Essie." That was one of my guys. I knew it even if I couldn't figure out who. His voice was sharp with fear, not soft and sensual.

Then the darkness swept around me, again.

Let me in, Kol whispered.

More searing agony.

Essie. Kol's face materialized out of the darkness, only a breath separating our lips. *Let me in.*

Yes. You, too. Yes.

Sensual heat flooded me and my thoughts stalled. There was only Kol... which wasn't right. There was Marcus and Jacob and Gideon, too.

But I couldn't keep my thoughts focused on them. I kept drifting back to Kol... back to dark, soft nothing... back to Kol and his magic... back to...

KOL

I CLUTCHED ESSIE'S BLOODY HAND AND FOUGHT TO CONCENTRATE ON pushing my magic into her. She wasn't so injured that I needed to give her my life force energy — thank God, because I didn't want to do that again let alone with a whole bunch of people watching — but once again I was in the back of an ambulance with her, racing to the hospital, trying to ease her pain.

Except this was so much worse than the first time. Her body was in better shape, but her mind and soul had been shredded by the zip, while my heart was shredded by what she'd said. She didn't make sense. She shouldn't have been there. And from the way she'd tried to burn herself up, she hadn't meant trapped under that building. She'd thought she shouldn't have been alive.

Jacob and Marcus had screamed at her. They loved her, needed her, didn't want to live without her.

And I didn't, either.

The thought of losing her, never being able to talk with her, hang out with her, or hold her had opened a black pit in the center of my being. I wanted more of what we'd done last night.

And, God help me, I wanted more than just that.

The ambulance pulled up behind Gideon's ambulance already parked beside the emergency doors, and the EMTs hurried Essie's gurney out of the vehicle. Gideon's EMTs and Amiah rushed past, racing him to surgery, and I could only pray he survived. I'd never seen someone so badly burned before. He was almost unrecognizable.

Our JP SUV screeched to a stop a few feet away and Cassius jumped out, running through the sliding emergency doors after Gideon. Behind us, Jacob staggered around the front of the SUV and Marcus rushed to help steady him. Was he using his brand with Essie to keep her alive? Was she giving Gideon everything she had to save him?

I ran with the gurney, staying by her side until I was told I couldn't go any farther, then I stood staring through the window in the security door, watching her get farther and farther away. Each hurried step squeezed tighter and tighter around my chest.

Her body convulsed, drawing a mangled, gasping cry from her lips, and my pulse lurched. I pressed against the door, willing my power to ease her pain even though she was too far away.

Her cry turned into a groan and she went limp, her head lolling to the side. Her eye lids fluttered partially open and a glimmer of light flickered in her eyes, making my pulse stop altogether.

The spell on her contacts, hiding the angel glow she'd gotten from defeating the archnephilim that had never gone away, was failing. I hadn't known how much time she'd had left on the spell when I'd caught her in Squatters' Row, but after the power she'd channeled tonight, it was a miracle the spell was still holding.

Someone huffed beside me and I realized I stood beside Cassius. He, too, was watching Essie be wheeled away, his face a mask of horror and I could only pray it wasn't because he'd seen the glimmer in her eyes — because even though we should expect magical changes in Essie because of her mating brands, reminding Cassius of that was a complication none of us needed.

"She nearly killed him," he whispered and I couldn't tell if he was talking to me or not. I wasn't even sure he was aware I was there.

"No," Marcus growled as he helped Jacob hobble down the hall towards us. "She nearly killed herself because Gideon's been fighting the mating brand."

"Because she's in love with you," Cassius said, having heard Gideon's confession over the coms, like all of us had. He was falling in love with Essie but didn't want to get in the way of her and Marcus.

"Because he assumed I wouldn't share my mate," Marcus growled back.

"You're a wolf," Jacob said, easing away from him and leaning against the wall to steady himself.

"And he's her mate, too," Marcus huffed. "Mate bonds are irreversible. You honestly think I'd battle it out with my mate's other mate?"

Cassius stared at him as if he couldn't understand what he was saying.

"She comes with him. That's who she is. That makes him mine, too."

Jacob was his as well... but not me.

Because Essie and I didn't have the same connection. The thought crushed me until I could barely breathe. I didn't belong. I never really had. It had never bothered me before, but now, having survived that horrifying moment when I thought I was going to lose her, I wanted that connection more than anything. I wanted to be hers. I wanted her to look at me with the love and desire she looked at the others.

Except she never would. Not for real. Even if I locked my power away completely — which was impossible — my nature would still influence her. No one loved an incubus and an incubus couldn't love in return. That was just the way it was.

Cassius drew in a shuddering breath and squared his shoulders. "There's nothing we can do for them right now."

"I'm not letting her wake up alone," Marcus said.

"We're staying until we know they're out of the woods," Jacob insisted, his hold on his vampiric intensity slipping and filling the hall with his cold, enveloping stillness.

"Agreed," Cassius replied, surprising me. I was sure he'd want to jump back into work. I didn't know him well, but if he was anything like Gideon, he didn't like standing around and waiting. "But once we know they're going to make it, I'm not sitting around while I know the bastards that did this are still out there." Fire burst from his hands, sending smoke billowing around him and sparks hissing on the floor, but somehow not setting off the fire alarms. With a growl, he yanked his magic back under his skin. "You're the most experienced agents we have. I need you— Gideon and Shaw need you on this."

"She won't wake alone," Marcus snarled.

Cassius's fire flared around his hands again and his expression tightened as he fought to control his power... and I wasn't entirely sure he wanted to control it.

"We take shifts," I said before the two started fighting in the middle of the hospital. "I can take the first shift. It'll take a while for the zip to leave her system and I can help keep her calm."

That and it would give me a chance to fix her contacts before the others noticed. I didn't know if Cassius had accepted Essie or not, but I didn't want to risk adding to her problems — and glowing eyes with a human's essence was a problem. Even if we could convince Cassius to accept her, others who didn't know her, might not. Everyone thought glowing eyes in a human meant nephilim and a lot of people, me included, had a lot of horrible memories about that.

Cassius opened his mouth to argue, likely assuming I'd try to get Essie to have sex with me, but Marcus cut him off before he could get a word out.

"Good idea," Marcus said and Jacob nodded his agreement.

Cassius huffed but didn't argue and turned his attention back to the now empty hall on the other side of the security door. The decision had been made. The conversation was over.

"I need some air," I said as I retreated down the hall back to the sliding doors, and out into the midday sun. It felt so strange to be standing in daylight when everything inside me was suffocating in darkness. The sun shouldn't have been so bright, so happy, when Essie and Gideon were fighting for their lives.

Except they would pull through. They had to. *She* had to. And when she did, she'd have time to recover before she was forced to show the world her glowing eyes.

I pulled out my phone and found Bane's number in the JP records. I might not be her mate and have the same connection with her that Gideon, Marcus, and Jacob had, but I was still her friend. Friends protected each other, too. I didn't have to be her mate to be near her and just being near her was enough. It had to be.

ESSIE

Cold swept around me, but this time the pain that followed wasn't a blazing agony, but a throbbing that radiated pain through every nerve into the core of my being. I yearned to go back to the warm darkness, the nothingness, but the pain persisted.

God, just take me back to the nothingness.

The pain dimmed and swelled, dipping me deeper into the darkness and back out again. Dimmed and swelled. Dimmed and swelled. Floating, bobbing, surrounded by water.

No, not water. It was thicker, warmer, comforting. I was safe in the not-water. I could stay in the not-water forever.

A boom cracked far off in the distance. A flurry of booms followed. It sounded like gunfire. I dragged my eyes open, and met warm brown eyes flecked with gold— Except his eyes weren't flecked with gold, the angel glow in his eyes was. The flecks danced, little pops of light, only noticeable because he stood so close. Gold. That was important. I just couldn't remember why.

He glanced over his shoulder then turned back to me, his hand pressed against something between us.

Gold flecks...

My mother had said my father had brown eyes with gold flecks.

Gold flecks...

The gold melted from his eyes and the brown shifted to warm

summer-sky blue. Gideon's eyes. So beautiful. I could spend a lifetime soaring in those eyes, imagining I had the wings to join him in the sky.

But I didn't have wings. I'd never fly. All I'd have was the sky in his eyes. Eyes that watched me with worry and ice. Eyes in a face with an expression so hard, it hurt to look at him.

My consciousness clawed at the soft darkness around me. He was watching me, arms crossed, head tipped back against a window. A harsh beep sliced through the silence, and the rush of air in vents and the hum of machinery followed.

Fire consumed me, my buzz an inferno trying to burn and bite its way out of me. My heart broke at the look in Gideon's eyes, and my throat tightened as my thoughts tripped over what I was looking at. His hair was too short, his eyes farther apart, and his nose was narrower.

"Where's Gideon," I croaked.

Cassius's expression grew grim, and I bit back a sob. It had to be horrible. *God, please let him be alive.* My pulse on the heart monitor beeped faster. I tried to remember what had happened, but everything was a blur of pain and fear. We'd been trapped. I'd been burning up— Hell, I was still burning up. Then I'd gathered all my power, every last bit and—

A sob broke free. "Did I kill him?" *Please, no. Oh, please, no.* "Is that why you're here? To arrest me? Please, don't let me hurt anyone else. Please. I—"

"I'm not here to arrest you," Cassius said. "And no, you didn't kill him."

Oh, thank God. Relief flooded me for a second, but my grief rushed back in. A tear leaked from my eye, trickled across my temple, and soaked into the pillow.

"He told me what you did."

Another tear rolled across my temple. "I'm sorry. I'm so sorry."

Cassius frowned. "What do you think he told me?"

"That I hurt him or killed him or—"

"I already said you didn't kill him."

Right. But I couldn't stop the flurry of terrified thoughts and tears. "What's wrong with me?"

"Severe depression and anxiety is one of the side effects of coming down from zip." He rubbed his face, and his expression shifted from grim to exhausted. "You know, that drug you got splashed with so Gideon wouldn't."

"The mortality rate for supers is so high," I sobbed. "I couldn't let her throw it at him."

"Now, about the team—"

"I know. I don't belong." More tears leaked from my eyes. "I'm too weak. I'll never be strong enough to take down a super." Which was ridiculous. I'd already taken down a couple of supers. But I couldn't think past the dark, malignant cloud oozing into my thoughts.

"Given that Gideon is still in surgery and has already drained two of the hospital's three healers to deal with the third-degree burns you gave him, I'd say you're more than powerful enough to take out a super."

"I burned him? I—" More sobs broke free. I couldn't hold them back, and my body shook as my skin blazed with fiery agony, thousands of bees stinging over and over again. I could have killed him. I almost had. Three healers and they were still working on him. God, I was a monster.

"Shaw—"

I turned my face into the pillow and cried. I just wanted to curl into a ball and die. A part of me knew this wasn't me, it was the zip, but I wasn't strong enough to fight the overwhelming sorrow.

"Shaw, you didn't— Come on, Shaw," Cassius said. "Jeez—" Metal like the legs of a chair on a linoleum floor screeched, and his footsteps hurried to the door. "A little help in here."

Soft footsteps rushed to me, and someone murmured something, but I couldn't drag my thoughts away from my grief or my burning skin to understand them. *Please, just let me die.* It was best for everyone if I just died. But then Gideon and Jacob could die. *Oh, God!* I'd almost killed Gideon.

The warm darkness from before swelled at the edge of my senses, and the beep from the heart monitor slowed. I floated again in the not-water, but I couldn't open my eyes to catch a glimpse of the angel with the gold flecks in his eyes. My father.

I'd never dreamed of my father before. Even after my mother had told me about him, her expression soft with wistful sadness. He'd always just been a reminder that I wasn't normal, that I had to hide who I was from everyone, always be on guard and ready to run at a moment's notice. He was the reason the angels would come for me. Except I wanted the angels to come— or rather, one angel. I wanted Gideon. I belonged with Gideon, just like I belonged with Jacob and Marcus.

I bit back a sigh, my pulse tripping at the thought of my guys. I loved them. It was crazy. We barely knew each other, but I did.

The heart monitor beeped at the edge of my senses, and I dragged my consciousness toward it, praying when I opened my eyes, I'd see one of my guys instead of Cassius.

Pale icy eyes stared at me, framed in a face also so pale his skin seemed translucent.

Sebastian Bane.

Soft white-blue light radiated from every inch of visible skin, giving him an ethereal appearance, and his mouth quirked with the hint of a wicked smile.

I frowned, trying to think past my still-blazing buzz. "What are you doing here?"

"Maybe I like to wander Mercy Memorial's ICU," he said, sitting back in his chair.

"The what?" I'd thought I was in a room in Operations, but beyond the window behind him lay a nurse's station, and now that I was paying attention, I could hear the rumble of many voices and someone being paged over speakers somewhere farther down the hall.

"Yeah, nothing but the best for JP agents. And since they don't want to have to keep an eye on two different floors, you're in the room beside Gideon's... when he isn't in surgery draining yet another healer. Not that you weren't touch and go there for a while. First time on zip?"

Grief swept through me, followed by an intense yearning to have all that power back. If I just kept taking it, I'd be strong, I could stay on the team.

I clenched my jaw and fought those thoughts. If I took zip again, I'd kill someone. I'd almost killed Gideon.

"God, Gideon!" I jerked up, sending agony blazing through me.

"Whoa." Sebastian grabbed my shoulders and urged me to lie back. "Gideon is fine. All your guys are fine."

Thank God. They were fine. Everything was fine. Wait— "Why are you here?" He still hadn't answered my question, and it was still so damned hard to concentrate.

Movement in the doorway at the end of the room caught my attention, and my heart skipped a beat at the thought that my guys were coming. But it was two shifters in nurse's scrubs peeking into the doorway, watching me.

Sebastian frowned and followed my gaze to the door. "Don't you have something to do?" he snapped at them.

The nurses mumbled apologies and hurried away as an orderly walked past the window, blatantly staring at me as he passed.

Sebastian tugged on the cord by his head and released the horizontal blinds, covering the window. "Apparently as the human half of an angelic mating bond, you're a real curiosity."

"You sure they're not looking at the faekin?" Being half human and half fae had to be just as rare as someone with an angelic mating brand.

"No, Kol warned me I'd have to shoo away your audience." He ran his hands through his spiky white and silver hair, drawing my gaze to his delicately pointed ears. "And before you ask again, I'm here because Kol paid me to top up the spell on your contacts."

"You can do that?" Maybe I didn't have to pay Mavis's exorbitant fee. Of course, I didn't know how much Sebastian charged.

"I can only top them up. I can't respell them, and my top up will only last a few weeks unless you do something stupid like channel all your power and fry your angel again."

My throat tightened at that, but tears didn't form in my eyes this time. Guess the consuming grief from the zip was fading. Now if only my buzz would fade. I kicked a foot out from under the blanket, trying to cool my inflamed skin, but the fire kept burning. "So my light strike is what's burning through the spell?"

He huffed and leaned back in his chair. "Obviously."

"Not obviously. How was I to know?" Jeez, if I'd known that, I wouldn't have used my light strike.

"It's basic concealment magic one-o-one. Everyone knows more powerful internal magics will affect any spell concealing something on the spell caster."

Except if I'd refused to use my light strike, Ibizual would be free or Floyd would have killed me.

Sebastian rolled his eyes at me. "How do you not know this?"

"I never had powers before I got this." I pushed my arm out from under the cover, revealing the delicate, shimmering angelic mating brand, the skin underneath red from my scratching.

"Hunh. Well, it's going to be expensive to keep hiding whatever you're hiding." He ran his hands through his hair again. "I can't believe I'm saying this, you're guaranteed business, but it'd be better for you if you came clean."

"What makes you think I haven't?"

"Because Kol made sure I did this top-up during his shift to watch you, which tells me he doesn't want the others to know." Sebastian frowned, and his gaze grew intense with that look that always made me feel as if he were seeing deep inside my soul. "But I get the feeling even your incubus doesn't know the whole truth."

I shivered under his scrutiny, afraid he'd discover my secret and use it against me. "He's not my incubus."

"You might not have a soul bond with him, but he paid a lot of money to protect you."

"Doesn't mean he's mine."

"So there's room for me, then?" Sebastian's lips quirked back into his wicked smile. "For when you get tired of your other three."

"Not going to happen. Never—"

The temperature plunged, making me gasp. One second it was normal, the next freezing, and frost rushed over my exposed foot, leg, and arm even though my skin still burned with my buzz. Someone was terrified. So scared that the frost swept over all skin not covered by the blanket.

Sebastian's eyes widened, and I yanked my limbs back under the covers as Cassius — strangely now in hospital scrubs when he hadn't been in them before — stormed into my room.

"Essie," he said, his voice ragged.

My heart lurched. Not Cassius. Gideon. Except his hair was cut close to his scalp.

Desperation tightened his expression, and his gaze locked onto mine, capturing my soul. All the ice in his eyes from before was gone, replaced with a heartbreaking fear that clenched my chest.

"Tell me you're okay," he said.

Sebastian rolled his eyes. "You know she's okay. You can feel it in your brand."

Gideon's attention leaped to Sebastian, light blazing from his eyes, and the temperature snapped to blistering hot. "Get. Out."

"Sure thing." Sebastian jerked to his feet and rushed out the door, pulling it half closed behind him.

The frost reformed — it had barely had time to start melting — and my soul ached at Gideon's pain and fear.

"Tell me you're okay," he said again.

"I'm okay." I raised my hand, inviting him to come to me, needing him to come to me. I trembled with hope that things were different, and yet feared they were back to the way they were before. I needed him to accept me, all of me, and that included Marcus and Jacob.

He collapsed into the chair Sebastian had just left and took my hand. My heart sang at the contact, and my fiery buzz vanished. I groaned in relief, until I realized that under all that fire, my head still burned with the pain of raw magical channels.

"I know the brand says you're physically fine, but Cassius said you wouldn't stop crying." He pressed the back of my hand to his forehead, reminding me of when he'd sat at Zella's bedside. He looked just as raw and haggard now as he had then.

"I'm okay," I repeated. I wasn't, not completely, but there wasn't anything he could do about it. Him being here, beside me, was more than I could have hoped for a day ago.

"He said it was the zip affecting you, but I had to see for myself."

"Gideon, I'm okay." I'd only ever seen him like this for me when I'd been shot and woken up to hear him talking with Amiah about how he couldn't have a relationship with me and didn't want one. And now I had no idea what else to say to him. I ached for him, for his touch, his kiss, and more. We were still two people, destined to be together, who didn't know anything about each other. Our attraction didn't sizzle like what I had with Marcus, but a part of me wondered if that was because both of us had been trying to keep our distance from each other. What would it be like for both of us to accept our destiny?

I searched his face for signs of desire for me, but all I could see was raw fear in his strong, sculpted features, a reminder that, even though I couldn't see signs of the horrible burns I'd given him, I still almost killed both of us. "I didn't mean to hurt you."

"No, you meant to hurt yourself," he said, his tone darkening. "I thought I could ignore the brand and everything would be okay, but the zip took you straight to suicidal grief. Just like the grief the surviving half of a mating brand would experience."

"You thought you were doing the right thing." I huffed a bitter laugh. "I probably could have endured it if I hadn't gotten a face full of zip." Not that I'd wanted to.

He raised his eyes and captured my soul again, his pupils dilated with a hint of desire.

Please, let him feel how I feel. Except I wasn't sure how I felt. Logically I shouldn't feel anything for him, and yet I yearned for him.

"Don't ever do that again," he said, his voice gruff.

"You sound like Marcus." This was a fierce, protective side to Gideon that I'd had no idea existed.

"Sometimes Marcus is right."

"Probably shouldn't tell him that," Kol said from the doorway. He flashed me a panty-melting smile, and my pulse tripped, embarrassingly obvious with the heart monitor. "The doc says Essie is free to go as long as one of us stays with her for the next twenty-four hours. Do you guys want a moment?"

"No—"

"Yes," Gideon said, cutting me off. His grip on my hand tightened. "Please."

A hint of hellfire flickered in Kol's eyes, and he left, fully closing the door behind him.

Gideon opened his mouth, and my pulse stuttered in anticipation. But then he snapped his mouth shut and pursed his lips. His gaze dipped away from me and an awkwardness sank into the silence between us.

ESSIE

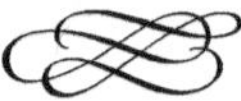

.I ached for Gideon to hold more than just my hand. He'd been part of my dream, had slid his hands against my core and begged to solidify our bond, and I could feel his yearning for me in the rising temperature.

The memory of my desire made my pulse pick up, but Gideon didn't seem to notice the faster beeps from the monitor... or he was pretending he didn't. And if the latter was the case, I had no idea why and didn't have the emotional energy to figure it out. His gaze rose and along with a building heat in his eyes, I could see pain and uncertainty. It had to be that uncertainty making him hesitate, even though he'd asked Kol for a private moment to talk with me. And if one of us didn't say something soon, Kol was going to be standing outside the door for a long time.

I shifted to my side and reached to brush my free hand over his too-short hair, but fear he'd pull away stopped me from making contact. "You look like your brother."

He stared at my free hand, but I still couldn't tell how he felt about me not touching him.

"The healers used all their magic dealing with my trauma and the burns, so it was easier just to buzz what remained of my hair," he said. "They'd never seen a light strike that powerful before. It was stronger than what you channeled when you destroyed Ibizual's key."

"Jacob was added to the mix—" Oh, shit. I snapped my mouth shut. I shouldn't have reminded him of our complicated situation. It was awkward enough with just the two of us, and I held my breath, afraid that pointing out I was also bonded with Jacob would make him put his icy walls back up. But all I saw was relief.

"He's the reason we're alive," he said. "His strength, through your bond, kept us both alive long enough for Amiah to stabilize us."

"Is he okay?" Sebastian had said all my guys were fine, but that didn't mean Jacob wasn't running on fumes. A shiver of desire swept through me at the thought of Jacob's magic.

Gideon's gaze darted to the monitor, noticing my change in pulse this time. "He'll need to feed, but he can wait until you've recovered."

"Yeah, about that—" If we were going to build any kind of relationship, I needed to tell him about the whole situation with Jacob.

"I already figured out he's stuck on you after all four of you showed up in the garage this morning. Victoria wouldn't have needed you if that wasn't the case." Gideon gave me a sad, rueful smile. "Which means you're bite locked, aren't you?"

"Yeah."

Realization suddenly flashed across his expression, and he burst out laughing, the change in emotion so quick it stunned me. "So that's why Kol has been dazed the last few days."

The door flew open and Marcus pushed in a wheelchair.

"I said she's having a moment," Kol said.

"They can have their moment after I get Essie out of here." Marcus shot him a fierce look and Kol raised his hands with a chuckle.

"Sorry, guys." He winked at me. "I know you were trying to build up to it."

"She's in a hospital bed," Gideon said. "Anyone could walk in, as just demonstrated."

"That's what makes it so exciting." Kol flashed another sexy grin, and the heart monitor gave me away again.

"Stop teasing her," Marcus said.

"Yes," Gideon agreed.

I laughed and Kol joined me. "I'm pretty sure he's teasing you two." I reached out my other hand to Marcus, strangely joyful. Perhaps it was another mood swing from the zip, but in this moment things were okay. I knew everything would go back to being complicated as soon as we got back to Operations, hell, with my luck, probably before we got to the parking lot, but there was hope for whatever lay between Gideon and me, and I was going to take it.

The guys wheeled me out of the hospital to the SUV. It was dark out, which meant I'd been in the hospital for at least twelve hours. I doubted it had been more than twenty-four, since Bane had said JP agents got nothing but the best, but still, I had no idea what day it was.

Which was a problem for tomorrow.

We drove the few blocks back to Operations, where Jacob met us in the garage. My pulse fluttered at the sight of him. He looked exhausted, but okay. Thank God, he was okay.

He lifted me out of the SUV, separating me from Gideon and setting my skin on fire, but I didn't complain and managed not to scratch too much. In that moment, he needed me, just like Marcus and Gideon did. I leaned against his chest, savoring the cold radiating from his body, while also keenly aware that his low temperature meant he needed to feed, and soon.

Jacob carried me up to my room, the rest of the guys following, and for a second I had a moment of wishing everyone would just pile into my bed with me so I could fall asleep with all of them close.

"The docs said we need to keep an eye on her for the next twenty-four hours," Kol said, pulling back the covers on my bed.

Jacob set me on the mattress. I'd made the transfer in my hospital gown since no one knew where my clothes were, and I didn't want to bother trying to hunt them down, so I didn't have anything to do except pull up the covers and pass out.

"Gideon should take the first shift," Marcus said.

Gideon's eyes widened with shock. "Marcus—"

"Pretty sure we've already discussed this." Marcus crossed his arms, as if daring Gideon to disagree.

"We have. You're right," Gideon said. "Still, it might not be the best idea. I might look fine, but I'm exhausted. I'm going to fall asleep, too."

"Then it's perfect." I held out my hand to Gideon. As much as I ached for Gideon, I didn't have the energy for much of anything, either.

"Not for me," Kol said with an exaggerated pout. "All you're going to do is cuddle."

"Pretty sure you and Jacob won't be running low for long," Gideon said, sagging onto the edge of the bed and absentmindedly placing a hand on my calf.

My buzz vanished. Yeah, he was the one I needed to be with right now.

Jacob brushed a kiss across my forehead and headed to the door.

Marcus's piercing green eyes darkened, his wolf coming to the surface. He tipped my head up and captured my lips in a fierce quick kiss then left. Kol followed him out.

"I still don't understand how Marcus just accepts this," Gideon said, his gaze on the closed door.

"Marcus knew before I did what our situation was." I laid down and shifted over so Gideon could join me.

He moved his hand from my calf, and my buzz blazed back to life. I swallowed a gasp as he kicked off his shoes and eased in beside me. But he didn't reinitiate contact, and his uncertainty twisted inside me. At least this time I could feel it.

"I'm confused about all this as well." I pressed my hand over his heart, easing my buzz. His pulse raced, but I couldn't tell if it was fear or desire.

The muscles in his jaw flexed and the glow in his eyes billowed. The temperature flickered with a whisper of heat, but I had no idea what that meant.

This was a mistake. As much as I wanted him near, and not just to ease my buzz but because our bond couldn't withstand the distance between us any more, this was too much too soon. Our emotions were just too confused. Even though we were destined mates, we were going to need time to figure out how we fit together.

I pulled my hand from his chest, but he captured it and pressed it back over his heart. "Why did you think killing yourself was the answer?"

Because I'm a monster. Whether I want to be or not, and you're all going to find out. "That was the zip."

"But it came from somewhere." The light in his eyes dimmed and his uncertainty melted into a soft sadness, forming a delicate mist around me. "Even without me, you have everything to live for. Your connection with Marcus and Jacob should have helped you with the grief of our almost-broken bond."

My throat tightened with a mix of his sadness and mine. "I kept trying to tell myself that. I don't understand why you keeping your distance hurt so much."

"I'd thought it was only hurting me. That what you had with Marcus was stronger because you had it first, but I guess it wasn't. Our bonds are equal. You don't have three parts making a whole. You have three wholes joined inside you, each as significant and consuming as the other."

"Do you still think the brand is a beautiful thing even though you're mated with a human with two other mates?" Did he feel— did any of them feel like I wouldn't have the time for them because of the others? Not to mention I didn't know if it was worse that they were all co-workers and friends or not.

The light returned to Gideon's eyes. Breathtaking summer sky that made me feel like I was flying. "It's the most beautiful, amazing thing." He brushed his fingers from my hand pressed over his heart to the delicate gold sigil on my forearm. "Just this little touch, and I know this is where I belong, who I belong with. Marcus and Jacob are a part of who you are, just like being a cop or your need to protect us." His eyes narrowed. "Even if that need makes you do dangerous things."

Stupid would be more like it. I knew exactly what he was talking about. "Cassius said you saw that I tackled the demon with the zip."

"That was foolish." His hand trailed up my arm, tracing the lines of Jacob's brand, and clouds passed over his summer-sky eyes, dimming his light again. "It probably saved my life."

"I couldn't let you die."

He brushed his thumb across my jaw, drawing a shiver of desire, and slid his fingers into my hair. His pupils dilated with desire, a desire I'd been aching to see for days now, and his gaze dipped to my lips.

"I couldn't risk that you'd be one of the supers that poison killed," I said, my voice breathy, my pulse racing.

"And yet you were going to burn yourself up with your power." He leaned closer to me, his gaze still locked on my lips.

"I thought I was going to hurt you." *Please kiss me. I need you to kiss me.* God, even exhausted, I needed him to hold me and fill me. Desire heated me, rushing through my body as if Jacob's bite magic was surging through me, or Marcus's wolf was undressing me with his ferocious gaze.

"Pretty sure killing yourself would have hurt me, too." He raised his eyes, and I was falling into a summer's sky.

"I didn't say it made sense." He was so close. If I just leaned in, our lips would meet. But would that be too soon for us? Would that scare him back into his icy demeanor? "I didn't want to hurt any of you. I make everything complicated with you and the team, and—"

He dipped in and kissed me with a tender, aching softness. It made my pulse flutter, and pricks of lightning teased through his brand. The connection between us swelled in my chest, seeping into my cells with desire and certainty, and a sigh of satisfaction escaped my lips. Yes, this was the way it was supposed to be between us.

With a groan, he deepened the kiss, his tongue teasing the seam between my lips, urging me to open to him. I let him in, and his power grew, turning my skin beneath his brand hypersensitive. The sensation sizzled past my elbow into Jacob's brand and swirled into a pulsing intensity that stole my breath.

I moaned and let the power rush through me. The temperature turned sweltering, and every brush of fabric or whisper of breath or shift of Gideon's fingers in my hair sent me gasping. My breath came fast and the room started spinning.

Darkness shuddered at the edge of my vision. My chest tightened and I couldn't breathe. Everything lurched in and out of focus. The power turned sharp and threatened to roar out of control. I was going to lose my hold on it and hurt him again. *God, no, please.*

Gideon jerked back, frowning, but his expression snapped to worried when he saw my face. "Essie?"

Tears stung my eyes. "I can't control it."

"Control what?" He brushed a lock of hair from my eyes, his expression so tender it broke my heart.

"The power," I said, my throat tight. "There's so much power. I'm going to hurt you again."

"Hey." He pulled me close, resting my head on his chest and holding me tight. His scent of fresh springtime and sun-warmed skin enveloped me. "It'll be all right."

Except I wasn't sure it would be. I fought to concentrate on the sure, strong beat of his heart, and slowly the power from his brand melted back into my skin.

"We have all the time in the world." He pressed his lips against the top of my head. "We'll figure it out. All of us. You're not alone."

A tear broke free. It had to be the zip still affecting me. His words filled me with such hope, and yet they also reminded me of how alone I'd been and how alone I'd be if they learned the truth.

"Just rest, now. Things will look better in the morning."

I sobbed into his chest and didn't fight my exhaustion when it pulled me into a soft, warm darkness. I floated without thought or dream. There was only love and fear. Pure, radiant, soul-affirming love, fighting the terror that I'd hurt Gideon and my guys.

Gentle knocking pulled me out of the darkness, and I dragged my groggy attention to the door as Marcus entered. Gideon, his arms still wrapped around me, stirred and tensed, as if he was expecting Marcus's wolf to lose his shit on us, but Marcus just sat on the edge of the bed and set a hand on my thigh.

"Cassius is summoning us to your office."

Gideon's grip on me tightened. "Can't it wait?"

"Doesn't sound like it," Marcus said. "Cassius sounded more uptight than usual."

Gideon drew in a sharp breath, and the whisper of emotions that had been teasing the temperature around me vanished.

"Okay. We're coming." He eased out from under me and sat up, but I managed to keep a hand on him. I wasn't ready to deal with my buzz just yet.

"Does Cassius's summoning also include me?" I asked. At the moment, I had mixed feelings about the team. I really wasn't strong enough to do the job safely. As much as I could summon a powerful light strike, I couldn't just fry every super we came across.

"I don't care if Cassius's summons doesn't include you. You're part of the team," Marcus said.

"Agreed." Gideon kissed the top of my head, making my pulse trip with a mix of heart-stopping desire and fear, before he slid out of bed.

My buzz exploded, setting my skin on fire, and I bit back a gasp. I wasn't sure why I was still hiding it. I could now easily say my buzz was because of the zip or the archnephilim or the mating brand, but a part of me feared if I said something the guys would want to fix it, and then people would start asking questions and running tests to find out what was going on.

"I'll go change and meet you in the hall." Gideon shoved his feet into his boots and left me with Marcus.

Marcus leaned over me, his wolf's ferocity radiating in eyes filled with desire. I slid my hands over his sexy scruff, tangled my fingers in his hair, and pulled him to me. We'd been intimate and I hadn't lost control. It was safe to kiss him, and I really needed the reassurance of our connection.

Our lips met, and Marcus groaned. He captured the back of my head and plunged his tongue into my mouth, fueling my desire. God, I didn't think I'd ever get enough of him, of his ferocious passion and his searing desire for me. It stole my breath and left me dizzy — and thankfully not in the terrifying I'm-going-to-lose-control-and-burn-you-up kind of dizzy.

With another groan, he pulled away and pressed his forehead to mine, his breath fast. "I really want to stay. God, do I want to stay. But Cassius has been surprisingly subdued about the team since we pulled you and Gideon out of the warehouse, and it would be best if we kept it that way."

"Pretty sure me showing up to a meeting will change all that."

"Not sure." Marcus eased back, leaving me aching at even that small distance between us. "You risked everything to save his brother—" He glared at me. "Stupid move, by the way. Zip can kill humans, too."

"I know." I rolled my eyes at him, only half meaning my exasperation. "I shouldn't ever do that again. Gideon has already told me."

"Maybe you'll listen to him, since you're not listening to me."

I gave him my driest look.

"Yeah, didn't think that would work. At least you have one hell of a light strike. Cassius lost his shit when he saw Gideon."

"So you all know?"

"That the zip made you try to kill yourself? Yeah." Marcus's fear and sadness swept a cold mist around me. "Jacob felt you pulling power from him, said it was the strangest feeling because he didn't know he had that kind of power, and Gideon was yelling at you to fade it away, don't blast it."

"He said that?" I didn't remember any of that.

"You weren't in your right mind." He pressed his hand against my thigh. "Now, come on. Hurry up and get changed. I'll meet you in the hall."

"You can stay. It's not like you haven't seen me with my clothes off."

"If I stay, your clothes will stay off and we won't leave your bed."

He left and I sat up, trying to figure out what if anything hurt beyond my raw magical channels and my burning skin. I couldn't tell and that worried me. I was pretty sure the healers at Mercy Memorial would have mended any broken bones, but even if I had slightly enhanced healing from Jacob's vampiric claim, I was still also human — or at least they thought I was human — which meant they couldn't heal me as fast as they could a super.

I shrugged out of the hospital gown, not surprised that I didn't have anything else on underneath, only surprised I'd been too exhausted to notice, and grabbed a change of clothes from my duffle bag. An old pair of runners waited by the door, and I could only assume one of the guys had gone to my apartment and brought me back a pair of shoes. I didn't have another light workout jacket and my skin was too hot for me to even think about covering up the angelic mating brands curled around my right arm, so I was just going to have to accept whatever looks Cassius gave me. Not to mention the looks I'd get from my guys, since it was clear I'd been scratching my arms to the point of bleeding.

After splashing some water on my face — a face that was back to being too pale with shock — I hurried into the hall. Gideon, now dressed in slacks and a dress shirt, waited for me with Marcus without a hint of tension between them, as if that moment when Marcus had first walked in and not reacted badly had been enough to reassure Gideon.

And God, did they look good. Marcus with his piercing green eyes, making my insides sizzle by just standing near him, and Gideon, all ice gone from his expression and the stiffness gone from his posture. He was back to the confident, strong angel I'd first met.

They noticed my scratch marks but thankfully didn't say anything. Although it was clear in their looks that we were going to have a conversation as soon as the meeting with Cassius was over.

We hurried to Gideon's office, where Cassius sat behind Gideon's desk, Jacob perched stiffly on the edge of the couch, radiating vampiric intensity, and Kol leaned against the wall near the door, his arms crossed, looking anything but relaxed. The guys were worried and ready for a fight. This wasn't good.

ESSIE

Cassius studied me as I entered, but with my buzz blazing, I couldn't sense any change in temperature, and his expression remained hard so I had no idea what he was thinking.

Marcus ushered me to the chair — it was slightly farther from Cassius than the couch — and I grabbed Gideon's hand, making my buzz vanish and leaving me cold. I wouldn't be able to concentrate on anything Cassius said with my buzz blazing, and I wanted a clear head, to face whatever was coming.

Gideon's eyes widened in surprise, as if he hadn't expected me to fully embrace our bond right away and in front of everyone, but he stepped up beside me and tightened his grip on my fingers.

Surprise also flashed across Cassius's expression, and he jerked his attention to the open file folder on the desk.

"So?" Marcus growled, drawing up beside Gideon and resting a hand on my shoulder.

"We're being summoned to the mayor's office," Cassis said. "He wanted to call you in yesterday to discuss the events at the cemetery, but, well, yesterday happened." The muscles in his jaw tightened.

"Screw the political crap," Marcus said. "We all need a day to get our shit together, and if we should be doing anything, it should be hunting down whoever blew up that warehouse and shut down whoever's distributing zip."

"We're a day behind them, and Summer didn't find anything in the rubble that would give us a lead," Jacob said. "And you didn't pick up any scents to follow."

"So we're back to the beginning," Kol said. "The sooner we get back to digging, the sooner we can shut these guys down."

"I agree," Cassius said, "but you can't put off meeting with the mayor. Even if you're all running on fumes and have better things to do, we need to go to City Hall and smooth this over."

"How can we smooth over what happened?" Kol asked. "It's not like we can go back and do things differently."

"Pretty sure the mayor just wants to yell at us and feel like he's in control," Jacob said with a warm glance at me. His still intensity pulsed from his brand, slow and sure, and helped to settle more of my unease about my place on the team and the danger I put my guys in.

"Exactly." Cassius turned a page in the file. "Although it would be better if we didn't have to call in over a hundred citizens for DNA samples to identify the remains of everyone who'd been reanimated."

"There's a lot about the last few days that could have been better," Marcus said.

"But there's nothing we can do about it." Gideon squeezed my hand. "Put on your most diplomatic smiles. We're going to the mayor's office."

"With Essie," Jacob said.

Cassius's eyes narrowed. "Agent Shaw needs more time to recover. The healers couldn't purge all the zip from her system so she's still in the tail end of withdrawal. Not to mention she needs a lot more training."

My thoughts tripped over that. "Are you saying I'm still on the team?" I wasn't sure if that was a good idea or not. Yes, it was what I wanted, but the last two days had proven how unprepared I was for the job.

"If you don't go with us, you won't be on the team," Gideon said. "The mayor will tell the chief of police you didn't show and you'll be reassigned."

"Fired," I corrected.

"So you're going." Marcus glared at Cassius as if daring him to disagree.

"We'll put you on modified duty and start your training when we get back." Gideon released my hand and stepped toward Cassius, adding his glare with Marcus's.

My buzz screamed to life, burning and biting and twitching. I drew in a sharp breath, which didn't help at all.

Jacob said something, I heard his voice rumble, but couldn't make out his words. Kol jerked away from the wall and his mouth moved. I clawed at my arm, unable to stop myself even though I knew it wouldn't help ease my buzz.

Someone else said something, but I couldn't make out the tone well enough to figure out who'd spoken, since neither Jacob's nor Kol's lips moved and I wasn't looking at the others. My hand now dug into my thigh and I noticed I'd changed body parts.

I squeezed my eyes shut and fought to concentrate. The buzz was so much stronger than before. The muscles in my thigh spasmed and I pressed my nails in deeper, desperate to make it stop.

"—of police will have to, except she won't be fully in the field until—"

Cassius's mouth moved in response, but his expression wasn't argumentative, as if he were agreeing with what the guys were saying.

The muscles in my shoulder clenched. I wasn't going to be able to do this.

"I don't think I should go," I said.

They all looked at me. Every one of them, even Cassius, was surprised.

"I'm not— I can't—" God, I had to tell them about my buzz, but I couldn't force the words out. Too many years of hiding in fear held them prisoner. "I'm still shaky from the zip."

"You're coming," Gideon said, his tone clear he wasn't going to argue with me about it. "We'll get you through this. You're a member of this team, and I can't have you fired from the UCPD before the paperwork officially transferring you to the JP goes through."

"Let's go," Cassius said as he stood.

We headed to the garage, piled into an SUV, where I managed to claim the seat beside Gideon and hold his hand, and we drove into the heart of Union City to City Hall.

It felt so strange, driving with the guys without any tension making the temperature lurch between hot and cold. I got a sense of determination and certainty from everyone, and I was pretty sure that was from real empathy and not my screwy version. I'd been having moments of that for a few days now, and as much as I wanted to pretend it didn't mean I was changing, I couldn't.

When this meeting with the mayor was over, even if Cassius hadn't left town, I was gathering my guys and revealing all my magic. I couldn't keep it a secret any more. I'd have to be careful to frame it in terms of recent events and not make them suspect I'd had magic before being claimed by the archnephilim, but I had to tell them. It didn't matter if they started digging, searching for a solution to my buzz that didn't involve being in constant contact with Gideon — I had to come clean.

Gideon laced his fingers between mine and offered me a soft, reassuring smile, warming my heart. This was the way it was supposed to be between us, not the icy distance.

Marcus turned onto the busy four-lane street that crossed through the heart of Union City's downtown core. The core always struck me as odd, with its strange mix of old and new buildings, and the bustle of people acting as if the new buildings weren't because half of the city's core had been leveled by Michael's nephilim.

We drove past two twisted metal beams — post-war urban art — curled together and standing upright in the middle of a new building's courtyard. A constant reminder of what humanity and supers had survived. Benches and potted trees around it created a welcoming area to sit outside and enjoy the unusually warm early summer day. Over a dozen people in suits were doing just that, even though it was only midmorning.

Marcus parked in a reserved spot on the street in front of the new glass-and-steel sixteen-story City Hall. It wasn't the tallest building in the downtown core, but it was the most impressive, with a large glassed-in rotunda in the front and a wide outside public square with a fountain.

Gideon gave my hand a quick squeeze then let go, and as much as I needed to keep holding his hand, the fewer people right now who knew I was intimate with my coworkers, the better. Marcus flipped the sun visor down to show the JP credentials and got out. Gideon did the same.

I clenched my jaw and fisted my hands at my sides in hopes I wouldn't start clawing at my skin.

People stared, gasped, and pointed at us as we gathered beside the SUV. Only human witches could sense a super's essence, but it was obvious we were supers. There weren't a lot of angels in Union City and they rarely left the Quarter, so the glow in both Gideon's and Cassius's eyes was a dead giveaway as to what they were.

An elderly woman sagged onto a bench and crossed herself, while others gawked with awe. Those who looked away from Gideon and Cassius gave Marcus and me cursory glances — we were the least impressive of the group — and then turned to Jacob.

Jacob had his vampiric intensity pulled back, so most people probably couldn't tell he was a vampire, especially since it was the middle of the day, but he was a big, bulky, dangerous-looking guy.

A moment later, every female eye — and a few male — jumped to Kol, and the awe from the angels turned to lust. He wasn't even radiating his usual sexual grace. In fact, his posture was tense, as if he were trying to hold back like Jacob. But again, like Jacob, even without radiating his magical nature, he would have drawn attention. His small horns poked through his dark hair, making it clear he was a demon, and he was drop-dead gorgeous. Pure sex walking in low-riding jeans and a tight T-shirt.

None of the guys seemed to care they were being stared at, and they headed straight to the building's front doors. I, however, had every alarm in my head screaming at me. Not because people were looking at me, but because they were looking at me and wondering what kind of super I was, and I'd spent my entire life avoiding that. No one was supposed to wonder anything about me. I was a nothing-to-see-here human. And just by getting out of the JP's SUV with my guys, the world looked at me differently.

We marched across the public square with its wide, shallow fountain, and pushed through the revolving doors. The lobby inside was packed with people, and a few hundred foldout chairs had been set up in the rotunda for some kind of event. Janitors and sound technicians talked with two women in crisp navy suits, who pointed at various spots around the rotunda and checked their phones.

Someone gasped. Slowly every eye turned toward us and the roar of voices became silent.

"This is why I hate coming to City Hall," Marcus growled as he glowered at the crowd.

"If you stop looking like you're going to rip someone's head off, maybe they wouldn't look so terrified," Cassius said, his voice low, only audible to our group.

"I don't look like I want to rip someone's head off," Marcus replied, his voice just as low.

"Yeah," Kol said, "You kind of do."

I caught myself scratching my shoulder and jerked my hand back to my side.

Marcus said something else and I strained to focus past the buzz.

A woman a few feet away sighed and sank into a foldout chair, her face flushed.

"At least you don't make people faint just by walking past them," Kol said as we headed toward the hall at the back of the rotunda, where the elevators were.

Marcus snorted. "Don't even try to tell me you don't like it."

"Normally I do. But my shields are still in tatters and all this energy is overwhelming," he said between clenched teeth, hellfire blazing in his eyes. "So can we walk a little faster?"

Two more women and a man had to sit before we reached the back of the rotunda, and I'd never seen Kol so tense before. The tension didn't leave his body when we stepped out of sight, and I had no idea when all those women would stop being excited about him and give him a break.

I shifted closer to him and dug my nails into my ribs, fighting a twitching muscle. "Sorry." It was my fault his shields weren't at full strength.

"Not your fault." He brushed my hand, as if he wanted to hold it, but didn't.

And now all I could think about was the biting agony in my hand. "Kind of is."

"Nah." He flashed me a teasing grin. "It's Marcus's fault."

"Pretty sure it's Jacob's," Marcus said.

Cassius stopped in front of a bank of four elevators, two on either side of the hall. He hit the call button and slid an exasperated look at Gideon.

Gideon shrugged. "We have an incubus on the team. Roll with it or it'll drive you crazy."

"There are rules of conduct for JP agents," Cassius said.

"It's a code, so that's more like guidelines instead of rules, right?" Kol's grin turned mischievous, although I could still see the tension around his eyes and in his shoulders.

"A code *is* a set of rules," Cassius said, as if the idea that the code was merely a suggestion horrified him.

Marcus bit back a laugh, and Kol snickered.

Cassius glared at them, and Kol batted his eyelashes with exaggerated innocence. Jacob snorted, and even Gideon's lips quirked into a smile.

"I should write you up," Cassius said.

"If that deserves a write-up, you're going to spend all your time filing paperwork." Gideon shook his head at him. "But by all means, go ahead."

Cassius sighed. "This is why I don't work with demons. You're all—" His mouth kept moving, but I couldn't concentrate on his words.

God, when would the buzz end? How the hell was I supposed to do anything?

The guys all turned to face the other way, and I couldn't figure out what they were doing.

"—Essie." Marcus grabbed my hand, jerking my attention to him. "The elevator."

I dragged my gaze to the open elevator behind me. Everyone else was already inside, with Jacob holding the door.

"Right—" I stepped toward them, but a swell of power crackled over me, ratcheting up my buzz.

Marcus's lips moved, and he frowned. He'd told me or asked me something, and I hadn't responded.

"Yeah, sorry." But God, that power. Except it wasn't my buzz. My buzz was responding to it, and it felt familiar. I clawed at my upper arm. *Please, just stop.* I wasn't sure how much more I could take.

Marcus grabbed my hand, blood under my nails, and all the guys had stepped out of the elevator.

Cassius frowned.

"—wrong?" Gideon said. "Are you—"

The power grew stronger, as if it were getting closer, and my whole body was on fire. *I know that power. How the hell do I know that power? And how the hell can I feel it?*

"—back." Worry darkened Jacob's expression.

I gritted my teeth and jerked my attention down the hall past the elevators. The power was close. It came from over there. And now I knew who it was. The woman from the warehouse.

She rounded the corner thirty feet away and jerked to a stop. Her gaze landed on me and her eyes widened with surprise. Yeah. I was still alive. And buzz or no buzz, I wasn't letting her get away this time.

<h1 style="text-align: center">ESSIE</h1>

THE WOMAN JERKED AROUND TO RUN BACK THE WAY SHE'D COME, BUT A group of people in suits came around the corner, blocking her way. With a hiss, she wrenched back to face me and bolted for the door to the stairwell instead of trying to push through the crowd.

I ran after her. Jacob, with his enhanced speed, got there first.

"Marcus. Kol. You're with me in the elevator," Cassius said.

I caught the metal security door before it closed. Somehow the woman had already climbed past the second floor landing, and I could still hear the sound of her feet pounding up the stairs, which meant she hadn't run into the hall. My buzz seared through me, and I gritted my teeth against the pain.

"Past floor two," Gideon said into his phone, coordinating the chase most likely with Cassius in the elevator.

Jacob hit the second floor landing. "Stop. JP agents. There's no place to go."

The woman barked a harsh word I didn't recognize in response, and my buzz exploded into an inferno for a second. Jacob jerked, his body seizing as if hit by a Taser, but I couldn't see any barbs.

"Glyph witch," Gideon said. "With lightning strike. Stay back, Essie." He shouldered past me, the palm of his free hand blazing with divine light.

He passed Jacob, who was still stiff, his expression tight with pain, and glanced up the stairwell, but I could hear the woman running again.

I reached Jacob and waved Gideon on. I'd left my sidearm at Operations. It hadn't even occurred to me to bring my weapon, which only emphasized the point that I wasn't ready to go back to active duty. And while I could cast a light strike, I had no idea how to control it. I was more likely to kill the woman or someone else than I was to stop her. That would make interrogating her impossible. Even if she was in charge, there were still a lot of people in her operation, and we needed to round up as many of them as we could.

Jacob sagged against the railing, his chest heaving with desperate breaths and his complexion gray. "I'm fine. Back up Gideon. I'll catch up when I can."

"I'm unarmed."

Jacob gave me his driest look. "You know you're not, and if Gideon needs you, he'll need your light strike. Go."

God damn, he was right, no matter how much it scared me at the moment to release my power.

"I'm on your six, Gideon," I called up to him as I bolted up the stairs.

"Past the fourth floor," Gideon said.

The woman's footsteps just kept pounding up the stairs. Why wasn't she getting off on a floor and hiding in one of the many offices?

My buzz blazed again, stealing my breath, and Gideon wrenched to the side, pressing his back tight to the cinderblock wall. Lightning burst over the wall at the bottom of the landing ahead of me, and he sent a blast of divine light up at her in response.

The woman barked another strange word that made fiery agony snap over me. Gideon's light exploded against an invisible wall, showering me with stinging sparks. Then the woman was running again before all the sparks had even faded.

She kept running, flight after flight, never getting off at a floor. Fire consumed me, and my legs screamed at the exertion. I fought to breathe, my breath sawing in my lungs.

At the tenth floor landing, she sent another blast of lightning at Gideon. He tried to dodge it again, but it clipped his right shoulder. With a grunt of pain, the lightning shot through his brand into me, leaving him free to keep chasing. My muscles seized, and for a second I thought I'd go down, but cold from Jacob's brand washed through it, bringing a swell of strength from him that consumed the spell.

A part of me wanted to yell at Gideon for using our brand that way. But he was the best person to chase the woman. We both knew that. If he went down, there was no way I'd be able to apprehend her.

She reached the top of the stairwell and ran out onto the roof.

"On the roof," Gideon said and shoved his phone into his pocket.

He slowed, glanced out the door, then ran through.

I reached the top, gasping for air, my body on fire. I glanced out the door as well and couldn't see or hear any fighting. Of course, with my buzz making my thoughts spin, that only meant they weren't fighting just outside the door. A warm wind gusted in my face and the sun beat down on the concrete rooftop. I hurried out and rounded a tall steel HVAC unit near the edge of the building.

Gideon stood with his back to me, facing the woman with long, wild bright-red locks. Power crackled over the tattoo on her arm. Even if I couldn't have seen it, I'd have known it was there from the roar of my buzz. Two other women, with swarthy skin and dark hair, a stark contrast to the pale-skinned redhead, stood on either side of her. They wore tank tops that exposed the colorful tattoos around their right arms, a match to the redhead's.

"Not smart, taking a fight with an angel to a rooftop," Gideon said.

Hurried footsteps pounded across the roof behind me, and I wrenched around, a flicker of my power blazing in my palms, but I heaved the power back as the rest of my guys and Cassius arrived.

"Make that two angels." With a flash of light, Cassius released his massive white wings.

"Angels are so arrogant," the redhead said.

"They think they're the only ones with wings." The woman to the redhead's left pressed her hand to her biceps and hissed something. Black batwings unfurled from her back, and she shot up into the sky.

Cassius shot up after her as Gideon released his wings. His were also a brilliant white, but unlike Cassius, his glowed with his divine light, as if more than his innate angelic power radiated from them.

He dove for the remaining two women, but jerked out of the way at the last second as the redhead grabbed her wrist and barked the harsh word, releasing her lightning strike.

Marcus grabbed my arm and wrenched my attention away from the fight. "Just stay back, Essie."

On any other day, I'd have argued with him. But I was a mess right now and more likely to get in the way than help.

He didn't wait for a response and dashed across the rooftop to help Gideon. Kol raced after him, drawing his daggers from the sheaths on his back. I didn't know if I should be surprised or not that he'd decided to go to the mayor's office armed.

Jacob drew up beside me, his complexion still too pale.

"How bad is that lightning strike?" I asked. If one hit knocked Jacob out of the fight, this battle could be over as soon as it started.

"The guys can probably take a few hits if they don't get slammed with something else while they're down," Jacob said. "I was low before we went to the warehouse, took a beating during that fight, and just haven't had time to recover."

Because of me. "You should have fed before we left."

"No one expected a fight—" He huffed a bitter laugh. "Well, not this kind of fight."

Marcus lunged at the redhead, slashing at her with his claws, but she pressed a tattoo and he slammed into her invisible wall. The other woman twisted out of the way of Kol's whirling blades, which impressed the hell out of me because he was damned fast, and grabbed her forearm. At this distance, I couldn't tell what image she'd touched, only that it took up as much of her forearm as Gideon's brand did on me and was bright green.

Massive vines shot out of the roof and twisted around Kol. He slashed at one around his leg and jerked out of the way of another about to seize his arm.

A vine shot toward Marcus's back, and I jerked forward, instinct taking over. Jacob bolted past me and grabbed the vine before it grabbed Marcus. Marcus glanced back at Jacob, gave him a tight nod, and lunged at the redhead with his claws again.

Above, the bat woman absorbed Cassius's fire whip into her skin and shot it back at him as a ball of fire. He yanked his wings back, dropped below the blast, and swooped up at her, while Gideon, hovering in the sky, twisted out of the way of another lightning blast from the redhead and shot a light strike of his own down at her.

The power from all three witches roared through me. Every time they activated a glyph hidden in their tattoos, my buzz flared. It made my muscles twitch, threatening my balance, and I staggered to the HVAC unit and leaned against it to keep standing.

The guys lunged and dove, twisted and slashed, but the witches' power didn't fade. Surely, as humans, they'd run out of juice. But I couldn't sense it diminishing. In fact, it felt as if it were still growing, as if they were tapping into a deeper source than just themselves.

My thoughts stuttered and whirled. One minute Cassius was in the sky, the next he slammed into the rooftop with a powerful boom. Marcus still fought the redhead, but Gideon now sliced at the vines holding both of Kol's arms.

I squeezed my eyes shut. My breath still sawed in my chest as if I hadn't had a few minutes to recover from running up sixteen flights of stairs.

Someone yelled. My eyes flew open. Everyone was in a different position again, and I had no idea how much time I'd lost. A vine wrapped around Cassius and slammed him onto the rooftop again. Gideon now flew in the sky, his hand wrapped in the front of bat woman's tank top. Marcus and Kol slashed at vines that just kept growing, and Jacob punched at the redhead's chest.

The world darkened and spun faster. I pressed a hand to the side of the HVAC unit and my pulse stuttered at the divine light blazing from my palm. My skin was already burned and oozing, but with the witches' power, I couldn't feel anything. Not my light or the pain.

Another scream and strength swept from Jacob's brand in my arm into him. My knees gave way, and I sank to the rooftop. Another lightning strike had hit Jacob, and while he was still alive, he was on his knees in front of the redhead, his head bowed, his face filled with agony. Cassius shot a blast of fire at the redhead, and Marcus hauled Jacob back.

I fought to breathe past the agony. My light blazed around me, and the rooftop under my hands blackened while a part of me screamed that if I didn't get my power under control, I was going to hurt someone.

Gideon yelled, jerking my attention up, as he careened toward the fight on the rooftop with bat woman. He slammed his weight down on her, drawing a strangled scream. Cassius pulled a red zip tie from his pocket, leaped at them, and grabbed her hands.

Bat woman's wings vanished the moment the tie was around her wrists, and the roaring power from the glyph witches contracted as the spell on the zip tie suppressed her magic. The redhead screamed and grabbed the tattoo on her wrist. Cassius wrenched to the side, but he wasn't fast enough, and his body jerked with the full force of her lightning strike, yanking his hand from his pocket and scattering red zip ties on the rooftop.

Marcus tackled the redhead, and Gideon grabbed a tie. A vine seized Marcus's neck and yanked him off the redhead as Gideon seized the woman's arm and secured a tie around one of her wrists.

The witches' power contracted again, but my buzz flared, blazing stronger, spinning my consciousness on the edge of darkness.

Someone yelled and I fought to keep my eyes open. Kol lunged in, his blade severing the vine around Marcus's neck, and he skidded across the rooftop.

"It's over," Gideon said to the remaining swarthy witch, as Cassius wrenched the redhead onto her stomach and secured a second tie, connected to the first around her other wrist, binding her hands behind her back.

"Never," she screamed, and a flurry of vines shot toward the guys. A large one slammed into Cassius, but he'd already finished securing the redhead. Marcus slashed his claws at two threatening to capture his arms and Gideon leaped into the sky, his divine light sword forming in his hands and severing the vine shooting toward him.

Kol sliced through three thin ones, his blades whirling, and rammed his shoulder into the vine witch. All her vines wrenched toward him with a roar of power and darkness rushed across my vision.

One of my guys yelled.

The woman screamed.

My power burned hot within me, blazing bright behind my lids and stealing my breath.

Another scream. This one masculine.

I wrenched my eyes open. Vines crushed Jacob and Marcus against the rooftop, and vine pieces littered the area around Kol. Gideon dove toward the vine witch, a zip tie in his hand, twisting midflight to dodge a shooting vine, and seized her wrist.

She howled and wrenched against his grip. Her vines flailed around her, pounded against Jacob and Marcus, while another grabbed Gideon's neck and choked him.

Kol cut the vine holding Gideon as another thick vine slammed into Kol and sent him flying. He crashed over the rooftop toward me, the vine following and tossing him up and over the edge behind me.

I screamed and lunged for him. He could survive a lot of damage, but I didn't think he'd survive a sixteen-story fall. The vine tripped me as I reached the edge. I caught his wrist, but his weight jerked me forward. Wind rushed around us. Terror filled Kol's eyes, and my buzz snapped into a supernova in my chest, the pressure threatening to tear me apart, even as I felt the last of the witches' power being suppressed with the zip tie.

My power ripped another scream from my throat and exploded with fiery agony, tearing out my back. White flashed behind me. Something jerked me up for a second. My grip on Kol slipped, and I dug my nails into his wrist and seized him with both hands. We plummeted across the street, the wind jerking me up, twisting me to the side. My shoulder clipped the edge of the building across the street from City Hall, and we crashed into an alley.

The impact tore Kol from my grip, and I slammed into a large garbage bin, the world spinning, a trail of white feathers littering the asphalt. Oh, shit. One of the guys had to be hurt.

I twisted to see if Gideon or Cassius were all right and was batted in the face with a wing.

My body spasmed and the wing hit me again.

My wing.

I had wings.

I. Had. Wings.

How the hell did I have wings?

Oh, fuck.

Kol staggered to his feet, his face a mask of pure horror. His body trembled and his breath was ragged, his gaze never leaving my wings.

"You're one of them." His voice broke.

Frost swept over me with his fear, and terror and rage — *his* terror and rage — exploded within me. God, I'd known the war had scarred him, but he'd put on a good face and hadn't revealed just how deep those scars went.

"Kol, I'm not going to hurt you." I raised my burned and bleeding hands. Just the slight movement sent screaming agony through me and twisted the world around me.

"You're one of them." Fury filled his eyes and the frost vanished, consumed by a searing heat and ferocious fury.

"Kol, I'm not going—"

"I won't go back," he snarled. He wrenched a knife from his boot. "You can't take me back. I won't go back. Ever!"

He dove at me. There was nowhere to go. The world still spun, and I was trapped against a garbage bin.

"Kol. No, please."

He rammed his knife toward my chest as Gideon swooped in and jerked him back. Cassius lunged in, taking Kol's place. He clamped a hand around my throat, seizing both my wrists with whips of fire, and yanked me to my feet.

The world twisted and darkened. White-hot pain swept through me from my buzz and the fall, and the ferocity of everyone's emotions.

He pressed his face close to mine, his eyes filled with a fury darker and more ferocious than Kol's. His hate for me turned the air to fire and blazed through my chest. I was one of the monsters who'd tortured Kol and slaughtered thousands upon thousands of humans and supers. I was an abomination, a monster that wasn't supposed to exist, and I'd made his brother fall in love with me.

DESTINED STORM

NEPHILIM'S DESTINY, BOOK 4

MMY SENSES REELED FROM THE POWER CHANNELED BY THE GLYPH WITCHES we'd fought on top of City Hall moments ago and from my crash into the alley, while my body burned with pain and power and Cassius's rage. His grip on my throat tightened, and his fire, searing bands of flame securing my wrists, burned my skin and controlled where I pointed my palms, as if he feared I'd blast him with divine light.

With a snarl, he pressed me harder against the garbage bin, drawing agony through ribs that had to be broken. The reek of the alley's bin in the early summer's heat, even perpetually shaded in the alley across from City Hall, made me gag. Wings I didn't know I'd had until a few seconds ago twitched and slapped against the metal side with a dull thud, as my pulse roared and my thoughts whirled.

I had wings.

I. Had. Wings.

I couldn't make my mind work past that thought.

I had wings.

I wasn't supposed to have wings. I was a powerless nephilim, more human than angel. How the hell did I have wings? Wings ruined everything. Made me a liar, and a monster.

I didn't want to believe I was more like Michael's nephilim than I was human. I didn't want my nature to change, to become violent or bloodthirsty. All I wanted, all I ever wanted, was to help others.

Behind Cassius, Kol howled and wrenched in Gideon's grip, swiping his blade at me, desperate to kill the monster. Me. His face was a mask of pure panic and rage, and his emotions turned the air frigid.

All sense of the flirtatious, wicked incubus was gone, and my throat tightened with grief and anger. A reaction like that meant his experience with Michael and his nephilim had been worse than he'd made it out to be. Horrifyingly worse.

Cassius pulled a red zip tie with a power containment spell on it from his pocket and, with his fire whip, yanked up one of my hands, burned and bleeding from my own power. He slipped the tie over my wrist, and the world darkened and snapped cold. My buzz's stinging inferno stuttered along with the lurching temperature from Cassius's fury and Kol's fear, but that only made me more aware of the pain in my body, adding a dislocated shoulder to my broken ribs and the agony in my back where my wings had ripped free.

"Her wings aren't magical constructs. The zip tie would have dispelled them. They're real." Cassius's gaze locked on me, his angel glow blazing in his eyes. "Get Kol back to the roof to guard the witches then get the SUV."

"Cassius—" Gideon started.

"She's a nephilim."

From the corner of my eye, my vision lurching in and out of focus, I saw Gideon stiffen. But I was afraid to look at him and see the same hurt and betrayal in his eyes that I'd seen in Kol's the moment my wings appeared.

"She's my mate." The force of Gideon's words made my soul sing, but when I raised my gaze, my vision darkened and his expression was strange. Had he really said that with conviction or was that just what I wanted to hear? God, it was so hard to focus.

"And she's a war criminal," Cassius said.

"Cassius—"

"We'll deal with this back at Operations. In private," he said, cutting Gideon off again. Then his tone softened a bit. "Get Kol to the roof and get the SUV. We have to get her back to Operations before someone sees her."

Gideon opened his mouth to say something but another billowing wave of spinning darkness swept over me and when my vision cleared, he was hauling Kol, still out-of-his-mind screaming, out of the alley.

Then Cassius wrenched back to me, his fury so strong it snapped to cold. "Where are the other nephilim?"

"There are no others," I gasped. I still couldn't figure out what had happened. The guys had been fighting the witches. Kol had been knocked off the roof. I'd tried to catch him and—

"There are always others. Your kind can't be alone. You don't know how to be alone. You're pack animals."

"There are no others." I was alone all the time. I had been for so long I hadn't realized how empty I was until I'd found my guys. God, my guys—

Cassius jerked me forward and slammed me back against the full garbage bin with a thud. Hot white agony shot through my chest and the world darkened. I fought to catch my breath but couldn't, each inhalation blazing torment through me.

A part of me prayed I'd pass out, in part to stop the pain, but more because I wasn't ready to face my guys. Kol had been instantly horrified. I was still confused about Gideon's reaction, and I had no idea what Jacob's would be. Marcus's, without a doubt, would be furious. He, above all, had completely believed I was human and that I wanted nothing to do with the supernatural world. He'd sacrificed years being apart from me because he'd thought that was what I wanted.

Except now the truth was out. Would his wolf still see me as his mate? Was that a bond that could be broken, unlike the unbreakable angelic mating brand I shared with Gideon and Jacob?

My throat tightened and tears stung my eyes. It had all happened so fast, and it was all too soon. Maybe if I'd had time to show them who I was, they'd have been able to forgive the lie. But they barely knew me, even Marcus. I was a monstrous abomination, my kind responsible for the torture and death of so many people, and Gideon, Jacob, and Kol all had first-hand experience with nephilim.

Cassius slammed me against the garbage bin again. "I said, what's your plan?"

I dragged my whirling thoughts back to him. "No plan."

"Tell me your plan. You infiltrated Operations. You branded my brother." His grip on my throat tightened, and I fought to breathe. "I can't kill you, but I can make the rest of your life miserable. Without your magic, you won't be able to kill yourself to end it or my brother." His fire whips tightened around my wrists, and I panted against the pain.

"Didn't your siblings tell you to kill yourself the second you were caught?"

"I don't have siblings. I'm natural." *God, please just believe me.*

He barked a bitter laugh. "There's no such thing as a natural nephilim."

"Please," I begged, the alley spinning faster and growing darker.

Cassius said something, but I couldn't focus past the pain to understand him.

Time lurched and Cassius shoved me into the SUV — I had no idea how I'd made it to the mouth of the alley. I tried to drag my gaze up to Gideon in the driver's seat, but couldn't raise my head. My heart was breaking. I had to know how he felt. I couldn't be alone again, an outcast without a family. Please. I needed them, needed to belong, needed to be loved for who I was.

Except I hadn't been loved for who I was. Not all of me. I'd never be fully accepted and it had been foolish to think I could keep my secret and my guys. Now I had neither.

The darkness surged again and my stomach churned. I had to have a concussion. It was the only explanation for why I couldn't think straight, couldn't get my vision to clear.

Another lurch in time and we were in the Quarter. I'd missed the entire ride from City Hall.

"Go around to security," Cassius said. "Let's not parade her in front of every angel in Union."

Gideon parked on the other side of the building in front of a metal door instead of pulling into the garage, and Cassius hauled me out of the SUV. He pressed his thumb to a fingerprint reader and marched me into the secure part of Operations where they kept the holding cells and interrogation rooms. I leaned my forehead against the cool cinderblock wall and squeezed my eyes shut, but the world wouldn't stop spinning.

"Go back to City Hall. Deal with those witches." That sounded like Cassius.

"Chris and Nathaniel are—"

"Not the team's leader." Cassius's voice was strangely gentle, with no sign of the fury I'd seen in the alley. "You have an optics problem already. You can't afford to let head office think they should replace you. I've got this."

Someone said my name. I was pretty sure it was Gideon. Or maybe

I'd just imagined it. Then there was a long pause... or I blacked out again. I wasn't sure which.

"God damn it," Gideon hissed. "Fine."

I forced my eyes open and managed to raise my gaze to look at him, but he'd already strode halfway out the door.

Cassius unlocked the interrogation room beside us, shoved me into the plain gray space, and down onto a metal chair. He cuffed my hands to the bar in the middle of the stainless steel table, and a freezing, aching hollowness filled my chest as the magic containment cuffs locked away my power. Without a word or a second glance, he stormed out of the room.

I sagged forward, leaning my forehead on the cool table, trying to draw a breath that didn't hurt and fighting my tears. I was a survivor. I could survive this.

Except I couldn't. Even if a miracle happened and I managed to escape, Gideon and Jacob would be able to find me through the brand. And even if they let me go, I was broken without them. I didn't want to be. I wanted to be strong, independent, but the magic that bound our souls together was stronger than me. I couldn't fight it for the rest of my life. Hell, I could barely fight just thinking about fighting it.

Come on. There had to be a way out of this, a way to break the bonds, to escape, to—

But I didn't *want* to do any of that. I wanted to stay. I wanted things to go back to this morning when I'd woken in Gideon's arms, and Marcus had kissed me, and all my guys loved me.

Didn't they still love me? They had to sill love me. Didn't they?

But I was now a monster, a war criminal. Unless I could convince Cassius otherwise, I was going to be locked up for the rest of my life even if they did love me.

This couldn't be my fate. I couldn't live like this.

Please, love me.

I knew I was being irrational, that my emotions were going crazy, but I couldn't get them under control. It was as if a dam had broken and I couldn't stop the flood. I bit back a sob. Even if my guys did want me, the best I could hope for was magical stasis. Cassius would put me to sleep, and I'd never wake up.

Which wasn't God damned fair. I wasn't one of the nephilim from the war and I didn't have an ulterior plan. But I already knew life wasn't fair. My mom gave up everything for me and she'd died too young. My father had given me up completely. I'd never known him and I'd like to have thought he'd have wanted to be in my life if it hadn't risked revealing my half-angelic nature.

The door banged open, and instinct jerked me up, my wings slapping against the back of the chair. Blazing white agony sliced through my chest and my throat tightened again. Cassius. Not one of my guys.

Jeez, come on. Get a grip. Focus.

"Gideon—"

"—is none of your concern now," he snapped, and I knew there was no way in hell he'd get any of my guys for me no matter how much I begged... if they even wanted to see me.

He sat in the chair across from me, fire licking over his hands as if he were so angry he couldn't fully control his power. "It'll be easier on you if you just tell the truth."

I sucked in a shallow breath. "I'm a natural nephilim." I forced out the words, words I'd never thought I'd ever say out loud, let alone twice and to an angel. "I was born before the war. I was seven when Michael fell."

Please believe me.

"The truth." Cassius's fire snapped from his fingers and brushed my knuckles. I jerked back, yanking my wrists in the cuffs securing me to the table and slicing more agony through me. "You bound my brother's soul to yours," he snarled. "You've poisoned something beautiful and sacred. For what? What's your plan?"

"There's no plan." He *had* to believe me. My *guys* had to believe me. *Someone* had to. But my mother had warned me. No one would. I was impossible, and no one wanted to risk letting one of Michael's monsters go free by believing a lie.

"There's always a plan." Cassius's fire flared, making me jerk back again. "Tell me."

"There's no plan." There never was a plan. All I wanted was to live a normal human life. All I wanted was to not be alone.

"I'll get it out of you," he said, his voice dark.

Except there was nothing to get, and he wasn't ever going to believe the truth. No one would.

My eyes burned, my tears threatening to release. I had no idea why I fought them. It didn't matter if Cassius thought I was weak. I couldn't convince him of the truth, and my emotions were just too overwhelming.

God, why did I have to have wings? Why couldn't they have shown up later when Cassius was gone and my guys truly knew me?

But that wasn't the way it was and I had to pull my shit together.

"Tell me the plan." His fire swept over my hands and up my wrists.

A strangled scream escaped my clenched jaw. The room darkened again, but I didn't pass out. I had to think. *Come on, think.*

"Lawyer," I gasped.

"You're a terrorist. I can hold you indefinitely without cause."

"Lawyer." There wasn't anything else I could say, although I didn't believe for a second he'd get me a lawyer or that a lawyer would even believe or, hell, represent me. All I could hope was that I'd buy some time while waiting for a lawyer to arrive… if a lawyer arrived, for my head to clear. "I have rights."

"JP law doesn't recognize nephilim as people. You don't have rights," he said. "Tell me where your siblings are. How many of you are left? What's your end game?"

"Lawyer." I couldn't lie about having nephilim siblings to get him to leave me alone. He'd just come back more enraged. A part of me wanted to say I'd only tell one of my guys, but that would only add to Cassius's belief that I had a plan.

He jerked to his feet and slammed his palms on the stainless steel table. His flames swept around him. "Tell me your plan or you'll wish you never perverted the mating brand and hurt my brother."

And that was what hurt the most. Even if I hadn't meant it, I'd betrayed Gideon and Marcus and Jacob in a way that couldn't be forgiven. I'd let them believe I was something I wasn't, and it didn't matter if I'd shown them my true self or not. That one fundamental lie put everything else in doubt, most of all whether they'd really fallen in love with me or if I'd manipulated them.

"Tell me." Cassius leaned closer, his fire searing over my arms.

I jerked against the cuffs, unable to stop myself, and blazing agony sliced through my chest, forcing me to pant shallow, ragged breaths.

"Tell me or I'll bring in Yadveer and have him tear into your memories."

My pulse skipped. He thought that was a threat, but having the lethe demon see the truth and then show it to Cassius might convince him I wasn't lying.

"I consent," I gasped. "I consent to the lethe demon reading my memories."

"You're not a person. I don't need your consent." He shoved back from the table. "Don't think you can give consent and then hide the truth from Yadveer. You can't hide anything from him. He's cracked more powerful supers than you."

He stormed from the room, and I sagged my head onto the table, sobbing. A flicker of electricity, the gentle hum I recognized as Gideon's power, whispered through our brand, finally noticeable past my buzz because the containment cuffs had silenced it. Guess the containment cuffs didn't affect the magic of the mating brand.

But that only made me ache more. I yearned to talk to him, to see him, but feared to at the same time. We'd finally agreed to start figuring out our relationship. Hell, I was just starting to figure out my relationship with all my guys.

And now—

My throat tightened and more tears plopped onto the metal table.

Gideon's electricity, still filled with warmth, affection, honor, and determination, the part of him that resonated core-deep with my essence, grew stronger. It slid up my arm into Jacob's brand, and I felt his powerful stillness and intense certainty.

My guys were coming closer. *Please open the door. Please tell me every-thing is going to be okay.*

But a small voice, the voice I'd lived with all my life, said that they wouldn't. And even if they did, what did I say to them? What *could* I say to them?

It always came back to that. I couldn't possibly be what I was. And even if I was, I'd still lied.

The minutes ticked by. Cassius didn't storm back in. He was probably trying to make me sweat, building up my fear about what was to come in hopes I'd confess. But having my memories read was my only salvation. Gideon and Jacob got a little closer, but not close enough to open the door. They probably weren't even in the secure section of Operations. And, now that I'd had time to think about it, the strange tone of Cassius's voice earlier had been calm and consoling. Without a doubt he'd lied to Gideon. Which, for a second, shocked the hell out of me, because that was a very unangelic thing to do. But Cassius was more emotional than the typical icy angel, and I didn't doubt he'd lie to protect his brother. Except that meant none of my guys knew where I was. They were prob-ably going along, business as usual, dealing with the glyph witches and the mess at City Hall.

My thoughts muddled, and my body grew heavy. I dreamed of Gideon arguing with Cassius, the light in his eyes blazing, his expression furious. In fact, all of my guys stood up for me and demanded my release. Gidcon was yelling, his voice hard and icy, Marcus barely had his wolf contained and was snarling, Jacob radiated more vampiric intensity than I'd ever felt before, and Kol—

Wasn't there. Even my psyche knew no matter what I wanted or craved, I'd lost our friendship by just being what I was.

Besides, it was just a dream. I was a monster.

Except I wasn't a monster. I was a naturally born nephilim.

But that didn't mean I wasn't a monster.

And that was the fear the zip overdose had brought to life, the fear I'd been hiding from myself my entire life. What if Michael's nephilim weren't monsters because that was how he'd made them, but because that was just what nephilim were? Human DNA twisting angel DNA because the DNA of a being of celestial light was supposed to be incompatible with anything else. Except if that was true, then I shouldn't exist—

Or I wasn't natural.

JACOB

Gideon paced his living room, his body tense and his angel glow blazing. Divine light glowed around his hands, a dangerous nimbus on the verge of exploding and as much as I should probably tell him to pull it back, I couldn't. His mate— *Our* mate had been hauled into an interrogation room like a criminal. And from what Gideon had told me, Cassius hadn't asked questions, just shoved her into the SUV and got her into Operations before dismissing Gideon.

"He lied," he spat out through gritted teeth. "He just outright lied. To my face." He reached his kitchenette and jerked around, glaring at me as he stormed back our way. "You should have let me hit him. I would have knocked him on his ass and she'd be out of that interrogation room right now and getting medical attention."

Marcus snarled in agreement and fur swept over the back of his hands and up his arms. I'd had to hold the shifter when he'd learned the truth about what Cassius had done, and I still wasn't sure he'd stay where he was and not go storming down to the secure section of Operations to break her out.

It was a miracle that he'd learned about Essie's situation after the fact and hadn't been in the hall with me and Gideon when we'd talked with Cassius. I wouldn't have been able to calm down both him and Gideon, and then we'd be running for our lives right now instead of being smart and coming up with a plan.

"We can't just take her," I said. "We need a plan."

"She's hurt," Gideon shot back. "I know you can feel her draining strength from the brands."

"And we're keeping her alive." Everything within me screamed to go and save her and I knew Gideon was feeling the same call. She was in danger. We had to protect her. Save her. Now now now.

My fangs extended and my grip on my vampiric nature slipped, filling the room and making Marcus snarl, his wolf sensing my need for a fight. He would egg me on or force my hand if we didn't make a move soon. So would Gideon, something I'd never thought he'd ever do. He was always in control, always ready to take a beat and make a plan before rushing in.

But the pull of the mating brand was powerful, stronger than anything I'd ever encountered before, and Gideon had waited to seal his bond with Essie. His soul was already being torn apart and if he and Essie didn't have sex soon and finish bonding, he'd lose his mind or die just as if she'd died.

"We have to be smart about this," I insisted. "She's a nephilim. Even if we could make your brother see reason—"

The light around Gideon's hands blazed brighter. Shit, wrong thing to say.

"He's not my brother," Gideon spat out. "My *brother* would never arrest my mate. He'd *know* she wasn't a monster."

"Even if he accepted that," I said, fighting to stay calm, "we'd still have to deal with the rest of Operations. Hell, the rest of the world. We need a plan before we break her out, a place to go, resources, a way to hide."

"I know that!" Divine light blasted from his hands, tearing through his bedroom door beside me, hitting the far wall, burning through the drywall, and exploding on the cinderblock firewall between his unit and Kol's. "Damn it!"

"We can come up with a plan once she's out of there," Marcus growled, his fur rolling the rest of the way up his arms and his canines extending. "You said she's drawing strength from the brands. Cassius has had his hands on her for over half an hour. If he was going to get Amiah to heal her, he would have done that by now. We can't assume he's going to try to keep her alive."

"He wouldn't risk Gideon's life," I said for the— God, I had no idea how many times I'd said that, only that I felt like I was a broken record. "We have time. We can't fuck this up."

"He's treating her like a criminal. She's not a God damned criminal and if you won't do something, I will." Marcus stormed to the door and I grabbed his wrist.

He jerked toward me and slammed his fist into my gut. My breath exploded from my lungs from the impact but I still managed to wrench him farther from the door. With a snarl, he punched again and I twisted out of the way, his knuckles skimming my ribs. I tried to heave the wrist I still held around to his back, but he jerked with the movement and slammed me against the wall, cracking the drywall.

"Enough!" Gideon barked.

Marcus glared at him, his pupils slitted, his wolf in full control. "She's your mate, too. You're just going to let Cassius interrogate her. We know she's not one of Michael's nephilim. She couldn't be."

Gideon sagged onto his couch and rubbed his face, suddenly looking exhausted. "She has to be."

"She's not a fucking monster," Marcus snarled.

"No, but she has to be one of Michael's nephilim. It's the only way she can exist."

"So what? You're just going to let Cassius interrogate and imprison her?" Marcus demanded.

"You know I'm not." The light in Gideon's angel glow blazed and his divine magic roared around his hands. "Damn it." He clenched his jaw and fought to get his magic back under control. "Michael may have made her, but she's not a monster like his other nephilim. Destiny wouldn't have bound any of us to her if that was the case. But Jacob is right. We have to be smart about this."

"Fine then," Marcus snarled.

"Once we've gotten Essie out of holding, we'll need to hide," Gideon said. "Ideally out of town. But to do that we'll need concealment charms so the JP can't find us."

"Do we have any money?" I asked. "I have some cash, but not a lot."

"I don't tend to carry cash," Marcus replied.

"Neither do I." Gideon released a heavy, shuddering breath. "I'll sell my light magic. That should get us more than enough."

My pulse leaped at that. "That would endanger Essie. Even if we could get Kol on board with our escape plan, we'd still have no way of siphoning off your magic without your essence in it. If anyone got a hold of it, they'd be able to control you."

Gideon's expression turned grim at the mention of Kol. He'd said Essie's wings had triggered a meltdown and he'd attacked her. Gideon had sent Kol back to Operations, but he wasn't here and that worried me. I didn't know if he was still in the middle of reliving his nightmares or if he'd come out of it and realized he'd tried to hurt Essie — and I wasn't sure which would hurt him more.

He and Essie had become close and he'd been more at peace with himself than I'd ever seen him before. The kid already carried so much guilt over what Michael had forced him to do. I could only pray that attacking Essie in the throes of a flashback wouldn't push him to hurt himself or, in the very least, that we could get to him in time to help him. I also knew he'd feel even worse if we helped him before Essie, which meant we needed to get a move on with getting her out of custody.

"Selling my light magic is the best solution. We can't use our accounts. The second we break her out, they'll either freeze our assets or use them to track us," Gideon said, his voice starting to sound like its usual in-control self. "If I seal the bond with Essie there's a chance no one will be able to control me through my essence."

"That's not a risk we should take," I said. Sure, creating a soul bond with Essie broke my sire bond with Victoria, but that didn't mean if someone else got a magical hold of my essence the bond would stop them from using my essence to control me and there was no guarantee the bond would protect Gideon, either.

"The other option would be raiding the armory and selling the weapons," Marcus suggested, his tone clear he didn't like the idea.

I didn't either, but it was better than having some shady witch controlling Gideon.

"Essie wouldn't want that," Gideon said.

"She wouldn't want you controlled, either," I insisted. "What's more dangerous? A bunch of guns in the wrong hands or you?"

"I hate that these are our options. Fine." Gideon rose and rolled his shoulders, his expression hard and determined. This was the man I'd followed into battle during the war, the man who put his emotions and desires aside to do what needed to be done — and likely why Essie's determined, generous soul had been bound to his. She did the same thing, unfortunately that usually involved her trying to sacrifice herself for the good of the many.

Well not today. Not ever. I'd just found her. I wasn't going to lose her. It didn't matter if Michael had made her or not. I knew who she was, knew her heart and soul were good, and I would do whatever it took to keep her safe.

THE DOOR BANGED OPEN, AND I JERKED AWAKE, THE SUDDEN MOVEMENT again shooting agony across my chest and stealing my breath.

Cassius stormed in again, fire still licking over his hands and now curling up his forearms to his elbows. Yadveer, Operations' resident lethe demon, shuffled in behind him, looking as elderly and weathered as I remembered. Pricks of red light glowed in his dark eyes, the only indication — at this distance — that he was anything other than human.

He settled on the chair across from me and held out his hand, radiating the telltale heat of a demon. "You want to know everything?" he asked Cassius.

I shuddered at the question, even though I already knew that if Cassius went ahead with his plan for Yadveer to read my memories, my entire life, every hope and dream and fuck-up, would be exposed. I wasn't sure if it was a good thing or not that I hadn't slept with Gideon. If I had, then Yadveer would be able to show Cassius how much I cared for Gideon and how connected we were... and how much his rejection was going to hurt.

"Make it fast." Cassius crossed his arms and glowered at me. "My brother's life is in danger. All of Operations could be in danger."

"Fast will be painful." Yadveer's gaze dipped to my burned and bleeding hands cuffed to the bar at the center of the table. "She's already injured. She could lose consciousness."

"Will it kill her?"

"Not likely," Yadveer said.

"Then my only concern is learning the truth and keeping my brother and everyone in this facility safe. You do what you have to do."

Yadveer's gaze rose back to mine, not a hint of sympathy in his eyes. "As you wish."

A hard ball of ice formed in my gut as Yadveer took my hand, and I tried to fight my fear. This was the only way to prove my innocence. Hopefully it would be enough so I wouldn't be locked up like a criminal for the rest of my life. Except the alternative was to be studied like a lab rat to learn how I was even possible.

Yadveer closed his eyes, and fire, not the gentle heat from when he'd read my memories before, scorched into my hand and up my arm with a pain as powerful as my buzz. I tried to bite back a scream but couldn't stop it. The inferno seared into every cell of my being, diving deep into me, threatening to control me like the archnephilim had—

I slammed against an alley wall, agony shooting through my chest. The archnephilim wrenched me close, his power and darkness whirling around me, turning my buzz into an inferno. Then he poured his smoke into my mouth, and I fought to breathe, to move, to do anything. But the archnephilim kept pouring his essence into me, trying to control me. *No, please. I won't let him. He can't take me—*

Except he *had* controlled me. He'd made me burn Kol—

I wrenched around as divine light burst from my hands and slammed into Kol's chest. He staggered, and everything lurched into terrifying slow motion, every detail crisp, perfect, as if Yadveer's magic enhanced everything I'd seen but hadn't noticed.

More divine light blazed from my palms, and terror filled Kol's eyes as I grabbed his head, sending all that power into his face, burning his skin, the charred bitter smell of blood and burnt flesh filling my nose.

Kol screamed. The sound tore at my soul, making the part of me that knew this was a memory, that Kol was all right, writhe against Yadveer's power. This wasn't who I was. The archnephilim had made me do it. I hadn't wanted to hurt Kol.

Please. Look at the good I've done, the people I've helped. I strained to direct Yadveer to the years I'd been a cop, but my memory jumped to a dark dusty living room.

My thigh was on fire. A shifter, his eyes filled with wild feral intensity, dug his claws deeper into my leg and yanked me close, while a massive gray wolf snapped its jaw around Marcus's arm. Marcus screamed and the wolf wrenched him to the floor.

My memory lurched again. Blood dripped from Marcus's elbow onto a floor with a thick layer of disturbed dust.

Another lurch. A vampire with pale skin, black eyes, and animalistic hunger in her gaze snarled at me. Blood, so much blood, smeared down her chin and soaked into her filthy torn shirt from the zip addict she'd just killed. Her fingers were extended into short, sharp claws, and the reek of rotting human flesh made bile burn the back of my throat. I had a magazine of enspelled ammunition in my hand, ready to load into my Glock, but lightning, like a Taser blast on its highest setting, shot through me. My thoughts jerked to Gideon. He was in trouble, hurt, dying, and I couldn't lose him. God, please. I couldn't lose him.

The thought crushed me and I couldn't breathe, but my memories jerked again, not releasing me.

I sat in a bland beige hospital room, my mother's frail hand held gingerly in mine. Her skin was so thin, so pale, like fragile gauzy fabric, and the monitor beeped, loud, slow, horrible chirps. She'd collapsed again and against her wishes I'd called 911. I knew it was too late to save her, but I couldn't sit by and watch her suffer any longer. She hadn't wanted me to spend my escape money on her, hadn't wanted to burden me with medical bills or questions, and we'd fought about it the last couple of days. My last words to her had been frustrated and angry.

Please wake up so I can tell you how much I love you. I slid into bed beside her and wrapped my arms around her. *Please don't die. You're all I have.*

My memory lurched again. We still lay in bed, but this time Mom had her arms around me, and I had my pink princess comforter pulled up to my chin. I was warm and safe and Mom smelled fresh and sweet. It was a few days before we'd had the first JP agent scare — or at least the first one I could remember. I was eight? No, seven, and I'd known nothing about the Joined Parliament or nephilim.

"Tell me again about Dad." It was a childish request, one I'd asked over and over again, but I couldn't help myself. Joy and awe always lit up Mom's eyes with a look I never got tired of seeing. True love. Love I'd hoped to have one day.

"He's the most beautiful angel I've ever seen. His hair is brown but looks like copper if the sun hits it just the right way, just like yours." She pressed her lips to my forehead. "And his eyes are warm and brown with flecks of gold. Angel glow radiates from his eyes even when he sleeps and his wings—" Her voice turned wistful and sad, like it always did when she talked about Daddy. "His wings are pure white, and he'll fly back to us soon."

Except 'soon' turned into 'someday', which turned into 'couldn't' because it was too dangerous. Daddy would never be able to hide his true nature and look human, while Mom would never be anything but human, and that would make too many people ask too many questions about me.

My memories lurched again, whirling faster and faster, the fire of Yadveer's magic searing into my cells. Hiding in an abandoned house, shaking with fear. Playing with three other kids on the banks of a shallow creek beneath an overpass, bright with wonder. Teased by Marcus while on patrol, hot with desire.

I fought to breathe, to think, to do anything other than feel the blaze of my memories, each one growing stronger, the emotions more powerful, as Yadveer yanked me around in my mind. Frost covering the backs of my hands, scared. Lying on soft grass in the backyard, safe. First day at the police academy, determined. Burying my mother by myself, empty. Seeing my guys for the first time, dread. Gideon. Jacob. Kol. Marcus. Anger. Joy. Desire. Fear. Whirling and lurching and burning and—

Nothing. No pain, no memory, and no magic. Just peaceful black oblivion. For a second, no longer than a fluttering heartbeat, I floated in a water that wasn't water. I was safe... but still alone. I ached for my guys. This wasn't where I was supposed to be. Except I no longer knew where to go or how to get there.

A thread of agony blazed through the darkness, and I gasped shallow breaths, desperate to ease the pain.

"—didn't get it all, but—"

"Then wake her up and finish it," Cassius snapped.

Another slice of pain cut through my chest.

"The block is magical," Yadveer said. "I think it's crumbling, but it's still too strong for me to break through. It also doesn't feel like her magic."

"So someone else put it on her?"

"Yes."

"Who?"

"I won't know until the block comes down," Yadveer said.

I cracked my eyes open to see an out-of-focus table edge and floor.

I'd passed out on the table, putting pressure on my broken ribs and dislocated shoulder. Blood darkened the side of my T-shirt and hip and dripped off the side of the chair into a pool on the floor. I couldn't figure out how I was bleeding. Yadveer's magic was purely mental and it didn't make sense that Cassius would hurt me while Yadveer worked.

With a snap of mental fire, residue of Yadveer's magical intrusion, my memory leaped back to the alley. Kol had attacked me. I must have been in too much shock to notice he'd actually cut me before Gideon had yanked him back. I tried to concentrate on my brands to see if I was drawing strength from Gideon and Jacob, determine if they were in danger of my dying, but couldn't focus past the pain.

"We're not waiting for the spell to fail. Call Bane. Tell him we need a spell broken, and I don't care what it costs." Cassius's feet strode into sight, and he grabbed my arm with the dislocated shoulder.

I screamed as agony exploded in my shoulder and chest. My wings jerked, hitting the back of the chair, and the room went dark.

"—and how could you not know she was bleeding?" That sounded like Amiah and she sounded pissed.

I cracked my eyes open again. My head was back on the table, and pain flooded every inch of my body. I must have passed out again.

"I know now, so heal her," Cassius said.

Amiah's black practical shoes came into sight. I tried to raise my head to look at her and Cassius, and hell, anyone else in the room, but couldn't find the strength. She grabbed my shoulder and the lightning of her magic erupted inside me, blazing through my body until darkness enveloped me again.

"—her essence."

I strained against the darkness, trying to figure out who had spoken, where I was, and what was going on. There'd been pain, so much pain, and—

I bit back a sob. My guys knew the truth.

"We'll deal with it when Bane gets here." That sounded like Cassius.

I'd passed out again? At least this time, although I could still feel the world spinning even with my eyes closed, the pain of my injuries was gone.

"He's a mercenary," Amiah said. "Do you honestly think we can trust him with this?"

"The replacement spell-break charm is still on backorder. He's the only one in Union City who might have quick access to one and be powerful enough to break the spell on her," Cassius said.

I forced my eyes open as he grabbed my upper arm and hauled me to my feet. The room darkened and lurched and my wings bashed against him, but I didn't pass out again.

He jerked me around the table, my mind stumbling over the fact I was no longer handcuffed to the bar. Amiah glared at me—

No, not a glare. Something else. I couldn't read her expression. It was hard and concerned... and something...But with the containment cuffs still around my wrists — at some point the zip tie had been removed — I had no idea what she was feeling.

She stepped away from the door to let us pass, and Cassius hauled me into the hall and deeper into the secured section of Operations. The fluorescent lights above were too bright and even though Amiah had healed me — or at least mostly healed me — I still couldn't get my head to stop spinning.

We reached a T-intersection and turned left into a long hall with half a dozen metal doors on either side. Cassius marched me to a door halfway down and unlocked it with his thumbprint. Inside was a narrow gray cell with a stainless steel toilet and sink and a hard, wide bench running along one side.

I shuffled inside — thankful he didn't push me — and the door closed with a heavy *thunk*. With a groan, I eased onto the edge of the bench, since my wings wouldn't let me sit back. And while I really wanted to lie down, I didn't want to deal with the frustration of figuring out *if* there was a good position to lie with them sticking out of my back.

Cassius hadn't removed the containment cuffs, probably because he didn't want me to turn my power on myself and commit suicide. Not that I'd ever consider hurting Gideon and Jacob that way. He probably thought the cuffs would piss me off, but I was grateful they were still on because they silenced my buzz. And once the cell stopped spinning from the blast of Amiah's healing magic, I was going to feel better than I had in days... physically, at least.

My back still stung, though, so I rolled my no-longer-dislocated shoulder, confirming it was back to normal, and felt my ribs and side for tenderness. Nothing. Guess Amiah's healing hadn't dealt with the effects of whatever magic had ripped my wings out from inside me.

I shifted, and my wings extended and banged into the walls on either side. Jeez, they were going to take some getting used to, and not only did my back still sting, but the muscles ached as well. I contemplated trying to pull the damned things back into my body, but I had no idea how to do that or if the containment cuffs would even let me.

Wonderful.

Okay, think. There's a way out of this. There had to be. *Please let Cassius believe the memories Yadveer pulled from my mind and let Sebastian confirm that whatever spell was on me wasn't my doing.*

My thoughts tripped over that. Someone had put a spell on me. Was that why my eyes hadn't glowed until after I'd blasted myself with divine light? Or why I barely had any magic? I'd thought I was more or less powerless because my human half was stronger than my angelic half, that it was just the way nature had combined my parents' DNA in me. But maybe nature had nothing to do with it.

Sebastian had said that every time I'd used my divine light, I'd burned through the concealment spell on my contacts. That was basic concealment magic one-o-one. What if my father had placed a powerful spell that concealed my true nature and my magic even from me?

I had no idea if that was even possible or the kind of power it would take for a spell to last thirty years without failing. Which made me wonder who my father was and just how much power he possessed.

The lock on the door clicked, and I jerked awake. Somehow I'd managed to lean my head and shoulder against the cell wall without twisting or crushing my wings too much and passed out. I rubbed my face, emotionally and physically exhausted from everything that had happened in the last couple of days, and knowing I needed to stay calm. Freaking out wouldn't help Cassius believe I was harmless and meant what I said when I claimed to be a naturally born nephilim.

Except it wasn't Cassius who stepped into the cell but Sebastian. His nearly translucent skin glowed with cold white-blue light, and his eyes, such a pale blue they were almost clear, leaped from my wings to my face. His lips curled back in a wicked smile, still filled with sexual invitation even though I was clearly a nephilim, and for the first time I didn't sense there was something else going on behind his smile.

"So that's what you've been hiding." He let the door close behind him but didn't draw closer. Which bothered the hell out of me.

"I don't bite."

"What if I ask nicely?" He still didn't move from the door.

"I'm—" My throat tightened and I snapped my mouth shut. I'd been about to say I was taken. But I didn't know if I was any more. I sagged back, painfully pinched my wing between the wall and the bench, and jerked forward.

God damn fucking wings. How the hell had I ever dreamed of having them so I could fly like Gideon? They ruined everything, and now I couldn't sit or move the way I wanted to. "Just do whatever Cassius is paying you to do."

"He wants to know why you have no memories of your siblings or your plans to infiltrate Operations."

"Because I have no siblings or plans." I don't know why I kept saying it. No one was going to believe me. "I'm an only child, naturally born."

Sebastian crossed his arms, straining his white button-down against his muscular shoulders and showing the shadow of his black tattoos twisting over his biceps. "Angels claim that's impossible."

"So I've been told."

"Did you have a spell put on you to hide your nature?"

"You mean the spell that Yadveer says is blocking my memories?" He wasn't going to believe the truth, either. "Just go digging around or spell breaking or whatever it is you're supposed to do. Cassius doesn't believe me. Why would anyone else?"

"I do." Sebastian eased onto the edge of the bench beside me. "I knew you were hiding something, but I never sensed insincerity from you."

He pressed a hand to his ribs, activating one of his magic glyphs. Light blazed from a swirl of black tattoo, making his white shirt see-through, revealing thick black tattoos covering his entire chest and abs and disappearing past the waistband of his slacks. "Take a breath and close your eyes."

I drew in a breath — an honest-to-goodness deep breath — and closed my eyes. Sebastian pressed his palms to my temples and lightning shot into my brain while power clenched inside my chest. I gasped and instinctively opened my eyes, meeting Sebastian's gaze.

A universe of icy light snapped in his irises with blazing power. It poured into every cell within me just like Yadveer's fire and the arch-nephilim's smoke, but instead of burning or consuming, it lit me up. My skin glowed, my divine light bleeding not just from my palms but every pore, and for a moment I felt like a true being of celestial light. I wasn't just half angel and mundane human. I was living, breathing light. It crackled along my nerves and radiated around my heart. My angel brands blazed a brilliant gold, swirling from my forearm to my shoulder, the light shining through the fabric of my T-shirt.

Sebastian's eyes widened and the icy power flared, the weight of the universe in his gaze crushing me, making my own light blaze brighter with a pressure that kept growing. It threatened to rip me apart, disintegrate my physical form until all that remained was light.

Tears raced down my cheeks, but I couldn't close my eyes, couldn't look away from all that power. I'd never felt anything like it before and doubted I would ever again.

A scream tore from my throat and my light erupted into a blinding explosion. My body went limp, but Sebastian caught me, pulling me against his chest before I could fall back and twist my wings. His breath came too fast and his body shook.

"You're not at all what you say you are," he gasped.

More tears rolled down my cheeks and soaked into his shirt. "So I am one of Michael's puppets and didn't even know it?" Were my mating brands with Gideon and Jacob even real? I loved them. I knew I loved them. But that didn't mean it wasn't part of some greater plan that I knew nothing about.

Oh, God, even my memories could be fake, magical constructions. All the time I'd spent with my mom, the heartache of losing her, my whole life up until I'd been assigned as Marcus's partner. I had no idea how any of that made sense, how anyone could have known being Marcus's partner four and a half years ago would get me close to the JP team, but I no longer knew what was true.

"Esther, you're not a puppet." He cupped my cheeks with his palms and nudged me back to look him in the eyes. The icy universe and his enormous power were gone. His eyes were back to their unusual, almost-clear blue. "You're not human."

ESSIE

My thoughts tripped over his words. "Of course I'm human." How could I not be human? "My essence says I'm human." My whole life, every super I'd come across who could read essences had thought I was human. Except my whole life might have been a fabrication.

"You're not. Someone hid your true essence with a powerful spell—" Sebastian frowned and his grip on my cheeks tightened as he drew nose to nose with me. "Gold flecks."

"Gold what?"

"Flecks. In your angel glow."

"What does that mean?" I tried to keep my voice steady while my thoughts spun. I didn't think I was ever going to feel steady again. I had to have gotten the flecks from my father, the man I'd dreamed about yesterday. Maybe Sebastian knew who my father was.

"It means you're at least half archangel," he said, a tremor racing through him. With a strangled groan, he pressed his forehead to mine, as if it were too heavy to hold up. "It's going to take at least another attempt, probably more, to break the spell on you."

"My father was an archangel?"

"Your mother, too, possibly."

"My mother, too?" I couldn't wrap my mind around that, especially since he was saying my mom couldn't possibly be my mom.

He had to be wrong. I couldn't be a full angel. My mom *was* my mom.

A human. Angels didn't die from cancer and the doctors had been clear, cancer had killed her, but— "I'm an angel, not a nephilim?"

"Yes," Sebastian gasped. "There's nothing human about you."

The cell door banged open, making me jerk back from Sebastian, who stayed sagged forward, hands on his thighs to keep himself from collapsing face-first into my lap.

Gideon stormed in, the glow in his eyes radiating brilliant white light, and my heart stuttered with yearning and fear. Even with his beautiful blond hair buzzed short like his brother's, he was breathtaking with his chiseled jaw, broad muscular shoulders, and narrow hips.

Except I'd never seen him this cold before, every inch of his posture screaming death and vengeance. This was an avenging angel, the kind people had talked about from the war. Powerful, brutal, and if they possessed any emotion at all, it was hard and icy.

A shiver swept over me, and a vise squeezed around my heart. I yanked my gaze to the floor. He was furious. I'd lied to him, and as far as he knew, I was an abomination. Our bond wasn't enough for him to love me. I knew it wouldn't be, not faced with the truth so soon, but that reality crushed me, making my soul hurt even more than my body did.

"Move away from her, Bane," Gideon said, his voice low, hard.

Because I was a monster.

Sebastian shuddered, groaned, and didn't move.

"Bane!"

The sharpness of his tone yanked my attention to Gideon as Sebastian gasped and jerked back, falling off the edge of the bench onto his butt. "It's not what it looks like."

"Then what is it?" Gideon growled. "The brand lit up with power."

"All her power."

Gideon leveled his gaze on me, and I shrank back, squeezing my wings against the wall. "Nephilim don't possess that kind of power."

"Yeah, about that—"

Jacob and Marcus shoved into the doorway, pushing Gideon further into the cell. They were opposites in size, Jacob bulky and big with his barrel chest and bulging biceps, and Marcus with his wiry compact form. Jacob's complexion was too pale, but I couldn't see any injuries and his clothes were clean. He must have changed after the fight on City Hall's roof with the three glyph witches while I was in the interrogation room. Marcus also looked like he'd changed, and he must have shifted and healed his injuries because he looked fine. At least they'd gotten through the fight okay.

My heart swelled with joy, then plummeted a second later as my brain caught up with my situation. I yearned for Marcus to wrap his arms around me, pull me tight to his lean-muscled body, and tell me everything was all right. But it wasn't all right. If Gideon was furious with me, Marcus certainly was as well. He, out of all of them, had the biggest reason to be livid.

"The brand started burning." Jacob turned all his vampiric intensity to Sebastian, who shuddered and groaned again.

"Not my power."

"He says the power was Essie's," Gideon said.

Jacob shifted his gaze to me, and for the first time the strength of his vampiric intensity terrified me. "Nephilim don't have that kind of power."

"No shit," Sebastian snapped.

"For fuck's sake." Marcus shouldered past Jacob, knelt in front of me, and grabbed my hands. His wolf darkened his eyes, its feral intensity threatening to take over, but not with rage. No, with ferocious, protective love.

My thoughts tripped over that and my throat tightened.

"Are you all right?"

Was I all right? He wanted to know—

Tears burned my eyes. One simple question and I knew Marcus didn't care what I was. He didn't care that I'd lied to him and we'd wasted years apart because of my fears. He still loved me.

"I'm getting you out of here." He pulled a handcuff key from his pocket and unlocked the cuffs.

My buzz exploded with a fiery agony, stealing my joy that Marcus was still my mate. Every inch of my skin burned, and my muscles twitched and clenched. It was worse than it had ever been before, and it had been overwhelming while standing on City Hall's roof.

"Marcus, please. Put the cuffs back on." I wasn't going to be able to stand, let alone think straight. And with Gideon still looking like he wanted to run someone through with his divine light sword — most likely me — I wasn't going to beg to hold his hand.

Jacob dropped to his knees beside Marcus. "We're not letting you stay here. We know *who* you are, what kind of person you are. We don't care *what* you are."

"Then you won't care that she's a full angel with at least one archangel parent," Sebastian said.

Gideon glared at him, the strength of his anger turning the air sweltering. "You should have led with that."

"You try breaking a spell designed to permanently hide even half of an archangel's power."

"Marcus, please," I gasped. The muscles in my back contracted, and my wings smashed against the wall and buffeted the guys.

Marcus's grip on my hands tightened, sending his frosted fear curling over my wrists and up my arms. "Pull your wings in."

"How?"

His eyes widened with surprise. Yeah, bet he'd never had an angel ask him how to pull her wings in. "You just— Don't you know?"

"I didn't even know I had wings until this morning."

"Concentrate on drawing them into your body," Jacob said.

Sure. Concentrate. A muscle in my thigh clenched, and I yanked my hand from Marcus's grip and dug my knuckle into my leg, trying to get the spasm to release. But the movement only sent more stinging fire up my arms that did nothing to burn away Marcus's frost.

"Take a breath, Essie," Marcus said, "and pull them in."

I tried to take a breath, but my shoulders seized, cutting off my air with a sharp snap.

Come on. Concentrate. Pull them in. I fought to imagine my wings drawing into my body. The muscles between my shoulder blades seized again, and my wings slapped Jacob and Marcus. "Just put the God damn cuffs back on."

Gideon grabbed Sebastian by the arm and hauled him to his feet. "What's wrong with her?"

"Hell if I know."

"It'll be easier to get you out of here if you pull your wings in," Jacob said. "Gideon. Help her."

"I can't concentrate. I'm on fire." I was going to burn up— No, I was going to combust and take all my guys with me. The thought made my pulse trip and my gut clench with fear.

"Oh, fuck." A shudder raced through Sebastian. "The concealment spell must finally be weak enough that her power is trying to break through. Get her wings in and get those cuffs back on."

"I'm not handcuffing my mate." Light flared from Gideon's eyes.

"Please," I begged.

"Until we can figure out how to contain her, it'll be safer for every-one," Sebastian said.

Gideon glanced at Marcus and Jacob and the cell's temperature plummeted. The frost on my hands and arms thickened.

"Fine." Gideon shoved Sebastian toward the door. "Everyone out."

Marcus jerked to his feet and snarled at Gideon. "I'm not leaving her."

"Then duck when she turns around and keep your wolf under control." Gideon lifted his gaze to mine and beneath the rage I saw absolute terror.

I wrenched my gaze from his, stood, and turned, trusting the guys to get out of the way. "I'm sorry. I—" The muscles in my side clenched, making me whimper.

Gideon brushed trembling hands along the top of my wings. My buzz dimmed at the contact, but didn't vanish like it had when he'd touched me before. I fought back a sob of frustration.

"We'll deal with the power after we get your wings in," he said, his voice low and soothing, no sign of the fear I'd seen in his eyes or felt in his hands. "Concentrate on the spot between your shoulder blades."

His fingers grew steadier and skimmed closer to the base of my wings. The muted fire of my buzz turned sultry with desire, but the pressure inside me still threatened to explode.

He shifted closer. Gentle warmth radiated from his body that did nothing to melt the frost on my arms, and his breath feathered across the back of my neck.

"Imagine a spark of magic right here." He slid his thumbs along the base of my wings, the movement slow and sensual.

My breath hitched, desire rushing low within me. I hadn't known the base of an angel's wings was an erogenous zone, but just one touch and I was melting with need. I ached for him to draw closer and press his body against mine, preferably without our clothes on. So far we'd only kissed, but I needed him as much as I needed my other guys, and I had to solidify our bond before a part of my soul completely shattered and couldn't be fixed.

His lips brushed the hollow behind my ear. I gasped at the sudden kiss and tipped my head back against his shoulder. A low moan escaped his lips and vibrated to the core of my being. The pressure of his thumbs against my wings grew, the movement rougher, faster, as his breath picked up. But just like the last time we'd kissed, the force of my magic inside me grew with my desire. It swelled and mixed with the electric crackle of Gideon's power radiating from his brand, taking it and entwining it with mine.

His magic surged up my arm into Jacob's brand, who gasped as the surge pulled power from him into me. It rushed around my heart, churning stronger and stronger, filling me, burning through every inch of my body, seeping into every cell, and threatening to erupt in a violent explosion. Fear soured my desire and the knot in my gut tightened. I was going to hurt Gideon again. I was going to hurt all of them. I couldn't control myself.

"I can't do it. Put the cuffs back on." I jerked forward to put some distance between us, but he shifted forward with me, pinning my legs with his against the bench.

"Focus right here," he whispered.

"I can't. I'm going to hurt you."

"Right here." He ran a sensual firm stroke across the base of my wings again, making my breath catch and my attention jerk from my roaring power to my back. As if thinking about it refocused it, my power surged to where he touched me. "Fill the area with power and squeeze your shoulder blades together."

My stomach churned. *Pull in your wings. Come on. Please. I can do it. Just pull them in.* That was all I had to do. Just pull them in. *Please. Don't let me hurt them.*

"Squeeze your shoulder blades, Essie."

My power burned hotter, crackling along the top of my wings and sparking from the tips, and my muscles clenched and snapped. I couldn't make them work, couldn't draw my shoulder blades together.

Just pull them in.

The frost on my skin thickened into ice, but I couldn't feel the cold any more. There was only fire, burning me up, threatening to explode and burn my guys up, too.

Come on. Come on. I could do this. I *had* to do this.

I clenched my jaw and with a strangled scream wrenched my shoulder blades together. Gideon snapped electric power from his thumbs into my back, and my body flexed. Light blazed behind me, and my wings contracted and slammed inside my chest.

Oh, thank God.

But my power, without me trying to focus it, rushed to my palms and filled them with blazing, burning divine light.

Shit shit shit.

"The cuffs," Jacob said.

Marcus grabbed my hand and snapped a cuff around my wrist. All my power leaped to my free palm and blackened the cell wall.

God, no. I fought to hold it back, the pressure threatening to rip me apart and turn everything to ash. I was going to turn all of them to ash.

Marcus snapped on the other cuff and my power vanished, whooshing out of me, taking all my strength and leaving me shivering and hollow. My knees gave out and Gideon caught me before I fell, lifting me with ease, and cradled me against his chest.

I pressed my face against his neck, my pulse racing and tears burning my eyes. I couldn't do this. I'd almost lost control again, almost killed my guys.

"Put me down. I have to stay here," I said. The last time I'd kissed Gideon, my magic had blazed out of control. Just having him stroke me made it worse. It wasn't safe for me to leave this cell. "I'm too dangerous. I'm going to hurt someone."

"You're not," Marcus growled. "We're leaving and—"

Cassius stormed into the doorway. "What the hell is going on?"

Gideon's arms around me tightened, and he turned to face Cassius, whose fire crackled over his hands, his anger just as strong as it had been before. Behind him, looking around his shoulder, was Amiah, her eyes narrow and gaze hard.

Marcus raised his chin in defiance and his fingers extended into claws. "We're taking our mate out of here."

"You're not taking her anywhere," Cassius said.

Jacob shifted to stand beside Marcus. "It's three against one."

Cassius's gaze jumped to Gideon. "Is it?"

"You lied to me," Gideon said.

"I said I'd take care of it and I did."

The light in Gideon's eyes flared. "You arrested her."

"Of course I did," Cassius snapped. "She's a war criminal. A monster."

"No, she's not," Gideon snarled, and Marcus growled a warning.

The muscles in Cassius's jaw flexed. "That's the brand talking."

"It's a true brand. Fate would *never* bind me with a monster." Gideon clutched me tighter. "Besides, she's not a nephilim."

Cassius turned his glare to Sebastian.

"Look at her eyes," Sebastian said with a shudder, his body still tight with pain.

With a huff, Cassius strode into the cell toward me. Gideon held his ground as his brother approached, but his body tensed and his electric power crackling up my arm swelled.

I met Cassius's gaze, praying he'd see what Sebastian had seen, and there wouldn't be a fight. If I wanted to look stronger, more in control, I should have asked to be put on my feet, but I needed Gideon's embrace right now more than I needed to convince Cassius of my power.

"Gold flecks." He didn't sound happy about that.

"So she *is* an angel, even if her essence doesn't say so," Amiah said, also not sounding happy.

"Glad you're so excited she isn't a nephilim," Marcus said, his tone thick with sarcasm. He turned to Gideon and Jacob, who gave him a tight nod, before returning his glare to Cassius. "We're leaving."

Cassius, his expression still hard, reached into his pocket and pulled out the handcuff key. "I'll remove the cuffs."

"No!" the guys said in unison.

Cassius's eyes widened with surprise.

"Not until I can figure out how to contain her power," Sebastian said. "She—"

A blast of all-too-familiar magic slammed into me, stealing my breath and blazing under my skin, as if the containment cuffs hadn't cut off my buzz. I was on fire again, my whole being caught in a whirling inferno of power, just like when I'd been on City Hall's rooftop and the guys had been fighting the three glyph witches. Except this was ten times more powerful.

Sebastian released a strangled cry and dropped to his knees. "What the fuck is that?"

"The glyph witches," I gasped.

Sebastian shuddered and hugged himself. "A glyph witch isn't that powerful."

"There are three of them," I said.

He groaned. "That's more power than even three glyph witches can summon."

"It's not the glyph witches. They're locked up under power containment wards," Cassius said. He looked fine, as if he could handle all that power pounding into him—

No. As if he couldn't feel it. I dragged my attention to Marcus and

Jacob. They didn't look as if they felt it either, and Gideon's posture hadn't changed, so...

"Sebastian and I are the only ones who can feel it?"

"If she can feel glyph magic with the cuffs on, she must be an archangel," Amiah said.

"They're either not glyph witches," Sebastian said, "or they're getting outside help."

The pressure from the power swelled, and I bit back a whimper.

"We have to get to their cells." Cassius jerked to the door, his fire crackling over his hands and up his forearms.

"No. Get back here!" Sebastian pressed his hands to his chest and light burst from a swirling glyph hidden in his tattoos, making his shirt see-through again. The glyph curled from his right hip across his chest to his left shoulder and, when he leaned forward and pressed his hands to the floor, I could see the tattoo finished in the center of his back. "As close to me as possible. Now."

Gideon knelt beside Sebastian, still holding me, and Marcus and Jacob pressed close. Amiah gave Cassius a questioning look.

The witches' magic swelled again. I panted, trying to catch my breath around the agony, and Sebastian doubled forward in pain.

"Move. Now!" Gideon said.

Cassius grabbed Amiah's hand and jerked close to Jacob. Marcus caught Amiah as she stumbled into the group. She locked gazes with him, and the shadow of something dark and sad passed across her expression, before the witches' power exploded and I was blinded by agony.

ESSIE

THE FORCE OF THE WITCHES' SPELL RIPPED THROUGH MY ESSENCE, STEALING sight, breath, and thought. One of the guys screamed. Someone else yelled something, but power rushed in my head, stealing the words.

"—the hell was that?" Marcus asked. "Bane? Bane!"

I blinked black specs from my vision. Gideon still held me, his forehead pressed to mine, his body curled forward, protecting me. Sebastian had collapsed on the floor, his cheek against the concrete, his eyes half closed, his breath shallow. Amiah dropped beside him and grabbed his shoulder. Light flashed from her hand as she used her healing magic, and he jerked up with a strangled gasp, his pale eyes jumping to her in shock.

"What was that?" Cassius asked, his expression dazed.

"One fucking powerful spell." Bane stood, but his legs shook and Marcus grabbed him before he collapsed.

"I have to check on the witches." Cassius raced into the hall, his fire curling over both his arms, dripping from his hands, and sparking on the floor.

Gideon rose. "Jacob, you're the weakest right now. Take Essie."

"I can stand," I said. The roar of the witches' power was gone and so was my buzz again.

"Gideon," Cassius yelled in the hall. "I need you."

Gideon set me on my feet and rushed to help Cassius. Marcus and

Jacob followed him. Amiah helped Sebastian stand, and I shuffled to the doorway, dizzier than I'd expected.

Power flickered at the edge of my senses, and Cassius tumbled past the door. Then a thick vine seized his leg and yanked him out of sight.

"Amiah, call for back up." I peeked out the door. With the cuffs on, I was powerless, even if it seemed I could still feel when the witches were activating the glyphs on their bodies. Only Marcus and Cassius had a key, and I wasn't sure I wanted to release my power. I was just as likely to blast one of my guys as one of the witches.

All three glyph witches were out of their cells, and had made it to the main hall leading to the double set of security doors separating the secure section of Operations from the rest of the building. Vines from one of the dark-haired swarthy-skin witches squeezed Jacob, pinning his hands to his sides and drawing a scream. Gideon sliced through the vines with his divine light sword, while Marcus lunged at the witch with bright red hair, his fingers extended into claws.

The vine, still wrapped around Cassius's leg, slammed him against the ceiling. He sliced the vine with a whip of fire and crashed to the floor. The third witch, with similar dark hair and skin to the vine witch and a dark tattoo covering her entire right arm, raced into the hall toward the doors.

"Stop her," Gideon yelled. "Don't let her get out."

Marcus shoved past the red-haired witch, but she pressed a hand to her forearm, activating a glyph hidden in the colorful tattoo on her arm, and yelled a guttural word. More power shuddered against my senses, stronger this time, and a flicker of buzz sliced through the magic of the containment cuffs as Marcus slammed into an invisible wall.

"I don't think so." She pressed a different tattoo and lunged in, a blade of ice forming in her hand.

Marcus jerked to the side. The blade skimmed his ribs, slicing shirt and skin. A vine shot from the floor, seized his leg, and tossed him into Gideon. They slammed into the wall and sagged to the floor. Cassius leaped past them and snapped a whip of fire at the vine witch, who blocked it with another vine.

Jacob dove for the vine witch as well, slicing through a vine that wrapped around his wrist with his short, sharp claws. But another, bigger vine seized him around the chest and squeezed, drawing another scream.

Bane staggered to the doorway beside me. "They're so powerful. How the hell did you apprehend them the first time?"

"I have no idea. Kol was with them and Jacob wasn't as hurt, but—" Even if Kol was fighting now and Jacob was stronger, the witches would still be kicking our asses.

Cassius roared and snapped a whip of fire around the vine witch's neck. She screamed and he yanked her to her knees. Marcus sliced through the vine holding Jacob, who gasped for air and staggered to the wall to keep standing, while Gideon swung at the red-haired witch, who shot shards of ice at him. He deflected the blasts with his sword and swiped at her. She wrenched back, his blade nicking her side, but the vine witch heaved a vine in Gideon's way and tripped him.

"Stop the witch from getting out," Gideon yelled. "Marcus. Cassius."

But neither could get past the vine witch. Even with the four of them, they weren't strong enough to subdue the witches.

A vine speared through Cassius's shoulder. His fire flickered, going out for a second, then flared back to life. The red-haired witch blasted a pillar of ice at Gideon, too big for him to dodge. I screamed as it slammed him into the wall. I had to do something to help them. I couldn't just stand by and watch.

"The witches should be out of magic by now," Sebastian gasped.

I glanced back at him and Amiah. "Where's the back up?"

"No one is answering their phone," Amiah said.

The red-haired witch leaped around the corner, and the vine witch sent a flurry of vines to cover their retreat. One vine seized Jacob's leg and slammed him against the wall, another speared Cassius through the gut. Marcus twisted out of the way and slashed the vines coming after him, while Gideon shoved aside the ice pillar.

The guys staggered around the corner after the witches. Someone screamed and my pulse froze. The witches were going to kill them. Even if I couldn't control my power, I had to use it. It was the only thing that might tip the balance of the fight in our favor. "Sebastian, can you uncuff me?"

"That's not wise," he said. "You can't control your magic."

"So you *can* uncuff me."

Another scream. Jacob flew back into the hall I was in and crashed against the wall, leaving a blood smear. His head lolled forward and he didn't move.

"Sebastian, please." I couldn't just stand there and watch. I had to do something.

"It's too dangerous."

Even with the handcuffs, my buzz was growing under my skin, making it hard to tell if Gideon or Jacob had started pulling strength from me through our brands. "My power is going to break free whether you unlock the cuffs or not."

"Fuck," Marcus yelled, his voice strangled and filled with pain.

Divine light swelled in my palms and Amiah's eyes widened.

"Sebastian!" I couldn't let them die. I had to save them.

He activated a glyph on his wrist and grabbed the cuffs. They popped open and my buzz screamed through me. I gasped, the agony dropping me to my knees.

"It's too much, Essie. Put the cuffs back on," Amiah said.

"No." I had to help them.

Jacob had regained consciousness and was trying to stand. Marcus swore again, and my divine light swelled, turning both my hands into blazing white nimbi. I fought to hold it back, to make sure I didn't hurt my guys in the blast. The agonizing pressure swelled within me, and I rushed to the T-intersection and turned my attention to the fight in the hall. But my thoughts tripped at what I saw.

Chris and Nathaniel stood by the first of the security doors, frozen in mid step, unaware of the chaos approaching them.

"So that's what they were casting," Sebastian said at my shoulder. "A time spell."

Between me at one end, and Chris and Nathaniel at the other, were my guys and the three witches. Blood wept from dozens of cuts on Gideon's body and he held his arm tight to his ribs as if they hurt. His breath was shallow and fast, and his divine light sword flickered in and out of existence. Marcus had somehow managed to get close enough to the vine witch to slice four deep gashes in her cheek, but her vines now crushed him against the ceiling, while Cassius had a fire whip around the other witch's neck.

She howled in pain and pressed a tattoo near the inside of her elbow, making my buzz blaze in response to the rush of her magic. Hundreds of spiders surged from the floor and swarmed over Cassius. He screamed, dropped to his knees, and his fire vanished.

Gideon turned to help him, but the red-haired witch shot another pillar of ice at him. He jerked to the side but there wasn't enough room to get out of the way.

I wrenched my palms up, straining to focus my divine light. My power blasted from my hands into the pillar. It exploded in a shower of ice shards and water and all three witches jerked toward me.

"Kill them," the red-haired witch said, shooting a spear of ice at me.

Marcus leaped up, taking the spear in his shoulder before it could hit me. I jerked my hands away at the last minute before I hit him, sending my blast into the ceiling above the vine witch. She made a canopy of vines that protected her, and seized the larger chunks of concrete from the ceiling and tossed them at Marcus. He twisted to the side but wasn't fast enough to get out of the way of all of them.

Gideon grabbed Cassius's arm and yanked him back. Cassius staggered but couldn't get to his feet.

"Defensive position," Gideon gasped.

"No, to me." Sebastian dropped to his knees beside Jacob, pressed both hands to his thighs, and power erupted from the floor in a circle around him. "We're getting the hell out of here."

Gideon's eyes widened with surprise before his attention locked on me.

"Get in the circle, Essie," he said. "Close to Bane."

I didn't know what Sebastian was doing, but if Gideon said get close, I was getting close.

Marcus grabbed Cassius's other arm and helped Gideon heave him into the circle as magic sliced into my body.

I screamed, my power erupting from me, but Sebastian's magic devoured it as it also devoured me. The spell tore into my cells, ripping me apart until I was nothing but blinding pain, a bolt of white agony blazing through black emptiness.

Then the pain tightened, grew, reformed me with my buzz burning me from the inside out. My knees slammed onto the floor, my wings tore from my back, and my power threatened to explode again from my hands. I pulled my palms to my chest, unable to see anything with the bright specks of light snapping across my vision and terrified I'd hurt one of my guys.

"Everyone okay?" Gideon asked.

"Get the cuffs back on Esther," Sebastian gasped.

Someone pressed a hand to my spine between my shoulder blades. "Pull your wings in," Gideon said.

With a moan, I fought to concentrate on sending power to my back. I imagined yanking my wings back into my body, and Gideon's magic snapped, stronger than the last time, with a painful bite. My wings slammed into me as if I'd been punched in the chest, and the cold metal of the containment cuffs clicked around my wrists.

I raised my gaze, my vision clearing, and met Jacob's dark eyes. His fangs were fully extended and he radiated his full vampiric intensity. Blood soaked his T-shirt and jeans from dozens of gashes, and his complexion was even paler than before and tinged gray. Strength seeped from me through his brand on my biceps into him. It also seeped from Gideon's brand into him as well. Both of my guys were seriously hurt.

I shifted to look at Gideon behind me, who groaned and pulled his wings into his body. He too was covered in gashes, his breath shallow as if it hurt to breathe. Beside him, Amiah and Cassius also had to pull in their wings. Cassius's skin, beneath nasty red, swollen spider bites, was grayer than Jacob's. He collapsed face first to the marble floor, making my thoughts stutter. Marble. We weren't in Operations anymore.

Instead, we were in a large, opulent living room with a vaulted ceiling covered in a white and silver fresco. Sunlight, tinted slightly purple, blazed through gauzy curtains hanging across tall windows along the back wall, reminding me that it was still the middle of the morning. A large silver and crystal chandelier hung from the center of the ceiling, catching the sunlight and sending refracted light onto a conversation area consisting of two blue-gray couches and a pale-wood coffee table.

"Where are we?" Amiah asked.

"My place," Sebastian said, not moving from the floor, his eyes unfocused. His skin was even more translucent, his glow brighter, colder, and his ears were more pointed than I remembered.

"In Rouge?" Jacob asked.

A massive black wolf drew up beside him and snarled at Sebastian.

"Hey, I didn't have a whole lot of time to think when I cast the spell," he said.

The wolf huffed and turned a piercing green gaze to me.

My breath caught. "Marcus?"

Yeah.

I wrenched back. "Holy shit, you have telepathy!"

Sebastian groaned. "She's the most powerful super in the room and doesn't even know shifters have telepathy in their shifted form. Have you been living under a rock?"

His tone broke something in me and I wrenched to face him.

"I've been trying to," I snapped. I'd tried so fucking hard. "As far as I knew, I was a powerless nephilim. So yeah, I stayed as far away from the supernatural world as humanly possible. And now I'm a— a—"

My anger lurched to confusion and grief. I couldn't catch my breath. I wasn't a despised, unnatural nephilim. I was an angel. And I had no idea who I really was or who my parents were. The woman who'd raised me, loved me, and left me too early wasn't my mother.

My throat tightened, and I heaved my gaze back to Marcus's.

He limped to me and bumped his head into my chest. *It's okay. You're okay.*

I don't know if I am. I sank my fingers into his thick ruff and pressed my cheek against his. I needed to feel him, to feel all of my guys, to reassure myself they were all still alive.

"Why did you shift?" I asked, trying to think of anything but my situation.

"It's the teleportation spell," Gideon said, his attention locked on Sebastian. "It reassembled us in our supernatural forms. Something a glyph witch shouldn't be able to cast."

"Yeah, well, you can tell by the ears and glow I'm not a faekin glyph witch." Sebastian groaned and pressed his forehead to the floor. "And if you tell anyone I'm full fae, I'll kill you."

"Depends on how much you plan to charge us for that rescue." Gideon coughed, the sound wet and rattling in his chest.

"I'll let you know how much when I can see straight."

I should have been surprised and awed that I was sitting next to a full fae, but I must have been numb from the cuffs and my new reality and, quite honestly, I was exhausted. All I wanted was to hold all my guys and cry with joy and grief. My whole life, I'd been terrified that my true nature would be discovered, only to learn I'd had no idea what my true nature really was, and that my guys loved me regardless. On top of that, we were all seriously hurt, the witches had cast some kind of freezing time spell, and the cop in me wouldn't just let that thought go.

"Those witches had wanted to be caught," I blurted out.

"Agreed," Jacob said. "We have to figure out their plan before people get hurt."

Amiah looked up from Cassius, who groaned, his eyes squeezed tight in agony, a thick sheen of sweat slicking his face and neck.

"You mean *more* people get hurt," she said.

"Okay." Gideon rubbed his face, coughed again, and drew in a ragged breath. "Healing first. Bane, have you got a guest room Essie and Jacob could use?"

"I live above a vampire nightclub. I've watched them feed." Sebastian grabbed the edge of his couch and climbed to his feet.

"I'm sure, but—" Gideon glanced at me. His summer-sky eyes filled with yearning and uncertainty captured my soul, and the pieces that were still fractured from fighting our bond ached for him, for his touch, his body, his love.

Then he blinked and his desire disappeared behind a mask of professionalism. He wasn't trying to avoid me, not like he had before, but healing our bond wasn't a priority. Healing Jacob was... and before I'd fallen into his gaze, he'd been asking me if I wanted Bane to know I was bite-locked.

My body and soul hurt too much to keep anything secret. Besides, Sebastian had already seen me naked. "I'm bite-locked, so even if I didn't want to give you a show, you're getting one."

"I would love a show," Sebastian said with his usual wicked grin, but it didn't reach his eyes. "Except I suspect your mates would then kill me. So... I'm going to my office to try to figure out how to deal with your magic without you destroying the building. Take any room except the one at the end of the hall, and call me when you want to talk about the witches." He staggered to a hall on the other side of the room near a grand piano, and opened the first door on the left.

"I'll call Kol." Gideon stood, drew in a ragged breath, and coughed blood into his hand. "With luck, he was still melting down over Essie and hadn't returned to Operations when the witches cast their spell. I'll tell him to avoid Operations and bring us clean clothes."

Amiah pointed to the couch. "No, you're sitting here until I heal you. Then you're calling Kol, then having a shower, *then* you're planning your next move." She snapped her attention to me and held out her hand. "And you. Hands."

I shifted closer to her and raised my hands. They were bloody and oozing from blasting my divine light at the witches. She grabbed my wrist, thankfully not touching my burned hands, and sent an agonizing blast of magic into me. I gasped and while I couldn't tell for sure beneath the blood if my hands were healed, they no longer hurt — and hell, I hadn't even realized how much they'd hurt.

"Come on," Jacob said to me as he climbed to his feet, his face contorted in pain.

Gideon caught my attention, the light in his eyes flaring for a second, making my pulse skip a beat. "Make it quick. We don't know what the witches are planning but they clearly wanted to disable Operations."

Are we even strong enough to stop them? Marcus asked.

Gideon coughed more blood. "I have no idea."

And that was what terrified me. The witches were more powerful than anything we'd faced before and my guys were duty bound to confront them.

ESSIE

Jacob shuffled into the hall and headed toward the end. I hurried to his side, helping him catch his balance against the wall as he staggered. His skin was freezing, proving just how serious his injuries were, and my pulse tripped with fear.

"Thanks." He drew in a breath almost as ragged and wet as Gideon's had been and left a thick blood smear on Sebastian's white wall.

I opened the closest door, even though it was clear he was trying to pick a room away from Sebastian in his office. *Please let this be a bathroom so we can clean up.*

Inside lay a bedroom with en suite bathroom, just as opulent as the living room. It was decorated in the same white, silver, and blues as the living room, and I was starting to feel like Sebastian lived in one big, icy crystal.

I helped Jacob inside, ignoring the king-sized bed with its pristine white duvet and pillows, and turned straight into the white marble bathroom with its large vanity, fluffy white towels, and shower that would have been big enough for a normal person but a tight fit for the two of us.

Trembling, he sagged onto the closed toilet lid. I pulled off my runners and knelt before him to help him unlace his boots.

"I was hoping things wouldn't be so dire the next time we had sex."

His dark gaze met mine, filled with sorrow and love, making me ache with a confusing mix of emotions.

My throat tightened and tears burned my eyes. I didn't want to have a breakdown. Really, I didn't. But in the blink of an eye, I'd thought I'd lost everything, and in another blink saw that love could conquer everything... and then had almost lost them again fighting the witches. I'd run out of strength and just couldn't hold it together.

"Hey." He cupped my cheeks with his large hands.

"If Sebastian hadn't been able to cast that spell—"

"We're okay."

"I'd hate to see your definition of not okay."

"Not okay is not being with you."

He dipped in and brushed his lips against mine. It was a tender whisper of a kiss that made a tear break free, not because I was sad but because there was just too much emotion and all of it was mine.

"Marcus was going to raid the armory then break you out," Jacob said, "and I was going to help him while Gideon distracted Cassius when the brand lit up."

"Even though I'm a nephilim."

"You could have been a hellfire prince and we would have come for you." He brushed the tear from my cheek. "I meant what I said. We know who you are. Fate would never bind us with someone evil."

"You didn't doubt the bond? Didn't think I'd falsely branded you like the archnephilim had branded me?"

"Never. None of us." Jacob chuckled then gasped in pain. "You should have seen Gideon lose it on Cassius."

"You need to feed." I grabbed the hem of his T-shirt and rose, peeling off the wet, sticky fabric. Deep gashes covered his massive chest, oozing blood over his bulky muscles and into the waistband of his pants.

"And you need to know how I feel about you." He tugged me into his lap, tangled a cold hand into my ponytail, and captured my lips with his.

Even without my empathy, I could feel his desire and love for me in his kiss. It was tender and certain. He had no doubt about having his soul forever bound to mine.

Need swelled within me, and his kiss deepened as if he knew exactly what I craved. His tongue slid into my mouth, languid strokes that fueled my desire, making my breath pick up.

"I wish I didn't have to feed," he whispered against my lips, "that I could use my magic to bring you pleasure because I want to, not because I need to."

I kissed my way along his jaw, sliding my neck closer to his lips. "I love you, too."

It was crazy that I'd fallen in love with him so quickly, but the thought of losing him, of losing any of my guys, filled me with absolute panic. And I knew as soon as I said the words that they were true. I was in love with him and Marcus and Gideon.

And, God help me, I thought I was in love with Kol. It broke my heart to have seen and felt his horror when he'd realized— or rather, *thought* I was a nephilim. I could only hope my full angel status would be enough to save our friendship.

Jacob slid his hand up my back and tightened his grip in my hair. His fangs slid into my neck with a sharp bite of pain and then bone-melting desire rushed through me. I moaned and leaned into him. Just like Marcus's ferocious passion, I didn't think I'd ever get tired of Jacob's tender touch combined with the rush of his magic.

He took a long pull on my neck, and his magic surged. Another pull, and his erection swelled hard under my thigh, revealing he was just as turned on as I was. His fangs still in my neck, he lifted me, carried me into the shower, and set me on my feet.

I eased back, drawing his fangs from my skin, as he turned on the shower and protected me from the cold spray with his body. Not that I would have felt the cold with the heat of my desire flooding me. Blood caked his chest and crusted the line of fine hair disappearing into his pants, but the gashes were already starting to seal shut.

His dark, intense gaze locked on mine and a warm smile curled his lips. My breath caught. God, he was stunning. Powerful and strong, every inch of him sculpted, hard muscle.

"You're so beautiful," he said, his voice that low rumble that made my cells thrum, aligning my essence with his.

He pressed close, capturing me between the shower wall and his massive body, and kissed me again. His lips tasted coppery with my blood, and his magic rushed in my core. He hooked his nails into the neck of my T-shirt, one on either side, and ripped the fabric along my shoulders, so he could draw my shirt down my body without it getting caught on the containment cuffs.

With a groan, he sank his fangs into my neck again and skimmed a hand over my too-sensitive skin into my bra. He tweaked my nipple in a tight bud, sending bites of pleasure racing through me, then moved to the other breast. His magic throbbed, growing stronger. My pulse roared and I ached for satisfaction.

I undid his pants and slid my hands inside, wrapping my fingers around his thick, hard erection and drawing a groan. The sound vibrated against my skin and more of his magic flooded me, melting me with pleasure, forcing me to use the wall to keep standing.

Hot water sprayed around us, a glimpse of the sultry heat I knew I'd feel if the cuffs were off, and my desire twisted tighter, teasing me with the promise of a release that I couldn't have until Jacob brought me to climax.

He sliced the straps of my bra and unhooked it, letting it fall to our feet. His fangs left my neck, and he slid down my body, sucking on my nipples as he undid my jeans. Then he slid them and my underwear down my legs, and knelt before me.

My breath hitched, my soul captured by the intensity in his gaze. It held a hunger for me that was more than just a vampire's need to feed. It was deeper than that. Light flickered from the brand on his arm, catching in the water running over his body.

I ached for him, body and soul, not just because of his magic whirling in me. I needed him in me, filling me. I needed him feeding, taking his fill, and healing. I couldn't feel my strength seeping into him through our bond anymore, but his complexion was still gray. He hadn't taken enough.

"You have to take more." My breath came faster with the anticipation of his magic building until I burst, and his erection driving into me.

"I don't want to take too much." He brushed his fingers over the angry red line in my side where Kol had cut me and Amiah had done the bare basics to heal it shut.

"I trust you. You won't." I hooked my fingers under his chin, urging him to rise.

But instead he nudged my legs open and sank his fangs into my thigh. I gasped, his magic jolting through me. With a groan, he slid a finger into my wet core and my muscles clenched around him, already on the edge of climax.

He took a long, hard pull, and slowly slid in a second finger. I dug my nails into his scalp, my head spinning as he drew out and slowly pushed back in. Sensation roared in every cell, building and twisting tight. He teased my clit with his thumb, making me jerk, my climax trembling on the edge. Then he stilled and let me tremble without crashing over. My breath stalled in my chest and I squirmed my hips, flexing, trying to drive his fingers deeper into me, rub my clit, anything to satisfy the pressure building inside.

He kept me teetering on the edge, drawing long sips of blood, until I was panting and moaning. Then a whisper of healing magic sealed the bite on my thigh shut, and he rose and pulled off his pants. His erection slid between my open thighs and brushed my folds.

God, yes.

With a low guttural moan, he grabbed my hips, lifted me, and slid inside, slowly burying himself to the hilt. He filled me, so big he stretched me with a whisper of delicious pain. Then he slowly drew out, building my pleasure beyond what I thought possible. I hooked my legs around his waist and my arms over his head and hung on, giving him control over my body. There wasn't anything I could do but ride this glorious wave.

The promise of my climax tightened until every cell within me strained for release. His pace grew faster, his breath as ragged as mine, until he was driving into me with delicious force. With a roar, his body tensed, his climax seizing him, and he sank his teeth into my neck.

My climax ripped through me and his magic exploded with blazing ecstasy through every cell. I screamed his name and our brands lit with golden light. For a second, no more than a rapid beat of my heart, I feared the screaming frozen pain from that last time we'd had sex would devour me, but another wave of pleasure swept through me instead, leaving me trembling and dizzy.

Jacob sagged to his knees. His healing magic warmed my neck as he pulled out his fangs and wrapped his arms around me in a tight embrace. His love filled me, an honest to goodness emotion that somehow seeped past the power of the containment cuffs. Maybe it was because of the brand. The cuffs didn't seem to affect that. But a part of me knew it was because our connection was that powerful. My empathy would be able to seek him out no matter what magic tried to contain it.

KOL

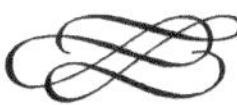

with Essie yesterday.

God, had it only been yesterday?

It felt like a lifetime ago. A lifetime where I'd been starting to regain control of my nightmares after the archnephilim — or as much control as I'd ever had — and was pretending to be a normal person.

And then everything had changed. I was back in that nightmare, trapped, scared, tortured, desperate, and angry, so God damned angry.

I'd been falling and then there'd been a flash of angelic light and wings. Essie, with her human essence, had released her angel wings, and suddenly I was back in the darkness, crushed and drowning, desperate to escape, hurting innocent women to stop my own suffering.

I hadn't even been sure what had happened until Gideon had dragged me out of the alley. I'd only known that I hadn't been a cowering child like I'd been back then, that I'd drawn my weapons and I'd attacked. I'd been determined to fight, to protect, to not give in like I had before.

Cassius had ordered me back to City Hall's roof, but Gideon had shoved me into a taxi instead and sent me back to Operations. Except the thought of going back there, of being surrounded by all that celestial light energy only deepened my panic and I'd redirected the taxi to the place where I'd felt the safest. It was light energy that was at the root of my nightmares, and I just couldn't go back. Not to Operations. Not to Michael's lab. I couldn't.

I won't. Don't make me.

I'd die before I ever went back. I'd fight with everything I had and now I could. I was no longer a scared, weak teen. I had training and strength and power, and I'd used all that to attack the nephilim, to kill it... except that nephilim was Essie.

God, how could I have done something so horrible? She'd saved me from a sixteen-story fall and I thanked her by attacking her. It didn't matter that I'd been trapped in a nightmare. I'd tried to kill her and that was unforgiveable. A small part of me had *known* it was Essie when I'd attacked despite knowing she'd never hurt me. For all I knew it was the mating brand and the divine light she'd blasted into herself that had changed her and given her wings and she wasn't really a nephilim.

Even if she was a nephilim, I knew her heart. She was good and kind. Gideon, Marcus, and Jacob would never be soul bonded to a monster.

My cheeks burned with shame. Essie wasn't the monster. I was.

One glimpse of wings with a human essence and I was a maniac willing to kill anyone and everyone to protect myself.

I needed to leave, ask for a transfer, quit the JP, whatever it took to get as far away from her as possible. If she had wings then she'd want to learn to fly and I couldn't risk falling back into the nightmare again and losing all reason. She wasn't safe around me.

The thought squeezed around my chest, stealing my breath. I could have killed her. If Gideon hadn't stopped me I would have. She was the one person I'd felt safe with, who I wanted to be with, who I lo— *cared* for.

I shouldn't have any more moments with her, not even ones where everyone was around. I could fall back into the nightmare at any moment. I'd been on the verge of being triggered since the archnephilim had started murdering my rescuers weeks ago and I'd finally completely broken.

The guys wouldn't understand and neither would Essie. They'd think I was okay, that I looked fine, so I was fine. But I wasn't. Not even close.

My phone rang.

I knew it was someone from the team since they were the only friends I had in the human realm, so I left the phone in my pocket. I wasn't ready to face any of them. They were all mated to Essie and while I deserved Marcus and Gideon yelling at me, Jacob would probably offer me help while I deserved to be yelled at. I didn't have the emotional strength to just take their anger and I certainly didn't deserve anyone's kindness.

I let it go to voicemail but it started ringing again.

Fuck. They weren't going to give up until I answered.

Fine.

I pulled out my phone. Gideon. Good, I could ask him to transfer or fire me. Get it over and done with and then I'd never have to face Essie again.

My heart pounded at the thought.

God, why did that hurt so much? I could have killed her. I didn't deserve to be friends with her.

The phone started the last ring before it would go to voicemail and I swiped my thumb across the screen.

"Senior Agent in Charge," I forced out, using his title instead of his name.

"Good. You're not in Operations," Gideon said, his words coming out in a rush, his relief confusing the hell out of me. I was sure he'd be pissed that I wasn't where he'd sent me on top of, you know, trying to kill his mate. "I need you to pick up clothes for the team and meet us at Bane's."

"Meet you at Bane's?" He wasn't making any sense.

"He has an apartment above Rouge. Don't go to Operations. It's caught in a temporal freeze and we're the only ones who made it out."

"A temporal freeze? Is Essie—?" *Caught in it? Is she safe? Did someone hurt her? Did I?*

God, I didn't deserve to be worrying about her, but I couldn't stop the rush of wild, painful thoughts.

"She's with us. Kol, " Gideon said, his tone growing... softer? He hadn't used that tone since he and Jacob had dragged me out of Michael's lab. "She's an angel who's been enspelled to look like a human. She's not going to hurt you."

But I could hurt her.

I already had. I might not have cut her this time, but I could, and I'd shown her and everyone exactly what I was. A monster. The monster I'd let Michael and his nephilim turn me into. I made women compliant, made them want to be assaulted by his angels again and again. But I couldn't keep my magic going forever and when I faltered, they knew the truth, knew what had been done to them. I'd never stop hearing their pleas and cries or the dead look in the eyes of those who'd been there the longest. And I'd been a part of that. I was responsible.

"I need you, Kol." Gideon's voice cut through the swelling darkness, pushing it back... a bit. "These witches are more powerful than we thought and we're the only JP agents left in town. We have to stop whatever they're planning."

And that *we* included Essie. Because human, nephilim, or angel, she'd want to fight for what was right. I couldn't let her and the guys face that alone. I owed them and her that much.

"I'm in the wolves' park—" I was about six blocks from Rouge and there was a store on the way where I could pick up clothes in sizes as small as Essie and as big as Jacob. They wouldn't be fashionable clothes, but if they needed me to pick something up then they had nothing. "Give me—"

A blast of sexual energy slammed into me. It tore through mental shields that I'd thought were finally solid after the last time Essie and Marcus had had sex and flooded into me. So bright. So powerful.

So Essie.

It stole my breath. Her desire was so deep, so radiant. It made me feel like I was weightless and sparkling, as if I was a being of celestial light and not a monster from the darkness.

Powerful stillness followed Essie shimmer. Jacob. And it wasn't just the release of his bite-lock, it was his orgasm as well. He and Essie were having sex. The thought made my insides twist. I wanted to be the one she was having sex with. I didn't want to feed on the aftermath of her release, catching it as it swept past me. I wanted to be in the center of that supernova, feel it focused entirely on me because I'd made her come, *I* was the one she desired.

Except that desire wouldn't be as deep as it was with her mates. She loved them and even if she thought she loved me, it wouldn't be real. Even if there was a hope in hell that it could be real, I couldn't let that happen. I'd never be able to love her back like the others could and I could snap at any moment and hurt her.

The best thing I could do for her was to keep my distance and remain professional at least until this current crisis was done. After that I'd go. It would be better for everyone.

ESSIE

AFTER COMING SO HARD WE COULDN'T STAND, WE SAT IN THE SHOWER'S spray, holding each other and trying to catch our breaths. I knew we needed to finish up and get back to the rest of the team, but I didn't want this moment to end. I wanted to stay in Jacob's arms forever.

Someone knocked on the wall, and I dragged my attention to the still open bathroom door.

"You guys alive in there?" Marcus asked. He stood in the doorway looking as ruggedly handsome as ever, without a hint of jealousy or anger in his expression.

He was dressed, which meant Kol had arrived with a change of clothes, since the magic that let him shift had destroyed his clothing when Sebastian had teleported us. A part of me ached to reach out and invite him into the shower to join us. But we didn't have time. Not to mention I didn't know what either guy would think about that, and the shower was too damned small.

"Yeah," Jacob said. He pressed a kiss to my forehead. "Can you stand?"

I had no idea.

Marcus set a stuffed plastic bag on the floor and grabbed a towel as I stood on shaky legs. The bathroom darkened and spun a bit, reminding me that Jacob had taken a lot of blood, and I shouldn't make any fast movements.

"Kol's here," Marcus said, "and Amiah's gotten Gideon back on his feet."

"Which means he wants to get back to work," Jacob said, using the shower wall to steady himself.

Marcus wrapped the towel around me and pulled me into a firm embrace. "You're too pale. You told him to take too much."

"He didn't take more than I could handle, and right now the only thing I'm good for is keeping you guys alive."

"That's not true."

I eased out of his embrace and raised my handcuffed hands. "I'm not taking these off until we can figure out a way to control my power, which means I can't go into the field with you."

"You'll always be more than just keeping us alive, even if you couldn't ever go into the field again." He turned his attention to Jacob, who was scrubbing off the blood from his now-healed injuries. "And you, you should know by now that she has no sense of self-preservation."

I grabbed Marcus's jaw and urged him to look at me. "I'm fine. Now help me at least put my pants on, since I'm not going to be able to pull on a shirt."

"I'm hoping you can hold your power in for a few seconds." He pulled a handcuff key from his pocket. "I'd rather you not be hanging out at Bane's in a towel."

"It's not like he hasn't seen me naked," I said.

Marcus groaned. "I'm not sure I want to know."

I pulled a pair of cargo pants out of the bag that were way too big for me, and set them on the vanity for Jacob. "Didn't Jacob tell you he helped us flee Rouge when our brand formed?"

"I left out the bit about you being naked." Jacob shut off the water and grabbed a towel. "Although if Marcus had been thinking about it, he'd have figured it out. He knew I'd brought you home wearing nothing but a sheet."

"I was a little distracted at the time by my mate being in dire need of an incubus's body heat."

"Speaking of our resident incubus..." I fished a lacy white thong and matching bra out of the bag. Not in the least practical for field work, but at least he'd thought to bring me underwear. I didn't know if that meant he wasn't freaking out over me being a nephilim or if Gideon had ordered him to buy them.

"He just arrived and he's feeling no pain right now." Marcus chuckled. "Even being a few blocks away wasn't enough to protect him from the release of your bite-lock."

"I hadn't realized it was that powerful." I stepped into the thong and a pair of cargo pants that were my size.

"Not sure he realized that, either," Marcus said.

Jacob toweled off and grabbed his pants. "We're going to need to figure something out for him if we want him to be able to do his job."

"Does he know I'm not a nephilim?" I didn't want him looking at me like he had in the alley ever again. All that pain and horror. I didn't want to think about what he'd gone through to have a reaction like that.

"Gideon told him." The muscles in Marcus's jaw flexed. "Not sure if he believed him."

Great. I didn't want to hide in the bedroom and wait for the team to leave. I wanted to be part of figuring out what we were going to do about the witches, even if I couldn't help in the field.

"He's here. Means he's had a chance to cool down since you saved him from a sixteen-story fall," Jacob said.

"I just don't want to trigger him again." Except right now, if I didn't want to hide in the bedroom, there wasn't anything I could do about it.

But maybe I should hide. I was exhausted, and if I was being honest with myself, still reeling over everything that had happened.

I bit back a sigh and held out my hands. In the very least, I could put a shirt on. And I was God damn going to hold my power back long enough for that. "Let's do this."

Marcus unlocked one of the cuffs. My buzz exploded into agonizing pain and my knees gave out. Marcus's eyes flashed wide, and Jacob grabbed me and steadied me on my feet.

"Just put me down," I gasped. "It'll be easier to get dressed without you holding me." Divine light blazed from the palm of my free hand and I clenched it in a fist, fighting to hold it in. The pressure inside me swelled, and my whole body blazed with fiery stinging bites.

Marcus put my arms through the bra straps — not bothering to hook it behind my back — then grabbed the T-shirt.

I strained against the agony, desperate to hold my power in. I could do this. I could hold it in. I wouldn't burn him like I'd burned Gideon. I wouldn't do that to anyone again.

The pressure grew stronger and darkness clouded my vision, then Marcus snapped the cuffs back on and my buzz vanished. I sagged into Marcus's arms, panting, my throat tight with tears.

"Come on, what's the hold-up?" Gideon asked, striding into the bedroom. "Kol and Bane are wait—" His gaze locked on mine and his angel glow flared as he dropped to the floor close behind Marcus. "What's wrong? What happened?"

"We needed to uncuff one hand to get her shirt on," Jacob said, his tone grim.

"I'm okay." I tried to push out of Marcus's embrace, but he held tight. "Marcus, I'm okay."

He growled and his grip relaxed, but I could still feel the tension in his body.

"Tell me Bane has figured out how to help Essie," Marcus said, his pupils slitted and his canines partially extended, his wolf threatening to take over.

I cupped his cheeks and forced him to meet my gaze. "I'm okay. He'll figure it out." My clothes were still just on my arms, so I settled the bra over my breasts. Jacob hooked it behind me before I could even ask for help — since I couldn't reach behind my back with the cuffs on — and I pulled my T-shirt over my head. I was still exhausted from feeding Jacob and terrified of hurting my guys, but this was the best I was going to get for the moment. "Tell me Kol isn't going to freak out if I step out of this bedroom."

"You're part of the team. You're not hiding in the bedroom." Gideon held out his hand to help me up, and I met his gaze. The warmth and worry in his eyes stole my breath. It was so different from how he'd been looking at me before that it almost didn't seem real. He didn't hate me. I wasn't the worst possible thing that could have happened to him. And while I knew he still loved and mourned Zella, I also knew he wanted our bond as much as I did.

We belonged together.

That was a destiny we couldn't deny, and we had to solidify our bond. The need crackled along the fractured edges of my soul, an aching desire I wasn't going to be able to resist.

The muscles in his jaw tightened. His worry slipped into a need as powerful as mine, and made my buzz whisper under my skin, reminding me that my desire for Gideon was dangerous.

With a quick breath, he shoved his desire back under a mask of professionalism, reminding me that no matter what I ached for — even if my power didn't release and burn him up — we were in the middle of a crisis.

Right. Jeez. We were adults. We could resist the pull of the bond long enough to figure out what we were going to do about the witches.

I took his hand, my fingers sliding over his palm, making his breath hitch and my pulse trip, and rose unsteadily to my feet. The room darkened and spun, and Marcus grabbed my hips to steady me.

I leaned into him, in part because I needed his support, but also because his wolf needed comfort. If the situation wasn't what it was, I'd tell Jacob to get out, and take Gideon then Marcus to bed. But pressing close to Marcus and holding Gideon's hand was the best I was going to be able to offer them.

We left the bedroom and headed down the too-short hall, my pulse picking up with each unsteady step. I needed Kol to not fear and hate me. My need was so deep it scared me. He wasn't one of my mates, I didn't have a connection to him like I did with the others, but I still desperately needed him.

He and Bane were both on the blue-gray couch facing me, but my attention instantly locked on Kol, looking sexily disheveled and exhausted and strained. It made my heart ache. I wanted to ease his pain, tell him everything would be all right, but I didn't know if it would be.

His gaze locked on mine and hellfire blazed in his eyes. His expression was strange, hard, but without my empathy I had no clue what he was feeling. Whatever it was, it wasn't good.

ESSIE

HE HELD MY GAZE AND A HINT OF HEATED DESIRE UNFURLED WITHIN ME. IT made my pulse trip with hope. Maybe he'd believed Gideon and knew I wasn't a nephilim, or maybe, after the initial shock of seeing what I was, he'd remembered *who* I was.

The desire swelled, the hellfire in his eyes burning brighter. My thoughts leaped to the dream I kept having of him caressing and kissing me, begging to satisfy me like my other guys could. To hell with it being his incubus nature influencing me. I wanted him sexually and emotionally as much as I wanted my other guys. Yes, we didn't have a magical bond, we weren't destined to be together, but I wanted him in my family. From the moment we'd met, he'd always been there for me, supported me, held me, made me laugh. We could make this work. We could—

He jerked his attention to the floor, his body tense and his heated desire vanishing, leaving me cold and aching. So much for being high and happy on my sexual release. My throat tightened, and I stumbled. Marcus growled and lifted me in his arms, carrying me the rest of the way to the seating area.

"This is a bad idea," I whispered against his neck. Especially if I was going to start crying every time Kol gave me a hard look. I hadn't even cried this much when Gideon had been trying to keep his distance and I'd had our bond slowly shattering inside me.

I needed time to still my whirling thoughts and regain my bearings, and the best way to do that would be sleep. Lots and lots of sleep. Something I hadn't really gotten in a long time.

"Deal with your shit later, Shaw," Marcus growled. "We need to figure out what the hell we're doing about these witches." He sat on the couch, but kept hold of me as if he couldn't bring himself to let me go, belying his harsh words.

Gideon sat beside us and placed a hand on my knee. It was a small gesture, but it spoke volumes to anyone who knew our situation. He was onboard with everything I was and everyone I was mated to. His electric power whispered over our brand, making my nerves thrum with need. I fought to concentrate past that, as well as the feel of Marcus's hard body against mine, determined to be a useful member of the team.

Sebastian shifted beside Kol, his icy eyes filled with worry, and jerked his thumb over his shoulder. "There's juice in the fridge."

Jacob strode past him to the far side of the living room area and disappeared through a wide archway into a room just as white as the living room.

"Have you found a way to deal with Essie's power?" Gideon asked.

Sebastian rolled his eyes. "It's been what? Less than twenty minutes? I haven't even pulled all the books I want to look at from my shelves."

"And that's not the issue," I said, as much as I really wanted my power under control and the cuffs off. "The witches let us arrest them and cast whatever they'd cast on Operations. They've got to be planning something. You said it was a time spell?"

"A temporal freeze," Sebastian said. "It temporarily stops time on every organic thing within the spells radius. Which I bet is all of Operations. And while I managed to protect us from the initial blast, if we'd stayed at Operations much longer, we would have been caught in the spell as well."

"We know what a temporal freeze is," Marcus said.

"If Esther didn't know you have telepathy in your wolf form, I'm pretty sure she doesn't know what a temporal freeze does."

"Glyph witches aren't powerful enough to cast a temporal freeze spell," Kol said, his words slightly slurred, the only hint so far that he'd been flooded with too much sexual energy. His gaze lifted for a second then jerked back to the floor. His breath picked up, and he leaned forward and tightly clasped his hands.

Sebastian rubbed his face. He looked as exhausted as I felt, and I couldn't help wondering how much magic he'd drained protecting us from the temporal freeze and then teleporting us to safety. "Obviously they're not glyph witches or they got help."

"Obviously," Jacob said, striding across the living room toward us with a huge glass of orange juice. At least he finally looked better. He'd been running on low for days now, barely recovering because I was barely recovering. I was sure he still needed more blood and sooner rather than later, but maybe I could convince Marcus to allow Jacob to feed on him and use his magic this time. Surely we could spare enough time to bring Jacob up to full, and I could spend some quality time with my angel and my wolf.

Jacob pressed the glass into my hands, sat on the arm of the couch beside Marcus, and rested a big hand on my shoulder. I wasn't sure if he'd done it on purpose to reinforce to Kol where they stood with me, and if he did, it didn't matter because Kol hadn't looked at me since I'd entered the room.

I shoved that thought away before my emotions overwhelmed me again and took a sip of juice. "On City Hall's roof, it felt like the witches' power kept growing, as if they were tapping into a source outside of themselves."

"That's what it felt like to me in Operations," Sebastian said. "They should have been out of magic after casting the temporal freeze, but they just kept casting stuff."

Marcus's grip on me tightened. "So even if we figure out what they're planning, they have an unlimited supply of magic?"

"Possibly. And you're going to want to hurry," Sebastian said. "The temporal freeze will only last for about twelve hours, no matter how much power is put into it."

Marcus groaned. "That's just fucking great. They're planning something that's going to happen in less than twelve hours and we have absolutely no clue what."

"We must know something," Gideon said, "or they wouldn't have needed to freeze Operations."

"Well, I have no fucking clue what that would be." Marcus's wolf darkened his eyes. "And we still have no way to stop them. I'm not letting you guys endanger Essie's life by running blindly into trouble. The dangers of mating brands go both ways, you know."

"We need an area containment master ward," Gideon said.

"We don't have an area containment master ward," Marcus growled.

"Only head office has an area containment master ward and I wouldn't want to bet on us being able to get it in time."

They glared at each other, then turned their attention to Sebastian.

He raised his hands in defense. "I don't have one, either."

"But can you find one on short notice?" Gideon asked.

"With enough money, I can find anything." He flashed a smile, but it was a ghost of what it usually was.

"What about dispelling the temporal freeze?" Jacob asked.

"It'd be easier to find an area containment master ward." Sebastian's gaze dipped to mine. "But that means Esther's problem will have to wait."

"That's fine. The cuffs are holding my magic back," I said. Keeping the city and my guys safe took priority over my comfort every time.

Kol raised his head and for a second I thought he'd look at me again, hoped, prayed, *please, look at me again*. But his hands clenched tighter and his gaze remained locked on the bowl of large clear marbles in the center of Sebastian's coffee table.

I fought back tears. Jeez. I really was exhausted if him not looking at me made me want to sob. But it was because I knew just looking at me caused him pain. As much as I couldn't get the memory of my sexy dream of him out of my head, I also couldn't get rid of the look on his face when he saw my wings.

Time. Just give him time. I could get back the easy friendship we'd had. I just had to be patient. Except a part of me feared I wouldn't get it back, that my wings had permanently changed everything between us. No more cuddling on the couch watching movies, no more jokes or teasing or playful wicked smiles.

"Okay." Gideon rubbed his palm against my knee, reminding me that we were working things out. And things would work out with Kol, too... even if we didn't share a soul bond. "In City Hall, the red-haired witch came from that back hall by the elevators. Let's go back there and see if we can figure out why they were there. With luck, it'll be connected to whatever they're planning in the next twelve hours."

"I'll start hunting down an area containment master ward." Sebastian stood with a groan and headed back to his office.

"How do we get out of here without Victoria or her offspring seeing us?" Jacob asked before Sebastian made if halfway across his massive living room. "I don't want to run into her, and I don't want her to know Essie is under her roof."

And if I hadn't been so exhausted, I would have thought about that already. I'd severed her link with Jacob when our brand formed two days ago, and while I didn't know how she felt about that, I'd place my bets on pissed.

"I have a private entrance." He jerked his thumb to a heavy door inset with a large frosted white and blue stained glass window. "Take the stairs to the left."

"I didn't know you had a private entrance," Gideon said.

"You're not paying me enough to know I have a private entrance."

"We pay you a lot," Marcus said.

"Yeah." Sebastian opened his office door. "So think about how much you'd have to pay to get prime customer service and go beyond the office I rent two floors down." He stepped inside his private office and closed the door.

The door on the other side of the hall opened and Amiah stepped out, quietly closing it behind her. "A word before you go, Gideon."

Gideon's strokes on my knee shifted higher, sliding up my thigh. My pulse picked up and a whisper of my buzz tickled my skin.

His gaze lifted to mine for a second, stealing my breath, then he realized what he was doing and jerked away to talk with Amiah.

A part of me ached at his absence, even though he was only a few feet away.

Jeez. Be an adult. But it wasn't that I couldn't be responsible. It was that my bonds with all my guys were too new, and the one with Gideon was still in danger of shattering. Except if my powers blazed out of control every time he touched me in a sensual way, we might never fix what we'd broken.

"Sebastian's going to hold this mess over us for a long time, isn't he?" Marcus said to Jacob. "I don't want to see what head office says when they see the final bill."

Jacob sighed. "One problem at a time."

"You're going out?" Amiah asked Gideon as he drew close, her voice low, only audible because Jacob's claim enhanced my hearing... or was it because I was really part archangel? I had no clue what powers an archangel possessed beyond those of a regular angel, only that they were powerful.

"How's Cassius?"

"Not good," she said, her gaze darting to the door she'd just closed. "I've managed to stabilize him, but the poison from those spiders is magical. I'm having trouble purging it from his system and it's still slowly killing him."

Kol stood, unsteady on his feet, and Jacob hopped off the couch arm and grabbed his elbow, steadying him before he banged his shins on the coffee table. "You're going to need to bleed off some of that excess magic."

"When I'm away from *her*," he mumbled, and headed to the door with the stained glass.

Marcus pressed his lips to my forehead. "Finish the juice." His warm breath caressed my skin, drawing a shiver of desire. "And get Amiah to heal you."

"She's probably running low as well. I'm fine." I lifted my lips to his and kissed him.

He groaned and slid his tongue into my mouth, adding fuel to my desire. His ferocious passion thrummed in his body, his muscles tense, his hold on me firm. I ached for all that power and desire to take me, fill me, send me spiraling with bliss.

"Come on, Marcus," Gideon said, his expression strained. "You can give her a few minutes to recover from Jacob."

"Yeah, I know," he mumbled against my lips. "But part of my wolf still feels like he has to protect her from Cassius."

Gideon's angel glow darkened, clouds passing over his summer-sky eyes. Cassius might have brought the full force of his rage against me when he thought I'd wrongfully and permanently bound his brother's soul to mine, but he was still Gideon's brother. I'd watched my mom die, so I could imagine how much Gideon hurt right now — and I didn't need my empathy to figure that out.

With another groan, Marcus slid me from his lap onto the couch cushion and followed the rest of the guys out of Sebastian's apartment.

I sagged back, tugged the elastic out of what was probably a disastrous ponytail so I could comfortably lean my head back, and took a long sip of juice. I wanted to comfort Marcus and Gideon, but given our deadline to who-knew-what disaster, there wasn't time for either. But Gideon and I had lasted apart for this long, so another day or so couldn't hurt, and Marcus already knew how I felt about him. He could wait, too — a shiver of desire swept over me — as much as I craved his ferocious passion.

My thoughts drifted to the last time we'd had sex. His wolf had been anxious, afraid I would choose Gideon over him, and I'd made a point of showing him how I felt. The attraction sizzling between us had been there from the moment we'd first met. It had survived my biggest screw-up, and I knew with certainty that we were mates. Just like I knew Gideon and Jacob were my mates, as well.

The electricity in Gideon's brand tickled over my forearm and sank into the intense stillness of Jacob's. A whisper of emotions that weren't mine ghosted through me, love, fear, determination, certainty. I couldn't tell which of my guys they came from, probably a bit from everyone, and I let myself sink into it, allowing sleep to drag at my senses. There wasn't anything else I could do right now, as much as that drove me crazy. Even if I could control my power, I was still exhausted. That made me a liability, and with our lives as entwined as they were, it was too dangerous to put me in the field. The best thing to do was get some sleep.

Something creaked, it sounded like a door opening, and soft footsteps drew close. They didn't sound heavy enough to be Sebastian's, so it was probably Amiah headed to the kitchen or something.

"You're pale," Amiah said, her tone brusque.

My eyes flew open and I jerked, nearly dropping my half-drunk glass of orange juice.

She stood near the couch, her arms crossed, her expression hard. "I've heard it can be difficult to say stop when they feed, for both of you, but that's why you need to set ground rules before you get started."

"He needed as much as I could give."

"I'm sure you'll say that every time," she said.

I met her glare. "For all of them. You'd do the same."

"Don't assume to know me. I'd never lie to my mate. Ever."

"You have a mate?" I hadn't seen her showing affection to anyone other than Marcus, but then I'd been trying to avoid all the angels at Operations in the short time I'd spent there.

"Of course not." Her angel glow flared, turning her summer-sky eyes, so similar to Gideon's, icy. "But if I did, they wouldn't have been blindsided by something as important as not being human."

"Oh, and you would have just come out and told them you were a nephilim?" Easy for her to say. She hadn't spent her entire life fearing that everyone wanted her dead.

"But you're not a nephilim. Even your essence has changed. It's muddled and still doesn't say you're an angel, but you're clearly not human."

"Except I didn't know I was a full angel." I set my glass on the coffee table, forcing myself not to slam it down. "I wasn't going to break Marcus's and Jacob's hearts by telling them I was a monster."

"You're still going to break Marcus's heart. You've branded Gideon and Jacob. If you were truly Marcus's mate, you'd have branded him, as well."

For the love of— Get over him already! I jerked to my feet. The room darkened and spun, but I gritted my teeth and kept standing. "What I have with Marcus is as strong as what I have with Gideon and Jacob. And who I love is none of your God damned business."

I grabbed the glass and wrenched around to head to the bedroom where Jacob and I had cleaned up to lie down, when blazing white lightning exploded from Gideon's brand. All my muscles seized, like I'd been hit with a Taser. My thoughts leaped to Gideon, my pulse racing. He was hurt. Oh, God, he was dying.

MY THOUGHTS WHIRLED, TRAPPED IN A BODY FROZEN IN AGONY. I HAD TO save Gideon. I couldn't lose him. *Please, God.* I could feel his life draining from him, the brand consuming my strength to keep him alive. *Save him. Save him.*

The lightning suddenly stopped and all my muscles went limp. The glass shattered on the floor, the juice an orange spray on the white marble, and I slammed down onto my knees, falling forward and narrowly catching myself on my hands before smacking my face.

"Sebastian!" I screamed.

I had to get to Gideon. Now. He wasn't going to last long. There wasn't anyway I could get to City Hall... if he was even at City Hall. I had no idea how long I'd been dozing. A few seconds? A few minutes?

"Sebastian!"

I scrambled to my feet. *Please. I can't lose him.*

Another blast of lightning ripped through me, blazing from Jacob's brand. I crashed back to the floor, every muscle seizing. *Not him, too.*

Amiah dropped to her knees beside me, all anger at what I was doing to Marcus gone, her eyes filled with terror, her expression hard, as if she were trying to lock away all that fear.

Every cell in my body screamed. *Do something. Save them.*

The second blast released me, and I tried to stand, but Amiah placed a hand on my shoulder. Her magic flared to life and I jerked away.

"Save it for them. Please." She was already low. I couldn't let her waste her magic on me. "Sebastian." I could barely get his name out. My ragged breath sawed in my lungs as if I'd run a marathon, and I couldn't get my muscles to support me even to rise to my hands and knees. "Sebastian."

He rushed into the hall, his exasperated expression snapping to shocked. "What?"

"You have to save them," I gasped. *Please, God, save them.* "I can't lose them. They're dying. Teleport them. Please."

Amiah reached for me again, and I managed to shove her hand away. "No. They need you."

Strength poured from both of the brands on my arm into Gideon and Jacob. Their injuries were bad. They weren't going to last. And God, I had no idea if Marcus or Kol were as badly hurt.

"Please, Sebastian." He was the only one who could get to them fast enough. My throat tightened and tears spilled down my cheeks.

"I don't have the power to teleport." He dropped to his knees beside Amiah. "I'm too magically exhausted to draw that much raw magic from the Realm of Celestial Light."

No. No no no. He had to help. He was the only one who could. I couldn't lose them, I wouldn't survive their deaths, and I didn't want to.

"I'll call—"

"Sebastian," I begged. "Now. They need help now." *Save them. Save them.*

A sob broke free. Divine light blazed from my palms even with the containment cuffs. Maybe I could teleport, maybe that was a power I'd inherited from my archangel parent. Except I had no idea if archangels could teleport or, even if I could, how. I had so much God damned power, it blazed through me, filling me with agony, screaming at me to use it, save them, and there wasn't anything I could do. All I could manage was to focus it on them, send it through the brand, and pray it was enough for them to hold on until they could get back here.

But it wasn't going to be enough. They weren't going to last. *Save them. Save them.*

"Esther, I can't draw in enough power."

My thoughts stuttered. I was bursting with useless power. "Take mine."

"I—"

"Sebastian, please. Take mine, take it all. Save them."

"Can you do that?" Amiah asked.

"I'm not tapping directly into the power from the Celestial Realm of Light, there's less chance of burning up, and her magic is divine light," he said. "That's the O negative of magic. Any being can use it."

"Sebastian, please."

Gideon's electric magic flickered in his brand and chilled. My pulse froze, my whole essence froze while my soul wailed. I shoved magic through the brand and his power flared, searing through me, ripping a scream from my clenched jaw. He was out of time.

"Let me get the charm for the transfer."

"No time." I grabbed Sebastian's hand and imagined the rest of my magic flooding into him, not burning — *please don't let me burn him* — but pouring into his essence and igniting it into a roaring magic.

His head jerked back with a howl of pain and divine light blazed from his eyes. "Slow it down," he gasped. "It's too much, Esther."

I tried to stem the flood, to pull some of it back, but my desperation had control. Sebastian needed it to save my guys and he was getting it all.

My power screamed through my body and poured into him, searing my magical channels. Sebastian wrenched his head down and squeezed his eyes shut, but divine light blazed from under his lashes, hell, it blazed from every inch of his exposed skin. "Call one of them. I need a living connection to know where to teleport."

Amiah pulled out her phone.

"Call Kol." My hands blistered and bled. So too did Sebastian's, but I kept hold of him, kept pumping magic into him. "He's the fastest healer. If they're all mortally wounded, he's the most likely able to answer."

They can't die. I can't lose them.

Amiah dialed.

"Amiah—" Kol moaned.

"Got it." Sebastian wrenched his bleeding hand from mine. A small circle of light burst around him, swarmed over him, and tore him to miniscule pieces.

"Bane is coming," Amiah said into the phone.

"How?"

"Essie." Amiah stared at me with a mix of horror and fear.

A ball of light exploded on the other side of the couch by the front door. Gideon appeared on his knees. His wings shot out with a burst of light and he collapsed, face first onto the floor, his wings splayed. Jacob lay on his back and blood rushed onto the marble around him the moment he'd fully materialized. Marcus materialized as his massive black wolf lying on his side, panting fast and shallow breaths, while Kol curled into a ball moaning as his phone clattered to the floor.

Sebastian took a staggering step forward then his eyes rolled back and he dropped, cracking his forehead on the arm of his couch.

"Oh, my God," Amiah said as she scrambled to the group.

"Save Gideon and Marcus." *Please save them.* I stood, making the room darken and whirl, and seized the back of the couch to keep standing. "I can save Jacob and Kol."

My stomach clenched, fear and physical weakness churning into nausea, and I staggered to Jacob's side. A massive hole had been punctured through his chest, terrifyingly similar to the injury he'd taken fighting the archnephilim.

I shoved half of what little strength I had left into his brand — praying he wouldn't need more in case Gideon also needed help. His eyelids fluttered opened and his gaze locked on me with the crushing power of his vampiric intensity.

I can't lose you. I can't lose any of you. Please let me have enough in me to save them.

I shoved my wrist against his mouth. For a second he hesitated, probably thinking about how much blood he'd already taken from me, then sank his teeth into my flesh.

His magic swept into me, muting my panic and making every terrified cell thrum with instant desire. I shoved my free hand under the back of Kol's T-shirt and pressed my burned palm to his skin, then set my forehead on the marble floor and closed my eyes, giving in to the sensation. I was exhausted liquid bliss. Jacob's power rushed to my core, and I ached for satisfaction, but I was also too weak to do anything about it.

My strength continued to bleed through the bonds, but it slowed from a torrent to a stream. A little more and they were going to make it. A sob broke free. I tried to raise my head to check on Marcus and Kol, but couldn't. *Please let them be okay. Please.*

Jacob groaned against my skin, and his magic twisted tighter within me. My breath came too fast, adding to my dizziness, but his magic wouldn't let me pass out. I needed a release so much it hurt.

A whisper of warmth caressed my wrist and Jacob sealed his bite shut, but he hadn't taken enough. Strength still seeped from our brand. I tried to tell him to take more blood, but my lips were numb.

"Will Gideon live?" Jacob asked.

"He's stable," Amiah said. "And Marcus, don't you dare shift."

I'm not as hurt as they are, Marcus said, his mental voice tight with pain. I knew he was talking to Amiah, but he'd included me in the conversation to reassure me.

Another sob ripped from my throat. *Thank God. Oh, thank God.*

You need to release her, Jacob.

"I know. Just—" He sat up, groaned again, and picked me up, his skin radiating cold through his clothes. "Just working up the strength to move us."

He trembled as he staggered to his feet and shuffled to the bedroom we'd used before. My eyes kept fluttering open... or did they keep fluttering shut? I wasn't sure. Everything spun with pain and exhaustion and need.

He sagged on the bed and propped himself against the headboard, cradling me in the V between his legs. His massive body wrapped around me, strong, secure, and deliciously powerful. Even seriously injured, his erection pressed hard against my back.

His hand slid down my abdomen and into the front of my pants and underwear. I shuddered, the promise of a climax taunting me, and the bedroom spun faster.

"You need to take more."

"No," he said, his voice rumbling through his massive chest, making my essence vibrate.

"You're still pulling strength through the brand. Please, Jacob." I might be weak, but I could handle this. "Amiah can't really heal you, but she can heal me. I'm not going to lose you."

He growled and sank his teeth into my throat. I gasped at the bite of pain and violent explosion of magic in my core. It rocked my hips, pushing his fingers into my curls and closer to where I needed him.

Every cell in my body throbbed, painful and full with his magic. I couldn't catch my breath, and I squeezed my eyes shut before the whirling room made me throw up. I could handle this. I had to handle this. He just needed a little more, just to stop the brand from pulling my strength into him.

He took a long pull on my vein, twisting his magic tighter. I moaned, bucking up again, urging him to release the climax clenching within me.

Another pull, and he slid two fingers inside me, slowly pumping in and out as he swept his thumb over my clit. The pressure of my climax grew. I panted, desperate, but knew I'd shatter and never recover if he didn't release me gently.

His breath came fast, too. Hard exhalations sweeping over my neck, ratcheting up my desire. His free hand slid under my T-shirt, and he roughly kneaded my breasts as his hips rocked beneath me.

My climax trembled, faded, trembled again, and with a final rock of our hips, rushed through me, blazing through my cells and sending sparks flashing across my vision.

Darkness followed, and I yearned to sink into it, but his brand still sucked my strength.

"It wasn't enough," I said, fighting to stay conscious. "Take more."

"No. Amiah can't heal you if you're dead."

"Jacob—"

He wrapped his arms around me and held me tight to his massive chest. "We can wait for her to help Gideon."

I concentrated on Gideon's brand. Weak electric magic danced under my skin, not nearly as powerful as it should have been. He wasn't pulling strength, but he was on the very edge of needing it.

"She has helped him."

"Then we can wait for her magic to recover." Jacob drew in a ragged, wet breath and groaned.

"Or I could help," Kol said from the doorway. He looked like shit, his body bloody and bruised. A massive gash, only partly healed, sliced from his forehead to his jaw, barely missing his left eye, and the front of his T-shirt was shredded, revealing more partially healed gashes all over his chest. Hellfire blazed from his eyes, and he gripped the doorframe with both hands as if he needed the help to keep standing.

My breath caught with hope that we were going to be okay, then he dropped his gaze.

"I can give Essie a boost," he said, his voice heartbreakingly soft.

"Don't. I don't want you doing something you don't want to do." Especially since giving me a magical boost meant he'd have to kiss me.

"You're also still weak," Jacob said. "Last time you saved her, it knocked you out for hours."

"Release your bite-lock again, and I'll get it back and a bit more." His knuckles turned white, his grip on the doorframe tightened.

"Kol, don't." It was clear just being near me hurt him.

His gaze rose and captured mine, the hellfire in his eyes stronger than before, bleeding light across his cheekbones. "I know you're not one of them. I just—" He swallowed hard and took an unsteady step into the room. "You saved us. Let me help you save your mates."

"No more than you can handle," I said.

A hint of his wicked smile pulled at his lips, but it didn't reach his eyes. "You should talk."

He staggered to the bed, one arm held tight to his body as if his ribs hurt, and sagged to the mattress beside Jacob's leg. The hellfire fully consumed his eyes and with the gash on his face, he looked dangerous, not the playful, devastatingly handsome incubus I'd come to know.

I wanted to tell him I wasn't going to hurt him, that I thought what had happened to him had been horrible, but the words wouldn't form in my muddled mind.

He leaned forward and cupped my cheeks between warm, trembling palms. A whisper of his heated power slid under my skin, and my pulse picked up in anticipation. His gaze dipped to my lips, and he squeezed his eyes shut, his face tight with pain.

This wasn't right. I couldn't ask him to do this.

"Kol, don't—"

His lips captured mine and his magic swept into me. I gasped, and he deepened the kiss, sliding his tongue against mine, pouring his power down my throat. It rushed, blazing liquid desire straight to my core, and spun my nerves into breathtaking sensitivity.

Instinctively, I grabbed his wrists to hold on, the flood of his magic overwhelming, but he tensed and his trembling increased. My throat tightened. I couldn't let him do this to himself. Jacob and I would find another way. Kol didn't have to fight his fear to help us.

I tried to pull away, but his hold on me tightened. "Don't fight me."

I wasn't, not like I had when I'd been shot and he'd stabilized me enough for Gideon to get me to Amiah. "You don't have to do this."

"Just take the magic," he said against my lips. "Please." His voice was thick with emotions. I just couldn't figure out which. Pain? Desire? Fear? I wasn't sure I'd be able to figure it out even with my empathy.

"Okay." I clutched the comforter to keep from reaching for him again and gave him full control.

His magic rushed into me, sweeping me into desperate aching need. It was similar to Jacob's magic, powerful, twisting, bone-melting, but so much more. It poured into my cells and made every inch of me hypersensitive. His lips were firm and hot and hungry. His grip on my cheeks tightened, sending more swelling power into my core. Beneath me, Jacob's breath picked up as if touching me connected him to Kol's magic.

Every breath I took sent the promise of a climax trembling through me, rubbed my body against Jacob's, brought me closer to Kol with his glorious heat. I was caught between hot and cold and wanted them pressed against me, capturing me with their bodies.

Kol's magic surged, rushing fast down my throat and entwining with my magic. He started to shake, and with a groan, he pulled his lips away. My magic clung to his for a second, curling wisps of red smoke between our lips, before he jerked back, putting too much distance between us and severing the connection.

I squirmed with need, no longer bone-weary. I was still tired, but I felt more like I had when they'd first arrived. Marcus padded into the doorway, still in wolf form, and his green gaze slid over the three of us.

"I didn't even pass out this time," Kol said. He stood, and his eyes rolled back and his knees gave out.

With a growl, Marcus lunged for Kol, shifting as he moved, catching him before he cracked his head on the floor. He leaned him against the wall, close to the bed but out of the way, then turned to me. Without his clothes, I could see every gash and bruise on his beautiful body, now partially healed because he'd shifted. I could also see his desire for me.

"You're still too pale," he said.

"Jacob is still too weak. We're running out of time to stop the witches and I—" Panic from almost losing my guys snapped through the desire from Kol's magic. "I can't lose you. Any of you."

"It'll be okay," Jacob said. "I'm okay."

"I can feel you're not." I pressed my hand against the delicate gold threads of our brand on his biceps.

The muscles in Marcus's jaw flexed. "Feed on me."

Jacob tensed beneath me. "Not without my magic like last time. And you're hurt, too. I wouldn't be able to take a lot from you."

"Then both of us," Marcus said.

"I still might not be able to get up and leave when—" Jacob said.

"That's not what I'm proposing." Marcus's piercing green gaze, filled with desire and need, locked with mine.

Holy shit, he'd been serious about the threesome.

ESSIE

MY MOUTH WENT DRY WHILE THE REST OF ME THROBBED IN ANTICIPATION of two of my guys in bed with me.

"I'm in if Essie is," Jacob said, his voice a low, sensual rumble.

I held out my hand to Marcus, unable to speak, inviting him to join us. His wolf darkened his eyes and his breath picked up. With a low growl, he crawled onto the bed and captured my lips in a fierce kiss.

His fear and love and need filled my chest, the magic of our connection, even without an angelic mating brand, defying the power of the containment cuffs. Amiah was wrong when she'd said Marcus wasn't my true mate because I hadn't branded him. I loved and needed him as much as Jacob and Gideon.

I dug my nails into his scalp, his passion making the remains of Kol's magic swell low and sultry. He leaned closer and reached past my head, offering Jacob his wrist. Jacob shifted, digging his still-hard erection into the small of my back, sending a thrill of pleasure racing through me, and sank his fangs into Marcus.

Marcus froze, his lips pressed against mine, his breath ragged. "Good Lord. I thought I knew what you felt when we released his bite-lock, but this—"

He moaned into my mouth and trembled with what I knew was an aching, twisting need. His hips dropped, and he ground his erection against me. I shifted so he hit my clit, shooting sudden pleasure to my core and nearly coming again.

"Not yet," Jacob said, placing a heavy hand on my head and tilting it to give him better access to my neck.

I shuddered, and Marcus deepened his kiss as Jacob sank his fangs into my neck.

Consuming desire swept through me, stealing all breath and thought. There was only the feel of hard muscle capturing me between them and the ferocity of their desire for me. Jacob took a long pull on my neck. His magic overwhelmed me, and I tipped my head back, knowing my guys had me, that they'd satisfy me. Marcus scraped his nails down my body with enough pressure to make me squirm but not enough to tear my T-shirt. He skimmed the sides of my breasts, my skin hypersensitive from Kol's and Jacob's power.

Jacob took another pull on my vein, twisting his magic tighter. My breath came fast, my body aching for release.

Marcus hooked his fingers into the waistband of my pants and pulled them and my underwear off. He sat back and swept his gaze over me, his eyes filled with awe and desire. His erection jutted from his body, thick and hard, and I shuddered, knowing how he'd feel sliding into me, driving me over the edge.

Another pull on my neck, and my eyes rolled back. Jacob's magic teased me with the promise of another mind-blowing climax, and Marcus trailed his claws up the insides of my thighs. I squirmed, pushing my legs wider, inviting him in, and he settled between me. His erection brushed my folds, and my breath hitched. *Yes, oh please, yes.*

Jacob's grip on my head tightened, and he pushed his other hand under my shirt and palmed my breast. He ground his erection into my back and rumbled with pleasure, a low vibration that radiated through me. I arched into Marcus, and his tip slid into me. Jacob's magic jerked, a sudden almost blast of climax, making all of us gasp.

Marcus slid in deeper. I squirmed, rubbing against Jacob's erection. His rumble turned to a groan. He needed a release as much as Marcus and I did, but with my hands handcuffed together, there wasn't much I could do.

Then Marcus thrust into me in a hard, fast stroke, and Jacob rocked his hips, pushing mine up and driving Marcus in deeper while grinding his length against me, and all thought vanished. There was only sensation.

I shuddered, my climax teasing me, my body aching for release. Slowly, agonizingly slowly, Marcus withdrew until just his tip was inside me, then he thrust again. Jacob matched him with another rock of his hips, and the pressure of Jacob's magic swelled. I squirmed, deliciously trapped between them. Another withdraw and thrust, faster this time, and another.

Marcus's wolf rose to the forefront, darkening his eyes and slitting his pupils. His canines extended and his thrusts grew more ferocious. He grabbed my hips for more control, and Jacob's hand left my breasts and dipped into my curls to rub his thumb against my clit. The pressure of his magic and Marcus's wild passion pounded tighter and tighter until my climax ripped through me, shooting stars across my vision and making me scream with pleasure.

Both guys tensed with their own release, and Kol jerked upright as if he'd been struck by lightning.

"Holy fuck," he gasped, then his dazed gaze focused on us. "Holy. Fuck."

I murmured my agreement and slid into a warm darkness. My guys were safe, and I was boneless and thoroughly satisfied. God, I loved them — and not just for the pleasure they'd given me. They were the family I'd never known I'd ached for. I yearned to lie, safe and loved, in their embrace forever. And now that I wasn't a nephilim, I could.

GIDEON

I PRESSED MY PALMS AGAINST THE SLICK WHITE TILES IN THE SHOWER OF Sebastian's second guest room, letting the hot water beat against my back and shoulders, unable to work up the energy to properly shower. Everything hurt. Amiah might have stopped me from dying, but she hadn't been able to do much more, not with having drained herself only a couple hours earlier when the witches had almost killed us the first time.

But the pain in my body was nothing compared to the pain in my soul and there were too many things threatening to tear it apart. Cassius lay on the bed just outside the bathroom, his skin gray, his expression tight with pain even though he was unconscious.

I'd told Jacob and Marcus that he was no longer my brother because of what he'd done to Essie, but I'd been lying to them and me. I was still furious that he hadn't even given her a chance, hadn't immediately known that I'd never be mated to a monster, but he was still my brother.

I'd already lost Dominic to Michael's war. I couldn't lose Cassius, too.

And, if I really thought about it, his reaction to Essie was because of Dominic. I hadn't seen enough of Cassius during the war to be certain, but I suspected our younger brother's death had broken something inside him that had yet to be healed. He'd never admit it, and he'd always been cold toward people — even colder than most angels — so it was hard to tell what exactly was wrong, but from the moment he'd returned to Operations and taken over my team, it had been clear he'd been trying to protect me.

Except the thing threatening to bring me down wasn't something he could protect me from, and it was my own damned fault. And while my fear that I'd lose Cassius was strong, my crumbling soul because I'd yet to seal my bond with Essie was stronger.

I'd been an idiot to think that I'd be able to resist the pull of the mating brand for sixty or seventy years. I'd barely lasted a few weeks.

Of course my resolve might have stayed strong if she hadn't shown me how much keeping my distance from her hurt her. The zip OD had made her try to kill herself, her grief at our unsealed bond over-whelming her.

Except it hadn't just been that we hadn't sealed our bond. It had been the fact that we were destined mates and she'd thought she was a nephilim. And while I wanted my mate to have automatically known that I'd accept her no matter what she was, I hadn't let her get to know me. I'd given her no reason to trust me and had purposefully kept my distance from her and as a result she'd been afraid I'd reject her if I knew the truth.

Except the truth was that no matter what she was, she was a good person. I'd fought against angels who were monsters and demons who'd upheld justice. Even if she had been one of Michael's creations that wouldn't have changed who I knew in my heart she really was.

Good... and mine.

And Jacob's.

And Marcus's.

I hadn't thought I'd share a mate— Of course I hadn't really thought about having a mate at all, and I certainly never thought I'd be one of the few angels gifted with a rare angelic mating brand. But sharing her didn't bother me like I feared it might. I'd only been upset by seeing Jacob's brand because Cassius had been breathing down our necks and it added another complication to Essie's relationship with Marcus... which I'd been doing my damnedest to respect.

I still didn't understand how Marcus's wolf accepted that Essie was going to be intimate with me and Jacob. It went against everything I knew about shifters. But he hadn't blinked an eye when Essie and Jacob had taken a shower together, and he'd almost looked pleased when her scream of pleasure had reached us in the living room. Of course maybe he felt the rightness of her bonds and accepted them like I did.

And now she and Jacob were in the other bedroom having sex. Again.

Her moans had twisted my insides so tight I could barely breathe, the need to seal our bond screaming through me. And I'd known when she'd come because Kol had released a low, sensual groan, and took in a deep, pain-free breath. He'd then headed into their bedroom with Marcus, still in wolf form, following close behind, and I'd made a beeline to Cassius's room to have a shower.

I couldn't listen to Jacob pleasing her. Not when I couldn't be with her the way I wanted. Jacob needed her more and it was best if I didn't get in the way. But I also had no idea how Marcus could stand to watch them... unless of course he wasn't just watching.

My cock grew hard despite the pain in my body. The image of Essie, her head thrown back in ecstasy as the two of them pleasured her, flooded my mind's eye. She'd be radiant, her brown eyes with gold flecks rolled back, her eyelashes fluttering against her pale cheeks, and her body moving in rhythm with them.

I'd yet to see her naked, but last night I'd held her while she slept, and I'd brushed against the soft swell of her breasts and the curve of her hips. I ached to touch her without clothes in the way, to memorize every inch of her body with my lips and find every sensitive spot. I burned to hold her, bury myself inside her, join our souls the way destiny demanded, and worship her into blazing, sensual bliss.

With a groan, I wrapped my fingers around myself and squeezed, fighting to regain control of my body. But that only made me harder, my body burning for her. My soul was going to shatter, the compulsion to seal our bond was going to tear me apart if we didn't join our bodies like our souls had been joined.

But more importantly, I needed her to know that I was hers, that I'd been an idiot for resisting and hurting her, that like Marcus and Jacob I would do anything to protect her and love her.

Except now wasn't the time. Cassius was dying, the glyph witches had something big planned and had almost killed us twice to ensure their success, and we were running out of time. I couldn't afford to lose myself in Essie. I could try for something quick just to seal the bond, but she deserved better than that, and with the state of our bond, I doubted it would let me get away with something quick.

No, our bond needed to be healed and that didn't come from a quickie, and I couldn't afford to let it overwhelm me and distract me from the current situations. Too many lives were at stake.

I jerked my hand up and down my length. Maybe if I relieved some of the pressure, I'd be able to hold out a little longer.

My thoughts leaped back to the fantasy of Essie captured between Marcus and Jacob. I'd never shared a woman before, hadn't thought it was something I was into, but the idea of watching those two making love to her brought me even closer to the edge.

I imagined them bringing her to climax, leaving her satisfied and dazed, and then I'd work her back up again. I'd go slow, building the fire of her desire into an inferno with my lips and hands before sinking into her heat.

My balls clenched tight and I came hard and fast, not at all surprised that I'd barely gotten into my fantasy before coming. And not at all surprised that making myself come had done little to ease the screaming need to join with Essie.

ESSIE

My dreams drifted from the warm darkness to the warm water that wasn't water. I gently bobbed, up and down, up and down, the motion calm, relaxing. A handsome angel with brown hair and gold flecks in his angel glow smiled back at me. My father. Now I knew he was an archangel. I just didn't know which one... and I didn't want to think too hard about that, given that I'd been hidden my entire life and my father hadn't come back for me once the war was over. Which meant he'd died, either defending humanity or trying to exterminate it.

A bang thudded far off in the distance, then another. My father glanced over his shoulder, but I couldn't see where he was looking. Only foggy darkness lay behind him, distorted by the not-water.

He pressed his palm against something between us and the warmth in the not-water swelled. It wrapped around me with a gentle embrace and the foggy darkness billowed until it was all I could see. A masculine voice murmured something to me. I wasn't sure who, but it had to be one of my guys. *My guys.* God, I loved thinking about them like that. I lay caught between two hard, muscular bodies, boneless from an amazing climax and craving more.

I slid my hand out to caress whichever of my guys lay in front of me but didn't touch muscle, only mattress. My mind stuttered. I wasn't embraced between my guys. I was alone—

"Agent Shaw," the voice murmured again from close behind me.

That made my pulse skip. Had Gideon stopped using my name? Was he back to addressing me formally? Perhaps old habits died hard? Or he'd changed his mind about being one of my many mates? The fractured part of my soul ached at that thought.

"Gideon, please." I rolled over, my sight blurry with sleep and my eyes sore from still wearing the contacts I no longer needed. I blinked my vision clear enough to see eyes with a pale angel glow.

Except they weren't blue and his hair wasn't buzzed short or blond. Not Gideon.

My pulse lurched. He wasn't Gideon, and this angel didn't know I wasn't a nephilim. I needed to run. Find my guys. Now.

"Agent Shaw." The man pressed a warm hand to my forehead and gentle heat seeped into me, easing my panic. "I'm Priam. Amiah asked me to help heal you."

My pulse returned closer to normal. Amiah knew I wasn't a nephilim... unless she was trying to get rid of me to save Marcus.

Except I was still in the same white and blue bedroom in Sebastian's apartment. The blankets had been pulled over me, while the white comforter, bloody from Jacob and Marcus's injuries, lay in a heap on the floor where Kol had been sitting.

"Is she awake?" Amiah asked, striding into the room.

"Just," Priam said. He was handsome — like most angels were — but in a casual, boy-next-door kind of way, not strikingly handsome like Gideon.

"Good." She looked pale and haggard, and my stomach plunged for a second before I realized she was probably just exhausted, physically and magically. Neither Gideon nor Jacob were drawing strength from the brand, Kol had gotten a pretty big infusion of sex magic, and Marcus had been healthy enough to help with that amazing orgasm.

"Are *you* okay?" I asked her.

She looked surprised that I'd even ask. "I just need to recover my magic, maybe sleep for a week."

Priam gently squeezed her elbow and gave her a warm smile. "Just like the good old days when we worked emerg at Mercy Memorial."

"Which I left for this very reason." She squared her shoulders, her angel glow billowing. "The guys are waiting for you in the living room. I'll give you a minute to get dressed."

She and Priam left. I retrieved my underwear and pants from the floor and put them on. My shirt was bloody from lying on Jacob's ravaged chest, but I didn't have a spare and didn't want to risk taking off the cuffs to change. I also really wanted to pull my hair back in a pony-tail, but I had no idea where my hair elastic had gone, so I did a few quick combs with my fingers then left the bedroom.

At least I felt a hundred times better than I had before. In fact, save for a burning headache that came from having used too much magic too quickly, I felt better than I had in days. The cuffs contained my buzz so my skin was no longer on fire, and Priam must have healed me completely because I couldn't feel a hint of having been drained of blood, twice, in the last handful of hours.

Everyone except Priam and Cassius sat in Sebastian's living room, and all eyes turned to me the moment I stepped out of the hall. My guys rushed to my side, and relief flooded me. They all looked healthy and well. Gideon's expression was strained and his face was still bruised, but at least the bruises looked a few days old instead of a few hours. Jacob looked fine, and when he wrapped his arms around me in a firm hug, his body was even warm. Marcus took over when Jacob released me, capturing my cheeks between his palms and kissing me with one of his ferocious, quick kisses that always left me breathless. There wasn't a hint of bruising on his face, and while his new, clean clothes made it impossible to tell if he was still covered in wounds, he didn't move as if he were still hurt.

Marcus released me, but threaded his fingers between mine as Gideon brushed a kiss over my forehead. God, I needed him to kiss me in full. But if his kiss had been as deep as Marcus's or his embrace as encompassing as Jacob's, my need to solidify our bond would take over and I'd drag him back into the bedroom. He hesitated, his body close, his power humming through his brand. I could feel his need to stay close, and hear his struggle with his ever so slightly too-fast breath.

Please kiss me.

Please don't.

I wanted both. I wanted him. I didn't want to be responsible for people getting hurt.

With a groan, he stepped back and crossed his arms, as if he were trying to keep his hands to himself.

Kol had risen from his seat on the couch but didn't approach. The nasty cut on his face was gone, and he no longer pressed his arm against his ribs. Hellfire flickered in his eyes, banked and contained, but his expression was tight. Things still weren't right between us, but it was complicated and not easily fixed.

Heat swept up my neck and across my cheeks. He'd seen me with Marcus and Jacob. Which had been amazing, and satisfying, and something I wouldn't mind repeating. And while I doubted Kol would judge my sex choices, I still couldn't help feeling awkward and embarrassed about desires I hadn't known I had.

Sebastian, still sitting, watched me from the seat beside Kol with that calculating look that made me feel like he was seeing into my soul. He didn't have a welt on his forehead from where he'd smacked his head and his hand was no longer burned, so Amiah or Priam must have healed him, too. But my divine light still bled from his eyes in tiny droplets that, every couple of blinks, rolled down his cheeks then sank back under his skin.

"How long was I out?" I asked as Marcus led me to the couches, sat, and pulled me onto his lap, even though there was space for both of us.

Jacob pushed the coffee table aside and sat on the floor at Marcus's feet, Amiah took the seat beside me and Marcus, while Gideon perched on the couch's arms — close but not touching.

Please, just touch me.

Jeez, my willpower just wasn't going to last the day, let alone the next couple of hours.

"Less than an hour," Marcus said. "So we've still time to deal with the witches."

"Tell me you've called for backup." I didn't want them to face the witches again, but I knew my guys wouldn't give up. It was their job to arrest the witches, and it wasn't in their nature to quit.

"The closest team in Los Angeles is dealing with their own problems, and head office doesn't know when they can get agents to us," Gideon said. "We're on our own."

Jacob rested a hand on my calf, his still intensity helping me to focus past the yearning of my bond with Gideon. "And we still don't know what they're planning or where they are."

"Even if we get backup, we still need a way to cut off their power before we face them again." Kol's gaze jumped to mine for a second then slid away. "That ambush in City Hall nearly killed us."

"Like I said five minutes ago," Sebastian said, his tone exasperated, "I'm still waiting to hear back from a few sources about your area containment master ward."

"That wasn't a criticism," Kol said. "Just a statement of fact. I'd rather not have those witches hand me my ass again. I doubt you'll be around next time to teleport us out of there."

"I don't know. I might be. Essie made one hell of a payment to save you, and she hasn't come close to spending it all." He shuddered and wiped a trickle of divine light from his cheek. "Archangel divine light is some potent shit."

"And you're never getting her power again." Gideon glared at him.

He raised his hands. "Never going to ask for it."

Something passed between the two men, a warning from Gideon to Sebastian, but I couldn't figure out for what. Gideon didn't strike me as the jealous type. He'd only been concerned about me having multiple mates because of Marcus's possessive wolf.

"So," Marcus said, breaking the tension. "What's the plan?"

Gideon opened his mouth to respond, but his phone buzzed. He checked the display and didn't answer.

"Apparently it involves continuing to avoid the mayor," Kol said.

Gideon set the phone to silent and shoved it back into his pocket. "I'll deal with him when we have a plan."

"And to do that, we need to figure out what the witches are planning," Jacob said. "I doubt they're still at City Hall."

"Sure, what are the odds they'll ambush us twice in the same place?" Marcus barked a bitter laugh.

"City Hall was a lucky guess," Jacob said.

"I'm not willing to risk that it wasn't." Gideon's angel glow flared. "These witches are powerful. I wouldn't put a scrying or tracking spell past them."

"It takes a shit load of power to cast anything like that," Marcus said.

Gideon met his gaze. "I know."

I didn't like the sound of that. "So if they're watching us right now, they know where we are and what we're planning. Whatever we do next, we could be walking into a trap."

"Not right now," Sebastian said. "I have a concealment glyph on my apartment."

"But as soon as we leave..." Kol ran a hand through his hair, mussing it and no doubt not realizing how sexy it made him look. "We need our concealment charms."

"But they're in Operations and even if we could get them, we don't have a witch who can set them." Jacob glanced at Sebastian. "Unless you can set a concealment charm, among all the other things you can do."

"I can't set charms, but I know who can." Sebastian pulled out his phone. "So long as you promise not to arrest her."

"I promise not to arrest her for giving us concealment charms," Gideon said, since only the JP and certain branches of the army were allowed to have those — although that didn't mean there weren't witches willing to make and set them for enough money.

Sebastian gave Gideon a dry look. "You can be a little less specific than that."

"Fine," Gideon sighed. "I promise not to arrest her for anything seen or done during this one exchange with her."

"Better." Sebastian typed in a text. "You'll have to go to her. She won't come to you."

Gideon pulled out his phone and checked the text.

"You know where that is?" Sebastian asked.

Gideon gave a tight nod. "I do."

"Good. You'll also need the right payment to cover all five of you."

"Four," Marcus growled. "Essie isn't going."

Sebastian turned his icy gaze on Marcus, and another divine light tear rolled down his cheek then melted into his skin. "You'd be an idiot not to take her. If things get bad, take off the cuffs and point her in the right direction."

That sounded like a terrible idea. "I agree with Marcus. I can't control my blast. It's too dangerous."

"If things get bad for your guys, it's really bad." Sebastian's attention jumped back to Gideon and his expression turned grim. Whatever Sebastian had teleported into when he'd rescued my guys, it had scared him. "You'll need a bomb, not a scalpel."

He had a really good point. My chest squeezed, remembering how near death they'd been when Sebastian had brought them back. Even if my blast incapacitated me, it could be enough for my guys to drag me out of there... if I didn't hit them, as well.

Marcus's eyes narrowed. "She's just about killed herself twice in as many hours trying to save us."

"And she'll lose her mind if you go down and she's not there." The muscles in Sebastian's jaw flexed. "Trust me. That wasn't pretty to watch."

I shifted to look Marcus in the eyes. "I'm getting the charm. We can decide if it's safe for me to go into the field after that. I'd rather not find ourselves wishing we had it."

"Agreed," Gideon said. "What type of payment do we need and what's it going to cost us?"

"Nothing. Essie's already paid, remember?" Sebastian grabbed a marble from the bowl on the coffee table and pressed his free palm to the center of his chest.

Icy blue light blazed beneath his white button-down as he activated a glyph. The divine light flared in his eyes and his body stiffened, the veins in his neck and arms bulging. Light raced along those veins and swept into his hand, then twisted into a miniature vortex in the marble, whirling faster and faster.

My buzz whispered just under my skin, the promise of a biting, searing fire, barely trapped by the containment cuffs. I tried to bite back a groan, but couldn't, and Marcus tightened his grip on me

"Bane?" he growled.

Gideon and Jacob also tensed. Even Kol shifted to the edge of the couch, his hands sliding to his back where he hid his sheathed daggers.

Sebastian ignored them, his attention locked on the marble. His breath grew ragged, sweat beaded on his forehead, and large divine light tears rolled down his cheeks and splattered onto his thighs before sinking back into his body.

The pressure from the vortex grew. Fire crackled under my skin, my buzz no longer just a whisper, and light billowed over my hands. I was going to burst into flames and take my guys down with me.

"Sebastian, stop," I gasped. "I'm going to lose control."

ESSIE

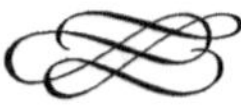

My breath turned ragged and my buzz sliced deep, seizing my muscles and threatening to consume me. The power in my hands grew, and I fought to hold it back. *Come on. Control it. Please, God, let me control it.* But the power kept building and my mental grip started to slip. "Please, Sebastian. Stop."

Gideon jerked toward Sebastian as his power surged, making the light in my hands flare, searing my palms. I screamed and yanked the power back under my skin, praying I'd be the only one I'd hurt this time. Then the power snapped off, and my buzz and magic vanished.

Oh, thank God.

Trembling and breathing hard, I leaned into Marcus. I needed his warmth and strength. In just a few seconds, Sebastian had demonstrated why taking me anywhere was a terrible idea.

Marcus rubbed his hands over my arms, trying to help me warm up. He glared at Sebastian, who held out the marble to Gideon, his hands shaking and his breath as ragged as mine.

"Your payment," he said.

Gideon glowered at him. In fact, all my guys looked like they wanted to rip his head off, even Kol. But Gideon took the marble instead and handed it to Kol. "It better be clean."

"My essence would be in there, as well." Sebastian sagged back, his icy gaze meeting mine. A tear of divine light, not as bright as before, trickled down his cheek and melted back into his skin. "It's the light magic you pumped into me, so both our essences are entwined in it. If I didn't strip it down to pure magic when I put it in the marble, a strong enough witch could use that to influence us."

"That's why angels don't sell their divine light," Jacob said. "They don't want to risk leaving a hint of essence behind."

And that had to be why Gideon had told Sebastian he was never getting my magic again.

"Angels also don't usually have access to someone who's magically sensitive that they trust, or who's sensitive enough, who will tell them if the magic is pure." Kol's attention flickered to me then jumped to Gideon, and he handed the marble back. "She's safe."

"Good." Gideon pocketed the marble. "Let's make this quick."

I stood on shaky legs and checked my hands. They were sore but thankfully not burned. So while I might be going out in a bloody shirt with my hands cuffed together, at least I wasn't injured.

"What are we going to do about Essie's cuffs?" Marcus stood, drawing up close behind me and steadying me. "It's dangerous for her to be hampered like this."

Except his tone made it clear he was really saying it was just plain dangerous for me to be doing anything.

"Can you do anything with the containment spell with all that extra magic Essie gave you?" Gideon asked Sebastian.

"I think I can split it if you can cut the links." Sebastian rubbed his face and sat forward. He met my gaze and pointed to the edge of his coffee table. "Sit."

I sat and Gideon created a small blade of divine light. Sebastian activated three small glyphs on his right arm, took a cuff in each hand, and gave Gideon a nod. Gideon sliced the chain holding my hands together, leaving the cuffs around my wrists, and Sebastian's power snapped over them. It curled up my arms, the right side sinking into Gideon's brand and drawing a hiss of pain from both of us.

With a groan, Sebastian closed his eyes. The muscles in his jaw flexed, and he took a slow breath as if to steady himself, but at least this spell didn't look as difficult as putting my magic into the marble and didn't reawaken my buzz.

"There." He sat back. "That'll hold for about a day."

"How long is *about*?" Jacob asked.

Sebastian cocked an eyebrow and gave him a dry, exhausted look. "If

I knew exactly, I would have said so. Esther burns through non-personal magic like it's dry tinder, so it could be a day or half a day. Depends on what she's doing."

"So that might not last until we've dealt with the witches," Marcus said.

"Let's hope it does." Gideon headed to the door. "Because we don't have a second set of cuffs and once that spell fails, nothing is containing her magic."

Which meant everyone near me would be in danger.

"This is a terrible idea," Marcus growled.

Hell, yes. In fact, I shouldn't be anywhere near my guys if I wanted to keep them safe.

Except that thought made my pulse stall. So far, not being near them hadn't kept them safe.

"We haven't been hiding our brands, so the witches know we're connected to Essie," Gideon said. "If we disappear from their magic sight, they might start looking for her."

Marcus groaned. "I hate when you make sense. Let's go."

"You should change first," Jacob said to me, grabbing a shirt from a bag on the floor near the hall and tossing it to me. "You'll draw enough attention with the cuffs as it is, even if they are separated."

"Yeah." I looked at everyone in the room. They'd all seen me in my bra, or less, no point in hiding in a room just to change my shirt. I took off the bloody one and pulled on the new one.

We left Sebastian's apartment, stepping into an opulent hall with a marble floor and gilded frescoes, just like the hall outside Victoria's suite.

Sebastian's private stairs were just as upscale, with marble steps and a crystal chandelier that gleamed in more gilded frescoes — these ones of winter scenes — as well as in the polished dark-wood railing. The stairs led up to the roof and directly down to the first floor, with no doors to any of the other floors, and took us to a small patio with a bistro table, two chairs, and four evergreen shrubs in planter boxes. Beyond lay a clean, narrow walking path, cobbled as if we were in an old town in Europe, that led to a side street as far away from Rouge's main entrance as possible.

The sun sat high in the sky, it had to be around noon, and even in the walking path's shadows the air was too warm and muggy. It might have been early summer, but it felt later in the season, and I was sweating by the time we reached the JP SUV sitting at the curb on the street at the end of the path.

We piled into the hot vehicle, everyone except Kol taking their usual seat. He sat in the back with Jacob, leaving me the entire second row. My heart ached at the distance he put between us, making it hard to remind myself that I'd awoken terrible memories for him and healing our friendship was going to take time.

Gideon, sitting in the front passenger seat, showed Marcus the address Sebastian had texted him as he put all the windows down to let what little breeze there was alleviate the heat before the AC could kick in.

"Really? Her? This plan just keeps getting better by the second," Marcus said, his tone thick with sarcasm.

He drove across the Quarter to Squatters' Row, straight to the mouth of Mystic Mavis's back alley, and my heart sank.

Of course Sebastian would send us to Mavis. She was the most powerful non-registered witch in the Quarter. Jeez, I'd hoped I wouldn't have to remind everyone, especially Kol, that I'd lied to them, but now I didn't have much of a choice.

"So, ah... Just so you're not caught off guard, I've done business with Ma—" Crap. No specifics, in case we were being spied on. "—this witch."

Jacob's vampiric intensity swelled, filling the car and sitting heavy in my chest, and I got out of the SUV, desperate for relief.

"Jeez, Essie. Why would you do business with her?" Marcus asked.

"To hide what she really was," Kol said, his voice soft, making my throat tighten.

I *needed* to make things right. How the hell did I make things right? I wasn't going to apologize for being who I was, and I wasn't sure if apologizing for lying would fix anything.

"The spell that made your essence look human is hers?" Marcus asked. "I didn't think she was that powerful."

"She's not. I just needed to hide my eyes. They never stopped glowing after fighting the archnephilim."

"Blasting all that divine light into your body must have been the first crack in the spell hiding your real essence," Gideon said.

Or at least the first big crack, since I'd already had my buzz for a few years. "I didn't know what to do. I thought I was a nephilim."

"Probably because whoever enspelled you knew that was the best way to ensure you'd keep yourself hidden even after they were gone."

Jacob's eyes grew dark and the muscles in his jaw flexed. "To tell that to a child, make them think the world hated them and was after them—" He clenched his hands and strode into the alley, the heat of his anger breaking through the containment cuffs and swirling in my chest, half real emotion and half my weird empathy.

The strength of his reaction shocked me. Yes, my guys accepted who I was and supported me, but I hadn't expected any of them to be furious about how I'd grown up nor to realize so quickly what my life had been like without me even telling them.

"Best way to piss Jacob off," Marcus said, glancing at Kol. "Hurt a child."

Kol jerked away from us and hurried after Jacob.

"So what does she know about you? Does she have leverage we should know about?" Gideon asked, drawing close but not touching me

Please touch me.

His gaze dipped to mine and the angel glow in his eyes flared. For a second I was drowning in a summer-sky, my breath and pulse stalled, hell, my whole essence stalled, focused entirely on him. I needed him, body and soul.

I gritted my teeth, crossed my arms, and shifted closer to Marcus. Maybe being near him would help ease my need to rip my clothes off and beg Gideon to take me.

"What kind of leverage are you talking about?" I forced out. "I bought enspelled contacts to hide my angel glow. I didn't know that every time I used my light strike it ate through her spell, so I had to go to her yesterday for a top-up." I hadn't looked in the mirror — I wasn't sure I wanted to see how stunned I looked this time from everything that had happened — but given everyone's reaction to me, I was sure the spell on the contacts was well and truly done. "She wanted more money than I could afford, or my light magic."

The muscles in Gideon's jaw flexed and his pupils dilated, but I got the feeling it wasn't just because I'd bought enspelled contacts from Mavis. "What did you give her?"

"Nothing. I thought I had a day to figure it out, then a building fell on us, and I found out I had wings." A part of me still couldn't believe that. I had wings. And I wasn't a nephilim.

We followed Jacob and Kol toward Mavis's door, the back entrance to a now abandoned building that used to have apartments upstairs and a restaurant on the main floor. A small Eye of Horus, glimmering with a hint of magic, had been drawn in black ink near the top of the solid metal security door. I hadn't noticed the glow before, but that could just mean new powers that weren't completely affected by the containment cuffs were breaking through the spell that had hidden my true essence and abilities all my life.

Jacob opened the door, releasing an impossible gust of cool air — since the building didn't have electricity and could only be air conditioned with magic — and Gideon took the lead. He was the agent in charge. This was his negotiation to handle. Kol went next, and Marcus and I followed, while Jacob took the rear.

The same thick incense filled the air with a purple haze, making it hard to breathe, and the sense of unease that I'd gotten the first two times I'd visited Mavis churned in my gut. The large black glyphs covering the walls also glowed when they hadn't before, and the urge to turn around and get the hell out of there swelled, making me tremble.

"Did you think bringing friends would scare me into changing the price?" Mavis asked, her raspy alto making the hair on the back of my neck stand up.

We stepped into what used to be the restaurant's kitchen. Most of the stainless steel counters had been replaced with dark-wood bookcases, filled with books and boxes and strange things I didn't want to look at too closely. The counters that did remain were crowded with vials and jars and bowls, and stood between a sink filled with dirty dishes and a stove that had a pot of something boiling on a burner that was powered by magic. Dozens of candles illuminated the space, casting dark shadows into all the nooks and crannies, and catching on Mavis's necklaces, bracelets, and multi-chain headpiece.

She sat in a high-backed chair in front of an intricately carved table, still looking like a gypsy from an old movie, wearing a billowy shirt cinched with a corset — this one gold instead of yesterday's black — and a dark red gauzy skirt. Her dark eyes took in every inch of my guys, her perusal slow and sensual, and her blood-red lips curled into a wicked smile. "They are nice to look at, though. All that muscle. My offer might change if one of them is on the table."

"We're taken," Marcus growled.

"The angel and vampire are, that's for sure," Mavis said, tapping her nails up her right arm. "Although I'm surprised the brand is enough to protect you from the angel, given you've been hiding your nephilim nature." She squinted and leaned forward. "Hunh. I was sure your essence said you were human."

Gideon shifted slightly in front of me, but I wasn't sure if he was consciously trying to protect me from Mavis's gaze or not. "My mate's essence isn't your concern. We need five concealment charms to protect against magical spying."

Mavis's eyes narrowed, her expression turning calculating. "A concealment charm will only get you so far and last for so long. If you're going to hide from the JP, you're going to need something more powerful."

"We just need the charms," Gideon said.

"Even if her essence isn't quite human anymore, you know they'll come after her, lover boy." Mavis's grin turned dangerous. "Especially if word so happens to slip out."

"And you'll be the one to tell them if we don't pay you?" Jacob released more of his vampiric intensity. His power wasn't fully revealed, but it was close, since he hadn't pulled anything back after getting pissed about my childhood.

"Something like that." Mavis sat back and crossed her arms, her expression dry. Guess Jacob wasn't powerful enough to scare her, which made me wonder just how powerful she was. I knew from the search I'd done on the dark web that her magic was strong, but she didn't seem at all worried about my guys.

"We're a little short on time," Kol said, "and you really don't want to play this game with us."

Mavis's smile deepened. "Of course I do. They'll do anything to protect her, which means they'll pay anything."

Kol shifted to the stove and took a sniff at whatever was boiling in the pot. "Love potion."

"Didn't think you'd be interested, unless..." Mavis said with a dark chuckle, "you're not powerful enough to break an angelic mating brand." She sat forward, a wicked gleam in her eyes. "You want the girl, too, don't you?"

Kol stiffened, making me ache. He wasn't mine. I wasn't supposed to want him like I did my mates. And he hadn't reacted to Mavis's words because he wanted me.

"I count at least twenty magic violations." He slid his fingers over a jar on the counter. "And this one's serious."

"So *you're* going to call the JP on *me*?" Mavis sneered. "Oh, honey, you shouldn't make a bluff no one's going to believe."

"And you shouldn't try to strong-arm an angel protecting his mate." Gideon pulled his ID from his pocket — I had no idea how he'd managed to keep it in this morning's chaos — and held it up so Mavis could see it. "We are the JP."

Her eyes flashed wide and her face paled.

"Now about those concealment charms," Marcus growled.

"You know it's illegal to make them," she said.

"Which is why we've come to you and not a registered witch." Gideon pulled the glowing marble from his pocket. Her expression jumped from fear to hunger in an instant. "For the charms and your silence."

"They'll still come after her." She held out her hand, her gaze locked on the marble, my divine light reflected in her eyes.

"The charms and your silence," Gideon pressed.

"Yes yes yes." Mavis flicked her fingers, her attention never leaving the marble, and a long metal box with a thick, complicated glyph on the lid floated off the shelf behind her and landed on the table. "Who's first?"

"I'll go," I said. It really didn't matter what order we went in, but I got the feeling the guys would feel better about not being enspelled while I was vulnerable to Mavis. "What do you need?"

"Just your wrist." Mavis pointed to the stool across from her, but Marcus grabbed my arm before I could move.

"I'll go first," he said. "If she fucks with us, better me than you."

"Yeah," Kol said, his back to us and his voice so quiet I wouldn't have been able to hear him without my enhanced hearing. "Marcus can't level a building."

Marcus sat on the stool and placed his hand on the table, palm up, and Kol stepped up beside him.

Mavis ignored Kol and opened the box. Inside, nestled on red silk, was a thin knife, a small jar filled with something dark, a paintbrush, and a half-dozen coins the size of a penny with a complicated glyph etched on them. She opened the jar, dipped in the brush, and drew a simple glyph on Marcus's wrist in black ink. Then she reached for the knife.

"Yeah, I don't think so," Kol said. "We don't know where that's been."

"Well, I need to make a cut," Mavis huffed.

"You can use this." Kol drew the knife from his ankle sheath and set it on the table.

Mavis glared at him, but took the knife, grabbed Marcus's hand, and made an incision through the glyph.

Marcus's shoulders tensed and his wolf darkened his eyes, the only sign he didn't want to just sit there and take it.

A whisper of red mist, demonic magic, curled up from the glyph for a second then vanished. Mavis hissed a word I didn't recognize and set one of the coins on the bloody glyph.

More red mist curled from the glyph. It wrapped around the coin and my buzz tickled under my skin.

Mavis's gaze slid to mine, and she hissed three more words.

The red mist billowed and so did my buzz. She raised an eyebrow as if she could see the effect her magic had on me. Another hissed word, and the coin sank into Marcus's wrist, drawing a grunt of pain. Then the mist vanished and so did my buzz.

"The spell is clean," Kol said.

Marcus stood, rubbing the spot where the cut and glyph should have been, but there wasn't a hint of ink or blood or even a pink line where she'd cut him. Jacob sat on the stool next, and Mavis sank a coin into his wrist, watching me through veiled lashes as she cast the spell.

My buzz blazed a little hotter this time, and the wicked gleam in her eyes that had vanished when Gideon had revealed he was a JP agent returned. She sank a coin into Gideon's wrist, and my buzz flared stronger, reaching a post-nicotine level —at a time when the nicotine patches had actually worked. Her gleam melted into worry as she enspelled Kol and my buzz burned at pre-nicotine levels.

"Last one," she said to me.

I sat, set my hand on the table, and pushed the handcuff up to make sure it didn't get in the way of the spell. My pulse beat a little too fast. So far my divine light hadn't flooded my palms, and my buzz had vanished the second the demonic magic had, but I had no idea how I'd react with the spell sinking into my body.

Mavis's worry turned to outright fear when she saw the cuffs. "They're containing your magic."

"Yes." No point in lying. She could probably see or sense the spell on the cuffs, and quite frankly there weren't any other reasons for me to wear handcuffs, even if they were separated.

"They're afraid of you." She painted the glyph on my wrist, my buzz burning without a hint of red mist, and grabbed my fingers with a trembling hand. "They should be."

My buzz burned hotter, snapping under my skin, as Mavis picked up Kol's knife. All she'd done was paint the glyph on my wrist and my magic was already growing past the power of the containment cuffs.

"We're not afraid of her," Jacob said.

"Then you're idiots," Mavis said, and slid the tip of the knife across my wrist.

The blade was so sharp — or my buzz was so strong — I didn't feel anything. For a second I worried Mavis's fear had stopped her from actually cutting me, then blood welled on my wrist. My buzz roared under my skin, and a whisper of red mist curled up from the glyph.

Mavis picked a coin from the box, but it slipped from her trembling fingers and clattered onto the table. Her fear frosted my hand where she held me and curled up my arm. She hadn't reacted this way the last time I'd seen her, so whatever scared her had to have been previously concealed by the now-crumbling spell hiding my true essence. And a part of me feared it had everything to do with how I reacted to demonic magic... which I wasn't sure had anything to do with archangels.

Her grip on my hand tightened. She grabbed the coin, pressed it into my blood, and hissed the first word of her spell. Red mist swept up from the glyph, and my buzz surged.

I gasped, the force of the flare stealing my breath, and Kol tensed, his hands sliding to his hips and closer to the hilts of the daggers on his back. Out of everyone on the team, he was the only one who could see the demonic magic... unless it was powerful enough for them to see... which I doubted, because this wasn't nearly as powerful as Ibizual's magic.

"Kol?" Marcus growled.

"Still good," he said, but he didn't sound certain.

Mavis hissed the next word and the mist surged. My buzz exploded, snapping and slicing under my skin and seizing my muscles. I bit back a groan, and light radiated from my palm. Mavis's fear swept frost to my elbow.

She gasped out the third word and red mist burst from Mavis's necklaces and bracelets, something that hadn't happened with the guys. The magic raced down her arm and over mine, sinking into my skin. My buzz blazed and my divine light swelled to encompass my entire hand.

"What the hell?" Marcus barked.

Mavis gritted her teeth and hissed the final two words of the spell. Agony exploded in my wrist as the coin sank beneath my skin, dragging a stream of demonic magic from Mavis, not just from her jewelry, with it.

With a strangled scream, she jerked close, red mist pouring from her eyes and mouth. It rushed around her head, spinning into a vortex that whipped up her wild black locks, and ripped off the chain headpiece, tossing it across the room.

Fire and ice, my magic and Mavis's fear, roared through me. My divine light filled the room with stark white illumination. It devoured Mavis's magic, twisting it tight in my chest, threatening to rip me to pieces from the inside out.

Kol seized Mavis's hand, still gripping mine, and yanked us apart. Jacob grabbed me and hauled me off the stool into his arms, while Gideon and Marcus shoved in front of me, ready for a fight.

The stream of magic pouring from Mavis into me snapped. My buzz blazed, and for a second there was a supernova within me on the verge of eruption. Then cold blasted into me, and the power and buzz vanished, once again contained by the cuffs.

I sagged in Jacob's arms, shivering and gasping, while Mavis stared at me, her eyes wide, her face pale.

"What was that?" Gideon demanded.

Her gaze darted over my guys, ready to defend me, then returned to me. "I helped you."

"Did you?" Marcus growled.

"Remember I helped you," she begged.

Gideon glanced at Kol. "Is the concealment spell good?"

Kol stared at my wrist where the coin had sunk under my skin, his gaze slightly unfocused. "It's good."

"Great, let's go," Gideon said.

Marcus stiffened. "I want to know what the fuck just happened."

"We don't have the time." The muscles in Gideon's jaw flexed and he met Marcus's glare, daring him to argue about it. And as much as I was sure everyone wanted to know what had happened, we couldn't risk staying there and being found by the witches.

Marcus snarled and jerked away, heading to the door. "Fine."

Gideon turned to Mavis and set the marble with my divine light on the table. "You say anything about Essie, and I'll bring the full force of the JP down on you."

"The JP is the least of my worries." Mavis jerked back in her chair and stared at the marble like it was going to bite her. "I don't want it. I don't want her essence in my shop."

"Have it your way." Gideon grabbed the marble, not arguing with her that the magic in the marble didn't hold any of my essence. He shoved it in his pocket and headed to the door.

We followed him out, and while I managed to walk on my shaky legs, Jacob kept an arm around me to steady me.

"What the fuck?" Marcus growled as he stormed into the alley.

Gideon glanced up and down the alley, then turned a worried gaze to me. "Are you all right?"

"I'm a little shaky, but fine." And physically I was. Mentally my mind whirled. Once again my magic had sucked in demonic mist. I really needed to read up on archangels... hell, I needed to figure out who my parents were. I didn't even know if an angel's power was hereditary or not.

"We have to get moving," Jacob said. "If the witches have a tracking or scrying spell on us, they know where we are and we've already spent too much time here."

"And now that we've disappeared to their magic, they know why." Kol drew his daggers and rushed to the mouth of the alley where the SUV sat.

Jacob moved to pick me up, but I waved him off. "I'm okay."

He didn't look convinced and neither did Marcus, but they didn't argue with me.

We hurried to the SUV, quickly checked the street, and got in. Marcus pulled away from the curb and drove to the far side of the Quarter.

"I don't know if it's a good thing or not that they didn't come after us," Marcus said.

Gideon turned in the front passenger seat so he could see everyone, sweat from the heat in the SUV slicking his forehead. "They must be busy with whatever they're planning."

"Which we still need to figure out," Jacob said from his seat in the back.

Kol shifted beside me. He still had his long daggers drawn, and he still sat as far away from me as possible, but at least this time he hadn't made a point of sitting in the back with Jacob. I wasn't sure if that was an improvement or just because choosing where he sat hadn't been a priority when we'd hurried to the vehicle. "We're going to have to go back to City Hall." He raised his gaze to meet Gideon's. "Unless we know someone who can get us the security tapes."

Marcus barked a bitter laugh. "Assuming the witches haven't destroyed the tapes."

"I'd rather not risk more civilians," Jacob said, "especially human civilians."

"Neither would I, and I don't want to face these witches unarmed again." Gideon's pale gaze met mine, capturing my soul and stealing my breath for a second. I couldn't lose him. I couldn't lose any of them, not even Kol. But I would if we didn't figure out how to deal with these witches.

"Is there anyone else we can go to?" I asked.

"For weapons, yes," Jacob said. "But that still leaves us risking civilians by going to City Hall to follow the only lead we have."

"We have to go to Operations." The muscles in Gideon's jaw tightened. "I took a moment to talk with Bane about the temporal freeze. We can be within the radius of the spell for about five minutes, so if we work fast enough, we can raid the armory as well as use Operations' systems to access and copy City Hall's security footage. The freeze only affects organic material, so the computers and door locks aren't frozen by the spell."

"I'm fast," Jacob said, "but I doubt I can access Summer's computer *and* raid the armory before the spell captures me."

"We'll split into two teams." Gideon jerked his chin at Marcus, who put the SUV in gear.

"Essie's not going in, right?" Marcus asked.

"I'd rather she didn't," Gideon said. "But it isn't safe for any of us to be by ourselves, even with the concealment spell. Jacob and I will go to Summer's lab. The rest of you go to the armory."

Marcus turned onto the main street leading through the center of the Quarter. His nails extended into claws, his wolf fighting for control. Tension radiated from all my guys the closer we got to Operations. The light in Gideon's eyes blazed brighter and Jacob's hold on his vampiric intensity started to slip. By the time Marcus parked in front of Operations, their combined power filled the SUV with a physical, crushing weight.

Kol and I staggered out of the vehicle, while Marcus, Gideon, and Jacob stormed out, their power rolling off them in a great wave.

"Jeez, guys," Kol said. "She's not helpless." His gaze jumped to me for a second, the look in his eyes saying there wasn't anything helpless about me. Then he yanked his attention back to Operations' closed garage door.

Jacob squeezed his eyes shut, and the weight of his power eased. "I know you're not helpless," he said to me. "I just—"

"It's the brand," Gideon said, his voice strained.

"The soul bonds," Marcus corrected. "I feel it, too, and I don't have a brand. You've almost died twice today. My wolf is still losing his shit over that."

I wanted to argue with him, point out that they'd almost died twice today, too, but my power was unpredictable and dangerous, even with the cuffs on. If something were to go wrong right now, odds are I'd be in the middle of it.

"It's still safer for her to go with you to the armory." Gideon pulled out his phone. "Set a timer for five minutes. Jacob, let's use the door closer to Summer's lab."

He and Jacob strode around to the other side of the building, while Marcus pulled out his phone and set a timer as well.

I didn't know the layout of Operations well, but given that Marcus and Kol didn't suggest entering through another door, the garage was the closest entrance to the basement stairs.

Marcus unlocked the heavy metal security door beside the big garage door with his thumbprint and we hurried inside. An invisible weight hit me halfway to the glass door leading into the building. It dragged at my limbs and thoughts, as if I were moving and thinking in molasses.

"How didn't we notice this when we were first fighting the witches?" Marcus gasped, heaving the door open and hurrying into the hall.

"The spell must have taken time to fully form." Kol leaned forward as if he were running into a wind storm.

I struggled to keep a quick pace as my buzz whispered under my skin with the promise of overwhelming fire and power. The hall had never seemed so long before, even during the times I'd been seriously injured and was lying on a gurney headed to triage.

We rounded the corner, and Marcus led us past the elevator and down the few steps into the cafeteria. A guy in dusty overalls stood on the scaffolding at the large decorative rock wall that was being rebuilt after the fight with the archnephilim, while another guy bent over a pallet of small plants. A few feet away, Cassey, one of the doctors who worked with Amiah, half stood and half squatted over a chair, as if she'd been in the middle of standing or sitting when the spell had hit. Another woman in scrubs sat across from her, a mug raised to her lips. Behind them, the squat man who'd served me lunch the day before yesterday held a lid over a tray of food, the steam frozen in the air, curled around his hand.

I shivered. If Sebastian hadn't cast that protection spell, that would have been us.

If we didn't hurry, that *would* be us.

Except each step grew harder and harder, and by the time we took the stairs down to the basement, I was sweating and gasping for breath, my buzz burning hotter.

I staggered around the corner and past the wide wooden table and couch just outside the elevator doors. The fluorescent lights hanging from the ceiling flickered on, filling the cold space with harsh white light, our movement tripping the motion sensor. Beyond the table stood the archives with row upon row of shelves filled with books, while opposite us was the locked armory door.

Marcus pressed his thumb to the keypad and lurched to the locker just inside the door.

"Sixty seconds, no more," he said. "We need time to get back up those stairs."

He tried to toss a duffle bag to Kol, but couldn't move his arm fast enough, and it fell to the floor halfway between them. I grabbed it and another one from Marcus and met Kol at a locker at the back of the narrow room.

Inside the locker were sheathed bladed weapons of all shapes and sizes. Kol dropped in three swords — thankfully one short enough for me... not that I had any skill in using it — and a dozen knives and daggers of varying lengths. I turned to the shelf beside him and emptied the ones with boxes of 9mm and 5.56mm rounds for the sidearms and M4 into my bag, not wasting time checking to see if any of them were the special enspelled ammunition or not.

"Thirty seconds, then we leave," Marcus gasped.

I heaved around to the sidearms and tossed in a few Glocks and a couple Berettas — since those were Jacob's weapon of choice — then grabbed two M4s from the rack.

"Time."

I wrenched against the spell and my buzz flared. It stole my breath and made my knees give out. Kol reached for me as I fell, but wasn't fast enough to catch me. My knees hit the concrete hard even though I was falling in slow motion.

"Shit, Essie." Marcus took a staggering step toward me.

"I'm fine." I grabbed the narrow work table in the middle of the room and hauled myself to my feet. My muscles screamed with the effort to rise against the spell. God, how the hell were we going to climb the stairs?

Kol groaned and grabbed my arm, helping me steady myself. We staggered out of the armory and back to the plain concrete stairwell. My chest burned, each breath an agony as my lungs fought to move against the spell. Power crackled under my skin, my magic responding to the magic of the spell just like it had when Mavis had cast the concealment spell or when the witches had activated their glyphs, although thankfully not nearly as painfully.

"We need to move faster," Marcus growled, reaching the first floor landing and heaving open the security door.

"Trying," Kol gasped.

I didn't bother saying anything. I barely had enough breath to move, let alone speak. We still had to make it out of the cafeteria and down the hall, and I had no idea how I'd manage it. The spell's pressure kept growing. Each step, each breath, hell, each blink of my eyes, had become an agonizing effort.

Gritting my teeth, I fought my way up the few steps out of the cafeteria, past the elevator, and back into the God-awfully long hall. Marcus's wolf had risen to just under his skin, darkening his eyes, elongating his canines, and even starting to change the shape of his jaw. His claws had fully formed and fur darkened the backs of his hands.

We reached triage's frosted-glass door. Almost there. I could hold out for just a little longer. Please, God. I just needed a little more strength.

My body burned, the agony from my muscles stronger than the burn of my buzz. A part of me hoped my buzz would flare and I'd magically have the strength to fight the final few feet through the spell, but I had no idea if that was what would happen or not.

We reached the end of the hall and the door to the garage. Dark specks and brilliant flashes danced across my vision. I couldn't catch my breath, couldn't breathe deeply enough. I took another step forward, my leg refused to hold me, and I went down again.

Kol grabbed the back of my shirt, not bothering to help me stand, and dragged me. The darkness swarming my vision thickened. Marcus turned back and grabbed my arm and they ripped me out of the spell.

The pressure vanished, but lightning roared through my mating brands and strength swept out of me into Gideon and Jacob. Ice clenched in my chest and every cell in my body screamed to save them, protect them, get them the hell out of there.

I gasped and the pull of strength to Gideon and Jacob grew stronger, except the desperate screaming need to save them that I'd expected when they'd been fatally wounded didn't overwhelm me. They weren't in dire need, but they were exhausted and low on strength.

I tried to stand, feeling like I should do something, but not sure what. Except my muscles were too weak and my body wouldn't obey my commands. All I could do was sit there and fight to draw breath. Which made me want to scream. My mates, even if they weren't dying, still needed help. I was supposed to be able to help them, supposed to be just as powerful and competent as them. I was tired of being useless, tired of my buzz and fear controlling me, and tired of being the weak link.

My buzz flared and light blazed in my palms, defying the containment cuffs and reminding me that I *was* as powerful as them, more so, dangerously so.

I focused on my magic, drawing it into me, willing it to give me the strength to stand, march around to the door where Gideon and Jacob had entered, and find them, wherever they were. I climbed to my feet, took an unsteady step, and my legs promptly gave out.

"Jeez, just take a moment," Marcus said.

Gideon's lightning crackled into Jacob's brand and the pull of strength swept over me. The garage darkened and spun, and my worry deepened. They might not be dying, but they were still in trouble. If they didn't get out soon, they were going to be trapped.

I tried to stand again, unable to resist the need to protect them, but Kol grabbed me and pulled me back down. "Just stay put. You're going to hurt yourself."

I jerked against his grip but didn't have enough strength to pull free. "They're still in there. I have to help them."

"You can't even walk. Getting caught in the spell won't help," Marcus growled at me.

The pull of strength grew and the black specks now completely devoured my vision. "Please, Marcus. They're pulling strength from the brand. They're in trouble. Maybe they're in the doorway and all we have to do is yank them free." But I knew Marcus was right. Gideon and Jacob weren't dying and no matter how much power I had, it wasn't enough to help me stand, let alone walk around the building.

The lightning crackling up Gideon's brand into Jacob's snapped, an agonizing slice, then the pull of strength vanished, the change so sudden it made me gasp.

They were out. Thank God, they were out. I sagged against Kol, my breath heavy as if I'd just pulled free of the spell again.

"I think they're free," Kol said, sitting me forward and putting distance between us that made me ache. "I'm mostly recovered. I'll go check on them."

Marcus pulled a small black box from his duffle bag and took out an ear piece. "Take this and let me know when they can walk."

Kol put the com in his ear and staggered out of the garage, while Marcus inserted another one into his ear and crawled to my side. He wrapped his arms around me, and I melted into his embrace. I ached for him and Jacob right now almost as much as I ached for Gideon... and Kol, but my bonds with them were secure and it was easy to just savor Marcus's warmth and strength.

"You're allowed to ask for help, you know," he said.

"I feel like all I do is ask for help." I felt like I'd run a marathon uphill and through water. Every muscle burned and trembled and I couldn't catch my breath. But I also felt as if my world had blown up and I didn't know what I was doing or where I was going, or hell, even who I really was. "I'm a mess right now."

Marcus snorted. "But you're my mess, and once we deal with the witches we'll have time to figure things out."

Except there was a lot to figure out and it seemed like every time we dealt with one thing, something else happened.

I wasn't sure how long I sat there with Marcus just holding me. The exhaustion from the temporal freeze spell eased, but my thoughts continued to whirl. And really, they'd been whirling since I'd fallen from City Hall's roof and my wings had appeared.

Kol told Marcus he, Gideon, and Jacob were on their way to the SUV, so Marcus and I stood, staggered the rest of the way out of the garage, and climbed inside the vehicle to wait for them.

My pulse beat faster as I sat there. Logically I knew they were okay. They weren't pulling strength from the brand, Kol had said they were out of the spell, and yet a part of me was still holding its breath, waiting to see them.

Then they rounded the corner, still gasping and trembling, but safe.

The pressure in my chest released.

They were all safe.

"Let's get back to Bane's and figure out what we're going to do," Gideon said as he got into the front passenger seat.

Jacob got in the back and Kol joined him. Swell.

We returned to Sebastian's and collapsed on his couches. Kol sat on the couch across from me — as far away from me as possible while still staying in the conversation area — while Marcus and Jacob squished in on either side of me. With a groan, Gideon settled in beside Kol and set a USB key on the coffee table, then turned to Marcus.

"What did you get?" he asked, jerking his chin to our duffle bags sitting on the floor a few feet from the couch.

"Coms, containment cuffs, enspelled zip ties," Marcus said, "and various holsters and belts."

"A handful of sidearms, two M4s, some ammunition, and a variety of blades," Kol finished.

Jacob turned on one of the two laptops they'd taken from Operations and inserted the USB key. "This could take a while."

"And even if we do figure out what they're doing, we still have no way to stop them," Marcus said.

"We just have to hope Bane can find us an area containment master ward in time." Gideon rubbed his face.

"Will that be enough?" I wasn't going to go through the pain of feeling them die again. Ever. Except with their job, I wasn't ever going to be able to guarantee their safety.

And God damn it, there wasn't anything I could do to help. Marcus might have said I wasn't useless, that even if I couldn't ever go into the field again I'd still be more than just away to keep them alive, but I'd never felt more useless in my life. If my emotions got out of control or someone used powerful magic, my magic blazed through the containment cuffs and endangered everyone.

Pointing me in the right direction and using my power like a cannon was only useful in certain situations. If the witches' plan involved a populated area, then that was too dangerous. I wasn't going to risk hurting bystanders, be they super or human... which I wasn't anymore... had never been.

I shoved that thought back and stood. "I'm going to help Bane look for answers for... whatever it is he's looking for." My problem, the witches' problem, I didn't care. I just couldn't sit there and do nothing.

"Get something to eat first," Gideon said. "We missed breakfast."

"And you missed dinner yesterday." Jacob frowned. "And lunch."

Marcus's eyes narrowed. "When was the last time you ate?"

I had no idea. A lot had happened in the last couple of days. If I really thought about it...

"I got healing in the hospital after the zip OD." As well as healing after feeding Jacob for the second time that day. That had to be why I wasn't starving now.

"Come on." Marcus stood and headed to the kitchen. "Let's see if Bane has more than orange juice in his fridge."

Sebastian's kitchen was as white and shiny as his living room, with white marble counters, stainless steel appliances, and decorative tin ceiling tiles that reflected the light of yet another crystal chandelier.

"He certainly has a specific style," Marcus said, heading straight to the fridge.

"I feel like I'm in a snow globe. A really expensive snow globe."

"At least his fridge is stocked. How about an omelet?" He set a carton of eggs on the counter, and pulled a red pepper and half a dozen stalks of green onion from the crisper, not waiting for me to answer.

"What if I said no?" I headed to the coffee machine, a complicated, single-serve appliance that made specialty coffees with the press of a button.

"You'd still get an omelet. It's the only thing I can cook." He flashed me a tired smile, and my heart squeezed.

It hadn't just been a stressful couple of days for me. Sure, I'd ODed on zip, had a building fall on me, fell sixteen stories then was arrested, but Marcus had dealt with that, too.

"When was the last time *you* ate or slept?" I checked the coffee machine's reservoir and hopper. Already filled with water and beans.

He snorted and rolled his eyes at me as he rummaged in the cupboard beside the stove and pulled out a cast iron frying pan. "You would ask that."

"What?" I opened the cupboard above the machine in search of mugs.

"You just had your life turned upside down and you're asking me how I'm doing?" He grabbed my hand and pulled me into a firm embrace. "You're allowed to think about yourself for a minute."

I stiffened in his arms, my throat suddenly tight, my eyes burning with tears. "If I think about myself, I'm going to start crying again, and I'm tired of crying."

"We already know you're tough." He rubbed gentle circles on my back. "Crying won't make you look weak."

"It's not that, it's—" A tear rolled down my cheek. "All my life I was told no one would understand. I was sure no one would. I've seen all the videos. Michael's nephilim were monsters. I thought I was a monster."

I hadn't realized how alone and scared that had made me. I thought I'd compartmentalized it and was able to carry on as if everything was normal. It had been hanging over me all of my life. I was used to it. But just like I'd spent all those years pretending my supernatural nature didn't exist, I'd also pretended my fear didn't, either.

Marcus's grip tightened. "Anyone who's spent more than a minute with you knows you're not a monster. Even if you were a nephilim, you're nothing like them."

"Cassius didn't think so."

"Cassius is an idiot."

Except I couldn't fool myself and think anything would get easier now that my eyes glowed and my essence still didn't say I was an angel. If I was smart, I'd find a way to respell or replace Mavis's contacts and pretend I was—

What? I had no idea. If my essence didn't say I was human, I couldn't pretend to be a human. Maybe I could get away with pretending to be a half demon. That would at least be easier for the world to accept.

Sure, my guys had stood by me, but that was only because of our soul bonds. I didn't have a bond with Kol and he'd tried to kill me. "Cassius reacted like a lot of people would, like Kol did."

"Kol's experience with Michael's nephilim was extreme." Marcus pressed his lips to the top of my head. "I don't know the details, but I heard he'd spent a long time in self-isolation after Gideon and Jacob rescued him. Kind of like you."

"I wasn't isolated."

"Sure you were." He captured my cheeks with his hands and tipped my head up to look me in the eyes. "That's why you never really socialized or became friends with the other officers when you were off duty, or why you never told me anything about yourself. I bet that didn't change in the four and a half years we've been apart." His lips quirked in a smile. "Hell, you didn't have a plant. Still don't."

"I've been meaning to get one in my new place." And by new I meant the one I'd rented two years ago, with the amazing skylight and roof access... for the wings I hadn't realized I had.

"It all makes sense now, why you fought so hard to stay away from the supernatural world, why every time I mentioned it you got a terrified look in your eyes." He brushed his lips against mine, a tender whisper of a kiss. "You're not a monster. You don't have to run anymore. You're not alone."

Which was something I still couldn't wrap my mind around. Marcus hadn't even thought twice about staying with me. Even believing I was a monster, all my guys had fought to protect me.

Except Kol.

Which only made me more heartbroken for the horror he'd experienced at Michael's hands.

Marcus turned back to making our omelets. "So if you were going to buy a plant... what would it be?"

"Are you trying to figure out what to buy me?" I reopened the cupboard above the coffee machine, grabbed a mug, and set it in the machine.

"Maybe. Although we're going to have to figure out where to put it. You can't stay in your room at Operations forever, and there isn't enough room for all of us in any of our apartments." He opened the cupboard in front of him, frowned, and moved to the next one.

My thoughts jumped to all of us trying to squeeze onto Marcus's bed. Hell, even Jacob's, which was huge, wasn't designed for five... er, four people. And would all of them be interested in that? Sure, Marcus had joined me and Jacob in bed, but that had to have been an extenuating, amazing, sexy, satisfying circumstance.

Marcus chuckled, and I jerked my attention back to him. His piercing green eyes lit up with a smile wicked enough to compete with Kol's. "Wow, that's a look. What are *you* thinking?"

Heat swept over my cheeks. "Nothing."

He pulled out two plates, slid the first omelet onto one of them, and held it out to me. "That didn't look like nothing."

"I... ah..." The memory of being pressed between his and Jacob's hard bodies flashed through me, flooding my face with more heat. I grabbed the plate and started pulling open drawers looking for cutlery.

"She was thinking about sex," Kol said, striding into the kitchen and heading straight to the coffee machine.

Marcus snorted. "Already figured that out from the blush. Need another top-up? I'm sure if I ask nicely, Essie and I could accommodate you." He cracked eggs in the pan to make another omelet.

Kol's gaze jumped to mine. The hellfire in his eyes smoldered, bright red pricks in his dark eyes, and heated desire slid across my senses. My pulse tripped at the memory of his magic pouring into me, bone-melting liquid yearning. Need swelled low within me. I craved more of his magic, of him, and not just on a human-craving-an-incubus level, but deeper. Soul deep.

ESSIE

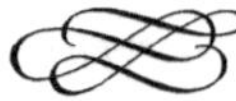

My breath picked up, and everything within me begged to hold him, kiss him, tell him I'd give my life to protect him. He was family. He belonged. I didn't care if he was a soul mate or not. I didn't want to give him up, and I didn't want him to give up the team. It'd been clear from the tour he'd given me of the Quarter the other day that the team meant everything to him. I couldn't take that away from him.

He blinked, releasing my soul for a second, then recaptured me again. The hellfire burned brighter, but now as well as hunger, I could see exhaustion in his eyes. I didn't know how much sexual energy he needed to properly heal, but it didn't look like he'd gotten enough.

"I'll finish breakfast and see how Jacob is doing. Pretty sure he didn't get enough, either."

"Well, that backfired." Marcus rolled his eyes at me. "I was trying to get you back into my bed, but there you go, thinking about what's best for all your mates again."

"Who said it has to be just me and Jacob?" I asked.

Oh, man. Did I just say that?

Ah, yup. And I'd meant it. When we had a moment, I was going to need a frank conversation with my guys about what I wanted and what they wanted.

"Well, then," Marcus said, his voice husky, indicating the threesome with Jacob wasn't a one-shot deal for him.

The hellfire fully consumed Kol's eyes and he jerked his attention to the counter beside me. "Don't bother," he said, his tone flat as if he'd just remembered who he was talking to. "I'm fine."

He pushed past me, set the first coffee on the counter, and put a new mug in the machine. Even with the cuffs suppressing my empathy, the emotional chill froze all the way to my heart. God, I just wanted to fix this, help him, help all of them.

Except right now the best way I could help Kol was to give him space. No matter how much that hurt. Jeez. Even if taking no action was the best action, it still drove me crazy.

"I'll go see if I can help Sebastian."

Marcus gave me a sad smile. He might not know exactly how I felt about Kol, but he knew everyone on the team was dear to me. Funny how everyone thought Marcus with his possessive wolf was going to be a problem, and he'd been the first to fully embrace all of me.

I found a fork and hurried out of the kitchen.

Gideon was gone but Jacob still sat on the couch, working on the laptop. He looked a little tired, but not nearly as bad as he'd been the last couple of days. A pressure that I hadn't realized had been in my chest eased. The witches might still be more powerful than us, but at least the next time we wouldn't be fighting with serious injuries.

"Where's Gideon?" I didn't need to talk to him, just wanted to see him and reassure myself he was okay, or as okay as he could get with his brother slowly dying, three powerful glyph witches threatening the city, and — if he felt like me, which I was getting the impression he was — the aching urge to solidify our bond.

"He stepped into one of the other rooms to talk to head office, trying to get an ETA on backup." Jacob jerked his chin to a second closed laptop on the coffee table. "But he'll be back in a minute if you want to talk with him."

"I'm fine."

"Okay." His eyes narrowed. "You should eat more than that."

"This is round one. I might as well eat and read at the same time."

"So long as it *is* round one." He released some of his vampiric intensity, making me shiver with desire.

I forced myself to head to the hall before I climbed into his lap and asked him to satisfy me again. We needed to solve problems. My desire could wait, but damn, it was difficult to resist the pull of our bond. It was still so new. All of my bonds were, and all I wanted was to keep them close and strengthen our connection.

I knocked on the first door in the hall and opened it without waiting for a reply.

Sebastian lounged on a couch, a massive book in his lap with more books piled around him. My divine light still radiated from his eyes, although no longer rolling down his cheeks like shimmering tears. Amiah sat behind a desk near the back, framed by a tall, slightly purple window. She was also reading and also surrounded by books. A fireplace — not in use since it was so damned hot out and Sebastian had his air conditioner running — sat against the right-hand wall and, along with the window, was the only other break in the wall-to-wall floor-to-ceiling bookshelves. Sebastian even had a floor-to-ceiling narrow ladder on a track to access the top shelves.

The room smelled of wood smoke and old leather. A heavy rug covered most of the marble floor, and even though the color scheme was still wintery, it felt comfortable and warm. I hadn't thought of Sebastian as a bookworm, but the room made me wonder if buying and selling hard-to-find magical items satisfied a personal need as well as a financial one.

Sebastian glanced up from his book. "Who's making omelets?"

"Marcus."

Amiah's shoulders stiffened.

"Great. I'm starving." He stood and set his book on his seat, leaving it open to the page he'd been reading. "If you're here to help, start on the pile on the floor by the desk. You're looking for anything that might explain what kind of magical poison is killing Cassius."

He left and Amiah raised a chilly glare at me.

I hadn't expected a warm welcome, but this was frigid.

Just great.

Well, no way was I going to let her cold-shoulder me out of the room, especially since this was the only way I could be useful at the moment.

I grabbed the book at the top of the closest pile. It was big and thick, with a swirling design etched in the leather cover on the front and back, and the edges of the pages were ragged, as if the paper had been handmade.

Power whispered across my senses, not strong enough to make my buzz flare, but enough to remind me that it was still there, contained by the handcuffs. Whatever this book was, it felt old and powerful, and ever so slightly alive.

I fought a shiver, shifted to sit on the floor with the book beside me but not touching me, and balanced my plate in my lap. "Anything specific I should be looking for? Certain words? Symptoms?"

Amiah continued to glare at me, and a heaviness joined the ice in her eyes. I had no idea what that meant, and, funnily enough, was once again wishing I had access to my weird empathy. Although with my luck, the heaviness, whatever it was, would still probably manifest as cold, and then I'd just be cold and slightly tired.

"Fine." I opened the book, ignoring another whisper of magic. The title page was handwritten in faded black ink in big flowing letters, and the paper was thick and stained with age. *Theories on Magical Healing.* That sounded dry.

I turned to the table of contents — a little surprised that a handwritten book would have a table of contents — and ate some of my omelet, which was really good. Although that could have been because I was starving.

Amiah shifted in her chair, her lips pressed tight, the tension in her shoulders growing to encompass her torso.

According to the book, angels weren't the only ones with healing magic. Which surprised me more than the book having a table of contents, since I'd never heard of any other super with the ability to heal others. Yes, Kol had helped me twice now by giving me some of the magic that sustained him, but I hadn't thought of that as healing. Except there it was, chapter fifteen, *Succubi and Incubi Energy Conveyance.*

When I'd been shot and dying, none of the guys had known Kol could help me that way, and Kol had said incubi didn't like anyone knowing that they could. Which only added to the evidence that this book was old and rare.

I scanned the rest of the table of contents. While I was curious to know more about how Kol could just give his life energy to me, I doubted it would help us figure out what kind of poison was killing Cassius or how to save him.

The light in Amiah's eyes grew and her hands curled into fists. Jeez, just sitting in the same room with me made her angry.

I fought to focus my attention on the book and not the rising tension. Aside from the chapter on incubi healing, there were a dozen chapters on angels, two on fae, and one on humans. I flipped to the human chapter. Maybe Amiah and Priam couldn't identify the poison because it wasn't angelic. Since the glyph witches were human, that seemed like the best chapter to start with. But the first few pages were exactly what the book's title claimed, theories on if it was even possible for humans to possess healing magic.

I was barely one book in, but my gut said I was looking for the wrong thing. I shouldn't be searching for healing, but trying to identify the type of magic used to poison Cassius. Glyph witches had a bit of demon blood somewhere in their family tree, either biologically or because of a demon-deal they or an ancestor had made for their power. They had the ability to permanently bind spells in glyphs that had been etched or drawn onto an object or inked onto their bodies and then activate the spells with their magic.

The spiders that had poisoned Cassius had been summoned by a glyph, which meant they had to have been some kind of spell. And that was as far as my magical knowledge went.

I took another bite of my omelet. Sebastian hadn't returned, so I couldn't ask him about spells. What were the odds that Amiah would actually talk to me? Probably zero. She was radiating so much tension, it made me squirm.

Best to go find Sebastian or one of my guys. I moved to stand, and Amiah's icy gaze captured mine.

"The mating brand is supposed to be sacred."

This again? Yeah, I got it. I wasn't worthy, I'd never be worthy, and I was ruining Marcus's life. "You're just going to have to get used to the idea that I'm branded and move on. It's not like I can get rid of them." Which I never would. Funny how just a few weeks ago that was all I wanted. Now the idea of losing my bonds made my heart pound.

"That's what's so terrifying," Amiah said, the heaviness in her gaze shifting, revealing her struggle to contain her fear. "You can't get rid of it. Your fate is controlled by someone else."

"None of the guys control me." Although I could see her point, and given how in control Amiah always was, losing any kind of control probably terrified her. Did little angel girls and boys dream of soul mates just like some little human girls and boys? Had Amiah? Angelkind had the possibility of a rare magical bond, making that dream of destined true love all the more possible. And now she'd seen the truth. An angelic mating brand wasn't as wonderful as it had been made out to be.

"They don't mean to control you, but they do. I hadn't realized how consuming the bond was." Her hands shook, and she clenched them tighter. "You just dropped to the floor the moment they were in danger. Helpless."

"They have to be mortally wounded for that to happen." Something I prayed would never happen again.

"You couldn't stand. You couldn't breathe." A shudder swept over her. "I've treated the angel half of a broken angel-human bond and it was difficult, but that—" Light flared from her eyes. "How could anyone ever think that was beautiful and sacred?"

"That's only one part of it." I didn't know why I was bothering to defend my situation with Amiah, but I just couldn't seem to help myself. My connection with my guys, all my guys, *was* beautiful and sacred. It was also terrifying and dangerous and amazing and nothing I could have ever imagined.

"How can you just accept the control the brands have on you?"

"I don't know. I don't think about it as being controlled. I just know I belong with them." I couldn't fight it if I wanted to. In fact, Gideon and I had fought our bond and that had been a disaster. I still felt broken, my soul cracked in a million pieces because we hadn't fully solidified our bond.

"You're independent to a fault. You'll recklessly do what you think is right." She huffed a bitter laugh. "Just like a lot of angels."

"Except I can't seem to follow the rules." Which, for a second, made me wonder if I really was all angel. Although Gideon and Cassius had demonstrated that when their emotions were strong, the rules didn't matter.

"Not all of us follow the rules to the letter like most humans believe. Yes, we need order, although some of us more than others." She spread her hands over the desk with the messy pile of books. Her office had been messy as well, completely opposite to Gideon's organized-within-an-inch-of-its-life space. "But almost all of us need justice. However we justify it. Michael thought ridding the world of humans and supers was justice for the destruction you'd wrought on the world."

"Any way you look at it, taking billions of lives isn't justice."

"Billions of lives that willfully hurt this planet."

"It sounds like you agreed with Michael."

"Never." The fearful hardness in Amiah's eyes bled into pain. "My magic is the gift of life. I couldn't have watched your slaughter from the Realm of Celestial Light if I'd wanted to. If Michael had attacked the

Realm of Celestial Darkness, I would have gone to help." She ran her hands over the open pages in front of her. "But I at least get to choose how and when. The brand gives you no choice."

Except even if the brand did give me a choice, I'd choose my guys every time.

Someone screamed and the door flew open, revealing a wide-eyed Priam in the doorway. "Amiah. I need help. It's Cassius."

Priam rushed back into the hall, and Amiah bolted from her seat. She ran into the room across from Sebastian's office, not bothering to shut the doors. I hurried after her, but froze at the sight of Cassius on the bed.

Black veins bulged on his neck and arms and he panted as if he couldn't catch his breath. His back arched off the mattress and he screamed, a strangled cry of agony. Priam pressed his palms to Cassius's temples. Light, not the brilliance of divine light, but a gentle healing glow, radiated from his hands, but with another scream, Cassius's back arched again.

Amiah dropped onto the bed beside him and pressed her hands over his heart. The glow from her hands wasn't as strong as Priam's, but I doubted that was because he was more powerful. Amiah had spent all of her magic saving my guys, and she'd barely recovered enough to help Cassius.

Gideon hurried into the room. A whisper of cold swept around me, his fear so strong it defied the containment cuffs. He hugged himself, staying back in case Amiah or Priam needed to move, but Sebastian, who entered next, didn't hesitate. He shoved past me and slapped his hand against his shoulder. The activated glyph lit up under his shirt, more brilliant than I'd ever seen any of his other glyphs glow.

"Both of you let go for a second," he said.

Amiah and Priam pulled away, and Sebastian pressed his hands over Cassius's heart.

Cassius gasped and his body went limp.

Amiah put her hands back on Cassius, but she stared at Sebastian. "What did you do?"

"Sleep spell." Sebastian shuddered and a weak divine light tear rolled down his cheek. "Hopefully with Esther's extra juice, it'll buy you and Priam more time."

Marcus, Jacob, and Kol crowded into the room behind Gideon.

"Have you found anything?" Gideon asked, his gaze locked on his brother, asleep but still gasping quick shallow breaths.

"Not yet," Sebastian said.

Priam closed his eyes and the light from his hands billowed. "It's getting harder to keep him stable. We're running out of time."

"When did the black veins show up?" Jacob asked. "It looks like blood poisoning, but I know it can't be because he isn't a vampire."

"Could it be something like that, though?" I asked. There had to be a way to figure out what this was and stop it. I couldn't accept that there wasn't anything we could do to save him. Cassius might not have treated me well, but he didn't deserve to die.

"There are a number of spells that behave in a similar manner, but I've searched for them in his body," Sebastian said. "Even with your extra power, I can't identify the poison."

"Do you have to know what it is?" Marcus asked. "Can't you just pull it out?"

"No," Amiah said, her voice soft. "It's in his essence. If we pull it out without dispelling it, we'll end up taking his essence with it."

And if too much of a super's essence was taken, he'd die.

The muscles in Gideon's jaw flexed. "Do what you can. Jacob, do you still need Marcus's and Kol's help reviewing the security footage?"

Jacob glanced at Cassius, his expression pained at the choice he had to make. If he said yes, then some of us weren't searching for a way to save Cassius. If he said no, then the witches could succeed and who knew how many lives could be in danger.

The glow in Gideon's eyes dimmed for a second, and he drew in a ragged breath. "Marcus and Kol, keep helping Jacob," he said, taking Jacob's hesitation as an affirmative. "I'll help Bane."

Marcus frowned. "Gideon—"

"We can't endanger the lives in this city. Not even for Cassius."

Gideon pushed past us and strode into Sebastian's office, his eyes, his body, everything about him hard, except his expression. That was tight with fear and desperation.

I hurried after him. "Hey."

His back stiffened and he fisted his hands. "Don't tell me to get everyone on saving my brother. We're JP agents, we have a job to do, and if you ask, I'll do it."

"I wouldn't ask that." I drew close, needing to touch him, comfort him, but knowing if I did the bond would overwhelm me.

"Marcus would," he said.

"Of course he would. His first loyalty is to the ones he loves." He'd shown me that time and again. "He'd sacrifice anything and everyone for them."

"Just like you would," Gideon said.

"I couldn't sacrifice anyone." Not anyone from Union City and certainly not any of my guys. "The only thing I have to offer is myself." And that wasn't an option, because my life was entwined with my guys.

"Don't you dare." Gideon turned on me and grabbed my shoulders, his grip so hard his fingers dug painfully into my biceps. Terror filled his eyes and frost swept over the backs of my hands. "Don't you do that to Jacob or Marcus."

His power crackled through our brand, little bites of electricity, so similar to my buzz and yet so different. It sizzled through my nerves, filling me with strength and yearning.

"Stop putting yourself in danger," he begged. His gaze dipped to my lips, and my pulse picked up.

I had to step back, pull out of his hold before I lost control, but the draw to be with him surged and my nerves thrummed with desire.

"Stop giving more than you have," he said, his voice breaking with need.

I gritted my teeth. "I'm not helpless."

"No, I am." His fingers tangled in my hair, his pupils dilated, and he shook, his struggle to control himself making his angel glow flare. "I need you, Essie. Our bond is too fragile, and I feel like I'm going to fall apart. I can't lose you, I can't see you hurt. I thought I could, thought I could resist the bond a little bit longer, but—" His chest heaved with rapid breaths and the tendons in his neck flexed. "I can't do it. There's just too much. Too many hard choices. Save our bond, risk the city. Save my brother, risk the city. I need to do all of it, but I can't."

His churning emotions sliced through the containment cuffs, and our bond squeezed my chest and tightened my throat.

I tried to focus on anything other than the need to ease the pressure of our bond, because for both of us the lives of others came first. They always did. Gideon would never forgive himself— hell, *I'd* never forgive myself if we let the bond take over and people died. Even just for a quickie. Because it wouldn't be quick. If I released my hold, I'd want all of him, completely. I knew in my heart that for our first time I'd lose myself in him, join with him, body, essence, and soul, and not care about anything else. We couldn't afford to get caught up in that, not when every minute might count.

"Our bond will survive," I said, as the bond within me screamed to draw closer, kiss him, shove him onto Sebastian's couch and take him.

More of his power crackled through his brand, and he tipped his forehead against mine, his breath ragged, desperate gasps. Warmth radiated around my hand —not with the burn of my divine light just my magical strength — and I pressed my palm over his heart and sent a trickle of power into him. He needed it more than I did. I had Jacob and Marcus helping me resist the bond. He didn't have anyone.

A moan escaped his lips and his breath feathered across my face.

God, kiss me. Please.

No. Focus.

We had to deal with the immediate issues first.

"Let's save your brother," I forced out, really wanting to say *take my clothes off*.

"You can take a few minutes in the guestroom next door," Sebastian said behind me.

"That's the problem." Gideon jerked back, releasing me and squaring his shoulders with a force of will that hurt to watch. "I resisted the bond for too long."

"I thought the brand was all that wonderful sacred angel crap." Sebastian picked up the book he'd set on his couch and sat. "Why would you resist it? Especially since resisting a soul bond like that is akin to losing your mate. It'll drive you crazy or kill you."

"Essie was in love with Marcus first." Gideon's angel glow flared and he took two more steps back, putting more distance between us.

"Ah," Sebastian said, as if that explained everything. And in a way it probably did. No one thought it was possible for Marcus to accept me with other mates, since wolves didn't share well with others.

"Okay." I shoved that thought aside and fought the urge to draw close to Gideon again. "You said you looked for spells in Cassius. Is there a type of magic you're not familiar with?"

"There always is. There are two basic types, light and dark, but there are variations, different ways of manipulating the magic, within both the light and dark spheres. So it's possible the spell on Cassius is in one of the variations I'm not as familiar with, or a whole new variation." His gaze grew unfocused and he frowned. "Some witches can create their own way of casting... And these witches have access to an outside power source, like they'd been saving their power up in a reservoir... but it feels more powerful than that and the spell on Cassius doesn't feel like a regular spell..."

He set his book back on the couch, pulled his ladder in front of the door, and grabbed a thin book from the top shelf.

"What are you thinking?" Gideon asked, his gaze locked on Sebastian.

"That I, of all people, should have looked past the fact that those women were glyph witches."

"But they're witches, aren't they?" I'd felt it every time they'd activated one of their glyphs.

"And so am I. My glyphs are real," Sebastian said, hopping down from the ladder and leaning against it. "I keep power stored in them, but I can also channel the raw light magic that comes from the Realm of Faerie and shape it to my will without burning up."

"Now it makes sense." Gideon's attention, filled with need, flickered to me for a second then jerked back to Sebastian. "You didn't just use your fae essence to teleport us."

"No matter how good Amiah is, I'd still be unconscious if I had. That would have drained me too deeply."

"And that means?" I asked.

"Most fae cast spells using their own magical essence." Sebastian pointed to his glowing skin. "Some supers like angels and witches have their own internal battery to power their magic, while others, like fae and vampires, use the magic in their essence. All of which, essence and battery, slowly refill through a passive connection to the primal energy in the realms. Some supers can transfer power from their internal battery to an external one, like what you did with your light magic into me and then I did into the marble."

"But that also gives another person access to the essence of the super who donated the magic to the external battery," Gideon said.

Sebastian raised his hands, his expression fully sincere. "And I have no intention of using Esther's essence against her."

"You better not."

Realization hit me and a small knot of fear tightened in my gut. The guys hadn't made a big deal about it, probably because they recognized there'd been no other option, but if the situation hadn't been so serious I was sure all of them would have given me an earful. Pouring my power into Sebastian had given him access to my essence. And when Jacob had woven his essence in mine, he'd been able to command me even if that command put my life in danger. I didn't want to think about what Sebastian or someone else could do to me holding my essence.

Sebastian rolled his eyes at Gideon. "There are also a small few of us who can open ourselves to the energy in the realms and shape it into anything we want... if we have the strength of will to do it and our magical channels haven't been burned raw."

"The harder the spell, the more dangerous it is for the sorcerer," Gideon said.

"So you're one of the fae sorcerers who helped with the war?" I couldn't believe I was talking with one of them. Humans and supers talked about them with whispered awe. Few had actually seen them, and they'd always worked behind the scenes. Some people didn't believe they were real, that the fae had locked the portals to their realm until the war was over, and since travelling to a realm other than the human one or your own required extreme amounts of magic, many thought the fae portals were permanently locked. "I thought all of you returned to your realm."

Sebastian shrugged and flipped open the book.

"Thank God you have a teleportation glyph that you keep charged," Gideon said. "We wouldn't have been able to get out of Operations without it."

"Oh, I have the glyph, but it's just to focus my magic. I never keep it charged. It's too big a spell," Sebastian said casually, scanning a page then turning to the next one.

"You don't keep it charged?" Gideon's eyes widened. "How could you not keep it charged? That's the only way you could have cast it without— Even with the glyph to focus—" His gaze leaped to mine, his eyes filled with fear. "You channeled enough magic to teleport seven people? Do you know how dangerous that is?"

Sebastian's expression snapped to serious. "I'm very aware."

The knot in my gut tightened into a frozen stone. "And you think these witches have that kind of power?"

"I think they're channeling an outside source, but it's not raw magic and it's not theirs saved up in a reservoir." He flipped a few more pages in the book then stopped. "It's worship magic. Followers drain their essences over and over again in worship of a god or idol. Some don't even know that they're doing it. Essence magic is different than light and dark magic. It's usually locked to the person's essence and is difficult, if sometimes impossible, to manipulate by someone else unless they've already been given a way in. With worship magic, the followers' essences go into a reservoir and the god — if it's a living god — and his or her priests or priestess can control it."

The muscles in Gideon's jaw flexed. "So there are more of them?"

"Possibly. And maybe a god," Sebastian said, scanning the next page.

"I didn't think gods existed." How the hell did I not know gods existed? And why hadn't any of them shown up to help fight Michael?

"There aren't any gods in the sense you humans usually think of them, like all powerful and all seeing. They're supers pumped up on worship magic." Sebastian turned the page. "And as far as anyone knows, there hasn't been a significant god for two, maybe even three thousand years. It takes a pretty strong super to control an essence-draining ritual and remain lucid. Usually it's a powerful priest or priestess who uses a super to power the spell, which puts them in a catatonic state. But whether it's just the priestess or the god or both, they're all bound by the same restrictions I am."

"Too much power, too quickly," Gideon said, "and you burn up."

Jeez, and I thought my power was scary.

My thoughts stuttered. Every time I used my divine light, I burned my hands. Except I was pretty sure there was no such thing as an angel sorcerer, even an archangel one, so my magic had to be something different. Which was something I could worry about once we'd figured out how to safely release it.

"So," I said, shoving aside the thoughts of my power, "now you know what it is. Can you stop it?"

Sebastian's pale gaze rose to meet mine. "I could have all the magic in the world, and I wouldn't be able to unwrap the spell from Cassius's essence. The essence in the worship magic is controlled by the god or the priest. No one else can use it without permission." He glanced back at the page and pursed his lips. "The only positive is that this kind of poison, at least if it's like all the other non-worship magic spells like it, pulls power from the witch who cast it, and will continue weakening her until it's run its course."

"That's not a positive," Gideon said. "The outcome of the spell is Cassius's death."

"There has to be something we can do." I couldn't accept that there wasn't anything we could do.

"Kill the root of the spell. But that could be the witch, or the god, or both." Sebastian snapped the book closed. "Or find a sin eater."

"Kill a god, or find a demon Michael made extinct on the slim possibility that they had the power to consume the spell keeping his nephilim alive." The light in Gideon's eyes dimmed, and more of my soul fractured at his grief. "There's no other way?"

"No." Sebastian climbed the ladder and put the book back.

"A shaman could unravel the spell," Amiah said from the doorway, unable to enter the office because of the ladder. Her complexion was gray, and she clung to the doorframe to keep standing. She must have given Cassius everything she had left. "Shamans use a form of worship magic. They take the essence naturally sloughed off by all living things and channel it into spells."

"Maybe." Sebastian pressed the balls of his feet to the ladder's rails and slid to the floor. "They are the only super able to channel someone else's essence for their magic."

"Not maybe," Amiah corrected, making Sebastian scowl at her. "Shamans have the innate ability to manipulate essence no longer within a body. It doesn't matter where it comes from."

"But the essence powering the spell on Cassius is locked with the god or priest." Sebastian pushed the ladder aside. "It can't be done. Besides, there isn't a sane shaman left on the planet."

I glanced at Gideon. "Pretend I'm an idiot and don't know anything."

"You're not an idiot," he said, shifting toward me but stopping himself before he could make contact. "You've just spent your life avoiding everything super."

"All the shamans went insane from the flood of power of billions of deaths during Michael's war," Sebastian explained, his gaze never leaving Amiah, his expression daring her to argue with him. "Looking for a sane shaman is as much a waste of time as looking for a sin eater."

Amiah huffed. "And here I thought you were the man who could get anything, given enough money."

"If it exists."

"There's a shaman a quarter of a mile past the Pinebrook Forest wall," she said.

Sebastian rolled his eyes at her. "Bull shit. If there was, I'd know about him."

"Her," she corrected, "and she had the misfortune of being a child and infected with lycanthropy at the beginning of the war."

"So her power wasn't fully developed and her DNA was being rewritten when the power flood happened," Sebastian said. "Well, shit, that would do it."

Amiah turned her attention to Gideon. "If you hurry, you can get her here within the hour. Tell her it's for me."

A phone rang. Sebastian pulled his from his pocket and strode to the back of his office. "Yes."

"I'll gather the guys," Gideon said, heading to the door.

Amiah grabbed his arm, stopping him before he passed. "She might not react well to the whole team."

"Nothing happens outside of this apartment without the whole team." His attention jumped to me for a second, the fear still in his eyes along with a hint of his aching need. And by whole team, he meant the guys. Not me.

Well, I was a liability and powerless, and while I could now go out armed to the teeth, that probably wasn't the best idea to pick up this shaman. The woman lived past the wall of Pinebrook Forest. That was the smallest shifter forest at the farthest end of the Quarter on the other side of Squatters' Row. Kol had said during my tour of the Quarter that only a handful of shifters used that forest because it wasn't in a convenient location. If she lived out there, more or less isolated, then it meant at best she preferred her privacy, and at worst, she was afraid of people.

"Then go in gently. Willow is a firebird. Their nature is sensitive enough. And while she's not insane, she's still fragile."

Gideon pressed a hand to Amiah's shoulder. "I'll be gentle," he said, and turned to go.

"Wait." Sebastian pocketed his phone. "I've got your area containment master ward, but you have to go now."

"It can't wait until we've picked up this shaman?" Gideon asked.

"Not if you want it, and you're not going to like all the terms." Sebastian leveled his icy gaze on me.

ESSIE

From the look in Sebastian's eyes, I knew I wasn't going to like the terms of the deal, which meant Gideon was going to hate them.

"What are the terms?" Gideon asked, his voice low, dangerous.

"You have to bring Esther along."

"It's a risk to take her out in the field, but not an unreasonable one," Amiah said. "Especially if you're just going to buy a master ward, even if that master ward is rare and powerful."

I had to agree, which meant, given Sebastian's expression, there had to be a catch.

"Bane doesn't always do business with the nicest people," Gideon said.

"I'm aware," Amiah huffed.

Sebastian flashed his wicked smile. "And yet you still do business with me."

Gideon glared at him. "The terms."

"You're meeting Voth at his office right now. The price is half a million, cash, non-negotiable, and yes, I'm willing to loan you the money until you have time to transfer it back to me. He also wants to see, and I quote, the mated couple for himself. Also non-negotiable." Sebastian looked at me and his smile turned apologetic. "There are disadvantages to being rare. And just wait until people realize you've got two brands."

That made my insides squirm. Even if I no longer needed to fly under the radar, that didn't mean I'd lost the urge to do so. Except we didn't have time for me and Jacob to get long-sleeved shirts — and that would look weird with the summer's heat — so there wasn't any way for me to hide Jacob's brand. But if getting gawked at and talked about meant I could stop those witches, so be it. "So we go, pick up the master ward, and get the shaman. Back within the hour."

"I'm not taking you to a hotel for supers owned by a greater demon. Especially one who reveled in his war assignment to take out as many nephilim as possible. Any way possible. Not with your essence unreadable and your eyes glowing." The room's temperature dropped a few degrees, Gideon's fear strong enough to bleed past the containment cuffs. "They'll think you're a nephilim."

"And tonight he's got that big fight," Sebastian said. "Smaller fights all afternoon leading up to the big bout."

"So even though it's the middle of the afternoon, the hotel will be packed." Gideon shook his head. "No way."

"At least he's banned all media and you won't get caught on TV," Sebastian said.

"No," Gideon snapped, his voice sharp, whatever control he had over his emotions starting to crumble.

"We don't have much choice." If we didn't get the master ward, the witches would win, except— "Will the area containment master ward even shut the witches off from their power?"

"Nothing in or out, not even worship magic. The witches will still have access to their personal magic inside the contained area," Sebastian said, "it's not like the handcuffs, but it does create a barrier impenetrable by magic."

"Essie isn't going. I won't— I can't—" Gideon's breath picked up. "What if we paid double? What if—" Gideon pulled the marble with my light magic out of his pocket. "What if we paid with this?"

"Whoa, Mavis didn't take the marble?" Sebastian asked.

Gideon shoved the marble toward Sebastian. "Will this double the payment?"

"It'll cover the payment and then some, but Voth's terms were clear. No mated couple, no master ward."

Shit. If Gideon feared I'd be mistaken for a nephilim, I really didn't want to leave the apartment, not until I figured out how to deal with that. "What about my contacts? Can you top up the spell?" Perhaps if I just went in with a weird essence, we could claim it was the effect of my brands... although I had no idea how we were going to explain the brand I shared with Jacob. We'd just have to hope no one would think about it until after we were gone.

"I can only top it up if you haven't completely destroyed the spell," Sebastian said.

"Do it," Gideon snapped.

"Only if the spell is still there." Sebastian shot Gideon a hard look, sat on the couch, and pushed the book aside. "Sit. If I can top up the spell, this might make you dizzy."

I sat, and he pressed his palms over my eyes. Heat radiated from his hands and my buzz whispered under my skin. I drew in a deep breath, trying to steady myself and keep my magic under control.

"Are you okay?" Gideon asked, his tone sharp with worry.

"Fine, just trying to contain my magic."

"Even through the cuffs?" Amiah asked.

"I did say she was the most powerful super in the room," Sebastian said.

Which scared me, especially since Gideon's reaction to Sebastian teleporting seven people with raw magic implied he was a big, powerful deal. Sure, I wanted to be able to hold my own with my guys, but I didn't want to be so powerful that people were afraid of me. I didn't want to lose myself to that kind of power. Knowing I could bring justice, instantly punish anyone, would make it too easy to lose perspective. I could fall into the same trap Michael did, thinking that killing billions of people was the right decision.

Except I had my guys. They wouldn't let me get away with any of that. That thought eased my fear. A bit.

"The spell is still there." The heat from Sebastian's hands grew and sank into me, making my buzz bite harder in response. It wasn't close to what it had been after Mavis had cast the concealment spell on all the guys, but it'd be there soon if Sebastian's top-up took much longer.

White light shot past my closed eyelids and drove into my skull. I gasped and Sebastian's hands tensed.

"She's fine, Gideon," he said, a little too quickly.

"She better be."

"Jeez," Sebastian huffed, his power still pouring into me. "Mated angels are a pain in the ass. Just as bad as wolves. How do you put up with it, Esther? Or is he just on edge because he hasn't gotten any?"

"Bane," Gideon growled.

"You'd be on edge too if you'd ignored your bond for weeks," Amiah huffed.

"I'm not stupid enough to ignore a bond like that." The light swelled and I bit back another gasp. "Of course, I'm also not stupid enough to get trapped in a bond like that."

Another brilliant swell and then the light and the heat — and my buzz — vanished with a whoosh. Sebastian drew his hands away and sat back. Another weak divine light tear rolled down his cheek and sank back under his skin.

"How long will that keep happening?"

"No clue. I've never had raw power pumped into me like that before. And you gave me a lot," he said. "I'm surprised you had power left to respond to my top-up."

I was surprised as well and a part of me was afraid to know the reason.

"All right," Gideon said, his body so tense it made me ache to look at him. "Let's go."

Amiah grabbed his wrist, her expression grim. "I think you should take me and Cassius to Operations first."

"Why—?" Realization flashed across his expression. "You want to take him into the temporal freeze."

"And be there with him when the spell ends."

Gideon pressed his hand over Amiah's. "Amiah—"

"Getting Willow here within the hour might have been tight to begin with," she said. "If you have to go to Voth's first, Cassius might not last."

"Will the temporal freeze stop the spell?" I stood and the room tilted.

Sebastian grabbed my arm and steadied me until the dizziness passed. "Yes. Most magic is considered biological, so the freeze will keep him at the state he's at."

"Will it also freeze the drain on the witch?" I wasn't sure how spells worked. Would she know the spell was frozen or would she think Cassius was dead?

"The spell will stay active but stop draining," Sebastian said. "She'll know we put Cassius in the temporal freeze."

"So she could go after him." I hated to think that way, but putting Cassius in the freeze spell made him a helpless target.

"It's a risk we're going to have to take." Gideon gave Amiah's hand a squeeze. "Trapped in the spell, he'll no longer be a threat to their plans.

We have to assume they won't do anything about him until after they've completed their goal."

"And we still don't know what that is," I said.

"One thing at a time." Gideon shot me a look filled with yearning, then jerked his attention away and strode into the living room. "Gear up. We're going to Voth's to get the area containment master ward."

"Light weaponry?" Jacob asked Gideon. "They're going to confiscate everything at the door, but it'd be better if we were armed when we're on the move."

"Agreed," Gideon said. "And while I really want Essie in a vest, I'd rather not have JP on her chest making her a bigger target than she already is."

Marcus jerked to a stop mid-step on his way to the duffle bags with our gear. "Essie is *not* going."

"This isn't a democracy," Gideon snapped. "Voth wants to see the mated couple as part of the buy, non-negotiable, and we need that master ward."

"I'm with Marcus. Essie's essence is muddled and her eyes—" Jacob's gaze froze on mine. "What happened to your eyes?"

"Enspelled contacts," Kol said without looking up at me. "Bought them from Mavis, remember?

"Everyone take a com." Gideon glanced back at Amiah. "You too. Jacob, when you're armed, get Cassius. We're taking him and Amiah to Operations to buy him time with the temporal freeze."

Marcus swore. "Still no way to save him?"

"We have a possible solution but we have to get the master ward first." Gideon turned to Sebastian. "Are you coming?"

"No. I'll get working on figuring out Esther's problem." Sebastian looked at me. "Try not to take down a building or anything while you're out."

"Gee, thanks." Except a part of me feared that, even with the cuffs, that could happen. While the rest of me was trying to figure out how to not draw attention to the fact that I wore separated handcuffs while I was being *seen* by Voth.

Everyone got a com, and those of us who needed weapons geared up. I really wanted to bring an M4, but arriving to buy a rare magic item armed to the teeth probably set the wrong mood. I was just going to have to trust that Mavis's concealment spells would keep us hidden, that the witches wouldn't attack while we ran our errands, and be happy with a Glock and two extra magazines.

Priam stayed behind with Sebastian. He'd been supposed to start his shift at Mercy Memorial in a few hours, but Amiah, as chief physician at Operations, commandeered his services for the JP for an indefinite amount of time.

As we got ready, Gideon, his posture tight, his gaze constantly darting back to me and making my pulse trip with need, gave the rundown of what we needed to do: buy the master ward and find Willow. The guys still didn't know what the witches had been doing at City Hall, only that one of them had stopped the mayor's assistant and briefly talked with him. So far the assistant hadn't answered his phone, and as soon as we got back from getting the master ward and picking up Willow, Gideon was going to breakdown and return the mayor's call. That, however, wasn't going to be a short conversation, since the JP had been involved in yet another public fight with supers. And at City Hall.

We hurried out of Sebastian's apartment and down the alley to the SUV. The sun was still pretty high in the sky but was now partially obscured by clouds, as if even the weather was starting to worry. We piled into the blazing hot vehicle with me sitting between Kol and Amiah on the middle bench. Kol leaned as far away from me as possible, while Amiah sat with her back stiff and her attention locked ahead of her — and I wasn't sure if she was staring at Marcus's headrest or out the windshield. Thank God it was a short drive to Operations.

Kol jumped out of the SUV before it had come to a complete stop at the curb, and I resisted the urge to scream at him and demand we work out whatever the hell was wrong. I knew what was wrong. I just needed to stay patient. God damn fucking patient.

We gathered outside the security door beside the garage's big door, everyone tense and worried.

"The spell starts about halfway to the inside door," Marcus said to Amiah. "It'll take about five minutes before the spell captures you, but moving through it is tough."

Amiah nodded.

Marcus's wolf darkened his eyes. "You don't have to go in with him."

She reached to take his hand but stopped and crossed her arms instead. "I need to be at his side the moment the temporal freeze ends."

"We'll have Willow ready and waiting," Gideon said.

"I know." She gave me an icy glare and marched into the garage.

Jacob hefted Cassius on his shoulder and followed her. My stomach churned at the idea that he was going back in there.

"Keep it fast," Gideon said, his voice beside me but also in my ear over the coms, drawing a shiver of need. "Get him on a bed in triage then get out of there, even if Amiah doesn't make it all the way."

"Copy that," Jacob said.

A whisper of power, perfectly still and intense, crept through his brand. He'd stepped into the spell. I drew in a slow breath. He'd been in the spell before. Putting Cassius on a bed in triage wasn't going to take as much time as going up to Summer's lab and downloading City Hall's security footage.

Marcus shifted closer to me. Gideon started to join him, then forced himself to stay put, which only made my yearning for him stronger.

"You're going to need to deal with that," Marcus said to Gideon.

"It can wait until we've dealt with the witches." The muscles in Gideon's jaw flexed.

Marcus's eyes narrowed and he wrapped his arms around me. "I'm not so sure about that."

I wasn't so sure, either, not on him *or* me being able to focus on the job and resist the brand.

"It's going to have to," Gideon said.

The whisper of intense power in Jacob's brand grew. He'd only been in there a few seconds, and he wasn't drawing strength from me, but I could feel him fighting the spell's pressure. My pulse picked up... or was that Jacob's? I wasn't sure. I didn't think my connection with him was that deep, but then it had started before our brand had formed, when he'd woven his essence into mine and claimed me.

He grunted across the coms, and I drew in another slow breath.

"Hurry up, Amiah," he said.

"Just go," came her strained reply. "I'll make it."

Another grunt. Someone was breathing heavily. Amiah? It didn't sound deep enough for Jacob.

I strained to hear anything past the breathing. Had I sounded that exhausted trying to get to the armory? Amiah wasn't a fighter, but she also wasn't a pushover. She was an angel and that automatically came with more power than the average human.

Come on. Come on. God, was the temporal freeze slowing time around Operations as well? Seconds were ticking away too slowly. Jacob was taking too long.

Marcus pressed his lips to the top of my head, as if adding more physical contact would help steady my nerves. Kol stepped farther away from us and leaned against the SUV, his posture stiff, not his usual sexy, dangerous grace.

"Jacob? Status?" Gideon asked.

The heavy breathing turned into slow gasps.

"Jacob? Amiah?"

"In triage," Amiah said.

"Almost— Out." The power in Jacob's brand melted back into my body.

Oh, thank God.

A few seconds later, Jacob staggered out the door, and I rushed to him, unable to stop myself.

"It was harder this time," he gasped, leaning on me to keep standing. "I think the spell is getting stronger."

"How long will it take you to recover?" Gideon asked.

"You mean, will I be ready by the time we get to Voth's?" Jacob shuffled toward the SUV. I stayed at his side. I couldn't hold his weight, he was just too big, but I could help him keep his balance. "I have no idea."

Jacob and I got in the back and he leaned forward, his chest heaving with deep breaths. "I thought the last time was bad."

"We wait until he's good," Marcus said.

"We could miss our chance to buy the master ward." Gideon turned in his seat to look at Jacob. "We've already pushed our luck by taking this detour."

"Then drive," Jacob gasped. "I'll be fine."

He wasn't, and I didn't know how dangerous Voth — or rather how more dangerous — he was, given that he was already a greater demon. I also didn't know what the situation we were walking into was like, but no way was Jacob going anywhere while still recovering from fighting that spell. I'd given Gideon extra strength even when he wasn't pulling it from the bond. I should be able to give it to Jacob.

My buzz flared at the thought, tickling against the magic of the containment cuffs. I ignored it and concentrated on gathering some of my strength. I didn't need all of it. The situation wasn't dire, but I still needed to be mindful. It wouldn't help anyone if I was out for the count.

The power warmed my palms, and I pressed them over our brand on his biceps.

"Essie," he said, his voice that low rumble that always made me ache with need.

"I've got lots." I let my strength seep into him until his breath steadied. I didn't even feel weak afterward. His love for me warmed my chest with real emotion, defying the handcuffs, and he dipped in and kissed me.

"Thank you."

Out of the corner of my eye, I saw Kol shift.

"We good?" Gideon asked, his voice and posture tight.

"Jeez, man, *you* aren't," Marcus said. "You've got to finish sealing your bond."

"We've already had this conversation." Gideon pointed down the street. "Drive."

"Fine," Marcus growled, and he put the SUV in gear.

We drove to the other side of the Quarter and through Squatters' Row to a massive, beautifully restored 19th century hotel. It didn't look like it had been touched by the war, and maybe it hadn't. Most of the buildings in Squatter's Row hadn't been touched, merely abandoned.

The ten-story yellow brick building sprawled on a hill at the very back of the Quarter, with a long, circular driveway leading up to a grand front entrance. Only the bottom five stories of windows had the telltale purple hue of UV-blocking glass, indicating that it catered to vampires but they weren't the hotel's only clientele.

Marcus drove to a parking lot at the side of the building, partially hidden by the hill. It was packed with vehicles and we were forced to take a spot at the far end of the lot.

"Do the vampires just stay until dark?" I asked, getting out of the SUV and following the guys across the hot parking lot to a set of double doors that, while not as grand as the front entrance, were still impressive.

"Voth had a subway built connecting the hotel to the vampire section of the Quarter," Jacob said.

"Which we should avoid at all costs," Gideon added. "We still don't know how Victoria is taking you taking Jacob from her, and anyone we run into in that tunnel will be a vampire."

I fought a shiver despite the day's heat. Yeah, that was another problem I didn't want to think about. I hadn't meant to sever her link with Jacob. Hell, I hadn't even meant to bind his soul with mine and brand him. But fate hadn't given me a choice, and if it had, I still would have picked Jacob.

Marcus fell into step beside me. "Don't forget, most supers are more aggressive than humans, and these supers will be riled up by the fights."

"So keep my head down." I rolled my eyes at him. "I was already planning on it. My power is restricted. I'm more vulnerable now than I've ever been."

His pupils slitted as his wolf tried to push to the surface. "Really didn't need that reminder."

"If I can keep it together," Gideon said, his body tight with strain, "you can."

ESSIE

WE REACHED THE DOUBLE DOORS AND STEPPED INTO AN AIR-CONDITIONED grand vestibule with a wide, sweeping staircase to our right, a long hall leading deeper into the hotel straight ahead, and a coat check, or rather weapons check, to our left. People packed the space, the roar of their voices echoing off the marble floor and walls, and the sense of power squeezed within me. Not just the force of vampiric intensity, although I could feel that in the mix, but the power of witches and demons with an innate ability, even the wild ferocity of shifters. There was so much magic crammed into the space it stole my breath.

"You okay?" Marcus asked.

I fought to make my lungs work against the pressure. This had to be part of what it meant to be a super, how they sensed essences or something. But man— "How long does it take to get used to it?"

Marcus frowned. "Used to what?"

"All the power of so many supers in one place. It's crushing."

"What power?" Gideon asked.

"You can't feel it?" How the hell couldn't they feel it? Except he didn't look affected at all. None of my guys did—

No, that wasn't true. Kol's posture had tightened even more and his expression was edged with pain, although if you didn't know him you probably wouldn't have noticed. I had thought the tension was because he was holding back his power to avoid turning on every woman and gay man in the vestibule, but maybe there was more to it.

"It'll get better in a month or two. Maybe more," Kol said with a shrug, confirming my suspicion. "Depends on how sensitive you are."

"Shit, right, she's a sensitive," Marcus said.

Jacob's gaze slid over the crowd. "Then this isn't the best place for her right now."

"So let's do this quickly." Gideon headed to the weapons check, where a bulky demon stood by the wall and a pretty demon stood behind the counter.

The bulky guy was about as tall as Gideon but twice as wide, with onyx colored skin that looked more like stone than flesh. He wore a white suit, a stark contrast to his black skin, and radiated danger. The pretty demon was his complete opposite. Petite, delicate, pale, with small horns poking through her long golden locks, she wore a barely-there dress, oozed sexual grace, and had a hint of hellfire in her eyes. Without a doubt, she was a succubus.

Her lips curled in a sultry smile and she wiggled her fingers at us. "Hi, guys."

None of my guys reacted to her — which surprised the shit out of me, because I knew how difficult it was to resist the pull of Kol's magic.

Mr. Muscles beside her counter straightened. Guess if seduction didn't work, then they'd make us check our weapons with force.

"We're here to see Voth," Gideon said.

I handed over my Glock, but kept the magazines in my back pocket. The girl gave me a flirty smile and a chip for my gun, then turned her flirty smile to Marcus and Jacob as they handed over their sidearms. Attempt number two and she still didn't get a reaction from my guys.

Her lower lip curled into a soft pout and the hellfire in her eyes flared. Sensual heat swept over my skin, and Gideon's breath picked up. Her pout shifted into a wicked smile, and she leaned forward, showing off more of her cleavage and trying to get Gideon's attention. But instead of turning from Mr. Muscles to her, he turned to me with aching desperate need in his eyes, a need that fueled my own. God, we needed to solidify our bond before I shattered, and my soul cried for me to do it now, here, to hell with everyone else.

Kol slid up to the counter and flashed her his own wicked smile. "Keep trying." His expression snapped to deadly, the hellfire in his eyes brighter than hers. "I dare you."

The succubus jerked back, her hands raised. "Just having a little fun."

The heat vanished and Gideon drew in a ragged breath.

"Have fun with someone else." Kol drew the matching daggers hidden on his back and set them on the counter, not bothering to take his shirt off to keep the blades in their sheaths. He turned to leave and Mr. Muscles cleared his throat.

"And the other ones."

For a second it looked like Kol was going to deny having them, but Gideon shot him a hard glare, and with a sigh, he drew a blade from each boot and another hidden in his jeans at his hip.

"Voth is expecting us," Gideon said through clenched teeth.

Mr. Muscles jerked his chin at the succubus, who was back to pouting. She picked up a phone, called her boss, and a few seconds later a wiry man in the same white suit as Mr. Muscles strode down the stairs and wove through the crowd to the weapons check counter. He looked completely human, not a hint of feralness, or vampiric intensity, or hellfire. His brown hair had been buzzed, making him look like a soldier, and if I added the confidence of his stride and the way he carried himself, I'd have guessed he'd been military before the war — and not just a volunteer like the thousands of others who'd signed up when humanity realized we were in the fight of our lives.

He gave us a cursory glance then turned on his heel and marched toward the hall. We fell into step behind him, Gideon leading the way, Marcus at my side, and Kol and Jacob taking up the rear. The hall didn't have as many people as the vestibule, but the crush of power didn't ease up. In fact, the closer we got to the end and an enormous set of gilded doors, the more the pressure squeezed me.

My buzz tingled under my skin, and I gritted my teeth. *I will not lose control. I will not lose control.* I could hold out until we'd gotten the master ward.

Two women giggled and another one fanned herself, but the reaction wasn't as strong as it had been when we'd walked into City Hall. I didn't know if that was because these women weren't human, or if Kol had regained control of his magical shields and wasn't leaking excess magic.

Our escort heaved open one of the doors and a wave of roaring voices and power crashed into me.

I gasped, and Marcus grabbed my arm to steady me.

Inside was a spectacular theater like the big fancy ones in Las Vegas, with a fight ring in the center and stadium seating all around, going down half a story and up at least one. Supers filled the seats, yelling and cheering. One man, or rather demon who looked a lot like Mr. Muscles, stood in the caged ring, wearing nothing but shiny shorts, his hands raised, making the crowd cheer louder.

A deep masculine voice announced someone else, the name flashing on the big screen hanging over the ring, then the image switched to a man with the intensity of a shifter jogging out of a tunnel between the aisles. The roar of voices swelled and so did the power crushing my chest.

People from the hall crowded in behind us and pushed past to take the stairs to their seats. Our escort led us along a wide hall ringing the theater, through more people, around a slight corner, and to a plain, glossy black door. We were led into a luxurious private box, complete with plush carpet, black leather couches, and a fully stocked bar. The noise of the crowd vanished as our escort returned to the hall, closing the door behind him, leaving us alone with a massive demon.

He wore an all-black suit and stood at the front of the box, one enormous hand pressed against the glass, the other holding a glass of amber liquid. Physically he looked human, with the exception that he was taller and broader than Jacob, if not seven feet tall then awfully damn close, with bulky muscular shoulders. But the waves of heat and crushing power radiating from his body, and the delicate tendrils of red mist curling over his skin then sinking back into his body, said in no uncertain terms he was a powerful demon.

"I don't see a bag," he said, his voice low and threatening, like powerful thunder heard in the distance. "The deal was cash. Non-negotiable."

"I don't see an area containment master ward," Gideon replied.

Voth glanced over his shoulder at us. Pricks of red hellfire smoldered in his black eyes and the force of his power swelled. "This isn't a game you want to play, angel."

My buzz grew stronger, and I strained to keep my breath even.

"This isn't a game." Gideon drew the glowing marble from his pocket.

Voth's eyes narrowed. "Put that on the bar and step away."

"Show me the master ward." Gideon squeezed the marble and the light in his eyes blazed brighter.

"Put that on the bar," Voth snarled. His red mist swept around him, his canines extended into fangs and horns grew from his forehead. The hellfire in his eyes didn't surge, but the crush of his power did.

Holy hell. I bit back a groan and grabbed Marcus's arm to keep standing. Light stuttered from my hands and he winced, but didn't pull away. Thank God, because I would have dropped to my knees if he did.

Voth's lips curled into a sneer. "Your brand has made her sensitive, and the spell on those containment cuffs isn't enough to prevent her from sensing my power."

"It's not," I gasped. We didn't have a lot of time to begin with and, God, if I didn't get out of there soon, I was going to collapse. Maybe if I stroked his ego, we'd move past the posturing. "I've never felt anyone as powerful as you." Which actually was the truth. Even Victoria with her enormous power hadn't affected me like this. "Just put the marble on the bar, Gideon. If he's going to break his word, there isn't much we can do."

Voth's sneer deepened. "Except he can't put it on the bar, because that would leave you defenseless."

Marcus snorted. "She's hardly defenseless."

"You don't count, puppy. I could crush you with a thought."

Except I was pretty sure that hadn't been what Marcus was thinking.

"None of you count." His power surged and my knees gave out.

Marcus grabbed me before I hit the floor and light blazed around Gideon's hand. Jacob and Kol stepped ahead of me, and Voth howled with laughter.

"Careful, angel. Looks like you've got some competition from your team for your mate." The misty magic twisted around Voth's fingers and over his hands. "Is your mating brand strong enough to survive that?" His gaze landed on Jacob and he frowned.

"It's not really a competition." Jacob shrugged his branded shoulder. "You've seen our brands, you know we've got the money, so are we doing this deal or not?"

"But I haven't really *seen* the brands."

"That's it," Gideon said. "We're leaving."

Kol grabbed the door handle but the door wouldn't open.

"What makes angels so special?" Voth set his glass on the bar and stalked toward Gideon, his power growing, stealing my breath and making the room darken.

My focus narrowed to Gideon, with his light blazing around his hands and from his eyes.

"How can your souls bond and a demon's can't?" Voth asked.

Marcus swept me into his arms, his body tight and trembling. "Kol?"

"It won't open."

"I'm going to fucking kill Bane," Marcus growled.

"Tell me," Voth hissed.

Red mist exploded from Voth's back and he released enormous leathery wings in the same way angels released their wings. He lunged at Gideon, who jerked back and shot him with a blast of light. It scorched Voth's chest, burning fabric and flesh, filling the room with a coppery acrid scent, but Voth didn't even stumble. He seized Gideon's arm and red mist poured into the brand.

Gideon screamed and dropped to his knees. Jacob leaped toward them, but red mist shot out of his brand, and he howled and collapsed.

"What's so different about your souls?" Voth knelt before Gideon and grabbed his chin, forcing Gideon to look at him. "What makes you so special?"

Fire and pressure whirled inside me. The misty demonic magic wept from my brands, curled around my arm, and sank back into my skin. My buzz snapped, making my muscles seize and my power gather in my palms.

"Tell me," Voth growled.

Gideon groaned. "I don't know."

"She has an angel and a vampire. Even a vampire's soul is worthy, but mine—" Voth howled, the sound filled with rage and pain.

With a moan, Marcus sagged to the floor. He struggled to keep hold of me, but couldn't and I rolled out of his arms into a heap on the floor.

"She has the puppy, too. What makes her so special?" Voth shoved Gideon out of the way and grabbed my head with one big too-hot hand. His mist swept down his arm and into me, whirling into a supernova in my chest.

I squeezed my hands into fists and clutched them to my chest, desperate to hold my magic back. The containment cuffs heated, turned red, and burned my skin and the front of my T-shirt, but I kept my hands closed. There was too much power inside me, like there'd been too much power when I'd fought Ibizual. The hellfire prince had tried to flood me with magic until I exploded, but we'd managed to stop him in time. I had no idea how we were going to stop Voth. All my guys, even Kol, were prone and gasping. I could blast him, but who knew how many people could be hurt?

Voth lifted me to my knees, the hellfire consuming his eyes, the heat radiating from him like a sauna. "Why you? Why them?"

He blinked and for a second his eyes were filled with heartache. What he was really asking was 'Why not me?'

"I don't know."

"You must. You bound them to you with your power." He pressed his palm over my heart. "You're strong, but I'm stronger."

I seized his wrist. I had to do something. Maybe if I focused my blast, I could get him to let go and not hurt anyone else.

But his grief crashed into me. So much pain. So much heartache. So much loneliness. My concentration slipped and my power roared from my palms. But instead of a fiery blast, it surged into Voth and wrapped, warm and tender, around his heart with my love for my guys.

It glowed golden like the swirling threads of our brands, a pure connection of souls with a magic more powerful than all other magics. It wasn't light or dark or essence-based. It was primal, the core of everything within the universe. I hadn't believed true love or destined mates was real, but I couldn't deny the truth. I belonged with them and they with me, and nothing could change that.

Voth gasped and a red misty tear rolled down his cheek. The demonic magic whooshed out of my chest into Voth, and his crushing power vanished. He released me and sagged back, clutching his hands over his heart, his expression stunned and sad. "So that's the truth."

"Yes," I gasped, even though I wasn't entirely sure what truth Voth had seen.

Gideon groaned and rose unsteadily to his feet. He clutched the marble in his fist and pointed it at Voth. "Let. Us. Go."

I wasn't sure what Gideon was going to do, since his first blast had barely affected Voth, but I knew he'd fight until his last breath to save me.

Voth stared at him, his expression still stunned.

The marble's light glowed brighter, and Gideon's body trembled.

Voth blinked away his shock, straightened, and with a billow of misty magic, pulled his wings back into his body. "You came for a master ward and you've more than paid for it." He pulled a phone from his pocket and sent a text, then leveled his dark gaze on me, only a hint of hellfire in his eyes. "People won't understand you. But I've seen your truth. You're nothing like them. If you call, I will come."

What the—? I had no idea what he was talking about or what the hell had just happened. The ferocity of his attack, the depth of his heartache... none of it made sense.

The door opened, bumping into Kol, who crawled out of the way, and the guy who'd escorted us to Voth's private box entered with a briefcase. He set it on the bar, opened it, and left. Inside was a small silver plate etched with glyphs. *Please, God, let this be the area containment master ward.*

"The master ward activates with a drop of blood and the word *vade*. Stay as long as you'd like. Watch the fights. Have a few drinks on me," Voth said, as if he hadn't just flattened us with his power and there wasn't a hole burned in the front of his suit. "And leave the marble on the bar."

He strode out of the room and Gideon sagged onto the arm of the closest couch.

"What the fuck just happened?" Marcus growled, sitting back on his heels. "I didn't think a greater demon was that powerful?"

"He used our soul bond with Essie against us," Jacob said, his palm pressed to his brand as if it hurt.

Kol crawled to the bar, used it to help him stand, and looked in the briefcase. "It's got power, and it could be the real deal, but the spell's too complicated for me to properly identify. You'd have to ask Summer to be sure."

"Except we can't ask Summer," Gideon said, "and we're running out of time."

"We're in no condition to move." Jacob squeezed his eyes shut. He didn't look hungry or hurt, just exhausted. They all did.

I considered standing but thought better of it. I was still shaky from all the power and pressure. At least my buzz was gone, not even a whisper like when I'd first entered the hotel. Maybe I was getting used to the power. And maybe I was just too magically worn out. The containment cuffs, however, looked like they'd barely survived Voth's attack and had melted painfully into my wrists. I could only hope I wouldn't face anything like that again, or that Sebastian would be able to figure out how to help me, before they melted off.

And since there wasn't a damned thing I could do about it, or my burned wrists, I wasn't going to think about it. "I think I can help everyone but Marcus."

"Even if all I do is shift and shift back, it'll help." Marcus reached for his right boot and started unlacing it.

"It's not helpful if you exhaust yourself," Gideon said to me.

"Better me than all of you."

"I'm not going to bite you," Jacob said. "I'm not that weak."

"That wasn't what I was thinking." And while I craved my guys, I wasn't interested in having exhausted sex with them in a greater demon's private theater box. "Let me use the brands to give you a little strength." I pointed to the floor in front of me. "Come here. I think it'll be easier if I can touch you."

Gideon glanced at Jacob, who sighed and eased within arm's reach.

Marcus pulled off his T-shirt, and my pulse tripped at the sight of him. I forced myself to turn my back on him so I could concentrate, and laid my hand on Jacob's arm on top of his brand. I drew in a steadying breath and imagined my strength seeping into him. My buzz didn't even flare like it had in the SUV, making me wonder even more if I was finally out of juice. For a second, I feared I wouldn't be able to give my guys some of my strength, but then heat swept over my palm, and the quiet intensity that always came from Jacob's bond strengthened and grounded me. Thank goodness my soul bond with my guys wasn't completely connected with my personal magic.

Jacob leaned closer to me, his eyes dark with desire. He pressed his cool hand over mine and brushed his lips across my temple, then pulled my hand away. "Just enough to keep us going."

He placed my hand on Gideon's arm, and my strength slid from him to Gideon.

The light in his eyes flared, his pupils dilated, and his breath picked up. "This is a bad idea."

"Just give it a minute," Jacob said. "Then we'll get this shaman and get back to Bane's."

Gideon's jaw flexed and his body started to tremble. With a groan, he clenched his hands and bowed his head.

Kol hesitated for a second then staggered from the bar, eased to the floor behind Gideon, and grabbed his other arm. His eyes rolled back and he drew in a deep, shuddering breath, his reaction the complete opposite to Gideon's.

Gideon groaned again and lifted his gaze to mine, capturing me in his clear, perfect summer-sky eyes. My breath hitched. I ached to close the distance between us. No, *needed* to close it. Now.

"Aaaand that's where we should stop," Kol said as he yanked Gideon away from me.

Gideon panted, his expression hungry and desperate. He squeezed his eyes shut and his whole body tensed.

"Okay," he said, his voice husky. "Jacob, Kol, are you good?"

"Yeah." Kol glanced at me, a strange look in his eyes before he jerked away and strode to the door.

"I'm good." Jacob stood and helped me to my feet. The world swayed a bit, but not any worse than when I'd fed Jacob.

Marcus secured the fly on his pants and pulled his T-shirt back on. He still looked tired, but not nearly as exhausted as a moment ago.

"Okay. Protect Essie and the master ward." Gideon set the marble on the bar, closed the briefcase, and handed it to me. "Let's get out of here."

With Jacob steadying me, we hurried into the hall. The crush of power of all the supers in the theater squeezed inside me. It wasn't nearly as painful as Voth's fully released power, but it wasn't pleasant, either. At least my buzz didn't tingle under my skin. There wasn't any threat of me hurting anyone or doing serious property damage.

We rounded the slight corner in the hall ringing the theater, and a group of vampires peeled away from the walls, blocking our way.

"Victoria is pissed with you, Jacob Lockwood," a rake-thin man said. He had sallow skin, stringy brown hair, and wore jeans ripped on both thighs along with a T-shirt fraying at the neck. Gus. The vampire who'd tried to claim me the first time I'd been to Victoria's nightclub.

Marcus groaned. "You got to be fucking kidding me."

ESSIE

My mind raced through our options, which were pretty much fight or run since no one was letting Gus take Jacob to Victoria.

The vampires released their intensity and the other supers in the hall either hurried away or drew to the side to watch. Only a few of the vampires had the weight of Jacob's power, but we were outnumbered three to one and we were tired.

"So you're her messenger now?" Jacob asked. "Tell her thanks for the invite but no thanks."

"This isn't a request," Gus said, flashing his fangs. "And I'm not Victoria's messenger, but I will be her new favorite once I bring her you and the bitch."

Gus jerked forward and the hall erupted into chaos. Gideon barreled toward Gus and slammed his fist, glowing with divine light, into Gus's chest. In a flash, Jacob had grabbed the vampire who'd been beside Gus and tossed him into the two vampires behind him, while Kol pounced on another vampire. He dodged that vampire's punch, seized his extended arm, and broke his elbow.

I met Marcus's gaze to confirm we were thinking the same thing. Yep. Make a run for it.

We bolted through the opening in the center of the pack the others had made for us, and had almost made it through when a vampire lunged at me. I wrenched the briefcase up and smacked his hand away just before he grabbed me. His eyes flashed wide with surprise that I'd moved that fast — I was surprised, too — and I clocked him across the face with the briefcase.

Marcus punched another vampire in the chest, shoving him into a naga with scaly red skin standing by the wall watching. The naga hissed and shoved the vampire back toward Marcus, who punched him again in the chest.

Another vampire seized my arm and wrenched me around. I swung the briefcase at her head, but she jerked back and I missed. With a snarl, she reached for my throat, and I heaved the briefcase up, smacking her hand away and buying myself time to scramble back.

A flicker of buzz whispered over me. I didn't know how I still had power left after everything that had happened, but I sure as hell couldn't let it blaze out of control.

The vampire lunged at me, and a blast of divine light shot from across the hall and hit her in the head. She howled, the side of her face burned, but it was nothing a vampire couldn't heal with a feeding. Gideon met my gaze for a second, the look in his eyes wild, before he wrenched his attention back to the fight.

Beside him, Jacob punched another vampire, but a bulky demon took his place, ramming his shoulder into Jacob's chest and shoving him into the wall. Behind them, more supers had joined the brawl. Kol fought with a shifter and another vampire, while two of the vampires who'd stopped us fought with a group of twisted-horned demons.

"We have to get out of here," Marcus gasped over the coms. "People are just joining in for the hell of it."

A shifter punched out a wiry demon and wrenched around to find another target. His gaze locked on me. *Shit.* I tensed, ready to fight, but Marcus shoved the guy aside into a squat demon, who seized the wiry demon and tossed him into another group of shifters.

"Get to that maintenance door," Gideon said. "Fifty feet up the hall."

I twisted out of reach of another demon, my buzz crackling stronger, and squeezed between two separate fights between vampires and demons, determined to get to the maintenance door. Marcus followed, but a green-skinned demon wrenched him back and the vampire/demon fights shifted, closing the path between us.

Jacob rammed his elbow into the chin of the bulky demon who'd pinned him to the wall, knocking him back, while Kol bounded off that demon's back to gain height and gravity to strengthen his punch into a vampire's face. Gideon slammed another divine-light enhanced strike into a demon's chest and shoved closer to me.

A vampire stumbled out of a fight with a shifter and bumped into me. She turned, her lips curling into a wicked smile as she recognized me.

Oh, shit.

My buzz flickered again. I gritted my teeth and jerked back, running into someone behind me. The someone, a bulky demon with onyx skin in a slinky gold dress, wrenched around and snarled. I ducked down, praying the demon would focus on the vampire. She did, and I scrambled to the side as the two women went at it.

Only a few more feet to the door.

Except Gideon had been pushed farther away again, and Jacob and Kol had only managed to move about five feet forward. God, even moving fifty feet was impossible. Where the hell was security? I would have thought Voth wouldn't have wanted fighting in his hotel's halls, but then I had no idea what amused a greater demon. Maybe all this chaos was exactly what he liked.

The guys grunted and panted and yelled over the coms. My breath burned my lungs and my body trembled. I was too tired for this kind of a fight. Hell, even if I'd been at full strength and hadn't been dealing with the pressure of everyone's power, I wouldn't have wanted to find myself in a brawl with supers. And my buzz — my God damn buzz — was at it again with tiny bites under my skin. Post-nicotine levels, so it was manageable, but that didn't mean it couldn't blaze out of control at any minute.

A few feet away, Marcus snarled and dug his claws into the gut of a vampire. She screamed and seized his throat. Her eyes gleamed with wicked cruelty as she squeezed. Marcus gasped, yanked his claws out of her gut, and drove them back in, but she didn't let go.

I lurched toward them. I didn't know how I could stop her without my magic. All I knew was that I had to try. But someone grabbed the briefcase and jerked me back. I stumbled, not letting go of the case, and the woman, a vampire in biker leathers, grabbed my ponytail and wrenched my head back.

"You really pissed off Victoria." She grabbed my chin with her other hand, taking full control of my head.

I heaved the briefcase back, but didn't have a good angle. The case skimmed her side and didn't even draw a grunt, let alone loosen her grip, and none of the guys were close enough to help.

Gideon punched a thin demon in the chest, knocking him back, his chest burned and oozing from Gidcon's divinc light. Kol kickcd out thc knee of the demon attacking him and rammed his elbow in her temple, while Jacob fought against the two vampires who'd had the strongest intensity among the original group who'd attacked us. Their movements were fast, almost a blur, and I couldn't tell if Jacob was winning or just holding his own.

Marcus growled and clawed at the wrist of the vampire choking him, but she held tight even though blood poured from her arm. With a snarl, she heaved him around and slammed him against the wall. His head snapped back and he gasped.

I wrenched against the vampire holding me, my buzz biting stronger. Marcus couldn't die. Not today. Not if I could help it. Except I couldn't break free. Not without using my magic and endangering everyone.

"They say you're delicious," the vampire hissed in my ear, her breath hot against my neck.

I rammed my elbow back, drawing an *oomph*, but she didn't let go.

Marcus gurgled and his movements grew weaker.

"Jacob, Kol," Gideon barked. "Protect Marcus and Essie."

But the guys, like Gideon, were caught fighting multiple people and could barely shove forward, let alone move the thirty feet to us.

"They say that's why Jacob left Victoria for you." She raked her fangs across my throat, not hard enough to pierce skin, but enough to let me know what she planned — as if I hadn't already figured it out.

Fuck no. Panic seized my chest and my buzz exploded out of my control into a fiery inferno, blazing from my whole body, not just my hands.

Oh fuck oh fuck oh fuck. I scrambled to hold my power back, but it roared through my mental grip and filled the hall with blinding white light, forcing me to squeeze my eyes shut. The vampire screamed and collapsed at my feet, panting and moaning, and thank God, not dead. The roar of the fight snapped to silence, and for a second I feared I'd killed everyone. Except if I hadn't killed the vampire who'd been holding me, surely those farther away had taken a weaker blow. Then screaming and yelling filled the hall, and my vision returned.

The vampire holding Marcus looked at me with horror. Everyone who wasn't running looked at me with horror.

My whole body shook and I fought to breathe. The buzz was gone and so was the fire, replaced with a bone-deep chill.

"You wanted a fight," Jacob said, his voice low, dangerous.

The vampire released Marcus and bolted. So did everyone else.

Marcus grabbed the wall, steadying himself and leaving a bloody smear. "Your eyes are glowing," he said, his voice raspy.

"We need to get the hell out of here before someone comes to the wrong conclusion." Gideon glanced down the hall behind him. "Jacob, help Marcus. Kol, take Essie."

Kol opened his mouth as if he were going to argue, then snapped it shut. Save for Marcus, none of my guys looked too hurt, but Gideon had an edge in his eyes and a tension in his body and we all knew it was because our not-yet-solidified bond, when he'd seen me in danger, had filled him with fear.

Jacob threw Marcus over his shoulder, and Kol swept me into his arms without giving me warning.

"Keep your eyes hidden," he said without looking at me. "That fight was bad enough. I don't want to deal with the rest of the hotel."

I wrapped my arms around his neck and buried my face in his shoulder, savoring the warmth radiating from his body. I wasn't freezing, not like I'd been when my brands had formed, but I was still cold, hollow.

He held me as if I didn't weigh anything, but his body was too stiff, his discomfort at carrying me clear. I ached to go back to the time before my wings had appeared, to the time when cuddling with him was safe and comforting.

We hurried down the hall and rounded a corner — best guess was we'd left the theater and were back in the main hall leading to the vestibule, but I wasn't going to risk someone seeing my eyes to take a peek. The rumble of voices returned, filled with excitement and fear and curiosity.

"Go straight to the SUV," Gideon said over the coms. "I'll grab our weapons."

Kol hurried out of the hotel, and sunlight and muggy summer heat wrapped around me. Sweat beaded on my forehead and between my breasts, but I didn't care. We were out of there and all my guys were safe.

"Can you walk?" he asked, shifting to set me on my feet without waiting for an answer, even though we were only halfway across the parking lot and not at the SUV.

"Yeah." I didn't know if I could, but I didn't want to make Kol more uncomfortable than he already was.

He put me down, but surprisingly held my shoulders to steady me. Hellfire and pain blazed in his eyes, breaking my heart.

I pulled my com out of my ear and swallowed against the lump in my throat. "When this is over, I'll take a break from the team," I whispered. And the break wasn't just for him. I needed a moment to catch my breath and figure out how to deal with my magic.

He took out his com. "You know none of them will accept that." He pulled his gaze from mine. "I can manage. Be a professional."

Gideon hurried out of the hotel and caught up to us. Kol put his com back in, took his blades, and strode toward the SUV.

I holstered my Glock, frustrated at my disappointment. *He just needs time. And he isn't mine.* No matter how much I wanted him to be.

"You okay?" Gideon asked, his voice husky, sending a shiver of need through me.

"Are you?"

He reached to cup my cheek, his breath a little too fast.

Please touch me. Please kiss me.

But if he did I wouldn't be able to stop myself, and we'd end up having sex in the parking lot.

He jerked his hand away. "I can still work."

Marcus grunted over the coms but didn't argue.

We headed to the SUV. Jacob had set Marcus on the middle bench behind the driver's seat and had started the engine, while Kol had climbed into the back. Gideon took his usual seat and I climbed in beside Marcus.

"How are you?" I asked him.

"I'll shift when we get to Pinebrook. That'll help." He threaded his fingers between mine and I leaned into him.

Jacob drove to a major cross street in the middle of Squatters' Row, and turned away from the rest of the Quarter and the human part of Union City, heading to the outskirts of town.

This part of the city had been expropriated by the plan for population growth of the supernatural community, and Pinebrook had been a part of that multi-year development. So while it wasn't near much of anything at the moment, that didn't mean it'd always be that way.

It sat on the other side of a small, abandoned single-story public school. Weeds grew out of cracks around the foundation, and all the windows were either broken or boarded up. Those boarded up had been tagged with graffiti, and so had every inch of the school's dirty-gray siding. Jacob drove around back and parked near the rusted shell of a portable building, as close as the SUV could get to the forest without off-roading.

Marcus had already taken off his boots and T-shirt, and he climbed out of the back and shed his jeans. God, he was gorgeous. Ripped muscles, a tight ass, and those piercing green eyes. His neck was red with little runnels of blood that had trickled down his throat from where the vampire had punctured his skin with her nails, and a massive bruise was forming on his chest.

He flashed me a tired smile, took a step forward, and his body turned to liquid flesh, morphing in one fluid movement from human to wolf.

I'll run ahead and see if I can find a break in the wall, he said in my head.

"Go. We're right behind." Gideon gathered Marcus's clothes as Marcus bounded off, then Kol and Gideon hurried after him, while Jacob offered me his arm.

"Thanks." I was still weak and unsteady, and didn't know how well I'd manage running through the forest. Especially since we still didn't know when the witches were going to do whatever they were going to do and had no idea how much time we actually had.

The hollowness in my chest hadn't eased in the five-minute ride from the hotel, and while a part of me was worried I didn't have any magic to defend the guys if we ran into trouble, another part of me was relieved. There wasn't any chance I'd accidently hurt someone if things got stressful.

I took Jacob's arm and he drew in a sharp breath, his gaze on my wrist. "We need to get these cuffs off you."

The metal containment cuff had melted, not just in a circlet into my skin, but had dripped runnels down my forearm, and my skin was raw and blistered.

"Not until we figure out how to control my magic," I said, pushing through the tall grass and weeds that used to be the school's football field. "It's too dangerous. I think I'm out of power now, but for how long?"

"Every super recovers their magic differently. Archangels have a deeper connection to the Realm of Celestial Light, so they tend to recover pretty fast," he said.

"So I'm going to return to being a bomb sooner rather than later. Just great."

We reached the edge of the forest. Gideon and Kol were already inside, jogging down a narrow path, and Marcus was out of sight.

"You'll get control," Jacob said. "You just need time to get used to it."

"It's all just so overwhelming." I'd been running on adrenaline, trying — and failing — to keep hold of my emotions. But the adrenaline was about to run out and I was afraid what my reaction would be. "I keep trying to tell myself it's fine. I'm fine. But I'm scared of what I can do, of all the people I can hurt. Of hurting all of you."

"You won't hurt us."

"I burned Gideon to a crisp a few days ago." My throat tightened at the memory of Gideon screaming as he sucked in all my power, stopping me from killing myself. "The power within me now feels stronger than that. The cuffs can barely contain it." I bit back a bitter laugh. "They can't contain it. Not when I'm scared."

"And you'll get control. You're one of the strongest people I know." He grabbed me, making me yelp in surprise, and swept me into his arms. "Give yourself a break."

"I can walk, you know."

He tightened his grip on me. "Break, remember?"

Fine. I leaned into him, resting my cheek against his massive chest. As a vampire he didn't have a heartbeat, but I could feel something gently pulsing inside him. It pulsed inside me, too, through our brand. A thrumming certainty that we belonged together, that we'd have each other's back.

"You might not be in transition like a shifter," he said, his low voice rumbling through me, "but you're changing. And any supernatural change is hard." A whisper of sadness crept into his certainty.

Had he had trouble? He'd once been human. I didn't know how difficult it was to become a vampire, although it didn't strike me as easy since one of the steps was dying. Marcus had also had trouble. He'd said it had taken him over a year to feel right in his own skin again. But my transformation wasn't anything like that. My DNA wasn't being rewritten, turning me into something else. It felt wrong to compare my struggle with theirs.

"Except I'm not actually changing, not like you or Marcus did. I've always been this. I just didn't know it."

"You thought you were a powerless nephilim. Your body felt like a powerless nephilim's. Now you have power you can't control. You're afraid of hurting people. You're scared," Jacob said. "Sounds like you're changing to me."

"How did you deal with it?"

"You should probably ask Marcus. I didn't handle my death well." Jacob's eyes darkened, his control on his intensity slipping. "I wasn't exactly willing, but Logan wanted more power and Victoria wouldn't turn him without turning me as well."

"So your brother coerced you?" That was horrible. Even though we'd had to kill Logan to prevent the hellfire prince Ibizual from escaping his cage, that didn't mean Jacob hadn't loved him. Logan's family had taken Jacob in, and the two had grown up together like brothers.

"Back then I would have done anything for Logan," he said. "I let him convince me that I could accept being a vampire. That a life of darkness and blood was an acceptable price for vengeance. It took me a long time of fighting my new nature, starving myself, feeling sorry for myself to come to terms with the new me. I fought my transition every step of the way, drew out the torture." He stopped walking and met my gaze, his quiet stillness radiating from the brand. "Don't fight it. It won't be easy, but you can get through it."

My emotions swelled and I turned my gaze to a large break in the canopy above as I fought back irrational tears. The clouds were starting to thicken and the wind was picking up. A storm was building, just like the one that was building within me.

"We'll help you," he said.

"I know you will." And that was part of what scared me. They weren't going to leave me alone, and I was an explosion waiting to happen.

ESSIE

WE JOGGED FOR ABOUT FIFTEEN MINUTES AND REACHED A SIX-FOOT BRICK wall half covered in moss and vines, with trees and bushes growing against it. It marked the edge of the Quarter's limit and had been magically put there, along with all the other features that had been magically added to the Quarter, when it had first been created. Not all the walls in all the forests were this tall, but, by request from the shifter community, there was always something to let a shifter caught up in the excitement of a chase know where the Quarter ended.

Thankfully this was the narrowest part of Pinebrook, although while this was the easiest way to get to it, it didn't mean that Willow lived close by. Gideon was looking along the wall off to the right, while Kol leaned against it, his posture relaxed and languid until he saw me.

Marcus loped toward us, bounding over a fallen log and skirting a thick bush. He reached us and shifted, one step as a wolf, the next as a human.

"There's a gate in the wall about ten yards that way." He pointed the way he'd come and took his jeans from Gideon. "It opens to a path leading to a cabin on a hill."

"All right." Kol pushed away from the wall, heading in the direction Marcus had pointed. "Let's do this."

"Amiah said to be gentle." Gideon dropped Marcus's boots in front of him and Marcus shoved in his feet. "Kol, I want her to see you first."

"And I should be the last," Jacob said.

"You know we already know this, Gideon," Kol said over the coms, not stopping or looking back at us.

"Give the man a break. He's not at his best right now." Marcus laced up his boots and pulled on his T-shirt. "And you and Essie are fixing that the moment we get back to Bane's." Gideon opened his mouth and Marcus glared at him. "The *moment* we get back. I'll get you two once we know what the witches are up to."

"Don't I get a say in this?" I asked.

"Would you prefer the SUV? I didn't think that was your style, but then—" Marcus glanced at Jacob and offered me a wry smile, making me instantly think of being in bed with both of them. "You did surprise me."

"I surprised you?" I asked as he hurried after Kol. "You surprised the hell out of me."

Jacob chuckled and easily fell into step beside Marcus with his enhanced speed. "I think we can agree the most surprised was Kol."

"Can we *please* stop talking about sex," Gideon begged, the tendons in his neck straining.

We reached a tall wrought-iron gate in the wall that swung on well-oiled hinges, and followed a gravel path through a field of flowering weeds to a log cabin. The sun fought to slice through clouds that did little to alleviate the summer's heat, and while the guys had to be exhausted even with the extra strength I'd given them, they didn't slow their pace. Yes, we didn't need Willow right away because Cassius was in the temporal freeze, but we did need to confirm her help and get back to stopping the witches. Because once we'd dealt with the witches — and we sure as hell were going to deal with them — Cassius would need immediate help.

The one-story log cabin wasn't very big, probably just a single room. Overgrown bushes with big dark leaves and bright red flowers crowded the front door and the single window and carried around the side of the building. Beside it, ten feet away, sat a shed made up of a patchwork of siding and a tin roof with a large, healthy vegetable garden stretching behind it. A single, massive maple offered shade behind the house and just about every possible flower bloomed in a chaotic jumble around the tree, edging the garden, curling past the shed, and even trailing back to an outhouse.

"Do you think she's out here because she's a shaman and wants to be with nature or because she's a firebird and fragile?" Although I wasn't quite sure what exactly a firebird shifter was.

We reached a front door that, while weathered, looked solid and secure. Jacob set me on my feet and moved back, while Gideon and Marcus took up position behind Kol. Even with Kol's sexy smile they were still going to be intimidating. I slipped past Marcus and stood beside Kol. I didn't know if this made us look any less intimidating, but at least she wasn't opening the door to a wall of muscular men.

Kol knocked.

A sparrow on the shed's roof chirped and took off.

Kol knocked again.

A gust of wind caught a loose strand from my ponytail and tickled my cheek.

"How long do we wait?" he asked. "We've only got about six hours left until the witches' temporal freeze ends."

"We take five minutes. Search the area," Gideon said, his voice icy and hard, even though the idea that we couldn't get Cassius help had to be eating him up. "Then we have to head back."

"I'll call in a favor with the pack. Get someone to sit on the house." Marcus headed to the shed.

"Thanks." Gideon pushed through the thick bush to peer in the windows.

Someone screamed, and a small, pale, feminine face appeared on the other side of the window directly in front of Gideon, making him jerk back. She had yellow, orange, and pink spiky hair and a small mouth and nose. Sparks danced off all of her exposed skin, and her eyes were blue... no, brown... no, green... no, purple?

"No no no no," she said, her words fast, her voice high-pitched and soft, softer than it should have been with how angry she looked and how thin the glass appeared. "You've ruined my bush!"

"Willow?" Gideon asked.

"Get out of my bush! I'm not talking to you," she snapped. "I didn't answer the door and that means I don't want to talk to you."

"We need your help," Gideon said.

"Did I open the door? No, I didn't," she said, without giving Gideon a chance to answer, more sparks bursting around her. "That means I'm not talking to you."

Kol bit back a snort. "Except she *is* talking with us," he said under his breath.

"We don't have time for this." Marcus shouldered Kol aside, and tried the door. It opened without him forcing it and he stepped inside. "Now, listen—"

"Get out! Get out!" Willow squawked, her voice rising an octave and gaining a little more volume.

I hurried in after Marcus. "Amiah sent us."

Willow froze, tilted her head to the side, making a lock of pink hair sweep over her shoulder, and blinked her green, yes, green— blue?— something eyes. She didn't have any of the feral intensity I recognized as a shifter's magic, but she did have power. It half fluttered and half unfurled in my chest, as if it couldn't decide what it was. It wasn't crushing like Victoria's or Voth's, but it wasn't weak, either. Just... different.

Kind of like the rest of her. She looked to be about my age, was thin, five foot nothing, and had multi-colored hair of a variety of lengths and kaleidoscope eyes. She wore men's boardshorts with a yellow and red Hawaiian pattern on them that came halfway down her calves, and her top was a billowy, short-sleeved blouse with fringe and sequins and dotted with snowflakes and stars.

I took a tentative step toward her. "Our friend has been enspelled with worship magic and Amiah thinks you're the only one who can help him."

"We really need your help," Kol said from the doorway.

She narrowed her eyes and glared at him. A single spark jumped from her cheek and vanished in a small puff of smoke. "The angel ruined my bush."

"I'm sorry about your bush." Gideon stepped past Kol and drew close to me. "My brother is dying. Please."

"My bush could have died."

"Willow," Kol said, his voice sliding across my senses, soft and sensual. A whisper of heat unfurled within me, but I knew the sliver of power wasn't for me.

"It. Could. Have. Died." She crossed her arms and raised her chin, not even a flicker of desire for him in her now yellow eyes.

"For fuck's sake. We're on a bit of a time limit. He said he's sorry." Marcus took a step toward her, and her defiance vanished. With a squeak and flurry of sparks, she scrambled to the far side of the cabin, heaved open the back door, and bolted outside.

"Wait." I ran after her, but she'd only gotten ten feet away when she skidded to a halt, her attention locked on Jacob on the other side of her vegetable garden.

"He won't hurt you," I said. *Please, calm down so we can talk to you.* I tried to will her to listen to us, to help us, but her gaze never left Jacob. "None of them will hurt you."

She extended a hand to Jacob and wove her way through the garden, slow and careful, as if she were afraid *she'd* spook him. He crouched so he wasn't towering over her, and waited for her to come to him.

I followed a few feet behind her and Gideon stayed back, motioning to Marcus and Kol to do the same.

"I've never seen one in the daylight before," she said, as if Jacob were a rare animal or bird that she was finally getting a glimpse of. She glanced back at me, a flicker of eye contact before returning to Jacob. "I don't know why you bother with the others when you have him. So still. So calm. How can you be in the sun?"

"I have a special charm." Jacob sat in the grass and raised his wrist, showing the thick silver bracelet with prongs every eighth of an inch digging into his skin.

Willow shifted closer to him and reached out with a tentative hand. She brushed her finger over the charm then jerked her hand back, her expression filled with wonder.

"Amiah said you might be able to help us," he said, his deep voice soft, filled with a tenderness that made my heart swell. "Our friend has a worship magic— an essence-based spell on him."

She drew a little closer and sat, her hand darting out again to touch his charm. "The turbulent angel's brother. But that isn't why he's breaking."

"No." Jacob's gaze rose to mine, filled with love and worry.

Willow followed his gaze to me. "But you're not breaking because you have him. So much stillness."

I knelt in the soft grass near her, but out of reach, hoping she wouldn't feel threatened. "We were confused and now—"

"Now the angel is breaking." She frowned, blinked, and did another bird-like tilt of her head. "You're broken, too, but not *breaking* and not because of him."

I wasn't sure what to say to that. A part of me was broken because I hadn't solidified my bond with Gideon, but I had a feeling she was talking about my magic and not my love life.

"And not because of all that—" She waved at my guys and scrunched her nose. "So much activity, noise. So so loud."

"Is that why you live out here?" I asked.

"People have too much life." She tentatively pressed a finger to the back of Jacob's hand. When he didn't move, she took his hand between her tiny ones and turned it palm up. "It vibrates too fast, charged with emotion." She traced a line in Jacob's hand. "You have emotions. Deep emotions. But you're so still. The angel and wolf and demon are blinding, grating."

"Am I grating?" I asked Willow. "I'll move back." I didn't want to jeopardize getting her help because I was grating to her magical senses.

"You burn brighter than all of them." Her frown returned. "But there's something I need to tell you."

"What?"

Her eyes flashed through the rainbow with gold and silver thrown in. "I can't remember. You should leave."

I glanced at Jacob, who shrugged.

"Can you help us? Can you break an essence-based spell? Will you come into the Quarter and remove the spell on Gideon's brother?" I asked as I stood.

Jacob started to rise, but she tightened her grip on his hand. "No."

"No you won't come to the Quarter?" Jacob asked. "Or no I shouldn't leave?"

"Correct."

"What the fuck?" Marcus growled.

She looked up at me. "Yes, yes, no, yes, and yes."

Ah...?

"Did she just answer your questions?" Kol asked.

"So you can break an essence-based spell and you will help us, but you won't go into the Quarter?" Except once Cassius was out of the temporal freeze, I doubted he had the time to be hauled through the forest. "Cassius can't be moved."

"If I'm with you, can you handle being in the Quarter?" Jacob asked.

She turned a brilliant, adoring smile to Jacob. "Can I have him? Please? So still and calm and kind. He's perfect."

"I belong with Essie," Jacob said.

She stroked his hand as if petting an animal. "She can visit."

"Is this the price for saving Cassius?" I wasn't sure I wanted to know.

So far every super I'd come across traded in something other than money.

She blinked at me. "Should it be?"

"No," Jacob said quickly. His gaze rose to mine and captured me with its dark intensity. My pulse picked up with need and awe for the love in his eyes. "I'd start breaking if I stayed with you. Just like the angel."

"That's why she can visit," Willow huffed.

"It he stays, we all stay," Marcus said, raising his voice so she could hear him.

"Marcus—" Gideon hissed.

Marcus shot him a dark look. "We'll be crammed in your little cabin. All the time. Killing your bushes. Being emotional."

Her eyes widened in horror and a spark jumped off her cheek. "You'd let him do that?" she asked Jacob.

"Essie wouldn't be able to leave me, and Marcus and Gideon can't leave her," he said.

"Then you *can't* stay." She jerked to her feet and stormed farther from the cabin with a trail of sparks and smoke. "No no no. You can't stay."

"Damn, Marcus," Gideon snapped. "We need her."

I scrambled to my feet. "Please. You're the only one who can help."

"But you have to promise not to stay." She whipped around to face me, her body tense and vibrating as if she needed to fight, her eyes deep purple. Sparks snapped and popped around her. "None of you stay. Promise."

"Promise." Jeez, so much for Willow being the last sane shaman on the planet.

She stomped her foot. "And I'm not leaving my cabin."

"But we need you to remove the spell." The conversation was going around in circles and we really didn't have the time. How the hell did I convince her to come into the Quarter?

"I don't need to leave to do that." She rolled her now blue eyes at me as if I should have known that and held out her hand to Jacob. "I can give you a door and a bell. Just ring and open and I'll work through you."

Jacob took her hand. "Thank you."

She closed her eyes and the strength of her power swelled.

"Wait—"

Her eyes flew open and the power dimmed. "What?"

"Is it permanent?" The answer wouldn't change Jacob's decision. Even if it was permanent, he'd say yes — I would have, too — but I wanted to know everything we were getting ourselves into. We'd already walked blindly into Voth's attack, thinking we were just there to buy a master ward. I wasn't sure why I'd thought it'd be a simple deal, nothing so far with the supernatural world had been simple, but I wasn't going to be caught off guard twice in one day.

"Permanent? No." Horror flooded her face again. "Permanent means you'll stay and you can't stay. You'll kill my bush." Her eyes snapped closed and her power swept over me like a giant wave.

I dropped to one knee and Jacob tensed, but I waved him off. I was fine. Willow's power wasn't nearly as crushing as Voth's.

"I can handle it," I said, hoping the others would stay back as well.

Her strange fluttering power beat against my ribs as if trying to escape, and heat swelled in Jacob's brand.

Willow clicked her tongue and did another bird-like tilt of her head. Golden light blazed from our brands, both my arm and his, and the fluttering grew faster. My buzz stayed quiet, making my stomach queasy. I really was out of magic and defenseless, and my fear of not being able to protect myself and my guys grew beyond my fear of accidentally hurting someone.

"You can't be in here," Willow said, the fluttering pounding harder in my chest. "The door is just his. Only his."

"How do I get out?" I gasped.

"Just get out," she snapped.

Sure. Just like that. I tried to open myself up and release the flutter, but it turned into desperate slamming strokes inside me. Maybe I needed to imagine distance between me and Jacob. I thought about drawing away from him, imagined a great void between us.

The heat and light in my brand blazed stronger and Jacob's power, calm and intense, swelled around my heart.

Willow scrunched her face in concentration, and a piece of the fluttering, still smashing inside me, snapped off. Jacob gasped and Willow fell back onto her butt.

"Is it done?" Gideon asked.

"No thanks to you." She whirled around and glared at me, sparks bursting off her. "You shouldn't have been in there. You—"

Her head snapped back and the fluttering exploded inside me. Her power burned along every nerve and seared into every cell, stealing my breath.

Jacob leaped to my side and caught me as I toppled over. Willow grabbed my hand, her eyes no color and every color, wide with fear, her sparks showering around us, stinging my skin.

"Hide. You have to hide. You must hide." Her tiny nails dug into my palm. "She's looking for you!"

"Who's looking for her?" Marcus asked, his voice right beside me and in my ear.

"Mommy," she said.

My mom? How could my mom be looking for me? She's dead. But the moment I thought that, I knew Willow hadn't meant the woman who'd raised me. "My birth mother. She's looking for me? She's still alive?"

Willow's hand trembled... or was that me trembling? My thoughts stuttered at that. I hadn't realized until now that I'd assumed if both of my biological parents were angels, then they'd died in the war. If they'd lived, surely they would have come for me by now.

"What do you know about Essie's mother?" Gideon asked, his voice also close.

The fire of Willow's power sputtered, with sparks that stung my skin as well as inside me jerking my essence. On off. On off. On—

"Too much power. Too much emotion." Sparks flashed off her cheeks and hands. "It's in everything. Woven into the heart of every flake of essence. You have to hide. You must hide. She lost the war but she's not dead, and when she finds you, she'll take you."

Ice swept into me as Willow's heated magic sputtered off and stayed off. My mom— my biological mom was looking for me. She wasn't dead. And she'd lost the war.

She'd fought with Michael against humanity and the Angelic Defense.

"You can't stay here! Hide!" Willow hissed at me and bolted into her cabin with a flurry of sparks.

I dragged my gaze from Jacob's intense stare, to Marcus's piercing green gaze, to Gideon's summer sky, to Kol's hellfire. They looked as scared as I felt, and Willow's fear had shaken me to my core. I hadn't thought I had enough magic for my empathy to work, especially with the containment cuffs on, but her fear terrified me.

"What just happened?" Marcus asked, his wolf slitting his pupils. "Who the hell is your mother?"

"We'll figure that out later." Gideon straightened. "Did we get what we needed to save Cassius?"

"Yes." Jacob adjusted his grip to carry me, his hold a little too tight, his body trembling.

"Then let's move." Gideon hurried back toward the forest and we followed.

I didn't know if we were running to get away from the threat of my biological mother or because we needed to get back on track with figuring out what the witches were doing. I couldn't get my mind to work enough to think straight. I had to hide. I couldn't let her find me. I—

Jacob climbed into the back of the SUV, still holding me, while the rest of the guys piled in. I hadn't even noticed us running into the forest or leaving it.

If my mother had fought for Michael, did that mean he was my father? God, could I be the child of the angel who'd slaughtered billions of people? Sure, I'd had nothing to do with that, but— Maybe I was still a monster, just not a nephilim.

Except maybe Michael wasn't my dad. Rafael and Lucifer had also fought for him. But that thought didn't make me feel any better. Rafael had been Michael's right hand during the war, and Lucifer was... well, Lucifer.

"Who the hell am I?"

Jacob pressed his lips to the top of my head. "You're Esther Shaw."

"Am I? My mom fought for Michael. My dad—" I tried to focus on the calm within Jacob's brand, let it seep into me, ease my panic, but couldn't still my whirling thoughts enough to draw in his stillness.

"Your dad could have fought for the Angelic Defense," Gideon said. "If your mom chose Michael's side and your father didn't, it'd make sense he'd want to hide you until the war was done."

"But he didn't come back for me." My throat tightened with all the hurt that I'd spent years pushing deep inside me. It was like I was nine again and realizing for the first time that no matter what my mom said, he was never coming back for me.

And now my mom wasn't my mom. But of course, I already knew that. If I was a full angel, the woman I loved, who'd given everything for me, was just some woman. Except she wasn't *just* some woman. She was the only parent I'd ever known. The only one who'd known my secret— although maybe she hadn't known. Maybe my father had lied and told her I was a nephilim.

But then why would she have lied to me about being my biological mother? Why lie about loving my father?

It was all a lie. My whole life had been a lie.

MARCUS

I drove back to Bane's, my gaze constantly jumping to Essie's reflection in the rearview mirror. She was too pale, shaken from what Willow had said.

Except it wasn't just from what Willow had said. It was from everything that had happened to her today. Things had finally seemed right this morning. She'd woken in bed with Gideon, been accepted onto the team by Cassius, and in the blink of an eye, everything had gone to shit.

It broke my heart seeing her so uncertain. The determined, confident officer I'd first met, the one who'd raced in to save a little girl against four werewolves without backup was now overwhelmed, turned into a woman afraid of herself because she didn't want to hurt anyone. And with her terrifying power, a power so strong it was able to break through the magic of the containment cuffs, there was a good chance she would.

On top of that, she'd just been told her biological mother had fought for Michael during the war and while Jacob had said her father had probably fought for the Angelic Defense and that was why she'd been hidden, there was still a chance her father was Michael or Rafael or, God forbid, Lucifer.

There were only so many archangels and I had no idea if those who'd fought for the Angelic Defense had had children before the war. It also didn't explain why he, or someone else from his family, hadn't returned for her when the war was over, why she'd been left to grow up afraid of everyone discovering she was a nephilim.

No, the more logical explanation was that her father was one of those archangels and she'd been stolen and hidden away and whoever had done it had died before he could retrieve her, which would explain why she'd been enspelled to look like a human and why her mother was now searching for her.

And Essie was smart enough to have figured all that out, as well as the fact that if her mother did find her, she'd have to arrest her as a war criminal.

Willow's warning likely hadn't helped either. The shaman had sounded terrified and saying that Essie had to hide or her mother would take her suggested her mother wasn't just an ordinary angel.

Bane had said that *at least* one of Essie's parents was an archangel, but that might not have fully sunk in until now and that just piled on top of everything else she was dealing with.

Beside me, Gideon shuddered, his expression tight with pain, his skin gray, and his angel glow dimming then flickering back to its regular brightness, reminding me that we had to deal with one problem at a time. And right now, he was the biggest problem.

There was no way he was going to be able to last until we'd dealt with the witches, which meant he and Essie had to have sex as soon as we got back to Bane's. It was going to have to be quick and wasn't what either of them deserved, but it had to be done.

My wolf huffed at that, not because our mate was going to have sex with someone else but because Gideon was an idiot to have put off sealing their bond.

If he'd just accepted it, they'd have had all the time they deserved, sensual showers, long drawn-out lovemaking, and cuddling in bed afterward... not that I'd gotten much of that, either, but I'd at least had the satisfaction of having her fall asleep in my arms. And by falling asleep with me, she showed me that she trusted me and my wolf implicitly, something I hadn't known I needed.

My gaze darted to Essie again, wrapped in Jacob's arms in the back of the SUV. They hadn't had enough time together, either, but at least they'd sealed their bond.

A flicker of hellfire caught my eye and my attention jumped to Kol on the seat behind Gideon. The incubus's posture was almost as tense as Gideon's, and while I'd first thought it was because Essie had triggered his PTSD when she'd released her wings, I was beginning to wonder if it was something else.

Every time I looked at him, he was either pointedly not looking at Essie or staring at her with an expression that was filled with an aching longing instead of fear. Then he'd remember himself and wrench his attention away. It was probably because we kept getting the shit beaten out of us and Essie was an easy source to refuel his life force.

But of course, knowing him, he didn't want to ask her to have sex with one of us so he could feed. Sure, he flirted and teased all of us, but he was the most tentative incubus I'd ever met. His line between appropriate and inappropriate was solidly on the modest side, and he always tried to keep a tight rein on his magic when around people, especially women.

And while I didn't know the details, I knew his behavior had everything to do with what that sick fuck, Michael, had done to him.

Hell, he was probably feeling guilty just riding the high he got when Jacob or I made love to Essie, except I had a feeling he wouldn't believe any of us if we told him we didn't mind — and I had no doubt all of us, including Gideon, were fine with it.

But again, one problem at a time.

I couldn't fix Kol with a single conversation, no one could, and I couldn't make Essie regain her confidence and come to terms with her parentage with a single conversation, either. Those things took time and Gideon resisting his bond and whatever the witches were doing took priority.

I could only hope that once everything was said and done we'd all be alive to deal with the rest.

Marcus parked in the alley near Sebastian's private door and we got out of the SUV. Jacob reached to pick me up again but I pushed his hands away. I couldn't let him carry me. I had to take action. Do something. Anything. Hide. Cry. Scream.

Pull your shit together.

Gideon needed me. The whole team needed me. Even if I physically couldn't help with the fight against the witches, they wouldn't be able to focus if they were worrying about me.

We climbed the stairs, but even knowing that freaking out wasn't helping them, I couldn't push it all down.

It was all a lie.

The words kept whirling around and around in my head.

A lie, and my mother was powerful and terrifying and looking for me.

We reached the top floor, but I couldn't bring myself to step into the hall and head to Sebastian's apartment. It was too much. I had to think, draw breath, do— God, I didn't know what.

"Essie?" Jacob asked.

I glanced up the stairs leading to the roof. "I just need a minute."

Marcus shot a look at Gideon. He didn't look well and we needed to solidify our bond, but—

A minute, that was all I needed. Sky. Quiet. A moment to mourn a life that had all been a lie.

"Take as much time as you need," Gideon said.

I pulled out my com, not wanting to hear the guys, shoved it in my pocket, and fled up the stairs. Tears burned my eyes and tightened my throat. Fear, hard and cold, squeezed my chest.

The door at the top of the stairs opened onto a barren rooftop with a tall metal HVAC unit. The UV-blocking canopy angled down and attached to the far side of the roof, marking the edge of the vampires' part of the Quarter. It tinted the brilliant sunlight purple, making it feel off. Just like I felt off. Add a lack of breezes, particularly with the clouds above racing by, and the roof didn't feel freeing or comforting.

A tear broke free and rolled down my cheek. Standing on a rooftop had always made me feel safe. Which was crazy, since Mom had always told me angels attacked from above. But now I knew why. I was an angel. And my mom wasn't my mom.

And I was trapped on this roof. The glass canopy was less than seven feet above me. Even if I could release my wings and knew how to fly, it'd be a challenge to take off. I'd have to go to the other side and jump.

Maybe I should. Run. Get the hell out of there. Hide like Willow had told me to do.

But that was the panic talking. When things got bad, I'd been taught to run. And I didn't want to run anymore.

I wanted to be with my guys. They'd stood by me even when they'd thought I was a nephilim. Which I wasn't. Because I was an angel and—

Come on. Pull it together. I could do this. I'd dealt with lots in the last couple of weeks. This was just one more thing. I could handle it. They'd said I was an angel and at least half archangel. I knew my father could have been on the wrong side of the war. I knew my mother could have been, as well. Deep down I had to have known Mom had lied to me. And really, did any of that change who I was? What kind of person I wanted to be?

Another tear rolled down my cheek, and I drew in a ragged breath.

I couldn't give in to my fear and grief. There'd be time after we'd dealt with the witches for that. Perhaps then I'd have calmed down and would be able to think straight.

I squared my shoulders and wiped my cheeks.

Right now my first priority was Gideon.

I drew another breath to steady myself. My guys had my back. They loved me regardless. With them, I could deal with anything.

My attention slid to my brands. Gideon's lightning gently crackled over my arm, and Jacob's powerful stillness seeped into me. I was stronger than I'd ever been before, and that had nothing to do with my growing magical power. I'd faced monsters and survived. I'd faced monsters and saved my guys. Even exhausted and fighting to contain my dangerous magic, I could handle whatever came next.

"I've been looking for you," a familiar sultry alto said behind me.

I jerked around, and Victoria rushed toward me with her enhanced vampiric speed, faster than humanly possible. I turned to run, and she clamped a hand around my neck and squeezed.

"You took what's mine." Her gaze jumped to my eyes. A hint of hesitation flickered over her expression, but then she released her power with an intensity that stole what little breath I had left. "And now you have the nerve to enter *my* house."

I clawed at her hand, my lungs screaming for air. Her lips, painted blood red, curled into a sneer, revealing the tips of her fangs. She was horrifying and beautiful, with her hunger filling her gaze and her voluptuous curves barely covered in a tight black dress.

"Thought you could sneak in?" She raised me up with her enhanced strength.

My toes skimmed the rooftop. I clutched her wrist with both hands, and darkness swarmed the edge of my vision. My thoughts jumped to my light strike, but my buzz didn't even whisper under my skin.

"You think you can do anything," she snarled.

The words of the light strike spell rushed in my head, something I hadn't needed for a while now. But still no buzz. Not even a glimmer of light in my palms.

Come on. Please. I had to get free, but I was too physically weak to make her let go and I didn't have any power to blast her with light.

"You think the mark on your arm protects you." She slammed me into the side of an HVAC unit, cracking my head and shooting stars across my vision.

Her grip eased, and I drew in a ragged breath before she tightened it again.

"He was mine." With her free hand she grabbed my hair and dug her nails into my scalp. "Mine." Her fangs extended in full and her intensity swelled, the pressure of her power crushing inside my chest.

Fear pounded through me. Still no light, no buzz. The words of the light strike spell muddled. My thoughts muddled.

"No one takes what's mine." She released my throat, and I gasped in another ragged breath as she sank her fangs into my neck with slicing pain.

With a snarl, she dug the nails of her now free hand into my chest and pinned me to the HVAC unit. She took a long pull, not using her magic, sending screaming pain through my neck.

No. Please, God, no.

I yanked my leg up to knee her in the groin, but she pressed close, her body tight against mine, making it impossible to land a good blow with knees or hands, not that I had the strength to move her. But I couldn't just stand there and let her kill me.

"Now I know why they want you," she said against my neck. "All this power. You're delicious. Should I drink you dry or save you for later?"

"The angels will come after you." I wrenched against her grip. "I'm sacred."

Her nails dug deeper into my chest and she took another agonizing pull. "Then I guess I can't drink too deep."

She ripped open my shirt and bit down hard. I screamed, making her purr with pleasure, and she pressed her palm over my heart, just like Jacob had done when he'd claimed me.

My pulse stuttered. I couldn't let her entwine her essence with mine. I might have been able to resist Jacob's claim after only a few weeks, but Victoria was a master vampire and so much more powerful than him.

I wrenched harder, but couldn't break free. My buzz sparked under my skin. *Yes!* And vanished. *No, please.*

"When you're mine, I'll make them watch you fuck me."

"Never," I gasped. *No. Please, no.*

My buzz sparked again and I mentally clutched at it. I couldn't draw enough breath to scream. It was the only thing that could save me. But it sputtered out, dying in my mental grasp.

"With my claim on you, you'll be begging for it."

Please, God. Help. "I don't consent."

"I don't care." Her crushing intensity slid into my veins, forcing my cells to thrum to her desires, just like they'd aligned with Jacob's when he'd claimed me.

She took another long pull on my vein and her palm heated. My soul screamed. I'd fought possession by the archnephilim and a hellfire prince. I had to be able to fight Victoria.

"The more I take, the stronger the claim." Another long pull.

The rooftop darkened and spun and a weight swept through my limbs. I strained to stay conscious. If I passed out, I became hers, and no way in hell was I becoming hers.

"Touch me," she purred.

My hand slid from her arm to her ribs.

God, no.

She moaned against my neck, the sound vibrating through me like Jacob's voice did, and my hand plunged into the front of her dress.

Get out of my soul. Get the fuck out.

My buzz sparked and I seized it, willing it to stay alive and grow stronger. I needed to release it. All of it. To hell with having any kind of control. I needed to get her away from me and force out her essence.

"I didn't say you could stop." She took another agonizing pull and her essence sank deeper into me.

I had to get it out. Even if I managed to blast her back, she'd still have control.

My hands started to move back to her breasts, but I yanked them away and slapped them against my chest. I released my buzz and fire erupted in my body, burning from my hands, through my skin, and into my cells. It surged against Victoria's essence, but with a snarl, her power grew stronger. The force of her magic stole my breath with its crushing weight and her essence roared, stronger than ever inside me.

I strained to hold onto my power, burn her out of me, but it wasn't enough. I barely had any magic left and I was fighting the containment cuffs on top of that. She was going to take control of me and there wasn't anything I could do. I just didn't have enough power.

My hands dipped under her skirt and skimmed her thighs.

No please. I didn't want to do this. *Fight. Flee. Please. Help!* But I couldn't draw breath, couldn't make my mouth work to yell.

Except I didn't have to yell. I had a connection with my guys. The cuffs didn't affect the brands.

Which meant I also had access to Gideon's power.

I concentrated on the lightning crackling over my right forearm, barely noticeable against Victoria's crushing power. I seized it and yanked it into me, letting it surge into my body.

Victoria tensed, her teeth digging deeper into my neck. I whimpered against the pain and gave in to Gideon's power. It seared every cell in my body with screaming agony and consumed Victoria's essence.

She howled and heaved away from me, her eyes wide with shock. "How did you do that?"

My knees gave out and I sagged to the rooftop.

"How did you—?"

The light in my palms stuttered and went out. My buzz vanished again and so, too, did Gideon's power.

Her shock snapped to rage. "You'll still pay for taking him. Even if I can't have you, you'll still pay."

She lunged at me. I tried to get out of the way, hit her, block her attack, anything. But she was too fast and I was too weak, and she sank her teeth back into my neck.

I FOUGHT AGAINST VICTORIA'S GRIP, BUT I HAD NO MORE STRENGTH AND NO more power. Her claws dug into my scalp and shoulder, pinning me against the HVAC unit, and sharp pain cut through my neck where she bit me.

I screamed to Gideon and Jacob in my head, begging for help over and over again, but had no idea if they could hear me. We hadn't communicated telepathically before. It might not even be a power we'd develop with our bonds. But it was the only thing I could do. Surely Gideon had felt me take his magic. Surely he knew I was in trouble.

The world darkened and spun, and I wondered how many times a person could be drained by a vampire in one day and survive. I tried to raise my arms but couldn't, and my breath slowed.

A faraway part of me realized I was sucking strength from my brands, but Victoria was consuming it as fast as I got it. It wasn't going to be enough to save me.

"Step away from her, Victoria," Gideon said from somewhere far away... or was I far away?

Victoria snarled, bit down harder and tore her teeth out of my throat. Hot blood gushed over my neck and down my chest. I gurgled and tried to clamp my hands over the wound but I was too weak to raise them.

"Oops," Victoria said with feigned innocence.

Someone yelled.

A blast of divine light slammed into Victoria and knocked her away from me.

Then Jacob appeared before me.

I hadn't seen him move, but I didn't think that had anything to do with his enhanced speed. He was fast. But not that fast.

"Get Priam," he yelled as he clamped a hand over my neck. "My magic isn't powerful enough to heal this."

I fought to breathe, each gasp an agony while blood raced down my chest, seeping into the lacy white bra Kol had gotten me.

"On your knees," Gideon said, his tone frigid. His divine light sword blazed in his hand brighter than I'd ever seen it before.

"She took what's mine. So I took payment in blood," Victoria hissed. "This is my house. My rules."

"Not for murder." The light in his eyes flared.

"Where's Priam?" Jacob's voice cracked. "Come on, Essie. Hold on."

I dragged my attention to Jacob, who swam in and out of focus. I wanted to tell him I loved him, I loved them all, but I was trapped in a body that wouldn't obey me, every thought and moment slow, stuttering, and heavy.

"Payment in blood is permitted," she said. "She took Jacob. It's not my fault she's not strong enough to pay the price."

"You tore open her throat," Marcus growled.

"Prove I did it on purpose." She cocked a sculpted eyebrow. "You surprised me. My fangs slipped."

"I'll fucking surprise you," Marcus snarled, prowling into my line of sight to stand beside Gideon, his fingers extended into claws and his eyes dark, his wolf on the verge of taking over.

She threw her head back and laughed. "I'm a master vampire, little wolf. None of you can take me."

"Sure, separately," Kol said. He was somewhere out of sight.

Priam dropped to his knees beside me, his face white, his expression tight with concern.

"You attacked a JP agent." Gideon pointed to the rooftop. "On your knees."

"There are no human agents." Victoria wiped a trickle of blood from her chin with her thumb and sucked it clean.

"Head office would beg to differ," Gideon said.

Priam captured my cheeks in his palms, forcing me to look at him.

"You're losing too much blood too quickly. I have to heal you fast. This will hurt."

Lightning exploded through me. I screamed and the rooftop vanished into darkness. Jacob's grip on my neck tensed, Victoria released her crushing power, and I fought to breathe.

"My house. My rules. Your delicate sensibilities don't matter. It doesn't even matter if she's really an agent. The JP will have your head if you illegally kill this master vampire."

"Maybe I don't care," Marcus said. "You tried to kill her."

"Prove it."

Light blazed from Gideon's eyes and he drew in a ragged breath, visibly trying to regain control of himself. "Her house. Her rules."

"Gideon—" Marcus snarled.

"We can't prove anything. She's in her right to claim a blood price for Jacob."

"Which has been paid in full," Jacob said, his hold on his vampiric intensity releasing, adding to the crush inside me.

She raised her chin. "You're worth more than what she can offer."

Marcus snarled. "Paid in full."

She huffed, her dark gaze sliding over my guys.

Jacob stood, murder in his eyes. "In. Full."

A hint of fear tightened her expression.

"Fine. Consider it paid." She squared her shoulders, pushing out her breasts, and sauntered past them with a seductive sway of her hips as if she hadn't just tried to kill me or they were ready to kill her.

Priam's magic turned into a blazing heat. Darkness enveloped me for a second then I dragged my eyes back open. My guys now crouched around me, bodies tense, eyes filled with fear. Sebastian muscled his way between Marcus and Priam, and dropped to his knees beside me. He activated the sleep glyph on his shoulder and pressed his hand over my heart.

Exhaustion swept over me, and I couldn't keep my eyes open.

Feet and bodies moved on the rooftop around me. Jacob wrapped me in his massive arms and lifted me while Priam's hands left my cheeks.

The guys argued as more heat blazed through me, and I drifted in and out of the dark nothingness. The not-water embraced me, but my father didn't appear. My guys drew close, stroking and caressing me, but the dream didn't fully form, leaving me aching with want. Then Kol's magic whispered through me, and the heat of his body pressed against me.

"We can't leave you for a minute," he said.

"This wasn't my fault." Pain crept into my body.

A curl of his magic unfurled in my chest. "You broke her link with Jacob."

"She was hurting him." There hadn't been anything else I could have done. Whether she'd wanted to or not, she'd almost killed Jacob and I'd had to protect him.

"So she hurt you back." His voice slid soft and sensual across my senses and his magic sank low within me. "They can't live without you."

"I can't live without them." I ached for more of his magic, for him to touch me. "Without any of you."

The magic in my chest swept away like fog in a sudden wind. "I'm not yours."

"But I want you to be." Jeez, sexy dream Kol wasn't being very sexy. He'd never been so hesitant before, but I guess even my subconscious realized what I had with him was broken.

"It's just my nature influencing you," he said, and his body heat drew away from me, leaving me cold.

KOL

I PRESSED MY LIPS AGAINST ESSIE'S FOREHEAD, SENDING ANOTHER SOFT thread of my magic into her, easing her pain. Bane had used his sleep spell on her again, but Priam hadn't had enough magic to fully heal her and in her sleep her expression was tight and she kept making little strained mewls and gasps as if even unconscious she could still feel the pain.

I wanted to do more — God, did I want to do more — but I had to stop with just easing her into a soft, blissful dream. She wasn't mine and she'd never be mine. She shouldn't be... no matter what she'd mumbled in her sleep.

Except every time one of the others touched her, I wanted to scream. *I* wanted to touch her. *I* wanted the look she gave them, the one filled with not just desire but love.

Look at me like you do them. Desire me like you do them... and mean it.

Because she did desire me. I could feel it taunting me, filling me, caressing me, and twisting me tight, but I knew she didn't mean it.

She shouldn't have still wanted to work with me after I'd tried to hurt her, and she sure as hell shouldn't have desire for me. But that only proved her desire was because of my magic and it wasn't real.

When she'd first walked out of the bedroom, leaning on Marcus and holding Gideon's hand, I'd expected her to yell at me. In the very least, I'd expected her to physically avoid me. But she hadn't and then when

I'd offered her my life force energy so she could save Jacob a second time, she'd acted as if I was the one who'd been wronged.

Which only made my heart hurt even more. It felt as if she saw me, the real me, not the sex demon, but the broken man with all the sharp ugly edges that Michael had torn into my soul, and she still cared.

Except it didn't mean what I wanted it to mean. It couldn't.

I forced myself away from her and into the hall of the high-end hotel suite Bane had taken us to. When she hadn't yelled at me, I thought that even though I was ashamed that I'd attacked her, I could eventually get over it and make things work and I wouldn't have to leave the team.

I'd told her I'd be a professional.

But I couldn't do it anymore.

God, I didn't want to leave. The team was the only place where I'd ever felt like myself, but Victoria ripped open Essie's throat and I hadn't been able to breathe. Then Victoria had fled and the others had rushed to her side as Priam worked to save her and all the oxygen left me. I wanted to shove them aside and tell them to get their hands off her. I wanted my turn and I knew in that moment I would never get it. I didn't belong. Not with her, not the way I wanted, and that crushed me.

But after trying to hurt her, I didn't deserve to be with her. Even if she did accept me and reciprocated my desire, she wouldn't really mean it.

And for the love of God, I didn't need her to reciprocate my desire. I didn't even need a turn by her side, holding her. I was an incubus. I could take another lover to feed, hell, I could be within a six-block radius of Essie while she had sex with the others and never need to search for sustenance again.

My chest tightened at that thought.

Fuck!

I punched the wall, managing at the last second to pull back my strength so I only cracked the drywall instead of putting my fist all the way through.

Something was seriously wrong with me. I was acting like Marcus. No, I was worse than Marcus, angry and jealous, and—

Fuck fuck fuck. I was losing my mind.

"She'll be okay," Jacob said, coming out of the bathroom, his bloody shirt in a heap on the floor. "She's weak but she's got me and Gideon giving her strength."

My gaze leaped to the delicate gold lines swirling over his right biceps and shoulder, the proof that he'd always been meant for her.

The vise around my chest squeezed tighter and I tried to look away but I couldn't.

Why was it so hard to breathe? Why couldn't I stop thinking about her? Why did I want her desire and emotions for me to be real... like mine were for her?

My pulse stuttered.

Oh, shit.

I really had lost my mind.

I was in love with Essie

Fuck no.

This couldn't be happening. I couldn't be in love with Essie. Incubi didn't fall in love and no one fell in love with an incubus. Our magic only made them desire us. That was all.

But I wanted Essie. I loved her.

God, there was so much wrong with that and if I was smart, I'd get the hell away from her.

ESSIE

THE PAIN TAUNTED ME, PROMISING TO SCREAM BACK TO LIFE WHEN I WOKE, and the soft darkness and the not-water no longer wrapped around me. I was suspended between everything and nothing. The guys said things. The world whirled by. Kol's magic unfurled in me for a moment, but my dream-Kol didn't visit again. More heat sank into my body, vanquishing the pain, and then I heard voices, far off, arguing.

No, not far off, whispering... and I could only hear them because Jacob's claim enhanced my hearing.

"You can't put her to sleep again." That sounded like Marcus.

"She's in no condition to solidify our bond." Gideon. "She's still pulling strength from the brand."

"She's going to have to be. We need you when we face those witches." Marcus again.

"Marcus—" That was Jacob's low rumble.

"I've recovered a bit of magic." For a second I didn't recognize that voice then remembered it was Priam's. "I can give her a little more strength."

"Let her rest." Gideon.

"The temporal freeze ends within the hour. We've run out of time," Marcus said. "Give her as much as you can."

"This isn't the way it's supposed to happen," Gideon replied.

"It's okay." I tried to open my eyes but my lids were too heavy.

"Do it," Marcus said. "You go into a fight like that, you're going to get killed, and that will be worse for her."

A door opened with a soft shushing as if it brushed against carpet, and a weight settled beside me. A warm hand — although not as warm as Kol's — cupped my cheek. Heat and strength seeped into my body. It wasn't much, but it was enough for me to open my eyes.

I lay under a light downy comforter with a big burgundy and green pattern on it. Priam sat on the bed beside me, pouring his healing magic into me, but his complexion was gray and his body shook. He'd already helped heal all of us this morning and had been working to stabilize Cassius. I doubted he had much left, especially since he'd just saved me from Victoria.

The light in his eyes stuttered and darkened and he pulled his hand away. "That's the best I can do. How do you feel?"

Achy and exhausted and dizzy. "Okay."

Marcus snorted. "You're not okay. But you're alive."

I dragged my gaze past Priam. Marcus and Gideon stood in the doorway, but the door was wrong. The doors on Sebastian's rooms had been white, this was dark brown. The walls were also cream and the carpet was burgundy, a match to the comforter. Not at all Sebastian's color scheme.

Marcus's hair was mussed as if he'd kept running his hands through it. His wolf looked like he would take over at any moment and he was keeping himself together by willpower alone. Gideon was gray and trembling. He looked worse than Priam and the glow in his eyes was barely there.

"How long was I out?" How long had Gideon been trying to hold it together while his soul was shattering because we hadn't solidified our bond?

"Over four hours," Marcus said, his expression grim.

"And Victoria?" I wanted to believe that it was over, that she was satisfied with almost killing me, but I doubted her anger was so easily quelled.

"Still fucking alive." Marcus shot a hard glare at Gideon. "But we're about as far from Rouge as we can get."

"We're in a suite in the Addington Inn," Priam added. "Courtesy of Mr. Bane."

Well, that was about as far away from Rouge as we could get. The Addington was on the opposite side of town from the Quarter, and I wasn't going to ask how many strange looks we'd gotten walking into the most expensive hotel in the city.

"We'll catch you up after." Marcus jerked his chin at Priam and nudged Gideon into the room, his expression turning apologetic. "We're short on time and I know this isn't what either of you want, but—"

"It's okay." I reached out my hand to Gideon, my heart breaking for him. I needed him so much it hurt, my soul just as splintered as his. I had my bonds with Marcus and Jacob helping me, but Gideon didn't have anything. I couldn't imagine how much he hurt.

Marcus and Priam left, and Gideon stared at my hand. "You're still pulling strength from the brand. You're too weak."

"And you're about to fall over. If we wait much longer, neither of us will be able to do anything."

"This isn't how I wanted our first time together to be." He eased onto the bed where Priam had sat.

"Neither of us are dying, so it's already better than my first time with Jacob." I traced my finger over his forearm along the gold thread of his brand, drawing a soft sigh from him. "And we're not having sex in Victoria's bed. Another plus."

"Your first time with Jacob was in her bed?"

"And I kicked her out of her own room."

He captured my hand, his palm pressing mine to his brand, making heat and power flutter in my forearm. "Marcus was right. You don't have any sense of self-preservation."

Not when it came to my mates. "I'd do anything for you, for all of you."

It was crazy that I'd fallen in love with them so quickly. Perhaps it was the soul bonds, but I didn't think so. The bonds were merely a representation of what was fated to be. Even if they hadn't formed, I would have fallen in love with them. Even Gideon. Most of all Gideon. He was the one whose soul best fit mine. We were both willing to do anything and sacrifice it all to do what was right and protect innocent lives.

Marcus I needed for his ferocity, his wild passion that made me feel alive. Jacob grounded me, strong and steady. And Kol—

My throat tightened. Even if Kol wasn't my mate, he was my joy. Playful, mischievous, a reminder to enjoy life. And I'd taken that away from him, reminded him of the horrors he'd experienced during the war.

"Hey." Gideon brushed my hair away from my temple. "We don't have to do this."

I cupped his cheek, my body and soul aching for him to hold me, kiss me, fill me. "But I want to."

He closed his eyes and leaned into my hand. The tension melted from his body, and the fear I'd been holding that we'd never figure things out, that I'd always have a broken part of my soul, released from my chest. We still hadn't figured anything out yet, but we were making the first step.

He pressed his lips to the inside of my wrist. The kiss was tender, soft and sensual at the same time. It reached something deep within me, and my ache for him swelled, my heart and soul overflowing with a love so deep there was no beginning or end. It was all-encompassing, unconditional, warm. There'd never be another lonely, cold night. I would never be alone again. I'd never need to hide or fear for my life. It was comfortable, secure, and sure.

He raised his gaze to mine and sizzling desire swept into the comfortable warmth. His summer-sky eyes were perfect and clear, radiating a brilliant white angel glow. Need as intense as Jacob's and as ferocious as Marcus's dilated his pupils.

I'd thought I'd already seen the full intensity of his emotion, his desperation when the zip OD had made me try to kill myself, his anger, his determination, but this desire was consuming. It sucked all the air from my lungs, from the room, and crackled, teasing licks of electricity through his brand on my arm. In this moment the world outside this room, hell, beyond his perfect blue eyes, didn't exist. There was only him and his desire, an aching, throbbing match to mine.

"Kiss me," I breathed.

Groaning, he leaned in and pressed his lips to mine. The kiss was soft, as if he was afraid to release the passion I'd seen in his eyes. And given that I was still weak, that didn't surprise me.

For a second I feared my buzz would return. It had the last time we'd kissed. My power had threatened to overwhelm me and hurt him. But I was exhausted and magically spent. The hollowness in my chest where my power blazed was still there. And if Sebastian couldn't figure out how to keep me from exploding, this might be the only chance I'd get with Gideon.

God, please, don't let this be it. I wanted time to explore his body, savor the feel of him pressed against me, and we didn't have the time for that now.

I ran my palms over his buzz cut and drew him closer. He teased the seam of my lips. I opened, and he deepened the kiss, stroking his tongue against mine, building the desire already blazing within me. My breath picked up. So did his and his body trembled with restraint. My head spun, dizzy with blood loss and need.

He tugged the comforter away from me and shifted to lie beside me. Someone had cleaned me up and I wore a baggy T-shirt and the white lacey thong Kol had gotten me. My bloody T-shirt and cargo pants were gone.

Gideon slid his hand inside my shirt and skimmed his fingers along the side of my breast. I gasped into his mouth and arched into his hand, shifting his thumb to brush my nipple. My bra was gone as well.

He groaned, a low sound rich with masculine desire that thrummed through me to my core. The electricity in his brand curled over my elbow and danced over Jacob's brand. The pull of strength from Jacob to me increased, granting me the strength to fully embrace being with Gideon.

"Now there's a trick," he said against my lips.

"I hope Jacob doesn't mind." I grabbed the bottom of Gideon's T-shirt and drew it up.

He leaned back, shrugging out of his shirt, and my breath caught, all thoughts of taking strength from Jacob gone. I'd seen Gideon with his shirt off before, but now I could run my hands and lips all over that sculpted muscle. I traced my fingers down his washboard abs to his waistband.

He moaned and captured my mouth again with a demanding kiss, his restraint crumbling. Heat unfurled in my chest and licked blazing desire over my skin, his yearning so strong it defied the containment cuffs and could be sensed with what little magic I had left.

His need and love filled me, and his power danced over my arm, through Jacob's brand, and across my chest. I clung to his waistband, overwhelmed by sensation. He tugged off my shirt and drew my nipple into his mouth, rolling it with his tongue. *Oh, God, yes.* Even with Jacob's extra strength, I was dizzy again, my breath too fast.

He skimmed his hand down my belly, pushing his fingers inside my underwear and brushing through my curls. My breath hitched in anticipation. He captured my mouth again with his and grazed my clit with his thumb.

I gasped and he plunged into me, his tongue in my mouth and his finger between my folds. My hips bucked, drawing him deeper into me.

His breath picked up, matching mine. I grabbed his waistband again, but all I could do was hold on. He added a second and third finger, stretching me, and ground his thumb against my clit, while his lips, still locked on mine, breathed in every gasp and moan.

My desire spiraled tight, need thrumming through me, racing me to climax. The electricity from his brand danced over my skin, so much like my buzz, and yet I knew the power wasn't mine. But even with Jacob's extra strength, darkness danced at the edge of my vision, and I struggled to steady my breath. I needed Gideon inside me, needed to seal our bond, before I passed out.

I opened his fly and pushed his pants off his hips. He released me long enough to pull off his pants and my thong, then settled between my legs, his full erection brushing my folds. His summer-sky gaze captured mine, filled with desire and certainty, and he pushed into me with a steady, firm stroke.

Sensation rolled over me, my muscles contracting around him, a whisper of climax rippling through me. He withdrew and drove back in, again and again, slowly building his pace and my need. The fractures in my soul where Gideon's bond belonged warmed and melded together. I rocked my hips into his, matching his rhythm, taking all of him inside me. His soul filled mine and mine filled his, our essences woven together in a blazing bond, now a match to the bonds I had with Marcus and Jacob.

Gideon's gaze never left mine, connecting us completely. My pulse picked up, our breaths grew ragged, and my desire swelled. It wasn't the wild ferocity of Marcus's passion, or the twisting need of Jacob's magic. It was a rising wave, seeping into every cell in my body with sensation and light, building and building until I was alight with it, unable to contain it all.

It swept me over the edge, my orgasm rushing through me with glorious, breathtaking pleasure, sending stars sparking across my vision and racing through my body. He cried my name with his release, and his electric magic seared my skin.

My buzz roared in response, merging with his magic, suddenly fierce, powerful, out of control, and exploding out of me with a terrible blast.

ESSIE

My back arched and I screamed, the power tearing through me. I couldn't control it, couldn't hold it back, couldn't even breathe. It made my pulse stall, and fear seized my chest.

Not again. Please, no. I couldn't burn Gideon again, and my magic was stronger than ever before. I didn't know where this blast had come from, but it exploded out of me like a super nova. He'd never survive. And God, the last time my power had exploded after sex, I'd branded Jacob, severed his bond with Victoria, and incapacitated myself.

But I couldn't stop it. It ripped at my soul, burning through my cells and blazing out of me. My wings burst from my back and my head jerked back. Power poured from my mouth, my eyes, my skin. My heart pounded. I couldn't catch my breath, and every muscle in my body clenched.

Someone screamed. The world shook and twisted. I was trapped in blinding white agony for a second... an eternity... I had no idea how long.

Then the power released me and I collapsed onto my back, my wings flattened against the mattress and bumping the bedside tables on either side of me. Gideon grasped my shoulders, divine light radiating from his thankfully not-burned skin, but his expression was stunned and his breath too fast. The door crashed open and the rest of my guys, along with Priam and Sebastian, rushed in.

"What the—" Marcus's gaze landed on me, his eyes wide with fear, his fingers extended into claws.

Jacob held his biceps, his brand pulsing with golden light. He'd lost hold of his power and radiated dangerous intensity, his fangs fully extended, while Kol clung to the doorframe, panting, the hellfire in his eyes so strong it licked across his cheeks.

"Esther, your hands," Sebastian said, his voice sharp with warning, his eyes as wide as Marcus's. "Control your power."

"My power?" I couldn't figure out what he was saying, couldn't drag my thoughts past the explosion.

Gideon reached for my hand, and I dragged my gaze to follow his movement. A whisper of light radiated from my palm and—

My pulse skipped a beat. The containment cuff was gone. My wrist was still raw and burned, with the nasty red trail where the metal had melted down my forearm, but all trace of the cuff was gone.

I glanced at my other wrist. That cuff was gone as well.

Panic stole my breath and clenched cold in my chest. "You have to— I'm going to—" I squeezed my hands into fists. The hollow feeling in my chest was still there... sort of. As if I had some power, but not a lot. I had no idea where that blast with my climax had come from, but I needed those cuffs. I was dangerous. I was—

Gently pulsing with power.

A soft thrum, halfway between Gideon's electricity and Jacob's intense stillness, pulsed within me. And no grating buzz.

"Esther, can I touch your hand?" Sebastian asked, dragging my attention back to him, but I got the impression he was really asking my guys, since I was naked with Gideon still inside me.

Well, this was embarrassing. "Can I... we... ah... cover up?"

"Is anyone hurt?" Priam asked, his face pale and stunned on top of his gray exhaustion from before.

I met Gideon's gaze, his angel glow so bright I couldn't see his blue irises.

"You didn't burn me," he said. "I'm okay."

Oh, thank God. And in fact he looked good, better than when he'd entered the room. His complexion had returned to a healthy hue and he no longer trembled.

"Then I'll just step back into the hall." Priam eased past Kol and shut the door.

Marcus grabbed the comforter and tugged it over me and Gideon, while Gideon slid out of me and helped me sit up, making sure I stayed covered. My wings twitched, brushing the headboard, and I shifted to try and find a comfortable position with them.

The room looked like the center of a tornado, with the window blown out and the heavy curtains ripped from their rod. They lay half crumpled on the floor by the window and half hanging out of it. A sharp wind yanked at a scrap of the window sheer, caught in a shard of glass, whipping and twisting it with the promise of a wild summer storm. The TV, its screen cracked, and the bedside lamps, also broken, were on the floor, while the burgundy reading chair by the window lay on its side. A chunk of something metal — the containment cuffs? —had lodged in the ceiling... and in the wall across from me... and the wall by Kol's head.

Jeez. Sex with my guys was getting dangerous and expensive.

Sebastian knelt beside the bed and held out his hand. I extended mine and he took it.

Still no buzz. I didn't know if I should be thrilled or terrified. At least my buzz had given me some warning when my new, powerful magic was about to erupt.

"Gideon, can you give her a little power?" Sebastian asked.

My heart skipped a beat and I tried to yank my hand back, but Sebastian held tight. "Are you sure that's safe?"

"Just a little," he said. "In the very least, you need it to pull your wings in."

Gideon took my other hand and closed his eyes. The electricity in his brand swelled for a second and warm light filled me. I held my breath, waiting for my buzz to roar to life, but my skin didn't even tingle.

"Try pulling in your wings," Sebastian said.

Gideon ran his thumb over the sensitive skin between my shoulder blades. I gasped, desire heating me again, and concentrated on pulling my wings into my body, not straddling Gideon and taking him deep inside me like I wanted to.

Light flared and my wings sank under my skin with a strange overly full sensation in my chest. I didn't think I'd ever get used to that. And my buzz was gone. No stinging or biting or miniature muscle seizures. I didn't ache or itch or anything. My buzz hadn't even been reduced to post-nicotine levels — not even those early days when the nicotine patches had worked really well. I wasn't wearing the containment cuffs and it was gone. "I don't feel like I'm holding an electric fence anymore."

I couldn't get past that. How could it just be gone? I'd had it for years.

"So what does that mean?" The muscles in Jacob's jaw flexed and some of his vampiric intensity eased away. The glow in his brand had vanished and it no longer looked like it hurt him.

Sebastian's lips curled into a wicked smile. "What do you see?"

"What do you mean, what do we see?" Marcus said with a huff of frustration.

"What do you *see*," Sebastian pressed.

Marcus glared at him. "My mate."

"An angel," Kol said, his gaze unfocused, his expression still stunned, high on the sexual energy Gideon and I had just released. "Her essence now says she's an angel."

"You've broken the spell hiding your essence and power." Sebastian squeezed my fingers then released my hand. "Your magic is no longer trying to break free, so you're no longer going to explode. Although you still have no control and you're dangerous."

Gideon wrapped his arms around me. "Oh, thank God."

"I'll send you my bill if you survive the witches," Sebastian said.

"Of course you will." Marcus rolled his eyes at Sebastian.

"Didn't I already pay with all that extra magic?" I couldn't believe my buzz was gone and—

I mentally reached inside myself, searching for the fractured part of my soul where Gideon's bond had been. I couldn't find it. The ache of our unfulfilled bond was gone, and my connection to Gideon was strong and sure and flooding me with love.

In fact, I could feel love from Marcus and Jacob as well. Kol was still dazed, and Sebastian... I had no idea what Sebastian was feeling. His emotions were a strange, sliding mix that raced through me too quickly to figure out what they meant. But the emotions from my guys were real, not the weird temperature changes I'd been used to. And while the room's temperature was on the warm side, I couldn't tell if that was just the way it was or my unusual empathy.

Gideon captured my lips in a quick kiss that stole my breath, and pressed his forehead to mine. "I really want to stay, but—"

"You have to stop the witches." I ached for him to stay, as well. I hadn't gotten nearly enough of him, or any of them, but my desires could wait.

"We think we might have figured out what they're after," Marcus said.

"The mayor's close personal friend Ambassador Hollaway is stopping in town for a private dinner with him and quick refueling for her jet before she continues on to Rome," Jacob said. "Her plane is landing in twenty minutes at Landry Airport."

"Have you called to warn her?" Gideon asked.

"We were about to when—" Marcus slid his gaze over the room.

"We'll call on the way." Gideon captured my soul with his summer-sky gaze. "Essie, I—"

"Go," I said, my voice breathy. If he didn't leave, I was going to lose what little restraint I had.

"I'll keep an eye on her," Sebastian said, his wicked smile gleaming in his eyes.

Marcus huffed. "That doesn't make me feel better."

"Ah... guys?" Kol staggered closer to me, his eyes still unfocused as he pointed at my arm. "Her wrist."

Jacob steadied him and shot Gideon a worried glance. "We know, her cuffs are gone."

"You need to bleed that excess off before we go," Gideon said to Kol.

"No— Well, yes, but—" Kol shook his head. "It's not that, it's—"

Seductive heat swept through me, filling me with sudden, desperate desire. I ached for my guys. All of them. In bed with me. I moaned and leaned into Gideon. He was the closest. I'd start with him. I needed his hands and lips on me. I needed him in me. Now.

Kol squeezed his eyes shut, and the heat vanished but not all of my yearning for satisfaction. I drew in a ragged breath, trying to focus. The guys needed to leave. Sex could wait.

"Sorry." He tipped a bit and Jacob caught him before he fell over. "Just... Essie's concealment charm is dead."

"You must have burned out Mavis's spell when you broke the one concealing your true nature," Sebastian said.

Kol dragged his gaze to his wrist with exaggerated concentration. "My charm's dead, too." He grabbed Jacob's wrist. "So is yours."

"Shit," Marcus said. "The witches can find us."

"And you're not going to stop us!"

The witch with the deadly spider tattoo and the bat wings flew through the broken window. Her wings vanished with a billow of black shadow laced with red demonic magic, and she rammed her shoulder into Marcus, shoving him back into Jacob.

Fear licked cold around me, but I couldn't tell who it came from.

Kol lurched toward her. "Stop." A wave of his seductive magic exploded within me with a full-body climax that seized every muscle with glorious contractions and shot stars across my vision. *Oh, my God. That was— Oh. My. God.*

I sagged into Gideon's arms, dizzy and gasping, boneless with bliss and unable to move.

The witch, the real target of Kol's magic, moaned with pleasure. Sebastian grabbed her arm and Marcus grabbed the other so she couldn't activate any of her glyphs, but she jerked her head back and screamed.

Power crashed into me. Kol and Sebastian gasped and dropped to their knees, also sensitive to the witch's magic. Then a physical, invisible force exploded from her and slammed into us. My head and shoulder smacked the headboard, slicing pain through my temple and my collarbone.

Gideon's cheek slammed into the wall beside me, and his eyes rolled back. Sebastian hit the bedside table, arm-first, with a sickening crack, and screamed in agony, and Kol smashed his face into the wall, breaking his nose. Marcus's head snapped back with enough force to crack the wallboard, while Jacob's big body indented it before he sagged to his knees.

The fear swelled, clenched in my chest as a real emotion, and curling over my forearms with frost.

The witch teetered, barely able to stand. She drew in ragged wet gasps, as if casting a spell with so much power had hurt her more than it had hurt my guys. I couldn't figure out her plan. In a few seconds, at least a few of my guys would regain their bearings and they'd have her again. I didn't think she had any power left, and didn't know if she could channel magic from her outside source in her condition. But she dropped to her knees and pressed one palm over her heart and the other to a web tattoo on her biceps. She gasped two words in a language I didn't understand.

"Shit. No." Sebastian, his expression still dazed, heaved toward her, but another wave of power crushed my chest as Sebastian's fear frosted past my elbows, stung my cheeks, and misted my breath.

The blast wasn't as powerful as the first one, and it didn't pound any of us into the walls, but it shot thick, heavy spider webs out of the witch's body.

The door jerked open. "What was that?" Priam asked, taking a step into the room. His eyes flashed wide as thick strands of web seized him, capturing him in the doorway.

Sebastian was caught mid-grasp, his hand outstretched, only a few inches away from the witch, straining to reach her. Jacob was halfway to his feet, while Marcus had crawled to his hands and knees. Kol tried to turn his head, but the webs had trapped him with his cheek against the wall. Gideon wrenched against the strands, pulling against the ones stuck to my face and shoulders and jerking me toward him.

My mind raced and my teeth chattered. Most of me was under the comforter and not stuck, but without a weapon and almost no magic, there wasn't anything I could do.

The witch's eyes rolled back, and the webs twisted around her body and lifted her off the floor. Blue lightning crackled from her and raced along the strands. It sliced into me, and all my muscles seized as if I'd been hit with a Taser, then released, leaving me twitching and gasping.

Holy crap. If that was what the spell did, I needed to figure out something fast. I wasn't sure how many more of those I could take.

"What the hell is this?" Marcus growled.

"Give it a second," the witch said, her voice ragged and wet, a wild gleam in her eyes.

Sebastian strained to reach her. "If you stop the spell now, you'll still live."

The witch jerked her head to face him. Billowing shadow and demonic mist wept from her eyes, like the magical tears Sebastian had cried when I'd given him too much magic, except hers were made of darkness instead of light. "I'm willing to die for my cause. Are you willing to die for theirs?"

Come on. Think of a way out.

But another blast of lightning swept through the web, stronger than the last, stealing my thoughts. It poured into my body, raced along my nerves, and sliced into my heart. The witch's body seized with ours, and the spell, when it released us, left her panting as well.

Except the spell didn't fully leave me. It crackled in my chest and wrapped tight around my heart. I couldn't draw a full breath and still had no idea how to use the fact that I wasn't fully restrained.

"You think you'll be a martyr, but you won't." A divine light tear rolled down Sebastian's cheek, but before it could sink back into his skin a strand of web curled over his face and the tear sank into it.

"My sisters... will remember me," the witch gasped with a sneer. "Are you... going to tell your friends... their fate?"

Pressure imploded inside me, the power sucking in tight around my heart then rushing into the spell. I gasped, my limbs suddenly weak, my head spinning as if I'd let Jacob feed and then stood up too fast. My magic poured out of me through the web, with little crackles of blue lightning that raced along the strands and into the witch.

"It's a draining spell," Gideon said, slicing a blade of light through the comforter. He wrenched his hand up and slashed through the web holding him, but the webs reformed, captured his hands, and pinned it above his head to the wall.

Kol moaned, his face tight with pain. He'd managed to get his hand a few inches from his boot, but didn't draw his knife. If the webs could reform, we needed to get smart with cutting them. But how the hell were we going to do that? I was getting weaker by the second and it looked like the guys were as well.

ESSIE

ANOTHER MINIATURE IMPLOSION POUNDED IN MY CHEST AND THE STREAM of strength from me into the web turned into a flood. Fear frosted my body and made my pulse race, the emotions inside me so strong it was hard to think straight.

Light flared in Gideon's eyes and his palms glowed with a divine light strike, but the witch glanced at him and the webs encased his hands.

"It's not just a draining spell. It's a full leach," Sebastian said, the web gathering more divine light tears as they welled in his eyes and slid down his cheeks. "It's going to take everything. Magic, essence, and soul. Hers as well."

"And it's going... straight to my sisters," the witch said, her body trembling.

"So killing her won't stop the spell," Jacob said.

The witch laughed a weak, manic laugh. "My sisters have control now. They'll carry on our mission to kill the ambassador. We will win the war."

"What war?" Gideon asked.

The witch's head lolled to the side as if it was too heavy for her to hold up. The billowing shadow and demonic mist leaking from her eyes twisted around her neck and down her body. "Did you honestly think killing Michael and Rafael would stop us?"

"But you're human." At least I thought she was human. The guys hadn't said the witches were anything other than glyph witches with a connection to worship magic. And God damn it, the fear inside me, which I knew was a combination of everyone in the room, was overwhelming.

I clenched my jaw and concentrated on locking the guys' emotions deep within me. I had to get control, do something. There had to be a way out of this. It didn't matter that I knew next to nothing about magic. I couldn't give up.

"If we win... I'll be more than human. My goddess... will transform me," she said.

A whisper of my own fear swept through me, and I prayed her *goddess* wasn't actually alive and was, like Sebastian had said, a super in a catatonic state used to power the worship magic spell.

"You'll be dead," Marcus growled.

"I'll be alive... in my sisters and my goddess." Her eyes rolled back and her head dropped forward, but her chest still rose and fell with quick, desperate breaths.

"Sebastian, is there a way to break the spell?" Gideon asked.

Sebastian strained to get closer to the witch. "If I could touch her—"

The witch gasped and her head jerked up as the webs yanked Sebastian back, pinning him to the bedside table beside me. "I can feel what you are, sorcerer."

Lightning shot over the web, and we all jerked taut, our muscles painfully contracted for an agonizing... second? Minute? God, it felt like forever. It released me and I lay limp, my head and shoulders still caught in the web, every muscle twitching. More of my magic and strength were sucked from me and even the guys' frosty fear started to melt. My empathy was fading and so was I.

"You think by touching me you can break this spell?"

"You seem to think so," Sebastian said.

Weak electricity flickered through Gideon's brand, but it didn't pull strength and I didn't pull strength from him or Jacob. We were all too weak.

The webs jerked Sebastian forward, capturing his hands behind his back and bringing him nose to nose with the witch.

"I'll drain you... first. Your touch doesn't scare me." She planted her lips on his and inhaled.

Sebastian screamed and brilliant white light poured out of his mouth into the witch. Her body shook and the lightning in the web crackled and snapped, slicing agony through me.

Marcus growled and wrenched against the strands, his fingers turning to claws, fur covering the backs of his hands, but he couldn't get enough movement to slice through the web.

Sebastian's complexion turned gray, and he gasped and choked on his power. But the witch also was choking. Her body wracked with strangled coughs, desperate for air, and her muscles clenched and unclenched. The webs tried to jerk her away, but she grabbed Sebastian's head and clung to him.

"I'll have all... of your magic. I'll take every last drop."

The strands holding me trembled, the biting lightning and the sucking pressure sputtering and flaring with painful jerks to my body and soul.

Jacob heaved against his strands, but even with his enhanced strength he couldn't break free. Kol slid out the knife from his boot and flicked the blade so fast I almost didn't see it move, slicing through one of the strands on his arm. The strand didn't reform.

Tears of divine light poured from Sebastian's eyes. The webs sucked it up, and the sputtering and flaring grew jagged.

"Essie, flood the spell with your magic," Sebastian gasped, light blazing from his mouth into the witch. "Burn the spell from the inside out."

"No," the witch screamed, and the pull inside me wrenched at my essence.

Another snap of agonizing lightning, and Kol flicked his blade through another strand of web that didn't reform.

"More power and it'll be too much for the spell to transfer," Sebastian said.

I strained to reach my power, but even my empathy was gone. "I'm out. Gideon?"

"I can't transfer like you can. I can only—" He squeezed his eyes shut and his brand on my arm blazed as his power flooded me, drowning me with magic. "Take it."

I fought to catch my breath. It was too much, too quickly. My body was on fire, but my buzz still didn't make an appearance. The room turned frigid, frost covering every exposed inch of my skin, and the guys' fear and determination crushed around my heart.

"Pour it into the web," Sebastian said.

"It won't be enough," the witch screamed, and she opened her mouth wider, the stream pouring out of Sebastian swelling.

The web's lightning sliced into my body and the pull reached into my soul, hollowing me out. I fought to focus Gideon's power on the web around my head and shoulders, send it pouring through those strands, but the magic raced to my palms caught under the comforter instead.

Shit. Refocus it. Come on. Move to the strands.

"Essie—" Sebastian gasped. The glow in his skin was gone and he looked fragile, like he was made from tissue paper. "Now. Do it now."

I fought hard to move the power to the strands, then realized that was stupid, shoved my hands from under the comforter, and seized the closest strands on my shoulders. Power surged from my palms into the webs. Lightning roared through me and all my muscles seized again. The suck from the spell sputtered and surged.

The witch howled and her manic laughter returned. "That's all you've got?"

"No," Gideon said, and more power blazed through me into the web.

Kol sliced through one last strand of web and lunged, driving his knife into the witch's heart. She screamed, and light erupted under Sebastian's skin. He lit up like the sun, too bright to look at. Magic roared from him and blazed along each strand of the web. It merged with mine, stealing all breath and thought with its force, and together it was enough to ignite the web.

Fire raced through the strands and engulfed the witch, burning her and the spell into ash.

Sebastian fell to the floor and didn't move, and Priam took a staggering step from the doorway toward him, but sagged against the wall before he could take another step. Marcus, already closer to Sebastian than Priam, crawled over to him and checked his pulse.

"He's alive."

Gideon wrapped his arms around me and I leaned against him, shaking, my skin blazing with fiery agony. I was afraid to look at my hands to see how badly they were burned, and couldn't tell if they were because all of me hurt. Maybe all of me was burned, but Gideon wasn't reacting like I was so I just had to trust that I wasn't. Jacob didn't try moving, just slid down the wall, gasping, and Kol collapsed to his knees beside the witch's big pile of ash.

The wind whipped through the window, tossing the ash around us.

Kol coughed, turned away from the pile, and covered his mouth and nose. "That's just gross."

"Who can move?" Gideon asked.

"Give me a minute," Jacob said, his head between his knees and massive chest heaving with deep breaths.

"I need more than a minute," Priam said.

Marcus sat back on his heels and pressed his hands to his chest. "I don't think I can shift this away."

"You can't," Sebastian said, still lying face down on the floor. "It's your essence and soul that's been injured, not your body."

"If one of you could hold my hand and make out with Essie, that would be great," Kol groaned.

"All you, Gideon," Marcus said. "You're the closest."

Jacob grunted his agreement.

Sebastian half raised his hand — still face first in the floor. "I'm close, too."

"Really?" Jacob lifted his gaze, his eyes dark with warning. "You want to make out with Essie?"

Sebastian snorted. "Jeez, you guys are so easy. You honestly think I would with all her mates in the room?"

Marcus rolled his eyes at him. "You can't even raise your head and you're already fucking with us. You sure you're not part demon?"

"Not the last time I checked," Sebastian said.

Gideon held out his hand to Kol. "Come on. We were already short of time before that witch arrived."

Kol climbed onto the bed, knelt beside Gideon, as far away from me as he could get, and took his hand.

Gideon shifted so I wouldn't have to strain my neck to kiss him. "Not sure how much you'll get out of this with our current... mood."

"It'd be better if Jacob bit you," Kol said to me, a whisper of hellfire in his eyes, "but we don't have time for that."

Yeah, and I didn't think I was up for that. And yet the thought of Jacob's bite still sent a shiver of need racing through me. A whisper of heat, one of my guy's desire, licked across my skin.

Kol raised his eyes. "Okay, maybe just thinking about Jacob's bite will help."

Well, hey. Bonus for Kol. Just thinking about sex with any of my guys turned me on. I was still exhausted and sore, but that didn't mean I didn't desire them... and that included Kol.

I shoved that thought away and slid my naked body against Gideon's, drawing a low moan of desire. He tangled his free hand into my hair and kissed me. For a second the kiss was tender, uncertain, then he groaned and released his desire, sending a wave of heat over me. His tongue stroked mine and his fingers dug into my scalp with delicious pressure. I rubbed my hands up his muscular chest and slid my leg over his to get closer, brushing my already slick core against his thigh.

His breath picked up and his erection pressed against my hip, taunting me, begging me to straddle him. God, even sore and exhausted I still wanted to have sex with him. But we didn't have the time. Jeez, why was that so hard to remember?

"Tonight," I gasped against his lips. "After the witches."

He tipped his head back and drew in a ragged breath. "After the witches."

"Are we good?" Marcus asked.

"Yeah," Kol said, but he was curled forward, his forehead pressed to the mattress, his breath fast and body trembling.

"You sure?" I asked. He should have looked satisfied and relaxed, like he had in Voth's theater box, not... whatever the hell this was.

"Un hunh. Just. Need. A minute." He shuddered, and a whisper of mist filled the air.

"Kol—" Instinct made me reach for him before common sense kicked in

He jerked back, the hellfire in his eyes doing nothing to hide the pain. "Please. Don't."

"Jeez, man, she's not going to hurt you," Marcus said.

"I know." But the look in Kol's eyes and the gathering mist said I was already hurting him. Except, for a second, it didn't feel as if the hurt came from reminding him of the war, but from somewhere else. A desire, maybe? A yearning? Mist usually meant grief or regret.

I had no idea, and then he blinked and that vulnerability vanished.

"It's okay." I drew away from him, now more confused than ever, and turned to Gideon. "Go get dressed and stop those witches. We can deal with everything else when you get back."

"You're coming, too." Gideon pushed the comforter aside and climbed out of bed, not seeming to care that the room was crowded and he was naked and turned on. "Everyone is coming. No one is left alone."

"I'm in no condition to fight," Sebastian said.

"And even if I was in good condition," Priam added, "I'd be useless in a fight."

"I don't care." Gideon grabbed his boxer briefs and shook out the ash. "We're all going. You can wait in the SUV. If you're targeted, then at least someone will be close by to help."

"I'll go get Essie's new clothes." Kol hurried off the bed and into the hall, taking his mist with him. Physically he looked the best out of everyone. Guess there was a lot more sexual energy with my kiss with Gideon than he'd expected.

Gideon pulled on his briefs and shook out his pants. "Priam, have you got anything to bolster our strength?"

"You're kidding, right?" Priam said.

"Do angels actually kid?" Sebastian asked as he struggled to sit up.

"No," the guys said in unison, Priam with a sigh, Gideon as if it were a matter of pride, Jacob like it was fact, and Marcus with an eye roll.

If I hadn't been so exhausted, it would have been hilarious.

"Anything you can give us," Gideon said. "I'd like everyone to survive this fight."

Kol reentered with a bag of clothes. "I'm not one of Essie's mates, but I can still give Jacob a bit of a top-up, so you only have to worry about Gideon and Marcus," he said to Priam.

Priam glowered at him, shuffled over to Marcus, and grabbed his shoulder. Light radiated from his hand and Marcus drew in a deep, relaxed breath.

"That's all you're getting," Priam said.

"It's better than before. Thanks."

Gideon moved to him, his pants still in his hand, and Priam gave him an infusion of energy. I could feel it starting to seep into me through the brand and mentally clamped down on that. I was good enough to sit in the SUV. Gideon needed every ounce of strength he could get.

He leveled his pale gaze on me. "Take half."

"You need it more than I do."

"Take. Half." Strength surged into me, breaking through my will to hold it back, and evened the imbalance between us so the brand no longer wanted to pull strength.

Priam stared at us wide-eyed for a second, then shook his head. "So it's true. The brand lets you share vitality."

"And takes it from the other if things get bad," I said. "You better not need it back."

"Love you, too," Gideon said, shocking the hell out of me, and he strode from the room.

"Did he just say—?" Sure, we'd had sex, but that didn't mean we knew each other yet. And while I knew in my soul that I loved him, it hadn't occurred to me that he'd come to that realization as well.

"We all do," Marcus said, brushing his lips across my forehead and leaving as well.

Kol set the bag of clothes on the bed without making eye contact with me, and everyone filed out — Priam helping Sebastian to stay upright. The clothes were a repeat of what he'd gotten me before. White lacy bra and matching thong, a T-shirt, and cargo pants. I changed, strode down a short hall with three other doors, and met them in a living room as opulent as Sebastian's, although this color scheme was gold and burgundy.

Wide patio doors led to a large balcony, complete with built-in barbeque and lounges that looked more like inside furniture than patio furniture. Beyond my haggard glowing-eyed reflection, dusk tried desperately to shine through dark storm clouds with thin weak bands of pink light. We were high enough to have a spectacular view of downtown and Unity Park, where I'd been shot in the chest.

I fought back a shiver and forced my attention away from the place where I'd almost died, as Jacob slid his teeth from Kol's wrist and the incubus sucked in a shuddering breath. I caught a glimpse of blazing hellfire in his eyes before he turned away, and could only assume Jacob had used his full magic to feed.

Marcus set aside an empty duffle bag that had held the gear we'd gotten from Operations and started unloading the other one, adding to the lineup of equipment and weapons on the floor.

Gideon ran a hand over his buzz cut and tossed a phone onto the couch behind him. "Yours is dead, too," he said to Marcus.

"They're all dead?" Marcus asked.

"The leach spell drains every bit of energy. Even batteries. If all of our phones were in that room, all of our phones are dead." Sebastian, who sat on the couch with his head between his knees, glanced up at us. "Did anyone think to grab a charger when you raided Operations? I didn't think to grab mine when we left Rouge."

"Just great," Marcus growled, picking up the room's phone. "Do you know how hard it's going to be contacting the ambassador or mayor from a number that hasn't been approved?"

"Just try," Gideon said.

"At least we can call for backup," Priam said.

Kol shook his head. "JP backup isn't close. They'll never arrive in time."

"Essie, take a Glock, an M4, and a sword." Gideon selected the weapons from Marcus's rows and set them aside.

"I should stay in the SUV with Sebastian and Priam."

"You should still be armed," Marcus said.

"Actually, she's in as good a condition as you and me, and she's not going to magically explode," Gideon said.

Marcus's back stiffened. "She's not going toe to toe with these witches."

"No, but she can ensure the mayor's bodyguard gets the mayor to safety, and with the M4 she can help keep the witches within the radius of the area containment master ward."

He had a point. Even though I was completely drained of magic, I still had combat training. So long as I kept my distance and stuck to using my firearms, I'd be helpful. And with these witches, my guys were going to need all the help they could get.

I knelt beside Gideon and accepted the sword, the sheath already secured to a belt. "Not sure how useful a sword will be, though."

"It's just a precaution," Gideon said.

Jacob secured two sidearm holsters to his belt and picked two of the Berettas from the row of guns. "The sword will be more effective against the vines than the Glock or the M4."

I was outfitted with my assigned weapons, extra magazines, and a bulletproof vest, along with one set of containment cuffs and a pocketful of zip ties with the one-hour containment spell on them.

The rest of my guys geared up with sidearms, extra magazines, and swords. Even Gideon took a sword, which worried me. It meant his magic was low enough that he feared he'd run out and wouldn't be able to manifest his divine light sword in the middle of the fight.

All the guys took a pair of containment cuffs and a handful of zip ties, and Jacob took the area containment master ward. He was the quickest of the group and would be able to run into the center of the fight and activate it. Then it was a matter of subduing the witches long enough to secure the cuffs or zip ties or both... if we could subdue them.

Gideon made it clear that subduing them was second to stopping them, since they were too powerful for us to not match their lethal force with our own. We couldn't afford to pull our strikes. That could get the ambassador, a civilian, or one of us killed.

Given how our last fight with the witches had gone, I had a feeling we were going to need everything we had just to keep them inside the master ward's radius, let alone subdue them long enough to cuff them.

ESSIE

Kol had no luck reaching the ambassador's office or the mayor's, so we left, taking the stairs down to the SUV in the hotel's parking lot. There wasn't anything else we could do.

Wind yanked on my ponytail and the clouds above rushed across the sky, the storm on the horizon growing larger by the minute.

My nerves thrummed with fear. The last time my guys had faced these witches, they'd almost died — and even knowing they were down one witch didn't ease my worries. It didn't help that I had just enough power for my empathy to curl a whisper of my guys' fear over my skin, chilling me despite the evening's humid temperature, nor the fact that none of us were at perfect health.

Kol and Jacob, who sat in the back, looked the best, while Priam looked gray and Sebastian kept flitting in and out of consciousness. Marcus and Gideon, sitting up front, looked like how I felt, tired and achy. I still had some fight in me, but I didn't know how much I could take.

Marcus flipped down the SUV's JP credentials and gunned it out of the parking lot. Rush hour was long past, but there was still a fair amount of traffic on the road.

"Okay." Gideon turned in his seat to look at me. "What do we know?"

Marcus swerved around a slower-moving sedan, jerking us in our seats. The driver stared at us wide-eyed as we sped past, and I didn't want to imagine the conversation we were going to have with the mayor when this was all over.

"Ambassador Hollaway's private jet is supposed to land at Landry Airport," Jacob said as he took a com from the com box and handed it to Kol.

"Which is about all we know." Kol took a com and handed the box to Priam.

Priam took a com, turned to Sebastian, who was unconscious, then passed the box over to me. "At least that witch confirmed they're after the ambassador."

With a squeal of tires, we made a sharp turn to the right, got off one of the busiest streets in the downtown core, and took a narrower, less busy street to get out of downtown. There were still streetlights to slow us down and vehicles to swerve around, but a fraction of the number on the other street.

"We also know that this isn't a public meeting," I said, taking a com and passing the box to Gideon. "That means no media and likely low security, even though she's an ambassador. The mayor probably didn't even request a bigger UCPD detail, since dinner and refueling can happen at the airport."

"Exactly." Gideon handed Marcus a com, took one for himself, and set the box on the floor by his feet. "So we need to get to the airport before Ambassador Hollaway's plane lands and subdue those witches."

"And all we'll have to worry about is the mayor's safety." Marcus slowed at a red light, glanced both ways, then gunned it through the intersection.

Kol huffed. "Given how he feels about us right now, he's going to *love* that."

"Let's just make sure he lives to yell at us another day," Gideon said.

We left the tall high rises of the city core, sped past strip malls and big box stores and car dealerships to the outskirts of town, and turned onto the airport's well-maintained country road. Even though the private airport didn't see a lot of traffic, that traffic usually had a lot of money, some of which the city hoped would be reinvested locally, hence the road's pristine condition.

Tall, wide hangars lined the left side of the road, and the light beacon on top of the control tower strobed across the dark clouds. We turned onto the airport's main drive, then took a quick right to go around the main building and head straight to the tarmac, but skidded to a stop in front of a closed gate with a small guard station.

A young man with freckles dusting his cheeks, wearing a security uniform that was a little too big for him, stared at us, his gaze locked across Marcus on Gideon — the most obvious super in the SUV with his glowing eyes, since Kol with his horns and hellfire was sitting all the way in the back and hard to notice with the low light.

Marcus lowered the window, and Gideon leaned across him and showed his credentials.

"JP," Gideon said. "I need you to call to the tower or your boss or whoever, and divert the ambassador's plane that's about to land."

The man frowned, but I couldn't tell if it was a frown of concentration or confusion.

"If the plane can't be diverted, the pilot needs to be told to stay at the end of the runway and keep the ambassador secure until it's safe. Do you understand?"

"Divert the ambassador's plane or secure the ambassador on the runway," the guy said as he raised the gate and reached for his radio. "Is UCPD coming?"

"Yes," Marcus lied, and he put the SUV in gear and drove away before the guy could ask anymore questions.

"But UCPD isn't on their way," Priam said, thankfully out of earshot of the security guard. "We didn't call them."

"You saw what it was like fighting one of those witches," I said. Someone's fear, probably Priam's by the size of his eyes, swelled for a second, just enough to give me goosebumps. "UCPD is all human. They'll get slaughtered if they show up." Hell, we were all supers and our chances weren't good.

Priam pursed his lips. For a second it looked like he was going to argue. Most angels didn't lie and they didn't disregard protocol, and even though I wasn't familiar with JP protocol, I was pretty sure calling in the local police for a situation of this size was required.

"I don't know how you do it, Gideon," he said. "Just the idea of disregarding protocol makes me uncomfortable."

"Me, too." The light in Gideon's eyes flared. "But the idea of slaughtered cops is worse."

We sped to the side of a large hangar and stopped in the shadows between the lights in front and behind it. With the spider-witch dead and her leach spell overpowered, the other witches had to know we were on our way. We had no element of surprise. But with Priam and Sebastian staying in the SUV, we couldn't just drive onto the tarmac.

"Priam, get in front," Gideon said as he got out. "If things go sideways, get Sebastian out of here."

Marcus shut off the engine but left the keys. Priam took the seat behind the wheel, and the fearful chill swelled again. Yep, definitely Priam's fear.

I got out, chambered a round in my Glock, and reholstered it, then shrugged my M4's sling over my head.

"You good?" Marcus's piercing green gaze darkened with his wolf's ferocious intensity, and he drew his Glock.

A gust of wind whipped my ponytail into my face and stole my breath for a second. "As ready as I'll ever be."

Jacob drew both of his Berettas, and Kol unsheathed the long daggers hidden on his back under his shirt. Another swell of chilly fear made me shiver. It looked like Priam wasn't the only one who was scared. In fact, if I concentrated, I could feel, ever so slightly, real anxiety from all my guys. I could even feel it from Kol, even though we weren't connected with a soul bond. The worry bled into my own fear and churned in my gut.

A thin streak of lightning sliced through the clouds and a few seconds later thunder rolled, low and ominous.

Swell. I gritted my teeth and locked down my emotions. I wasn't as good at doing it as an angel — although maybe I was, since I was an angel — but I could at least do it well enough to focus on the job at hand. I was a cop— no, I was a JP agent. This was my job and I could handle this. *Please, God, let me be able to handle this in my condition. Let all of us.*

Gideon and Marcus took point while Jacob and Kol took the rear, securing me in the center of our formation. A part of me, the part of my soul bound to them, wanted to argue that they were in just as much danger as I was, but they also had soul bonds compelling them to protect me and it was three against one.

We hurried around the edge of the hangar. The tarmac stretched ahead of us, a wide expanse of concrete. Two more hangars sat beside the one where we'd parked. The farthest one had an open bay door and light splashed out the wide entrance in a stark white rectangle stretching over the concrete ground. Beside that hangar sat the main building with most of the lights on and more hangars beyond creating a gentle arc embracing the tarmac.

A black sedan was parked about a hundred feet from the main building's glass back doors. A squat man with a large bald spot that caught the light leaned against the sedan's door, while a tall lanky man in a dark suit stood beside him. A few feet away, standing at the nose of the car to easily get to the mayor or hop back into the driver's seat, stood a bulky guy with a buzz cut. The mayor, his assistant, and his UCPD bodyguard Officer Brant Keels.

My stomach flip-flopped. It was just my luck the UCPD officer assigned as the mayor's bodyguard tonight would be someone who knew me and knew I'd gotten two partners seriously injured. He'd seen my partner Hank bleeding to death after the feral vampire attack, and had been there four and a half years ago for the aftermath of the fight with the werewolves that had made Marcus a super.

And now he was going to see me with glowing eyes. Would he think I was a nephilim? God, would everyone who knew me before I'd broken the spell on me think I was a nephilim?

I shoved that thought aside. Brant was a professional. No matter what he thought about me, he'd do his duty to protect the mayor.

"The mayor is still waiting," Kol said. "Looks like the ambassador's plane wasn't early and has yet to arrive."

I scanned the area around them. No sign of the witches. But there were a lot of places to hide: inside one of the hangars, in the shadows between the hangars, hell, even in the main building.

"Eyes open, everyone," Gideon said as we left the relative safety of the hangar's shadow and hurried across the tarmac.

The mayor jerked away from the sedan before we were halfway to him. He stormed toward us, and his assistant — clutching his jacket to keep it from flying open — hurried after him. Brant followed as well, using his longer stride to catch up, and dropped his hand to the grip of his sidearm, but didn't draw. His eyes, however, widened with surprise when he saw me and cold snapped over my skin, then vanished. Shit. He was afraid of me.

"What the hell are you doing?" the mayor demanded.

"Mr. Mayor, there's a situation," Gideon said calmly, no indication of the tension that radiated from him through our brand.

Brant's posture stiffened, but I didn't know if it was because Gideon had said the mayor was in danger or because of me.

"Of course there's a situation. There's always a situation." The mayor threw his hands up in frustration.

"You need to leave. Agent Shaw will escort you to your car." Gideon gestured to the sedan.

The surprise in Brant's eyes grew. Guess the chief hadn't told anyone I'd been reassigned to the JP, or perhaps his surprise was because Gideon had referred to me as agent, not officer. He, like everyone else, had probably figured I'd already been fired.

"What's it this time? More feral vampires? Zombies? A wild wolf pack?"

The muscles in Marcus's jaw clenched, but he kept his attention on the shadows between the hangars, letting Gideon deal with the mayor.

Brant yanked his gaze away from me to the mayor, and his surprise vanished behind a cool professional mask. "Mr. Mayor—"

"Ambassador Hollaway will arrive in a few minutes and I have every intention of telling her what kind of disaster you are." He turned to his assistant. "In fact, Allen, make this an official memo to the Joined Parliament."

The assistant, Allen, glanced at Brant, who shook his head no, but Allen pulled out his phone anyway. "Recording."

"Can you please make your official memo in your car, as you leave," Gideon said, the light in his eyes growing brighter.

The mayor raised his chin in defiance. "I cannot."

"You should listen to the JP agents." Brant shifted to scan the area to his right and behind him.

"You need to get into your car," Marcus growled. "Now."

I forced my attention across the tarmac. Most of my guys had the hangars and the main building, so I joined Jacob watching the runway.

The wind yanked on my ponytail and tugged at my T-shirt and cargo pants. Small snaps of electricity crackled through Gideon's brand, while tense stillness radiated from Jacob's, and I fought to keep my grip on my M4 relaxed.

Lightning flashed, illuminating the dark sky and revealing a small jet coming in for a landing.

"The ambassador wasn't diverted," Jacob said.

Marcus swore.

Thunder rumbled in the distance, louder and closer than before. My pulse picked up. The tension of the team was palpable, chilling my skin and squeezing around my heart.

We knew the witches were out there. We knew they knew we'd killed their sister. Their attacks would be more ferocious now than before, and we had no idea which direction they were going to strike.

"Sir." Gideon grabbed the mayor's elbow and jerked him around to face the sedan. "You need to leave. Your life and the ambassador's life are in danger."

"Because you can't do your job," the mayor huffed.

"I can't believe I voted for this asshole," Marcus said. He jerked his attention to the mayor, his wolf threatening to break free. "Get. In. Your. Car."

The mayor yelped and Allen's face went white. Gideon yanked the mayor's elbow, getting him moving, and marched him back to the sedan, with Allen hurrying to keep up but keeping his distance from Marcus. I fell into step behind Gideon and Marcus, and Brant fell into step beside me.

"Shaw?" he asked, his voice low, his attention like my guys' on the area, searching for trouble.

Cold whispered across my skin, and I was grateful I was so low on power. I didn't doubt that Brant's fear and my guys' worry would have already formed ice on my hands and cheeks despite the humidity.

"It's complicated," I said, straining to see anything in the shadows. God, they were here. They were going to attack. Just where?

Something flickered at the edge of my vision. I tensed and jerked my gaze to it. The wind gusted and a plastic bag tumbled across the concrete.

"Are you a—?"

"She isn't," Jacob said. "We're dealing with two extremely powerful glyph witches. Get the mayor and his assistant out of here."

"We don't care how you do it," Kol added.

Another shift of shadow, but I couldn't see anyone or anything by the far hangar. Jeez, now I was jumping at shadows. I had better control of my emotions than this. But it was my fear for my guys and the memory of how they'd looked the last time they'd fought the witches that made my emotions so hard to control.

Lightning flashed again and a heavy raindrop splattered on my cheek.

The mayor jerked against Gideon's grip, but he held tight. "I'll have you written up! You'll be fired before you even get back to the Joined Parliament Operations Building."

"You go ahead and do that," Marcus growled.

Allen's face grew paler and he dropped back from the mayor to walk with me, taking Brant's place as he hurried to the sedan and opened the back door.

"Reckless risk of *human* life—" the mayor said.

"Ah, guys?" Kol said.

"What do you see?" Gideon asked, reaching the car and releasing the mayor.

"I sense—" Kol frowned. "I thought— Essie, do you sense anything?"

The mayor turned to Gideon, his finger raised. "Reckless destruction of city property—"

"I don't sense anything," I said, but then I wasn't concentrating.

"Do you know how much it cost to clean up Unity Park?" the mayor demanded.

Thunder cracked, explosive and sharp, making Allen jump with a yelp, and the clouds released rain that pelted me, instantly soaking my clothes and leaking into my eyes.

"Get in the car," Brant said.

The mayor didn't look away from Gideon. "Do you know how much it cost to clean up the cemetery?"

"Essie? Kol?" Gideon asked.

I closed my eyes and focused on how I felt. The witches' magic had been a pressure that had crushed me from the inside out and sent my buzz blazing. Except my buzz was gone. And the crush—?

A weight slammed into my chest, stealing my breath.

"And don't get me started on City Hall!" the mayor said, grabbing the car door. "Do you know how much—"

A massive pillar of ice dropped from the sky. It slammed onto the hood of the car with a crunching, squealing boom, and the mayor started shrieking.

ESSIE

I JERKED MY GAZE AROUND, TRYING TO FIND THE WITCHES. ANOTHER weight crashed into me and shards of ice shot from the shadows between the two closest hangars. With a yell, the red-haired witch barreled toward us, ice blasting from her palms.

Brant yanked the shrieking mayor down and hurried him around the crushed front of the car. I grabbed Allen and did the same. My guys took cover behind the car as well, and Jacob fired two quick shots, but they slammed against an invisible shield protecting her.

"Jeez, she can have two spells going at the same time," Marcus said. "We need to get the area containment master ward out."

"Not until we've got eyes on the other one," Gideon said. "Essie, get the mayor into the main building. Jacob and I will lay down cover fire."

"She's protecting herself with a force field," I said. She wasn't going to care if the guys were shooting at her or not.

"She's not protecting her ice," Gideon said, sending a blast of divine light into a volley of ice shards and destroying them. "Go."

I met Brant's gaze, who gave a tight nod, and we hauled our civilians to their feet. The mayor's shrieking grew louder and Allen's fear made him trip over his feet.

Allen went down.

I grabbed the back of his suit jacket and wrenched him up as another weight slammed into me.

Holy crap. I forced my legs to keep moving, praying that whatever was being cast, my guys could deal with it, but a flurry of vines exploded from the concrete in front of the main building's doors.

The mayor screamed. Brant yanked him out of the way of a thick vine and fired one-handed, point blank, but the shot didn't destroy the vine and it kept surging toward them.

I drew my sword and hacked at it with all my strength. The blade sliced through and it burst into dust, but more vines were surging toward us.

"Gideon, do you see the other one?" I shoved Allen away from a vine and sliced another one in half.

Gideon leaped up beside me, cutting and hacking with his divine light sword. Rain pasted his T-shirt to his muscular chest and torso and made his cargo pants cling to his thighs. "No."

There had to be some place we could go, but without knowing where the other witch was, we couldn't make a run for it or we risked running straight to her.

Another crash of magic.

I gasped, stumbled, but managed to catch my balance.

Red's volley of ice stopped and another massive pillar of ice crashed from the sky.

Gideon yanked me back. Allen dove to the side, while Brant wrenched the mayor, whose shrieking rose in pitch and volume, out of the way. The ice exploded as it hit the concrete, shards slicing my right cheek and arm.

Lightning lanced overhead and thunder roared around us. The mayor gasped shallow, desperate breaths. If he didn't get himself under control soon, he was going to hyperventilate. His eyes were wide and his fear, mixed with everyone else's, tipped my empathy over the top and turned the water slicking my body into a thin layer of ice.

"Second witch at four o'clock," Jacob said over the coms as Kol leaped past me, slicing vine after vine, his blades a water-spraying whirl of steel.

Gideon wiped watery blood out of his eye from a gash in his forehead and glanced to his four o'clock. I hacked my sword through another vine and scrambled around a piece of ice to get to Brant and the others.

"To the hangar," I said to Brant, jerking my chin to the open one in the opposite direction from the vine witch.

More vines surged toward us. One grabbed Brant's arm and I sliced through it, somehow managing to keep my grip on my sword with my wet, icy hands. The mayor had his arms over his head and was sobbing, and Allen looked frozen with fear.

"Get moving," Gideon said.

But we couldn't, the vines surrounded us, blocking our escape, and no matter how much Gideon and Kol sliced at them, we weren't breaking through. The only way to stop the vines was to take out the witch.

"Jacob, target the vine witch." I hacked at a vine about to wrap around Allen's leg.

He fired at Vines, two quick shots, but Red jerked her hand up and her invisible shield sprang up in front of her sister, deflecting the rounds.

Shit—

Except the shield had shimmered on the second shot. Had it weakened?

Jacob fired again. The first shot deflected like the other first one and the second and third shots made the shield shimmer again.

"It's going to take more than a few shots to break through." I fumbled to shove my sword back into its sheath without cutting myself. "Jacob, save your ammo. I've got the larger magazine."

A vine swept toward me and I sliced it with my blade. No way was I going to be able to sheathe the damned thing. "Brant."

He turned to me, and I tossed him the blade, sliding it over the concrete for fear if I actually threw it, I'd hurt someone. He caught the weapon and hacked through a vine wrapping around the mayor.

I wrenched my attention back to Vines, flipped the M4 to fully automatic, and fired.

The rounds slammed into the shield. It shimmered and flashed. Red yelled a word I didn't understand, and another knee-weakening *thu-thud* of power slammed into my chest. Her shield in front of Vines flared, suddenly visible, and the rounds clattered to the ground.

I fought to keep standing and hold my finger on the trigger. A vine seized my ankle. Gideon sliced it, while Brant severed another one racing toward my arm.

The shield shimmered again and a round broke through, driving through Vine's shoulder. She screamed and grabbed a tattoo on her forearm. The ground shook and another *thu-thud* of magic hit me.

I dropped to one knee and struggled to breathe and keep firing. But a stone pillar shot up from the ground, giving her protection, and her vines surged toward me. The mayor shrieked and Brant rescued him from a vine, while Gideon sliced through the vines coming after me.

But he wasn't fast enough and a thin vine slipped past his guard and seized my arm. I wrenched against it, but without a blade, I couldn't break free. Another vine twisted around the M4. Shit. If it pulled me down, I was done for.

I hit the sling release on the M4, but the vine had also wrapped around the sling and heaved me forward.

Shit shit shit.

"Essie—" Gideon gasped. His blade of light flashed at the edge of my vision, but wasn't close enough to save me.

I twisted, sliding the sling off over my head and arm. It caught on the vine around my arm, but Brant freed me, and I scrambled to my feet, abandoning the rifle.

Red, now almost at the car, raised her hands and hissed words I didn't understand. Another crush of power stole my breath, and lightning lanced through the clouds above us. It filled the air with electricity, and my pulse stalled. Back in City Hall, she'd used a lightning strike to temporarily immobilize the guys. That strike had been invisible and not overly powerful, but this—

"Lightning strike! Move! Move now!" I yelled.

Allen stared at me, still wide-eyed and frozen in fear. It was a miracle none of the vines had taken him down, while the mayor was the complete opposite, flailing and screaming.

I shoved Allen to get him moving — *please God, move* — and a surge of power swept from Jacob's brand down my hand and into Allen. He jolted and the frozen panic vanished. I had no idea what I'd done and there wasn't any time to think about it. We had to get out of the way.

A blast of lightning exploded from the sky. Jacob and Kol bounded away, Gideon released his wings and leaped into the air, and Marcus gritted his teeth and took it — thankfully he wasn't as close to the epicenter and had been twisting and slashing through the mess of vines to get to Vines.

Red took in ragged gasping breaths and Kol bolted toward her. My pulse stuttered, everything within me screaming to call out to him, to stop him. If Red had another lightning strike ready, Kol was dead. But this was the job and my guys had to stop the witches.

And my job was to get the mayor and his assistant out of there.

Marcus reached Vines and slashed at her, and Gideon shot a massive blast of divine light, burning a path through the vines and giving me, Brant, Allen, and the mayor an escape route.

"Get to the hangar." We bolted toward it while Marcus thankfully distracted Vines long enough for us to run through the path.

"Jacob, the master ward," Gideon said over the coms.

Another crush of power. One of my guys grunted. All of their breaths were heavy.

"*Vade*," Jacob said, and a swell of magic, not the same crushing power from the witches, washed over me.

One of the women screamed. Something small thudded in my chest and I realized it was one of the witches casting a spell. But without being able to access their worship magic, the spell wasn't nearly as powerful. *Thank God.*

"Keep them in the containment area," Gideon said over the coms.

I reached the edge of the hangar, drew my Glock, and wiped water out of my eyes. The mayor, Brant, and Allen, all panting, took cover behind the wall, with growing puddles of water forming around their feet.

"What the hell was that?" Brant gasped. "Are glyph witches really that powerful? They didn't say anything about falling pillars of ice or lightning from the sky in the advanced training for supers."

"They had access to extra magic." I glanced out the hangar door to cover our backs, but both of the witches were busy fighting my guys.

"Nine one one," a quiet voice said— no, not quiet, on the other end of a phone call.

Crap. I wrenched around to stop whoever was calling. If UCPD showed up, there'd be serious human casualties.

"Supers—!" the mayor said, his voice pinched and desperate.

"Don't—"

"Landry airport. Send everyone. I'm the mayor!"

"We need backup," Brant said to me.

"No." I shot him a glare and he flinched, afraid of me. That stung, but if it got people to listen to me, so be it. "You honestly think UCPD can help? A human fighting against supers is a death sentence. Trust me."

"Is that why you're now a super?"

The mayor gasped. "You're the human officer—?"

"Officer Esther Shaw," Allen provided.

"Are you her? The one who was assigned to the JP team?" He wrenched away from me, his fear freezing the water on my body, making my pants and T-shirt stiff and my teeth chatter. "Your eyes are glowing."

"I'm not a nephilim. It's complicated." We didn't have time for this. The guys were still battling the witches, and while they were holding their own, it was by the skin of their teeth.

But first I had to get the mayor to safety. Then I could go back and help.

I scanned the hangar. A metal security door sat at the back, past a stack of large plastic shipping crates and a small office area with three desks and half a dozen filing cabinets. "Brant. Take the mayor out the back. Priam?"

Please let him be paying attention to the coms.

"Yeah?" he asked.

Thank God. "We're in the first hangar beside the main building. Come around and get the mayor, his assistant, and bodyguard."

"Okay."

One of my guys screamed and fear clenched my chest. I didn't sense anything from the brands so it had to have been Marcus or Kol. I glanced out, looking for a shot that could help them, but Gideon was in hand-to-hand combat with Red, Marcus and Kol were fighting with Vines too far away for a good shot, and I had no idea where Jacob was.

Crushing pressure exploded in my chest. What the hell? Had the master ward lost power?

"What are you doing?" the mayor yelped.

"Brant. Move the mayor to the back of—" I wrenched my attention to Brant and my words stalled.

Allen had dropped his soaked suit jacket to the concrete floor and shoved up the sleeve of his button-down, revealing a colorful tattoo curling over his right arm that was far too similar to Red's. He clutched his wrist, covering whatever tattoo he'd activated, but whatever it was, it wasn't good. Brant, his body trembling, his eyes wide, had the sword raised and pointed at the mayor, while the mayor stood shaking in a puddle of water with his hands up.

"Drop your gun or I make Officer Keels here kill the mayor," Allen said.

"If I drop my gun, you'll still make Brand kill the mayor."

Allen's grip on his wrist tightened, his knuckles turning white, and I realized his tattoo wasn't exactly like Red's. It wasn't as complicated. There were blank spots where his skin showed through. Did that mean he wasn't as powerful? It probably meant he didn't have as many spells, but that didn't necessarily mean he wasn't just as strong as the women.

Another chest-crushing *thu-thud* weakened my knees, but they locked, keeping me up, and my body wrenched my Glock up and pointed it at Brant.

Panic stole my breath. *My body. No one else's. Please.* I couldn't have someone control me again. I couldn't be forced to hurt someone again. The memory of blasting my divine light into Kol's face made bile burn my throat. *No. Please God, no.*

I wrenched against Allen's magical hold, but all I did was tremble.

"Better yet, I'll make you and Keels kill each other, and then *I'll* kill the mayor."

Brant dropped the sword, drew his Glock, and pointed it at me, his eyes wide with terror.

"Stop. What are you doing?" the mayor cried.

"They say you're a deadly incident waiting to happen, Officer Shaw," Allen said with a dark chuckle. "What would everyone think if you killed Brant?"

My trigger finger flexed, and I mentally heaved at Allen's control, stopping myself from shooting Brant.

Brant's breath picked up, his chest heaving with desperate gasps.

Allen glared at me. "I said kill him."

His magic surged, squeezing around my heart. My trembling grew, my muscles painfully contracting as I fought him. But I wasn't going to hold out much longer, and I didn't have my buzz to help me this time. God, the last time the archnephilim or Ibizual had tried to control me, my buzz had saved me, burning through their magic.

Now, I had nothing.

Water in my hair trickled over my temple and dripped from my jaw. Brant's gasps turned to shallow pants. Another trickle of water slid down my temple and froze.

The mayor's gaze leaped over the three of us and he jerked to bolt to the back of the hangar. But Allen's power thudded into me and the mayor froze as well.

The power seizing my muscles shuddered for just a second, relaxing them then jerking them taut again.

"Shoot him," Allen snarled.

"No," I forced out.

No.

No. No. No.

I wouldn't and he couldn't make me.

Even if I didn't have my buzz, I still had some magic, and I was God damned going to use it to break Allen's control of me instead of freezing water on my face. I knew what my magic felt like. It was a thrumming electricity. Like Gideon's. It always blazed through my body and curled tight around my heart and in my back where my wings — my wings! — were.

"Shoot him." Fire erupted inside me, threatening to burn up what little control I had. "Shoot. Him."

I ground my teeth — me, I did — and mentally dove into the core of my being where my magic curled tight within me. With a scream, I seized it and wrenched my aim to Allen.

Shock flashed across his expression and the fire in my body surged. My hands trembled and shifted away from Allen. I heaved them the fraction back to aim at the center of his chest.

"Fine. If you won't kill him, he'll kill you." Another powerful *thu-thump* pounded in my chest. My fingers went numb and my Glock clattered to the ground.

Brant whimpered and fired. I fought to move, to drop, to do anything, but knew I'd never be fast enough to dodge a bullet.

Agony exploded in my shoulder, stealing all breath and thought. Fear shot adrenaline through me, and my power erupted. It raced into every cell, consuming Allen's magic. I dropped to grab my Glock, but the mayor yelped, jerked forward, grabbed the sword, and awkwardly swung it at me, forcing me back.

Brant groaned again, the precursor to another shot. I dropped to the concrete and pain sliced across my cheek. The mayor, sobbing and gasping with tears streaming down his cheeks, swiped at me again.

I rolled out of the way and scrambled to my feet. I needed cover— No. I needed to stop Allen. If Allen was down, Brant would stop shooting, but I wouldn't be able to take Allen down without first dealing with Brant.

I dove for Brant. The muscles in his face twisted in agony, and he heaved his Glock aside just enough for the round to roar past my cheek.

The slide stayed back.

Out of ammo. Thank God.

I slammed my fist into his face with a quick jab that broke his nose and stunned him. His head snapped back, and I rammed my other fist into his temple with all my might. It wasn't easy to knock someone out with a few punches, and I prayed whatever damage I'd done could be healed, but I needed Brant out of the picture.

Please God, let knocking him out break Allen's control.

Brant's eyes rolled back and he collapsed.

I wrenched to face Allen, and he bolted for the back door.

Oh, fuck no. I raced after him, my muscles burning from having fought his possession magic.

Another *thud-thump* made me stumble. *What the fuck now?*

The mayor's sobbing turned to desperate howls. A gunshot roared behind me and blazing agony sliced across my shoulder.

"My spell might not be powerful enough to make the mayor kill himself," Allen snarled at me. "But I can make him kill you."

"I don't think so." I dove for him. He was a little too far away for a tackle, but with my momentum there was a chance I could make it.

I would God damn make it.

My wings burst from my back, catching just enough air for me to slam into Allen. We crashed to the floor. Allen shoved me off him, painfully twisting one of my wings, and the mayor's footsteps pounded toward us.

"Please stop. Please stop," he sobbed.

Another gunshot exploded, the sound monstrous in the mostly empty hangar. The round sliced through my right wing and pinged off a metal filing cabinet.

Allen scrambled to his feet. I grabbed his ankle, yanked him back to his knees, and he wrenched around to punch me in the face, but I hit first.

I slammed an uppercut, palm open, against his chin, and a blade of divine light burst from my palm. My power blazed through every cell in my body and shot out the top of Allen's head.

My power vanished, leaving me cold and trembling, with agony screaming through my shoulder and throbbing across my cheek. Allen crumpled to the ground, his eyes wide and lifeless, and I gasped out a relieved breath.

The sobbing mayor sagged onto his knees and tossed my Glock away. It skittered across the concrete and everything within me screamed that I needed to go after it, secure my weapon, but I didn't have the strength.

"Essie. Sit rep," Gideon said, his voice ragged. "Essie."

"Son of a—" Marcus growled.

"Just stay there," Kol said. "You too, Jacob."

I strained to hear past the coms and my rushing pulse for any kind of fighting outside, but I couldn't concentrate. All I wanted to do was pass out. At least this time only my shoulder was on fire, not my entire body. That was an improvement over the last couple of times, but I was having trouble focusing my thoughts to enjoy that and a hollow chill had seeped into my bones.

"I'm fine. Essie, answer," Marcus said.

"You're not fine," Jacob groaned.

Marcus snarled. "Well, neither are you."

They were all alive. All of them. They'd all spoken. And no one seemed to be in the middle of a desperate fight.

I staggered to my feet and stumbled to my Glock. Off in the distance, sirens screamed. Backup was arriving, thankfully not in time to join the fight.

"Essie." Gideon again.

Right. He'd asked a question. "Here," I gasped. "The mayor is secure."

"Good," Gideon said, his voice filled with relief. "Priam, where are you?"

"In the SUV, waiting behind one of the hangars." Which was where I'd told him to meet us.

The sirens grew louder, but the mayor didn't rush out of the hangar to his human help. He stared at me wide-eyed, his face white, tears streaming down his cheeks. "I couldn't stop myself. I just couldn't. How could you?"

"I have magic."

His gaze slid to my wings. "Because you're an angel?"

Yeah, duh. But if he was in as much shock as I was, I should give him a break for stating the obvious.

"Officer Keels couldn't do anything, either," the mayor said.

"You're human. Unless you made a demon-deal to become a witch, the odds of you winning a fight with someone like Allen are next to impossible."

Cruisers sped onto the tarmac and red and blue lights strobed into the hangar. Gideon limped to the hangar's mouth and my heart swelled. The rain had soaked his clothes and blood still wept from the gash over his eye, as well as from dozens of other gashes and punctures all over his body. His left arm was badly burned, his right was hugged tight to his side, and his face was pinched with pain. He looked like shit. He'd gotten worse than I had, but he was alive.

Half a dozen cops rushed in behind him, and someone radioed for EMTs. A few seconds later two paramedics rushed in. One went to the mayor, the other to Brant. Allen was clearly dead, his head in a growing pool of blood, his eyes vacant.

The JP SUV pulled up in front of the hanger and Priam hopped out. "Are the witches dead?" he asked.

"Yeah," Gideon said, his tone strange, but I was too exhausted and numb to figure out what it meant. "Take the team to Operations so Jacob can heal Cassius."

"Do we think the poison is still killing him? We killed the witch who cast it," Jacob asked over the coms.

"I don't want to risk it," Gideon said. "I'll stay here and coordinate with UCPD until Chris can get here."

"No, if Priam has enough magic to stabilize me, I'll stay," Marcus shot back, his voice strained. "You should be with your brother."

"Jeez, Marcus," Kol said. "You're bleeding out and your leg is broken. You're not staying."

"You took a full blast of lightning," Marcus gasped.

This was getting us nowhere and I was too exhausted to let it go on. I made eye contact with the closest officer, who thankfully wasn't from my precinct and didn't know I was supposed to be human. "We all need medical attention. A JP agent will be on scene shortly. Pass that on to whoever's in charge."

He gave a tight nod. "Yes, agent."

"We're all leaving," I barked at my guys. "Get in the car."

I staggered to the SUV, blood racing down my arm, leaving a trail on the pale concrete. A paramedic hurried after me.

"Agent," he said, "I know angels heal quicker than humans, but you'll still bleed out before you get to the hospital." He pulled thick wads of gauze from his bag, painfully packed both the entrance and exit wounds in my shoulder, and taped more gauze over that. "Apply pressure."

The rest of my guys staggered into sight, all bloody and all soaked from the storm still pelting rain. Jacob was covered in gashes, and Kol's whole body had been badly burned. Even with the burns, he was still helping Marcus — who had a calf bone protruding through his pant leg — hop to the SUV. God, I couldn't imagine how much pain all of them were in.

"Jesus," the paramedic gasped.

Priam scrambled out of the SUV and pressed his hands to Marcus's chest. "I don't have much," he said, his voice soft and quick over the coms as light flared from his hands. "But this should stabilize you."

Marcus drew in a sharp breath, and his wolf's intensity flared.

"Don't shift," Priam said. "Not yet. You're still too injured."

"I know," Marcus growled.

With Gideon's help, I pulled my wings back into my body and climbed into the SUV. Sebastian was out cold, but his breath was steady and a hint of light, still weaker than it should have been, was radiating again under his skin.

Rain rattled the windshield and the wipers swiped the glass clear, revealing the destruction from the fight. Black marks scorched the pale concrete where it hadn't been ripped up by vines that were no longer around because the spell that had created them was gone. All of the windows of the main building had been shattered, and the mayor's car had taken more damage and looked like it had been crushed with a compactor.

The glyph witches lay among the dirt and broken concrete. Red's battered and burned face was turned toward me, her eyes vacant, and the vine witch's neck was cocked at an unnatural angle, clearly broken. They were both dead.

The rest of the guys piled in and Priam raced us to Operations, driving not nearly as fast as Marcus, but faster than the speed limit. Medically none of us were out of the woods, and we could only pray that he and Amiah had enough to stabilize us so we could wait until their healing magic had been restored.

We were halfway to Operations when our coms were close enough to connect with Amiah's. Cassius was stable and most of the poison was gone, but there was still a thread woven into his essence. Priam gave her a heads-up about our condition, and she and Cassey, along with two other human-looking guys in scrubs, were waiting for us at the garage door with two gurneys.

Jacob and Kol helped Marcus onto a gurney and he was whisked away, while Priam and Gideon put a still-unconscious Sebastian on the other gurney. The rest of us staggered down the white hall with the pale gray vinyl floor to triage, leaving trails of water and blood.

We entered as Amiah put a hand on Sebastian's head. "He's just drained," she said to her team, and they hurried him deeper into the mini hospital, likely to put him in a room to recover.

One of the guys returned with another gurney and Gideon insisted I take it — there was only room for three in triage — and he sagged against it, using it to help him stand while Jacob went straight to Cassius and pressed his hands over Cassius's heart.

Green light with orange sparks burst around Jacob's hands and his head jerked back. A shudder of something fluttered through me and I wondered if I was always going to be feeling spells and magic as a pressure in my chest, not to mention if I'd ever get used to it. But I was too exhausted to really feel anything about that right now.

The powerful stillness in Jacob's brand swept over me and my thoughts drifted — and I hadn't realized they had until I blinked and noticed that Jacob no longer stood beside Cassius. He now sat on the tan leather couch in the waiting area. Cassius groaned and his eyes fluttered open for a second before he sighed and passed out again.

"Is he—?" The light in Gideon's eyes dimmed with worry.

Amiah turned away from examining Marcus's fracture and laid a hand on Cassius's chest. "All trace of the poison is gone."

"Thank God." Gideon pressed his forehead to mine and squeezed his eyes shut. Relief flooded me and I pressed my palm to his cheek. We were alive. All my guys were alive and that was all that mattered.

Amiah stabilized me enough for fresh tightly packed gauze in my gunshot wound to stop me from bleeding to death, and I was wheeled to a hospital room where she told Jacob in a stern voice that I was too weak to heal him. He said he could wait, sagged into the bedside chair, and held my hand as the sedative Amiah gave me helped me fall asleep.

I drifted into darkness, floating in the warm not-water. Panic seized me, so unlike my not-water dreams before that it shocked me. But I had to see my father and know who he was. And yet I already knew I didn't recognize him. I'd dreamed of him before and had no idea who he was.

Far off in the distance something boomed. That something... I knew what it was... why couldn't I remember? It sounded so familiar. I knew I'd recognized it in a previous dream, but now I couldn't remember.

All I really knew was that something wasn't right. *I* wasn't right. The not-water was no longer comforting and I had to get out of this dream and—

And what?

I had no idea. I didn't know what was wrong. I didn't know how to fix it.

Just talk to me. Kol's voice slid like silk over my senses, drawing a shiver of desire.

I don't know what to say. You won't look at me. You don't want to talk to me.

Because I'm afraid.

I know.

Of what I want. His lips whispered over mine. Just a breath of a kiss, but it slipped liquid bliss down my throat and into my heart.

You don't really want me. It was me who wanted him, needed him, just like I needed Marcus and Gideon and Jacob.

How do you know? His lips slid across my jaw to my ear, his breath caressing my neck. The swell of his magic sank low, heating my core, and he brushed his hands up my naked body, the motion slow, sensual, and making me squirm. His thumbs skimmed my nipples on the way up, but didn't stop like I wanted. Instead, he captured my face and kissed me with a wild, almost desperate passion, and his magic flooded me, making my nerves instantly thrum on the edge of climax.

My dream filled in, revealing the hellfire blazing in his eyes with a need for me and only me. His naked body pressed against mine, his heat radiating from his flesh. My breath picked up, my thrumming nerves hypersensitive to every miniscule shift. Each breath brushed my flesh against his.

I ached for him, like I ached for all my guys, needing him body and soul.

He hooked a leg over my hip and pulled me tight, my back to his chest. The length of his hard erection pressed against my butt, and I squirmed against him, drawing a moan of desire from both of us. He trailed a hand down my belly, another whisper of flesh against flesh, that alone almost had me coming, and his fingers—

I was God damn not going to wake up before his fingers reached me, before his magic flooded me. Not like the last dream.

How do you know? he asked against the back of my neck.

The tip of his index finger brushed my clit and shot the first tremor of a climax through me.

How do you know unless you talk to me?

A miniature climax rushed through me, sweeping away Kol, my yearning, everything, leaving me to drift in a darkness that was no longer warm or comforting.

I wasn't sure how long I slept, but when I woke, Gideon had replaced Jacob in the chair beside my bed, and my heart swelled with joy and relief at the sight of him. He looked perfect. His complexion was back to normal and there wasn't a scratch or bruise on him.

"How is everyone?" I asked, my voice setting off a low-level throbbing headache.

"Good." Gideon offered me a gentle smile and took my hand. There were two puncture marks on his wrist. He'd let Jacob feed from him, which meant Jacob wouldn't be up to full, but better than when I'd passed out. "Amiah has finally finished with Marcus and he's giving his wolf a run. Jacob—" His gaze dipped to his wrist. "Marcus and I took turns with a little healing help from Priam, and he's finally back up to full."

"And Kol?"

"He's come and gone and back to full."

And I wasn't going to acknowledge the sting of disappointment at that, because it was selfish and irrational. Kol survived on sex. Even if we were in a relationship, he'd still need to sleep with other people so he wouldn't end up killing me.

Jacob knocked on the open door. His complexion was finally back to normal, and I hadn't realized I'd been beginning to fear that his health would never be fully restored. But there he was, with his vampire intensity mostly hidden and yet radiating powerful stillness.

He sat on the foot of the bed, revealing Marcus standing in the hall behind him, dressed in his jeans and boots but holding his T-shirt in his hand, making my pulse trip at the sight of his beautifully sculpted, undamaged body.

"I told you she was awake," Jacob said.

Marcus hopped onto the bed, squirmed in behind me, propped himself up with the pillow, then helped me settle, my back to his chest, his legs on either side of me. He wrapped his arms around me and pressed his lips to my head. Gideon shifted his chair closer and pressed his palm over his brand on my forearm, while Jacob rested his hand on my calf.

Their love and warmth surrounded me and filled me. This was where I was supposed to be and who I was supposed to be with. There was just one person missing.

Kol peeked in through the door, and a part of my soul sang.

I shoved that as deep down as I could.

Not mine.

"I thought I felt something," he said.

He looked as he always did, breathtakingly beautiful, his black hair ever so slightly mussed and making me think of wild sex — *yes please!* — with a flicker of red hellfire in his eyes.

I yearned to reach out to him, invite him to join us.

He crossed his arms, didn't draw closer into the room, and slid his gaze away from me.

Really. Not mine.

The only thing that had been right about my dream was that we needed to talk. But he and everyone could have time to recover, regain their equilibrium that had been upset when my wings had first appeared — God, had it only been this morning...?

None of the guys looked like it was still the day I'd fallen off City Hall's roof.

"How long was I out?"

"A full day," Gideon said.

"Amiah wanted to keep you out long enough for your magical channels to heal a bit," Marcus said. "How's your head?"

"Still a little sore." But given how much it had hurt after channeling massive amounts of magic to destroy the key that would have freed Ibizual, I was probably the best I'd ever been.

No buzz. Barely any headache. And there wasn't a single part of my body that hurt.

I had no idea how I'd managed to get through the last few days alive, let alone unscathed, and I really had no idea how I'd gotten so lucky as to have four— er, three soul mates who'd proven they'd accept me even if I was a monster.

"So it's a party in Esther's room," Sebastian said, and Kol shifted from the doorway to lean against the wall so Sebastian could enter. Sebastian was still dressed in the shirt and slacks he'd worn yesterday, his complexion was still gray, and his internal light wasn't as radiant as I remembered, so I could only assume Amiah hadn't released him from her mini hospital.

"Dude, Amiah will kill you if she catches you out of bed," Kol said.

Sebastian rolled his eyes at him. "Let her try."

"Well," Gideon said, "I'm sure you'll still send us one enormous bill, but thank you. We wouldn't have gotten out of that alive without you."

Sebastian shrugged and gave me a wicked smile that made Marcus tighten his embrace. "Esther did make a large down payment."

"Still," Gideon said. "You didn't have to help. But you did and we prevented an assassination."

"About that." All wickedness vanished from Sebastian's expression. "You know it isn't over, right? We might have killed four witches, but the source of their worship magic is still out there."

"I know." Gideon's grip on my hand tightened and Marcus shuddered behind me. Jacob's hold on his vampiric intensity slipped a little, revealing his deadly nature, and the hellfire in Kol's eyes flared.

It wasn't close to over. There were more witches out there and worse, a goddess. And it was our job to stop them.

DESTINED RADIANCE

NEPHILIM'S DESTINY, BOOK 5

THE WORRY IN MY HOSPITAL ROOM AT OPERATIONS DROPPED THE temperature. All my guys stared at Sebastian standing in the doorway, his posture casual, his hands in the pockets of his slacks, as if he hadn't just reminded us that there could be a powerful goddess out there determined to finish Michael's war and kill all humans and supers.

"You've already lost a day," he said, leveling his pale, exhausted gaze on me. Even the soft blue-white glow that usually emanated from his translucent skin was dimmed. He didn't look like he was made from tissue paper any more, not like he had after pouring all his magic into the glyph witch's power-leaching spell to save us, but he didn't look close to being recovered, either.

Marcus, who lay behind me in the bed — my back against his bare chest — tightened his grip around my waist, shifting my hospital gown under the blankets a little higher up my thighs, and growled low in his throat. "Not Essie's fault."

"Hey." Sebastian raised his hands in defense. "Not saying everyone didn't need a day, but you don't even know the true extent of the source of the glyph witches' worship magic. How many followers are there? How many witches have access to the source?"

"Not to mention whether their goddess is awake or merely a catatonic vessel for the worship magic spell," I said, fighting a shudder.

I didn't want to think about the source of the glyph witches' power.

We'd barely managed to survive stopping them from assassinating Ambassador Hollaway, and God, couldn't I just get a day with my guys when nothing happened?

But that wasn't how the team worked and the angel half — or rather, my angel entirety — couldn't ignore the danger.

And yeah, I still wasn't sure what I thought about being a full angel. Learning the truth had happened so fast and during so much chaos that I hadn't had time to let that really sink in. And it seemed I still wasn't going to have the time.

Jeez, I didn't even have time to give in to the need thrumming through all my soul bonds. A need that was still so strong, I ached for them. Especially Gideon. Yes, we'd solidified our bond yesterday, and the pieces of my soul bound to his were no longer fractured, but I needed more, needed to give myself over to the magic binding us together. I needed to give myself over to the magic binding me to *all* my guys. The urge was overwhelming, and it took everything I had not to turn in the bed and start making out with Marcus. Especially since I could tell I was in a hospital gown and nothing else.

Angels said the mating brand was beautiful and sacred, and while I had to agree — I was still in awe at how amazing having my guys felt — it was also a pain in the ass right now. How was I supposed to do my job when all I wanted was to take my guys to bed and stay there?

My job.

As a JP agent.

Which was another thing that shocked me... and was possibly uncertain... since I'd been assigned to the team as their required human agent.

I pulled my gaze from Sebastian and slid it over to Kol. Much to my surprise, he was actually making eye contact with me.

The hellfire in his eyes flared for a second, sending a thrill of desire mixed with hope through me. Maybe we could work things out, get our friendship back... get more. But realization slid over his breathtaking features and his hellfire snapped to barely-there pinpricks, his magic and emotions grasped tight as he pulled his attention back to Sebastian.

My hope wavered. Yesterday's issues hadn't been forgotten. Thinking I was a nephilim had still triggered horrible memories, and I'd still lied to him. And really, it was too soon. Shock and betrayal, especially around what had to be PTSD, wasn't something that someone just got over.

But God damn it, I just wanted to grab him and scream at him. Sure, we didn't have a soul bond, but I couldn't help feeling like we were supposed to have something more, like he was as much mine as Marcus and Jacob and Gideon.

And that wasn't just a human— er, woman craving an incubus.

But screaming at him wouldn't help. As much as I wanted everything to go back to the way it had been, that wasn't going to happen right away... if ever.

Jacob shifted from his position sitting at my feet, sliding his hand on top of the blanket higher up my calf and drawing my attention. His vampiric intensity sent a shiver of desire racing over me and made my pulse pick up, which made Marcus release a soft, sensual growl that vibrated through my back and shot heat to my core. Gideon, who sat in the chair beside the bed, squeezed my fingers, a mix of yearning and worry in his summer-sky eyes, clearly torn between protecting innocents and giving in to the urge of our bond.

I was just as torn. My guys weren't seriously injured, we weren't fighting for our lives, and I finally felt good. Yeah, my inner magical channels were still a little raw, but I didn't feel like my magic was going to explode and take out the building, and my buzz was gone. Gone! It had been years since I hadn't felt like I was holding a low voltage electric fence. In fact, I felt powerful, like a light had been turned on inside me and it radiated heat and strength and magic through every cell in my being.

And those cells wanted my guys. Now.

"So," I forced out, my voice embarrassingly breathy, "what's the plan?"

"You're going to take care of that." Kol gestured at the three of us, his whole body tense. "And I'm going to take a walk on the other side of the Quarter."

Gideon's gaze captured mine, and my pulse stuttered at his heated desire, then the muscles in his jaw flexed and he yanked his gaze away. "What we *need* is to figure out how to find the source of the witches' power."

Sebastian sighed. "I can help with that."

"And how much is that going to cost us?" Marcus asked.

"*You're* not helping with anything," Amiah said as she stormed into the doorway, her voice sharp. "You're going back to bed."

"I'm fine," Sebastian said.

"Oh, don't tell her you're fine," Kol warned. He'd told Sebastian that

Amiah would be upset seeing him walking around, and... well... as predicted—

She grabbed Sebastian's elbow. "You're not fine, and I don't even need my magic to see that. Your essence is still low and your magical channels are raw. Do I need to sedate you?"

Sebastian glared at her. "I'm not an agent, so I'm not a patient."

"You're in my hospital."

"I'm visiting a friend." He jerked his chin at me.

Amiah followed his motion and glared at me, probably because I was in Marcus's embrace. A strange, honest-to-goodness emotion, not a temperature change, whispered through me, but it came and went so fast I had no idea what it meant, even if I could clearly tell — how, I didn't know — that it was Amiah's emotion.

She yanked on Sebastian's arm with enough force to make him stumble a step into the hall. "You came in on a gurney. That makes you a patient."

He jerked his elbow free. "I'm fine enough to do this."

"No, you're not."

"I am. Especially if Esther is going to supply the juice." He flashed his wicked smile, the sexual invitation clear. All of my guys — including Kol — shifted and the temperature rose to ever-so-slightly too warm.

"What are you proposing?" Gideon asked, his tone edged with ice.

Sebastian's smile deepened — as if his invitation hadn't been clear before — and his eyes filled with mischief. "Well..."

"Bane," Marcus snarled.

Sebastian laughed and Amiah huffed.

He rolled his eyes at her. "I propose casting a spell to locate the source of the witches' magic."

"No doubt the source is hidden. You're going to need to channel too much magic." Amiah grabbed his elbow again. "No one is burning up in Operations on my watch."

"That's why Esther is going to do most of the hard work," he said.

Marcus's snarl turned into an outright growl and a whisper of his cold fear swept over me. "I don't think so."

"She's not a spellcaster," Jacob added.

"But she's got power and she's magically sensitive," Sebastian said.

"Her sensitivity hasn't been trained." Gideon frowned. It was clear he was weighing the pros and cons of going ahead with the plan.

And I couldn't blame him. If it was the fastest way to find the source of the witches' power and it stopped them from killing any more people, the angel in me was going to agree to it no matter how dangerous. Of course, it was also better to know exactly what I was getting into. Jacob's vampiric claim on me being a perfect case in point. I hadn't known exactly what being claimed by a vampire meant, and now Jacob's hunger was focused entirely on me and I was bite-locked.

"How dangerous is it?" I asked.

"Very," Jacob said as he turned his attention to Kol. "Unless you have help."

"But I've never assisted with a tracking spell before," he said.

"You know how to hone in on a magic source?" Sebastian pursed his lips, his gaze going unfocused. "I can make that work. I'll link the three of us and—"

"That's a terrible idea." The muscles in Kol's jaw flexed and the air around me chilled.

"No, it's perfect," Sebastian said. "I cast the spell and you guide her. The danger will be minimal."

"To her," Amiah said. She leveled a hard glare on Sebastian. "You're still going to need to manipulate raw energy and risk burning up or draining your essence to unconsciousness. Neither is acceptable in your condition."

"You saw what three of those witches could do," Gideon said. "We need to move on this." He stood, the yearning in his gaze deepening, making my pulse stutter, and glanced at his phone. "The team from head office is just about to leave. I'll tell them to stick around."

"Just great," Marcus said. "We're never going to hear the end of it from them."

"Put your pride and ego aside. We need all the help we can get." Gideon shoved his phone back into his pocket. "Essie? Kol? You up for this?"

"Yes," I said. We had to know if there were more of those glyph witches out there.

But resignation tightened in my chest.

What the hell was I resigned about?

Then Kol shifted and I realized the emotion wasn't mine.

"Fine." His gaze started to slide back to mine, but he jerked it to Gideon instead, his body so tense it hurt to look at him. "But I can't do it until the four of you release some energy."

"We don't have the time for that," Gideon said.

A whisper of Kol's seductive magic slipped over my skin. He shuddered, which made me shudder, which make Marcus's breath pick up and his hands slide down to my hips.

"If you want me to be able to concentrate enough to guide Essie during the spell, make time. I'll be back in an hour." Kol rushed out of the room and down the hall.

"I need to pick up a few things from my apartment," Sebastian said, shooting Amiah a just-try-and-stop-me look, and followed Kol out the door.

"Idiot," Amiah huffed, and she headed down the hall in the opposite direction, leaving me with Marcus, Jacob, and Gideon.

The temperature rose and Marcus's breath didn't relax. Gideon and Jacob turned their attention to me, one bright and filled with light, the other dark and filled with intensity. Both blazing with need.

My pulse stalled and heat pooled low within me. These were my guys and they wanted me as much as I wanted them.

"We shouldn't do this here," Marcus said, his voice husky.

His hot breath feathered across the back of my neck, sending a tremor of desire racing down my back, and I bit back a moan.

"We have an hour. How do we want to work this out?" We hadn't had a chance to talk about our situation, or how sex with the four of us was going to work. What were everyone's boundaries? Had the moment yesterday with Marcus and Jacob been a one-time thing?

If I was being honest with myself, I hoped it wasn't. I didn't want to have to pick, or keep a schedule. I wanted my guys, now, all of them. And I *really* wanted more than just an hour.

The guys glanced at each other, and a flicker of uncertainty cut through my desire. They'd had a conversation without me. But what had they decided on?

"Was the threesome yesterday because of extenuating circumstances?" Gideon asked me.

Jacob's intense stillness billowed, radiating through his brand, and Marcus stiffened behind me. The temperature in the room rose a few more degrees with their desire, but their uncertainty grew stronger.

"I won't ask any of you to do something you're not comfortable with," I said.

"For fuck's sake. Be more direct, Gideon. We're wasting time," Marcus growled. "Essie, I'm taking you up to have a shower. I'm sure Gideon and Jacob would like to join us. Are *you* comfortable with that?"

The temperature jumped to sweltering and a need as strong as mine, a mix from all my guys, rushed into me. I gasped and bit back a groan. "What are we waiting for?"

"Finally." Marcus climbed out of bed, dressed only in his jeans — since he'd just come back from a run in his wolf form — looking sexy as hell, and picked me up, cradling me against his firm muscular chest.

"I'll go tell the head office team to meet us in the cafeteria in an hour," Gideon said.

"Meet us in my room," Jacob said. "My shower is bigger."

"And your bed," I added.

Marcus's piercing green eyes darkened, his wolf rising to the surface, and he released a low, sensual growl. God, I loved that sound, loved his ferocity. I slid my hand along his jaw, savoring the rasp of his sexy scruff on my skin, and captured his lips with mine. His grip on me tightened and he raked his tongue into my mouth, fueling my desire, kissing me with a breathtaking kiss that left me panting.

"Jesus, Essie," he gasped. "If you keep that up, we're not going to leave the room."

"The bed isn't big enough for the four of us." I sucked on his lower lip, drawing a throaty moan from him.

"And it doesn't have a shower." Jacob pulled me out of Marcus's arms and strode out of the room.

With a groan, Gideon ran a hand over his buzzed blond hair and marched in the opposite direction. Marcus, his T-shirt clutched in his hand, hurried after us as we took the smaller halls to the elevator and hit the call button. Thankfully the halls were empty. Gideon had said I'd been unconscious for a full day. That meant it had to be after nine at night.

Jacob's grip on me tightened as we waited, his breath coming a little too fast. If he'd had a pulse, it would have been racing. The air around me simmered, hot and muggy, slicking my skin with sweat, and flickers of electricity from Gideon's brand nipped up my right arm into Jacob's brand and swirled with his powerful stillness.

"I can walk, you know." I pressed a hand against his chest and his gaze, his eyes intense black pools, captured mine.

"I need to do more than just hold your hand," he said, his voice a low rumble that sent my essence into glorious resonance with his.

The door opened and he carried me into the elevator, his attention still locked on me. My pulse picked up, pounding in a chest overflowing with desire, mine and theirs.

"I need more, too," I said, and he dipped in and kissed me, the kiss slow, sensual, lingering. It flooded heat through my body, ratcheting up the temperature even more, and left me just as breathless as one of Marcus's ferocious kisses.

The elevator door slid open and we hurried past my assigned room to Jacob's suite. He unlocked his door with his thumbprint and opened it without barely shifting my weight, and carried me straight to his cream-and-gray bathroom with his large standup shower.

Something flashed at the corner of my eye and I jerked my attention to my reflection in the mirror. My thoughts stalled. Brilliant white light with gold flecks radiated from my eyes, and I had no idea if the glow was at its usual bright state or brighter because of my heightened emotions.

The stunned, scared nephilim I'd seen in the mirror the last few weeks no longer looked back at me. In her place was an angel radiating tremendous power. I brushed a finger over the scar along my cheek where I'd almost been shot, then slid it over the ugly ragged scar on my neck where I'd been bitten.

A lot had happened in a little while and so much had changed.

"Amiah might be able to remove those," Jacob said, sitting me on the counter. He cupped his massive hand over my neck, capturing my hand and covering the feral vampire bite. A whisper of regret and worry slid through me. He thought my scars upset me, made me think I was less attractive. But it wasn't the scars bothering me. My whole life had been turned upside down, ripped to shreds, and set on fire.

And I had the scars to prove it.

I also had the soul bonds.

I tangled my free hand into Jacob's shoulder-length hair, pulling it free from the elastic holding it back, and leaned forward.

He captured my lips with another slow, breathtaking kiss. His hand slipped under my hospital gown and skimmed a teasing trail along the top of my thigh. I shifted forward, spread my legs apart, and tugged him close, pressing myself against the bulge in the front of his pants.

With a groan, he deepened the kiss, his tongue raking against mine, his desire weakening his control. I pushed my hands under his shirt and ran my nails over his bulky chest. God, I loved the feel of all that powerful muscle. I didn't think I'd ever get enough of it. Behind him, Marcus had taken off his clothes and started the shower. His wolf's ferocity filled his eyes, capturing my soul, as he stepped into the spray and pumped a hand down his full erection.

A shudder swept through me at the thought of all that ferocious power focused on me. Jacob's hand on my thigh shifted inward, teasing oh so close to my core, and my breath hitched.

Marcus growled and slid his hand back to his tip and pumped again, and I imagined it wasn't his hand he was thrusting into. I squirmed against Jacob, brushing myself against his fingers, sending a shiver of need racing through me. Now all I could think about was getting him out of his clothes and dragging him into the shower with Marcus.

I grabbed his T-shirt. "You should take this off," I said, my voice husky.

"You should take *that* off," he replied, his gaze raking over my body.

"You should both get in the fucking shower," Marcus snarled, his heated desire mixing with the steam from the shower.

A wicked smile, almost as wicked as Kol's, tugged at Jacob's lips. He slowly dragged off his T-shirt, his body still tucked tight against mine, making it impossible for me to get out of the three-sleeved hospital gown.

"Essie—" Marcus said, his voice low.

Jacob slid both of his hands under the gown, teasing close to my core again, but not making contact.

God, just touch me already.

"Possessive shifter sex," he rumbled in my ear. "How wild do you want him?"

Holy fuck. "You sure you're not Kol?" Getting Marcus riled up was definitely something Kol would do.

The memory of my dream of Kol and his magic sliding into me sent another shiver racing through me.

"I may have asked for a few pointers when our brand first appeared." His thumb whispered against my clit and I gasped in surprise.

"You asked Kol for pointers?" And he gave suggestions? I didn't know if that made our sooner-rather-than-later necessary conversation more awkward or not.

"I like to learn new things." He bit my neck hard and plunged a finger inside me.

ESSIE

Sensation shot through me, pain and pleasure. A rush of aching hot need on a giant wave of Jacob's magic. I tipped my head back, my eyelids fluttering shut, and Jacob took a long pull on my vein, tugging all the way to my core. He slid a second finger into me, drew them out, and slid them back in, slowly. My breath picked up and his magic spiraled tighter within me.

God, this was what I needed. Sure, we only had an hour, but the world wasn't going to end and I wasn't going to explode and take out a building. I could give in to the pull of our soul bonds.

Another thrust of his fingers, matched with another pull on my neck. My essence throbbed, a breathtaking mix of my desire, Jacob's magic, and surging need from Marcus. I felt all of it with my empathy, a mix of heat and steam and honest-to-goodness emotions.

I shoved my hands down the front of Jacob's pants and grasped his erection, drawing a moan from him and a growl from Marcus.

Jacob ground his thumb over my clit and his fingers worked faster, spiraling his magic tighter within me. My breath picked up. I was flying on blazing need, spiraling higher and higher.

A whisper of a climax shuddered through me, not enough to release his magic, and he tugged me off the counter. His healing magic sealed the bite on my neck shut, and with my head still spinning with desire, he backed me into the shower, the hot spray soaking the hospital gown and pasting it to my body.

My back hit hard muscle, and another whisper of climax made my muscles clench in anticipation. Marcus grabbed my shoulders and wrenched me around. He seized a fistful of my hair and slammed his mouth against mine with a possessive, demanding kiss. The ferocity of his passion stole my breath, blazed across my skin, and flooded me with emotion.

He shoved me against the tiled wall, his free hand raking up under the gown. I hooked my leg around his waist and ground against his erection, showing him how much I needed him inside me.

"Mine," he snarled, and for a second, all I could see in his eyes was his wolf. His pupils had slitted and his canines had started to extend. He was incredible. The attraction that had been sizzling between us from the moment we'd first met had nothing on this. I was burning up with his need and I couldn't get enough.

I dug my fingers into his scalp and snarled back. "Mine."

"Fuck, Essie, you're incredible." He crushed his mouth back against mine and thrust into me, burying to the hilt in one powerful, glorious stroke. With a growl, he grabbed my hips, forcing me to wrap both legs around him and driving him deeper inside me.

Jacob's magic swelled, stealing all breath and thought. There was only sensation. The soaked gown clinging to my skin, the tile at my back, Marcus's fingers digging into my butt, the feel of him filling me, and his passion blazing around my heart.

He pounded into me with forceful, wild thrusts, making Jacob's magic twist tighter and tighter. Every cell sang with it, spinning into a supernova until it ripped my orgasm free. Every muscle in my body contracted. I cried Marcus's name as he tensed within me, his own climax seizing him. Stars danced behind my eyes, I couldn't catch my breath, and magic swelled around my heart, strengthening our mating bond.

Marcus gasped and his body trembled, but Jacob, now fully naked, drew up tight behind him and steadied us against the wall. The intensity in Jacob's eyes sent another shuddering climax through me, making Marcus groan.

I slid my legs from Marcus's waist, and he wrapped his arms around my back and turned us, capturing me between him and Jacob. One lithe muscular body thrumming with passion even after he'd just come, and the other bulky, powerful, encompassing, radiating an intensity focused entirely on me.

"You're still wearing too much clothing," Jacob said, his voice rumbling through me, reigniting my aching need.

"I can help with that." Marcus yanked a claw through the thin fabric, ripping it open.

My pulse tripped, and Jacob tugged the gown off. A low, sensual growl rumbled in Marcus's throat and his pupils dilated. He slid his hands up my belly and cupped my breasts. I leaned into him. God, I'd just had a mind-blowing orgasm and I wanted more with him, with Jacob... with all of them.

Jacob pressed tight behind me and I ground my butt against his huge erection. He reached around and found my clit as Marcus rolled my nipples, pinching them into tight, aching buds.

I moaned into Marcus's mouth, and Jacob's tip brushed my folds, teasing me.

Oh, fuck, yes.

I arched my back, giving Jacob a better angle. He slid inside me, slowly, stretching me with his girth, his thumb rubbing my clit while Marcus pinched my nipples and plunged his tongue into my mouth. It was sensation overload. I'd never experienced anything like it before.

Jacob drew out and agonizingly slowly pushed back inside. My breath picked up and my body trembled. I didn't even have his magic inside me, and I throbbed with a burning, consuming need.

"Jacob, please," I begged, grinding against him and pressing my hands against the wall on either side of Marcus's head to keep my balance.

He drew out again, and Marcus slid lower down the wall and sucked hard on my nipple. I gasped and Jacob pushed back in. He built up his pace, growing my desire until I was trembling on the edge again. Then he drew me back and sank his teeth into my neck.

His power exploded through me and another glorious climax crashed over me, stealing my breath and sending stars snapping across my vision.

More heat seared around my heart and strengthened my bond with him, and his intense stillness surged from his brand, rushing up my arm, his magic manifested in my body.

He tensed with his own climax, sending glorious aftershocks rippling through me, and we breathlessly sagged to the shower floor with Marcus.

"Wow—" It was all I could think of to say. "Oh, wow."

The bathroom door opened with a whirl of mist, and Gideon stepped in. His angel glow blazed from his stunning blue eyes, and a flicker of electric magic crackled through our brand.

"You're just in time," Jacob said.

Marcus rumbled a satisfied agreement. "But you're wearing too much clothing."

Gideon's gaze locked with mine and I could sense uncertainty and need. A need that made my pulse trip as if I hadn't just had another amazing orgasm.

"Essie?" he asked, his uncertainty breaking my heart, sending miniature fractures through my bliss.

"I agree. You're wearing too much clothing." I reached out a hand to him. "Help me to bed, Gideon. I'm not sure I can actually stand any more."

Marcus captured my lips in a quick, fierce kiss. "You're welcome."

"You can't stand either, buddy," I said back.

"Oh, I'll be able to stand again soon enough." He shifted, drawing my attention to his already growing erection.

Oh, my!

Gideon's uncertainty flared stronger. In a way, he was the newest to the relationship, even though we'd shared a brand first. And just like I'd needed to reassure Marcus's wolf that he was mine, it looked like I needed to reassure Gideon that he was mine, too.

I turned my attention back to my angel and started to stand. My legs trembled and — as I'd hoped — Gideon rushed forward to steady me. For a second, I was soaring in a blazing summer sky, my soul captured by Gideon's gaze. And now I really did have wings. Flying with him was no longer just a dream.

"Mate," I breathed, and pressed my lips to his.

He groaned, swept me still dripping wet into his arms, and carried me to Jacob's bed. More electricity nipped through our brand as Gideon stared down at me, laid out on Jacob's comforter, waiting for him to join me.

"You're so beautiful." He flicked open the top button of his shirt. The front was wet from carrying me out of the shower and clung to the perfect contours of his chest. "And generous." Two more buttons. My breath hitched. "And brave." Another button. "And strong."

I squirmed. Good lord, he was just unbuttoning his shirt, but with the searing desire in his eyes focused entirely on me, he was lighting me up and making me ache.

I sat up and slid my hands inside his shirt and across his sculpted pecs, making him draw in a sharp breath, and pushed his shirt off his shoulders.

He ripped open the last button and shrugged out of the shirt, his gaze never leaving mine. "Even if fate hadn't bound us together, I still would have fallen in love with you."

He cupped my cheek and brushed his lips against mine. Desire shivered through me at that whisper of a kiss, and our bond throbbed inside me. I could feel how much he wanted me. The room was practically a sauna, and his emotions flooded my chest.

"But fate *did* bind us together," I said.

His uncertainty flickered through his desire.

"Because we were destined for each other all along." I pressed my hand over his heart, willing him to feel how much I wanted him, how much I cared for him.

Heat swept down my arm, picking up some of Jacob's stillness and Gideon's electricity, and swelled around my palm. For a second I feared I was going to blast him with divine light, but the power felt different, not the blazing, roaring magic I always felt when I shot a light strike. Yes, it was still warm, but not burning. Still strong, but not destructive.

It sank into Gideon's chest and his eyes widened with surprise. "You feel that for all of us," he gasped. "For me?"

"Yes." I returned his kiss and he took the invitation, leaning forward and kissing me in full.

I let him nudge me back to the bed and plunge his tongue into my mouth. His passion wasn't as ferocious as Marcus's nor intense as Jacob's, but there was a certainty in it that made the divine light in the core of my being light up. And his control was insane. I knew how much he ached for me. It made my desire burn hotter, and yet he kissed me as if we didn't have less than an hour left. He kissed down my neck to my breasts, sucking on one nipple and teasing it into a tight bud before turning to the other one in a slow, sensual way that had me squirming and panting beneath him.

Then he sat back and undid his pants. Marcus climbed onto the bed beside us and stole a kiss as Gideon undressed. Jacob knelt on my other side. I turned my head to kiss him, and Marcus switched his mouth to my nipple.

The weight on the bed behind my legs shifted and I returned my attention to Gideon, gloriously naked and ready for me. He grabbed my hips and slid into me with a slow powerful stroke, his gaze never leaving mine. We were connected, body, magic, and soul, and our power crackled over our brands, divine light dancing over our forearms.

He pumped into me as Jacob made love to my mouth and Marcus sucked on my nipples. My desire ratcheted higher, my breath so fast I was dizzy, and I rocked my hips, meeting Gideon, driving him as deep as he could go.

My climax built fast in part because I was already aching for Gideon and his desire flooded me, and because of Marcus and Jacob caressing and kissing me.

Gideon's pace picked up and grew frantic, then Jacob rubbed his thumb over my clit and I shattered. Light blazed from my brands and eyes, hell, my whole body. My bond with Gideon surged strong and sure. He came, his body tense, his wings exploding from his back, at the same time the full force of my climax made every muscle clench.

With a shuddered groan of satisfaction, Gideon pulled his wings back in and Marcus shifted so he could collapse beside me.

"That was—" Gideon gasped.

"Amazing," Marcus finished.

"Yeah," Jacob said.

That was one way to put it. It'd also been incredible, sexy as hell, and utterly satisfying. This was the way it was supposed to be. I could feel my guys, their bonds pulsing around my heart and their emotions filling me.

Jacob nudged me — then I nudged Gideon who nudged Marcus — and we all shifted over to make room for Jacob on his bed.

I could lie with the guys like this, naked and boneless, forever. Add Kol and it would be perfect—

Jeez.

I fought to shove that thought aside.

Kol wasn't mine.

I had to remember he wasn't mine.

Except a small voice kept whispering, *he should be.*

Gideon ran his hand over my belly, drawing a shiver of renewed desire — which surprised me since I'd just had three amazing orgasms

— and pulled me close. He planted a soft, lingering kiss on my lips that made my breath pick up again, then, with a sigh edged with regret, he sat up.

"We have to get back to work," he said.

Marcus groaned. "I hate those glyph witches more than I did before." But he too sat up and headed into the bathroom.

Gideon grabbed his pants off the floor and stepped into them. "I brought you a change of clothes." He set my duffle bag on the bed.

I sat up and reached for the bag. "Are there actually clean clothes in there?" I couldn't remember if I had any remaining changes that I'd originally brought from my apartment yesterday...? The day before...?

Jeez. I had no idea when I'd last been home.

"I ran over to your place and grabbed a few things earlier today," Jacob said. He hooked a finger under my chin, raised my head, and kissed me before getting off the bed and heading to his closet.

"Thanks." I returned to the bathroom, was kissed senseless again by Marcus, and had a quick proper shower, since a lot had happened between now and my last shower at Sebastian's.

With my wet hair pulled back in a ponytail, and dressed in a clean pair of jeans and a T-shirt that revealed all of Gideon's brand and most of Jacob's, I joined my guys striding down the hall to the elevators. I'd never felt more sure about my place. It was here with my guys, helping people as a JP agent. And yet I had no clue if I was still an agent.

The elevator door slid open and we stepped in. Marcus snaked an arm around my waist and drew me tight against his body, while Gideon and Jacob pressed close on either side.

"So am I just helping out with this spell or am I still an agent on the team?" I asked.

Marcus huffed. "Of course you are. Why would you ask something like that?"

"Because I was assigned as the *human* member of the team and I'm no longer human. I really want to know where I stand."

"Beside us," Gideon said. "Your paperwork went through this afternoon while Amiah had you sedated. You're officially a JP agent assigned to our team."

"Even though I'm your mate?" That was the other issue. Although I wondered how Cassius felt about that now that I was actually a full angel.

"Head office knows everything," Jacob said. "And the mayor has rescinded his demand that a human be assigned to our JP team."

Thank God. Because I didn't know how any human would survive chasing the city's most dangerous supers. I had some power and I'd barely managed to survive the last few weeks.

Gideon gave me a warm smile that made my soul sing. "Once we've found the source of the glyph witches' power, we'll get you proper training."

Once we'd found the source. That sounded suspiciously like I was going to help with the spell and nothing more. I resisted the urge to fight him on that. I might now be a powerful super, but I still had no idea how to control that power, or the best way to apprehend supers. There was a lot I needed to learn before I could be a good agent.

"Hopefully now that the spell blocking your magic and true essence is gone, you'll have more control over your light strike," Jacob said.

"So my essence now says I'm an angel?" It was going to be even more challenging to be an agent if my essence still said I was a human and my eyes glowed. Everyone would mistake me for a nephilim. And while I knew my guys had my back, the average-Joe-super wouldn't.

"More or less," Marcus said.

"What does that mean?"

"If you look closely, there's still something a little wonky with it, but it does say you're an angel," Jacob said.

"Bane says it's just the remnants of the spell," Gideon added. "It'll eventually pass."

Well, that was a relief. Finally something was going right. There was just one more thing—

"What about Cassius? Is the team still under review?" He'd been against me since the beginning... then he'd arrested me and been poisoned and nothing with him had been cleared up.

Jacob shot Gideon a worried look.

Oh, that wasn't good. Maybe nothing *would* be cleared up and he'd always hate me.

"Cassius is still unconscious," Gideon said, his angel glow dimming with worry.

"But we removed the magical poison," I said. "And the glyph witch who cast the spell died." Surely that had been enough to destroy the spell poisoning him, and, although things were a bit of a blur, I thought I recalled Amiah saying the poison was gone. As much as I didn't like

Cassius and he'd been a real asshole to me, he was still Gideon's brother — and all that assholeishness had been a misguided attempt to protect Gideon, something I could fully understand.

"And Willow worked through me to pull it all out." The muscles in Jacob's jaw flexed, but I wasn't sure if it was because Cassius hadn't woken or because he'd let Willow use him to save Cassius.

Gideon squared his shoulders. "He'll wake eventually." But I could feel his worry.

The door slid open and we headed the short distance down the wide hall to the shallow steps leading down to the cafeteria.

It was empty. Thank God.

I wasn't ready to face all of the angels in Union City, as well as my non-angelic co-workers, as a full angel. Especially since everyone had believed I was a human. Just the thought of how much attention that was going to get made me shudder. I'd spent my life hiding, striving to not be noticed, and now I was sure everyone was talking about me.

The rock wall feature was still under construction, surrounded by scaffolding, the water still off, and only half of the decorative plants were in their crannies. But the bank of windows at the back and the door leading to the patio had been replaced. If I ignored the rock wall, I could pretend the archnephilim hadn't destroyed the room and murdered Zella.

I slid a glance at Gideon, threaded my fingers between his, and gave his hand a squeeze. I knew he was in love with me. I could feel it in our bond. But that didn't mean he hadn't been in love with Zella. Love was complicated. There wasn't just one person — my bonds were proof of that — nor was there one way to love someone.

Jacob headed to our usual six-seater table while Marcus, Gideon, and I went to the fridge containing the wrapped sandwiches and salads. I picked a turkey club sandwich and a bottle of water, and took the chair beside Jacob as he slid his phone back into his pocket.

"Just letting Kol and Bane know where we are," he said as Gideon sat at the head of the table and Marcus sat across from me.

"Good." Gideon cracked open his water bottle. "We need to figure out what we're going to do once we locate the source of the witches' magic."

"Let the professionals handle it," a raspy alto said, as a tall woman strode down the steps toward us. She was strikingly beautiful, even with the sneer curling her lips. Not quite succubus beautiful, but close, with black hair pulled back into a long braid, sculpted cheekbones, and large black eyes that glowed with a prick of hellfire. She wore a tight tank top that showed off her muscular arms and gave a hint of what had to be a perfect six-pack. But what shocked me was her power. It filled the room, pushing out the air and crushing inside me. Whoever she was, whatever kind of demon she was, she was powerful.

ESSIE

THE FORCE OF THE WOMAN'S POWER STRENGTHENED AS SHE DREW CLOSER, and I could barely breathe by the time she stood beside Gideon and stared down at him.

"Would you mind pulling it back?" Marcus growled, his anger curling tight in my chest. "Our mate can't breathe."

The woman cocked a black eyebrow. "I didn't think you were sensitive, agent."

"You *know* I'm not." He and the others looked fine. But then they weren't magically sensitive and couldn't feel the woman's power like I could. "But that doesn't mean you can just let it all hang out."

Wisps of red demonic magic curled around her forearms and sank back under her skin, and the force of her power billowed. It stole what little breath I had left, and I clutched the edge of the table to keep from collapsing.

"Zuri." Gideon shoved out of his chair, the light in his eyes blazing, his emotions turning the air hot.

"I outrank you," she hissed. "Sit back down."

Black specks crept around the edge of my vision. She was doing it on purpose. I had no idea why, but it pissed me off. I was sick and tired of being in pain and out of breath and the weak link.

Well, no more.

My magic roared inside me, ignited by my determination. It seared in my chest, shoving the woman's power out of my body, and blazed from my palms. I drew in a deep, ragged breath and stood, my chair's leg screeching on the floor.

The woman's eyes widened, her hellfire flared, and her power pounded with enormous force, but couldn't get back inside me.

"I'll give you a pissing contest if you want one." I met her raised eyebrow with my own. I had no idea if I could win a fight against this woman, but all the frustration and fear from the last few weeks now burned in a powerful rage inside me. I was done running and hiding. My guys had stood by me even when they thought I was a nephilim, and now it was time for me to stand my ground.

The woman's sneer deepened and with a flash her crushing power vanished. "Strong enough to withstand a greater demon. She *is* an archangel. I'd say a full one, too." She grabbed a chair from the table behind her, pulled it beside Gideon's, and sat in it backwards.

Gideon glared at her and the temperature stayed hot. "Was that really necessary?"

"Head office requested it," a broad-shouldered guy with angelic glowing eyes said from the top of the cafeteria stairs. Beside him stood a rake-thin woman radiating the feral intensity of a shifter, and another guy, who looked to be in his mid-twenties and was built like Marcus with a lean-muscled body. I couldn't sense any power radiating from him, and he didn't give off vampiric intensity or shifter feralness, so I had no idea what kind of super he was.

"I really want to tell head office to fuck off," Marcus said under his breath.

"It's not that they don't believe your reports..." the angel said as he headed down the stairs toward us.

"But there hasn't been a new archangel in generations." Gideon sat back down. The temperature eased a bit, but didn't fully return to normal. In fact, if I looked closely — because I could also *feel* it with my magic — all of my guys were tense with anger and worry.

"Just like there's only been one other mated pair in over a hundred years," the demon-woman said. Her gaze slid to Jacob's arm and his brand. "Mated trio?"

"Plus an extra," the female shifter said with a sniff. "Your incubus must be in heaven."

"Or he's stoned out of his mind," the demon-woman said. "You said he'd be back in an hour."

"There are still a few minutes left," the angel said, taking the empty chair beside Marcus.

The demon-woman rolled her eyes at him.

"I'm sorry about your welcome to the JP," the angel said, holding out his hand to me. "I'm Ephraim, Zuri's second in command, that's Regan —" He jerked his thumb at the shifter, who took the other empty chair, leaving the human-looking guy to grab one from another table. "And that's Xavier."

"Who can just as easily cast this location spell as your guy," the demon-woman, Zuri, said.

"I don't know about that." Xavier rubbed the back of his neck, looking embarrassed.

"You're powerful enough to be on an elite team, kid. Start acting like it," Regan growled at him.

"I just mean Sebastian Bane is known in witching circles to be powerful and he's already felt the magic we're looking for. I'd need even more power just to figure out where to start looking."

"He's also rumored to sell illegal goods to known criminals," Ephraim said. "We can't look the other way because he's helpful."

"Rumored," Sebastian said as he entered the cafeteria with Kol at his side. They were both breathtakingly sexy, Sebastian the ice to Kol's fire, but I couldn't keep my eyes off of Kol.

"Are we finding the source of the worship magic or not?" Sebastian asked.

"We're waiting on you." Zuri shoved out of her chair and marched right past Sebastian to the stairs, as if she knew exactly where she was supposed to be headed.

Her team fell in line behind her, and Gideon rose and glanced at me. Love and desire swept across his expression before he gave me a nod of encouragement and squared his shoulders.

"Always great to have an elite team visit," Marcus growled, his voice low.

"We need them," Gideon said. "Especially if those weren't the only witches able to access that worship magic. Those glyph witches nearly killed us twice."

I shuddered at the memory of my guys bleeding and gasping, my soul screaming that they were dying, while I'd been unable to help them. I was never going through that again.

"Three times," Jacob said. "We didn't fare too well at the airport."

Marcus shot him a dark look. "Don't remind me."

"Come on." Gideon jerked his chin to the cafeteria stairs. "Let's not keep the *elite* team waiting."

"Just give me a minute with Esther and Kol," Sebastian said, his gaze leaping past Gideon to the hall where Zuri and her team had gone. "I want to set up the necessary links without the audience."

"I'll go keep them distracted." Jacob headed out of the cafeteria.

"Marcus, go with him," Gideon said.

"Really?" Marcus asked. "They're not a threat."

"Yet," Sebastian said.

Marcus glared at him. "They're assholes, but we're all on the same side."

"Come on, Marcus." Gideon's angel glow flared. "Given how we were greeted, I don't want any of us alone with them."

"You think we're still under review?" Kol asked.

"Cassius—" Gideon said, and a swell of grief misted the air around me. "Cassius is still unconscious and we called for help. It's not a question of whether we're under review or not. It's for how long. And we can't risk being reassigned to different teams. I don't want any of us to have to choose between Essie or our jobs."

"Then why the hell did you ask them to stay?" Marcus asked. "They were supposed to be on a plane by now."

"Someone else would have shown up in a day, probably less, and I'm not going after the source of the glyph witches' power with just one senior agent. I want that team." Gideon ran his hands over his buzz cut. It was a little longer now, but not anywhere close to what it was before I'd burned him to a crisp during a drug-induced suicide attempt.

"Are you coming?" Jacob asked from down the hall. I could still see his legs, so he hadn't gotten far. He'd probably heard the debate and waited for Marcus.

"Yeah." Marcus shot me a heated look that sent a shiver of desire down my spine, and hurried to catch up with Jacob.

Kol dropped his gaze to the floor for a second, his body tense, then raised it, his expression tight, his hellfire still small, barely there, pinpricks. "So how does this tracking spell work?"

"First," Sebastian said, sitting in the closest chair and placing a large coin with a complicated glyph on it on the table, "Essie needs to connect to the link charm."

"Kol?" Gideon asked, and Kol picked up the coin and shut his eyes.

"Feels like a temporary link with nothing else attached," Kol said, opening his eyes.

"You still don't trust me." Sebastian gave an exaggerated sigh. "I've already had access to her essence. If I wanted to control her, I would."

Gideon's eyes narrowed. "That doesn't make me feel better."

"And it doesn't mean we shouldn't be careful," Kol added.

"They don't trust me." Sebastian flashed me a wicked smile filled with heat and mischief. He took the charm from Kol and held it, resting it in his palm.

"Probably because you keep messing with them," I said.

"Everyone has to have a hobby." He cocked a white eyebrow, drawing my attention to a gaze so pale blue it was almost colorless. A flicker of his power danced across his eyes. Even with his essence low, I could glimpse the vast, icy universe of magic in his pupils. "Place your palm on top of mine and we'll get this link set."

"So I'm *not* giving you magic?" I asked. I'd thought I was going to transfer power into him like I had yesterday, when my guys were dying and he needed to teleport them to safety.

"You're not," he said. "I'm not dumb enough to try a transfer with an untrained archangel who's used to using extra force to get her power out. I'd be fried before I could blink."

"Which means I'm still a bomb waiting to explode." Just great. I thought I was past that. My buzz was gone and I couldn't feel my power threatening to erupt, and while my head was still sore from channeling too much magic, I'd thought I was finally fine.

"You're not going to explode," he said. "The pressure building within you as your magic was trying to break the spell on you is gone."

"But an energy transfer to a person is a delicate thing, and you don't have that kind of control yet," Gideon said.

"If you weren't as powerful as you are, it wouldn't be a problem." Sebastian shifted his hand closer to me, reminding me I was supposed to place my hand on his. "If I wasn't in my... *current* condition, your lack of control wouldn't be a problem, either."

Great. So I wasn't a ticking bomb, but that still didn't mean my light strike wasn't going to accidentally hurt someone.

"We should get on with this," Kol said, shoving his hands in his pockets. "Zuri isn't going to wait forever."

Right. We were supposed to be playing nice with her so she wouldn't break up the team.

I placed my hand over Sebastian's. He captured it, setting his other hand on top, and murmured something, his voice so low I couldn't make out the words even with my vampire-enhanced hearing.

A shiver of ice, somehow soft and sensual, crawled over my hands and snaked up my arm. Miniature magical ruptures sparked under my skin, frozen and powerful. This was what Sebastian's power felt like. Or at least this was a glimpse. I got the feeling this was merely a fraction of the whirling power that lay inside him.

He turned my hand so the charm lay in my palm and looked at Kol. "Your turn."

"Yeah," Kol said, his tone sharp.

He pressed his warm palm to mine, the heat from his demonic body temperature sinking into my skin and swirling with Sebastian's ice. My gaze lifted to his of its own volition. The hellfire in his eyes grew, simmering and stealing my breath like it always did, and for a second, the connection between us felt like it had before my wings had appeared. Warm. Sensual. Right.

Then frustration cut into the feeling. The muscles in Kol's shoulders stiffened, his hellfire tightened, and he shifted his gaze to Sebastian, who captured our hands between his and murmured the spell again.

A caress of heated desire entwined with Sebastian's ice, and need swelled in my chest and lower. I bit back a moan. I was pretty sure this wasn't supposed to turn me on. There wasn't even close to enough of Kol's magic to fill me with yearning, but I remembered what the full force of his power felt like, hell, what even half of his power had felt like when he'd poured it into me to save my life, and my body craved him.

Maybe Kol wasn't really mine. Maybe my reaction to him *was* just a woman, reacting to an incubus.

The heat swelled and another slice of frustration cut through it.

Kol pulled his hand back and my yearning billowed, aching with the loss of his skin against mine. The curls of his magic and Sebastian's were still there, but it felt as banked as the hellfire in his eyes.

Sebastian sat back and ran a hand over his face, looking exhausted. "Okay. When we get to—" He turned a questioning look at Gideon.

"The clean room," Gideon said.

"Good call. Lots of wards and no magical residue. We might need those." Sebastian drew in a sharp breath and squared his shoulders. "When we get to the clean room, I'll initiate the spell and link you to it.

Essie, just relax into it and let Kol guide you." He stood and shoved the charm into his pants pocket.

I stood and Gideon threaded his fingers between mine. I hadn't thought he'd be a handholding kind of guy, but perhaps he was trying to make up for the weeks he'd tried to stay away from me.

We headed out of the cafeteria and down the hall, going past the elevator and deeper into the 19th century warehouse half of Operations. The first time I'd been there, I'd been in pain and afraid my secret would be discovered. I'd just had the crap beaten out of me by the arch-nephilim and Gideon had all but gotten a court order to have my memories read. I hadn't wanted to go to the place where every angel in Union City lived and I certainly hadn't wanted to get close to Marcus again, not with the attraction still sizzling between us.

Just a few weeks later and everything had changed. Now I walked hand-in-hand with Gideon, craved all of Marcus's ferocious passion, yearned for Jacob's intense stillness, and ached for Kol.

I'd dreamt again of Kol while doped up on Amiah's sedatives, of his embrace, his kiss, his caress. Dream Kol had told me that he craved me as much as I craved him, that I should talk to him and shouldn't assume it was all in my head.

Which, ironically, had *been* all in my head.

But every interaction I'd had with him so far indicated he wasn't ready to talk. Even if it was to just tell him I understood his reaction when I'd triggered his PTSD and was there for him when he was ready.

We reached a nondescript door in a hall of nondescript doors and entered the all-black windowless room where I'd first had my memories read. The light was still low, the room illuminated by a single-bulb fixture in the center of the ceiling, and the four benches, one along each wall, still the only pieces of furniture.

Jacob and Zuri stood by the door. It looked like they'd been talking but their conversation had stopped the moment we'd entered, and I felt Jacob's essence focus on me. It was subtle — I was pretty sure no one else noticed — and it settled nerves I hadn't realized were thrumming.

The rest of the elite team sat on the bench on the right-hand wall, Ephraim posture-perfect, Regan managing the lotus position on the narrow bench, and Xavier leaning against the wall. He sat up when Sebastian — who'd been behind me — entered.

Marcus, sitting on the bench on the other side of the room from the elite team, sat forward as well, his gaze locking with mine for a second, his wolf slitting his pupils. A wave of fierce protectiveness flooded my chest and the temperature rose a few degrees.

Sebastian went straight to the middle of the room, sat cross-legged, and motioned for me and Kol to join him. We sat, and Xavier leaned forward, his elbows on his thighs, as if he wanted to get closer but had been told to stay where he was.

"Just let the spell work through you," Sebastian said, leveling his icy gaze on me. "Don't fight it."

I didn't like the sound of that. "Will I want to fight it?"

I'd had the archnephilim, a hellfire prince, and Victoria try to control me, and I'd hated that feeling. I never wanted to go through that again, the helplessness, the terror. Thinking about it still made my stomach churn and my pulse race. I really hoped this spell wasn't anything like that.

Sebastian pressed two fingers to his neck, activating one of the glyphs tattooed on his body. Light burst from it, turning his white button-down see-through and revealing that the glyph snaked down his chest, between thicker glyphs, in a thin, complicated design. More glyphs covered his torso, a mix of thick and thin mesmerizing black swirls. "Just concentrate on relaxing."

"Sure," I said. No problem. Even if concentrating seemed the opposite of relaxing.

He activated another glyph that curled over his right biceps, and a third at his hip, at the waist of his slacks.

"He's combining spells," Xavier said, his voice breathy with awe.

"Take a breath and release it, Esther." Sebastian held out his hands, one to Kol, the other to me.

I drew in a slow breath and took his hand as Kol took Sebastian's other hand.

Just relax and let the spell flow. That was all I had to do.

Sebastian jerked his chin at the space between me and Kol. "Now complete the circle."

Kol grabbed my hand before I could reach for him and a blast of ice, Sebastian's frozen magic, sliced into my chest. My power erupted in response, exploding into a consuming inferno that threatened to burn Sebastian and his magic into ash.

ESSIE

My pulse raced and the twin fears that I was going to hurt someone and I was being controlled by someone seized me. My power roared stronger, blazing through magical channels still raw from the last couple of days, fighting the thread of ice determined to wrap around it and control it. I couldn't let it. Never again. The ice had to get out.

Get out. Get out get out.

My heart slammed in my chest and I couldn't catch my breath.

Get out. Please, get out.

Except this was what was supposed to happen. Sebastian had told me not to fight it.

I gritted my teeth and struggled to give in to his magic. We needed to find the source of the glyph witches' power and this was the only way to do it.

But God, everything within me howled against the feeling of being possessed, of letting someone take over.

"Just take a breath." Sebastian's grip on my hand tightened. The glow from his glyphs now radiated so brightly he was engulphed in their light and looked like a being of pure illumination.

On my other side, Kol had bent forward, his forehead pressed to the floor, his face scrunched with pain.

"Take. A. Breath," Sebastian gasped.

I forced myself to take a slower breath. It wasn't as long and calming as it could have been, but it was the best I could do.

Sebastian's ice twisted, sliding against my blaze, trying to gain purchase inside me. He rolled his shoulders as if he, too, was trying to relax, and his icy blue-white glow rippled down his body. "Another."

I drew in another breath, slower than before, willing my power to calm. It didn't have to be an inferno. It could be a banked fire, or an electric blanket, or something God damn calm and controllable.

Just let him in. That was all I had to do. My power heaved, and I imagined the swell as a great wave sweeping over me, followed by a smaller wave, and then an even smaller one. There were still swells, I didn't think the magical burning ocean within me was ever going to be a perfectly still lake, but I managed to wrench it back so it was now no longer a ferocious storm.

Sebastian's ice curled into my ocean, twisting my power into his spell. The sensation grated on my nerves and made my soul scream to push him out, keep control. He didn't belong. He wasn't supposed to be inside me.

Then a whisper of sensual heat blended with the ice and my essence instantly focused on it. The ice, the fear, the inferno, were gone. There was only Kol's magic, warm and aching and right. I didn't want to kick him out, felt no need to fight him... because he wasn't trying to control me, not like Sebastian. But I couldn't help wondering if it was because I wanted Kol as much as I wanted Marcus and Jacob and Gideon.

The ice and heat wove deeper inside me, bringing with it a flood of emotions from them. Sebastian was exhausted and worried. Kol was afraid and hurting, a pain that reached soul deep. I gasped, drowning in feelings that weren't mine, fighting to breathe, to think, to do anything beyond *feel*.

My power surged again, instinctually defending me from the *emotional* attack. I scrambled to control it and managed to refocus the blast into a rope and twist it deeper into Sebastian's spell. The sudden burst of power shot my consciousness out of my body and into the sky floating above Operations.

Below lay the helicopter pad and the rooftop patio where Gideon had first agreed to let me be on the team. Ahead stretched the park ringing the Supers' Quarter and beyond that lay the rest of Union City. Fifteen minutes to the north was my apartment in its four-story walkup in its neighborhood of four-story walkups.

This is what the glyph witches' source feels like, Sebastian said in my head, his voice strained as he struggled to keep the spell together. *Kol, guide her.*

Kol's heat sank deeper into me, his essence entwining with mine like how Jacob had entwined our essences when he claimed me. My soul sang with joy and grief and a churning mix of emotions that I wasn't sure were mine, until his sensual magic overwhelmed it all with bone-melting desire. I swallowed a moan, my pulse picking up again, and strained to concentrate.

We were supposed to be doing a spell. Weren't we?

Can you feel the witches' magic? Kol asked.

God, I couldn't feel anything but Kol's strong, aching, liquid desire flooding my every cell.

Esther, Sebastian gasped. *Concentrate. You might be powering this, but I'm still holding the spell together.*

Which meant I needed to hurry up. He was still weak, and out of all of us in this spell, he was the one risking burning up by channeling too much magic.

I fought to mentally push past Kol's magic but couldn't make myself leave him. I wanted to stay embraced in his heat forever.

An aching slice of frustration cut through my desire and Kol's heat turned brittle, losing its sensual slide through my essence.

Reach out with your senses, he said, his voice tight as he gave me a mental shove.

My senses spiraled out. For a second, all the magic in the city flooded me, bright, dark, cold, burning. There was so much. The Quarter was one big churning ocean threatening to drown me, but there was also magic in the human part of the city. Protective wards and charms and a few supers who'd chosen to live outside of the Quarter. So much magic, all if it calling to me.

And then I plunged into a sticky black crushing smoke. It clung to me, threatening to ooze into my magical pores and foul the brilliant light at the core of my being. It was more powerful than anything I'd encountered before, even when sensing the glyph witches' magic. It was as vast as the universe in Sebastian's eyes and more, a swirling, writhing force that could devour me and everyone in the room in an instant, which awed and terrified me, since I hadn't thought I'd ever encounter anything more powerful than Sebastian.

That's it, Kol said. *Hard as a rock and impossible to access.*

Rock hard? It didn't feel hard or inaccessible at all. It curled in and around me, cajoling and begging me to embrace it, draw it in. I'd be more powerful than anyone alive. I could right all the wrongs in the world. I'd be worshiped, adored, feared.

Except I didn't want to be worshiped and I certainly didn't want to be feared. And how had I so easily forgotten the threat of being consumed by it? It mesmerized and terrified and spun my thoughts until I wasn't sure what to think.

Esther, please, Sebastian groaned. *Find its source so I can end the spell.*

I struggled to push out of the smoke, but it wouldn't let me go.

Esther.

I'm stuck. I mentally wrenched harder, and the smoke thickened, grating against my magic with a shifting buzz, faster one moment, slower the next, as if trying to find my core resonance. My internal light dimmed and my pulse stalled. It was trying to gain a hold within my soul, trying to take over.

How can you be stu— Kol's heat swelled, but the smoke hit the grating burn of what my buzz used to be and a wave of darkness crashed inside me.

Shit. Bane. What the hell is happening? Kol asked, his voice small and far away.

Esther, fight it, Sebastian yelled, sounding as if he were standing on the opposite side of a great chasm. And that chasm was getting bigger by the second.

His and Kol's fear sliced frozen inside my chest. So, too, did Gideon's, Marcus's, and Jacob's.

The smoke flooded my essence, pounding into me and drowning me in darkness. It tossed me, a soul adrift in a sticky miasma, each second staining my cells darker and darker.

I heaved and yanked and clawed, but couldn't find my way out. There was no up or down, and no light. Only a clinging, exhausting darkness.

My thoughts stalled. For a second I was in the water-that-wasn't-water of my dreams. Asleep but not asleep. Then I was back to drowning in a black void, my soul screaming, my power stuttering.

Blazing white.

Darkness.

Blazing white. Dark—

Blazing fucking white.

I grasped at my light and pumped every bit of my willpower into it. I pulled strength from Gideon and Jacob and even Kol. I could sense extra power from Sebastian but I could also feel the fiery agony inside his head and the strain on his body to keep the tracking spell active so I left him alone.

I spun all that power into a supernova, twisting it tight, and released it in a massive blast inside my body. Sebastian screamed and his magic clenched around mine. Kol's magic faltered and started to fade away. I mentally seized it and it shot me out of the smoke, racing through floor after floor of some kind of building and rushing out the top of a shiny copper peak.

Got it, Sebastian gasped, and his spell burst apart.

I slammed back into my body, staring up at three—? one—? four—? light fixtures, with the room spinning around and around and around.

Out of the corner of my eye, I saw Kol bent forward with his forehead on the floor. With a groan, he sagged to his side and rolled, spread eagle, onto his back.

"What the hell?" Marcus said as he appeared above me, blocking out the too-many light fixtures. He cupped my cheeks with his strong hands, his eyes filled with worry. "Are you all right?"

"Bane?" Gideon asked, and I caught a glimpse of my angel past Marcus's shoulder as he drew close. "How come Essie and Kol are down, but you're not?"

Marcus raised his gaze — presumably glaring at Sebastian — and I managed to turn my head enough to look at the fae sorcerer. He held his head in his hands as if it hurt, his glow dimmer than before, but he didn't look as if the room was spinning and he hadn't collapsed.

"I'm not sure. Something happened and for a bit they were caught up in the worship magic spell, not just the power it's collecting," he said.

"Which is where?" Zuri asked.

"The Cromer Building," Kol gasped.

"Shit." Marcus's wolf rose under his skin, threatening to break free. "We have to assault the mayor's pride and joy, the jewel of Union's newly built downtown?"

"We're not assaulting anything until we have more information," Gideon said.

"That's not your decision, agent." Zuri stepped into sight and glared at Gideon.

The light in Gideon's eyes flared. "You're here on my request. Pretty sure it is."

"I outrank you."

"Not in this situation," Jacob said as he knelt beside me and brushed a strand of hair that had slipped out of my ponytail off my forehead. His dark eyes were filled with concern, and his worry wormed chilly around my heart. "Are you okay?"

"I've been worse."

"Not helpful," Marcus growled.

"Bane, how long will Essie and Kol be down?" Gideon asked. I could feel his need to touch me, reassure himself that I was okay, conflicting with his certainty that he had to stay in control of this situation, not look weak or distracted, and make sure Zuri didn't think she could take over.

"The effects of the worship magic spell will leave their system in about twenty minutes since the spell isn't focused on them." Sebastian rubbed his face. "Given that they're close to passing out, I'd say the spell has also knocked out the super it's focused on, which means we're just dealing with juiced-up witches and not also a goddess."

Which was good. We'd been looking at two outcomes with the source of the witches' power, a comatose super used as a vessel to store the worship magic or a super strong enough to stay conscious while maintaining the spell, along with having access to all that extra power.

Marcus looked up at Gideon. "We should call Amiah."

"No." I grabbed Marcus's wrist, drawing his attention back to me. "We need her at full." Especially if the team was going up against any more witches powered up like yesterday's witches.

"She can spare a little right now. We're just going to start with surveillance," Marcus said.

I gave him the driest look I could muster, which probably just came out as exhausted. "And what happened the last time we just did surveillance?"

Marcus's pupils slitted. "Right." The last time we'd done surveillance, we'd gotten into a fight and a building had been dropped on me and Gideon. "Let's just wait twenty."

"Okay." Gideon nudged Marcus aside, knelt, and offered me a gentle smile. "Are you good to stay here while we go to Summer's lab and figure out the op?"

"As long as I'm not required to stand." The room had stopped spinning and my vision was no longer double, but I was so exhausted I didn't know if I could raise my head.

Gideon's gaze lifted. "Kol?"

"Sure thing." He raised his hand, thumb up, then dropped it back to his side, as if it were too heavy to hold up.

"Meet us in the lab." Gideon brushed his thumb along my jaw, his gaze wistful. "If we're done before you're up, we'll come get you."

"You're not taking those two anywhere," Zuri said.

"We'll discuss this in Summer's lab." Gideon straightened and marched out the door.

My guys, Sebastian, and the elite team followed, leaving me alone with Kol.

Stillness filled the room, the only sound the soft buzz of the overhead light and Kol's slow, ragged breathing, both dragging me closer to sleep. I couldn't feel anything from Kol, not inside me or as a temperature change, and I didn't know if that was because he'd locked down his emotions or if I was just that tired.

This was the first time we'd been alone together since my wings had appeared, and I knew I needed to talk to him, but I didn't know what to say. I couldn't just say I was sorry I reminded him of the monsters who'd tortured him during the war, but I was madly attracted to him.

And even if he was attracted back, how would that work? He'd said incubi didn't have romantic relationships like humans or other supers, and I got the impression what he'd really meant was that they didn't have romantic relationships at all. I suppose you couldn't really have one if you didn't know if your partner was actually in love with you or if her feelings were just your magic influencing her.

He also still acted like he didn't want to talk to me, hell, he'd barely looked at me since I'd woken in my hospital room, and I was torn between broaching the subject to get it out of the way and giving him more time to sort out his emotions.

"Kol?"

A whisper of hurt and longing and frustration slid across my senses. I rolled my head, almost too heavy with exhaustion to move, to look at him, but his face was turned away from me so I couldn't read his expression.

"I'm sorry I lied to you."

His breath shuddered.

The bulb in the fixture continued to buzz and my thoughts grew fuzzy, except I didn't know when we'd have another moment alone to talk. I had to say something. Now.

"I thought— I wanted—" Him. I wanted him. Marcus, Jacob, Gideon, *and* Kol. That was the way it was supposed to be. But I didn't know how to fix what I'd broken between us.

My enhanced hearing picked up the mumble of voices in the hall, a conversation between at least two people. But they weren't close enough for me to make out who they were or what they were saying.

"Kol, please." I fought to keep my eyes open.

He released another couple of shuddering breaths, each one coming farther apart, slowing with the same exhaustion that pulled at me. I wanted to think that was why he wasn't answering me, but I feared it was because he didn't want to talk with me.

Now just isn't the time. And really, it was selfish of me to try to force this on him. He was the one with the PTSD. He was the one who'd been triggered. Just like facing Marcus's rage over turning him into a werewolf, my conversation with Kol had to be on his terms. Which was going to drive me crazy.

I dragged my eyes open, not realizing I'd closed them. They slid shut again and with a heavy sigh I gave up trying to stay awake.

I drifted into a warm darkness, bobbing up and down... up and down... in the thick water that wasn't water. I was safe, secure, and alone. For the second time in as many days I felt empty in my not-water dream. I was missing something.... or someone. I didn't know which, and my mind just kept bobbing with my body, soft and out of focus, unable to figure it out.

The handsome angel with the light brown hair and the gold flecks in his angel glow appeared before me. My father. He *had* to be my father. We had the same hair, the same gold flecks. Everything within me *said* he was my father.

He pressed his hand on something between us, and said something, but I couldn't make out his words.

A boom sounded far off in the distance. My father glanced over his shoulder, but I could only see darkness behind him and I had no idea what he was looking at.

Another boom and a flurry of sharp cracks.

A sob quickly followed, coming from the darkness.

The sharp cracks drew closer and my thoughts clicked. Gunfire. I was hearing gunfire.

More cracks. Another boom.

The sobbing grew louder, heartrending, and I strained to see in the gloom, find whoever was crying, help them.

Please, he sobbed.

My father vanished. So too did the not-water, and the sobs turned into ragged pleas.

Stop, please. Please. No.

My pulse picked up. I needed to help him. I couldn't just lie there and listen. But I couldn't see him. I couldn't see anything.

No! The sobber begged and released a raw, desperate scream. It tore into my soul and wrenched me out of the darkness as Kol screamed again.

I yanked my gaze toward Kol, who was still asleep, as another sharp, panicked scream tore from him. Curled in the fetal position, he whimpered and pleaded with his nightmare, his breath desperate gasps, tears leaking from his eyes.

Real fear and agony poured into me, while also frosting my hands and arms and making my breath mist. So much pain and terror. I could barely breathe against its crushing weight. God, how could he even live with it?

"Please. I promise I'll be good," he begged, his voice raw and cracking, sounding shockingly young.

I had guessed he'd been young when Michael had manifested him in this realm to control the women used to create the nephilim army. Kol could have been as young as thirteen or fourteen, fresh into his power to enthrall multiple people at the same time. And now I had proof.

"Please. I promise. I promise."

Bile burned the back of my throat. To do that to a kid. To—

"I promise," Kol sobbed.

"Kol, wake up." I pressed my hand to his warm back, not wanting to startle him but needing to wake him and unable to resist the desire to comfort him.

He stiffened, still asleep, his breath catching, his fear turning the frost on my hands and arms into a thick ice despite the warmth radiating from his body. His pain slammed into me, and my power flared with the strange heat that wasn't my destructive light strike but that something else I'd used when I'd shown Gideon how I really felt about him. It flowed out of my hand into Kol and spun a gauzy golden net around his terror.

He drew in a ragged breath but didn't wake and didn't stop sobbing. The ice on my arms cracked and fell off, and the net thickened, ever so slightly softening the edges of his fear.

A shuddering sigh escaped his lips, and the ice on my hands crumbled.

My pulse skipped a beat. My magic wasn't just a strange energy. This was my empathy easing his emotional agony. I could make his memories of the war seem like a dream, take away all of his fear. I could make him feel relaxed and joyful—

I could make him fall in love with me.

But I didn't want to *make* him love me. I wanted him to love me because *he* loved me.

"Kol, wake up."

My magic seeped deeper into his essence and soul, drawn to a horrible, infected darkness. A ragged tear that had never healed, and made me want to scream at the injustice.

Beautiful, mischievous, amazing Kol carried such pain, every day, and no one knew. I wondered if he even knew. The tear was buried deep, hiding among emotional and psychological scar tissue. He probably knew there was something wrong, but not what, and thought it was something he just had to live with.

Heat fluttered around me, Kol's magic caressing mine, and aching desire sank into my core. He groaned, the sound low and sensual, making my nerves thrum in anticipation, and his eyes cracked open. His hellfire blazed in full, dancing along his cheekbones, and accentuated an expression that was filled with an aching yearning. A yearning that stole all breath and thought. There was only him, his passion, his need, and that tear in his soul that I wanted— no, *needed* to mend.

My magic swelled, curling around the tear's edges, and his heat flared in response. His breath picked up, his desire fueling mine for a breathtaking second.

Then he wrenched his gaze away from me and squeezed his eyes shut. "Essie, stop."

But I hadn't even begun to mend the tear, hadn't even managed to soften the painful ragged edges. "Kol—"

"Please," he begged, his voice heartbreakingly similar to when he'd been begging in his nightmare, his emotional pain overwhelming.

I pulled my hand away and released my magic. I didn't know how I was causing him harm, but it was clear I was. "You were screaming in your sleep."

"Sometimes I scream," he said, panting, his pain still raging through me. "Don't do that again."

"But I can help you." My empathy was finally good for something. He'd helped me so much, dealing with Marcus and Gideon, and had welcomed me with open arms to the team. Now I could help him in return.

"Let it be."

"Kol—"

"I've worked with empaths to ease the emotions and lethe demons to dampen the memories," he said, his voice tight, his whole body tight. "It's fine."

"It's not fine."

"The nightmares will pass in a week or so. You're not the first to trigger me and you won't be the last." He sat up, drawing farther away, the hellfire in his eyes back to barely-there pinpricks. "It is what it is. The sooner I move on, the better."

"Pretty sure that's not how it works."

"Just let it be." He stood and headed to the door, taking a page out of Gideon's book and walking away to end the conversation.

I scrambled to my feet, surprised that I still wasn't completely exhausted, and hurried to catch up with him. I could help him. I knew I could. He didn't have to suffer. "Kol—"

His back stiffened and a mix of yearning and horror swept through me, confusing me even more.

"Leave it," he snapped.

"Wasn't what I was going to talk about," I snapped back, even if it was. A part of me was frustrated that he didn't want help, but another part, a part that had lived through a few horrible events — although not nearly as horrible as Kol's — understood the desire to just shove everything down deep and carry on. Not to mention right now he was probably still reeling from that nightmare. Better to bring the conversation up when he wasn't feeling on edge.

"How much do you know about Zuri and her team?" I asked, jumping on the first topic change I could think of.

The tension didn't leave his body and he kept walking down the hall toward the elevator. "I've met them a couple of times before but never worked with them. They think they're the best, probably because they are."

"So they can back up the attitude?"

"Oh, yeah." Kol hit the call button and we waited for the elevator door to open.

My whole essence yearned to step closer to him, not just to let my empathy heal the wound in his soul but to be close to him, while his stiff posture and averted gaze said in no uncertain terms *keep back.*

"They're the best of the best," he said, his gaze locked on the closed elevator door. "Zuri's elite team is the best of the elites. I'm surprised they have that new guy, the human witch. He's awfully young to be an elite."

"And he didn't strike me as powerful."

"I think he is. I just think he's really good at hiding it." Kol gave a sensual shrug and a bit of tension eased from his posture for a second. "Of course, after seeing past Sebastian's concealments to his true essence, every witch you come across is going to seem weak in comparison."

The door slid open, revealing Jacob inside. His dark gaze leaped to mine and quiet certainty flooded me through our brand.

"You're up," he said with his soft low rumble that always made my essence thrum with desire.

"They send you down to get us?" Kol stepped into the elevator and I followed.

Jacob wrapped an arm around my waist and drew me tight against him. He didn't scold me like Marcus would have, but I could feel his worry for me. "It's been half an hour. Gideon and Zuri have agreed on the op and we're getting ready."

Kol shoved his hands into his pockets.

"What's the plan?" And was I going to have to fight to be a part of it... and did I want to? Even if I now had incredible power, I was still untrained.

Except no way in hell was I letting my guys face anyone as powerful as those witches again without me.

Guess I'd made my decision. I was fighting for my place on the op.

"Xavier is setting us up with short-term concealment spells, then we're gearing up and going in through the Underground."

"I didn't think the Underground had been restored all the way to the Cromer Building." The Underground had been a series of underground halls between some of the bigger buildings in the downtown core and a couple of the downtown subway stops. It used to be just as busy as above ground, with shops and restaurants, but only a fraction of it had been restored when the downtown had been rebuilt. And while the original building in the Cromer Building's location had access to the Underground, it sat on the very edge of the core. Access had been cut off halfway between it and the next high rise and had yet to be restored. Or at least I thought it hadn't been restored.

"Construction started middle of last week," Jacob said.

So just about the time when things had really gone to hell for me. No wonder I didn't know about it — because I was sure the mayor would have been all over the local news the moment anything with the Cromer Building had come up.

Although I suppose I couldn't say any more that things had gone to hell. Sure, I'd been attacked by a feral vampire and that had just been the beginning, but I had my guys, I wasn't alone any more, and I'd found where I belonged.

I leaned into Jacob, savoring the feel of his massive body against mine. I always felt so safe when I was in his arms. Even before our mating brand had formed, he'd made me feel that way.

"An access tunnel was established for the construction workers," Jacob said. "We'll go in through there."

The doors slid open and Kol hurried out. "How many are going in?"

"All of us," Jacob said as we followed Kol down the hall to Summer's lab. "Those were Gideon's conditions. You, Essie, even Bane. It's a ten-man team."

"If I didn't know what we were up against, I'd say it was overkill for just surveillance," Kol said. "How did Gideon convince Zuri?"

Jacob's expression darkened. "He reminded her that Cassius is still unconscious and showed her the surveillance footage of our arrival at Operations last night after the fight at the airport."

"That would do it," Kol said.

We reached Summer's lab, a large room with stainless steel tables and shelves and humming machinery. The petite angel stood at a computer, her fingers flying across the keyboard, her expression tight with concentration. Beside her, the large screen hanging on the wall had its image split between a satellite picture of downtown with the Cromer Building dead center, a map of the Underground, the halls colored red, yellow, or green — no access, partial access, full access — and a muted news report about the preparations for this year's unification ceremony.

Jeez, the last time I'd looked, the ceremony marking the day the treaty between supers, humans, and the Angelic Defense had been signed and turned the tide of the war against Michael had been over a week away. That had been before I'd been thrown back into the supernatural world by running across that feral vampire's nest. God, it had only been a week and yet it felt like a lifetime ago.

Gideon, Zuri, and Ephraim stood staring at the screen, discussing the advantages and disadvantages of different search options and splitting the teams into groups. Regan sat on an empty table beside them, and Sebastian leaned against it, his weak glow belying his relaxed I-don't-give-a-shit posture. Behind them, Marcus sat on a foldout metal chair at another table across from Xavier. He turned to me the moment I entered, even though his back was to the door, and his wolf gave a soft huff of contentment.

Xavier raised his gaze to me and Kol and tapped the butt of a permanent marker on the table. "Next."

"I'll go." I headed to the table and Marcus gave up his seat, sliding his palm across the small of my back as we traded places and sending a shiver of attraction racing over me.

"Hold out your wrist," Xavier said.

I set my arm on the table wrist up, my stomach churning. Mavis's spell yesterday, where my power had roared out of control and started devouring her magic, had scared me, and I didn't want a repeat of that, especially not with Zuri's team watching. I needed to prove I could control my power, at least well enough not to hurt an ally.

Xavier quirked an eyebrow, making him look even younger than the mid-twenties I'd originally assumed. "You don't have to hold your breath. It's not going to hurt."

"You sure?" While I didn't see a knife or a box of coins, I wasn't going to assume it wouldn't hurt. So far almost everything in the supernatural world had hurt.

He held up the marker. "It's just a temporary glyph. I draw it on and the spell will last about six hours."

"What about topping up the concealment charm we got yesterday?"

Xavier's other eyebrow joined his first. "You got charms yesterday? Who set them?"

"It was kind of an emergency." Marcus placed a hand on my shoulder and gave it a reassuring squeeze. "The glyph witches had a tracking spell on us, and he can't top up the charms because once the spell ended, the coins disintegrated. Besides, he's casting a concealment against magic *and* video surveillance, which the charm didn't have."

"But if you got them yesterday..." Xavier said.

"Trust me," Kol said, "they're dead."

"Pretty sure you would have sensed them," Sebastian added over his shoulder.

Xavier's gaze dipped to the table. "Not if a more powerful witch cast them."

"Jeez, man," Regan growled. "Grow a pair."

"And no," Sebastian added. "I can't set charms. So you've got one up on me, kid."

"Not even close," Xavier said under his breath, only audible because Jacob's claim enhanced my hearing... or was that because I was part archangel? I wasn't quite sure which.

"You're obviously powerful enough to be on an elite team." I nudged my hand closer to him, reminding him he was supposed to be casting a spell on me — as much as I was afraid I'd react badly to his magic.

"I specialize in support magic." He took my hand and drew a complicated glyph on my wrist with his extra-fine tip black marker. "Concealment charms, wards, extra power, that kind of thing. Trust me, you don't want me beside you in a fight. You want me about six feet back. But Sebastian Bane is—" His voice dropped low but I was pretty sure everyone in the room could still hear him. "Sebastian Bane is a legend. A faekin with more glyphs than any known glyph witch."

I bit my tongue against telling him that was because Sebastian wasn't a faekin but a full fae and a sorcerer able to channel raw magic power, something most witches and supers couldn't do.

"He just combined glyphs to cast the tracking spell. I've never seen a witch do that before." Xavier set the marker aside and grasped my hand with both of his.

I instinctually tensed.

"Just take a breath," Marcus said, releasing my shoulder and stepping back. Guess he couldn't be touching me while Xavier cast the spell.

I drew in a slow breath, willing my power to remain calm. I wanted this spell. I needed the spell.

Jeez, maybe if I thought about it hard enough, I wouldn't lose control.

Xavier said two soft sibilant words I didn't recognize, and a gentle heat swelled over my wrist.

My power didn't blaze out of control.

In fact, it didn't react.

Finally!

Xavier said another soft word. The heat grew a little and a wisp of white smoke, just a breath of magic, curled from the glyph's lines and wrapped around my forearm in a gentle gauzy net.

Another word and the net swelled, brushing the bottom of Gideon's brand. The brand lit up with brilliant golden light that surged past my elbow into Jacob's, making it glow as well and filling me with glorious, brilliant power. I was alight with it, filled with the promise of being a super of pure light, like when Sebastian had first discovered I was a full angel. Both of my guys gasped as the brands on their arms lit up, and Xavier's eyes widened with awe.

"Amazing," Ephraim said, his voice breathy.

Zuri huffed. "Yeah, yeah. Beautiful and sacred. Finish the glyph. We need to get a move on."

Xavier rushed through three more words. The power in my brands grew stronger, filling me with Gideon's certainty and Jacob's calm, and the smoke of the concealment spell sank into my skin, taking the marker's ink with it.

I pushed out of the chair, a little stunned, my inner light blazing. I hadn't felt that good in a long time, years, and I could feel the strength of my bonds with not just Gideon and Jacob, but Marcus as well, powerful and sure and right.

Marcus pulled me into his arms and Kol took my place, sliding into the chair without his usual sensual grace. His body remained tense for the whole time Xavier was casting the concealment spell, and then he shoved out of the chair and headed toward Gideon.

"Gideon, a word," Kol said, his voice low.

"All right." Zuri squared her shoulders, distracting me from Kol and Gideon's quiet conversation, and swept her gaze over everyone in the room. "Get your gear and meet in the garage."

Gideon glanced past Kol, met my gaze, and jerked his chin toward the door. "I'll take you to the armory."

"Grab the faekin a vest while you're down there," Zuri said as she strode from the room.

I turned to Sebastian. "Are you sure that's a good idea?" The light that usually radiated from his skin was still dim — I barely caught a glimpse of it from the corner of my eye — and exhaustion still pinched his expression. "You're running on fumes."

"Oh, I've got more than fumes." He flashed his wicked smile, making Regan snort as she, Ephraim, and Xavier followed Zuri out of the lab. "There's still magic stored in some of my glyphs and if things go south, I can use Xavier's magic to power my bigger glyphs." His expression snapped to serious. "We know what we're up against. The elite team doesn't. This dangerous source of magic needs to be eliminated and I'm not going to sit by and let their egos fuck this up."

"Hunh," Marcus said. "Didn't know you cared."

"These witches are still fighting Michael's war and if his side wins, I'm going to have to go home—" His expression darkened and he shoved past us. "I've a lot invested in this realm. I'd hate to lose my money," he said, his tone flippant. But I got the impression his grim look hadn't been because of the money.

"Well, Agent Shaw," Marcus said, kissing the back of my head and releasing me from his embrace. "Let's do this."

"Meet you in the garage." Jacob gave me a warm smile that heated from his brand to my heart and lower, and he and Marcus left.

Kol hurried after them and I joined Gideon, taking the stairs two floors down into the basement so the guys could take the elevator up to the top floor to get their gear from their rooms.

We emerged from the plain concrete stairwell, rounded the corner, and stepped into the study area just outside the elevator doors. With a soft *click*, the overhead fluorescents flickered on, the sensor registering our movement and illuminating the wide wooden table, old couch, and shelves upon shelves of books in the Operations' library. Directly across from us sat the armory's metal door, with its thick security glass and fingerprint reader.

Gideon pressed his thumb to the reader and unlocked the door.

I hurried inside and headed to the locker with the sidearms, but he grabbed my wrist as I passed him and tugged me around to face him. "Are you up for this?"

Really? I rolled my eyes at him — as much as a part of me did wonder if I was up for this. "You didn't just ask me that."

The muscles in his jaw flexed. "I'm team leader and it's my job to ask." His expression softened and a hint of worry dimmed his angel glow. "I'm also your mate and you've had a tough few days."

"And so has the whole team." I thought he knew me, knew I couldn't sit this out. "Are we going to have the you-can't-be-on-the-team argument again?"

"No. I'm just checking in. I can feel through the brand that you're worried, but I don't know why or over what."

"Gideon, three witches kicked our asses and we don't know what we're walking into in the Cromer Building. Of course I'm worried."

"Well, yes." He frowned. "But it feels deeper than just that."

"Deeper than maybe losing one of you?"

The concern in his expression grew and he pulled me into a firm embrace. "We've just found each other. No one is dying." He said it with such conviction that I desperately wanted to believe him. Except this wasn't a situation he could control.

I leaned into him. Just thinking about losing any of them made my heart pound. But our job was dangerous, and if I couldn't even consider giving it up, I couldn't ask them to give it up, either.

And while that was a huge concern, if I was being honest with myself, my most immediate one was Kol. He wasn't acting like himself and I feared being off his game would endanger him.

"What do you think about Kol?" I raised my gaze to Gideon's. "You know him better than I do."

Gideon's angel glow dimmed even more and the air around me misted.

Damn. My heart sank. "What?"

"He just asked for a transfer," Gideon said.

My essence stalled, my mind unable to fully register what he was saying.

"He'll help us deal with the source of the witches' power," Gideon continued, "and then he wants to be reassigned. Out of town."

"Reassigned? Out of town?" My throat tightened. He couldn't leave. Not now. Not when things were working out. He belonged on the team. I knew that meant everything to him. He belonged with my guys. With me.

I also knew I was the reason he was leaving.

That, and the horrible scar Michael and his nephilim had left on his soul.

The urge to find him, convince him to stay, God, just fix that tear in the core of his being before he left for good, made me push out of Gideon's grasp before I could stop myself. "It's because of me, isn't it?"

"He didn't give a reason and I didn't press."

"Does the rest of the team know?" I asked, forcing myself not to rush out of the armory. Kol had already refused my help. I had to respect that. Just as I had to respect his desire to leave. But I'd thought I'd have more time, that I'd just have to wait it out and things could go back to the way they were. The way they were supposed to be. Not him leaving.

"I haven't told them. I'm hoping he'll sort himself out by the time this op is done." Gideon released me and opened the locker with the bullet-proof vests, pulled out three vests, and set them on the long, narrow standup table in the center of the room. "I haven't seen him this shut off since Jacob and I pulled him out of that hellhole. It took over two years before an angel could get into the same room with him without him completely shutting down."

"That's horrible." I stared at him, stunned. I didn't know why. I already knew whatever Michael and his nephilim had done had left a festering hole in Kol's soul. And then I'd brought up all those memories again.

Gideon must have seen something in my expression because he wrapped his arms around me again.

"It's not your fault. It's Michael's." A whisper of his anger slid through me. "And mine. I didn't realize how bad Kol was. I thought with how well he'd handled the other day with the witches that the trigger had been manageable and he was pulling himself together. I wouldn't have asked him to help with the tracking spell if I'd known."

I wanted to scream with frustration, at the injustice of what he'd suffered, and, selfishly, at how much it hurt me. I didn't want him to leave, and I didn't want him afraid or hurting. I wanted my Kol back. And there wasn't a damned thing I or Gideon, or anyone, could do about it right now. He needed time and therapy and—

God, I didn't know what else. He needed everything I could give him and more to take away this hurt. And even then, none of it would matter if he didn't want my help.

The thought stung, but it was the truth. I couldn't force help on him and he'd decided getting away from the situation was best for him. And if I wanted my guys to get through dealing with any more witches alive, I couldn't be distracted by that. Focusing on Kol's PTSD right now would only get someone hurt.

I eased out of Gideon's embrace and squared my shoulders. "Do you think he'll be able to hold it together during the op?"

"He's assured me he can and he handled the other day fine." The temperature dipped and worry slid through me. "If push comes to shove, I know he'll have our backs."

"And if push comes to shove, we might need everyone." A shudder of fear swept through me.

"Exactly," he said. "Which is why I've reluctantly agreed to keep him on. Now, before we head up to the garage, prove to me you can make a blade of divine light. It's not as powerful as a light strike, but it's safer for the rest of us and I'll feel better knowing you've had a little practice forming one."

I doubted it was a good idea to keep Zuri waiting, but I could sense that confirming the divine light blade that I'd only summoned twice before was important to Gideon. Both of the times I'd formed the blade, I'd been desperate, with my adrenaline pumping, and had been working purely on instinct. But that didn't mean I'd be able to summon one next time I was desperate.

"Hold your hand as if you're holding a knife," Gideon said.

I clenched my hand and held it out. Gideon clasped his hands over mine and I met his warm gaze. A shiver of desire swept over me along with the memory of how he'd kissed, caressed, and filled me only a few hours ago.

"Aren't you supposed to be behind me?" I asked, my voice suddenly breathy as I imagined him tucking up close, his body hard against mine.

The warmth in his eyes turned sizzling. "We'd never make it out of the armory and I really don't want Zuri walking in on us."

He had a point. If he got any closer, I'd give in to the yearning of our bond and rip his clothes off. Hell, he didn't have to get closer. My pulse had already picked up and the rising temperature was revealing his.

"Just like when you pulled in your wings, flood your hand with power," he said, his voice husky. "Imagine it turning into a blade."

"A blade." I could do this. I'd done it before. I imagined my magic rushing to my hands and raised my gaze from our joined hands to his eyes. For a second I was drowning in his perfect summer-sky, captured body and soul. It stole all breath and thought and filled me with warmth and certainty and need. This was where I belonged and who I belonged with. I could do anything with him and Marcus and Jacob and Kol—

My thoughts tripped, stuttering over that, and my power exploded in a blazing inferno in my palm, and Gideon released a strangled cry.

Shit.

Shit shit shit.

I slammed my power back into the core of my being, fear making my pulse pound. "Did I burn you?" *Please say I didn't hurt you.*

"I'm fine," he said, but didn't release his hands so I couldn't tell if I'd burned him or not. "Flood might not have been the best word. Try imagining your power as a marble in the palm of your hand."

"Not until you show me your hands." I'd hurt him. The sultry heat that had been warming the air around me was gone, replaced with an ever-so-slightly unnatural chill and a whisper of real-emotional worry.

"You didn't burn me."

"Gideon."

"I'm fine." He peeled back an unblemished palm, letting me see, then retightened his grip. "Just should have been thinking about what we were doing and not—" He cleared his throat. "Marble. Blade. We don't have a lot of time and I know you can do this."

Right. Zuri was waiting.

I drew in a breath and imagined a pinprick of power, not even a marble. Just a spark. If it wasn't big enough, I'd add another spark and another until it was, but I wasn't going to risk a blaze again.

The spark formed, bigger than I expected, and Gideon's face lit up with a stunning smile.

"Good." His electric magic swelled in my brand and slid into my hands, making my skin tingle. "Imagine that marble forming into a knife. Just something small to start."

I closed my eyes and concentrated on stretching my spark into a blade.

"Yes," Gideon breathed.

My concentration slipped, the spark flickered, and my eyes flew open. Gideon's lips quirked in a smile and he sent a pulse of magic into my hands. I regained control of the spark and it lengthened into a three-inch blade.

"Good." He released my hands and stepped back. "Now do it again without me."

I fought to ignore my disappointment at the distance he put between us — now wasn't the time to give in to the brand — released my hold on the blade, letting it disappear, and reformed it.

Gideon made me form it four more times as he grabbed a Glock from the locker securing the sidearms and an M4 carbine from the rack. If I hadn't already known how dangerous anyone we might meet in the Cromer Building could be, I'd have said all the weapons were overkill, just like the ten-man team.

But just like making sure I could form a light blade when I needed to, I also knew Gideon wasn't taking any chances with our weapons. And since I'd yet to be fully trained in my powers — hell, we might not even know all the powers I possessed — I was going to be armed as before, which was just fine with me. Even if it meant causing another incident with the mayor if I was spotted, armed to the teeth, in his pride and joy.

With my Glock holstered, the M4 on a sling across my chest protected with a bulletproof vest, and two extra magazines with ammunition enspelled to stun for each weapon, I left the armory with Gideon.

We took the elevator up to the first floor and headed down the long hall to the garage where everyone waited for us.

Everyone, even Zuri's team, wore vests. Of my guys, Jacob was the only one with visible weapons, with his paired Berettas at his hips, but I knew Marcus wasn't unarmed because of his wolf's claws, and Kol, without a doubt, had at least half a dozen blades — probably more — hidden on his body.

Marcus took a step forward as Gideon and I entered the garage, his wolf slitting his pupils, and Jacob's hold on his vampiric intensity slipped a little. My soul sang, my bonds making me ache for them. Kol, leaning against the side of an SUV, crossed his arms and kept his attention on Zuri, with not even a glance in my direction.

"Let's go," Zuri said with a jerk of her chin to the medium gray JP SUV behind her. Her team piled in and we, plus Sebastian, got into the SUV parked beside it.

"Did you figure out your blade?" Jacob asked as he got into the back.

Gideon reached between the front seats and handed Sebastian his vest. "Yes."

Kol got into the back with Jacob, and I slid onto the seat beside Sebastian, keeping close to my door to avoid getting an elbow in the face as he put on the vest.

"You should have taught her how to fly." Marcus, in his usual spot in the driver's seat, shot me a dark look in the rearview mirror and pulled out of Operations' secure garage. "I'd rather know you can get the hell out of there."

"We already know I'm terrible at running if it means I'm leaving someone behind," I said. "Learning to make a blade was a better choice." Even if I really did want to learn to fly.

"And we're going into underground hallways," Sebastian said. "Flying wouldn't be very useful."

"I *know* that," Marcus growled, driving through the Quarter toward the human part of Union City with the other SUV following. "But my wolf really disagrees."

Kol shifted, the tension radiating off him making my stomach churn.

"You're going to need to learn to get it under control." Jacob opened a small black plastic case with the team's coms, pulled one out, and handed it to Kol.

Kol took a com and handed the case to Sebastian.

"This is why soul bonds are a bad idea." Sebastian took a com and passed the case to me. "No one can think straight. You guys need a month to fuck and get the crazy out of your system."

Kol stiffened.

"Gee, what a beautiful way to put it," Marcus said.

Sebastian raised a sculpted white eyebrow. "Don't tell me your wolf doesn't like that idea."

Marcus growled.

"So the source of the witches' magic." I took a com and passed the case to Gideon. "Did you get a better idea of where it might be instead of just in the Cromer Building?"

Sebastian rolled his eyes at my not-so-subtle change in topic. "Underground."

"Like a basement office?" Marcus asked.

"Deeper." Sebastian frowned. "I think. I'm hoping because I've cast the spell that once we get close, I'll be able to sense the magic even if it's concealed."

"Below the expected basement means less chance of accidentally being seen by civilians," Jacob said.

"But that means if we run into someone," Gideon said, "they're most likely involved with the worship magic. That might make it harder to get in, get the lay of the land, and get out."

Jacob's hold on his vampiric intensity slipped a little more, building a pressure inside my chest. It wasn't crushing, not yet, but if I didn't get out or he didn't pull it back soon, it would be. "Zuri will want to split us up to cover more ground."

"I've already told her that isn't a good idea," Gideon said.

"Yeah, well, let's just hope she believes you," Marcus growled.

GIDEON

As we drove to downtown, my gaze kept sliding to Essie, despite knowing I needed to focus on the op. I felt like I had when we'd first sealed our bond: stunned, amazed, awed by the incredible woman who'd claimed me as her mate — and without a doubt, since Jacob was also branded, she was the one who'd done the claiming.

It was like a piece of my soul that I hadn't known was asleep had been awakened and I was now whole. Not because she completed me or I her, but because she was the spark to awaken a dormant shard of light within me that had been waiting just for her.

Marcus, in the driver's seat beside me, huffed a soft satisfied rumble. He'd been doing that since the three of us had made love to Essie and had only stopped momentarily when it looked like Bane's spell to track the witches' power was going sideways. Then once he'd known she was okay, his wolf had settled again. He was still tense with what we were about to face, I think we all were, but it was clear he felt a certainty and contentment about how his life had unfolded despite Jacob and me also being mated to Essie.

I was actually stunned with how comfortable he was first sharing her with Jacob in the shower and then with me on Jacob's bed. Sure, his wolf might have accepted that Essie had other mates, but that didn't mean he wanted us around while they made love.

Of course, I was also a little stunned with how comfortable I'd been during our foursome.

I didn't have any experience with group sex and hadn't really known how I felt about it. I also hadn't been sure how Essie would respond to adding me to her intimate interactions with the others and had been hesitant of my reception. I'd held her at arm's length even after our mating brand had formed and hadn't done nearly enough to atone for unknowingly hurting her.

But she and the others had welcomed me into their intimacy without hesitation and it was like everything just clicked.

I'd been an idiot to think Essie would only want to love Marcus for the short lifetime they had together, that she wouldn't want me butting into their relationship. I'd thought I was doing the right thing for them — and me — and had thought there was no way she could love me with the same intensity that she loved Marcus. But she did. She'd shown me with her body when we'd sealed our bond the other day and again a few hours ago in Jacob's bed.

We belonged together. The four of us a single unit with Essie the sun at the center of our solar system.

Kol, sitting behind Essie in the back with Jacob, shifted positions, drawing my attention and ratcheting up my worry. His expression was tight but I now knew it wasn't because of the op.

I'd been an idiot about so many things in the last couple of weeks, and Kol was one of them. The appearance of Essie's wings had triggered his PTSD and I should have paid more attention to him. And while he'd put up a good front and held himself together yesterday, I should have noticed he was struggling. But, no, I'd been consumed with the compulsion to seal my bond with Essie and hadn't noticed that Kol was barely holding on.

If I'd just accepted the brand and actually talked to Marcus instead of assuming what was best, I might have noticed Kol struggling, and now I prayed that if I just gave him space to figure himself out, a transfer wouldn't be necessary.

I didn't want to lose him. He was a valuable member of my team and I trusted him with my life and Essie's, and much to my surprise, I liked him.

I hadn't thought I'd ever like working with an incubus and certainly didn't think I'd ever befriend one. But when Jacob had approached me and said being on the team might help the kid we'd pulled out of Michael's lab, I'd agreed.

Kol had been eager to learn new skills and had taken to agent training as if he'd been born for it. He also had a stranglehold on his magic — as if he were afraid to actually use it — so I hardly ever had to worry about him misusing his enthrallment, but he could still charm just about anyone without it. Getting information and compliance from people became infinitely easier with Kol on the team, not to mention he was incredibly skilled as a fighter.

It had only taken a few weeks of active duty for him to feel as if he'd always been on the team... just like how Essie now felt like she'd always been with us.

His attention slipped to Essie and the hellfire in his eyes flared. For a second it didn't look like he was afraid of Essie or that her presence brought back his nightmares. It looked like he desired her. But it wasn't the sexual hunger of an incubus, it was something more raw and desperate and heartbreaking. Then his attention jumped to Jacob and the look turned sour before he jerked his gaze out the back window.

He practically lived for the team with no other social life. Did he think because three of us were mated to Essie he'd be pushed out?

None of us would allow that, especially not Essie. She'd been distraught to hear he wanted a transfer and not just because she believed her presence caused him pain, but because she knew, like we all did, that Kol belonged with us.

But there was something else in his look, something that didn't make sense. If he hadn't been an incubus, I'd have said he was jealous, that he wanted Essie as well.

But that was impossible. Incubi didn't have relationships, they didn't fall in love, and they didn't get jealous.

And not something I could let distract me right now. We were about to walk into the heart of the witches' power and everyone's lives depended on me being focused and in control.

ESSIE

Twenty minutes later, we drove into the downtown core and reached the most discreet and easiest access point into the Underground: the entrance to the subway four blocks from the Cromer Building.

I didn't like that we were so far away. If things went south and someone got hurt, we were going to have to drag them four blocks to get them to a vehicle. But if there were a lot more witches connected to the glyph witches' cause to restart Michael's war, we couldn't risk them seeing us enter the Cromer Building. Just because we couldn't be seen by magic or security cameras didn't mean we were invisible.

Marcus parked on a shadowy side street around the corner from the busier street where the subway's entrance lay, and we gathered in the shadows as Ephraim pulled up behind our SUV. Tension from my guys crackled against my senses and the summer night was cooler than I'd expected given how hot the last couple of days had been — and I couldn't tell if that was because of my empathy or not.

Zuri's team, however, was more relaxed. In fact, Zuri and Regan looked more than ready for a fight. Even Xavier, with his Glock drawn — the only one of Zuri's team who had a weapon — looked more 'ready to do business' than worried.

They had no clue what we were up against.

And I prayed they wouldn't find out. Not until we had more information, like how many witches remained, and how many worshipers were sacrificing their essence into the pool of magic controlled by those witches.

"Com check," Zuri said as she swept her gaze over the area, and we all sounded off. "Form up as planned."

She gave Jacob a tight nod, and together they headed around the corner to the stairs leading down into the subway.

Kol and Regan were next, followed by Xavier and Sebastian. Marcus jerked his chin at me and we fell into line, leaving Gideon and Ephraim to take the rear.

As I hurried onto the brighter main street, I glanced up and down the road looking for possible danger as well as bystanders. Thankfully the street was empty. Most of the downtown clubs were on the other side of the core and at this hour there was little traffic, which was one of the reasons Gideon had picked this subway stop.

So far, so good.

I wondered if Gideon had followed protocol and alerted the UCPD of our operation or if, like at the airport, he'd decided breaking protocol was better than endangering human cops — which a few weeks ago would have shocked the hell out of me. Angels didn't lie. They followed the rules. But Gideon, at least, understood that sometimes a rule had to be ignored to save lives.

Zuri and Jacob hustled down the stairs. I took another glance up the street, then followed. This subway stop had miraculously managed to avoid destruction, even though most of the buildings around it had been damaged beyond salvation or outright leveled during the war.

But that meant the stop hadn't received revitalization money, and while it wasn't in rough shape, it still looked old and tired. Grime had built up on the corners of the stairs and the tiled floor at the bottom was chipped in a few places and scuffed all over. A ghost of black graffiti stained the wall, either bleeding through a too-thin layer of paint or not completely scrubbed away, a strange contrast to the large, bright poster beside it touting tomorrow's unification ceremony in Unity Park.

There wasn't a soul in sight, but a rumble far off down the tracks told me a train was on its way and we might not be alone in the station for long.

To my right stood the turnstiles and self-serve ticket station separating the Underground from the platform, and ahead lay a wide, dim hall, most of the lights off, blocked off by a floor-to-ceiling metal security gate.

"Xavier," Zuri said as she swept her gaze past the turnstiles to the platform.

Xavier holstered his sidearm and hurried to the lock on the far side of the gate. With a few hissed words and a pulse of power that rippled through my chest, he unlocked the gate and stepped back.

Jacob pushed it open just wide enough for him to slip through — which was more than wide enough for everyone else since he was the biggest member of the group — and hurried inside.

The rest of us followed in order, reformed our formation on the other side, and Gideon pulled the gate closed, covering our tracks. The only way someone would know something was different was if they tried to open the gate and discovered it was no longer locked.

Half a dozen small stores, also locked behind security gates with only a light or two on inside, lined the hall on either side. Beyond stretched a long expanse of plain hall leading to the next section of the Underground, half a block over in the basements of a pair of twin office towers.

I peered into the darkness ahead of us, seeing farther than I would have if I was a normal human. Thanks to Jacob's claim — or my angelic nature, I wasn't sure which — I didn't need help seeing in the dark.

There wasn't a soul around. Which was expected, since we were in an area closed down for the night.

Except I couldn't shake the feeling that something wasn't right.

I brought the scope on the M4 to my eye and searched the hall for heat signatures.

No one.

We reached the next building over, crossed an area with a food court, and headed into a narrow, concrete service hall. Zuri must have memorized the route because she took us without hesitation down four more narrow halls to one blocked off by a temporary security gate.

A large plastic sheet, with multiple slits in it to allow access but keep dust in, hung just past the gate, and a mess of dirty footprints led to and from the entrance.

I continued to scan everything with my scope, confirming we were alone.

But I just couldn't shake the sense that something was wrong.

Except I didn't know what, and just saying something was wrong without giving actionable intel was useless. Everyone was on guard. Even if Zuri and her team didn't fully understand the danger we were in, my guys and Sebastian did. No one needed to be warned to watch for danger. They already were.

Xavier unlocked this gate and we pushed past the plastic, hustling down a dark hall with construction equipment and crates and rubble.

The worry in my chest grew the closer we got to the end, and I still couldn't see any heat signatures with my scope or explain what was off.

We reached another locked security gate and stepped into a wider, cleaner hall. A few feet down stood a solid metal security door with a glimmer of light seeping under the crack at the bottom.

"Eyes open, everyone," Gideon said. "This is the Cromer Building."

Jacob opened the security door a crack and Zuri peeked out.

"Clear," she said, and without making a sound, she hurried into the main basement of the Cromer Building.

The guys ahead of me followed her and fanned out into an area that was still dim, but brighter than the maintenance halls. It was a big space, with a large food court with five wide halls branching away, a restaurant — still under construction — and a dozen shops. A large set of metal and glass stairs trailed up the far side to a glassed-in second-story — or rather main floor — promenade that ringed the area, and the ceiling rose at least two stories above that.

Pale moonlight shone into the area through the many large windows above on the first-floor lobby. Most of the food court kiosks were covered with plastic tarps, empty spaces waiting to be finished, and only two stores looked like they had businesses in them. The floor was plain concrete not yet tiled, and half of the drywall had yet to be painted.

I hustled out of the hall with Gideon and Ephraim close behind, and the massive weight of the witches' power slammed inside my chest, stealing my breath.

My knees buckled and I fought to keep standing. Kol gasped, Sebastian groaned and sagged to one knee, while Xavier screamed, clutched his head, and dropped to both of his knees.

Zuri jerked around to look at us. "What the hell?"

"Ambush." Gideon grabbed the back of my vest and hauled me back as a massive ball of fire exploded in our midst.

Sebastian slapped his chest, activating a glyph, and a shimmering magical shield swept around him and Xavier. Kol leaped back, and the rest of the group scrambled to get out of the way. The fire seared the air then vanished in a flash. Regan's pants caught on fire and she dropped and rolled as Marcus slapped at the flames, putting them out.

Gasping for breath, Sebastian sagged forward, down to both knees, his hands pressed against the floor. "Fucking hell."

"Here." Xavier grabbed Sebastian's arm and hissed a quick word. Sebastian's head jerked back and light blazed from his skin for a second, turning his button-down see-through, revealing all the black tattoos covering his arms and torso.

Another *thu-thud* of power crashed into me, and six people — four men and two women — with bat wings flew down at us, shadowy swords of darkness in their hands. Their wings vanished with a puff of black smoke and they attacked Zuri and Jacob, two on each, while the remaining two went after Kol.

Regan and Marcus lunged into the fight with Zuri and Jacob, and Ephraim shot a whip of water at one of the bat-witches on Kol.

More witches, a mix of men and women, barreled out of the shadows from down the halls and out from behind the counters of the unfinished food court kiosks. They all had tattoos on their right arms, indicating they were glyph witches. Some had more complicated tattoos than others, but while those with less ink likely had fewer spells at their disposal, that didn't mean they were any less dangerous.

I turned to the group coming from my left, while Gideon shifted to cover my back and take the other side.

A witch with an all-red tattoo curling up her arm screamed and raced toward me. I fired my M4, set to a single shot, and hit her in the chest, the stun spell activating and dissolving the round before it punctured flesh. Red lightning crackled around her, but she didn't drop.

Crap.

They were like the other supers I'd come across. One shot didn't take them out.

I flicked the switch on the M4 to a three-round burst.

The red-tattooed witch was almost on me, and another big guy was close behind. I fired again, dropped the woman with a larger blast of red lightning, and aimed at the big guy. But another *thu-thud* of magic slammed into me.

The world shuddered. A wisp of sticky, smoky darkness crawled against my soul and my magic flared in response, blazing through the miasma and pressure.

Out of the corner of my eye, I saw Kol stumble and barely get out of the way of a shadow blade, and Xavier bit back a strangled scream, his body trembling.

Gideon shot a blast of divine light at the big guy barreling toward me, knocking him back.

Two of the witches who'd rushed out of the shadows grasped hands and in unison yelled a harsh word. A writhing mass of smoky tentacles erupted from the concrete, very much like the vines the glyph witch had summoned at the airport but without all the damage to the floor, and shot toward us.

My pulse stalled for a second at the memory of the archnephilim and all his writhing smoke, but I shoved that thought aside. I'd handled him. I could handle this.

Sebastian dragged Xavier back to me and Gideon, and activated a tattoo on his neck. Marcus snarled and tossed the witch he was fighting into one of the witches on Jacob, who swiped his short vampire claws at another witch. But a tendril of smoke seized Jacob's wrist and yanked him off balance before he could strike.

The witch, a bulky guy not quite as broad or tall as Jacob but close, jabbed his shadow blade at Jacob's heart.

Jacob jerked away with his enhanced speed and wrenched free of the smoke tendril.

I shot a three-round burst at one of the hand-holding witches, a squat woman with a thick colorful tattoo. Red lightning burst around her. She sagged to her knees and her partner, an average looking guy in every way, screamed. But she didn't go down, and the smoke tendrils whipped toward me.

"Really? More than three?" Shit.

I fired another burst, but the smoke devoured the rounds and the tentacles didn't vanish.

I hadn't hit my mark.

A tendril seized my leg and the sticky smoke, the source of the witches' power, oozed around my cells, trying to gain purchase inside me like it had during the tracking spell.

Gideon swept his divine light sword through the tendril around my calf then severed another one going after Sebastian.

"Call your blade," he said to me, slicing through a third tendril reaching for Xavier. "Anyone got eyes on the smoke pair?"

"Little busy," Kol gasped.

Someone else grunted, but I couldn't tell if that was an affirmative or a negative.

The witches' power thudded again, and my knees buckled.

"Xavier, pull up your extra internal shields and give Esther one," Sebastian said, and a pulse of his power, wild and icy, crashed through my back and out my chest.

I dropped to both knees, my legs too weak to hold me.

Sebastian's magic whirled into a raging vortex and swept into the smoky tendrils. It wrenched the smoke to the ceiling high above and ripped it apart.

Xavier scrambled to my side and grabbed my arm, but his eyes widened with surprise. "You don't have any shields?"

"That's why I asked for one," Sebastian said, and another pulse of icy power shuddered through me, making the world darken and my power roar in response. It swelled in my palms, blazing divine light, and I shot the blast at a wiry man with a thin tattoo on his arm before it could build up.

The blast hit him in the chest and slammed him back into an empty store's security gate fifty feet away. The gate ripped free, buckling around him, and he skidded deeper into the store's shadows.

"Oh, my God!" Xavier gasped.

"Shield," Gideon snapped at him, and Xavier mumbled a longer sentence than he'd used before in a language I didn't understand.

Heat wrapped around me as another *thu-thud* of power pulsed into me, but this time the thud felt far away, like it had when the witches had been within the area containment master ward at the airport. The force didn't steal my breath and I had no trouble standing. Thank God.

"Thanks," I said to Xavier as I stood.

But the sense of inky dark magic oozing against my soul and searching for a way in grew. I could put an end to all of this if I just let the power in. I'd be powerful, feared, adored if I just embraced it.

I'd be consumed and there'd be nothing left.

I gritted my teeth against its begging and fired my M4 at a witch barreling toward Regan.

Lightning exploded around him and he dropped. Regan raised her gaze to me, gave me a tight nod, and lunged at a woman with a long black ponytail.

Beside him, Kol sliced the hamstring of a bulky man, while Ephraim seized another man with his water whip and slammed him into a third man.

Above, witches lined the promenade, shooting blasts of shadow at Zuri, Jacob, and Marcus. Their magic thudded softly, like an explosion far off in the distance.

With a burst of misty red demonic magic, Zuri released her massive leathery wings — not the magical constructs like the glyph witches. Twisted horns extended from her forehead, and red wisps of magic whipped around her. Snarling, she flew up to the promenade, grabbed the closest witch, and threw her over the railing.

The witch screamed and landed with a sickening crunch on the concrete floor. Blood pooled around her body and her half-open eyes were vacant.

The other witches on the promenade turned the force of their shadow blasts on Zuri, but she buffeted them away with a ferocious flap of her wings and wild gust of demonic smoke. And while she knocked the four witches in front of her to the floor, the three farther back merely stumbled.

More witches rushed out of the darkness, and with a strangely distant thump, and seductive swell of inky magic inside me, another fireball exploded around Marcus and Regan, encompassing them and the witches they were fighting.

Xavier yelled something. His power rippled through me, and Marcus and Regan screamed.

My pulse stalled. *No, please.* I couldn't lose him. *Please be alive.*

I ran toward them before the fire had fully dissipated, the heat threatening to burn my skin.

Both of them were on the ground, their clothes burning, along with the five witches they'd been fighting. Everyone was screaming, their gut-wrenching cries filled with agony.

Ephraim doused Marcus and Regan with his water magic, putting out the fire on their clothes. Somehow — it had to have been what Xavier had cast — they weren't completely burned. A nasty burn scorched up Marcus's ribs on his left side, his shirt nothing but blackened tatters. The burn ran along his left biceps, with a small trail up the side of his face, but other than that he was unharmed. Regan was in similar shape, with her hands and most of her back burned.

"We need to take cover," Gideon said. "Regroup."

"No, we stay," Zuri snarled, leaping into the air and jerking out of the way of a blast of lightning.

A swell of Sebastian's icy magic pulsed, and the witch with the lightning collapsed. I didn't know what he'd done, but that was at least one more witch down.

"Clear this coven out for good," Zuri said.

"Are you crazy?" Marcus gasped. "Didn't you listen to anything we said?" His ferocious gaze met mine before he wrenched a still-stunned Regan out of the way of a witch's shadow sword.

She staggered, and I scrambled to her side, catching her as she crumpled to the floor.

"Regan is down," I said.

"Xavier, to Regan," Zuri snapped. "Ephraim, to me."

Light exploded from Ephraim's back as he released his brilliant white wings and swept up to the first floor balcony.

Xavier scrambled to my side, and I pulled my attention from Regan and searched for a witch to shoot that was far enough away from my teammates that I wouldn't accidentally hit them.

"There are too many," Gideon said. "We need to pull back."

"There are only thirty." Zuri dove for a witch and tossed her over the railing to join the others. "And most can only summon shadow swords, so they're not that powerful. Take out your share and we'll be done with them."

The witches' power thudded again, the sign of a more powerful spell, and I wrenched my attention over the chaos, searching for the spellcaster.

There. Half in the shadows down one of the halls. A man, close to my age, with stylishly mussed blond hair, wearing a black robe, holding his hands above his head.

The inky magic in my soul swelled as his mouth moved, saying the quick words of his spell, and something inside me sparked. My pulse lurched and a massive ball of fire exploded around me, Marcus, Xavier, and Regan.

Fiery agony seared my skin for a blazing second, then my magic roared through me. It exploded from my body with a massive wave of power and light that consumed the inky magic inside and the fire searing my skin, and slammed into anyone not standing close to me.

Everyone, including Gideon, Jacob, Kol, and Sebastian, was tossed to the ground, stunned. Zuri and Ephraim hovered at the top of the ceiling two stories up, while Xavier and Marcus — who hadn't been hit with my wave of power while propping up an unconscious Regan — stared at me, wide-eyed.

Ice, not just frost, swept over me, snapping my inflamed, thankfully not-scorched skin, from burning with heat to burning with cold, and overwhelming fear squeezed tight in my chest.

Shit.

Gideon, who I'd slammed against the wall beside the security door and who'd sagged down the wall onto his butt, blinked, his angel glow flickering for a second and making my pulse stall. "Pull back. We're getting out of here."

"Copy that," Jacob said, crawling to his hands and knees, his breath ragged.

All around us the witches I'd knocked to the ground moaned. But the inky power thudded again, still a far-off feeling, and they all drew in a quick, reviving breath and stood.

Shit shit shit.

I pumped strength into Gideon and Jacob through our brands to get them standing. There wasn't anything I could do for Kol, who was climbing to his feet, using a pillar to keep his balance, so I shot the witch closest to him.

Behind him, still partially in the shadows, the fire witch sneered.

"Stand your ground," Zuri yelled. "They're down, cuff or kill them. I don't care which."

Gideon jerked to his feet, his gaze leaping to me, and the strength pouring through our brand hit a mental wall. "Don't."

He'd blocked me off.

I mentally pushed, but he held firm.

"You need it," he said.

"I wasn't just slammed onto my ass." I shot at a witch lunging for him, missed the woman's torso, but nicked her shoulder with one of the rounds. The strike and small flicker of red lightning was enough to make her stumble, giving Gideon time to ram his light blade through her chest.

"Thanks for that," Sebastian groaned, lying face first on the floor, his tone thick with sarcasm.

"No one got burned to a crisp. Deal with it," Marcus snarled, lunging at a witch and ramming his claws into the man's gut. "Xavier, get Regan to Gideon."

Xavier slung Regan over his shoulder and staggered under her weight. Jacob ripped out the throat of another witch and grabbed the arm of a woman, stopping her from running Kol through the back with her shadow blade.

Three witches on the promenade above shot a barrage of shadows at me, and I jerked out of the way. A blast slammed into my shoulder. Screaming agony ripped through me and my whole arm went numb. I fought to keep hold of my M4, but my hand slipped away and my arm hung limp at my side.

The inky magic seeped deeper into me.

Embrace me. Use me. Be powerful.

I could end it with a thought, flatten everyone. My magical blast against the ball of fire had been powerful, but the inky magic was stronger.

The witches fired another barrage and I dove out of the way. A shot hit my thigh. More agony. Darkness teased my vision for a second. My leg went numb, and I sprawled, face first, across the concrete. Another blast skimmed Kol's back. He stumbled and the witch fighting him rammed his shadow blade into Kol's chest as if he weren't wearing a Kevlar vest.

He screamed and dropped to his knees, blood gushing from his chest and splattering on the floor. The witch swept his sword up to decapitate Kol, and instinct wrenched my good hand up. Divine light shot from my palm and tossed the witch across the courtyard.

Kol clutched his chest, but blood still rushed through his fingers. He staggered to his feet, lost his balance, and I hurried to help him, but Marcus pushed me aside, catching him before he fell.

"You've got the range weapon," he said, wrapping one of Kol's arms across his neck and taking the incubus's weight.

I reached to draw my Glock. It was easier to shoot one-handed than the M4... but still, not as accurate as a one-handed divine light strike. I left my Glock holstered and raised my palm.

Zuri and Ephraim dove into the witches on the promenade and Gideon shot a light blast at a witch running toward me. The blast hit the woman in the center of her chest. She screamed and dropped to her knees, bent forward in agony.

"I said stand your ground," Zuri yelled.

Jacob bolted up beside me, helping me cover Marcus's and Kol's retreat. He gave me a grim glance, his worry flooding me and stealing my breath for a second.

Sebastian was back on his feet, a long tattoo curling over his left arm blazing under his shirt. He raised his hands and his icy magic swept over me, but a blast of searing magic engulphed it, killing whatever spell he was going to cast.

I wrenched my attention to the fire witch and shot a bolt of divine light at him, but the witch's magic thudded stronger, almost as strong as it had been before Xavier had given me a shield, and wrenched me to my knees.

The inky magic, desperate to get inside me, howled. *Use me and end it. Let me in. Let. Me. In.*

Kol screamed and Marcus dropped to his hands and knees beside me. Jacob went down on one knee, while Zuri and Ephraim dropped from the air and crashed onto the concrete.

Xavier went down face first with Regan and all the witches went down as well.

Gideon and Sebastian staggered forward a step, but the weight of the fire witch's spell pulsed again, pounded them to their knees, drawing screams from everyone already down.

The power crushed me to the floor. I couldn't move, couldn't think, and couldn't draw breath. Something in my chest snapped and agony sliced through me.

My power erupted and blazed against the spell, but the fire witch's power just kept growing, squeezing me tighter and tighter, and I couldn't push past it like I had with the ball of fire.

If I just let the inky magic in, I'd be able to stop him.

But if I let the inky magic in, it'd take over.

I couldn't forget that. No matter how much it cajoled and begged and promised me unimaginable power, my essence and soul would be devoured.

The fire witch strode out of the shadows, his dark eyes filled with malice, and he wove his way between his fellow dead and unconscious witches, and crouched in front of me.

"That's it, fight it," he said, his voice a raspy hiss.

His magic swelled and mine surged in response, raging through every cell, burning at the inky magic, pressing against the fire witch's crushing spell. But I couldn't blast free. He was stronger than me—

No, the external source he was drawing from was stronger. I could feel the same sticky magic desperate to possess me also inside him, pouring into him without end. And while I still had power and could draw from Gideon and Jacob if I needed to, it wasn't going to be enough.

Except it had to be enough. If we didn't break free, the witches would kill us.

Behind him, a stunningly beautiful woman, with skin so pale it was pure white and long black hair, dressed in a black body-hugging gown, stepped out of the shadows.

Red demonic mist curled from her skin, caressing her, and hellfire consumed her eyes. Heat filled the room as if a massive furnace had been turned on, and the witches' crushing power swelled.

Whoever this woman was, she was the most powerful super I'd ever come across, and that said a lot, given the supers I'd encountered in the last couple of days.

The ice on my arms evaporated in her heat, and the heart-stopping fear from my guys and the rest of the team squeezed tighter.

I fought to breathe against the power and fear as darkness danced at the edge of my vision.

The woman knelt before me, her radiating heat making the air ripple around her, and grabbed my chin with a searing hot hand. Agony screamed through my face and neck and the acrid sent of burning flesh filled my nose.

"I bring you sacrifices," the fire witch said, "my goddess."

ESSIE

Oh, fuck.

My whole essence stalled, pulse, breath, and thought, and that one word raced over and over again in my mind. Goddess. We were up against a real goddess. The super— or rather demon powering the worship magic spell was strong enough to contain it *and* remain conscious. How the hell were we supposed to stop a goddess? We couldn't even stop her witches.

The goddess's power surged, slamming into me, and the darkness at the edge of my vision engulfed me.

The fire witch hissed something else and the woman murmured a reply, but crushing pressure muddled my thoughts and I teetered on the edge of unconsciousness. If I'd heard what they'd said, I didn't remember a second later.

People moved around me, groaning and shuffling. The crushing magic continued to squeeze my chest and I struggled to breathe.

For a second I was in the not-water, but the bobbing wasn't soothing. It was jerky and shot through with slicing agony.

My eyes fluttered open. Pain screamed through my chest and along my jaw and pounded in my skull. I stared down at someone's butt, legs, and bootheels as they walked across granite flagstones, and with slug-gish thoughts, I realized I'd been slung over someone's shoulder.

He shifted my weight, digging his shoulder into my ribs, slicing more pain through me. I had no idea if the crush in my lungs was from my position or the witches' magic, and I was in too much pain to care.

Out of the corner of my eye, I caught a glimpse of two bulky men, each holding one of Jacob's arms, dragging his unconscious body across the floor. I couldn't feel past the pressure and dizziness to tell if he was pulling strength from me or not, or if Gideon was, and I couldn't get an empathic sense of emotions from anyone.

Please let him be okay. Let them all be okay.

I strained to raise my head and look for the others, but a wave of dizziness swept me back into the darkness and I was bobbing again in the painful no-longer-comforting not-water. I couldn't breathe, when, like with the strangeness of dreams, I'd been able to breathe in the water before. A vise squeezed my chest and the inky magic, the clinging miasma of the witches' power, taunted me.

If I'd just let it in, my guys would be safe.

If I'd just let it in, I wouldn't be in pain.

If I'd just—

Someone called my name, but I couldn't tell which of my guys it was, only that it was one of my guys.

I shoved at the inky, sticky magic, but couldn't get it out of my head and could feel my resistance to it weakening. It was going to take over and I was going to lose myself.

Embrace me. Let me in.

No.

My guy called me again, and a whisper of warmth from my brands strengthened my soul for a moment.

Let me in.

I whipped my power around the inky magic, but couldn't force it out and could feel myself slipping away.

I strained to focus on my connection with my guys, and my sense of self returned.

Let me in.

Except I didn't have enough power to force it out right now.

Fine.

I'll wrap you up so tight I won't be able to hear you.

With a mental scream, I spun my power, tighter and tighter, squeezing the voice of the inky magic until I could barely hear it.

"Essie."

I jerked awake, shooting agony through my head, chest, and neck. The pain stole my breath and made my vision waver.

Holy hell. I knew that feeling all too well. Broken rib. At least one. Probably more. The fiery agony in my head felt like my magical channels had been scorched raw, and the pain in my neck felt like...

I wasn't sure.

My memory lurched to the demon-goddess grabbing my chin with her too-hot hand.

She'd burned me. Her internal demonic power was so strong, her touch had burned my skin.

This was bad.

"Essie," Jacob said from behind me, but not in my ear through the coms. "Wake up."

"I'm awake," I gasped, knowing the longer I stayed silent, the more my guys would worry.

I dragged my gaze around me, my thoughts still whirling and my vision clouded with darkness.

I sat, propped up against a metal wall in a plain, all-metal, ten-by-ten box with a stainless steel single-unit toilet and sink, very much like the cell in Operations. Harsh fluorescent light, from an exposed fixture in the ceiling on the other side of narrow metal bars and a solid metal door, glared off the metal floor and walls. My weapons, extra magazines, cell phone, and vest were gone. So too was the com that had been in my ear.

Across the hall, Regan and Ephraim lay on the floor of their ten-by-ten cell, but I sat too far back in my cell to see into the other cells or down the hall.

"Thank God," Jacob said from the other side of my cell wall, his relief creeping into my chest.

But my chest didn't feel right. The agony of broken ribs aside, there was something wrong. I was cold and hollow and—

My stomach bottomed out. A hollowness in my chest meant I was either out of power or cut off from it. And that hint of emotion had to have come from the soul bond I shared with Jacob, not my empathy.

"How badly are you hurt?" Gideon asked, his voice tight, also coming from somewhere to my right. Except he sounded farther away than Jacob so most likely in the next cell over.

"How badly are *you* hurt?"

He snorted, which turned into a ragged wet cough, and then gasping shallow, rattling breaths.

That didn't sound good. I closed my eyes and fought to concentrate past the pain on my brands. Neither Jacob nor Gideon were pulling strength, and I wasn't pulling from them, but that didn't mean we weren't seriously injured. The brand wouldn't pull strength if it jeopardized a mate's life, even if the other mate was in critical condition.

"I asked you first," Gideon gasped.

"At least one broken rib, my head throbs from all the magic I used, and—" A shudder swept through me at the memory of the power and heat radiating from the demon-goddess. "My neck is burned."

"I think we all have broken ribs," Jacob said. "That spell that took us out literally crushed us."

"Yeah." Another shudder shook me. With all that power, the goddess could have smashed every bone in our bodies and killed us. Which scared me even more. She wanted us alive.

You can be stronger than her.

But that was a lie. I couldn't be stronger than her by tapping into her worship magic like her witches did... could I? No, it was still her magic. She controlled it.

"How long was I out?" I asked, struggling to ignore the inky magic's lure. "And who's in which cell?"

"You weren't out much longer than us," Jacob said.

"But we have no idea how long we were out," Gideon gasped. "As for who's where... Zuri is with me. She's still out and in rough shape. I haven't been able to stop her bleeding. She might have only taken a one-and-a-half-story fall, but with that spell and from the look of how many bones she's broken, I'd say the impact was more like a five- or six-story fall."

"Greater demons heal quickly," Jacob said.

"Not *that* quickly," Gideon shot back. "Anyone in the cell with you, Essie?"

"No."

"I don't have anyone, either." Worry darkened Jacob's tone. "Bane and Marcus are across the hall, and I can see Regan and Ephraim across from you."

"They're both unconscious," I said.

"We figured, since they weren't answering us." Sebastian groaned. "Your wolf is also still out of it and is pretty beaten up. His burns are serious and he was stabbed a few times during that fight. I've managed to stop most of the bleeding for now, but..."

My pulse lurched and I fought to slow it down.

Come on. Control your fear and think straight. Fear wouldn't help us out of this mess and we needed to get out of there. Everyone needed medical attention and—

Oh, God.

"Where are Kol and Xavier?" No one had said they were in a cell.

If they weren't in a cell, where were they? Were they dead?

I lost what little control I had on my emotions and my breath turned to desperate pants that sliced agony through me.

Please don't be dead. Please. Kol couldn't be dead. I needed him. Just like I needed Marcus and Jacob and Gideon. *He had to be alive. He had to.*

I didn't know what I do if he wasn't.

My throat tightened, and a whisper of inky magic broke free from my mental hold and crept along my senses.

He could be alive if I just let it in.

Which was a lie. It was all lies. Only a master vampire could bring someone back from the dead and only if they performed the ritual to turn him into a vampire.

"Where is he?" We had to get out of there. Find him. Now.

Now now now.

And the only way to do that was to fucking focus!

I gritted my teeth and tried to draw in a slower breath, but that only shot more agony through my chest. The only way out, the only way to find him, was to get more information. Hell, even just answers to basic questions like where we were would be useful.

"What do we know?" I forced out.

"We're all injured," Jacob said.

Sebastian huffed. "And our magic is contained with one hell of a powerful containment spell."

Which was why I felt so hollow. But I knew that already. "Will it affect personal magics? Like Kol's healing or Marcus's shifting?"

"No, but that's about it," Sebastian said.

"We also don't know where we are or why they've kept us alive, how many of them are left, or even how powerful they are," Gideon added, his voice grim.

Jeez, this was bad. Beyond bad. Even if we could figure out how to get out of those cells, we were running on no information. We could just as easily be captured again. "And that doesn't even take into account their goddess."

"Oh, fuck," Sebastian hissed, reminding me that they'd all been knocked out before she'd stepped into sight. "Let me guess. She isn't asleep."

"She isn't."

Someone groaned, the sound a low, throaty growl. Marcus. A glimmer of relief rushed through me, but it was squashed by the fear that Kol was missing, possibly dead.

"Don't move," Sebastian said. "You'll start bleeding again."

"Essie? Where's Essie?" Marcus gasped.

"I'm right here." I shifted closer to the bars at the front of the cell to try to look at him. He lay with his head close to his bars and I could see the oozing burn trailing up the side of his face, mixed in with red, swelling bruises. "I'm in better shape than you."

"Thank God." He rolled his head to look at the ceiling. "Where the fuck are we?"

"Better question," Gideon corrected. "Why aren't we dead?"

Sebastian shifted into sight, his glow barely there, his skin like tissue paper. "I'd rather know how to get out of here. Anyone know how to pick a lock?"

"Sure," Jacob said, his voice a dark rumble. "If I had something to pick it with."

"We have to wait for someone to show up and unlock our doors," Gideon said, breaking into a fit of wet coughs that made my heart stutter again with worry.

I concentrated on our brand and imagined strength seeping into him, but there wasn't even a flicker of electric magic or heat or anything to indicate it was working.

"I hate waiting," Marcus groaned. "Come up with a better plan."

Footsteps sounded down the hall, at least two people, men from the weight of their tread, but possibly more, and with them was a strange *shushing* sound that I couldn't identify.

"Someone's coming," Jacob said.

Marcus started to sit up and Sebastian pressed a hand to his chest. "I said don't move."

"You going to jump whoever opens our door?" Marcus growled.

"I've got more than magic up my sleeve, wolf," Sebastian shot back as he stood and grabbed the bars.

"Get ready," Gideon said.

I clutched the bars in front of me and staggered to my feet, the pain in my chest overwhelming. Darkness flickered at the edge of my vision, but I was God damn not going to pass out.

Someone moaned, and I strained to see farther down the hall.

The first of the glyph witches stepped into sight, a thin woman, her right arm covered with a thick tattoo, her expression hard, unreadable. Behind her, two burly guys gripped a barely conscious, moaning Xavier under the armpits, his feet dragging on the floor.

The woman slid a key into the lock on Jacob's cell door and opened it.

Jacob wrenched toward her but she grabbed her forearm and her power thudded in me. My knees buckled and I slid down the bars as Jacob gasped and did the same.

"Fuck," Sebastian snarled, and he too sagged down.

"Jacob, get up," Gideon said.

"Can't," Jacob gasped.

The woman sneered at him and the men holding Xavier tossed him into Jacob's cell. Her sneer deepened, and she closed that door and opened mine. I clutched the bars, fighting to stand, but another thump of magic swept through me and a massive weight pressed me to the floor.

Another pair of guys dragged Kol into sight, and my heart stopped. His head lolled forward and blood oozed from the gash in his chest — clearly visible because he too had lost his vest — leaving a trail on the metal floor. He wasn't even moaning like Xavier was, and I couldn't see his chest moving. I couldn't tell if he was alive.

Oh, please.

The men tossed Kol face first onto the floor beside me and the woman slammed my cell door shut.

I grabbed Kol's shoulder and rolled him over as our captors left. His complexion was gray and blood dampened the entire front of his T-shirt, pasting it to his body. I pressed my hand over the wound, trying to stop the bleeding, and everything lurched inside me. He was cold.

"Oh, God. His heat is gone." I didn't think demons could ever have a cold body temperature. I thought the coldest they got was close to human normal.

I strained to feel his pulse beat or his chest rise under my palms, anything to tell me he was alive.

"Essie, is he alive?" Gideon asked.

"I don't know." I pressed two fingers to his neck.

Gideon coughed, the sound ragged and gasping, and his fear joined mine and tightened inside me. "If he's alive, cold means his essence has been drained."

"Which would be why they took him," Sebastian said, as if he'd just realized the obvious. "It's worship magic. And their goddess is awake. She can probably drain someone even if they're unwilling, and he's got the strongest essence out of all of us."

"He won't be able to heal," Jacob said. "Not with his essence drained to the point that he's cold."

Which meant he needed sexual energy to regain some essence.

I pressed my lips against his, praying my desire for him would be enough for me to feel a pulse, a breath, anything. But my heart pounded and not with desire.

Please, take a breath.

I tried to imagine the feel of his sensual magic sliding into me, or Jacob's bite twisting in my core, and push that sensation into my kiss.

But his lips didn't move, just squished against mine, and my throat tightened, taking me farther from any sensual thought that might help him.

I still couldn't feel a pulse or breath. His chill seeped into my hands. Even his blood was cold. How the hell could his blood be cold?

"Essie?" Gideon gasped. "Is he dead?"

Tears burned my eyes.

"Is he dead?"

He couldn't be dead. I wouldn't allow him to be dead. *Please, God. Don't let him be dead.*

ESSIE

I panted, unable to slow my breathing and stop the shooting agony in my chest. My hands trembled, the cold radiating from Kol's too-still body deepening my fear. It was impossible to focus and tell if he had a pulse.

Jeez. I had to calm down. Concentrate. But I couldn't. I just couldn't accept that he was dead and it didn't matter if I couldn't feel a pulse. He was alive and I could save him. I just needed to get turned on.

Except my fear was so strong my teeth chattered.

A tear leaked down my cheek. I couldn't lose him like this. Not before he knew how much he meant to me. It was like Jacob all over again. Except Jacob had been alive. I'd been able to do something.

"Essie?" Gideon pressed. "Is he dead?"

"I don't know!"

God, do something. Anything.

Sebastian had said the containment spell didn't affect personal magics. That meant Jacob's bite could still turn me on. I wouldn't be able to release the bite-lock myself, but Kol could do it with his magic when he revived. Because he was God damned going to revive.

Gritting my teeth against the pain in my chest, I crawled to the bars, pressed my face against the metal wall between my cell and Jacob's, and reached around. "Bite me."

"No," Jacob said.

"Jacob, bite me. It's the only way."

"If he's dead, the bite-lock will keep building within you," he said.

"Jacob, please," I begged. "He's not dead. He can't be dead." He was family. He belonged.

He was mine.

"I'm too scared," I gasped. "I can't draw enough desire to help him. Jacob, ple—"

Marcus jerked forward and seized the bars as Jacob grabbed my hand. "Don't—"

Pain sliced into my wrist, and more tears rolled down my cheeks with a mix of fear and hope. His teeth sank into my flesh and with a gentle pull, bone-melting desire shot up my arm and straight to my core.

I gasped at the sudden surge, my body instantly throbbing with need.

Marcus snarled and his wolf turned his expression fierce. "God damn it, Jacob. She's not just *your* mate. If he's dead, we all get to listen to her lose her mind."

Jacob took a longer pull, sinking his magic deeper into me. It twisted around my heart, burning away all fear and thought, leaving only aching, desperate need. Then as fast as he bit me and flooded my essence with his magic, he withdrew his fangs, sent a whisper of healing magic into his bite, and released my wrist.

I sagged against the metal wall, my breath too fast, each inhalation slicing sharp agony through me. But the pain didn't diminish Jacob's magic. It kept growing, twisting until I could barely feel it

With a shuddering groan, I crawled back to Kol, pressed my hands against his wound — not that it'd help slow the bleeding, I just couldn't stop myself — and kissed his too-cold lips again. The memory of his magic pouring down my throat when he'd saved me, and again when he'd helped me save Jacob the other day, made me shudder and twisted Jacob's magic tighter.

Come on. Work. Please work. Please don't be dead.

Kol's blood continued to ooze through my fingers.

"Please," I begged against his lips. "Come back to me." *Don't leave me.*

But he *was* leaving. He'd asked for a transfer because I'd reminded him of all the horrible things he'd gone through during the war. And because of that terrible tear in his soul that I had to heal before he left. That I'd never be able to heal if he was dead.

"You can't be dead."

A tear fell from my lashes and plopped onto his face. It rolled over his breathtakingly beautiful cheek and trailed a line along his jaw. I'd been attracted to him the moment I'd seen him, but that wasn't why I desired him, why he belonged. It was everything else after the moment I'd woken in the hospital. All his wicked smiles, his playful teasing, his unwavering support and kindness.

Something fluttered under my hands. Was that a breath? His pulse? He was still so cold.

I sat back on my heels. Jacob's magic billowed and sank low, teasing me on the edge of a climax I knew wouldn't come. I fought to concentrate on Kol's chest, desperate to feel another flutter, terrified it had all been my imagination.

The ragged, shallow flutter under my hands came again.

It was a breath. He'd taken a breath.

"Oh, thank God."

I yearned to embrace him, kiss him, rub my aching body against his, but I forced myself to take his hand in mine and lean against the wall. I didn't have his consent to keep kissing him, and holding his hand and letting him feed off my desire from Jacob's bite would be just as effective as anything else.

"Is he alive?" Gideon asked.

"Yes," I said, my voice breathy. "He's going to be all right." I just needed to wait until he'd gotten enough sexual energy to warm up and seal the gash in his chest shut.

"Will you be?" Marcus asked.

"I'll be fine." A shudder swept through me, surging Jacob's magic and making my breath hitch. "I just need to wait."

I tipped my head back, but that made me think of Jacob sinking his fangs into my throat and the glorious rush of his magic. A magic that twisted tighter and tighter.

Seconds... minutes... an eternity dragged by, trapping me on a razor's edge of pain and pleasure, and not the good kind. I just needed to wait it out. I could wait it out.

Please, God, let me be able to sit here long enough for Kol to wake up.

Then Kol groaned and my pulse leaped, the urge to throw myself on him and beg him to take me overwhelming. I fought to stay put and another shudder taunted me with a climax that wouldn't come. I ached with need, every nerve hypersensitive, every breath and twitch and thought ratcheting up my desire. My breath kept speeding up and was now short, sharp gasps, and the small cell spun around me.

"Essie," Jacob said, his voice rumbling through me, twisting his magic tighter. "Slow your breathing. You're going to pass out."

But I couldn't slow anything. The only control I had of my body was to stay where I was. *Just God damn stay put and hold Kol's hand.*

I tightened my grip on his hand and added my other hand, clinging to him as if that would somehow ease my pain.

"Focus on my voice, Essie," Jacob said, his voice that sexy, deep rumble I loved so much, sending another shudder of need through me.

"I can't. Stop talking. Please."

Marcus pressed his face to the bars, his eyes wild. "Gideon, use your brand. Do something. Kol isn't waking up fast enough."

A hint of Gideon's electric magic whispered over my right forearm, adding to my agonizing desire. "Oh, fuck, Gideon," I whimpered.

Kol groaned again and his hand twitched, shooting another taunting tremor through me.

I squeezed my eyes shut. I couldn't fight or ignore the feeling of Jacob's magic, because that was what was saving Kol, but God, I was going to shatter into a million pieces and there wasn't going to be anything blissful about it.

"Kol," Marcus said, "wake the fuck up."

Kol groaned again.

"Wake up!" Marcus barked. "Please, God, wake up."

Kol gasped and his hand on mine tightened. My eyelids flew open and I was drowning in hellfire. It blazed in his eyes and licked across his cheeks. Cheeks I wanted to lick. *Needed* to lick. *Oh, God.*

"What did you do?" he gasped, his eyes filled with horror.

A whisper of his sultry magic slid up my arm, drawing another whimper.

"You have to release the bite-lock," Marcus said.

"I what?" Wild emotions — fear, anger, pain — flashed across his face and he jerked away from me. Just the idea of releasing Jacob's magic hurt him.

"Kol, please," Marcus begged.

The anger deepened, and Kol squeezed his eyes shut and dragged in a deep breath that didn't seem to calm him. He dragged in another breath and the muscles in his jaw flexed. The frustration and anger deepened and he glared at me.

"Fine."

But it wasn't fine. I didn't know what Michael and his nephilim had done to him, but they'd forced him to do things he hadn't wanted to do. And now so was I, and he hated me for it.

"Just use your magic and release it," I gasped. Then he wouldn't have to come any closer. Hell, he wouldn't even have to look at me.

"It doesn't work that way," he snapped, shifting farther away from me. "The bite-lock will absorb my magic before your body can use it to set you free."

"You mean you have to—?" My breath hitched with a mix of yearning and dread at the thought of Kol doing more than just using his magic and releasing Jacob's power.

"It's fine. I'll deal with it." He dragged his gaze up his body, over his bloody T-shirt and arms, then jerked it around the cell, stopping at the toilet-sink unit. "I'll fucking deal with it," he said again, his tone hard, breaking my heart, as he crawled to the sink.

But it wasn't fine and there wasn't anything I could do about it. My throat tightened and even that made me gasp with another torturous tremble of climax.

God damn it. All of me, body and soul, burned with a desire soured by heartache at what needed to happen. He didn't want to touch me. Just being near me hurt him deeply. And still I yearned for his touch, his kiss, his body filling me.

He scrubbed the blood off his hands and arms. The water ran over his skin, making me think of sex with my guys, all of my guys, in the shower.

I squeezed my eyes shut, but that only deepened the fantasy. Water running over their sculpted muscles, slicking their erect—

Fuck.

I forced my eyes open to find Kol glaring at me, his body tense. "Let's get this over with." He stood and, using the wall to keep his balance, shuffled the few steps to my side and glared down at me. "Just— look away or close your eyes or something. I can't— not with that look on your face."

"What look?" But I knew what look. I ached for him and I ached for more than just releasing Jacob's bite-lock. He belonged with me and the guys. He needed the team and quite frankly the team needed him. I needed him.

"The look you give *them*," he snarled, his voice low and dark. "It's not real. It's Jacob's bite and my magic and you don't mean it."

"What are you talking about?" The magic in my chest billowed, the sensation fierce and painful. *Oh, fuck.*

Please, yes.

He sagged to his knees beside me. I wanted to scream at the anger and pain in his eyes, at being just as bad as Michael and making him do something against his will. And yet my body didn't care. It begged for his touch, for his kiss. For God damned anything. *Just please touch me.*

"You don't actually want me," he said between gritted teeth. "You don't really love me."

My thoughts stalled. Even my desperate need for release caught on that one word.

Love.

He thought I didn't love him?

"You want me to love you? But I triggered you, I reminded you of—" Of all the horrors he survived. "You asked for a transfer."

"And I'm God damned taking it." His expression hardened and filled with frustration. "I have to get away from you. You've fucked everything up. You've fucked me up." He slammed his fist into the wall beside him. "I want to scream every time they touch or kiss you. Every time they make love to you."

The hellfire in his eyes flared, and a shot of searing, sensual magic whipped into Jacob's magic and blazed through my core, making me whimper.

"Incubi don't get jealous. It's not in our nature. You're a free meal. Fuck, with the four of you, I'm going to be riding high for the rest of my life with no risk of draining anyone to death. But I can't do it."

His breath picked up and frustration and need swelled in my chest. His emotions were so strong I could feel them despite the containment spell, and they merged with the agonizing pleasure in my body.

"I can't keep riding your desire for *them*." He raked his hands through his hair. Hands that needed to be on me, caressing me, releasing me. "I want your desire to be for *me*. I want you to love *me*," he yelled, his voice breaking. "Like you love them."

"But I do love you." I was more certain now than I'd ever been before.

The thought of him leaving— God, of him dead or dying, filled me with as much panic as it did for the rest of my guys.

"That's just my nature influencing you. You only think you love me. No one loves an incubus. They only think they do." The pain in his eyes turned to full, desperate grief. "And incubi don't fall in love. How can we? It'll never be real. We don't need it to be real. But I want it to be fucking real. I want something I'm not supposed to want or can ever have."

"Kol." I captured his cheeks with my palms, still sticky with his blood, and forced him to meet my gaze. "I do love you. And it is real."

I smashed my lips against his and kissed him, willing him to feel all my love and desire and need for him. A desperate kiss had convinced Jacob how I felt about him. It had to be enough to convince Kol. I had no other way of proving to him that I cared for him as deeply as I cared for Marcus and Jacob and Gideon, that he was just as loved and desired. He was a part of the family I'd ached for, the love I'd been missing since my mom died and more, and no way in hell was I letting him go without a fight.

He stiffened, his body trembling. He was going to reject me. I could feel it in my soul. Fear and hurt and a certainty of what he was supposed to be was going to take over. I'd lose him forever if I didn't do something. But I had nothing else to offer that could convince him of how I felt.

My thoughts leaped to my power, even though I didn't have access to it, and my imagination took over. I envisioned my empathic magic flooding into him, just like it had flooded into Voth the other day when I'd shown the greater demon my love and connection to my guys to get the area containment master ward.

In my mind's eyes, I saw the same gold strands, the primal, brilliant source of the universe that was neither light magic nor dark magic nor essence-based magic and yet all of it. A pure power that recognized true mates and bound souls together.

The power swirled through Kol's soul and essence, then swelled into a ball of dazzling magic around his heart.

He sucked in a startled gasp, his breath stealing mine through our kiss, and my magic surged. I could almost feel it now, a blazing fire in the center of my being, pouring into him.

With a moan, he tangled his hands into my hair and deepened the kiss, sliding his tongue against mine. His hold on his magic slipped and it rushed into me, but my power pulled it in before it could twist into Jacob's magic, adding to the imagined blaze in my body—

No. Not imagined blaze. It was real. Kol's cheeks were cool to the touch but it wasn't because his essence was low. It was because every cell in my body was on fire.

And that fire kept growing, trapped within me, squeezing around my heart. It ignited Gideon's brand, gold light blazing from it, and swept up my arm into Jacob's. The power roared through me, poured over and through my chest, and surged into a supernova about to rip me to pieces.

ESSIE

THE PRESSURE OF MY MAGIC TORE OUT OF ME WITH FIRE AND AGONY. EVERY muscle in my body seized, every cell on fire for a torturous eternity, before it vanished with a whoosh.

I collapsed into Kol's arms, the room spinning, my breath fast, painful gasps with my broken ribs. Jacob's bite-lock still held me captive, my body desperate for release, but I was too weak to do anything about it.

The hollowness in my chest returned, along with a bone-deep cold that went beyond just being cut off from my magic. But I knew what that cold meant and my soul sang with joy.

"See. I do love you," I gasped.

"What the hell was that?" Ephraim groaned, his voice weak and filled with pain. Guess he'd finally woken up. My thoughts tripped on that for a second, but with my mind whirling, I couldn't focus on that detail long enough to figure anything out.

"Another one just bit the dust," Sebastian said. "Even with the containment spell on us."

I tried to raise my hand and place it on Kol's heart, but couldn't make my muscles work.

"What did you do?" Kol shifted and looked me in the eyes, his expression stunned. The movement sliced agonizing pleasure through me, drawing a half moan, half whimper from my numb lips.

"Please," I begged. But I couldn't tell if I'd actually spoken, because his expression didn't change.

"Essie?" He moved to hold me with one arm and cupped my cheek with his palm. "Essie, talk to me."

I unclenched my jaw — so I guess I hadn't spoken — and my teeth started chattering. I wanted to tell him it would be okay. That this was what had happened every time I'd claimed one of my guys, but I couldn't pull my focus from my desperate need long enough to form coherent thoughts.

"What's wrong with her?" He clutched me to his warm chest. So warm. Gloriously warm. And yet even the cold flooding me from bonding my soul with Kol's was nothing compared to the agony of Jacob's bite-lock.

"She was stupid enough to bind your souls together within the containment spell," Sebastian said. "She's in shock. Again."

"Pretty sure she didn't have a say in when their bond formed," Gideon said, his voice low.

"Are you saying she just claimed another mate?" Ephraim asked.

"Check her brand." Jacob's voice rumbled through me, and the world spun faster, my not-climax tearing into me.

Tears leaked from my eyes and my twitching made everything worse, an aching, freezing, desperate need.

"No, check if the bite-lock is released," Marcus said.

Kol closed his eyes for a second and sensual heat roared through me. Darkness shuddered across my vision, but Jacob's magic wouldn't let me pass out. All I could do was pant and twitch, my mind begging, my body numb and weak.

"Shit." Kol shifted, his body sliding against my too-sensitive nerves. *Oh fuck oh fuck oh fuck.*

He braced his back against the cell wall and settled me in the V between his legs, my back against his chest. Heat seeped from him into me and a hint of the chill melted from my bones.

"I've got you," he said, just like the times before when he'd held me and I'd been in shock from binding my soul with Gideon's and Jacob's.

He reached down with one hand, undid my jeans, and slid his hand inside. My breath picked up so fast I was certain that this time I would pass out despite Jacob's magic. Just a brush of Kol's fingers into my curls, and I was on fire, the taunting climax trembling within me. Except my body still shivered, and I couldn't get the tears to stop leaking from my eyes.

"We need to do this gently," he said, his breath hot against my neck and cheek. "There's too much magic trapped in the bite-lock."

I weakly squirmed against him, desperate, spinning, freezing and on fire at the same time. Then he brushed his finger over my clit and every muscle in my body clenched in anticipation, but the magic didn't release.

No, please.

"Just let it go, Essie."

He brushed my clit again. My body clenched tighter, every cell screaming in pain, drawing a whimper.

Another gentle brush. The promise of my climax trembled and twisted so tight I couldn't breathe. I jerked in his embrace, unable to draw breath, every muscle seized, and on the edge of a climax that wouldn't come.

"Essie, breathe. Release it." Kol's voice grew sharp and his frozen fear spiraled into my agony.

Tears streamed down my cheeks and I still couldn't draw breath. The darkness creeping at the edge of my vision promised blissful unconsciousness, but it wouldn't come, teasing me like my climax teased me.

"Shit," he hissed. "I'm sorry. Gentle isn't working." He thrust two fingers into me, my body already slick and ready for him, and ground his thumb against my clit.

I shuddered. He withdrew and thrust again and again, the strokes fierce and fast, his thumb hard against my clit until my climax exploded with a blazing agony that threatened to tear me to pieces.

Blinding light burst across my vision, and all breath and thought vanished, consumed by pain. Someone screamed. A great, heartrending wail, and I realized it was me.

Kol stiffened and his magic roared through me. For a second there was only sensual, agonizing pain, then his power rushed out of me into him, taking the destructive release of Jacob's bite-lock with it and leaving me limp in Kol's arms.

Someone gasped. Not me. But with all the whirling darkness, I couldn't figure out who.

Marcus growled, the calm stillness in Jacob's brand shuddered, and a single snap of lightning surged through Gideon's brand.

"What the hell?" Marcus asked with a throaty groan.

Gasping, Kol pulled his hand from my pants and cradled me against his chest. I should have been bothered by the fact he was still covered in blood and getting it on me, but I didn't care. The pain from Jacob's magic was gone, leaving just the agony of broken ribs, and I was right where I needed to be, wrapped in Kol's warmth and love.

"What was that?" Gideon gasped.

"It was too much," Kol said, his voice ragged. "I needed to send it somewhere. Her soul bonds were the easiest way to disperse the bite-lock's release."

"I owe you a serious apology if that's what you feel every time my bite-lock releases," Jacob said, his words slurred.

"That was a lot stronger than usual. There was just too much magic built up this time." Kol pressed his lips to the top of my head. "You okay?"

I opened my numb lips to respond, but footsteps clattered toward us from down the hall and Kol tensed.

"They must have felt Essie form her bond with Kol," Gideon said.

"Gee, you think?" Sebastian huffed. "Anyone sensitive in a ten-mile radius probably felt that."

Kol shifted out from under me and leaned me against the wall.

"Which one of them released the power?" a male voice asked from down the hall.

"Check all of them," a woman replied.

Three men and a woman rushed into the prison. The first man, a bulky guy with a buzz cut, opened my cell door, and Kol dove at him, moving as if he were completely healed.

The woman reached for her arm, but Kol's magic surged, sending a shudder of desire through me, but not enough to reignite my passion. The woman, the real target of Kol's magic, dropped to her hands and knees, panting, as Kol slammed his fist into Buzz Cut's throat and snapped his heel into the next man's temple. Buzz Cut staggered back choking and the other guy dropped to the floor unconscious. With a snarl, Kol seized the front of the third guy's shirt, but the woman reached for her arm again.

Kol tossed the man in his grasp at her, sending both of them crashing to the floor in a heap. But Buzz Cut had recovered and lunged at him. Wrenching around, Kol slammed his palm into Buzz Cut's nose and his eyes rolled back. Kol was turned around and facing the remaining two before Buzz Cut's body hit the floor.

The man Kol had thrown into the woman scrambled back and

grabbed one of his tattoos, but Kol whipped a key at him — he had to have gotten it off of one of the witches, although when, I had no clue. The small piece of metal embedded in the man's eye and killed him before he could cast his spell.

The woman screamed and her power thudded into me. Kol lurched forward a step and dropped to one knee.

"They can cast within the containment spell?" Sebastian groaned. "We're fucked."

"No," Kol barked, his determination to save me blazing through my chest. "We're getting out of here."

He fought to rise, his body shaking with the effort. He was almost up. I couldn't believe it. But it wasn't going to be enough to get to the woman. He needed more strength.

And he was God damn going to get it.

I concentrated on my new connection to him and flooded him with what little strength I had left. It rushed out of me with a strange sticky heat, unlike the gentle warmth I usually felt when I gave my guys strength. But the hellfire in Kol's eyes flared, demonic magic misted around him for a second, and he heaved to his feet.

He grabbed the woman's head, breaking her neck, and the pressure crushing me vanished.

"Thank God for too much sex," Sebastian said.

Kol grabbed another key from beside the woman's body and unlocked the rest of the cells.

I crawled to the front of the cell and stood. The world tilted and darkened, and I clung to the bars to keep standing. I might have released the pain of Jacob's bite-lock, but I was still freezing and weak from binding my soul with Kol's and couldn't take a full breath without slicing agony through my chest.

"Who can walk?" Gideon asked, staggering into the hall, his face pale and pinched with pain. "We need to get out of here now."

"We just need to get away from the containment spell," Sebastian said, supporting Marcus.

"Even *you* don't have enough power or strength of will to teleport ten people," Jacob said, heading into Ephraim's and Regan's cell. His complexion was gray, his eyes a little unfocused, but he wasn't bleeding, so the little bit of blood I'd given him must have helped.

"I'm willing to risk Essie frying me to a crisp with a direct power transfer to get the hell out of here," Sebastian said. "She's probably still low on juice, so the odds of her burning me up are less than if I channel directly."

"There's not going to be ten of us," Ephraim said. "I can't feel my legs. My back has to be broken. And Regan is still unconscious. Too many of us are down."

"We're not leaving anyone behind." Jacob knelt beside Regan and pressed his fingers to her neck. "She's still alive."

"I can walk on my own," Marcus said, pushing away from Sebastian but clinging to the closest bars to keep standing.

"You can't." The muscles in Gideon's jaw flexed. "And Essie can't give you strength like she can for the rest of us."

And like I could take the strength from them, as well.

Marcus glared at Gideon, his wolf darkening his eyes. "Thanks for reminding me."

If I could pull some strength from Kol, no one would need to carry me.

"If we don't have to go far, I can probably carry one person," Gideon said. "Jacob, can you carry two?"

"Yes, but we're still short one," Ephraim said. "You have to leave. Now."

I concentrated on my brand with Kol. I'd given him strength to defy the witch's spell, but I had no idea how I'd done it. I couldn't seem to push or pull anything through it any more. My trembling increased, and I lost my grip on the bars and slid to the floor.

Kol rushed to me and picked me up.

"Why can't I pull strength from you?"

"Your bond is too new," Gideon said. "It might form quickly, but it's not instant. You can't give or take strength from him right away."

"But I just gave him strength to break through the witches' spell."

Sebastian narrowed his eyes, his look that soul-deep appraising look he'd given me before my angelic nature had been revealed. "Are you sure?"

Well... was I sure? I'd thought I'd given Kol strength... but... it had felt weird. Maybe it had been my imagination.

Jeez, it was so hard to think. All I wanted to do was fall asleep wrapped in Kol's warmth.

"We don't have time to figure this out." Gideon stepped back into his cell and, with a grunt of pain, hefted Zuri over his shoulder. "Jacob, grab Xavier and Regan."

But that left Ephraim. "You can't just leave him," I said. Anyone left behind was dead or kept alive to have their essence drained to the point of death. And I had no doubt the witches would drain Ephraim again and again until he wished he was dead.

"We have to leave someone and he's agreed." Gideon met Ephraim's gaze and a shadow passed through both of their angel glows. "Do you want rescue or death?"

My pulse tripped. Did he just ask—?

"You're going to kill him?"

"If that's what he wants. His back is broken. He can't heal that on his own and we can't get him out. Death is a kindness," Gideon said, but I could feel his horror at what he'd asked through our bond. "The angels Michael captured never got that kindness."

"Rescue," Ephraim gasped. "I might learn something important." But his grim expression said the rest: if the witches kept him alive.

Gideon gave him a tight nod. "We'll come back with a full squad."

"Given what we just faced, bring at least two," Ephraim said.

Gideon coughed, the sound still wet, and grabbed a nearby bar to keep standing and holding Zuri. "Kol, lead the way."

Kol's grip around me tightened, and even with the pain in my chest, I fought to keep my eyes open against the lulling warmth of his body.

We headed out of the small, ten-cell prison into a long hall with the same metal floor and walls. The only lights shone at the entrance of the prison and at the far end at a T intersection, leaving thick shadows in between, and with no other hallways or doors, the only place we could go was the T-intersection.

I strained to listen for anyone nearby, but my teeth kept chattering with the bone-deep cold of magical shock and my thoughts kept drifting back to Kol. My mate. Thank God. Finally. His pulse pounded strong, the release of Jacob's bite-lock having brought him back to full, and his warmth embraced me.

For a second I was drifting in the not-water with my father staring at me, the flecks of gold in his angel glow mesmerizing. He pressed his hand against something between us and glanced over his shoulder.

Far off in the distance, gunfire popped and hurried footsteps pounded closer.

Shuddering cold sliced through the warm not-water, and I gasped. My eyes flew open, but the footsteps didn't stop.

"They're getting closer," Kol hissed. "Which way?"

We were at the T-intersection and both directions looked identical to where we'd come from: metal floor and walls with low light and a long stretch to the far end. Although this time there were two doors on either side of each hall to break up the cold sleek metal.

"Bane, do you feel anything?" Gideon gasped.

"Until I'm out of the containment spell, I won't be able to tell you its radius," Sebastian said.

"To the right." Jacob jerked his chin toward the right-hand hall. "The witches are coming from the left."

Kol hurried down the hall as the footsteps grew louder. I peered around his shoulder at the others behind us. Jacob's chest heaved with heavy breaths. Even just hurrying down the hall while carrying Regan and Xavier — one on each shoulder — was too much for him in his condition. Marcus didn't look any better, clinging to Sebastian as if that were the only reason he was upright, and the tendons in Gideon's neck were bulging with the strain of carrying Zuri and his face was ashen — and I doubted Zuri would normally be too heavy for him.

The footsteps drew closer. I couldn't see whoever was coming at the far end, but they had to be close and we still had at least fifty feet to the next intersection.

"We're not going to make it," I said. "They're about to round the corner."

Kol raced to the closest door and opened it, taking a huge risk by not stopping to listen for anyone inside. We rushed in and he set me on my feet, just inside the door, clinging to the wall for balance, then stepped back into the hall to cover the rest of the team's retreat.

A cold air swept around me and the only light came from the hall, a weak splash of illumination on a metal floor. The rest of the room lay in complete darkness.

Jacob hurried in through the doorway, and I staggered along the wall to make room for him so he didn't have to move too deeply into the dark.

My hand hit a light switch as Gideon, Sebastian, and Marcus hustled inside. Kol stepped in last, shutting the door behind him, and I turned on the lights.

The fluorescent lights flickered on blindingly bright. I slapped my forearm over my eyes — since my hands were bloody — and squeezed them shut as the guys hissed and groaned.

"A little warning next time," Sebastian said, his voice echoing, indicating we were in a large room. "Better yet, don't."

Marcus huffed. "Or you could go bashing into whatever is in here."

"Or we could just wait for the witches to run by," Sebastian shot back.

I dropped my gaze to the floor and shifted my arm, letting in a little light, trying to get my eyes to adjust as quickly as possible. I could barely stand or breathe or hell, even think. I didn't want to be even more useless by being blind.

Shading my eyes and squinting, I blinked back tears and raised my gaze to check our surroundings. We stood at the edge of a platform with a waist-high metal railing that stretched across the front of a vast room. The unfinished ceiling with exposed metal girders towered above us and the main floor sat one floor down, accessible by stairs on either end of the platform. A massive black circle surrounded by large swirling glyphs had been drawn in the center of the metal floor below, and tables, cabinets, shelves, and tall stacks of crates crowded against the walls on either side. Most of the tables were covered in thick plastic, protecting whatever equipment lay beneath, and with that, along with the lack of electric hum, my best guess was that this was a lab that wasn't yet in use.

It was a lot like the zip lab we'd stumbled across a few days ago that the red-haired glyph witch had brought down on us, except this looked four times bigger and more sophisticated. If this was their new lab, we were in serious trouble. There were already too many deaths from the magically enhanced upper, and an influx of the drug would only make things worse.

"Oh, Jesus," Jacob gasped, his attention on the back of the room.

"No." Kol's back stiffened and frozen fear shot through my still-hollow chest. "We have to destroy them. We can't leave without destroying them."

"Are those—?" Marcus staggered to the railing and pointed to a dozen large glass tanks standing at the back. They were big enough to hold a single person, sealed at the top and bottom with metal caps, and had dozens of pipes and wires trailing out of them.

"Nephilim maturation tanks," Gideon said.

My pulse stalled and more frozen fear from my guys slid through me, defying the containment spell.

A wave of dizziness washed over the fear and I bobbed in the not-water. The inky dark magic that I'd tried to lock away started laughing.

The footsteps in the hall pounded closer, and we froze. Then a soft wet plop filled the silence and everyone's gaze dropped to the floor and the splattered blood on the landing by Jacob, Gideon, and Marcus, then jumped to the trail leading to the door.

Marcus groaned. "Shit."

"There's a door at the back," Jacob said, pointing to a narrow metal door in the corner half hidden by a tank.

"Move." Gideon shifted Zuri's weight on his shoulder, groaned, but still hurried to the stairs with Jacob close behind.

"With luck, we won't need the door. The tanks and the circle require a lot of magic." Sebastian slung Marcus's arm across his shoulder and they followed Gideon and Jacob. "They can't be within the containment spell."

Kol flipped the deadbolt on the door — not that the witches wouldn't have a key, but it might slow them down long enough for us to escape — and swept me off my feet into his arms. Agony sliced through my chest, my head spun, and for a second, I was lurching again in the not-water. Then my vision cleared and Kol's gaze locked on mine, his fear twisting in my chest. The edge in his eyes, the one I'd seen when my wings had first appeared, was back.

We rushed down the stairs and reached the magic circle, but the hollowness in my chest didn't ease up.

"Come on," Sebastian said, staggering with Marcus around the outside edge of the circle, careful not to touch the glyphs. "There's got to be a break. There's got to be—" The light under his skin flared then dimmed again, and with a groan, he sagged to his knees, taking Marcus with him.

We were right beside the tanks, with just a narrow strip between the edge of the magic containment spell and the tanks.

Gideon's back straightened as he crossed the invisible threshold of the spell, and the light in his eyes blazed bright and kept glowing. Zuri groaned and he set her on the floor beside Marcus, while Jacob knelt and rolled Regan and Xavier off his shoulders beside Zuri.

Then Kol stepped out of the containment spell and fire rushed through me. I gasped, filled with power, my head throbbing, my body still trembling from magical shock, and freezing with a fear that wasn't mine.

"All right, Esther." Sebastian held out his hand. "Don't burn me up."

Someone said something outside in the hall and Jacob jerked to face the front. "How fast can you do this? They're going to find the blood trail."

Kol set me on the floor beside Sebastian and hurried to the narrow back door. My gaze followed him for a second, but slid back to the tank beside me. It was bigger than I'd first thought, able to easily hold someone Jacob's size. This was how Michael had made so many of his monsters so quickly. It took magic to speed up maturation, and he'd figured out how to do it in the womb in the human women he'd enslaved to create his army, and, once his nephilim had been born, in tanks like these. And he'd had hundreds of women captive and hundreds of tanks.

A shudder swept through me and the inky magic's laughter grew.

Michael had used dark magic to create his monsters. That had to be why they were so monstrous. It hadn't just been demonic magic, but magic warped by pure evil.

Just like the inky magic trying to worm its way into my soul.

You'll be powerful. Worshiped. A goddess.

My thoughts whirled, and I raised a trembling hand and pressed it against the glass of the maturation tank.

"Esther," Sebastian said, grabbing my other hand and jerking my attention away from the tanks. "Think of a stream—" He frowned. "Better yet, think of a very thin thread of magic sliding from you into me."

"The door is locked," Kol said.

"Jacob, can you force it?" Gideon asked.

Sebastian's grip on my hand tightened, dragging my attention back to him. Again. "Esther, focus. We don't have a lot of time."

Right. Escaping.

The voices in the hall rose in volume, and I struggled to block them out. They were at the door, they knew it was locked, and our only means of escape was me giving Sebastian enough power to teleport us.

But there's no escape. You're not powerful enough.

Shut up.

I imagined a thread like Sebastian had said, and connected with my power. The moment I did, my magic erupted into an inferno and roared out of my hand into Sebastian. A scream tore from his throat and his head jerked back. Light blazed from his skin and poured out of his eyes and mouth, and the inky magic howled with pleasure.

I fought to pull my power back, control it, but the guys' fear and the strain to ignore the inky magic, along with the bone-deep exhaustion of binding my soul to Kol's, kept ripping it from my mental grasp. My power was consuming me and I was going to take Sebastian along with me.

My pulse leaped to a rapid tattoo, giving me a blast of mental strength. I wrenched my power out of Sebastian, and it slammed into my chest, stealing all breath and thought. I was a supernova erupting and it took all I had to keep the explosion inside my body and protect those around me.

The inky magic surged, slipping into my cells while I struggled with my power. It consumed my inferno, leaving me trembling and cold and desperate to keep it from sinking into my soul and taking over.

Sebastian sagged forward, his forehead pressed to the metal floor, and I started to fall over and join him when the inky magic seized my body and heaved me to my feet.

My breath caught. *No, please, no.* Not again. I couldn't be possessed again. I mentally clawed at it, desperate to regain control of my body. I had to get it out, had to get free, but I couldn't get rid of it.

My body jerked, slicing agony through me. I clenched my teeth, fighting the movement, but I wasn't strong enough to resist the inky magic's control of my muscles while also keeping it from controlling my soul, and turned to face the front of the room. My guys were a few steps ahead of me on their hands and knees, their heads bowed, their bodies trembling. And on the landing stood ten witches and the demon-goddess.

ESSIE

"That's better," the demon-goddess said, her voice dark, filled with the promise of excruciating pain. Wisps of red mist curled around her and the hellfire in her eyes licked her cheeks, releasing little sparks that snapped around her.

"Ah, fuck," Sebastian gasped, his voice ragged. "That's Lilith."

"What?" Zuri asked.

"The Hellfire Queen herself." Sebastian groaned. "Who the hell let her out of her cage?"

"Now let's have a look at you," Lilith said, raising her hand.

My body stepped forward into the containment spell, and the chill in my soul swelled as the sickening hollow feeling filled my chest again.

"Fight it, Essie," Marcus gasped, and a tear leaked from my eye. He didn't even have to question me, he already knew I was being possessed, knew I wasn't stepping forward of my own free will.

I strode between Marcus and Jacob and stopped in the center of the magic circle, my body trembling as I fought to regain control. I had to get free—

Or I had to buy Sebastian enough time to recover and get my guys out of there.

"Fight," Gideon said, and I instinctually connected with... I wasn't sure what in his brand. It wasn't like the physical strength we shared when one of us was weak, and it didn't feel as if it flowed from him into me. It was more like a strength of spirit that connected our souls and rooted mine deeper within myself, making the inky magic's hold on me weaken. Just like that same strength had weakened it before I'd regained consciousness in the cell. It lasted a second before the inky magic seized control again, but I'd weakened it. I was sure I had.

"Well," Lilith said, her voice thick with disgust, "you look like *him*."

Look like—? My pulse stuttered. Had she just said—?

"Who?" I asked, even though I had a sinking suspicion I knew who she was talking about.

"Your father." The hellfire in Lilith's eyes flared, showering red sparks around her that hissed when they hit the metal floor. "I should have seen the resemblance the moment you were presented as a sacrifice. Your father's spell hiding you was powerful. I didn't notice the truth until you used your power a moment ago." Her lips curled into a wicked smile. "But even he can't hide all of your magic forever."

"All of my magic?" That didn't make any sense. I'd already broken through the spell hiding my magic.

Oh, you think so? the inky magic inside me asked.

"I know it's in there. Not as locked away as he'd hoped." She flicked a finger and the inky magic inside me jerked me to my knees, jarring my broken ribs and stealing my breath.

Out of the corner of my eye, Jacob tensed, and I concentrated on the spiritual strength in his brand, bolstering my hold on my soul. The inky magic's grip on me faltered again, and I mentally held onto my bond with Jacob, making my body tremble... but because it was partially back in my control. My bonds were the key to pushing the inky magic out.

"He thought he could keep you from me," Lilith said, "thought he could break our bargain."

The image of my father, with his hand pressed on something between us, flashed through my mind's eye. Fear tightened his expression and he glanced over his shoulder.

The red mist curling from Lilith's skin whipped into a vortex around her, and her witches shifted back, their postures tense.

I added concentrating on Gideon's bond along with Jacob's and pushed the inky magic back even further. A little bit more and I'd be free. But when I reached for Marcus, nothing happened.

I tried again.

Nothing.

Crap. Whatever it was that strengthened my soul against the inky magic, it only came from my brands.

"You might be half his," she snarled, "but you're also half mine, *my weapon*, and he'll regret the day he stole you. I'll make him worship at my feet with the rest of them."

She snapped her hand out, and her demonic mist shot across the room and slammed into me. Every muscle in my body seized with fiery pain. My concentration on my soul bonds slipped and her magic, both demonic and worship, ripped through me, tearing into my essence.

Behind me my guys yelled, their fear and anger a churning mix in my stomach.

"All that trouble that he went through, and you still came back to me. And just when things are about to get good."

Specks of shadow and light snapped across my vision. I fought to breathe and stay conscious. I couldn't pass out. If I passed out, Lilith would turn her attention to my guys, and while they might be able to hold off the witches long enough to escape, they wouldn't stand a chance against the demon-goddess.

Please, let Sebastian be okay to cast. Please, they have to get out of here.

"I know it's in there," Lilith said. "I've already felt it."

Her demonic magic reached the core of my essence and my brands lit up. Power from my guys surged into me, and I scrambled to hold onto it, use it to fully force Lilith's magic out of me. But I was too weak from having claimed Kol and her demonic power incinerated it, burning deeper and deeper until all of me was on fire. It scorched my insides and exposed a ball of radiant magic within my heart.

There you are, Lilith hissed in my head. *All that beautiful darkness.*

Her magic contracted around the ball and the pain turned to screaming agony. Tears streamed down my cheeks, my chest heaved, but I couldn't manage to draw a full breath.

Darkness swept over me, stealing all sight and sound, and I bobbed again in the not-water. Gunfire popped off in the distance, and my father glanced over his shoulder. In the shadows behind him stood row upon row of human-sized tanks.

Then the radiant ball of magic hidden in the core of my being exploded and more demonic magic, *my* demonic magic, roared through me.

No. Oh, please, no. It couldn't be true.

I *was* a monster.

I was an impossible creature, born of evil magic. Michael *had* created me, and even if I wanted to deny my memories of being in the maturation tank, I couldn't deny my demonic magic now writhing inside me.

"Now you're a *real* weapon." Lilith flicked a finger and her worship magic, the inky magic howling with laughter inside me, pounded in my chest.

I focused everything I had on my brands, Gideon's crackling magic, Jacob's calm stillness, and even managed to sense sensual heat from Kol. I had to force the inky magic out.

I gritted my teeth. I would God damn force it out.

With a scream, I wrapped the spiritual strength from my guys around my soul and then swept it out from my core in a massive wave and pushed against the inky magic.

The inky magic howled and clawed, but I clenched everything I had, and shoved it out.

I toppled over, too weak to hold myself up, my mind whirling. I'd been made to subjugate and kill. That was my entire reason for existing.

"Get them back in their cells," Lilith said. "I don't care what condition they're in so long as they're alive, since *someone* forced me to change my plans and make my move today."

I hadn't been born to help people or fight for justice. I'd been made to murder and destroy and force people to worship Lilith, the Hellfire Queen and — God! — my mother.

"The ambassador's funeral was going to send the perfect message, and now I have to make do with second best, so I'll take payment for your transgression from your essences."

I dragged my attention back to Lilith. She sneered, her gaze locked on me. "I'm glad you're finally home, daughter. My war can now begin."

She left with another body crushing thump that made my head spin.

"Surrender," a guy said as he and the other witches stormed down the stairs and raced to the edge of the magic circle to face us.

"Fuck, no," Marcus snarled behind me.

"Zuri," Gideon gasped. "Get Bane steady. We need that spell."

I pushed up to my hands and knees. Demonic mist curled around my forearms, licking around Gideon's brand.

I really was a monster.

Would they still love me?

I shoved that thought aside. It didn't matter. I loved them and they were getting the hell out of there. They had to warn the JP about Lilith, and above all, they had to live.

I jerked my head up and gathered the mist around my hands.

The witches grabbed their tattoos to cast a spell and the *thu-thud* of their magic pounded in my chest. With a yell, I released my power. The force disrupted their spells and crashed them into the tables and crates, drawing screams of pain.

The mist weeping from my skin thinned, and the cold hollowness in my chest where my divine light should have been sank heavier into my soul. My body shook and the unconsciousness I'd been fighting before threatened to overwhelm me. I was running out of strength and magic.

"Sebastian, cast the teleport spell," I yelled without looking behind me. My guys had to go. Now. I couldn't let Lilith drain their essence. "She has to be stopped. You have to get out of here."

A strong arm wrapped around my waist. "Not without you," Kol said, and he hauled me out of the containment spell.

My magic didn't even flare, and the strength of the bone-deep chill of magical shock crashed over me and stole my breath.

Zuri looked at me with horror and shifted away as Kol dragged me closer. Sebastian, his glow so bright it hurt to look at him, had his head down and his burned and bleeding hands pressed against his thighs, so I had no idea what he thought about me. Regan and Xavier were thankfully still unconscious, and Marcus, Jacob, and Gideon stood with their backs to me, facing the witches.

"Bane," Gideon snapped.

"Almost... got it." The muscles in Sebastian's shoulders tightened and his breath grew ragged. A circle of light flickered around him, but had yet to fully form.

One of the witches, still lying on the ground, screamed something and grabbed a tattoo on his arm.

His magic thudded, making the room lurch around me, and I jerked my hand out, praying that I had enough magic left to stop him. Red mist sputtered out of my palm and blew apart in the air. I couldn't get hold of it. I could barely focus.

Just a little more. That was all I needed. I could do this.

The witch's magic thudded again, and a blade of ice shot from his hand straight for my heart. Shit. Without my magic, I had nothing to stop him.

I wrenched my trembling body to the side, but knew as the agony of my broken ribs screamed through my chest that I wasn't going to be fast enough to get out of the way.

With a yell, Marcus dove at me. He tackled me to the ground. White lightning exploded in my chest and for a second, time froze.

It was just me and Marcus and the ice spear protruding from his back. Then the ice exploded, tearing open the wound and drawing a gut-wrenching scream from both of us.

No no no. Please, no.

Blood rushed over me, instantly soaking my shirt, and he went limp, his weight crushing me, each breath agonizing. But I could barely feel the pain. He couldn't die. None of them could die.

My demonic power burst from my skin and swept into him. It flooded his cells, wove into his essence, and clenched around his soul. I would save him. If Kol could give me his strength through his essence, I could give it to Marcus. Being half whatever-type-of-demon Lilith was had to be good for something.

"Got it." The light around Sebastian flared bright, creating a wide circle on the floor around him. "Everyone get over here."

Gideon and Jacob raced to Sebastian's side, and the teleportation spell tore me to pieces with an agonizing mix of light and darkness and raging red storm.

I was everything and nothing, hurtling through an emptiness as hollow as the feeling in my chest and as searing as my pain. A pain that grew tighter and tighter, until my wings burst free and my back hit something hard.

The air lurched from hot to cold and a wild mix of emotions flooded my chest then vanished as frozen emptiness filled me. The guys hissed and groaned, and Marcus, still on top of me, screamed and convulsed.

Oh, God!

I rolled him off me and pressed my hands over the wound in his chest. My demonic magic still churned inside him, clinging to his wound and slowing the rush of blood onto the floor, but not stopping it. Mist curled over my forearms and sank into him, burst free from his skin, and sank back in again.

Out of the corner of my eye, I caught a glimpse of my wings, and clenched my jaw in resignation. The tips of my feathers were red. My essence had probably changed, too. I wouldn't be able to hide what I really was.

Beside me, Sebastian, his skin dull with no glow at all, both arms burned past his elbows, threw up blood and collapsed. Gideon tucked his wings back but didn't pull them in, and Jacob's vampiric intensity surged, while Kol's seductive magic caressed my soul, stealing my breath.

Zuri, her horns and fangs revealed because the teleportation spell reformed us in our supernatural states, flapped grit into my face with her leathery wings as she scrambled away from me.

My pulse stalled. We were supposed to be reformed in our supernatural state. Marcus was supposed to be a wolf and he wasn't.

"Oh, my God," a feminine voice gasped. "What is that?"

We weren't alone.

Shivering from adrenaline and shock, I jerked my attention from Marcus to see where we were, and my gaze landed on the shallow cafeteria steps in Operations leading up into the hall. They were only a few feet away, so we had to be at the front of the room. All around us, the tables and chairs had been pushed back and toppled over, the force of Sebastian's spell shoving them aside to make room for us, and half of the scaffolding on the rock wall beside us had collapsed.

There wasn't anyone in front of me, so I turned to the rest of the room. All of the lights were on, but the sky out the back windows was dark, so it was still before dawn. At the far end, a dozen people, along with Cassius, stood around two large tables that had been pushed together, their chairs shoved back, a few toppled over, as if they'd quickly stood up. Half-eaten sandwiches, empty sandwich wrappers, various bottled beverages, folders, phones, and laptops littered the table, indicating we'd interrupted some kind of meeting.

Amiah and Priam, who'd been near a table halfway between us and the others — clearly not a part of whatever late night meeting had been taking place — rushed toward us.

Thank God. Marcus was going to get help.

"Cassius," Gideon gasped. "You're awake."

"That's an archnephilim," a broad-shouldered muscular man said, his eyes bright with an angelic glow. "Amiah, get back. Agents, secure it."

Marcus screamed again, his body jerking under my hands. Something crunched inside him and my demonic magic swelled, surging deeper into his essence.

Amiah stumbled to a halt a few steps from me, her gaze locked on mine. "So you're a—?"

"I am," I said, my teeth chattering and my body shaking so hard it was difficult to keep my hands on Marcus. And my mother was the Hellfire Queen, determined to restart Michael's war, except she didn't want to kill humanity, just subjugate them… and use me to do it.

I dragged my attention to Kol, afraid of what I'd see. He was the closest, still kneeling beside me, and the one most affected by learning that I really was a nephilim. And while his breath was shallow and the edge in his eyes had turned to full terror, he drew closer to me, making my heart swell with love and relief.

"I won't let her take you," he said. "I swear it."

"Who?" Amiah asked as Marcus screamed again and something tore inside him with a sickening wet sound. She dropped to her knees beside him and placed a hand on his leg, her palm glowing with her healing magic.

"Lilith," Jacob said.

Amiah gasped. "Lilith is free?"

My shaking grew stronger, but I didn't know if it was from the cold or fear. "We have to put her back in her cage before she gets stronger." *Before she can use me to kill people.*

"Get that abomination in a cell," the broad-shouldered angel snapped.

Another gut-wrenching scream tore from Marcus's clenched jaw and his body convulsed.

"They need to get to triage," Amiah said, her gaze sweeping over us. "All of them."

"In a cell," the broad-shouldered angel repeated.

"Director, wait," Gideon said, his breath wet and ragged. "Essie isn't a threat."

"But I am if Lilith gets ahold of me—"

"She's not getting ahold of you," Jacob said, taking a step ahead of me and releasing his full vampiric intensity with a breathtaking swell of power. "And neither are they."

Kol gave me a tight nod and stood, taking position beside Jacob.

Marcus gasped, and with another sickening crunch his jaw started to lengthen into his wolf's, then crunched back into a human's, as if his body couldn't figure out how to shift any longer.

"Amiah, please," I begged.

The light from her hand glowed brighter as she pumped more magic into him.

"Agents," the Director said, storming toward us with Cassius at his side, the others close behind, "secure the creature. It's dangerous."

"Lilith is the real danger," Gideon gasped, staggering to his feet, his right arm pressed tight against his side. His complexion was ashen, sweat slicked his forehead, but he squared his shoulders, ready to fight.

The Director's expression hardened and lightning crackled around his fists.

"Director, don't," Amiah said. "She's soul bound to half the team. If Lilith really is free, you'll need them."

"Gideon, listen to reason," Cassius said. "She's clearly an arch-nephilim."

"She's my mate."

"She's a war criminal."

"You know that's not true," Gideon said.

"It doesn't matter. The law is the law." Cassius took a few steps ahead of the Director and squared his shoulders just like Gideon, emphasizing their family relation. "She's a monster. An abomination. She only exists because of Michael's evil magic. I have to arrest her."

"No. You don't." A tremor shook Gideon, and a nauseating mix of his rage, fear, and exhaustion churned my stomach, mixing with the cold. "Even if you didn't know Essie, you know me. You know my mate would never be a monster."

"Gideon." The muscles in Cassius's jaw flexed. "Don't make this harder than it has to be."

"Listen to your brother," the Director said. "You're not thinking straight, agent. You're compromised."

Gideon's gaze stayed locked on Cassius's, his expression glacial. "You know I'm not."

"I know your bond is true, but it doesn't matter," Cassius said, fire curling over his hands and up his forearms. "It's the law."

"Then you're going to have to pick." The light in Gideon's eyes blazed in a brilliant nimbus around his head and his sword of divine light formed in his clenched fist. "The law or me."

ESSIE

CASSIUS STARED AT GIDEON, STUNNED, AS IF HE HADN'T EXPECTED Gideon's ultimatum, then anger and horror darkened his expression. In the brief time I'd spent with him, it was clear he needed rules, needed that certainty and structure possibly more than Gideon did. But he'd also shown me that he loved his brother and would twist his precious rules to protect him.

Now he had to choose. He couldn't twist this. The law was clear. Arrest me or don't. Those were his only options.

They glared at each other, Gideon's breath wet and shallow, and Cassius so tense he shook.

The Director shifted a step closer, the eleven others, a mixed party of six men and five woman — four with glowing angel eyes, the rest a mix of vampires, demons, and shifters — only a few steps behind. They stared at us, their expressions ranging from worried, afraid, to angry.

Tension filled the room with a palpable energy that set my nerves on fire and made my pulse race. Everyone waited, the whole room holding its breath to see what Cassius would do.

I didn't want Gideon to fight his brother, but I knew he'd never let Cassius arrest me. Even faced with Voth's enormous power, Gideon hadn't backed down from the greater demon. He'd give his life to protect me. Just like I would for him.

Marcus screamed, breaking the silence, and his shifter magic dissolved his shirt, revealing raw burned skin underneath and the ragged wound in the center of his chest, partially held together by my demonic mist. That was the only reason he was still alive, and I could only hope my power lasted long enough for Amiah to heal him. Patchy fur swept across his chest as his torso expanded, each rib cracking with a resounding snap, then sank back under his blistered skin.

"Gideon, we have to get him to triage," I said. I jerked my gaze over the rest of the group.

Zuri had dragged Regan — who, because of the teleportation spell, was now a sleek panther — and Xavier — still perfectly human — away from us, leaving a wide swath of blood on the cafeteria floor. Priam had rolled Sebastian over and pressed his palms to the unconscious fae's chest, his magic radiating around his hands.

Gideon was in rough shape, and Jacob was too pale with a small pool of blood at his feet. The blood trail we'd left while we were escaping hadn't just been from Regan and Xavier.

Kol was the only one who looked well, but by himself he didn't stand a chance against the Director of the Joined Parliament Bureau of Supernatural Law Enforcement, who was rumored to be one of the strongest angels in the mortal realm, along with eleven other supers, plus Cassius.

Gideon's eyes narrowed, his gaze still locked on Cassius. "Pick."

Cassius glared back.

Marcus screamed, more of his bones shattering.

"Pick!" Gideon yelled, and Cassius roared back at him, the cry desperate and primal.

"God damn you, Gideon." He jerked around, his fire exploding from his hands and sweeping into a massive burning wall that reached from the floor to the ceiling and all the way across.

Sweat instantly covered my body, and the air, blazingly hot, seared down my throat with every shallow breath. Zuri hauled Xavier and Regan farther away, her face a mask of horror, and the supers on the other side of the wall yelled.

"Pick up Marcus and get out of here," Cassius snapped.

Gideon turned to grab Marcus, but gasped in pain.

"I've got him," Jacob said, heaving Marcus, still screaming and writhing, onto his shoulder. My demonic mist surged around him, stretching between us, then split, still billowing and sinking under his skin as well as mine.

Amiah stood as well and placed her hand back on Marcus.

Cassius's eyes widened. "What are you doing?"

"They need medical attention." She turned to Priam. "Stay with the elite team."

"You don't have enough power to heal them all," Priam said.

She squared her shoulders. "I'll have to."

"Kol, get Bane," Gideon said. "He's not an agent. I'm not leaving him here to be interrogated."

I staggered to my feet and the cafeteria lurched, but Gideon grabbed the back of my shirt, catching me before I fell.

"Pull your wings in," he said, pressing his palm against my back.

I squeezed my shoulder blades together and his power exploded into me, forcing my wings back into my chest with an agonizing *thud*. The cafeteria lurched and darkened, and he swept me into his arms. Pain tightened his expression and his body trembled, but he didn't let go.

"Get moving," Gideon barked, waiting for the others to hurry up the stairs first.

"I've got your back." Cassius ran toward us and his fire wall shuddered, his power weakening, taking the searing heat with it.

My bone-deep chill returned and Gideon's body heat taunted me, warm enough for me to feel it but not warm enough to melt the cold inside.

Behind him, lightning shot through Cassius's fire wall and slammed into his back. He staggered, caught his balance, and kept running, but his fire vanished.

Through the smoke, the Director glared at us and barked orders. Half of the other JP agents, or whatever they were, ran after us. The rest summoned magic, their power swelling, crushing inside me and stealing my breath.

There was no way we were going to escape. We didn't have enough of a head start. Cassius needed to put up another fire wall or something to slow them down.

My demonic magic fluttered across my vision, gusting toward the rock wall.

Or *I* had to do something.

God damn it.

I mentally seized my red mist, along with every last flickering ounce of power in my soul.

Gideon and Cassius rushed up the steps, and I whipped my mist around the rock wall and wrenched, the effort burning through my body with glorious heat for a second. The rocks crashed onto the stairs with a boom and a thick cloud of dust, blocking the way behind us, just like they had when the archnephilim who'd started it all had pulled down the wall.

"That won't slow them for long," Cassius said as we barreled past the elevator and around the corner into the long hall leading to the garage.

"We just need a head start," I gasped, leaning into Gideon, desperate for warmth, any warmth.

We ran into the garage and straight onto the street, not taking a vehicle because the Director would be able to use its GPS locator to find us. Thankfully, it was early morning and we weren't near the vampire section of the Quarter, so no one was around.

Gideon's steps jarred my ribs, and the world spun around me with a mix of painful flashes of streetlight, enveloping darkness, freezing cold, and Marcus's gut-wrenching screams. I tried not to think about anything, but my thoughts kept jumping back to the truth.

I wasn't just an angel. I'd been made. My sole purpose was to kill and destroy. I wasn't supposed to exist. And my guys were risking everything, not just their careers, but their lives, to protect me.

We zigzagged from street to alley and street again, until Jacob staggered to a stop near the end of an alley, just deep enough to not be in the band of streetlight shining between the buildings.

"We can't keep running," he gasped. "We need a plan."

"We need to get off the street." Kol ran his hands through his hair. "Some place where they can't hear Marcus."

"Bane's is the closest, but I don't want to go back there," Jacob said, struggling to keep his hand over Marcus's mouth and muffle his screams while keeping him on his shoulder.

"We have to get out of the Quarter," Gideon said as he stumbled. With a groan and hacking cough, he shoved his shoulder against the alley wall and caught his balance.

"I'll take her," Cassius said, his voice gruff.

The light in Gideon's eyes flared and his grip around me tightened, putting pressure on my broken ribs.

I fought to hold back my whimper because he needed to hold me and I needed him to hold me, but it still escaped. He shot me a worried look, eased up his grip, but didn't hand me over.

"Wherever we go, it has to be good," Jacob said. "We're next to helpless in our condition."

And that was the problem. The JP would find us. There was no doubt about that. It was just a matter of time. If we hid well enough, we might have enough time for Amiah to heal all of us, but that was the catch. Where could we go where they wouldn't think to look? And who would help us?

I struggled to focus my whirling thoughts on our options. We could go to Willow, the firebird shaman. No one knew about her, but given how our last encounter with her had gone, the odds of her helping us were slim. I also doubted any of the shifter packs would go against the JP, and I'd destroyed whatever ties we had with Victoria, Union City's master vampire. Which left—

No one. There wasn't anyone else we could go to for help.

Except there was.

Please, God, don't let me be wrong. There was one other person who'd said if I called, he'd help.

The cold surged and my shaking increased, spiking agony through my chest. God, I was never going to get warm. "We have to go to Voth's."

"No." Gideon's angel glow burned brighter. "Absolutely not."

"Even I know that's a terrible idea," Cassius said. "He didn't earn the nickname the Angel of Death for nothing. Voth took great pleasure in killing nephilim during the war. He's going to love killing you."

"He said if I called, he'd come." The conversation flashed through my mind. He'd flattened us with his power, all to figure out why he didn't have a soul bond and we did. "He said they wouldn't understand me, but that he's seen my truth and that I was nothing like them. He already knows what I am."

"Are you sure?" Jacob asked.

Voth had been shocked when I'd shown him my connection to my guys, but then he'd been determined and certain. Not a hint of fear or rage. He had to have known I was one of Michael's creations... and if I really thought about it, Mystic Mavis's reaction to me when I responded to her demonic magic said she'd realized the truth, too. Except she'd been terrified of me and Voth hadn't.

"He knows," I said. He'd searched inside me and seen the truth... and so had Sebastian. Had he known that I was a monster as well?

Gideon's angel glow dimmed with worry and his eyes narrowed. I didn't need my empathy to know he didn't like the idea but knew we didn't have any other choice.

"If you're wrong, he'll kill us," Cassius said.

"I'm not wrong." A wave of darkness stole my vision, and I fought to remain conscious. I couldn't afford to pass out now, and I couldn't be wrong about Voth. *Please, don't let me be wrong.* We didn't have anywhere else we could go.

"He did say he'd help," Jacob said, his voice low.

"He's not an angel. He'll have no problem going back on his word. Especially since she's—" The muscles in Cassius's jaw clenched.

"What?" Kol snapped. "Smart? Determined? Beautiful? Mated to the four of us?"

Amiah gasped.

"He flattened us when he thought she had Gideon, Jacob, and Marcus," Kol said. "I don't want to know what he'll do when he realizes she's branded a demon."

Marcus convulsed and his mouth jerked free from Jacob's grip, his cry loud in the silence.

"We can't keep standing here," Jacob said, the muscles in his arms bulging as he fought to hold Marcus. "Voth said they, whoever they are, wouldn't understand her. He has to know she's an archnephilim. We've got no other place to go."

"Fine." Gideon drew in a ragged breath. "We go to Voth's."

Cassius threw his hands up. "This is insane."

"You can always stay here." Kol adjusted Sebastian's unconscious form on his shoulder, shifted to the mouth of the alley, and glanced out at the street beyond.

"You know I can't," Cassius said.

"Then suck it up, because we're going to Voth's and we're going to break another law to do it." He rushed out of the alley and disappeared from sight.

Jacob and Amiah hurried after him, and the sound of shattering glass followed a few seconds later.

Cassius stiffened and fire licked over his hands. "I'm going to kill your demon."

"Cassius," Gideon said, his voice gruff, jerking his brother's attention back to him. "Thank you."

"You would have died to protect her," he snarled. "I'm not losing another brother."

He stormed out of the alley, and Gideon staggered after him.

"You have— had another brother?"

"We did. Cassius doesn't like to talk about it," Gideon said. "Dominic accepted a mission to infiltrate Michael's army, but he stopped communicating with the Angelic Defense six months in." He pursed his lips. "We haven't heard from him since."

No wonder Cassius had been so determined to protect Gideon from me, and why Gideon had just about had a breakdown when Cassius had been poisoned.

"Cassius blames himself, although I don't know why. It wasn't like he had anything to do with Dominic's mission," Gideon said as he stepped out of the alley.

Kol stood a few feet down the street, reaching in through the now-broken back window of a late model minivan,

"You can't just steal a car," Cassius said.

"You and I might be able to walk to the other side of the Quarter, but no one else can." Kol unlocked the door, set Sebastian on the middle bench — since the back one was down — and climbed into the driver's seat. "Sit your ass down or we're leaving you behind."

Cassius huffed and took the front passenger seat. Gideon set me on the bench beside Sebastian, climbed in as well, and pulled me back into his arms.

Warm, so warm, and yet not warm enough. The world darkened and spun, and when it cleared, Amiah and Marcus were in the back, and Jacob was on the bench with us with Sebastian squeezed between us.

The engine sputtered and caught, and Kol put the minivan into gear. We sped away as another gut-wrenching scream tore from Marcus's throat, and my pulse lurched. His thrashing increased, and the demonic mist swirling around him grew thicker, more like strands than wisps.

"If it takes everything you have to save him," Gideon said to Amiah, "use it. The rest of us can manage."

"I'm sure you think that," she said, her tone sharp. "But it doesn't matter how much I have, it isn't going to help him. He's in transition, and healing magic can't help with that. I healed the injury in his chest, but now the most I can do is try to make him more comfortable and restart his heart if it stops. It's a matter of waiting and keeping him alive long enough to get through this." Her expression darkened, her worry clear. She didn't know if he would.

My throat tightened and tears burned my eyes. This was a nightmare. I couldn't stop shaking, couldn't do anything, and couldn't lose him. I couldn't lose any of them. "There has to be something we can do."

Marcus screamed and Amiah wrenched her attention back to him. "There isn't."

"How the hell can he be in transition?" Kol asked, speeding around a corner and heading toward Squatters' Row. "He's already a shifter."

Gideon raked his hand over his face. He looked exhausted, and his complexion was too pale and his expression haggard.

Please, God. Help me.

"Something must have gone wrong with the teleportation spell," he said.

Jacob turned in his seat to look at Marcus. "Nine people must have been too much for Sebastian in his weakened condition."

I dragged my gaze to Sebastian, and fought to focus my wavering vision. His breath was so shallow it was hard to tell if he was breathing. Blood crusted around his mouth and the left side of his face — he must have collapsed in a blood pool — and his skin was a flat white, tinged with gray with no hint of radiance.

"Then why weren't we affected?" Kol asked, taking two more quick turns.

"Because he's a shifter," Jacob said.

Marcus howled and kicked the back of my seat, jarring my broken ribs. A tear broke free. I had to do something, but I couldn't even give him strength, since we didn't share a brand.

Gideon drew in another rattling, wet breath. "Regan shifted with no problem."

"It couldn't be because he was injured," Cassius said. "You're all barely walking." His eyes narrowed. "Except you, incubus. How the hell are you all right?"

"Well," Kol said, his voice too bright, "when a man and a woman, or a woman and a woman, or a man and a man, or, well, a group of naked people love each oth—"

"Kol, please!" Gideon gasped, making Kol flinch.

"Sorry. Trying to hold my shit together. You know, because the Hellfire Queen is free and she has—" His voice broke and a wave of panic crashed through our newly formed bond, as if a wall inside him had just shattered. "She has nephilim tanks and I— The nightmares came back and—" His breath picked up, and his body started shaking almost as badly as mine.

"Just hold it together long enough to get to Voth's," Gideon said. "You can do this."

"I've been holding it together for weeks." Kol jerked the wheel, turning onto a narrow street, squealing the tires, and wrenching us in our seats. "First the archnephilim, then Essie's wings, then— I can't go back to that. I'd kill myself before I go back to that, but then I'd hurt Essie and I— Fuck, I—"

"Take a breath." Jacob reached around the driver's seat and squeezed Kol's shoulder. "You can do this. Think about why... why fate bound you to Essie."

"Because fate is fucked up, that's why. Now she's stuck with me." Kol's breath grew faster, sharp desperate gasps. "God, I love you so much." He released a manic hysterical laugh. "I'm so fucked up. I'm in love. How the hell does an incubus fall in love? And I could still snap again and hurt you. I could—"

"Hey." A tear leaked down my cheek. I couldn't help Marcus and I should have helped Kol. He'd been holding it together since we'd fought the archnephilim and I hadn't noticed. I didn't think anyone had. "You're not going to hurt me."

"You don't know that. I already did and—"

"This isn't working," Cassius growled. "He shouldn't be driving."

Another gut-wrenching scream ripped from Marcus's throat and I gritted my teeth, fighting more tears. Crying wouldn't help anything. But God, I was so tired and cold and my soul hurt for Marcus and Kol.

"Kol, please." Gideon's breath wheezed. "Take a breath and tell me why Sebastian's spell affected Marcus and not us."

"How am I supposed to know?" Kol yelled back.

"Your best guess," Gideon said. "Focus on that and not running off the road."

More of Marcus's bones crunched and the demonic mist sweeping around him billowed to the roof of the minivan.

"Well, I— Okay." Kol slowed to a safer speed, fighting his fear with an effort that made my heart hurt just watching him. He turned onto a side street at the edge of Squatters' Row, avoiding the main strip.

Just a few more minutes and we'd be at Voth's, who — *please, God* — would help us.

Darkness crept across my vision and the cold inside me started numbing everything, the physical and emotional pain, as well as my whirling thoughts.

I needed to hold on just a little longer, just until I knew my guys were safe.

Except if I was wrong about Voth, there wasn't anything I could do to protect my guys.

"We've ruled out being injured and being a shifter." Kol's grip on the steering wheel tightened, making the veins and tendons in his forearms stand out. "Maybe it's because he's not a natural shifter."

The red strands curling up from Marcus twisted and pulled apart, undulating in a breeze I couldn't feel, taunting me. All that power and I was still helpless.

Because that power wasn't in me at the moment. It was in him. Only pale, shuddering wisps drifted from my skin. I was hollow and just wanted to close my eyes. At least I'd put that magic to good use and saved Marcus. Amiah hadn't said he was dying from his injuries. I just had to hope he'd survive this transition. Had his first transition been this painful? This was horrible. I had no idea how anyone got through this kind of pain and came out the other end sane. But he'd survived his first one. He could survive this.

"Okay," Gideon said. "Anyone know if Regan is natural or not?"

"I don't know," Jacob said.

A strand curled over the back of the bench, wrapped around my arm, and sank under my skin, just like it was sinking into Marcus.

My thoughts tripped on that.

"So that could be it," Cassius said, not sounding certain. "But..."

Oh, no.

Oh, please, no.

But the moment I thought it, I knew it was true. I'd poured my demonic magic into Marcus, desperate to save him when Sebastian had cast the teleportation spell, a spell that ripped us apart and remade us. My magic must have melded inside Marcus during the spell.

I'd done it to him again. I'd made a decision and he was paying for it.

"It's my fault," I forced out between chattering teeth.

"It's not your fault," Gideon said.

"He was bleeding out." I raised my trembling blood-crusted hand and stared at the weak demonic mist swirling around it. There wasn't any other explanation. I'd fucked up. I shouldn't have used magic I didn't understand. I should have trusted Sebastian would have gotten us to Operations in time. But I hadn't. I'd just pumped raw magic into Marcus because I hadn't been thinking, I hadn't been able to lose him, and now he was transitioning into—

God, I had no idea what.

"I thought if Kol could help me with his magic, I could help Marcus just enough to get him to Amiah."

"You used your demonic magic?" Jacob asked.

"Yes." A sob broke free, the sharp breath slicing pain through my chest.

"It must have mixed with Sebastian's teleportation spell and reawakened the lycanthropy in his DNA." Gideon pressed his lips to the back of my head. "You were trying to save him."

Marcus howled, yanking my attention up, and I met Amiah's gaze, her expression hard. Even if my angelic magic hadn't been used up and I had my empathy, I'd have known exactly what she was feeling, and I couldn't argue against it.

Marcus was in agony and it was my fault. Again.

KOL

I FOCUSED ON THE FEEL OF THE STEERING WHEEL CLENCHED IN MY HANDS and the stretch of empty road ahead, illuminated only by the mini van's lights. The darkness of the unlit street crowded against my sight as the darkness inside me crowded everything else.

I just had to hold on a little longer. Just until Essie and the others were safe.

My heart lurched and power rippled from the brand Essie had seared into my body. It was proof I wasn't going crazy, that what I felt for her was true love and that the desire in her eyes when she looked at me was real and not because my magic was influencing her.

We were destined for each other and that was more fucked up then an incubus in love.

I was broken beyond repair and now she was permanently stuck with me.

They all were.

I might have thought I could pull myself together after the arch-nephilim had reawakened the worst of my nightmares, but I'd been fooling myself.

The terror that had seized me when Essie's wings had first appeared and I thought she was a nephilim had come back with a vengeance at the sight of Lilith's maturation tanks. I was barely holding it together and knew even though I loved Essie, I was a danger to her.

When I'd snapped in the alley the first time, I'd known who she was and that she'd never hurt me. Now with red demonic mist swirling around her while her essence still said she was an angel, it was blatantly obvious she was a archnephilim, and without a doubt when my night terrors took control, I'd hurt her.

And God, I'd probably watch myself doing it like I had the last time I'd attacked her and wouldn't be able to stop myself.

I glanced back at her in Gideon's arms, shivering from having bonded our souls together, tears leaking from her eyes. She was in shock and not just from using her magic. She'd just learned she'd been made to be a weapon to subjugate humankind and the instant someone other than our team had seen her, they'd turned on her.

It had played out exactly like she'd been told it would and that tore at my heart. I wanted to hold her and comfort her like I had when her bonds with Gideon and Jacob had formed, tell her that the world was wrong, that she wasn't a monster. But it was too dangerous. If I fell asleep, the nightmares could take hold and I would hurt—

"Hey!" Cassius barked and I jerked my attention back to the road, swerving around a parked car that I should have seen from a block away.

"I should have—" Essie gasped, but Marcus's scream cut her off and the rest of her words turned into a strangled sob.

"We'll figure this out," Gideon murmured, his lips pressed against the top of her head. "He'll be okay."

But we all knew that was only a hope. We might have figured out what had happened to initiate Marcus's transition, but we had no way of knowing if he'd survive it, or if he was even going to transition into a different kind of shifter at all. For all we knew Marcus's body was going to keep tearing itself apart, never finding a new form, until he died.

My chest tightened, the need to hold her stealing my breath. Essie would never forgive herself if that happened. Gideon could try to use logic for the rest of her very long life, he could beg and plead with her, but if Marcus died, she'd always believe she'd killed him.

Even if he managed to survive, his life was still in danger. All our lives were.

In the blink of an eye we'd become fugitives, hunted by the very agency that we'd devoted ourselves to.

God, it made me furious that the Director hadn't even given Essie a chance before proclaiming her a monster. Hadn't he read any of the reports about her?

She'd been willing to sacrifice herself to save us from that first arch-nephilim and again to stop Logan and Ibizual. She'd thrown herself into danger time and again to protect those who couldn't protect themselves. Did he think it was all a long con? Some kind of massive manipulation to worm her way into the JP?

It didn't make sense. Until Lilith had awakened her demonic magic, Essie's essence had said she was an angel. If she'd just presented herself as one, she could have joined the JP, plain and simple.

She hadn't needed to hide as a human who believed she was a nephilim. And adding angelic mating brands to the mix only complicated the situation even more. She could have gotten close to us just working on the team. There was no need to bond her soul with ours.

No, the Director hadn't thought at all. He'd just reacted. Like everyone else would.

We needed to find a permanent way to hide her true essence and identity and to stop the JP from tracking us. It was the only way she'd be safe. Get off the grid and go into hiding.

Except that would be lying and I had no idea if Gideon's angelic nature would allow him to do that. Hell, Essie was half angel. Would hers? Not to mention Lilith was planning on restarting Michael's war—

The image of the maturation tanks flooded my mind's eye and panic stole my breath.

Fuck.

I strained to relax, to draw breath, to not let the darkness overwhelm me. I couldn't let my fear take over.

Fucking concentrate. Stay on the road. Keep driving. Get to Voth's. Don't think about Lilith.

Except that made me think about her and how she'd ripped my essence from my body to add to her already immense power.

We hadn't stood a chance, even with the elite team as backup, and I had no idea how we were going to be able to defeat her without the help of the JP. But I knew Essie well enough to know she'd want to stop her. It didn't matter that the woman was Essie's mother. She was pure evil and Essie— No, *none of us* could let pure evil go free if there was even a slim chance that we could stop her.

The darkness inside me swelled, but I gritted my teeth and fought to keep my attention on the road. We wouldn't be able to do anything until we got to Voth's and got healing... if, of course, Voth didn't kill us for showing up with an archnephilim.

ESSIE

A FEW MINUTES LATER, WE REACHED VOTH'S HOTEL, A MASSIVE TEN-STORY 19th century building sitting on top of a gently sloping hill. We avoided the long circular driveway leading to the grand front entrance and headed to the almost as grand side door. Even at this hour, there were lights on in many of the rooms, and warm illumination glowed through the glass double doors at the side entrance. But then Voth catered to supers, including vampires, and likely had entertainment happening all night long.

Except that was going to be a problem. Even if it was weak, red mist wept from me, and given that the Director of the JP Bureau of Supernatural Law Enforcement had instantly known I was an archnephilim, there was a chance someone else would recognize what I was. In our condition, we couldn't handle any more fighting.

"Someone has to go in and get Voth," I said, as Kol parked at the back of the lot but didn't shut off the engine. And while the lot wasn't as full as it had been the other day, there were still plenty of vehicles.

"We have to get you and Marcus inside," Gideon said. "You're not getting warmer even with my body heat."

My eyes drifted shut and I forced them back open. "We can't risk someone seeing me."

And crap, if we lived through stopping Lilith, would I have to spend the rest of my life in hiding?

"Shit," Kol hissed. "And we better hope Voth has a more discreet entrance around back, because yeah, I'm not fighting who-knows-how-many supers when they see you."

"Pretty sure that's not a worry. Voth will kill us the moment we step through those doors," Cassius said.

Marcus screamed and the red mist billowed around him. I clenched my jaw, more tears leaking from my eyes, and the creeping darkness stole my vision for a second.

"Essie's identity is going to get out," Jacob said. "We're going to need to figure out what to do about that."

"First we need to hide and heal." Gideon glanced over the guys and frowned. We were all injured, burned, and covered in blood. We looked like we'd just stepped out of a horror movie. "Cassius, you're up. Tell Voth..." Gideon rubbed his face, smearing blood down one cheek, turning his haggard expression fierce. "Tell him the mated angel is cashing in on his promise."

"This is insane. And we have no idea he's actually in there." But Cassius got out of the minivan and marched across the parking lot.

"We also have to figure out what we're doing about Lilith," Gideon said, his voice soft and far away.

"Gideon, will your angelic nature let you run and hide for much longer?" Kol asked.

Amiah huffed. Guess she didn't think it would.

"If it protects Essie, yes." Gideon's embrace tightened, but thankfully not enough to squeeze my broken ribs. "But I don't think there's anywhere we *can* hide. You heard Lilith. Essie was supposed to be her weapon and she's ready to restart Michael's war. Do you honestly think we can buy a concealment spell strong enough to hide for the rest of our lives?"

The darkness swelled and I bobbed in the not-water... that was the viscous liquid in my nephilim maturation tank. But this time it wasn't warm and comforting. It was freezing, the cold seeping into every pore, every cell, chilling my soul.

"I doubt we could buy one strong enough to last the week," Jacob said from somewhere in the darkness beyond my tank. "I think the best we can hope for is that she's distracted by whatever she's planning long enough for us to come up with our own plan. And even then... Everything I've heard about Lilith said she was a powerhouse before she was imprisoned and now she also has all that extra worship magic."

My father stepped into sight and pressed his hand against the tank. He'd made a deal with Lilith to make me, then hidden me from her. Why had he changed his mind? And if he'd changed his mind, did that mean he wasn't Michael?

"Well, we can't stand up to her," Kol said. "We were literally crushed."

"The JP still has to be warned." Gideon rubbed his hands up and down my arms, trying to warm me up, but the cold was too deep, and his voice was getting farther and farther away. "They need to know Lilith is free and that she's planning something soon, and someone needs to go back for Ephraim."

Except would they even listen to us? The Director had said Gideon was compromised because of our angelic mating brand. Everyone else probably thought that, too.

My father's face re-materialized out of the darkness. Light brown hair with a hint of copper, just like mine, and gold flecks in his angel glow, also like mine. Fear tightened his expression. He glanced over his shoulder and the *pop pop pop* of gunfire sounded in the distance. Screaming drowned it out, tearing at my soul. I had to stop the pain. I had to get out of the tank, had to—

"—have to do something," Jacob said.

"For God's sake, none of you are doing anything," Amiah said, her tone sharp. "You're—"

I lurched back into the not-water. So cold. So damned cold. I was never going to get warm.

"—be ready to gun it, Kol." Gideon tensed beneath me.

Something was happening. We were in danger. I forced my eyes open and dragged my attention out the window to see Cassius running toward us, his expression hard.

"He said he'd help." Cassius hopped into the front passenger seat and glared at me. "Pull around back. He's meeting us at the loading bay."

"You don't believe him?" Gideon asked.

"We'll see what he does when he sees her," Cassius said.

Kol put the minivan in gear and drove across the sloping lot to a blocky modern addition at the back of the hotel. I fought to stay conscious, but the darkness stole my vision again and I was back in the freezing not-water.

One of my guys said something. The minivan stopped moving and the engine died. A door opened and closed and Marcus screamed, wrenching me awake.

We were in an enclosed loading bay, just big enough for one transport truck. Jacob had already gotten out and hefted Marcus — now completely naked — onto his shoulder. Across from me, Cassius leaned through the open minivan side door, the light from his eyes harsh, accentuating his hard glare at me, and hauled out Sebastian. Behind him, his expression just as hard, was Voth.

My pulse stuttered for a second. Even with his power contained — I wouldn't have been able to breathe if it hadn't been — the massive demon was terrifying. Cassius was right. In our condition, we didn't stand a chance against him.

"There's a clinic second door on the left." Voth pointed to an open door a few feet away.

"You have a clinic?" Amiah asked as Gideon lifted me out of the minivan.

"I ran my squad out of here for about ten years after the war. Then just kept it because it's useful for when a fight in my theatre goes a little too far."

Another wave of freezing darkness stole my vision, and another scream from Marcus jerked me back awake.

"—have a transition room, too?" Amiah asked. She sounded surprised.

"Like I said," Voth said, his voice a low, dangerous rumble. "I ran my squad here for a while after the war."

I dragged my eyes open. Voth's clinic was small with barely enough room for two gurneys, but it was packed with as much equipment as Amiah's mini triage in Operations. At the back stood a plexiglass wall, partitioning off the last eight feet of the room, and the only thing inside was a thin plastic-covered mattress on the floor. A shudder swept through me. It looked like a cell.

Voth opened the plexiglass door, and Jacob entered and set Marcus on the mattress, still screaming and writhing, smearing blood from the cuts and burns covering his body over the mattress's white surface.

"You're locking him up?" I said, my chattering teeth making it hard to get the words out.

"Transition isn't just dangerous for the shifter." Gideon set me on the closest gurney and sagged against it, struggling to breathe, while Cassius set Sebastian on the other one. "When his beast takes over, he could be dangerous."

A tear leaked from my eye and Gideon caught it with his thumb. "A transition only lasts a day or two at most. It'll be okay."

"His first transition lasted over a week," Amiah said, kneeling beside Marcus and placing a hand on his forehead. "Do you have sedatives?" she asked Voth. "Flurazepam or Midazolam will get him through the rest of the morning."

"In that cupboard by your head." Voth jerked his chin at Cassius, who opened the cupboard behind him and scanned the rows of boxes and vials. "There are also needles in the drawer."

"A week?" I could barely get the word out. "He suffered like this for a week?" With his bones breaking and rebreaking and his body ripping itself apart from the inside out.

"Yes." Amiah captured my gaze with hers, but her expression was so strange, or I was just so exhausted I couldn't figure out what it meant. Anger? Hurt? Regret? Sorrow?

No wonder she was so angry with me. She'd sat by his side, listening to him scream for over a week. I'd be furious too if all I could have done was listen and wait, especially when all this pain could have been prevented. I was furious now. Except I could only be angry at myself. Just like the first time, Marcus's agony was my fault.

God, how was he still in love with me? How could he have ever forgiven me? How could he now?

Cassius grabbed a vial and a needle and took them to Amiah, then helped Jacob hold Marcus down. She injected Marcus and a moment later he went limp, his breathing still ragged, but his body no longer seizing.

"He's strong," Gideon said, entwining his fingers with mine.

More God damned tears leaked from my eyes, and Jacob joined us and placed a warm hand on my shoulder. I shuddered. My insides were so frozen that even Jacob, who needed to feed and should have been cold to the touch, felt warm. "You won't lose him."

"You can't promise that," I said. And they couldn't promise I wouldn't lose him even if he survived.

"Okay." Amiah stood and raked her gaze over us, then strode to Sebastian and placed a hand over his heart.

Blinding light radiated from her palm, but I couldn't shut my eyes, couldn't take my gaze away from Marcus, bleeding, naked, and sprawled on the mattress. Beside me, Gideon's breath rattled wet and heavy, while Jacob's hand on my shoulder trembled. My teeth chattered and my shivering turned the once-spiking agony in my chest to constant gasping pain.

Voth said something and left. I was too dizzy and exhausted to pay attention to his words. I wasn't sure if Cassius went with him or not. One moment Cassius was in the clinic, then I blinked — I guess I'd actually closed my eyes — because when I opened them he was gone.

Amiah stepped into sight and placed a hand on my cold, empty chest above my heart. I had nothing left in me. I didn't even have faint wisps of demonic magic curling from my skin any more.

"Can you warm her?" Gideon asked. I couldn't hear the wet rattle in his breath any longer, so Amiah must have healed him.

"Not if I want to fix her ribs." For a second Amiah looked exhausted, then my vision wavered and her expression returned to hard and angry. "I haven't got much left. You and Sebastian were in rough shape. I have no idea how you've been running around carrying her."

Agonizing heat screamed through my chest as Amiah shot her healing magic into me, and the room vanished into darkness.

"—sedation won't help with her condition, she still needs to be warmed up," Amiah said, "and I don't know if Voth has heating pads."

"I've got her." Blazing hot hands slid under me and cradled me against a searing chest, his T-shirt sticky with blood. His blood. "But I shouldn't be alone with her."

"Kol." I pressed my hand over his heart. It beat too quickly, and his worry and fear seeped through our barely formed bond. "You're not going to hurt me."

"You don't know that," he murmured. "If Gideon hadn't stopped me in the alley outside City Hall, I would have killed you."

"But you didn't," Jacob said.

"I could have. I even knew it was you, knew deep down you wouldn't hurt me, and I still couldn't stop myself." The muscles in his jaw tightened and little pieces of my soul started to shatter. "It's like there's another me that takes over. The me that would do anything, kill anyone, to never go back to that."

"It'll be okay," I said.

"It won't be. That me is still in here. What happens when I wake from a nightmare and find myself in bed with a—" His breath picked up and his body shook. "With a—"

"A monster?" My throat tightened and I wanted to scream at Kol's heartache, at the tear in his soul, and all the things he'd suffered. And I wanted to scream at the truth. Michael had made me. I was a creature created from evil magic who shouldn't exist. I endangered the lives of all my guys, and there wasn't a damned thing I could do about that.

"You're not a monster," Gideon said, his expression stern. He turned to Kol. "And you're not going to hurt her."

"I wish I was so certain."

I raised my gaze to his, his hellfire mesmerizing, stealing my breath and filling me with sudden, aching need. But when I focused past the hellfire, the look in his eyes was so scared it turned my aching need to grief.

Gideon brushed another tear from my cheek — I hadn't even realized it had fallen. "Come on. We're exhausted and not thinking straight. Let's clean up and get some sleep." He turned to Amiah and set a keycard in a numbered cardboard sleeve on the gurney. "When Cassius is done with Voth, tell him to watch Marcus and get some rest."

Kol carried me out of the clinic, my soul begging to stay with Marcus. He needed me. God, I couldn't leave him when he was in such pain. But I could barely keep my eyes open and I couldn't stop shivering. I was useless to Marcus and everyone else. If I didn't get some rest and warm up, I'd continue to be useless. Amiah said the sedative would help him for the rest of the morning. I had a few hours at least to pull my shit together.

We headed down a plain hall, the exposed cinderblock walls painted white, the floor an institutional gray laminate, and the lights above long, glaring fluorescent bulbs. Jacob and Gideon walked ahead of us, Jacob's movements slow as if he were still in pain. At least Gideon looked better. Not perfect, but he no longer held his arm against his side as if his ribs were broken.

About halfway down the hall, Gideon stopped at a plain door with a card reader, unlocked it, and let us into a simple hotel room. The light on the table by the queen-sized bed and the one in the bathroom had already been turned on, revealing a clean and tidy room, decorated in beiges and browns with green accents. A thick curtain covered the window on the back wall, pulled tight to keep out the sunrise which was only a few hours away. The bathroom looked a lot like my bathroom in Operations, just big enough for a sink with some counterspace, a toilet, and — unlike my room in Operations — a walk-in shower instead of a tub. Given how opulent the side door lobby had been, I doubted Voth let guests stay there. If the room was used at all, it was most likely a room for visiting entertainers who were performing in Voth's massive theatre.

"Kol, you and Essie get cleaned up." Gideon looked at the bed as if he wanted to sit, then glanced at his bloody clothes and leaned against the wall instead and held out his wrist. "Jacob, let's see if we can't seal shut the wound in your side that you've been trying to hide."

I opened my mouth to offer my blood, but both Gideon and Jacob glared at me.

"Don't even think about it," Gideon said, and he jerked his chin to the bathroom. "You're barely conscious and you're shivering so hard I'm afraid for your teeth."

Kol's pulse picked up and I was certain it wasn't with desire. "We should wait, or I'll feed Jacob and Gideon, you—"

"She needs you right now," Jacob said, his expression exhausted and sad. "You're the warmest and there isn't enough room for all of us in that shower. Leave the door open. We won't let you hurt her."

"Kol," I said, pulling his attention to me, his face wavering through the encroaching darkness. "I trust you."

"Didn't you hear me in the clinic? You really shouldn't." But he stepped into the bathroom and sat me on the closed toilet lid. "You shouldn't have claimed me, either."

"Even if I'd had a choice, I would have claimed you." I leaned into him, drawn not just to his warmth but his soul. "You belong. You're mine, just like Marcus and Jacob and Gideon. And I will fix this. I promise." I knew I could help him with my empathic magic—

Except I didn't. Not really. I'd tried to save Marcus and now he was in agony. I didn't want to do that to Kol, too.

Shit. All right. Fine. Even if I couldn't help him with my empathy, I'd find a way to help him. Whatever it took.

He knelt in front of me, his eyes filled with yearning and heartache. "I can't be fixed."

With a sigh, he grabbed the bottom of my blood-encrusted T-shirt and drew it up over my head, but gasped, his gaze on my chest, his eyes wide with—

I had no idea, but it wasn't fear, so I couldn't be injured... especially since Amiah's magic would have healed anything serious.

Which meant my chest had shocked...? Surprised...? Jeez. It had gotten a reaction from an incubus. I didn't know if I should laugh or cry.

"Pretty sure you've seen breasts before," I said through numb lips.

Maybe if I made a joke, it would change the mood. "Mine are pretty average." That, and I still wore a bra. I was certain he'd seen me without my top on... hadn't he? Why couldn't I remember? But I could barely concentrate and—

"They're so much more than average," he said, a whisper of his usual wry smile pulling at his lips. "But I was looking at this. It's so beautiful." Kol brushed a tentative finger across my collarbone, drawing a shiver of desire that was quickly consumed by the cold and darkness threatening to overwhelm me. "And so wrong."

I dragged my attention down, my gaze moving in slow motion. Delicate gold threads curled from my shoulder along the top of my right breast. I reached for Kol's T-shirt but he nudged my hands away and took it off, exposing the breathtaking expanse of his sculpted chest and abs. The stab wound in his chest was gone, the only evidence he'd taken the deadly injury the hole in his T-shirt and all the blood crusted on his skin.

Just like me, he had gold threads curling from his shoulder across his collarbone and over the top of his right pec. The mesmerizing design shimmered as if the threads were real gold reflecting sunlight, and I pressed my hand over it, savoring the heat radiating from his body. So warm. I needed to get closer, needed him wrapped around me.

"God, I'm so in love with you," he said as he straightened, my hand sliding down his abs, before he stepped back out of reach. The distance made the cold grow stronger, and even with my jaw clenched, I couldn't stop my teeth from chattering. But he undid his fly and shoved his bloody jeans off his narrow hips, releasing his full thick erection, and for a second the cold and darkness vanished. There was only his breathtaking body and his desire for me.

Holy smokes. My mouth went dry in anticipation, even though I was really too weak to do anything about it. He was so beautiful, so...

The darkness surged, and the bathroom started to tip.

Kol's face lurched into sight, suddenly close — he'd moved and I'd missed it.

"Come on, Essie. Hold on just a little longer. Guys," he called over his shoulder, balancing my weight against his chest. "This isn't going to work. She's barely conscious. I doubt she can stand long enough to get her jeans off, let alone shower. She's been conscious now longer than she ever was when she claimed you two. We need to get her in bed."

Yes. In bed. With all of them. Finally.

Except I didn't have Marcus. He was in Voth's clinic, his body tearing itself apart because I'd fucked up again. I needed to go to him. Now. *Now now now.*

Not while you're useless.

My throat tightened and I wanted to scream at wanting to cry and scream.

God damn it, I could deal with it. All of it. Marcus *would* survive, even if, once I'd regained some strength, I had to go back to the clinic and brand him, knocking myself out for who knew how long. And I *would* stop Lilith. I didn't know how, but I'd figure something out... just as soon as I could stop shaking... and see straight... and—

"Go," Jacob said from out in the bedroom, his voice that sexy rumble I loved so much. "I can hold out."

"Okay." Gideon stepped into the bathroom and stripped. He was bulkier than Kol, his shoulders broader — although not nearly as broad and bulky as Jacob — and just as breathtaking. The light in his eyes blazed, capturing my soul, and I soared in a beautiful summer sky for a second... an eternity...

Kol's heat vanished, and when I dragged my gaze away from Gideon, my incubus was in the shower, quickly scrubbing away the blood on his body, the water and soap sliding over his sculpted muscles.

Oh, wow. My pulse picked up and desire unfurled, hot and needy within me. Gideon unhooked my bra, helped me stand, and turned me into Kol's now clean arms. My back slid against his wet chest and a shiver swept through me, although now I couldn't tell any more if the shiver was from the cold or my desire.

Gideon stripped me of my shoes, jeans, and undies, and Kol helped me stagger into the hot shower spray. He wrapped his arms around me, holding me close, and I leaned my head back, trying to press as much of my flesh against his as possible.

A whisper of his sensual magic slid across my senses, turning my nerves hypersensitive, as Gideon ran a soapy washcloth over my branded arm, sending a tiny tremor of climax shuddering through me.

"Jeez, sorry. I'll pull it back," Kol said, his voice gruff, and the heat of his magic vanished, making me shake with cold even though I was in a steaming shower and leaning into him, his demonic body temperature gloriously warm.

"Please don't. It's warm." And I wanted it. With Kol's magic, I could forget everything, just for a moment. Even if I couldn't do much about the desire it inspired, I could savor the feel of being captured between the hard, slick bodies of two of my guys.

"Okay." Kol's sensual heat swept back in, and a moan escaped my lips.

Gideon stepped closer, his erection brushing my belly, and ran the cloth over my other arm, scrubbing away Kol's and Marcus's blood.

I gave in to the sensation of the pulsing water and the washcloth against my skin, and of Kol's heat and hardness, and Gideon's as well, pressed against me.

Gideon ran the cloth up my belly and circled the soapy fabric over my right nipple and across my new brand. My breath hitched and he dipped in and captured my mouth in a slow, sensual kiss that made me throb. God, I needed him.

I needed both of them.

I needed all of them.

"Gideon," I murmured against his lips, my voice breathy, the darkness flickering over my vision.

"I thought she was going to kill you." He tangled his hand into my hair. "I thought we were going to lose you." The wash cloth landed on my foot with a wet *plop*, and he ran his free hand up my belly to my breast as his kiss turned rough and desperate.

My breath picked up, and Kol shifted his grip to slide his fingers down my abdomen and into my curls. His magic swelled, heating me from the inside out. Gideon kissed me with a desperation that made my soul ache, like if he kissed me hard enough and long enough everything would be all right.

I kissed him back with the same need. I couldn't lose him or any of them. And it had been so close.

Kol brushed his finger over my clit, back and forth, as Gideon stole my breath with his lips. The shower spun with my exhaustion and need until Kol's power swelled into a gentle climax that swept through me, bringing with it a soft, warm darkness.

After that, my consciousness flickered between darkness and fuzzy flashes of reality. The guys rubbed me down with a thick towel. Kol carried me to bed, drawing me tight against his hot body and pulling up the heavy comforter. Gideon fed Jacob, showered, then climbed into bed under the covers with us, settling in front of me. Jacob showered as well, and fell asleep on the floor propped up against the side of the bed.

The flashes dimmed and I bobbed in the not-water, a wisp of inky magic curling around me. I needed to push it back, not let Lilith's magic control me. I needed to be at Marcus's side, even if there wasn't anything I could do for him. My soul cried. Our soul bond was different than what I shared with the other guys, but just as strong, and knowing when he woke he'd be in agony shattered me.

My father's face materialized out of the darkness, his eyes filled with fear, and I tried to ask him why. Why had he made a deal with Lilith? Why steal me from her? Why hide me and leave me with a human woman?

But the moment I opened my mouth to ask, a scream tore through the darkness and heart-stopping terror stole my breath.

ESSIE

Everything within me froze with a fear so absolute I couldn't breathe or move or think. There was no light or joy or salvation. The inky magic and the worry about Marcus was gone. There was only fear and emptiness, and screaming, gut-wrenching cries of desperation.

No, please. I promise. I promise. Kol begged. *Please. I won't go back. I can't go back.*

I fought to wake up. This had to stop. He couldn't carry on like this. I had to do something, and my empathy hadn't hurt anyone... yet—

No. I had to try. I couldn't let him suffer any longer. I had no idea how he'd survived like this for so long and how he'd managed to hide it from everyone.

You can't make me. I won't, Kol hissed, and his terror turned to searing anger.

Something heavy crushed my chest.

I won't.

My body burned and I fought to breathe. His rage was overwhelming, threatening to consume me.

I wrenched at my consciousness. If I didn't wake, his emotions were going to shatter me.

My eyes flew open, but the crushing fire didn't vanish. It grew stronger.

I still lay with my back against Kol's chest, but his arms were vises around my ribs. Gideon — lying in front of me — opened his eyes, and a second of panic flashed across his expression before Kol screamed again and Gideon's attention snapped to me.

"I won't go back." Kol's voice broke and his grip tightened. "Please. I can't. I can't."

"Kol, wake up," I gasped, grabbing his wrist and trying to pry at least one of his arms off me.

"I promise. Don't hurt her. Don't—" He tensed and screamed as if he were in agony, and the fire of his rage snapped back to freezing terror.

"Kol, I can't breathe."

Gideon's eyes widened and he shoved the comforter back, exposing all of us, in bed and naked.

"No. You can't— I won't—" A heartbreaking sob escaped his lips. "Don't make me."

"Kol." Gideon grabbed Kol's arm, but Kol wrenched away, yanking me with him, and pressed his back against the headboard, his arms still so tight around me I was afraid he'd break my ribs.

"No," Kol gasped. His eyes were open but unfocused, as if he were seeing something else. "You can't make me. I won't hurt her."

His terror lurched back to rage then snapped cold again, his emotions heaving inside me, freezing and burning, and always with pain, so much emotional pain. I gasped in short, sharp breaths, and specks of darkness danced at the edge of my vision, a sure sign I was about to pass out.

"Jesus." Jacob scrambled onto the bed — also naked because we'd all showered and hadn't had clean clothes to change into.

Kol curled around me, as if he were protecting me from his nightmare, and snarled like an animal, his face a mask of primal desperation and rage. Jacob hesitated, his expression tight, his complexion still a little too pale. He wasn't fully recovered.

"No. I won't let you. Please." Kol's snarls turned to sobs again, his voice so painfully young and broken. God, I had to help him, had to stop this. "Please, don't. Please."

Another lurch of emotions and the heat inside me tightened, whirling into a ball of blazing divine light. Wisps of my demonic magic burst from my skin and the darkness in my vision deepened.

"Kol, please." I clawed at his arm. I wouldn't be able to help him if I passed out. "Let go."

"I'll kill every last one of you," Kol spat. "I swear to God, I'll kill you."

Gideon grabbed Kol's shoulder, and Kol wrenched around and rammed his fist into Gideon's chest, shoving him off the bed.

Jacob lunged in and seized Kol's arm before he could grab me again.

Kol screamed. His fingers dug into my skin and a blazing agony exploded through the new brand on my chest.

"I'll kill you. You can't take me back. I won't go back."

I wrenched out of Kol's grasp and fell off the bed onto my butt as Jacob yanked Kol around and wrapped him in a bear hug, Kol's back against his massive chest.

Kol howled and kicked. His hellfire barely glowed, miniscule pinpricks of red light in his dark eyes, and his breath was too fast. Golden light blazed from his brand, bathing half his face in light and half in shadow from the dimly lit hotel room, and his lurching emotions made the room spin. The burning mix of his rage and my power seared my skin, and the agony in our brand flared, releasing a burst of red demonic mist from my skin.

"Don't touch her. Don't hurt her," Kol begged.

"Kol, wake up." Jacob's intense gaze met mine over the top of Kol's head, his expression clear. This was bad. And I couldn't help wondering if he'd ever seen Kol like this or had realized the depth of his pain.

"Please. Essie. Please," Kol sobbed. Grief slammed into me, stealing my breath, and a thick mist filled the air. My angelic magic surged, swelling to my palms with the gentle heat of strength, not destructive divine light, and I climbed back onto the bed before I realized what I was doing.

"Essie, get back." Gideon jerked to his feet and grabbed my arm, yanking me away from Kol. "Jacob, hold him until I can get Amiah and a sedative."

Kol wrenched in Jacob's grip and slammed his head back, but wasn't high enough to hit Jacob in the face with the back of his head. My demonic mist swelled, whipping around me in a wind I couldn't feel, and Kol's eyes widened. Frozen terror turned the mist to snow that vanished before it hit the comforter.

"No, please. Stop. Stop!" Kol cried.

"Kol, it's okay." I mentally grabbed some of the stillness that always radiated through Jacob's brand and pushed it into Kol's new burning one.

He tensed, his expression stunned.

"Gideon, let me go." Sedating Kol would only prolong his agony and

I had the power to help him right now. Except my brand with him was too new, and I couldn't risk it not being strong enough to help him. I needed to touch him.

"No," Gideon said. "He's going to hurt you. We need to sedate him."

"If this doesn't work, then yes."

Gideon glared at me. "He'll never forgive himself if he hurts you."

I pressed my hand over Gideon's, the one that still gripped my arm, and pushed a little of Jacob's stillness into him.

He shuddered and yanked his hand back. "Don't do that. I can't protect you if I'm zoned out."

"Whatever you're going to do, do it, Essie," Jacob said. Kol's breath was picking up again and the wild desperation had returned to his eyes, along with his lurching fear and rage.

I lunged forward before Gideon could stop me and captured Kol's cheeks between my palms. My magic surged. *Please work. Please let me be able to help him.*

My heat flooded him and his body seized. I fought to keep hold of his face while Jacob strained to hold his body.

Kol kneed me in the ribs, and Gideon scrambled in behind me and pinned Kol's legs to the bed.

"Jacob, don't encourage her," Gideon said.

"She's an empath—" The seizure released Kol and he rammed his elbow into Jacob's gut, drawing a grunt of pain. "Maybe she's strong enough to heal him."

"He's already been to all the best empathic healers," Gideon said.

"And he didn't have a soul bond with any of them," Jacob shot back.

Kol snarled and dug his nails into Jacob's arm, drawing blood.

"Essie—" A shadow passed over Gideon's summer-sky eyes. "He just needs time to regain his balance. It's all we can do for him."

"No, there's a tear in his soul." And I was going to fix it.

God, please, let me be able to fix it.

I closed my eyes and gave in to the angelic light within me. My demonic magic swirled around it but didn't meld with it, as if my empathy was purely angelic. The light poured into every one of my cells until I was nothing but light, a being of pure illumination... with a writhing core of darkness—

I pushed that thought aside and let the light and warmth sweep deeper into Kol, filling him like it filled me. It reached all the way to the core of his being, where the horrible infected darkness lay. A darkness so different than what lay within me. Faced with the horrendous tear in his soul, it was easy to see that my darkness was primal, celestial, neither good nor bad, just like my light. Kol's tear was gangrenous, as if the horrors he'd experienced had warped his core essence, and he'd been holding himself together — probably without even knowing it — by force of will alone.

Please, he cried. *I can't go back. I can't live like this.*

You won't. I promise. My pulse stalled as realization hit me. All this time, I hadn't just been dreaming about Kol. When I'd been shot, he'd poured his essence into me to save me and my magic had held onto it and picked up on his heart's desire. And while I might have just branded him, it was clear my soul had chosen him weeks ago. Perhaps from the moment I'd first seen him, just like I had with Marcus, and, if I was being honest with myself, just like with Gideon and Jacob.

Please, Essie. Please love me.

I do. I always did.

My magic swelled in and around the tear, curling over the edges and burning into the infection. The darkness shuddered. I was doing it, mending the agony he'd been living with for over twenty years. Finally, my empathy was good for something.

But then Kol jerked. I didn't know if it was just his soul or his body as well. He released a heartrending scream, and the darkness surged. It whipped into me, consuming my light and infecting my essence with a sudden ferocious blast. Horror and agony stole my breath. I was drowning in terror, too small and weak to fight.

No, please. I can't hurt them. I won't hurt them. But I would. I couldn't withstand the pain. I would beg them to stop, tell them I'd be good, let them use me, hurt me, hurt any one they told me to, do anything to make it stop.

I struggled to break free, but Kol mentally clung to me and the infection ripped my essence to shreds, whirling it around and around, giving Lilith's inky magic, magic I'd thought I'd gotten rid of, room to push back inside me. I was no longer a being of light, but of pain, screaming, consuming pain. I couldn't breathe, couldn't think. All I could do was suffer.

No.

I seized a piece of my essence from the infected darkness and clung to it. I was stronger than this. I had to be. For Kol's sake. For all my guys.

Lilith's inky magic whispered the promise of immense power, the power of a goddess, but I concentrated on my brands and kept my soul strong. Becoming a goddess was a lie. I'd only become Lilith's puppet if I let her magic in.

I grabbed another piece of my essence and another, rebuilding myself against the whirling vortex. With each piece, my power grew stronger, brighter, hotter. It squeezed Lilith's inky magic deep inside me until I could barely sense its presence again, and I flooded my light back into Kol, spinning it around the edges of the tear in his soul.

The infection snapped, its darkness slicing at my essence, but I gritted my teeth and pumped in more power. All of my power. I drained myself of my angelic magic, flooding it into Kol, until he was the being of pure light, the infection gone, and I was a being of celestial darkness, not a glimmer of light left.

The tear sealed shut, leaving an ugly scar, but one I knew wouldn't give him night terrors like the infection had, and I collapsed forward, my body too weak to hold me up.

"How did you do that?" Kol gasped as he hugged me tight. He shook as much as I did, his pulse racing. "You didn't just push it back to where I'd tried to lock it away. You took its power. No one's ever been able to do that."

"Half archangel empath," Jacob said, wrapping his arms around both of us.

"For the love of God," Gideon said. "Stop doing things like that."

I turned my head just enough so I could look at him. His eyes were wide and his fear, barely felt with the sliver of angelic magic I had left, cold in my chest... which felt weird. Hollow yet not hollow at the same time. I'd drained myself of my angelic magic again and my weaker demonic magic couldn't fully take its place. I was pretty sure my head would start pounding soon. But it was so worth it.

"Gideon." I held out a trembling hand to him.

He took it and Kol released me enough so I could shift and capture Gideon's lips with mine in a slow sensual kiss that told him how much I cared for him. Strength seeped from him into me and a crackle of electric magic shivered up my arm.

"You know I had to," I said.

"Doesn't mean it didn't scare me." He kissed me again, his passion fueling my desire. I hated that I'd scared him, but I didn't mind the kisses that came with it.

Kol groaned and shifted, his erection digging into my hip. "We need to make some decisions before things go too far."

Right. I was exhausted and naked in a bed with almost all my guys.

And the moment I thought that, the urge to jump up and go to Marcus, sit with him, suffer with him, squeezed in my chest. Except I had no idea when Kol and I would have a chance to seal our bond. There might not be another opportunity any time soon, and I wasn't going to allow a repeat of what had happened with Gideon.

Lilith's inky magic, still clinging to my cells, whispered and cajoled. If I let it in, I'd be able to help Marcus. He wouldn't have to suffer.

No. I concentrated on my brands, rooting my soul deeper inside my body, and held it back, then returned my attention to my guys. After yesterday, I knew both Gideon and Jacob were fine with all being together in bed, and I doubted Kol would argue. But—

I pulled away from Gideon.

"I know we don't have a lot of time, but Kol and I are going to seal our bond." And this was something I wanted to do with only him. "Just us."

Gideon flashed me a warm smile, no hint of jealousy in his expression or radiating through our bond. "We'll give you two some privacy." He lifted his gaze to Kol. "Treat her gently. She almost died yesterday."

The hellfire in Kol's eyes flared. "I'll treat her exactly the way she wants."

"Please don't." Gideon climbed off the bed and grabbed a towel from the floor. "We all know she has no sense of self-preservation."

"She can draw strength from three of us now. She can have it anyway she likes," Jacob said, pulling me closer to Kol so he could reach past the incubus and kiss my forehead. My vampire still looked pale and exhausted and I was going to need to help top him up — since his hunger was stuck on me and my blood was more potent than any of my mates — but we could deal with that after Kol and I sealed our bond, and after I went to Marcus, and after we figured out a plan to deal with the JP and Lilith, and—

"You two have fun," Jacob said. "We'll leave clothes outside the door."

The guys found robes in the small closet by the bathroom and left, closing the door with a loud *click* that made my pulse jump.

I was alone, naked, and in bed with Kol. My incubus.

"So," Kol said, his voice husky, his gaze capturing mine. "How *do* you like it?"

ESSIE

A SHIVER OF ANTICIPATION SWEPT THROUGH ME, AND THE AIR TURNED HOT and humid. His hellfire filled his eyes with an intense sultry desire, and all thought of being cold and exhausted vanished. He might not be able to do anything about the hollow feeling in my chest, but I already wasn't cold.

"Do you like slow and sensual, like Gideon?"

He skimmed his fingers up my jaw, drawing another shiver, cupped my cheek, and dipped in. His lips brushed against mine, just a whisper of a kiss, making my breath hitch before he pulled away.

His awe and love swelled through our brand, and I leaned into his touch. He pressed his lips back to mine, this time with a full, soft, tender kiss, and the warmth from his brand deepened, turning sensual and unfurling a breath of his magic within me. But his kiss remained tender, reverent, slowly, oh so slowly building my passion, until I was alight and floating with desire.

"Or," he said against my lips, "do you like fierce, like Marcus?"

He cupped my other cheek, capturing me between his palms, and the kiss turned ferocious. His tongue invaded my mouth, and the air around me grew steamy. The desire radiating through our brand surged, making me gasp. He devoured my gasp and stole the rest of my breath as his magic sank lower, drawing a delicious ache. Except his power didn't grow stronger, as if he was waiting to see what I truly desired.

I tangled my fingers into his hair, unable to do anything but hold on and give in to the ferocity of his desire. My insides seared with need, mine and his. The room started to spin and he pulled his lips away and pressed his forehead to mine, his chest heaving, his breath just as fast as mine.

"Or," he gasped, "do you prefer a little pain, like Jacob."

He grabbed my hair, his nails biting into my scalp, and jerked my head back to a painful angle. But a sliver of his magic turned the pain to exquisite need, and my whole body throbbed. He crashed his mouth back onto mine, dominating me with his strength and passion. His free hand scratched down my neck to my breast, and he pinched my nipple, spiking more pain and another bone-melting curl of magical bliss.

Holy fuck.

I moaned into his mouth, every nerve aching for him, my head spinning with sensation. Pain and pleasure, wild dominance, sensual awe. I'd take it all, anyway he wanted it.

His hold on his magic slipped and a whisper of a climax shuddered through me, making me gasp.

He wrenched his lips away and released me, his hellfire licking his cheeks, and I clung to his shoulders to keep steady, lightheaded from his kiss.

"Jesus, Essie." He clenched the comforter on either side of him as if he wanted to touch me but needed to control himself. "It really wasn't sex magic, just the strength of your soul bonds."

"I told you," I said, breathless.

"And your desire is just as strong no matter how I kiss you."

"Probably a good thing, given I'm in love with all four of you."

A hint of a wicked smile pulled at his lips. "Variety is the spice of life."

"So—" Another whisper of a climax shivered through me. "How do *you* like it?"

"Whatever way satisfies you the most," he said, his voice husky.

I bit back a moan. "Whatever way?"

"You want it different every time, I'll do my best." His hands, still clenching the comforter, shifted closer to my legs, his gaze holding me captive.

My pulse picked up with just the anticipation of him touching me again.

"You want to dominate me, you want me to dominate you, you want pain, just ask." His thumbs brushed the outsides of my knees, and my breath stalled.

Jeez, just a touch. On my knees. God, he could just look at me, he wouldn't even need to use his magic, and I'd come.

"If you want to watch me do one of the other guys—" He flashed a wicked smile that made his eyes light up, and his hands slid to the top of my knees, sweeping a shudder of need through me. "Not sure how they'd take that. It'd probably be better if they did me. But I'm game for that."

I wasn't sure what the others would think of that, but I had a feeling Kol had found a new thing to tease them about.

His fingers brushed up the top of my thighs. "If you want me to watch while you do the other guys—" He frowned as if he were considering taking that back, and given how he'd been so desperate to get away from me because he couldn't have me, I wouldn't have blamed him.

How ironic that out of all my guys, he'd be the one who wasn't okay with group sex.

"It's okay if you can't watch," I said.

He pressed his palm against my collarbone atop his brand. "You want me, too."

"Yes."

"I'll give you the stars if you ask for them."

"I wouldn't ask for it if it hurts you," I said.

"Watching you with them won't hurt me." He traced a line in his brand with his index finger, his thumb dipping dangerously close to my nipple.

Oh, God. I was going to lose my mind, and I was loving every second of it.

"Because I don't have to just watch any more and *I* can make you come, too."

"Yes, please."

He captured my mouth with his again, his love and passion for me swelling through our brand, and he urged me to lie back on the bed.

His emotions were overwhelming, bright, hot, pure, and amazed. He'd never been in love before, and given what he'd said to me in Lilith's prison, he probably hadn't thought he'd ever be in love.

I tangled my fingers into his hair, deepening the kiss, and let my love for him course through our brand, drawing a startled gasp. Then his sensual magic swelled and all thoughts of love vanished. There was only aching, glorious need.

He kissed me until the room spun again, trailed his lips across our brand to my breast, and worked my nipple into a tight bud with his tongue. He worshiped one breast then the other, sucking and stroking until I was panting and squirming underneath him, teetering on the edge of climax.

"Definitely not average," he murmured against my breast, then kissed his way down my belly. "Nothing about you is average."

His breath teased my curls and I bit back a moan. Every nerve thrummed for him, my body heavy, liquid bliss. He slid his hands up the insides of my thighs, urging my legs to spread wider and make room for him. With a low masculine hum of pleasure, he slowly — so fucking slowly! — kissed a trail from my knee up my thigh.

"Kol," I gasped. "You're driving me crazy."

"That's the plan." He teased his tongue along the seam where my hip met my torso, making my breath hitch. Another lick and I tangled my fingers in his hair, desperate for his mouth and tongue on me, satisfying me.

"Kol, please." My thumbs brushed the base of his horns, drawing a moan and sending a rush of hot breath over my core.

Oh, God. My climax twisted tighter and another wave of sensual bliss swept over me.

Another teasing lick, so close. I stroked the base of his horns again. Two could play this game, and with a shuddering groan, he swept his tongue over my clit.

Sensation shot straight to my core. I gasped and jerked, unable to hold still. He grabbed my hips and swept his tongue over my clit again. He licked and sucked, building the pressure and speed. I writhed against his grip, every nerve alight, drawing closer and closer to climax. Then he added his fingers, sliding two inside me with a firm stroke and hitting just the right spot.

Stars snapped behind my lids and I hadn't even climaxed yet. He stroked and sucked, his magic whirling into a massive wave that crashed over me with thundering bliss.

He continued to gently stroke me, bringing me down, until the glorious tremors released. Then, with a soft kiss on my clit, he shifted to lie stretched out beside me, his head propped in his hand, staring at me with a slightly dazed smile.

"That's one." His love pulsed through our brand, sending an aftershock trembling through me and stealing my breath. "If it were just me,

I'd make you come all day long. But I have a feeling the others might object to that."

And I couldn't stay away from Marcus for much longer. Even riding the bliss of an amazing climax, my insides were twisting with the need to be by his side. He, out of all of my guys, needed me the most right now.

Another aftershock shivered through me, drawing a gasp from me and a heart-stopping smile from Kol.

"I love that sound." He brushed a lock of hair away from my face, and a curl of his magic slipped into me, making me gasp again.

"Just that sound?" I asked, breathless.

"You also make amazing sounds when I touch you." His smile turned wicked and he teased a finger down between my breasts to my abdomen. "And when I kiss you."

His wicked expression grew hungry. Every nerve within me ached, suddenly hyperaware of his touch, his breath, his erection against my thigh.

"You scream their names when you come with them inside you." His hunger deepened and my insides turned to molten desire. "Scream my name."

Oh, yes. I crashed my mouth against his, my need for him making me wild. I didn't think I'd ever get enough of him, of any of my guys. And while a part of me knew that the frenzy of our newly made bonds would fade, my desire for them wouldn't.

Kol grabbed my knee, drew my leg up over his, and teased his fingers through my wet folds. I moaned into his mouth. He was going to drive me insane. Slow and sensual was nice, and I'd take it again, but right now I needed something harder.

With a growl, I pushed him onto his back and straddled him. "You want me to scream? Make me."

"Challenge accepted." He thumbed my clit and sent a shock of magic through me.

My head jerked back and my muscles clenched on the verge of climax again. But he yanked his magic back. It whooshed out of me, taking the climax with it, then surged in again, stealing my breath.

Holy shit.

My hips bucked, grinding against his erection. His eyes rolled back in pleasure, and he sent another pulse of bliss sweeping through me then took it away. With a groan, I wrapped my hand around his length, savoring his girth, knowing he'd fill me completely, and aligned him with my opening.

He gripped my hips, his gaze locked on mine, his desire flooding me. I slid him into me with a strong, sensual stroke, and he curled his magic into the whisper of pain as I stretched around him. Then he urged me into a hard, sensual rhythm, building the climax within me, taunting me, pulling his magic away and teasing it back in, until I was panting and moaning.

The love in his eyes and through our brand was intoxicating. My soul sang at the rightness. This was the way it was supposed to be, who I was supposed to be with.

He was mine.

Marcus, Jacob, Gideon, and now Kol. Mine.

Kol's expression turned fierce and he rolled us over, pinning me under his lithe, sculpted body. He captured my mouth, possessing me with his lips, stealing all breath and thought, and his magic whirled hotter and hotter, making our brands blaze with golden light.

Our breaths ragged gasps, he picked up his pace, his thrusts growing more ferocious, driving me closer and closer to the edge, until my climax slammed into me and I screamed his name.

He thrust again, my name on his lips, and tensed with his own climax, sending a wave of his magic rushing into me, soaring me to new heights. Every muscle seized with a glorious, shattering contraction, and stars exploded behind my lids. All breath and thought vanished. There was only bliss, mind-blowing searing bliss, crashing through me over and over and over again.

When I opened my eyes, I lay in Kol's warm embrace, my head on his chest, my whole body heavy and relaxed and thoroughly satisfied. "Jeez, did I pass out?"

"Yeah." He pressed his lips to my forehead. "Means I did my job right."

Affection and awe seeped from his brand into me, and a wisp of red demonic magic curled from my arm. He trailed his fingers through it, breaking it apart, before it sank back into my skin.

"We're going to need to deal with this," he said, and sadness and fear crept into his affection. The tear in his soul might have been healed, but that didn't mean everything was all right. He'd been living with so much pain for so long. That wasn't something anyone got over in an hour, let alone days or even years.

I could, however, at least try to alleviate some of his fears before I got dressed and sat with Marcus... who I had to go to. Now now now. Even if he got through his transition and despised me for causing all that agony again. I had to go.

The bedside clock read 11:33 a.m. Amiah had said the sedative would get him through the morning and that was almost over.

I gritted my teeth. Ease Kol's fears, then go to Marcus.

Except we had more problems than just that.

Jeez. One thing at a time.

"You know when you were caught in your nightmare, you didn't try to hurt me."

He traced his fingers from my arm across the heavy bruise forming around my ribs where he'd crushed me. "I have evidence to the contrary."

"You were trying to protect me. You wouldn't let Gideon or Jacob get near me." I raised my gaze to meet his, determined to will him into believing me. His hellfire was banked, small red pinpricks, but it felt forced, as if he were trying to keep hold of his emotions and had forgotten or didn't know I could feel them through our bond, no empathy needed. "You won't snap like that again."

"I know." The hold on his emotions slipped and his hellfire swelled, along with a wave of desire. "I don't know what you did, but it's gone. The weight and sludge and darkness is gone. I still—" He shuddered and his sadness misted the air around me. "I still remember. I don't think I'll ever forget. But I feel like I can breathe again."

Another red wisp curled from my arm, and he twisted it around his index finger.

"I understand if you need time." I didn't want to give him time. I wanted him with me just like I wanted my other guys. God, I needed him to help me get through whatever was going to happen with Marcus. But pushing him wouldn't help. "I'm—" My throat tightened and I forced out my words. "I'm a nephilim, and you have every reason to fear and hate what I am."

"Archnephilim," he corrected. "The daughter of Lilith and..." His sadness swelled.

"You can say it. Michael is probably my father." I sat up, pulling my gaze away from him, unable to look into all that love knowing the horrible truth. The gold flecks in my angel glow said I was half archangel — that, and only an archangel's DNA was strong enough to be magically combined with a demon's. Michael had been willing to do anything to win his war. Deciding to sleep with Lilith to create a powerful weapon would have been an easy choice for him.

I didn't want it to be true, but my other paternal options were just as bad and less likely.

Except why did he steal me away from Lilith and hide me with my mom?

"You're not your parents. Even if my soul wasn't bonded to yours, I'd know that." He sat up as well and hooked his finger under my chin, urging me to look at him again. "You'd do anything, fight anyone, to protect the ones you love. Hell, to protect complete strangers. That isn't you *trying* to be good. It's who you are. It's woven into your soul. But until we can figure out how to convince the JP and everyone else of that, you're going to need to pull your demonic magic back."

"Won't my essence still give me away?"

"Unless you look at it closely, it still says you're an angel." The muscles in his jaw flexed and while he didn't say it, I knew he was thinking: for now. "Actually it'd be better if you pulled all of your power back. You're radiating so much power, it's starting to push through the high of your release. And that was so strong I had to feed some of it to the guys again."

"Really? My chest, where I feel my divine light, is almost hollow. I've got almost nothing left after healing your soul."

Kol groaned. "Now you're really going to have to learn to pull it back. If you're almost empty now, I'm going to be in agony when you recover."

"But how is that possible? I wasn't this powerful before." But I already knew how. Lilith had destroyed what was left of my father's spell containing my magic. I'd thought she'd just released my demonic powers, but there must have been more archangel power locked away with it.

And if I let the inky magic in, I'd be even more powerful.

Which wasn't going to happen.

"You also just branded your third mate." Kol traced a line swirling over my shoulder. "I doubt our bond is old enough for me to add to your strength, but you and Gideon have been bonded for over three weeks. You could be starting to feel the effects of that now."

"Please tell me I'm not going to go back to being a bomb." That was the last thing I wanted. It had been bad enough when everyone joked about me taking down a building. A part of me hadn't really taken that seriously. But now, if I was that much stronger... I probably could. And I had no idea what I could do with my demonic powers.

Something I'd have to figure out later.

My first priority was going to Marcus and—

What? Sitting there and worrying. It was the only thing I could do for him.

My insides squirmed. *Get up. Go. Now.*

No. It would be best if I learned to pull my power in so Kol and anyone else around me who was magically sensitive wouldn't be in pain. And given that I was in a hotel for supers, there could be any number of supers nearby who'd noticed someone powerful was in the building. Which was a complication we didn't need. *Then* I could be with Marcus.

But that didn't address the JP or Lilith.

I drew in a steadying breath, fighting the twisting ache to be at Marcus's side when there were so many other things I also needed to deal with. "How do I pull it back?"

"I imagine I have a box inside me where I keep my magic. Depending on how much I want to use determines how wide I open the box. But others think of it behind a wall, or in a vial. Whatever they need to think about to contain it."

"Okay." The moment Kol had said it, I knew the box idea wasn't right. My magic, when I was at full — or what I'd thought had been full — was a wild blazing sun in the core of my being. I didn't think I'd be able to shove it into a box or be able to imagine a box big enough inside me to contain it. Perhaps a wall?

Whatever I picked, I needed to do it now, get out of bed, and deal with... well, everything else.

No. Marcus. I *needed* to go to Marcus.

I imagined a circle of heavy cinderblocks around me. I had a lot of power, I'd need a strong, solid wall. But my pulse began to race the moment I added the next row of blocks. And it beat faster and faster the higher and thicker the wall became.

My angelic power, what I'd thought had been a faint glimmer, flared and exploded against my mental wall. With a burst of light, my wings released and Kol's eyes flashed wide.

ESSIE

"Well, that didn't work," Kol said.

"No shit." I shifted back so I wouldn't hit him while I figured out how to get my damned wings back into my body. Which — *ah, crap* — I had yet to do without Gideon's help.

"What were you imagining?"

"A wall." I squeezed my shoulder blades together and imagined my magic flooding into my back.

My wings twitched.

And stayed right where they were.

"Claustrophobic? It's pretty common in angels."

"I hadn't thought I was." I strained to push more magic to the spot Gideon always touched when he helped me. "But I did get an apartment with roof access and a skylight before I'd even known I had wings."

"Which you've only had for a few days." Kol's expression softened. "How are you handling that? I'm sorry, I should have asked earlier. We've had our lives turned upside down, but yours..."

"Was doused in gasoline and set on fire?" I finished for him. I squeezed my shoulder blades harder, straining to get whatever natural angelic reflex I had to work.

Come on.

Pull them in so you can contain your magic and get to Marcus.

Jeez. Just do it.

The urge to go swelled and my breath picked up. My wings jerked and magic flickered along my spine, then vanished without pulling my wings back in.

"God damn fucking wings." I didn't have the time to deal with this. Marcus needed me, and we had to figure out what we were going to do about Lilith and the JP.

Let me in and you'll have enough power, the inky magic hissed.

No.

I heaved with everything I had and imagined a massive blast of power crashing into my back. Light blazed around me and my wings slammed into me, stealing my breath as if I'd just been punched in the chest.

Kol cocked an eyebrow. "That well, hunh?"

"I'm sure I'll love them more when Gideon teaches me to fly. Until then, they keep getting in the way and messing things up."

"I think they're beautiful," Kol said, and his smile grew wicked again. "And I've heard the base of an angel's wings are really sensitive."

A shiver of desire swept through me at the memory of Gideon stroking my wings the first time he helped me pull them back in.

"Oh, ho!" Kol's eyes lit up. "So they are and you already know. That's going on the list of things we should try. And with Gideon and his wings..."

My body heated at the thought and my breath grew ragged again, this time with desire.

Jeez. I wasn't going to get anything done now that I was bonded with a incubus.

"Later," I forced out. "I promise. First, I need to get my power pulled back." Then Marcus. *Please, God, let him be all right.* I didn't care if he hated me so long as he lived.

"I'm holding you to that," Kol said. "Okay, so the wall didn't work. How about a shield or a vial or a jar?"

But those didn't sound right, either. Even if I tried to imagine just locking up my magic and not all of me like I'd done with the wall, I had a feeling my power would fight it. The only idea that kept popping in my mind was twisting it tight like it had been when my father's spell had contained it. What were the odds that I could twist it back up again?

Given my luck, probably terrible. But it was the only thing that felt right. So I drew in a steadying breath and imagined the sun at the core of my being. It burned, a blazing whirling supernova of half light and half darkness.

I mentally grabbed a thread of each, entwined them into a single strand, and dragged them in the same direction until it whipped into a raging vortex that threatened to tear free from my mental grip, but was at least all moving in the same direction. Clinging to my power with every-thing I had, I forced the vortex to tighten and curl in on itself, creating a ball.

The ball strained and swelled, and Lilith's inky magic surged and oozed between my cells, sensing a weakness in my concentration.

I mentally clenched down on it and my magic, and with a sharp contraction, my power compacted into a tight super-charged marble, pulsing in my heart, waiting for me to summon it, as if this was how it was supposed to be. I had no doubt it would roar to life the moment I called on it, but I couldn't help the glimmer of pride at successfully containing it. It also didn't hurt that I could feel Kol's pride rushing through our brand as well.

The inky magic's seductive whisper also dimmed, but it wasn't out and I didn't know how to get it out. Which scared the shit out of me.

"What did you pick?" he asked. "You feel like an ordinary angel now."

"I spun it tight into a ball."

His eyebrows rose and surprise flickered through his pride. "No container?"

"It didn't seem right."

"Well, okay then." He blew out a heavy sigh, the whisper of sadness returning. "We should return to real life."

Yes. Go. Go.

Kol got out of bed, strode to the door still naked — God, he was gorgeous — and retrieved a bag of clothes from the hall.

"There's a note," he said, dumping the contents of the bag on the bed. White T-shirts and tan cargo pants. Not really tactical team attire, but wearing all black wouldn't help us blend in with everyone else's summer clothes if that was what we needed to do... not that it wasn't going to look odd with all of us wearing the same thing. "We're to meet the guys in the conference room at the end of this hall, opposite end from the clinic. There'll be breakfast."

"I need to check in on Marcus first." I needed to *stay* with him. Except our troubles weren't going to wait and we needed a plan.

Why couldn't I focus on that? I wouldn't be able to help Marcus if the JP arrested us or Lilith found us.

I grabbed the two T-shirts, tossed the bigger one to Kol, and set mine aside. Focus on the immediate problem. I couldn't do anything for Marcus — God, I had to do something! — so how did we deal with Lilith? We couldn't let her restart Michael's war and if she was gone, so too would be her inky magic. "We have to figure out what to do about Lilith."

If there was even anything we could do. We hadn't stood a chance the first time we'd fought her. What made me think we'd stand a chance now?

I picked up a pair of cargo pants, looking for more clothes, namely underwear. "We won't be able to stop her without the JP's help. Which is a whole other problem, since all of you just set your careers on fire and became fugitives for me."

Where was the God damned underwear? I needed underwear so I could go to Marcus—

No, come up with a plan for Lilith—

No, figure out how to get my guys' lives back.

"You shouldn't have run," I said. "If you'd let the Director lock me up, we'd have an army to stop Lilith. Hell, we'd have *the* army."

"Essie—"

I picked up the cargo pants I'd already set aside. Undies my size were small. Maybe they'd been caught in a pocket or something.

I needed to get dressed. I needed to go. "We'd have resources and magic and healing. Marcus would be in one of the best transition facilities in Union and—"

I shoved my hand into all the pockets and shook out the clothes. Whoever had purchased the clothes hadn't thought to buy any underwear. And while I doubted Kol minded — in fact, if I recalled correctly he hadn't been wearing any when he'd stripped in the bathroom last night, or rather earlier this morning — I didn't want to be running around without a bra and chafing down there.

"Essie—"

"Where the fuck is the God damned underwear!"

Kol grabbed my hands. "He'll be okay."

"I *know* that," I snapped. But I didn't, and even if he was going to be okay later, he was still suffering now, and I had to fucking think about other more pressing problems.

As if Marcus's pain wasn't pressing.

"You're freaking out over underwear."

I sucked in a sharp breath. What the hell was wrong with me?

But I knew what. Even if Marcus and I didn't share a brand, we were still bonded, and my soul was panicking as if it were Gideon or Jacob in danger. Healing Kol's soul and sealing our bond had distracted me momentarily, but now I had to think about so many things, and yet all I could think about was Marcus.

I could see why Amiah had been distraught over realizing *this* was what it meant to share a soul bond. If all her life she'd thought the soul bond through the angelic mating brand was all beautiful sunshine and fuzzy kittens, seeing this ugly truth would have been a shock.

I sucked in another breath. *I could not freak out. I could not freak out. Please, God, don't let me freak out.*

I squeezed Kol's hands and pulled out of his grip. "I'm okay."

He frowned. Yeah, I didn't believe me, either.

"Fine. I'll *be* okay." I got off the bed and grabbed my dirty underwear and bra from the bathroom.

See. I could think straight.

Thankfully not a lot of blood had soaked through my jeans and T-shirt, so my undies and bra were mostly blood free, and what blood there was had dried while I'd slept.

I put them on, returned to the bedroom, and finished getting dressed. "I'll check in on Marcus then meet you in the conference room," I said, since I was pretty sure I wouldn't hear a word anyone was saying if we made our plans in the clinic. "We have to figure out our next move."

Kol dipped in and brushed his lips over mine with a whisper of a kiss that shivered desire all the way down to my toes. "I'll let the guys know."

We went down the hall in opposite directions, my stomach churning with worry for Marcus and my heart a confused mix of whispering emotions, joy, grief, anger, desire, and not all of it mine. My powers might have been pulled back, but it looked like that didn't mean my empathy had turned off, and I still had enough angelic juice to *feel* things.

I pushed open the clinic door and a wave of heartache swept over me.

Oh, crap. My legs trembled and I staggered to the now empty first gurney to catch my balance. Sebastian must have been moved to a room.

Amiah, sitting on the floor in front of the plexiglass door of the transition room, jerked her head up to look at me. "What do you want?"

Her blue eyes, so much like Gideon's, were red and filled with ice — had she been crying? The heartache would suggest so — and her face was haggard and pale.

"When did you last sleep?" Cassius was supposed to have given her a break, and given that she'd also been in the cafeteria when we'd teleported back to Operations in the early morning, she probably hadn't gone to bed last night. She clearly hadn't changed. She still wore the thin hospital scrubs she'd left Operations in and they still had blood on them. She was running on less sleep than I was. It shouldn't surprise me that her emotions were overwhelming.

"I'm fine."

"Yeah, you look fine," I said, the insensitive words jumping out before I could stop them. Crap. Even if Amiah had been a bitch, I could still take the high road and not be a bitch back. Especially since it was clear the ice and anger right now was hiding emotional pain and exhaustion.

The light in Amiah's eyes flared and she jerked her gaze back to Marcus, who still lay on the thin, bloody mattress with the billowing cloud of demonic mist weeping from and sinking back under his skin. His naked body was a sickening mix of man and beast, his limbs still breaking and changing even though he was unconscious.

"Don't make this harder than it has to be," she said, her tone icy but her heartache swelling.

"You're right. I'm sorry. I'm just having trouble controlling my emotions." And ignoring hers. I clenched my jaw and mentally pushed back the pressure of her feelings and the twisting urge to be closer to Marcus. I shuffled past the gurneys and pressed my hands against the plexiglass wall.

Marcus whimpered and his back arched. His left arm snapped and expanded into a wolf's foreleg, his flesh bleeding and blackened, but fur didn't sweep over it. The red mist whirled faster as if the wind blowing through it had picked up.

God, even unconscious he was in agony. "Is this what transition is always like?"

"Most don't have it quite as bad," Amiah said, a wave of anger cutting into her heartache. "But this is just like Marcus's first time."

"For over a week?" My stomach bottomed out. God, I couldn't

imagine surviving this kind of agony for a few days, let alone a week, without losing my mind.

"The first couple of days were the worst. I suspect it'll be the same here. His body didn't want to accept the change then, and it doesn't want to accept it now," Amiah said. "Then it'll be on and off for the rest of the week."

"And there's nothing I can do?" There had to be something. But a divine light strike and empathy wouldn't help and my demonic magic was the reason he was in this mess. I sagged to the floor beside Amiah. "He's never going to forgive me, is he?"

"If we don't tell him the truth, he might never know."

I jerked my gaze to Amiah, surprised. I'd have thought she, out of everyone, would want Marcus to know that his suffering was my fault, again.

Her angel glow dimmed and her heartache melted into sorrow. "If you hadn't used your demonic magic, he would have died the moment you arrived in the cafeteria," she said matter-of-factly, her tone hiding even a hint of her emotions. "He's alive because of you."

"He's also in agony because of me." Again. And, if Amiah had been telling the truth, he could still die.

Marcus whimpered again and his wolf-like right leg crunched and turned back to a human leg, his flesh torn and bleeding.

"There has to be something." I couldn't just sit there. And really, I had to meet with the rest of the guys and figure out what we were going to do next. It wouldn't help if he recovered to find the situation still just as dire. Except my soul wouldn't let me leave. "What if I branded him? Could I take his pain?"

"Angelic mating brands don't work that way. You have to be destined to be together. Just because you want it doesn't mean it's going to happen." Amiah's sorrow swelled but a shudder of fear swept through it. "Your life already isn't your own. Why trap Marcus, too?"

"You're probably the only angel around who doesn't think the angelic mating brand is a beautiful, sacred thing." But then, when we'd talked in Sebastian's office the other day, she'd been horrified thinking that I'd lost all control of my life. And maybe I had and just couldn't see it.

How did I explain to her how right my bonds were? That I belonged with Gideon, Jacob, Kol, *and* Marcus. Even if we didn't share an angelic mating brand, Marcus was mine and I was his. I knew it in my soul. Every cell in my being knew it.

"If you love him, let him go." Her heartache churned stronger, now cut with a thread of yearning and regret as well as fear. I'd always known there'd been something between them, but this didn't feel like a jealous ex-girlfriend. This was softer, like she desired him, but above all, she wanted him to be happy whether it was with her or not.

"Even if I could let him go, you know he'd never leave me. His wolf has made its choice." I pressed my lips together. Did I say it? Did I push the subject and find out exactly what had been between the two of them? Did I want to face the fact that my reappearance in his life had ended their relationship and I hadn't even given that a second thought until now? "He'd never go back to you."

"He never really was with me," she said, her voice small and tired, the icy mask she'd put up starting to crumble. "I thought if I was patient enough — thought his wolf's mating call couldn't be that strong for you because he wasn't a naturally born shifter and eventually he'd see me in that way. I just needed to be patient. And then you branded Gideon and Jacob and not him. I thought—" Her eyes grew glassy, but frustration snapped through me, and her mask hardened her expression again. "You caused him so much pain. He used to scream your name when the lycanthropy was ripping him apart— I know now he's not my destiny, but without a brand, he's not yours, either. If you love him, let him go. Your brands will make you love the others more than him whether you want to or not, and he doesn't deserve that."

Marcus groaned, and his chest rose and fell with rapid, shallow breaths, his expression twisting in agony. The unfelt wind blowing his demonic mist gusted, whipping it around for a second before returning to its uneasy undulations.

"You brand men left and right." She glared at me, but her frustration and heartache belied the anger in her eyes. "Did you really brand Kol?"

"Yeah."

Marcus groaned and the wind gusted again.

"Then that's proof. If you and Marcus were supposed to be mates, you'd have branded him."

Marcus's body jerked taut, and he screamed as both of his legs shattered with a sickening crunch.

"Damn." Amiah jerked to her feet and rushed to the counter, her fear swelling within me, but her body language and expression sternly professional. "He's metabolized the sedative faster than he should have."

My pulse stalled. That didn't sound good. "What does that mean?"

"It means the lycanthropy is more aggressive than a standard transition." She grabbed a needle from the drawer and inserted it into the vial of sedative that had been left on the counter. "He's going to come out of it soon, and it'll be better if he's partially sedated for his transition."

"Partially sedated?" I didn't like the sound of that, either. Even fully unconscious, he'd been in pain. Partially conscious would be torture.

"He has to be at least semi-lucid to get through it. If we keep him knocked out, he'll never finish transitioning."

"So why did you fully sedate him last night— earlier— whatever."

Marcus screamed again. His chest expanded and ridges formed in his skin, a swirling design of angry red welts cut into his chest.

"If he wasn't out, you'd have never left the clinic, and the rest of the guys wouldn't have left and you all needed to get some sleep." She measured out the dosage she wanted then pocketed the vial along with another capped needle. "Now hold him down for me."

I opened the door as Marcus released another heartrending scream. The welts thickened and turned black. He thrashed onto his chest and the welts rolled over him, crawling over his sides onto his back.

"Roll him over and hold him steady," Amiah said. "I need a vein."

I hurried inside, dropped to my knees beside Marcus, and grabbed his still-human shoulder. His mist whipped around us, and he wailed and heaved against my hold.

"Get him over."

I hauled him onto his back. His arm swept out and the back of his fist slammed into my face. Pain exploded in my cheek and the world spun. Half blind, I threw myself on top of him, pinning him with my body.

Amiah grabbed his arm and captured it under her knees.

His breath heaved and his ribs shattered beneath me. The skin under my hands grew bumpy, the swirling ridges sweeping over his shoulder, and he bucked, my weight not enough to keep him down against his strength.

"Keep him still," Amiah said, fighting to keep his arm steady enough to insert the needle.

But he was too strong. I wasn't going to be able to hold him down, let alone get him still. Not unless I used my magic.

I sucked in a quick breath that did little to steady my nerves and reached for my empathic magic to help push some of Jacob's calm into Marcus. My power flared, rushing out of the tight ball in my heart, sputtered, and vanished.

Shit. I had just enough to feel Amiah's emotions and nothing left to push into Marcus. I'd used everything I had healing Kol.

"Essie, hold him."

"I'm trying."

Marcus bucked again, knocking me off, and howled, the cry half human and half beast. Bones shattered and muscles tore. I jumped back on him and his eyes fluttered open, revealing burning red hellfire.

Everything within me froze. *He's a demon? I made him a demon?* My magic hadn't just reawakened the lycanthropy in his DNA, it had changed it.

Amiah gasped and her fear turned the air frigid for a second before she locked down her emotions. She tightened her grip on his arm, but he wrenched free, his arm half human half... I had no idea what. His whole body was disfigured, his skin covered in swirling ridges and turning black. What the hell was he becoming?

Another scream and he heaved onto his side. His demonic mist whipped around us, sucking all the air into a wild vortex.

"Just hold him. I'll have to do this intramuscular," she said.

I reached for him, but he wrenched to his hands and knees and snarled at me, his jaw misshapen, extending into a snout, the hellfire in his eyes licking across his blackened cheeks.

"Marcus, it'll be okay." I raised my hands. Maybe if I didn't look like an aggressor he'd calm down.

"You can't reason with him in this condition." Amiah grabbed his shoulder, and he jerked toward her, his body breaking and twisting, growing into a massive, furless, muscular mastiff the size of a pony.

Her eyes widened and her fear spiked, no longer under control. She scrambled back.

He swiped an enormous paw at her, his claws tearing into her arm and sending the needle flying across the room.

With a scream, she wrenched her arm tight to her chest, blood oozing between her fingers. She twisted to the side out of the way of another paw swipe and her back hit the plexiglass wall. Nowhere else to go.

He snarled, no sign of humanity in his eyes, and lunged, his massive jaws going for her throat.

AMIAH'S FEAR COATED ME IN FROST AND TURNED THE AIR SO COLD MY breath misted. She wasn't going to get out of the way fast enough and without her, he might not have a chance of surviving the rest of his transition.

"Marcus, stop." I shoved her out of the way, taking her place in front of Marcus.

His jaws snapped, his canines grazing my throat, and my pulse lurched.

Oh shit oh shit oh shit.

"Marcus, please."

He slammed a heavy paw on my chest, pinning me to the wall, and growled, the sound low and dangerous.

"You can't reason with him. It's not him. It's his beast. He won't be him again until his transition is over." A gut-churning mix of horror and grief joined her frozen fear. She was mourning his loss, as if there was a strong chance we'd never get him back.

His lips curled back giving me a close-up look at those massive teeth that had almost ripped out my throat, and his hot breath blasted my face, each huff fast and flecked with spit. The hellfire blazed in his wide, wild eyes, but there was a glimmer of piercing green in their core, a pinprick of the humanity still deep in his soul.

He was still in there.

He had to still be in there.

Amiah scrambled to the needle and Marcus jerked his head toward her.

"Marcus." I grabbed his head. His body was covered in a short velvet-like fur and not naked flesh like I expected, and his skin was searing hot. I wrenched his attention back to mine with a strength I didn't know I possessed. The red mist sweeping around him curled around my arms and sank into my skin, making my demonic magic burn in my chest. "Marcus, come back to me."

He jerked forward and snapped at me. I flinched, unable to help myself, and his teeth grazed the side of my face but didn't break flesh.

"Marcus, please." My mist whirled into his, swirling around and around.

"He's not in there." Out of the corner of my eye, I saw Amiah slide her hands into her pockets and pull out the vial and extra needle.

But he was in there. I knew it. I could *feel* it. "I'm not giving up on you."

Amiah shifted closer and he wrenched his head out of my grip, his hind legs bunched, ready to leap. The hellfire in his eyes surged, devouring the glimmer of green and any sense that Marcus the man was inside the beast.

My pulse stalled.

I was losing him. If I didn't do something now, the beast would take over and never let him go.

"Marcus." I seized his head again and shoved my forehead against his, his flesh burning hot to the touch in painful contrast to Amiah's frozen fear. "Fight this. You're stronger than your beast."

He wrenched in my grip but I held tight. I would *not* lose him. Not now. Not ever.

"Come back to me."

His claws dug into my flesh, and in the back of my mind, I knew I was bleeding again, but I couldn't feel anything past my desperation and the frigid air.

"Marcus, please." *I can't lose you.* "You're mine."

He howled, the sound deafening and heartbreaking. So much pain and fear and rage.

"You're. Mine." I dug my nails into the thick skin under his jaw and heaved back to meet his gaze, while still trying to hold on. The hellfire raged in his eyes and our demonic magic snapped, stinging my skin.

"Both of you," I growled, my voice, body, hell, my whole essence radiating my determination to keep him and that I loved him. *All* of him. He was my soul mate, and I would *not* lose him. Ever. "Mine."

He stiffened, the fire in his eyes flaring before dimming, exposing the glimmer of piercing human green again.

Essie? he asked, his voice in my mind weak.

Then he collapsed, his weight dragging me to my knees, and melted back into a man, his body temperature returning to normal.

Oh, thank God.

The red demonic storm that had raged around him vanished, now only a few thin wisps seeping from his skin and disappearing in the air. Beneath the blood smeared on his body, his skin was smooth and swarthy, no longer pitch black.

I pulled him into my arms and clung to him. I'd almost lost him. Again.

My throat tightened and tears burned my eyes.

Forgive me. Please forgive me.

Amiah knelt beside us, her eyes wide, and I was hit with a wave of awe and sorrow, the ice of her fear gone. "You really are soul bonded with him. Only his mate could control his beast like that." She pressed a hand against his back, blood rushing down her forearm from four deep gashes, and closed her eyes. Light radiated from her palm for a second, then she sat back on her heels. "Only his mate could have quickened his transition like that."

"What does that mean?" I tightened my grip around him, afraid the answer meant more pain for him.

"It's over. Just like that. You helped him accept his beast, by accepting both of them." Another wave of heartache swelled inside me, but her expression revealed nothing. "Help me move him back to the mattress. He could still be out for a while."

We half carried, half dragged him back to the mattress, and I sagged down beside him. A tear broke free and rolled down my cheek. I had too much emotion churning inside me, not all of it mine, and I couldn't contain it any more.

"He'll be all right," Amiah said.

I brushed a lock of hair from his forehead.

"I know you want to stay with him," Amiah said with a sigh, "but..."

"But I can't? It's too dangerous?" I snapped. To hell with what she thought. Marcus's beast could have killed me and it hadn't. I wasn't the one in danger. And hadn't she just said it was over?

I yanked my gaze to glare at her and tell her I was staying by his side, but my words stalled at the pain tightening her eyes. She held her arm against her chest, her blood soaking into her shirt.

"But I could use a little help. It's hard to bandage your own arm." She forced the words out as if it hurt to say them, and given how in control she always was, asking for my help must have been painful.

"What about your magic?"

"I have enough left so you won't need to stitch me up, but that's about it."

Jeez. Why hadn't I remembered that? I really wasn't thinking straight. We'd been in rough shape when she'd healed us only a few hours ago, and she'd looked haggard when I'd walked into the clinic. She probably didn't have much left. She didn't even have a career any more. In the blink of an eye, she'd decided to come with us and made herself a fugitive as well.

"Why?"

"Because I don't want to bleed on everything." She rolled her eyes and a wave of frustration swept through me.

"No, why did you help us? You didn't have to come with us. You know I'm a—" God, why was it so hard to say? Everyone knew it. It had been clear the moment I'd appeared in the cafeteria and again just now when I'd been with Marcus and my demonic magic had entwined with his.

Except none of her fear had been because of me.

Her expression hardened. "You might be reckless, but it's always to protect people who can't protect themselves. I understand that now. I don't know why you're not like Michael's other nephilim, but you aren't, and I've staked my freedom on that."

"Which still doesn't explain why. The JP will charge you with treason like the rest of us."

"Because I know you and the rest of the team well enough to know you're going to go after whatever beat the hell out of you." A whisper of her fear chilled inside me. "And if you're going after it, then without a doubt it's evil and *needs* to be stopped."

Yes, but how? I shifted, suddenly uncomfortable with just sitting there. I needed to do something, figure out how to save everyone, and I couldn't do it sitting there with Marcus, since all I could think about when I was with him was him.

"In your previous condition, you wouldn't have stood a chance," she said.

Except I didn't know if we had a chance against Lilith and her witches even if we were at full power. Not without the JP's help. How did I stop Lilith and keep my guys safe? There had to be a way. We all had to get through this alive.

"Helping you was the only sensible option. Now, please." She dipped her gaze back to her injured arm, her emotions a mix of heartache and frustration and resignation. "Even if I had more power left, I'd still need help. My magic is for others. It takes a lot more power to heal myself than someone else."

"Well, that must suck." I forced myself to ease away from Marcus, picked up the original needle — which was only a few feet away from me and farther from her — and followed her out of the transition room.

"I don't usually need to heal myself." Her eyes narrowed, her attention on my chest. "And you're bleeding too."

I followed her gaze to the bloody puncture holes in my new T-shirt. The bleeding wasn't bad and I could hardly feel the pain, so Marcus's claws mustn't have dug in too deep, but I'd ruined another shirt and I hadn't even been wearing it for an hour. Not to mention my cargo pants were also bloody from brushing up against Marcus's body.

My heart squeezed, and I struggled not to think about him. I wouldn't be able to function if I did, and I had to function, had to figure out a way to stop my mother.

I shuddered.

Yeah, not going to think about that, either.

"There are bandages in that drawer." Amiah pointed to the drawer beside the needle drawer and closed her eyes. Light blazed from the hand keeping pressure on her wound and her body tensed. Then the blaze vanished and she sagged, clutching the counter by the sink with her good hand to keep her balance. Her expression was even more haggard than when I'd first entered the clinic, and with trembling fingers, she turned on the tap and ran her bloody arm under the water.

Behind me, Marcus moaned, making my pulse lurch and my attention jump to him. The urge to take action, to help him, stop Lilith, do something, made my breath pick up even though Amiah had said he was going to be okay.

Except he was only going to be okay from the transition I'd forced onto him. Not from Lilith.

But what could I do? Maybe the other guys had figured something out. Which meant leaving Marcus's side, and what if something happened while I was gone? What if Amiah had lied to me? What if—

Amiah grabbed my chin and forced me to meet her gaze. "He's through the transition," she said, as if she'd been able to read my mind.

A surge of heartache and yearning swept through me. I needed Marcus to be okay above all else... except he was okay. I ached for him, yearned for him—

No, Amiah did. God, it was getting difficult to tell which emotions were mine. She loved him even though she'd known he was in love with me. And now she had absolute proof that I was Marcus's mate. All hope was lost. Even if I never branded Marcus, he was as much mine as Gideon and Jacob and Kol.

"Amiah, I'm—"

A sudden quick blast of her healing magic seared through my body, stealing what I'd been about to say — which was probably best, since I really had no idea what I could say to her.

"I promise. He's going to be okay," she said with another wave of heartache that she kept hidden behind an icy mask of indifference. "Now get something to eat. You won't do him any good if you collapse."

"You should talk." But she was right. I needed to eat and think, and I wouldn't be able to do either if I stayed in the clinic.

I made myself step out into the hall, but instead of going to the conference room, I turned in the other direction, heading to the loading bay and the outside door, away from the weight of Amiah's emotions, and, now that I thought about it, the ocean of feelings coming from the entire hotel.

I just needed a moment. I needed air and sky and a few deep breaths. Then I'd be able to go back in and figure everything out.

Except the truth was that if my guys went up against Lilith again, she'd kill them.

On top of that we were fugitives, wanted by the most powerful law enforcement agency on the planet, and without a doubt they'd use a tracking spell to find us sooner rather than later.

I had to do something.

The emotions from the hotel churned inside me, the pressure building.

Come on, think of something. Save them. Protect them.

How?

I shoved open the security door at the back of the empty loading bay and staggered onto the driveway behind Voth's hotel, momentarily blinded by the hot late-morning summer sun. Before me stretched the vast swath of manicured lawn behind the hotel, and beyond that the forest at the edge of this side of the Quarter. Above, the sky was clear, the same stunning blue as Gideon's eyes, but it did nothing to steady me against the emotional storm inside me.

Come on, Essie, pull your shit together.

But it was all too much. I couldn't ignore it any longer. I couldn't steady my thoughts or emotions, and I sure as hell couldn't get a grip on everyone else's. The pressure grew, raging into a crashing storm, swirling and lurching, hot and cold, burning humidity and freezing mist, all threatening to pull me apart, and Lilith's inky magic chuckled.

Soon I'd give in. Soon I'd be Lilith's. Soon my guys would die.

I screamed, a primal cry of pain and frustration, desperate to get out all my heartache and fear and anger. God, I was so angry. Angry that I wasn't a full angel, angry that my mother was a monster, angry at feeling helpless, and angry that I couldn't figure out how to face Lilith without losing any of my guys.

My demonic magic blasted from my clenched fists and exploded into the ground at my feet, sending chunks of asphalt into the air.

"Feel better?" Gideon asked from behind me.

Gasping, I turned to the door and was captured by his summer-sky eyes. So beautiful. So certain. Our connection instantly righted my internal equilibrium in a way I couldn't. His gaze always mesmerized me. I could look into his eyes forever and never come up for air.

But his angel glow dimmed, a summer's storm settling in his sky, and I dragged my focus to the rest of him. His arms were crossed, stretching his white T-shirt across his broad shoulders, showing off his muscular biceps. He looked well, but his expression was tight with worry.

"Do you?" he pressed, his gaze taking in my bloody clothes. His worry seeped deeper into my chest and a flicker of lightning crackled through our brand. "You didn't come get breakfast and you weren't in the clinic."

"I just needed—" My gaze dropped to the holes I'd made in Voth's driveway.

"To scream?" Gideon crossed the few steps to me and wrapped me in a strong embrace. "He's strong."

I leaned into him, my ear pressed over his heart listening to his steady sure pulse, embracing his love for me and letting that push out all the other emotions, mine and the ones that weren't mine. All except the one that really stung, the one I'd been avoiding to even think about. "I made him a demon."

"A hellhound," he murmured, his lips against my forehead. "He'll forgive you. You saved his life. And Amiah says you quickened his transition and he's already through it. So you'll have saved him a second time, too."

"Only for what? To die facing Lilith?" We couldn't let her restart Michael's war, but we weren't strong enough to stop her. "We have to tell the JP about Lilith and get their help."

"I know." Gideon's resignation seeped into me. "Even with Amiah and Cassius on our side, I don't know if the JP will accept you."

"If that's the price I have to pay to ensure Lilith is stopped, I'll pay it," I said. "I'll convince the JP that I manipulated all of you."

Gideon grabbed my shoulders and stepped back to look me in the eyes. "You'll do no such thing."

"I'm the only one who has to be incarcerated. You can get your life back."

"You *are* my life." His love for me surged, overwhelming all his other emotions. "Stop with the self-sacrifice. There's a way around this. We just need to figure it out."

His gaze jumped past my shoulder and he stiffened, his emotions lurching to fear. "Oh, God."

I wrenched around, my demonic power rushing to my fists.

A tall, broad-shouldered angel in jeans and a T-shirt strode across the lawn, his angel glow so brilliant I could see it clearly from almost a hundred yards away in the full sunlight, sunlight that that also shimmered in jaw-length light brown hair with a hint of copper. This was the angel I kept seeing in my dreams, the man who'd pressed his hand against the glass of my maturation tank, looking exactly the same as if over twenty years hadn't passed. My father.

Except Michael and Rafael were dead, which only left one other archangel who'd tried to eliminate humanity.

Lucifer.

ESSIE

Gideon stepped in front of me, his divine light sweeping over his hand, ready to be blasted. "That's far enough."

"You really think you can stop me, angel?" Lucifer said, his voice a sensual tenor edged with steel.

Oh, shit. Lilith was bad enough, but now we had to deal with Lucifer?

Except I sensed hesitation and worry from him, not rage or ferocity or whatever murderous psychopaths felt. And he had stolen me from Lilith and hidden me.

So what did that mean?

I had absolutely no idea.

"I won't let you take her back to Lilith." Gideon's fear and determination to protect me swelled, overwhelming what I felt from Lucifer.

The archangel narrowed his eyes. "You know what she is. Why are you protecting her?"

"I won't let you take her." Gideon widened his stance and formed his divine light sword. A glimmer of light flared from the brand on his forearm and his electric power crackled up my arm.

"You branded her?" Lucifer's expression flashed from shock to anger and his horror and rage slammed into me, along with a fierce need to protect that was strangely similar to Gideon's.

Had Lucifer really done everything he'd done to protect me?

"You son of a bitch. You branded her." He stormed toward us, his gaze locked on Gideon, murder in his eyes. "And you've done a shitty job protecting her. Look at her. She's covered with blood and has a black eye."

I stepped up beside Gideon and Lucifer's attention jumped back to me with another rush of conflicting emotions and a need to protect.

"You weren't supposed to have anything to do with this world," he said, jerking to a stop a few feet away.

He really *was* trying to protect me.

"What's he talking about?" Gideon asked, his voice low.

Why the hell had Lucifer done what he'd done? He was the original angel who'd fallen and slaughtered thousands. He was evil.

Except the angel standing in front of me didn't look evil and his emotions didn't feel evil.

"Why?" I asked. "Why break your deal with Lilith? Why hide me? Why make me think the world would hate me?" Why God damn everything?

"Because the world *will* hate you, save for maybe me and your angel." He frowned, his attention on my right arm. "Your brand is bigger than his."

"Essie?" Gideon shifted beside me, his fear growing stronger.

Lucifer's gaze jumped back to mine, and I caught a glimmer of gold flecks in his angel glow. "Is that what she called you? Essie?"

"Esther. You didn't even name me?" I don't know why that hurt so much. He might have donated his DNA to make me, but he wasn't my father. He hadn't raised me, hadn't had anything to do with my life.

"If I did, I wouldn't have been able to let you go." His anger and frustration melted into regret. "If you stayed with me, she'd have found you. But it looks like she will anyway. I'd feared the spell wouldn't be strong enough to contain the power of an archangel and the Hellfire Queen, but it was the only thing I could do."

"That and hiding my memories and manipulating some human woman into thinking she loved you."

His surprise spiked through me. "That wasn't supposed to happen."

"She waited her whole life for you, died thinking you loved her and that you had to stay away because of me." My mom had spent all of my life heartbroken over a lie because she'd been magically manipulated. "She used to cry herself to sleep when she thought I couldn't hear her. She could have been happy. She could have had real love."

"That wasn't my intention," Lucifer said, his voice gruff.

"Well, what was?"

"To give you what neither I nor Lilith could give you. Life. Love. Anything but Michael's fucking war."

"Says the angel who fought for him," Gideon said.

"Not willingly." A shadow passed over Lucifer's angel glow.

"It was *your* war," Gideon said. "You started it. Michael just picked it up years later. I'm sure you jumped at the chance to get out of your cage and finish what you started."

"I jumped at the chance to get out, but it wasn't Michael who freed me." Lucifer's regret swelled and realization hit me.

"It was Lilith. That was the deal you made with her. Your freedom for her weapon."

A whisper of surprise from Gideon sliced through me then disappeared, and he shifted closer to me. He'd just figured out the horrible truth and without a word, reassured me that he stood by me.

"Michael would fuck just about anyone but her. Probably to drive her crazy. Or rather more crazy than she already was." Grief twisted into Lucifer's regret and he rubbed his right forearm, drawing my attention to the pale, delicate scar swirling over his skin. "She'd learned the secret to making nephilim and leveraged Michael by offering her help in the war to use one of his maturation tanks. I'd been locked away from the Realm of Celestial Light for too long. I had no power. Agreeing to Lilith's terms was the only way she wouldn't kill me."

"So why steal me?"

"Because the Angelic Defense was moving in and Michael was destroying all the tanks, killing all of his nephilim." He shifted closer and Gideon tensed. "And you weren't a thing or a weapon. None of Michael's nephilim were until he finished his process by pulling them from their tanks and shattering their souls. You'd barely had any time in the tank and you were just a little girl. My little girl. And you deserved everything I couldn't give you."

"Because you were a fugitive?"

"Because my soul is broken." He held out his arm, giving me a clear view of the delicate white lines swirling over his forearm.

Gideon drew in a sharp breath. "You survived the death of your mate?"

"I went insane and tried to slaughter not just the humans who'd killed her but every last one of them. I deserved to be locked in that cage. Now you're bound by the same curse." His gaze rose to Gideon, his expression fierce, but his fear surged inside me. "I'll bring you back and kill you again in the most painful way possible if you die on her."

Gideon glared back.

Tension filled the air and I opened my mouth before my father — an archangel, so clearly more powerful than Gideon — flattened my mate. But the door behind us banged open and we all jerked to see who it was.

"Hey, Essie—" Kol froze mid-step, his eyes wide, his fear flash-freezing over my skin. "Oh, shit. Lucifer."

"Jeez," I said. "I should have drawn a picture. Everyone seems to know who you are except me."

"Drawn a picture?" Lucifer asked.

"I've been dreaming about you for a week now."

"Ah," Lucifer said. "That's how you knew who I was."

Kol's gaze jumped from Lucifer to me to Gideon. "You should be freaking out. You know who you're standing beside, right?"

"Lucifer," Gideon said, and a wicked smile flashed across his face, along with a burst of mischief. Oh, that was a feeling I never thought I'd feel from Gideon. "Meet your father-in-law."

Kol gasped, his jaw dropped open, and his surprise hit me.

Gideon snorted. "That's payback for how you told me about Jacob."

"Jesus, you've two mates?" Lucifer asked. "And an incubus? Really?"

"Four, actually. And I love him for his personality."

Lucifer rolled his eyes and looked heavenward. "God, help me."

"So, if you're not here to take me back to Lilith, why are you here?" A part of me wanted to believe everything he'd said, that he'd done what he'd done to protect me. But I didn't know him. He could have some other motive in mind, no matter what his emotions were telling me. I was still, after all, a weapon.

"I felt the spell on your angelic magic shatter a day and a half ago, and the spell on your demonic power this morning." Lucifer raked his hands through his hair. "Lilith is going to come after you and you're— I *thought* you were helpless." His gaze dropped to my hands, where demonic mist billowed and a glimmer of divine light heated my palms. "That isn't the control of someone who's had power for less than two days. How long has my spell been failing?"

"At least three weeks," Kol said from the doorway, not drawing any closer. "That's when you bought the enspelled contacts to hide your angel glow, didn't you?" he asked me.

"It was before then," I said. "Blasting myself with the divine light made the biggest crack, but my buzz started about two and a half years ago and my weird empathy manifested before then."

Lucifer frowned. "Buzz?"

"It was like I was constantly holding an electric fence. Nicotine patches worked to calm it for a bit, until we fought the archnephilim— the *other* archnephilim. And then—" I entwined my fingers with Gideon's and looked up at him. "Being near you used to calm it until the zip OD."

"You ODed on zip?" Lucifer's eyes narrowed, his gaze growing fierce again. "You're the worst mate in all the realms. How could you let her take zip?"

Gideon met Lucifer's gaze head-on again. "She didn't take zip, she got dosed, and you've never met your daughter so you have no idea how stupid telling me I should or shouldn't *let* her do anything is."

"Can we please not tell the *archangel* Lucifer he's stupid," Kol said.

Lucifer shifted his attention to me. "The spell was designed to gain strength and further suppress your powers the closer you got to an angel. But if it was already breaking... The zip must have twisted it. Now come on." He held out his hand to me. "Summon your other mates and let's go. I need to get your powers contained before Lilith realizes you're still alive."

A part of me wanted to take his offer. If my powers were contained again and my essence looked like a human's, we could change our names and live a normal life — or as normal a life as a nephilim-in-hiding with an angel, a vampire, a were— hellhound, and a demon could live. We wouldn't face Lilith and my guys would be safe.

But then no one else would be safe. Lilith was planning something that would restart Michael's war and there was no guarantee that the JP would believe us or send enough agents to stop her.

I glanced at Gideon. His emotions had become a strange churning mix of hope and regret, desire and fear, the same as mine. And all from the choice of keeping me safe or saving others. We couldn't have both.

"I have your back," he said.

"So do I. And I'm sure Marcus and Jacob do, too," Kol added.

I turned to meet Kol's dark gaze. His hellfire was banked, but his love radiated through our bond. He was more certain than Gideon about following me down whatever path I chose. Of course, unlike Gideon, he wasn't as psychologically bound to follow the law and protect people.

"We can't let Lilith go unchecked." I turned back to Lucifer. "She already knows I'm alive. She's the one who broke the spell on my demonic magic. She's planning on reigniting Michael's war. Face her with us."

The muscles in Lucifer's jaw tightened and his frustration returned. "I can't."

"Can't or won't?" I asked.

"I was locked away from the Realm of Celestial Light for a long time. I have almost no power. I'd be a liability in a fight, not the asset you want. Come with me. I'll hide your true nature. You're still young, not fully into your power. You won't stand a chance against her as you are."

"If you have no power, how are you going to hide Essie's?" Gideon asked, his emotions turning wary. "And how did you contain it all those years ago?" He frowned. "And are you implying that you can cast spells? That you're a sorcerer?"

"I'm not a sorcerer, I can't channel power directly from the Realm of Celestial Light, but I can weave a spell and use my own essence to power it. I spent a long time in that cage, not unconscious like everyone said I was, and my powers weren't completely locked away. One of my innate magics is to enter and manipulate minds."

"Which is how you locked away my memories and convinced my mother I was her child." Was he manipulating me now? I didn't feel like I was being influenced by him, but I wasn't sure if I'd know if I was.

"Yes. But I couldn't influence anyone in my cage, I could only go along for the ride, and I had a lot of time to kill."

"That still doesn't explain how you cast the spell to hide Essie's true nature," Gideon said, his suspicion growing. "If you don't have any power now, you likely didn't have any power when you pulled her from the tank."

"It doesn't take a lot of power to weave a spell. The big power suck is when you activate it. I wove the spell to hide you and tied it to your magic," Lucifer said, "You were the one maintaining it. That's why the zip OD twisted it. I'll show you, if you don't believe I'm nearly powerless."

He extended his hands, one to me and one to Gideon.

I glanced at Gideon, who gave a tight nod. We took Lucifer's hands, and he gasped, his head jerking back and his angel glow blazing.

"Oh, fuck, I was wrong," he said, his body trembling. "You're more powerful than even she imagined. Once you recover the magic you've spent, you *will* stand a chance against Lilith, even now."

"And you?" Gideon asked, his voice dark. "Stop hiding your power."

"I'm not." Lucifer's frustration grew and he mentally tugged my essence deeper into his, where the whisper of his magic lay. I could sense his essence held the potential for enormous power, a power as crushing and terrifying as Lilith's, but it was like an atrophied muscle, withered from lack of use, and was going to take a long time to recover.

"You're an archangel," Gideon said. "How does that happen?"

Lucifer gently pushed us out and released our hands. "No contact with the Realm of Celestial Light. I don't recommend it."

So he really couldn't help us. Damn. And as much as Lucifer thought I stood a chance against Lilith, I already had proof I couldn't. "So we're back to where we started. Helpless against Lilith and fugitives from the JP."

Lucifer's worry returned. "They know about you, too?"

"We should probably do something about that," Kol said. "I've no doubt they've called in someone who can cast a tracking spell. If our luck holds, they'll have to bring that someone in from Rome."

But if our luck didn't, the spell could be cast at any moment.

"And I think the only reason Lilith isn't coming after Essie is because she's busy preparing for whatever she's planning," Gideon said. "I have no doubt once she's done, she'll hunt us down."

"You're sure you won't come with me?" Lucifer asked.

"Lilith can't be allowed to restart Michael's war."

He held my gaze, the gold flecks dancing in his angel glow mesmerizing. His worry churning in my stomach slowly shifted to resignation.

"There's too much angel in you." He blew out a heavy breath. "Fine. I'll take care of the JP—"

"No killing," Gideon said.

"Wasn't planning on it. I might have a powerful charm that hides me from magical tracking, but the moment I show my face, every agent will be assigned to find me. You'll no longer be their priority. That should buy you some time. And this—" Lucifer drew close and Gideon tensed. "Jeez, I'm more likely to hurt you than her, lover boy."

"Doesn't make me feel better," Gideon said.

Lucifer huffed and brushed his lips against my forehead. A burst of heated magic snapped in my head and the image of a complicated glyph filled my mind's eye.

"This will give you an edge against Lilith," Lucifer said. "Share that glyph with a witch, any witch, she or he doesn't have to have a lot of power and doesn't need to set it, because you'll only need it once. It just needs to be drawn on your body with enough power to seed it."

"What is it?"

"The spell that made my cage. I had a lot of time to study it. You're going to need to touch Lilith when you cast it, so cast it fast so she doesn't have time to counter it. But then you don't need to hold on to her, just put every ounce of power you have behind it to imprison her and contain her magic." His eyes narrowed. "Waiting until you've recovered your angelic magic is your best chance at success."

Except I was pretty sure I wasn't going to be recovered by the end of today, which meant going ahead without the necessary strength or sitting back and letting Lilith hurt people.

"And remember to focus. Too much power too quickly will burn you up." His emotions turned sad and he brushed his lips against my forehead again, giving me another complicated glyph.

"What's this one for?"

"It's the spell to contain your powers. I'll always have to hide from everyone, but you don't have to." He shot Kol a hard glare then turned it on Gideon. "If my daughter dies and it doesn't kill you, I will."

"If Essie dies, it means I'm already dead," Gideon said.

Lucifer turned his attention back to me, his emotions returning to sad and misting the air. This was goodbye, and he had no intention of ever seeing me again. "I'm glad I got to meet you. When you figure out what Lilith is doing, call in an anonymous tip saying you saw me there. The JP will send every agent they have."

With a burst of determination, he turned on his heel and strode away, regretting every step he took that put distance between us.

"Well, that was—" Kol's emotions whirled, too mixed up for me to tell what he was really feeling. "I have no idea what that was."

Jacob stepped into the doorway behind him. "Who was that?"

"Daddy," Kol said with a shudder.

"Lucifer." Gideon squared his shoulders. "Did he really give you the spell to imprison Lilith?"

Jacob's eyebrows rose in surprise and his vampiric intensity deepened.

"I don't know," I said. It felt like he had, but I knew nothing about spells and the only person I knew who did was Sebastian. "Is Sebastian awake?"

"He is," Jacob said. "And he managed to get to the conference room for breakfast, but he should probably still be in bed."

Which meant asking him to weave the cage spell was a bad idea. But since I didn't trust any witch Voth might bring in, he was all we had. Here was hoping, given everything we'd been through, that he was still willing to help and that helping wouldn't kill him.

MARCUS

I awoke with a start, my eyes snapping open and my body jerking me up to my hands and knees. A ferocious inferno roared through me, burning in every cell in my body. It sang in my blood, a song of feral, primal power that was so much stronger than my wolf's original nature.

It should have overwhelmed me, should have made me feel like a stranger in my own skin like I had the first time I'd transitioned into a shifter, but it didn't.

Because this was who I was supposed to be.

The other half of my soul had never really been a wolf. I'd always been a hound, I just hadn't known it. No one had. How could they? Hellhounds had disappeared from the mortal realm long before Michael had started his war, and clearly a bite from a werewolf hadn't been strong enough to fully awaken all my dormant DNA. I'd needed the help from Essie's demonic magic to properly complete my metamorphosis and that never would have happened if I hadn't been critically wounded.

My pulse skipped a beat.

Essie.

She'd saved me.

Most of what had happened after Lilith had revealed Essie's true nature was a blur, but I remember diving in front of an ice spear to save her and that magic exploding in my chest, tearing me open.

I'd known I was dead, could feel my life rushing from me, the world darkening and growing cold, and I remember thinking it was a good thing Essie hadn't branded me. My death would hurt her, but it wouldn't kill her or drive her crazy like if one of the others had died.

Then her demonic magic had plunged into me. It burned into my cells seconds before Sebastian's teleportation magic had ripped me apart and reassembled me, permanently searing Essie's blazing demonic magic into my essence and soul.

Agony, fire, and darkness had followed as my new hellhound nature had fought to be born. It ripped into my soul, consuming my wolf, and strained to tear out of my body. It battled me for dominance, its will more powerful than my wolf's had ever been, and the primal part of my soul that was human screamed with terror that my hound wasn't going to share. It was going to consume all of me.

And it could have. A human susceptible to a shifter's bite was rare, but there had been cases where a balance couldn't be found between the two halves of the person's soul and the newly awakened animal half had taken over. And that had just been with a human to regular shifter transformation, not into a hellhound.

On top of that, my human soul was terrified that Essie would never accept us if our hellhound was fully born. It hadn't mattered that she'd already accepted I was a wolf. My wolf was tame compared to the ferocious monster now taking over, and if she rejected it, it would hurt her.

But then she'd appeared right in front of me while my hound had been on the verge of fully taking over. She'd captured my head in her hands, locked gazes with me, accepted him and me, and everything clicked into place.

Of course, my hound huffed inside me, its essence a strange mix of contentment and roiling blazing energy. *She's mine. I'd never hurt her.*

What about her other mates? I asked, uncertain of the answer. Even though her acceptance of us had instantly found the balance between the two halves of my soul, I had yet to learn what changes this new feral energy had made within me. Maybe I was now the possessive beast everyone had originally thought I was and I wouldn't be able to share her.

Mine, he snarled, the energy turning fierce, demanding. *All of them.*

Three simple words and there was no more doubt in my mind. They belonged to me. I didn't want to have sex with them, what I was attracted to hadn't changed, but they were mine. I would protect them with my life and that meant standing the fuck up and finding them.

My hound heaved inside me and soft short black fur rolled over my hands and up my forearms before sinking back under my blood-crusted skin.

Once again my body had ripped itself apart to become something new and I was covered in blood, stained with the cost of my excruciating rebirth... which would have been a lot worse if it hadn't been for Essie—

Oh, shit. Essie.

She'd help me come out of this transition, which meant she'd seen how painful and bloody it was.

My attention jumped to the blood-streaked floor and thin, plastic mattress beside me.

Really bloody.

And it was her magic that had awoken the transition.

She was never going to forgive herself, and because I didn't share a mating brand with her like the others did, I couldn't just tell her I wasn't mad. She'd always have doubts.

No, I wouldn't allow her to feel guilty. I would show her how I felt about her. I would brand my essence into hers as deeply as any angelic mating brand, prove she had nothing to feel guilty about, and that she was mine and always would be.

My hound's ferocious blaze surged inside me. We needed to reclaim our mate and we needed to do it now.

"You're awake," Amiah said from behind me.

"Where's Essie?" I snarled, as I turned to her.

She stood in the doorway of a plexiglass wall that separated me from a clinic that looked a lot like triage in Operations but clearly wasn't. Her expression was haggard and her angel glow was barely noticeable, revealing bloodshot eyes as if she'd been crying.

I'd never seen her so emotionally raw before. Usually she had better control, always striving for a professional expression. But her lack of angel glow meant she'd drained herself, likely healing the rest of the team, and she probably hadn't gotten any sleep while I'd been going through transition. She was also probably under a great deal of stress since Essie was an archnephilim and about to become a fugitive — if she wasn't already — and there was a good chance the JP would consider her a traitor for helping us.

"Essie," my hound snarled even though I should have probably asked Amiah if she was okay, what had happened, or even where the hell we were. But I couldn't think past the need to claim our mate and prove to her that she was still ours. "Where is my mate?"

Amiah's gaze dropped to my already hardening cock and her expression darkened with a strange mix of grief and frustration and fear before she turned her back to me and headed to the counter a few feet away.

"You have to accept it," I said, trying to soften my tone, even though my hound wanted to snap at her.

She'd been against Essie from the beginning. She'd been rude and cold to her and I hadn't done anything to stop her because I'd thought forcing Essie away from me by any means possible would protect her.

But once I realized that I couldn't push Essie away even if I wanted to, I hadn't had a chance to tell Amiah to back off.

Something I needed to set straight, right now.

"I might not have a brand," I growled, "but I'm as much her mate as the others."

And I was going to prove it to her and everyone as soon as I found her.

"I know she is," she replied. "Your bond is so strong she pulled you through your transition in a matter of minutes." She released a shuddering breath and gripped the counter, still facing away from me as if she couldn't look at me. "But I knew you were mates before your second transition. I just didn't want to accept it, because..." She pressed her palm against her hip and released another shuddering breath as realization hit me.

"You have feelings for me." Fuck, I was such an idiot. I'd just thought because our flirting had been so mild and infrequent that she hadn't been interested in anything more... and because my wolf had picked Essie from the moment it had seen her, we never would have considered Amiah or anyone else. "Were you waiting for me to forget about her?"

She looked at me, her eyes glassy with tears. "I was so certain you would. I—" Her hand returned to her hip. "I have a not-yet-awakened mating brand that started to ache when I first met you. I thought—" She swallowed hard and fear bled into her grief. "I thought you were my destined mate and if I was just patient enough you'd fall out of love with her and— But after seeing what the brand is like, how Essie has no control over her life anymore—" She shuddered then squared her shoulders and her cold, if exhausted, mask of professionalism slid over her face, as if she hadn't just dropped that emotional bomb on me.

She had an angelic mating brand and she'd thought I was her mate?

No wonder she was so mean to Essie. I'd do anything for my mate, alienate anyone and everyone to protect her, and she'd thought Essie was going to break my heart.

I'd had no idea that Amiah was in love with me and I was probably an idiot for not having seen it. But she was an idiot for not speaking up and asking for what she wanted.

But then I still wouldn't have accepted her and asking for something for herself wasn't who Amiah was. She was frosty and bitchy and scolded you when she thought you were being reckless because she couldn't understand that there were some things you couldn't control. But she never did it because she wanted something for herself. She just didn't want to see you or others hurt.

"If you have a brand, then you have someone amazing waiting for you." Just like I did... who I needed to get to. Now now now.

She barked a bitter laugh. "The mating brand isn't beautiful or sacred. My destined mate could be anyone." Her lips curled back in disgust and she shuddered. "It could be that arrogant, lascivious fae, Sebastian Bane."

"Fate wouldn't be so cruel," I said, giving her my driest look as my hound heaved inside me, fighting to take control. We'd talked for too long and I needed to reclaim my mate. "Now where's Essie."

"Everyone should still be in the conference room having breakfast and coming up with a plan. It's at the end of the hall." She picked a keycard off the counter, held it out, and gave me her own dry expression. "But she'd probably appreciate it if you showered first."

No, my hound snapped.

Yes. I gritted my teeth, refusing to let it take over. As much as I hated to wait even a second, Amiah was right. I was a powerful demonic shifter now and I couldn't risk our mate thinking I was any more of a monster than I already was by trying to reclaim her looking like a psychopathic murderer who'd bathed in my victims' blood.

ESSIE

After finding out Lucifer was my father, we headed back inside the hotel and were now gathered in the conference room. It was a plain room with a large conference table and a dozen uncomfortable-looking chairs. A platter of pastries and fruit sat at the edge of the table, along with a carafe and a cluster of coffee mugs.

Sebastian sat in the chair closest to the door, picking at a half-eaten croissant, his skin still dull gray without its usual glow, and his emotions radiating exhausted worry. He wore a white T-shirt and tan cargo pants, like the rest of us, as if whoever had bought the clothes had just purchased a variety of sizes of the same thing. And I really hoped they'd purchased extra so I wouldn't have to continue running around in bloody clothes.

It was strange seeing him in something other than a button-down and slacks, and he really didn't look like himself.

"How many supers does it take to get an archnephilim to breakfast? Three, apparently." A ghost of his wicked smile pulled at his lips, but his emotions didn't change. "Or did you stop for a little fun on the way? If I'd known, I would have joined you."

"Sure, you could have met Daddy, too." Kol grabbed the carafe, poured a cup of coffee — his hands shaking — and handed it to me.

Sebastian quirked an eyebrow.

"Lucifer." I pulled out the chair beside Sebastian and sat. "And while he can't help us fight Lilith, he did give us a spell."

Sebastian's worry deepened. "What kind of spell?"

"I'm hoping you can confirm it." I met Sebastian's gaze, staring into his almost colorless eyes, searching for a glimmer of the power I'd seen before. But they were icy and dull. He looked like shit. Still breathtakingly handsome, but handsome that had had the crap beaten out of him. I really couldn't ask him to do anything more than look at the glyph and confirm it was actually a cage spell. "And do you know a witch we can trust to seed it?"

Gideon sat in the chair on my other side, his worry also growing, while Jacob leaned against the wall beside the door, his complexion still too pale. Both of them gave off the sense that they didn't like the idea of bringing anyone else into this, although I wasn't sure if it was to protect whoever we wanted to bring in, since that would make them a fugitive as well, or to protect me and my now-no-longer secret.

"Given your... nature and the fact you're wanted by the JP, I'm not sure I trust anyone," Sebastian said.

"And did you know about my nature?" I asked. But if he had known, why hadn't he said anything?

Sebastian pursed his lips.

So he had known. And he hadn't been afraid of me or turned me in. "Why didn't you say anything?"

Although if he had, I wasn't sure what I would have done. I probably would have figured out how to leave my guys to protect them.

"You weren't ready to know." He glanced over my shoulder at Gideon. "*They* weren't ready to know. I've never felt evil intent from you and I like to judge a person on *who* they are, not *what* they are." His gaze dropped to his half-eaten croissant, and with a sigh, he set it on the plate and held out a shaking hand. "Since you're not holding a piece of paper and Lucifer's power is memory magic, I'm assuming he embedded it in your memory."

"Yes." I took his hand.

A shiver of cold magic caressed my skin and vanished.

Sebastian frowned. "He didn't transmit it through touch?"

"No, he kissed her," Kol said, taking a muffin from the tray and sinking onto a chair.

"Really?" A flicker of mischief flashed through me. "A kiss, hunh? You know they say, once you've kissed a fae—"

Kol cleared his throat. "Dude, you can't compare. Don't even try."

"Right. Soul bonded with an incubus. Because three bonds weren't crazy enough." Sebastian rolled his eyes at me. "All right, lay it on me like Lucifer did."

I leaned in, imagining the first glyph Lucifer had given me, and pressed my lips against Sebastian's forehead. A flash of heated power swept from my lips into Sebastian's head.

He groaned and grabbed the edge of the table, his breath suddenly fast. "Jeez, that's one hell of a spell. Give me a week or so to recover and I can cast it."

"We don't have a week," Jacob said. "Lilith is planning on restarting Michael's war today."

"Well, I don't know of any witch who's powerful enough to cast it." Sebastian picked up his croissant but set it back down again.

"I'm told I just need the witch to draw the glyph and seed it," I said, still not entirely sure what *seeding* meant, only that it required a little magic and not a lot. "Do you have enough power to do that?"

"To seed it for a one-time use, yes. But it would be better if it was fully set. If you're not careful, this spell will burn you up. Setting won't protect you from that, but it's better than not setting it." Frost crept over the back of my hands, the fear coming from all my guys as well as Sebastian.

"You saw what Lilith can do. She has to be stopped." And the fact that she was my biological mother wasn't going to deter me.

Sebastian glanced past my shoulder to Gideon. "You can't possibly be okay with this."

"I'm not." Gideon shifted my chair so he could wrap an arm around my waist and pull me close. "But if not us, then who?"

Sebastian glanced at each of my guys, their expressions grim and determined, before returning his attention to me. "You're all insane. But you're right. If you don't burn yourself to a crisp, you're probably the best ones to go up against Lilith."

"Okay." Kol shoved up from his seat. "So how do we do this?"

"The bigger the glyph, the easier it'll be to control." The mischief returned to Sebastian's expression, and his emotions turned to heated desire. "So it looks like I take Esther back to my room and get her naked."

"You just don't know when to quit," Jacob said, rolling his eyes at him.

"Hey, maybe I'm Esther's fifth soul mate." He flashed me a seductive smile, but surprise snapped through me, as if he hadn't expected to say that, and his fear dropped the temperature.

Interesting. He desired me, but was afraid of being my mate. And while I was physically attracted to him — who wouldn't be? He was as hot as any of my guys — I didn't have the same pull, the same certainty that I did with the others. I knew in my soul they were mine. And Sebastian wasn't.

I leaned in and trailed a finger along his jaw, bringing my lips close to his. He shuddered again, both his desire and fear deepening. The emotions from my guys swelled into a confusing mix, then one by one settled on acceptance. They didn't know Sebastian like they knew each other, and yet if Sebastian was another mate, they'd accept him.

Sebastian's fear grew, overwhelming his need, but he hummed low in his throat, a sound of sensual masculine desire.

Jeez, he'd do anything to hide his true emotions.

"You know I'm an empath, right?" I breathed against his lips.

"Well, shit," he breathed back. "So, am I doomed or can we just fuck for fun?"

Gideon shifted closer, Jacob's intensity swelled, and the hellfire in Kol's eyes flared.

"Pretty sure I won't need to look beyond my mates for sex. And I'm more than sure that you're not one of mine."

He sagged back with a heavy sigh. "Oh, thank God. Bound to someone for eternity—?" He shuddered. "I don't care how good the sex is, that's a nightmare."

"Okay." Gideon stood, his relief surging into me. "What do you need to seed this spell?"

"A permanent marker and some time." Sebastian glanced at his croissant as if he were going to continue eating then shoved the plate farther away. "How are we dealing with the JP? They've got to have a tracking spell on you by now."

Gideon opened his mouth as Cassius stormed into the conference room. His gaze jumped to me and a wash of mixed emotions swept through me: confusion, fear, relief, and a fierce protective love that I was pretty sure was for Gideon.

"Things just got worse," Cassius said. "Lucifer has been sighted."

Gideon pursed his lips and Kol drained his coffee mug.

"I'll go find that marker," Jacob said, and he strode out of the room.

Cassius frowned. "Why do none of you look surprised?"

"He's running interference with the JP so we can figure out how to deal with Lilith," I said.

Cassius's eyes narrowed. "Why would he do that?"

For a second I contemplated not telling Cassius the truth — and given how I had no problems lying when necessary, I should have known I wasn't all angel. But I was already Lilith's daughter and none of the paternal archangel options were good. Lucifer being my father didn't make things any worse.

"He's my father and doesn't want Lilith or the JP to get their hands on me." I glanced at Sebastian and stood. "Let's get this spell seeded."

Cassius threw his hands up in resignation. "Of course he is. So what's the plan? I can't decide if I want him to lend us his power or not. An archangel would be useful in a fight. A murderous psychopath, not so much."

"The plan is to put Lilith back in her cage." Sebastian stood, using the table to steady himself. His expression tightened with pain, and fear snapped through me then vanished as he locked his emotions down.

Damn, maybe I shouldn't have told him I was an empath. I was sure that was the last I'd feel from him.

"And to do that, we need to figure out where she's going to be," Kol said. "Any ideas?"

Sebastian shuffled to the doorway, sweat beading on his forehead before he'd even made it into the hall.

"You sure you're up for this?" Gideon asked, falling into step beside him.

"I can sit and draw on Esther's back." He huffed. "If you give me a few hours I could probably manage more, but given we don't know our timeline, the sooner I seed this spell, the better."

We stopped at a door halfway down the hall, and Sebastian unlocked it and let us in. The room was identical to the one I'd shared with the guys. The bed had been slept in, the comforter and sheets crumpled, and the bathmat lay on the floor in front of the shower, but other than that it was the same plain, clean room.

Kol propped the door open with a rolled-up towel so Jacob wouldn't have to be let in and leaned against the wall at the foot of the bed as Sebastian sagged onto the mattress.

"So what do we know?" Gideon asked, also leaning on the wall and crossing his arms.

I tugged the comforter and sheets up to make a smoother surface to lie on and pulled off my bloody T-shirt.

Cassius's eyes widened. "I'm not sure I should be here for this."

"He's drawing a glyph," Gideon said. "You're fine."

"You're mated to an archnephilim whose parents are the two most dangerous supers on the planet. I'll let you know when I'm fine."

"Well, if you keep thinking about it that way," Kol said, "you're never going to be fine."

Cassius glared at him.

"So, about the plan." I laid face down on the bed, unhooked my bra, and Sebastian set his hands on my back. Ice trickled into my skin with a whisper of his power, and I turned my head to meet his pale gaze. "Just enough to seed it."

He rolled his eyes at me. "Not a self-sacrificing idiot like your mates."

Jacob returned with the marker and handed it to Sebastian, and the trickle of ice vanished, replaced by the maker's cool tip.

Kol's gaze slid up my body. The heat in his eyes grew and stole my breath, and his seductive power slipped into me and shivered down my spine.

"Jeez," Sebastian huffed. "If you don't want me to mess this up, hold still."

With his lips quirked in his usual wicked smile, Kol mouthed "sorry" to me, although I was pretty sure he wasn't sorry at all. He did, however, slide down the wall and settle on the floor where I couldn't make eye contact with him.

Gideon rolled his eyes at Kol, but a hint of heat darkened his gaze as well when he turned his attention back to me. "Okay, we know Lilith wants to make a statement. She tried to assassinate Ambassador Hollaway so she could attack the funeral and take out as many high-ranking JP members as possible."

"She also said she'd had to move up her plans to today," Jacob added.

"So what does that mean?" Cassius asked, his gaze jumping from Jacob to Gideon to Kol.

"Hey, don't look at me," Kol said. "The only thing I remember from the fight in that lab is freaking out over the maturation tanks. And I'm pretty sure the only reason I didn't have a complete breakdown was because I was in shock over being branded. That whole fight is a blur for me."

Cassius sighed. "Do we know for a fact that she hasn't used the tanks?"

"Nothing is certain," Jacob said. "But the tanks were empty, they didn't look like they'd been used, and all of the equipment was covered up."

"I also couldn't sense any magic in them," Sebastian said, "and those puppies need a lot of magic, magic that would leave a residue for a long time."

"So no nephilim, yet." Cassius pursed his lips and frowned.

Yeah, that was the key word: yet.

"And thank God for that," Kol said. "Her witches feeding off her worship magic are powerful enough. They took out us and an elite team at the same time."

"So is it one or the other for her right now?" I asked. "She can have her army of witches *or* create her nephilim. She doesn't have enough power right now for both?"

"That has to be her plan," Gideon said. "She wasn't going to just kill the JP members at Hollaway's funeral. Most of them are powerful supers with strong essences. She was going to drain them. Probably kidnap them and drain them over and over again until she had enough power for both witches and nephilim."

Sebastian slid the marker over the invisible sensitive spot by my shoulder blade where my right wing formed. Desire shivered through me, and I squirmed, wiggling my toes, fighting to stay still.

Kol groaned. The temperature in the room rose, and Gideon shifted, his breath a little too fast.

"If the funeral isn't happening, where would she go to get an influx of power?" Jacob asked, his voice low and raspy.

"And what would be just as much of a statement as draining JP members?" Cassius added.

Gideon tipped his head back and closed his eyes. "That's also happening today?"

I turned the questions over and over in my mind. If she couldn't drain a handful of powerful supers, would draining a lot of not-powerful supers or even humans give her the power she wanted? What was just as much of a statement as attacking the ambassador's funeral?

Oh, shit. There was only one thing happening today that might fit that bill. "Lots of people and a statement? She's going to attack the unification ceremony. The supers in attendance won't be as powerful as those at Ambassador Hollaway's funeral, but there'll be more of them, and what better statement for restarting Michael's war than attacking a ceremony marking the beginning of its end?"

Gideon glanced at the bedside clock. "That's in just over two hours."

The marker trailed along my ribs, then curled into the small of my back.

"The ceremony takes place in the middle of Unity Park," Jacob said. "There aren't a lot of good places to hide. And even if there were, Lilith would still be able to sense us."

"Well, we can't just walk up to her and take her out," Cassius said.

Except I needed to touch Lilith to cage her and that meant getting close. "I think I *have* to walk up to her. We're not going to be able to catch her unaware with me close enough to touch her, so there's no point in trying to be stealthy."

Gideon ran his hand over his hair, thankfully now not quite as short as Cassius's, and worry but also consideration swelled into me. He was seriously thinking about it.

"Gideon, please," Cassius said. "Don't go through with this. You were all barely alive when you teleported back into Operations. You can't just walk up to Lilith."

"He won't be. I will. I'll hold my power back so hopefully she won't realize how much I have left until it's too late." I wasn't going to mention how I had no idea if I could pull that off. Especially since I also had to concentrate on my bonds with Gideon, Jacob, and Kol to resist the inky magic from taking over my soul, which I was sure would gain strength the closer I got to Lilith. But it was really our only option.

"Are you sure about this?" Jacob knelt by the bed so he could look me in the eyes, his expression tight, his complexion still a little pale. "With a spell this size, you'll need everything you've got, both angelic and demonic magic. If you walk into the middle of the unification ceremony and use both, everyone will know you're a nephilim. You won't be able to get your life back."

"I haven't lost my life. I have you guys." And I wasn't going to think too hard about how I might not have Marcus any more. "I'll tell Lilith I want to join her."

"I'm not sure she'll believe that," Kol said.

"She only needs to believe it long enough for me to touch her," I reminded him. "You'll need to stay out of sight until I can start the spell, but then you have to take care of her witches. As soon as Lilith realizes what I'm doing, they'll come after me."

"We'll always have your back," Gideon said. "And you're right. If she thinks you're an enemy, she won't let you close, but if she thinks you're her daughter coming to join her cause, you might get close enough to touch her."

"I hate that the plan revolves around a might," Cassius said.

"We all do." Jacob offered me a sad smile. We could all do the math. Even if Lucifer believed I was strong enough to imprison Lilith, that only meant the odds were marginally less terrible. "So we have two hours. We should probably get some rest."

"First I want to check on Marcus," I said. "Then I'm bringing you back to full."

Gideon gave a tight nod and pushed away from the wall. "I'll go talk to Voth and see if he has, and is willing to loan us, anything that might help."

"No, Gideon." I held out my hand to him. I might want Jacob at full health, but I wanted him near me, too. I wanted all my guys. If this didn't go well, if Lilith killed me, or worse, her magic possessed me, this might be my last chance to be with them. "Stay. You, too, Kol."

"And by stay, she means in your own room," Sebastian said.

"I'll talk to Voth." Cassius turned on his heel and left, taking a strange mix of garbled emotions with him. For a moment, I wondered if I'd be able to sort out his feelings if I concentrated, but it was probably rude to be feeling his feelings as it was — something I supposed I'd have to work on if I survived.

Sebastian pressed his palm against the center of my back, sending another whisper of cold magic into me, then sat back.

"Done. Just touch here and think about activating the spell." He brushed a cool finger over a black swirl at the top of my left shoulder. "As long as you have a hand on Lilith when you activate it, it won't matter if she pushes you away. The spell will be locked on her. You just have to pump in enough power to break through her defenses without burning up."

"Gee, it sounds so easy when you say it," I said, not even trying to hide the sarcasm in my voice.

"There's nothing easy about it." Sebastian groaned and bowed his head. "Now get out of here."

I rehooked my bra and reached for my bloody T-shirt with its four claw holes. "Please tell me I can get another one of these. New cargo pants as well would be great."

I really didn't want to put the dirty shirt back on. It was bad enough I'd had to wear my dirty bra and undies. But I couldn't go walking around the halls without a shirt even if it seemed we were the only ones down here, so I pulled it on and stood.

Jacob stood with me, taking my hand in his, and we stepped into the hall. Gideon followed, falling into step on my other side, and Kol drew up close behind me, his body heat radiating against my back.

Their emotions were a mix of worry, desire, and heartache, so I gathered a little of my angelic magic — still not close to being recovered from healing Kol — and pushed my love for them through our bonds.

Kol drew in a sharp breath. His surprise and awe at feeling love made me smile. Gideon turned his gorgeous blue gaze on me, while Jacob's grip on my hand tightened.

"I love you, too," Jacob whispered, his voice that deep rumble that made my soul's vibration align with his.

Forty feet down the hall, the door to our room opened and Marcus stormed out in only a pair of cargo pants hanging low on his hips. Water dripped from his wet hair, trailing a sensual runnel over his chest and making my breath stall. God, he was sexy. All the blood that had caked his skin was gone, and only a red ugly scar the size of my fist lying too close to his heart proved he'd nearly died.

I froze and his piercing green gaze jerked to me, as if he instantly knew where I was. The feralness in his eyes was stronger than before, brutal, as if he could rip me to shreds with just a look.

The temperature jumped to sweltering, sweat instantly slicking my body, but with his hard, ferocious expression, I was certain the heat wasn't desire but rage. We might be mated, but that didn't mean what I'd done to him was forgivable. I'd taken away his humanity and turned him into a demon. He wasn't a despised monster like me, the world didn't hate him, but I didn't know if he'd see it that way.

His stance widened. A whisper of hellfire flared in his eyes and his breath picked up.

"Hey, Marcus," Jacob said, his voice calm and even.

But Marcus growled, his gaze never leaving mine, and he stormed toward me.

Oh, shit.

I squared my shoulders. Marcus's rage seared my skin, every ounce of him radiating deadly ferocity. "I did what I had to do."

"I know," he snarled, picking up his pace.

"Marcus." Gideon stepped in front of me, and Marcus shoved him aside, tossing him into the wall with a resounding crack.

His hands dug into my biceps and he slammed me against the wall, crashing his mouth against mine. I gasped, surprised, and he devoured my breath, kissing me with a wildness that made my senses reel, blazing through me until every nerve was on fire, desperate and needing.

With a snarl, he grabbed my hair, painfully digging his fingers into my scalp, and yanked my head back to deepen the kiss. A whisper of Kol's magic slid into me, turning the pain to delicious pleasure, and I groaned into Marcus's mouth.

He growled back and ripped open the front of my T-shirt with the claws of his free hand. My breath picked up as he shoved his fingers inside my bra and clenched my breast. His erection ground against me, his need for me overwhelming, and another whisper of Kol's magic twisted the pain into pleasure.

"Marcus." Gideon grabbed Marcus's shoulder.

"Mine," he snarled against my lips, his body trembling as if he were struggling to restrain himself. "You have to know you're still mine and I still want you."

"But I hurt you. Again."

"And you're an idiot to think I won't still love you."

"But all that pain—"

"You saved me. And I knew you wouldn't just take my word for it. We don't share a brand. So I'm cutting to the chase and *showing* you exactly how I feel," he said, his wolf— or rather *beast* darkening his eyes, straining to take over, his rage actually a wild, uncontrolled primal passion. "We both have to show you."

Kol snorted. "Perhaps you could show her in our room. Not out in the hall. You know I'm all for a good display of public indecency, but I'm not sure about Essie and I'm certain this one—" He jerked his thumb at Gideon. "—would hate it."

Jacob unlocked our door and held it open. "We'll give you the room."

"Only if that's what you want," Marcus said to me, not a hint of hesitation or regret in his voice or a change in his searing emotions. "I love *all* of you. Everything you are. Angel and demon and multiple soul bonds. Don't get me wrong, I'll never say no to just the two of us, but I won't say no to anything else."

We only had two hours until the unification ceremony and while I wanted to let Marcus show me that I'd been an idiot to think he'd hate me, I wanted to spend every minute I had left with all my guys.

"I want all of you."

With a growl, Marcus grabbed my hips and urged me up. I wrapped my legs around him and he captured my lips in another breathtaking kiss as he carried me into the hotel room. The rest of the guys followed and I motioned to Jacob.

"Let's get you closer to full."

Marcus turned us and pinned me against Jacob, who brushed my hair away from my neck and pressed his lips against my vein.

My breath hitched, half in anticipation and half in fear. The last time Jacob had bitten me, I'd almost lost my mind.

Jeez. What was wrong with me? I loved the feel of Jacob's magic. Really. But I couldn't seem to push back the memory of what had happened.

"Essie." Kol drew up close and met my gaze, the hellfire in his eyes blazing. "I've got you."

His magic slid into me, melting my fear, and Jacob sank his fangs into my neck. I gasped at the pain and Kol's power grew until Jacob took a gentle pull and flooded me with his seductive magic.

Marcus deepened our kiss and his grip on my butt tightened, his passion fueling mine and adding to the aching need inside me. Another pull on my vein and Jacob's magic twisted tighter.

But my breath picked up, and the fear returned. What if I couldn't release it? What if it built up beyond what I could handle again?

Which was ridiculous. My guys had me. They'd never let it go that far again, and it hadn't been their fault in the first place.

"Hey." Kol gave Marcus a look, and Marcus jerked away with a snarl, his emotions fighting with his beast to give me what I needed even if that meant it wasn't him.

Jacob wrapped an arm around my waist, pulling me tighter against his massive chest and supporting my wobbly legs, and Kol drew close. He kissed me, slowly, sensually, making my head spin, then trailed his lips down my body. He sucked each nipple into a tight peak, drawing all my focus to his mouth on me and away from Jacob's mouth on my neck. With a low hum of pleasure that radiated to my core, he sank lower and slid my pants and underwear down my legs.

Jacob took another bone-melting pull and his magic spun tighter as Kol's lips trailed up my thigh, weaving his magic into Jacob's and sinking both of their powers into me with a seductive, sultry need. I gasped as Kol's tongue brushed me, then I melted into the pleasure of his hot mouth on me. It was glorious, the rasp of his tongue, his hands clutching my hips to keep me in place, and his magic combined with Jacob's throbbing inside me.

Kol caressed and licked as Jacob slid a hand to my breast, his magic spinning tighter and tighter, until I was drowning in sensation.

My orgasm crashed into me, sudden and hard, stealing all breath and thought, before I fully realized what had happened. My knees gave way completely, and Jacob tightened his grip, securing me against his muscular chest, his healing magic warming my neck.

Kol's grip on my hips tightened, the only sign my release had affected him, and he slowly brushed his tongue against my clit, drawing out shuddering aftershocks as Marcus stepped close again. He grabbed my chin and turned my head to capture me with a searing, possessive kiss.

The heat of his desire blazed across my already heated skin, and Kol worked me back up to squirming, desperate need with his tongue. I wrapped my arms around Marcus's neck, needing him closer, needing to feel his ferocity driving inside me.

Kissing me breathless, he pulled me from Jacob's arms. Darkness and hellfire and wild desire filled Marcus's eyes. He threw me on the bed, grabbed my ankles, and yanked me to the edge close to him. His gaze locked with mine, the question in his eyes. Did I want this? His beast had more control than he did and there wasn't going to be anything gentle or slow about this.

Just the thought made me throb, aching for all his ferocity focused on me. "Yes." *Oh, yes please.*

With a snarl, he seized my hips and thrust into me, plunging in all the way to the hilt.

A ripple of an orgasm swept through me, my muscles clamping around him already on the verge of release again.

The hellfire in his eyes burned brighter, and his canines extended into fangs. Little wisps of demonic magic curled from his hands and forearms and sank into my skin with glorious, searing sparks.

He pulled out and thrust back in again, hard.

Oh, fuck, yes.

The muscles in his sculpted arms and shoulders flexed as he controlled my body, pounding into me with a wildness that stole my breath. I was awed at how powerful he was and on fire with need. Even without a brand, I could feel the strength of our soul bond blazing in my chest, surging with his love and desire.

Gideon settled on the bed above me, hooked his finger under my chin, and urged my head back. For a second, time stalled and there was only him and his strong, sure love, then Marcus slammed back into me, twisting my desire tighter, and Gideon kissed me. He devoured each gasping cry of pleasure, making love to my mouth slowly, sensually, as Marcus drove me to climax.

The orgasm ripped through me, shooting stars behind my lids and making my head spin. Moments later, Marcus growled and tensed with his own release, his erection pulsing inside me and making me clench tighter around him.

Gideon paused for a second, his lips brushing mine, letting me catch my breath, and the weight on the bed between my legs changed. Large strong hands slid over my hips and along my ribcage to my breasts. Jacob. His erection brushed my wet swollen entrance and I squirmed, my desire picking up again.

Oh, yes, please.

Kol chuckled. He lay on the bed beside me, the hellfire in his eyes so strong it licked his cheeks, his expression blissfully dazed.

"Can't hide anything from you," I said, my voice low and husky.

"You never could before and now I'm free to enjoy it." He nudged Jacob's hand aside and flicked his tongue over my already sensitive nipple.

Oh, yes. I tipped my head back, and Gideon deepened our kiss as Jacob rubbed his tip against my opening. God, I wanted Jacob in me, filling me, but he captured my hips and held me in place, teasing me with his tip as Kol sucked my nipple into his hot mouth.

Gideon palmed my other breast and Jacob slid slowly — so damned slowly — into me, filling me completely. Kol increased the pull on my nipple, twisting pleasure and pain again with his magic, driving me wild, and Gideon commanded my mouth. With a groan, Jacob withdrew just as slowly, drawing out the sensation, then pushed back in.

I writhed against their grips, my senses on overload, their mouths and hands and bodies searing me with their desire. Every nerve, every cell, hell, my whole essence was on fire with need.

Jacob pushed back in again and tightened his grip on my hips, and Gideon and Kol pulled away. With one fluid movement, he rolled us over so I straddled him, and our gazes locked. The depth of his passion swelled through our brand, solid and eternal, and he tangled his fingers in my hair and pulled me down to kiss him.

I melted into his embrace, his hips still rolling in a slow sensual rhythm, sliding his erection out to the tip and driving back in, each thrust drawing out as much pleasure as possible.

Then Kol's hot slicked fingers caressed my back entrance, and my pulse leaped. I had no idea where he'd gotten the lube, but he was an incubus. It shouldn't have surprised me. His fingers teased me, testing my interest, drawing glorious tremors of pleasure and making me gasp.

My breath picked up even faster. The idea of both of them inside me, filling me, almost made me come again right there, but Kol snapped a thread of magic into me and stole my climax, taking me back to the aching edge without letting me crash over.

I groaned, and he slowly pushed his finger into me. Jacob kept his rhythm, and with his thumb rubbed circles over my clit as Kol stretched me, adding another finger, drawing out the anticipation.

God, I ached for him, for more. I almost cried in grief at the loss of the glorious pressure when he pulled out his fingers, but he pressed his thick, slick tip against me, and the cry turned into a moan.

He pushed inside, turning that first moment of pain into sultry pleasure with his magic. Jacob held steady for me, his thumb skimming my clit, keeping me on the edge until Kol was buried deep, his hips flush with me. It was almost too much to bear, the pleasure mixed with pressure mixed with Kol's bone-melting magic.

"Jesus, Essie," Kol gasped, running his hands up my chest and teasing my nipples. "You feel so good."

Panting, I leaned back into him and gave in, riding their rhythm, my skin growing more and more sensitive with each swell of Kol's power. Every caress of Jacob's thumb or pinch of Kol's fingers or stroke deep inside me spun my desire tighter and tighter. My body was on fire, teetering on the edge of climax. Their rhythm grew faster, turning my breath to gasping moans. Then Jacob tensed with his climax, and my body shuddered, my orgasm swelling in response.

Kol surged a mind-blowing blast of magic into me, and all of my muscles contracted. His grip around me tightened, pulling me close, and he gasped my name, his breath hot in my ear. Bliss crashed over me, shattering me. It was the most amazing feeling, coming with two of my guys inside me, their love and satisfaction coursing through our brands.

I didn't know how long we stayed connected, but too soon, Kol was pulling out and easing me onto Jacob's massive chest. He wrapped his arms around me, and I drew in deep ragged breaths.

"Holy fuck, guys."

Kol flashed me a wicked, satisfied grin and Jacob gave a contented sigh as Gideon stretched out beside me, a whisper of electric power crackling through our brand. He drew me from Jacob's arms into his, and kissed me in his slow, sensual style, drawing out every second, his hard erection digging into the crux between my thigh and torso. Oh so close and oh so far away from where I wanted it.

"You're so beautiful," he murmured against my lips. "I love the way you look when you come."

"Then make me come," I said back, my voice breathy.

"As my mate commands." He settled between my legs, his gaze never leaving mine, and thrust inside me.

The force of his invasion and the intensity in his summer-sky eyes surprised me. His desire for me was just as fierce as my other guys, his love just as sure, but was more reserved than the others. Funny how he was the one I'd been the most afraid of, the one I feared would never accept me, and all I could see in his eyes and feel from his brand was unconditional love.

He trembled, holding himself still, and the anticipation, waiting for him to move, to do anything, twisted my need tighter until I was squirming.

With a breathtaking smile, he dipped down, kissed me, and started to move inside me. His rhythm was slow and powerful, building my desire until I was writhing and gasping underneath him.

The light in the core of my being flared, resonating with the light in his, and all my brands lit up. I could feel all of their love, and the certainty that we belonged together. Fate hadn't led us astray. This was destiny, and even if I'd wanted to fight it, I couldn't.

Gideon's thrusts grew faster, whirling me closer and closer to a climax not just fueled by physical sensation but emotions as well.

Then he tensed, his climax tearing through him, and mine slammed into me a second later, hard and fast, drawing a scream and shattering me again.

My essence and soul spun on light and bliss, and I was no longer a being of flesh, but one of pure glorious sensation.

After a moment to catch our breaths, Gideon withdrew from me and shifted to draw me onto his chest. Marcus stretched out in front of me and pressed the length of his body against mine, even with Gideon's arm between us, as if he needed as much flesh-to-flesh contact as possible. Kol curled above me, his forehead against the top of my head, his eyes glazed over, and Jacob lay at my feet, his big hand just above my knees between my thighs.

I drifted on boneless pleasure with their bonds — all of their bonds, not just the branded ones — radiating love, satisfaction, and certainty.

I could stay this way forever. I wanted this forever. But if we hid away from the world, Lilith would destroy it, and no matter how much I craved my guys and being satiated like this, none of us could allow Lilith to restart Michael's war.

My love for my men swelled, filling my chest, but so too did my fear.

Please, God. Don't let me lose any of them.

ESSIE

A GENTLE KNOCK ON THE DOOR WOKE ME, AND GIDEON'S GRIP AROUND ME tightened as Marcus groaned, his breath feathering warm across the back of my neck.

"I know you're sealing bonds and all that," Cassius said, "but you're out of time. We have to go."

"Fuck," Marcus growled.

Kol mumbled something and a trickle of his magic swept through me, making me gasp.

"Fuck," Marcus said again, his voice raspy, his erection hard against my thigh. "Do you have to make that sound, Essie?"

"Blame Kol," I said as another trickle teased me. "He hasn't got full control of his magic."

"Still?" Jacob asked, his hand sliding higher up my inner thigh, although I suspected he wasn't fully awake, either. "He sent a big surge through the soul bonds before we passed out."

"A couple of surges," Marcus added.

Cassius knocked again. "Anyone? I have clean clothes for Shaw."

Gideon groaned, sat up, and gave Kol a shake, waking him.

"What?" Kol asked, his words slurred.

"You're going to need to bleed that off." Gideon slid off the bed, found his pants in a pile of clothes on the floor, and pulled them on.

"Yeah, sure," Kol said, rolling away from me and drawing in a shuddering breath. "I never thought this would be my problem."

"Who'd have thought we'd find an incubus's limit on sexual energy," Jacob said with a chuckle.

"Only because our soul bonds make everything more powerful." Kol squeezed his eyes shut and more magic swept through me.

A mini orgasm clenched my muscles and I moaned, grinding against Marcus.

"I like this." Marcus pulled me closer and kissed me, his beast's hellfire flickering in his eyes.

I liked it, too, but we didn't have time for more. If we didn't move now, Lilith would kill a lot of innocent people.

With a groan, I eased away from Marcus. Once we'd stopped Lilith, then we could spend all day in bed... because we were all unemployed... and fugitives.

Which was a problem for another day.

Cassius handed off a bag of clothes through a crack in the door just wide enough for the bag without letting him see all of us naked in bed, and Gideon tossed the bag to me. No underwear. Swell. I put my dirty bra and undies back on and pulled on the clean T-shirt and cargo pants as the rest of the guys dressed as well

Kol still leaked sensual magic that heated my skin and made Marcus stand distractingly close, but it wasn't unmanageable, and his eyes were starting to clear. Thank goodness, because I didn't feel good about letting him go into a fight high.

We strode into the hall where Cassius waited. His angel glow flared when he saw us, and his emotions swirled in a strange mix before settling on fear.

"Voth has Berettas and M4s for anyone who wants them. He also has vests," he said, shoving away from the wall and leading us down the hall toward the clinic and the door to the loading docks.

"We'll take whatever he's got," Gideon said as we hurried into the loading bay. "Anything magical that might be useful?"

Voth, standing at an open locker filled with tactical gear and weapons, looked at us. "The only thing magical I have to offer is this." He held up a glowing marble that looked a lot like the marble imbued with my light magic that we'd used to buy the area containment master ward.

"Is that my power?" I asked. I was still low, so any extra magic would help. Especially if I was going to need everything I had to reimprison Lilith.

He shrugged and handed it to me, as if he wasn't just giving up an extremely expensive power source. "Thought it might be helpful."

The marble warmed my palm, resonating with me even though Sebastian had stripped all of my essence from it before we'd handed it over.

"You're not radiating a lot of power now," Voth said.

I glanced at Kol, who nodded his agreement and took a pair of sheathed knives the length of my forearm out of the locker. So far, I was still managing to contain my power, but I didn't know how easy it would be once I'd recharged.

"Cassius told me your terrible plan. I'd wait until the cage spell is activated and I'd gotten away from Lilith before reabsorbing your power. If you absorb it now, it'll be harder for you to hide it from her."

"And Lilith won't be able to sense the marble?" I asked, pocketing the marble.

"Not unless it's awakened or absorbed." Voth pulled two bulletproof vests out of the locker and handed them to Gideon, who handed one to me.

"I can't." No matter how much I wanted to take a vest and a Beretta. "I can't look like I'm ready to fight. I have to look like I've given in and want to join her."

Marcus growled and Kol tensed.

"This plan just keeps getting worse." Cassius threw his hands up and strode to the front of the loading bay by the security door.

"It's the only way she'll get close," Jacob said.

The muscles in Gideon's jaw tensed and he gave the vest back to Voth.

Yeah, I didn't like it either.

"The SUV is parked outside," Voth said. "I'll give you fifteen minutes then call in the anonymous Lucifer sighting. I also have business I have to take care of, but I'll come as soon as I can." He tossed Cassius a set of keys and strode back into the hotel, passing Amiah who stood in the doorway.

She stared at us, her arms crossed, her expression icy and her fear chilling the air and churning in my stomach. Her gaze darted to Marcus, who was putting on a vest, and a whisper of heartache curled around me before she jerked her attention back to Gideon as he walked over to Cassius.

Jacob belted on a pair of Berettas, drew close, and pressed his large hand against the small of my back. "Are you ready?"

"Nope. But I don't think I'll ever be ready to reimprison my mother the Hellfire Queen."

"I really hope I don't regret this," Cassius growled, and he strode out the door.

We followed him to a silver SUV parked just outside the loading bay door. It wasn't as spacious as a JP vehicle and didn't have a third row of seats, but it was big enough for all six of us if Jacob sat in the back, so it would do the trick.

Fear from my guys chilled me inside and out even in the sweltering SUV, which had clearly been sitting out in the summer sun all morning, but they all kept their expressions tight. If I hadn't been an empath, I wouldn't have known just how worried they were. And I didn't know if that made me feel better or not.

I shifted, unable to keep still as we drove out of the Quarter to Unity Park. Marcus, who sat beside me, squeezed my knee, drawing my attention. His beast lay just under the surface, a prick of hellfire flickering in his piercing green eyes and sending a mixed shudder of desire and worry down my spine.

"You can call this off any time you want," he said.

"You know I can't." I leaned in and kissed him, savoring the feel of his lips against mine.

Kol, on my other side, shifted closer, and Jacob, sitting in the back, reached over the seats and pressed his big palm against the back of my neck.

Gideon glanced back, the light in his eyes dim with worry, before he sucked in a quick breath and squared his shoulders. "Okay. Essie needs to convince Lilith to trust her long enough to get within grabbing distance. That means we need to stay out of sight. No matter what."

Cassius shot him at hard look. "I really hate this."

"We all do," Jacob said.

"I'll get to her as fast as I can. Hopefully we can get to her before she starts anything."

"There's another word I hate." Cassius stopped at a stop light, his knee nervously bouncing as he waited for it to change. "Might and hopefully. This is a terrible plan."

"You can stay in the SUV," Kol said.

"You know *I* can't," Cassius snapped back.

The light turned green and Cassius sped through the intersection, faster than the speed limit, but not so fast we'd get pulled over. I was actually impressed that his need to protect lives was stronger than the angelic urge to follow the rules. But then, he was Gideon's brother and more emotionally volatile than Gideon, so maybe it shouldn't have surprised me.

"This is the best plan we've got," Gideon said. "We should park on the far side of the park and make our entrance from there."

"Agreed." Cassius took a corner a little too fast, squealing the wheels, and slowed down a bit. "It'll take a little longer to get to the ceremony's location, but we're less likely to be spotted by any supers."

I didn't like the sound of that. Once again we were leaving our vehicle farther away than I liked and this time we didn't have anyone who could teleport us to safety. But I couldn't argue against it. Better to be farther away than caught before I could even get close to Lilith.

JACOB

EVERYONE WAS TENSE, OUR WORRY A PALPABLE ENERGY CROWDING AROUND us, as Cassius gunned it through the intersection the moment the light turned green. He was driving to the park almost as aggressively as Marcus usually drove, and this was a side of the uptight angel I'd never seen before.

Admittedly I didn't know him very well, we'd only met a few times during the war and a handful more times in the following years. But he'd always been strung tight and angry and deadly serious about his commitment to the JP, and I'd never thought he'd defy the director and abandon his career.

Of course, he'd barely survived the witches' attack on Operations and had seen our condition when Sebastian had teleported us into the cafeteria. He'd known if we'd escaped Operations we were going to do something stupid — like we were now — and eliminate whatever had nearly killed us and an elite team, because he knew Gideon. And in his heart, despite the fact that it was obvious she was an archnephilim, he had to know that Essie had the same serve and protect values.

We all did. Destiny wouldn't have bound our souls together if we hadn't.

A part of me was still stunned that I was blessed with something so amazing and even more stunned at how natural it had felt for the four of us to make love to Essie. There'd only been one tense moment at the beginning when she'd been afraid of my bite, and if she'd asked, I would have stopped. But Kol had eased her past her fear and when it was my turn to show her how much I loved her, she hadn't hesitated.

If only the tension now could be as easily overcome.

Essie shifted in the seat in front of me and entwined her fingers with Kol's. I'd pressed my palm against the back of her neck to reassure her with my touch just like Marcus and Kol were, trying to ignore my fear of what was about to come and focus on her, my mate, but really there was little any of us could do to ease the fear.

We had to face Lilith and our odds of success were slim.

But I was also worried about what would happen if we survived.

Even if we won, everything Essie had worked so hard for would be destroyed. She was going to walk into a crowd where there would be news cameras and everyone had a cell phone, reveal she was an archnephilim, and tell Lilith she wanted to joined her fight to restart Michael's war.

Even if we could convince the JP that Essie wasn't evil, there'd be video evidence to the contrary and she'd be convicted in the arena of public opinion.

It didn't matter what happened beyond this point. Her life as she knew it was over and it broke my heart. She was going to sacrifice everything for a world that was going to turn on her and I could only pray the four of us would be able to help her rebuild in some way and not spend the rest of our lives on the run.

Not that I was going to stop us from going ahead with the plan. Lilith needed to be stopped and we were the ones best able to do that. I just wished Essie didn't have to suffer anymore. She'd already been through so much. She'd lived in fear of being discovered during her childhood and now she'd learned she really had been created to be a weapon.

Everything was happening so fast, I doubted she'd had time to process. I doubt she'd even had time to fully process branding Kol even though they'd sealed their bond or that Marcus was now a hellhound.

My gaze jumped to Marcus and the red hellfire flickering in his eyes.

None of us had had time to process his transition or what it might mean for him.

There weren't any hellhounds in the mortal realm. I wasn't sure there were any in any of the realms. If by some miracle we could still stay in Union City, would his pack still accept him? Did he still need to have a pack now that he was a hound? Or had the four of us become his new pack?

He was strong enough to be a pack alpha. If he saw the team as his new pack, would he want to take control from Gideon?

The memory of him pounding into Essie only half an hour ago while Gideon kissed her jumped to mind. Aside from dominating Essie's body with his, he hadn't been upset that Gideon had stolen her cries with his lips, and he hadn't had a problem when I'd bitten Essie and she'd needed Kol instead of him to distract her from her fear.

No, the dynamic of the team would stay the same. Marcus hated paperwork and organizational politics — which was good because with his temper we'd be perpetually under review — and he hadn't wanted to take control of everyone in the bedroom. He'd be his usual obstinate self, but he wouldn't fight Gideon for leadership, which was good because we couldn't afford to have infighting especially if we were on the run from the JP.

Of course that only mattered if we survived the next however many hours against Lilith.

<h1 style="text-align:center">ESSIE</h1>

TEN MINUTES LATER, CASSIUS PARKED AT THE FAR END OF UNITY PARK. The tension in the SUV, and the power slipping from my guys with their worry, squeezed my chest, making it hard to breathe.

Kol and I jumped out of the vehicle before it had even come to a full stop, and I sucked in deep gasps of the hot, humid air, sweat instantly slicking my skin.

"Sorry," Marcus mumbled.

Jacob and Gideon gave us apologetic looks, and Cassius gave us a tight nod.

I glanced at the blazing sun. The clock in the SUV had said 3:26 p.m., and the sun still sat high in the sky. With the heat and no clouds, it was a perfect day for an outside ceremony — if possibly a little too hot — and that meant a lot of people would be in attendance.

Gideon and Cassius headed to the path leading into the park, and the rest of us followed. The trees were thicker here than the other side of the park, not so thick you couldn't see through them, but certainly offering better cover. We were a quarter of a way around Unity Lake from the wide, level green space where the ceremony was being held — which was about a hundred yards from where I'd tumbled to a stop after being shot.

I strained to see any sign of Lilith and her witches, but couldn't see or sense anything beyond the slight press of power from my guys and an even slighter pressure from the supers gathered up ahead for the ceremony. No crushing power from Lilith and not a hint of the inky magic inside me.

Were we wrong? Was she going to attack some place else? Was the inky magic gone?

No. I couldn't even pretend that I'd managed to push out her inky worship magic when I'd released my primal scream behind Voth's hotel, and I could only pray I'd be able to hold onto the connection in my brands and keep the inky magic from seizing my body and soul long enough to cast the cage spell.

And Lilith's plan had to be to attack the ceremony. It was the most logical, biggest statement. It had to be.

"Cassius, you, Jacob, and Kol go left," Gideon said. "Marcus, you're with me. Cover Essie and keep your eyes open for JP agents. If Voth timed this right, they should show up in about five minutes."

And me, I was to head straight down the path and draw everyone's attention.

Gideon grabbed my wrist and pulled me close. "If you don't think you can cast the spell, pull out."

"Do you honestly think we'll get another chance?" I asked.

"I don't care." Determination and fear sparked an electric zap through our brand, reminding me that we shared a soul bond and our lives were irrevocably entwined. "You pull out."

I wanted to argue with him, but if anything happened to me, all four of them were lost. Even Marcus. Sure, we didn't share a brand, but I had no doubt his soul would be just as damaged as if he did.

"You have my word." I leaned in, rose on my toes, and kissed him. "Stay safe."

"We need to get moving," Cassius said.

Gideon pulled away, his reluctance to leave me twisting my insides.

The guys hurried off the trail and wove in between the trees, not out of sight, but less obvious, and I carried on down the path. I didn't believe for a second that Lilith would think I'd left them behind, but we were betting it all that me being out in the open and not them would buy us enough time for me to get close enough to touch her.

I picked up my pace, jogging down the path and straining for even the slightest hint that Lilith and her witches were here, my nerves getting tighter and tighter the closer I got to the lake.

Given the time, the ceremony had already started and I only had four minutes to go before they reached the signing of the unification treaty part of the ceremony. If we were right, Lilith was waiting for the most dramatic moment — the signing of the treaty — to make her entrance.

As I drew closer, I caught bits of the mayor's speech, his voice carrying through the park on the loudspeakers, talking about the grim days when humanity thought all hope was lost. Too many angels and humans had already been slaughtered and Michael had just unveiled his terrible new army of monstrous nephilim.

I shuddered, the grief and horror from the crowd creeping into me even though I was still a fair distance away and my angelic magic was low. And I couldn't blame them. It had only been about twenty years since Gabriel had killed Michael, and the nephilim had been vicious. They hadn't cared for any life, because Michael's whole plan had been to exterminate everyone. Even I was horrified when I watched the videos of what they'd done. But then how did I convince anyone who didn't have a soul bond with me that I wasn't a monster?

My thoughts tripped over that. I still wanted this to work out, to be accepted. I wanted my guys to not have to face a life as fugitives when they'd devoted so much of their lives to upholding the law and protecting people.

And while Cassius, Amiah, and Sebastian trusted me, or seemed to, they'd seen my determination to protect people before they'd known the truth. No one else, when they saw me now, would believe I wasn't a monster. There'd never been a nephilim who hadn't been one, and everyone thought it was the magic that created us that made us evil, not Michael.

I shoved those thoughts aside.

Deal with Lilith, then the rest of the world. And I wasn't even going to hope anyone would be grateful if me and my guys actually stopped her.

The path curled down a hill and around the squat, red brick public bathrooms. I hurried around the corner just as the crush of enormous pressure pounded into me and the inky magic roared back to life, calling and cajoling and oozing.

I stumbled and caught my balance before I crashed face first to the ground.

Shit.

The mayor started screaming, high-pitched panicked cries that carried over the loudspeaker.

Shit shit shit.

I still had over two hundred yards to go and I couldn't even see the ceremony. The time for a cautious approach was over.

I focused on my brands and my soul's connection to Gideon, Jacob, and Kol, and raced down the path. The pressure from Lilith, her witches, and the gathered supers up ahead swelled, and a blast of smoke shot up from behind the trees where the ceremony's greenspace was. The mayor's screams grew louder, more desperate, and now I could hear others yelling and crying as well, even though they weren't crying into a microphone.

The familiar *thu-thud* of power from a witch casting a spell crushed inside me, threatening my balance again, but I gritted my teeth and kept going.

Another *thu-thud* and another. The magical pressure continued to grow, squeezing until I couldn't draw a full breath and my lungs burned.

I raced past the trees to the edge of the lawn and staggered to a stop, the air freezing around me, covering my arms and cheeks with frost. People screamed and ran, knocking over each other and the white foldout chairs for the important city leaders and the elderly. A toddler screamed for his mommy and a guy picked him up and bolted away. I didn't know if the man was related to the kid, but he was going in the right direction: away from the danger.

Lilith stood at the front on a small stage, red demonic mist whipping around her in a wild vortex, the hellfire in her eyes dripping sparks that hissed when they hit the stage floor. The air around her shimmered as if she stood in the middle of a parking lot on this hot summer's afternoon and not in the park, and the mayor cowered on his knees, his face red and dripping sweat, the mic still clutched in his hand catching every gasping whimper.

A dozen glyph witches with tattoos covering their right arms attacked those fleeing, forcing them back toward the stage with shadow swords and pressure waves and blasts of fire, into the grasps of more witches who snapped shadow whip after whip around the bystanders' necks. They ensnared human and super alike, until each witch had easily captured a dozen people. Half a dozen bat-winged witches lobbed blasts of shadows from the sky, and Lilith cackled, her eyes wild.

The pressure of power grew the closer I got to the fray, and so did the swell of inky magic. If I let it in, I'd be able to stop this. I'd be powerful. I'd be worshiped. I'd—

I skidded to a halt fifty feet from the edge of the chaos.

Lilith threw her head back and raised her hands. Magic pounded in my chest, stealing my breath, and everyone with a whip around their neck screamed. Most collapsed to their knees, a few larger supers staggered a few steps closer to Lilith then collapsed, and another *thu-thud* of power wrenched at my very soul. She was draining their essences, gaining more power. I could feel the pull of the spell even though it hadn't leeched onto me. No one with a whip around their neck stood a chance.

"I see you've come to my party." Lilith's burning gaze jerked to me and her lips curled back in a wicked smile. With a hiss, she flicked her wrist and her whirling demonic mist swept toward me.

ESSIE

I forced myself to take a step forward and let Lilith's power curl around me. It burned where it touched my flesh, leaving angry red welts, and sank inside me. It made the inky magic surge and strained my hold on my connection with my guys.

"And here I thought I'd have to go looking for you when I was done with this," she said, her voice dark. "It's always nice when your toys come back without an effort."

I squared my shoulders. "I'm more than just a toy."

And you could be a goddess if you let me in.

No.

One of the witches snapped a shadow whip at me. I jerked my hand up on instinct and a blast of red demonic magic shot from my palm and ripped through the whip. The witch's eyes flashed wide and he shot a bigger whip at me.

I sent another blast of magic through that one as well, then twisted my power before it dissipated and slammed it into the witch's chest, knocking him off his feet.

Lilith watched with narrowed eyes. I couldn't tell what she was thinking from her hard expression, or feel what she was feeling through the frozen fear of everyone else. I could only pray I'd intrigued her enough to get close.

The people around me screamed, their fear thickening the frost on my arms despite the summer's heat, while bursts of pleasure from the glyph witches churned my stomach. I needed to get close. Now. The guys wouldn't do anything until I started the spell and they were probably feeling just as sickened as me.

"I'm your weapon," I said, striding past the witch I'd knocked over. "Your right hand."

She raised a sculpted black eyebrow and the fire witch turned to face her, as if he'd sensed she wanted his attention. He wore dark shorts and a white T-shirt, blending in perfectly with the people attending the unification ceremony. With the exception of the tattoo on his arm, which gave him an edgier appearance, he looked like an ordinary guy.

He tossed the man he was holding into the arms of another witch and stepped into my path.

"You're not my right hand," Lilith said.

"Isn't that why you made me? You wanted the power of both an archangel and the Hellfire Queen at your side?"

The mayor gasped, his eyes growing even wider with his horror.

The churning in my stomach grew and my throat tightened. I'd never had anyone look at me like that. Sure, there'd been frustration, hate, and fear when I was a beat cop, but never absolute terror. Kol had been the closest when I'd triggered his PTSD, but his reaction had also been filled with rage.

God, I never wanted anyone to look at me like that, like I was a monster.

You're not a monster. You're a goddess, the inky magic cooed, oozing against my soul, seeping in deeper and dragging my attention from Lilith.

I wrenched my gaze back to her — I didn't know when I'd looked away and I could only pray it hadn't been for long — and forced myself to sneer. The only way I'd get within touching distance of Lilith was if she believed I was just as evil as her.

And to do that, I needed to get the fire witch out of the way as fast as possible before this turned into a real fight. Please let a preemptive strike catch him off guard.

I shot a blast of demonic magic at the fire witch, but in the blink of an eye, he grabbed a tattoo on his arm and hissed the words to activate it. His magic thudded and flames raced through my mist, burning it up just before it reached him.

Shit.

"You're going to have to do better than that if you want to be my right hand," Lilith said.

Shit shit shit. I couldn't afford to get into a magical pissing contest with this guy. I needed everything I had to cast the cage spell.

Unless you let me in.

The fire witch matched my sneer.

A few feet away, a human woman with a shadow whip around her neck collapsed to the ground, her eyes wide and vacant. My pulse stalled. She was dead. They were draining these people to death. Lilith had no intention of taking prisoners to drain and redrain.

"You know my potential." I slowed my pace, now only thirty feet from the fire witch and sixty from the stage. The air was so hot from Lilith's power, it was difficult to breathe, and sweat plastered my T-shirt to my body. How the hell did I convince her to accept me before anyone else died? "Do you honestly believe I won't surpass him? I've had demonic magic for less than twenty-four hours and I've already started to control it."

The fire witch slid his hand higher up his arm and touched a different tattoo, and time stuttered into slow motion. Two more people nearby collapsed. A woman with the feral eyes of a shifter wrenched free of a shadow whip, transformed into a tiger, and leaped at her assailant. All around me people continued to scream and die and the *thu-thud* of the witches' power pounded again and again inside me.

God damn it. I didn't want to waste power.

But if I didn't make a decisive move against this fire witch, Lilith would never let me get close. The only positive was that the witch couldn't create a massive ball of fire around me without killing the people Lilith wanted to power up from.

And no, I wasn't letting the inky magic inside. Its promises were lies. It would possess me—

Shit. The inky magic was as powerful as it had been in Lilith's lab when it had possessed my body. Lilith might not have my soul, but if she could already control me... unless of course Kol's brand had developed enough that adding it to the other two now helped to protect me.

The fire witch opened his mouth to cast whatever spell had been tattooed in his skin.

This needed to end now.

His magic thu—

I wrenched my hand up, clinging to the connection with my guys to keep the inky magic at bay and focusing on the core of power inside me. Heat and light burst from my palm and a blast of divine light — the last of my divine light until it replenished — slammed into him with all the force I could muster. He flew back, crashing into the side of the stage and taking out all the legs on that end.

Lilith hopped off as the stage collapsed and strode toward me, the hellfire in her eyes flaring.

"Teach me," I said. "I'll be your sword, your vengeance on all who refuse to worship you."

Her wicked smile deepened and the mayor, lying on top of the broken stage, whimpered.

The fire witch crawled to his hands and knees and I hit him with a blast of demonic magic — trying to hold back as much power as possible and yet still send him tumbling.

"I might look like *him*," I said. "But I'm also half yours."

"That you are."

Just one more step. That was all I needed to get within grabbing distance. But God, it felt like I was standing in the middle of an inferno.

I fought to keep my expression hard and concentrated on twisting my demon power tight. I couldn't let her realize just how much power I had—

Which won't be enough.

It will. It had to be because I wasn't going to get another chance to do this.

She held out her hand to me. "Be my highest disciple, daughter."

Behind me, someone yelled, but it didn't sound like a cry of fear or pain. It sounded like a battle cry.

Lightning shot toward us, and Lilith wrenched her hand away and redirected the blast into the ground at our feet.

JP agents from the late-night cafeteria meeting, along with Zuri and Regan, barreled across the lawn toward us, and above flew the Director and the four other angels, their massive white wings brilliant in the summer sun.

"You know the JP won't stop me," she said as the Director threw another bolt of lightning toward us.

"I didn't bring them."

"Oh, no? I saw you wearing their letters when you first entered my temple." The inky magic swelled in my muscles, but my hold on my brands kept it from possessing me. Adding Kol had been enough to help me.

With a snarl, she twisted her demonic magic around my neck and hauled me up until my toes skimmed the ground, even though she stood a few feet away.

Fear sliced through my chest, radiating from my brands, and I fought to break free from Lilith's grip. We couldn't risk my guys being noticed before I'd cast the spell. Except I wasn't sure I'd be able to get within arm's reach now.

I gasped, trying to breathe, and clawed at her mist, but my fingers kept sweeping through it while it still clenched tight. "I didn't bring them. I swear," I said, trying one last time to convince her. "They betrayed me. They learned what I was and turned on me."

"They'll always turn on you, because they fear your power," she hissed, stepping closer.

Just another step. Please. God.

"I'm yours. I swear."

Her gaze drilled into mine as if she could see into my soul and she shifted closer.

Just a little more. If I strained, I might be able to reach her.

"You made me," I gasped. "I was always destined to be yours."

The Director dove toward us and Lilith's attention jerked up. A massive wave of power exploded from her, stealing what little breath I had left and slamming the Director and the other angels into the ground.

Darkness swarmed my vision. I had to grab her now before I suffocated and passed out.

I heaved against her magic and grabbed her arm, the heat radiating from her flesh burning my hand. With a scream, I slapped my other hand to my shoulder and imagined the cage spell bursting to life. Power exploded within me, blazing through every cell in my body, and crackled around Lilith with blue-white lightning.

She screamed, and a massive blast of power tossed me across the grass. Specks of light and darkness snapped across my vision, and the inky magic surged, determined to take over.

I fought to breathe and keep hold of my connections through my brands and the cage spell.

The witches dropped their shadow whips and barreled toward me, as the JP agents reached the green and entered the fray.

My guys and Cassius bolted out from wherever they'd been hiding, Gideon striking the witch closest to me with his divine light. Kol killed the witch closest to him before I'd fully registered that he'd drawn one of his blades and was on the next witch an instant later. Red demonic mist burst around Marcus's arms and his fingers extended into claws, and Jacob fired four quick shots, taking out two more witches, while Cassius created a fire whip and yanked another witch to the ground.

The Director staggered to his feet and screamed orders to arrest all of us, his gaze filled with rage and locked on me.

But his rage wasn't as terrifying as Lilith's. "You think you can cage me? You think you're strong enough to stop me? You're even more of a fool than your father."

I scrambled back. I didn't need to get to my feet to reimprison her, I just needed to grab the marble in my pocket, but Lilith blasted more power into me, slamming me into a tree trunk. My head snapped back and the specks of darkness in my vision thickened.

ESSIE

THE CAGE SPELL WAVERED, SHUDDERING AROUND HER, THREATENING TO melt away, and I mentally clenched at it, pushing more of my demonic magic into it.

"You're not stronger than me. You'll never be stronger." She jerked her hand and her magic crashed into me, burning into every cell and threatening my concentration.

The inky magic howled with laughter and surged, seizing my muscles. I couldn't breathe, could barely think.

The spell stuttered. I was going to lose it. I needed more magic, except I couldn't move to grab the marble.

I'll give you more power, the inky magic said, oozing against my essence. *Embrace me. Let me in.*

No.

You'd be stronger than her. You could replace her.

"I'm the Hellfire Queen," Lilith said. "The power of every full demon is mine to control." The cage spell's lightning sparked and sputtered, and she pointed at Kol.

He screamed and his body seized. Agonizing lightning exploded through our brand, and red mist erupted from his skin and poured into Lilith.

He crashed to the ground, writhing in pain, and for a moment, my mind jerked to him and only him. There was no fight, no spell, nothing but him, and the strength pouring out of me into him through our brand. He was dying. And fast. She was tearing the life out of him, and I had to save him. He couldn't die. *Please.*

Except the only way to save him was to stop Lilith.

With me, the inky magic cooed.

No. I ground my teeth against the inky magic's lure and the agony tearing through my brand, and strained to refocus on the spell. I pumped more of my demonic magic into it, the ball in the core of my being growing smaller and weaker by the second.

The spell flared around her but her powers swelled, ripping into the cage spell, as if my effort meant nothing.

It is nothing. Nothing compared to her.

"I'm the Hellfire Queen," she roared, and Marcus stumbled.

He screamed as the demonic mist curling around him swept to Lilith and his body jerked, forced into a painful, body-tearing shift. Now that he was past his transition, his shift should have been smooth, painless, but it was like he was still in transition, his bones crunching, his muscles and tendons ripping.

No. Please, no.

Embrace me. You could be the Hellfire Queen.

No. I'd just be the Hellfire Queen's pawn.

I needed to absorb the magic in the marble. It was my only chance.

I heaved against her power and she howled with laughter.

A blast of fire erupted nearby and bystanders, JP agents, and a few witches screamed. The Director shot lightning at the fire witch, knocking him to his knees, but the witches flying above barraged him with blasts of shadows before he could finish off the witch.

Gideon and Cassius sent fire and light up at them, while also trying to protect Kol and Marcus from the other witches, and Jacob had holstered his sidearms — likely out of rounds — and was tearing into more witches with his short, deadly claws.

Lilith clenched her hands and both Marcus and Kol screamed again. "You will bow to me or you will die."

"If I bow to you, I *will* die," I gasped.

"Bow to me,"

"Never." I strained against the inky magic's hold on my muscles to shove my hand into my pocket. The marble was my only hope. The cage spell was sucking up my demonic power. Soon I'd have nothing left and it didn't even look like Lilith was having problems.

Embrace me. Become a queen. Become a goddess.

No.

The spell stuttered.

You can't do it without me. Give in.

God, I wanted to. I could sense the strength of the inky magic, feel it waiting for me to welcome it in. In fact, it was already in. It had hooked into my soul when I'd been in the Cromer Building. All I had to do was embrace it.

"No," I gasped again.

"Then you get to watch them suffer," Lilith snarled, jerking her hand again. Her mist blasted into Jacob, tossing him into the center of the lawn and ripping off the bracelet embedded in his skin that protected him against sunlight.

His skin burst into flames and he screamed. More agony exploded from Jacob's brand, joining Kol's, and my muscles seized tighter, my hand at the opening of my pocket. More strength raced out of me into Jacob.

No. God, no! He couldn't die. I couldn't lose him. I had to save him, do something, God damn fucking do something.

I'm waiting, the inky magic taunted.

Gideon swore and bolted toward him, as Cassius stopped the three witches barreling toward him with a blazing wall of fire.

Jacob staggered toward the closest shade, his skin blackening, the flames fully engulfing him, the strength pouring out of me the only thing keeping him alive.

"He has such strength." Lilith's manic laugher grew. "Or is that yours? How much more can you take?"

Gideon grabbed Jacob despite the flames, and Lilith slammed a blast of demonic magic into Gideon's back with a resounding crack. He screamed and crumpled, taking Jacob down with him.

My whole right side was on fire with pain.

Cassius howled and bolted toward Gideon, but Lilith shot another blast and he went down, too.

"Do you think an angel with a broken back can fly?" she sneered. "Now I've got three of a kind to play with."

A witch shoved his shadow sword into Gideon's gut, not a killing blow, but still painful, and more strength poured from me into him. Jacob dragged himself into a shadow, his bulky body barely recognizable as human.

"I'm going to drain them and drain them and drain them again," Lilith said with a manic laugh. "And you're going to feel all of it until you give in to my will."

My soul wailed, the agony overwhelming.

All around us, people screamed and yelled. Half of the JP agents were battling the witches, the rest gathering around the Director, who stood in a patch of blackened grass, his lightning magic snapping around him.

I could barely think past the pain, barely keep the cage spell in my mind, and even that was starting to slip. The inky magic was going to take over and then all would be lost.

I was out of time. If I couldn't finish this spell, we were all dead.

With a scream, I moved my hand against the pain deeper into my pocket. My fingers brushed the marble, but Lilith snapped a blast of demonic mist at me. Her power ripped open my pocket and tossed me tumbling to the other side of the lawn. The marble landed on the grass at her feet, too far away from me to even try to scramble to it.

"Did you think this would be enough?" She clenched the marble. Light burst from between her fingers then vanished, and she opened her fingers and let the shattered remains of the marble fall into the grass.

Fuck. No.

I couldn't finish this without the marble.

You can finish it if you embrace me.

Wicked pleasure filled her eyes. She'd won and she knew it. There wasn't anything I could do to stop her.

Embrace me. Become a goddess. Be worshiped. Be feared.

A blast of lightning shot through Lilith's chest and sliced into my side. White agony stole my breath. The cage spell sputtered and the inky magic wormed its way deeper inside me.

Shit shit shit.

Lilith wrenched around to face the Director and the JP agents, all powerful supers, the hole in her chest sealing shut as she turned.

The ground was littered with bodies, both victims and witches, and less than half of her witches remained.

"It's over," the Director said.

She laughed at him. "It's just begun."

He wrenched his hand up and shot another blast of lightning at her. She twisted out of the way and the bolt sliced through my shoulder.

I screamed and panic shot through my brands.

Two JP agents with the feral intensity of shifters turned their fingers to claws and leaped at the closest witches, and the Director pressed his attack, shooting more lightning and barreling toward Lilith.

Another JP agent, a woman with glowing angel eyes, whipped a vortex of wind around Lilith, knocking her off balance, and another lightning blast cut through her chest. She stumbled and the cage spell swelled, Lilith's resistance weakening.

A moment of hope flickered through me before her power surged. I didn't have enough magic. Not even if the Director hurt her.

With a howl of rage, her demonic magic tore through the wind and she shot out a crushing blast of power. Everyone fell to their knees, screaming, including her witches. I fought to breathe. Another surge of power and her witches staggered to their feet, half of them attacking the Director and the agents while they were down, the others seizing my guys and Cassius.

She jerked toward me, her power building, the tattoos on all of her witches' arms glowing red.

"You're mine," she spat at me.

"Never."

The agent with the wind magic seized me with a powerful vortex and tossed me farther away from Lilith as the Director shot another blast of lightning at her, cutting into her.

The gash sealed shut and her gaze leaped over the chaos before wrenching back to me.

"You will submit. I'll torture your mates until you come crawling back to me." Her magic exploded with a chest-crushing *thud* into a massive teleportation spell. She vanished with a blinding flash of red light while light rushed from the witches' tattoos. Those holding my guys tightened their grip and her spell ripped into them, taking Cassius and my guys with them.

ESSIE

I COLLAPSED TO THE GROUND, MY BODY TREMBLING, THE GUYS' AGONY STILL blazing through my brands, my strength pouring out of me into them. The inky magic threatened and begged, fighting my concentration on my brands — which only made me feel my guys' agony more — and the cage spell sputtered. I clutched at it, twisting it tight into the hollow core of my being, praying I could keep it active with what little magic I had left until I could figure out what the hell I was going to do.

Because I *was* going to do something. I was going to get my guys and end this before Lilith killed more people, and I was going to need the spell to do it.

The Director grabbed the front of my T-shirt, hauled me up, and slammed me against the tree, the force knocking the air from my lungs. The light from his eyes blazed and his lightning crackled with white-blue snaps over his forearms.

"Get her secured and into interrogation." He tossed me into the arms of two other JP agents that I recognized from the fight in the cafeteria. Both men had hellfire simmering in their eyes, but they were complete opposites. The one was so thin he looked like a skeleton with pale skin stretched over his narrow frame, and the other was big and bulky with dark red skin.

I sagged in their grips, my legs too weak to hold me up.

Okay. Think. I needed a plan. I had no idea how long I could keep the spell activated, linked to Lilith, and captured inside my body, and the longer I waited to make my move, the stronger Lilith got, draining my guys over and over again. I also didn't know how much more my guys could take. Sure, Lilith had said she was going to keep them alive and torture them, but she didn't need all of them and she didn't need me sane to be her weapon. In fact, breaking my soul by killing one of my soul mates might become her new plan if I waited too long to go to her.

A third agent, a woman with the feralness of a shifter, pulled out a pair of containment cuffs and my pulse stalled. I wrenched in the men's grips. If my power was cut off, I'd lose hold of the cage spell.

"Please," I gasped. "I'll go willingly. You don't need to cuff me."

Her expression tightened and her gaze slid to my right arm. Blood stained my T-shirt where I'd been hit by one of the Director's lightning blasts. It trailed over my bicep, into the flickering gold light of my brand, and dripped from my elbow.

"She has my mates." My throat tightened and the inky magic pressed against my senses, reminding me I couldn't get distracted for a moment. "I have the spell to stop her, but the cuffs will dispel it."

"What are you waiting for? Cuff her," the Director barked.

The woman grabbed my wrist and I wrenched against the demons' grip, too weak to break free.

"Please. I can't lose the spell."

The demons, Skeleton and Red, shoved me face-first to the ground, and the woman yanked my hands behind my back and secured my wrists. The frozen hollowness in my chest swelled as the containment spell cut me off from my magic.

The cage spell sputtered and shrank, and I strained to pull magic from my brands. Both Gideon and Jacob had given me magic before. But the drain of strength from me to them was too strong. I couldn't pull anything from them, not even magic, without endangering their lives, so the brands wouldn't let me.

Desperate, even though I couldn't feel any power inside me, I imagined shoving everything I had left into the spell to keep it active. My force of will had been strong enough to break through the containment spell on Lilith's prison to claim Kol. It had to be enough now.

Please. Let it be enough. I couldn't lose the spell, not when my guys were in danger. Lilith had to be stopped and the cage spell was the only way.

A spark of demonic magic glimmered in my heart and spun into the spell.

Oh, thank God.

Now I just needed to hold onto it while I figured out a plan.

Except it didn't matter if I had a plan. Not if I didn't have any power.

Skeleton and Red hauled me to my feet, dragged me to a JP SUV, and shoved me inside, one on either side of me. Their power squeezed in my chest, revealing just how magically strong these men were, and their red demonic mist curled from their skin and caressed me.

I followed the wisp of mist as it slid down my body. I bled from both the gash in my shoulder and in my side, and I was sure my burned hand was bleeding. Which wasn't good. If I had any hope of saving them, I'd need medical attention first. I wasn't rapidly bleeding out, but the longer I sat here unable to apply pressure to my wounds, the more blood I lost. Except I couldn't feel any of my injuries because of the agony screaming through my brands.

I'm coming for you. I promise.

I just had no idea how the hell I was getting out of this mess, and the urge to go to my guys, now — now now now — without thinking things through was overwhelming.

But I couldn't take on Lilith alone. I had less power now than I did before and she still had many of her witches and was regaining power as I sat there. I couldn't just find power and shove it into the cage spell from wherever I was... well, maybe I could. I wasn't sure how the spell worked. But if I didn't have eyes on Lilith, I couldn't guarantee that she wouldn't kill my guys before I finally caged her.

I promise, I'm coming for you.

The pain in my brands flared. My muscles seized and a strangled scream escaped my lips. Skeleton and Red grabbed my arms, their eyes wide as if they were afraid I was going to attack them.

My soul cried. Save them. Do something—

With a whoosh, the pain swept out of me, and the blazing agony was replaced with an overwhelming heartache and a numbing cold that still made it impossible to feel my other injuries. Everything within me stopped: pulse, breath, and thought. The connection with my guys had cut off.

It was gone. Their presence, the pull of strength, and the whisper of desperation, fear, and determination, which I hadn't realized had been seeping through the brands, was gone.

My soul started to shatter and the inky magic swelled.

Gone. They were gone. Another sob threatened to break free and I glanced at my right arm. My brands were still golden. Did that mean they weren't dead?

Please don't be dead. Please.

The inky magic roared with laughter and surged, straining to take over.

I clenched my jaw and desperately reached for my bonds, praying they were still there. They had to still be there. I just had to reach deep enough, concentrate hard enough—

There. Deep inside me. A whisper of our connections.

Oh, thank God. Thank God.

They were far away and cold, but still there, and still rooting my essence and soul within my body, keeping the inky magic out... barely, and that could change at any time.

They had to have shut me out just like when Gideon had blocked me off during the first fight with the glyph witches in the Cromer Building.

Except then I'd still sensed my connection to him. This was absolute. Empty. Crushing. A complete blockage. And they had to have done it to protect me. It was the only reason I could think of for cutting me off like that. Gideon knew the soul-wrenching effect of having his mate mortally wounded. He had to have told the other guys to shut me out, too, but God—!

The female agent and the Director got into the front seats of the SUV and we drove toward Operations. The pressure of magic inside the vehicle swelled, and the demonic mist from the guys on either side thickened.

A whisper of heat sank into my skin and the spark of demonic magic keeping the cage spell alive grew bigger.

Skeleton shifted, and I watched a curl of his magic trail from his hand and sink into my arm. It added to my core of power, just like when I'd been immersed in Ibizual's magic, or when I'd consumed the spell of the demon who'd attacked me behind Hacksaw, or taken it from Mavis while getting the concealment charm.

Lilith had been able to suck the magic out of Kol and Marcus. It hadn't felt as if she'd tried to suck it out of me. She'd said she could only affect full demons and had probably assumed she couldn't pull it out of me. But that didn't mean I hadn't inherited the ability to feed off of demons from her.

Crap. I didn't know how much power I could get from these guys, but if I consumed their magic, I'd look more like the monster they thought I was.

Except if that was the cost for stopping Lilith and saving my guys, so be it.

But even if I drained these demons, would it be enough?

You know it won't, the inky magic whispered. *You need more. You need it all. The only way to be more powerful than her is to embrace me.*

I turned the problem over and over again as we drove to Operations, fighting the heartache of my frozen bonds and the inky magic's lure. How could I get more power, enough power, and soon? Was I willing to drain every demon in Operations? Could I?

More heat sank under my skin, refilling the core of my demonic power, but I resisted the urge to actively draw it in. So far neither demon had noticed, and I didn't want to alert anyone to the fact that I could quickly regain magic and I was strong enough to resist the containment cuffs. Not until I had a plan.

And the best one I could come up with was to somehow convince the Director to help me. It was the only way I could get enough power and enough people to confront Lilith again.

Which I had to do now now now. I had to save my guys, break through the block they'd put up between us and give them everything I had—

Jeez. Focus.

I fought to steady my breathing and control my panic, but it was nearly impossible with my concentration torn in too many directions.

Lilith had gained a lot of power draining the people at the unification ceremony, but she'd also expended a lot teleporting her witches and my guys. If she was ever at her weakest, it was right now.

The woman pulled the SUV up to the side entrance by the secure section of Operations, and the demons hauled me inside and shoved me into the hard metal chair in one of the interrogation rooms.

At least this time I was more conscious, even if I was still bleeding… which I still couldn't feel. And, from the blood trail I'd left staggering into the room, it was too much to hope that I'd also inherited a little of Lilith's super-fast healing.

The Director stormed in and glared at me while Skeleton and Red took up position by the door and the shifter woman left. I didn't know if they were now too far away for me to consume their magic or not, and didn't want to risk notice by trying, not until I'd exhausted every other option.

"So this was your plan all along," the Director said. "Compromise the city's agents and open the door for Lilith to attack."

"We were trying to stop Lilith."

"It didn't look like that to me," the Director said.

"My guys were fighting Lilith's glyph witches and I was fighting her." I shook with the effort to hold myself together and not break down crying at not being able to feel my guys. "I have a cage spell that can reimprison her, but I can't do it by myself and we have to do it now before she regains her magic."

The Director barked a harsh laugh. "You think I'm going to believe that you actually want to stop Lilith? I know you're her daughter. The agent in charge of the elite team has already made a full report. You're an abomination made from evil magic. You'll say anything."

They're not going to believe you. You're a monster.

I'm not a monster. I might have feared for a bit that being a nephilim meant I was evil and I'd turn into a monster whether I wanted to or not, but I now had Lilith's inky magic trying to worm its way into my soul and I knew what real evil felt like. My soul was nothing like that and never would be.

"Finding out I'm an archnephilim and that Lilith is my mother doesn't make me evil." If he was this certain I was a monster, how the hell was I going to convince him to help me stop Lilith? "It doesn't change the fact that my soul is good, and it doesn't erase all the good I've done as a Union City cop."

The door opened and Yadveer shuffled in.

Oh, thank God.

I clenched my jaw, fighting to not show my relief. If Yadveer read my memories, the Director would have absolute proof of my intentions. But I couldn't look like I wanted it. That would only make the Director think I had a way of deceiving Yadveer's magic.

The elderly lethe demon stared at me with wide eyes containing only a pinprick of hellfire. Even without my empathy, it was clear he was terrified of me.

"You can say whatever you want, but we'll know the truth soon enough." The Director stepped back from the table and crossed his arms. "Read her memories and find out what her plans are."

Which were to stop Lilith. Now. Get my guys. Renew my bonds. Please. I didn't know how much more of the numb chill I could take.

Yadveer glanced at the other chair, but didn't sit. My arms were secured behind my back and he'd have to reach across the table to make contact. Instead, he rounded the table, his breath a little too fast. He didn't want to be this close to me even if I was handcuffed and my magic — supposedly — contained.

They won't care when they learn the truth, the inky magic hissed.

They will. They had to. It was my only hope.

He pressed his palms against my temples, his skin radiating the tell-tale warmth of a demon, although it was nothing compared to Lilith's burning heat. His body tense, he raised his gaze to the Director.

"I want to know everything," the Director said.

"Fast?" Yadveer asked, his voice hopeful, making it clear that the faster he got my memories, the faster he could get away from me.

"Yes."

Before I could take a breath and steady myself, searing power exploded in my head. I fought to keep hold of my frozen bonds and the cage spell while letting Yadveer see everything. He had to see it all, no matter how ashamed or embarrassed I was. If he didn't see everything, the Director would still suspect me.

His magic burned into my essence and lurched me from memory to memory. Fear. Love. Anger. Joy. My guys. Life before my guys. Bobbing in the not-water. Whirling faster and faster, turning my insides into a raging inferno.

The inky magic swelled, doing nothing to quench the fire, and oozed around my cells, sensing a weakness in my resistance. If I let it in, I'd be powerful.

You've told me that already. No.

I gritted my teeth and clung to the cold connections in my brands. Yadveer and the Director had to believe me. *Please.*

The cage spell sputtered and I forced more demonic magic into it.

Be a goddess.

No.

Be powerful.

No.

Be—

I won't be Lilith's puppet.

My essence heaved and spun. Burning, always burning. And yet the core of my being remained frozen with the absence of my guys. There wasn't a memory or thought or embarrassment or screw up that wasn't seen. My life, with all of my imperfections, was laid bare and Yadveer's power hungrily blazed through it all.

I clung to the cage spell and myself. It was all I could do. I just had to hold on. Just a little longer. The Director needed to know I wasn't a monster, that I was more angel than anything else and that the main thing that drove me was protecting people who couldn't protect themselves.

Someone screamed, and Yadveer's power swept out of me with a whoosh. My body went limp and I tipped out of the chair as Yadveer jerked out of the way, letting me crumple to the floor.

"You—" he gasped.

I dragged my gaze up to him. His shock cut through my chest, his emotion so strong that whatever wisp of angelic magic I'd managed to recover in the short time I'd been in the interrogation room had picked it up through the containment cuffs.

"Show me," the Director said, as if he knew asking Yadveer questions would be useless in his state of shock. He pulled out the chair across from me, nudged Yadveer to sit, and knelt in front of him.

Red hurried to my side and hauled me back into my chair. I dragged in ragged breaths, trying to get the room to stop spinning and my stomach to stop churning.

Please believe me. Please help me. I didn't know how much longer I could hold myself together, not without my full bonds, and I had to save my guys. I had to.

The only way is to let me in.

"How?" Yadveer asked, his gaze locked on me.

The Director grabbed Yadveer's chin and turned his head to face him. "Show me."

Yadveer pressed his palms to the Director's temple, and the Director's head snapped back, his angel glow blazing so bright I had to squint to keep looking at him. His breath picked up and his body trembled.

Please believe me. Please.

With a strangled cry, the Director sagged forward and pressed his forehead against Yadveer's knees.

Red tensed, and more mist curled from him and melted into me.

Yadveer yanked his hands away and the Director groaned, turning his brilliant gaze to me.

"This—" He clutched the edge of the table and used it to help him stand. "This— I need to think about this."

He staggered to the door and my pulse stalled.

He was going to leave and waste time thinking? I didn't have time for him to think about this. My guys didn't have the time.

"Wait." I jerked to my feet and Red shoved me back into the chair, a flicker of his fear chilling my skin. "We have to make our move now. Lilith doesn't just have her own power. She's also using worship magic. She can regain her strength faster than normal."

"Your memories might say you have nothing to do with Lilith or Michael, but I'm not going to make a snap decision. You still had recent contact with Lucifer and used his name to get us to the park."

"Because we couldn't stop Lilith by ourselves."

"I'm aware." The muscles in his jaw flexed. "I can't accept even the slightest risk of letting a monster go free."

"I'm not a monster." God damn it. "I can't do this alone."

You can't do it at all. Not with your amount of power.

The Director's eyes narrowed, his emotions seeping into me. "*You're* not doing anything." He was suspicious and worried. He didn't believe— No, he didn't *want* to believe.

Red tightened his grip on me and more of his magic heated my skin.

"Her witches are down in power and so is she," I pressed. "At full strength, they took out our team plus an elite team. This might be the only chance we get."

God, how did I make him believe me? He'd already seen the truth, that I'd been a child during the war and had nothing to do with it, that I'd dedicated my life to helping others.

"There is no *we*."

He'll never trust you. You'll never get enough power.

And he'd never release me to do it myself.

No power, no help, and I was running out of time. I had no other options. Lilith needed to be stopped and I had the spell to stop her.

There was only one thing I could do.

ESSIE

I HAD TO LET THE INKY MAGIC IN. IT WAS MY ONLY OPTION. IF I COULD GET close to my guys, get them to unblock our connection and concentrate on our bonds, I might be able to hold onto my soul long enough to imprison Lilith. Then...

Then, I had no idea. If imprisoning Lilith didn't end the worship magic spell, and her inky magic didn't disperse, I didn't know if I'd ever be able to get it out of me. I could already feel it clinging inside me, so sticky that I feared it wouldn't matter how hard I scrubbed, it would never go away. I wouldn't be able to live like that, always fighting the inky magic, resisting the evil that everyone believed was inside me. But if my guys could shut me out this completely, maybe with enough power I could make a strong enough block between us that my death wouldn't kill them or drive them insane.

It was a terrible plan.

And the guys would never agree to it. It also depended on a lot of luck, and even then the odds weren't good that any of us would get out of it alive or sane. Not to mention I desperately wanted to be wrong. I wanted to be able to burn the inky magic out of me when I was done and get the life I craved with my guys.

But it was the only plan I had.

Which still didn't address fighting off all of Lilith's witches. If I was concentrating on caging her and holding onto my soul, I'd be open to attack. No matter what I did, I still needed the Director's help.

And the only way I'd been able to convince someone I wasn't a threat was to let them see my soul, like I'd done with Voth.

The Director turned to open the door and I sucked in a thick strand of demonic mist from Red, making him yelp in surprise.

Please let this work. Please let me have enough angelic magic for this to work.

I blasted the demonic magic around my hands, shattering the handcuffs, and rammed my good hand into Red's stomach. His breath burst from his lungs, a blast of hot air in my face, and I shoved him back with a gust of demonic power.

The glimmer of angelic magic I'd felt while handcuffed grew a little stronger, filling my chest with the Director's and the demons' fear and anger. *Please, let it be enough.*

Skeleton jerked forward, his magic rushing around him. On instinct, I twisted my hand, and his power flooded into me, but my concentration on the cage spell started to slip.

Crap.

I heaved the extra power around the spell and twisted it tight, while also trying to release my divine light.

The Director snarled and jerked toward me, lightning dancing over his hands, but I slapped my burned and bloodied hand over his heart and pushed the heat of my empathy into him.

"This is who I am," I said, my good hand wrapped in the front of his shirt, holding him close.

I pushed every ounce of angelic magic I had into him, exposing my soul, my true essence, and the radiant gold threads binding me with my guys.

He gasped, his fear and anger melting into awe, and he held up his hand, stopping Skeleton and Red from hauling me away.

What I had with my guys was pure and primal, and that wasn't something that could happen if my soul was corrupted by evil magic. Yes, I was a being of celestial light and darkness, an impossible creature, but I wasn't a monster. I was a destined being. Evil had conspired to make me, but fate had set me on my path. And that path was to end Michael's war once and for all. Lilith couldn't be allowed to remain free, and I would do everything in my power, sacrifice my life to stop her, even knowing that could irrevocably hurt my guys.

The little angelic magic I had weakened and I strained to hold onto my connection with the Director. I might have changed his emotions about me, but I didn't know if I'd changed his mind. He had to understand I wasn't trying to make him make a rash decision. This was our best, maybe our only chance to stop Lilith from slaughtering millions of people like Michael had. I had to ensure he saw my truth, my need to save my guys, my anger and frustration and fear over how I'd grown up, always afraid, and my overwhelming need to protect people.

"Help me," I begged. "Please."

I had to save them. I couldn't live with this ache inside me. I had a chance to save everyone and I had to try.

Let me in now and you won't have to worry about it.

No. I had to wait until the last possible moment before I let the inky magic in. Anything sooner, and Lilith would know what I was planning. And if I could get the Director's support, I might not need to let the inky magic in at all.

"I'm holding a spell that will reimprison her, but I can't do it by myself." Not even with all of Lilith's inky worship magic.

The Director's eyes narrowed. "You're not strong enough to cast a spell to contain her. I can feel the pressure of your power weakening, and there aren't any divine light crystals in this operations building to give to you to power up."

Shit. That meant I had to let the inky magic in. And I still needed his help.

"Please. I can't do it alone. My guys shut me out of our brands—"

"They can do that?" His surprise whispered through me.

My angelic magic was almost gone. The cage spell wavered and the cold in my chest billowed. I gritted my teeth. I just needed to hold on a little longer. "If they see me, they can give me magic."

Believe me. Just God damn believe me.

"Vampires don't have magic," the Director said. "And can you pull magic from an incubus through your brand?"

I could pull magic from any demon, but I wasn't going to remind him. "We can discuss the finer points of angelic mating brands later. Do you trust me?" *Just fucking say yes.* If he didn't, I'd have to come up with a plan B and it had been hard enough coming up with a plan A.

He hadn't moved since I'd flooded him with my empathic magic and he hadn't hit me with his lightning. That meant he didn't see me as a threat, but that didn't mean he trusted me with his life or the lives of his agents.

Skeleton and Red stood a few feet away, still ready to strike on the Director's command.

The Director frowned.

God, he still had to think about it?

"Do you trust me?" I pressed. There wasn't anything else I could do to convince him.

"Everything I know says I shouldn't, and yet you've shown me your soul. I *know* you. My soul knows yours. Even if I refuse to help, you'll still go after Lilith."

The interrogation room door banged open and Voth stormed in, with Zuri close behind. They had their powers contained — thank God — but from Voth's dark expression, it wasn't going to stay that way for long.

"You want to let Essie Shaw go," Voth growled, his voice filled with danger.

Lightning crackled over the Director's hands. "You don't have the authority to make demands, and you—" His attention jumped to Zuri, standing in the doorway. "You let a civilian into Operations' secure area?"

"If the Angel of Death has come to defend her, then there's nothing evil about her even if she is an archnephilim." Zuri squared her shoulders. "I already told you when I made my report that Agent Shaw had no idea what she was or who her mother was. I don't believe that knowledge will suddenly turn her into a monster."

A swell of magical pressure shuddered inside me and demonic mist curled around Voth, his hold on his power slipping. "Michael was one of yours, angel. You don't get to judge her on what she is."

"But the only way she's possible is because of black magic," Skeleton said.

"She's proven beyond a doubt that she doesn't have evil intent," the Director replied.

More power rippled off of Voth, straining my hold on the cage spell. "So you're standing here letting her mates suffer because...?"

"Because we were discussing the plan." The light in the Director's eyes flared.

Skeleton and Red stiffened. I could no longer sense emotions, so I wasn't sure if they were surprised or upset. These men had been in the cafeteria when we'd teleported back to Operations, which meant even though they were acting as regular agents during this interrogation, they were still two of the top leaders of the JP Bureau of Supernatural Law Enforcement.

"Director, are you sure?" Red asked.

"Without a doubt," the Director said. "Agent Shaw, you say we have to make our move right now. What's the plan?"

"That you see Priam," Zuri said to me, her attention jumping to the floor then back to me.

I followed her gaze to the blood splattered at my feet. I was still bleeding from my injuries even though I couldn't feel them past the frozen numbness in my soul.

"How are you not screaming in agony right now? You're bleeding out. Slowly, but still bleeding out."

"The guys shut me out, blocked off our bonds." And if I thought about that, I'd break down. And I would *not* break down. "But I started the cage spell and I'm trying to keep hold of it."

"How long can you hold it?" Voth asked.

"As long as I have to," I said between gritted teeth. "But releasing it sooner rather than later would be better."

But only if you let me in.

"Call Priam and tell him we're meeting him in triage," the Director said to Red, and he grabbed my elbow and tugged me toward the door. "I want a full sit rep, Agent Shaw."

The Director helped me stagger out of the secured section in Operations, with Voth following close on my other side and Zuri and Skeleton behind us.

I repeated how Lilith was using worship magic to become more powerful. "But as I understand, teleportation spells use a lot of magic. If we're lucky, she spent whatever she gained during her attack on the unification ceremony to make her escape."

"But," Voth said, "she now has three angels, a vampire, an incubus, and a hellhound. She's going to be able to replenish her power the moment they're strong enough to drain."

We reached triage, where Priam and Xavier waited for us. Xavier's face paled the moment I walked in the door, even though I was with the Director and Voth and clearly not in custody. Even if I wasn't public enemy number one when this was over, it was going to be a long road, maybe an impossible road, of convincing people I wasn't a monster.

Except the odds of me surviving this were slim. The best I could do was fight to save my guys.

Priam, thankfully without a hint of fear in his eyes, helped me onto a gurney and quickly cut away my bloody T-shirt.

"Is fast okay?" Priam asked, meaning did I mind the burning pain of being healed quickly.

"We don't have a lot of time," I said.

He placed a gloved hand over the wound in my shoulder and lightning roared through me, searing through the hollow chill with blazing agony and threatening my hold on the cage spell.

Darkness swarmed my vision and the inky magic swelled and laughed. Then Priam's magic vanished with a whoosh, leaving me gasping for breath, shivering with cold, and desperately pushing more magic into the cage spell.

"So what's the plan?" Voth asked, placing his enormous hand on my ankle and sending a warm wave of power into me, helping me steady myself.

"Can all demons absorb each other's magic?" I gasped.

"Not many," he said. "But I sensed your ability when we... first met."

And by met he meant when he'd flattened me and my guys in an attempt to understand how an angelic mating brand worked and why he didn't have a soul bond. It was strange to look at the big, bulky, powerful demon and how he looked like he was always on the verge of wanting to rip your head off, knowing his soul ached for a true bond.

But that only made me think of my bonds, drawing my attention back to the frozen numbness of being shut out.

I shoved that thought aside. I had to focus to save them. Just focus.

"I'm guessing Lilith is back in the Cromer Building," I said, as Priam doused some gauze in saline and wiped away the smeared and caked blood around my now healed wounds. "She's expecting me to return to her, so she wouldn't be hiding, but I'll try to use my bonds to confirm their location."

"Can you do that if they've shut you out?" the Director asked.

Priam drew in a sharp breath and met my gaze for a second. Yeah, every angel would probably be shocked to know my guys could block our connection. Well, every angel except Amiah. She'd probably do a happy dance.

"I'm hoping I can. Then I have to walk up to Lilith's door, give myself to her, and finish casting the cage spell."

Zuri frowned. "But if the spell is strong enough to reimprison Lilith, I doubt you'll be able to do anything else. That will leave you wide open to attack."

"I believe that's where we come in," the Director said. "We can't show up with Agent Shaw, and in fact we'll have to keep a few blocks away to avoid detection, but on your signal, we can make our assault and draw most, if not all, of the glyph witches away from you."

"Exactly. I suspect Lilith will think she's strong enough to deal with me on her own." And at the moment she was.

Voth's eyes narrowed. "How do you plan on finishing the spell? You've got almost nothing left."

"I'm going to use Lilith's worship magic against her," I said.

"You can access her worship magic?" Xavier asked, his curiosity, stronger than his fear, pulling him into the conversation. Realization flashed across his expression. "Of course you can. You hold part of her DNA and she always intended for you to be able to access it. She could have attuned the worship magic to include you without ever having met you."

The inky magic howled with laughter. *Soon. Soon.*

"Yes." *Please let my guys have enough strength left to hold me together to cast the spell.* Then, if I couldn't be saved, I could embrace the inky magic fully, shut them out, and burn myself up.

Except I really wanted to be saved.

ESSIE

Skeleton, left to inform the rest of the JP Bureau's top agents of the plan.

The inky magic kept laughing and laughing, and it took everything I had to keep hold of myself and not let it take over. I was giving it exactly what it wanted and I could only pray I could resist it long enough to not give Lilith what she wanted. But there was no other way. I had no angelic magic left and I wasn't willing to drain demons on the chance that I'd get enough power.

A flicker of agony shot through Kol's brand and my pulse leaped, but the pain vanished as fast as it had appeared, reminding me of how aching and cold I was without them.

My pulse stalled with the realization that whatever was happening, it was horrible enough to weaken his will.

But this was a chance to confirm where they were.

I scrambled to regain hold of our connection. I just needed a moment, just enough to confirm where they were. The frozen numbness swelled, and I shoved at it, determined to break through.

Just give me a glimpse.

The numbness trembled.

Please.

Then the agony roared back into me, stealing my breath and making my muscles seize. But instead of breaking the block between me and Kol, I was connected with Gideon... and he'd let me in on purpose.

His pain, rage, and determination pounded through me. But so too did the knowledge that he knew I wouldn't be able to leave them to Lilith, no matter what he or the other guys wanted. He knew I'd come after them no matter what and he was showing me where they were and what I was walking into.

The foggy image of a vast room filled my vision, blocking out everyone in triage. Its stone floor, walls, and ceiling were covered in glyphs. About a hundred people in robes lay prostrate on the floor in front of Lilith who sat on a large stone throne raised up on a wide dais. Power whirled around her in a wild vortex, tugged at her hair and the hem of her gown, and sent the sparks from her hellfire whirling up to the ceiling to rain down around her, snapping and hissing when they hit the stone floor.

Her fiery gaze slid to me— or rather Gideon's gaze, and captured my soul, her essence burning into me as if she were looking at me through Gideon's eyes.

With a wicked smile that made the inky magic purr with pleasure, she flicked her finger.

Oh, shit.

More searing agony exploded through me, consuming the frozen numbness, and Gideon screamed. She tore into his essence, ripping away chunks, adding it to the vortex, and I fought to breathe.

I'm coming for you. I promise.

The connection snapped closed, engulfing me in darkness and then frozen numbness. I sobbed, my soul shattering at his pain and the distance between us, and blinked my vision clear.

Voth and Priam stood on either side of the gurney, their expressions tight with fear.

"What the hell was that?" Priam asked, pressing his hand against my forehead and sending a warm thread of magic into me, looking for physical injuries.

"Gideon let me confirm where they were." And everything within me cried that I had to go. Now. I couldn't wait for the Director to gather the other agents. Every second meant Lilith gained more power and my guys grew weaker.

"And?" Zuri asked, her expression just as tight.

Xavier returned with a T-shirt and handed it to her, who handed it to me.

"They're under the Cromer Building." I dragged on the new T-shirt, even though Priam hadn't finished helping me clean off the blood, and I slid off the gurney.

The room tilted and Voth grabbed my arm, steadying me. He sent another wave of magic whirling around my heart and easing my trembling muscles.

"Thanks."

"You shouldn't face Lilith alone," he growled.

I took an unsteady step toward the door. "Take care of her glyph witches fast and I won't have to."

Voth's expression darkened.

Yeah, we both knew I couldn't count on that.

"Whatever happens, Lilith and her witches must be stopped." I drew in a ragged breath and tightened my hold on the cage spell. "Whatever the cost."

I took another unsteady step, and another, straining to look steadier and more confidant than I felt. My insides squirmed with the need to go to my guys, to finish this, to — *please, God* — survive this.

Zuri fell into step beside me and pulled out a set of keys from her pocket. "It's the blue sedan. I didn't have time to return the keys after the disaster at the park."

"Thanks." I took the offered keys and strode into the garage, each step taking me closer to my guys and giving me more strength.

I *would* save them. I *would* reimprison Lilith. I *would* do what I had to do to ensure the safety of the city, the world, and my guys.

The Director and half of the high-ranking agents he'd brought with him from Rome were gathered around the SUVs. Some wore tactical gear. Many didn't. Their conversations stopped the moment I stepped through the door, and all eyes turned to me.

Even without my empathy, I could tell the emotions were mixed. Which actually surprised me. Some of the agents — most of them angels — looked at me with disgust. Given that I was an abomination to beings of celestial light that didn't surprise me. I broke their rules. Most angels had trouble with that. But the three demons, Red among them, and the one vampire present watched me with cautious appraisal, as if waiting to see what I'd do.

They're still never going to trust you, the inky magic hissed.

So be it.

"Tell us when you're ready to strike." The Director handed me a com, and one of the angels stiffened while the vampire's posture relaxed even more. "We'll go in on your word."

"The glimpse I got looked like she had about a hundred witches." I inserted the com in my ear. "Check."

"You're good," he said, as bits of the other agents' conversations filled my ear.

My hold on the cage spell flickered, and I gritted my teeth. "Can you put me on a separate channel?"

"Are you sure?" the Director asked.

Yeah, being put on a separate channel meant I wouldn't have the reassuring chatter of my backup, but— "I'm kind of concentrating on a lot of things right now. Blocking everyone out on top of that is just going to make everything more challenging."

He gave a tight nod. "I understand. Switch agent Shaw to a separate channel," he called out, then turned and barked orders at the agents.

The chatter in my ear cut out, and I got into the blue sedan and drove out of Operations' secured garage, my soul sobbing while I strained to hold myself together. The late afternoon summer heat turned the car sweltering and sweat slicked my body, but my insides were so cold and numb I could barely feel the heat and didn't bother to put the windows down, let alone turn on the air conditioning.

So much had happened in so little time. It hadn't even been a month since I'd walked into Abe and Pam's pharmacy and got caught up in my worst nightmare — permanently soul bound to an angel and immersed in the supernatural world.

Now I didn't want to imagine my life without Gideon, without any of them. I craved Marcus's ferocious passion, Jacob's intense desire, Kol's sensual playfulness, and Gideon's unwavering devotion.

God, I loved them so deeply. There was a chance I might be able to live without them, but I didn't want to. They were a part of my soul, and blocking me out cut to my core, even if it was just to protect me.

Just like I knew blocking myself from them and burning myself up was the only way to protect them if the inky magic didn't dispel once I'd imprisoned Lilith and if I couldn't push the magic out of me.

I tried not to think about that as I drove out of the Supers' Quarter to the heart of downtown, the churning in my stomach growing the closer I got to the Cromer Building.

By the time I parked on the side of the road across the street from my destination, I had a death grip on the steering wheel to keep my hands from shaking.

I had to help them.

I had to stop Lilith.

I wasn't going to be strong enough.

My mind kept whirling — *save them, save them, whatever it takes* — and my insides ached, my body strangely frozen and numb, and yet covered in sweat from the heat in the car. I got out of the vehicle, hoping the breeze would at least make my hands feel less clammy.

But there wasn't even a whisper of wind, as if the world held its breath, waiting to see if everyone in this city and in this realm could carry on, healing the wounds of a war that had only ended about twenty years ago, or if they were going to go back to fighting for their lives.

I dragged my gaze over the street. Even though it was dinnertime, the area should have been busy. Unity Park was only a few blocks away and the restaurants and shops in the areas were still open—

The sign in the store window beside me said CLOSED and only the night security lights were on. In fact, all of the stores and businesses around me looked closed. There were also no pedestrians and very few cars on the road.

A cruiser rounded the corner and pulled up beside my sedan. For a second, panic made my pulse trip. I didn't want to have to deal with anyone who knew me when I'd thought I was human. That was time I couldn't afford to waste.

I tried to roll my shoulders without looking like I was rolling my shoulders to ease some of the tension in my neck. The odds the officer knew me were slim. This part of the city wasn't in my old precinct. And — thank God — when the officer put down her window, I didn't recognize her.

"There's an evacuation order for downtown. It's not safe to be out here—" The woman's gaze locked on my face and her eyes widened. Guess she'd finally noticed my glowing eyes. "I'm sorry, agent," she said, assuming because I was an angel in the human part of town that I was a JP agent.

"That's okay, officer." I fought to not show my fear and desperation. "You'll want to keep a secured perimeter around this area. The rest of the JP team will be here shortly."

"We haven't gotten word of an operation."

Crap. Of course they hadn't. Jeez. I'd spoken on auto pilot. I should have just kept my mouth shut. Because it was best if she and the rest of the UCPD kept their distance. There wasn't any way a normal human would stand a chance against Lilith's glyph witches. Of course, I wasn't sure if the top leaders of the JP Bureau of Supernatural Law Enforcement stood a chance, either. Not without me imprisoning Lilith and terminating her worship magic spell... if imprisoning her ended the spell.

Except if I failed, there wasn't any way I could keep Union City's humans out of the fight. We'd needed everyone, supers and humans, to defeat Michael. Lilith's war would be the same.

Be a goddess. Be strong.

Save them.

The cage spell flickered.

"It's nothing that requires UCPD backup." I gave her a tight nod and strode across the street to the Cromer Building. It wasn't great that she knew where I was going, but I couldn't stand there any longer and wait for her to leave.

I pulled open one of the many glass doors and marched into the building's empty, spacious, multi-story glass and metal lobby. Unlike the level below, the main floor's construction had been finished to sleek and modern perfection, glass and steel and marble, in white, grays, and black.

The weight of enormous power crushed inside me and the inky magic swelled, pressing against my essence and straining my will the moment I crossed the threshold into the building. All this power could be mine if I let it in. I wouldn't have trouble holding onto the cage spell if I just let it in.

Ahead of me, in the center of the lobby, stood the fire witch with his arms crossed and his lips curled in a sneer.

He wore the same dark shorts and white T-shirt he'd worn at the park — the T-shirt now with a large grass stain. His dark eyes narrowed and he released his hold on his power, adding to the crush inside me

"I thought you said you were something," he said, his voice a raspy hiss. "You didn't even last an hour before you came crawling back to her."

I fought to breathe and look like I wasn't affected. "And I thought you were her right hand. Looks like you're just her errand boy."

Come on, just take me to Lilith. I didn't have the willpower to stand there having a pissing contest with him.

"I'm whatever my goddess needs me to be. Just like you." He turned, strode deeper into the lobby to a bank of elevators, and pressed the call button. "You can't fight it. But I'm glad you did."

I followed, pushing through the power as if it had physical mass. The elevator door opened as I got there and I staggered inside with him.

"I'm going to enjoy watching her break you." He opened the panel with the floor buttons, revealing a single button, and pressed it.

"Well, that's handy," I said. "A button behind the buttons."

I didn't know if the Director and the other agents would be able to deal with Lilith's witches before I had finished the cage spell... or was dead... but on the off chance, he needed to know how to get to me and my guys.

The fire witch shot me a dark look, and the elevator went down, deep under the building, the pressure of Lilith's power, along with the fire witch's caught within the confines of the elevator, growing by the second. The strain of concentrating on my freezing, aching bonds, and holding the spell, made me tremble, and my breath turned into shallow gasps that I couldn't hide from him, making his sneer deepen.

When the door finally opened, I staggered out into a long, wide hall without waiting for the fire witch. The floor was large polished granite flagstones, and the walls were stone with swirling glyphs carved into them. Torches in wrought iron holders placed on both sides of the wall about thirty feet apart illuminated the way with a mix of light and writhing shadows, making me feel like I'd entered some ancient temple.

But then this *was* a temple. I'd already seen Lilith sitting on her throne in her throne room, the walls covered in glyphs and the witches bowing to her. They referred to her as their goddess, and with all the worship magic at her disposal, she *was* a goddess.

And *I* needed to be stronger than her.

The inky magic chuckled. *Embrace me, and you will be.*

I'd also be Lilith's puppet if I couldn't keep hold of myself.

The fire witch led me all the way to the end of the hall to a pair of enormous metal doors.

My pulse pounded. I needed to get eyes on my guys, then find a way to call in the Director without giving myself away. If I pushed power into the cage spell first, Lilith's witches could just blast me into submission before I'd even started.

The fire witch flicked his finger and released his magic with a crushing *thu-thud,* and the doors slowly opened inward, revealing the enormous chamber, the floor, walls, and ceiling covered in glyphs, exactly as I'd seen it through Gideon's eyes.

Wrought iron chandeliers with dozens of candles lit the room with the same flickering illumination as the hall, their smoke making the air hazy, and the acrid reek of sweat, blood, and desperation filled my nose. The hundred witches still lay prostrate on the floor in perfect lines, leaving a wide center aisle and drawing my gaze up to Lilith, sitting on her large stone throne, radiating enormous power, heat, and darkness.

ESSIE

THE THRONE SAT ON A RAISED DAIS WITH FIVE WIDE STONE STEPS, AND THE glyphs behind her pulsed with a mix of red demonic magic and smoky black worship magic. Marcus, in his massive hellhound form, lay on the floor at the foot of the dais, a thick chain around his neck securing him to a metal ring attached to the floor.

He stiffened, and for a second I worried that Lilith had a containment spell on the chamber that only allowed her and her witches to cast spells.

Shit. That was something I should have thought of. I wouldn't stand a chance against her if I was also trying to push the cage spell through a containment spell. I'd barely been able to hold onto it with the cuffs on and I doubted the spell on the JP's cuffs was as powerful as the spell on Lilith's prison.

Except I still didn't have any other option but to confront Lilith and I couldn't back out now.

I tried to draw in a steadying breath, but could only manage a shallow gasp that made the fire witch chuckle with dark pleasure as I stepped across the threshold into the room.

No chill or hollowness. At least not any more than what I already had with my guys blocking their bonds.

Thank God. My chance went from none back to slim again.

The hellfire in Marcus's eyes grew as I took another step, but he didn't get up or move. I couldn't tell if he was injured or not, but if Lilith had control of his ability to shift, then Marcus needed to be smart about when he made his move... if he *could* make a move.

Up at the front of the room on the right-hand wall hung the rest of my guys, along with Cassius and Ephraim.

The churning cold and fear in my gut hardened, a whisper of emotions: agony, rage, and terror made my throat tighten. I gritted my teeth. I couldn't attack Lilith. Not until the glyph witches were out of the room.

Yes, my guys were alive, but they were in rough shape, bleeding and bruised and barely breathing. They'd been chained with their hands above their heads, high enough that only their toes skimmed the floor, making it difficult to breathe, and the glyphs behind them pulsed with demonic and worship magic in time with the glyphs behind Lilith.

Jacob looked the worst, his skin blackened and oozing blood. What I could make out of his charred T-shirt was half burned, half pasted to his bulky body, and so, too, were his cargo pants. Beside him, Kol raised his head.

I gasped, unable to stop myself.

His face was one big ugly bruise, with one eye swollen shut. They'd beaten him after they'd captured him and drained him so deeply he couldn't heal. Which meant Lilith was already well on her way to regaining the power she'd spent to teleport out of the park.

Gideon hung beside Kol, his face almost as battered, his clothes also bloody from dozens of gashes. He trembled, the muscles in his arms flexed, the tendons and veins raised as he fought to hold himself up so he could breathe. With his back broken, he wasn't able to support himself with his toes like Jacob and Kol.

Cassius, beside him, was in the same situation, arms bulging, his face red with exertion, while Ephraim, at the end of the line, had collapsed. His head lolled forward, and I couldn't tell if he was alive and was in no position to check.

Lilith leaned back, her magic sweeping through her hair, the pressure increasing in my chest and straining my hold on the cage spell. "You're not crawling."

I strode to the middle of the room. "Let them go and I'm yours."

She flicked her finger, the glyphs behind her exploded with red light, and the glyph behind Gideon burst to life. He screamed and his body jerked, his muscles seizing. His gaze locked on me and the connection through our brand grew colder. He wouldn't let me take his pain, wouldn't let me give him strength to survive this.

God. I wanted to yell at him, at all of them, and at Lilith. But shutting me off was the only way Gideon thought we could win.

Except Lilith was expecting me to be writhing in agony at Gideon's pain. She had to be. She knew the effects of the angelic mating brand and if I didn't react, she'd know everything wasn't as she expected.

With a strangled cry, I dropped to my knees and bowed my head.

"Your bonds make you weak," she said.

Another *thu-thud* of her power, and Jacob screamed. The chill in our bond deepened as well and my throat tightened, my thoughts whirling. They were in pain. They were dying. I had to save them. I had to—

"Move in now," I whispered, praying Lilith wouldn't be able to hear me over Jacob's and Gideon's screaming.

The inky magic laughed with gleeful anticipation. I was going to let it in. It would have my soul and I'd be Lilith's puppet.

No. Not yet. Not until Lilith sent all her witches to confront the Director. My guys and I just needed to hold on a little longer.

Kol started screaming and everything within me joined him. I could stop this. I had the power inside me to stop this. I just needed to let the inky magic in.

God damn it, just wait. Just a little longer.

"I'm yours," I gasped to Lilith. *Please, stop.*

"What was that?" Lilith asked. "I didn't hear you."

Another scream from Gideon and I pressed my forehead against the carved granite floor. The plan wouldn't work if I didn't look like I was in agony and weak, and it took everything inside me not to pump every ounce of power I had left into the cage spell right now.

"You need to speak up over the screaming, daughter," Lilith said.

The fire witch grabbed my hair, digging his fingers into my skull, and yanked my head up.

"What are you?" Lilith snarled.

"I'm yours. I'm your weapon."

"You're mine to do with as I please. Just like your mates," Lilith said.

"Thank your goddess for using you." With a thud of magic that stole my breath, the fire witch sent flames burning down my neck, searing my skin. I fought my scream, but it tore free, a strangled sound that made Jacob heave against his shackles.

I gritted my teeth. Where the hell was the Director? Putting me on a separate channel from the rest of the op might have been good for my focus, but I had no idea what was going on unless the Director made an effort to communicate with me.

Except it hadn't been that long since I'd given him the signal and he'd had to stay a few blocks away to avoid notice.

"Thank your goddess," the fire witch pressed.

"Thank you," I gasped.

Lilith jerked to her feet, her hellfire flaring, sending sparks showering around her. "Not good enough."

The prostate glyph witch beside me tensed, and the fire witch's sneer deepened.

"You need to learn your place." Lilith gave a nod so slight I almost missed it.

The fire witch wrapped his arm around my burned neck and hauled me to my feet, choking me. I rammed my elbow into his gut and heaved forward, tossing him over my shoulder onto the stone floor.

Lilith barked a harsh laugh. "Oh, you're going to have to do better than that, Bates."

The fire witch, Bates, snarled something and grabbed a small tattoo on his right arm as the other glyph witches bolted out of the way, gathering by the pillars at the sides of the room. His power thudded in my chest, stealing my breath.

What little demonic magic I had left swelled, ready to blast at him, but the cage spell sputtered.

Shit.

I scrambled to bolster the cage spell as Bates's spell slammed me into a pillar.

Agony sliced through my chest and my head cracked against the stone, sending flashes of light and darkness dancing over my vision. The cage spell sputtered again and so too did my hold on my frozen bonds.

The inky magic dug in deeper, grinding against my will, begging, cajoling, promising I'd be strong if I'd just let it in.

Let me in. Fight back.

Not yet. I had to wait. I'd fail if I didn't wait.

But I was going to have to let it in soon. Holding the cage spell active inside me had drained almost all of my remaining demonic magic. If the JP didn't arrive soon, I was going to have to go ahead with the plan whether the other witches were there or not, or I'd lose the spell.

Bates pressed a red tattoo on his shoulder and hissed a quick word.

Fire roared around his hands like Cassius's fire magic, and he snapped a whip of fire at me.

I wrenched out of the way, shooting agony through my chest — another God damned broken rib — and the whip sliced into the pillar. Sparks flew through the air from the impact, stinging my skin. I scrambled to get to cover around the pillar, but Bates jerked his hand. The whip sliced into my shoulder. Blood rushed down my arm and the acrid scent of burned flesh filled my nose. The cage spell sputtered.

Shit shit shit.

Bates snapped the whip again. I heaved to the side and the whip hit the floor with another shower of sparks. I couldn't keep this up. My lungs burned, desperate for more air, but I couldn't draw a full breath against the pressure of magic power inside me and out.

Jacob and Kol screamed and heaved against their shackles, while Gideon gasped, still fighting to keep himself up so he could breathe.

Come on, Director. Any time now.

I shifted to put the pillar between me and Bates, but his whip seized my ankle, searing my flesh, the pain stealing the rest of my breath and straining my hold on the cage spell.

With a snarl, he yanked me out into the open.

"Your place is bowing before your goddess," he said, flicking his wrist and wrapping his whip around my neck. I tried to scream, but I had no breath left. I barely had enough thought to hold onto the cage spell. The inky magic swelled and its power seeped into me, the fiery pain burning away my resistance.

A ghost of demonic mist rushed around my hands, ready to strike Bates, but I shoved it back.

Not yet. Not yet. Just a little longer.

He wrenched me across the floor, too fast for me to get to my feet, grabbed my hair again, and shoved my face against the flagstones. "Thank your goddess for letting you live. Thank—"

"My goddess," a reedy masculine voice said from somewhere behind me, his words coming out fast and sharp. "The JP have entered the building."

"About time," Lilith snapped.

The inky magic roared with laughter.

Shit, I should have thought of that. Why didn't I think of that? But I'd been focusing on too many other things at the time. Of course Lilith expected me to lead the JP there. She had to have assumed they'd arrested me in the park, so I'd either escaped and they'd followed me, or I'd made a deal and shown them her location.

Bates yanked my head up, his fire whip digging deeper into my neck, the flames searing agony over my jaw and cheeks and down my chest.

Lilith gave me a sickeningly sweet smile, her eyes filled with malice. "The Joined Parliament's bureau will be in chaos when I kill their top leadership, and then I'll release you on the world."

"Never," I gasped.

"You don't have a say in the matter." She flicked her finger and light burst from the glyphs behind my guys. Their muscles jerked taut and they screamed.

I heaved in Bates's grip. I had to get free, had to stop her—

I had to wait for her God damned witches to get out of the room.

Come on. Tell them to go. Please.

The inky magic churned as whispers of rage and fear ghosted through my chest, my guys' pain so strong I was picking up their emotions through our blocked bonds. The cage spell flickered, snapped back to life, then flickered again.

I was out of time.

Lilith swept her gaze over the witches gathered by the walls. "Kill the JP agents."

The witches threw off their robes and raced to the door, and Lilith turned her gaze back to me. "Bates, break her. She's a weapon. She doesn't need a whole soul or mind."

"As my goddess commands." The fire in his whip surged and so did the agony. Darkness danced across my vision and the cage spell burst into smoky nothingness inside me.

No. Please no.

I screamed, and let the inky magic in.

ESSIE

THE INKY MAGIC EXPLODED INSIDE ME, A FEROCIOUS POWER THAT STAINED my soul. Every cell was blackened with its malicious intent and filled with Lilith's essence. I was finally hers to command, and she'd been waiting for this moment all along.

"That won't save you," Lilith taunted, and my body jerked up to my hands and knees. "That's my worship magic. I control that power."

"I know." I heaved at the power and spun it into the cage spell. I needed to save it above all else.

"You're not strong enough to take it away from me."

"I am with my bonds." The cage spell flared, a blazing ball inside my chest, but the inky magic whirled into a vortex of overwhelming power, too strong for me to grasp hold of and push fully into the cage spell. It tore at my soul and essence, consuming pieces and adding them to Lilith's inky reservoir.

"Your bonds make you weak."

My body crawled toward her, blood from my burned neck splattering on the floor. I fought to keep myself in place, control the inky magic, anything to keep hold of myself. Please, God, I couldn't let her possess me.

Bates released his whip from around my neck, and snapped it down onto my back. I screamed. Every nerve was on fire and I couldn't catch my breath. Too much pain and pressure and inky magic. And I had to hold onto the spell. Just. Hold. On.

Marcus jerked to his feet and snarled, wrenching and clawing at the chain around his neck, but couldn't break free.

"Stay," Lilith hissed, and red demonic mist twisted around him and yanked him down to the floor, drawing a yelp of pain. "You're all weak."

The glyphs glowed blindingly bright, making my guys scream, and a flicker of electric magic cut through my arm as agony tore through me.

Save them. Save them. They're dying. I have to save them.

The inky magic's hold on me weakened and I jerked to a stop before Gideon clamped down on our bond again, the sudden aching cold stealing my breath.

I wrenched my head against the inky magic's control and looked at him. "Release it."

"No," he gasped. "It'll kill you."

"It'll save me. I can't resist her without you and the connection within our brands."

"You can't resist me at all," Lilith said. I heaved forward, back onto my hands, and Bates kicked me in the ribs, knocking me over.

White lightning shot through my chest, and the inky magic's vortex tore more pieces from my soul. I was losing myself, who I was, what I remembered, who I loved.

"Please, Gideon, Jacob, Kol. Focus on our brands."

"I love you," Gideon said, and lightning exploded inside me. My muscles seized and for a second there was only him and his pain.

Then Jacob and Kol released their hold on our bonds and I was burning in the center of the sun, my soul ignited, their brands pulling strength from me. But in that center with me were my guys — Gideon, Jacob, Kol, and a whisper of Marcus because we didn't share a brand — and the raw primal power binding us together.

The surety of our bonds filled my burning soul, holding it together against the inky magic's vortex. I clung to my guys, their love, their determination, and used that strength of spirit to weave my essence into the inky magic and spin its vortex into a tight supernova in the core of my being, just like the rest of my power. A supernova more powerful than anything I'd ever contained before that threatened to burn me up.

Lilith howled, and the inky magic strained to control my body, but my guys held me steady.

I heaved to my feet and shoved power into the cage spell. It burst around Lilith in a crackling nimbus of blue-white lightning, but her demonic magic roared with a chest-crushing *thud* that weakened the spell.

I gritted my teeth, fought to stay standing, and pushed more power into the spell to keep it going.

Bates jerked forward and snapped his whip at me, but I sent a blast of demonic mist, powered by Lilith's inky magic, into him. It threw him to the back of the room, slammed him into one of the enormous metal doors, and took it off its hinges.

"You think you can cage me?" Lilith's demonic magic tore into me.

I staggered. Behind me, I felt the *thu-thud* of magic, but couldn't move to get out of the way.

A fireball exploded around me. The heat started to sear my skin but my power roared stronger, rushing out of me in a great wave and sweeping Bates's fire away from me.

My hold on the cage spell weakened and Lilith's demonic magic surged. I wasn't going to be able to fight Bates and cage Lilith at the same time. I needed all my concentration on the cage spell. I needed my guys to be fighting.

"Brace yourself," I yelled at them, and shoved power into the bonds. Gold light gleamed from their brands. Jacob's vampiric intensity swelled, his monster fully released, and the light in Gideon's eyes turned into a blinding halo and his wings burst from his back. With a gasp, Kol's head jerked up and his hellfire flared from his good eye.

I shot a blast of demonic magic into the chain securing Kol as Gideon sliced through his restraints with a blade of divine light.

Oh, thank God. They'd either kept some power back in reserve, or my surge into them hadn't just given them strength but replenished some magic as well.

"We've got Bates," Gideon said, sagging to the floor and sending a blast of divine light into Jacob's chains. "You cage Lilith."

"You can't cage me," Lilith snarled. "I'm the Hellfire Queen. I'm more powerful than you. You think stealing my worship magic will make you more powerful?" She clenched her hands and the inky magic seized my body and dropped me to my knees. "It just makes you mine."

"No," Jacob said, and the power in our bond grew stronger. "She'll never be yours."

"Never." Kol glanced at me, his one eye still swollen shut, and the power in our bond grew stronger as well.

Another *thu-thud* of power from Bates behind me, and Gideon blasted divine light as Jacob and Kol charged toward him, somehow moving with speed and power even though I knew they were still seriously injured. Marcus snarled and lunged toward Lilith, but her demonic magic wrenched him back, making him whimper.

I clung to my bonds, anchoring myself in the raging power burning inside me, and pushed more magic into the cage spell.

The blue-white lightning around Lilith flared and thickened, the spell gaining strength, but she squared her shoulders and whipped more demonic magic around her, burning through the lightning as fast as it formed.

Out of the corner of my eye, I saw Jacob slash at a fire whip with his short sharp claws, breaking it apart, as Kol leapt in, ramming his fist into Bates's face. Gideon blasted more divine light, hitting Bates in the chest and knocking him back.

Bates grabbed a tattoo and a massive invisible weight slammed into me. Jacob and Kol staggered and dropped to their knees, and the next blast of light from Gideon fell short, exploding on the floor at Bates's feet.

I wrenched my attention back to Lilith. This would end if I caged her, and I fought to strengthen the spell.

"That power belongs to me." Lilith heaved at the inky magic and my grasp on it weakened. The cage spell sputtered.

Shit. I scrambled to regain my grip on the inky magic. My muscles trembled and my insides burned. I couldn't afford for her to take back her worship magic.

Screaming, I shoved my soul fully into the inky magic. It twisted around my essence and I wrenched the power out of her grasp and shoved it into the cage spell.

Lilith hissed and clenched her hands, yanking demonic magic from Marcus and sucking out his essence. With a howl, he collapsed on his side, writhing on the floor, his massive black chest, covered in all those swirling glyphs, heaving with shallow, ragged breaths.

"Release the cage spell and I'll let him live." Lilith reached out her hand and Kol screamed, his demonic magic rushing out of him into her. "I'll let them both live."

But the moment I released the spell, we were all dead. I had to cage her before she killed Marcus and Kol. It was the only way to stop this.

Please, God, let me stop this.

I pushed more power into the spell. All the power I had as fast as I could. The inferno inside me burned into my essence and soul, and poured out through my body. My skin blistered and burst, the agony excruciating, but I had to overpower Lilith and finish the spell.

Lilith roared, a primal cry of rage, and wrenched her power out of Bates. He gasped a strangled cry and collapsed, and her strength started to overpower mine.

I fought to hold on. Darkness swam across my vision and the inky magic tore away more pieces of my soul, but Lilith's skin also blistered and burst. Blood trailed down her face, and her expression grew wild, and yet still she pushed more power into her defense.

"You will not cage me," she yelled as she released a massive blast of power, burning it into the inky magic.

But I shoved my magic against hers, pushing it back into her, and her eyes flashed wide with surprise.

Fire exploded from her body. With a scream, she spun her power into a whirlwind, sucking at the flames, but the fire kept burning, brighter and hotter. Wailing, she thrashed against the inferno, but it consumed her, burning her into a smoldering pile of ash.

She'd chosen death over imprisonment.

I sagged forward, my insides still burning, and the inky magic grew.

Mine. All mine.

It tore the rest of my soul to shreds, sweeping it around in its vortex. I fought to cling to my bonds but they kept slipping out of my mental grasp. I wanted to kill, to rule, to be worshiped—

No. Please. That was the inky magic. That wasn't me.

Of course it's you. You're a monster.

I'm not. My soul is good.

Not any more, the inky magic laughed.

I fought to pull my soul back together, but my bonds were no longer strong enough to keep me whole. I was drowning in sticky, malicious magic and was too exhausted to resist. The only thing I could do was shut my guys out and finish burning myself up.

I heaved my head up and locked gazes with Marcus. I couldn't do this alone. I wouldn't be strong enough. I loved him so much. All of them. I had to do this to protect them. If I let the inky magic take over, I'd become a monster just like Lilith, and I'd take them with me.

Tears streamed down my cheeks. There had to be another way, but I could already feel the magic taking over, and soon I wouldn't have enough strength to finish this.

A small, distant part of my mind found it funny that once again I was going to sacrifice myself to save my guys, as if my final battle with the archnephilim had been practice for this very moment. I'd proven I'd had the nerve once before. I just had to do it again. Except now I had so much more to lose.

"I love you. All of you."

I clamped down on my bonds. An icy hollowness snapped through my chest and the guys started yelling. Kol grabbed my arm, but I tossed him back with a blast of magic.

"Essie, stop," Jacob begged.

"I can't fight it. I won't become like her." I gathered the power inside me. One quick blast and, please God, let that be enough to end it. "Our connection isn't strong enough. It's taking over."

"No, please." Kol's heartache cut through my block and my throat tightened.

"Block me out. You'll survive if we both block the bonds."

I shoved another wave of power out around me and pushed my guys farther back, then released the rest of the magic inside me.

Marcus howled and lunged toward me, shifting at the same time as Gideon snapped the chain securing him to the floor with a blast of divine light.

"Don't you fucking dare," Marcus growled, cupping my cheeks.

"No." I tried to shove him back, get him out of the way of my inevitable fiery explosion, but all of the inky magic was already released and burning through me.

No, please. He's not supposed to die with me.

Flames licked over my skin, making both of us scream, and I fought to pull the magic back, change its direction, anything to save him. The block I'd put in my bonds shattered and the strength of my guys' souls flooded into me.

They yanked the inky magic into our brands, and the primal magic binding our souls together consumed it. Gideon's brand lit up, then Jacob's, then Kol's. The magic poured into my chest, and roared around my heart.

Marcus groaned and his grip on my cheeks tightened. Golden magic burst from his bare chest over his heart, and twisted into a beautiful complicated sigil, binding our souls together with an angelic mating brand.

With the combined strength of all my guys and the primal magic binding us together, 1 burned out every last speck of inky magic, and collapsed into Marcus's arms.

ESSIE

Two weeks later, I sat on a blanket in the shadow of a large maple with my back against Jacob's broad chest and his arms around me. It was a glorious summer's day, hot and humid, and I'd decided to wear shorts and a barely-there body-hugging halter top that showed off almost all of my brands.

The sky above was a perfect clear blue, just like Gideon's eyes, and less than an hour ago, I'd been soaring with him — after a lot of stumbles and help — for my first flying lesson. He, along with Kol, was now at the Tasty Tacos food truck ordering lunch while we waited for Marcus to finish letting his beast loose in the wolves' forest.

The last few days had been a strange mix of writing reports, being interrogated— or rather *interviewed*, and doing nothing because we'd all been put on medical leave until the JP decided otherwise.

I didn't remember much after Lilith had burned herself up by channeling too much magic and I'd branded Marcus. It had all been a frozen, agonizing blur. My burns had been so bad, and there'd been so many other serious injuries between my guys and the other agents, that the angels with healing magic had kept me sedated while they drained, regained, and drained their magic again and again to heal me and everyone else.

So when I'd woken, it had been almost a week later, and much to my surprise, I hadn't been handcuffed to the hospital bed. All of my guys had been in the room with me, waiting for me to wake, none of them in handcuffs, either.

My head had been pounding and was still a little sore. My magical channels had been burned so badly that both Amiah and Priam had said it would take months, maybe years... maybe never to regain all of my magical strength. Which didn't leave me helpless, just not as likely to accidentally take out a building, and I could live with that.

I'd learned the team, along with Cassius and Amiah, had been reprimanded but not arrested or fired, and that I was still an agent.

That shocked the hell out of me. I hadn't thought it was possible for the JP to completely accept me. Sure, the Director had been willing to support me to stop Lilith, but that didn't mean he trusted me.

Except I'd shown him my soul and he'd become one of my strongest supporters. With the help of an angel with an empathic power, he'd shared the experience of my memories and empathic soul-baring, and the rest of the surviving members of the JP Bureau of Supernatural Law Enforcement's leadership were on my side as well... and I wasn't going to think about all the people who now knew a lot of really embarrassing things about me.

It also didn't hurt that Voth, the Angel of Death — a moniker he'd picked up during the war for all the nephilim he'd killed — was another strong supporter and he'd threatened the lives of any JP leader who thought to arrest me. He'd also told them they were idiots if they didn't keep me on as an active agent. I'd already proven I'd go up against terrible odds and face anyone — even my mother — to save lives. If that didn't prove my soul was good, he said, he had no idea what did.

Unfortunately, video from the fight in Unity Park had gone viral. The only saving grace was that one of the many videos released included the whole fight: both the horrible part where I'd told Lilith I was hers and wanted to join her, as well as when I'd denounced her and swore I'd stop her.

I wasn't surprised at the fear and hate the video received. The inky magic hadn't been wrong. People were afraid of me. They might always be afraid. I reminded them of the worst time in their lives and was the same kind of super that had slaughtered thousands.

But the inky magic hadn't been right, either. There were a lot more people who'd commented positively on the video, and many — mostly shifters but surprisingly a few angels, too — were furious on my behalf that Lilith had vowed to torture my mates. Soul bonds were sacred and rare, and many of them were amazed I hadn't completely lost it under those conditions.

It also didn't hurt that the JP had, at the Director's insistence, agreed to have their most powerful empathic angel judge my soul. A process which thankfully wasn't as intrusive or embarrassing as what I'd done to prove my innocence to the Director.

It did, however, confirm with irrefutable evidence that I didn't have evil intent, and the Joined Parliament had made an official statement about me, providing the evidence the empath had gathered. And while the JP technically didn't lie, they did leave out certain details which I had no doubt made the public assume they'd had a bigger part in my life than they really did.

They'd said I'd been a nephilim taken out of her maturation tank as a child, and had had nothing to do with the war. True.

Except there was no mention of *who* pulled me from the tank.

They'd said I'd been raised to help and protect people. Sort of true.

But they certainly hadn't mentioned who raised me, likely hoping the public would assume they'd had a hand in my upbringing.

They'd said — after the Director shared my conversation with Lucifer with them — that they'd learned nephilim became monsters because Michael shattered their souls, and because Michael had never gotten his hands on me, my soul was still whole. True.

And then they provided the evidence from the empathic angel.

I was, without a doubt, not a danger and would never be a danger to the law-abiding citizens in the earthly realm. The empathic soul examination and the video of me vowing to stop Lilith were proof.

I was certain not everyone believed them, but Voth, a notorious war hero known for killing nephilim, had made numerous television appearances spreading the JP's official statement.

It wasn't a guarantee that everything would go smoothly from now on — nothing in life was guaranteed — but it certainly helped having the JP's official and very public support. And for the most part, shocking me even more, the world accepted the JP's statement.

I was not a threat, or a monster, or a war criminal.

Yeah, I also got that in writing. Best to have as many bases as possible covered.

The Director, along with Zuri and her team, including Ephraim who'd barely survived, had returned to Rome shortly after the empathic angel had proven my innocence, and I'd tried to come to terms with everything that had happened.

I wasn't a naturally born nephilim. I didn't even have any human DNA in me. The world of the supernatural was still terrifying, but, given that I was the daughter of the Hellfire Queen and the archangel Lucifer, I was one of the scariest things out there now.

That didn't make me feel better. But it did make me feel more confident in my ability to protect those who couldn't protect themselves.

I ran my finger over the new thick silver bracelet around Jacob's wrist with the prongs digging into his skin every eighth of an inch. His charm protecting him against sunlight had been replaced, he'd recently fed, and the calm certainty of his love for me radiated around my heart.

"It's almost a shame they reinstated us," he said, his soft low voice rumbling through me. "I could spend every day sitting in the sun with you."

"Pretty sure you'd eventually get bored."

"Of you?" His arm around my waist tightened. "Never. And I'm sure we wouldn't just be *sitting* every day."

He brushed his lips across the back of my neck, drawing a shiver of desire.

Yeah, there wouldn't be much sitting at all, and if he kept that up, there wouldn't be any sitting right now. But then Kol would want to join and he'd convince Marcus to join, too, and Gideon would get angry and everyone in the park would see a whole lot more of me than I really wanted.

"Well, Kol would be happy." I leaned back and kissed him, letting my love and desire for him swell through our bond.

"I have a feeling Kol wouldn't be the only one," he groaned, his breath fast.

"Yeah," I sighed as I leaned my head against his shoulder, savoring the feel of his large body against mine, his arms embracing and protecting me.

The giggles of a young child carried over the rumble of cars on the busy street nearby and the conversation of the half dozen other people standing in line at the taco truck. Marcus, in his massive hellhound form, burst out of the underbrush on the other side of the lawn with a naked child, probably about five or six, clinging to his back. Two more kids about the same age, also naked, chased after him, and three wolf pups nipped at his heels.

He tipped the child off his back onto the grass and gently headbutted another kid as six adult wolves, half the size of Marcus, broke through the trees. They shifted back into their human forms, a mix of men and women, laughing and chatting and pulling on the clothes they'd left with their picnic baskets.

"Okay, that's enough," one of the women called to the kids. "I'm sure Marcus didn't come here to play with you." Her gaze jumped to me and I tensed.

Everyone in the Union City wolf pack knew Marcus was mated to me, the archnephilim. My face had been plastered on every newscast for the last two weeks — which meant I was never going to be doing undercover work again. But that was a small price to pay for not being public enemy number one.

Except I still couldn't stop the instinctual reaction of anticipating hate and fear. I'd spent my entire life hiding what I was without even knowing *what* I really was, and had been told over and over again that the world wouldn't understand me. Now I kept expecting to wake up and find that my amazing new life had all been a dream.

The woman waved and gave me a warm smile, shocking me, then turned back to the kids. She knew what I was and didn't care.

"I feel your surprise through our bond every time someone welcomes you," Jacob said. "Is it that shocking that someone would see you for who you really are? You stopped Lilith. You prevented another war. Most of the supers in Union City think you're a hero."

"Yeah." Although I suspected my positive welcome had a lot to do with Voth. I had a feeling he was the one who'd spread all the extra details about my fight with Lilith. The tale had grown to near epic proportions and it had only been floating around for a few weeks. Even those who lived and worked in Operations whispered it with awe. The one detail, however, that always remained true, because in retrospect it was pretty epic — or pretty foolish, depending on how you looked at it — was that I'd been willing to do anything, even burn myself up, in order to stop Lilith... my mother.

Something I didn't think I'd ever fully come to terms with. I was the daughter of the Hellfire Queen and the most notorious fallen angel in human and angelic history. And yet I didn't feel any guilt over Lilith's death. She'd been determined to kill everyone, and every cell in my being knew she'd needed to be stopped. That she'd chosen to burn up instead of being caged wasn't something I'd had any control over, and while I might have half of her DNA, she hadn't been my mother. My mother had been a kind, protective human woman who'd given me everything she could. Just like Lucifer had hoped for when he'd left me with her.

Marcus nudged an eager child out of the way. He'd been worried that the Union City wolf pack wouldn't accept him because he was no longer a werewolf, but the pack had welcomed him with open arms... although some of the single ladies had been disappointed that he was off the market.

He strode toward us, his powerful muscles bunching and releasing, the sun catching in his short velvety fur, accentuating the swirling glyphs in his skin. As far as anyone knew, he was the only hellhound in the mortal realm, and now one of a few remaining hounds in all the realms.

Tests had proven his DNA had completely changed from human with the lycanthropy infection, to fully demonic, and no one could explain it. And I didn't care. He was alive, healthy, now with the extended demonic lifespan, and still mine.

He shifted, the movement fast and smooth, as if his body turned to liquid from one step to another and then back to flesh again. His piercing green gaze captured mine, making my pulse stutter, and I dragged my attention away from his eyes to appreciate his lean-muscled body and the delicate golden glyph above his heart before he put on his clothes.

He cocked an eyebrow, his beast's feral intensity rising, and pulled on a pair of shorts, covering his growing erection.

With a low growl, he knelt before me and captured my lips in a fierce, breathtaking kiss. "God, I love you."

"Ooo, are we showing Essie our love for her again?" Kol asked as he sat beside me, handed Marcus the tray with our food, and kissed me, building up my barely-contained desire for him and the rest of my guys. A whisper of his heated magic unfurled low within me and a moan escaped before I could stop it.

He sat back on his heels. The hellfire in his eyes licking his cheeks revealed his desire, while his lopsided grin revealed his awe and joy. It had only been a few weeks since our brand had formed, but I had a feeling he'd always be a little surprised that he, an incubus, had fallen in love.

He'd been in the worst shape when I'd woken in Operations. Amiah and Priam — and a few other angels who worked at Mercy Memorial and had been reassigned to Operations by the Director to deal with all the wounded — had taken care of Gideon and Marcus, and they, in turn, had helped Jacob. But Kol had been unwilling to go to someone else to get the sexual energy he needed to properly heal.

I'd yelled at him over that. I understood his nature, and while I didn't exactly like the idea of him turning to someone else, the idea of him spending almost a week sitting at my bedside in agony bothered me more.

He had shrugged and changed the subject with a kiss that turned into more and went a long way to healing him.

And here I'd thought Marcus would be the most stubborn of my mates.

Gideon, also carrying food and drinks, sat by my feet and set the tray on the blanket between us. A crackle of electric power teased over my forearm and his desire seeped through our bond.

He was the most reserved of my guys, at least when it came to large displays of public affection, but that didn't mean he didn't crave me. His love radiated through our bond as strongly as the other guys, and the moment we were out of the public eye he freely kissed me in his sensual, languid style that always awakened the divine light within me and made me squirm for more.

He'd said he and Cassius had talked during the week I was unconscious, and while Cassius no longer looked at me like I was going to murder his brother, his demeanor toward me remained cool, verging on icy, and his emotions seethed with anger and frustration.

But he was icy and angry with everyone, not just me, and really, the anger was probably at himself. Gideon had forced him to make a choice and he'd gone against what he believed in to protect his brother. That kind of choice could make a person question everything he thought was true about himself, and that wasn't something easily dealt with.

Amiah also remained brusquely professional, her emotions harder and icier than Cassius's. But her world had been rocked as well. She'd been determined to protect a man who could never have loved her back, and now, with my angelic mating brand on Marcus's chest, any last shred of hope was gone. My empathic healing magic kept flaring up when she was near, desperately wanting to help her, but I was the last person she'd want help from so I kept my power restrained.

"So we have a decision to make," Gideon said, handing me a paper-wrapped burrito. "Head office approved our request to renovate the fifth floor."

"You're kidding." Kol grabbed a cardboard tray with his brisket tacos. "What did we have to give up?"

"Nothing." Gideon opened his bottle of water and took a long sip.

"Nothing?" Jacob asked. "The reno is going to be expensive. I was sure they'd negotiate."

We'd proposed a plan to strip the suites on the fifth floor in the southwest corner of Operations to create an apartment for us. We wanted a main bedroom as well as individual rooms so each of us had our own space. We'd also thrown in some fancy bathroom plans for multiple bathrooms, private access to the roof, along with a private rooftop patio — because hey, if we were going to ask, why not start by asking for everything — and a skylight over the open concept living room/dining room/kitchen area.

None of us had expected head office to say yes. In fact, I had been expecting them to outright refuse us. I'd already caused them an enormous amount of trouble with my very existence, and I was pretty sure they considered the debt for stopping another war paid by ensuring the townsfolk didn't come after me with pitchforks.

"We're a mated quintet." Gideon's love for me swelled in my chest. "That's never happened before, and despite me being the only full angel in the group, we're still sacred."

"I wonder what else we can get out of that?" Kol's eyes lit with a wicked gleam, and I could just imagine all the crazy requests he'd make just to see if they'd say yes.

Gideon rolled his eyes at Kol, probably thinking what I was. "We're not going to abuse this," he said. "The only other thing we should use this for is leverage to leave the JP if that's what we want."

Which was the other option on the table. Yes, we were still a JP team, but was that what we really wanted? The job was dangerous and the JP wasn't without politics. With the second spell Lucifer had given me, I could hide my true nature and we could move someplace where no one knew us. There'd still be a chance someone would recognize me, but without my glowing eyes and a new haircut, people would be more likely to think I *looked* like the infamous archnephilim and wasn't actually *the* infamous archnephilim.

I hadn't asked Sebastian if he would cast the spell, but as a full fae sorcerer, I was sure he had more than enough power to do it.

He'd popped by two days after I'd woken up, looking like his usual sexy self. The soft glow radiating from his skin was back to normal, or rather normal for the faekin he was pretending to be, and his ears were a little less pointy than a real fae's. He hadn't gotten close enough for me to look into his eyes and see the vast universe of power, and he'd kept his power and emotions locked down tight, but I had no doubt he was back to normal. After a brief hello and a wicked smile, he'd given Gideon a bill that Gideon had said head office would never pay, then he'd left.

"So?" Marcus said.

"Do we stay or go?" Jacob asked.

But I didn't want to run and hide any more. I couldn't. That life was over. I wasn't the same Officer Essie Shaw whose only goal had been to help people while flying under the radar. Hell, I wasn't even the same species, or at least the species I'd thought I was. I no longer had to keep everyone at arm's length for fear they'd learn my secret, nor hide from all things supernatural. For the first time in my life, I was free to choose whatever path I wanted.

And I was in a position where I could help so many people.

I knew my guys would give up everything and follow me to the ends of the earth, just like I would for them. But I'd never ask them to. They'd joined the JP to serve and protect, just like I'd joined the UCPD.

"I made a promise to myself to help those who couldn't help themselves," I said. "I want to keep that promise."

I met Marcus's piercing gaze, his feral passion making my pulse pick up, and Kol released a shuddering breath, drawing my attention to him. The hellfire in his eyes flickered and danced, and his sensual magic whispered low within me.

Leaning back, I looked into Jacob's eyes, black still pools focused entirely on me. His yearning merged with the heat building within me, and then Gideon's magic crackled through our brand, stealing my breath. I slid my attention to him and soared in a perfect summer sky, wrapped in desire and love and trust.

I wasn't despised, I wasn't weak, and I was no longer alone. I belonged with these men and they loved me for who I was, the good and the bad. Destiny had conspired to give me everything I'd thought I'd never be able to have. I'd just needed to accept myself, both my darkness and my light, to attain it.

OTHER BOOKS BY TESSA COLE

NEPHILIM'S DESTINY

Destined Shadows, prequel story

Destined Darkness, book 1

Destined Blood, book 2

Destined Fire, book 3

Destined Storm, book 4

Destined Radiance, book 5

ANGEL'S FATE

Fated Bonds, book 1

Fated Winter, book 2

Fated Fear, book 3

Fated Despair, book 4

Fated Resolve, book 5

Fated Heart, book 6

THE GRECIAN GODDESS TRILOGY

written with Clara Wils

Kiss of the Goddess, book 1

Power of the Goddess, book 2

Bonds of the Goddess, book 3

ENSNARED BY THE PACK

Wolf Deceived, book 1

Wolf Denied, book 2

Wolf Desired, book 3

Wolf Distressed, book 4

Wolf Decided, book 5

9 781990 587269